The MAGE STORMS

A VALDEMAR OMNIBUS

The MAGE STORMS

A VALDEMAR OMNIBUS

MERCEDES LACKEY

TITAN BOOKS

The Mage Storms Omnibus
Print edition ISBN: 9781783293810
E-book edition ISBN: 9781783293827

Published by Titan Books
A division of Titan Publishing Group Ltd
144 Southwark Street, London
SE1 0UP

First edition: September 2015
2 4 6 8 10 9 7 5 3

A CIP catalogue record for this title is available from the British Library.

Printed and bound in Great Britain by CPI Group Ltd.

The MAGE STORMS

A VALDEMAR OMNIBUS

STORM WARNING

A VALDEMAR OMNIBUS

BOOK ONE of
The MAGE STORMS

Dedicated to Elsie Wollheim with love and respect

1

Emperor Charliss sat upon the Iron Throne, bowed down neither by the visible weight of his years nor the invisible weight of his power. He bore neither the heavy Wolf Crown on his head, nor the equally burdensome robes of state across his shoulders, though both lay nearby, on an ornately trimmed marble bench beside the Iron Throne. The thick silk-velvet robes flowed down the bench and coiled on the floor beside it, a lush weight of pure crimson so heavy it took two strapping young men to lift them into place on the Emperor's shoulders. The Wolf Crown lay atop the robes, preventing them from slipping off the bench altogether. Let mere kings flaunt their golden crowns; the Emperor boasted a circlet of electrum, inset with thirteen yellow diamonds. Only when one drew near enough to the Emperor to see his eyes clearly did one see that the circlet was not as it seemed, that what had passed at a distance for an abstract design or a floral pattern was, in fact, a design of twelve wolves, and that the winking yellow diamonds were their eyes. Eleven of those wolves were in profile to the watcher, five facing left, six facing right; the twelfth, obviously the pack leader, gazed directly down onto whosoever the Emperor faced, those unwinking yellow eyes staring at the petitioner even as the Emperor's own eyes did.

Let lesser beings assume thrones of gold or marble; the Emperor held court from his Iron Throne, made from the personal weapons of all those monarchs the Emperors of the past had conquered and deposed, each glazed and guarded against rust. The throne itself was over six feet tall and four feet in width; a monolithic piece of furniture, it was so heavy that it had not been moved so much as a finger-length in centuries. Anyone looking at it could only be struck by its sheer *mass*— and must begin calculating just how many sword blades, axes, and lance points must have gone into the making of it...

None of this was by chance, of course. Everything about the

Emperor's regalia, his throne, his Audience Chamber, and Crag Castle itself was carefully calculated to reduce a visitor to the proper level of fearful respect, impress upon him the sheer power held in the hands of this ruler, and the utter impossibility of aspiring to such power. The Emperors were not interested in inducing a *groveling* fear, nor did they intend to excite ambition. The former was a dangerous state; people made too fearful would plot ways to remove the cause of that fear. And ambition was a useful tool in an underling beneath one's direct supervision, but risky in one who might, on occasion, slip his leash.

There was very little in the Emperor's life that was not the result of long thought and careful calculation. He had not become the successor to Emperor Lioth at the age of thirty without learning the value of both abilities—and he had not spent the intervening century-and-a-half in letting either ability lapse.

Charliss was the nineteenth Emperor to sit the Iron Throne; none of his predecessors had been less than brilliant, and none had reigned for less than half a century. None had been eliminated by assassins, and only one had been unable to choose his own successor.

Some called Charliss "the Immortal"; that was a fallacy, since he was well aware how few years he had left to him. Although he was a powerful mage, there were limits to the amount of time magic could prolong one's life. Eventually the body itself became too tired to sustain life any longer; even banked fires dwindled to ash in the end. Charliss' rumored immortality was one of many myths he himself propagated. Useful rumors were difficult to come by.

The dull gray throne sat in the midst of an expanse of black-veined white marble; the Emperor's robes, the exact color of fresh-spilled blood, and the yellow gems in the crown, were the only color on the dais. Even the walls and the ceiling of the dais-alcove, a somber setting for a rich gem, were of that same marble. The effect was to concentrate the attention of the onlookers on the Emperor and only the Emperor. The battle-banners, the magnificent tapestries, the rich curtains—all these were behind and to the side of the young man who waited at the Emperor's feet. Charliss himself wore slate-gray velvets, half-robe with dagged sleeves, trews, and Court-boots, made on the same looms as the crimson robes; in his long-ago youth, his hair had been whitened by the wielding of magic and his once-dark eyes were now the same pale gray as an overcast dawn sky.

If the young man waiting patiently at the foot of the throne was aware of how few years the Emperor had left to him, he had (wisely) never indicated he possessed this dangerous knowledge to anyone. Grand Duke Tremane was about the same age as Charliss had been when Lioth bestowed his power and responsibility on Charliss' younger, stronger shoulders and had retired to spend the last three years of his life holding off Death with every bit of the concentration he had used holding onto his power.

In no other way were the two of them similar, however. Charliss had been one of Lioth's many, many sons by way of his state marriages; Tremane was no closer in blood to Charliss than a mere cousin, several times removed. Charliss had been, and still was, an Adept, and in his full powers before he ascended the Throne. Tremane was a mere Master, and never would have the kind of mage-power at his personal command that Charliss had.

But if mage-power or blood-ties were all that was required to take the Throne and the Crown, there were a hundred candidates to be considered before Tremane. Intelligence and cunning were not enough by themselves, either; in a land founded by stranded mercenaries, both were as common as snowflakes in midwinter. No one survived long in Charliss' court without both those qualities, and the will to use both no matter how stressful personal circumstances were.

Tremane had luck; that was important, but more than the luck itself, Tremane had the ability to recognize when his good fortune had struck, and the capability to revise whatever his current plan was in order to take advantage of that luck. And conversely, when ill-luck struck him (which was seldom), he had the courage to revise plans to meet that as well, now and again snatching a new kind of victory from the brink of disaster.

Tremane was not the only one of the current candidates for the succession to have those qualities, but he was the one personally favored by the Emperor. Tremane was not entirely ruthless; too many of the others *were*. Being ruthless was not a bad thing, but being entirely ruthless was dangerous. Those who dared to stop at nothing often ended up with enemies who had nothing to lose. Putting an enemy in such a position was an error, for a man who has nothing to lose is, by definition, risking nothing to obtain what he desires.

Tremane inspired tremendous loyalty in his underlings; it had been *dreadfully* difficult for the Emperor's Spymaster to insinuate agents into Tremane's household. That was another useful trait for an Emperor to have; Charliss shared it, and had found that it was just as effective to have underlings willing to fling themselves in front of the assassin's blade without a single thought as it was to ferret out the assassin himself.

Otherwise, the man on the throne had little else in common with his chosen successor. Charliss had been considered handsome in his day, and the longing glances of the women in his Court even yet were not entirely due to the power and prestige that were granted to an Imperial mistress. Tremane was, to put it bluntly, so far from comely that it was likely *only* his power, rank, and personal prestige that won women to his bed. His thinning hair was much shorter than was fashionable; his receding hairline gave him a look of perpetual befuddlement. His eyes were too small, set just a hair too far apart; his beard was sparse, and looked like an afterthought. His thin face ended in a lantern jaw; his wiry body gave no hint of his quality as a warrior. Charliss often thought that the man's tailor ought to be taken out and hanged; he dressed Tremane in sober browns and blacks that did nothing for his complexion, and his clothing hung on him as if he had recently lost weight and muscle.

Then again... Tremane was only one of several candidates for the Iron Throne, and he knew it. He *looked* harmless; common, and of average intelligence, but no more than that. It was entirely possible that all of this was a deeply laid plan to appear ineffectual. If so, Charliss' own network of intelligence agents told him that the plan had succeeded, at least among the rest of the rivals for the position. Of all of the candidates for the Iron Throne, he was the one with the fewest enemies among his rivals.

They were as occupied with eliminating each other as in improving their own positions, and in proving their ability to the Emperor. *He* was free to concentrate on competence. This was *not* a bad position to be in.

Perhaps he was even more clever than Charliss had given him credit for. If so, he would need every bit of that cleverness in the task Charliss was about to assign him to.

The Emperor had not donned robes and regalia for this interview, as this was not precisely official; he was alone with Tremane—if one discounted the ever-present bodyguards—and the trappings of Empire did not impress the Grand Duke. Real power did, and real power was what Charliss held in abundance. He *was* power, and with the discerning, he did not need to weary himself with his regalia to prove that.

He cleared his throat, and Tremane bowed slightly in acknowledgment.

"I intend to retire at some point within the next ten years." Charliss made the statement calmly, but a muscle jumping in Tremane's shoulders betrayed the man's excitement and sudden tension. "It is Imperial custom to select a successor at some point during the last ten years of the reign so as to assure an orderly transition."

Tremane nodded, with just the proper shading of respect. Charliss noted with approval that Tremane did not respond with toadying phrases like "how could you even think of retiring, my Emperor," or "surely it is too early to be thinking of such things." Not that Charliss had expected such a response from him; Tremane was far too clever.

"Now," Charliss continued, leaning back a little into the comfortable solidity of the Iron Throne, "you are no one's fool, Tremane. You have obviously been aware for a long time that you are one of the primary candidates to be my successor."

Tremane bowed correctly, his eyes never leaving Charliss' face. "I was aware of that, certainly, my Emperor," he replied, his voice smoothly neutral. "Only a fool would have failed to notice your interest. But I am also aware that I am just one of a number of possible candidates."

Charliss smiled, ever so slightly, with approval. Good. Even if the man did not possess humility, he could feign it convincingly. Another valuable ability.

"You happen to be my current personal choice, Tremane," the Emperor replied, and he smiled again as the man's eyebrows twitched with quickly-concealed surprise. "It is true that you are not an Adept; it is true that you are not in the direct Imperial bloodline. It is also true that of the nineteen Emperors, only eleven have been full Adepts, and it is equally true that I have outlived my own offspring. Had any of them inherited my mage-powers, that would not have been the case, of course..."

He allowed himself a moment to brood on the injustice of that. Of all the children of his many marriages of state, not a one had achieved more than Journeyman status. That was simply not enough power to prolong life—not without resorting to blood-magic, at any rate, and while there *had* been an Emperor or two who had followed the darker paths, those were dangerous paths to follow for long. As witness the idiot Ancar, for instance—those who practiced the blood-paths all too often found that the magic had become the master, and the mage, the slave. The Emperor who ruled with the aid of blood-rites balanced on a spider's thread above the abyss, with the monsters waiting below for a single missed step.

Well, it hardly mattered. What *did* matter was that a worthy candidate stood before him now, a man who had all the character and strength the Iron Throne demanded.

And what was more, there was an opportunity before them both for Tremane to *prove*, beyond the faintest shadow of a doubt, that he was the only man with that kind of character and strength.

"Your duchy is in the farthest west, is it not?" Charliss asked, with carefully simulated casualness. If Tremane was surprised at the apparent change of subject, he did not show it. He simply nodded again.

"The western border, in fact?" Charliss continued. "The border of the Empire and Hardorn?"

"Perhaps a trifle north of the true Hardorn border, but yes, my Emperor," Tremane agreed. "May I assume this has something to do with the recent conquests that our forces have made in that sad and disorganized land?"

"You may." Charliss was enjoying this little conversation. "In fact, the situation with Hardorn offers you a unique opportunity to prove yourself to me. With that situation you may prove conclusively that you *are* worthy of the Wolf Crown."

Tremane's eyes widened, and his hands trembled, just for a moment.

"If the Emperor would be kind enough to inform his servant how this could be done——?" Tremane replied delicately.

The Emperor smiled thinly. "First, let me impart to you a few bits of privileged information. Immediately prior to the collapse of the Hardornen palace—and I mean that quite precisely—our envoy returned to us from King Ancar's court by means of a Gate. He did not have a great deal of information to offer, however, since he arrived with a knife buried in his heart, a rather lovely throwing dagger, which I happen to have here now."

He removed the knife from a sheath beneath his sleeve, and passed it to Tremane, who examined it closely, and started visibly when he saw the device carved into the pommel-nut.

"This is the royal crest of the Kingdom of Valdemar," Tremane stated flatly, passing the blade back to the Emperor, who returned it to the sheath. Charliss nodded, pleased that Tremane had actually recognized it.

"Indeed. And one wonders how such a blade could possibly have been where it was." He allowed one eyebrow to rise. "There is a trifle more; we had an intimate agent working to rid us of Ancar, an agent that had once worked independently in Valdemar. This agent is now rather conspicuously missing."

The agent in question had been a sorceress by the name of Hulda— Charliss never could recall the rest of her name. He did not particularly mourn her loss; *she* had been very ambitious, and he had foreseen a time when he might expect her value as an agent to be exceeded by her liabilities. That she was missing could mean any one of several things, but it did not much matter whether she had fled or died; the result would be the same.

Tremane's brow wrinkled in thought. "The most obvious conclusion would be that your agent turned," he said after a moment, "and that she used this dagger to place suspicion on agents of one of Ancar's enemies, thus embroiling us in a conflict with Valdemar that would open opportunities for her own ambitions in Hardorn. We have no reason for an open quarrel with Valdemar just yet; this could precipitate one before we are ready."

Charliss nodded with satisfaction. What was "obvious" to Tremane was far from obvious to those who looked no deeper than the surface of things. "Of course, I have no intention of pursuing an open quarrel with Valdemar just yet," he said. "The envoy in question was hardly outstanding; there are a dozen more who are simply panting for his position. The woman was quite troublesomely ambitious, yes; however, if she uses her magics but once, we will know where she is, and eliminate her if we choose. No. What truly concerns me is Valdemar itself. The situation within Hardorn is unstable. We have acquired half of the country with very little effort, but the ungrateful barbarians seem to have made up their mind to refuse the benefits of inclusion within the Empire." Charliss felt a distant ache in his hip joints and shifted his position a little to ease it. A warning, those little aches. The sign that his spells of bodily renewal were fading. They were less and less effective with every year, and within two decades or so they would fail him altogether...

One corner of Tremane's mouth twitched a little, in recognition of Charliss' irony. They both knew what the Emperor meant by that; the citizens of what had been Hardorn wanted their country back, and they had organized enough to resist further conquest.

"In addition," Charliss continued smoothly, "this land of Valdemar is overrun with refugees from all the conflict within Hardorn and from the wretched situation before Ancar perished. Valdemar could decide to aid the Hardornens in some material way, and that would cause us further trouble. We know that they have somehow allied themselves with those fanatics in Karse, and that presents us with one long front if we choose to fight them. Valdemar itself is a damned peculiar place…"

"It has always been difficult to insinuate agents into Valdemar," Tremane offered, with the proper diffidence. Charliss wondered whether he spoke from *personal* experience or simply the knowledge he had gleaned from keeping an eye on Charliss' own agents.

From beyond the closed doors of the Throne Room came the soft murmur of the courtiers who were waiting for the doors to open for them and Court to begin. Let them wait—and let them see just whose business had kept them waiting. They would know then, without any formal announcements, just who had become the Emperor's current favorite. The little maneuverings and shifts in power would begin from that very moment, like the shifts in current when a new boulder rolls into a stream.

"Quite." Charliss frowned. "In fact, that *Hulda* creature was once one of my freelance agents in the Valdemar capital. I was rather dubious about using her again, despite her abilities, until I realized just how cursed difficult it *is* to work in Valdemar. As it was, her progress there was minimal. Most unsatisfactory. She was never able to insinuate herself any higher than a mere court servant's position, and she had more than one agenda and more than one employer at the time."

The corner of Tremane's mouth twitched again, but this time it was downward. Charliss knew why; Tremane never knowingly worked with someone who served more masters than he.

"Why did you trust her in Hardorn, then?" the Grand Duke asked in a neutral tone.

"I never *trusted* her," Charliss corrected him, allowing a hint of cold disapproval to tinge his own voice. "I trust no agents, particularly not those who are as ambitious as this one was. I merely made sure that this time she had no other employers, and that her personal agenda was not incompatible with mine. And when it appeared that she was slipping her leash, I sent an envoy to Ancar's court to remind her who her master was. And to eliminate her if she elected to ignore the warning he represented. That was why I sent a mage, an Adept her equal, with none of her vices."

"Your pardon," Tremane replied, bowing slightly. "I should have known. But—about Valdemar?"

Charliss permitted his icy expression to thaw. "Valdemar is peculiar, as I said. Until recently, they've had next to no magic at all, and what they had was only mind-magic. There was a barrier there, according to my agents, a barrier that made it impossible for a practicing mage to remain within the borders for very long."

"But how did Hulda—" Tremane began, then smiled. "Of course. While she was there, she must have refrained from using her powers. A difficult thing for a mage; use of magic often becomes a habit too ingrained to break."

Charliss blinked slowly in satisfaction. Tremane was no fool; he saw immediately the solution and the difficulty of implementing it. "Precisely," he replied. "On both counts. And that was *why* I continued to use her. In business matters, the woman's self-discipline was remarkable. As for Valdemar—though they have begun again to use magic as we know it, the place is no less peculiar than before, and many of the mages they seem to have invited into their borders are from no land that *my* operatives recognize! Well, that is all in the past; what we need to deal with is the current situation. And that, Grand Duke Tremane, is where you come in."

Tremane simply waited, as any good and perfectly trained servant, for his master to continue. But his eyes narrowed just a trifle, and Charliss knew that his mind was working furiously. A current of breeze stirred the tapestries behind him, but the flames of the candles on the many-branched candelabras, protected in their glass shades, did not even waver.

"Your Duchy borders Hardorn; you will therefore be familiar with the area," Charliss stated, his tone and expression allowing no room for dissension. "The situation in Hardorn grows increasingly unstable by the moment. I require a personal commander of my own in place there; someone who has incentive, *personal* incentive, to see that the situation is dealt with expeditiously."

"Personal incentive, my Emperor?" Tremane replied.

Charliss crossed his legs and leaned forward, ignoring the pain in his hip joints. "I am giving you a unique opportunity to prove, not only to me, but to your rivals and your potential underlings, that you are the only truly worthy candidate for the Wolf Crown. I intend to put you in command of the Imperial forces in Hardorn. You will be answerable only to me. You will prove yourself worthy by dealing with this situation and bringing it to a successful conclusion."

Tremane's hands trembled, and Charliss noted that he had turned just a little pale. How long would it take for word to spread of Tremane's new position? Probably less than an hour. "What of Valdemar, my Emperor?" he asked, his voice steady, even if his hands were not.

"What of Valdemar?" Charliss repeated. "Well, I don't expect you to conquer it as well. It will be enough to bring Hardorn under our banner. However, if during that process you discover a way to insinuate an agent into Valdemar, all the better. If you take your conquests past the Hardorn border and actually *into* Valdemar, better still. I simply warn you of Valdemar because it is a strange place and I cannot predict how it will measure this situation nor what it will do. Valdemar can wait; Hardorn is what concerns me now. We must conquer it, now that we have begun, or our other client states will see that we have failed and may become difficult to deal with in our perceived moment of weakness."

"And if I succeed in bringing Hardorn into the Empire?" Tremane persisted.

"Then you will be confirmed in the succession, and I will begin the process of the formal training," Charliss told him. "And at the end of ten years, I will retire, and you will have Throne, Crown, and Empire."

Tremane's eyes lit, and his lips twitched into a tight, excited smile. Then he sobered. "If I do not succeed, however, I assume I shall resume nothing more than the rule of my Duchy."

Charliss examined his immaculately groomed hands, gazing into the topaz eyes of the wolf's-head ring he wore, a ring whose wolf mask had been cast from the same molds as the central wolf of the Wolf Crown. The eyes gazed steadily at him, and as he often did, Charliss fancied he saw a hint of life in them. Hunger. An avidity, not that of the starving beast, but of the prosperous and powerful.

"There is no shortage of suitable candidates for the Throne," he replied casually, tilting the ring for a better view into the burning yellow eyes. "If you should happen to survive your failure, I would advise you to retire *directly* to your Duchy. The next candidate that I would consider if you failed would be Baron Melles."

Baron Melles was a so-called "court Baron," a man with a title but no lands to match. He didn't *need* land; he had power, power in abundance, for he was an Adept and his magics had brought him more wealth than many landed nobles had. His coffers bulged with his accumulated wealth, but he wanted more, and his bloodlines and ambition were likely to give him more.

He also happened to be of the political party directly opposite that of Tremane's. Tremane's parents had held their lands for generations; Melles was the son of merchants. Melles was, not so incidentally, one of Tremane's few enemies, one of the few candidates to the succession who did *not* underestimate the Baron. There was a personal animosity between them that Charliss did not quite understand, and he often wondered if the two had somehow contracted a very private feud that had little or nothing to do with their respective positions and ambitions.

Melles would be only too pleased to find Tremane a failure and himself the new successor. This meant, among other things, that if Tremane happened to survive his failure to conquer Hardorn, he probably would not survive the coronation of his rival, and he might not even survive the confirmation of Melles as successor. Melles was the most ruthless of all the candidates, and both Charliss and Tremane were quite well aware that he was a powerful enough Adept to be able to commit any number of murders-by-magic, and make them all appear to be accidents.

He was also clever enough *not* to do anything of the sort, since his political rivals would be looking for and defending against exactly that sort of attack. Melles was fully wealthy enough to buy any number of covert killers, and probably would. He was too clever not to consolidate his position by eliminating enough rivals that those remaining were intimidated.

That was, after all, one of the realities of life in the Empire; lead, follow, and barricade yourself against assassins.

And the first in line for elimination would be Tremane—if Melles were named successor.

Charliss knew this. So did Tremane. It made the situation all the more piquant.

Interestingly enough, if Tremane succeeded and attained the coveted prize, it was not likely that he would remove Melles. Nor would he dispose of any of the other candidates. Rather, he would either win them over to his side or find some other way to neutralize them—perhaps by finding something else, creating some other problem for them, that required all their attention.

Charliss had used both ploys in the past, and on the whole, he preferred subtlety to assassination. Still, there had been equally successful Emperors in the past who ruled by the knife and the garrote. Difficult times demanded difficult solutions, and one of those times could be upon them.

The entire situation gave Charliss a faint echo of the thrill he had felt back at the beginning of his own reign, when he first realized he truly *did* have the power of life and death over his underlings and could manipulate their lives as easily as the puppeteer manipulated his dolls. It was amusing to present Tremane with a gift of a sword—with a needle-studded, poisoned grip. It was doubly amusing to know that Melles, at least, would recognize this test for what it was, and would be watching Tremane just as avidly from a distance, perhaps sending in his own agents to try and undermine his rival, and attempting to consolidate his own position here at court.

The jockeying and scrabbling was about to begin. It should produce hours of fascination.

Charliss watched Tremane closely, following the ghosts, the shadows of expressions as he thought all this through and came to the same conclusions. There was no chance that he would refuse the appointment, of course. Firstly, Tremane was a perfectly adequate military commander. Secondly, refusing this appointment would be the same as being defeated; Melles would have the reward of becoming successor, and Tremane's life would be in danger.

It took very little time for Tremane to add all the factors together to come to the conclusions that Charliss had already thought out. He bowed quickly.

"I cannot tell my Emperor how incredibly flattered I am by his trust in me," he said smoothly. "I can only hope that I will prove worthy of that trust."

Charliss said nothing; only nodded in acknowledgment.

"And I am answerable only to *you*, my Emperor? Not to any other, military or civilian?" Tremane continued quickly.

"Have I not said as much?" Charliss waved a hand. "I am certain you will need all the time you have between now and tomorrow morning, Grand Duke. Packing and preparations will probably occupy you for the rest of the day. I will have one of the Court Mages open the Portal for you to the Hardornen front just after you break your fast tomorrow morning."

"Sir." Tremane made the full formal bow this time; he knew a dismissal even when it was not phrased as one. Charliss was very pleased with his demeanor, especially given the short notice and the shorter time in which to make ready for his departure. There were no attempts to argue, no excuses, no plaints that there was not enough time.

Tremane rose from the bow, backing out of the room with his eyes lowered properly. Charliss could not find fault with his posture or the signals his body gave; his demeanor was perfect.

The great doors opened and closed behind him. Alone once again in the Throne Room, Emperor Charliss, ruler of the largest single domain in the world, leaned to one side and chuckled into the cavernous chamber.

This would be the most enjoyable little playlet of his entire reign, and it came at the very end, when he had thought he had long since exploited the entertainment value of watching his courtiers scramble about for the tidbits he tossed them. But here was a juicy treat indeed, and the scramble would be vastly amusing.

Charliss was pleased. Entertainment on this scale was *hard* to come by!

2

Steam curled up from the water as An'desha gingerly lowered himself into the soaking-pool of Firesong's miniature Vale. *A Vale in the heart of Valdemar—no larger than a single Gathering-tent. I would not have believed that such a thing was possible, much less that it could be done with so little magic—yet here it is.*

It was amazing how much could be created without the use of any magic at all. Most of this enchanted little garden had been put together by ordinary folk, using non-magical materials. There were only two exceptions; the huge windows, and the hot pools. The windows were not the tiny, many-paned things with their thick, bubbly glass, that An'desha had seen in all of the Palace buildings, which would not have done at all for the purpose. These eight windows, two to each side of the room, went from floor to ceiling in a single flawless triangular piece. Each had been made magically by Firesong, of the same substance used by the Hawkbrothers for the windows in their tree-perching *ekeles*. He had also created a magical source for the hot water for the pools. The rest, this garden that bloomed in the dead of winter, and the pseudo-*ekele* above it, was all built by ordinary folk, mainly due to Firesong taking shameless advantage of the Queen of Valdemar's gratitude and generosity.

Firesong felt that if he *must* remain here as the Tayledras envoy to primitive Valdemar, then by the Goddess, he would have the civilized amenities of a Vale!

Valdemar. An'desha had never heard of this land until a year ago. As a child and even a young man among the Clans, he had not heard of much beyond the Walls; indeed, the only places beyond the Walls he had learned of as a youngster were the Pelagiris Forest and the trade-city of Kata'shin'a'in. The Shin'a'in as a general rule cared very little for the world beyond the Plains; only Tale'sedrin of all the Clans had any measure of Outland and outClan blood.

In some Clans—such as An'desha's—such foreign breeding was occasionally considered a minor disgrace—not a disgrace for the child, but for the Shin'a'in parent. "Could he not draw to him a single woman of the Plains?" would come the whispers, or "Was she so unpleasant that no Shin'a'in man cared to partner her?" So it had been for An'desha, child of such an alliance—and perhaps that was why his own Clan had never so much as mentioned the lands outside the Dhorisha Plains. Perhaps they had feared that talking about the lands Outside would excite an un-Shin'a'in wanderlust in him, a yearning for far places and strange climes.

Well, I found both—without really wanting either.

The blood-path Adept who had flamboyantly named himself Mornelithe Falconsbane had never heard of Valdemar, either, until the two white-clad strangers from that land had come into the territory of Clan k'Sheyna of the Hawkbrothers.

An'desha had been a silent, frightened passenger in his own body, which Falconsbane had usurped by magic and trickery. With the Adept possessing him, he had learned just who those strangers were and something of their land. He'd had no choice in the matter, since he was a hidden fugitive within the body that Falconsbane had stolen years ago.

He should have died; that was what always happened before, when Falconsbane took a body. But he hadn't; perhaps the reason was that he had fled, rather than trying to resist the interloper.

A prisoner in my own body... He closed his eyes and sank a measure deeper into the hot water. So odd... the memories of those years of hiding, when he had no control over the actions of his own body, seemed more solid and real than this moment, when the body he had been born into was once again his.

An'desha's had been only the last in a long series of bodies Falconsbane had appropriated as his own. All that was required, or so it seemed, was for the victim to be gifted with mage ability and to have been a descendant of a mage called Ma'ar. If those remote memories were to be trusted, Ma'ar had lost his first life—or body, depending on

22

your point of view—in the Mage Wars of so long ago it made An'desha dizzy to think about the passage of years between that moment and this.

He slipped down to his chin into the hot water, and closed his eyes tighter, letting the steam rise around his face. *His* face now, and not the half-feline face of Mornelithe Falconsbane. His own body, too, for the most part, though it was more muscular now than it had been when Falconsbane helped himself to it and tried to destroy the original owner. Falconsbane had made a hobby of body sculpting, trying out changes on his daughter before adopting them himself. He had indulged in some extensive modifications to An'desha's body, changes An'desha had been certain he would have to endure even after Falconsbane had been driven out and destroyed.

But his own actions, risking real soul-death to rid the world of Falconsbane, had earned him more than just his freedom. Not only had he regained his body, most of the modifications had vanished when the Avatars of the Goddess "cured" him of what had been done to him.

There were only two things they could not give him again; the original colors of his hair and eyes. His hair was a pure, snowy white now, and his eyes a pale silver, both bleached forever by the magic energies that Falconsbane had sent coursing through this body, time and time again. So now, when An'desha gazed into a mirror, it always took a moment to recognize the reflection as his own.

At least I see the face of a half-familiar stranger, and not that of a beast. However handsome that beast had made himself.

The hot water forced his muscles to relax some, but he feared he would have to resort to stronger measures to release all the tension.

This place is so strange... Let Firesong wallow in being the exotic and sought-after alien; An'desha was *not* comfortable here. The only people he really knew were Nyara, the mage-sword Need, and Firesong, the Tayledras Adept. Of the three, the only one he spent any time at all with was Firesong. Nyara was very preoccupied with her mate, the Herald called Skif—and at any rate, it was hard to face her, knowing she was the offspring of his body when Falconsbane had worn it, knowing what his body had done to hers. Now that the crisis was over, Nyara seemed to feel the same way; although she was never unkind, she often seemed uncomfortable around him.

As for the ancient mage-sword that housed the spirit of an irreverent and crotchety sorceress, the entity called Need had her nonexistent hands full. She was engrossed in training Nyara, helping *her* adjust to this new land. Need was quite used to adjusting to new situations; she had been doing so for many centuries; in this, he had nothing in common with her.

After seeing changes over the course of a few hundred years, I would imagine that there is very little that surprises her anymore.

And as for Firesong—

He flushed, and it wasn't from the heat of the water cradling him. *I don't understand,* he thought, his logic getting all tangled up with his feelings whenever he so much as thought about Firesong. *I just don't understand. Why this, and why Firesong?* Not that the Shin'a'in had any prejudice about same-sex pairings, but An'desha had *never* felt even the tiniest of stirrings for a male before this. But Firesong—oh, Firesong was quickly becoming the emotional center of his universe. Why?

Firesong. Ah, what am I to do? Is he my next master?

His thoughts circled, tighter and tighter, like a hawk caught in an updraft, until he physically shook himself loose. He splashed warm water on his face and sat up straighter.

Don't get unbalanced. Concentrate on ordinary things; deal with all of this a little at a time. Think of ordinary things, peaceful things. They keep telling you not to worry, to rest and recover and relax.

He opened his eyes and deliberately focused on the garden around him, looking for places that might seem a little barren, a trifle unfinished. He had discovered a surprising ability in himself. It was surprising, because the nomadic Shin'a'in were not known for growing much of anything, and Falconsbane had been much more partial to destroying rather than creating when *he* had been active.

I never thought I'd be a gardener. I thought that was something only Tayledras did. He *loved* the feel of warm earth between his fingers; seeing a new leaf unfold gave him as much pleasure as if he had created a poem. Though the plants were cold and alien, in their own way they were like him. They struck a chord in him the way open sky and waving grass inspired his ancestors, and the scent of fresh greenery renewed him. An'desha had an affinity with ornamental plants, with plants of all kinds now, and a patience with them that Firesong lacked. The Adept enjoyed the effect of a finished planting, but he was not interested in creating it, nor in nurturing it. Though Firesong had dictated the existence of the indoor garden, planned the general look of it, and sculpted the stones, it was An'desha who had filled it with growing things, and given it life. In a sense, this fragile garden was An'desha: body, mind, and soul.

An'desha had not confined his efforts to the indoor garden surrounding the pools, hot and cold, and the waterfall that Firesong had created here. He had extended the plantings to cold-hardy species outside the windows, deciding that as long as the windows were that tall, there was no reason why he couldn't create the illusion that the indoor garden extended out into the outdoors. So, for at least the part of the year when the outside gardens were still green, this could have been a shady grotto in any Tayledras Vale.

The illusion was not quite perfect, and An'desha studied the intersection of indoors and outdoors, frowning slightly. He had matched the pebbled pathway between the beds of ornamental grasses indoors and out, but the eye still saw the windowpane before the vegetation outside it. He moved to the smooth rock edge of the pool and laid his chin down on his crossed arms to study it further.

There must be a way to make the window more of an accidental interruption to the flow of the gardens, the sweep of the planting.

Bushes, he decided. *If I have some bushy plants in here, and more that will outline a phantom pathway beyond the glass, that will help the illusion.* With just a little magical help, he'd accelerate the growth of a few more cuttings, and he'd have them at the right height in a week or two.

If I use evergreens, perhaps I can even take the edge off the transition between indoors and outdoors even in winter.

He had worried when Firesong came up with these clever ideas that the original "owners" of this bit of property might object to all the changes. Firesong's little home was in the remotest corner of a vast acreage called "Companion's Field," and the horselike beings that partnered the Heralds of Valdemar could very well have objected to their privacy being invaded. But they didn't seem to mind the presence of the Adept and his compatriots; in fact, they had contributed to the landscaping with suggestions of their own that made the *ekele* blend in with the surroundings, just as any good *ekele* should. From outside, the mottled gray and brown stone of the support pillars blended with the trunks of the trees masking it, and the second story was hidden among the branches. Firesong had chosen this particular place after he had heard of a legend that told of a Herald Vanyel, supposedly Firesong *and* Elspeth's ancestor, trysting with his beloved in this very grove of trees; after that, nothing would do but that his own *ekele* be here as well.

Firesong had insisted on building his "nest" in Companion's Field in the first place, rather than in the Palace gardens, precisely because he did not want any hint of the alien buildings of Valdemar to jar on his awareness.

Strange. I would have thought that Darkwind would be the one to feel that way, not Firesong. Darkwind was a scout; at one point, he could not even bear to live within the confines of a Vale! But Darkwind dwells quite comfortably in the Palace with the Queen's daughter, and it is Firesong who insists on removing himself to the isolation of this place.

Then again, Firesong was a law unto himself; he could afford to dictate even to a Queen in her own Palace how he would and would not live. Firesong was the most powerful practicing Adept in this strange land, and he did not seem to have a moment's hesitation when it came to exploiting that fact. Eventually Elspeth and Darkwind might come to be his equals in power, but he had been a full Adept from a very tender age, and had a great deal more experience than either the k'Sheyna Hawkbrother or the Valdemaran Herald.

And perhaps he has isolated himself for my sake, and not his own. That could very well be the case. An'desha stared into the tree-shadows on the other side of the window, and sighed.

He, more than anyone else, knew just how tenuous his stability was. For all intents and purposes, he was *still* the young Shin'a'in of fifteen summers who had run away from his Clan in order to be schooled in magic by the Shin'a'in "cousins," the Hawkbrothers. For most of his tenure within Falconsbane's mind, he had no more than brief glimpses of what Falconsbane had been doing. He had no real experience of those years; he might just as well never have lived them. In a very real sense, he hadn't. Most of the time he had been hidden in the darkness, snatching only covert glimpses of what Falconsbane was doing. *I was afraid he'd sense me watching through his eyes—and what he was doing was horrible.*

If he chose, he *could* delve into Falconsbane's memories now; mostly, he did not choose to do so. There was too much there that still made him sick; and it all frightened him with the thought that Falconsbane might *not* be gone after all. Hadn't *he* hidden within the depths of Falconsbane's mind for years without the Dark Adept guessing he was there? What was to keep the far more experienced and practiced Adept from having done the same? He had only Firesong's word that Mornelithe Falconsbane had been destroyed for all time. Firesong himself admitted he had never before seen anything like the mechanism Falconsbane had used for his own survival. How *could* Firesong be so certain that Falconsbane had not evaded him at the last moment? An'desha lived each moment with the fear that he would look into the mirror and see Mornelithe Falconsbane staring out of his eyes, smiling, poised to strike. And this time, when he struck at An'desha, there would be no escape.

Firesong was teaching An'desha the Tayledras ways of magic, and every lesson made that fear more potent. It had been magic that brought Falconsbane back to life; could more magic not do the same?

But by the same token, An'desha was as afraid of not learning how to control his powers as he was of learning their mysterious ways. Firesong was a Healing Adept; surely he should be the best person of all to help An'desha bind up his spiritual wounds and come to terms with all that had happened to him. Surely, if there were physical harm to his mind, Firesong could excise the problem. Surely An'desha would flower under Firesong's nurturing light.

Surely. If only I were not so afraid...

Afraid to learn, afraid not to learn. There was an added complication as well, as if An'desha needed any more in his life. The first time he had voiced his temptation to let the magic lie fallow and untapped within him, Firesong had told him, coolly and dispassionately, that there was no choice. He *must* learn to master his magics. Falconsbane never possessed a descendant who was anything less than Adept potential. That potential did not go away; it probably could not even be forced into going dormant.

In other words, An'desha was still possessed of all the scorching power-potential of Mornelithe Falconsbane, an Adept that even *Firesong* would not willingly face without the help of other mages. The power remained quiescent within the Shin'a'in, but if An'desha were ever faced with a crisis, he might react instinctively, with only such training as he vaguely recalled from rummaging through Falconsbane's memories.

On the whole, that was not a good idea. Especially if the objective was to keep anything in the area alive.

To wield the greater magics successfully, the mage must be confident in himself and sure of his own abilities, else the magic could turn on him and eat him alive. Falconsbane had no lack of self-confidence; unfortunately, that was precisely the quality that An'desha lacked.

I cannot even bear to meet all the strangers here, and it is their land we dwell in! Stupid of course; they would not eat him, nor would they hold Falconsbane's actions against *him.* But the very idea of leaving this sheltered place and walking the relatively short distance to the Palace, crowded with curious strangers, made him want to crawl under the waterfall and not come out again.

27

So he remained here, protected, but cowering within that protection.

He found it difficult to believe that no one here would hold against him the evil Falconsbane had done. *He* had such difficulty facing those stored memories that he could not imagine how people could look at him and not be reminded of the things "he" had done.

And I don't even know the half of them… the most I know are the things he did to Nyara. The truth was, he didn't want to know what Falconsbane had done—never mind that Firesong kept insisting that he must face every scrap of memory eventually. Firesong told him, over and over again, that he *needed* to deal with every act, however vile, and mine it for its worth.

He decided that he had stewed enough in the hot water; any more, and he was going to look like cooked meat. There were no helpful little *hertasi* here in Valdemar to attend to one's every need—a fact Firesong complained of bitterly—but An'desha had grown up in an ordinary Shin'a'in Clan on the Plains. That was a place where if a person did not do things for himself—unless he was incapacitated and needed help—they did not get done. He had brought his own towels and robes to leave beside the pool, with extras for Firesong when he should reappear, and made use of those now.

This hot pool was the mirror image of a cold one on the other side of the garden. It had a smooth backrest of sculptured rock, taller than the user's head; hot water welled up from a place in the center of the pool, and a waterfall showered cooler water down from above, from an opening at the top of the backrest. The whole was surrounded by screening "trees" and curtains of vines; Firesong did not particularly care if someone wandered by and got an eyeful, but An'desha was not so uninhibited.

Firesong's white firebird flew gracefully across the garden room as he climbed out of the pool and dried himself off. It landed beside the smaller, cooler pool that supplied the waterfall, in a bowl Firesong had built for it to bathe in. It plunged in with the same enthusiasm as the humblest sparrow, sending water splashing in all directions as it flapped and rolled in the shallow rock basin. When it finally emerged from its bath, it looked terrible, as if it had some horrible feather disease, and its wings were so soaked it could scarcely fly. It didn't even bother to try; it just hopped up onto a higher perch to preen itself dry with single-minded concentration. Hawkbrothers usually had specially-bred raptors as bondbirds, but in this, as in all else, Firesong was an exception.

An'desha got along quite well with the bird, whose name was Aya; especially after he had coaxed some berrybushes the bird particularly craved to grow, blossom, and bear fruit out of season in this garden. Aya was happy here; he did not seem to miss the Vales at all.

Even the firebird felt more at home here than he did.

He recognized the fact that he was feeling sorry for himself, and he didn't much care. The firebird paused in its preening, as if it had read his thoughts, and gave him a look of complete disgust before shaking out its wet tail and turning its back on him.

Well, let it. The firebird had never had its body taken over by a near-immortal entity of pure filth, had it?

He dried his hair and wrapped himself up in his thick robe, then went off to one part of the garden he considered his very own.

In the southwestern corner of the garden, near the window, he had planted a row of trees screening a mound of grass off from the rest of the garden. In that tiny patch of lawn he had pitched a very small tent, tall enough to stand in, but no wider than the spread of his arms. It wasn't quite a Shin'a'in tent, and it certainly wasn't weatherproof, but that hardly mattered since it was always summer in this garden. Here, at least, he could fling himself down on a pallet, look up at a roof of canvas, and see something that resembled home. And as long as he made no sound, there was no way to know whether or not the tent was occupied. Firesong had made no comment about the tent, perhaps understanding that he *needed* it, even as Firesong needed some semblance of a Vale.

A strand of his own damp white hair tangled itself up in his fingers as he pushed open the tent flap, and he shook it loose impatiently. White hair—he looked Tayledras. Just as Tayledras as Firesong or Darkwind. There was no way that anyone would know he was Shin'a'in unless he told them. Was there a reason for that? Firesong had told him it was because of the magic, but if the Star-Eyed had chosen, She *could* have given him back his native coloring. For a little time, at least.

He sat down on the pallet; it was covered with a blanket of Shin'a'in weaving—a gift from a Herald, who'd bought it while on her far-away rounds—and it still smelled faintly of horse, wood smoke, and dried grasses. The scent was enough, if he closed his eyes, to make him believe he was home again.

If the Star-Eyed could remake my body, couldn't She have taken away the magic, too?

Magic. For a long time, he'd wanted to be a mage. Now he wished She had taken his magic away, but there was always a reason why She did or did not do something.

He stared at the canvas walls, glowing in the late afternoon sun coming through the windows, and chewed his lower lip.

If She left me with magic, it is because She wants me to use it for some reason that only She knows. Firesong keeps saying it's my duty to do this, to Her as well as to myself. He felt a flash of hot resentment at that. Hadn't he risked everything to defeat Falconsbane—not just the pain and death of his body, but the destruction of his soul and his self? Wasn't that *enough?* How much more was he going to have to do?

Then he flushed with shame and a little apprehension, for he was not the only one to have risked all on a single toss of the dice. What of those who had dared penetrate to Ancar's own land to rid the world of Ancar, Hulda, and Falconsbane? If Elspeth had been captured, she would have been taken by Ancar for his own private tortures and pleasures. Ancar had hated the princess with a passion that amounted to obsession and, given the depravities that Falconsbane had overheard the servants whispering about, Elspeth would have endured worse than anything An'desha had faced.

Then there was Darkwind. Falconsbane hated Darkwind k'Sheyna more than any human on the face of the world, and only a little less than the gryphons. If Darkwind had been captured, his fate would have been similar to the one Elspeth would have suffered. And as for Nyara—

Nyara's disposition would have depended on whether or not King Ancar had recognized her as Falconsbane's daughter. If he had, he would have known she represented yet another way to control the Dark Adept, and she might have been kept carefully to that end. But if not— if Ancar had given her back to her father—

She would have been wise to kill herself before that happened. In her case, it would not have been hate that motivated atrocity, but the rage engendered by having a "possession" revolt and turn traitor. Motivation aside, the result would have been the same.

As for Skif and Firesong, the former would have been recognized as one of the hated Heralds and killed out of hand; the latter? Who knew? Certainly Falconsbane *and* Ancar would have been pleased to get their hands on an Adept, and given enough time, anyone could be broken and used, even an Adept of the quality of Firesong.

No, he was not the only person who had risked everything to bring Falconsbane down, so he might as well stop feeling sorry for himself. Still, it hurt.

That was precisely what Firesong would likely tell him, if Firesong had been there, instead of teaching young Herald-Mages the very basics of their Gift.

Firesong... Once again, a wave of mingled embarrassment and desire traveled outward in an uncomfortable flush of heat. Somehow Firesong had gone from comforter to lover, and An'desha was not quite certain how the transition had come about. For that matter, he didn't think Firesong was quite sure how it had happened. It certainly made a complicated situation even more so.

Not that I needed complications.

He flung himself down on his back and stared at the peak of the tent roof. How did a person sort out a new life, a new home, a new identity, and a new lover, all at once?

It only made the situation more strained that the new lover was trying to be part of the solution.

Would it be easier if Firesong had been nothing more than a concerned stranger, perhaps even a tentative friend, as Darkwind or the two gryphons were?

He's being awfully patient, I suppose. Anyone else would have given up on me by now. Surely a stranger would have blown up at him more than once, have cursed him for his timidity, and consigned him to the ranks of those that could not be helped because they would not help themselves.

On the other hand, sooner or later Firesong's frustration was going to overcome his patience. He *wouldn't* be able to be impartial; he made no secret of the fact that he wanted, badly, for An'desha to reach his potential as a mage so that the two of them could enjoy a relationship of two equal partners, the kind that the gryphons had.

But is that what I want? Part of him longed for it with all his heart. Part of him shied away from the very idea. Firesong frightened him sometimes; the Healing Adept was so very certain of himself and what he wanted. *Sometimes I don't think he's had a single doubt in his life. How could I ever have anything in common with someone like him?* Powerful, charismatic, blindingly intelligent, and handsome enough to be a young god, Firesong was everything An'desha had imagined he *could* be, back in that long-ago day when he had run away from his Clan. No longer; he had endured too much, and he could never be that naive or hopeful again.

But Firesong *was* all those things. He would *never* lack for bed partners. An'desha could not imagine someone like Firesong being willing to wait around on the mere chance that a frail Shin'a'in half-breed *might*, one day, regain some of the spirit he had lost. Why should he? Why should he waste precious time that way?

And yet—

He's kind, he's patient. In fact, Firesong had been coaxing, courting, and cajoling him with a gentle awkwardness that seemed to bespeak a distinct lack of practice in those three skills. *Then again, why would he ever need to coax or court anyone? He could have anyone he wanted, I'd think. They must be throwing themselves at his feet, over there in the Palace.* So it was all the more confusing that Firesong was willing to take the time to lead An'desha along like a spooked and frightened colt, time he could, without a doubt, spend more pleasurably elsewhere, with other people.

His thoughts muddled together at that point. He didn't *want* to consider all the ramifications of this. He didn't *want* to think that Firesong meant everything he had said in the dark of the night. He certainly didn't want that kind of devotion.

Did he?

This was getting him nowhere. Rather than face further uncomfortable thoughts, he rose from his pallet and took himself back out into the garden.

The firebird had preened all the water from its feathers, and busily fluffed them, holding its wings away from its body in order to make certain that they dried fully. The bird paid no attention to him as he passed it and went to the far side of the garden, and the wrought-iron staircase that led to the second floor and the *ekele* he shared with Firesong.

He climbed the stairs and emerged in the middle of the central room of the *ekele,* a room intended for socializing. This room looked exactly like the "public" room of any Tayledras *ekele;* it was light and open despite little free floor space, furnished with a number of flat cushions for sitting and lounging, a pair of perches for bondbirds, and some low tables. The floor was a herringbone pattern of two different hardwoods, amber and pale honey.

An'desha passed through this room to reach his own room, one draped with cloth against all the walls, and gathered up in the middle of the ceiling, supposedly to resemble a Shin'a'in tent. Firesong's idea, and he couldn't spoil Firesong's pleasure by telling him it no more looked like the inside of a Shin'a'in tent than the Palace gardens looked like a Vale. It contained the chests that held his clothing, the few personal possessions that he had managed to accumulate, and a more comfortable bed than the pallet in the tent in the garden. He didn't use the bed much, except to lie on and think.

He pulled aside the cloth covering the windows on the outer wall, and looked out into the branches of the tree just outside. He found himself wondering if that story Firesong had heard was true—and if it was, how had it ended? In tragedy, or in happiness?

And how could it matter to me, either way? Oh, I think too much.

He turned back into the room, dropped the robe, and pulled out a shirt and breeches from the chest that held his clothing, pulling them on and trying to ignore the slightly odd cut. These were not Shin'a'in, and there was no getting around the fact. They would never feel exactly "right."

But it was clothing, and it worked very well; it didn't matter if it felt like Shin'a'in clothing or not.

He turned back to the window—

And suddenly, out of nowhere, *the fear* came again. Not one of the stupid, personal fears, but something much, much greater. He clung to the windowsill with both hands as the sunlight turned as chill as a blizzard sweeping across the Plains, and his teeth chattered as he shook from head to toe, unable to move, scarcely able to draw a breath. His stomach clenched; his jaws locked on a cry of anguish. His heart thundered in his ears, and he wanted only to run, mad with terror, until he couldn't run any farther.

Something is wrong...

Then, abruptly, the fear left him, gasping for breath, as it always did.

But the message remained.

Firesong sat under a crocus-patterned lantern in the gathering dusk, scratching the crest of his firebird. The bird weighed down his other arm, its eyes closed with pleasure, and Firesong's eyes were distant as he concentrated on An'desha's hesitant words.

"...it was the same as the last time," An'desha concluded, the memory of that terror calling up a chill all over again. "That's three times now, and the circumstances I was in were different all three times."

Firesong nodded slowly, brushing a lock of white hair back behind his neck. The firebird slitted one sleepy eye in disapproval, until Firesong's hand came back to scratch his crest again. "I don't think this is coming from within you," he said, as a night-blooming flower beside An'desha released perfume into the air. "I believe your own impression is right; there is a menace approaching that we are not yet aware of, and this feeling of fear of yours is a presentiment."

An'desha sighed with relief; the first two times that this had happened, Firesong had been inclined to think it was nothing more than a delayed reaction to all that An'desha had been through. Still, he was troubled. "F-F-Falconsbane had no such prescience," he stammered.

Firesong only shrugged. "Falconsbane never wished to know the future," he pointed out. "He assumed it would follow the course that *he* set. And you are not he; the Star-Eyed could well have granted you such a gift along with all else."

A very real possibility and, if so, it was yet another "gift" he wished that She would take back. His face must have reflected that thought since Firesong smiled slightly.

"The most likely direction for threat is east, of course," he continued. "This Empire that the Valdemarans fear so much is rich with mages; I think it likely that they will not end their conquest at the Hardorn border."

As An'desha sat there dumbly, Firesong expanded his speculations. The Empire *was* a good prospect; the Adept was right about that. But An'desha could not rid himself of the surety that the danger was not coming from the Empire.

This was something more than mere warfare; something much, much worse.

When I was still hiding in Falconsbane's body, and the two Avatars of the Star-Eyed came to teach me the way toward freedom, did they not say something about this?

Now that he came to think about it, he believed that they *had*. He had been guided by a pair of spirits, who had once been fleshly. One had been a Hawkbrother, the other, a Shin'a'in shaman. They had helped and taught him how to gradually insinuate himself into his enemy's mind in such a way that Falconsbane thought the thoughts directing his actions were his own. They had also taught him how to gain access to the memories of Falconsbane's many pasts.

At least once, and perhaps more often, they had hinted that if he succeeded in regaining the use of his own body again, there was an even greater peril to be faced.

If only he could remember what they had said! But he had been too busy worrying about his own survival to pay much attention to vague hints of terrible danger to come. He'd had quite enough terrible danger on his plate at the time!

Firesong continued his speculations concerning the threat of this Empire, and he tried in vain to suggest that the peril *might* be coming from elsewhere. Finally, he just gave up; when Firesong had the bit between his teeth about something, there was no hope for anyone else to get anything in. It was best to just nod thoughtfully and let him continue to expound.

But inside, his thoughts had a new target to circle around in worried, dizzy spirals. The danger was *not* from the East, but from where? What could be worse than an army, full of powerful mages and larger than anything Valdemar had ever seen, bearing down on the border?

If only he could remember...

3

Karal patted his horse's damp neck nervously and tried not to be too obvious about watching the Valdemaran Guards out of the corner of his eye. The horse fidgeted and danced in place as it picked up his unease, and he dismounted to hold it by its halter, just under the chin. It snuffled his chest but calmed as soon as he got down on the ground beside its head; a light, warm breeze played across both of them, gradually drying the horse's sweating neck.

He continued to stroke it, his nose full of horse scent, the familiar aroma calming his own nerves. Nothing really bad had ever happened to him when he was around horses, and he kept reminding himself of that, holding it to him as if he held to a luck-talisman.

This was a good little gelding, and someone had trained it well before tithing it to Vkandis Sunlord. The sun shone on a perfect, glossy coat, skin without scars or disease, an eye bright with intelligence. Karal had no idea why the gelding's first owner had sent it in as part of his tithe, but it was obviously someone who took his duty to the Sunlord seriously, sending "the first and best fruits of his labor" as the Writ urged, rather than trying to cheat as so many did, sending only the unwanted and unusable.

A good thing for both of us that they did, Trenor.

The gelding was too small and light to go to the cavalry, and too nervous for a scout or skirmisher, so it had gone to the Temple. Karal had known quality horseflesh when he saw it, and requisitioned this youngster the moment his master and mentor suggested that he was entitled to a mount of some kind from the Temple herds.

This gelding was a lovely bay, otherwise perfect except for the slight flaw of high-bred nerves, and he'd named it after his little brother Trenor, who danced in place in much the same way when he was nervous. Trenor the gelding was, without a doubt, the best piece of horseflesh currently in the novices' stables, and every time he rode the gelding, Karal gloated a little under the envious eyes of his fellow novices. None of them were mounted nearly as well as he, although the horses they had requisitioned might look more impressive than little Trenor. *They* were gentlemen for the most part, and were certainly above choosing their own mounts—assuming any of them could tell a spavined breakdown from a sweet little palfrey like this one. And none of them would have stooped to asking for *his* advice. Doubtless, they had sent servants down to the stables, with orders to select beasts "suited to their station." Well, they paid the penalty of pride in their rumps, every time they rode, for the rest of the horses in the stables were a collection of sorry misfits. Most of them were showy pieces, huge creatures with long manes and tails, rejected from some noble warrior's string. Yes, they were lovely to look at, shiny and high-stepping, but they had iron mouths, bad tempers, or gaits that were pure torture to sit.

Not that all these traits were incurable. Karal could have settled an iron mouth or a bad temper quickly enough—but why should he, when his fellow novices neither asked for his help nor deserved it? Let the others suffer; Sunlord knew they'd made *him* suffer in other ways all through his training.

But that was behind him now. By the time he completed this assignment as his mentor's secretary, he would be a full Priest of Vkandis, and the equal of anyone in Karse save the Son of the Sun herself. *No one* could deny him that rank, no matter what his antecedents were.

He squinted up at the sun in the cloudless sky above. *We are all equal in Vkandis' Light,* he reminded himself. *Oh, surely, and cows will take to the air and soar like falcons any day now!*

Trenor tried to dance, this time with impatience, but Karal held him steady, and soothed him with a wordless croon. How long had it been since he'd seen the human version of this fidgeting bundle of nerves? Three years? No, it was only two.

But if this Valdemaran escort doesn't show up, he may be grown before we ever see home again!

It was an exaggeration, of course, but it felt as if he had been standing here for days beneath the carefully dispassionate gaze of these two young men in their blue and silver uniforms. He and Ulrich waited on a stretch of newly-cut road that was only a few leagues long, one of the tangible evidences of peace with Valdemar. These bits of roadway linked Karse and its former enemy, bridging the distance from a Karsite road to a Valdemaran one, and giving real traffic a place to cross. On the Karsite side was a gatehouse and a pair of guards where the old road joined the new one. On the Valdemaran side were facilities and guards nearly identical to their counterparts at the Karsite border-crossing behind him, except for the color and cut of the uniforms. The Valdemaran version seemed rather severe to Karal, accustomed as he was to the flowing scarlet and gold of the Karsite regulars, with the embroidered sashes of rank, feathered turbans, and brocaded vests. Plain tunics, plain breeches, only the tiniest bit of silver trim and braid... these men might have been mistaken for someone's lowest-rank servant, a stable sweeper or horseboy.

Like I was... even Father dressed more handsomely than these men do.

Karal's father had never worn such unadorned clothing in Karal's memory; the Chief Stableman of the Rising Sun Inn could boast beautifully embroidered garments from the hands of his loving wife and daughters. His pay might be meager enough, but he could put on a show fit to match anyone of his own station and even a little above. The clothing Karal had worn before the Sun-priests came for him had been plain enough, but he *had* been a stable sweeper, and anyway, he had only been nine. Not nearly a man, and in no way needing to prove his worth the way a man did.

I wish that there was some shade here. The sun that was so kind in the mountains, countering the chill of the breezes, was a burden here. His dark robes soaked it up and released none of the heat. But the situation was too new, too delicate, for any real amenities for the few who wished to cross from Valdemar to Karse. All brush and trees had been cut back from the road for a distance of twenty paces, so that the guards at either gatehouse had a clear view of anyone coming or going. Karal could understand that. This was not a job he would care to have, himself; the guards at the Karsite side were clearly nervous, and the ones here probably were as well. This was only the second time that he had seen a real Valdemaran up close, one of the Hellspawn themselves—

No, not Hellspawn. Her Holiness, the Son of the Sun, High Priest Solaris has said that was all a fiction created by corrupt priests. They are not Hellspawn, they never were. Just people, different from us, but people.

Hard to undo the thinking of a lifetime, though, and if it was hard for

37

him, it must be incredibly difficult for people like the officers in the Army. How must that be, to go to sleep, only to wake up the next day and find that your demonic enemies had become, by Holiest decree, your allies? To learn that they were not demonic at all, and never had been?

To discover that a terrible war that had killed countless thousands over the course of generations should never have taken place and *could have been ended* at any time?

Karal sighed, and his master Ulrich dismounted from his mount, a placid and reliable mule. Ulrich was no horseman, and moreover, he was a most powerful Priest-mage. He might need to work magic at any time, and needed a riding beast that would stand stock still when the reins were dropped, no matter what strangeness it heard or saw. The mule—which Ulrich called "Honeybee," for she was sweet, but had a sting in her tail in the form of a powerful kick when annoyed—was older than Karal, and looked to live and carry her master for the same number of years. Karal liked her, trusting her good sense to bring Ulrich through any common peril. Storms didn't spook her, uncanny visitations could not make her bolt, she knew when to fight and when to flee, and she was surefooted and wise in the way of trails and tracks.

But she was boring to ride, and while he could not have wanted a better mount for his master, she was the last one he would have chosen for himself.

"Patience, Karal," Ulrich said in an undertone. "Our escort is probably on his way this very moment, and will be surprised to see us waiting. We are early; it is not even Sunheight yet. You may worry when it lacks but a mark or two before Sundescending."

Karal bowed his head in deference to his master's words. Ulrich was surely right, yet—

"It seems ill-mannered, sir, to have us cool our heels at the border-crossing, when you *are* the envoy from Her Holiness," he said doubtfully. "And to send only a single escort—it seems a deliberate slight to me. Should we not have many guards, perhaps a Court Official, or—"

Ulrich raised his hand to halt his young protégé in mid-thought. "We are two, coming from the south, wearing the plain robes of some sort of priest," he pointed out. "If the Queen sent an escort of a score of her Guards, what would the obvious inference be? That we *are* envoys of Her Holiness, of course. There are perils along the way, not the least of which are those who will not believe that the war between our lands is over."

Ulrich waited patiently while Karal thought out the rest of the perils for himself. Mobs of angry border people, or even a single, clever madman could plan to kill old enemies; assassins hoping to eliminate the envoys and thus the alliance were a real possibility. Even mercenaries could try to slay the envoys, hoping to start up the war again and thus ensure continued employment. For that matter, the threat need not come from a citizen of Valdemar; it could come from someone from their own land, hoping to rekindle the flames of the "holy war against the Hellspawn."

Karal shook his head mournfully, and Ulrich just chuckled. "That, my son, is why I am envoy and you are a novice. *I* requested that we be met by but a single escort, though I also requested one who could be trusted completely. I fear that it takes years of being steeped in deception and infamy to recognize the possibility for both."

Ulrich patted Honeybee's neck, and she sighed. Ulrich nodded at the mounts, at their own equipage. At the moment he and Karal were wearing only the plainest of their robes for travel. "As we are, with a single escort—yes, we are dressed well, and clearly Priests from a foreign land, but we could be from *any* foreign land. Unless we have the misfortune to come across someone who has seen a Sun-priest, we should meet with no one who will recognize our robes or our medals. Valdemar is awash with foreigners these days, many of them being escorted to Haven even as we. I think that we shall not draw undue attention to ourselves."

Karal did not answer his mentor, but in this case, he thought privately that, for once, Ulrich might be wrong. He took another covert look at the Valdemaran guards, compared the Sun-priest with them, and came up with an entirely different answer than Ulrich's.

They were both dressed with relative modesty, compared to the magnificent garments they would don once they were in the capital city and the Palace, but there were still a myriad of ways that anyone who had ever seen a Karsite would know who and what they were.

They both wore their Vkandis-medals on gold chains, first of all, round gold disks blazoned with a sun-in-glory—and how many people of moderate importance ever wore that much gold? For that matter, *was* there another sect that used that particular blazon? Their garments had a cut peculiar to Karse; certainly Karal had never seen any foreigner attending Her Holiness who wore anything like the Karsite costume. And if they were of moderate importance, why send an escort at all?

Oh, I suppose I worry too much. Ulrich is right; if what we have heard is true, there are foreigners arriving daily who are so outlandish that we shall not even attract a second glance.

Ulrich was certainly not particularly remarkable; many novices passed him by every day, thinking him a Priest of no particular importance. He was, in fact, utterly ordinary in looks and demeanor—of middling height, neither very young nor very old, neither handsome nor hideous, neither muscular nor a weakling. His gray hair and beard and perpetually mild expression belied the sharpness of his eyes, and his expression could change in a moment from bemused and kindly to implacable. These Valdemarans seemed to be of no particular physical type; one of the guards was lean and brown, the other muscular and blond. Not so with the two Karsites, for both were typical of anyone from their land; Ulrich could easily have been Karal's hawk-faced father; they were two from the same mold, dark-haired, dark-eyed, sharp-featured.

Perhaps that was all to the good, too. Outsiders might assume that they *were* related. Better and better, in fact, since Karal doubted anyone outside Karse knew that the Sun-priests were *not* required to be celibate or chaste, though many of them swore such oaths for various reasons. So if he and Ulrich appeared to be father and son—it might be that no one would think they were priests of any kind.

Karal rubbed his temple; all this thinking was giving him a headache. Ulrich patted his shoulder with sympathy as the guards continued to ignore them.

"Don't worry about it too much, young one," the Sun-priest said, with a kindly gleam in his black eyes. "Try to get used to the new land first, before you devote any time to learning about intrigue and hidden dangers. There will be enough that is strange to you, I think, for some few days."

The Sun-priest—the Red-robe who was once one of the feared and deadly *Black*-robe priests of the Sunlord, a wielder of terrible power and commander of demons—looked back down the road they had come and sighed. "You have seen so many changes already in your short lifetime, I should think you will cope better with this new place than I. To you, this must seem like a grand new adventure."

Karal choked back a reply to *that;* little as he wanted to be sent off into this voluntary exile, he wanted still less to be sent home in disgrace. But he did *not* think of this as a "grand new adventure," nor any kind of an adventure; at heart, he was a homebody. His notion of a good life meant achieving some success as a scholar, perhaps finding a suitable partner among the ranks of the female Priests, growing older, wiser, and rich in children and grandchildren. Yes, he had seen changes aplenty since he had been taken from his own family at nine, and being subject to having his world turned upside down before he was twelve had not made him any readier for having it turn again at thirteen, fourteen, fifteen, or now, at sixteen.

In fact, most of the time lately he was just plain bewildered, and there were moments when the stress was so great that he feared it was visible to anyone who looked at him.

Is there not some barbarian curse that wishes your life be interesting? If so, then he should find the barbarian who had visited such a curse on him and persuade him to remove it! He found excitement enough in books for anyone's lifetime.

At nine, he had been his father's apprentice; a horseboy and stable sweeper, and supremely content with his position and the world. He loved horses, loved everything about them, and looked forward to rising to take his father's job when he was old enough. He had three sisters, two older and one younger, to tease and torment as any small boy would, and a little brother who toddled after him at every opportunity with a look of adoration on his chubby face. There was always food enough on the table, and if it was plain fare, well, there were folk enough who had not even that, and he knew it even then. He had been *happy* as he was. He had not wanted any changes that he could not foresee.

By now he had seen enough of other families to know how idyllic, in many ways, his own had been. Both his parents were as ready to praise as to reprimand, and no matter what mischief he had been into, he could count on forgiveness following repentance. His father was proud of him, and was teaching him everything *he* knew about horses and horseflesh. His world was full of things and people he loved; what more did any boy need?

There was only one cloud in all their lives—the annual Feast of the Children, when parents were ordered to bring their children to the Temple to be inspected by the Sun-priests. The examinations began when a child was five, and ended when he was thirteen. The Feast always brought suppressed terror to every parent in the town, but it was especially hard on Karal's father and mother, for both of them had had siblings who were taken away by the Priests, and were subsequently burned for the heresy of harboring "witch-powers." There was always the fear that one of their children might be taken—and worse still, might be given to the Fires. Even those who were not thrown to the Fires never saw their homes and families again, for that was the way of the Sun-priests. So it had "always" been.

For four years, the Priests had passed Karal over, and his father and mother had begun to lose a little of their fear, at least for his sake, if not for the sake of his younger siblings. Even he began to feel a cocky certainty that the Feast would never mean more to him than an occasion to claim a double handful of spun-sugar Vkandis Flames from the Priest's servants when the inspection was over.

But then, the year he was nine, his world and his certainty shattered.

A new Priest came to the Feast; a new Priest in black robes, rather than red, a Priest who watched him with narrowed eyes—

—and claimed him for the Sunlord.

One moment he had been standing with the others in a neat line, the next, a heavy hand came down on his shoulder, and two servants seized him before he could react, ushering him into the Temple, pushing him past the altar into the rooms beyond, where the townsfolk were never permitted, only those belonging to the Temple.

He didn't remember much of that day, or even of the following week, which might have been due to shock, or to the potion the Priest gave him to drink when he launched into hysterical tantrums. He had been the only child chosen from his town, and there was no one else he knew to share his ordeal and his exile. He vaguely remembered a long ride inside a dark wagon, which paused now and again so that another blank-eyed, stranger-child could join him on the bench. No spun-sugar for him or for them; only a bitter cup, a long period of shadow-haunted daze, and then the awakening in a strange and hostile place—the so-called Children's Cloister, where he and the others would live and study until they were accepted as novices or given duties as Servants.

Or until someone said they had witch-powers. He shuddered, cold creeping over him for a moment, as if the sun had lost its power to warm him.

In time, Karal came to accept what he could not change. He was told that he would never see his family again; that he was reborn into a new and greater family, the Kin of Vkandis. They allowed him time to rebel, one chance to *attempt* to run away. This was unsuccessful, as were all such attempts as far as he ever learned. A terrible creature of flame caught him at the gate, and chased him back to the Cloister. *He* never made a second attempt, though he heard that others did; he resigned himself to his fate.

Then began the lessons, hour after hour of them.

Most of the children did not master much more than the barest skills of reading and writing; those were sent, at ten, to become Servants. Some, a fraction of the rest, were taken off by the Priests for "special training" that had nothing to do with scholarly pursuits.

Some few of *those* were given to the Flames, later, as witches. Karal and the rest were required to attend the burnings, and he was told that the ashes were returned to their families as a mark of the disgrace to their bloodline. The three burnings he had witnessed still gave him nightmares.

For some reason, Karal did well in scholastic pursuits and did not again attract the attention of those who meted out "special training." He found a pure pleasure in learning that was as great as his pleasure in anything he had ever experienced. He soon outstripped most of the others who had originally been "collected for Vkandis" with him. This gained him admission to another group of young pupils—the offspring of nobles and the well-to-do, sent as their parents' tithe to Vkandis, children who had the advantage of tutoring from an early age. These had never before been forced to share teachers or quarters with those of the lower classes… they resented this new development in their lives, and needed someone to take their displeasure out on.

And that had opened him to a new series of torments—not overt, but covert. He pleased his teachers, and the young nobles could not cause him trouble in his classes, but *outside* those classes, he was fair game for any prank they could invent that would not call down the wrath of their Keeper on them.

He shook his head, driving away the unpleasant memories for now. *None of that mattered, then or now. I have to remember that.* What mattered was that he had graduated into the ranks of the novices with high honors, despite the opposition of the other students, and when the time came to be taken by a mentor, he was selected by that *same* Black-robed Priest who had singled him out at the Feast of the Children.

Only now he *knew* what those ebony robes meant. His new mentor was a Priest-mage, a user of magic in Vkandis' name, and a summoner of demons.

He would have been terrified, if Ulrich hadn't immediately shown his kindly nature. And every morning since that day, he had offered up a paean of gratitude with his other prayers that it had been Ulrich who had chosen him. His Master had rank enough that not one of his fellow novices dared to torment him further, though they could, and did, shut him out socially.

Not that he cared. His Master was a scholar, and set him scholarly tasks that suited his nature. When his Master learned of his background and his love of horses, he suggested he find himself a mount early enough that the horses and mules were not all picked over. Ulrich *made certain* he had time out, every day, to spend at least a mark or two with his beloved gelding, Trenor. For a week or two, everything was well; he thought for certain that the future was again predictable.

He had already suffered two upheavals in his life—being torn from his family and being shoved, will-he, nill-he, into the ranks of those born far, far above his station. Now he suffered the third, but this time, the entire Kin of Vkandis "suffered" along with him.

Vkandis—the God Himself—selected a *woman* to be the Son of the Sun, in a fashion that brooked no denial of the validity of her claim to the position. That woman, High Priest Solaris, proceeded to set the entire established hierarchy on its side, declaring things that *had* been established orthodoxy for generations to be perversions of Vkandis' Word and Will.

And Ulrich not only approved, he was in the thick of it all, as one of Solaris' most trusted aides and assistants. So, perforce, was his protégé.

Not that I was unhappy about that initially—not when one of the first things she did was to order that all novices and under-novices were to be permitted the same contact with their families that Army recruits had! Until that moment, no one taken by the Priests was ever permitted any contact with his family, even the most casual. Now he was able to write to them, even visit them twice a year, something that would have been unthinkable under the old Rules. In fact, when Solaris appointed Ulrich as her special envoy to Valdemar, she had taken the effort to order that Karal also take a week of special leave to see his family before he left with his Master. And when had a Son of the Sun ever concerned himself with something as trivial as the needs of a mere novice?

He stroked Trenor's neck soothingly, smiling to himself. The very first time he had gone home, the entire fortnight had been a wonderful visit. His mother had been so proud of him—and his father had been beside himself with pleasure. *His* son was secretary to a powerful Priest! *His* son was privy to all the secrets of the high and privileged! *His* son would see people and situations his father could only dream about.

But that had come later; no sooner had Solaris staged her internal revolution and he had returned from his first Familial Visit, than Karse acquired a new enemy, in the person of King Ancar of Hardorn. Ancar staged a major attack on the border; not in living memory had there been anything in the way of a concerted attack from Hardorn. The shock of the attack had reverberated throughout the entire country; to be honest, most Karsites were used to scoring small covert victories and raids against Hardorn and Valdemar, not having a concerted attack staged on their own borderlands.

The skirmishing had become all-out war, with Karse very much the weaker of the two. Not even the Black-robe Priests and their magic could counter Ancar, his army, and his mages.

Solaris had predicted this. Very few had believed her. Now, with her star in the ascendant, she made the most unprecedented move of all.

She recruited a new ally; one not even Ulrich could have predicted.

Valdemar. Valdemar, home of the White Demons and their Hellhorses. Valdemar, land of Hellspawn, land that had given shelter to the heretic Holderkin, sworn enemies of Vkandis and all he stood for.

And once again, Vkandis showed by signs that could not be counterfeited that He approved.

Suddenly, by decree of Solaris and Vkandis Himself, Valdemar had become the abode of the slightly misguided, but noble-minded allies of Karse. It was nothing short of a miracle that Solaris managed to get just enough cooperation out of her own folk to rush the alliance through. It was just in time, just barely in time to keep Ancar of Hardorn from squashing Solaris and Selenay like a couple of insects, and their lands and peoples with them.

As Ulrich's secretary, Karal had been in the midst of everything, from the initial plan to the complex negotiations to the investiture of a woman from Valdemar as a Vkandis Priest. It left him breathless, and so bewildered before it was all over that all he could do was to hold onto his sanity with both hands and watch with wide and often confused eyes. Now, with the advent of peace, it was harder than ever to encompass the notion that the Evil Ones were now to be Karse's best friends...

"I believe our escort is here," Ulrich said, breaking into Karal's thoughts.

He looked up, shading his eyes with his hand, staring past the gate and the two Guards to the roadway beyond. For a moment, he saw nothing against the glare of the sun on the dust of the road. Then he caught a glimpse of movement; his focus sharpened, and he spotted a rider coming around a far-off bend in the road.

The man could hardly be missed even against the sun glare; he was clad all in white, with a horse as white as the clouds in the sky above him.

This was no ordinary traveler; the quality of his clothing was very high—white garments were expensive to keep pristine. The garments he wore had the feeling of a uniform about them; Karal knew that the colors of Valdemar were silver, blue, and white. Was this Royal livery of some sort? As the man drew nearer still, Karal noted the extreme quality of his tack, specially dyed and constructed, of the same colors of silver and blue that the Guards wore. The Guards themselves were waiting for the man with a deference they had not shown the two Karsites, which in itself was interesting. Did this mean their escort was of higher rank than an envoy, or did it mean that no one had told these two Guards anything at all about Ulrich and his young secretary, not even that they were Solaris' envoys?

Well, it probably didn't matter at this point.

The man paused at the Gate, but he did not dismount; instead, he leaned over the neck of his mount to talk to the two Guards. Now Karal stole a moment to admire the horse he rode. The head was quite broad across the forehead, which argued for high intelligence. Aside from that—which some might consider a flaw, though Karal would not agree with them—the beast was breathtakingly beautiful. He had never seen a horse so perfectly white as this one, which gleamed as if someone had just washed it—and how on earth did the Valdemaran manage to get that silver sheen to the horse's hooves? Not paint, surely—paint would damage the hoof and deform it. No one but a fool would paint the hooves of a horse like this one.

As the rider spoke with the Guards, the horse shifted slightly, as if to watch the two Karsites. Its movements were as graceful as the horse itself was beautiful; it arched its neck so that its flowing mane fell just *so*, for all the world as if it knew how stunning it was.

Perfect. That was Karal's thought, and he reveled in the fact that he would be spending the next several days in the company of such a beast.

After a brief consultation with the Guards, the man in white beckoned to them. Now that he'd had his fill of watching the horse from afar, Karal was perfectly willing to mount Trenor and rein in behind Ulrich; he'd had enough waiting around to last him for quite a while!

It probably isn't going to be the last time I have to stand around and wait, though.

The escort had blond hair going to gray at the temples, a good, square jaw, deep-set, frank, hazel-colored eyes, and a nose that had obviously been broken more than once in the past. He sat his horse rather stiffly, which struck an odd note, given the grace of the horse itself.

The man hesitated for a moment, then held out his hand to Ulrich as they approached the gate. "Envoy Ulrich?" he said, as his horse stood rock-steady beneath him, showing no more inclination to shy away from strange beasts than if the horse were carved of pure alabaster. "I am your escort. Call me Rubrik, if you will."

It has blue eyes, Karal saw, with a surge of disappointment. Most blue-eyed, white creatures were stone deaf. Was this the flaw in this otherwise perfect mount? Certainly deafness would account for the horse's apparent calm.

Ulrich took the man's hand and shook it, as Honeybee eyed the blue-eyed white horse dubiously, probably expecting a nip or a kick from it.

The man's Karsite was excellent; much better than Karal's Valdemaran. He had very little accent, and when he spoke, there was no sense that he was stopping to translate mentally before saying anything.

"You speak our language very well, sir," Ulrich replied with grave courtesy, "and I hope you will accept my apology for not returning the compliment, but the truth is, I am nowhere near as fluent in your tongue as you seem to be in ours. This is my secretary, Karal."

The man held out his hand to Karal, who followed his mentor's example and shook it. Rubrik's clasp was firm and warm, without being a "test." Karal decided cautiously that he liked this Valdemaran.

Rubrik squinted up at the sun once he had released Karal's hand. "You have come a long way, and as I am sure you realize, there is a longer journey still ahead of you, Envoy," he told Ulrich. "Weather in Valdemar is still not so settled that I'd care to wager on clear skies for more than a day. I'd like to make as much distance as we can while the weather holds, if you've no objection."

Ulrich shook his head. "No objection whatsoever," he replied. "You are limited only to the number of leagues our two beasts are able to travel in a day; my secretary and I are good riders, and have no trouble spending dawn to dusk in the saddle, if you like."

Karal winced at that; *he* was not so sure of his endurance as Ulrich seemed to be. Hopefully, the man would not take him at his word.

Rubrik smiled warmly. "Your High Priest Solaris has chosen her envoy well, my lord," was his only reply. "If you would follow me?"

The trio passed the silent Guards, went through the open gate, and for the first time in his life, Karal entered a foreign land.

* * *

47

Karal had expected to feel—something—once he was across the border and in a new land. Some kind of difference in the air, or in himself. He'd expected that this alien place would *look* different from Karse somehow, that the grass and trees would be some odd color, that the people would be vastly different. There was no reason to have expected anything of the sort, of course—

—but emotions don't respond well to logic, I suppose.

As they rode northward all the rest of the day, there was literally no way of telling that they were not in Karse. The hills were virtually identical to the ones they had just traversed; covered with the same trees, the same grass. The scents in the air were the same; sun-warmed dust, the occasional perfume of briar-roses blooming beside the road.

The few people that they encountered were not really all that different either, except that it was obvious they were *not* Karsite. Their clothing was different; plain in the extreme, severely styled, in muted grays, browns, and tans. Mud-colors, really; no Karsite would ever wear such nothing-colors unless he were too abysmally poor to afford anything else, or unless he intended to do some truly filthy task and didn't want his proper clothing ruined. Even for work in the fields most Karsites wore good, strong saffrons and indigos—but not these folk.

They passed a number of folk cutting hay, one herding swine and another with a flock of geese, a few weeding fields of cabbages or other vegetables. The animals turned to watch the trio pass; the people themselves blatantly ignored the travelers, turning away from the road, in fact, in stiff and disapproving attitudes that bordered on rudeness. "Holderkin," Rubrik said, after the third or fourth time that someone deliberately turned his face from them. The escort sighed and shook his head. "I'm sorry about this. They don't like those of us who represent the Queen, much—hardly more than they like you Karsites. I do believe that if there was any way to manage it, they'd create their own little country here, build a high wall around it, and shut Valdemar *and* Karse outside forever and aye."

Ulrich laughed at that, and his eyes crinkled up at the corners with sympathetic good humor. "In that case, sir, I think my land well rid of them. I am marginally familiar with them, in a purely historical sense. They seem to have made themselves something of a thorn in your side."

Rubrik shrugged ruefully and rubbed the side of his nose. "I can't say that *no* good has come from them—the Queen's Own, Lady Talia, is of Holderkin breeding. But aside from that, they are a damned unpleasant people, and I've had occasion more than once to wish them somewhere far, far away."

Karal kept silent through this exchange, watching their escort, and trying to deduce why the man rode so stiffly. How was it that someone who seemed to be such a clumsy rider had such a fine mount? How was it that the mount was so used to the rider that the horse itself actually accommodated the rider?

Finally, as Rubrik turned to point out a wedge of geese flying overhead, pursued by a goshawk, the answer to all those questions came to him.

Rubrik's right arm moved stiffly; he could not seem to raise it above his shoulder. There was a "dead" quality to the right side of his face. And although his *right* knee stuck out woodenly, his left leg showed the perfect form of an experienced rider.

Rubrik was injured somehow—or he'd had some kind of brainstorm. He was partially paralyzed; the stiffness of his right side and the little tic in the corner of his right eye were the last clues that Karal needed.

Rubrik would have to have such a mount, one trained to compensate for *his* weakness, if he was to be at all mobile. Now Karal's admiration for the stunning horse increased a hundredfold, for a horse so trained must be as intelligent as one of the legendary Shin'a'in beasts.

His admiration turned to more surprise when he realized that Rubrik's horse was not a gelding as he had assumed, but a full stallion. A full stallion—one which showed no interest in Honeybee who, although a mule, was still a mare? What kind of training could ever give a horse that kind of self-control?

He would have asked just that question if Ulrich had not engaged their escort's attention completely, asking about some complex situation at the Valdemaran Court. A good half of the names Ulrich bandied about so casually completely eluded his secretary, although Karal recognized most of the rest from all the correspondence he had handled over the past few weeks.

I guess there was a lot more going on in those private conferences than Ulrich led me to believe. Not that *that* should surprise him!

He suppressed his own curiosity and simply listened to the two men talk, for this, too, was part of his job—to learn as much as he could by listening.

Eventually, either Ulrich tired of asking questions, or the envoy decided that he wanted to think about what he had learned before he asked anything more. By this time, the last of the farmlands were behind them; if anyone used the hills on either side of the road for anything, it was probably to harvest timber and for grazing. Silence fell on the party, broken only by the sounds of wildlife out in the forested hills, and by the sound of the hooves of their mounts.

That was when Karal noticed something else. While Trenor and Honeybee had perfectly normal, dull, clopping hoofbeats, the sounds of the white horse's hooves striking the ground had a bell-like tone to them.

Maybe the Valdemarans *did* treat the beast's hooves in some way; how else could they be silver and have such a musical sound to them?

The road they were on generally followed the contour of the land itself, staying pretty much in the valleys between the hills. Once in a while Karal caught a whiff of he-goat musk, or spotted the white blobs of grazing sheep among the trees. Forest rose on either side of the road; tall trees that had been growing for decades at least. In places the limestone bones of these hills showed through the thin soil; the trees themselves were mostly goldenoak with a sprinkling of pine or other conifers, and the occasional beech or larch.

What the forest lacked in human inhabitants, it made up for in animals. Squirrels scolded them as they passed, and songbirds called off in the distance, their voices filtering through the leaves. Jays and crows followed them with rowdy catcalls, telling all the world that *interlopers* were passing through. Once a hawk stooped on something right at the edge of the road, and lumbered up out of the way just as they reached the spot, with a snake squirming in its talons.

The road met the path of a wide river as the sun westered and sank below the level of the treetops. Karal caught glimpses of the water through the screening of trees, reflecting the light in shiny bursts through the brush.

By this time, despite his master's assertion that the two of them could stay in the saddle as long as need be, he was getting saddle sore and stiff. His buttocks ached; his back and shoulders were in knots. He began to wonder just when this Rubrik intended to stop—or did he want to ride all night?

There was no sign of a town or village, though, so there didn't seem to be any place they *could* stop. *I don't mind camping out—but Ulrich is too old for that sort of thing,* he thought, a bit resentfully, but telling himself that concern for his master was more important than his own aches and pains. *We don't have tents, we don't even have proper blanket rolls. Surely this man isn't going to expect the envoy of the Son of the Sun to sleep in leaves, rolled up in his own cloak like a vagabond!*

"There's a village I expect to reach just after sundown," Rubrik said, startling Karal. It was almost as if the man had just read his own thoughts! "If you don't think you can make it that far, please tell me, but I've made arrangements there for a private suite for you two." He made an apologetic grimace. "I hope this doesn't seem boorish, but I would rather that no one know your exact origin or your mission here until we reach Haven, and the best way to keep quiet is to keep the two of you away from people who might be a bit too curious about visitors to Valdemar."

Ulrich waved away any apologies. "Those are my thoughts, precisely," he replied. "The fewer folk who even know there are two Priests traveling here, the better. That was why I requested that Queen Selenay send only a single escort. But I must confess, I am not as confident of my stamina as I was when we met you." He shook his head at his own weakness, then shrugged. "We are used to riding most of the day, but I have just begun to realize that 'most' of the day is not the same as 'all' of the day."

"If it helps any, I have requested that a hot dinner be served in the suite as soon as you arrive," Rubrik answered with an engaging smile. "And hot baths to follow."

"I wouldn't say no to a bottle of horse-liniment as well, sir," Karal ventured, a little shy at inserting himself into the conversation.

"That I can supply myself—muscle-salve, and not horse-liniment, young sir," the escort said, turning to look at him, as if surprised that he was back behind his master. Perhaps Rubrik had forgotten him?

Karal was far more pleased than offended, for if that was what had happened, it meant that he had achieved his end of being "invisible." Ulrich had told him that a good secretary would develop the knack of vanishing into the background; that would make him less intrusive, especially to people who might be nervous about a third party being present at a delicate negotiation.

"That would be very much appreciated, my lord Rubrik," Karal replied, ducking his head in an approximation of a bow.

But Rubrik shook an admonishing finger at Karal. "Not 'my lord,' youngling," he chided gently. "Just 'Rubrik.' Among Heralds, there are no titles—with the sole exception of the Lady Elspeth, the Queen's daughter. My father—was something of a landowner, a kind of farmer."

"Ah?" That clearly caught his master's attention. "And what did he farm, if I may ask?"

"Root crops, mostly, though he had some herds as well," was the ready answer. That set the two of them off on a discussion of the condition of farms and farmers in both Valdemar and Karse, and it was Rubrik's turn for questions, mostly about the weather, and whether or not it had affected the Karsites as badly as it had their Valdemaran counterparts.

Karal wondered if Rubrik realized how much information *he* was giving with the way he phrased his questions.

The moon rose, silvering the road before them. Karal listened and made mental notes for later. If all that Rubrik told them was true, Valdemar had been suffering from truly horrible weather until very recently—storms and disturbances out of season that were somehow connected with the magics Ancar of Hardorn had been working.

"But now that we've got a few mages doing weather-working, things are getting back to normal. In time to save the harvests, we hope," Rubrik concluded.

If he hoped for a similar statement from Ulrich, he was not going to get one. "Vkandis has always cared personally for the welfare of His people," Ulrich replied, and Karal was very glad that it was dark enough that he did not have to hide a smile. *That* was certainly a double-edged statement, and quite entirely the truth as well! It could be taken by an outsider as the simple pious mouthings of a Priest—but the bare fact was that Vkandis *did* care *personally* for the welfare of His people. What His Priests could not deal with, using the powers of magic He had granted them, He might very well take care of Himself. Karse had not suffered more than inconvenience from what Ulrich called "wizard weather," precisely because Priests who could control the weather had been sent out to make certain that people, crops, and property were safeguarded properly.

If Rubrik was taken aback by this bland statement, he said nothing. Instead, he described some of the damage that had occurred in Hardorn, which was evidently much worse than that in Valdemar or what had been prevented in Karse.

Ulrich had taught his pupil that unshielded use of powerful magic disrupted the weather, but Karal had never had that lesson demonstrated for him. Now he *heard* what had happened, and he was appalled at the level of destruction that had taken place. And Ancar had done *nothing* to prevent it.

"Ah, look!" Rubrik said, pointing ahead of them. Karal squinted against the darkness and thought he saw lights. "There's our inn at last. We'll be there in less than a mark!"

"And it won't be too soon for me," Ulrich sighed, with feeling.

Nor for me, Karal added silently. His behind hurt so much he was sure that he had saddle-sores, something that hadn't happened since he was a child. The lights in the distance grew brighter and more welcoming with every moment, and the aches in his legs and back grew more persistent. No one had ever warned him that being the secretary to an envoy was going to involve *this* kind of work! *I hope this is the last time I ever have to ride like this for as long as I live!*

4

Karal didn't get his wish, of course. He did, however, get possession of a bottle of muscle-salve that had such near-miraculous properties that he suspected magic, or the talents of a Healer-Priest in preparing it. When he woke the next morning, his aches were mostly gone, and the little pain that was left eased as he rubbed in a new application of the salve. It had a sharp scent somewhat like watercress, not unpleasant, but nothing he recognized. Ulrich helped himself shamelessly to the potion as well, leaving the jar half empty.

They met in the courtyard of the inn, in the thin gray light of false dawn. Rubrik was already waiting, his cloud-white horse saddled and ready to ride. Rubrik himself looked quite disgustingly rested. One sleepy stableboy presented them with their mounts, already saddled, and a cook's helper, powdered with flour, came out from the kitchen with a tray of buttered rolls and mugs of hot tea. Karal was glad he'd used that salve after he helped Rubrik to mount and climbed aboard Trenor. "Stiff" simply wasn't an adequate description for how he felt when he tried to actually make his muscles do some work. That reminded him of how little salve was left in the jar in *his* saddlebag—between himself and Ulrich, it wasn't going to last more than another day or two.

The kitchen helper reappeared with a pair of cloth bags, and handed them to Rubrik, who slung them over his saddlebags. "Our noon meal," their escort explained. "I hope you don't mind eating on the road, but I want to make as much time as possible."

Lovely. Which means we'll probably be riding even longer today. Somehow he managed not to groan. "Excuse me, sir," he said instead, anxiously. "But that salve you gave me last night worked very well—so well I don't have much left. And—"

"And there's more where that came from, young man," Rubrik replied with a wink. "It's very common in Valdemar; I have more, and I can make sure to *get* more when we stop for the night."

"I can tell already that we both will require it," Ulrich put in, with a rueful smile. "I purloined some of it myself. Perhaps you are used to riding all day, but we are not as sturdy as you. I fear the scholars' life has left both of us ill prepared for this situation."

Karal smiled at his mentor, grateful for Ulrich's little comment. It made *him* look like less of a weakling. After all, how did it look, that a man who was half-crippled could ride longer and harder than a fellow half his age?

They left with the rising sun, completely avoiding any of the other guests at the inn by leaving before anyone else woke up. They didn't stop until late morning, and by that time Karal and his master were both ready for another application of salve. How Rubrik managed such a pace, Karal could *not* fathom. Once they had stopped last night, he'd demonstrated his own physical weakness by needing help to dismount. On the ground, he had limped along with the help of a cane, his bad leg frozen with the knee locked, so that he had to swing it around from the hip, stiffly, in order to use it at all.

This morning he'd needed help to mount as well—help that Karal had provided, since the stableboy had vanished as soon as the lad brought their horses to them. Rubrik's horse had also helped on both occasions, much to Karal's surprise, by lying down so that Rubrik could get his bad leg swung over the saddle with a very little assistance. Karal bit his lip to keep from commenting or asking questions, since this went far beyond any horse training he had ever seen. Rubrik saw his expression, though, and simply smiled, without offering any explanation or inviting any inquiry, so Karal said nothing.

Once the sun actually rose, it looked as if (despite Rubrik's warnings) they were going to have another day of good weather. The sky held dark clouds to the east, but not many were close. It would probably be fairly warm later in the day, but the cool of morning was still in the air and riding would be very pleasant.

Provided my calves aren't tying themselves into knots by the time we stop next.

The second day was a repeat of the first; steady riding with brief stops to stretch, relieve themselves, and eat something. By the afternoon of this second day, the steep and forested hills gradually changed to gentler slopes; the fields beside the road showed signs of agriculture.

They began to meet greater numbers of people, both on the road or working in the fields beside it, none of which looked anything like the surly Holderkin of the first day. These people, at least, wore clothing of bright and varied colors, and most were cautiously polite, waving or calling out a greeting as the three of them rode past.

There was curiosity in their expressions, but they kept their distance when Rubrik did not stop or encourage any closer approach. No one seemed terribly concerned or alarmed over their appearance, which eased at least one of Karal's anxieties. He was not anxious to be driven out of Valdemar by that mob of angry peasants he had envisioned. He'd had uneasy moments yesterday, when the Holderkin turned to stare with open hostility, just before averting their faces just as pointedly.

As some of his anxieties disappeared, more surfaced, however. All his life he had heard stories about the Hellspawn of Valdemar, the White Demons and the Hellhorses they rode. Did Rubrik wear white, and ride a white horse, as an honor to the White Demons? Surely all those tales had not been made up out of whole cloth. Certain Karsites—the Black-robe Priests in particular—had enough experience with real demons to know them when they saw them! So where *were* the creatures out of the tales his mother and every other mother told her children? Where were the demons that would *get him* if he wasn't good?

Magic isn't stopped by borders or boundaries, he thought, watching Rubrik's back cautiously. *Our Black-robe Priests could control demons, so it stands to reason that the people here have mages who can, too. So where are they? If this escort of ours intends to impress us with the power of Valdemar and the Queen's mages, now would be the time to trot out a few horrors. He wouldn't want to frighten anyone in a really populated area, after all. He'd want to make sure we were the only witnesses to his private show.*

But they rode up to yet another inn after sundown, tired to the bone, without any sign of horrors, monsters, or, truly, any magic at work at all. So now, were they being insulted by not being shown any magic at all?

By the time they reached the promised inn, Karal was so bone tired that it was all he could do to stay awake. The hot bath waiting for them *did* help the aches and cramped muscles, but once he'd climbed out of the tub and rubbed more of that salve into himself, he could barely keep his eyes open. He ate, but only because he was starving as well as exhausted. He helped his master Ulrich to bed, but he didn't recall falling into his own cot at all. He simply woke there to the sound of knocking on the door.

Once again, they rose before sunrise, leaving the inn behind them still shrouded in darkness. This time the breakfast included fresh berries as well as bread and whipped butter, but otherwise the routine was the same.

Ulrich didn't seem upset by what seemed to Karal to be unseemly haste in getting them north, so Karal held his peace as they ate their meal in the saddle and set out into the gray of predawn. It did occur to him that if it was Rubrik's intention to keep their very existence a secret without going to extreme lengths, such as riding at night and sleeping by day in hiding places, this was a good way to accomplish that intention. Certainly they hadn't had a chance to speak to anyone in the two days they'd been in this land! They arrived so late at their inns last night and the night before that no one would think twice when they ate in their rooms and went straight to sleep without going to the taproom to socialize with the rest of the guests.

And if it was Rubrik's plan to keep them from noticing pertinent military details about Valdemar—well, Karal, for one, was too tired by now to take note of much of anything. He wasn't likely to have known how to tell if something was strategic or not. Ulrich was exactly what he appeared to be, a scholar. The Priest had spent his life in studying magic and the Writ and Rules of Vkandis; Karal was at the beginning of those very same, intense studies, and the very thought of having *time* to study military strategy as well made Karal want to laugh.

Then again, how could Rubrik possibly be sure of that? True, he was only sixteen, but that was the age many young men were commissioned as officers in the Army. He *could* be a military spy; a successful spy presumably would look like something harmless.

Like some Priest's rather young, green, and confused secretary, I suppose.

He knuckled his foggy eyes and stifled a yawn, while Trenor walked briskly behind Honeybee. What was truly mortifying was that Ulrich, who *should* have been in worse shape than he was, actually seemed fresh and alert after his night's sleep. He talked at length with Rubrik, in Valdemaran this time, supposedly in order to refresh his memory and increase his proficiency. Karal listened while their escort rattled on about the people who lived along this road, what crops they grew, what beasts they herded. Pretty boring stuff, but it did sharpen *his* Valdemaran. And for the first time in any language study, they *did* have a reason to ask "how far to the Palace?"

The landscape gradually flattened until, by afternoon, there was nothing on either side of the road but farm country, and the terrain had turned to gentle, rolling hills. Trees lined each side of the road as a windbreak, and more trees were planted in windrows between each plowed or fallow field. A warm breeze crossed their path; warm enough to make him sleepy all over again. He caught himself nodding more than once, jerking awake as he started to lose his seat.

They couldn't avoid people now; every time they stopped to rest, there would be some curious farmer or passing merchant who wondered who they were and what their business was. Rubrik was friendly, but close-mouthed, describing them only as "foreigners." For most people, that seemed to be enough of an explanation.

"Been a mort'o foreigners, lately," said one old man, as he drew water from his well for their horses. Rubrik agreed and did not elaborate, so the old man's curiosity went unsatisfied. Karal and Ulrich politely pretended that they had not understood him.

But Karal watched their escort closely all during the afternoon after that. He set himself a mental exercise to keep himself awake, trying to determine what choosing *this* man as their escort meant to their status, and hence, their ongoing mission. Of course, this was not technically anything he needed to worry about, but Ulrich would probably be asking him questions, sooner or later, to see what he had reasoned out for himself.

So while Ulrich talked in Valdemaran about the weather, the corn harvest, the other "foreigners" that had been in Valdemar because of the war, Karal watched and listened and thought.

While "crippled" Rubrik might look unsuited to this position, he was certainly bearing up under all this hard riding better than the two "able-bodied" people he was escorting. He didn't need all that much help, really; just what Karal or the occasional common horseboy could provide. His white mount took care of the rest. His command of Karsite was excellent, as Ulrich had already noted; how many people *were* there in Valdemar who were fluent in Karsite? There couldn't be many.

Rubrik was well-versed enough in the current situation in the Valdemaran Court that he had been able to answer most of Ulrich's questions so far. This business of hurrying them on their way could be a very clever means of making certain they didn't do anything really impolite—or politically unfortunate. Limit the contact, and you limit the chance of mistakes. After all, they were the first envoys from Karse to Valdemar in hundreds of years—and no one in Valdemar had any idea how they were likely to react.

57

We could just as easily be two of the "old sticks" that Solaris complains to Ulrich about; stiff-necked and stubborn and ready to make a stupid fuss about anything that might possibly be considered heresy—fighting the things she has restored to the Writ and Rules because there've never been Rules like that in their lifetime. Someone like that would probably cause an incident as soon as he got even half an excuse to do so, just out of sheer spite. He can't be sure yet that we aren't like that, and the Valdemaran Court would plan on it if they have any foresight.

Rubrik probably *was* the best man for this job.

This third day out, Karal found himself warming to the man. Rubrik *could* have been sitting around wallowing in self-pity, recounting past glories to uninterested passersby on Temple steps somewhere; instead, he was performing an important duty, perhaps freeing someone more able-bodied for some other task, certainly seeing to it that he and Ulrich had someone in charge of their journey who was not only competent, but fluent in their language, and at least marginally friendly.

As the sun sank on their third day of travel, it also occurred to Karal that finding someone who fit the criteria of "competent, fluent, and friendly" in the case of a former enemy must be a rather difficult task. Perhaps, rather than trying to figure out if the choice of Rubrik had been meant as an insult, he should assume it was a compliment and should be *grateful* that they had him!

Exhaustion impaired his reasoning fairly quickly after that. As the lights of the next village neared, Karal found himself thinking of nothing more than the bed he expected to fall into.

Soft bed, clean sheets, a hot bath... sleep. Not in that order, of course. Food. Lots of fat feather pillows. Sleep. Some more of that salve. Sleep.

They rode into the courtyard of the inn Rubrik had chosen. The courtyard was lit with lanterns and torches, the windows glowed from the candles within, and wonderful aromas of cooking meat and baking bread drifted out through the open door.

A stableboy helped Rubrik dismount, then moved to hold Honeybee and Trenor as Rubrik limped into the inn to arrange for their lodging.

But he hurried right back out again, a serving-boy hovering at his elbow, just as Karal helped his master dismount, and the stormy look on his face made Karal's heart sink. Rubrik was angry, and was keeping his temper carefully in check. Something must have gone wrong here.

Is it us? Has someone recognized that we're Karsite, and refused to grant us shelter? It was a real possibility—and the opening for a potentially damaging incident before their mission had even begun!

"I'm afraid this place is already full up," their escort said apologetically, while Ulrich steadied himself with one hand on Honeybee's shoulder. The flickering light from the torches did nothing to mask his chagrin and annoyance, and Karal felt his own face fall, but Ulrich seemed undisturbed. "This idiot of a landlord claims that he misunderstood the day; it's not a deliberate insult, I insisted on seeing the register, and they really have let out all the rooms. They can give you dinner while I see about some alternate arrangements, if you don't mind waiting for me to manage something."

"I do not see that we have much choice in the matter," Ulrich replied, with a philosophical shrug. "Personally, I simply can't ride any farther. No journey ever proceeds exactly as planned, and after all, the world does not arrange itself to suit our particular whims."

Rubrik grimaced, the torchlight turning his face into an ugly mask for a moment. "In this case, it should have," he said, annoyance overcoming his chagrin, "since I specifically stopped here on my way to the border to arrange rooms for us on this date. I—well, it doesn't matter. I managed to throw a good fright into the innkeeper himself, and he'd rather slit his own wrists now than inconvenience us further. I *do* have a private parlor for you to dine in, and I threw out the dice game some of the innkeeper's cronies were playing to get it, too. If you'll follow the boy, he'll see that you're served, and I'll see what I can arrange for the night."

Ulrich nodded as graciously as if this were all his idea, and put Honeybee's reins into the hands of the stableboy. He brushed off his riding robes, shook out a few wrinkles, and followed the serving-boy inside.

Karal trailed along in Ulrich's shadow, through the door into the inn itself, and crossed the crowded taproom.

Across the *very* crowded taproom. Every bench was full, every table loaded with full and empty plates and tankards. The floor underfoot was sticky with spilled drink, and there was just enough room for the servers to squeeze in between the patrons. He was just as glad they weren't going to eat in here; the room was hot and stuffy, and his nose was assaulted with far too many odors at once to make his stomach happy. On top of that, it was noisy, and the babble was all in Valdemaran; it made him feel three times the foreigner, and between the confusion and his exhaustion, he found his grasp of the language slipping away.

The boy brought them to a door on the other side of the crowded room, opened it quickly, and motioned them inside. Even if he had tried to say something, he could not have been heard above the babble. Ulrich went in first; Karal followed on his heels.

The very first thing he noticed was the relative silence as the boy closed the door behind them. His ears rang for just a moment. The walls must have been incredibly thick for that much of a difference in the noise level.

The "private parlor" was a smaller version of the larger room, without the noisy crowd or the heat. The table in the middle of the room showed signs of the dice game Rubrik had presumably disrupted; a scattering of gaming counters and a few empty cups, which the boy swept aside as he gestured anxiously for them to take their seats. He produced a pitcher and a pair of cups, and poured cold fresh ale for both of them before vanishing out the door.

He returned in moments with two girls behind him, both of them bearing laden trays of food. At this point, Karal would have eaten the scraps usually thrown to the dogs, but it looked as if Rubrik must have given this innkeeper a stout piece of his mind, for the repast the two girls spread out on the table was a fine one, and there was enough there for half a dozen people. Platters steamed temptingly as the servers uncovered them, watching the faces of the two Karsites anxiously for a hint of approval.

Karal approved of it all, and couldn't wait to tuck into it. A tasty broth, thick with barley and vegetables, began the meal, and a berry tart with a pitcher of heavy cream concluded it. Karal didn't realize *how* hungry he was until he wiped up the last of his berry-flavored cream with a bit of crust, and looked up to see that he and Ulrich had done a pretty fair job of decimating a meal he had *thought* would serve six.

He hadn't been paying any attention to anything except the food in front of him. Now he looked around the room, following Ulrich's faintly ironic gaze.

There were no windows in the plastered white walls; this room must have been in the very center of the building. There was plenty of light, though, from a series of lanterns around the walls, in addition to the candles on the table. There was no fire in the cold fireplace, but it was hardly needed in this warm weather.

Besides the table and half a dozen stiff-backed, wooden chairs, there were three couches upholstered in brown leather placed on three sides of the room, couches of an odd shape. They had no backs, and only one fat, high arm.

"I think perhaps this room is used for other games than dicing," Ulrich said quietly, still wearing that ironic little smile. Karal blinked at him for a moment, then stared at one of the couches again—

And blushed, the blood rushing to his face and making him feel as if he was sunburned. He was *not* the naive horseboy he'd been when he was first taken from his parents. Between what he'd learned among the other novices, and the odds and ends he'd picked up while serving Ulrich, he had an amazingly broad education in worldly matters. Oh, he knew what those couches were for, now that Ulrich had pointed it out.

Still, a couch was a couch, and Rubrik still wasn't back. He shoved away from the table, the chair legs scraping on the polished wooden floor, and got up.

"I don't think anybody's going to bother us until Rubrik returns, Master Ulrich," he said, gesturing to the couch nearest the table. "I think you ought to get a little rest while we wait. I certainly intend to."

Ulrich's smile widened a little, and he rose, a bit stiffly, from his own chair. He took the couch that Karal indicated, lowering himself down onto it with a grimace, and took a more comfortable, reclining position. Karal waited until his master looked settled, then chose one of the other two couches and sat gingerly down on it.

The cushions were certainly soft enough, and a faint, musky perfume rising from them as he lay down confirmed his guess as to the purpose they usually served. Small wonder they were covered in smooth leather; that kind of leather was easy to clean, easier than fabric.

On the other hand, he was *not* going to sit around on one of those straight-backed wooden chairs until their escort returned, while there was something a lot more comfortable in the very same room.

Besides, while he and his master were in here, the careless innkeeper was *not* able to use the room for any other purpose. Karal found himself almost hoping that Rubrik would not be able to make any other arrangements. These couches would not make the most comfortable beds in the world—unless you were accustomed to sleeping in certain positions—but they weren't the floor, or a pile of hay, or the ground under a tree. They certainly were softer than the pallet he'd been given in the Children's Cloister.

He didn't think he dared sleep, though, much as his body cried out for rest. They were alone and unarmed, and it could be presumed that the innkeeper was not altogether happy with their presence here, whether or not he knew anything about who or what they were. So Karal decided that this very moment was a good one to review his Valdemaran vocabulary, including all the tenses of all the verbs, in alphabetical order.

He had gotten as far as the third letter of the alphabet when Rubrik returned. His arrival woke Ulrich, who had been dozing. The priest sat up slowly and moved more stiffly than he had when he went to sleep. Karal frowned; that was not a good sign. Not only because it meant his master was very, very tired, but because Ulrich generally suffered from stiff and aching joints when the weather was about to change for the worse.

"I have good news of a sort," Rubrik began. "I have excellent accommodations for you—the problem is that you might wish to decline them. Your host—is actually a hostess. She is the local Commander of the Guard; as it happens, this village is her home, she has her command-post here, and she has offered her guest room to you."

Ulrich considered this for a moment, as Karal blinked, and tried to imagine a *woman* in a position of military command. Women were not even permitted to serve with the Karsite army as Healer-Priests; only men could serve with soldiers. The *old* laws said that women who took on the "habit and guise" of men were demons, to be controlled or destroyed—whichever came soonest. Female mercenaries captured by the Karsite Army had fared rather badly, historically, something that Ulrich had never tried to conceal from his pupil.

For that matter, in Karse, the law still forbade women to hold property on their own; all property, whether it be land or goods, must be owned by a male. By Karsite standards, this Commander was doubly shocking.

On the other hand, Her Holiness had been making it clear that the days of laws forbidding women to do anything were numbered. Vkandis had made His will clear on the subject.

I guess that eventually we'll even have women fighters in our *Army, given the way that things are going.* Somehow, he did not find that as horrifying as he should have. Maybe he was just tired.

Maybe being around Her Holiness Solaris had taught him he'd better *never* underestimate the competence of a woman.

"If the lady in question is not offended by us, I fail to see why we should take offense at her offer of hospitality," Ulrich said, finally. "I would be very pleased to meet our hostess. I have never met a female warrior face-to-face before. I believe the experience will be enlightening."

He rose carefully and smoothed out the front of his riding robe with both hands. Karal scrambled to his feet, realizing belatedly that Ulrich had just accepted the unknown woman's invitation.

"I *did* tell her precisely who and what you are," Rubrik replied, with a twitch of his lips. "Since she is the local Commander, I had to inform her anyway. She said something similar about you, sir."

"No doubt," Ulrich replied dryly, but followed their guide out the door, through the taproom (which was still just as noisy and crowded as it had been when they entered), and back into the night, with Karal trailing along behind.

Evidently someone had already seen to their mounts, either stabling them at the inn or bringing them on ahead, and Rubrik had (correctly) judged that, weary as they were, neither Ulrich nor his secretary were ready to climb back into a saddle again. Instead, they left the courtyard of the inn, turned into the street, and walked the short distance along a row of shops and homes to the large house at the end. The narrow two-storied buildings seemed abnormally tall and thin to Karal; each had a workshop or store on the ground floor, and living quarters above. The house at the end of the street differed in all ways from those lining it; this building had no commercial aspect to it, and it was as broad as three of the others.

It wasn't as big as the homes of several high-born nobles that Karal had seen, nor even as large as the inn, but it was quite sizable compared to its modest neighbors. The main door was right on the cobblestone street, with a single slab of stone as a step beneath it. Torches had been lit and placed in holders outside the white-painted door to light their way, and a servant opened the door before Rubrik could knock on it.

The servant ushered them into a wood-paneled hallway, lit by candlelamps. It was less of an entryway, and more of a waiting-room. They were not left to wait for the lady on the benches however; as soon as the servant shut the door, he directed them to follow him down the wide, white-painted hall to a room at the end.

Karal expected a lady's solar, or a reception room of some kind, but what the servant revealed when he opened the door was an office; businesslike, with no "feminine" fripperies about it. Their hostess was hard at work behind a plain wooden desk covered with papers; she nodded at the servant, who saluted and left. Rubrik gestured to them to go in, following and closing the door behind them.

The lady set her papers aside, and looked them both over with a frank and measuring gaze. Karal flushed a little under such an open appraisal, but Ulrich only seemed amused by her attitude. If she was as high an officer as Rubrik had indicated, there was nothing of that about her costume, at least not as Karal recognized rank-signs. Their hostess wore the same Guard uniform that they had seen before, with perhaps a bit more in the way of silver decoration.

Personally, she was quite attractive, and could have been any age from late twenties to early fifties. She had the kind of face that remained handsome no matter the number of her years, a slim and athletic build, and an aura of complete confidence. This was someone in complete authority; someone who *knew* that she was good at her work, and did not bother to hide that fact. Karal was intimidated by her, and he realized it immediately. The only other woman who had ever had that effect on him was Solaris, and the Son of the Sun was relatively sexless compared to this Valdemaran commander. He was very glad that *he* was not the one that most of her attention was centered on.

"Well," she said, slowly, lacing her fingers together. "I've faced your lot across the battlefield, my lord Priest, but never across a desk. I hope you'll understand me when I say that I find our situation a great improvement."

"I, too," Ulrich replied smoothly. "Few Valdemarans would have such understanding, however, I think. Or is it forgiveness?"

"Huh." She smiled, though, and nodded. "I don't know about your Vkandis, sir Priest, but my particular set of gods tells me that past battles are just that: past. I am something of an amateur historian, actually. I like to know the causes of things. Some day, I expect, I'll have the leisure to sit down with one of your scholars and find out just what started this particularly senseless war between us in the first place. For now—" she waved one hand at the door, presumably indicating the house beyond it, "—allow me to do my part to cement the peace by offering hospitality." Her brow wrinkled for a moment, then she recited, in heavily accented and badly pronounced Karsite, "To the hearth, the board, the bed, be welcome. My fires burn to warm you, my board is laden to nourish you, my beds soft to rest you. We will share bread and be brothers."

Karal's jaw dropped. The very last thing he had ever expected to hear from this woman was the traditional invocation of peace between feuding hill families!

She smiled broadly at his open-mouthed reaction but said nothing.

Ulrich, for his part, remained unperturbed, although Karal thought he saw his mentor's lips twitch just a little. "For the hospitality, our thanks. Our blades are sharp to guard you, our horses strong to bear you, our torches burn to light your path. Let there be peace between us, and those of our kin." He then added to the traditional answer, "And I do mean 'kin' in the broadest possible sense."

"I know that," she replied. "If I hadn't, I wouldn't have offered you the blessing." She nodded, as if she had found Ulrich very satisfactory in some way. "Well, I think I've kept you standing here like a couple of raw recruits long enough. You've covered a fair amount of ground today, and I won't keep you from your baths or beds any longer. You'll find both waiting in your room, and my servant will show you the way."

And with that, the servant opened the door again, and she nodded in what was clearly a dismissal.

It occurred to Karal that a real diplomat might have been offended at her blunt speech and curt manner, but he was just too tired to try to act like a "real diplomat."

Then again, anyone who would be annoyed at a soldier acting like a soldier is an idiot. No, she didn't mean anything more or less than she said.

Instead of trying to analyze the encounter, he followed the servant, who led them to another room on the same floor, but on a different hallway.

It was tiled, floor and walls, with white ceramic, and contained two tubs, one a permanent fixture, and one smaller one obviously brought in so that Karal would not have to wait for his bath, both with steam rising from them. He and Ulrich had shared bathhouses often enough; they both shed clothing with no further ado. The servant came to collect their clothes as soon as they had both gotten into the tubs, indicating by pantomime that their beds lay in the next room.

Karal soaked his sore muscles, then wrapped himself in one of the towels and followed Ulrich into the bedroom. Valdemaran sleeping robes were laid out for them, a nice touch, he thought. He found his baggage, rubbed in his salve, and fell into the cot in the next room in a complete fog. Once his head touched the pillow, the fog became total darkness that did not lift until the servant woke them in the morning.

5

After three days of what could only be described as endurance riding, Karal was finally getting used to the pace. He was also getting used to Rubrik, and it seemed that their escort was getting accustomed to them as well. His formal manner loosened a bit, and during the fourth day of travel, he began to talk with Karal directly.

At that point, Karal had to revise his opinion of their escort sharply upward, for Rubrik was even more of a scholar than he had guessed. He spoke four languages besides his own, and his rattling on about the geography, husbandry, and economics of the places they passed was no mere prattling to fill empty ears. He knew this area and the conditions in it as well as its own overlords did.

And that only made Karal more curious than before. Who *was* this man, that he had so much information at his very fingertips? Surely he had not memorized it just to impress or occupy them.

When they left the home of the lady Guard Commander, clad in riding gear that had been freshly washed and cleaned by the lady's servants, gray skies threatened rain. The rain did not actually materialize in the morning or even the early afternoon, but toward late afternoon the clouds thickened, and the wind picked up. Ulrich's joints hurt him quite a bit at that point, so they actually stopped *early* for once, at least two marks before sunset.

Their stopping place was yet another inn, this one with a courtyard surrounded on three sides by the inn itself, and on the fourth by the stable. A gate in the middle of the stable led into the courtyard, and this arrangement cut the wind completely. Ulrich descended from his saddle with a gasp of pain, and Rubrik was concerned enough to ask the Priest if he thought he would require the services of a Healer.

"Not unless your Healer can give me the body of a man three decades my junior," Ulrich replied with a ghost of a smile. "No, this is simply the result of old age. I shall retire to my bed with a hot brick and some of your salve, and with luck, this rain will move on so that we can follow suit as soon as possible."

But the rain didn't move on; in fact, no sooner had Karal seen his master settled into a warming bed than it began to drizzle.

The taproom of the inn was mostly empty; the miserable weather was probably convincing people to stay by their own hearths tonight. There was a good fire in the fireplace, though, quite enough to take the chill out of the air, and on the whole it was a pleasant place, all of age- and smoke-blackened wood. Heavy beams supported the ceiling, and below their shelter, gently curved tables and benches polished to satin smoothness were arranged in an arc around the fire. As the drizzle turned into a real thunderstorm, Karal found a perch at a window-seat table and watched the lightning dance toward the inn through the tiny panes of a leaded window.

"Impressive, isn't it?"

The eyes of Rubrik's reflection met his in the dark and bubbly window glass. The man smiled, and Karal smiled tentatively back.

"Would you prefer I left you to your meditations?" Rubrik asked politely.

Karal shook his head. "Not really," he replied. "You can join me, if you like. I've always been fascinated by storms; when I was a boy at an inn like this one, I used to sneak away and hide in the hayloft to watch them move in."

"And let me guess—you used, as an excuse to go to the stable in the first place, that the horses were frightened by the thunder and needed soothing, no doubt," Rubrik hazarded, and grinned, taking the seat on the other side of the table. "My father never believed that one, either, but his stableman was always on my side and backed me up with specious tales of how I had kept the prize mounts from hurting themselves in a panic."

Karal realized that at last their escort had just let something fall about his own past. Up until now Rubrik had been very closemouthed about anything of a personal nature. *His father's stableman. So that means he comes from a well-to-do family, if not of noble blood. So his father was no mere farmer as he implied.* He responded in kind. "My father never minded too much; there's less work at an inn during bad weather. It's a lot easier for people to stay at home, watch their own fires, and drink their own beer. And of course, once the few travelers who wanted to try and beat the storm got in, no one else would arrive until it was over, so we stableboys didn't have much to do either after we'd dealt with their beasts." There. It was out. If Rubrik was going to be offended by his low birth—

"That's probably the *only* time you didn't have much to do," Rubrik said, with a conspiratorial grin. "I've always felt a little sorry for inn folk during wonderful weather. They never get a holiday like the rest of us do. It hardly seems fair, does it, that in the very best of weather, when everyone else is out enjoying themselves, people in an inn have to work three times as hard tending to the holiday-makers? I would guess that storm watching was the closest thing to a holiday you ever got."

Karal chuckled and brightened. "I never thought about it, actually. It wasn't as bad as you might think, so long as you like horses. Father never made it easier on me than it was for the other horseboys, but he was a good and just taskmaster." He clasped his hands together on the tabletop and stared out at the rain. "I never really saw the heavy work, when it came to that; I wasn't old enough for anything other than light chores, like grooming. The Sun-priests took me at the Feast of the

Children when I was nine, so I was never big enough to do heavy work."

Rubrik looked at Karal for a moment, then stared out at the lightning. The silence between them grew heavy, and Karal sensed that he was about to ask something that he thought might be sensitive.

Probably something about us, about Karse and the Sun-priests. That's not a problem; Ulrich already told me what I can't say. No reason to avoid his questions, especially not if the information he wants is common knowledge at home. I think he's been looking for an excuse to talk to me alone, figuring that I will be less wary than Ulrich. He felt himself tense a little. He would have to be very canny with this man. It would be easy to trust him; hard to remember to watch what he said.

Rubrik coughed politely. "I—ah—suppose you realize we have all kinds of stories, probably ridiculous, about the reasons why the Sun-priests took Karsite children—and what they did with them afterward—"

Karal only sighed, then rested his chin in his hand. "The stories probably aren't any worse than the truth," he said at last.

Rubrik nodded and waited for him to go on. Encouraged, Karal told him all about his own childhood, what there was of it—how the Priests had taken him, how he had been educated, and how, finally, Ulrich had singled him out as his protégé. He told their escort about the Fires, too, and caught an odd expression on his face, as if what Karal had told him only confirmed something horrible that he already knew.

"The children taken are either extremely intelligent, intelligence that would be wasted in a menial position, or are children with the God-granted ability to use magic, of course. Ulrich told me later that I had both qualifications, but my ability to use magic is only a potential, rather than an active thing. He called me a 'channel,' but I've never found out what that means, exactly. I was absolutely terrified that at some point I'd start showing witch-powers like my uncles did, and a Black-robe Priest would come for me and that I'd end up going to the Fires," he concluded. "But I never did—though in one sense, I suppose, a Black-robe Priest *did* come for me."

Rubrik waited for him to say something; out of pure mischief he held his peace. Finally the man gave up. "Well?" he said. "What's that supposed to mean?"

Karal grinned; at least this would be one thing he could surprise the man with. "Ulrich was a Black-robe—that is to say, a Demon-Summoner—before Her Holiness Solaris made the Black-robe nothing more than a rank. And now, of course, there *aren't* any Fires. The

Cleansing ceremony has gone back to what it *used* to be. Ulrich and I found the original Rite in one of the ancient Litany Books." He didn't make Rubrik ask for the answer this time. "It's a Rite of Passage, that's what it originally was, before it was perverted; children who are about to become adult bring something symbolic of their childhood to be burned as a sign that they are ready to take on adult responsibilities. Ulrich says it's easy to change holidays and rituals to suit a purpose, since they're usually subjective anyway. Harvest festivals and fertility rites are coming back, too, the way they were a long time ago."

Rubrik took all this in thoughtfully. "Solaris has made many changes, then?"

"Her Holiness certainly has! Mostly she has reversed changes that had been made by corrupt Priests seeking nothing more than power," Karal corrected. He wasn't certain why, but for some reason he felt that point needed to be absolutely clear. Solaris was not some kind of wild-eyed revolutionary, despite what her critics claimed; what she had done in the Temple thus far was restoration, not revolution. "Ulrich is not precisely certain how long things have been wrong, but we know that it has been several centuries at the least. True miracles ceased, and the illusions of miracles were substituted. The God-granted power of magic that *should* have been devoted to the wellbeing of Vkandis' people and to His glory was perverted into the use of that power to bring temporal power and wealth to the temple and the Priests. And Vkandis is very real, not an imaginary God like some people have!"

Rubrik smiled, but not mockingly. "I know."

Oddly enough, Karal believed him. "Ulrich believes we will know the date the corruption started when we learn just when the rank of Black-robe Priests was created. They were the heart and soul of the corruption."

Lightning lashed the top of a tree not too far away; Karal winced at the thunder but enjoyed the atavistic thrill it sent up his spine. *And I am glad to be in here, and not out there.*

"I thought you said that Ulrich was a Black-robe," Rubrik replied, slowly. "Your robes are *still* black, in fact."

"He was," Karal agreed. "His duty in the former days, according to the Writ and Rule, was to summon demons on the orders of the Son of the Sun and send them against the enemies of Karse. It was not a duty he took any pleasure in. He also frequently brought danger down on himself by refusing to counterfeit miracles." He turned his head a little so that his eyes met Rubrik's. "He showed me every counterfeit he knew, so that I would not be taken in by the tricks of the higher-ranked Priests," he told the man, whose eyes widened at his serious tone. "And that alone might have gotten him burned had I betrayed him. Some of the tricks were so simple anyone who paid attention could have seen through them—but that's the power of belief."

He turned his attention back to the storm. There were other things Rubrik might do well to learn about Ulrich, but Karal would rather that it was his master who told the Valdemaran.

Besides, how could I tell him about the times that Ulrich returned from a summoning, troubled and heartsore—how he hinted that the definition of "enemies of Karse" was becoming broader and broader? No, that should come from my master and not from me. I do not want this Valdemaran to think that I am in the habit of betraying my mentor's confidences.

"You said something about Solaris changing all that," Rubrik ventured, after several long moments filled only by the boom of thunder and the pounding of rain on the roof. "Was that when she became the head of Vkandis' religion?"

Karal nodded, and smiled a little. *This* was the part of the tale he really enjoyed. "That was what gave her the office, in fact. It was a miracle—a *real* one, and no fakery. I was there, I saw it myself. For that matter, so was Ulrich, and *he* is certainly an expert at spotting something that was not a God-produced miracle. I do not believe that there is any kind of fakery, either sleight-of-hand and illusion, or magic masquerading as a miracle, that he cannot detect."

It had been a very strange day to begin with; the day of the Fire Kindling Ceremony at Midwinter, when all the fires of Karse were relit from the ones ignited on the altars of Vkandis. It should have been bitter cold—

"It was the strangest Midwinter Day I have ever seen," he said slowly. "Hot—terribly hot and dry. Hot enough that the Priests had all taken out their summer robes for the Fire Kindling Ceremony. There was not a single cloud in the sky above the city, but outside the city the sky was covered with dull gray clouds, from horizon to horizon. Ulrich and I were at the front of the Processional; Solaris was no more than three people away from Ulrich." He closed his eyes for a moment, picturing it, and chose his words carefully, trying to set the scene for his listener. "We Priests and novices surrounded the High Altar in a semicircle; the beam of sunlight—called the Lance of Hope—shining through the Eye in the ceiling above us slowly moved toward the pile of fragrant woods and incense on the Altar. The golden statue of Vkandis-In-Glory, wearing the Crown of Prophecy, shone like the sun itself behind the Altar, and Lastern—the False Son—stood beside it, ready to kindle the flames by magic if the sunlight didn't do the trick promptly enough."

Rubrik nodded. "I take it that this was a fairly common practice?"

Karal snorted with disgust. "I never once saw the False Son bring forth a single true miracle. For that matter, he was so feeble in magic that the most he could do was to kindle flame in very dry, oily tinder. Well, that day, he never got the chance for his deceptions."

He turned toward Rubrik, and lowered his voice like a true storyteller. "Imagine it for yourself—the crowd of worshipers filling the temple, the golden statue of Vkandis shining behind the Altar and the False Son standing beside it like a fat, black spider. The Processional ended just as the beam of sunlight crept up to the Altar platform; Solaris was no more than five paces away, watching, not the False Son, but the beam of light, her face mirroring her ecstasy."

Was that a little too florid? No, I don't think so.

"Most of the important Priests only looked bored, though, on what *should* be an important day for them, the Holiest of all of Vkandis' Holy Days. They couldn't wait to get back to the Cloister and the feast that waited there for them." Ulrich and a great many of the low-ranked Priests avoided the feast when they could. It was little more than an occasion for those in favor with the Son of the Sun to lord it over those who were not. Hardly Ulrich's choice of a way to spend a Holy Day. He preferred to spend his rare free time reading.

"The beam of sunlight slowly moved onto the Altar itself, while the Children's Choir sang. I saw the False Son's hands moving as he prepared to trigger the fire-starting spell if the wood didn't catch. Then, just before the beam touched the kindling in the middle of the Altar—"

As if he had triggered it himself, a tremendous bolt of lightning lanced down right beside the inn, and as they both jumped and Karal squeaked, the thunder deafened them and everyone else inside the inn.

He sat there for a moment, waiting for his ears to clear, and very grateful that he had not been looking out the window at that moment. If he had, he'd have been blinded!

Rubrik laughed shakily. "Next time, tell me when you are going to produce a surprise to liven up your tale!"

"I'm *not* responsible for that one!" Karal retorted, with a shaky chuckle of his own. "Perhaps you ought to ask Vkandis if He has widened His lands to include Valdemar! Because that was precisely what happened in the Temple—a bolt of lightning shot down through the opening in the Temple's roof, out of the cloudless sky, and completely evaporated the False Son of the Sun."

Rubrik stared at him skeptically, as if he suspected that this was just more tale-telling.

But Karal shook his head emphatically. "I promise you, I was there, and so was Ulrich. He'll corroborate what I've said. There was literally nothing left but the man's smoking vestments and boots, too—I've never seen anything like it, and neither had anyone else. But that wasn't the end of the miracle, it was only the *beginning!*"

"What next?" Rubrik asked, his tone conveying that even if he was not quite convinced, he was certain that Karal was telling the truth as he saw it.

"Next, was that when we could see again, every stone column in the Temple had been turned upside down, and since they all had carvings on them, it was pretty obvious that they'd been inverted. We didn't know it at the time, but we found out later that every cloud vanished from over the whole of Karse, and the First Fires on every Altar blazed up and burned for a full week without any additional fuel." He left out the other, smaller miracles—about the children waiting to be burned who had vanished from the hands of the Black-robes, only to be discovered long afterward, hidden in the homes of their families. He eliminated the story of the Priests' Staffs—how some of the staffs turned brittle and disintegrated at a touch, while others put out green branches covered with flowers.

And the Staffs that turned to dust were the ones that belonged to the False Son's favorites and cronies, and those Black-robes who had truly enjoyed the demon-summoning and the burnings... He himself had held Ulrich's Staff, which had so many tiny red flowers covering the branches at the top that the wood could scarcely be seen. It had remained that way for a week, the flowers sending out a heady perfume. Ulrich and every other possessor of a flowering Staff had planted their Staffs in the various Temple meditation gardens, where they remained as flowering bushes, living reminders of the day of the miracles.

"But none of that would have gotten Solaris made Son of the Sun," he continued. "No woman had *ever* been named Son of the Sun, the very idea was absurd. No, if that had been all that happened, the Priests would have convened and elected a new Son, perhaps one a *little* more pious than the old one, but still—"

"It would have been business as usual," Rubrik supplied, his ironic nod showing that he understood the situation all too well. "So what *did* happen?"

"Another miracle. The last, and greatest of all. Silence hung over the entire Temple, for the worshipers were too stunned to cry out or even move. Then, before anyone could recover enough to say or do anything to break that silence, the golden statue of Vkandis began to move." He closed his eyes to picture it again in his mind, and described the vivid memory as best he could. "It moved exactly like a living man—there was nothing stilted or jerky about the way that it looked about, then stepped slowly down out of the niche behind the Altar. That convinced me it couldn't be some mechanical thing substituted for the real statue. I remember staring up at it, and thinking how *much* like a man it was; the skin moved properly over the muscles; the muscles rippled as it stepped over the Altar and stopped in front of Solaris. *She* was staring up at it, with that same enraptured expression on her face, even though most of the Priests were groveling and babbling out a litany of every sin they'd ever committed."

That had been rather funny, actually. For some reason, it never occurred to him to be *afraid* of the image, and there were a few more, like Solaris and Ulrich, who actually seemed to be in a trance of ecstasy as they gazed upon it. The face of the statue wore a look of complete serenity, as it always had—yet there seemed to be a hint of good humor in the eyes, a ghost of a smile about the lips, as if Vkandis found the groveling Priests just as funny as Karal did.

"The statue took the Crown of Prophecy off its own head; once the Crown was in its hands, it *shrank*. It dwindled until it was small enough to fit a human. Then the statue bent down and placed the Crown on Solaris' head."

The eyes of the image and of Solaris had met and locked. *Something* passed between them; Karal didn't know what it was, and on the whole, he would really rather not find out. *I'm just not ready for the personal attentions of Vkandis. I would be very happy to stay with Ulrich and work researching the old Rites and never have Him notice me.*

"Then the image went back to the pedestal behind the Altar; that was when the fire there on the Altar in front of it blazed up so quickly and so high we thought another lightning bolt had hit it. When the flames died down so we could see the niche again, the statue was exactly as it had been, *except* that it wasn't wearing the Crown anymore. Solaris was."

"And you're sure that there was no trickery involved?" Rubrik persisted.

Karal nodded. "Absolutely. It wasn't an illusion, or how would Solaris have gotten the Crown? It wasn't a mechanical device, because no mechanical could have moved as the statue did. And besides that, how would a mechanical creature make the Crown shrink like that? And Ulrich says it definitely wasn't human magic, or he would have known immediately; even without summoning demons, he's still one of the most powerful mages in the Priesthood. None of us have ever seen Solaris work *any* magic, before or since, except for the demon-summoning she was required to perform because she was a Black-robe. Ulrich says he doesn't see how any mage could have delivered a lightning strike like that, animate the statue, and light the First Fire and still be standing afterward. Even if she or a confederate, or even a number of conspirators, *could* have done all that with magic, there's still one question—*how* would she have gotten the Crown off the statue, and shrunk it down to fit her? The Crown wasn't just some piece of jewelry that had been made to fit the statue—it was *part* of the statue, part of the original casting. The Crown is part of the statue's head. It was deliberately cast that way to discourage thieves."

"Huh." Rubrik stared at the rain which was coming down in a solid sheet. Karal watched his expression very carefully, trying to guess his thoughts. "Well," he said, very slowly, "I would have said that I didn't believe in miracles, if I hadn't seen one or two lately with my own eyes. Smallish ones, mind, compared to your moving statues and shrinking Crowns, but they definitely qualified." He paused, and Karal had the sense that he was choosing his words with the utmost care. "The Lady-Goddess of the Hawkbrothers and Shin'a'in seems to intervene now and then on behalf of her own people, so why not the Sunlord, right?"

Karal nodded cautiously. He wasn't entirely certain he ought to be agreeing to anything that compared Vkandis with some outlandish heathen Goddess—but Rubrik *said* he'd seen this Goddess working miracles...

Vkandis was supposed to have a Goddess-Consort in the oldest records, but she seemed to have gotten misplaced somewhere far back in the past. Or had the Priests in that far past been right to eliminate her?

This was getting more confusing by the moment. "Goddess?" he replied weakly. "What Goddess?"

Rubrik shook his head, and chuckled. "Oh, this theology business is too much for a simple soul like me! Let me order us some dinner, and you tell me just what Solaris did once she had that crown on her head, all right?"

Karal agreed to that with relief. Rubrik summoned a serving-girl, who eyed Karal in a way that made him blush and wish secretly that he wasn't sharing a room with his master. *He* was only a novice; he hadn't taken any oaths yet, much less oaths of celibacy and chastity...

Rubrik must have ordered something that the kitchen already had prepared, for the girl returned with laden platters in short order. Karal's stomach growled as the aroma of hot sausage pie hit his nose. The scent was unfamiliar, as unfamiliar as most of the Valdemaran food, but even if he hadn't been starving, it would have been enticing. He felt ready to eat the pie and the plate it was baked in.

Rubrik dug into his own portion without hesitation. "So," he said, gesturing with a fork, "what did your Solaris do next?"

"There was no question of naming anyone else the Son of the Sun, of course," Karal replied, around a mouthful of sausage and crust. He swallowed; the pie was wonderful, and the spices weren't *too* different from the ones used at home. "Everyone who would have protested was there for the Miracles, and they were terrified that any more miracles would target *them*. Solaris was invested right then and there with the White Robes—she already had a Crown—and the acolytes swept what was left of the False Son out with the ashes of last year's Fire. The next day she called a convocation, and told everyone that the duties of the Black-robes would change from that moment. She ordered that Black-robes would retain their rank, but they would serve exactly the same duties as the Red-robe Priests. Demon-summoning was declared anathema, forbidden, and the texts that taught the means of summoning the creatures were to be burned."

"That's a good start, though normally I don't hold with burning books," Rubrik observed. "But destroying something so open to misuse instead of burning innocent people was a pretty good way of beginning her rule."

Karal nodded enthusiastically and had another couple of bites before continuing. "She said that she had been having visions for some time now, and that the event in the Temple merely confirmed that her visions had been from Vkandis and not mere dreaming and vainglory. She told us all that she had been shown that the ways of the Writ and Rule were not the ancient and true ways of worship."

"I'd hardly expect her to say anything else," Rubrik pointed out dryly.

"If she was going to establish herself as an authority, she would have to shake up things in your Temple right from the beginning. First day."

Karal bit his tongue to keep from making a sharp retort, and took a little time eating before continuing, lest he say something he shouldn't. No matter what Solaris was, one thing she *wasn't* was a mere political creature. Yes, she understood politics, but it was only to take them into account. When politics didn't agree with what she was going to do, she worked around them.

"She made quite a few changes in the first week," he told the Valdemaran. "And later, when Ulrich and I were doing research into the older ways, we found out that the changes she had made *were* nothing more than a reestablishment of those ancient paths. 'The Sunlord has always been a God of life, not destruction,' she said. 'His Fire is the life-giving Fire of the Sun, not the Fires that eat the lives of children.' She decreed an end to the Cleansing Ceremonies as we knew them. She declared the Feast of the Children to be a time of testing youngsters for their powers and intelligence, but ordered that no child was to be dragged away from its family; children must come to the Temple by consent of their families and their own will." He answered Rubrik's slightly raised eyebrow with a sardonic smile of his own. "She also pointed out that in families with many children and limited resources, telling the child and its parents that from now on the Priesthood would feed and clothe it would get them to at least give the Cloisters a try. I have to admit that I was fed and housed better than my parents could afford when I was in the Cloisters, and on the whole I had less work to do. I'm told now that children sometimes cry when they *aren't* taken, instead of crying when they are."

"Ah," Rubrik said, with a twitch of his lips. "As we say in Valdemar, presenting the apple instead of the stick."

"Precisely." He finished off his portion of pie and took a long swallow of ale. "The changes she made with the children and the novices were that they were to be allowed full contact with their families and annual leave to visit them if they wished, just as if they were recruits in the Army. But that all came later; it was part of the changes she made that were really restorations of the old ways."

"The old ways…" Rubrik finished his own food thoughtfully. "So, just how did she come to know all these 'old ways'? More visions?"

Karal laughed. "Oh, no, not at all! She appointed a number of friends of hers among the former Black-robes to find them in the archives!"

"Don't tell me—" Rubrik said quickly, holding up his free hand. "One of the places where she used to spend a lot of her free time was the archives, right? And I already know that she is a linguist and a scholar and can read all the oldest records for herself. So that was how she just happened to know that the 'old ways' weren't exactly the same as your current—what did you call it?"

"The Writ and Rule." Karal shrugged. "I don't know, but does it really matter? The point is that she knew that there was a record of the old ways in the archives, and everything we found confirmed or added to what she had already declared. Ulrich was one of the former Black-robes she assigned to the archives, and since I was his secretary, I worked beside him."

The serving-girl came to clear away their empty plates, refill their cups, and bring them a dessert of fruit and cheese. Rubrik said nothing while she was there, and spent some time carefully cutting up an apple without continuing the conversation. "None of this ever got to Valdemar," he said at last. "We only heard that there had been some disturbance, and that suddenly the ruler of Karse was a woman. Then we learned nothing at all for a year or two." He looked up from his apple dissection, and cocked an eyebrow at Karal. "Is there any connection between your Solaris and the other woman that called herself 'the Prophet of Vkandis' about ten or fifteen years ago? The one that decided she was going to be the head of your army and damn near got herself a big chunk of Menmellith?"

Karal shook his head. "No—and in fact, that woman is the reason the original Crown of Prophecy went missing. It was lost with her when she vanished."

No point in getting into that; the story was much too complicated. And if Rubrik did not know the part of Solaris' story that his own countrywoman Talia figured so prominently in—he wasn't as well-informed as Karal had thought.

Rubrik ate his apple thoughtfully. "I can't imagine that the rest of your priesthood just rolled over like cowed dogs and let Solaris rule as she wanted."

Indeed they didn't, Karal thought quietly. But this was one of the subjects Ulrich had instructed him to say nothing about. There had been a great deal of opposition to Solaris' new Writ and Rules, and to her decrees as well. Not only from the Priests, either.

There had been plenty of people in Karse who liked the corrupt ways very much indeed. A number of the highly born resented the intrusion of the Priests into areas of governance they had always considered their private preserve. There had been a kind of understanding between the Priests and some of the nobles that certain—excesses—would be ignored if gifts "to the Temple" were valuable enough. There had been Priests who were as corrupt as some of those nobles; they had shared in those excesses.

Solaris put an end to those "understandings." And an end to the slave trade, to a profitable market in deadly intoxicants, and a number of other unsavory trades that had been ignored or even given tacit sanction by the Priests.

This did not earn her friends in some quarters.

There were Priests and the favorites of Priests who lost prestige and position with the change in stature of the Black-robes—those who were no longer permitted to call demons did not inspire the same fear. This didn't earn her any goodwill from those factions, either.

There were even those at the borders who *wanted* the demon-summoners back. At least when demons roamed the night, the bandits stayed hidden, and conducted their raids only by day, when it was somewhat easier to see them coming and to fight them. There were plenty of border dwellers who feared the Rethwellans, the Valdemarans, and the Hardornens on the other side of those borders, and wanted the demons and their summoners to keep the "foreigners" away.

The two years that followed the Miracle were not easy ones, and Solaris had fought a grim and mostly-silent battle against a number of enemies. But Karal was not going to tell Rubrik any of that. If the Valdemaran spies weren't good enough for their Queen to have learned *that* much, too bad. And if no one had bothered to inform this agent of the Queen of these things, that was not Karal's problem.

"So, at some point after Ancar stole his father's throne, he decided that Karse was an easy target, hmm?" Rubrik took the hint, restarting the conversation with something obvious.

Karal shrugged. "I suppose so. I've never talked to anyone from Hardorn. Those who were trying to escape went across your borders. I suppose they didn't want to chance the demons; they had no reason to know there weren't any demons anymore. All I know is that suddenly we had an army trying to run over the top of us. Solaris was very good at picking brilliant generals, but good generals were obviously not going to be enough. Ancar's fighters didn't seem—human."

"They weren't, exactly, anymore," Rubrik replied, and it was obvious from his expression that *he* was not going to elaborate on this point. Well, fine. So they both had things they weren't supposed to share.

"You should know the rest," Karal continued. "Solaris retreated to the Sun Tower and came back down with a new decree from the mouth of Vkandis Himself."

"Truce with Valdemar." That was a statement, not a question, but Karal nodded anyway.

And if the situation hadn't been so bad, that would have been the end of Solaris. As it was, Ancar's fighters and mages committed so many outrages that even her worst enemies were convinced that she was right. There hadn't been a single family in all of Karse that didn't know of *someone* who'd been affected. Torture and rapine were the least of the vile deeds Ancar's followers had perpetrated, although they in themselves were quite bad enough.

Rubrik shook his head with an expression of wry sympathy. "You know, when your messengers reached our people, and we were finally convinced that Solaris meant what she said, there were some of us who thought the world had surely come to an end. I mean, truce with *Karse?* How much crazier could things get? And most people were certain it wouldn't last."

A flicker of expression on Rubrik's face, quickly suppressed, told Karal that this man was in the group of those in Valdemar who had felt that way. "I don't imagine your people were terribly happy about the idea, especially anyone in your Guard."

Rubrik grimaced. "Well, when those Priest-mages of yours came north and helped hold Ancar's armies to a crawl, it pretty well convinced even the most skeptical that you meant to hold by the spirit of the truce and alliance as well as the letter of it. At this point, we've got acceptance—if a grudging acceptance—of the situation. There are still people who can't keep up with the changes in the land, though. So much has changed so quickly inside Valdemar—and outside her borders—that probably half of the population is in a whirl."

Karal sighed, and then caught himself in a yawn. How late was it, anyway? "I suppose you could say the same about us," he replied. "Except for two groups, that is."

Rubrik raised an eyebrow.

"Those who support Solaris without reservation, like Ulrich, purely because she *is* the Son of the Sun by Vkandis' Own hand," Karal said, "and those who are simply too young to have fought Valdemar personally, and so have no personal grudges to bear. When you're young enough, the world is new every day."

"Ah." Rubrik considered this for a moment—perhaps noting that Karal did not say which group *he* belonged in—and straightened a bit in his seat, stretching and flexing his shoulders. "And on that optimistic note, I suggest we both find a nice warm bed," he said.

Optimistic? Well, I suppose so—if you consider that he means that eventually all the old fossils will die and the new generation, presumably without the prejudices of the old, will take over. "That sounds like a good idea to me," Karal agreed. "And forgive me if I hope that your bad weather holds long enough to prevent us from leaving until the sun is properly *above* the horizon!"

Rubrik only laughed. "I won't promise anything," he replied. "But I think this is a wizard-storm, and if it is, it will be cleared up before midnight at the latest." Karal sighed.

Ulrich was still awake when Karal came in, and Karal reported the whole conversation faithfully. As Ulrich's secretary, he had learned how to memorize long conversations verbatim, when they had been in a situation where taking notes would have been impolite or impolitic. Ulrich listened without comment, then nodded approval.

"You did very well," he told his protégé. "You told him nothing he should not know—and perhaps, having been told of the Miracles by an eyewitness, he will be reporting them as fact rather than hearsay to his superiors."

Karal stretched his knotted muscles and grimaced. "Master, I have to tell you that although I do enjoy this man's company, I had almost rather be facing an armed enemy than have another of these conversations with him. He is *very* good, very subtle. I think that if he tried, he could probably have gotten much more out of me than I intended to tell him. I believe he was hoping for just this sort of opportunity to catch me alone and question me. He knows what will be good for Valdemar to know of Karse now, but if I spent too much more time in his presence I think it might be that I would tell him too much—or something he would misinterpret."

Ulrich considered this for a moment, staring into the fire in the tiny fireplace in their room. "I think you are probably right," he replied, his expression thoughtful, though not at all apprehensive. "It was probably not coincidental that he began asking all these questions of you at the moment when I was out of reach and earshot. I think that the next such conversation should include me."

Karal heaved a sigh of relief at that. He had been concentrating so hard on telling only the truth, and yet not *all* the truth, that he had not realized how tense he had been under Rubrik's scrutiny until he got back to the room he shared with his mentor. Now, he found he had to go through every stretching and relaxing exercise he knew just to get himself unknotted enough to sleep!

This Rubrik was subtle, very subtle. And although he had not consciously been aware of the fact, something instinctive had reacted to that. Among the Priests, "subtle" frequently meant "dangerous."

And among the Priests, "subtle" *always* meant that the man must never be underestimated.

But as Karal blew out the candle and climbed into his own bed, he found himself hoping only one thing—that in this case, "subtle" did not mean "treacherous" as well.

6

R egrettably, Rubrik was right about the weather. A tap on their door at an absolutely unholy hour proved that the storm *had* cleared, before dawn, if not by midnight. Karal pried himself out of his warm cocoon of blankets with a groan of regret that was only slightly softened by the fact that the servants who woke them also brought breakfast along with wash water and a candle. A *real* breakfast this time, not just bread and drink.

I might be able to face the day, he decided, after a decent meal of eggs and bacon, hot bread and sweet honey-butter, with plenty of freshly pressed cider to wash it all down. The hastily-snatched meals on horseback tended to wear very thin, long before Rubrik would decree a halt for further food.

"I think that our escort has probably forgotten how much a young man needs to eat," Ulrich observed with an amused smile, as he watched Karal devour the remains of his mentor's breakfast as well as his own. "I shall remind him."

"Thank you, Master Ulrich," Karal said with real gratitude. "It's not as if he hasn't been very reasonable, but—"

"But he is probably as many years removed from the age at which one devours one's weight in food every day as I am," Ulrich replied. "One forgets."

Karal only smiled, and washed his hands and face clean of the sticky honey he had devoured so greedily. If there was one thing he had a weakness for, it was sweets.

Which means I'd better never take a real scholar's position, or I'll soon resemble Vkandis' own seat cushion.

"Are you sure you can ride?" he asked his mentor anxiously. Ulrich had been moving with the slow, deliberate care that meant his joints were still stiff. Karal had more than a duty to Ulrich as his mentor, he was under *orders* to make certain Ulrich remained healthy during his tenure as Karse's envoy.

He was fairly certain Ulrich was not aware of this, however.

Solaris had called Karal into her Presence just before they left, to make him promise he would take particular care of his mentor. One session with that formidable lady's will concentrated on him and him alone was more than enough. He could not imagine that the Eye of Vkandis Himself would concentrate any more force than did His earthly representative's. Karal did *not* ever want to report to her that Ulrich had come to any kind of grief.

"Oh, I shall live," the Priest said, sighing. Then he smiled wanly. "Don't be too concerned, Karal. These joint aches are not a sign of anything dangerous."

But Karal continued to stare at his mentor with a frown of worry on his face until Ulrich grimaced. "I swear to you that I will ask our escort to stop for the day if I need rest. Will that suit you?"

"I suppose it will have to," Karal told him, trying to sound as severe as one of his own instructors had, when *he* had tried to avoid making pledges. "Since I doubt I'm going to get anything more reasonable out of you."

But Ulrich only raised a quelling eyebrow at him. "Don't try to sound like Ophela, child; it doesn't suit either your years or your personality."

Suitably rebuked, Karal flushed with embarrassment and quickly turned his attention to his packing. Not that there was much to pack—most of what they would be needing at the Court had been sent on ahead with a merchant pack train, and should arrive shortly before they did. Ulrich had not wanted to attract attention by traveling with the number of wagons they would need to maintain their proper state as Officials of the Court. Wagons would mean armed guards, and guards would imply importance or value—and they would end up with the same problem that a large escort would have caused them.

By way of simultaneously showing his contrition and his rebellion, he packed up Ulrich's gear as well, before his mentor could get to it himself. Ulrich only raised his eyebrow even higher at this implication that he was too feeble to deal with it on his own.

With packs assembled, Karal shouldered both, and stepped aside for his master to lead the way out to the courtyard.

As usual, Rubrik was already there, waiting for them in the gray light of false dawn, this time already astride his lovely white horse. Karal fastened the packs behind Honeybee's saddle first, then Trenor's, and swung quickly up onto Trenor's back so that he could watch while Ulrich mounted.

At least Ulrich didn't seem to be in any great difficulty. Maybe he *was* overreacting.

And maybe I really don't ever want to have to face Her Holiness and confess to carelessness. Better safe than sorry, as the saying goes.

They were some few leagues down the road, when Rubrik pulled up his mount beside Ulrich, and motioned to Karal that he should stay abreast of them as well. "I had a rather interesting conversation with your young secretary last night," he said, and waited for Ulrich's reply.

"I know," Ulrich said calmly. "He told me."

"I rather thought he might," came Rubrik's amused response. "You and your leader have chosen well. If I may venture a guess, he told me *exactly* what he was permitted to—no lies, but nothing more and nothing less than what he had been granted leave to reveal."

Ulrich laughed out loud. *"Very* good, friend! And now, since your appetite—or that of whomever it is you are reporting to—has been whetted, you are coming to me for more information than you think he is allowed to give, in the hopes that I have permission to tell you more. And knowing that young Karal would not have been permitted to tell you *anything* if we had not intended for you to come to me."

Rubrik made a slight bow from the saddle, full of amused irony. "Now that we have both agreed that we are too clever for the usual diplomatic half-truths, if you will allow me to give you a starting point, perhaps you can tell me how the Karsites reacted to the alliance with Valdemar, especially after we got rid of Ancar. Do feel free to ignore anything *you* haven't got leave to answer."

"I shall," the Priest replied with urbane courtesy. Then Ulrich nodded, as if to himself, and while the steady sound of hoofbeats filled the silence, spent a moment in thought. "Many of the Karsites felt the alliance would not endure past that moment," he replied. "There was a sizable number, though not a majority, who believed that the alliance had *never* been a good idea. But then the army of the Empire appeared, already well into Hardorn, and heading for Karse and Valdemar."

Rubrik snorted mirthlessly. "Indeed. An unpleasant surprise for all concerned."

The sky to the east showed a hint of color; sunrise would be spectacular—which did not presage a very pleasant ride today. A colorful sunrise, at least in Karse, meant that there would be storms during the day. There was no reason to think that the weather had changed just because he was across a border.

"We knew of the Empire, of course, but probably no more than you," Ulrich said after a moment. "Some had even dismissed the power of the Emperor and the size of the armies he controlled as nothing more than myth or exaggeration. But then—there he was, or rather, there his army was, even bigger than all the stories had claimed. Suddenly there was nothing standing between us and an Empire fabled for gobbling up entire countries. We had nothing that could stop them—except, perhaps, our own resourcefulness, our God—and that insignificant, inconvenient little alliance with Valdemar."

"Which probably didn't seem so insignificant or *nearly* so inconvenient, all things considered, when troop estimates came in," Rubrik replied. And if there was a hint of smugness in his voice, well, Karal could hardly blame him.

"There was another side to all of this that you probably had no hint of," Ulrich said, after another moment of thought. "And that is what the appearance of the Empire did for Her Holiness' credibility."

Ulrich nodded at his secretary, and Karal couldn't resist the invitation to have a word of his own in the discussion. "She'd been saying all along that Vkandis was warning her of an even greater peril to come," he offered proudly. "There weren't too many people who believed her, Son of the Sun or not, except Ulrich and a few other Priests."

He stopped then, afraid he might have overstepped himself, but the look Ulrich gave him was approving rather than the opposite. "Precisely. *Now* she showed that she was a true prophet, for no one could have predicted that the Empire would take an interest in Hardorn—and everything beyond it, one presumes. There is not a soul in Karse who doubts her now."

Well, that wasn't quite true, but it was near enough.

"Now our people as a whole are somewhat—bewildered," Ulrich

concluded. "They are having some difficulty with the various changes she has decreed, but it is obvious even to the worst of her detractors that she *knows*, in the broadest sense of the word, what must be done to save us. It is very clear that if her instructions—or rather, the instructions of Vkandis, as passed to her—are not followed, Karse will not survive the attentions of the Empire. For the people, it is a difficult time. For those of us who believed in Solaris and in our land and God, it is a time of vindication."

"Interesting," Rubrik replied, softly. "I hope you won't mind if I think all this over for a while."

"Be my guest," Ulrich told him, with a hint of a smile. "I believe you might be having just as much difficulty with some of this as some Karsites I could mention."

Rubrik gave him an oblique look but did not reply. Karal felt immensely cheered. It looked as if his mentor had given the Valdemaran more to chew on than he had reckoned possible. Karal had the feeling that the Valdemaran, for the first time, actually believed that Solaris truly was the Son of the Sun, and not just another power-hungry Priest. The Valdemarans would have been perfectly willing to deal with another False Son—provided he (or she) set policies that benefited Valdemar. Karal was not so naive as to think otherwise. But a ruler with the *true* power of the One God behind her—now *that* was another proposition altogether.

Seeing Vkandis as something other than an empty vessel or a puppet for the Priests to manipulate was something Karal guessed Rubrik had not been prepared to deal with.

One point scored for us, he thought with satisfaction, and settled into the ride.

Rubrik inevitably came back with more questions, of course, but they were not about the political situation in Karse, but rather, about Ulrich himself. Gradually Karal came to see the pattern to those questions. Rubrik was trying to discover what the envoy *himself* was made of, the kind of man that the Valdemaran government would be dealing with— and just how much trust Solaris placed in the hands of that envoy.

It was sometimes hard to tell what Rubrik was thinking, but Karal judged that on the whole he was satisfied—and rather surprised to *be* satisfied. Whatever he had been expecting, it had not been a pair like Karal and his master.

Karal found it amusing to speculate on what he *might* have been expecting. An oily, professional politician like the last False Son had been, interested only in power and prestige? An ascetic, like Ophela, with no personal interests whatsoever, blind and deaf to anything other than God and Karse?

Throughout the morning, storm clouds had threatened to unleash another torrent; by the time they stopped at an inn for a meal at noon, it was obvious that they were going to ride right down the throat of another storm like the one yesterday.

This time their escort had found them a decent inn, which had its own share of travelers, and none of them paid any attention to a pair of black-clad clergy and their white-liveried escort. Most seemed too concerned with eating and getting on their way again to waste any time in idle curiosity about other travelers. While Karal and his master lingered over a final cup of ale, Rubrik went out to the courtyard, brooded over the state of the weather, then stared at his horse's head for a long time.

Finally he signaled to the stableboy to come and take his horse, Honeybee, and Trenor to the shelter of the stables, then limped back to the inn. "There's no use going any farther today," he said, clearly annoyed, but not with them. "This storm reaches from here past the inn where I intended us to stop. I wish that Elspeth had a few more Herald-Mages to go around. It seems that this so-called 'wizard-weather' is getting worse, not better."

Now how did he know all that? Karal wondered. He hadn't spoken to anyone. Then again, he was very familiar with this area, as he had already demonstrated more than once. Maybe he could tell what the weather was doing by looking for clues too subtle for Karal to catch.

"I can't speak for your situation here," Ulrich replied carefully, "but I can tell you that in magic, sometimes things do have to get worse before they get better."

"*Not* the sort of thing that your escort cares to hear, my friend," Rubrik replied with a weary laugh as he turned to look at the lowering clouds. He shook his head for, if anything, they were darker and thicker than before. Even Karal could tell they were in for a blow. "I was hoping to make up some time—"

"Not today, friend," Ulrich said with regret. "If we do not stop here, we would *have* to stop soon. I'm afraid that my old bones are not dealing well with this weather of yours."

Inwardly Karal cheered. At least Ulrich was going to keep his promise!

Rubrik looked around for the innkeeper. "Well, I might as well bespeak some chambers. At least we are well ahead of anyone else."

So it seemed, for he returned to them in a much more cheerful frame of mind, just as the stableboy brought up their packs from the stable. "I think you'll enjoy this stay. This may make up for the fool who sold our rooms out from under us," he said—then told the boy, "Bard Cottage."

The horseboy led them around to a door at the rear of the inn, which seemed a little odd to Karal. Such doors were normally used only at night, by servants, and he could not begin to imagine why the boy had taken them this way.

Then the boy led them outside, and there, connected to the inn by a covered walkway, was a neat little building standing all by itself. It was *probably* supposed to look like a farmer's cottage, but no farmer had ever built anything like this. Toylike, cheerfully painted, and far too perfect; if Karal was any judge, it had probably cost more than any three real cottages put together. *It's more like the way a highborn would think a farmer's cottage looks,* Karal decided, regarding the gingerbread carvings, the window boxes full of flowers, and the freshly-painted, spotless exterior with a jaundiced eye.

"This place is usually taken," Rubrik said with satisfaction. "It's very popular with those with the silver for absolute privacy. There's a small bedroom for each of us, beds fit for a prince, cozy little parlor, private bathing room, and they'll bring dinner over from the inn. If we're going to have to wait out a storm, this is the way to do it."

The rooms were tiny, but the beds were as soft as promised; Karal had the absurd feeling that he was sequestered in a doll house, but the place was comfortable, no doubt about that. The cottage would be hideously confining for a long stay, especially for three adults who did not know each other very well.

By the time they'd each taken a turn at soaking in the huge bathtub, however, Karal was quite prepared to agree with Rubrik's earlier statement. For waiting out a storm, this was the best of all possible venues. He was the last to take his bath, and when he got out, the smell of fresh muffins and hot tea greeted his nose.

He followed his nose to the parlor, where a servant from the inn had just set a tray on the table. Ulrich looked up at his entrance and chuckled at his expression. "Evidently our innkeeper has several young men of your age," the Priest told him. "His cook sent this over before I could even ask Rubrik to find a servant to get you a snack."

Rubrik turned around in his chair and grinned at Karal's expression. "Your master reminded me that young men your age are always hungry, and I pointed out this simple fact to our host. He is good at taking hints."

Karal entered the parlor and took the third chair in front of the newly-lit fire just as the storm broke outside. A crash of thunder shook the cottage, and rain lashed the roof in a sudden torrent, making Karal very glad that they were all inside, and not out on the road.

The windows in this pseudo-cottage were small, and not very satisfactory for storm watching, so Karal contented himself with listening to the thunder and the rain pouring down on the roof, as he helped himself to muffins and tea. He'd always enjoyed watching flames dance in a fireplace, anyway. It would be nice to spend a couple of nights here, if it came to that. Ulrich could use the rest, and he had some papers Ulrich had suggested he study that he hadn't had the time for.

But Rubrik is never going to wait that long, he decided, listening to the conversation with one ear. *He wants us in Haven as soon as possible. I wonder what could be so urgent?*

Ulrich had turned the tables on their escort, and was asking personal questions of *him*. Rubrik didn't seem at all reluctant to answer them now, although he had not been so forthcoming before this. Perhaps he had decided that not only was Ulrich worthy of trust as an envoy, he was to be trusted with other things as well.

Ulrich had just asked him—with the Priest's customary tact and delicacy—how he had come to be injured. Karal stopped listening to the rain outside, and devoted his full attention to the conversation.

"That is—an interesting question," the envoy replied measuringly.

"I hope you'll forgive such impertinence," Ulrich told him, with sincerity that was obvious, "but I couldn't help but think, since from the scar it is a recent injury, that it occurred in the war with Ancar. I thought perhaps it might have a bearing on why *you* are our escort, and not—someone else. And I wondered if something in that tale might account for your astonishingly good command of our tongue."

"It's not all that impertinent. I find stares a great deal ruder. And oddly enough, it does have something to do with why I am here—and why I know Karsite so well," the Valdemaran said, after a pause to examine Ulrich searchingly, as if he was trying to ferret out some hidden motive in asking such a question. "It happened while I was trying to protect one of your fellow Priests of Vkandis."

Ulrich nodded gravely. "You did seem to know a bit too much

about us." He raised his mug of tea and sipped. "More than could be accounted for by your presumed acquaintance with a certain Master of Weaponry that we both know is in your Queen's employ."

"Correct." Rubrik smiled crookedly. "Your fellow Priest was not particularly happy to have *me* guarding him, at the time. Not that I can blame him, since at the time *I* was not particularly happy to be there. We had something of a cautious truce, but neither of us really trusted the other."

Why does that not surprise me? Karal thought, with heavy irony.

Rubrik closed his eyes briefly and set his cup down. "We went through several encounters without much trouble, but then our lot got hit hard, by a company of Ancar's troops that not only included *a* mage, but *several* mages. Good ones, at that. He agreed to hold the rear in a retreat—damned brave of him, I thought—counting on me to keep him from getting hurt while he set up the magic that would take care of that. He got wrapped up in working some complex bit of magery, and couldn't move—"

"Tranced," Ulrich replied succinctly. "Many of the young Priests cannot work magic without being entranced."

Rubrik coughed, picked up his cup again, and sipped his own tea. "Yes, well, the line moved back, and we didn't move with it, and no one noticed for a long, critical moment. And since I'd been assigned to guard him, well, I did."

"And?"

He coughed again. "There were several of them, and only two of us, Laylan and me. I'm not a bad fighter, but I'm no Kerowyn. One of the biggest got through my guard, and I went down, right about the time *his* magic finally started working. That was when someone behind us noticed we weren't with the group anymore, and came back to get us."

Ulrich tilted his head to one side. "A glancing blow? But obviously one that did a great deal of damage."

Rubrik shivered, in spite of the warmth of the fire. "It was closer than *I* ever want to come again. I will say the Priest stood by me until the others got to us, right along with Laylan. And he was touchingly grateful, and dragged another one of your Priests over to Heal me as soon as we were hauled back to safety, since there wasn't one of our Healers around that could handle a wound like this one. I'm told that's why the only lasting effect of what could have killed me is this bit of stiffness and an uncooperative leg. Your Healer-Priest was a damned fine human being, treated me as if

I was Karsite—and your other lad not only thanked me when I woke up, but acted like he *believed* in the alliance from then on. That's when my view of your lot changed to something a bit more charitable."

Ulrich refilled his mug from the teapot and nodded. "As his did of you Valdemarans, I expect."

Rubrik chuckled. "I won't say we became the greatest of friends, but we got along just fine after that. He did express a great deal of surprise that a White Demon would take a life-threatening injury to save him, and that the Hellhorse would then proceed to guard both of us."

Karal paled a bit. White Demon? Hellhorse? Rubrik?

Ulrich grinned broadly. "I daresay. Perhaps some good came out of the bad, then—"

"I just wish it hadn't happened to *me.*" Rubrik sighed. "Ah well, the life of a Herald is not supposed to be an easy one. I could count myself lucky that the ax went a bit to the left. To end the story, that's why I'm your escort, and not someone like—oh, Lady Elspeth. I was impressed enough with the way that stiffnecked youngster turned around, and with the Healer-Priest that helped me, that I specifically requested assignment to any missions dealing with Sun-Priests. I wanted whoever met you two to be someone who would at least treat you like human beings."

Herald? White Demon? Hellhorse? Oh, glorious God—

Rubrik was a Herald. A White Demon. And that beautiful horse that Karal had admired so much was no horse at all.

He stared into the fire, stunned, quite unable to move. It was a good thing he wasn't holding anything, or he'd have dropped it, his hands were so numb. He didn't even realize that Rubrik had excused himself and gone back to the inn for something, until the door closed behind him.

"Child, you look as if someone smacked you with a board," Ulrich observed dispassionately. "Are you all right?"

Karal rose to his feet, somewhat unsteadily, and stared at his mentor, trembling from head to foot in mingled shock and fear. "Didn't you hear what he said?" Karal spluttered. "He's one of *them!* Demonspawn! The—"

"I know, I know," Ulrich replied, with a yawn. "I've known all along. If that 'here I am, shoot me now,' white livery of theirs wasn't a dead giveaway, the Companion certainly *is.*"

"But you didn't say anything!" Karal wailed, feeling as if he'd been betrayed.

"I thought you knew," Ulrich told him, a hint of stern rebuke in his voice. "We *are* in Valdemar. We *are* envoys from Her Holiness. The

Heralds *are* the most important representatives of their Queen, and the only ones she trusts fully to accomplish delicate tasks. We've always called them *White* Demons. It should have been logical."

Karal just stared at him.

"Then again," Ulrich said, after a moment of thought, "I apologize. I should have told you, you're correct. I suppose I shouldn't be so surprised that you didn't recognize our friend for what he is—you've only had those ridiculous descriptions in the Chronicles to go on. I should have said something."

"But—" Karal began, wildly. "He—"

"—is the same man he was a few moments ago, before you realized what his position in Valdemar was," Ulrich pointed out, sipping his tea. *"He* is still the same. You are still the same. The only thing that has changed is how you see him, which is not accurate."

Karal tried to get a breath and couldn't. "But—"

"Does he eat babies for breakfast?" Ulrich asked, with a hint of a grim smile.

Karal was forced to shake his head. "No, but—"

"Do he or his mount shoot fire from their nostrils, or leave smoking, blackened footprints behind them?" Ulrich was definitely enjoying this.

Karal wasn't. "No, but—"

"Has he been *anything* other than kind and courteous to either of us?" Ulrich continued inexorably.

"No," Karal replied weakly. "But—" He sat back down in his chair with a *thud*. "I don't understand—"

Ulrich picked up Karal's tea mug and leaned over to put it back in his hands. "Child," he said softly, "he has heard the same stories of us that we have heard of the Heralds. The trouble is—I fear that the stories about us were partly true. We *did* have the Fires of Cleansing. We *did* summon demons to do terrible things, often to people who were innocent of wrongdoing. And yet he has the greatness of heart to assume that you and I, personally, never did any such things. What does that say to you?"

"That—he's the same man whose company I enjoyed this morning," Karal finally said, with a little difficulty. His mind felt thick. His thoughts moved as though they were weighted. And yet he could not deny the truth of what Ulrich had just said.

"I suggest that you relax and continue to enjoy his company," Ulrich replied, leaning back in his chair. "I certainly am, and I intend to go on doing so. In fact, after hearing his story, I am inclined to trust him to live up to every good thing that Her Holiness told me about Heralds."

But—Karal's thought froze right there, and he clasped his mug and stared down into the steaming tea as if he would somehow find his answers there. Ulrich was right; nothing had changed except for the single word.

Herald. Not such a terrible word. Just a word, after all. A name—and Karal had, in his own time, been called plenty of names.

That never made me into anything that they called me.

Yes, well, the word "Herald" in and of itself was nothing terrible either. What word really was?

Ulrich was right about the rest of it, too. *He* had never seen a Hellsp— *A Herald.*

Right. He had never seen a *Herald* in all his life. The descriptions in the Chronicles were infantile, really—composed of all the horrors mothers used to frighten little children into obedience, rolled into one and put into a white shroud. Not a neat uniform, a livery like Rubrik's, but a tattered, ichor-dripping shroud of death. And no matter what other things he'd learned that had been *wrong* about their former enemies, somehow he had still expected Heralds to be monsters.

If you want to make your enemy into something you can hate, you first remove his humanity... Had Ulrich said that at one point, or had that been something he'd heard during one of Solaris' speeches? It was true, whoever had said it, and the Chronicles had certainly tried to remove all vestige of humanity from these Heralds. *Make them only icons. When they are seen as a type, and not as individuals, they are easy for a fanatical mind to grasp—and hate.*

Karal didn't *think* he was fanatically-minded, but then again, what fanatic ever did? It was going to take a while to get used to this.

"I think I'm going to go—ah—meditate for a while," he said to Ulrich, who was staring into the fire with every evidence of utter contentment. The Priest waved a lazy hand at him.

"Go right ahead," his master said. "I believe you ought to. You've just had a shock, and you need to think about it. I'm sure your nose will tell you when dinner arrives, if your stomach doesn't demand it first."

Karal put down his mug and retired to his room, flushing in confusion, and wondered how things in his life had managed to become more complicated than he had ever dreamed possible.

And how was he ever going to make all the scattered pieces of it fit again?

* * *

He still hadn't quite wrapped his mind around the concept of "Rubrik-as-Hellspawn, Hellspawn-as-Herald" by the time dinner arrived. He ate quickly and quietly, listening, but not participating in the conversation at all. Ulrich and their escort continued their chat as blithely as if nothing whatsoever had changed, although Rubrik did ask, with some concern, if Karal was feeling all right.

"You look pale," he observed, as Karal bolted the last of his dinner. "If you're getting sick, please tell me—this is a good-sized town, and there are real Healers here. Healer-Priests, too, and there may even be one of the splinter Sunlord Temples here—"

"Ah, I meant to ask you about that," Ulrich interjected. "Later, that is."

"It's nothing, sir, my master already knows about it," Karal said hoarsely, taking the proffered excuse for what might be considered rude behavior. "It's just a headache. I—I think I'll go to my room, and sleep it off."

Karal fled before Rubrik could ask anything else. His dinner lay in his stomach like a ball of cold, damp clay. It had probably been excellent; he'd bolted it so fast he hadn't really noticed.

He spent part of the night staring sleeplessly at the ceiling, the murmurs of conversation in the next room scarcely audible over the pounding rain. He wasn't able to make out what the other two were saying, and he wasn't sure he wanted to. He just couldn't handle this. How could he act normally around Rubrik ever again?

But the soft, comfortable bed and the rhythmic pounding of the rain overhead seduced him into a dreamless sleep, and in the morning his anxiety seemed pretty stupid. He lay there in his bed, sheepishly wondering why the "revelation" had seemed so terrible last night. Ulrich was right; Rubrik was still the same man—and Heralds, as Karsite myth painted them, couldn't possibly have been anything like the reality. After all, there were plenty of things that had "always been True" or had been "the Will of Vkandis" that Solaris had proven were lies. So why should anything the False Ones taught about the Heralds be true?

He rose and went into the parlor, to find Ulrich already there and in high good humor, which meant his joints no longer pained him. The doors and windows were standing open wide to a wonderful warm breeze, there was a meal waiting on the table for him, and Rubrik was nowhere in sight. This storm had swept through cleanly last night, leaving behind a morning like a new-minted coin, the air washed so clean and pure that it was a pleasure to breathe. Rubrik had *not* sent servants to wake them up, and had let them sleep until after the sun rose. After a truly excellent breakfast, they joined their escort in the courtyard of the inn beneath an absolutely cloudless blue sky.

"Headache better?" Rubrik asked, as the horse-boy led Trenor up to Karal and held him so that Karal could mount easily.

"Yes, sir, thank you," Karal was able to reply, with a smile.

"Good. I get a touch of one myself in these wizard-storms. They say most people with any hint of mind-magic do." He gazed searchingly at Karal, who had no idea of what he was talking about. Karal shrugged his incomprehension.

"Yes, but how does that explain my poor, aching joints?" Ulrich put in, with a faint smile. "I certainly do not hear thoughts with my knees!"

Rubrik laughed heartily. "A good question, and one that probably proves that, as always, the nebulous 'they' are probably as foolish as the things 'they' are reputed to say!"

On that cheerful note, he led them out to the road, heading north again, under a brilliant sun.

That seemed a good enough omen to start, and as the morning wore on, Karal managed to dismiss the rest of his lingering fears as absolutely groundless. The Herald and Ulrich must have shared a great deal of personal information after Karal went to bed, for now they acted like a pair of real friends.

Huh, he thought, with astonishment, for Ulrich had never been *friends* with anyone that Karal had ever noticed. But there it was, as they rode side by side, there was an easiness between them that could not be anything but friendship. *Ulrich respected him as soon as we met—and after that, there was a kind of—fellowship, maybe? Something like that, anyway; like he'd have with, oh, one of the Army Captains. Someone who deserved respect and was an interesting and intelligent person, a man he had things in common with. But this is different. I'm not sure how, but it's different. Ulrich seems happier, more open, and the tone of his voice is warmer than it usually is around other people.*

He found that Rubrik was taking pains to see that Karal was included in conversation as the day wore on. And somewhat to his astonishment, he realized that he had begun to actually relax around the Herald. If anything, Rubrik reminded him of his favorite uncle, the one who'd been a guard with a merchant caravan and had a wealth of tales about strange places and the wonderful things he had seen.

Rubrik was evidently in the mood to tell some of his own tales this morning, for he began to describe some of the other "foreigners" that they would meet once they reached the capital of Haven and the Court of Queen Selenay. Some of them, Karal would not have believed under any other circumstances, but Rubrik had absolutely no reason to lie and every reason to tell them the whole and complete truth.

But if he *was* telling the whole and complete truth—some of the other envoys weren't human at all...

Ulrich didn't act at all surprised, though, as the Herald described some of the strangest creatures Karal had ever heard of. The Hawkbrothers were bad enough, with their white hair, intelligent birds, and outlandish clothing. But then he described the gryphons—Treyvan, Hydona, and their two youngsters. It was the little ones that made Karal decide that the Herald was *not* trying to play some kind of elaborate trick on them. Why make up that kind of detail if it was only a jest? The adult gryphons would have been more than enough.

"I'd been warned," Ulrich said laconically, when Rubrik ended his description. "After all, several of our Priests actually worked with these gryphons. Including one young lady who learned a valuable lesson in—hmm—"

"Cooperation?" Rubrik suggested with a wry smile.

"I was thinking, humility, but that will do." Ulrich's eyes actually twinkled. "Karal, you'll remember her, you were schooled with her. Gisell."

Karal's mouth dropped open with astonishment. "Gisell? *Humility?*" The two simply did *not* go together! Gisell had been one of the most stiffnecked little highborn bitches he'd ever had the misfortune to meet. Nothing could induce her to forget her lofty pedigree or her many important relatives.

Rubrik laughed heartily, and his smile reached and warmed his eyes. "Oh, a gryphon can bite you in two and have your legs shredded while your top half watches. When he tells you that you *will* work with the son of a pigkeeper and *like* it, you learn to be humble very quickly."

"If Gisell can learn to be humble, then I *can* believe in gryphons," Karal said firmly, provoking another burst of laughter, both from the Herald and from his master.

"Gryphons are just as real as my Companion Laylan, I promise you," Rubrik assured him. "And no more a monster than he is."

Now that triggered another thought, one that had sat in the back of his mind, pushed aside by the pressing dilemma of Rubrik-as-Herald.

His horse—or rather, his Companion. Karsite legend had plenty to say about the creatures that Heralds rode, too! And now his behavior, which had seemed to be "only" remarkable training, had an explanation.

Laylan wasn't a horse. Obviously. *"No more a monster than he is"* he said—*but he isn't, can't be, even a magical horse like the Hawkbrothers' birds. Even if back home they'd call him a Hellhorse. So what is he if he isn't a horse?*

He held the question back, but it irritated him like an insect bite he couldn't scratch. Laylan himself seemed to know that it was tormenting him, too, because he kept *looking back* at him, and now he saw what his assumption that he was an animal had not let him see before. He *watched* him, watched Ulrich, and he had the sense that he was somehow participating in the conversation, even if he couldn't say anything in words.

Finally he couldn't stand it anymore. "Sir? Your—Laylan—what *is* he?"

Rubrik blinked, taken quite by surprise by the breathless question. "I suppose you *wouldn't* know, would you?" he said, finally, turning in his saddle and squinting against the bright sunlight. "Ah—the best explanation we have is that Companions are a benign spirit in a mortal body. In some ways, rather like gryphons, except that they deliberately ally themselves with Heralds in order to help us help our land. They choose to look like horses, we believe, because horses pass without notice practically everywhere."

"Ah!" Ulrich's exclamation of delighted understanding made both of them turn toward the Priest. "That is the *best* explanation I have heard yet; I never had heard any reason why your Companions should have that particular form. It seems an inconvenient one."

Rubrik snorted, and so did Laylan. "Say that some time when you see him in full charge! This is several stone of muscle and *very* sharp hooves, my friend, and he knows how to use both to advantage! I'd rather have him in a fight than twenty armsmen, and that's a fact." He tilted his head to one side and added, as if it had never occurred to him before, "Odd though, that you Karsites don't seem to have anything like Companions, with your Vkandis being so—"

He flushed, and cut the sentence off, but Ulrich chuckled. "So much of a divine busybody in our lives, is that what you were going to say?" Rubrik winced, but the Priest only grinned. "Oh, don't apologize, even Her Holiness has been known to comment on that from time to time. Actually, though, Vkandis *does* have two supernatural manifestations that ordinary Priests—which are the closest thing we have to your Heralds—can experience. The sad part is that one of those was and is tragically easy to feign."

Ulrich gave Karal a prompting look.

"The Voice of Flame?" Karal asked with interest, taking the look to mean that Ulrich meant him to supply the correct answer.

Ulrich nodded. "Good, you recall what I told you." He turned back to the Herald. "The Voice of Flame is a sourceless nimbus of fire; it appears above the head of a Priest and speaks through him. It is, by far, the most common manifestation of Vkandis' Will. Since we Priests are often mages as well as clergy, I'm sure you can see how easy this particular manifestation of the Will was to counterfeit."

Rubrik made a sour face. "Not a chance you could counterfeit a Companion—" he began.

"Ah, but this is what is interesting," Ulrich interrupted eagerly. "There was, traditionally, *another* manifestation that was impossible to counterfeit—and it was one that had not been seen in so long that it had fallen almost into myth. Until recently, that is. And it seems to me that the Firecats are *very* like your Companions."

"Firecats?" Rubrik shook his head. "I've never heard of them."

"Not likely anyone has, outside of Karse," Karal put in. "In fact, until one showed up with Solaris, I'd say most of the Priests didn't believe in them anymore, either!"

"A cat?" Rubrik's skepticism was quite clear. "How could an ordinary cat—"

"No more an *ordinary* cat than your Laylan is an ordinary horse, my friend," Ulrich told him gleefully. "First of all, there is the color— Firecats are unique. They are a pale cream in color, with red ears, facial mask, paws, and tail. And like your Companions, they have blue eyes. Then there is the *size*—they are as tall as mastiffs. And they talk."

"Talk?" Rubrik was incredulous for just a split second. "Wait—you mean, in Mindspeech?"

"Mind-to-mind, yes," Ulrich agreed. "They can, and do, speak to whomever they choose, however, and I believe your Companions speak only to their selected Heralds?"

Rubrik nodded, and Ulrich went on.

"Firecats historically appeared at significant times to offer advice, not only to the Son of the Sun, but often to anyone else who was of crucial importance. In ancient times, the Son of the Sun was always accompanied by at least one, and often two Cats." Ulrich shrugged. "Now, the Cats stopped appearing, I believe, about the time that the Fires of Cleansing were begun; I also believe that there has not been a genuine manifestation of the Voice since that same period, at least not among the Priests in the capital and the larger cities. Until recently."

Rubrik sat as bolt upright in his saddle as his infirmity would allow. "Are you telling me that—"

"I, myself, have seen Her Holiness speak with what I believe to be the genuine Voice," Ulrich told him. "But far more important, Solaris has a Firecat. He calls himself 'Hansa'—and that *is* the name of one of the most ancient Sons of the Sun, a name not even a demon would claim with impunity—he is not only seen sitting beside her, but he actually appeared *shortly after Vkandis struck down the False Son.*" He nodded as Rubrik's eyes narrowed in speculation. "His appearance served to further confirm her in the eyes and minds of the populace. But if you have any doubt, I have heard it from her own lips—and from Hansa's mind—that *he* is the one who advised her to make Herald Talia an honorary Sun-priest to cement our alliance."

Rubrik's mouth formed into a silent "o", but Ulrich wasn't quite finished yet.

"All the Firecats have traditionally referred to themselves by names of former Sons of the Sun. We have always believed that they *are* the spirits of former Sons who have taken on a material form in order to guide and advise us." He cast a significant glance down at Laylan, who looked up at him blandly and actually batted his eyelashes at him. "Obviously, they are exactly like your Companions, except that there are fewer of them. I assume that is because there are fewer deceased Sons than there are deceased Heralds."

Now it was Rubrik's turn to look as if someone had hit him in the back of the head with a board. And there was a whicker from Laylan that sounded suspiciously like a snicker.

"Of course—" Rubrik replied weakly. "Obviously." As if it wasn't obvious at all, and the thought had *never once crossed his mind.*

Rubrik's astonishment was so total, and so blatant, that Karal came very near to disgracing himself completely by blurting out the question, *"Do you mean that hadn't ever occurred to you?"* He stopped himself just in time.

In the first place, such a question would be twenty leagues beyond rude, and Ulrich would be completely within his rights—even his duty—

to send him back in disgrace on the spot. One did not ask questions like that if one was a diplomat.

In the second place—

It's possible that the Companions actually have been keeping Heralds from even thinking just that. The Firecats were known to be what they were *only* to the Priests—the rest of the Karsite populace simply regarded them as signs of Vkandis' favor. Most ordinary folk were not even aware that the Cats spoke to the Priests; after all, the Priests had the Voice, what did they need with a talking feline?

I can think of several reasons why Companions would not want it known that they had once been Heralds, Karal decided, rather grimly, after a moment of silence that gave him plenty of time to really examine the idea. For instance, there had been one infamous attempt to destroy a Firecat by the traitor who had brought about the assassination of the Son of the Sun whose name the Firecat bore.

Not that that *worked. Firecats can protect themselves very nicely. The assassin made a lovely bonfire, so the story goes.* But surely, there were people who would be very unhappy if certain Heralds were to reappear after their demise—and Companions, unlike the Cats, *could* be killed.

And even a Karsite knows that if you kill the Hellhorse—the Companion—you'll probably kill the Herald.

There could be emotional conflicts among the Heralds as well. *How* would a loved one feel, knowing that the beloved ex-Herald *could return if he chose,* even if in a rather—inconvenient—form? It would be devastating if he *did,* and nearly as bad if he *didn't.*

As he was mulling all this over, he caught sight of Laylan staring back at him over his shoulder—and when he caught his eye, he nodded as if he had been following his very thoughts.

As if—like Hansa—he can see what is in my mind—

Once again, he sat frozen in place, stunned. *Like Hansa. The Cats* are *like Companions—*

Once again, he nodded; gravely, but unmistakably.

Only one thought floated up out of the shock.

If the Cats are like the Companions, then we are not so different from our ancient enemies after all.

And he could not for the life of him decide if that realization was a reassuring one.

7

An'desha stared unhappily out the window of his provisional home. Late afternoon sunset streamed through the branches of the trees around Firesong's *ekele,* and left patches of gilding on the grass beyond the windows. The silence that must surely be outside was not mirrored within. The indoor garden was full of laughter and talk, even to the point where the burbling of the waterfalls and fountains was overwhelmed by human chatter.

An'desha sat on a rock ledge in the farthest corner of the hot pool, dangling his feet in the water and trying not to sulk. He could not suppress his bitter unhappiness, though, and by the gods, he wasn't sure he wanted to! Firesong had *not* consulted him on this; he hadn't even been warned that there were visitors coming this afternoon. Firesong had simply showed up with all of them in tow, some of whom An'desha had never even met before. It was rude, it was unfair, and he was not in a mood to make the best of it.

This was *supposed* to be his retreat away from all the strangeness of Valdemar—so why did Firesong have to bring half of Valdemar into the retreat and spoil it?

Well, maybe not half of Valdemar, but it certainly sounded like it. The garden *felt* overcrowded, and the fragile peace he had been trying to cultivate was shattered.

An'desha had not had a very good day today; not that everything had gone wrong, but nothing had quite gone *right.* Firesong kept telling him that he needed to get out and interact with other people, to *meet* some of these foreigners, so today he had gritted his teeth and made an attempt, hoping for Firesong's approval. Hoping for *some* success to show him, however small that was.

He'd gone off on his own this afternoon while Firesong taught the young mages. A few days ago he had volunteered to help a group of those youngsters who wore the rust, blue, or gray clothing with one of their lessons in Shin'a'in, and their teacher had gladly accepted his offer. Today was to have been the first of those lessons, and An'desha had some vague idea that he might socialize with them after the lesson. Wasn't that what these strange children did? First have lessons, then socialize?

The lesson had gone on all right, but afterward, when they accepted his hesitant suggestion that they could ask him questions and he would try to answer them, he'd retreated in bewildered confusion within a few stammered sentences. They were just too—weird. They weren't anything like the Shin'a'in of his Clan; they seemed avidly, greedily curious about everything, at least to him, and they asked things he considered terribly callous and horribly intrusive. Of course it was possible that they had no idea that they were being so intrusive—and it was possible that with their limited grasp of Shin'a'in they simply didn't know what they were asking, but why ask him all those prying questions about Firesong? And what in the name of the Star-Eyed was a "Tayledras mating circle?"

Rudeness was bad enough, but they were also shallow, or at least their questions pointed in that direction. To him they seemed selfish and preoccupied with trivialities. He found himself getting angry at them for being so cavalier and carefree, then was appalled at himself for being angry with them simply for acting like children.

A Shin'a'in child was an adult the day he (or she) could ride out on the horse he had trained from a colt, and survive on his own on the Plains for one week. That could be any age from nine up. These Valdemarans, raised in cities, had no such measuring stick for maturity. They *were* children—more to the point, for all that they were not all that much younger than his apparent age, they were sheltered, protected children. He gathered that most of them had never personally been touched by the war that had threatened their land, and certainly none of them could ever even imagine, in their worst nightmares, the kinds of things *he* had gone through. How could he fault them for being what they were?

But they not only had nothing in common with him, they were so very different from him that they might just as well have been gryphons or *kyree*. For that matter, he had more in common with the perpetually ebullient Rris than he did with any of *them!* At least he understood why Rris was always asking questions; he was a historian, and he wanted not only the facts, but the feelings and reasoning that brought the facts about. *Kyree* oral histories took these factors into account; they were important parts of the tale. These children had no such excuses for *their* greedy curiosity.

So he returned in confusion and some distress to the only shelter he had anymore—only to find that Firesong had led an invasion of Valdemar into the place where he sought tranquillity, an invasion planned without his knowledge or consent.

Oh, granted, there were only half a dozen of the strangers, but it seemed like more, three times more. They poured into his garden and inserted themselves into his heated pool, barely stopping long enough in their ongoing conversation to greet him. And if he sequestered himself upstairs, Firesong would want to know why and probably be disgusted with him for not even trying to be polite and sociable. So he stayed and found himself virtually excluded from the conversation anyway, simply because he had no idea what was going on or what they were talking about.

To his right were Elspeth and Darkwind; well, at least he knew them. Elspeth was the daughter of the ruler of this place, and a Herald—she had a spirit-creature called a "Companion" that looked something like a horse and spoke in the mind. A lithe and lively young woman, her dark hair was now more silver than sable, and her eyes a soft blue-gray, turned that way by her use of the node-energy from the Heartstone beneath her mother's palace. She was that unique creature among humans, strong *and* beautiful, and perfectly self-confident, if rather headstrong. Darkwind was another Hawkbrother, an Adept, though not the equal of Firesong, with the raptoral features of most Tayledras, and the pure silver hair and blue eyes all Tayledras grew into eventually, simply by living around Heartstones. Both Elspeth and Darkwind knew Firesong long before An'desha had met any of them; he got the impression that Firesong had been their teacher at one point.

Beyond them, up to their necks in hot water, were a tall blonde woman they called "Kero" and a man whose name An'desha hadn't even caught. It had sounded something like "elder" and that surely couldn't be right. Both of them were older than anyone else here, but An'desha wouldn't have challenged either of them to a fight. Their muscles and the way they moved told him that they were a lot more dangerous than they looked. The clothing that the man had shed was of the white kind worn by the Heralds, and though the woman had been wearing dark leather gear, they both seemed to have those same kind of spirit-beasts that Elspeth partnered.

Beyond them was Firesong, holding court, and beyond him, the Shin'a'in envoy and some mage or other this "Kero" knew who looked to have a lot of Shin'a'in blood in him. He was a little younger than Kero was, and although he had the dark hair and golden skin of a man of the Plains, he had emerald green eyes. Besides, he was definitely a mage, and An'desha knew from personal experience that no Shin'a'in could be a mage, unless he was a shaman as well. He seemed comfortable in this strange gathering, anyway. A lot more comfortable than An'desha, who *belonged* here.

Not a huge group, after all—only six, eight if you counted An'desha and Firesong, but they were all such vivid personalities that An'desha felt smothered, ignored, or both. They were all chattering away like old friends, which they probably *were*, but they seemed to have forgotten that An'desha didn't know any of them, really.

This invasion of his private preserve, coming at the end of an uncomfortable afternoon, made him want to throw a very childish tantrum. He wanted to be alone with Firesong—no matter how hard it was to reconcile his feelings about the young mage, at least Firesong was one person he could *understand*. Firesong would make excuses for him and help find answers! An'desha wanted the music of falling water, not insistent chatter. Or, if there must be talk, he wanted to talk to Firesong about his difficulties with these strange, intrusive people of Valdemar. They were nice enough, but *nosey*.

He would have said that he wanted to go home, except that he had no home, and this was the closest he was likely to get. Now these strangers had just proved that it wasn't *his* home, and never would be, simply by being here.

He didn't want to share Firesong *or* his place with the group of laughing, splashing invaders.

They were talking like mad things in three languages, only two of which he understood at all well; his own Shin'a'in and Tayledras. They chattered about *more* people and doings he knew nothing about.

That was not all that upset him. There was something about this gathering that set his nerves on edge, something intangible that had nothing to do with the invasion of his place. There was a frenetic, feverish quality to the conversation he sensed, but couldn't fathom. They acted as if they were trying to drive something unpleasant away by sheer volume of talk.

And as if that wasn't bad enough, it was becoming increasingly clear to him by the moment that Firesong was *flirting* with Darkwind. In front of everyone!

Was Firesong *trying* to humiliate him?

He pulled his feet out of the water in a fit of sullen fury, and snatched up a towel and his clothing. Furious, he began to dry himself off, ignored by the others. Ignored even by Firesong, who was engrossed in his flirtation.

Oh, gods. How could he not have guessed that something like this would happen? Weren't the Hawkbrothers supposed to be as light-in-love as their feathered companions?

But must Firesong take on a new conquest in front of him and everyone else? And why Darkwind?

Well, naturally, they are both Tayledras Adepts, and Darkwind is attractive and clever and mature, and I'm a half-Shin'a'in freak with more problems than twenty sane people. I'm a cowardly fool who doesn't understand most of what Firesong tries to show me.

"...and now that you're properly silver-haired, as an Adept should be, with a *decent* wardrobe, you're actually a credit to k'Sheyna instead of a disgrace," Firesong teased, while An'desha struggled into his shirt and breeches; a difficult proposition with still-wet skin. "I don't know how Elspeth was ever attracted to you, with your hair dyed the color of mud and full of bark. You looked like a mad hermit, not a proper Hawkbrother."

"Oh?" Darkwind arched his eyebrows and grinned, then splashed Firesong with a handful of water. "Really? And *who* was it told Elspeth he wanted to braid feathers into my hair? I thought perhaps you liked the rustic look. You might have found me challenging."

"Hmph." Firesong sent the droplets flying back at Darkwind with a flicker of magic. "If I did tell her something like that, it was because I was *hoping* to induce some sense of proper grooming into you."

Darkwind pouted. "And here all the time I thought you *wanted* me!"

"We-ell, now that you look like a civilized human being and not a patch of brush—" Firesong fluttered long, silver eyelashes at the lean and muscular k'Sheyna Adept, who smirked and fluttered right back at him.

An'desha stared, aghast, embarrassed, humiliated. Oh, he *knew* that the Hawkbrothers were free enough with their favors, but—

—but how could they carry on like this! And *right in front of him!* They *were* trying to hurt him! He hadn't done anything to deserve treatment like this!

He felt his skin grow cold, then hot; his throat choked, and his stomach knotted. As he struggled to control himself, astonishment turned to something darker, in the blink of an eye.

He flushed again, hotter this time. From "how could they," the thought turned to another.

How dare they!

His hands knotted into fists; his stomach cramped. He clenched his jaw so hard he thought his teeth would shatter. He choked back an exclamation of pain and outrage.

Firesong continued to flirt, without a single glance at him.

His heart pounded until he shook with the rhythm and blood roared in his ears. His jaw ached as he clenched it tight. Firesong leaned closer to Darkwind and murmured something that made the other Adept laugh aloud, throwing his head back and showing a fine set of white teeth. Firesong laid one elegant hand on Darkwind's shoulder.

Rage flared, fed by jealousy, into an all-consuming conflagration which left room for only one thought.

I'll—I'll eviscerate him! Though which "him," he couldn't at that moment say. He struggled with his numb, impotent anger, fought with the feelings that threatened to bind him where he stood.

Something dark uncoiled like a newly-awakened snake, deep inside him. It oozed through his veins and tingled along his nerves.

For a brief moment, his rage lacked a target, torn as it was between Firesong and Darkwind equally. But then, as Darkwind made to snatch at a feather from his bondbird's tail to give to Firesong, it all turned against the interloper.

How dare he!

And suddenly, as soon as he *had* the target, his anger was no longer impotent.

The darkness filled him, burned his fingers, longing to be unleashed. He felt power rising in him, rushing to his summons eagerly, flowing into him, all too familiar from the anger-fueled mage-attacks of Mornelithe Falconsbane; power that was poised to tear the guts right out of Darkwind's treacherous body and fling them back in the bastard's face—

—tear the guts from—

—tear—

Realization froze him in place, just before he let the power loose to turn the interloper inside out.

What am I doing?

He stopped himself, appalled, before the power got away from him; hauled it back and quashed it; dispersed it, let it drain out of him in a rush that left him trembling, this time not with anger, but with horror.

I nearly killed him—

—nearly—

—oh, gods—

Rage turned inward and ate itself, and with a strangled sob of terror, he whirled and fled the garden.

He dashed up the stairs to the second story, blinded with panic, with fear, and with tears of shame. There was only one thought in his mind.

I could have killed him. I could have. I almost did.

Panic gave his stumbling feet the strength his body lacked. He had to get away, away from everyone else, before something worse happened. What was he? What had he become?

Worse yet—*what was he still?*

A monster. I'm a monster. I'm the Beast...

Falconsbane was alive and well, and living inside *him.* Waiting for a chance to get out, or better still, looking for a way to make An'desha into the kind of sadistic, perverted, twisted horror he had been.

He heard the running footsteps of someone following him, and turned at the top of the stairs, intending to send whoever it was away, far away from him—away from one irrevocably contaminated with the lurking shadow of Mornelithe Falconsbane. He wasn't thinking any more clearly than that; he only knew that no one should be near him.

But he didn't get a chance to say anything, for it was Elspeth who had followed him, hard on his heels. He had been misled by the soft sound of her bare feet into thinking she was farther behind him. She didn't stop when he did; she ran up the last three stairs and caught him up in her arms and in an impulsive embrace as soon as he turned and faced her, ignoring the fact that she was dripping wet and so was the brief tunic she wore. That simple embrace undid him completely.

Oh, gods...

He collapsed against her without a thought and began to weep, hopelessly; she held him against her damp shoulder, and stroked his hair as if he had been a very small child caught up in a nightmare. In a moment, it didn't matter that her tunic was wet; tears of pain and panic burned their way down his face and into the sodden cloth, and his throat ached with the effort of holding his hysterical sobs back. He simply clung to her, a shelter, a sure refuge, and she supported him.

"An'desha, it's all right," she said quietly, over his strangled sobbing. "Dearheart, it wasn't what you thought it was! Darkwind and I are bonded and Firesong knows it, and Darkwind knows how Firesong feels about *you!* They were only teasing each other, dear, truly, and they would never, ever have done that if they had any idea how hurt you were just now. We just all thought you were tired and wanted to be left alone, and Firesong's had mischief in him all day."

"But you—" he got out, through the tears. "You—"

How she knew he was trying to ask why she had followed him, he had no idea—but she knew, or guessed right, and gave him the answer.

"I was the only one close enough to see your face, *ke'chara*. It was only play, and now they're teasing Kero. You were so quiet that we all assumed you'd join in after you revived a little. No one else knows you ran off. You mustn't let things like this bother you so much!" She held him very tightly for a moment, and he felt the warmth of her concern flowing over him. He *wanted* it to help; he wanted to feel comforted.

It did nothing to thaw the frozen center of his fear.

Worse, she only thought he'd fled, like some stupid jilted lover, like an idiot in a ballad. She hadn't a clue why he was falling apart like this.

He had to tell her. She had to know. It might be her life he threatened next. *Would* be, if Falconsbane got loose.

"That's not—" He fought the tears back as they threatened to choke him into incoherence. "Elspeth, it wasn't *that*—didn't you feel it? I was angry, and power just—took over and I almost struck Darkwind! I almost killed him!" He pulled away from her, afraid that he would somehow contaminate her as well. "It's Falconsbane!" he choked out. "He's still—here, he *must* be, he's still controlling me and I—I—"

He began to shake, trembling with absolute terror. How could he have done that? How could it not have been the Beast within?

Yet she did not draw away from him as he was certain she must, and when she pulled him back against her shoulder he did not resist.

"Is there somewhere up here we can go to sit for a while?" she asked quietly, as the tears began again. He waved vaguely to the right, and she supported him as she steered him away from the staircase and into the sitting room with its view from among the tree branches. She helped him down onto a cushion and sat beside him, still holding him, until his shaking stopped.

"Let's start over," she said quietly as the sun set somewhere beyond the trees, and thick, blue dusk gathered about them. "You were obviously tired, out-of-sorts, and we thoughtlessly came trampling in to destroy what little peace and quiet you had. That put you further out-of-sorts, right?"

He nodded, his stomach churning, only half of his mind on what she was saying. How could any of this matter now?

"Then, already unhappy and angry with us, you *thought* that Firesong was trying to seduce Darkwind. What you really saw was just Firesong teasing someone who is a good enough friend to tease back." He heard a definite tone of wry amusement in her voice. "I was told by a—a Shin'a'in friend that Hawkbrother teasing usually involves a lot of innuendo and flirtation. She told me that I might as well get used to it, since it's as stupid to get upset over something *they* grow up with as it would be to become upset because birds fly. So—I got used to it, and I've been known to give as good as I get."

"S-s-so I've got no choice but to get used to it, too?" he said, with a touch of anger getting past the tears, momentarily distracted from his deeper and weightier fears.

He felt her shrug. "If you don't, you're only setting yourself up for more pain," she replied logically. "An'desha, I don't know if you've ever felt strongly about anyone before, but there is one thing you had better get into your head right now. You *don't* go into a pairing intending to try and change someone to suit you. They were themselves long before you came along. You *do* go into a pairing ready to compromise."

He shook his head numbly, his entire soul rebelling at the idea that she thought his troubles were no more serious than simple hurt feelings, and once again she divined what he meant though he could not say it.

"Huh... it's not that?"

He nodded, then shook his head helplessly.

"It's not that, and it's more than that?"

He sniffed, and nodded.

She paused for a moment, and thought, her brows creased. "All right. I'll start with what's simplest. Now, listen to me and *believe* me. Darkwind and I are lovers, partners, and friends; there isn't much that is going to come between us, and Firesong *knows* that. He also knows that I am not Tayledras, and that I would be very, very hurt if what you saw and heard was anything other than friendly teasing. So does Darkwind. That's one of the compromises *we've* made." Then she laughed dryly. "More than that, he knows that there is a very real possibility that *he* would be very, very hurt as well—physically! I have quite a few faults, An'desha, and I have a very bad temper. I do *not* care to share Darkwind with anyone, and I will *not* be humiliated, especially in front of others. If I thought that was going to happen, well, someone would need a bandage or splint."

"Oh," was all he could say.

"So—for the answer to the situation that made you angry in the first place and triggered all this, if I don't have a reason to feel jealous or humiliated, and I'm the most jealous wench in Valdemar, certainly *you* don't!"

Uncertainly, he rubbed at his burning eyes with the back of his hand and coughed. A certain Shin'a'in proverb sprang immediately to mind. Not a flattering one, either. "But they say that the—"

"The lady is always the last to know." She snorted, a most unladylike sound. "Yes, but 'they' don't reckon on bondbirds and Companions, both of whom would tell tales, I promise you. Vree doesn't much care for Firesong's bird Aya, and he likes me and Gwena both; he'd babble like a scarlet jay either to me or to her if Darkwind got up to something with Firesong that I didn't know about."

An'desha wiped his eyes again. It certainly sounded logical. "But—"

"But that's giving Firesong no credit whatsoever for any kind of feelings, honor, or decency; that's assuming that he *is* as shallow and light-minded as he would like us to think. That is not fair to him, and you know better. For that matter, so do I." She took his chin in two fingers, and angled his face towards hers so that he had to look into her eyes. *"Ke'chara,* he is a *Healing Adept.* Don't you realize what that means? Of all people, you should. For all that he seems light-minded on the outside, he *cares,* more than anyone I have ever seen. He cares for *you,* and I think he has surprised himself by how much he cares for you. He has put a great deal of himself into the Healing of *you,* and he will literally empty himself for you if you let him, right down to the dregs. He is as decent and honorable as any Herald I know, and that is the greatest compliment I could give anyone."

An'desha swallowed slowly past the great lump in his throat. "I—"

"He has his faults, plenty of them, but failing to care about you and what happens to you is not one of them. He and I are rather alike when it comes to matters of the heart. Maybe it's the blood we share, I don't know." She looked very stern, and he was forcefully reminded of Need. "Give the man some credit. He has the capacity for great love, and he's not going to risk great love for something trivial. It was nothing more than a game. He would never, ever jeopardize anything having to do with you."

He had to believe her. *She* knew; she knew people, and she knew Firesong and Darkwind. He blinked, his eyes feeling gritty and sore, and nodded. Then his fear rose in him again, worse than before, when he realized what he could have done *for no cause.* Somehow that made it all worse.

"But Fal—" he began, with a wail of despair.

She cut him off with a look and a finger placed against his lips. "Falconsbane had nothing to do with the way you reacted. Being far too ready to think yourself hurt *did,* but not Falconsbane. He is gone, and good riddance."

"No," he replied, with heat. "This time *you* don't understand! Even if he's gone, he's still a part of me, he's corrupted me, he's gotten into the way I think and react and—"

"Hell, no," she said firmly. "Horseturds. For one thing, I doubt that Mornelithe Falconsbane ever cared enough about anything or anyone to *ever* feel jealousy! In order to become jealous, you have to care for and value something besides yourself, you know."

That took him aback; it was something that had never even entered his mind. He had to nod cautiously. Falconsbane had certainly never cared for anyone—only valued them as prizes.

She smiled grimly. "As for your own reaction and how strong and irrational it was—perfectly ordinary people have moments of jealousy as terrible as anything you just experienced. It happens all the time." Her smile turned into a grimace of pain. "Unfortunately, Heralds see the aftermath of that kind of jealousy all the time, too."

"I'm *not* ordinary," he began.

"No," she agreed readily. "You aren't. Ordinary people do not have the ability to rend people limb from limb with little more than a thought. But ordinary people *do* have the ability to rend other people limb from limb, period, if they are angry enough. It just takes a little more effort on their part, and as I said, Heralds see the aftermath of those episodes of jealousy and rage all the time. The gods know that in this city alone there are plenty of beatings and knifings and other kinds of mayhem inflicted every day to prove that perfectly ordinary people can be driven to kill over jealousy. The only difference between them and you is that they will use perfectly ordinary physical means against the object of their rage." She coughed and rubbed her nose. "It's horrible, it's tragic, but there it is."

"But my point—" he tried to interject.

"What makes you *different* from those stupid, ordinary people," she continued inexorably, "is that you stopped yourself from acting. You *controlled yourself.* You were horrified by the very idea you could have hurt Darkwind, even though *you* were already hurt *by* him."

"But I might not have!" he cried, panicking again.

"But you *did,*" she replied with emphasis. "You did, even when you didn't know it was a game and meant nothing. You did control yourself, when you thought you had every reason to strike back. *Now* you know what the silly teasing-game looks like between two very good friends, and you won't make that mistake again. You know how much *we* value you, and that we would never knowingly hurt you, and I hope that you will *ask* one of us before you jump to any conclusions."

"I…"

He stopped and never completed the sentence, because he frankly did not know what to say. She *had* an answer for every one of his fears and his arguments. She could even be right. He had no way of knowing.

She waited patiently for him to say something, then shrugged. "Right now I think we ought to do something to salvage this situation. I don't think you want anyone else to know that you came running up here, hurt. If I were you, I wouldn't."

Well, he had to agree completely with that, anyway. He felt enough like a fool; the last thing he wanted was for everyone else in the gathering to *know* he was a fool.

"In that case, we need to think of some logical reason for both of us to have come up here." She nibbled a fingernail for a moment, deep in thought. "Food, maybe? Or something to drink? Do you two keep those things here?"

"Yes," he replied, nearly speechless with gratitude at her quick thinking. "And surely everyone is thirsty by now."

"Good. Let's go get some drink and bring it down to them; maybe something in the way of a snack as well." She rose to her feet and gave him her hand. He took it and she helped him to his. She was a lot stronger than she looked.

Her brief tunic had dried, and so had her hair; it curled around her face in a wispy silver-streaked cloud. He wondered how it was that she could be so earthy and so unearthly, all at the same time.

"Lead the way, *ke'chara*. I'm not a lot of good as cook, but I can carry a tray with the best of them." She winked at him, and he found himself smiling back at her as he led the way to the tiny kitchen where he prepared meals from time to time.

They assembled enough food and drink to have accounted for their absence, and she used a damp, cold cloth to erase any lingering traces of his hysteria. He allowed her to persuade him to rejoin them all by promising that she would make *certain* he was not left out of things from now on.

But he did not go back down those stairs without an invisible load of misgivings along with his other burdens. She was very likely right when it came to her assertions about Darkwind and Firesong—but when it came to himself, he was not so sure.

And despite Elspeth's kind words, Falconsbane *had* left traces inside him, in the form of knowledge and memories. Even if he was able to control his emotions forevermore, there were things he could never have faith in again. There were too many things he could not blindly believe in now, after hosting a madman in his body. No, when it came to the future, he could not seem to muster Elspeth's level of hope. There was no blind optimism left in him, no confidence that he'd control his rage next time, and he was very much afraid of that uncertainty.

There was more than one way for a madman to be born.

8

*H*orses were never suited to traveling by night, especially moonless nights. Karal was a good rider, and the gelding's tension communicated itself to him through a hundred physical signals he felt in his hands and his legs; the horse was nervous as well as tired, and all of his nervousness stemmed from the fact that he couldn't *see.*

Trenor stumbled on the uneven road, and Karal steadied him with hand and voice. The gelding whickered wearily, and Karal wondered if he ought to tell Herald Rubrik he was going to have to dismount and lead the poor horse before he took a tumble and ruined his knees.

"We're almost there. Just over the next rise, Karal, you'll see it in a minute," Rubrik's voice floated back through the moonless dark. He could have been a disembodied spirit or hundreds of paces ahead; there was no way of telling. "Or rather, you'll see the lights. Once your horse can see where he's going, he'll have an easier time of it."

"I'm not foundering Trenor," he replied stubbornly. "I'm not going to ride him to exhaustion, and I'm not going to let him take a fall with me on his back. One more stumble, and I'm walking him in."

A white shape loomed up in front of him, and he realized that Rubrik and Ulrich had pulled up on the road verge to wait for him. "No one is asking you to hurt Trenor, lad," the Herald said in a tired voice. "I'd spare you both if I could, but there's nowhere to stay but hedges between here and Haven, and once we reach Haven we might as well go to the Palace. I'm sorry I had to push you like this, but I had word there's more wizard-weather coming in, and that last bridge was about to go."

He's repeating himself; that's the third time he's told me that. He's pretending to be in a lot better shape than he really is. I'll bet he's in a lot more pain than he's letting on, too.

Since they'd passed that last bridge right at sunset, and Karal had been able to see for himself just how shaky the structure was, he hadn't argued with going on at the time, and didn't now. And since he had also seen the remains of the huge tree that had caused the damage to that bridge mere hours before they had reached it, he also didn't ask why such an important bridge hadn't yet been repaired.

Thinking back on it, he recalled something else he hadn't paid a lot of attention to at the time. That tree, which had a trunk as big around as two men could reach with their arms, had been torn up by the roots. It hadn't simply washed down into the river, it had been torn up and flung there. He really didn't want to think about the kind of weather that tore up trees by the roots and sent large rivers into flood in a matter of hours.

Once they'd crossed the bridge, they'd found there were no rooms to be had at any of the inns. Everything was full up, in no small part due to the effect the weather was having in disrupting travel during the heaviest months for trade in the year.

So they had pressed on, knowing that once they reached Haven, at least there would be rooms and meals waiting for all of them. But once the sun set, the going had gotten a lot rougher than Karal had thought it would. It was a moonless night, and heavy clouds obscured the stars; that might not trouble a Companion, but poor little Trenor found it rough going, and so, probably, did Honeybee. A couple of handfuls of grain and some grass snatched as they rested was not a satisfactory substitute for his dinner and a good rest in a stall.

Karal's mood matched his horse's, even if he knew the reasons why they were moving on through the middle of the night. At least it was better for Ulrich to ride than to rest beside the road, perverse as it might sound. Honeybee had carried him on all-night rides in worse conditions than this, and while he was riding, his joints stayed warm and flexible because they were being exercised. If they stopped beside the road to rest until the sun came up, he'd be too stiff to move after a night without shelter.

The thick darkness smothered sounds because there were so few visual reference points; even the insects by the side of the road sounded as if they were chirping behind a wall.

"I promise, I've sent messages on ahead of us," Rubrik continued. Karal believed him, even though there was no way *he* knew of that messages could be racing ahead of them. Except magic, of course, there was always that possibility. Ulrich had been taking it for granted that their escort was reporting regularly to his superiors *somehow*, so it must be by magic. "There are servants waiting for us, and the Queen's own farrier will be taking care of your gelding as soon as we reach the Palace."

Karal patted Trenor's neck without replying. Tired as the gelding was, he wasn't winded or strained yet. For all of his stumbling, he hadn't actually taken a fall or an injury. A good hot mash inside him, a good blanket covering him, and a warm stall to sleep in, and Trenor should be all right in the morning.

For that matter, I wouldn't turn down a hot mash, a good blanket, and a nice thick bed of straw right now.

"Thank you," he said at last. "I'd rather take care of him myself—but I'm as tired as he is, and I'd do something stupid, like let him drink too much or too fast."

I'm babbling. I'm too tired, and I'm babbling. It's a good thing Rubrik's probably too tired to notice, or he could get anything he wanted out of me right now, just by starting a conversation and letting me run on. Ulrich is too tired to pay any attention to anything I say.

"This is the last rise," Rubrik promised. "It's a long slope downhill from here."

Well, I hope so. Or I will get off and walk.

Rubrik's promise was good; a few moments later, from his vantage point in Trenor's saddle, the lights of Haven appeared as they crested the long hill they'd been climbing for the past half mark and more. There weren't many of those lights, late as it was, but it was obvious from how spread out they were that Haven was a good-sized city. It was possible to guess the general shape and size from here, in fact.

Large. Quite large.

A few years ago, Karal might have been gaping with amazement, but that was before he'd been taken to Sunhame, the capital of Karse and the site of the first and biggest Temple, as was proper for the Throne of Vkandis. Sunhame was at least the size of Haven, and might even be bigger. So he wasn't impressed, except by the fact that the city was closer than he had thought.

"Not long now," Rubrik repeated. "We're almost at the outskirts. With no traffic, we should make excellent time through the city streets once we're within the walls."

Trenor lifted his head and sniffed; he must have liked what he scented because he arched his neck tiredly and picked up his pace a little. Beside him, Honeybee did the same, though her call was not a soft whicker but an asthmatic bray.

"They probably smell the other horses, and possibly the river down there," Ulrich murmured to himself, clearly not even aware that he had spoken aloud.

He's babbling, too. Well, good, if he's that tired, he won't be up first thing in the morning. I may get a chance to sleep in.

The first building that could properly be said to belong to the city appeared on the right; it was too dark to make out what it was, but from the scent of cold, damp clay, smoke, and heated brick, Karal guessed it might belong to a large-scale pot maker or something of the sort.

That, too, was similar to the way that Sunhame was set up; a lot of tradesfolk on the outskirts, warehouses, even mills and the like. Smiths and manufactories. Not too many people wanted to have their houses where there was noise from people going about their trades, so those trades tended to get shoved to the outskirts of the city.

Other buildings appeared soon after, mostly just unlit shapeless bulks against the sky on either side of the road. One or two candles or lamps burned behind curtains, but not enough to cast any kind of light. The hooves of their beasts echoed dully in the silence, a silence broken only by the occasional bark of a dog or creak of wood from an unseen sign swaying in the scant breeze. A few insects called, but no birds, and no other animals. They might have been riding in a city of the dead.

Karal shivered; he did *not* like that particular image at all.

A few more lights appeared up ahead, lights which proved to be lanterns mounted on posts outside closely-shuttered shops. There were still more of these lanterns up ahead, evidently placed along the road at regular intervals. As they passed the third set, Karal finally saw a living, waking person approaching—a young man leading a small donkey laden with a pair of stoppered pots and a short ladder.

Now what is that all about?

Karal's question was soon answered. The man took the ladder down off the donkey's back just as they neared him, and propped it against the lantern-post. He waved as soon as he spotted them.

"Evening, Herald!" the man called in a soft, but cheerful voice, without pausing in his climb up to the lantern.

"And a fine evening to you, sir lamptender," Rubrik called back. "They told me wizard-weather is coming in tonight—"

"So I was told, so I was told. I'll be finishing here in a candlemark, I hope. I'd like to be indoors when it hits." The man lifted the pierced metal screen that shielded the lamp wick from wind, and carefully trimmed it, then filled the base of the lamp from a smaller jug at his hip. "This is like to be a nasty storm, the mages say. At least we've got warning now, though they don't seem to be able to do much about it. More's the pity."

Huh. Well, maybe that's why everything is so quiet; everybody's shut their houses up, waiting for the blow. They passed the man as he started down his ladder. He waved farewell to them, but was clearly anxious to finish his job for the night.

Why can't the Valdemaran mages do something about the weather? We can...

"Too much to do, and not enough mages," Rubrik said, his shoulders sagging. "For some reason, weather-working seems to be one of the abilities *we* don't see often. Weather-witches, the people that can predict weather, we have in plenty now that we know how to train them, but not too many that can fix problems without making them worse elsewhere."

"We have something of a surplus of weather-workers," Ulrich said, very carefully. "It seems to be a talent we Karsites have in abundance. Perhaps it is because our climate would be so uncertain without them."

"I know," Rubrik replied, his voice so tired that Karal couldn't read anything into it at all. "That is one of the first things that Selenay wants to discuss with you. We thought that we would have everything under control once Ancar stopped mucking about with unshielded magic, but things are getting worse, not better. You saw the bridge—"

"Hmm." Ulrich said nothing more, but Karal knew what he was thinking. Aside from all other considerations, Valdemar was a wealthy land by Karsite standards—in the only real wealth that counted, arable land. Karse was hilly, with thin soil that was full of rocks. Valdemar had always had a surplus of grain, meat, animal products. Karse would not be at all displeased to acquire some of that surplus in return for the service of a few weather-workers. *That* sort of thing hadn't come up in the truce negotiations, and the tentative arrangements for the alliance that followed.

That sort of thing was why he and Ulrich were here now.

That sort of negotiation would be impossible if it weren't for the presence of the Empire looming in the East, an Empire whose magics were legendary.

Not even for food would some of those stiff-necked old sticks be willing to negotiate anything with the Demonspawn. Only Vkandis and the threat of complete annihilation managed to get them to agree. Well, if we start getting these little incidental negotiations through, perhaps by the time the threat is disposed of, either the

*old sticks will be dead, or they'll be so used to having deals with the "Demonspawn"
that it won't matter to them anymore.*

Still, it seemed odd that Valdemar should be having *more* magically-induced problems, not less. They had Adept-level mages enough to teach the proper ways of handling and containing magic, and now that Ancar wasn't spreading his sorcerous contamination everywhere, things *should* have been settling down. Shouldn't they?

Unless there was something else stirring things up.

"I wonder if the Empire has anything to do with this," he wondered aloud, not thinking about what he was saying before he said it.

"To do with what?" Rubrik asked sharply.

Karal flushed hotly, glad that the darkness hid his embarrassment. Stupid; that was twice in a row, and he was going to have to watch himself. And school himself not to talk when he was so tired—his thoughts went straight to his lips without getting examined first. "The—this bad weather, sir," he replied. "The Empire is full of mages, so they say. Could they be sending bad weather at you, to soften you up as a target?"

"It's possible—it's more than possible. I just didn't know something like that could be done at such long distances." Rubrik cursed quietly for a moment. Then he stiffened, stifling a gasp, and Karal realized that the man must still be in a tremendous amount of pain. This business of pressing on was as hard on him as it was on any of them, for all that his Companion seemed as fresh as when he started out this morning.

"It can be done in theory, though no one in Karse ever tried that I know of," Ulrich told him. "There's some mention of such things in older texts on magic, but using magically-induced or steered weather as a weapon is generally considered too unreliable to count on, since it is too easy to counter."

"Unless, of course, your enemy is known for *not* using magic." Rubrik cursed again. "The Empire's spies surely picked that up, at the very least. They must be laughing up their sleeves at us, if this *is* their doing. I'll make sure and mention it, just so that someone considers the idea."

"Even if it's sent-weather, a reliable weather-worker can deal with it," Ulrich offered. "The worker doesn't even need to be particularly powerful. I can't tell you if your 'wizard-weather' is sent or created myself; at least not at the moment. I'm too tired, and the probable distance between us and any Empire mages is too great. But if it is something the Empire is causing, that very distance works for us far more than it does the Empire. As far away as they'd be working, they wouldn't be able to stop a minimally-talented weather-worker from getting rid of anything they could send at us. In fact, a *minimally* talented worker, casting close to the target, can disperse the sendings of someone much more powerful than he is."

"That is good to know." For all his weariness, Rubrik sounded grateful. "Please, in case I forget to tell this to someone, make sure you do."

"Take note, Karal," Ulrich told his aide, who filed it carefully away in his memory. He would, some time within the next two days or so, make certain that this whole bit of conversation was included in the notes that Ulrich would take into a discussion with Valdemar's leaders.

"What is *that?*" Ulrich asked, as Karal repeated everything to himself once, just to be certain he had it all. Karal looked up; there seemed to be something awfully large across their path, and it was much too big to be a building. There were lights across the top of it, lights that might be torches or lanterns. How high was it? Several stories, at least. Well, *this* part of Haven rated some admiration, at least.

"The old city walls," Rubrik replied, with relief in his voice. "They mark the boundary of the original city of Haven. We are almost home."

The walls *were* impressive; quite thick, as demonstrated by the tunnel beneath them with gates at either end.

And manned by competent, alert Guards, as demonstrated by the ones that stopped them. They were detained at the gate long enough for the Guard Captain to look through a set of papers, scratch something with a stick of graphite, and wave them through.

"Efficient," Ulrich noted. Rubrik only nodded.

Looks as if they really were waiting for us—

By now the lights along the side of the road were frequent enough that neither they nor their mounts had any trouble seeing, and once inside the walls, there were further signs of life. Taverns were still open; music and the sound of voices came from windows open to whatever breeze might happen by. Here and there an industrious tradesman burned candles to finish a task. The scent of baking bread told Karal that bakers in Haven were no different from those in Sunhame; they did most of their work late at night, when it was cooler. Here and there they even crossed paths with a huge, heavy cart hitched to a team of four or more enormous draft-horses, hauling wagonloads of barrels and huge crates about that could not be transported during the heavy traffic of full day.

The streets here were paved, covered with something smooth that didn't resemble cobblestones or any other form of pavement Karal recognized. Rubrik looked around at the fronts of the buildings, though, and frowned.

"This storm is likely to be worse than I was told," he said, after a moment or two. "Look how all the shutters are up, and I think they've been latched on the inside."

Karal nodded, finally realizing why the place had seemed so dead and so quiet. Most windows *were* firmly shuttered against whatever weather was coming; shutters that would shut out light and sound from within as well as weather from without. "Is that unusual at this time of year?" he asked.

"Very," Rubrik said shortly.

Well, if they are expecting the kind of storm that ripped a huge tree up by the roots, if I lived here, I'd shutter my windows too. Better a night spent behind shutters than to have a window blown in—or worse, find something storm-flung coming through it.

It seemed to Karal that they were spending a lot of time winding back and forth; far more time than was necessary. He started looking around, craning his neck, trying to see if there was a shorter way to the Palace anywhere. Great Light, he hadn't even *seen* the Palace, and if this was Sunhame, they'd be looking right down the Grand Boulevard straight *at* it!

"Haven wasn't built like Sunhame," Ulrich said in a low voice, as he continued to search for some sign that they were nearing their goal. "It was built on strictly defensive lines. I'm told that the Palace was originally a true fortress, that it's not a great deal taller than many of the homes of the high-ranked and the wealthy. And the streets here were planned to make invasion difficult, even if an army penetrated the outer walls. The streets all wind around and around the city; there is no direct way to the Palace or to any other important building."

Where Sunhame was built as a place of worship first; the Temple is the center of the city, the Palace of the Son of the Sun a part of the Temple, and all roads lead directly there. Sunhame was planned as a stylized solar disk, in fact; the main buildings were placed in a circle in the center of the city, and the main streets all radiated from that circle. He could only hope that the minds of these Valdemarans were not as twisted and indirect as their streets.

At least the quality of shops and houses was steadily increasing, which was a good sign that they *were* nearing their goal.

Eventually the shops and taverns vanished altogether, leaving only the walled homes of the great and wealthy. Finally, just when he thought for sure that Rubrik was leading them in a circle, that they were hopelessly lost in this maze and that they would never find their way out again, they came to another wall.

This one was much shorter than the first, a bare two stories tall. If it was manned, Karal saw no signs of guards, although there were lanterns hung high on iron brackets. They were high enough to be above the heads of any riders who followed the street beside the wall, and seemed easily within the reach of someone walking along the top to service them.

There was a large building on the other side. Before Karal could ask anything, however, they came to a small gate—so *very* small that he could easily have passed right by it.

"Heyla, Rubrik!" a cheerful young man in a livery of lighter blue than any Karal had seen before hailed their escort. "What, bringing the envoy in by the kitchen entrance? *That's* hardly the way to treat an ally!"

Karal stiffened at the implied insult, but Rubrik just aimed a kick at the Guard. "You insolent idiot! This isn't the kitchen entrance, it's the Privy Gate, and well you know it, Adem! What are you trying to do, start another war with Karse for me?"

Karal relaxed. The Guard just laughed and unlocked the gate. "Come now, those stiff-necked fellows probably don't speak a word of our—"

"Oh, I speak your tongue well enough to know that you mean no harm, but you ought to learn to mind your manners, young lad," Ulrich said in a casual tone. "With so many foreigners coming to your Queen, you should learn *never* to assume they are ignorant of your language, and guard your tongue accordingly."

The Guard whirled, turning as pale as the bleached stone of the wall, and started to stammer an apology.

But Rubrik interrupted him, turning in his saddle to look fully at Ulrich. "Well, my Lord Priest? It was you who he insulted by his cavalier manner, so I leave it to you to decide how many weeks he is suspended."

He spoke in his own tongue so that there could be no misunderstanding by the Guard. Ulrich pondered the question for a moment and answered in the same language. "I believe you should report him—but do not repeat his exact words," the Priest said, very carefully. "Say only that he was not—ah—professional, and that he acted that way on the assumption that we did not know your language. He means no harm, I think, but such behavior *could* be construed as an insult. In fact, I believe that the *best* punishment to recommend would be that he must learn the rudiments of *our* tongue!"

Rubrik looked down at the trembling Guard, who Karal now saw was certainly no older than *he* was. "You heard him, Adem. You'll be on report in the morning, and they'll probably put you on stable duty for a fortnight, but that's less than you deserve. You represent the Queen at this post, whether or not it's the dead of night and you never see anyone, and you had better remember that."

The Guard saluted smartly, and pushed the gate open for them, standing aside and keeping his eyes straight ahead. "Yes, sir!" he said, his voice still shaky, but relief obvious in his eyes. "Absolutely, sir!"

Rubrik went through the gate first, followed by Ulrich. The Guard looked up as the Priest passed.

"Thank you, sir," he said, very softly.

Ulrich nodded, and allowed a ghost of a smile to cross his lips as he nudged Honeybee through the gate.

Karal followed, and the Guard closed and locked the gate behind them with a creak of iron hinges and the clatter of a key in a massive lock. Ahead of them was a long, stone-surfaced path that led to the enormous building Karal had glimpsed above the wall. This structure was illuminated on the outside by carefully placed lanterns.

Very carefully placed lanterns; guards on patrol would be able to see every corner of the outside, there would be no place to hide. And they don't blend in with the exterior—I wonder if the Queen has had some unpleasant visitors in the recent past?

It was apparent now that the area enclosed by the wall was far larger than he had supposed. It was huge, in fact—it looked even bigger than the city itself. There even seemed to be a forest of some kind off to the left—

But it was to the right that his attention was drawn, to the multistoried, gray stone building there, and the group of people coming up the path to meet them.

At least four of these were servants, but there were two men dressed in rich clothing, and two more in the white uniforms that Karal now knew meant they were Heralds.

Rubrik turned to Ulrich as the group approached. "Thank you for your understanding, sir. Young Adem is well-intentioned, and as you surmised, he meant no harm, but he's also known me since he was a babe, and he's highborn and inclined to be very cavalier about rank.

He volunteered for the Guards, but I'm afraid he still thinks things like sentry duty are something of a joke."

Ulrich shrugged, but Karal could tell that he wasn't displeased. "Well, really, one can afford to be cavalier about rank when one has it, true? If he's going to be mucking out stables for a fortnight, I think that's likely to teach him all he needs to learn from this little experience."

Rubrik nodded, and the Companion tossed his head and uttered what sounded a lot like a laugh. "I'll be leaving you here, sir. It has been a pleasure escorting you. I hope we will be able to meet socially in the future."

"I have enjoyed your company, and I shall make a point of meeting you when leisure permits," Ulrich said with emphasis, then turned toward the group approaching them.

Rubrik straightened in his saddle as best he could; the group stopped just beyond his Companion's nose. Karal noted that he didn't dismount, and neither did Ulrich—but it didn't appear that anyone expected them to. "My Lord Priest Ulrich, Envoy of Her Holiness of Karse, Son of the Sun Solaris, the Prophet of Vkandis, may I present to you Lord Palinor, Seneschal of Valdemar and the Seneschal's Herald, Kyril—"

The two older men bowed; the Seneschal was marginally younger than his Herald, a trifle taller, and a bit less in shape. And every bit the diplomat. In body type he was neither thin nor fat, nor was he either exceptionally handsome or ugly. The grandeur of his robes made up for his otherwise unremarkable exterior. The Herald, on the other side, was as memorable a person as Karal had ever seen; from his erect carriage to his iron-gray hair, his chiseled features to his direct way of gazing straight into the eyes of the person he spoke to. Karal did not think too many people ever had the temerity to lie to this man.

"I am gratified that you meet me in person, my lords," Ulrich said, his own demeanor as professional and diplomatic as that of the Seneschal. "In fact, I am flattered, on my own behalf and on that of my ruler. It is *very* late, and—" he paused to gaze significantly upward, "—I am given to understand that there is unpleasant weather expected at any moment."

"Too damned true," muttered the other man in the Heraldic uniform. Then, despite the rising wind he stepped forward and bowed. Rubrik raised his eyebrows in shocked surprise.

He recovered quickly. "And the ah—entirely accurate gentleman, is Prince-Consort Daren, Queen Selenay's personal representative."

This was the Prince? In Herald livery? Karal was too well-schooled to gape with shock, but he very nearly bit his tongue. Rubrik had clearly not expected any of the royals to meet them out here, or he surely would have warned them. Karal was all too conscious of how shabby and unkempt he and his master must look after riding since dawn.

Prince Daren smiled, and echoed his gesture. "You are most welcome and well-come, my Lord Priest Ulrich. I was afraid that if I did *not* come in person, this initial meeting might degenerate into a minor diplomatic event, and if you will forgive my being as blunt as the soldier that I am—"

A chill wind screamed up out of nowhere, whipping their cloaks and making even the tired horse and mule dance and shy. Leaves torn from the nearby trees, and dust and sand pelted them. A growl of thunder in the distance warned that the storm was at hand; a flash of lightning told it was coming on as fast as the wind could blow it.

Thank Vkandis for the Prince! He's the only one here with rank enough to override diplomatic protocol without making it an insult, and he knows it!

"—that 'weather' you mentioned is going to drench us all if we *don't* get you under cover!" Prince Daren shouted over the howling of the wind.

Neither Ulrich nor Karal needed any further prompting; they dismounted as quickly as Ulrich's aged bones and Karal's weary ones permitted, surrendering their mounts into the hands of the servants. Then, as fat, icy drops of rain splattered onto the path, they surrendered all pretense of dignity, gathered their robes and cloaks around them, and *all* ran for the shelter of the Palace.

Prince Daren proved to be a far more graceful politician than he claimed; he cut through protocol with a smile and an eye to their comfort, sacrificing his own dignity to preserve Ulrich's. "I'm just a blunt soldier, and I don't hold with a lot of this political dancing about," were words that were often on his lips, and neither Karal nor his master believed them for a moment—but paying lip service to those words made it possible to retain the respect due to their office while at the same time getting things done with dispatch. By common consent, proper diplomatic maneuvering was deferred to the next day. Prince Daren showed them personally to their suite, and left them there after demonstrating the system of bells that summoned servants.

"It's late. You need food and rest in that order, my lords," he said as he departed. "And your proper reception will take place at *your* convenience. Selenay and I will make certain that one of us is free for you to make the appropriate presentation of your credentials tomorrow. When *you* are ready, send word. This alliance is very important to us, and it is equally important that everything be done properly so the quibblers have less to wag their tongues about."

All things considered, it was an auspicious beginning for continued relations.

The suite of rooms they had been granted, on the second story of the Palace and in the section reserved for other ambassadors, was far above anything that Karal had experienced, even as Ulrich's secretary. It was composed of a total of five rooms. They had their own bathing room with an indoor water closet, two private bedrooms, a casual sitting room, and a reception room quite elegantly appointed. The suite was arranged in an odd pattern; they entered at the reception room, which led to the sitting room to the right. Then came the bedrooms, with the bathing room between them. The reception room and the sitting room were rather longer than they were wide, which might prove useful. Someone had pulled the shutters closed over the windows, so there was no way to tell what kind of view they had—if any—but from the hideous noise of hail pounding the wooden shutters, Karal was just as glad. There was a fine five-course meal waiting for them in the sitting room, and a servant who spoke some rudimentary Karsite to serve them, a young man, strongly built, with a thatch of thick, black hair and a pair of bushy eyebrows as thick as Karal's ring-finger.

They settled into chairs on either side of a small table, and the servant filled their plates, then excused himself to draw a hot bath for his guests' comfort.

Karal was hungry enough to have eaten the plates along with the savory roast chicken and succulent steamed roots. Ulrich barely picked at his meal, though, which told Karal that his master needed that hot bath *very* badly, and bed just as much. He always lost his appetite when his joints pained him.

"Don't bother with that, sir," Karal said, as Ulrich brought the same forkful of food to his mouth and laid it back down for the third time. "Go get into the bath; I'll fix one of those little bread pockets for you, mix up your medicine, and bring both to you."

Ulrich did not even argue which told Karal that his master was in more pain than he had thought. He allowed the servant to guide him into the bathing room, help him disrobe, and get into the bath.

The servant took himself into the master bedroom; Karal ate

in silence for a little longer, then, when he reckoned that Ulrich had warmed and relaxed enough for his appetite to return, cut a slice of breast meat and laid it inside a sliced-open roll. A trickle of the white sauce followed it, and some thin slices of roots. Their saddlebags had arrived by that point, and before the servant took them to the proper rooms, he got Ulrich's medicines, poured a glass of sweet, white wine, and mixed the powders into it.

He brought both to Ulrich, who lay back in the bath with the lines of pain and strain slowly easing from his face. His master looked up at his footsteps, and managed a smile.

"Food first," Karal told him. "If you drink this, you might fall asleep before you manage to eat."

"Especially on an empty stomach." Ulrich accepted the bread pocket and managed to eat all of it, which surprised and gratified Karal. When Ulrich was truly exhausted, he often lost all semblance of appetite, and had to be reminded that he *had* to eat. When the last crumb was gone, the Priest held out his hand for the wine glass, and downed it in a single gulp.

"Be a good lad and call that servant to help me out now, would you?" his master said, when the last of the potion was gone. "You go finish your meal—and mine, if you've a mind to. I'll be going straight to bed, I think."

Karal went to the sitting room to do just that. "The Envoy needs some help getting to bed, please," he said in careful Valdemaran. "He's not young, and he has just had medicine that will make him sleepy."

The servant nodded. "Yes, sir," the young man replied. "Ah, I believe you should know that we servants assigned to you and your master are not precisely ordinary. We're Heraldic trainees."

Karal raised an eyebrow himself at that, but nodded, slowly. So, that explained why this young man's clothing, though gray, looked very much like the livery that Rubrik wore. "Well, neither of us is likely to offend any of you by being unreasonable or demanding; frankly, I'm more used to serving than being served, and my master is a Priest and does not usually have any servant other than myself."

Let him make what he will of that. It can't do any harm to be thought ascetic. It might make people think twice about trying to bribe us; a true Priest is as hard to sway by material offerings as the statue of Vkandis.

The young man smiled shyly. "My name is Arnod, sir. I'll be on night duty. Day duty will be either Johen or Lysle. Would you like a Healer to look at your master?"

Karal gave it a moment of thought, then shook his head. "No, he'll be all right once he gets into bed. It was just a very long ride, and this storm isn't helping matters any."

As if to emphasize that, the wind shook the shutters, a violent rattle that sounded for all the world as if an angry giant had seized them and was tugging on them.

"Let me get the Envoy into his bed, then, and I'll return to see if there's anything you need." With a glance at the shutters, Arnod left Karal alone with the half-finished meal.

Karal quickly made certain that it became a *finished* meal, although he ignored the rest of the wine in favor of water. He knew what would happen if, as tired as he was now, he drank wine.

I'll sleep for two days and wake up with the world's worst headache.

The sitting room was as well-appointed as it was comfortable; two chairs, a couch for lounging, the table, a desk, and a fireplace shared with the reception room on the other side of the wall. Hard to tell in the soft light from the candles, but he thought it had all been decorated in neutral tones of gray and cream. There were no rushes on the floor, but the hard wood was softened by attractive rugs with geometric designs woven into them.

It was interesting that Heralds-in-training should be assigned instead of Palace servants, however. That might be a good sign.

It might also be a sign that the authorities did not trust the servants around a pair of Karsites. Or these almost-Heralds could be a not-so-subtle way of keeping an eye on the Envoys, and an ear in their midst.

It is also possible that they are doing us some kind of honor, he mused. *It is hard to say.* The only thing he could be sure of was that this Arnod fellow—who was perhaps seventeen—seemed to be a likable enough chap on the surface, not at all put out by being made into a servant. That would make things easier on all of them. Arnod could make things uncomfortable for them if he resented his current position.

Arnod reappeared about the time Karal polished off the remains of Ulrich's custard. "The Envoy fell asleep as soon as I got him into the bed," the young man said, his black brows furrowing together with concern. "Is that right? Should he have done that?"

Karal mentally reckoned up the effect of the medicines when taken with Ulrich's exhaustion, and nodded. "It's mostly that we had been riding since before dawn; we've been almost twenty marks in the saddle, and that's hard on him."

Arnod winced. "It's a good thing you didn't stop, though, if you'll forgive my saying so. We got word that the bridge at Loden is out; if you'd waited there tonight, you'd have had to go clear up to Poldara to cross in the morning. You'd have been another week getting here." His brows knitted. "I'm not being too forward, am I? Tell me if I am, please—I'm not used to this serving business, but they thought you and I might have a bit in common, since my da raised horses."

Karal laughed, a little startled at the young man's open, easy manner, and Arnod gave him a tentative grin. "Oh, just be as respectful to Lord Ulrich as you would to any Priest that you honor, and I think it will be fine. Like I told you, I am *not* used to having a servant around, or to being served by anyone. The reverse, in fact." He shared a conspiratorial grin with Arnod. "You see, *my* father was the stablemaster at an inn."

It was a very good thing that he and Ulrich had a chance to practice their Valdemaran with Rubrik on the journey up here; Arnod's Karsite was barely adequate to manage simple requests. A conversation like this one would have been impossible.

The wind pounded on the shutters again, and sent hail pounding against it in a futile effort to get through. Karal felt more relaxed than he had been in a long time.

Unless these "servants" are far, far more subtle than anyone I've ever heard of before, they're probably nothing more than they seem. They certainly are not accustomed to the kinds of intriguing I've seen in Ulrich's service. No, I think that while they certainly will be reporting what we say and do to their leaders, Ulrich and I can assume they are not expert spies.

That was a relief, a great relief. So great a relief that he relaxed enough to yawn.

"Oh—I drew you a bath, sir—" Arnod began.

"Karal. Just Karal," Karal corrected. "My master is 'sir,' or 'my lord.' I'm just a novice, I haven't taken any vows, and I'm not highborn, so I'm just plain 'Karal.'"

Arnod nodded, earnestly. "Right—I drew you a bath, Karal, I figured you'd want it when you finished eating. Can I get you anything else, or shall I just clear the plates away and let you get that bath and some sleep?" He hesitated a moment, then added, "We have a pair of guards stationed on this corridor, outside your doors. Not just for your benefit, but all the ambassadors. You won't have to worry about your safety."

Oh, and by the way, don't try to get out to prowl around. Right, well, that's the last thing on my mind. If Solaris wanted spies here, she'd have sent someone other than us.

"Bath and sleep," Karal said firmly—or he would have, if he hadn't had to yawn right in the middle of the sentence. Arnod chuckled and began picking up the dishes even as Karal got up to go find that hot bath.

He was impressed all over again by the bathing chamber; tiled in clean white ceramic, it contained a tub large enough to relax in, supplied by heated water from some system of pipes and a wood-fired copper boiler. It also contained an indoor, water-flow privy, an amenity Karal had come to appreciate after living with Ulrich. *Especially* on a night like this one. Going out to a privy, or even to a jakes on the outside wall, would have required more courage than he thought he had. The mere idea of that cold, hail-laden wind coming at one's tenderest parts...

Wouldn't need to take a vow of chastity after that. I wouldn't have anything left to be unchaste with.

When he returned, warm and dry and relaxed in every muscle, Arnod and the remains of dinner were both gone, and all but one of the candles in the sitting room had been blown out. Karal made his way across the chamber to his own room, smaller than Ulrich's, and with one wall on the outer hallway where the guards supposedly prowled. His room would presumably shield his master's from any intrusive sounds from the hall—and any sounds from the hall would wake *him* up so that he could defend his master if need be. Of course, this meant that he had no window in his room, but tonight he didn't want one. The howling of the wind and the roar of rain on the shutters was *quite* clear enough.

Candles had been left burning in his room, and a set of bedclothes had been laid out for him—a sign that their luggage *had* arrived safely. Thanks be to Vkandis, indeed. If they did not have the appropriate clothing, they could not be formally presented without disgracing themselves and their ruler.

And besides, there were a dozen books in there he'd been wanting to read.

Good. One less thing to worry about.

He dropped the towel he had wrapped around himself and pulled the soft, loose shirt and breeches on, blowing out all the candles but one and climbing into bed. The bed had been warmed, a welcome, if unexpected touch, and the candle nearest the bed gave off a delicate fragrance as well as light.

I could get used to living like this, he decided. It was a far cry from sleeping in the stable, or the hard pallets in the Children's Cloister. There was a lot to be said for the life of an envoy. He blew out the bedside candle, and lay back in the warm embrace of what had to be a real featherbed.

This is beginning to feel like undeserved luxury, actually. I haven't done a thing yet to earn all this.

On the other hand, the real work was about to begin—not physical labor, but mental. Tomorrow, in addition to his work as a secretary, Ulrich would begin asking him to watch certain people, or take note of situations, and he would be expected to make accurate observations. When they were presented formally to the Valdemaran Court, it would be his job to remember the names, the faces, the positions, and the identifying characteristics. Then there would be long diplomatic meetings, during which he would be taking mental notes—and later, transcribing those notes into an accurate copy of what was actually said.

No, this was not unearned luxury after all, now that he thought it all over. He could foresee, without recourse to a mage-mirror or a scrying crystal, that there would be days when he would not see this bed until well past the midnight hour.

Then again—in some ways, everything in this world is paid for, in the end…

But before he could ponder that any further, he fell asleep.

"Watch the Heralds," Ulrich said, just before they left their suite the next morning. Only that, but it was all the direction that Karal needed. Ulrich had trained his secretary well; Karal did not need to be told the rest of his job.

Ulrich would be watching the Prince and the other officials of Valdemar during this first day of introductions and preliminary negotiations. He wanted Karal to keep a covert eye on the other power in this land, the power that never quite revealed itself openly but had a hand in literally everything.

The Heralds. Even a Karsite knew *that* much.

He was the perfect person to perform that particular task; it was not likely that anyone would pay a great deal of attention to *him.* He was only the secretary, after all, of no importance, and furthermore, no older than the callow lads who had been assigned to serve them. *He* could not possibly be hiding anything.

Well, he *wasn't.* He doubted that he could ever successfully conceal the fact that he knew something, if anyone ever entrusted him with a real secret. But he didn't have to hide anything; all he had to do was *watch* passively.

They rose late—for Ulrich, at least, who was used to rising at dawn.

A new young man, who introduced himself as "Johen" but otherwise was as silent as Arnod had been talkative, brought them their breakfast and took away Ulrich's request for the formal presentation.

He returned with the word that it would be agreeable to everyone if that presentation could be made at the regular Court session in a mark. Or "candlemark," as the Valdemarans reckoned time. Easy enough to judge, since the candle that had been left burning all night was a time-candle—marked off at regular intervals. As near as Karal could judge, the Valdemaran "candlemark" and the Karsite "mark" as reckoned by water-clock were about the same length.

Since immediate reception was precisely what Ulrich had hoped for, they sent Johen off with word of their agreement. They both dressed with care for the occasion; fine velvet robes that had been especially created for their roles as both Priest and Novice, and Envoy and Secretary. There was a great deal more gold and embroidery than Karal personally felt comfortable with; he rather liked the simple, short black woolen robes, sashes, and breeches that those who served Vkandis normally wore. But he was a representative of Her Holiness—it was right and proper that he should *look* like a representative of Her Holiness.

Besides, Ulrich was laden with three times the gold braid and embroidery that *he* had to endure. He didn't even want to *think* about the amount of ecclesiastical jewelry Ulrich was carrying; it was enough to make his shoulders ache just looking at it.

Johen brought a young Guard to serve as their escort to the Court chamber, or whatever it was that the Valdemarans called it. The Throne Room, Karal had thought he'd heard Johen say. This second Herald-in-training spoke a lot faster than Arnod, and it was harder to follow him.

The Guard left them at the door, which was wide open, and they simply took their places among the other people gathered there. They stood out among the Valdemaran courtiers like a pair of crows in an aviary of exotic birds. As they waited their turn to be summoned before Queen Selenay, there was a little space around them, a degree of separation from the rest of the Court that clearly showed that most Valdemarans were still not altogether sure of their new allies.

Watch the Heralds, Ulrich had said. Karal kept his eyes humbly down, but he watched the people around him through his lashes. There were not too many Heralds out here among the courtiers—one, standing beside a man who *looked* like a soldier, and a second, female Herald in a very *strange* and exotic white outfit, chatting with the first. There were three up on the dais with the Queen—well, five, if you counted the Queen and her Consort as well. Another surprise, that—the Queen wore a variation on the white livery, as well as the Prince. One Herald he already recognized; that was Talia, who had come to Karse herself as the representative of Selenay. Not a bad idea, really, although there were Guards in their blue and silver uniforms everywhere in this room, standing at rigid attention along the walls.

The last two he dismissed, at least temporarily. If they were standing there in any capacity other than as guards, it was probably to do the same task that Ulrich had assigned to him—*watch*. He would learn nothing from their faces which would wear the same receptive blankness that his would.

No, he would concentrate on Talia and the other two, the man who shadowed the richly-dressed warrior, and the fascinating, peculiar white-clad woman.

He would have watched the latter just out of sheer curiosity. If he was a gilded crow in this aviary, *she* was the exotic bird-of-prey. For all her fancy plumage, the deliberate way that she moved and the implicit confidence of her carriage warned him that she would be dangerous in any situation, and that very little would ever escape her notice. She looked far too young to have that mane of silvered hair, though; that was strange.

Then he recalled his magic lessons, rudimentary as they were. *Ah. She may be an Adept; handling node-magic bleaches the hair and eyes.* Ulrich's hair had gone all to gray and silver before he reached middle age, his master had told him. So, if she was an Adept, who was she? There weren't that many Adept-level mages in Valdemar, after all.

The reference points quickly fell together for him; the exotic garb, the age, the deference with which she was treated…

That's Lady Elspeth. The one who went away to find mage-training in far-off lands, and returned with more than mere magic.

There was some commotion at the door, and more people entered; people… and *things*.

The sea of courtiers parted with respect tinged with just a little fear, making way for an odd party indeed. There were two men, both silver-haired, both dressed in costumes as foreign and elaborate as Lady Elspeth's. Neither of the costumes was white, however, and compared to them, her outfit was quite conservative. The younger and handsomer of the two was the more flamboyant, in layered silks of a dozen different shades of emerald green; the second contented himself with garments cut more closely to his body, in the colors of the deep forest.

But they paled beside the creatures that followed; a huge, wolflike gray beast the size of a newborn calf, and—

—a gryphon—

Oh, my. Oh, Lord Vkandis.

He stared, his heart racing, as he took in the near-mythical beast. He felt very much the same way as he had when he had first seen Hansa—except that the Firecat was nowhere near this *big.*

Even after the descriptions, Karal realized he had not been prepared for the reality. For one thing, this creature was *huge,* as tall as a draft horse, and its crest-feathers brushed the top of the sill as it passed through the double doors to the Throne Room. For another, it was unexpectedly beautiful. It was not, as he had imagined, some kind of put-together thing, a bit of cat, a handful of eagle. No, it was *itself.* If he hadn't known any better, he would have said it had been designed by the hand of an artist.

It had a head that was something like a raptor's, except for the greatly enlarged skull, with a wicked beak he would not have wanted to get in the way of; the tightly-folded wings would be enormous when unfurled. The four legs ended in formidable talons; he noted with slightly hysterical amusement that someone had constructed talon-sheaths, wooden-tipped and laced across the back, so that the ends didn't damage the wooden floor. In color it was a golden-brown, with shadings of pure metallic gold and darker sable. And when it turned and he caught its huge, golden eyes, he lost any last bit of doubt that this was a creature every bit as intelligent as he was. There was not just *intelligence* in those eyes, there was humor there as well, and a powerful personality. It looked him over, unblinking, then transferred its regard to his master, pupils expanding and contracting a little as it focused its gaze.

The entrance of this little cavalcade seemed to be all that anyone had been waiting for; Court proceeded briskly from then on.

He and Ulrich were evidently the center point of this session of Court; there was some ordinary enough business, dealt with efficiently and quickly, and then the majordomo beside the dais called them forward.

Karal followed behind his master, keeping his mind blank and receptive. He already knew what Ulrich would be doing; there were documents to present, authorizations, copies of the existing treaties. Ulrich would be telling the Queen, in a suitably flowery and elaborate speech, just how much Solaris welcomed the opportunity to change the truce into a true alliance. The Queen would respond in the same way.

This time, at least, there would be truth behind the speeches, at least on the Karsite side of the equation.

Maybe on the Valdemaran, given that storm last night, and the Prince's assurances. From the damage he'd seen to the gardens from their window, the storm had been fully powerful enough to make people concerned. There had been at least one uprooted tree, and many thick branches broken and tossed about like wood chips. It appeared that Karse, in the form of its weather-mages, had something Valdemar needed very badly.

So, there would be truth enough on the Queen's part as well. Enough to overcome centuries of hatred?

From the thoughtful look on Herald Talia's face—yes. There, if anywhere, was the proof of sincerity. Talia was of Holderkin stock, and had grown up on the border with Karse. If she could forgive Karsite depredations enough to become an honorary member of their very religion, it was possible that anyone could, given enough incentive.

Ulrich made his graceful speech, the Queen made hers; Karal didn't pay much attention. He was watching Talia closely. *She* was paying no attention to Ulrich after the first few moments of his speech. Instead, her eyes wandered over the envoy's head, for all the world as if assessing the temper of the rest of the courtiers.

There wasn't much to read in her thoughtful expression, however; it seemed to be just as carefully blank as his own.

"If you have no objection, my Lord Priest," the Queen was saying as he pulled his attention back to the work at hand, "I should like to take this opportunity to present you to the other dignitaries of this Court, and the representatives of our other allies and friends."

So that's why the gryphon and the rest showed up! As Ulrich accepted—after all, this was precisely what the Priest had hoped would take place—the crowd of courtiers reshuffled itself, and Karal found himself standing at Ulrich's elbow in a formal receiving line.

Now I earn my good dinner and soft bed! Ulrich would be depending on his trained memory to keep track of everyone introduced to them. Well, that was why he was here.

The full Council paraded by first, beginning with the Seneschal, Lord Palinor, whom they had met last night. Then came the Lord Marshal, who proved to be the military-looking fellow that Lady Elspeth had been speaking with. He was followed by a horsey woman, Lady Cathan, who represented the Guilds, and she in her turn was followed by a relatively young cleric, Father Ricard, who turned out to be the Lord Patriarch, the putative leader of *all* religious organizations in Valdemar.

Huh. I'll believe that when I see it! Never yet saw two priests of two different religions able to agree on anything, *not even that the sun was shining!*

But it was not his duty to pass judgment; just to remember who these people were.

There were more representatives from the four "quarters" of the country, then came the other Powers. The Heralds—the ones with offices.

Kyril, the Seneschal's Herald. A man who appeared to be Talia's age, tall, and strongly built, named (oddly enough) Griffon, who was the Lord Marshal's Herald. Another older man, Herald Teren, Dean of the Collegium (whatever that was). Lady Elspeth, "Herald to the Outlanders," which was a title just as puzzling; he could not imagine why she was not titled "princess" or "heir." Another *very* formidable woman, tall, and blonde, who carried herself with completely unconscious authority, Herald Captain Kerowyn, a woman he had heard so many tales of he could not even count them all. Names he knew of from his briefings, and his discussions with Rubrik, names he could now put faces to.

Then the other envoys and ambassadors—from Rethwellan, J'katha and Ruvan, from the Hardorn court in exile (what there was of it), from the Outland Guilds, from the Mercenary's Guild, from the White Winds and Blue Mountain mage-schools—

And the most exotic. A hawk-faced woman, blue-eyed and ebony-haired with golden skin, dressed in deep blue trews and wrapped jacket, Querna shena Tale'sedrin, envoy from the wild Shin'a'in of the Dhorisha Plains. Behind her, the flamboyant, silver-haired beauty of a man in the emerald-green costume, who proved to be one Firesong k'Treva, Adept and Envoy of the Tayledras.

The wolflike creature was also an envoy—Rris, who represented not only his own species, the *kyree,* but others, *tervardi, hertasi,* and *dyheli.* Ulrich nodded, as if he knew precisely what those creatures might be, but Karal knew he'd be doing some quick scuttling about, to ferret out descriptions and, hopefully, pictures later.

And last of all of the ambassadors, the gryphon.

The magnificent creature bent his head to acknowledge Ulrich's bow of respect, and opened a beak quite sufficient to take the envoy's head off. "I am Trrreyvan," the creature said in Valdemaran, and Karal could have sworn that it smiled. "I am mosssst pleasssed to make yourrr acquaintance. I believe we have a mutual frrriend? A Red-robe Priesst called Sssigfrrrid?"

Ulrich's mask of polite geniality turned into a real smile. "Indeed we do," he replied warmly. "I had hoped to find someone here who worked with him, sir gryphon, but I did not expect it to be you!"

The gryphon *did* smile. "We ssshall trrrade talesss and trrrack down Sssigfrrrid, laterrr, I think," he said, and bowed again.

The gryphon moved off gracefully, leaving only the courtiers to be presented. None of these were especially interesting; Karal simply memorized names and faces as they moved past.

Finally, it was over. The Queen dismissed the Court and departed with her entourage, after inviting Ulrich to present himself to her privately after the noon meal. By then, the exotics had dispersed, leaving no one that Ulrich wanted or needed to speak with.

As the courtiers filed out of the Throne Room, Ulrich finally looked over at his young protégé. "I've had enough for an hour or two, at least," he said in Karsite. "Would it shatter your heart if we had our meal in our room, rather than with the Queen and Court?"

Karal thought of all those eyes, curious, occasionally hostile; thought of trying to choke down a meal with all of them watching him, and shuddered. This position was far more public than he had thought. Ulrich chuckled. "I will take that as a 'no,' and leave the arrangements up to you," he said. "Meanwhile, I will go consult with Herald Talia and discover if this is to be an informal or a formal meeting."

"I'll see to it," Karal said, taking that as his dismissal. Evidently they no longer required a Guard; he was allowed to leave the Throne Room and return to their suite without one.

After he rang the bell for the servant, he went to the desk in the sitting room, where he had just this morning laid out pen and paper. By the time the servant arrived, Karal had already begun on the list of dignitaries they had just met. He ordered a meal to be served in the room with all the absentminded confidence of someone who was actually used to having a servant at his beck and call, and it wasn't until after the young man disappeared that he realized what he had just done.

The thought made him stop in his tracks. For just a moment, he was stunned. He had only been in this land a few short days, and already it was changing him.

He could not help but wonder where the changes would lead.

9

Ulrich returned to their rooms about the same time lunch arrived. He ignored the food for a moment to fetch a brown-leather document case from his room; Karal took just long enough to bolt his portion, then returned to his frantic note-taking. Ulrich watched him for a moment, then said, "If you would be so kind as to take a change in direction, I'd like your notes on the business of offering the skills of our weather-workers as a trade measure, and please tell me any observations you made on Herald Talia. The meeting is to be an informal and closed one, and I was specifically asked to come alone."

Karal stopped writing, his pen poised above the paper. "Do you think they believe me to be a spy? Do you think my function offends them?" he asked.

Ulrich shrugged. "I am not certain; remember, these people are more familiar with mind-magic than with true-magic, and as a consequence might believe that you are actually somehow speaking mind-to-mind with an agent outside. I shall attempt to determine what it is they think you do; in the meantime, complete your notes on the Court dignitaries, then relax until I return." He smiled. "I saw some of your books; I do not think you will have any trouble passing the time."

Karal flushed, because fully half of his books had been nothing more enlightening than popular romances and tales of high adventure. Ulrich chuckled.

"Please, Karal," he chided. "A young man who buries himself in scholastic tomes is learning nothing of life—and a young man who knows nothing of life will find ordinary people baffling. We can't have that, can we?"

"No, sir," Karal replied, still flushing. He turned quickly to his work and took out a fresh sheet of paper, making neat notes in the short version of Karsite hieratic script. It would be enough for Ulrich to use as a guide; he just wished that he was going to be there for this initial conversation. He would have to make notes based on whatever Ulrich remembered.

As he completed the page of notes and dusted it with sand to dry the ink, he looked up at his mentor. Ulrich was standing with his back to the room, looking out the window at the gardens below.

"A copper for your thoughts, Karal," his mentor said, without turning back to face his aide.

He looked at his list, remembering all the conversations they had shared with Rubrik. "Not very original, master," he replied. "Only that, even though we are so very different from these Valdemarans, there are fundamental things we have in common. And some of them I never expected—the Companions being like Firecats, for instance."

"Yes, although personally I am just as glad that the Cats are fewer in number than the Companions," Ulrich said with a chuckle, as he turned away from the window. "I am not certain I would care to share as much of my life and inner thoughts with any creature, as Solaris shares with Hansa."

Karal had nothing whatsoever to say to that; he knew that Ulrich had been a good friend to Solaris before she became the Son of the Sun, but he had not known that she continued to speak as informally with him as his comment just implied.

How important is he, then? Karal wondered. From the sound of it, Ulrich might well be the one person in all of Karse that Solaris trusted to speak authoritatively with her voice. So the elaborate robes and badges of rank actually *meant* something. Did the Valdemarans know this?

"I was hoping you would be thinking along those lines by now," Ulrich continued, going to the mage-sealed case he had placed on the table. "I have something for you to read besides those old books of law you brought with you."

He unsealed the case with a whisper of invocation and a touch of his finger. The seal glowed briefly, then parted; he reached inside and brought out a handful of small, dusty books. The bindings had all faded to a mottled brown with age, and the edges of the pages were yellowed. He opened each of them, glancing at the first pages, and selected three, replacing the rest in the case and sealing it up again.

"I think you are ready for these, now," he said, placing them beside Karal on the desk. "Let me know if there is anything in them you want to discuss. I suspect there will be quite a bit."

And with that, serenely ignoring Karal's surprise, he gathered up the pages of notes his protégé had penned for him and left the room, allowing the door to close behind him with a quiet *click*.

Karal could not restrain his curiosity and snatched up one of the books as the door closed behind his mentor. To his vast disappointment, it was handwritten in very archaic Karsite, and difficult to puzzle out. The other two were similar, and it was quite clear that reading these things was going to require a lot of hard work on his part.

It was also going to take a great deal of time, and he did not have it to spare. With regret, he put the books aside and turned his attention back to his list of dignitaries. Duty must come before pleasure, or even curiosity, and his duty was to complete that list.

Several pages later, he put down the pen, feeling virtuous and ready for a little recreation. He thought about the adventure tales still buried in his luggage, but somehow the three dusty volumes still on his desk had more allure than the sword play and sorcery of "The Tale of Gregori."

He took the first of the books and moved over to the couch, curling up so that he got the full benefit of the sunlight.

A few moments later, he knew he had made the right decision. Not only was this a very old book, it was a copy of something that was much older, the personal journal of a Vkandis Priest.

With a shock of excitement that made his fingertips tingle, he spelled out the name of the Priest who had written the journal.

Hansa.

If what Ulrich believed was true, and the Firecat who sat at Solaris' side at this very moment had once been a Son of the Sun himself, then *this* book had been written by the same entity. And from the look of it, the Journal had been started when Hansa was a man no older than he, right after he took his vows as a Priest and long before he became the Son of the Sun. Was this very book where Ulrich and Solaris had found some of their revolutionary ideas? If so, how much more was in here that they had not yet revealed?

"The Tale of Gregori" could *wait!*

Several marks later, he put down the volume and rubbed his tired eyes. This was no scribe-made copy, but someone's handwritten version. The writing was tiny, crabbed, and barely legible in places; the archaic language more difficult to work through than he had thought. He hadn't read more than two pages so far, and he'd been forced to take notes in order to get that done.

On the other hand, there was still a thrill of excitement as he contemplated the closely-written pages of the book. It was definitely going to be worth working through this. The things he had already gleaned about the Priesthood back in those long-ago days were enough to widen his eyes. *When* had the order of the Priests of the Goddess Kalanel—the consort of Vkandis—disappeared, for instance? And when had Her statue vanished from its place beside Vkandis' in the Temples?

The door opened, and Ulrich walked in as Karal put down the

book with a slightly guilty start. His master only dropped his gaze to the little volume in his hands and smiled.

"I see you have been putting your time to some good use," he said. "But before you wear out your eyes, I have some other duties for you to attend to, while I am at private meetings."

He must have looked disappointed, for Ulrich only chuckled. "Don't fret, they have little or nothing to do with negotiations. I'm going to meet with Lady Elspeth and Darkwind on a regular basis to analyze our various magics. I'll be doing the same with the representatives of the White Winds and Blue Mountain mage-schools. *You* would find all that very boring, and there would be nothing you could record that would be at all useful."

Karal sighed but nodded his agreement. His own mage-craft was minimal; barely enough to light a fire, and that only if he happened to be particularly hard-pressed. In ordinary circumstances, he would be well advised to keep a firestriker on his person. "Yes, sir," he said with obedient docility. "What is it you wish me to do?"

"Attend classes," came the surprising reply. "I wish you to become as fluent in Valdemaran as you are in our tongue. There may be shades of meaning in our negotiations that I may miss otherwise. I do not have the time to spare for this, and you do."

Well, that was reasonable enough. He and Arnod had been able to make conversation last night, but it had been stilted and rudimentary, and both of them had paused often to search for words. Someone needed to be able to understand all the talk going on around them. For that matter, he could pick up a lot of information from idle conversation if no one realized that he was exceptionally fluent in Valdemaran.

He nodded, but Ulrich wasn't finished yet. "You are going to spend far too much time sitting at a desk," he continued. "You need exercise, and more than that, you need to learn how to defend yourself. *I* can hold off an enemy with magic, but if you were ambushed by someone, what would you do?"

Karal opened his mouth to reply, then thought better of it and closed it again. Ulrich was right; what had served him at the inn and the Children's Cloister would do him no good here. He was no longer just another child, and anyone who intended to attack him *here* was likely to be trained and practiced, perhaps even an assassin. Yes, the Valdemarans had provided guards, but anyone who had weathered the war with Ancar knew that guards were not always enough. For that matter, there were probably plenty of people in the Valdemaran ranks who would like to see him dead as a means of starting hostilities again.

"I've arranged for Johen to come and take you to your weaponry teacher in a few moments," Ulrich said. "So you ought to change into something like your riding gear; something you can sweat and tumble about in, and do it before he arrives."

"Yes, sir," Karal replied and stood up quickly. He was all the way to the door of his room when he thought to ask a question.

"Who is going to be teaching me these things, sir, do you know?" he asked, as he looked for a clean set of riding clothes in the chest at the foot of his bed. In a way, he was hoping to hear that Rubrik was to be his language teacher. It made sense, and Rubrik was the one friendly, familiar face here.

"Well, there's only one person who is equally fluent in Valdemaran and Karsite," came the easy reply. "Herald Alberich, the Weaponsmaster. He's already agreed to the idea."

Clothing dropped from Karal's numb hands, and he felt as if his stomach had dropped right out of his body.

Alberich? *The* Alberich? The Great Traitor? The man whose very name was used as a synonym for traitor back home?

The man whose intimate knowledge of the Karsite Army and the Karsite Border had prevented Karse from gaining so much as a grain of sand or a word of reliable intelligence for twenty years and more?

The man who was the first that Solaris approached to arrange the truce, he reminded himself. *The man she trusted to keep his word when she sent her agents in to negotiate for a Valdemaran envoy. He is not, cannot be, the enemy I was always told he was; if he was, Solaris would never have gone to him. She values honor above all else, except devotion to Vkandis. I have never heard the truth about him, nor why he deserted his post, all those years ago.*

But still—Alberich? The very idea turned his blood to dust.

"As for your weaponswork," Ulrich continued, blithely unaware of Karal's shock and dismay, since he could not see Karal from his seat in the next room. "I had a volunteer before I even asked for one. Herald Captain Kerowyn."

Karal dropped his clothes again.

"Karal?" Ulrich called, when he said nothing.

Karal tried to move, forcing his shaking hands to reach for his riding clothes. It took him three tries to pick them up, and when he put them back down on the bed, it took him an eternity to get the fastenings undone on his Court robes.

"Karal, there is nothing to worry about," Ulrich said into the silence, finally divining the fact that Karal was disturbed by these revelations. "She is not going to drive you the way she does the young Heralds-in-training. She knows that you are never going to have to do more than defend yourself in an emergency."

But she is eight feet tall, his mind babbled, ignoring the fact that he had already *seen* her just this morning, and she was nothing like the creature that reputation painted. *She eats babies for breakfast, and washes them down with nettles and wolves' milk! She can break warriors in half with one hand! She—*

"At any rate, she's waiting for you now," Ulrich said cheerfully, as Karal fumbled his breeches on. "I'm really very flattered; she doesn't take individual pupils very often."

I'm not! I'd rather have some nice, quiet little undertrainer—

Oh, calm down, Karal. It could be worse.

It could be Alberich!

He pulled his shirt on over his head, and came out into the sitting room. Ulrich had his back to him, examining some papers, as Johen tapped diffidently on the door and entered.

Ulrich looked up to see who it was, then waved absently at them, returning his attention to the papers. "Off you go, then. I'll see you later, Karal. Try not to get too bruised; we'll be taking our dinner with the Court, and I'll need you to be presentable. I'll get a bad reputation if it looks as if I beat my secretary on a regular basis."

Karal staggered after the silent Johen, incoherent with nerves.

Try not to get too bruised? Oh, lovely, I shall...

Johen led the way down a set of stairs and out into the gardens. Under other circumstances, Karal would have enjoyed the impromptu tour, for the Palace gardens were nothing like similar gardens at home, and were full of trees and plants he didn't even recognize. But he was too numb to pay a great deal of attention, and it was *far* too soon for his peace of mind that Johen brought him to a large wooden building, standing very much apart from the rest of the Palace complex.

It didn't resemble any building Karal had ever seen before—but then, he had never had any occasion to find himself inside one of the army training halls. The windows were right up near the edge of the roof, which seemed very strange to him. He couldn't imagine the reason for such an odd arrangement.

But he got no chance to ask Johen about it, for the young man hurried on ahead of him as if he could not get his escort duty discharged quickly enough. Arnod might be friendly, but this young man certainly was not.

He followed Johen into the building; once inside, it proved to house, in the main, one huge room. The closest comparison he could come up with was that it was like an indoor riding area with a sanded wooden floor; with mirrors lining the walls, and benches placed in between the mirrors, pushed up against the walls. The fourth wall held racks of wooden practice weapons, and those benches were laden with what even Karal recognized as protective padding. He sniffed; the place held the mingled odors of sweat and sawdust, leather oil and dust. At the moment, it was empty of everything else.

A door at the back of the room opened, and Herald Captain Kerowyn stepped out into the room. She was not wearing that white livery that every other Herald wore, which seemed very odd to Karal; there was no way of telling that she was a Herald without that white uniform, since her Companion wasn't with her.

Huh. Maybe that's the point?

She was, however, dressed in a way that would have scandalized most good Karsites and not just because she was wearing "men's clothing." No one could ever mistake her for a man, in a brown leather tunic and breeches, both so tight-fitting that they showed every curve and muscle of a quite spectacular figure.

Karal swallowed, hard; she might be old enough to be his mother, maybe older, but there was no sign of those years on her body or in the way that she moved. There was also no question but that she was just as attractive as she was dangerous. He was very glad that his own tunic was long enough to hide his inevitable reaction, but he flushed anyway.

Then he paled, and his body lost interest, as she shifted her weight in a way that reminded him of her profession and her history. This was *Kerowyn*, Captain of the Skybolts, mercenary fighter long before she became a Herald. If she didn't eat babies for breakfast, she certainly had a reputation for devouring certain parts of the conquered as a battlefield trophy feast!

She stood with her feet slightly apart, hands on hips, and studied him. Johen simply made a gesture toward him and left without a word. She tilted her head to one side, and he hoped that his trembling wasn't as visible as he thought.

"Be steady, youngster," she said at last, in heavily-accented Karsite. "I be not going to eat you. Not without good sauce, anyway; you be too stringy for my liking."

He flushed again as he realized that she was laughing at him. She knew he was afraid of her, and she was laughing at him! But his fear was a lot stronger than his anger, and his good sense at least as strong.

Let her laugh—if it keeps her from pounding me into the ground like a tent peg!

She paced toward him, slowly and deliberately. He stood his ground—mostly because he wasn't able to move. His feet were frozen to the floor, and he couldn't look away from her.

She circled him, looking him over from every angle, as if he was a young horse she was considering for purchase. He flushed even harder; he wasn't used to being given that kind of scrutiny by a woman, or at least, not by a woman like this one. *Solaris* had given him that kind of detailed examination, but there was nothing remotely feminine about Her Holiness; when Solaris sat on the Sun Throne, she *was* the Son of the Sun, and that was all there was to say about it. Kerowyn was as female as she was formidable.

"Right," Kerowyn said at last, as if answering a question, though he had said nothing. "Come here, boy. I be wanting to be testing the strength of you."

For a moment he hesitated. What was she going to do, feel his legs and arms, as if he was a young racing colt and she the prospective buyer? But she beckoned peremptorily, and he followed her, not daring to do otherwise.

She brought him over to the corner of the room, to a series of ropes and pulleys. The corner looked like a setting for some kind of arcane torture, or worse. But it turned out that what she had in mind *(thank the God!)* were only tests of how much he could lift, pull, or push; the ropes could be loaded with weights, and she would watch him as he tried to raise them from various positions. When she was done, *he* was sweaty, and she looked satisfied.

"Be better than I be *thinking*," she told him. "You be not spending all your time pushing paper around on desks. Now, here be what we be going to do. I not be making a fighter out of you, and I be not going to try. What I be going to do, is I be teaching you some things you be using to be defending yourself with, things that be buying you enough time for help to be getting to you. *Real* help, trained fighters."

"That makes good sense," he said slowly.

"Here be problem, that we be going to be making these things into ways that you be acting without thinking. And we be going to be making you stronger than you be already. So—" she waved at one of the things he had just been using, weights loaded onto ropes attached to pulleys, "—be doing what I be showing you, fifty more times, then we be working on the first move."

Not what he wanted to hear...

By the time she was done with him, he was weak-kneed with exhaustion, and quite ready to drop, but he already had one move down well enough to use against an attacker who wasn't expecting it. The likeliest scenario, as Kerowyn postulated it, was that he would be attacked from behind by someone who intended to strangle him. She showed him how to use the attacker's rush and momentum to tumble forward, throwing the attacker over as he did so, then get to his feet and run.

With enough practice, he *would* do just that without thinking.

When she dismissed him and sent him out the door with the admonition to return at the same time the next day, he realized that there had been another effect of the lesson besides exhaustion. He had absolutely, positively, not a single drop of desire in his veins for her, despite the fact that they had been tumbling all over each other, often ending tangled in positions that would have caused her father to issue Karal an ultimatum to marry her—had they been in Karse.

He wasn't certain how that had come about, but there was no denying the effect. If she had stripped herself stark naked and posed for him like one of the street women, he would not have been able to perform with her. She overwhelmed him. She was now, in his own mind, in the same class as Solaris, and therefore untouchable.

He was simply grateful to be allowed to escape.

He dragged himself back to his room; Ulrich was not there, but *someone* had had the foresight to fire up the copper boiler in the bathing room. Johen? If so, then perhaps that young man was not as unsympathetic as he had seemed.

After a hot bath, the world seemed a little friendlier, and he was ready to face Ulrich, the Court, and whatever else came up. And it was a very good thing that he *was* prepared for just that, for just as he finished dressing, there was a decisive knock on the door. Before he could answer it, the door opened.

There was a man standing there; a man wearing dark gray leather very like Kerowyn's except for the color. Tall, lean, and dark, Karal had never seen a human being who looked quite so much like a hungry wolf before. His hair was snow-white, and his face seamed with scars; he regarded Karal as measuringly as Kerowyn had, out of a pair of agate-gray eyes as expressionless as a pair of pebbles.

He was Karsite; his facial features and body type were as typical as Ulrich's and Karal's own. There was absolutely no doubt of that.

Which meant that there was only one person that he could be. Karal had forgotten that he was also scheduled for lessons in the Valdemaran tongue.

Karal swallowed, his mouth gone dry, and bowed. "H-herald Alberich, I-I-I am honored," he stuttered in his own tongue.

He rose from his bow; Alberich was smiling sardonically. "Honored? To be tutored by the Great Betrayer? I think not." The Herald strode into the room and closed the door behind him. "You are one of three things, boy—diplomatic, uninformed, or a liar. I hope it is the first."

Karal didn't know what to say, so he wisely kept his mouth shut. Alberich looked him over again, and the smile softened, just a little.

"The first, then. When you report, tell Solaris that I compliment her on her choice of personnel." He reached for a chair without looking at it, pulled it over to him, and turned it so that the back faced Karal. Then he sat down on it backward, resting his arms along the high back.

Karal took this as an invitation to sit, and took a chair for himself. He was weak in the knees again, but this time from the sheer force of the man's personality.

"First, we'll see just how much Valdemaran you really know," Alberich said—and then began a ruthless examination. Or rather, interrogation; he spouted off questions and waited for Karal to answer them. If Karal didn't understand or lacked the vocabulary to answer, he shook his head, and Alberich moved on to another question.

During this entire time, Alberich never once took those gray eyes off him, and whether or not it was by accident, the questions he asked revealed more about the man than Karal had ever expected to learn.

It was impossible to remember that this man was called the Great Traitor—no, not impossible to remember, but impossible to believe. Not when everything he said or did reinforced Karal's impression that Alberich lived, breathed, and worked beneath a code of honor as unbreakable as steel and as enduring as the mountains of his homeland.

"Come with me," Alberich said after about a mark's worth of this intensive questioning. He stood quickly and gracefully, and Karal scrambled to his own feet, feeling as awkward as a young colt and drained completely dry. "I'll get you some books to get you started."

He turned and led the way, Karal following behind him; eventually, after many turnings and twistings and sets of stairs leading both up and down, Alberich turned to open a pair of unguarded doors. Behind those doors—as far as Karal was concerned—lay Paradise.

Books. Floor to ceiling, and huge freestanding shelves full of them. The only other library Karal had ever seen to rival this one was the Temple library at home, and novices were never allowed in *there* alone. He stood in the door, gawking; he would never have known where to start, but Alberich seemed to know exactly where he was going. He went straight to the rear, and took down half a dozen small volumes, blowing the dust from them as he did so. He stalked back to where Karal was waiting for him, and handed them all to him.

"I don't think anyone has looked at these since I used them," he said, with another of those sardonic smiles. "There are a couple of Valdemaran-Karsite dictionaries, and a pair of advanced grammar books, and a history of the beginning of the war with Karse from the Valdemaran point of view, written by one of the Priests from the schismatic branch of the Sunlord. It's a little archaic, but it will give you some perspective and a good lesson in language at the same time. I'll question you on the first chapter or so tomorrow."

With that, he led Karal back to the suite; this time Karal tried to memorize the way, since he would certainly want to return to a library as impressive as that one, but for once his memory failed him. That was more than a disappointment; he *wanted* to be able to return there at will. He'd brought his own books largely because he was afraid he would not be permitted access to other books in the Palace, but there were no guards on that library door, which implied that residents in the Palace were free to come and go as they pleased.

If they could *find* the place, that is. Maybe the maze of corridors was enough to keep them out of it!

But Alberich might have been a reader of thoughts after all, for when he brought Karal back to the door of their suite and opened it for him, he paused.

"Any time you want to visit the royal library, ask a page to take you," he said. As Karal twitched reflexively in surprise, he added—again, with that peculiar softening of his normally sardonic expression, "I've seen book-hunger before, lad. There's nothing in there that's forbidden you, and you could do a great deal worse than learn how these people think from their own words. Feed your hunger and open your mind at the same time."

Then he turned on his heel and strode off down the hallway, leaving Karal clutching his books and staring after him.

Finally, Karal went inside and put his books down on his bed, then sat down beside them, wondering where he was going to find the energy to complete the day.

All this—and there was still the formal dinner with Selenay's Court to endure before he was allowed to collapse!

He'd never thought this was going to be an easy position to fill, but this was insane. How did Ulrich manage his schedule? It was at least as difficult as Karal's, probably much more so.

The same way he always tells me to take things, Karal decided. *One at a time...*

One thing at a time—and right now, that meant finding and laying out another set of Court clothes for Ulrich. He got to his feet with an effort, and let momentum and habit take over.

One thing at a time.

For the first several days he thought he was going to collapse at any moment. There were never enough daylight hours to complete all of his tasks, and he and his mentor spent long candle-lit sessions after dinner trying to catch up. Sometimes he attended meetings with Ulrich, but often Ulrich scheduled meetings during his lessons with Kerowyn and Alberich, probably a tactful way of excluding him without needing to manufacture an excuse. Ulrich was a diplomat, after all. Karal gave up trying to understand why the Valdemarans were so worried about *him* being present; it really didn't matter in the long run. And on the positive side, it *was* one less duty in a schedule that was already too full.

There were endless pages of notes to turn into something legible, Ulrich's postings back to Karse to write out properly from *his* hastily dictated notes, more pages of notes to transcribe from Ulrich's private meetings, preliminary drafts of agreements to put together; the work seemed never-ending. For a while, Karal despaired of ever getting any time to himself. It seemed as if the only time he was anywhere without a mindbending task in front of him was when he was in the bathtub!

Yet, after the first rush of activity, things *did* slow down. Initial agreements were drawn up, agreed to by Ulrich and the Queen's representative—usually Prince-Consort Daren—then sent off to Karse. The initial stage of setting up diplomatic relations was over; now it must all be approved by Solaris and then by the Queen's Council. Solaris would ponder Ulrich's suggestions long and hard before deciding on them, then make her own changes; the Valdemaran Council was like every ruling body Karal had ever heard of and must debate things endlessly before agreeing to them. Work for Karal slowed to a mere trickle; work for Ulrich was in getting to know those in power on a personal basis. That meant more meetings, informal ones this time, just between Ulrich and one or two of the people in power—meetings Karal didn't attend.

Karal found himself alone in the suite more and more often, with nothing to do but read his recreational books, study Valdemaran, and puzzle out the journals that Ulrich had given him. At first he welcomed the respite, but his own books were soon devoured, studying Valdemaran was *work*, and trying to make his way through the journals no less so.

He went out looking for company on several occasions, but the search didn't bring him any success. When he encountered the highborn offspring of Selenay's courtiers that were his own age, they ignored his presence as if he was another statue or a plant in the garden. Wherever he met them, they looked right past or even through him, and no one ever replied to his cautious greetings. The Heralds-in-training seemed mostly afraid of him and avoided his presence entirely; Arnod was the only exception to that, and Arnod was on duty only late at night.

He finally found himself sitting and staring out the window down into the gardens one afternoon, burdened by what could only be "homesickness." Whatever it was, it left him depressed and profoundly unhappy; aching with the need for something, anything that was familiar, and so enervated he found it hard to even think. He wasn't tired, but he couldn't find the energy to move, either. What he *wanted* was to be home, back in his familiar little cubicle near Ulrich's rooms; back in the Temple library, helping Ulrich track down a particular book, or copying out designated text. Oh, this place was very luxurious, but he would have traded every rich and exotic dish for an honest Karsite barley-cake. He would have traded his soft bed and private room for a breath of mountain air, every sweet, cream-rich cake and pudding for a mouthful of fruit-ice, and all their spiced wine for a good, strong cup of *kava*.

There was nothing about this land that was quite the same as in Karse, not the food, the scents, the plants that grew in the gardens, or the furniture. *Everything* had some tinge of the foreign to it; he couldn't even sleep without being reminded that he was not at home, for the herbs used to scent the linens were not the ones he knew, no bed he had ever slept in had been so thick that you were enveloped in it, and there were no familiar night-bird songs to thread through the darkness and lull you to sleep.

And there was no one he could confide in, either. Ulrich was too busy to be bothered with nonsense like this, and he would probably think him immature, unsuited for the duties he had been given. He was here to serve his master, not get in the way with his childish troubles.

I was able to talk to Rubrik—no. No, he has more important things to do than listen to some foreigner babble about how lonely he is. What would the point be, anyway? What could he say, "go home?" I was given this duty; there is no choice but to see it through.

Confiding in either Kerowyn or Alberich was absolutely out of the question. They would lose what little respect they had for him. They, too, would think that he was acting and reacting like a child. He was supposed to be a man, filling a man's duty—and furthermore, if they knew he was this unhappy, they would tell their superiors. This homesickness could be used against the mission; any weakness was a danger.

I knew what I was getting into when Ulrich told me where we were going, he told himself, as he stared out at the garden, wishing that he could make the bowers and winding pathways take on the mathematical radial precision of a Karsite garden. *I knew how alone I was going to be, and I knew that I was going where there were no signs of home.*

But *had* he known, really? As miserable and lonely as his years in the Children's Cloister had been, they were still years spent among people who spoke the same language as he did, who ate the same foods, swore by the same God. Here the only two people who even knew his tongue as native speakers were both men so many years his senior, and so high above him in social position, that there was no point in even thinking of confessing his unhappiness to them. Neither his master nor Alberich were appropriate confidants.

This was a marvelous place, full of fascinating things, a place where he had more freedom than he had ever enjoyed in his life—but it was not home.

It would never be home. And he despaired of ever finding anyone here he could simply *talk* to, without worrying if something that he might say could be misconstrued and turned into a diplomatic incident—or just used as a weapon of leverage against the mission.

If he couldn't have home—he needed a friend. He'd never really had one, but he needed one now.

He continued to stare out the window, feeling lassitude overcome him more and more with every passing moment. He was too depressed, too lonely, even to think about rereading one of his books.

This is getting me nowhere. If I don't do something soon, I might not be able to do anything before long. He'd just sit there until someone came along and found him, and then he'd be in trouble. Ulrich would want to know what was wrong, people would think he was sick, and he'd just stir up a world of trouble.

I don't think the Healers can do anything about homesickness. Not even here.

There was a section of the gardens, a place where kitchen-herbs were grown in neatly sectioned-off beds, that reminded him marginally of the gardens at the Temple. It had no rosebeds, no great billows of romantic flowers, no secluded bowers, so it was not visited much by people his age. Perhaps if he got out into the sun, he would cheer up. Maybe all this gloom was only due to being cooped up indoors for too long.

And maybe fish would fly—but it was worth trying. Anything was better than sitting here, feeling ready to drown himself in his own despair.

Feeling sorry for myself isn't going to fix anything either.

He managed to get himself up out of his chair; that was the hard part. Once he had a destination, momentum got him there. The kitchen gardens were deserted, as he had thought—with the sole exception of one very old Priest of some group that wore yellow robes. The old man sat and dreamed in the sun, just like any of the old Red-robes in the Temple meditation gardens; his presence almost made the place seem homelike.

With a bit of searching, Karal found a sheltered spot, a stone bench partially hidden by baybushes and barberry-bushes. He moved into their shade, and slumped down on the cool stone.

The depression didn't even fade, not the tiniest bit. Now that he was out here, the bright sunshine didn't seem to make any real difference to how he felt.

He closed his eyes and a lump began to fill his throat; his chest tightened and ached, and so did his stomach. Why had he come here? Why didn't he find a reason not to go? Why hadn't he let someone older, more experienced, come with Ulrich? He could have found a new mentor, couldn't he? And even if the new Priest wasn't as kindhearted as Ulrich, wouldn't dealing with a new mentor have been better than being this lonely? Did it matter that Ulrich was the only person who had ever been kind to him since he'd been taken away from his family? He had survived indifference and even unkindness before—and at least he would have been home! He would not have been stranded in a strange land, where everyone was a potential enemy.

"And lo, I was a stranger, and in a strange realm, and no man knew me. Every man's heart was set against me, and every man's hand empty to me."

He jumped, stifling an undignified squeak; he opened his eyes involuntarily. Who could be quoting from the Writ of Vkandis, and with such a *terrible* accent?

For a moment he did not recognize the woman who stood just in front of him, smiling slightly; she was dressed in a leather tunic and breeches like Kerowyn wore, though not so tight, and of white leather rather than brown.

A mature woman, rather than a girl, he guessed she was somewhere around thirty years old. She wasn't very tall; in fact, she would probably come up to his chin at best; her abundant and curly chestnut hair had just a few strands of silver in it, and her eyes were somewhere between green and brown in color. She gave an oddly contradictory impression of both fragility and strength.

Then his mind cleared, and his memory returned; he had been fooled by her clothing. He had never seen this particular Herald in anything other than formal Court costume before. Talia—the Queen's Own Herald.

Granted, she *was* a Sun-priest, but how had she learned the Writ? Why had she bothered? There was no real need for her to have done so; the office was only honorary.

"Thought I wouldn't take my office as Priest of Vkandis seriously, did you?" she said, with a smile that was full of mischief. "Maybe Solaris only meant the title to be honorary, but it seemed to me I ought to give the honor its due respect, and learn something about the one I was supposed to be representing. "

"Oh," he said, feeling very stupid and slow-witted. But then he realized that she was speaking in his tongue, and as bad as her accent was, the words soaked into him like rain into dry ground. He wanted to hear more; he needed to hear more.

"I thought that particular quote seemed awfully apt, given how you looked when I came up," she continued. "Not at all happy, actually. Of course, it *could* just be indigestion—"

She cocked her head to the side, as if inviting his confidences. He hesitated. She seemed friendly enough, but how much difficulty could he get himself into by talking to her?

On the other hand, she's not only a Herald, she's one of the Kin of Vkandis. If she did hurt one of the Kin, wouldn't the Sunlord do something about that?

She waited a moment more, then her smile widened a trifle. She had wonderful, kind eyes. "Or perhaps it's a peculiar kind of indigestion," she suggested impishly. "You've swallowed a great huge lump of Valdemar, and it isn't going down easily."

He had to laugh at that, it was so unexpected, and so vivid an image. "I suppose that's as appropriate an explanation as any," he replied, relaxing marginally. He had longed for someone he could talk to—and here was someone offering herself, someone it might even be safe to unburden himself to. What *did* he know about this woman? She was some kind of special advisor to the Queen—Solaris had spent an awful lot of time in her company—but there was something more, something important.

Hansa trusted her. That was it; he had the memory now. The Firecat had definitely trusted her; it was Hansa who had suggested she be made an honorary Priestess, if what Ulrich had told him was true.

She nodded at him in a friendly manner, and she did not seem inclined to move off despite his hesitation. Interestingly, she also made no attempt to intrude on him by sitting down on his bench uninvited. "I felt the same way when I first came here," she told him, as she shifted her weight from one foot to the other. "I was from a place so unlike this that it might as well have been on the other side of the world. You may find this difficult to believe, but my people kept their children very isolated from anything outside their farms. I had *no* idea what Heralds or Companions really were, other than the few things I'd been able to pick up from a bit of reading. I thought when Rolan Chose me that I had simply found a lost Companion. I thought I was supposed to bring him back to his owners, like returning a strayed horse!"

He had to laugh at that one with her; at least he knew a little more than she had! Rubrik had described the business of being "Chosen" by a Companion, that it was rather like being picked out for a Firecat's particular attentions. Hard to believe that anyone in Valdemar could have been unaware of a Companion's real nature.

On the other hand, it was easy enough to control a child, as she had pointed out. But being Chosen was supposed to be rather dramatic—he could well imagine someone trying to deny such a selection, for being Chosen would definitely put an end to any other plans one had for one's life, but Talia must have been unique in her ignorance of what being Chosen meant.

"Seriously, though, I was as out-of-place here as you are feeling now; I think you must have gone through Holderkin lands to get here—well, that's where I'm from." She smiled as he nodded, very cautiously. "They swear they escaped from Karse, but I'd be more willing to believe that your people threw them out; there can't be a more intransigent group of stoneheads in all the world. Personally, I think they're more trouble to deal with than they're worth."

"I don't know one way or the other," he confessed. "I never studied them, so I couldn't venture an opinion. But I can see how you would be feeling very—ah—foreign, when you arrived here. It was obviously very different here than among your own people. You probably *were* as foreign to Haven as I am." There. That was diplomatic enough.

She studied her fingertips, then looked back up at him. "I've heard you haven't been able to make any friends here, though, and that's where our circumstances differ. Of course, you are laboring under a double handicap," she pointed out. "You are with the envoy, which makes you dangerous to know, and you are from our former enemy, from a Priesthood known to be able to call up very powerful magic forces, which makes you *personally* rather dangerous to know. There's a Shin'a'in saying, 'It is wise to be remote in the presence of one who conjures demons.' Hard to make friends when people you meet are afraid you're going to turn them into broiled cutlets if you get annoyed with them."

"Ah—interesting," he replied, to buy himself time. It had not occurred to him that he might be frightening away would-be acquaintances; he never considered himself to be any threat to anyone. "I never thought of that."

"Yes, well, our younglings can be a rather timid and conservative lot," she said casually. "At least the children of the courtiers can. At the moment, I don't know of anyone in the younger set who would deliberately be rude or hostile to you. On the other hand, they've had a rather unsettled time of it; that can make even the boldest youngling into a mouse. Most of the youngsters here have lost at least one family member to the conflicts with Ancar, and there are a few who went from being fifth- or sixth-born to being second or third heir to their parents' holdings within the space of a few weeks. Many of them don't even have parents anymore; they're under the guardianship of older siblings. They don't like to think of any of that; to escape from their memories they tend to concentrate on some fairly shallow interests. The trouble is, no one has put you into the set that's actually doing something with their time—mostly because *they* are as busy as you."

That shocked him out of his own depression entirely. *How* many of the Valdemar elite had died in this war? Had Karse suffered as much at the hands of Ancar? Surely not, at least, not at first. Perhaps once the alliance had been made public—

"I'm sorry to hear that," he said at last, hoping his tone conveyed the fact that he really *was* sorry. "I don't believe we had nearly that much trouble with him."

"No, you didn't, not at first," Talia agreed. She ran her hand through her hair in what looked to be a gesture of habit. "For one thing, he really didn't want Karse all that badly, and for another, he was under the rather mistaken impression for some time that Solaris was male." She shrugged, and spread her open hands. "Once he learned she was female, it was only a matter of time before he included her in his vendetta against women. We guessed that was why Solaris sent messengers to Alberich, looking for a truce."

Then she smiled again. "But this gloomy talk is not why I stopped here! I saw you looking unhappy, and I hoped I could cheer you up. I don't think war-talk is going to achieve that, do you?"

"Probably not," he agreed.

"I did want you to know that once people realize that you aren't going to call up demons to avenge imaginary slights, they'll probably be more friendly," she continued. "I think I can count on at least a few of them being curious enough to start asking you questions. You certainly are not the most exotic creature gracing our Court, or even the most formidable; they'll get over their nerves soon enough."

He thought of the gryphons and found himself chuckling. "At least I walk on two legs," he offered. "And I am afraid that my ability at magic is very overrated. Not only can I *not* conjure a demon—even if Solaris hadn't forbidden the practice—but I can't even light a fire. Candles, yes; fires, no. My master Ulrich *is* a mage, but he didn't choose me for my magical abilities, he chose me for my scholastic bent. Your people are safe around me."

He meant it as a joke, but she took the joke a step further. "I wouldn't go so far as to say that," she replied, and if he thought he'd imagined a sly twinkle in her eye, he knew now it wasn't imagination. "You'd be a very handsome young man if you just didn't look as if you were about to deliver a sermon on Moral Life at any moment. If you smiled more often, I wouldn't wager on *any* of our young women being safe around you!"

Belatedly he remembered that if she knew enough to quote the Writ correctly, she also knew that Priests of Vkandis took no vows of celibacy and only a modified vow of chastity. Which meant she knew that he was as free to pay court to young women as anyone here. He guessed she was encouraging him to do just that, and blushed.

Still, he found her very easy to talk to, and more so with every moment. She invited confidences and made it easy to give them to her; a lot like his own mother, in fact. *Mother used to adopt every stray that happened by the inn, from motherless horseboys to kittens. Talia must be like my mother—that's why she stopped when she thought I looked unhappy.*

She chuckled at his flush and his slow smile. "I hope you don't mind my teasing," she said, then added wryly, "we aren't as far apart in age as you might think. It wasn't all *that* long ago that I was your age, and if I wasn't happily wedded and very much in love with Dirk—" She laughed and wrinkled her nose at him. "Well, consider my reaction representative of what the young women of the Court are probably thinking about you."

His cheeks heated, and he blinked. Her reaction? She considered him attractive? No female, girl *or* woman, had ever told him that!

She shook her head. "Listen to me—'if I was your age'—I sound like I think I'm an old crone! My, motherhood certainly has taken the ginger out of *me!*"

He had to laugh at that. "My mother says the same thing," he told her. "She swears that we each added five years to her age with every prank we pulled!"

"Some days I would agree with her," Talia replied, and sighed. "I don't remember littles being this much trouble to *my* parents! You have brothers and sisters?"

"One brother and several sisters," he told her, then found himself talking about his family while she simply stood there and listened to him with no evidence of boredom. She even asked him questions that proved she had really been listening, and not just pretending to pay attention.

He progressed from telling her about his family, to finally confessing his own depression and loneliness. It seemed natural, after the way she listened to him about everything else. After all, if Hansa trusted her, why shouldn't he?

"I don't even know where they took Trenor," he sighed, after talking for what seemed to be the better part of a mark. "He's Karsite, too, after all... and horses have always been as much my friends as people. I'd love to go riding, but I don't know where I would be allowed to go, even if I *could* find him, and I don't know what people would think if I asked for the stables." He shrugged. "They might think I was some kind of spy, looking for a way off the grounds to pass messages on, when all I want to do is ride my horse."

She brightened at that. "Havens, at least *that* is one thing I can help you with," she told him. "I certainly know where the stables are, and there are riding paths all through Companion's Field; there's no reason why you can't ride your gelding in there. Plenty of people ride their Companions on the paths. I can't imagine why anyone would forbid you riding Trenor in there. Would you like me to show you where the stables are right now, and get you acquainted with the stablemaster? Once he knows who you are, he can have Trenor set up for a daily ride for you, if you'd like."

He stared at her for a moment; this was the last thing he had expected, and the one thing that would help! He had a little trouble replying, until he got his wits back about him. "Thank you!" he exclaimed. "Oh, that is exactly what I *do* want! Thank you so much!"

But she waved away his thanks. "Not to worry, Karal. I'm glad that there is at least one remedy I can give you for your homesickness that will work right now. Time, I fear, is the only other remedy." She laughed at his grimace. "I know, I know, the one thing a young man hates to hear is that the only cure for *anything* is time! It can't be helped, though; it's a cliché precisely because it's so often true. When problems are big, it's usually because they're swallowing up everything else you would be thinking about. When you have some time, new things come up, and make the old problems seem smaller when you look back at them. So let some time pass, do a few things you really enjoy, and let your mind rest."

He stood up quickly as she gestured for him to follow her, and she led him off at a brisk pace, pointing out exactly where they were and what places they were passing. "Here's the rose garden, the maze is just through there; if you look through the rose trees you can just see the end of the Courtier's Wing of the Palace. That's where your suite is, though most Courtiers don't live here, they have their own manors outside the walls—" That helped him orient himself, and he began to suspect that Alberich had led him in circles that first day, when he had taken Karal to the library. Perhaps it had not been deliberate; perhaps it was simply in the man's cautious nature to attempt to confuse. Perhaps there had been work going on that required they make some elaborate detours.

But from the outside, at least, the Palace and the buildings around it were laid out in a logical fashion. He knew that the library was on the first floor of the wing that contained most of the other rooms used for "official" purposes, and that wing lay directly across from his, according to Talia.

But she was pointing out other buildings now, buildings that were separate from the Palace. "That's Healer's Collegium, and that's Bardic—look, there are the stables, you can see them from here, just on the other side of those trees."

But it was not the stables that caught his attention, but the huge wooded field to their right. It *seemed* to be full of horses.

Then he realized why his mind had phrased it that way, for the "horses" were all white. There wasn't another color of four-legged beast to be seen. Which meant, surely—

Talia saw where he was looking; she squinted against the sun in that direction. "That's Companion's Field. Do you want to go look over the fence for a moment?"

As well ask him if he wanted to fly! Of course he did—and at the same time, the idea terrified him. Companions! The beautiful creatures that Rubrik had so eloquently praised, and the Hellhorses of Karsite stories. His *head* knew that they were not the monsters from his childhood, but his stomach lurched at the idea of so many of them concentrated here. Still, he nodded numbly.

She must have guessed something of his thoughts from his expression, or lack of it. "You do realize that they aren't demons, don't you?" she asked, a little nervously. "Your escort surely explained what Heralds and Companions really are—didn't he?"

I must look as tense as a cocked crossbow. "Yes," he told her. "Our escort and my mentor had a number of conversations about the Companions. I think Ulrich plans to come out here one day when he isn't busy chasing diplomatic rabbits down holes." He moved closer to the fence, until at last he was leaning right up against it, staring at the beautiful creatures in their Field.

Not demons, he reminded himself; orthodox theology held that demons could be as beautiful as they pleased, but he still did not have to remind himself too forcefully. Now that he was here, watching them, his stomach settled again, deciding that maybe his head was right after all. There was something about the Companions that was so completely innocent that the idea of their being demons was absurd.

Not horses, either. He could see how they would excite lust in the heart of any horsebreeder, though. If only one could achieve lines like that with horses! They were easily the most elegant creatures he had ever seen; Rubrik's Companion was no isolated case. Well, rumor said that the Shin'a'in had bred horses to equal Companions, but who knew? Rumor also had it that the Shin'a'in rode naked and painted themselves blue, and he rather doubted either was true.

For one thing, riding naked is damned uncomfortable. You can get yourself such a set of blisters if you have a saddle, and such a rash if you don't…

"Well," he said at last, shaking himself out of the reverie the field full of Companions induced in him. "Your time is precious, even if I'm at leisure at the moment. And I am selfishly devouring it. So, if you can spare me a few moments more to take me to the stables—"

"I can spare you as much time as you need," Talia said firmly. "Come on, and I'll introduce you to the stablemaster."

Talia was no out-of-shape courtier; she set out again at a stiff walk, and he was glad he'd been working out with Kerowyn. The stable was huge, which was only to be expected; their luck was in, though, for Trenor was in the third stall from the door, and whickered as soon as he caught Karal's scent.

Karal let himself into the gelding's stall, while Talia went looking for the stablemaster. Trenor was overjoyed to see him and whuffled his hair and chest with such enthusiasm that he left damps spots all over Karal's clothing. When Karal looked him over carefully, he saw no signs of neglect, much less any of ill-use. That eased most of his worries; these Valdemarans were taking very good care of his "baby."

The stablemaster arrived while Karal was examining Trenor's feet and hocks. He was clearly pleased by the way Karal carefully examined his gelding, rather than being offended at the implication that the stable staff had been neglecting the horse.

"You know horses," the man said—a statement, rather than a question—as Karal finished his examination and stood up to be introduced. Karal nodded anyway, and the man turned and spoke to Talia in a dialect of some kind, too heavily accented and rapid for Karal to follow.

Then he turned away and went back to the work they'd taken him away from; shoeing a pretty little mare. It rather surprised Karal that the stablemaster himself would tend to a task like that, instead of assigning it to underlings. On the other hand—the mare had the delicate lines of a very highly-bred palfrey, and the nervous air of a horse that had been brought up to be high-strung. Better that the stablemaster handle a beast like that; that was what Karal's father would have said.

"Tahk says that you obviously are a good horseman, and that he'll arrange for Trenor to be readied for you for a daily ride if that's what you want. He also offered another option; if you prefer, he'll simply leave orders with the stableboys that when you show up, they're to fetch your tack." Talia scratched Trenor's neck, just along the crest, and laughed when the gelding leaned into her scratching. "I told him I thought you'd probably prefer to make less fuss than the highborns, and would take care of your own saddling, and he simply repeated that you were a *good* horseman."

"I would, and thank you," Karal replied sincerely. "I'd rather not have Trenor saddled up at any specific time, since I don't always know exactly when Ulrich will need me."

"Thought so." She moved her scratching to under Trenor's halter, and the gelding sighed with bliss. "You know, you could combine your lessons with Alberich with a daily ride; he has to make sure his Companion gets some exercise, and neither of them are anything but stiff first thing in the morning, which is when they *have* been going out." She tilted her head to one side, as if sensing his apprehension at trying to approach the formidable Alberich with any kind of a request. "Want me to suggest it? I can tell him it was my idea."

"Oh, would you?" He was appallingly grateful. "By the Light, I seem to be getting deeper and deeper in debt to you."

Once again she waved away any suggestion that he might "owe" her anything. "Don't mention it. I really just want you to be happier than you are. *That* would make a big difference to me, and if you're happier, your work will go smoother."

"And if the work goes smoother, my master will be likelier to be in a good mood, and if he's in a good mood, he'll make concessions, hmm?" He chuckled, and she joined in. "That I can understand! Everyone here is a diplomat."

Though why my being happier would make a big difference to her *in particular I can't fathom...*

"We'd better be going," he said, reluctant to leave Trenor, but feeling better than he had in days. "His blanket's damp, so they've obviously had him out for a good workout today, and from tomorrow on I can take over his exercise."

"I—I had one more thought," Talia said, hesitantly. "You were saying that you wished you could make some friends here, right?"

He hadn't *said* anything of the sort, but he'd certainly *thought* it, so he nodded.

She licked her lips. "There's another person here I would really like you to meet. He's in a similar position to yours, but without even the authority of being a secretary to an envoy. I know that he is very lonely, and even though you don't have anything at all in common in the way of background, you are still both from places that are so different from Valdemar that you are alike in your reactions."

He turned to stare fully at her, because he sensed that she was not even telling him a fraction of what she knew about this person—that describing this person as coming from a place that is "different" from Valdemar just might be the understatement of the millennium.

"What exactly...?" he asked. "What do you mean?"

She made a face of frustration. "I'm really not certain what I can and cannot tell you about him. His situation is—well, nothing short of what you would read about in a legend, and even then you would probably not believe it. The thing that the two of you have in common is that you're both—bewildered, I suppose is the right word. Bewildered and quite foreign to Valdemar. He *does* need a friend, and he is terribly shy. He is also very reserved, and tends to think of questions as being intrusive, which makes him unhappy when he is around our younger Heralds-in-training."

Karal nodded, grimacing. He had met one or two besides Arnod who hadn't been afraid of him—but both of those *children* had been full of questions that in Karse would have been considered dreadfully rude. He had answered them anyway, because they *were* clearly children and hadn't meant anything offensive by their questions.

"I will meet this person, if you like," he offered, feeling that he had to offer her *something* after all the help she had given him today. "I cannot promise anything after that. We might immediately hate one another, after all."

"Oh, I don't think that is very likely," she replied, looking quite satisfied. "I usually manage to find people who are going to enjoy each other's company, rather than the reverse." Then she bit her lip, as if something had just occurred to her. "There is just one thing—"

Karal looked at her sharply. "Which is, what?"

"Do you recall the Tayledras envoy? Firesong, the Hawkbrother Mage?"

Of course he recalled Firesong. Even if he did not have a secretary's trained memory, he could hardly have forgotten *that* flamboyant young man. He nodded.

Talia sucked at her lower lip, and her brow creased a little. "An'desha is with him, but he isn't exactly Tayledras, even though he looks like he is. Technically, he's Shin'a'in. And he's a lot younger than he looks, literally. He's really about your age, maybe a year or two older."

"Ah." Karal nodded again, even though that was more confusing than it was enlightening. That phrase though, "An'desha is with him..." Was she implying what he thought?

Could be. Then again, maybe not. There are probably those who think Ulrich is more than just my master and mentor.

In any case, did it matter? Despite the fact that such a liaison was supposed to be against the Will of Vkandis, there were plenty of situations, pairings like that in the Priesthood, something which had been made very clear to him and every other novice once they graduated from the Children's Cloister.

It was also made very clear to the entire Priesthood once Solaris came to power that *nonconsensual* liaisons, whether they be of opposite or same sex partners, were Anathema, right up there with demon-summoning. *You shall force no one,* seemed to be the whole of the law as far as Solaris was concerned.

And as for Karal—as long as this An'desha wasn't looking for a—

"He's devoted to Firesong," Talia said, as if she could read his mind. "He's going to be a very powerful mage, and Firesong is teaching him. I thought you ought to know about that, too."

Karal thought about any number of responses, and finally settled on a shrug. She might be implying what he thought, and she might not. It hardly mattered.

I have had so many things in my life turned upside down, why not this one as well?

"Good enough," Talia responded, looking cheerful again. "Come on, then, and I'll tell you more about him. If you thought *your* life was strange, you haven't heard anything yet!"

10

An'desha might not yet be even half the mage that Falconsbane had been, but he knew an Empath when he saw one, at least. He readily recognized that Gift in the Herald who came up the path to the *ekele,* black-clad stranger in tow. He thought he recognized the woman, vaguely, though he could not remember her name. Oh, Falconsbane would have *loved* to get his hands on a female like this one! That was one Gift he had been unable to simulate, and no real Empath would serve Falconsbane of his own free will.

No point in trying to force an Empath to serve, either. It's a Gift that can't be coerced, though Falconsbane certainly tried often enough.

He wondered if these were more of Firesong's friends, and at first he was put out at the prospect of yet another invasion of his home. He left his seat in the garden and went outside to meet them, torn between a desire to be polite and irritation at Firesong for bringing more strangers in without consulting him.

But the Herald brightened when she saw him, and approached with the young man a step or two behind her. "An'desha?" she said (and she gave his name the correct pronunciation, which was a wonder). "You don't know me, but I am Elspeth's friend, Herald Talia. She's told me a great deal about you—and to be honest, I *am* an Empath, and you haven't exactly been shielding yourself from me, so I've been learning a bit about you from that as well."

He started; he had not been aware that his emotions had been carrying that far. And when he thought about his predominant feelings since arriving here, he flushed. Mostly tension, unhappiness, even despair—he would not have wished that on *any* Empath.

But she was going on. "Elspeth said something about you spending a great deal of time alone out here, and what I picked up from you—well, it seemed to me you might like to try a little company. I thought that you and this young fellow probably have a great deal in common."

She turned to the young man. "An'desha shena Jor'ethan, this is Karal Austreben, secretary to the envoy from Karse. Karal, this is An'desha, who is an associate of the envoy from the Hawkbrothers." Not only was she an Empath, but she was a skillful one; he felt her exerting her powers to soothe him, and at this point, he was intrigued enough to let her do so.

He knew who she was, once she introduced herself to him. This Talia was the person Elspeth trusted most in the whole world, even above and beyond Darkwind. An'desha was more than ready to be soothed at the moment; he had tried once again to socialize with the Valdemarans yesterday, and once again had met with failure. Here, though, was an Empath, bringing someone she *wanted* him to meet. It stood to reason, given her Gift and her expertise, that she just might have found someone he *could* get along with.

"I thought you two ought to at least meet," she said to the handsome, dark-eyed, black-haired young man. She spoke slowly and carefully so that he—and presumably, Karal—could pick out every syllable. "I can't imagine two people who have less in common with most of Valdemar. Even Firesong knows more about us and feels more comfortable with us than you two do. I'm sorry I waited this long to introduce you—in fact, I'm sorry I waited this long to introduce myself to you—but I wanted to make certain your mutual vocabularies in our tongue had gotten beyond the basics."

An'desha had to laugh at that. "That was a good idea. You are probably right, that I feel less at home here than even Firesong," he said, just as carefully. "Although I do not think I would ever *fit in* with any place or person."

Just a cautious warning—*I hope she isn't expecting us to be instant friends.*

Talia shrugged. "You're probably right, An'desha, but at least Karal is familiar with magic, and he's not afraid of it. That makes him better company for you than most of my people; many of the—how shall I put this?—more reticent folk are afraid of both of you and your magics. Those who are not, or who pretend they are not, tend to be too forward. Oh, let me be blunt—they are *obnoxious.* They want to know everything about you, and they want to know it *now.* At least magic is hardly a novelty to the two of you."

An'desha's eyebrows raised at that. Karal nodded. "My master Ulrich is a powerful mage as well as a Priest," the young man said diffidently. "He *was* one of those who summoned demons, until the Son of the Sun, Her Holiness Solaris, forbade the practice."

"Demon-summoning?" Excitement thrilled along his nerves. Perhaps Talia had more in mind than simply introducing two lonely strangers. If *anyone* was likely to understand his dilemma, it would be one who was familiar with demons and their ilk.

"He never cared to practice that skill," was all Karal said, but An'desha sensed a great deal behind that statement that Karal did *not* say. "I, personally, have no magic to speak of. My skills lie elsewhere."

All the better, so far as An'desha was concerned; the last thing he wanted at the moment was another would-be "teacher." Firesong was quite enough in that department.

"It often causes more problems than it solves," An'desha offered tentatively. Talia watched both of them with a slight smile on her face.

Then Karal smiled himself. "That sounds like something my master would say," he replied warmly. "The people here do *not* seem to understand that, they keep wanting to know what magics can be done to cure this or that—" He stopped himself and shrugged. "Well, I suspect you know."

"I do," An'desha replied. The corners of his mouth lifted along with his heart; this Talia was right, he and Karal *did* have a great deal in common, even though their backgrounds were probably utterly opposite.

An'desha had not realized how hungry he was for a *friend* until this moment. An Empath as strong as Talia would have to have sensed the need even though he had not voiced it to her—sensed it even past the stronger and darker emotions that his fears for the future had been calling up in him. The fact that she had brought Karal here indicated that she had sensed that same need in him as well.

This was a good thing; one of the first unreservedly good things that had happened since he entered the Gate to this land.

"Well, I wasn't able to tell Karal a lot about you, because I didn't want to take liberties that I was not entitled to take, An'desha," Talia told him. "So why don't you explain your situation? Who you are, how you came here, that sort of thing."

An'desha groaned. "I am *not* so fluent in your tongue!" he exclaimed, in mock protest.

But Talia wouldn't hear any excuses. "You are better than you think," she said, as she nodded at the open door to the *ekele* garden, then raised an eyebrow in silent inquiry.

Well, if Firesong could invite people in, so could he! He asked them both into the garden, and described how it had been built—partially to buy himself time, and partially as a way of feeling Karal out. He was more than pleased; Karal's questions were as discreet and nonintrusive as those of the young Heralds had *not* been.

Talia quietly absented herself a few moments later, and he and Karal sat down next to the waterfall in the garden. He noticed only because he sensed the absence of her soothing "spell." He doubted that Karal had any idea that she was gone. The gentle gurgling of the waterfall created an atmosphere of peace and privacy; an ideal place to talk.

By then, Karal was describing his own background. An'desha listened with fascination—sometimes horrified fascination—as Karal explained what the Vkandis Priests had once done to the children, and to the enemies, of their land. While Karal's descriptions were no match for the things that Falconsbane had done, An'desha guessed that at least *some* of the Vkandis Priests had been well on their way to becoming twins of Ancar of Hardorn, and all under the guise of religion. The only thing they had not done was to poison and drain their own land for further power.

And given time, they might well have done that, too.

"That is over now," Karal concluded. "Solaris has decreed the Cleansing Fires and the summoning of demons to be Anathema—that is, completely forbidden, unholy. So, here we are, Ulrich and I, trying to forge an alliance with people we were once at war with. It is—rather unsettling. I was brought up to believe that the people and especially the Heralds of Valdemar were beasts of utter evil and depravity, and now I find that they are—just people." He shrugged. "I have seen so many changes in my lifetime, though, that I expect I will get used to this change as well. What of you?"

An'desha struggled to find the words to describe his own situation, and decided on the simplest possible explanation. "I was Shin'a'in," he said at last. "Longer ago, I think, than you realize, my body is older in years than it looks. I am—was—linked by descent to an ancient mage, an Adept. A very *evil* man, as evil as any of your demons. Because of that, he was able to—" *What to say?* "—to steal my body."

"Ah!" Karal nodded with complete understanding, the very first time he had seen that statement met with anything other than blank incomprehension. "Possession. That's what we call it. That was one of the powers the demons had, to be able to put on the body of a person as if it was a garment. The Black-robes used that power for ill. But Vkandis also has that power, and can use it with the Priests and sometimes with very holy lay people for good. It is called 'the Voice of Flame,' and Vkandis can use the voice of the person to deliver prophecy. But this Fal-cons-bane must have been a very strong demon to displace you; only the strongest and most evil of the demons had that power." Karal's voice and expression were quite sober. "You are a very lucky person, An'desha. Most people do not survive the touch of a demon upon their souls. You must be very strong as well."

"You *do* understand! Though I think it was luck that let me survive." For *once* he was talking to someone who didn't look at him as if he was half an idiot and all mad. "Strong," "evil," and "demonic" were certainly all words that could have been used to describe Mornelithe.

"He had lived in many other bodies, and I still am not certain how I remained alive after he took mine. Perhaps it was because I was a coward and tried to flee instead of fighting him."

"Perhaps he had grown careless," Karal suggested shrewdly. "Demons are known for their pride, and great pride makes for carelessness. So he stole your body. Then what occurred?"

"He did great evil with my body, and I could not stop him," An'desha continued, the words tumbling out of him now. "Then he sought to bring harm to my people, and to the Hawkbrothers, and these Valdemarans, all at once. But he was damaged by some of what he had done, and my Goddess sent to me two of her—" Now what Valdemaran word could he use to describe the Avatars? "—two of her spirit-beings. They helped me, a mage called 'Need' helped me, and Elspeth and Darkwind and Firesong helped me, and Falconsbane was cast out after much battle. When it was all over, the Goddess made me look the age I had been when he first stole my body, or nearly, returning to me the years he had stolen from me."

Well, it was oversimplified but fundamentally correct. Karal was looking at him with a sober expression on his face, and biting his lip as if he had something he wanted to say but was not certain how it would be accepted.

"Possession is a great evil, if it is not the Voice of Flame," he said finally. "I think it is a greater evil than even you know, and you were possessed in truth."

"How do you mean?" An'desha asked, hoping that perhaps, just perhaps, this Karal might have some real answers for him. He might be the only person in this whole country who truly *did* understand, completely, what had been done to him.

"Possession can hurt the one possessed," Karal told him earnestly, leaning forward with the intensity of a greyhound about to be loosed for the chase. "It can make deep wounds, unseen wounds to the spirit. It is wounds like these, though they are invisible, that are harder to heal than *any* physical wounding. Evil corrupts, like the touch of any foul thing; it corrodes, like acid. It can etch the shape of itself into a spirit."

That was exactly what the Avatars had said! An'desha nodded, not bothering to hide his astonishment. But Karal was still not through.

"I do not know you well, An'desha," he said, diffidently. "You are not of my faith, you do not swear by the Sunlord, and yet when the Voice of Flame possessed Solaris, Vkandis Himself laid the duty upon all of us to bring the breath of healing to *any* who needed it. *'He who does good in the name of another god, does it for Vkandis,'* He said, *'and he who does ill in the name of Vkandis does it for the darkest demons in hell. Let those of good will bring succor to one another, and dispense with the naming of Names.'"* Karal took a deep breath, and An'desha held his, every muscle tight, every nerve singing with tension. "Healing hurts to the spirit is something of what my training is about," he continued. "My master Ulrich knows far, far more than I. There are many who were hurt in this way by the Black-robes that my master and others have later helped."

He paused, and An'desha nodded, unable to speak. Karal took that as license to continue.

"I think that you are still in pain and fear, An'desha," he said, as somber as any shaman. "I cannot see you in pain and not offer to help. If it is your will, my master or I can try to help you." He smiled shyly when An'desha did not immediately reject the offer or turn away. "I do not know *if* we can help you, but I know that we would try. This—healing does not require that you swear by Vkandis; it only requires that you be willing to have it done. Even if we can do nothing, perhaps we can give you the direction to help you heal yourself."

For a moment, hardly more than the blink of an eye, young Karal was surrounded by a soft, golden glow—as if he sat in the midst of warm summer sunshine. But the waterfall was in shadow—

An'desha blinked, as he realized that there was something more about this young stranger that he had sensed but had not understood. After his own brush with the Avatars, he had become far more sensitive to those the shaman would call "god-touched." It did not even matter that the god in question was not his own Star-Eyed Lady. There was something about this Karal—a color, or a sense of Light about him—that was a great deal like the feeling he had when the Avatars were near, though it was much weaker. And now—this glow about him was clearly a confirmation of what he had felt. He had sensed similar Light about the Shin'a'in envoy, although he had been far too shy to approach her; she was sworn to the Goddess, marked so by her dark apparel, and he had not had the courage to speak with her after the way he had run off from his own Clan, so long ago. And this feeling Karal called up in him was also identical to the kind of feeling he had when he was around a Companion...

Whoever, whatever he is, he hasn't made this offer frivolously, or because he wants to impress me. He has *something that can help. And Firesong doesn't understand me when I try to tell him what's wrong with me...*

If there is *any hint of Falconsbane around me, surely someone like Karal or his master can banish it! And he talks as if he understands the horrible things I've been feeling and the terrible things I've almost done!*

He flushed with embarrassment and ducked his head a little. "Yes," he said softly. "Please. I don't know why you have offered, but—"

Karal patted his hand, that he had unconsciously clenched into a fist on his knee. "I have offered because it is my—my job? I suppose that is right. It is something I must do, as flying is something that a bird must do. I think I know now why Herald Talia brought me to meet you; if it was not of her will, it might well have been of the will of Vkandis. She *is* a Priest, and He can work through her, if He chooses."

"That may well be," An'desha began. *After everything I have seen, I am not about to say that there is anything a god may or may not do!* "And—"

Bells from the Collegium marked the hour, chiming clearly over the sound of the waterfall, and the young man started as he counted them. He said a word that An'desha did not recognize, though he *did* recognize the tone of annoyance easily enough. "Of all the times—" He shrugged helplessly. "I must go to attend my master at a Council session. Pah! I would gladly have it be some other day, but I have no choice."

"I understand," An'desha said quickly, and then he grinned. "Council sessions do not wait on the needs of such as you and I!"

"No, we are only poor underlings to dance to the bells." But Karal's answering smile took any hint of sourness out of those words. "I will return, I pledge you, and I will see what I can do for you then. I will send word when I may come, if that is well with you?"

"Very well, and I cannot begin to thank you," An'desha replied, rising to escort him to the door. Karal ran off with a backward wave, soon vanishing among the trees and bushes screening the trail; An'desha watched him go with a much lighter heart than he had ever expected to have.

I have a friend. And there was one other thing, small in the light of all that Karal had offered, but in its way just as comforting. *I did not—desire him, except as a friend.* He had been afraid that his desire for Firesong was yet another example of how Falconsbane had warped his spirit. In fact, now that he thought about it, he had found Talia rather comely... and Elspeth as well, though she was as intimidating as she was attractive.

What I feel for Firesong is not of Falconsbane's doing.

Yes, in a way, that was the most comforting of all.

* * *

Karal ran down the trail that led back to the Palace; his feet and heart felt as strong and light as the hero Gregori's on his way back from the Ice Mountain. He had not known what to expect from the silver-haired, gray-eyed young man that Talia had brought him to meet, and at first he had mostly been grateful that this An'desha was dressed *far* more conservatively than his friend Firesong. But then, as they talked, something unexpected had happened.

He found himself really liking the quiet man, so unlike anyone he had ever met before. This was very much akin to the liking he had felt for Rubrik, and yet it was different from that. His feeling for Rubrik had been in part because he had admired the man; they were too different in age and personality to be true friends. But for An'desha—there was the interest of kindred personalities. As they spoke, he realized they had much in common, from a love of learning, to a liking for the same kinds of music. But there was something more to it than that, as well, and although he did not understand it, he waited for the moment when the feeling would be explained.

Then An'desha had revealed that he had been possessed—and there was the explanation.

Ulrich had told him, all of his teachers had told him, that when he came upon a spirit that needed his help, he would feel that need and would respond to it. He was of the Kin of Vkandis, and Vkandis would guide him to those in need. *Now* he knew what they had meant.

If I cannot help him, surely Ulrich can, he thought as he ran. *Now I understand how Healer Priests feel, when someone nearby is wounded or ill, though they cannot see the person. There is a hunger to help, a hunger as strong as the hunger for nourishment. Yes, we can and will help him.*

He broke through the trees and began the sprint to the Palace buildings in the distance. Fortunately, he had heard the bells that gave him a half-mark of warning *before* the meeting. It would take him a quarter-mark to reach the Palace and get his note-taking supplies; that should give him enough time to catch his breath so that he didn't make an unseemly entrance.

Ulrich would much rather work the magics of healing the soul-sick than do any other kind of magic. He has said as much to me more times than I can count. Surely Vkandis moved subtly through Herald Talia today, to bring the two of us together.

There was a stile that went over the fence around the Field, and he headed for that instead of the gate, since it was nearer the Palace. He leapt from the top of the stile as if he was trying to fly and hit the ground running; a few of the gray-clad youngsters stared at him as he ran past them, but that was probably because they didn't recognize him. He only stopped at the outer door to wait for the guard there to acknowledge him and open it for him, then he was off again, running down the hall to the staircase. A few moments later, he burst into the suite, half expecting to see Ulrich there.

He was faintly disappointed to find the rooms empty. Still, nothing could be discussed until after that meeting anyway, and he put his impatience and his news aside.

Business first. An'desha has waited this long, a few marks or even a few days more will not matter a great deal. Patience. Isn't that what Ulrich always tells me?

Given that he had a few more moments than he had anticipated, he took just long enough to peel off his tunic and pull on another, more presentable one. Then he snatched up his pouch of paper and pens and headed for the Council chamber, walking slowly and taking deep breaths to ease his panting, so he would *not* look as if he had been running a quarter-mark ago. *Appearances. Always appearances. Something no foreign envoy can ever forget.*

He had been to this great Council Chamber several times before, but this was the first meeting he had been permitted to attend that would include all the envoys of all the allies. That meant, among other things, that one or both of the gryphons would be there.

He had not seen a gryphon since the formal presentation, although he suspected that Ulrich had spoken more than once with the male, Treyvan. The idea of seeing them again, closely, made him shiver with excitement. There were no magical creatures in Karse—unless one counted the Firecats, of course—and calling them simply "magical" seemed rather blasphemous. Gregori had rid the land of the last of the ice-drakes, and although there was a skull of a basilisk in the Temple, there had not been a living one in even the most inaccessible swamps since long before the first battle with Valdemar.

And ice-drakes and basilisks are evil creatures; Treyvan and his mate are anything but evil. I have seen gryphons listed in the Writ, among other creatures that Vkandis is said to love—sunhawks, snowhorns, scaled ones. They are said in the Writ to be special, "created without guile;" no one could ever tell me just what that was supposed to mean, but perhaps I will be able to ask them some time soon for myself.

Daydreaming aside, there were other good reasons to be here that had nothing to do with his duty to his master. *I will see a bit more of Firesong here, which will be a good thing. If I am to help An'desha, I must know something of the one he is "with."*

He got to the door of the Council Chamber to find that he was actually the first one to arrive; there were only a pair of guards and a young page on duty.

Well, that was convenient. He would have a chance to impress, not only his master, but the other dignitaries, with the diligence of those from Karse. Anything that could show Karsites in a good light was definitely to be pursued.

He had the page inside the chamber show him where Ulrich's seat was, and took the lesser one beside it. He opened his pouch and took out everything in it, sharpening his pens, making certain the ink was mixed, readying all his materials so that there would be no unseemly fumbling with pouch, pen, and papers when the meeting began.

Just as he completed his arrangements, the rest of those who were to attend the meeting began to filter in. He recognized all of the Councilors, of course, though they paid him no attention whatsoever. *Both* gryphons arrived with Firesong between them, and they took a place behind him, since they obviously would never fit at the table itself. The Shin'a'in envoy arrived as well, and with her, Ulrich.

Well, *that* was certainly interesting. Had Ulrich been engaged in a private discussion with her before this meeting? The way they were talking suggested that he had been. But Ulrich's seat was at one end of the horseshoe-shaped table, and the Shin'a'in's seat was at the other, next to Firesong.

Ah, I see—they have us grouped by geography—those who live near each other are seated next to each other. That's useful, and practical as well.

Ulrich sat down next to Karal with a smile of approval for his preparations. Karal was not the only secretary attending this meeting, but he was clearly the best organized of the lot. The others were fumbling out their supplies and trying to be unobtrusive at the same time, and it wasn't working.

The envoy from Rethwellan was supposed to sit next to Ulrich, but to Karal's astonishment, which he quickly cloaked, it was the Prince-Consort who took the chair there. A solemn-faced young man in sober blue took the seat next to Daren's, and prepared to take his own set of notes on behalf of the Prince.

So the Prince-Consort also plans to act as the Rethwellan envoy? That's just a little irregular, isn't it? But no one else seemed to mind, and only the Shin'a'in envoy raised an eyebrow. On the other hand, Daren had once been his brother's Lord Martial, and presumably could still speak with authority on military matters within Rethwellan. Perhaps he was the best choice for this meeting.

Eventually the Queen herself arrived with very little fanfare. Talia came quietly along behind her, and took up a special seat that Karal had *thought* was for the Prince Consort.

Evidently not. He studied the Queen's Own, wondering just what the basis for her position was here. Clearly she was some kind of advisor, but what did she do? *I'm going to have to ask someone some time soon.* These Valdemarans were so surprising that they might even tell him the truth!

When everyone attending the meeting was seated, and all the underlings had their papers and supplies in order, the Queen stood. Selenay wore only a circlet of gold on her head to denote her rank; otherwise her clothing was nothing more than a richer version of the Herald's livery. That in itself was fascinating, because Solaris of all of the Sons of the Sun in living memory was doing precisely the same thing with *her* robes of office. She seldom wore the Crown of Prophecy except when the Voice was going to possess her; as for the rest, the sole symbol of her office was the special Sundisk pectoral that only the Son of the Sun wore, a neckpiece as ancient as Karse itself. Her robes were the same as any other Priest; save only that the cloth was a little softer, of a slightly finer weave. This was very effective, as it made her seem much more approachable than any of her predecessors. Had she taken her cue from the Queen of Valdemar, or had she contrived the notion herself?

"The forces of the Eastern Empire are currently not moving forward through Hardorn," the Queen began, as soon as the murmur of talk was replaced by silence. It was odd, but she looked a lot calmer than Karal would have been in identical circumstances. He made note of that; impressions could be useful. "We have taken this opportunity to gather intelligence information, and we have called this Council to present it to the representatives of all of our allies at once. Much of this will be new even to me."

Ah. So she isn't using the royal plural; when she says "we," at least in this Council, she is talking about more people than just herself. Also useful to know.

And with that, she sat down and gestured to the first of a series of underlings to come forward and make his report.

Karal took copious notes. The first was a basic report on how much territory the Empire had already annexed, and the current situation with what was left of a government in that portion of Hardorn still held by loyalists.

The news wasn't good. The Empire held roughly half of Hardorn at this point. There was resistance, which became more organized with every passing day, but the question in the minds of those who had written this report was whether or not it would become well-organized enough in time to actually stop the Empire short of the Valdemar border.

"The current government consists of a Special Council," the clerk read, as Karal wondered who had been intrepid enough to ferret out all this information. It *had to* have been obtained at firsthand. "There are thirty surviving nobles, the heads of the Guilds, and someone who claims that he speaks for all the mages who are left. It is the opinion of those who have watched this Special Council in action that they are still disordered and demoralized, and a single leader has yet to emerge from the chaos."

The clerk presented his papers to the Queen and bowed himself out. She looked straight at Ulrich as she accepted them, but she waited until the clerk was gone before saying anything. "My Lord Ulrich," Selenay said smoothly, "has your leader any interest in this situation while it remains on the opposite side of her borders?"

Karal fully expected Ulrich to say nothing, but once again, his master surprised him. "I would be lying, and we both know it, if I said that this was *not* a very tempting situation for us, your Highness," he replied, just as smoothly. "The secular advisors to Her Holiness would like nothing better than to annex a bit of Hardorn while the situation is so very unstable, and they have, in fact, so advised her. We might already have done so—but for one insurmountable barrier." He raised his eyebrow. "The Voice of Flame spoke through Her Holiness and made His Will quite plain, to the public in general, and again to Her Holiness in her private meditations. Vkandis Sunlord does *not* approve of the notion of increasing Karse beyond the present border, and will make His displeasure clear to anyone who flouts His holy Will. Since that displeasure has been known to be fatal, no one has suggested any more annexations."

One of the Valdemar Councilors snorted in derision, but it was not Ulrich who answered that clear expression of disbelief.

"I do assure you, my lord," the Shin'a'in envoy said, in a tone of voice that put frost on the rim of every glass in the room, "while deities are not known for personally manifesting Their wrath inside your realm, we who live outside are quite accustomed to hearing our gods *and* obeying them. It is more than faith that governs us, it is *fact.*"

The Councilor in question flushed a painful scarlet and mumbled an apology in Ulrich's direction. The Priest bowed slightly in acknowledgment and acceptance, and the Queen took the floor again.

"It is just as tempting for Valdemar to act during this period of confusion," Selenay said gravely. "We are overcrowded with Hardornen refugees, for one thing. It would be very convenient for us to send them back into their own land again, under Valdemaran supervision. Sending military advisors, perhaps?"

The Councilor for the East asked for the floor. "We *have* been encouraging them to go back to Hardorn and take back their own land again, but it's very difficult to convince them to do so when *we* can promise them no help. Ancar drained his land dry, and times would be very hard there without an army of occupation holding half the country. They simply cannot do anything against the Empire without substantial aid."

"But if we offer them aid, we open up another bag of troubles entirely," the Lord Marshal said instantly. "At the moment, Hardorn is still a buffer between us and the Empire, and the Emperor seems in no great hurry to take the rest of the country. If the Emperor decided that offering aid to Hardorn was a direct act of aggression, he *could* escalate his occupation in order to get at us. Frankly, he can move more troops and resources faster than we can respond. I don't advise any kind of intervention, no matter what words or titles we cloak it in." His mouth twitched in a grimace of chagrin. "I may be a military man, but I know my facts. Fact one—we don't have the resources to take on the Empire. Fact two—we can't afford to antagonize them. We have no choice."

"What *is* the Empire doing right now?" Prince Daren asked. In answer, Selenay gestured to Kerowyn, who stood up with a sheaf of papers in her hand.

"I have an intelligence report on precisely that right here," Kerowyn said, her voice carrying easily to all parts of the room. "In essence, they've stopped moving forward. My agents say that there is a new commander in charge of the entire operation, someone reporting directly to Emperor Charliss. This new commander seems to have decreed a halt to further conquest while he builds a supporting infrastructure behind his lines. How long that will take—I can't tell you. They have more resources than we do, and anybody with a lot of resources can do quite a bit very quickly, barring bad luck and acts of nature or gods."

"Granted." Prince Daren nodded. "Then what happens?"

"Once that is in place," Kerowyn continued, "chances are he will order another push forward, then halt to build, and repeat that pattern until he has the entire country. It's my opinion that he'll hold to that pattern as long as there is little or no organized resistance."

"What will he do when he reaches the Valdemar border and the Karsite border?" the Guild representative, Lady Cathal, asked in a tone of quiet tension.

Kerowyn shrugged. "Frankly, he's got a big enough army that if I were in his shoes, I wouldn't stop. I'd keep right on going as long as losses were acceptable. And don't ask me what 'acceptable losses' are for him; the entire population of all our peoples could be less than a regional garrison to them. I don't know what counts as 'acceptable,' because he hasn't yet met with any resistance that's given him any palpable losses at all. I haven't been able to see the conditions that make his commanders pull back. For Ancar, *any* losses were acceptable as long as he took ground. For us—we're more inclined to retreat than lose lives. He could follow either pattern, but chances are he'll be somewhere in the middle. I can tell you this; 'acceptable losses' will be a percentage of his troops, rather than a hard number. One percent of *his* strength is a lot more in real numbers of men than one percent of *ours*."

"And our land is worn out from the conflict with Ancar," the Lord Marshal pointed out glumly. "We could mount some resistance, but how could it be enough to discourage an army like the Eastern Empire can field?"

"Karse is not in much better shape than Valdemar, although we took little direct damage," Ulrich added. "Indirectly—we did lose troops to Ancar, and mages that we sent up here to you."

"And speaking of mages," Kerowyn put in, taking over the floor again, "the Empire seems to have mages that do things differently than ours do. Many of you have heard Elspeth describe how the Imperial Ambassador to Hardorn created a Gate without any physical counterpart, and our mages have all reacted to *that* bit of news with dropped jaws. Maybe these mages are better than ours, and maybe they aren't. It hardly matters; they're *different*, and that's a problem. Vastly different approaches to mage-craft make it quite likely that they can hit us with something we would never expect in a hundred years."

"And there are," Firesong added smoothly, "many, many *more* mages in the Empire than the entire Alliance can currently supply. Again, that is a real fact. Herald Captain Kerowyn asked me to look at the section of her intelligence report that deals with magic. It is evident to me that much of Imperial infrastructure depends very heavily on mages. I would judge, from the descriptions in the report, that they use mages for communication, construction, and transportation, making their conventional supply-lines much different from what we would use. In layman's terms, I believe that all of their supplies come from deep within the Empire itself by means of Gates. If they can afford to use mages for tasks where we would use carts, workers, and messengers, what kind of offensive magics can they muster?"

"I'm not sure I want to think about it," someone muttered grimly, as shocked silence fell around the table.

Kerowyn is a good commander who does not shrink away from the truth, however unpleasant, Karal decided, and wrote exactly that down. *She has a talent for stating baldly the things that no one else truly wants to consider.*

Finally the Lord Patriarch cleared his throat, making no few of those sitting around the table start. "Well," he said, unsteadily, "what *are* our options, with such a force levied against us? It begins to look as if the only one we have is to pray!"

The Shin'a'in envoy looked at Firesong, and he nodded, deferring to her. She stood up, took a pointer from a page and went to the great map inlaid on the wall.

"The Shin'a'in and the Tayledras have agreed to establish safeholds in the west, in this line," she said, pointing out a line that began at the southern rim of Lake Evendim and continued down to the Dhorisha Plains. "We will hold a safe path of retreat at all times, just as we did during the war with Ancar. We can also receive some of your Hardornen refugees that are willing to take a chance on making new homes in the west, and we hope that this will take some of the strain from the resources of Valdemar."

She sat down again, and Firesong took up where she had left off. "I must admit to you all, however, that as reinforcements, both of our peoples are fairly useless. We are equipped to wage very small-scale battles at the best. The Shin'a'in excel as individual warriors, but they have no organization or structure above the Clan hunting party. The Tayledras have better organization among our scouts, but again, we field very small units. We can offer a place of retreat, we can offer some support, but as *armies* go—" his expression was rueful, "—we can't manage much that is going to be useful to you."

"What about mages?" the Guild representative called.

"Ah, mages." Firesong nodded. "First of all, the Shin'a'in do *not* have mages. However, the Kaled'a'in—that is an offshoot tribe of both our peoples—do practice magic, and the Star-Eyed has given them leave to use it up here, am I correct?" He glanced back at the gryphon called Treyvan, who chuckled.

"Betterrr sssay that Ssshe hasss given them theirrr marrrching ordersss," the gryphon said, with a glance over at the fellow who had expressed scorn over Vkandis' implied power. "Asss sssomeone elssse herrre pointed out, theme arrre *sssome* of usss who arrre usssed to hearrring dirrrectly from ourrr godsss."

"So, that's one group—and I have to admit that even I am not certain what these magic-users can and cannot do. They have been separated from us for a very long time, and casually use things that we had long considered lost arts. We, the Tayledras, are also prepared to strip the Vales of mages and bring them here. We will not endanger our Vales, but there are many projects that can wait a little longer while we aid you."

"White Winds, Blue Mountain, and any other school we can contact will be doing the same," the White Winds representative put in. *Quenten, I think. A friend of Kerowyn.* Karal noted that they appeared to be about the same age. "If the Empire moves this far west, we freelance mages cannot afford to stand by idly. The Empire will annex *us*, or destroy us. That has been their policy in the past, and it is what they are doing now in Hardorn."

Firesong nodded. "I did say that there is no way that we can even begin to equal the sheer number of mages that the Empire can bring to bear—and I still mean that. However, the fact that the Empire works in a different tradition from us can work against them as well. If we don't know what *they* can do, the reverse is true for them. Right now, absolutely the best thing we can concentrate on is to learn everything we can about the Empire and its mages."

"True, and we're working on that," Kerowyn replied, "but don't forget they'll be doing the same thing about us."

Karal was taking notes furiously, while fighting his wish to gawk at the rest of the table. Firesong was as flamboyant as the last time Karal had seen him, though this time his color of choice was scarlet with touches of bright blue; the Shin'a'in envoy was sleekly exotic, as quiet and deadly as one of her arrows.

Then there were the gryphons. Once again, hearing an intelligible, intelligent sentence emerge from those beaks gave him something of a start. If he had not seen the Firecat Hansa conferring with Solaris with his own eyes, he would have been even more startled—and inclined to suspect trickery, some kind of magic to make it *look* as if the "beast" was speaking.

Ulrich stood up, and all eyes went to him. "I am inclined to agree with the Herald Captain in principle," he said, carefully, "but there is another factor involved here. The Empire is enormous, very old, and has probably never met with serious opposition in a very long time. They are likely to be used to these favorable conditions. They may very well dismiss all of us as 'barbarians' and inconsequential. They may not pursue their own intelligence-gathering operations as vigorously as they should. We cannot *count* on this, of course—" he added, as Kerowyn looked ready to protest such hubris, "—but we should be watching for patterns that indicate this. In fact, I believe that we should pursue the notion of planting information that we are as disorganized on this side of the border as the poor Hardornens are, and as paralyzed with terror. If we see the attitude of complacence developing, we will then be poised to take instant advantage of it."

Kerowyn smiled broadly at that, and bowed a little in acknowledgment of Ulrich's cleverness. He returned the ironic little salute as he regained his seat.

"What about the mages of Valdemar?" Prince Daren asked into the silence.

Now it was Elspeth's turn, and she rose to her feet. "The obvious answer is that we should train as many, and as quickly, as we can—which we are doing. The second obvious answer is that we should also recruit as many freelance mages from the south as possible, just as we did during the last conflict with Ancar. The problem with that second obvious answer is that other than mages from the Kaled'a'in and Tayledras, and those coming from schools and teachers personally known to Quenten, we *have* to suspect that at least some of the mages we might recruit from the south are agents of the Empire. Most of the mages that Quenten knows and can vouch for are already up here. That leaves us with the first answer. We're training our own—but there are only so many of them."

"Whoa, wait a moment," Kerowyn interrupted, a look of concentration on her face. "I just thought of something. Why make so hard a push for mages at all?"

"But—!" someone cried, triggering a storm of protest from around the table; she waved the protests away.

"No, I'm serious. What put the idea in everyone's head that mages were the answer to everything?" she asked.

Well that certainly put a fox among the hens. Stunned silence reigned for a moment, until Kerowyn broke it.

"Yes, we *needed* them desperately when we were fighting Ancar, but that was because without them there were things he could field that we simply couldn't fight. But that's not the case now." More protests erupted; she waved for further silence. "Wait, hear me out!"

The Queen herself ordered silence when it was obvious Kerowyn was not going to command it herself. From the looks of suppressed panic around the table, unless Kerowyn made her point very well, the silence was not going to last very long.

"Look," Kerowyn said earnestly, leaning over the table to emphasize her point. "The things that the Empire is simply not prepared for are the factors that make Karse and Valdemar absolutely unique in their experience. In Karse—it's something *we* aren't even prepared for, the fact that Vkandis Sunlord can, will, and *does* intervene with and guide His people directly. For all I know, if the Empire penetrates the borders of Karse, He might even decide to lob a few firebolts at some select Imperial generals!"

"It would take more than simply penetrating our border to cause Him to do so," Ulrich murmured gently, as she looked at him with expectation, "but it is possible He could choose to intervene selectively."

"Yes, well, miracles do happen with predictable regularity in Karse," she retorted.

Ulrich simply smiled very, very slightly.

"That's going to make it difficult, if not impossible, for the Empire to attack successfully in that direction. And meanwhile, I'll bet your Sunlord is doing something else the Empire isn't prepared for. I'll bet He's feeding Solaris with better information than any of my agents can get," Kerowyn stated baldly, then smiled at Ulrich's cautious nod. "Well, I've got some good news for you and your people. As far as my spies have been able to determine, the people of the Empire have a state religion that venerates the current Emperor, his predecessors, and all his ancestors. I'm sure that's very nice for Charliss, but I've got no evidence that he has any special power that an Adept couldn't duplicate, which means that the Sunlord isn't going to be squaring off against another deity if He does decide to throw firebolts around."

Karal scribbled all this down furiously.

179

"Ah," Ulrich said, brightening. "That does put the likelihood of intervention, at least within the Karsite borders, much higher."

"Thought so," Kerowyn said, with an even bigger smile. "All right, then. In Valdemar, one thing that the Empire is not prepared for is the simple existence of the Heralds and Companions. We have brought mind-magic to a high art here; I don't think there's another place north of Ceejay that has people using mind-magic so—scientifically. For that matter, I don't know that there's anyone using it this way *south* of Ceejay either."

Quenten shrugged. "Not that I've ever heard of."

Kerowyn nodded. "That's what I thought. We had to do without magic from the time of Vanyel; we found ways to deal with problems that didn't require magic. *They* put a tremendous emphasis on magic— you all heard the report, they do things with magic we wouldn't dream of, but that makes them very vulnerable if they expect us to do the same and plan their magical attacks accordingly."

Firesong nodded vigorously, Ulrich cautiously; Elspeth simply looked thoughtful. "That sounds good for a working premise," Elspeth said at last.

"So, this time we have one thing that we didn't have when we were fighting off Ancar—we have time, while they're busy eating Hardorn a gulp at a time." Kerowyn shrugged. "I know it sounds cold-hearted, but just at the moment I can't recommend helping the Hardornens directly. My recommendation is that we study the Empire, we make diplomatic overtures to them to buy time, and we find out how we can counter their magic *without* using magic of our own—or with using mind-magic instead. We use what we can apply with confidence to the absolute limit, because they simply will not be expecting that."

More nods around the table, as Karal caught up with everything that had been said so far. He was *very* glad now for all those lessons from Alberich; without them, he'd have been lost long before this.

Prince Daren spoke up next.

"The Empire waited decades—maybe longer—before they moved on Hardorn," he pointed out. "They actually *attacked* only when they could do so with an absolute minimum of resistance. We know they had an agent at the highest levels to feed them accurate intelligence—we should assume that they have had agents there all along. If we convince them that it would be too expensive to take us, they may decide not to."

"We can hope for that," Selenay said. "We can work toward convincing them of that. But we cannot risk *assuming* that."

"Agreed," rumbled the Lord Marshal.

There was more discussion, a few more pertinent comments and additions, but on the whole the real work of the meeting was over at that point. When people had begun repeating what had already been stated, Selenay called a halt to it all, and declared the meeting closed.

It was not too soon for Karal; his fingers were beginning to cramp.

And none of this had driven An'desha and An'desha's plight out of his mind. He could not wait to get Ulrich alone, and see what his mentor had to offer.

"You're very quiet tonight," Firesong observed, as An'desha stared at lamplight reflected in the waterfall. "Are you well?"

"Just tired," An'desha replied truthfully. "I did some work in the garden, and then repeated all the mage-exercises you showed me until my control felt uncertain; then I quit."

Firesong looked pleased, and An'desha relaxed. He had made the conscious decision to keep this new friendship with the Karsite a secret from Firesong for at least a little while. That was partly because he was not certain how Firesong would react to such a revelation. Granted, Firesong had been encouraging him to be more sociable, but An'desha was not altogether sure what he would do if he learned that An'desha had made *a*, singular, friend. Especially when he found that friend was male.

It had occurred to him that under those circumstances, Firesong was very likely to come to the erroneous conclusion that his friendship with Karal was based on physical attraction, not mental attraction, and that it might go beyond mere "friendship" before too long.

No, it would be a good thing to keep his meetings with Karal between the two of them—unless Karal brought his master, Lord Priest Ulrich, along. Then it should be safe enough to reveal.

The oddest thing is, he'd never make the same assumption if my friend was female, and it would be far more likely that I'd—ah—get involved with a female than with another man.

"Any more of those premonitions of doom?" Firesong asked, a little teasingly. "They might be useful, actually; it seems that the mages in the Empire—"

Premonitions of doom—

An'desha gasped, as the ground seemed to drop out from underneath him, and Firesong's voice faded into a roar that filled his ears. He clutched at the rock he was sitting on, but his fingers didn't work. Darkness assaulted him—then blinding light. Then darkness again, filled with the twisting snakes of red An'desha always saw after a bright light. He tried to scream and couldn't. He couldn't even feel his jaws opening.

Then light, striking him in concentric circles. It was almost as if something had picked him up and was shaking him, waving him as a maiden might wave a scarf in the Rainbird Dance. And everywhere, everywhere, was terrible fear, filling him with icy paralysis. Then the darkness again, and then less light than before, then darkness.

Then it was over, as swiftly and without warning as it had begun. He found himself falling backward, still on his stone, Firesong clutching his shoulders and staring into his eyes, while *his* hands held to the rock underneath him, spasmed into rigidity.

"What—?" he choked out.

"You were in a trance," Firesong said, testing An'desha's forehead with the back of his hand for fever. "You cried out once, and grabbed for the stone—I saw how your eyes looked, and sensed power about you, and knew you were in a trance. You looked terrified."

"I was. Am." An'desha gulped. "It was terrible, horrible, yet there was nothing that I can describe. Light and dark in waves, disorientation."

Firesong looked into his eyes, and frowned. "It happened when I asked if you were still troubled by premonitions. This seems too well-timed a response to be simple coincidence."

Numbly, An'desha nodded. If anything, his sense of dread, his tension, had *increased* now.

"Listen, and I will tell you what was related at the Council," Firesong said at last. "Mornelithe Falconsbane was not given to prescience—but *you* are not he, and there is no reason why you should not have that Gift. For that matter, *She* might well have granted it to you; as we were reminded at the Council, there are more hands than the merely human working in this stewpot now."

I wouldn't be too sure that I am not Falconsbane, An'desha thought bleakly, but he listened quietly while Firesong recited what had transpired at the meeting.

"Did anything I spoke of wake a resonance with you?" he asked, when he was done. An'desha had to shake his head.

"Nothing," he said sadly. "You might as well have been telling me facts concerning cattle or sheep. It meant nothing."

Firesong tugged at a lock of silver hair, frowning. "I am at a loss," he said finally. "It would seem to me that our great enemy is at hand—that the Empire and all the Empire's mages should be the source of your fears, and yet——"

"It is not the Empire, peacock!" An'desha retorted, losing his temper. "I have been *trying* to tell you that! It is something else, something we have not even dreamed of! And I think——" he gulped and felt his skin turn cold and clammy as he voiced what he feared he must do, "——I think there is some key to it among the memories that the Great Beast left with me."

Firesong winced, but a moment later placed one hand comfortingly over An'desha's clenched fist. "Then we must examine those memories," he replied, with more gentleness than An'desha would ever have credited him with. "You and I. I have been remiss in forcing you to walk those paths alone, An'desha. I had been so certain that I knew what the answer to your fears was." An'desha stared at him, startled at this new and unwonted humility. "I do not know. Captain Kerowyn made it very clear to me in ways I could not ignore after the Council meeting that these Imperial mages were so very different from anything I have ever experienced that it was wildly unlikely I would be able to counter anything they brought to bear on us effectively." Then a ghost of his old self came back for a moment. "Or at least, it would be unlikely the *first* time they unleashed something upon us. I daresay once I had seen it, I could deal with it."

Then even that bit of arrogance faded. "Still, they need only keep changing their weaponry—and the Captain pointed out that what I cannot anticipate, I cannot *personally* guard against, either." His own face grew paler as he looked solemnly into An'desha's eyes. "For the first time in my life, I cannot be sure that I can guard *myself* from harm. That is—very unsettling. Even when wrestling the power of a renegade Heartstone I did not have such a sense of mortality as I do now. It makes me unsure."

Oh, most lovely. Now what?

"But if that is true, then it is also true that things I had assumed—things regarding you—might also be incorrect." He sighed. "So, now, at long last, I *am* listening to you. And I am asking you: what do *you* think we, together, should do?"

Run away! his cowardly inner self said. But he swallowed, took a steadying breath, and said, a bit shakily, "You must help me with those memories of lives that Falconsbane had before he took my body. We must go farther than I have dared to."

If only the Avatars would come again, he thought, stifling fear, as Firesong nodded his agreement. *They knew what it is I am floundering about in search of—*

Or did they? In all their warnings, they had seemed to bear a sense of frustration that they could not explain themselves clearly. Perhaps even *they* did not know. They were very near to the flesh-and-blood bodies they had once worn, after all, and in fact, Tre'valen and Dawnfire were not technically "dead" at all as they had explained it to him. That was *why* they had been able to help him, so far from the Plains and the Hills, and out of the range of the Star-Eyed's influence.

They are likely back where they might do some good, doing—whatever it is that Avatars do. Perhaps they are aiding the Kal'enedral, the Swordsworn. I do not think they have the power to aid me now.

But Firesong did. As frightening and as perilous as it might be to invoke *anything* connected with the creature that had once possessed his body, An'desha could not in conscience see any other choice.

"Perhaps we should begin tonight?" he suggested timidly.

Firesong nodded gravely. "I think it would be best, *ke'chara.* Before we both lose our nerve."

Ah, but mine is already lost, An'desha thought, yet he did not protest as Firesong helped him to his feet, and led him to their heavily-shielded circle in the garden where all An'desha's rumblings at magic took place. *But perhaps—perhaps now I can find new bravery...*

1 1

"So—there was *nothing* left of the False One?" An'desha had listened, completely enthralled, to Karal's tale of how the Son of the Sun came to power. There was something oddly comforting in the notion that there were other peoples whose deities tended to express themselves as directly as the Star-Eyed did. More directly, in fact, although An'desha could not even begin to envision how a false prophet could ever set himself up as sole authority to the Shin'a'in, much less how an entire succession of them could have. The Star-Eyed would have been much more likely to have arranged for the first fool to be eaten by something large and predatory before he ever became a problem.

"Nothing. Just a pile of smoldering ashes." Karal nodded. "It was quite—ah—daunting. It made me certain that I never wanted to find myself receiving the Sunlord's direct regard. I will be quite *happy* to remain in obscurity!"

"I can well understand that," An'desha replied. "The Star-Eyed is—a little more subtle." *That may be the understatement of the century. Kal'enel is not inclined to strike people dead with lightning even at Her angriest.*

The serene little indoor garden had become their meeting place; they were reasonably certain of being left alone there, and since An'desha and Firesong already practiced all magic there, it was one place where An'desha felt relatively confident. And no matter what the weather— which continued to be uncertain—it was always balmy summer in this miniature Vale.

He noted that Karal was no longer wincing whenever he mentioned the Shin'a'in Goddess, and his dark eyes no longer clouded with unease. *Poor Karal. He was so shocked at first to learn that Vkandis might not be the* One True God.

"But then again," An'desha continued with a shrug. "She and He are both gods, so who are we to say what they will and will not do? For all that I was touched by the Star-Eyed's own hand, I am still hardly qualified to judge Her or Her probable actions."

Karal coughed politely. An'desha took the hint.

"Speaking of probable actions—I spoke with Ulrich about you." Karal waited for An'desha's reaction.

His reaction would have been enthusiastic enough to satisfy anyone. Excitement sent a chill along his arms. "Will he come? Has he time? Does he think he can help?" An'desha had spent enough time delving back into the memories of Falconsbane's previous lives to feel as if the already uncertain ground beneath him had become a quagmire. He couldn't help thinking that only extreme good fortune had kept him from stepping into a bottomless pit that would swallow him up before he could cry out for help. He'd had a particularly hag-ridden nightmare last night, after yet another stroll through the memory-fragments of the past. He'd spent the rest of the night huddled into a blanket in a fearful ball of misery, and finally Firesong had thrown his hands up and lost patience with him after failing to calm him. Firesong had gone off to the garden to sleep, leaving An'desha to watch out the last of the night by himself.

I knew that he was right, that it had only been a nightmare, but what could such nightmares lead to? What if I fell into one and never came out again? That was what held me so terrified that he could not comfort me. I don't know how many more nights like that I can go through.

Karal nodded solemnly. "He said he would try to come this afternoon, unless I came to tell him otherwise. Shall I go see if he is free?"

"Please!" An'desha replied, with more force than he had intended. He made himself relax, though Karal gave no sign that he was alarmed by the violent response. "Please. Things are—I would truly like to speak with him."

"He'll come. I'll go find him now." Karal knew An'desha well enough by now to take him seriously. He got up and trotted off without another word, leaving An'desha alone in the garden again. Although An'desha was not normally given to pacing, he did so now. After all this time—someone who understood his pain and his peril, who was willing to help him—

What would this Ulrich be like? *Let him not be like the shaman of my Clan… that would leave matters worse than they are now!* He could not bear that—to have someone deliver a lecture to him on his own moral weakness, on how he should be showing some spine instead of cowering like a child afraid of monsters in the tent shadows. He *was* doing his best, he *was!* Even if Firesong didn't think so—

Now that the moment was at hand, he was rapidly tangling into a knot of tension.

"Here we are. I found him on the very path," said Karal cheerfully, from the door. An'desha spun about to see his friend entering through the doorway, with a much older man beside him, a man who walked carefully and a little stiffly.

As they neared, An'desha noted the calm expression on the older man's face—a face, thin and intelligent, with a sharp and prominent nose and matching chin. He and Karal were very much of a "type," as Shin'a'in, Kaled'a'in and Tayledras were of a "type." Interesting, since Valdemarans were as mixed in "type" as a litter of mongrel puppies.

The priest had probably seen some fifty summers or so; his silver hair had a few black threads in it, but not many. But more important to An'desha than his years was his expression; there was none of the querulous impatience An'desha remembered the shaman wearing more often than not.

"An'desha." The man bowed a little in greeting to An'desha, rather than extending his hand to be clasped as Valdemarans did. "Karal has told me something of you and your plight, but I would like to hear it all from your lips, as well." He smiled a little, and his eyes wrinkled at the corners. "Sometimes things can be garbled in the translation, as any diplomat will tell you."

The smile was enough to convince An'desha that, whatever Ulrich was, he was nothing like the shaman. The shaman had *never* smiled.

Ulrich listened to his history and his current fears with no sign of impatience, and even took him back over a few points to clarify them. As Ulrich questioned him, An'desha was reminded more and more of the spirit-sword Need, the blade that was now carried by Nyara. Need had coached him through his ordeal as he acted against Mornelithe Falconsbane from—literally—within. She had never promised more than a chance at his freedom; she had never given him pity or sympathy, only guidance.

Ulrich was of a similar mind. He did not want to hear excuses, and would not accept them if An'desha tried to make them—but as long as An'desha had clearly been doing his best, Ulrich would praise him for it, and make allowances for things that could not yet be helped.

He did spend quite a bit of time asking many questions about An'desha's experiences with the Avatars, after An'desha mentioned them. He had done so with extreme caution, remembering how shocked Karal had been at the intimation that there were more real deities in the world than his own. But to An'desha's relief and mild amusement, Ulrich was not only *not* shocked, he seemed to accept it as a matter of course.

"You do believe me, don't you?" he asked, when Ulrich fell silent. "I mean, you believe me about Dawnfire and Tre'valen, that they *are* Her Avatars, and not something I hallucinated, or something else."

Ulrich took a moment to think before replying. "I admit that such an explanation had occurred to me, when you first mentioned them," he said at last, steepling his fingers together. "You hardly qualified as sane under normal definitions. But after all you have told me, I am quite certain that they are exactly what you claim. And that your 'Star-Eyed' is what you claim Her to be."

Karal made a small sound, something like a strangled cough; An'desha glanced aside and saw him turning a fascinating color.

Ulrich chuckled and turned to his protégé. "What, surprised to hear me say that, young one?" he chided gently. "Did you think me so bound by the letter of the Writ? Here is another lesson for you. Most wise priests are well aware that the Light can take many forms, many names, and all are valid. It is there in the earliest copies of the Writ, for those who care to look."

He turned back to An'desha. "It is a man's deeds that define him," he said earnestly. "As I believe Karal has told you—Vkandis Himself

187

has passed that stricture to us, that a good deed done in the name of the Dark is still done for the Light, but an evil one done in the name of the Light is still quite evil, and a soul could be condemned to Darkness for it."

An'desha nodded, as much relieved by those words as by anything else Ulrich could have said or done. The tradition-bound shaman of An'desha's Clan would never have said anything like *that.*

"I have always felt," Ulrich continued thoughtfully, "that before I passed judgment on any man because of the god he swore by, I would see how he comported himself with his fellows—what he did, and how he treated them. If he acted with honor and compassion, the Name he called upon was irrelevant."

All very well, An'desha thought, after a moment of silence, *and I am glad he feels this way—but what about me? What about the dreams, and—*

"However, that has nothing to do with your predicament, An'desha," Ulrich said, startling him. Could Ulrich read his mind? "You have some very real fears that need to be addressed. Let me start with the one closest to your heart—the fear that you are still possessed by that evil creature that called himself Bane-of-Falcons."

An'desha leaned forward eagerly, misgivings forgotten. Point by point, with careful detail, Ulrich proved to him that he knew what he was talking about—and that, as Firesong and everyone else had said, Falconsbane was *gone.*

What convinced him was that Ulrich had a reason—a sound, believable reason, for some of the things he'd been experiencing. "There really is a simple explanation. You are only now able to feel the physical effects of your emotions, after so many years existing only as a disembodied spirit, so to speak," Ulrich told him patiently. "For you, such things are as fresh and startling as regained sight for one who was blinded, or hearing restored to the deaf! Think of how such a former deaf man would react to a sudden noise—and then think how you are reacting to a sudden surge of emotion. Not only that, you are feeling the sweat of your palms, flushing of the skin or paleness that come with emotions, for the first time in a very long time. They must feel overwhelming to you, easy to interpret as signs of possession. Yet you now feel them with your own body, and not one taken over by an evil spirit."

An'desha nodded, very slowly. This made such good sense, he hardly knew what to think.

"I'm not—I cannot seem to deal with all this," he began hesitantly.

Ulrich smiled. "If you were handling all this well, *then* I would suspect another possessing spirit, for no sane human could be taking your situation *well* at this moment!"

Weakly, An'desha returned his smile. "I suppose you are right, when you put it that way—"

"An'desha, not every soul is suited to being a Priest, or a conquering hero, or a serene Healer. You blame yourself for being a coward, when in fact you show more bravery than anyone should expect of you. Judge yourself, not what others would think of you, and be content with what you can do. This does not excuse you from learning how to control your emotions," Ulrich warned. "The shadow of your demon still lurks there. His taint is that it is much, much easier for you to feel anger than joy, hatred than compassion. These are old, worn paths through your body, which will react according to long habit—and old, worn paths through your mind, which experienced what Falconsbane experienced. It is always easier to take the well-worn path than the new one. You must overcome that taint. The scars upon your soul can be smoothed away, but it will take not only time, but your own will, that you will prove to be nothing like him."

That, too, made sense, and An'desha nodded, more comforted now than he could express. Granted, others—including Firesong—had said exactly the same things to him, though in different words, and with no explanations; but this time he felt he could believe them, since they came from an impartial source.

Perhaps Ulrich *was* a kind of Mind-Healer—or perhaps, a Spirit-Healer, if there was such a thing.

And who am I to say that there is not? Karal said so. I think that I must believe him.

"But this other—this great fear you have that there is danger for all of us that we cannot foresee—this troubles me," Ulrich continued. "This may be something you are sensitive to because of those ancient memories you carry; that would be *my* guess, at least." He chewed his bottom lip thoughtfully. "If you would like it put another way, part of you, the part of you that holds those ancient memories, *knows* what they contain, and knows that there is something going on at this moment that relates to those memories, or even matches them. But most of you does not want to face those terrible memories. So, that part of you that is aware and knowledgeable is trying to force the rest of you to become aware and knowledgeable." He cocked an eyebrow at An'desha. "Am I making sense to you, or is all this gibberish?"

"It is making sense," he replied dazedly. In fact, like the other explanation, it was making a little too much sense. He'd had a sense of being divided internally for some time now, but he had thought it was a sign of Falconsbane's continued presence. Now he had another explanation for the feeling, and it was one that did not cater to his fears and left him no excuse for inaction—

Which makes it more likely to be the right one.

"It is what the shaman called 'The Warrior Within.' The voice inside us that tells us what we must know," An'desha said slowly. "The source of all honor, faith, and prosperity under the Goddess is that voice, if we listen with wisdom, they say."

Ulrich studied his face as he sat there with all those powerful thoughts passing through his mind; at last the priest nodded, as if he was satisfied with what he read there. He raised an eyebrow at Karal.

"I have laid the foundation," he said to his protégé. "I think you can complete the work. Simply keep your mind as open as it has become, and I do not think you will misstep."

He turned back to An'desha. "The bulk of your solutions lie within you, I do think," Ulrich told him. "Karal will help you, but on the whole, you will be doing the real work to find them. I will do what I can, but there is nothing that I see in you now that requires my further help."

Which meant—what? That he *had* needed Ulrich's help until this moment?

"I would be the last person to assert that things cannot change, however," Ulrich continued. "If they do, I would be distressed if you did not come to me. Meanwhile, you may trust Karal. He is sensible, he has learned good judgment, he is not afraid of the strange or the powerful, and he has, most of all, a good heart."

Then, while Karal was still blushing a brilliant sunset-crimson, Ulrich got up and left the two of them alone again.

With Ulrich's encouragement, Karal spent as much of his free time as possible with An'desha. As the days passed, Karal became more and more convinced that Ulrich was right; the key to everything An'desha feared lay in those buried memories. Not only was there something in those recollections that was triggering An'desha's prescient episodes *and* his nightmares, but there were also things about An'desha himself that needed to be dealt with.

So Karal continued to work on the "foundation" that Ulrich had established; building An'desha's confidence, convincing him that he *had* passions and would make purely human mistakes, but that as long as he remembered to keep his *powers* under a tight rein, the mistakes he made would teach him how *not* to make other mistakes.

"Compassion and honor," he said, over and over again. "Those are what is important. So long as you have both, and act with both, you cannot make any mistake that will bring lasting harm."

"No?" An'desha replied with skepticism—a healthy sign, that he should respond with anything other than blind agreement. That meant he was thinking for himself. "But—"

"But good intentions count for something, else I'd have been condemned to Vkandis' coldest Hell long ago!" He grinned and hugged An'desha's shoulders. "If you have compassion and honor, and you made a mistake that harmed someone, must you not, out of compassion and honor, see that the mistake is *being* made and try to stop it?"

"Well, yes, I suppose," An'desha replied slowly.

"And having seen the effects of such a mistake, must you not also try to reverse them?" he continued, with purest logic. "Don't you see? Compassion and honor require that you *not* make excuses, nor allow yourself to say, 'nothing can be done.' So even if you make a mistake, you must fix it. You'll *want* to."

Perhaps because Karal had no great powers of his own, and yet was (relatively) fearless in the face of great powers, An'desha came to trust him, even as Ulrich claimed he would. And although An'desha was not told, Ulrich's interest went far beyond the one meeting. The priest questioned his protégé carefully every night, and asked Karal what his continuing plans were. He very seldom suggested any other course— Karal had the feeling that Ulrich was letting *him* make his own mistakes and rectify them as well—but it gave Karal a feeling of increased confidence to know that his mentor was keeping track of all this, though the progress came by infinitesimal increments.

But there was some measurable progress. An'desha *did* start looking at some of the older memories. He was already past the life of a strange creature that had called himself simply "Leareth" (which meant "Darkness" in the Hawkbrother tongue), a time that seemed to be several centuries ago.

And Firesong was a great deal happier with him, at least according to An'desha. An'desha carried some of his confidence back into his lessons with the Adept, and was making more and steadier progress toward using those powers he carried, instead of wishing them gone.

Success gave An'desha further courage to look farther and deeper into those dark memories, and to face what lay there.

And, just as important, An'desha was able to look at the terrible things in those memories and acknowledge, without flinching, that the hateful or jealous things *he* felt (and did not act on) could be considered a faint, far shadow of the dreadful things that the one who had been Falconsbane had done.

And Ulrich pointed out something that Karal had wondered about. The farther back those memories went, the *more* human, rather than less, that entity became. And the more "reasons" and excuses he made up to justify the unjustifiable.

Ulrich made no conclusions in Karal's hearing about the pattern, but it certainly left *him* wondering what it meant, and trying to come to a few conclusions of his own. He continued to read those ancient notebooks that Ulrich had given him, and found more than one place in the text that sounded familiar. Then he realized that Ulrich had been quoting extensively from these very texts when he had given An'desha that little speech about doing deeds in the name of the Light.

He was reading in his room, puzzling through another Valdemaran history that Alberich had recommended, when Ulrich cleared his throat from just outside his open door. He looked up, quickly, and sat straight up on his bed. His master wore an unusually serious expression, and his robes were not only immaculate, he was wearing one of his formal outfits, robes of heavy ebony silk that shone with full magnificence.

"I dislike ordering you out of your own room, Karal," his mentor said apologetically, "but I have only just arranged a meeting with someone very important, who wishes to discuss matters of a sensitive and theoretical nature. And if—"

"If I'm here, your important person won't talk, because I might overhear something. Yes, sir." Karal put a marker in his book and quickly got to his feet. "Since these discussions are theoretical, you won't need a record of them. I'm certain I can find something to occupy my time between now and—say—dinner? I'm already dressed for it, so I won't need to return."

"Excellent, and thank you." Ulrich stood aside to let him leave, with no further comment. Karal had been expecting something like this for the past few days; negotiations between his mentor and not only the Valdemaran government, but the Rethwellan government as well, had gotten to the point where some significant gains could be made. That meant private, one-to-one meetings, where both parties could discuss possibilities in total confidence and privacy.

As he walked down the wood-paneled hallway with a friendly nod to the guard patrolling there, he realized that he was, for once, completely at loose ends. An'desha would be with Firesong, in his magic-practices. There was no use going into the garden to be snubbed by the young nobles there—and it *was* snubbing, now; they had learned he was no noble, and saw no reason to treat him better than any other servant. The library, ordinarily enticing, was usually as full of young Heralds at this time of the afternoon as the gardens were full of young courtiers. *They* weren't snubbing him, but he wasn't in the mood for fending off questions and curious glances, either.

I'd ride, but I'm not exactly dressed for it, he thought wryly. Dressing for dinner early might not have been such a good idea. A pity; another workout wouldn't have hurt Trenor in the least. One simply did not go in to dinner with the Court smelling of horse, however.

That did give him an idea, though. He'd been passing through Companion's Field on a daily basis without gawking at the inhabitants, but he could spend whole marks watching real horses, so why not spend some time watching these not-horses? It might give him some insight into what they were.

With that in mind, he took himself down to the first door to the outside, and headed for the path that would take him to the Field.

While there were plenty of people about, none of them paid any attention to him. He leaned up against the fence and simply watched the graceful creatures, taking a completely aesthetic pleasure in the way they moved rather than consciously analyzing what they were doing. Within a very little time, though, he was aware that they did not act like horses at all. There was no sense of a "herd" at all; the closest to "herds" were small groups of foals playing together, with the mares standing or grazing nearby, very much like mothers keeping a careful eye on their toddlers while gossiping. There was no dominance-shoving or scuffling among the young stallions as there would have been in any other situation where there were mares present; rather, the young stallions were as calm as the mares, and the only way of telling one from the other was by the physical attributes. There *was* one stallion that every Companion there deferred to, but there was nothing of the submission to the dominant herd beast; they acted more like loyal courtiers with a genial and approachable monarch. It was rather fascinating, actually. Any person with a bit of knowledge of real horses would be well aware that this was not "normal" behavior. In fact, he had a disconcerting impression of a large group of people taking their ease in a park...

"There have been times when I would have been pleased to have traded places with any of them," said a familiar voice behind him.

"I can certainly see why, Herald Rubrik," Karal replied, turning to greet their former guide with a smile. "Perhaps one day you will also be able to explain to me how a creature as large as your Companion can succeed in creeping up behind someone, while making no noise whatsoever!"

Rubrik shrugged, gazing down on Karal from his vantage point in his Companion's saddle. "I have no idea, but the gryphons are just as good at it. I've had the male come up behind me unexpectedly and scare the wits out of me; he didn't intend anything of the sort, and he was very apologetic about it, but I can't imagine how he managed to do it in the first place." The Herald eyed Karal speculatively. "Think you could spare a few moments to help me down?"

"Surely. Here, or at the barn?" he replied readily.

"The barn, if you would be so kind." Rubrik chuckled. "You aren't dressed for grooming, so I won't ask you to help me, but I'd appreciate some company while I take care of things."

"Actually, so would I," Karal admitted, as the Companion started off toward the gate at a sedate walk, and he took up a position at Rubrik's stirrup. "I found myself at loose ends, and I was just thinking how few people I really know here. Most of the ones I know by name, I do not know well enough to speak casually to."

"Ah." Rubrik nodded sagely. "I can see that. In part, I would suspect that is the burden of being a diplomat, if only by association. Whatever anyone says to you is likely to be scrutinized from every possible angle. And—I understand as a 'commoner' forced to operate socially with highly born folk with an exaggerated sense of the importance of bloodlines, things are not as pleasant for you as they could be. Your master is protected and given status by his rank as ambassador, but you are no more than a lowly secretary, completely beneath their notice. It is rather difficult to have an enlightening conversation under those circumstances."

Karal sighed, and fidgeted with his Vkandis-medal. "I could wish that was less accurate, sir."

"At least your Valdemaran has improved significantly," Rubrik observed as they reached the barn and crossed the threshold into the cool and shadowed interior.

Karal managed a smile. "If it had not, your own Herald Alberich would be having some irritated words with me. As I'm sure you are aware, his irritation is not an easy thing to bear!" He helped Rubrik from the saddle, then assisted with removing the tack and handing Rubrik grooming brushes while they talked.

Rubrik succeeded in drawing him out, as he had so many times in the past. It wasn't hard; Karal desperately wanted someone to talk to, and he realized before too long how much he had missed the older man's insights and quiet observations.

"I suppose I'm lonely," he said finally, with a sigh, as he leaned against the wall of a stall and watched Rubrik comb out his Companion's mane. "I was so much of a loner at home that I wasn't expecting to be lonely here, but it's harder than I thought, being so much a foreigner here. It's partly because in Karse, one of the Kin would feel at home in any holy place, and they were everywhere. But here, there is only one strange place after another."

"I think I might have a solution for you, rather than a handful of platitudes, for a change," Rubrik replied; a completely unexpected response. Karal stared at him as he patted his Companion and sent him on his way out the door, then turned back to him with a smile that hinted of plans behind Rubrik's eyes. "What if I found you someone about your own age to talk to? The Court is far from being *all* there is to this place, and even Herald's Collegium is not the center of the universe—though we'd like to think it is!"

Karal wasn't sure how to respond, so he just smiled weakly at this sally. Rubrik didn't take any offense at this lack of enthusiasm.

"There are quite a few young people your age here—far more than either the Heraldic students or those conceited young nobles," he continued. "Would you care to meet people who are more concerned about your skills than your birth?"

"It sounds good, but I don't know, sir," Karal said carefully. "As you pointed out, I am a foreigner here and associated with the diplomatic mission. *They* might not care for *me.*"

But Rubrik was not to be dissuaded, and put forth a number of convincing arguments. It sounded too good to be true, actually, and entirely too idealistic, but finally Karal allowed himself to be swayed by Rubrik's enthusiasm and agreed, keeping his reservations to himself.

Rubrik still had tack to clean, and was quite prepared to talk more, but time got away from them. As the warning bell rang to signal that dinner was imminent, he walked back to the Palace alone, wondering who this mysterious group of people *was*. He certainly hadn't seen any sign of them in all the time he'd been here. And why would they be any different from—say—the Heraldic trainees?

Oh, well, he decided, as he entered the Palace itself with a nod to the guards at the door, and sought the Great Hall, joining the thin but steady stream of courtiers heading that way from the gardens. *It is certainly worth a try. I have more time on my hands now than I expected to, and much less to fill it.*

Dinner was the usual controlled chaos of conversation and Karal was at his usual place at Ulrich's right hand; and as usual, Karal understood less than half of what was said around him. On the other hand, he didn't expect to need to understand what was said; he was watching what was done. The subtle languages of movement, expression, and eyes told him more than speech did, anyway. He paid very careful attention to Ulrich's dinner companion, the Lord Patriarch, since his mentor seemed to be having a particularly intense discussion with that worthy gentleman. It seemed to be an extension of an earlier conversation but was couched in very vague terms; Karal couldn't figure out exactly what they were talking about. He wondered if the Lord Patriarch was the person Ulrich had been meeting with this afternoon. There were offshoot Temples of Vkandis here in Valdemar, Temples whose members had defected from the Mother Temple when war broke out with Karse, holding their allegiance to Valdemar—or the older Writ—higher than their allegiance to the Son of the Sun in Karse. Given all that Karal had learned about those times, it could be they had placed their allegiance correctly! But could Solaris be planning on bringing these strayed sheep back into the fold? That would certainly cause a great deal of upheaval in the offshoot Temples at least, and make for more diplomatic incidents at the worst.

He wasn't too surprised when after dinner he found himself alone again, excluded from the suite by more "confidential conversations." But this time the library was empty, so that was where he went.

And that was where Ruhrik found him.

There was someone else with him; a young woman dressed in a uniform very like that of the young Herald students, but colored a light blue rather than gray. She was thin and earnest, with a nose that was a match for Karal's, deep-set brown eyes, and short, straight brown hair—scandalously short, by Karsite standards. She was not exactly pretty, but her face was full of character and hinted at good humor.

"I thought I'd find you here," Rubrik said cheerfully, as he limped up to the desk where Karal was leafing through an illustrated book of Valdemaran birds. "This is the person I wanted you to meet. Natoli, this is Karal; Karal, my daughter Natoli."

Daughter? Oh, no—is this some kind of matchmaking ploy?

His eyes widened involuntarily at the thought, and he frantically tried to marshal some kind of excuse to get away, but Rubrik's next words collapsed that notion.

"She's one of what the Heraldic trainees call 'the Blues,' for their uniforms," Rubrik continued. "What that means is that they share classes with the trainees without being Heraldic, Healer, or Bardic trainees themselves. Some of these students are the children of nobles, but many are lowborn or of the merchant classes, young people with high intelligence who distinguished themselves enough to find patronage into the ranks of the Blues. Most of Natoli's friends are mathematicians and crafters, like Natoli herself."

The girl nodded briskly, with no attempt at flirtation, which relieved Karal immensely.

"I've asked her to give you a tour of the Palace and Collegia as a Blue would see it, then introduce you to some of her friends." Rubrik grinned. "You might be surprised. Some of them actually speak rudimentary Karsite."

Before Karal could stammer his thanks, Rubrik limped off, still chuckling to himself. His daughter examined Karal for a moment, with her arms crossed over her chest and her feet braced slightly apart.

Evidently she approved of what she saw. "Actually, Father doesn't really understand what I want to do," she said, with no attempt at making small talk. "I'm going to construct devices, *engines,* we call them, to do the work that several men or horses are needed for now."

"What, like wind and water mills?" Karal hazarded, and she grinned with delight.

"Exactly!" she replied. "And I want to build special bridges too, that would allow for the passage of masted ships and—well, that doesn't matter right at the moment. There's still some sunlight, would you like to take that tour now?"

She seemed friendly enough, even if she wasn't like any female Karal had ever encountered before. It occurred to him that he was meeting a great many women here in Valdemar who weren't like the females he knew at home. He nodded, and she motioned to him to get up and follow her. "You're in the Palace library, I'll show you the others, and the classrooms for the three Collegia first," she said—and proceeded to do just that, with a brisk efficiency that had his head spinning.

She pointed out things to him that he would never have had any interest in on his own—details of architecture and the mechanics that created the many comforts in the Palace itself. How the chimneys were structured so that the fireplaces in each room drew evenly for instance, or the arrangement of rainwater gutters and cisterns on the roof that put water in every bathing room. It was quite clear that she loved her avocation, and equally clear that flirtation was the farthest thing from her mind.

The sun set just as she completed her tour, and she marked the crimson glory with a nod of satisfaction. "The Compass Rose should be just about filling now," she said, a non sequitur that caused him to knit his brows in puzzlement.

"Compass Rose?" he repeated.

"Oh, that's the place where all my friends and their teachers meet, just about every night," she replied airily. "Father told me to introduce you around, so I figured that I'd take you there tonight and get all the introductions over at once."

"Tavern?" he echoed. "Uh—tonight? You mean, right now?" *I'm not sure I'm up to a strange tavern in a strange city full of strange people...*

"Of course," she said, and set off down the path that led to the small gate in the wall he had first entered when he and Ulrich arrived here, without waiting to see if he was going to follow her. "That's much more logical than trying to track them down tomorrow, one at a time. And much more efficient as well."

He had the feeling, as he trailed in her wake, that "logical and efficient" played a very large part in how she regarded the world. He could only wonder what some of his teachers back at the Temple would have made of her.

The gate guards let them out without a comment, and they made their way through the lamplit streets. Natoli threaded her way through the traffic with the confidence of someone who passed this way so often she could have done so blindfolded. The tavern lay just beyond the ring of homes of the highly born or wealthy, but Natoli knew shortcuts that Rubrik apparently hadn't, little paths that led between garden walls and across alleys he would never have guessed were there. By the time the last sunset light had left the sky, they were already at the door of the Compass Rose itself.

Karal knew what to look for in a good tavern, and he was pleased to find all of it in this one; clean floors and tables, enough servers to take care of the customers without rushing, decent lighting, and no odors of spoiled food or spilled drink. In fact, in the matter of lighting, the Compass Rose was as well-equipped as the Temple scriptorium, which rather surprised him.

Most of the tables were full, or nearly, but Natoli knew exactly where she was going. "Come on," she told him, as she peered across the room with her hand shading her eyes. "It looks as if everyone's here."

She started out across the crowded room, expertly dodging chairs and servers as she moved. "We form up in groups according to what we're interested in, and each group has its own tables," she explained over her shoulder, as he struggled through the crowd to keep up with her. "The teachers are all in the back room, of course—you know they've graduated you when they send you an invitation to join them. That's when you stop taking classes and start looking for work or a patron, or start teaching, yourself."

"Oh," he replied, which was really all he could say, for by that time she'd reached the table she wanted—a long affair surrounded by two dozen chairs at least, all but three of them filled with blue-garbed young men and a few young women, and covered not only with tankards and mugs, and platters of food, but with books and papers, water-stained and dotted with mug rings. Now the reason for the good lighting in here came to him. It looked as if these people were as accustomed to doing some of their work and reading here as in libraries or other quiet places! No few of the people who greeted Natoli were just as foreign-looking as Karal himself, though he was the only one wearing anything other than that ubiquitous blue uniform. They greeted her with varying degrees of enthusiasm, from boisterousness to carefully contained cheer.

"This is Karal," his guide said, when they'd finished. "He's with the Karsite ambassador. Secretary."

"Really?" One of the nearest, a young man with sharp, foxlike features and a wild shock of carrot-colored hair, raised his eyebrows in surprise. Then he grinned, and said in careful Karsite, "I would be grateful, good sir, if you could tell me the direction of the Temple."

"South, about four hundred *meiline* from here," Karal replied shortly in his own tongue, then continued in Valdemaran. "Your accent is really quite good, but you need to form your gutturals farther back in your throat, and they're like hoarse breathing, not like gargling."

"Ah! Alberich never could explain that properly, thank you!" the young man said, and he hooked the nearest empty chair with his foot, dragging it over. "Have a seat, won't you? Natoli, we need your help on the drawbridge project."

Karal took the proffered chair as Natoli helped herself to another, and was immediately engulfed in a technical discussion of which Karal understood perhaps half. The center of attention for the group was a huge piece of paper, covered with scribbles surrounding a drawing of a bridge, that they had placed in the middle of the table so that everyone could look at it at the same time. Someone got him a tankard of light ale, and someone else shoved a plateful of cheese-topped bread rounds at him, and everyone else at the table acted as if he *belonged* there, so he simply sat and listened while they thrashed out whatever the problem was. When the topic turned to other subjects—the problem of the drawbridge having been satisfactorily dealt with—on the occasions when he could contribute a word or two, he did.

To his pleasure, these people ignored what he looked like and where he came from in favor of what he thought and said. Granted, at the moment, that wasn't much—he was much more comfortable with simply listening to the others—but the few things he did say were treated with no more and no less respect than what anyone else said.

He drank his ale and kept his ears and his mind open, covering a great deal of astonishment by hiding his expression in his tankard. He had never before seen anyone with the kind of unbounded curiosity these young men and women shared. They talked and acted as if there was nothing that was impossible, from flying like birds to moving beneath the surface of the water without needing to breathe, like a fish. And they behaved as if there was nothing, no subject, that was "not meant for man to know."

He knew what *most* of his teachers would have said by now. At one point or another, every single one of the people sitting at this table uttered something that could be taken as blasphemous, and at least before Solaris' day, blasphemers met with the Fires.

By the time Natoli declared that they both needed to get some sleep and led him back out into the cold darkness, his head was swimming with so many conflicting ideas and emotions that it felt as if a hive of swarming bees had come to rest inside it. Excitement warred with nervous fear, and he was glad that the darkness hid his expression from Natoli as she led him back to the Palace. Her own excited monologue about some mathematical progression or other required only that he make vague noises in response from time to time and covered the fact that he *couldn't* have answered even if he'd known what it was she was talking about.

The guard at the gate knew her very well, it seemed, and shook his head when the two of them approached. "I don't know what I'm going to tell your father, young woman," he said, as soon as they came within earshot. "Out until near midnight, and with a young man!"

"Who is someone Father *told* me to introduce around, so you can curb your lurid thoughts," she replied smartly. "As for coming in late—if he doesn't ask, you don't have to tell him, do you?"

The guard continued to shake his head, but he opened the gate for them and locked it behind them without another word.

She left him on the path to the Palace, parting from him with a cheerful wave and a promise to meet him tomorrow. "I live in the dormitory with the Bardic students," she told him. "Most of the people you met tonight actually live in town, rather than on the Palace grounds, but since Father's a Herald, they let me live here. Will you be free right after lunch tomorrow?"

"Uh—yes," he said, responding before he could think.

"Good, then I'll meet you in the Palace library." And without giving him a chance to say anything else, she trotted off into the darkness.

He made his way back to the Palace in something of a dazed condition. The guards he encountered must have recognized him, since only two of them stopped him to ask who he was and where he was going. He managed to find his way back to the suite with a minimum of stumbling around in the dark, as most of the halls were lit by a minimum of lamps at this time of night.

He waved a silent greeting at the corridor guard, who grinned as if he had his own ideas about where Karal had been. The door was unlocked, and he pushed it open slowly, hoping that it wouldn't creak. The suite of rooms was dark but for a single candle burning in the nightlamp, and he made his way to his own room, stepping carefully to keep from waking Ulrich up.

He felt a certain amount of guilt at not leaving a note for his mentor. *I only hope Rubrik told him that Natoli carried me off... even if Rubrik didn't know where we were going.* He had the feeling that there was going to be a lot of explaining to be done in the morning.

At least he was used to staying up this late. When Ulrich didn't need his services, he generally read until just about midnight anyway. He didn't seem to need as much sleep as some people did, which was very useful, given the number of times Ulrich had needed multiple copies of documents at short notice.

He pushed open the door of his own room and closed it carefully behind him, heaving a sigh of relief as it shut with a minimum of sound. Only then did he turn around—

And froze.

There was someone waiting for him on his bed, a long, pale form that lay curled up against the pillows. It *wasn't* Ulrich, unless Ulrich had suddenly acquired a pair of green-gold eyes that glowed in the dark.

He gasped, and the lamp in the bracket beside the door lit itself with a little *puff* of sound.

As the lamplight steadied, a slender, cream-colored body uncurled itself gracefully from the place where it had been lying, near the head of the bed, cushioned by the pillows. The green-gold disks became the widened pupils of a pair of intensely blue eyes, surrounded by a brick-red mask. The otherwise pale-cream face was topped by a pair of brick-red ears, both of which were swiveled to face him. A red tail switched restlessly, curling up and curling down again, rather than *thudding* against the bed as a dog's would have.

:Well, you certainly have been enjoying a night on the roof,: the Firecat said in his mind. Its tone was amused, genial, and quite friendly.

It's a Firecat. A Firecat—in my room, on my bed, talking to me.

"I—uh—" He stared at the Cat with his mouth dropping open, unable to make his mind or his body work properly. What was a Firecat doing *here?* And why was it in *his* room?

:Close your mouth, child, you look like a stranded fish,: the Cat said, and purred with high good humor. *:I'm not here to drag you off to some kind of punishment. I've simply been sent here to give you some advice from time to time— advice your mentor wouldn't be able to grant you. That was what you wanted, wasn't it? Someone you could trust to advise you?:*

He was irresistibly reminded at that moment of an ancient proverb. "Be careful what you wish for—"

:Indeed. "—you might get it." Quite true, which is why it's a proverb, but in the current situation it's not entirely apt. I'd have come here even if you hadn't wished for an advisor you could trust. This is an unstable situation, and you are in the middle of it. You are central to a number of complicated problems, the confidant to several

key persons, and we simply couldn't have you walking about and chancing blunders without a little guidance.:

"Oh," he said, weakly, and could not help wondering if he had already blundered somewhere?

:Oh, Bright Flame, no! You've been doing just fine so far. And I'm not here to steer you into some kind of predestined future. Just at the moment, no one *knows what may be coming, how this situation will resolve itself. No, not even the Sunlord Himself. The advice I am to give you will simply be based on a little more information than you have access to. If we are all very lucky, we will all work to bring this to a good conclusion.:*

The Cat tilted its head to the side, waiting for his response.

"If that's supposed to be comforting," he replied with more bravado than he felt, "it isn't."

:Good. I'm not here to comfort you. I hope you're nervous; given what I know, you should be. Now, just shed those clothes and get into bed, you'll need the sleep.: The Cat moved down to the foot of the bed and sat there, watching him, its bright blue eyes fixed on him in a way that suggested if he didn't hurry up and do what he'd been told, the Cat would—help.

Probably by shredding the clothes right off my body.

He quickly stripped off his clothing, and slipped into bed. The Cat arranged itself comfortably near his feet, without weighing him down, and gave its paws a quick wash. *:By the way:* it said, as he put his head warily down on the pillow. *:That Herald with the limp did come by and tell Ulrich that his daughter had kidnapped you, and not to wait up. And my name is Altra.:*

Altra? But wasn't that the name of the Son of the Sun who—

He didn't even get a chance to finish the thought, for he fell asleep instantly.

Birdsong coming down his chimney woke him—which meant it must be a fair day, rather than a stormy one. Perhaps the Heralds had finally gotten their weather-magic working.

He stretched and yawned, without opening his eyes. *Odd. I dreamed that a Firecat was here last night. What a strange—*

He opened his eyes as his foot encountered a heavy weight at the foot of his bed. The Firecat raised his head and blinked at him.

:Good morning. As you see, I'm not a dream.: Altra yawned, showing a formidable set of teeth. *:You do have a very comfortable bed, and I am pleased to report that you neither toss nor snore.:*

"Uh, thank you." He racked his brain for something to say. *What* do *you say to an Avatar of your God? "Hello, heard any good Sunlord jokes recently?"* *"Good morning, how may I worship you?"* "Can I get you anything for breakfast? Uh—fish? Milk?"

:Nothing, thank you,: Altra replied loftily. *:Firecats are above such mundane considerations as eating.:*

Well that was something of a relief. If the Cat didn't eat, it probably didn't eliminate either, which meant he wasn't going to have to find a box of sand somewhere—or would a Cat be able to use facilities made for humans?

Oh, this was too much to think about—but how was he going to explain the presence of a huge feline in his room, when he hadn't arrived with any such thing? "It followed me back from the tavern"? And how was he going to explain the presence of a Firecat to Ulrich, who *knew* what they were?

:Don't be surprised if you don't see me very often,: Altra continued, getting up and giving a full, nose-to-tail stretch. His claws were as formidable as his teeth. *:I have other business to worry about. Your master is as much in need of that bit of advice now and again as you are. I'll just drop in discreetly whenever you require the extra information I'm privy to—and if you think you really want it, I'll also give you—ah—"fatherly" advice, in the absence of your real father, if you feel too embarrassed to ask Ulrich.:* Altra actually winked slyly. *:Meanwhile, I shall be—invisible.:*

The door to his room opened of itself. The Firecat stretched again and jumped down off Karal's bed. There was a patch of bright sunlight just beyond the now-open door; Altra strolled casually out the door and into the sunlight.

And vanished.

Karal collapsed back against the pillows, not sure whether he should be elated or frightened out of his wits. He settled for a mixture of the two, with a healthy dose of panic.

Oh, Bright Flames, the last thing I need is the personal attentions of the Sunlord in my life! And a Firecat! The Cats get into everything and anything—what if Vkandis finds out about all the strange things I've been learning here? What if He finds out about what goes on at the Compass Rose?

Wait a moment. Vkandis was a god, all-knowing, all-powerful. How could He *not* know what Karal had been getting into?

Altra said I was doing the right things—so—

A visitation from an avatar, warning that the situation was unstable and about to become perilous, a hundred strange and possibly blasphemous things to think about that he'd heard last night—

—a powerful mage who was frightened of his own memories, unsure of himself—and called him "friend"—

—and a young woman, bright, intelligent, and competent, and disturbingly attractive—

—*my head hurts.*

All this before breakfast.

If I go back to sleep, will all this go away? No, probably not. He might as well get up and deal with it, then. It certainly wasn't going to get any better. *I just hope,* he thought glumly, as he climbed out of his bed and started looking for a clean set of clothing, *that it doesn't get worse.*

1 2

Belief, however, is a fragile thing, when coupled with shock. By lunchtime, he had a hard time convincing himself that he had actually *seen* the Firecat; in the face of all of his everyday work and lessoning, the whole incident seemed more like something brought on by a little too much imagination—and ale—than anything real. Besides, it made no sense! After all, why would a Firecat come to *him*? How could *he* possibly be central to anything? Now—Ulrich, or even that Herald Talia, *that* he could believe, but there was no reason to even *dream* he'd get the attentions of a Firecat. He was nothing more important than a secretary; a good one, but no more than that. Oh, there was that mysterious business that Ulrich sometimes alluded to, that he was a "channel," which was presumably rare, but nothing ever seemed to come of it, and he doubted that anything would.

After a good, solid lunch of perfectly ordinary food, and when no further manifestations of the Sunlord's regard appeared in his path, he had just about put it all down to an extraordinarily vivid dream just before waking. When he returned to his room to change after his lesson and ride with Alberich, he had second and third thoughts. There were no celestial cat hairs on his bedspread, no glowing paw prints on the wooden floor of his room. There had never been a Firecat; it was all the fault of reading those notebooks. He'd had a vivid dream, then let his imagination take over, that was all.

Comforted by those thoughts, he headed for An'desha's home (his *ekele*, he reminded himself; An'desha was teaching him Tayledras to go along with his Valdemaran), with nothing more on his mind than gratitude for the lovely, fair day. Too many times of late he'd had to make his way across Companion's Field through drizzle, or worse, a downpour, just to visit his friend. Today, he might even be able to persuade An'desha to take their discussion outside. The young mage spent far too much time cooped up inside.

He was planning just where he would like to go, when he noticed that the Companions were not ignoring his presence the way they usually did. In fact, they were moving in on him from all directions, with a cheerful purposefulness to their steps. Some of them even seemed to be trying to block his path in a nonthreatening way. He stopped right where he was, and they continued to move toward him—but still not with any threat that *he* could detect. Rather, he got the impression of welcome, as if they had suddenly decided to play the gracious hosts.

This was decidedly strange behavior, even if he *knew* they weren't horses!

But before he could say anything to them—though he wasn't sure what he *would* say—or make any move to retreat, they took the initiative away from him.

They surrounded him completely, closing him inside a circle as they stood flank-to-flank. He couldn't possibly get past them unless he pushed through them, and he knew from handling horses that if they didn't want him to pass, he wouldn't be able to move them.

One of the nearest tossed its—his, it was definitely a young stallion—head, and made a sound that closely resembled a human clearing his throat. As Karal turned his attention to that particular Companion, it blinked guileless blue eyes at him.

:Ah—you're Karal, as I understand,: said a voice speaking into his mind, exactly as Altra had. *:I hope you'll forgive the informality of introducing myself. I'm Florian.:*

The "tone of voice" was as different from the Firecat's as a young man's high and slightly nervous tenor would be from an older man's confident and amused bass. But with no one else anywhere around, it was pretty obvious that the "voice" was coming from the Companion directly in front of him, the one with deep blue eyes it would be incredibly easy to fall into—

Twice in one day? Twice in one day that uncanny creatures decide they're going to speak in my mind?

Why now? And why me?

Karal shook his head to clear it, and wondered if he ought to sit down. He coughed, tried to think of something clever to say, and then settled for the first stupid thing that came into his mind. "Ah—Florian? Are you a Companion?"

:Last time I looked, I was.: The one who must be Florian switched his tail and cocked his head to one side. The other Companions had broken their circle and were moving away now, as if they were satisfied that Karal was not going to run screaming out of the Field.

That was probably only because his knees were so shaky he wasn't certain he could walk, much less run, screaming or otherwise.

"Why—why are you talking to me?" he asked, inanely.

:Well, partly because of Altra,: Florian told him, dashing his half-formed conviction that the Firecat had only been a dream. *:He's a stranger here as much as you are, and he doesn't know some of what we know. We're familiar with the entire history of Valdemar, including a lot that isn't in the books. We thought it was time you had someone around who could answer your questions about this place, the Heralds, and all. You never ask the questions that are in your mind; you keep trying to find the answers in books.:* Florian snorted. *:That's not always possible. People don't always write down important things.:*

Well, he had been a little reticent about asking questions. He hadn't wanted to look like a complete idiot...

:You hardly need to worry about looking stupid in front of a horse now, do you?: Florian flipped his tail playfully, and Karal got the impression that he was grinning.

"Well, couldn't An'desha have told me?" he replied, feeling stubborn. He hadn't *asked* for this—or for Altra, for that matter! "Or—Natoli, *she's* from Valdemar! And her father's a Herald, too!"

But Florian only stamped his hoof scornfully. *:Your friend An'desha is just as much a stranger to this place as you are, and while young Natoli is a very nice young lady, she doesn't know anything at all about politics.:*

"And you do?" he responded dubiously.

Florian snorted. *:Not me alone. We do. We, the Companions as a whole. Remember, our Heralds are up to their ears in politics, and we share their thoughts. There isn't much at all about us in the books, either, nor Heralds, the details of our partnerships aren't the kinds of things that get written down. I can tell you all about that, whatever you want to know.:*

"All?" He wasn't sure he believed that, either.

:Well, if there's something I can't tell you, at least I won't lie to you, all right? I won't mislead you.: Florian's mood was as mercurial as anyone Karal had ever seen; now it seemed as if he was pleading with Karal. His ears went

down a little, and his head sank a bit. *:Look, we just wanted to make certain that you knew where you could find someone to help you. Altra may be your guide, but you know cats. They show up when it suits them, and not necessarily when you need them. And they love secrets. He could withhold things from you just to appear mysterious. That happens all the time.:*

That did sound just like a cat, and he chuckled weakly in spite of his shock. "Still—I mean, I'm not a Valdemaran, I'm a Karsite. What's more, I'm sworn to Vkandis. Are you really, really sure this shouldn't be left to Altra?"

Florian snorted. *:Altra doesn't know near enough about Heralds and Companions, things that you* will *need to know—but being a cat, he'll act as if he does, and make up what he doesn't know. Really, Karal, I'm honestly here to help you. If you'll let me, that is.:*

Karal hardly knew which way to turn; he could only remember one thing. According to Ulrich, Companions were "just like" Firecats. That made them, in effect, speakers for the Sunlord—

Or Whoever, he reminded himself.

:Well, remember what Ulrich told you,: Florian reminded him. *:Does it matter who I speak for? We're both on the same side. Karal, this is important. You need to accept me. Please, trust me in this.:*

Wonderful. Now something else wanted him to trust it.

On the other hand—

:You need me,: Florian repeated stubbornly.

He sighed. "All right," he said at last, with resignation. "I'll trust you. But mainly because it's a lot easier coming to you for answers than it is to go look them up—or try to, anyway."

:Good!: Florian tossed his head and pranced in place. *:Excellent! I told them you'd see reason! Now—since I happen to know that your friend An'desha is still with Firesong, and I also know you have a head full of questions you haven't asked yet—:* The Companion nudged him with his nose in the direction of the barn, *:—you can groom me while you're asking those questions. I haven't got a Herald, and no one spends any amount of time grooming Companions who don't have Heralds. I itch.:*

"I'm sure you do," Karal sighed. "I'm sure you do."

He headed obediently toward the barn; after all, he might as well do the Companion that little favor in return for getting an easy set of answers to all his questions, starting with, "just what *does* the Queen's Own do?"

But if anyone had asked him, among Natoli, Altra, and Florian, he was beginning to feel as if he was suffering from a spiritual concussion!

* * *

Some people are born to greatness, Grand Duke Tremane thought glumly. *Some people stumble into greatness. And some people get all the responsibilities without the acknowledgment.*

From the moment he had walked through the Gate into the headquarters of the Hardornen Campaign, he had been forced to improvise. The situation was a complete nightmare, the worst campaign he had ever seen or read about. The only good thing about the disaster was the headquarters itself; the fortified manor of some nobly-born Hardornen his men had taken intact. Not even the paintings on the walls were disturbed, nor more than a handful of jewels and other small objects looted. If he must be in a perilous situation, at least he would endure it in comfort. This was the privilege of command and control.

Normally when the Empire moved in on a country to conquer it, the conclusion was foregone from the moment the troops first crossed the border. The situation within the target nation was always in a state of turmoil; the central government would be in chaos thanks to the internal machinations of Imperial agents, and generally the populace was in revolt as disorganization allowed greedy nobles to take liberties. That made conquest little more than defeating the few troops willing or able to oppose the Empire, and moving in.

Front-line Imperial shock troops always went in first to take a *precisely* calculated amount of terrain. They would take no more, and no less. At that point, they would stop and hold a line; consolidation troops would follow to mop up whatever weak resistance still remained. Once the commander was certain that the conquered territory was going to stay conquered, holding troops moved in. Their task was one of fortifying strongholds, establishing or repairing roads, mills, and whatever industries existed or needed to be built.

They were followed in turn by administrators and policing troops, whose *only* task was to maintain order and establish Imperial Law. By this time, the populace was always so dazzled with the superiority of Imperial life that they welcomed the establishment of Imperial Law and government with religious fervor.

And lastly, Imperial priests moved in, to establish worship of the Emperor and all his predecessors alongside the worship of whatever gods the barbarians kept.

With all that done, and a secure base behind him, the frontline troops could leapfrog out again.

This strategy had never failed—until now.

Mages were always part of every phase of the invasion, of course. None of this could be done without them. They were better and more reliable than spies, enabled all commanders to communicate with each other and with their general instantly, and their offensive magics usually terrified the enemy. Without the Portals they built, it would be impossible to maintain troops in the field; with the Portals, fresh soldiers and supplies were available at a moment's notice, and a general was able to return in person to the capital—or any other place, for that matter.

The mages were the keystone that made it all work—which was why every candidate for the Iron Throne must be enough of a mage that other mages would not be able to trick him by under- or over-stating their own abilities. Ideally, he would be First-Rank, but Second would do in a pinch.

Tremane himself was not only a First-Rank, but was a First-Rank Red; the only two degrees above him were Blue and Purple—and the only Rank higher than First was Adept. That was one reason why he considered himself the best choice for the Throne. And it was one reason why, after due reflection, he had decided that the conquest of Hardorn had simply been bungled by a general who did not understand how to utilize his mages properly.

He had discovered the instant he set foot on Hardornen soil that he had been completely wrong.

The conquest of Hardorn had begun with the usual Imperial efficiency. It should have continued that way. There was no reason—on paper—why everything should not have gone according to the plans.

Tremane rested his chin on his hands and glowered down at the map on the table before him. But not at Hardorn—at the land beyond its borders in the west.

Valdemar.

Valdemar was to blame; he knew it in his bones, although he could not prove it. There was only one agent inside Valdemar in a position to observe *anything* in the Court, and he was not terribly effective. He was not able to get close to anyone in the queen's councils, and as a commoner, he was excluded from anything but the most trivial of gossip. He had reported nothing in the way of aid from the Queen, but Tremane knew better.

The Valdemarans were, must be, offering covert support and

organizing the resistance, no matter how much they might pretend otherwise. It was a situation that simply should never have occurred, and what was more, it made no sense. Until the moment of Ancar's death, Valdemar had been locked in war with Hardorn. That state of war should have continued, even with Ancar slain. Valdemar should have been grateful to see someone else trouncing their enemy. They should have been as happy to see the Imperial troops marching into Hardorn as the poor oppressed citizens of Hardorn itself.

It didn't, they weren't, and we're bemired. And I can't even prove *it's Valdemar that's behind it all.*

As had been reported, the conquest of Hardorn had slowed to a crawl, and it had become much more expensive in terms of men and material than had been projected. The situation was worse than he had expected. The Empire ran by close accounting; sometimes he suspected it was the accountants that actually ruled it. Every unexpected loss meant resources would have to be reshuffled from elsewhere.

He buried his face in his hands for a moment. He was tired, mortally tired. He'd spent every waking hour since he had arrived trying to staunch the hemorrhage this campaign had become, and he had been awake for far too many hours in the day. Now, at least, they were no longer losing men and supplies at the rate they *had* been, but the situation had turned into a stalemate. They could not go forward, but could not go back, either. They could not even move in the support troops, for the countryside that had been "taken" had not yet been pacified.

I have to make a decision, he realized wearily. *I can try to press on, as General Sheda did, or I can make this temporary halt more permanent, consolidate what we have, and try to figure out how to break the deadlock.*

He had already made far too many command decisions that he was going to have to justify later. There were spies in the ranks; he knew that, and he also did not know who all of them were. He came into this too late to put enough of his own men inside to be really effective at ferreting out who belonged to whom. Some of the agents in place were spies for his rivals, some for the Emperor, some spied only to sell information to the highest bidder. That was the problem with Imperial politics; if you served in any official capacity, you had to worry as much about enemies from within as enemies of the Empire.

I didn't expect to have to make decisions this risky the moment I took command. His stomach burned, and there was a sour taste in the back of his throat no amount of wine could wash away. *And how is it going to look to the Emperor when the first major order I give is for a retrenchment? He told me to conquer Hardorn, not sit on my heels and study it! I'll look weak, indecisive. Hardly the qualities for an Imperial Successor.*

"Uncomfortable" was an inadequate description for the situation, although that was how he had politely worded it in his first dispatch back to the Emperor.

He took his hands away from his burning eyes and studied the map again, this time ignoring the taunting shape of Valdemar. *Ignore them. Pretend for the moment that they do not exist. Now study the tactical display.*

It showed far too many hot spots behind his own lines, areas where there were still attacks on the troops, where there were pockets of resistance that melted away like snow in the summer whenever he brought troops in to crush them. This was *not* pacified territory. He could not and would not ask support troops to come into a situation like this one. It would not be a case of risking their lives, it would be a case of throwing their lives away.

I will have to retrench, he decided. He took up a pen, and studied the map again, then drew a line. *Here—to here.* The Imperial troops would retreat until they were all behind the line he drew on the map. Most of the resistance was on the other side of that line; such pockets of trouble as still remained could *probably* be dealt with in an efficient manner.

I hope, he thought glumly, writing up his orders and ringing for his aide to take them to his mage. A great weight lifted from his shoulders the moment the boy took the rolled paper, although a new set of worries descended on him in its wake.

It was done; there was no turning back. In a few moments, the mage would have magical duplicates of the orders in the hands of the mages attached to every one of his commanders, and the retreat would begin.

He rang for another aide as soon as the first had left. "Bring me the battle reports again," he told the boy. "This time just for Sector Four. And set up the table for me. Leave the reports on it."

The boy bowed, and took himself out. When Tremane finally gathered enough strength to rise and go out into the strategy room, the reports were waiting, and the plotting table had been set up with the map of Sector Four and the counters representing Commander Jaman's troops were waiting along the side of the table, off the map.

At least he had this thick-walled, stone manor as a command post, and not the tent he had brought with him. The weather around here was foul—no, it was worse than foul. Out of every five days, it stormed on three. Outside the windows, a storm raged at this moment, lashing the thick, bubbly glass with so much rain it looked as if the manor stood in the heart of a waterfall. It would have been impossible to do anything in a tent right now, except hope it didn't blow over.

These people knew how to build a proper fireplace, and a sound chimney, which edged them a little more into the ranks of the civilized so far as Tremane was concerned. One of those well-built fireplaces was in every room of the suite he had chosen for himself. A good fire crackled cheerfully at his back as he lined up the counters and began to replicate the movement described in the battle reports.

He had chosen Sector Four because it was typical of what had been happening all along the front lines, and because Jaman wrote exceptionally clear and detailed reports. But this time, he did not put any of the counters representing the enemy on the table; Jaman had not been able to *really* count the enemy troops, and everything he wrote in those reports about enemy numbers was, by his own admission, a guess. Instead, Tremane laid out only the Imperial counters, and dispassionately observed what happened to them.

By the time he had played out the reports right up to today's, he *knew* why the Imperial army, trained and strictly disciplined, was failing. It was there for anyone to see, if they simply observed what was happening, rather than insisting it *couldn't* happen.

The Imperial troops were failing *because* they were trained and strictly disciplined.

If there was any organization in the enemy resistance at all, it was a loose one, and one which allowed all the individual commanders complete autonomy in what they did. The enemy struck at targets of opportunity, and only when there was a chance that their losses would be slim. The Empire was not fighting real troops—even demoralized ones. It was fighting against people who weren't soldiers but who knew their own land.

Disciplined troops couldn't cope with an enemy that wouldn't make a stand, who wouldn't hold a line and fight, who melted away as soon as a counter-attack began. They couldn't deal with an enemy who attacked out of nowhere, in defiance of convention, and faded away into the countryside without pressing his gains. The Hardornens were waging a war of attrition, and it was working.

How could the army even begin to deal with an enemy who lurked *behind* the lines, in places supposed to be pacified and safe? The farmer who sold the Imperial cooks turnips this morning might well be taking information to the resistance about how many turnips were sold, why, and where they were going! And he could just as easily be one of the men with soot-darkened faces who burst upon the encampment the very same night, stealing provisions and weapons, running off mounts, and burning supply wagons.

And as for the enemy mages—*his* mages were convinced there weren't any. They found no sign of magic concealing troop-movements, of magical weapons, or even of scrying to determine what *their* moves might be. But he had analyzed their reports as well, and he had come to a very different conclusion.

The enemy mages aue concentrating on only one thing—keeping the movements of the resistance troops an absolute secret. That was the only way to explain the fact that none, *none* of his mages had ever been able to predict a single attack.

They weren't keeping those movements a secret by the "conventional" means of trying to make their troops invisible, either. They didn't have to—the countryside did that for them. There were no columns of men, no bivouacs for Tremane's mages to find, no signs of real troops at all for FarSeeing mages to locate. That meant it was up to the Forescryers to predict when the enemy would attack.

And they could not, for the enemy's mages were flooding the front lines with hundreds of entirely specious visions of troop movements. By the time the Imperial mages figured out which were the false visions and which were the reality, it was too late; the attack was usually over.

In a way, he had to admire the mind that was behind *that* particular plan. There was nothing easier to create than an illusion which existed nowhere except in the mind. It was an extremely efficient use of limited resources—and an effective one as well.

Whoever he is, I wish he was on my side.

The only way of combating such a tactic was to keep the entire army in a combat-ready state at all times, day or night.

And that is impossible, as my enemy surely knows.

Try to keep troops in that state, day after day, when nothing whatsoever happened, and before long they lost so much edge and alertness that when a real attack did come, they couldn't defend effectively against it. They would slip, drop their guard, grow weary—and only *then* would the attack come. There was no way to prevent such slips, either; people grew tired.

The enemy wasn't using mages to predict when troops had gone stale; he didn't have to. The very children playing along the roads could do that.

Perfectly logical, a brilliant use of limited resources. The only problem was, it fit the pattern of a country that was *well*-organized, one with people fiercely determined to defend themselves against interlopers, not a land ravaged by its own leaders and torn by internal conflict.

He turned away from the tactics table and faced the window, staring into the teeth of the storm. *We never move in until and unless conditions inside the country we wish to annex are intolerable. The arrival of our troops must represent a welcome relief—so that we can be seen by the common people as liberators, not oppressors. King Ancar* certainly *created those conditions here!*

In fact, if half of what he had read in the reports was actually true and not rumor, Ancar would have had a revolt of his own on his hands within the next five or ten years. When Imperial troops had first crossed the border, in fact, they *had* been greeted as saviors. So what had happened between then and now to change that?

It can't be the tribute, we haven't levied it yet. Imperial taxes amounted to sixty percent of a conquered land's products every year—and the conscription of all young men between the ages of sixteen and twenty-one. But none of that had been imposed yet; it never was until after all of the benefits of living within the Empire were established. By the time the citizens had used the freshwater aqueducts, the irrigation and flood-retention systems, the roads, and most of all, the Imperial Police, they were generally tolerant of the demands the Empire made on them in return.

The taxes were adjusted every year to conform to the prosperity (or lack of it) in that year—the farmer and the businessman was left with forty percent of what he had earned, instead of having all of it taken from him—and he didn't have to worry about the safety of his wife, daughter, or sister. Women could take the eggs to market and the sheep to pasture without vanishing.

Which is definitely more than can be said for the situation during Ancar's reign.

If there was any grumbling, it was generally the conduct of the Imperial Police that changed the grumbling to grudging acceptance of the situation. Imperial citizens and soldiers lived under the same hard code as conquered people. Even in the first-line shock troops, the Code was obeyed to the letter. The Imperial Code was impartial and absolutely unforgiving.

The Law is the Law. And it was the same for everyone; no excuses, no exceptions, no "mitigating circumstances."

Assault meant punishment detail for a soldier, and imprisonment with hard labor for a civilian. A thief, once caught, was levied fines equal to twice the value of what he had stolen, with half going to the ones whose property he had taken, and half to the Empire; if he had no money, he would work in a labor camp with his wages going to those fines until they were paid. If the thief was also a soldier, his wages in the army were confiscated, and his term lengthened by however long it took to pay the fine. Murder was grounds for immediate execution, and no one in his right mind would *ever* commit rape. The victim would be granted immediate status as a divorced *spouse.* Half of the perpetrator's possessions went to the victim, half of the perpetrator's wages went to the victim for a term of five years if there was no child, or sixteen years if a child resulted. If the child was a daughter, *she* received a full daughter's dowry out of whatever the perpetrator had managed to accumulate, and if the child was a son, the perpetrator paid for his full outfitting when he was conscripted. That was a heavy price to pay for a moment of lust-anger, and rape was much less of a problem within the Empire than outside of it. The second Emperor had determined that attacking a person's purse was far more effective as a deterrent to crime than mere physical punishment.

And once again, if the perpetrator was some shiftless ne'er-do-well, who did not have a position, he would find himself in a labor camp, building the roads and the aqueducts, with his pay supplying the needs of the child for which he was responsible. And that responsibility was brought home to him with every stone he set or ditch he dug.

And if a perpetrator were foolish enough to rape again—*then* he underwent a series of punishments both physical and magical that would leave him outwardly intact but completely unable to repeat his act.

Tremane brooded as lightning flashed outside the window. *Compared to life under Ancar, all this should have been paradisiacal. So why the revolt and resistance now?*

Perhaps Ancar had not been allowed to operate freely long enough. *There may still be enough people alive who recall the halcyon days of his father's rule. They may be the ones behind the resistance.*

He grimaced. *Too bad they didn't have the good taste to die with Ancar's father and spare the Empire all this work!*

He would have to revise his plans to include that possibility, though. Somehow, he was going to have to find a way to counter their influence.

Perhaps if I fortify and protect select cities, and bring in the Police and the builders… no matter how golden the old times are said to be, the reality of Imperial rule will be right in front of these barbarians as an example. With Imperial cities prospering, and rebellious holdings barely holding on, the equation should be obvious even to a simpleton.

But what about Valdemar? The more he looked at it, the more certain he became that *they* were as much behind the resistance as these putative hangovers from an earlier time. But what could he do about them, when he knew next to nothing about them?

Then he gave himself a purely mental shake. *Stupid. I may know nothing now, and it may be very difficult to get current information out, but I have other sources of information.* He was a great believer in history; he had always felt that knowing what someone had done in the past, whether that "someone" was a nation or an individual, made it possible to predict what that someone might do in the future.

And I have an entire monastery full of scholars and researchers with me—not to mention my personal library. I can set them the task of finding out where these Valdemarans came from in the first place, and what they have done in their own past.

There was one rather odd and disquieting thing, however, that might concern the land of Valdemar. In all of the histories of the Empire, from the time of the first Emperor and before, the West was painted as a place of ill-omen. "There is a danger in the West," ran the warning, without any particular danger specified.

That was one reason why the Empire had concentrated its efforts on its eastern borders, taking the boundary of the Empire all the way to the Salten Sea. Then they had expanded northward until they reached lands so cold they were not worth bothering with, then south until they were stopped by another stable Empire that predated even the Iron Throne. Only *then*, in Charliss' reign, had the Emperor turned his eyes westward and begun his campaign to weaken Hardorn from within.

Tremane turned away from the window and walked back into his study in silence. The light from his mage-lamp on the desk was steady and clear, quite enough to give the feeling that no storm would ever penetrate these stone walls to disturb him. *Odd how comforted we humans are by so simple a thing as a light.*

There was an initial report on Valdemar from his tame scholars, hardly more than a page or two, lying in the middle of the dark wooden expanse of his desk. He picked it up without sitting down and scanned it over. He didn't really need to—he'd read the report several times already—but it gave him the feeling that he was actually doing something to pick it up and read the words.

The gist of it was that some centuries ago, a minor Baron of a conquered land within the Empire named "Valdemar" reacted to the abuses of power by *his* Imperial overlord in a rather drastic fashion. Rather than bringing his complaints to the Emperor, he had assembled all of his followers in the dead of winter when communications were well-nigh impossible, and instructed them to pack up everything they wanted to hold onto. Valdemar was a mage, and so was his wife; between them, they managed to find and silence all the spies in their own Court. Then Valdemar, his underlings, their servants and retainers right down to the last peasant child, all fled with everything they could carry. At last report, they had gone into the west, the dangerous west. Valdemar had probably known that the Empire would be reluctant to pursue them in that direction. *Presumably his quest for some land remote enough that he need no longer worry about the Empire finding him bore fruit.* The coincidence of names seemed far too much to be anything else, and according to the scholars, this present "Kingdom of Valdemar" bore the stamp of that original Baron Valdemar's overly-idealistic worldview.

That was all simple enough, and it could account for the animosity of the current leaders of Valdemar toward the Empire of which they *should* know very little. If they, in their turn, had a tradition of "fear the Empire," they would react with hostility to the first appearance of Imperial troops anywhere near their borders.

That much was predictable. What was *not* predictable was the shape that Baron Valdemar's idealism had taken. *Where in the names of the forty little gods did this cult of white-clad riders come from?* There was nothing like them inside the Empire or outside of it! And what *were* their horses? His mages all swore to a man that they were something more than mere horseflesh, but they could not tell him what they were, only what they *weren't*. How powerful were the beasts? No one could tell him. What was their function? No one could tell him that, either. There was nothing really written down, only some legend that they were a gift of some unspecified gods. Were they "familiars," as some hedge-wizards used? Were they conjured up out of the Etherial Plane? No one could tell him. Nor had the agent unearthed anything; the riders themselves, when asked directly, would only smile and say that this was something only another rider would understand.

That was hardly helpful.

I never liked the idea of employing an artist as an agent, he thought with distaste. *When they aren't unreliable, they're ineffectual.*

Not that he'd had any choice; the agent was an inheritance from his predecessor, and there hadn't been time or opportunity to get another in place.

White riders and horses were bad enough, but worse had somehow occurred before Ancar took himself out in some kind of insane battle with an unknown mage or mages.

Valdemar had somehow managed to patch up a conflict going back generations with their traditional enemy, Karse. And *how* they had managed to make an ally of that stiff-necked, parochial bitch Solaris was completely beyond him! He wouldn't have thought the so-called Son of the Sun would ally herself with anyone, much less with an ages-old enemy!

And *where* had all the rest of Valdemar's bizarre allies come from? He would hardly have credited descriptions, if he had not seen the sketches! Shin'a'in he had heard of, as a vague legend, but what were Hawkbrothers? And *who* could believe in talking gryphons? Gryphons were creatures straight out of legend, and that is where they *should,* in a rational world, have remained!

His agent's report credited most of this to Elspeth, the *former* Heir. Former? When had a ruler-to-be ever lost his position without also losing his life or freedom? Yet Elspeth had abdicated, continuing to work in a subsidiary capacity within the ranks of the white Riders, the Heralds. Elspeth was too *young* to have made alliances with so many disparate peoples! She'd have no experience in diplomacy and very little in governance. In the end he'd simply dismissed the agent's report as a fanciful tale, doubtless spread about to make the former Heir seem more important and more intelligent than she really was.

He wished he could dismiss the gryphons as more fanciful creations, but there were others who had seen them as well as the agent. The gryphons worried him. They represented a complete unknown; in an equation already overcomplicated, they were a dangerous variable. Were there more of them? A whole army, perhaps? The idea of flying scouts and spies working for the Valdemarans was not one that made him any happier.

He groaned softly and flung himself down in a chair. Useless to ask "why me?" since he knew why all this was happening to him. *I want the Iron Throne. An Emperor must be able to deal with situations like this. If I want the*

Throne, I must prove to Charliss that I am competent.

Of course, now that he had begun, it was impossible to bow out of this gracefully.

His nearest rival was also his nearest enemy, and if he failed here, or even gave it up and admitted defeat and resigned his position, his lifespan could and would be measured in months or years rather than decades. He *would* be dead, as soon as Charliss gave up the Throne. No new Emperor permitted former rivals to continue existing; the first few years on the Iron Throne were generally nervous ones, and it didn't make any sense to leave potential troublemakers in a position to make the situation worse.

No, now he must carry this through, or else flee—into the south, into the west, into those barbarian lands beyond even Valdemar, and hope to cover his tracks well enough that no agent of the Empire could find him.

I walk a tightrope above the vent of a volcano, he thought grimly. *And there is someone shaking the tightrope, trying to make me fall.*

Shaking? That was odd... For a moment it felt as if something had just picked up the building and dropped it; the unsettled feeling in the pit of the stomach an earthquake caused. But there was no earthquake, and this was no physical feeling; this was centered in the mage-senses—

—as if something strange, terrifying, and *huge* was looming over him—

Before he could move from his chair, it struck.

All his senses failed; sight, sound, hearing, all gone. He floated in an ocean of nothingness, bereft of any touch with the real world. Mage-energy coursed through him, without truly touching him. Once, as a child, he had gone to the Salten Sea on a holiday. A great wave had come in and picked him up, nearly drowning him, carrying him up onto the shore and leaving him gasping on the sand. This was another kind of wave, but he was just as helpless in its powerful grasp, and now, as then, he did not know if it would leave him alive or drag him under to drown. It tumbled him in dizzying nothingness, disorienting him further. He was lost...

He thought he cried out in terror, but he couldn't even hear his own voice.

Then it was over. He *felt* the chair he was in again, heard his own harsh gasps for breath as the breath burned in his throat. His body shuddered with the pounding of his heart, and his hands ached as they spasmed on the arms of his chair. For a moment, he thought he was blind, but lightning struck just outside and illuminated the room for a moment, and he realized that the mage-light had simply gone out.

Simply? It was not *that* simple; the kind of mage-light he had created was supposed to endure anything save having the spell canceled!

He blinked. There was light in the next room, dim red light from the fire. He unclenched his hands with a rush of relief; at least he wasn't left in the dark! Odd. All his life he'd had mage-lights about him; even in a room darkened for sleep there was leakage from lights in the garden, lights in the hallway or the next room. He'd never realized how *dark* a truly dark room could be.

With shaking hands, he felt in a drawer of the table next to him, found a candle, and took it into the next room to light it at the fire there. Some enemy had sent a magical attack at him, surely! Magical assassins had been blocked by the protections he kept constantly in place—or was this meant simply to disrupt his concentration? This attack, if attack it was, certainly hadn't been very effective! And yet—to cancel a mage-light spell *within* his protections meant that someone had incredible power. He controlled the trembling of his hands and forced himself to think of who might command that kind of power.

That was all he had time for; aides burst in on him, sent by every commander in the camp, all of them carrying messages of varying levels of hysteria.

That was when he realized that the effect of the—whatever it was—had not been targeted solely against him.

Somehow he managed to assemble all of his mages within a reasonable time the next day, gathering them all into his councilroom to assess the damage. "So it swept the entire country?" Tremane asked his chief mage, Artificer Gordun. The homely, square-faced man nodded, as he laced his thick, clever fingers together.

"As nearly as we can tell," Gordun replied. "It was like one of those enormous waves that carries right across the Salten Sea; it came from the east and north, and is traveling into the west and south. We think it also washed over the Empire, but just at the moment, it is impossible to tell. We can't get messages to the Empire, and I would suspect that the reverse is true."

Tremane grimaced. Like those great waves, this thing that had come and gone had left devastation behind it, and the more something was connected to magic, the worse the effect was. *Every* spell suffered damage to a greater or lesser extent. Lines of communication were all gone until the mages found each other again; the Portals were all down, and only the forty little gods knew when they would be reopened. Defenses were gone, or shaken. Little things, like mage-lights, magical cook-fires, weather-cloaks, timekeepers, all the tiny things that made life run smoothly for the troops, were gone, the spells that created them shattered. There would be dark, cold tents and cold meals all up and down the lines tonight, unless the various commanders quickly found nonmagical substitutes.

"It was a mage-storm, that much we are certain," Gordun continued. "Although it is not like any such storm we have ever encountered before. The storm itself did not last for more than a heartbeat or two. Mages encountered a physical effect, as you no doubted noted yourself. Non-mages experienced nothing."

"That was enough," Tremane muttered. "It's going to take days to set up all the spells it knocked down, and more time to inspect anything that survived for damage and repair it."

"That isn't all, my lord Duke." The thin, reedy voice came from the oldest mage with Tremane's entourage, his own mentor, Sejanes. The old man might look as if he was a senile old stick, but his mind was just as sharp as it had been decades ago. "This mage-storm has affected the material world as well as the world of magic. Listen—"

He picked up the pile of papers on the table before him, with hands that were as steady as a surgeon's. "These are the reports I have from messengers I sent out on horses to the other mages in the army. The tidings they returned with were not reassuring. From Halloway: 'There are places where rocks melted into puddles and resolidified in a heartbeat, sometimes trapping things in the newly-solid rock.' From Gerrolt: 'Strange and entirely new insects and even higher forms of life have appeared around the camp. I cannot say whether they were created on the instant, or come from elsewhere in the world.' From Margan: 'Roughly circular pieces of land two and three cubits in diameter appear to have been instantly transplanted from far and distant places. There are circles of desert, of forest, of swamp—even a bit of lake bottom, complete with mud, water-weeds, and gasping and dying fish.'" He waved the papers. "There are more such reports, from all up and down the lines, and from behind them as well. You are well beyond my needing to prompt you, Tremane, but this *cannot* have been an act of nature!"

"And it isn't likely that it is residue from King Ancar's reckless meddling, either," Tremane agreed.

"I cannot see how," Sejanes replied, dropping the papers again. "Ancar was not capable of magic on this scale. There *is* no mage capable of magic on this scale. I can only assume that it must have been caused by many mages, working together. Perhaps that would account for the variety and disparity of its effects."

Tremane racked his memory for any accounts of *anything* like this "mage-storm," and came up with nothing. Oh, there were mage-storms of course, but they all had purely physical effects, and were caused by too much unshielded use of magical energies. *Those* storms were real storms, weather systems, very powerful ones. This was not like any mage-storm *he* had ever seen, and yet the term was an apt one. It had struck like a storm, or a squall line; it had passed overhead, done its damage, and passed on.

And there was only one place this storm could have come from.

"There is only one place this storm could have originated from," Sejanes said, echoing his own thoughts. "Despite the fact that it began east of us—well, any fool knows that the world is a ball! What better way to surprise us than by sending out an attack to circle the world and strike from behind?"

"You're saying that Valdemar sent this against us," Tremane replied slowly.

Sejanes shrugged. "Who else? Who else has access to strange allies from lands we never even heard of? Who else uses magics we don't understand? Who else has reason to attack us from behind?"

"Who else indeed," Tremane echoed. "They lose nothing by making life miserable for the Empire and the Imperial allies, and they could have warned their friends to erect special shields. Except that—according to all of you, Valdemar has the absolute minimum in the way of magic!"

He cast an accusatory glance around the table. Most of the mages cringed and averted their eyes, but Sejanes met him look for look.

"We still don't know what those horses are," Sejanes pointed out acidly. "And we don't recognize their magics. So how could we tell what they had and didn't have? We made our best guess based on the fact that they simply do not use magic in their everyday lives. There are no mage-lights or mage-fires; they have only candles, lanterns and torches, and physical fires. There are no Constructors; they build contrivances with no magic at all to haul water, grind grain. There are no Replicators;

all documents are copied by hand, or printed with much labor. Messages are sent by those crude mirror-towers, or by human messenger. So what are we to think? That they have no magic, of course."

"But if they have no magic in daily use," Tremane pointed out, thinking out loud, "then they will not suffer from this attack as we have."

Sejanes nodded, his head bobbing on his thin neck like a toy on a spring. "Precisely. *As if they used this kind of attack all the time.* As if they planned for this kind of attack to be used against them."

It made sense. It more than made sense. If you expected someone to hurl fire at you, you built your fort of stone. If you expected catapults, you built the walls thickly. If you expected to be deluged with mage-caused thunderstorms, you built truly good drainage.

And if you expected to be attacked by something that twisted and ruined your spells, you didn't *use* any. Unless, of course, it was the spell intended to twist and ruin all other spells.

"But where did this come from?" he asked, thinking aloud again.

Sejanes shrugged, and the rest of the mages only shook their heads. "It passed roughly east to west, and at a guess I would say that if it came from Valdemar as we think, it truly *did* circle the whole world to get here. That is logical, and in line with the notion that it originated in Valdemar. Frankly, if I had such an attack, I would use it that way, because it would be at its weakest when it finally got back to me. It was certainly strong enough to wreak havoc for us when it reached us!"

That made sense, too. "You're saying you can't find a point of origin, though," he persisted. "If you could, we would know where their best mages were." *And that useless artist could find out who they are. Then we could neutralize them.*

"Not a chance," Sejanes said flatly. "At the moment, we're lucky to find the mages in the other camps, much less a point-of-origin for this thing. We are fundamentally disarmed at this point, and we'd better hope that neither the rebels nor the Valdemarans have anything planned for us, because we're so disorganized that we'll be lucky to hold the ground we've got."

The others chimed in with more tales of woe; he had already heard from his military commanders by now, and he was simply glad that so many of them were used to working under primitive and uncertain conditions. They had found substitutes for the magics that weren't working, but there was no substitute for the lack of communication. That was the worst.

Tremane was just grateful that he had called a halt to the attempt to advance *before* all this happened. If he had been in the midst of a military maneuver, it could have been a disaster.

Sejanes was the only one who really had anything useful to say, and what he had was all too meager. The rest simply floundered, out of their depth.

"I can only see one thing useful at this point," Tremane said at last. "Repair the damages, and armor the repairs against a repeat of this attack. Communications, first. Then the Gates; if this goes on too much longer, we'll be short of supplies in a week. Shield and reshield everything you do. Then check back with me; I'll determine what is most important."

Tremane finally dismissed his mages back to their work of repairing the damages after a little more exhortation, and slumped back into his chair, his temples throbbing. He hoped that he was the only one suffering from a headache, that it was caused more by stress than by the magestorm; if all his mages were working under the burden of an aching head, they'd only be about half as effective as they were normally.

He rang for a page and called for strong wine. He seldom drank, but at this point he needed at least one cup of fortification.

He stared at the polished surface of the table and turned the cup around and around in his hands. One question was uppermost in his mind: *How did they do this?*

It was not just that the attack was like nothing he had ever seen before. It was not only the sheer size and scope of the attack. It was the randomness of it all.

Insane. Absolutely insane. Not even Ancar had been crazed enough to have developed a spell like this one.

And the effects—what *possible* use was there in an attack that ripped up circles of land and planted them elsewhere? Were the Valdemarans simply hoping that there *might* be strategic targets inside those circles? Or were they just striking for the effect on mind and morale?

Was there a meaning behind it at all? Or was the chaos really the meaning? Was *this* representative of how Valdemarans thought? If so, they were more alien than the gryphons they courted!

If they can do this, he thought to himself, sipping the bitter, dark wine, *what else can they do? Have I taken on even more than Charliss himself could handle? Or is this another of Charliss' little tests?*

That, too, was possible. Charliss and the Empire were in the east, and the storm had come from the east. The Emperor could be testing him under fire, to see how he handled such an attack.

It *still* could have been one of his enemies who had sent this; or more likely, several of his enemies working together.

As he reached the bottom of the glass, another thought occurred to him, one even more bitter than the wine, and more frightening than the mage-storm.

What if Charliss *wanted* to be rid of him? How better than to embroil him in a conflict he could not win?

Had he been set up to fail from the beginning?

Tremane ground his teeth as he pursued that thought. He had been under the impression that he was the Emperor's own choice for successor. Charliss could have been lying, or he could have changed his mind between now and when he had left. He could not ignore the possibility that Charliss now favored one of his enemies.

Could Charliss realistically get rid of him if he succeeded, against all odds and the Emperor's own opposition?

Probably not. A victory here would make him too popular to get rid of. Charliss would be forced to name him as his successor. *And once I am back in Court, at his side, I think I can repair any damage that was done while I was gone.*

That left him with new problems, though. *I am going to have to assume that there will be interference with my orders and requisitions once the orders reach the Empire. Supplies will come in slowly, not at all, or not enough. Reinforcements may not come in time. So I will have to assume the worst and issue my orders well in advance, for more than I think I will need, once our communications are back.*

And if communications could not be restored? That was another possibility.

I will have to plan to at least hold my ground with no help. A grim prospect. *I have to find a way to throw as much interference in the ranks of the Valdemarans as I can...*

Well, what had made them able to turn the tide against Ancar? What was enabling them to hold their own now?

If this *was* their doing, where had the magic come from?

Allies.

He ran his finger around and around the rim of the empty goblet. The new allies—that was how Valdemar was holding her own. So find a way to make those alliances fall apart, and Valdemar would probably have enough trouble at home to prevent any more interference in the situation in Hardorn.

He grimaced again, but this time with distaste. He used spies, he gathered unsavory information, but there was one aspect of this game of empire that he hated. Nevertheless, to buy himself time, he would use it, because he must win the game or die. It was not only his own life that lay in the balance of whether he won or lost, but the lives of all of those who had linked their fortunes with his. If he fell, his family and all their retainers fell as well.

He rang the bell that summoned one of his servants. There was one certain way to ensure that the tentative alliance of Valdemar, Karse, and Rethwellan melted away like snow in the summer, and that was to put one of his own agents into play. It was time for his Spymaster to go to work.

It was time for his Spymaster to make use of those little copies of that souvenir of Valdemar that had come into the Emperor's possession.

"Send me Lord Velcher," he said to the man when the servant arrived. "Tell him that I finally have need of his *particular* services."

1 3

Karal sat quietly on his bed, his legs crossed beneath him, waiting. His eyes were closed and his breathing was steady.

Ulrich would have said he was "meditating," of course; in fact, that was precisely what most of his teachers would say he was doing. Karal felt uncomfortable with that word. It implied that he was trying to touch the Sunlord in some way. It also implied a certain quality of "holiness" he felt equally uncomfortable with.

He certainly didn't think he was very religious, even if he was an acolyte of the Sunlord. He hadn't really wanted to be in Vkandis' Service. It had just turned out that way, due to fate, Vkandis' Will, or luck.

Still, he *was* being visited by a Firecat, and he *had* agreed to give An'desha some kind of moral support. So while he really didn't want to call any further attention to himself, it seemed to him that if he was just quiet enough, and patient, Vkandis might, well, *dribble* some kind of guidance into him.

So he waited, keeping his mind as free of thoughts as he could, hoping for a dribble, and trying not to *ask* for one.

Nothing came, though, no matter what he thought of—concentric rings in a pool of water, raindrops sprinkling on a still pond—and he gave up when his feet began to go numb. He opened his eyes and stretched, and discovered that at least the mental exercise had relaxed his physical muscles, even if it had made his extremities pin-tingly.

He was just about to swing his feet down to the floor, when he was abruptly no longer alone.

Altra flashed into the middle of the room, every hair on end, eyes as round and wide as a pair of blue plates.

:*It's happening!:* the Firecat exclaimed. :*Brace yourself!:*

And then, as abruptly as he had appeared, Altra vanished, without telling Karal just what "it" was that was happening.

He sat there, staring stupidly at the spot where Altra had been, for two or three breaths. Then he didn't have to wonder what "it" was.

From his point of view, the entire room heaved and rolled for just a moment, as if he was a speck on a carpet someone had decided to pick up and shake. Even though there were no outward signs that any actual movement was happening, his stomach dropped, and he clung to the bed as a wave of dizziness overcame him for no more than three heartbeats.

Then it was over.

That was all? What had Altra been so excited about? It was strange, yes, and felt a little like an earthquake was supposed to feel, but nothing in the room was disturbed, so obviously the "quake" wasn't really physical. Unless—was this some symptom of a disease? Could he be falling ill? Could it be some kind of plague, and was Altra warning him that an attack was coming?

Could Ulrich have it? If Ulrich was sick—

He's not strong; something serious could kill him! Karal was trained in basic field surgery, as were all acolytes. If his mentor was hurt, he could at least diagnose major problems. He was off his bed and out of his room without another thought; he wrenched open the door to Ulrich's room, nearly separating his wrist from his forearm, to find his mentor sitting up so stiffly in his chair that he might have had a metal rod for a spine. Ulrich's face was pale, and beads of cold sweat trickled down his temples; his white-knuckled hands clutched the arms of his chair, and the pupils of his eyes were mere pinpoints.

Ulrich blinked and suddenly relaxed, slumping back into his chair. Color came back into his face, and he raised a trembling hand to wipe the sweat from his forehead.

"Master? Master Ulrich?" Karal said, uncertainly. "Shall I get you some help? A Healer? Are you ill?"

"No—no, don't bother, my son," Ulrich replied, his voice tremulous with fatigue and other things Karal couldn't identify. "This is nothing a

Healer can deal with. Did you feel anything, just now?"

"I was dizzy for a moment, and I felt like I was falling," Karal replied promptly. "Nothing more, though. Should I have felt something more?"

Ulrich managed a faint and tremulous smile, and shook his head. "Not necessarily. Altra warned me in time to brace myself. *This* is what he has been waiting for, what he has been warning all of us about, obliquely. And this may well be what your friend An'desha has been sensing would descend upon us. It was a mage-storm, Karal, but one unlike any we have ever seen."

"That?" Karal shook his head; Ulrich wasn't making any sense. "How could that be dangerous? It was no more than a little moment of dizziness!"

"For you, perhaps," the Priest replied sharply. "But for those of us who are mages—we just spent an eternity in that 'little moment' and for us, it was like being dropped into a cauldron and stirred! I suspect that the more mage-power one has, the worse one would be affected."

Karal gasped. "Then An'desha—"

"And Firesong as well," Ulrich replied, looking alarmed. "They will have suffered worse than I. They may well have injured themselves, falling—at the least they will be disoriented. Go to them! I can manage for myself."

Karal didn't need Ulrich to tell him twice; he shot off like an arrow from a bow, and ran all the way from the Palace to the secluded *ekele*.

It never occurred to him that he might find the two of them in an—embarrassing position—until he actually reached the door of the dwelling. He paused for only a moment, his hand on the latch, before going in anyway. After all, he would be embarrassed, and that hardly mattered, not when the other two might be hurt. He let himself into the garden.

There was no one there.

He headed for the staircase. "An'desha?" he called over the sound of falling water. "Firesong?"

"Here—" came a weak reply from above. It wasn't An'desha's voice; it had to be Firesong. He dashed up the stairs and found the silver-haired Hawkbrother lying in a heap with one leg twisted under him, his face as pale as his hair, and obviously dazed. His firebird was clenched to a chair arm nearby, scorching the wood in its agitation.

"My leg—" The Adept gestured at the offending limb. "I fell down."

"Don't move; I know some field surgery." This at least was something he could do. He knew enough to check for broken and dislocated bones, and if Firesong *was* hurt, he could go for a real Healer.

Firesong looked at him, and though his eyes were glazed, they held some recognition in them. And questions.

"What—who—" Firesong began. Karal answered the questions as best he could.

"My name is Karal, sir," he said, "I'm a friend of An'desha's. I'll tell you about that later. You've probably seen me during Council sessions, with my master Ulrich, the Karsite envoy. I think you've sprained your ankle, and it probably hurts like anything; can you flex your toes, then your foot, carefully?"

Grimacing with pain, Firesong did so. "I—ah!—if I can do this, nothing is broken. Find An'desha," the Adept ordered. "Tell me the rest when we know he's all right."

"Yes, sir." Karal left the Hawkbrother sitting on the floor of the *ekele* massaging his ankle, and sprinted up to the kitchen, calling An'desha's name as he ran. The third time he called, he got an answer.

"Here," An'desha said. "Here—" Karal found him in a small room, draped to look like the inside of a tent. His friend was curled up in a ball on the floor, but it didn't look as if he was hurt. Karal dropped to his knees beside the young mage.

"An'desha?" he said, touching the mage's arm tentatively.

"I am all right, Karal," An'desha whispered, slowly opening his eyes. "I believe it is over for now."

"You didn't hurt yourself, did you?" Karal asked anxiously.

"No; I felt it building, and something warned me to fall to the ground." An'desha blinked, as if he was forcing his eyes to focus again. "It is well I did so. I think—I think this, or something *like* this, is what I have been fearing." He blinked again, and astonishment and relief spread over his features. "Karal? That dread I was feeling, waiting for something terrible to come—it is gone!"

"Can you stand?" Karal asked anxiously. "Can you walk? Your friend Firesong is hurt, and—"

He was not able to get anything more out of his mouth; An'desha scrambled to his feet, unassisted, and was already out of the door and running before Karal was standing. By the time Karal reached the two of them, An'desha had supported Firesong over to a couch, and was making distressed sounds over his rapidly-swelling ankle.

Karal blushed, his face and ears hot. "I'll—ah—get a Healer," he stammered, leaving An'desha to explain where and how he and Karal had met.

By the time Karal returned with a Healer, he was also full of other news. In general, there was no real physical damage to anything in or around the Palace, and the worst physical hurt seemed to be a couple of bruises, bloody noses, and Firesong's ankle. From all he had been able to make out, some of the weaker magical defenses about the capital had been taken down by the storm and would have to be put up again, but there wasn't much more to worry about. If this was what An'desha's attacks of fear and dread had been about, it was certainly anticlimactic.

Besides the Healer, Karal brought orders for Firesong and An'desha to come to an emergency meeting of the allies and the Council, though, which tended to make him think that there had been effects outside of Haven that were a lot more serious than disorientation and the disruption of weak shields.

He was right.

"Once you are outside the shields that Elspeth, Darkwind, and Firesong erected to protect Haven, there are places all across the country where very *weird* things have happened," said Skif. "I went out for a fast reconnoiter with Cymry, and I saw some of them for myself. There are places where rock turned to liquid for an instant, places where circles of land have been cut out as if someone was making cookies, and circles of land from somewhere else were fitted into the holes! People brought me insects, plants, fish—even animals, all strange, all things I've never seen before in my life! People are scared."

"Surely this was the work of the Empire," the Seneschal began, but oddly enough, it was the Lord Marshal who shook his head, and Kerowyn who echoed that headshake.

The Lord Marshal deferred to the Herald Captain with a raised eyebrow and a nod, as if to say, "After you."

"It can't have been the Empire's doing, unless it was some new magic they were trying that backfired on them," Kerowyn told them all, drumming her fingers nervously on the table in front of her. "I already have short reports from two Mindspeakers behind their lines, and word is that their forces have suffered *much* more damage than ours have. They depend more than we do on magic, and right now they are working with most of their support systems reduced. By that, I mean they have no means of communicating between groups except by messenger, and no Gates back to the Empire for supplies and reinforcing troops. In a word, gentlemen and ladies," she said, with a certain satisfaction, "at the moment, they are well and truly flattened. The only thing that could have hit them worse would have been an army-wide outbreak of dysentery."

Silence followed that pronouncement, and Queen Selenay sat back a little in her seat. "I trust you'll forgive me if I take some pleasure in that news," she said dryly. "Base though such a sentiment is—"

"Forgive me, Majesty," Darkwind said, interrupting her. "As a mage and an Adept, I cannot help but be more concerned, rather than less. These physical effects—it seems to me that they indicate something very serious. They worry me more than the effects upon magic. How do we know this thing will not come again?"

He turned to Firesong as if for confirmation, and the handsome Hawkbrother nodded in complete agreement. "If we cannot tell what it is and from whence it came," Firesong said gravely, "we cannot hope to judge whether it will fall upon us again, nor when."

He glanced aside at Karal, who was busy jotting down notes. Karal had caught a couple of strange looks from him, but otherwise, he had said nothing about Karal's acquaintance with An'desha.

"And you don't think this will be an isolated incident." Selenay's inflection made that a statement rather than a question.

"Absolutely," Firesong replied. "And before we can make any guesses as to what it may be, we need to know more about these physical effects—what they are, at what intervals—"

As the other mages chimed in, Elspeth and Treyvan, Hydona and Master Ulrich, and even An'desha venturing a word or two, it became obvious to Karal that for this, the rest of the Council and allies were superfluous. It must have been obvious to the Queen as well, for after regaining order and promising all of the resources needed for whatever the mages required, she ended the Council session and left the chamber to the mages and Prince Daren as her representative.

Karal remained as well, in his usual capacity, but he soon found himself drafted to serve another purpose altogether.

"We need a view frrrom above," the male gryphon said, flatly. "If therrre isss a patterrrn, we may only sssee it frrrom above."

"That's true enough, old friend," Darkwind agreed. "But you should have a human with you. You two aren't familiar enough to the average Valdemaran that some poor farmer is going to be able to take the sight of you lightly. I'd hate to have to pick arrows out of your rump. And it should be someone with hands, and at least a mediocre talent at drawing sketches of what you see."

"Rrr." The gryphon ground his beak, then glanced around the table. His eye lighted on Karal.

"Him," the gryphon said. "He isss light and sssmall enough, and intelligent. He can take notesss. With yourrr perrrmisssion?" he added, nodding graciously at Ulrich.

The Priest looked the gryphon straight in the eye, as Karal shivered with mingled shock and apprehension. The gryphons wanted to *fly* with him? *Fly?* Like a bird?

"It is up to my secretary to speak for himself," Ulrich said, with a nod to Karal. "I have no objections, but rumors to the contrary, we of Karse do not make slaves of our subordinates. If he chooses not to volunteer, I shall not force him."

"Well?" the gryphon asked bluntly, turning his huge eyes on Karal.

Karal swallowed hard. "Ah—yes, sir," he replied, managing not to stammer. "If you think I will be of help. I've never done anything like this. I might only get in your way."

I might die of fright before we go a hundred paces.

"Good. It isss done." The gryphon turned his attention back to the other mages, leaving Karal feeling rather dazed.

And feeling as if he had somehow been bowled out of his path by a very heavy object. *Now what have I gotten myself into?*

He had occasion to ask himself that question again, a few marks later, when he saw the object that Treyvan casually referred to as "the carry-net." He had envisioned something a little more substantial; this was hardly more than a wicker laundry basket in a cradle of thin lines of rope, with laminated wood spars here and there above it. It didn't look as if it would take the weight of a child.

It sat in the middle of a patch of lawn in the gardens; there were no trees of any size here. He gathered that it would take the gryphons time to haul him above tree level. That did not comfort him much, either.

"It's stronger than it looks," said Darkwind, who had come to the Karsite suite to fetch him.

Karal held back a grimace. "I'm sure it is, sir," he replied instead, politely. He was past having second thoughts about this expedition— now he was into fourth and fifth thoughts!

"Heh. I distinctly heard a tone of 'It would have to be stronger than it looks,' Karal. There's magic in the making of it," Darkwind continued blithely, as if they *weren't* out to investigate the effects of the failure of magic! "Don't worry, you'll get used to it. Treyvan told me that k'Leshya use carry-nets like this all the time, that they're as safe as the floating barges."

As if I knew what a "k'Leshya" is. Or a floating barge, for that matter. He looked the "net" over dubiously; each end of the rope sling was meant to fasten to a harness worn by each gryphon, and the basket in the middle was evidently supposed to supply more stability to the rider than he would get from the kind of hammock this resembled.

The rope was a lot stronger than its light weight suggested, and Karal discovered when he tried to tilt the basket while it was still sitting on the ground that it resisted all of his attempts to turn it over, even though he could lift it straight up quite easily. So, there was a great deal more to this contraption than met the eye!

Maybe this wouldn't be so bad, after all. But still, *flying*?

"The gryphons will be along in a moment," Darkwind said, glancing up at the angle of the sun. "I need to start my own search pattern with Vree, Firesong, and Aya, so I'll leave you here to wait for them."

"Wait a moment." Karal hesitated, then asked the question he'd had on his mind anyway. "If what they need is someone to record what they see, why do they need me? They have perfectly good memories."

"But no hands," Darkwind reminded him. "They read, but they can't write or draw—not easily, at any rate. That lets Rris out as well—I promise you, he was terribly disappointed. He wanted a ride through the air very badly; he said he would be the first of his clan to do such a thing, which would mean he would *finally* do something famous-cousin-Warrl hadn't!" The Tayledras mage smiled, and clapped Karal on the back. "Don't worry. After a few moments, you'll be glad they asked you to come. You'll do very well indeed."

Karal could not imagine what it was about him that prompted such assurance on Darkwind's part, but he nodded bravely.

A few moments after Darkwind's departure, Hydona appeared from inside the Palace, wearing her harness. It was a sturdy affair of leather and brass, and it looked a lot more substantial than the basket. The gryphon clacked her beak in greeting to him once she was within earshot, and sauntered over to stand beside him.

"If you would fassten that clip herrre—" she said to him, indicating what he should do with a touch of her talon. "And that one herrre—"

She nodded with approval as he engaged the two fasteners. "That isss good. When Trrreyvan comesss, do the sssame on hisss harrrnesss." She cocked her head to one side and studied him for a moment, then added, "If it isss any help, I have carrried my little onesss in thisss verrry net. They may be fledged, but they arrre not trrruly flighted, yet. They tend to plummet."

If she trusted her precious gryphlets in this—Hydona's maternal qualities were one of the first things anyone mentioned about her. She wouldn't risk her little ones. Relief made him relax, and he managed a tentative smile.

How had she read his expression so accurately? And how had she guessed the very thing that *would* make him feel that the net was flightworthy? "Thank you, my lady," he replied humbly. "It does help. I have never flown before."

With that, she chuckled. "I would be verrry sssurrrprrrisssed if you had," she rumbled smoothly. "But I think you will enjoy it."

Treyvan appeared from above, backwinging gracefully to a landing beside the two of them. "I have been aloft, and therrre isss a patterrrn, I think," he said cheerfully. "Ssso—let usss sssee if I am brrrilliant, or deluded!" Caught up in his excitement, which radiated from him like warm sunshine, Karal snapped the hooks of the other side of the net onto the male gryphon's harness, and got into the basket, suddenly eager to be off. He arranged his stylus and waxboard, and didn't even think about being afraid until they were several stories above the ground, skimming the treetops.

And at that point, he was too caught up in the incredible feeling of power and freedom to be frightened.

Like most people he knew, he'd had dreams of flying before, but it had never been like this. He was buffeted by wind from all directions—from the backwash of both gryphons' wings, and the maelstrom of their passage. They were moving *much* faster than the fastest horse he had ever ridden. He clung to the edge of the basket—which did *not* tip over, even when he dared to lean out to look straight down—and stared at the city below.

Was this how the gryphons always saw things? From this vantage, the city took on an entirely new look. Patterns emerged that he would not have seen from below. Now he could judge what houses were built about the same time from the way the roofs were constructed, for instance. Now he could tell that someone who had an otherwise impressive house might be either very careless or falling on hard times by the dilapidated state of what did not show from the street level. People in the poorer sections *used* every bit of space, too, which was not the case with those who were better off; roofs in the poorest parts of town held plants, vegetables grown in carefully-tended tubs of soil, and were strung with lines for hanging out wash. People gathered up there, women and children mostly, who gaped and pointed at him and the gryphons when they passed overhead. Children stopped in their games, and one woman even shrieked and flung her wet laundry over her head to hide.

A moment later, they were over a district of warehouses—and a moment after that, they were outside the city walls.

The gryphons strained for altitude, and climbed higher into the cloud-strewn sky. Karal watched those clouds worriedly; this would be a very bad time for a lightning storm to blow up! But, even if he were struck from the skies, he would die knowing what it felt like to be so close to Vkandis...

"Look," Hydona called, over the thunder of her own wings. "Down therrre. That isss the firrrssst of the sssignsss."

Karal looked down obediently and saw exactly what she was talking about. Right in the middle of a green field was a circular space that held black sand. Sheep eyed it dubiously.

"We need morrre height to sssee the patterrn," Treyvan called back. She nodded and strained upward.

The sheep dwindled into white toys, then into clots of wool, then into small dots on the green field. The air got colder and thinner—not even while going through high mountain passes had Karal been this high up! His ears and nose were numb, and his eardrums popped again and again as they surged higher. Treyvan pointed, and Karal followed the direction of his talon.

A thrill of excitement touched him. There *was* a pattern! Beyond the circle of black sand, there was another discoloration in the middle of a field of grain, a place that appeared to be circular as well. And beyond that, a mere blot of color in line with the first two, there seemed to be a third at about the same distance as the interval between the first and second.

"Go down!" he shouted to Treyvan. "Land next to the sand-circle! I'll make some notes and take a sample; we'll go on to the next one and do the same. We'll measure that distance, and see if there really is a third and what the distance is to it—"

"And if therrre isss a fourrrth, and a fifth," Hydona added. "Good idea, Karrral!"

They dropped a lot faster than they had climbed. Karal clamped both hands firmly around the front of the basket, but felt like he would be better served by clutching at his stomach. Still, the basket landed with a controlled bump that rattled Karal's teeth but did no other damage. He hopped out and measured the circle of sand by pacing it, folded a bit of paper into a cone and scooped up a sample, then sketched and described the circle. There didn't seem to be anything alive in it; he stirred the center of it with a stick and came up with nothing but fine, black sand, completely uniform in makeup and texture. The sheep watched him with vague alarm on their silly faces but couldn't make up their minds whether to flee or stand. They were more afraid of him than they were of the gryphons and shied sideways, bleating each time he made a move toward them.

The gryphons watched, panting, sunlight glinting off their feathers. He made sure to take long enough at his tasks to allow the gryphons enough time to catch their breath.

"All right," he said, when he couldn't think of anything else useful to measure. "Are you ready?"

Treyvan nodded, and he climbed back into the basket. The takeoff was a little slower this time; with only sheep to impress, Treyvan didn't seem to be in as much of a hurry.

The next spot was, indeed, a circle—but this time, it wasn't of sand. This spot contained a short, wiry grass of an odd yellow-green; the soil beneath it was hard and full of reddish clay, so that the earth itself looked red. There were dead insects in this patch, but they didn't look any different from the ones Karal was familiar with. Nevertheless, he took a sample of the earth, the grass, and a little black beetle. Maybe someone else could make something of this.

The third circle held something quite unexpected; a section of ground that could have come from a Karsite meadow. The ground was exactly right; gray and full of stones. The plants were that tough gorse and mountain grass that only goats could eat, and in one side of the circle was a patch of kitten-paw flowers that Karal *knew* would not grow in Valdemar. He knew that because they were the common Karsite remedy for headache, and when he had asked for some, the Healers hadn't a clue what he was talking about.

Dutifully, he sampled this as well. He also took every kitten-paw bunch that was handy because he felt there would be a lot of headaches in his immediate future. He added notes and observations on the waxboard, and each page of paper. The distance between the first and second circles and the second and third was precisely equal.

They continued to follow a line of disturbances on away from Haven into the north; not all of the things they found were as obvious as those circles of alien earth. Several times they actually had to land to find that there *was* a transplant, for it was so similar to what surrounded it that only the neat circular cut-line around it betrayed that it was there. And once, they found, not a circle of transplanted soil, but a circle of fused sand.

Only once had Karal ever seen anything like *this*, and that had been as a child, in a place where lightning had struck sandy loam. That had left a mark about the size of his hand; *this* was a circle of blackened, cracked black glass, mottled and full of bubbles and irregularities, that was easily the size of a freight wagon. The three of them stared at the lumpy glass, and Karal wondered if the gryphons felt the same cold dread that he did. Something had certainly struck here with terrible force. What if it had struck within the city limits?

What if, somewhere out there, in Valdemar, Karse, or Rethwellan, it *had* struck within a populated area? What if it struck his father's inn, or Sunhame?

"Therrre werrre weaponsss that did damage like that in the old daysss," Hydona said softly. "Terrrible weaponsss, in the daysss of Ssskandrrranon. The Grrreat Adeptsss usssed them. We had hoped neverrr to sssee sssuch again in the lifetimesss of ourrr childrrren."

Weapons? It had not occurred to him that such a thing could be a *weapon*. What could possibly guard against such a thing?

But remember the Sunlord; Vkandis can strike like this. Surely Karse, at least, is safe. Surely He can protect His people. But somehow, with this before him, it was hard to have faith that Vkandis would protect His people. This seemed too random, like a cosmic event, and even Vkandis Sunlord was said to be a part of a greater universe.

"We have enough, I think," Treyvan said in a louder voice, shaking himself as if to shake the terrible thought from his mind. "It isss time to rrreturrrn."

Obediently, if more than a little disturbed, Karal climbed back into the basket. But he was much too preoccupied with the thoughts called up by that circle of crackled glass to take any pleasure in the return flight.

As night fell, the mages gathered again to compare their notes in the Council Chamber, and once again, An'desha prevailed on Firesong to let him come along. To his relief, Firesong had accepted his explanation of how he and Karal had met with outward calm. Pointing out that it was *Talia* who had introduced them seemed to make the difference; An'desha had noted more than once that Firesong, who rarely gave deference to anyone, gave an immense measure of respect to Lady Talia.

That was just as well; An'desha had a lot more on his mind than explaining a simple friendship to his lover. The mage-storm's first bluster had stirred something up from out of Falconsbane's deepest and oldest memories, and he was still trying to sort it out.

First and foremost, he was certain, as he had never before been certain of anything, that *this* was what both the Avatars and his seizures of fear had been warning him about. Secondly, he knew that a part of him recognized just what the mage-storm really was—or rather, what it was a symptom of.

There was a version of Falconsbane who called himself "Ma'ar" who was somehow involved with that memory, though without actually probing after it, he could not be sure just what that involvement was.

When Firesong went out with Darkwind to do a bondbird aerial sweep to the south, An'desha stayed behind in the reassuring confines of the tiny Vale. Although he would have preferred to have Karal to talk him through this, he had approached Karal's master, the Karsite Priest Ulrich, as a substitute to help him through another search through those dreadful memories. When Ulrich agreed, the Priest suggested his own quarters as the best place for such a search, and An'desha had taken the suggestion with relief. Then he had taken his courage in both hands, just as he had done when he had tricked Falconsbane into walking out into the trap that meant his death, and plunged into a trance to trace back the memory.

It had taken a long time, and when he emerged from it, he was too shaken by the experience to say anything. Ulrich did not seem in a hurry to make him speak, though; the Priest just sat there with him, pressing a cup of sweet tea on him, letting him take his own time in recovering.

But by the time An'desha felt ready to talk, Firesong came to tell Ulrich that the rest of the mages had already gathered.

"I should be there, too," An'desha said, as steadily as he could, and felt a little glow of warmth at Firesong's glance of approval.

He's been trying for so long to get me to accept my powers and responsibilities... I suppose this makes him feel very good. In spite of the soul-churning effect of wandering through the miasma of Falconsbane's evil memories, An'desha realized that it made *him* feel rather good, too. Shouldering the burden—at least at the moment—was actually less onerous than anticipating and dreading the need to shoulder it. It made him feel the way he did when the Avatars had come to him—that tremulous exultation, the sense of being a tiny but bright light in a great expanse of darkness. He accepted what he must do.

He followed the others into the Council Chamber again, and waited with them while pages went around the room lighting the lanterns set into the plaster-ornamented walls. The Court Artist, who had apparently been sitting there and sketching some of the mages under pretense of recording a historical event, was sent packing out of the room by a scowl from Daren. Karal was there, sitting with the gryphons this time, bearing signs of windburn and chapped lips. His friend gave him a shaky smile. He seemed very disturbed by something, and somehow An'desha doubted that it had been the flying that had set that expression on his face.

Karal is brave, braver than I am. He wouldn't be afraid of flying. Something else has frightened him.

"Let Karrral ssspeak forrr the thrrree of usss," said Treyvan, when all the shuffling of papers and settling into seats was done. The great gryphon raised his head into the light, and his eyes glinted with reflections. "We have dissscusssed thisss, and he hasss the feelingsss of all three of usss."

Karal cleared his throat self-consciously as all eyes turned toward him. "Well, what we basically discovered, is that there is a regular pattern to the disturbances, the ones that we saw, anyway. They are all the same size, the same distance apart, and in a straight line. We went as far as we could before turning back, and we didn't see an end to them. Most of them are—transplants, I suppose you would say. They are circles of foreign soil; they look as if a gardener cut circles of land and replaced them with circles of land from somewhere else. Most of them were so similar to Valdemaran soil that if we hadn't been looking for signs of disturbance we wouldn't have spotted anything wrong. Some were from places I couldn't recognize—the one nearest the city going directly north from the Palace is of black sand, for instance. There was one piece that I would swear was right out of a mountain meadow in Karse; it even contained an herb I know grows only there. I took samples from all of them. But one—there was one at the end that was different. That strange one—it was fused sand, like badly-made glass." He swallowed, hard. "I—it would be very terrible if whatever did *that* has done it somewhere where there are people."

"Did you see any of the strange animals some people have described?" Elspeth asked.

Karal shook his head. "No, nothing that didn't seem quite normal, just out of place where we found it."

"I found some of the strange animals, and even a bird," Darkwind spoke up. "Or rather, Vree found them and caught them. I had the impression that the disturbances were not regular and not in a pattern, but it hadn't occurred to me that many of them would simply look just like the land around them."

An'desha listened with a sinking heart. Oh, this sounded far too much like that ancient memory for his satisfaction! *I had hoped they would prove me wrong, but they are only proving me more and more right!*

An'desha simply sat and absorbed it all, unable to garner the will to speak. Not just yet, anyway.

Darkwind described the creatures that he had caught and brought back; the other mages who had gone in other directions added their observations. Karal offered more comments of his own, calmly, though with obvious deference to the others. He wouldn't venture any conclusions, but based on his own figures and those of the rest, he began to plot the rest of the observations on a larger map of the land around Haven. Karal's relative self-assurance—and his and Ulrich's occasional glances of encouragement—finally gave An'desha the courage to speak up in a moment of silence.

"You all know—what, who I was," he said softly, his eyes fixed on a spot in the middle of the table.

Every eye in the place turned toward him. Karal stopped writing.

"I still have Mornelithe Falconsbane's memories," he went on, haltingly. "And those of the lives he led before he was Falconsbane. I *knew* this mage-storm when it struck. I *recognized* it somehow, out of those memories, though I did not know what it was, exactly, nor how I recognized it." He swallowed; his throat and mouth felt terribly dry, and his hands were cold. "Please—please, do not think me crazy. What I say is true, as true as I can say it. With the help of Master Ulrich, I—I sought answers to that recognition. I believe I know what this storm was, what caused it, and even why."

The silence was so thick he heard the hiss of the lantern flames behind him. "Please be patient with me; this was the oldest memory I have ever touched, possibly the oldest that Falconsbane himself had. It came from a time when Falconsbane was a mage and a king called Ma'ar."

The gryphons hissed as one, hackles and crest-feathers smoothed flat to their heads, and sat straight up on their haunches. No one else moved.

"The memory of a storm like this one—it came after a Gate was destroyed. Not a temporary Gate like we know, but a *permanent* Gate—one that was held ready to be opened at any moment. It was a small storm, and the effects were limited, but they were very like what you have been describing here." He swallowed again; what followed had been very, very hard to cope with, even at the remove of several hundreds, if not thousands, of years. "But when Ma'ar—died—it was with the knowledge that *his* realm, and that of his enemy, were both about to fall to a suicidal cataclysm. Both realms, rich in magic, *built* with magic, were about to have every spell within them broken within moments of his death. *Many* permanent Gates, shields, devices, all—and all at once. He died before he himself experienced that cataclysm, but the effects would have been very like those we are seeing now, but much, much worse, lasting for days, and traveling across continents."

"Continents?" someone asked. An'desha nodded.

"Hence, that it is called 'the Cataclysm' in the old texts," Ulrich murmured as if to himself.

"But that wasss verrry long ago," Hydona said, puzzled. "What hasss that to do with usss?"

He took another deep breath. This was even harder to speak of, but for a different reason. "I do not often tell of this, but when I was entrapped within my body by Falconsbane, I was aided by two—presences." *Please, oh please, do not let them doubt my sanity!*

"Avatars of the Star-Eyed, he means," Firesong interjected, and reached under the table to squeeze his hand encouragingly. "The blade Need spoke to me of these, more than once. I believe they were what they claimed to be and so does she; after all, some of you saw them when they unmade both Nyara and An'desha, giving them back more human likenesses."

"An'desha has told me of these Avatars," Karal spoke up. "I believe them to be true Visitations also."

An'desha cleared his throat self-consciously, feeling his ears and neck growing hot with a flush he could not control. "They warned me then, several times, that there was something terrible in the future. Something that threatened not only Valdemar alone, but all our lands. *I* thought it was only Falconsbane, but I continued to have terrible dreams, and spells of great fear after he was gone. Now that this mage-storm has come upon us and I have searched out that old memory, I—I have—" he shook his head. "I am no great mage, for all the potential power that Firesong thinks I hold, but there are some things that are now making dreadful sense to me. The Avatars spoke to me once of 'power and chaos echoing back across time.' I thought that meant Falconsbane, but now I do not think so. I have the memory of *how much* power lay in all those spells that were released in that long-ago time of the Mage Wars. Ma'ar believed in his last moments that it was more than the fabric of the world could bear, to have it all released in a single moment— and as importantly, to have *two* such centers of power interacting with each other. I think that what happened *then* is about to echo back upon us *now*—but in reverse of the original. I think that the storm we just experienced is only the warning."

An'desha drew a halting breath, and summed it up as best he could. "What we experienced was the little chill breeze that presages a hurricane."

Firesong stared at him, stunned. Now it was Treyvan's turn to break the silence.

"It isss in the trrraditionsss of the Kaled'a'in k'Lesshya that therrre werrre weeksss of mage-ssstorrrmsss following the death of Urrrtho," the gryphon said with steady calm. "The old chrrroniclesss sssay that it wasss impossssible to dessscribe how terrrible they werrre, in effect, and in ssstrrrength. The verrry land wasss torrrn assssunderrr, and even time ssseemed to flow ssstrrrangely forrr the yearrr afterrr."

"There is an oral tradition of the same among the Tayledras," Firesong managed and shook his head. "I can't even begin to guess what effect the release of that much mage-energy would have. If it could turn the land around the King's Palace where Ma'ar was into a cratered lake, and the land around Urtho's Tower into a plain of glass, there is no reason to suppose it might not even travel through the fabric of time itself. So many spells and wards are linked to time as if it were a physical presence—and even small magical explosions wreck the latticework of magic for a dozen leagues around them."

The others turned their attention back to An'desha, who looked horribly pale. "I do not have the learning to guess at more," he said humbly. "And if you will please forgive me, I do not wish to delve more into those memories that might give me that learning—at least not tonight. They make me feel ill."

"I have knowledge of the old Kaled'a'in magicsss," Treyvan rumbled.

"Asss passsed to Vikterrren and Ssskandrrranon by Urrrtho himssself. The making of Gatesss warrrps time, asss waterrr warpsss wood; the making of perrrmanent Gatesss warrrps it morrre. Therrre werrre at leassst twenty sssuch Gatesss at Urrrtho's Towerrr, perrrhapsss morrre. Therrre werrre all the weaponsss that Urrrtho *would not* ussse, forrr they werrre too terrrible. Therrre werrre the prrrotectionsss on the Towerrr, and the magicssss of the placssesss we grrrryphonsss werrre borrrn."

Ulrich's brows knotted with thought. "I—this goes beyond what I have learned," he said at last, "but I can tell you this; I have myself had warnings from an Avatar of Vkandis that something of this sort portended."

Elspeth looked impatient. "You had *vague* warnings, An'desha had *vague* warnings, why didn't anyone get anything clear?"

An'desha winced. That was a perfectly reasonable question. And he didn't have an answer.

But Ulrich only smiled slightly. "Perhaps because even the Star-Eyed and Vkandis Himself did not know what the effect would be," he replied gently. "Hear me out. When the Gods granted mankind free will, They allowed uncertainty to enter the world. Some things can be predicted; others cannot. If I may make an analogy—I can tell you that a great storm is coming. With the knowledge I have that when the wind blows such-and-so, and the glass falls, and the sky looks thusly at this time of year, I can say that there will be a storm. But I cannot predict what places will flood, how high the floodwaters will rise, what homes will be battered to bits, and what keeps struck by lightning. As this power comes back to us, I think that even the Gods could not tell exactly what form it would take, *perhaps* because of what we and others have done with magic since then. They could only warn that there was danger."

"So—" Elspeth said slowly, after a long silence. "The good news is that this isn't anything we caused, and it isn't anything that the Empire is turning on us. The *bad* news is that this really isn't a 'mage-storm' as such. Not yet, anyway. It was—was one wave, created by the real storrn that is out of sight of the land. It swamped boats and wrecked docks, but the real storm still hasn't come in yet."

An'desha watched as the faces of all the mages around the table sank as they all accepted that conclusion. If it was not the truth, it was certainly the closest thing they had to the truth at the moment. No, it wasn't a weapon, or anything *they* had caused. But it also wasn't anything they could stop, any more than they could stop a real storm from sweeping in.

"I should point out that there may be a bright side to this," Prince

Daren said. "Kerowyn said it herself; the Empire relies *far* more heavily on magic than we do. The real mage-storm will hurt them *far* more than it does us."

"True." Elspeth chewed her thumbnail, a habit that made An'desha wince. "But it may destroy us all, Empire included. Well, there is one thing we *can* do, though whether it will do any good or not, I don't know. We *have* to get warnings out to every member of the Alliance about this, so that they will at least know what this last squall was, that it wasn't *us*, and that there's worse to come. There *is* worse to come, right?"

She looked at Firesong for the answer to that.

The Healing Adept shrugged. "My guess is that there will be. An'desha's prescient dreams were terrible things, and I do not think this little 'squall' as you called it could account for them. There were 'waves of mage-storms' before, and if the reverse of the past is happening, these squalls will build into a powerful climax."

"We have to collect every bit of information we can," An'desha insisted. "We have to know every spot of disturbance in Valdemar. If we have a pattern, maybe we can deduce the next places that will be struck."

"We—or, rather, the Tayledras—have another task before us first," Firesong interjected grimly. "Which is why I plan to send a mage-message to my parents as soon as we are done with this meeting. We *must* get the best shields ever created around each and every Heartstone, including the one here beneath the Palace. If that is not done, we, Valdemaran and Tayledras alike, could all find ourselves facing rogue Stones, and the storms will be immaterial for we will already be dead."

An'desha blinked in surprise as both Elspeth and Darkwind blanched. He had not thought there was anything that could rattle *those* two.

"Then Darkwind and I—all the Herald-Mages—had better get to work right now," Elspeth said, pushing away from the table and standing up. "Anything else can wait."

"I will help you, if you like," Ulrich offered. "I believe that I may know some shielding techniques you do not."

"We ssshall asss well," Treyvan said, with a dry chuckle. "Afterrr all, it isss *ourrr* tailsss in jeoparrrdy, too!"

"Shall—" An'desha began to add his offer to theirs, but Elspeth and Firesong both shook their heads.

"I know that you dread another walk through those memories, *ke'chara*," Firesong said quietly, "but if there is any more information in them, I wish you would look for it."

"I will be sssending a messsage to k'Lessshya, forrr accurrrate copiesss of the chrrroniclesss," Hydona told them. "Therrre may be morrre ansssswerrrsss therrre."

"Huh. *Rris* might even have something to add. But he's so selfish with his stories!" Darkwind raised an eyebrow as a chuckle of nervous laughter met his comment. "Well, he *is* a *kyree* historian; there might be an oral tradition about this among the *kyree.*"

"True enough," Prince Daren said as he stood up, smoothing his white uniform in a gesture of habit. "Well, I think we have wrung the last drop of water from this for now. I will go report to Selenay; I leave you to your various tasks."

He paused for a moment before leaving, as his troubled eyes met each of theirs in turn. An'desha could not sustain that contact for long; he felt somehow guilty about all of this, as if he were somehow the cause of it.

"As unpleasant as my task will be, giving Selenay ill news," Daren said at last, "I do not envy any of you *your* jobs. For once, I am glad I am no mage. You must all feel like oarsmen trying to outrun a wave you cannot stop."

With that, he took himself out, and the rest of them followed his example. An'desha wasn't certain how the others felt, but so far as he was concerned, Prince Daren had summed up the entire situation *far* too accurately.

Despite Prince Daren's gloomy words, Karal was not about to give up the fight before he had even started! Surely there was something they could do about this? Even if they couldn't stop the storm itself, well, people built houses against storms all the time; why couldn't they build shelters against this one?

They survived back then, or we wouldn't be here now. What we need is more information. The more we know, the better we'll be able to prepare.

Maybe he was no mage, but he did know exactly where to go to find people who were absolutely, precisely ideal for the task of gathering and categorizing information.

As Ulrich followed Elspeth, Darkwind, and the gryphons to some mysterious room in the cellars of the Palace, he went off in a different direction entirely.

The clouds of this afternoon had thickened, and the air smelled damp, so he stopped just long enough to fetch a cloak from his room before heading out the side door to the little postern gate in the Palace walls that Natoli had shown him. The Guard there tonight wasn't one he knew, but it didn't much matter; most of the Guards probably knew how to get to any tavern in Haven.

His supposition wasn't wrong; the Guard was only too happy to give him exact directions to the Compass Rose, directions that matched very well with his own hazy memory of the way Natoli had led him the first time.

By the time the Guard was satisfied that he had the directions straight, thunder rumbled off in the far distance, and he thought he glimpsed a flash of lightning against the dark night sky. He set off down the street just as the first few fat drops of rain fell onto the cobblestones in front of him with audible *splats*.

The few drops had become a downpour by the time he reached the tavern door, and just before he opened that door, he had a horrible thought. *What if the rain kept everyone away? What if I can't find them all? What am I going to do then?*

But the blast of sound and warmth that hit his face as he opened the door against the rising wind told him that his fears were groundless. The Compass Rose was packed to the rafters; rather than avoiding the tavern because of the storm, the storm seemed to have had the effect of driving every Blue in Haven into the taproom.

Mouthwatering aromas hit his nose and made his stomach growl, but he ignored his hunger for the moment. Karal waited just long enough to get his senses used to the noise and light before pushing his way through the crowded tables in the general direction of the one Natoli and her friends generally used. He heaved a sigh of relief as he spotted the back of her head; one of her friends saw *him* and waved to him. Natoli turned around, saw who it was, and beckoned to him to join them.

He didn't need any further prompting; he increased his pace, leaving apologies to those he had unceremoniously shoved aside in his wake, and wedged his way in beside their table.

"Karal! We've just been talking about all the *weird* things that happened today," Natoli said, as several of the others edged over on a bench to give him a place to perch. "Some of us got dizzy, and a couple even thought there was an earthquake—and now there are all kinds of strange things outside the walls! It has to be magic, but none of us can figure out what in the Havens' name happened, or who caused it all." She eyed him with speculation. "*You're* in the thick of things at the Palace; I don't suppose you have a clue, do you?"

Karal silently thanked Vkandis for providing him with the most perfect opening that anyone could ever ask. "I am, I do, and I came here precisely because I need to talk to all of you about this."

That got their attention, all right. He became the center of a little island of silence in the middle of all the noise.

He wanted to blurt it all out at once, for the words were just bubbling up inside of him—but these youngsters were logical people, and he knew that the better organized his words were, the more likely they were to believe him. He knew that *he* would not have believed any of what he was about to tell them, if he had not been present from the beginning of it all. He would have to place *them* at the beginning, to prove to them that he was not deluded, or worse, making it all up out of whole cloth.

So that was how he told them, laying out everything that had happened and been said from the very beginning—starting, in fact, with An'desha's prescient fits of fear. He left Altra out of it, and the Avatars; these students were familiar with ForeSight and ForeSeers, but not Visitations from the Gods. He did not want to stretch their credulity with tales of Avatars and their ilk.

To his gratification, they listened to him, carefully and soberly, and did not seem inclined to doubt him, even when he spoke of the effects of magic reaching forward through thousands of years to reach them now. "I know this all sounds mad," he said finally, "But that's the conclusion even Firesong and Elspeth have reached. Prince Daren believes them—"

Natoli covered his hand with hers to still his plea. "We believe you, Karal," she said, then looked around the table. "Right?"

Nods all around met her question. "You've got no reason to lie to us," one of the others said. "And besides, it matches up too damned well with all the weirdnesses today. So, I've only got one question. We aren't mages, and everything we do deals with the strictly physical. Why did you come to us with all this?"

He heaved a sigh of relief and felt a huge weight lift from his mind. "Because I think you can help," he told them all. "And this is why. Right now, we're looking for patterns, patterns that will let us predict what is going to happen next, and maybe even when it's going to happen. Patterns are mathematical, logical."

"So who better to deal with math and logic than us?" Natoli finished for him, her eyes bright with enthusiasm. "Right! I think you came to the right people. We—" She paused for a moment, frowning. "Hang on, though, this is too important for just one tableful of students. This is something everyone should hear, *especially* the Masters."

With that, she leapt to her feet and shoved her way over to the fireplace. There was a large bell hanging there; Karal had never seen anyone ring it, so he'd assumed it was only there for decoration. Now, as Natoli seized the cord hanging from the clapper and rang it with vigor, he realized it had a real purpose after all.

The entire room fell instantly silent, so much so that the only sounds were those of the wind and rain outside, and the shoving back of chairs in the next room where the Master craftsmen were. Soon they, too, crowded into the taproom, pushing through the door in the rear wall; some looking annoyed, but most wearing expressions of startlement and curiosity.

"We have a friend among us, secretary to the envoy from Karse," Natoli called out into the silence. "He was introduced to me by my father, Herald Rubrik, and I was told I could trust and believe him. Tonight he learned of things he felt we should all hear, and having heard them, I believed they were important enough to sound the bell so that all craftsmen and students could hear them as well." She waved at Karal, who got to his feet, flushing with embarassment. "Karal, could you repeat what you just told my table?"

Still blushing, but obedient to her wishes, he did so, concentrating on keeping his words in exact chronological order, clear, and precise. When he finished, there was more silence, but there wasn't a single doubtful or hostile face in the room.

Finally, a wizened little man stepped forward from behind some of the other Master Craftsmen. From the way they all deferred to him and made way for him, Karal guessed that he might well be senior to all of them. He couldn't have been any taller than Natoli; his gray hair ringed a bald spot that took up most of his scalp, and his clothing was no richer than anyone else's here, but he had an air of competence and authority that no wardrobe could impart.

"Young lady—Natoli, is it?—you were right to ring the Silence Bell," he said, his old voice cracking. "This *was* a tale we all needed to hear— and a task too important for one table of students to deal with! And young secretary, you were right to come here with your tale." His eyes disappeared in a mass of wrinkles as he squinted in Karal's direction. "Magic is not the answer to all problems, as I have said in the past."

"Repeatedly," one of the boys still seated at Karal's left muttered under his breath.

"Whether or not magic will be the answer to this problem remains to be seen," the old man continued. "But if it is careful gathering of facts and measures, and equally careful advice that you want, then *this* is the place to look to find your experts!"

"Here, here," murmured several of the other Master Craftsmen; from the tone of their voices, Karal had the shrewd notion that they resented this intrusion of *magic* and *mages* into their world and would be very pleased to show that they could solve a crisis that mages could not cope with.

The old man paused and looked out over the taproom. "I know that there are tasks you have all undertaken and may not in honor leave unfinished—whether those tasks be study and learning, or the building of a road, a mill, or a dwelling. Nevertheless, as I can see at this moment, we all have hours of leisure that are at *our* disposal, or we would not be here, drinking our hosts' excellent beer and telling lies to one another. Can I request that until this crisis is dealt with, that you devote those hours to your Queen and your land?"

Karal honestly expected that no more than a third of those in this tavern would volunteer—which, philosophically, would be more trained hands, minds and eyes than he'd had when he walked in here, and far more than he ever anticipated! But without warning, Natoli jumped to the top of the table nearest her. She waved once, seizing the attention of everyone in the room, and stood there in a defiant pose, with her feet apart and her hands on her hips.

"How many of you spent your student days in the Collegium?" she asked, before anyone could make an answer, yea or nay, to the old man's question. "And how many of you saw the highborn brats looking down their noses at us, because we were going to *work* for our livelihood? And how many of you just twisted with envy every time one of those Herald-trainees rode by on their Companions? The highborn, the trainees, *they* were going to be important! All *we* were going to do was make *their* lives a little easier! Just one short step up from peddlers, that's us!"

The students hissed and booed her words, and the sour looks on the faces of the Master Craftsmen said all that needed to be said,

"But now *we* can do something they can't!" Natoli cried out in triumph. "Even those fancy mages, *they* don't have the training or the organization—*they can't look at this problem logically.* I don't think they can solve it! But *we* can! Can't we?"

An angry chorus of "Aye!" and "Damn bet!" answered her. She grinned with satisfaction.

"And we're *going* to solve it, if it takes every spare moment we have, aren't we?"

Again, there was a chorus of assent.

"And how *better* to get the funding for our projects than to show the Palace that *we* are the ones with the answers?"

This time the chorus was even stronger. Natoli's grin widened, and she jumped down from the top of the table, bowing slightly to the old man as she alighted.

"I believe you have your answer, Master Magister Henlin," she said, and made her way back to her table.

The old man shook his head, but grinned anyway, and his eyes disappeared in his wrinkles again. He waited patiently for the noise to die away, then gestured to the rest of the Master Craftsmen.

"Gentlemen, select your helpers; I assume you'll all be selecting your own students, but don't overlook someone who wants to work for you, or who hasn't been chosen. Master Tam, Master Levy, please go with this young man to the Palace and present our services to the Queen. I will organize the groups for work tomorrow morning." He sighed and shook his head. "I am too old to be traipsing out into a tempest, I fear, or I would go myself."

"Master" Tam was actually a strong and squarely-built female of late middle age; she laughed and crossed her arms over her chest. "Henlin, you haven't once left the Compass Rose as long as there was a single drop left in the kegs in all the years I've known you. I hardly expect you to start now."

Master Henlin shrugged but looked unrepentant. The other Masters moved out into the taproom, but she and Master Levy headed straight for the table shared by Natoli's cronies.

"We'll take you scruffy lot, since you're already our students," Master Levy said, as soon as they got within an arm's reach of the table. "We're both used to you delinquents, and I wouldn't wish you on some poor, unsuspecting Master who has no idea what depravities you can get up to."

Natoli only nodded, unabashed. "Suits me. What *will* we be up to?"

"Dawn is what you'll be up to," Master Tam replied, and smiled evilly as the students groaned. "The logical, obvious thing is that first we'll divide up the area around Haven and each group will take one piece to study. We'll look at the obvious anomalies and look for ones the Heralds and mages missed, because I'll bet there will be some—once we've measured each anomaly to within a hair, we'll come here to collate the information. After that?" She shrugged. "My guess is that either we'll be sending individual students out with fast horses to get information from farther out, or we'll just make up a set of precise instructions based on what we find, and rely on locals to do the work. Then we'll start looking for answers that fit the information. We'll probably use the Rose as our headquarters, since it's set up to hold all of us."

"Just like a class problem," groaned one of the boys.

"Exactly." Master Levy fixed the offending party with a gimlet eye. "Don't you think you ought to cut the evening short, since you're going to be up so early?"

Obediently, the students started gathering up their cloaks; students at the other tables were doing the same, so evidently the other Masters had imparted the same set of orders to their groups. "I think Lady Herald Elspeth would be the one to take your offer, sir," Karal said to Master Levy, who was nearest him. "I know she'll still be awake. Would you like to go to the Palace now?"

"Between us, I'm pretty certain that Karal and I can get you both past the gate guard," Natoli added. "They've been letting me run tame at the Collegium since I could toddle, and every Guard and Herald there is my 'uncle.'"

Master Levy looked to Master Tam for advice. The woman nodded brusquely. "Sounds as good a plan to me as any." She slung her cloak around her shoulders and took a last swig of beer from a student's mug. "Let's go."

They slogged through rain that filled the gutters and soaked their cloaks; bent their heads against wind that drove the rain into their faces and threatened to pull their cloaks right out of their hands. The relatively short walk to the Palace was as exhausting as one of those dawn-to-dark rides he and Ulrich had endured on their way up here.

At long last they reached the postern gate, and the Guard there recognized all four of them. He waved them inside without any formality—which was a mistake, in Karal's opinion, for they could have been *anybody*, in very clever disguises. He resolved to tell someone about the lapse tomorrow. Alberich, maybe, or even Kerowyn.

Once inside the Palace, however, the Guards were a great deal more alert, to his relief. They were left to drip in front of a fire while someone went off to verify that they were who they *said* they were, and to fetch Herald Elspeth. Hot spiced tea arrived after a while, and towels, both brought by pages, who hung their cloaks over frames in front of the fire to dry them thoroughly. The air filled with the smell of wet wool.

Elspeth was not at all pleased to be fetched; she looked tired and rather frazzled. Her hair had escaped from its utilitarian braids, and her face was slack with exhaustion. But the moment that Master Tam and Master Levy introduced themselves to her and explained what brought them there, she brightened with relief, and actually apologized for her curt welcome.

"I'm dreadfully sorry I was so surly, but we just finished some very difficult work, and we're about to repeat it to double the effect," she said, pulling a damp curl off her forehead with an impatient gesture. "I can't even begin to tell you how much I appreciate this! Yes, we certainly *do* accept your offer, and I can't think of anyone better suited to try to apply logic to all of this." She favored Master Levy with a wry grimace. "Some of the others won't like it, but I can and will overrule them—and Mother will most *certainly* be relieved that someone is trying mathematics instead of intuition for a change!"

She continued for a little while longer, as both Masters glowed with satisfaction under the weight of her sincere thanks and praise. There was no doubt that she meant every word she said—and no doubt that both of them had been half-expecting to find opposition from someone who was a mage as well as a Herald. Not surprising; *they* didn't know her, after all.

I wonder if she's stretching all this thanks out a little—he thought, when she began repeating herself. Then he saw her take a surreptitious glance at the cloaks, and knew he was right. She was waiting for the cloaks to dry before sending them away!

Thoughtful, making up for being discourteous earlier? It could be. Elspeth, he had learned by watching, was like that.

"Well," Master Levy said, when Elspeth finished her speech, "if we're going to lead a team of unruly students out into the muck at dawn, *we* need to take our leave. As soon as we have anything of any substance, we will let you know, Herald Elspeth."

"Send me your measurements and charts, would you please?" Elspeth asked as the two Masters took up their now-dry cloaks. "They might help those of us who aren't applying strict logic to the problem."

"Certainly, my lady," Master Tam assured her, tossing the cloak over muscular shoulders. "Now, by your leave?"

"I've sent for a carriage; at least you won't have to walk back in this mess," Elspeth told her, and grinned at the gratified expressions they wore. "Masters, I promise you, no matter what you've heard, I didn't turn into a *complete* barbarian while I was gone!"

They laughed, and Elspeth called for a page to take them to the carriage she'd ordered up. Once they had gone, she turned her attention back to Karal, who was waiting quietly for her to dismiss him.

"Was this your idea, sir secretary?" Elspeth asked, with a stern expression that was entirely spoiled by her glow of amusement and the twitching of her lips.

"Yes, Lady," he replied. "I don't know a great deal about magic—but Altra, a friend, told me to trust my own good sense. You *all* said you needed measurements and facts, and my own good sense said that if you were going to need facts and figures, you ought to have people who specialize in them gather them for you."

"Well, your friend was right," Elspeth declared. "And I can't begin to thank you for going out and *acting* on your conviction. You do your order proud." And with that, to his immense confusion and embarrassment, she kissed him, much to Natoli's open amusement.

"Now, you've done more than anyone else but the mages tonight, and you deserve some rest, so you ought to go get it," she told him. Then she turned to Natoli. "You are just as much to be thanked for seeing that the task was too large for a small group of students and acting on *your* conviction," she added. "It isn't every youngling who'd sacrifice personal glory for seeing that the job is done right."

Natoli shrugged. "A Herald's daughter learns not to let self-aggrandizement get in the way of the job," she said.

"A Herald's daughter?" Elspeth looked at Natoli with speculation but did *not* ask *so why aren't you a Herald, too?*

"So that would be how you met Ulrich's young secretary?" she asked instead.

Natoli nodded. "Father was the one assigned to escort them. He thought I might be able to help Karal get settled."

Elspeth smiled. "I'd guess you succeeded, since he managed to find the Compass Rose and its taproom! Anyone could get settled with a couple of Rose pints in them!" Natoli lost control enough to giggle.

But Elspeth wasn't finished yet. "There's one thing I'd really like to tell you, Natoli. No matter what it may sometimes seem like, there are important, vital jobs that can't be done by Heralds, which is one reason why this land isn't hipdeep in Companions. You and your friends and Masters are and will be doing things as important as anyone who ever put on Whites, and don't ever let anyone tell you differently. We Heralds are there to be obvious symbols to the people, but the Guard and Bards deserve most of the glory we get."

As Natoli flushed with confusion, Elspeth gave her a little salute and then left.

"Well!" Natoli said at last. "What brought that on?"

Karal raised his hands and shook his head, although he had a good idea what had brought it on. Natoli's carefully veiled expression of envy on seeing Elspeth's uniform, and the flat tone of her voice when she mentioned that she was the daughter of a Herald. "Heralds. Who knows? It was something she thought you ought to hear from her directly, though, or she'd never have said it."

And given that little speech back there in the Compass Rose, I think you needed to hear it, he thought silently.

Natoli shrugged uncomfortably. "Well—I need to get back to my bed. Coming here isn't going to excuse me from going out with the others at dawn."

"Thank you," Karal said, very softly, catching her arm as she turned to go. "We couldn't do this without you. Elspeth was right. You did some very good things. I think you're going to do more of them. I really admire you."

Natoli blushed again and averted her eyes. "I've—got to go!" she blurted, and turned and hurried away. Karal watched her go and remained staring at the door for minutes after she was gone.

Karal made his own way back to the Karsite suite, his head so full he couldn't even begin to sort out his thoughts. He was only certain of one thing.

He'd better get some sleep, himself, no matter how much turmoil his thoughts were in. Whatever lay ahead of them—this was likely to be the last moment of peace any of them would have for a long while to come.

14

But the next morning, it might all have been a dream.

Except that Ulrich was up very early and left immediately after canceling all of his appointments, and when Karal took his usual lesson with Kerowyn, she was preoccupied and actually let him score on her without making him work himself into exhaustion to earn it. He waited for an opportune moment and told her of the Guard's laxness of the night before, which earned him a nod of approval.

But after that lesson was done, he found himself at loose ends. Ulrich had forsaken meetings and discussions in the face of this greater threat, which left Karal with nothing whatsoever to do as Ulrich plied his other avocation of Priest-Mage.

Ulrich reappeared for lunch, just long enough to snatch a hasty meal and ask Karal if he had taken care of the appointments that had been canceled.

"Yes, sir," Karal replied. "Is there anything else you want me to do?"

"Not really," the Priest told him. "Really, just take a rest; do whatever you want to do this afternoon. I'll be in conference with the rest of the mages. We're still mostly at the talking stage, now that we've reinforced all the shields and—well, never mind. Just take a little holiday."

With that he was gone, leaving Karal to trail forlornly around the suite, finally ending up in his own room.

For the first time in a very long time, he had leisure to be lonely— and, suddenly, homesick. Up until now, he'd been so busy that he hadn't had much time to think about himself. When he wasn't actually working, he was encouraging An'desha, learning as much as he could about the land and the Heralds that guided it from the library and from Florian, or discussing what he'd learned with Ulrich.

He hadn't even had a chance to talk about this latest crisis with his mentor, and that bothered him more than he had thought it would. He sat on the bed, staring at the wall, feeling very much left out. No point in looking for An'desha, he'd be with the others. Natoli was out doing whatever her Master assigned her. Florian was like Altra—you didn't go to the Companion, *he* showed up when he wanted to. Karal wasn't a mage—and he wasn't one of the Blues, either. That left him with no purpose at all, and nothing useful to contribute.

:Oh, do stop feeling sorry for yourself!: Altra snapped, appearing out of nowhere and jumping up onto his bed. *:You've taken the initiative before. What's to stop you from doing it again? You're an adult, Karal, an acolyte, not a novice! Of course you have a purpose! You're supposed to be Ulrich's assistant, aren't you?:*

"Ah—yes, but—" Karal began, starting a little at the Firecat's sudden appearance.

The Firecat snorted. *:Well, go assist him, then! Do your job! Who's going to remind him to eat and rest if you don't? Didn't Solaris tell you to take care of him? All of the rest of them are younger than he is; if they don't feel tired, they'll keep going, and he'll feel he has to keep up with them. Who's going to take notes? Even if you don't understand all that mage-babble, you can take notes, can't you?:* Altra's tail switched from side to side, annoyance in every twitch.

Karal nodded, tentatively at first, then with more enthusiasm. There was a very good chance they wouldn't exclude him if he presented himself at the door of the meeting. He *was* Ulrich's assistant, after all. And there probably *wasn't* anyone else playing secretary in all the mage-conferences.

:Besides, what you learn there, you can take to Natoli and the others,: Altra added, narrowing his eyes, which gave him a very sly, self-satisfied look. *:The Seekers need that information as much as they need measurements. They really don't know how magic works, and the more you can tell them, the better they can do their job. Right?:*

"Right." Karal got to his feet, and gathered up his pouch of note-taking materials. "Thank you, Altra."

:My pleasure.: The Firecat twitched his tail again, jumped down off the bed—and vanished before he touched the floor.

Karal shivered. He really wished that Altra would at least get out of sight before he pulled one of those disappearing tricks. Having the Firecat *there* one moment and *not-there* the next was decidedly unnerving.

Oh, well. He knew where the meeting was going to be, since Ulrich had let that drop—not in the Council Chamber this time, since they couldn't keep usurping it from governmental business, but in the gryphons' suite, since it was the only other set of rooms large enough to hold the gryphons comfortably.

He had never been there, but it was easy enough to find a page to show him the way; they *all* seemed to know where the gryphons were. The tiny child who led him down the maze of corridors confessed as they walked that he often played with the young gryphons. Karal had to shake his head at that; how in Vkandis' name had his parents been persuaded to allow him to play with meat-eating raptors that could easily bite his hand off? That said a lot for the ability of Treyvan and Hydona to convince Valdemarans that they were as friendly as they claimed.

The chamber was at the end of a long corridor that looked vaguely familiar to Karal. It looked as if it had been originally intended for some other use than as guest quarters, with its huge double doors of carved wood. Had it been a lesser Audience Chamber, perhaps? Tentatively, he tapped on the door and was a little surprised when Ulrich himself answered it.

"Karal?" the Priest said, when he recognized who was there. He held the door as if he was thinking about shutting it again, a frown just beginning to crease his brow. "Didn't I tell you—"

"You don't have anyone here to take notes for you all, do you?" Karal interrupted, before Ulrich could chide him. "You don't have anyone here to fetch things for you; you'll have to call for a page and wait until one comes. You don't have anyone to run out and have meals and drink sent up. I can do all of that, and you already *know* that I won't get in the way." He swallowed a bit, and let a little pleading creep into his voice. "Please sir, I want to help. I want to help *you*. It's not a duty, it's a pleasure."

Ulrich's frown faded when he heard Karal's intentions. "I didn't— think you'd care to be here," he replied, with a hesitancy he had never shown before. "You've been working hard, and I thought I'd been exploiting your good nature. I was afraid we'd overwork you—"

Karal coughed as his cheeks heated. "Master, one of my duties is to make certain that *you* don't overwork." He lowered his voice to a near-whisper. "You aren't exploiting my good nature, sir. I am proud to serve and honor you as I would serve and honor my own father."

Ulrich bowed his head, and he blinked rapidly for a moment. "Karal, you are a remarkable young man. I am proud to be here to help you when I can. Thank you. We can certainly use your services."

Karal slipped inside the door as Ulrich held it open just enough for him to get inside. There was no furniture, just the bare wooden floor and huge pillows and featherbeds; logical, actually, since this place was meant for the comfort of gryphons, not humans. Firesong was holding forth and did not even notice as Karal took a place on the edge of the gathering, got out his pens and paper, and began taking notes in the middle of Firesong's current sentence.

"—if all of you are really set on it, I can't see how it's going to hurt anything," the Healing Adept was saying, his voice full of contemptuous amusement. "But I repeat, I *don't* think that these—craftsmen of yours, these *engineers*, as you call them—are going to accomplish anything at all useful. Magic simply does not work the way they are used to thinking. Magic is a thing of intuition, of art; you can't dissect it, set down logic, make it march in step."

"But haven't *you* been teaching me the laws of magic?" An'desha objected stubbornly. Karal's eyebrows arched in surprise, though he kept quiet, true to his promise. Was An'desha actually *disagreeing* with Firesong? If so, it must be for the very first time!

"Yes, but—" Firesong floundered for a moment, then regained his poise. "But the 'laws' of magic are simply guidelines! Haven't Elspeth and Darkwind accomplished things the mages of k'Sheyna thought could not be done, simply because Elspeth was not aware that common thought was that they were impossible? That is because magic simply is not *logical.* It doesn't always answer the way you think it will. You can't call it to the glove like an imprinted falcon!"

"But you won't object if I assist the engineers?" An'desha persisted. "So long as I don't use time and energy we need to put into shields?"

He's opposing *Firesong? Has the moon started rising in the west?*

Firesong flung up his hands in defeat. "How can I object to what you do with your free time?" he asked sourly. "If you want to waste it, go right ahead. I simply don't see where you are going to accomplish anything concrete."

"Well, now that we have that out of the way, shall we get down to the business at hand?" Darkwind asked dryly.

Firesong shrugged and sat down again, settling into a more comfortable position against one of the huge pillows, a bolster of a green so dark it approached black. Karal noted with amusement that he had chosen the only pillow in the room that harmonized with his brilliant emerald costume.

"I asked Rris if there was any oral *kyree* tradition about the mage-storms that followed the Cataclysm," Darkwind told them all. "So here he is, and he's going to recite it to you."

Rris rose from his place at Darkwind's side where he had been lying like an obedient dog, stepped forward into the center of the room, bowed his furry gray head once to all of them, and sat down on his haunches with immense dignity. *:I trust you will not object if I tell it in the traditional manner?:*

"Go right ahead," Firesong said. "You might forget something if you break from tradition, else."

Rris nodded. *:Hear you all, from the times of the Change, from the times of the Falling of the Sky and the Stars,:* he began, his mental voice ringing in Karal's mind. It occurred to Karal at that moment, as he scribbled furiously to get all of the story down, that he himself had changed out of all recognition ever since he had come to Valdemar. Not that long ago, simply *seeing* the *kyree* would have put him into shock. Now he was taking down what the creature dictated into his mind, without a second thought.

Was this a good thing, or a bad one?

Neither, he decided, as his fingers flew across the page, filling line after line with meticulous script. *It's just change. You change, or you turn into a dry old stick.*

And another thing occurred to him.

Dry old sticks break under pressure. So maybe it was a good thing after all. The last thing they all needed right now was one of their number who would snap like a twig.

It had been a long day; it was going to get longer before Karal saw his bed. Nevertheless, when An'desha intercepted him on his way out of the gryphons' room and asked him to make a map of the way to the Compass Rose, he volunteered to act as An'desha's escort instead, after they both had some supper. Ulrich was to work with the Tayledras and Elspeth, strengthening shields again; that left Karal free to make a hasty copy of the day's notes and show An'desha the way.

That was why they both found themselves trudging through a night made darker by the clouds still overhead, splashing through puddles left by the rain, with the sounds of carousing coming from the lantern-lit taverns all around them.

"Thank you for coming with me to where these engineers meet," An'desha said shyly. "I would be very uncomfortable, going there alone."

Since this would be the first time, to Karal's knowledge, that An'desha had *ever* left the grounds of the Palace, he suspected that "uncomfortable" was an understatement. *Terrified* might be more apt.

But An'desha was set on going. He felt that someone was going to have to try to explain magic to those without it, and that he was the best person for the task. That was the argument Karal had walked in on this afternoon. An'desha had volunteered his services, and Firesong had objected.

Firesong might be jealous; he might be afraid that An'desha will find someone else he's attracted to. I wonder if that occurred to An'desha as an explanation for all his objections?

"I have all these notes from our meeting to deliver, and I need to get copies of what they've done for our mages," he replied. "And besides— An'desha, I know you're shy, and I just couldn't let you walk in there alone, face all those people you don't even know. That's what friends are about, right?"

"I had hoped so." An'desha smiled tentatively. "But you are stretching yourself very thin, running errands for all of us, transcribing the notes of our meetings for us. I hadn't wanted to ask you."

"Before this is over, we're all going to be exhausted, so don't worry about it," he told the young mage. At that moment, they reached the door of the tavern, and he paused for a heartbeat on the threshold. "Well, brace yourself. This is not going to be like anything you've ever seen before."

An'desha did visibly brace himself, but he still winced as the door opened and a steady stream of babbling voices poured out over them.

But the voices all stopped when people noticed just who it was that was standing in the doorway. Natoli hurried over to them, and Master Tam was right behind her.

"We've got notes and charts for you," Natoli began.

"And I've got notes from the mages' meeting for you," he replied. "And more than that, I've got a mage with me who wants to show you some of how magic works." An'desha clearly wanted to shrink back away from all the people, but only his trembling hands betrayed his nervousness. "An'desha, this is Natoli, and this is Master Tam. Ladies, this is An'desha; he's both Shin'a'in and Tayledras, and he's one of the mages that works with Lady Herald Elspeth."

"Very pleased to see you, Master An'desha," Master Tam said, folding her hands together and bowing a little to him, rather than seizing his hand to shake it. That was a rather tactful gesture on her part, Karal thought. "We badly need someone to help us understand how these magic powers of yours work. Right now, we're in the position of trying to read the wind."

"I can understand," An'desha replied, so softly that Master Tam had to lean forward to hear him. "I am happy to be of help."

"Well, come over with us, then. Karal, I think Master Henlin wants your notes so he can have copies made; join us when he lets you go." Master Tam took charge of An'desha as if she were used to shepherding shy youngsters all the time. Perhaps she was; it occurred to Karal that many of her students might be just as shy and introspective as An'desha. Intelligent children generally got into trouble with their less intelligent peers; it had happened that way to him when he'd been taken by the Priests, after all.

I only hope none of her students have had half so exciting a life as An'desha. I wouldn't wish that on anyone.

He brought the notes to Master Henlin, who was in the Masters' Room at the rear of the tavern, presiding over a sea of paper, hundreds of sheets of it, covered with figures and diagrams. Then, relieved of his burden, he hurried back out to see if An'desha was still holding up well under the scrutiny of so many strangers.

He was; in fact, he was deep in a discussion of where magic energy came from.

"—so some mage-schools have built up reserves, like a cistern or reservoir, and that is what *their* Master mages can tap into when they need it," he was saying. "It all comes from the same source, though—the energy of life that is all around us. All of us living creatures shed it as we breathe and move."

"And what about the Adepts you mentioned?" Natoli asked. "Do they use something special? Or are there other reserves only they can use?"

"There are," the young Adept replied, nodding. "But they are not the reserves that have been built up by other mages. Rather, they are the reserves that exist where two or more natural lines of force meet. These are called 'nodes,' and they are *so* powerful that only an Adept can control the energy that pools in them. Anyone else trying would either be unable to touch the power, or would be engulfed by it and devoured. Charred."

One of the boys shivered. "Not a pleasant prospect."

"No," An'desha replied soberly. "It is not. But you see, now, that this all *does* respond to natural laws. The power comes from somewhere, and goes elsewhere, like water flowing to the sea. Where it goes eventually, is to a place we call the Nether Planes, where everything is made of chaos and energy. And I suspect that it comes back into our World Plane from there, through the medium of living things."

"Time to speculate about that when we have the leisure," Master Levy interjected, spreading a map out on the table in front of An'desha. "We've been over every thumblength of ground a half day's ride from Haven, and this is what we've found so far. Transplanted areas are in green, blasted areas are in red, transformed areas are in yellow."

An'desha bent over the map to study it; Karal whispered to Natoli.

"Transformed areas?" he asked. "What are those?"

"Places where whatever was there was changed," she whispered back. "Everything in them is the same as it was, but inside those circles, it's another season. We're in late summer right now; there, it's fall, winter, or even spring. Plants that should be in fruit are blooming, or dormant, insects are dead or in cocoons or eggs, and birds or animals are in winter or courting colors."

He blinked at her in surprise; she only grimaced. "Don't ask me, I have no notion what could have caused something like that," she told him.

He turned his attention back to the map, thankful that there were fewer red dots than green or yellow. There definitely was a pattern there; the dots were spaced out at equal intervals, and if you followed a line of them, they would sequence as three greens, a red, and three greens and a yellow. But there didn't seem to be a center to the pattern, or a point of origin.

"I wonder—" An'desha began, then stopped.

"Go ahead," Master Tam urged. "You know magic, and we don't. If you can suggest some kind of meaning or interpretation, I for one would be happy to hear it."

"Well—I wonder if what has happened is that with the transformed and blasted places, there was *too much* energy brought to bear, and that is why the damage?" Then he shrugged. "I am grasping at straws."

"That's no more than we've been doing," Master Levy confessed to him. "Let's follow that theory for a moment."

Karal couldn't understand more than half of what either of them said, but they seemed to understand each other, and that was the important part. Since An'desha didn't seem nearly as shy of these people as he had when he'd first walked into the room, and since Natoli was immersed in the discussion and ignoring everything else, Karal finally left them and assigned himself to one of the desks where others his age were making copies of the same chart that Master Tam had unrolled in front of An'desha.

I can make a copy of this to take back with me; that will save these others from having to make a spare. He helped himself to pens, ink, and paper, and when he had finished that task, he began making copies of his own notes for the other Masters, just as the rest were doing.

When his tired eyes threatened to unfocus completely, he finished one last page, and rolled up his map and the pages of descriptions of the "magic circles," and went to find An'desha.

Despite the latter's promises to Firesong, An'desha *had* been giving demonstrations of mage-craft to the engineers, and he was tired and ready to go back to the Palace. When Natoli declared her intention to defect as well, the whole group broke up, yawning.

"I'll walk back to the Palace with you," she said, as Karal handed An'desha back his cloak. "I've got a room in the wing where they put some Blues who don't have patrons or aren't highborn, and who also don't live in town. We share it with the Healer- and Bardic-trainees."

"I'd wondered," Karal admitted, slinging his cloak around his shoulders, as Natoli found hers in the pile of student Blues. "You kept popping up in the Palace and you acted as if you belong there."

"In a sense, it's the only home I have," Natoli admitted. "Father was Chosen after my mother died of complications of childbirth. No, it wasn't me," she added hastily. "It was a stillbirth, and I was about four. He brought me with him to the Collegium since he hadn't any place else to take me, and I've spent all of my life here. When he went out on circuit, one or another of the Heralds would take care of me until he got back."

Well, it wasn't the worst sort of childhood, though it was nothing like the warm family situation Karal had enjoyed.

"It sounds lonely," An'desha said ingenuously as Karal opened the door and held it for the two of them.

Natoli only shrugged as she stepped out into the dark street. "Mostly, it was odd. When Father was *here*, he made sure I knew he wanted me there, and that he cared about me. For lack of anything else to do, once I got old enough, I took most courses in all the Collegia except the ones in Bardic that had to do with performing and composing, and the ones in Healer's that had to do with really *Healing* someone. Then one day I realized what I wanted to do; I went to Master Tam and asked to be taken on, and she asked *me* why I had taken so long to figure out what I was good at."

"She would," Karal said dryly. "I have the impression that Master Tam would never take an indirect route when there was a direct one available." Other students drifted along behind them, talking quietly to one another, voices murmuring across the otherwise silent street.

"She does tend to bludgeon things," Natoli replied, but smiled. "Father was just pleased that I'd found my avocation; he granted his leave, and I've been studying with Master Tam ever since."

"At least you had some choice in the matter," Karal replied, with some envy. "I was quite literally kidnapped by the Priests." He went on to describe his own childhood, while An'desha and Natoli both listened with interest.

"Odd that of the three of us, I am the one who had the most normal childhood," An'desha mused. "How very strange."

"Well, you made up for it." Karal slapped him lightly on the back. "Never mind; I've figured out that anyone who is more intelligent than the people around him has troubles as a child. The important thing is not to dwell on those troubles and make them into *all* you are. You should do what you can with what parts of your life you have personal control over!"

"That makes good sense," Natoli applauded, and changed the subject. "I wonder what late night food we can gain personal control over?"

Several days passed, with Karal serving double duty: to the mages and with the engineers. As the days went by, the engineers collected more and more information and added it all to their charts, tables, and maps. Florian passed on a great deal more of what Master Tam referred to as "data" from other Companions out in the field with their Heralds—all of it was pertinent, and most of it was much more accurate than the information coming from humans. After the third day of this, Karal paused in the midst of his copying, struck by the fear that all this might *not* be the sort of thing Vkandis would approve of his acolyte doing. After all, he hadn't seen Altra in days. Was the Sunlord annoyed with him?

At that very moment, Altra wandered through the room, tail waving like a banner in a light breeze.

Karal froze, and not just because Altra had appeared the moment Karal thought of him, but because it was here, in the middle of a crowd of—well—unbelievers. What were *they* going to think? Altra wasn't exactly inconspicuous!

But the others did nothing unusual. The other students and teachers *saw* him—they avoided trampling him when he was in their path—but they didn't seem to see anything odd about him. He jumped up onto one or two tables and surveyed the figuring and charting going on with aloof interest, and none of them stared at him. He might very well have been a perfectly ordinary tavern cat.

Considering that he was four or five times larger than any domestic housecat that Karal had ever seen, that was certainly strange!

But Altra eventually made his way to the back of the room where Karal sat staring at him, and gave Karal an approving wink.

:They see only what they are expecting to see,: the Firecat said cryptically. *:I have more information for you. The same patterns are in Karse and southward. Tell the others. You'll get the maps and so forth that Solaris has sent you in a few days.:*

And with that, Altra strolled underneath a table, and did not come out on the other side. Karal sat there with his pen still in his fingers for a long time.

Well—at least he approves, Karal thought, dazedly. That was, after all, one less worry.

But given his current luck, with every worry that he lost, four more rose to take its place.

A day later—and the half-expected second wave swamped them. It came exactly one day short of a fortnight, and at very nearly the same time of day as the first one.

This time the areas of disturbance were not as obvious until a few days had passed, and someone noticed that there were places where plants and insects had—changed. They weren't dead, but they certainly weren't the same anymore. The plants in particular had undergone a transformation that made them act like primitive animals. They reacted to the presence of other living creatures, some by shrinking away, but others by reaching toward whatever was near them. Some of the plants were observed trapping and presumably eating insects; others were growing strange new forms of defense; thorns and spikes, saps that had a terrible stench or were outright poisonous. And two days after the storm passed over, when a farmer found his child in a patch of the changed plants, crying hysterically, with hundreds of tiny thorns in her flesh that she swore the plants had flung at her, Selenay ordered that samples be sent to the Palace and the parent plants be destroyed wherever they were found.

The mages studied the changed plants without learning much—except that Firesong noted a definite resemblance to some of the dangerous "thinking plants" in the Uncleansed Lands of what Valdemarans called the Pelagir Hills.

One day short of a fortnight later, the third storm-wave arrived.

If this keeps up for much longer, I'd better think about growing gills. Karal trudged through yet another nighttime thunderstorm, his cloak already soaked, heading for the Compass Rose. But this time, he felt a little more cheerful than at any time before.

According to Firesong, this last wave was just a trifle weaker than the previous two. This time virtually no shields had gone down before the onslaught, and although even non-mages had experienced the disorienting effects of the wave, Firesong was positive that this mage-storm hadn't lasted as long as the previous two had. No one had reported in from the area outside Haven yet, but the mages were guardedly optimistic that the worst was over.

Such good news was more than compensation enough for a long slog through a driving rain, at least to Karal's mind. He couldn't wait until the others heard!

He opened the door of the tavern and stepped through into warmth and light, only to find virtually everyone clustered around a single table. They were ominously quiet, and when they all turned to see who had entered, there was not a single cheerful expression among them.

"I've got good news!" he said into the oppressive silence. "Firesong says this last storm was weaker!"

Their expressions did not change, and he felt his own spirits dropping. "It was weaker, wasn't it?" he faltered. "Firesong said so. We didn't lose any shields this time—"

Master Levy shook his head slowly. "I'm afraid your Firesong is mistaken," he replied. "Not only was it not weaker, it was actually a little stronger than before. The reason nothing magical was affected was because you've managed to build up good enough shields to protect everything magical that you still retain—and you've pared the number of magical things you need to protect that way to the absolute minimum. Come over here and look at this."

He gestured to something in a wooden box with a grate over the top of it. Karal couldn't see clearly what was in it, but it sat on the table next to Master Levy and had been the object they had all been clustered around. His mouth suddenly dry with trepidation, Karal edged over to the group and looked down into the box itself.

It was an animal, but no animal he had ever seen or heard of before. Mad red eyes stared up at him, and long, hairless ears flattened against a viperish skull covered with a thin coat of gray hair. It snarled at him, and he inadvertently backed up a pace.

"Don't touch it," someone warned. "It just about took Semon's hand off."

"What is it?" he asked, fascinated and repulsed at the same time. It looked vaguely familiar, somehow.

"Nearly as we can tell, it *was* a rabbit." Master Levy looked down at the creature and shook his head. "Or rather, most of it was a rabbit. We can't tell if this was just a case of several creatures being melded together into something new, or a rabbit that got turned into some sort of meat-eater. *That* is what your latest wave did; we've sent word to the Palace to warn people out in the countryside. We're just lucky that there generally aren't any large creatures inside those circles of change. I don't know what something as large as a dog would turn into. Just as a guess, I'd say our wave of disruption is now powerful enough to affect larger animals."

"Think what would happen if this hit a cow, or worse, a pig," someone added. Master Levy shuddered, and Karal didn't blame him.

"Or a human. Another evidence that this wave is stronger is the storm outside," Master Levy put in as an afterthought. "There's always a thunderstorm after the wave passes. This one is worse than the one before, which was worse than the one before that."

"There's always good news to go with bad news," Natoli said, as Karal finally shivered and turned away from the creature on the table. "With three waves, we have enough information to make some predictions. Now we know *when* the next wave will come, we know *where* the affected circles will be, and we know something else. We've been calling these storms 'waves' just as an analogy, but it turns out they really *are* waves."

"You can? They are?" The sick feeling in the pit of Karal's stomach cleared. "But that's wonderful! If we can predict these things, we can at least make certain nothing like *that* thing can happen!"

"For now," Master Levy said ominously. "The size of the affected circle is growing, too, as the duration of each wave increases with its power—"

"Wait!" Karal exclaimed. "Don't tell *me*. You'll have to tell the council of mages—and you ought to come with me and tell them *now*, while they're still congratulating themselves that Valdemar survived the worst of it and came through all right! They haven't told anyone else yet. We have to stop them before they tell Selenay."

"He's right," creaked Master Henlin, running a hand over his bald spot. "If we wait until tomorrow, they might not believe us, even with that *thing* in the box to back us up. Even if they did believe us, they might not want to appear like fools, telling the Queen this directly after telling her everything would be fine. Right. Levy, Norten, Bret; you all go with him. Take all the new charts and the wave-drawing, so they can see for themselves how the waves are acting. Go! We'll all stay here until you come back with word. Maybe now that we know *how* these waves are acting, we can work out a more effective defense against them."

Rolls of paper were carefully inserted into waterproof cases; cloaks were collected, and Karal found himself once again leading a group of men who otherwise would never have given him a second glance out into the teeth of a storm.

This physical storm was indeed *much* worse than the ones that had followed the last two waves. "This alone ought to show your mages that we're right!" Master Levy shouted over the thunder. "That An'desha showed us how unshielded magic-power can affect the weather, and if this isn't an example of just that, I'll eat my map case!"

Karal didn't think that the case was in any danger of becoming an entree, given the severity of the storm. He just hoped that the others were still where he had left them. The little parade struggled against wind and rain all the way to the Palace, despite the sheltering effects of the buildings on either side of the street. Several times Karal was afraid they'd be blown off their feet, but it never actually happened.

Kerowyn must have given the guards a fairly severe lecture; some time was consumed in verifying that everyone was who he said he was, but it was time that Karal didn't begrudge. Master Levy did, though; he stormed up the path to the Palace, grumbling under his breath, and Karal trailed in his wake, followed by the other two Masters. Norten and Bret were too busy trying to keep their cloaks around them to say anything, which didn't make Karal feel too comfortable.

But once they reached the doors of the Palace, Master Levy allowed him to take the lead again, even though the Master's expression was as stormy as the night outside. It was just fortunate that the gryphons' quarters were not very far; Karal feared that another delay might well cause the temperamental Master to explode.

But maybe it isn't just temper; maybe it's worry. Worry and fear made people sometimes act in ways that you wouldn't expect. Ulrich just got more clever when he was worried. Maybe Master Levy had fits of bad temper when he was concerned about something.

Never mind, he told himself, as he reached up to knock on the door to the gryphons' rooms. *Temper-fits are hardly our worst problems at the moment.*

As the door opened, Karal recognized the voice just beyond as belonging to Elspeth, which meant that the single most important person they needed to convince was still here. He waved the others inside first, and wondered for a moment if he just might possibly be able to get away and let the Masters do all the explaining.

No, he told himself sternly. *That would be cowardice.* And, reluctantly, he followed them inside.

Karal listened to Master Levy speak about mathematics and theory with great envy for Natoli, who had such a good teacher. If *he'd* had teachers as good as this man, he might have had more understanding of and love for mathematics. Instead, math was as arcane a subject for him as magic, and he remembered his mathematics lessons as being ordeals.

"...so you see," Master Levy said, with a certain grim satisfaction, "by using this mathematical model, I was able to predict the size and location of all of the areas of disturbance from this last wave. We will have parties out in the countryside verifying my predictions, of course, but the ones we were able to reach before darkness fell were all where I predicted they would be and the size I expected they would be."

"So these storms are really *waves;* they act like real waves?" Elspeth asked, weariness warring with the need to understand, both emotions mirrored in the set of her mouth and the tense lines around her eyes. Darkwind looked over her shoulder at the charts and maps, his brow creased with exhaustion and anxiety.

"In many ways," Master Levy told her and raised a sardonic eyebrow. "I take it that I have convinced you?"

"Just by virtue of the animal you found. I've seen the creatures in the Uncleansed Lands for myself," she replied. "This rabbit-thing you found sounds much too like them for me to disbelieve you."

"And I must agree, at least that the waves are growing stronger, not weaker," Firesong said with extreme reluctance. "They must be growing stronger to have had the effect of warping an animal in such a manner. But—still—mathematical models? Magic does not *work* that way!"

To Karal's surprise, the look that Master Levy bestowed on Firesong was one of understanding and sympathy. "Sir, I comprehend your feelings. Yours is an intuitive nature, and your understanding so deep that you *intuit* the formulas and laws. So must an artist feel when he picks up a shell, paints a sunflower or creates an image of a snowstorm—yet I can reproduce that sunflower in precise mathematical terms, and every snowflake is a mathematically exact shape. If I show you in such a way that you can understand me, will you believe that your magic *does* answer to predictable laws?"

Numbly, Firesong nodded. Master Levy had a force of personality—when he cared to exert it—that was easily the equal of Firesong's. This must have been a rare experience for the Hawkbrother Adept, to find someone who was his equal in personality and intellect.

"Look. This was your original Cataclysm," Master Levy said, pulling out a clean sheet of paper and a pen and drawing concentric circles on it. Karal marveled at that—there were not many people in his experience who *could* draw an even circle without the use of tools. Master Levy must be something of an artist in his own right.

"There were two centers of disruption," the mathematician continued. "One *here*, where the Dhorisha Plains are now, and one *here*, where Lake Evendim is. The force spread outward, in waves—each of these circles represents the apex of the wave—you see where they meet and touch as they spread outward? *That* is where your points of extreme disturbance are, where the apexes of two waves meet."

"So why were the areas of change so great in the original Cataclysm?" Firesong asked stubbornly. "They weren't little circles of devastation, they were huge swaths, reaching from Lake Evendim to beyond where the eastern border of Hardorn is now!"

Master Levy smiled patiently. "The very first waves had a period—a 'width,' if you will—that was enormous; roughly the equivalent of several countries. In areas of the apex of the wave, disturbance was powerful enough that there was no need for waves to interfere with each other to distort the real world, the wave itself was what did the initial damage, and created what we call the Pelagir Hills and what you call the Uncleansed Lands—and yet, entire nations who happened to be in the trough of the wave remained relatively unscathed. I suspect that you would find that where the apexes of the first two great waves met, you *would* find areas of such damage that nothing lived through it."

Firesong bit his lip, as if Master Levy had triggered a memory of something, but he remained silent.

"Now—this is another guess, but I believe that the first wave of shock, the one from the initial destruction of the two centers, was followed by waves of successively shorter period and lesser strength." He cocked his head at Firesong, as if to ask if Firesong understood.

"Perhaps—" Firesong murmured reluctantly.

Master Levy flashed Karal a conspiratorial glance. "Now look; I am drawing the circles closer together, for a reason. The next waves had a period that was shorter, and the next, shorter still. The areas of overlap were correspondingly more frequent, and smaller, until the last of the waves of disturbance passed. As the waves grew weaker, and the period smaller, the disruptions were confined to the places where the wave-apexes intersected. That is why we are finding little circles of disturbance at regular intervals; the intervals represent a combination of the period of the two sets of waves. And the periods presumably lessen due to effects analogous to how the troughs of waves in deep water reduce when they 'drag' the floor of the body of water. Expenditure of energy."

Firesong studied the rough diagram and nodded slowly, then

began twisting a lock of his long silver hair in an uncharacteristically nervous gesture.

Firesong? Nervous? The sun will surely rise in the west tomorrow!

"Now, if what I believe turns out to be the truth, these waves of disturbance are returning through time, in a mirror image of how they occurred in the first place." Master Levy waited, like the teacher he was, for someone to volunteer the next piece of the puzzle.

"Do you mean that they are beginning small and weak, and will end enormous and enormously powerful?" Darkwind hazarded.

"I do," Master Levy replied, nodding at Darkwind as if the mage was a particularly good student. "And I also mean that they are traveling in the opposite direction; instead of radiating *out* from the Plains and Lake Evendim, they are *converging* on the Plains and Lake Evendim. Which means that all their force, in the end, will be concentrated in those two spots."

"Oh." Elspeth held her knuckles to her mouth in stunned silence.

"And as the waves increase in strength, the areas of disturbance will no longer be confined to the points of intersection, but will be as wide as—" Master Levy paused for a moment, "—at a guess, I would say roughly a third of the wave's period. Once again, that could be an area the size of a country, or larger."

Firesong sat down slowly. "You have convinced me, mathematician," he said, his face blank. "Your proofs are too good. And you have told me that my people are doomed, mine and the Shin'a'in. They lie directly in the area that will be affected the worst. No shields can ever withstand the force of the kind that is mounting against them."

"Feh!" snorted Master Norten into the heavy pause that followed. He was a short, squat fellow who had remained silent during all of this. His exclamation pierced the ponderous silence, making all of them start.

"What?" Elspeth faltered.

"I said, begging your pardon, *Feh.* No one is *doomed,* young man." Master Norten favored Firesong with a sharp glare, as if he had caught Firesong being impossibly dense. "We have enough information to *predict* the period of the next waves! We have enough information to *know* what the strength will be, and where the intersection points are! Right now, the danger is only at the intersection points; we can keep people and animals out of them; we can destroy the plants inside them. But haven't you been paying attention? We *have* a temporary solution, enough to buy us time to find a real solution!"

"You have?" Elspeth gasped.

"We *have?*" Master Levy gaped.

Master Norten took the cane with which he had been supporting his bulk and rapped Master Levy with it. "Of *course* we have, you dolt! All you ever see are your damned mathematical models! *Think*, man! You're the one who pointed out that these spurts of magic are acting in a way we recognize! Can't you understand that these—these magic-waves— are acting *exactly* like waves of water? And can't we protect harbors and anchorages from *real* waves with breakwaters? So why can't these mages come up with magical breakwaters to protect important places, places like cities and those nodes of theirs and all?" He glared at all of them, as if he could not believe they had not seen what to him was so obvious. "Hell and damnation! Why can't they just build a magical breakwater to protect every country in the Alliance?"

"This is why I am a mathematician and not an engineer," Master Levy replied, with chagrin. Master Norton snorted again, and looked very pleased with himself.

"I—I suppose it ought to be possible," murmured Darkwind, his brows knotted as he thought.

"Well, then, you ought to damn well *do* it, boy!" Master Norten retorted. "We can surely give you the dates and times and interference points. We can calculate the strength and period if you help us establish scales. With all that, I don't see why you can't do the rest, instead of sitting on your behinds, whining about being 'doomed'!"

"But magic doesn't work that way," Firesong whispered—except that it sounded more like a plea than a statement of fact.

"I'm sorry, Firesong," Karal replied, not at all sorry to see Firesong at last convinced that he was not the greatest expert in all things. "It does." He handed Firesong a set of all of the tables for the last two waves, his own copies that he had been keeping with him. In the face of all the neat rows of dispassionate, logical figures and formulas, finally even Firesong had to concede defeat.

"All right," the Healing Adept said at last. "It does. And I promise that I will learn how to use all of this. How long do we have before the *real* mage-storm breaks?"

"We haven't calculated it yet," Master Levy responded instantly. "We only now have enough information to predict how much stronger the next waves will be from the ones preceding them. It would *help* if we had an idea how strong the original waves were, and what their period was."

"Farrr enough that the Kaled'a'in werrre engulfed in the rrresultsss of the Cataclysssm, dessspite the grrreat distancsse they had gone frrrom Urrrtho'sss Towerrr," Treyvan rumbled. "Howeverrr—we alssso trrraveled to a point outssside that, beforrre we finally found a placsse wherrre the land wasss clean. Therrre we ssstopped. Perrrhaps we can give you an essstimate."

"An estimate will do," Master Levy told the gryphon. He had started when Treyvan first spoke, but he seemed to have accepted the fact that the gryphons could speak with intelligence.

"I can send a mage-message," Firesong volunteered instantly. "And—wasn't there something in that history Rris recited about how long the original—ah, I suppose we could call them 'aftershocks'—lasted?"

"It was fairly vague," Karal replied after a moment, checking his notes from that first meeting. "I've got it here. He just said, 'many moons.' That's not much help."

Firesong blinked, as if he had forgotten that Karal had taken notes for all their meetings.

"Except that we know we have at least a few months to figure something out before the monster comes upon us," Master Norten was quick to point out. Then he yawned hugely and looked surprised. "Gods and demons, it *must* be late, or I wouldn't be yawning! Look, none of us are fresh enough to do any good right now. What if we three meet with you mages in the morning, and we'll see what we can work out from here?"

"That—would be good." Firesong bowed his head. "I hope you will forgive me. I am not used to being wrong. It sticks like a barb in my crop."

"I can understand that." Master Norten favored him with a sardonic smile. "I'm not used to being wrong, either, and I hate it like poison when I am."

"So we understand each other." Firesong gingerly took the Master's hand as Elspeth and Darkwind watched, the former with approval, the latter with amusement. "Tomorrow, then?"

"Tomorrow." Master Norten favored Karal with his stiletto glance now. "I trust you'll be there, with nimble fingers and sharp pens? I want notes on *everything*, even if at the time we think we've gone down a dead end. It might be useful."

Karal sighed. It was going to be a *very* long day.

"Yes, sir," he promised. That made yet another group he was taking notes for. At this rate, his fingers would be worn to the bone! It was just a good thing he had glass pens now, instead of the old quills or metal; the glass hadn't worn out yet.

Well, I did volunteer. And with luck, maybe Natoli will be impressed with all this diligence. I get the feeling that nothing impresses her quite like competence.

Only after he was well on his way down the corridor, walking next to his master, did he wonder why he'd had that particular thought...

Grand Duke Tremane listened to the tales of woe from his commanders with a blank expression and a churning gut. They had all ridden here—*ridden*, as if this was some barbarian army rather than the proud Army of the Empire. Most of them hadn't ridden any distance in years, but with all the Gates down—again—there was no other way for them to reach him.

It was very clear to everyone that the Imperial forces were in a state of barely-controlled panic. No sooner did the mages manage to fix all the things that had gone wrong, than another wave of disruption came along and knocked everything magical flat again. There wasn't even time to set up shielding around things! This was the third time, and it was worse than the last two; shields that had held through the first two waves had broken before this third onslaught.

Not one of his commanders cared a bean about gaining more ground in Hardorn anymore. All *they* wanted was for things to get back to normal! Even the weather-workers were having problems; they couldn't even begin to control the storms and were just trying to keep the worst effects off the camps themselves.

Add to that the panic and the disruption in services of all those terrible storms that dumped purely physical chaos down on the camps, and you had a recipe for disaster if he didn't *do* something to increase the troops' confidence. Rumors running through the camp right now were enough to cause even hardened campaigners to worry; new recruits were often panicking, and had to be restrained by their more experienced fellows. There were tales that Hardorn had bought the services of the Black Kings in the south, stories that some mage in the Empire itself had caused this by accident, rumors that Valdemar was unleashing the hidden powers of their Heralds and white horses. No one knew, but everyone had a theory. Most of those theories painted a grim picture of the first defeat that the Imperial Army was likely to face in centuries, if Tremane didn't pull some answer out of his sleeve.

The only trouble was, he hadn't the foggiest notion how to do that.

I pledge you a tonne of incense and a gross of candles each, he silently told the forty little gods, *if you will just grant me some inspiration on what to do in this situation!*

But inspiration and intervention, divine or otherwise, was clearly in short supply at the moment. None of the forty vouchsafed him a reply.

"We have to do something," General Harde said, at last. "No matter what your orders are, you have to order us to do *something,* or the troops will assume you've lost your nerve and we've lost the situation."

"Consolidate," he said finally. "Everyone pull your men in, and consolidate our forces around this keep. To the coldest hell with the battle plans; I want every soldier right here where we can stay in contact by runners if we have to. With all the men we'll have here, we can build purely physical fortifications. Abandon the front line; the Emperor is hardly in a position to find out what we're doing right now, anyway."

Oh, if only the Empire is suffering the same effects that we are! he prayed. *Chaos there will save the situation for me here. Chaos there will convince the Emperor that I am not exaggerating my troubles to cover my own incompetence. And if this is something that Charliss unleashed on me, on his own* loyal *soldiers—*

He did not finish that thought; it would be treason, no two ways about it. He was not ready for treason.

Not yet.

"But what about supplies?" one of the commanders asked. "How are we going to keep such a huge force fed?"

"I don't know yet; I'll have an answer for you when we finally bring them all in," he promised. "I have supplies here for the whole Army for about two weeks before we'd have to go on lean rations. Meanwhile, there are rebels out there, and they are still picking at us; we're better off with all the men in one place, rather than stretched out along a line that reaches across half this benighted country. I *don't* want to lose any units by having them cut off from me."

That put some spine back in them; with firm orders to carry out, his commanders were a lot more comfortable. And with a march ahead of them, followed by the physical labor of building fortifications, the men should remain tractable until the work ran out.

Better get the engineers to work on designing a wall using only the materials on hand, and mostly hand-labor. And after that, well, if I have to, I'll march the whole damned lot all the way back to Imperial soil, he thought grimly, dismissing his commanders. He turned his attention to the reply to last night's urgent request for information from his tame scholars. He'd literally ordered them out of their beds, and set them to work all night. *I may go down in disgrace, but I won't leave these men to be picked off two and three at a time by a pack of barbarians.*

At least he'd transported his whole library here before everything went to hell. Somewhere, some time, *something* like this must have happened in the past. He'd ordered his scholars to abandon their search for information on Valdemar and concentrate on looking for just that. He was, by the gods, going to find out *when* there were disruptions like this, where they occurred, and most important of all, what the people back then did about it!

My lord; the letter read—the Chief Historian had been impressed enough by the salty language of his order to keep his report concise and omit all the flowery nonsense usually pasted into such documents. Then again, the Chief Historian was now working without mage-lights, mage-fires, running water, or any of the other comforts he was used to. That alone must have impressed him that the situation was urgent. *These disruptions that we are now experiencing were unusual enough that we were able to eliminate most of the texts in your library immediately. I and my three colleagues are familiar with the history of the Empire, and we knew that there would be nothing in the Official Chronicles—which meant that we began our search in the copies of texts we had that predated the foundation of the Empire itself.*

Well! Tremane sat back in his chair, taken aback. He knew that the fact that he actually owned copies of pre-Imperial texts was something of a fluke, and due only to his own interest in history. Most people didn't own anything nearly so old; he'd paid a healthy sum in bribes above and beyond the cost of the books to get some of those books, too, and now he was very glad that he had.

First, I must caution you that these texts are a jumble of many archaic tongues, and it is going to take some time to translate them precisely. We have all agreed on the general gist of what we found, however.

Second, the texts themselves are the personal papers of a mixed group of ancient warriors. Some were—we think—mercenaries, and others were liegemen to a Great Lord of some kind.

Well, that certainly fit in with the official history of the Empire. Tremane cupped his chin in his hand and read on.

We have gathered from the papers that this group was part of a much larger force; that they were cut off from the rest when their enemy gained an unexpected and decisive victory. They were warned by their Lord that they must flee as far and as fast as they could, by means of a Gate.

Interesting. That was *not* part of official history, which stated that the group had marched off on its own to carve out conquest for themselves.

Why they fled, we do not yet know; our guess, and it is only a guess, was that the Great Lord intended his enemy's victory to be an empty one, and meant to ensure his enemy claimed only ashes by destroying everything before he actually took it. Be that as it may, it is clear that they did build a Gate to reach a location they knew was relatively safe, far eastward of the place where they had retreated after being cut off. Then something happened as they were passing through the Gate, and a catastrophe of—we believe—a magical nature, flung them farther away than they had ever intended to go. This landed them in completely unfamiliar territory—territory that became, as you have probably anticipated, the heart of our Empire. In the days that followed, a series of disruptions that one writer terms "magic-quakes" occurred; another writer describes them as "aftershocks." These disruptions seem on first blush to match the kinds of troubles we are experiencing now.

This was exactly what he had been hoping to find! Elation built in him——only to be crushed, abruptly, by the words that followed.

You were most urgent in your orders that once we found a match to our circumstances, we should discover what those ancients had done to remedy their situation. I have no good news for you, my Lord. Once again, my colleagues and I are unanimous in our understanding of these papers.

Our ancestors did nothing. They could do nothing. They simply waited for the magic-quakes—or aftershocks—to end, or destroy them. Eventually, of course, the disruptions ended, they consolidated their position, and the rest is official Imperial history.

Tremane buried his face in his hands.

They waited it out. This was not *good news.*

But I am going to have to deal with it. He was not one to try to pretend that bad news wasn't the truth. If anything, he tended to act as if bad news was only the shadow of worse to come. It would be a good idea to act that way now.

His mages were in a panic; the waves of disruption were growing stronger, not weaker, as each one passed. His instinct to get the Gates up *first*, and start hauling supplies through them as soon as they were up, had been the right choice. They had supplies enough to last them well into the winter at half rations, now, and if they could just get the Gates back up a few more times, they might get enough to last all the way to spring on *full* rations.

No. That was the wrong choice—get the supplies, yes, that should be the priority, but why waste time on getting *several* Gates up, when he only needed one? Just the one to the westernmost Imperial supply depot, the one for foodstuffs. Forget weapons; he wasn't going to allow his men to waste a single arrow until he had decided what his long-term plans should be. Forget reinforcements; he had all the men he needed to hold firm, and too many for an orderly retreat, if it came to that. He would have all his mages concentrate on getting that one single Gate back up, and he would forge the orders he needed to loot the depot, and to the coldest hell with honesty and procedure, and anyone else who might need supplies from it.

It's easier to apologize than get permission. He could make amends to the Emperor later, if he needed to.

At least he knew one thing; it was less likely now that Charliss was actively sending this against him. However, it was still possible that Charliss had known this would happen, and had sent him off on a doomed mission to be rid of him.

And condemned hundreds of thousands of good soldiers with me. That made him angry; the loyalty of the Army to the Emperor was legendary. To have that loyalty betrayed so callously was a betrayal of everything the Empire held sacred.

Which isn't much. When he thought back on the state of the Court, of the corruption deep in the bureaucracy, perhaps he shouldn't be angry *or* surprised.

He shook his head. It didn't matter. What *did* matter was that while he was maneuvering to get his army into a defensive position, there was Valdemar, virtually unscathed, poised, and waiting.

If I were the Queen, I'd strike right now. I'd bring in Karse, hit the Imperial lines at a dozen places and break us up into manageable pieces, and then wipe the pieces out at my leisure. I wouldn't hesitate. Just arm the natives, and they'd probably take care of most of it for me. That would give me Hardorn with a minimum of effort—and I might even be able to penetrate into Imperial territory before it got too expensive.

He had to do something to keep Valdemar so busy with its own troubles that it wouldn't have the leisure or the coordination to strike now.

Unfortunately, that meant using a weapon that he'd held in reserve because he hated it so much.

But a man threatened will use anything to stay alive. I am fighting for not only my life, but the lives of my men. I cannot hesitate. I will *not hesitate.*

He would not entrust this to an aide or a messenger. Instead, he unlocked a drawer of his desk, and removed a square of something heavy wrapped in silk. He laid the square in the middle of his desk and unwrapped it, uncovering a piece of polished black obsidian-glass, perfectly square and perfectly flawless.

This was another reason why all candidates for the Iron Throne should be mages. Some messages were too important for anything but personal delivery.

He reached into the drawer again, and brought out a hand-sized portrait of a man; it was an excellent likeness, though the man himself was hardly memorable. This was a good thing; it was not wise to employ a man who was distinctive as a covert agent. With the portrait was a lock of the man's hair; the physical link needed to contact him.

It was also the physical link that any decent mage could use to *kill* him if he became uncooperative, as all agents knew very well. There was nothing like having a little insurance, when one dealt with covert operatives.

Using the portrait, he fixed the agent's image in his mind, and reached for the energies of his own personal reserve of magic. He did not care to trust the lines of power hereabouts; his mages had already warned him that they were depleted and erratic. What these disruptions had done to them, he did not care to speculate. While he relied on his own protected pool of power, he should be immune to the disturbances around him.

He stared into the black glass, emptying his mind of everything except the agent and the need to speak with him, flinging his power out as if it was a fishing line, and he was angling for one fish in particular.

His power slowly drained out as he sought and waited; sought and waited. This might take a while; he was prepared to wait for as long as it took. His agent was not in command of his own movements, and it could be some time before he was free to answer the call. That was fine; a mage must learn patience, first and foremost, before he could build any other skills. A mage must learn concentration, as well, and Tremane had ample practice in both virtues.

The marks crept by and the candle burned down, and at long last, past the hour of midnight, the answer came to his call.

The agent's face formed in the glass, expression anxious and apologetic. Tremane thought, with a curl of his lip, that the fool looked even more ineffectual than he did in his portrait. *Why* had anyone ever chosen an artist as a covert agent?

"My Lord Duke!" the man cried, his lips moving in the glass, his voice as thin and weak as a fly's buzzing whine. *"I beg you to forgive me! I could not get away! I—"*

"You are wasting my time with apologies," Tremane said curtly. "Here are your orders. Release the little birds."

The agent's face went dead white. *"My—my Lord?"* he faltered. *"All of them? Are you certain?"*

"All of them," Tremane ordered, curtly. "See to it."

Before the fool could waste his time and resources further by arguing or pleading that this would place him in danger, Tremane broke the spell. The agent's image vanished from the glass, quickly as a candle flame is blown out. Tremane paused for a moment, massaging his temples, before he folded the silk around the obsidian and put glass, hair, and portrait back into the drawer.

Would the agent survive his appointed task?

He would if he was careful, Tremane decided. There was nothing about the job that left him vulnerable to discovery. The "little birds" should already be in place, and setting them free could be done at a distance. If he was stupid, he might be caught, though.

Then let him suffer the penalty of stupidity, Tremane decided with uncharacteristic impatience. *If he is caught, he has done all he need do, and he is expendable.*

He was rarely so ruthless with an underling, but this man was no agent of *his* choosing, and he had not been particularly useful until now.

He clenched his fist for a moment, as a pang of regret for what he had just ordered swept over him. This was—ugly, unclean, and underhanded. It was neither honest nor honorable. It would be the first real stain on his conscience or soul. He had ordered the deaths of men before, but they had always been death in battle or other circumstances where both sides knew what they were getting into. He knew that he would spend at least one sleepless night over this and probably more to come.

This was the death of innocents, noncombatants. Yet an Emperor had to be ruthless enough to order just such an action to save the lives of his own people.

But I had no choice, he told himself, staring up at the black glass of his window, so like the black mirror he had just used. *I must save my men. This is war, and I had no choice.*

So why did it feel as if he had betrayed, not only his honor, but some significant part of his own soul?

1 5

There were seven days left before the next wave, and Karal was not altogether certain he was going to live that long. There were simply not enough marks in the day to do everything he had to. Then again, he was not the only person working to exhaustion; the mages and the engineers were all walking around with dark rings under their eyes. The only reason *he* was getting any sleep at all was because he was seeing to it that Ulrich got a decent rest every night, and then dropping into slumber shortly thereafter.

The mages did their shielding work in the morning, when they were all fresh; then came a break for lunch, then their meeting with the Master Engineers, and then their own meetings. Karal was not always present at the latter; the mages needed his reports on what the engineers were doing, more than the reverse, since An'desha was making himself available to them for explanations and demonstrations. Karal had to wonder where *he* was getting the energy.

Generally he kept himself as unobtrusive and invisible as possible— except where Ulrich's health was concerned. It had taken a major effort of will to march right in on the mages and demand that Master Ulrich be allowed to get some rest, the first time he'd gotten back to the suite after returning from the Compass Rose only to find that Ulrich was not in his bed. He was nothing more than the merest secretary; *he* had no standing and no authority among such luminaries as Elspeth and Darkwind! But Ulrich's welfare was the most important job he had; *Solaris* had entrusted him with seeing that his mentor remained hale and well, and staying up until dawn, snatching an hour or two of sleep, and getting up to work complicated magics was going to wear him to nothing in a very short period of time. He didn't think the others, being much younger than Ulrich, were aware of how quickly he could be exhausted. So he had gathered up all of his courage, walked straight into the meeting, and respectfully "reminded" Ulrich that his master had left orders to be told when midnight arrived so that he could get enough rest to work the next day.

Ulrich had looked momentarily startled, then had given Karal a long, hard look. Karal had done his best to wear an expression of bland implacability.

I won't go away, sir, he'd thought hard at Ulrich. He'd never known whether or not his master could read thoughts as he had often suspected, but if Ulrich could, he was certainly getting an "earful" now. *Whatever it takes to persuade you to get some rest, I'm going to do it, even if I have to fabricate emergencies, even if I have to recruit Altra.* Though how he was going to persuade the Firecat to go along with the scheme, he hadn't had a clue at the time.

He still didn't know if Ulrich could read thoughts, but his mentor had risen with thanks for the "reminder," and had excused himself from the meetings whenever Karal appeared after that, and all without a contradictory word thereafter.

Still, if Karal felt as if he was constantly on the verge of exhaustion, how must Ulrich feel?

He knew what was driving them all; he felt it himself. Beneath it all, underscoring every waking moment, was the sense of urgency. *Hurry, hurry, hurry,* whispered a tiny voice. *Don't waste any time. You don't have time to waste. Find the answer; find it* now, *before it's too late.*

Some time, soon, too soon, scant months from now, it would *be* too late. The real storm would break over their heads, and Valdemar was closer to the center of one of the two places in peril than any other land and people—

Except for the Shin'a'in.

And except for the small group of Kaled'a'in that had made their new home on the very edge of the Plain. Those were the gryphons' people, and although Treyvan and Hydona said nothing about it, Karal knew that they were as grimly worried about their little group as the Shin'a'in ambassador was worried about her own people.

There was an option that no one liked, but which would at least save the lives of those in peril. Before the Storm actually hit, the people themselves could move. It wouldn't be easy, though; by then, disruption-waves would be arriving daily, making it impossible to set up Gates. They would all have to move the hard way; overland, by foot and horse, and even the Kaled'a'in "floating barges" would be useless unless the mages spent all their time and energy in holding shields against the disruption.

By then, though, the lands around the area would be the next thing to uninhabitable. There would be no possibility of anyone leading a normal life, not when your crop plants were suddenly warping into things that could kill you with flung thorns or poison, and the beasts of your fields had turned into rabid killers.

Karal had the latest maps spread out on the table in front of the fireplace and was studying them while he waited for Ulrich to return for lunch. These were the maps predicting the areas of effect from the next disruption-wave. It would come exactly one and one-half days short of a fortnight, and the circles of "change" would be twenty hands across— enough that now a large animal *could* conceivably be caught inside one.

A Shin'a'in horse, for instance. Or a Valdemaran bull.

Or a wild deer; it didn't matter. The "rabbit" had nearly taken off someone's hand; anything larger would be deadly to whatever was within its range of movement.

Karal shivered at the thought. With luck, and the help of all the Heralds out on circuit, they could warn people to keep their livestock at home that day, or confine them away from danger zones. That was in Valdemar, and it still left the possibility that some large game animal would be caught in a change. Altra had taken a copy of the map this morning as soon as he had made one, and had vanished with it; evidently now the Firecat had no problems acting as a messenger to Solaris. That took care of Karse—again, except for wild animals, and they would just have to chance that.

Presumably Firesong could send the information to the Hawkbrothers by magic—and they in turn would pass it to the Kaled'a'in and the Shin'a'in.

Prince Daren had sent a Herald off last night to Rethwellan, but there were no Priests or Heralds in Rethwellan to distribute the warning. There were none in Hardorn either, nor in the icy wilderness up above the Forest of Sorrows, nor in Iftel. There was no way to tell anyone farther south than Rethwellan, except if the Shin'a'in got around to it, nor were there any ways to distribute warnings there. *Their* only hope was that the wave centering on Evendim would be so weak by the time it got that far, that the combined effect with the one centered on the Plain would be negligible.

It wouldn't remain that way for long, though. Sooner or later the waves would be strong enough that the warping effect would be felt even farther away than Ceejay, and at that point, the waves would be coming more often, too.

Somehow, someone had to spread the word. Somehow, *they* had to find the answer to stopping this thing.

Hurry, hurry, hurry, before it's too late...

Nothing could be done about the Pelagirs or the northern mountains. What would happen when the beasts that were already strange and deadly, out in the Uncleansed Lands, encountered these warping forces a second time? One wag of a student had suggested that they *might* just go back to being rabbits, mice and tree-hares. That was an amusing thought, but unlikely.

And what about the Empire? There was still an army out there. What if whoever was in command decided that Valdemar, Karse, or both were the cause of all this? *They* had command of far more magic than either land did, and an unlimited supply of troops, or so it seemed. What if they decided this was an attack, and decided that it was worth carrying the battle to the enemy?

As if that thought had been a cue, the door opened, and Ulrich stepped in.

The sound of his limping footstep made Karal turn, with a frown of worry on his face. Ulrich should not be limping, not unless he was so exhausted that even walking was an effort.

His frown deepened when he saw the pale, translucent skin above Ulrich's beard, and the dark circles beneath his eyes.

"You've been overworking again," he accused.

"I've been undersleeping," Ulrich corrected. "I had troubling dreams last night, and this morning I urged that our work consist of sending out warnings, maps, and the formulae to calculate the schedules, not only to the Tayledras, Shin'a'in shaman, and Kaled'a'in, but to every mage-school any of us knew of. It occurred to me that in the schools there is *always* someone teaching or practicing a scrying spell, and we needed only to "interrupt" what was already in place. The Blue Mountain and White Winds mages were particularly helpful there." He smiled wanly. "We covered quite a bit of ground, so to speak."

"That's all very well and good, but—" Karal stopped himself in midscold, shaking his head at himself. "I'm sorry. I sound like your mother, or at least a nagging son, and I'm only your protégé and secretary. Forgive me, Master Ulrich."

But to his shock and delight, Ulrich not only did not take offense, but he smiled again, this time with real warmth. Wan sunlight reflected from the white plaster-adorned mantel fell on him, accentuating his pallor. "You have every right, and if I had a nagging son, or any kind of son, I would hope he would be precisely like you. You are a never-ending delight to me, Karal. I had thought when I first took you as my protégé that I would always be a little disappointed in you because you were not a mage. I was wrong."

"Wrong?" Karal replied vaguely, more than a little stunned by the sudden turn this conversation had taken.

"Very wrong." Ulrich limped across the floor to him and hesitantly put one hand on his shoulder. "You are something more important than a mage, and much rarer, my son. You are a warrior of the spirit and a healer of the soul. You have more compassion than I can begin to understand, and you are already showing the beginnings of true wisdom. People trust you instinctively, and instinctively you sense that and try to help them, even as you do your best not to betray that trust. You will be a great Priest in the purest sense one day, the sense that has nothing to do with magic, power, or politics; that, I think, is why Altra was sent to you."

Karal trembled under Ulrich's hand; this was *not* anything he had ever expected to hear, and he plainly didn't know what to think.

"Yours will not be an easy path, I fear," Ulrich continued. "But I can tell you one that you should make the time to speak to. Herald Talia is one who is very like you; her abilities differ in that she is a healer of the heart, rather than the soul, but otherwise she will understand you better than anyone else you are ever likely to meet."

"B-but—Solaris—" he faltered, blurting out the first thing that came to mind. *Why is he talking like this? He sounds as if he thinks he might not be here while I still need him—*

Ulrich shook his head. "Solaris is something else entirely; the Prophet and the Leader are concerned with the needs of the people as a whole, and not with the needs of individuals. Solaris will not be able to help you—although you may be called upon one day to help her."

Karal dropped his gaze to the floor, a lump in his throat, confusion in his heart. Ulrich put a finger under Karal's chin, and raised his face so that Karal was forced to look into his eyes. "In one thing, Talia will not be able to help you, and you will have to find your own way. The way of the true Priest is often solitary; he can sometimes tread a parallel road with another, but sooner or later, their ways must part, and they may not come together again. Your life belongs to others, and I think you already understand and accept that, although you have not put it into words for yourself. If you are very lucky, you may find a partner who can understand or accept that. If you are not, there will be heartache. If the heartache comes, *remember* what you are, and that if you may not be the lover of one, you *will* be beloved by many."

Karal blinked up into Ulrich's eyes, trying his best to understand what his master was saying, and not quite grasping it. Ulrich looked down at him for another heartbeat or two, then released him with a dry chuckle.

"Ah, my dreams have made me fey, a little mad, or both," he said lightly. "Either that, or I am so hungered that I am seeing shadows of a future that may never happen. Did you bespeak lunch?"

Karal released a sigh of relief and nodded. "And it's odd that you should have mentioned Herald Talia; she wanted to talk to both of us about An'desha. She says that he is all knotted up over something, and she thinks we can help him."

"Well, perhaps we can," Ulrich began, just as a light tap signaled someone at the door.

"Come!" Ulrich said immediately; the door opened and the Lady Talia herself stepped inside, followed by the page with their lunch. For a moment, there was a little confusion, as Karal quickly cleaned the papers off the table, the boy maneuvered the tray onto the waiting surface, and everyone sorted themselves out. The boy bowed quickly and left, Talia and Ulrich exchanged greetings, and Karal *started* into the other room to fetch a third chair.

He never even got as far as the door.

Something—some strange sound, or maybe not a sound at all, just a feeling—made him whirl around, every nerve afire with the certain knowledge of *danger*, deadly and imminent.

The fireplace was decorated with plaster ornaments much like the Council rooms and most of the other suites in the Palace. They were set into the wall on either side and above the mantel, a series of whorls and scrollwork, with four larger whorls, one just off each corner of the mantelpiece.

A shrill trilling sound split the air just as the plaster of those whorls split and shattered, releasing *something* that sprang out into the room and hung, hovering, in the air.

Karal didn't get a good look at them; they made his eyes hurt, and no matter how he concentrated, the very air blurred around them. He only had an impression of a diamond-shape of sharp blades, frightening and deadly.

He didn't think, he acted, instinctively flinging himself in front of Talia, keeping his own body between her and them. If anyone in this room was in danger, surely it was Talia!

In the next instant, Altra was in front of *him*. Every hair on the Firecat's body was on end, and the Cat howled a piercing battle cry that rivaled the whining trill of the devices.

The diamond-blades *moved;* the two nearest Karal flew at him as fast as a pair of glittering dragonflies. He flung himself backward, trying to knock Talia to the floor to shield her. He expected at any moment to feel one or more of those blades piercing his heart—

But there was a sharp *crack*, and two of the devices vanished altogether in a flash of fire, one that originated from Altra's extended claws. The third went careening sideways, into the path of the fourth, deflecting it—

But not enough.

The device slammed into Ulrich's chest with enough force to knock him to the floor, as the second device embedded itself in the wall.

The trilling stopped, leaving silence, and the sound of harsh, bubbling breathing.

"Ulrich!" Karal screamed, as he scrambled to his feet and flung himself down beside the Priest. Talia was right behind him, and stopped him before he could pull the damnable device out of Ulrich's chest. The Priest was still breathing, but he was unconscious, and a thin trickle of blood appeared at one corner of his mouth and ran down the side of his face.

"Don't touch him," Talia ordered. "I've called for help. I know some Healing, let me—"

Obediently, he moved aside and let *her* be the one to remove the device. Fearlessly, she pulled it out, and the wound whistled for a second until she slapped her hand over it, blocking it. "It's a lung-hit, that's bad," she muttered under her breath, distractedly. "Very bad—where *is* that damned Healer?"

Karal hovered beside her, in an agony of helplessness, wanting to do something, *anything*, and unable to aid her at all. "Ulrich, Master," he whispered, one hand on his mentor's forehead, the other on his shoulder on the uninjured side. "Please, help is coming, don't leave me, I need you, *don't leave me.*"

Time just did not feel like it was moving right. *Nothing* felt like it was moving right. This couldn't really be happening, Karal thought through a mental sludge. The sounds of their voices and movements seemed truncated, as if they were down a well, and Ulrich's halting, gasping breaths were too loud.

Then, finally, the door burst open, and a dozen or more people crowded into the room, at least two of them in the green robes that denoted a senior Healer in this land. They swarmed over Ulrich, shoving aside both Karal and Talia. A moment later, they carried the Priest away, leaving Karal and Talia behind, with one other person. Karal started to follow, but a hand on his shoulder stopped him.

"Let me go," he spat, grabbing the hand to pull it off. But another hand grabbed his wrist and made him turn, and he found himself looking into Kerowyn's sober green eyes.

"You can't help Ulrich, and you'll only get in the Healers' way," she said, bluntly telling him the truth that he didn't want to hear.

"But—" He looked at her, and unexpectedly burst into tears.

Talia put her arms around him—and strangely enough, so did Kerowyn. Both of them held him while he sobbed hysterically.

"Why?" he wept. *"Why?* He never hurt anyone! He was an old man! He never *hurt* anyone! *Why?"*

Neither of the women said anything to him, which was just as well, since he wouldn't have been able to hear them or respond. They simply made soothing sounds at him and supported him as time wobbled and spun. After a moment, or a candlemark, Kerowyn detached herself and left him to bury his head in Talia's shoulder while the Herald stroked his hair and swayed back and forth with him in her arms.

Terrible grief shook him; he couldn't see, couldn't hear, couldn't even think. The only things in his mind were the dreadful sound of the blade-device thudding into Ulrich's chest, never-ending, and the sight of Ulrich's body hitting the floor...

It was exhaustion that finally brought him back to himself. His tears stopped, mostly because his eyes were too sore and dry to produce another drop. Dully, he allowed Talia to lead him to a chair, and he sat down in it.

Kerowyn knelt in front of him, the two devices in her hands. "Ulrich wasn't the only one attacked," she said gently. "The Shin'a'in ambassador was killed outright, and it was just pure luck that the other mages were with the gryphons when more of these things came after *them;* they all managed to knock the things down, though Treyvan and Darkwind each took a wound. It looks, at the moment, as if someone hid these damned things in plaster ornaments in the rooms of every single one of the foreign mages."

He blinked at her, his eyes gritty and swollen. "Why?" he asked stupidly.

She shrugged. "Either *someone* wanted to eliminate all the ambassadors, or that same *someone* wanted to eliminate all the mages, and he settled for getting the foreigners because the rest of them live in the Herald's Wing and he didn't have access to that part of the Palace." She tilted her head to one side, and frowned. "Come to think of it, he wouldn't have access to Firesong's place, either. Maybe that's why there were four in here; the other two might have been meant for Firesong and An'desha."

He shook his head again. *"Why?"* he persisted. "Why try to kill anyone? And who would it be?"

Kerowyn's mouth tightened. "Figure it was the Empire that planned this, and you'll probably have your answer. Since I don't recognize these things, and I thought I knew every kind of assassins' weapon there was, the Empire would be my first choice for *who* did this."

Her words set his frozen mind in motion again, and almost against his will, a myriad of possibilities occurred to him. "If I wanted to break up the Alliance, I'd kill all the ambassadors," he said reluctantly. "If Valdemar couldn't protect the envoys in the Palace itself, the allies might assume it was too dangerous to ally with Valdemar against the Empire. It's possible that *some* of the allies, like Karse, might even blame Valdemar for the deaths. It might only be incidental that the targets were mages."

Talia's eyes went wide, and Kerowyn's narrowed in speculation. "That hadn't occurred to me," she admitted. "But it's an even better reason than killing them to lessen our mage-power."

His mind was still working, out of long habit and training with Ulrich—

Oh, Ulrich—I've lost you. We've all lost you—

"The Empire would believe that this is an ordinary alliance, especially with Karse and Valdemar," he continued; now that his thoughts were set in motion, they wouldn't stop until he followed them to the end. "They can't know that Solaris is working under a divine decree; they'd assume that the death of her envoy would mean she would go back to the old assumption of Valdemar-as-the-Land-of-Demons. That would be why there was a device in here for me, even though I'm not a mage—so that there would be no witness to the contrary."

Kerowyn's lips thinned, and she nodded once. "That makes the best sense of all. Good work, Karal. I'm going to take these to Elspeth and Darkwind, and maybe they can take them apart. *You* are being moved to another room, as quickly as I can get *my* people in here to move your things."

He saw immediately why she had said that. "There's an Imperial agent in the Palace, isn't there," he stated flatly. "Someone who had access to all the rooms, and the *ability* to hide those things in the plaster."

"And I bloody well don't know who it is," she agreed. "So I want you and the rest of the foreigners out of here and into the Herald's Wing. Or better yet, I'll move *you* in with An'desha and Firesong, if they'll take you. Firesong got at least five of those things all by himself."

He looked up at her as she stood, and he felt his lower lip starting to quiver, his eyes starting to burn. "What about—" he began.

"Ulrich's in the best of hands, Karal," Talia said gently. "It's too soon to tell—but he *is* an old man, and we both know that he's been overworking, putting himself under a lot of strain."

He nodded and looked quickly down at his hands, before Kerowyn could see the tears starting to form in his eyes again.

Kerowyn left, but Talia stayed, so that when he began to sob again, this time quietly, she was there to hold him.

Talia stayed with him for the rest of the day; later in the afternoon Kerowyn returned with her hand-picked crew of tough-looking mercenaries from her own Company, packed up everything in the suite, and carried it out—off to Firesong and An'desha's *ekele*, she said. Karal stifled his tears when they came in; he just didn't want to cry in front of these hardened soldiers. They'd think he was being childish; surely they'd look on him with contempt.

But one of the toughest-looking turned in the middle of the packing when Karal saw them carrying out some things of Ulrich's and choked back a sob. The man put down the robes he had draped over his arm and dropped down onto his heels in front of Karal's chair.

"Don' be 'shamed t'be a-grievin', boy," the man said, patting his hand awkwardly, his speech slow and so thickly accented that Karal barely understood him. "This kind'o thing don' get any nor easier e'en for the likes o' we. Gie yer tears t' a man who deserves 'em, an' take ye no shame i' the weepin', aye? Sure, an' we won' think th' less o'ye."

He stood up, as soon as Karal nodded numbly, and picked up his burden again. Karal just let the tears flow, then, and ignored all the comings and goings until the sun set, and the now-empty room filled with darkness.

"Do you want to go to the Healers' Collegium to wait, Karal?" Talia asked gently. "Or would you rather wait here?"

There was nothing for him here; the rooms held not even the scent of incense from Ulrich's robes—not that he could smell much after all the raw-nosed sniffling. "I'd like to go to Healers', I think," he said thickly. "If I won't be in the way."

"Of course you won't be," Talia replied warmly. She offered him her hand. "Come on, I'll take you there."

Somewhere he lost track of the walk, or else it was all swallowed up in misery. The next thing he knew, he was sitting down again, in another room, this one full of well-worn, ancient benches. The whole place had a sad air of *waiting* about it, interminable waiting. Talia was walking toward him as he looked up, suddenly aware of his surroundings again; she must have left him here without his noticing.

"There's no change, Karal," she said, and bit her lip. "I won't lie to you; you'd know it if I did. That's not a good sign. He hasn't even regained consciousness."

He nodded; she rested her hand on his shoulder.

"I'll stay with you if you want me to," she offered, and he knew that she meant it.

Just as he knew that she had much more important things to deal with than one boy's pain. Thanks to Florian, he knew what she was now, and how important she was. He knew that eventually he would be touched and grateful that she had given him so *much* of her time today, but right now, there was room for nothing but grief.

"You have to go," he told her. "I—I understand. I'll manage."

She searched his eyes for a moment. "You do understand, don't you?" she asked, wonder coloring her voice. "Thank you for that, Karal. If you can't bear it, send for me."

He nodded, and she walked off quickly, but with a slight limp. He watched her go, then turned his thoughts inward.

He prayed, even though he wasn't quite certain what to pray for. It would be no kindness to Ulrich to force him to live, if living meant he was trapped in a helpless body that held nothing but pain. Those blades were long—long enough to have pierced through the chest and damaged the spine. Perhaps that was why Ulrich had not awakened…

He tried to remember what Ulrich had taught him—that Vkandis was neither some cosmic accountant, who weighed and measured a man before deciding if he lived or died, nor was He a grand torturer, inflicting punishment after punishment upon the living to find their breaking points. *We have free will, all of us, and Vkandis interferes very little in our life in this world,* Ulrich had said. *He does not play with us as a child plays with toy soldiers or dolls, nor does He test us to see what we are made of. He allows us to live our lives and make our own choices, and only after we cross to join Him does He judge us on the basis of what we have and have not done with the life and free will we were granted at birth—and how well we have kept our word in promises made to Him. What we choose to do intersects with what everyone else in our lives chooses to do; sometimes those choices mean joy, sometimes sorrow, often a little of both. That may be why good things sometimes happen to evil people. Most assuredly, with no cause by the Sunlord's hand, bad things sometimes do happen to good people.*

So it was by free will that *whoever* it was had laid those deadly traps, and Ulrich and he had been the ones to encounter them. It was by sheer circumstance that there had been four of the things, one too many for Altra to deal with. In fact, had Altra not *been* there—by the Sunlord's own will—*he* would be dead right now.

But I wish it had been me and not him! he cried to Vkandis. *Oh, Sunlord, I wish it had been me!*

The marks crawled by, tedious and slow as an ancient tortoise, plodding painfully toward midnight, and then toward dawn. People came by at intervals, presumably to see if he was all right, but they did not disturb him, and he did not speak to them.

Finally, though, someone *did* stop, and touch his shoulder.

He looked up, and the sympathy in the Healer's face told him everything he needed to know.

He could not show his sorrow before all the strange faces, sympathetic though they might be, and he could not burden Talia further by asking someone to disturb her rest and bring her to him. Instead, he refused all offers of consolation and stumbled blindly away from the building, shaking with sobs he could not give voice to, throat so choked with grief he could not even swallow.

It was not yet dawn; frost-covered grass crunched underfoot as he wandered out into the waning hours of the night. He had to go somewhere... life *would* go on, and now he was the sole representative of Karse here. Where had Kerowyn said she was moving his things?

The ekele. *An'desha and Firesong*—

That was bearable. Better them than to try to make a place among strangers, Heralds whose names he didn't even know.

Now that he had a destination, he set off through the darkness. Once he was out of sight of the Healers and their unwanted, professional sympathy, he allowed the tears to come again. Blinded as much by his weeping as by the dark, he felt his way along the path to the gate in Companion's Field; got it open, and slipped inside—

And there he stopped; or rather, collapsed against the gate post, shuddering with great, racking sobs that did absolutely nothing to ease the agony of his loss.

:Karal—: the voice in his mind was hesitant, but the sympathy was real. *:Karal, I am not Talia, but I am here for you.:*

Blindly, he turned and buried his face in the white shoulder that lowered to meet his trembling body as the Companion lay down. His tears trickled through the silky white mane that presented itself to him. He clung to Florian's neck and wept and wept until his throat was sore, his eyes were nothing more than slits, and his nose was so swollen and stopped up that he *had* to stop sobbing because he couldn't breathe.

The breathing of the Companion at his side was steady and soothing, and after what could have been a candlemark, the pace of his own breathing matched Florian's.

:Karal, I am with you. This might not be the best time, but there is someone who sorrows as much as you do,: Florian said hesitantly. *:He needs you very badly, and right now he has no one to comfort him.:*

Unlike me… The unspoken implication had not escaped Karal. "Wh-who?" Karal asked dully, wiping his nose.

:Listen,: was Florian's only answer.

Obediently, Karal stifled his sniffling for a moment. As he strained his ears to listen over the sound of the river nearby, he heard what Florian was talking about—a high-pitched wail so much like a baby's cry that he was startled.

A baby? But what would a baby be doing out in the middle of the Field?

The wail came again, so full of heartbreak and pain that Karal had to respond to it; he walked in the general direction of the sound, Florian following behind. A few moments later, he knew what it was—not a baby, but a cat.

"Is that Altra?" he asked, incredulously.

:Yes,: Florian replied. *:He hasn't told you the whole truth, Karal. The Firecats are almost exactly like us—like Companions, except that they have magic to protect themselves, and they can move themselves the way someone who has the Fetching Gift can move an object. They are mortal, they eat—he's been stealing food from the kitchen— and they have no more idea about what is going to happen in the future than you or I do.:*

"That was why he didn't know that the disruption-waves were coming, he only knew *something* was going to happen," Karal replied absently, distracted for the moment from his grief by this revelation.

:Yes. And that was why he didn't know you were going to be attacked until it happened. Nor does he know who your attacker was. He blames himself.: Florian's mental voice was saddened and subdued *:I can understand that only too well. I had thought about urging you to take a break this morning and come out here for a ride on Trenor; you haven't seen him for days. I keep wondering what would have happened if I had* done *that instead of just thinking about it.:*

"What's the point in rasping away at yourself with might-have-beens?" Karal retorted. "All you do is make yourself hurt more—"

:*I know that. You know that. It is Altra who needs to hear that.*: They were practically on top of the wailing now, and Karal made out a white form curled into a ball of misery, wailing disconsolately into the night. Karal's heart and his resolve to stay controlled broke at the same time.

"*Altra*—" he cried, flinging himself down in the grass beside the Firecat. He took the Cat into his arms exactly as Talia had taken him into her comforting embrace, and his tears started again. "Altra, Altra, it wasn't your fault."

:*I had to choose,*: the Cat cried in his mind. :*I had to choose, and I was sent for you, so I had to choose you.*:

"And you almost saved both of us anyway," Karal told him, holding his furred body tightly, as the Firecat shivered with more than physical cold. "You aren't the Sunlord, Altra, you can't know everything or be everywhere at once. *You did your best.* I *know* that."

:*But I couldn't—save—him!*: The heartbreaking wail began again. Altra had no way to shed tears, so Karal did the crying for them both.

Florian stood vigil over them, a solid, comforting presence in the dark, until they were finally too tired to weep anymore.

In the end, Karal picked up the exhausted Firecat—who must have weighed nearly half what he himself did—and carried him to the *ekele*, with Florian walking beside them. Firesong was still awake, but he said nothing when he met them all at the entrance to his home, neither about the lateness of the hour nor Karal's odd burden. He only gestured for Karal to follow and led the way to that peculiar room draped to resemble the interior of a tent.

And this was where Karal talked to Altra until the sun rose, telling him all the things he had tried to tell himself, and in so doing, seeing the truth in those things. That was where they finally slept, spent and exhausted—but neither one alone.

When Karal awoke, he knew by the sun that it was well into the afternoon. He'd slept far later than he had thought he would, and Altra was still curled against him. The Firecat woke as soon as he moved, though, and raised his head to look at him with shadowed blue eyes.

"Altra?" he said, quietly.

:*I will be all right,*: the Firecat replied. :*The pain—it is bearable, now. We have things we must do, you especially, and he would not thank us for neglecting them.*:

Karal rubbed at his eyes; they were sore and gummy, the lashes all stuck together. His nose and cheeks were tender from scrubbing at them. Odd how such little discomforts distracted a person from grief, but not enough to be more than one more burden.

He had awakened with a heaviness of soul that cast a gray shadow over everything. He knew that he ought to be hungry, but he had no appetite whatsoever.

He scratched Altra's ears; the Firecat didn't seem to mind being caressed like an ordinary cat. All of his things were here, piled into baskets at the sides of the fabric-draped room. Was this supposed to look like the inside of a Shin'a'in tent? Probably. So this would be An'desha's room, though he doubted An'desha used it much.

Now he wondered what it was about An'desha that Talia had wanted to talk about. If she hadn't come to their suite, would things have fallen out any differently?

No matter. He should follow his own advice, and not torture himself with might-have-beens. The danger from the disruption-waves hadn't gone, just because Ulrich was—

His eyes stung.

There was still work to do. He should get changed and do it.

"Altra, you ought to stay here and rest." The fur under his hand felt harsh and brittle, and Altra looked in poor shape, as if the events of yesterday had completely depleted him. "I'll be back after I find out what everyone else is doing."

"Everyone else—the mages and the Prince, that is—is—are?— coming here," Firesong said from the doorway. Karal's head snapped up and he started; he hadn't heard anything at all to indicate that Firesong was in the hallway. "With an unknown agent somewhere in the Palace, the others are reluctant to trust that he or she might not be somehow listening. The *ekele* is safe enough; I supervised every bit of the building myself, and before you arrived I checked for more such little gifts as were distributed yesterday."

The Hawkbrother entered the room and sank down on his haunches beside the pallet that Karal and Altra shared. He studied Karal for a very long time without saying a word; Karal didn't say anything either. He was too tired, and too grief-laden to play at verbal fencing with the Healing Adept. If Firesong wanted to know something, then he could damned well ask it.

"I think I understand, now," Firesong said, out of the blue.

"What?" Still less was Karal ready to trade non sequiturs.

"What An'desha sees in you." Firesong continued to sit on his heels, watching Karal measuringly.

Karal traded him back look for look. Firesong was baiting him, and he was not going to rise to it. Maybe the Hawkbrother meant well, trying to distract him from his sorrow, but he'd chosen a bad tactic to use.

"Talia wanted to talk with you and—" Firesong hesitated, then went gamely on. "She had already spoken with me. An'desha is in the midst of a crisis, she thinks; he is afraid of setting his feelings free, and he is afraid of losing control of himself if he keeps examining those 'Ma'ar' memories. Evidently they are the most powerful and the most seductive of all. Falconsbane was mad, purely and simply, but Ma'ar was as close to sane as anyone of his ilk is ever likely to be. He had reasons and rationalizations for everything he did, and I suppose that is what makes his memories so seductive." Firesong shrugged. "An'desha is afraid of much, and I have lost patience with his timidity. Frankly, I do not think he is going to be of much use to us unless he can face what he has inside him without being afraid of it, and I know he will not be of much use— ah—to us, if he keeps shutting off how he feels."

"That's what you told Talia?" Karal asked.

"And now you," Firesong confirmed. "Now, more than ever, we cannot afford to have anyone handicapped, and at the moment An'desha is like a hooded falcon."

"Or a racehorse with hobbles and blinders." Karal nodded. "Let me think about this."

"Fair enough." Firesong stood; today he had chosen to dress all in white, as if to represent the winter that drew nearer with every passing day. "I—I am not always this insensitive. If I had a choice, I would not have mentioned it until you were feeling better. It is a burden you could do without."

"But we don't have the time for sensitivity," Karal acknowledged. "I understand."

"You can bathe in the pools below," the mercurial mage said then, changing the subject completely. "There is food in the kitchen. The others will be here shortly."

And with that, he turned in a swirl of long sleeves and crystal-bead fringe, vanishing as silently as he had arrived.

Food. No, he still didn't want to even think about food. Nor about all the times that Ulrich had teased him about how much he ate—

Wait. This is all wrong. I should *think about things like that.* He should remember as much as he could; there was good advice buried in nearly everything that Ulrich had told him, and now he was going to have to glean as much of it out of his memories as he could.

:He used to offer me cat-mint, you know, as a kind of joke, as if it would affect me as it does a real cat.:

Altra looked up at him from the pallet.

"And what did you do?" Karal asked obediently.

:Asked him to make it into tea, and serve it in a civilized fashion.: Altra sighed. *:It was funny at the time.:*

"It will be funny again," Karal promised warmly. "I'll bring *you* something to eat, if you like."

:So Florian spilled my secret, did he?: Altra actually snorted, and looked annoyed for a heartbeat. *:Ah, well, I couldn't stay mystical and inscrutable forever, I suppose. Please bring me something that isn't breadish or vegetablish.:*

"I'll be glad to, as soon as I have a quick bath." At least Altra still had an appetite. That was something, anyway, a sign that the Firecat was on the way to recovering.

He found that he felt better after a bath and a change of clothing. It did help that there was nothing at all here to remind him of Ulrich. He didn't think he would be able to maintain his own fragile stability if there had been.

He still had no appetite, though; rummaging around in the larder didn't do anything to remove the lump of cold grief from his stomach. He confined himself to taking care of Altra; he found some fish that was so fresh it must have been caught that very morning, and decided that someone in the two-person household had seen Altra for what he really was. And while the Firecat didn't precisely fall on the offering as if he was half-starved, he certainly polished every scrap off during the time it took Karal to change into clean clothing.

I'm the only Karsite representative, now, he thought, as he examined his clothing. *Until Solaris sends someone else—it's me or no one. I'd better look the part.*

He chose one of his formal robes, and carefully arranged his sun-disk pendant over the front placket. He wished there was a mirror.

:You look very impressive,: Altra observed from the bed. *:You've grown since you came here. You're a bit young for an envoy, but as old as some ruling nobles I've seen, even as old as some reigning monarchs. I've even heard of Sons of the Sun no older than you.:*

Karal tugged his tunic straight. "I'll have to do," he replied. "There isn't anyone else for the moment."

"You'll do very well." Once again, Firesong had appeared out of nowhere. He eyed Karal carefully and nodded with satisfaction. "No longer the retiring little secretary. Very good. Let's go down, the others are waiting."

:You'll be fine,: Altra murmured.

Well, he would, if appearance was all that counted. He only hoped he could be so confident of his abilities.

The subject, inevitably, was the attempt to uncover a presumed agent of the Empire.

"I've checked and rechecked the servants under Truth Spell," Elspeth told them all as Firesong and Karal took their places in the circle. Beside her, Darkwind nursed a bandaged shoulder, and the male gryphon had a stitched-up cut in his right wing. "They're all exactly what they seem to be, so it can't be one of the regular servants."

"It could be one of us, you know," Karal put in reluctantly.

Prince Daren grimaced. "That had not escaped me. It could also be any of the other ambassadors and envoys, including those of long standing. Whoever this agent is, it is likeliest that he has been among us for a very long time, and he could be one of a number of foreigners we trust. It is a bit difficult to persuade *them* to be examined under Truth Spell."

"Difficult?" Firesong put on his best sardonic look. "Only if you are not willing to risk an incident."

"Selenay is not," Daren replied flatly. "We have enough of an incident on our hands already, although mage-messages have come from Solaris this morning saying that she is aware of what happened and that it changes nothing."

Only that Ulrich is gone… and I promised to take care of him. Karal tucked his head down so that his grief would not show until he got his face back under control again. *Altra must have gone to her with the news, before* he *fell apart. No wonder he looked so depleted.*

"That leaves—what? Something like a hundred possible suspects?" Kerowyn hazarded. "And a good chance that whoever this is will do something again."

Karal frowned. Perhaps associating with the engineers had put an edge on his reasoning ability, but he was certain he could narrow the field down more than that. "Wait a moment. It can't be that many. It has to be someone who is *high* enough in rank that no one would question seeing him anywhere in the Palace, but low enough in rank—or *apparently* ineffectual enough—that no one would ever notice him. It also has to be someone who would have a reason to be in and out of people's rooms at least once this year. If this is an agent of long standing, then surely the Empire is using him to gather information—so it has to be someone who has a reason to receive and send packages at intervals of more than once a year. He *couldn't* have sent his information by magic-messengers before this year, remember? You had a guard against magic until then." Once again, his own intellect had seduced him into concentrating on something besides grief. "That virtually eliminates all of the Palace servants."

Kerowyn gnawed on her lower lip. "That does eliminate most of my suspects," she admitted. "It could be one of the personal servants of one of our own nobles, though."

"Yes, and it could *be* one of your nobles." Darkwind was quick to point that out. "It would not be the first time that Selenay had had her own intrigue against her."

"The weapon, though—it had a residue of magic that made me think it was targeted to a specific individual," An'desha said shyly. "That would imply that your agent is a mage himself, or more likely, found a way to gain access to something personal from each of his targets to imprint the weapons with their intended victims."

"Then planted them into the walls." Kerowyn looked baffled. "Now you open it up to everyone in the Palace *except* the servants."

Karal pondered his next words long and hard before speaking them. *How expendable am I Realistically, very. And I have Altra, who will try to protect me. I think that I must do this.*

"I can offer a possible trap," he said carefully. "With myself as the bait. Two of those weapons were meant to eliminate me; let me place myself where our agent can come at me. I honestly do not believe he will try to take me again, so soon. I think that he will try to ascertain what Solaris' position is, and whether or not the Alliance is in jeopardy, due—"

He couldn't say it; he choked up. The others gave him time to recover. After a struggle, he got control of his voice again. "If disrupting the Alliance was this agent's primary goal, he will want to talk to me almost as soon as I appear in the halls of the Palace. Let me go walk there, and see who comes to offer condolences and fish for information."

"And what if this agent decides to ensure the Karsite defection by eliminating you?" Kerowyn asked quietly.

He twitched his mouth in what was supposed to be a smile. "Have you not been training me in enough self-defense to keep myself alive until help can come? Magicked weaponry is difficult to come by; if this person wishes to strike again so soon, I think he will have to do so through conventional means. That requires skill, opportunity, and time. I will assume he has the first, I will give him the second, and I will deny him the third." There. Hopefully, he sounded like the self-confident Karsite envoy. He certainly didn't *feel* like the self-confident Karsite envoy.

Kerowyn continued to gnaw her lower lip. "I like it, and I don't like it at all," she said finally. "I don't like it, because it puts you in so much danger, Karal. I like it, because it has a good chance of winkling out our agent. I wouldn't ask it of you, but if you are volunteering—"

:As am I,: Altra said, for Karal's benefit alone. *:You were right in thinking that I can roam the corridors with you and protect you. I shall do better this time.:*

"I am," Karal said firmly. "What is more, I am ready now."

"Well I'm not—or rather, my men aren't." Kerowyn reached over and patted his knee. "Give *me* a chance to get set up, say, after dinner. Don't come to formal dinner; that will make it look as if there might be trouble with the Alliance. Then come on over and roam to your heart's content. Among other things, you can reassure some of our own people that things haven't deteriorated to the point of war quite yet."

Karal sat back and let them discuss the weapon itself; they were mages, he was not, and what they had found did not mean a great deal to him. At least he could *do* something now, though. That helped, a little.

Only a little, but it was a beginning.

In the evenings, after formal dinner, Ulrich had often strolled in the gardens with the rest of the courtiers. During inclement weather, the same leisurely strolls took place in the hallways and the small informal audience chambers. The weather was barely warm enough for both to be in use, so Karal resigned himself to a long evening with a great deal of walking.

Most of the Valdemarans did not seem to know quite how to treat him; he *had* been the insignificant secretary, and now he was the only Karsite representative at Court, and he had dressed to reflect that rise in position, though the velvets were too warm for the indoor venue and not warm enough for the gardens. Most of the courtiers eventually opted for brief and uncomfortable expressions of regret and condolence, approaching him, making graceful but painful short speeches, and scuttling away again.

For the first few marks, no one even mentioned the fate of the Alliance, and as Karal alternately sweated and shivered, he began to wonder if this had been a fool's errand.

The first person who did was the Seneschal, a situation so absurd that Karal almost burst into hysterical laughter. The only ones that were privy to Karal's little ruse were the mages; Prince Daren had decided that it would be better not to let any of the Councillors in on the subterfuge, on the grounds that they were very bad actors, and would probably give the whole thing away. The Seneschal was pathetically transparent in his attempts to divine Solaris' position from Karal's attitude, and to keep up the illusion that Solaris was still undecided, Karal was forced to be distinctly cool to the poor man. It took all of Karal's ability to keep from revealing the whole trick with his reaction to the poor fellow's disappointment in learning nothing.

He eliminated the next few "fishers" on grounds that they were not likely to have a pretext that would let them move in and out of private rooms at will. Then came another long, dry spell; his sober face and black robes seemed to put people off, making their expressions of sympathy hurried and nervous.

He resigned himself to a fruitless, boring evening.

Ah, well, at least I tried—

"Master Secretary?" said a squeaky voice at his elbow.

He turned, and had to think long and hard before he could identify the fellow who had greeted him. He was utterly nondescript to begin with, and had the demeanor and apparently the personality of a mole—

"—ah, my condolences, Master Secretary," the mole said, squinting at him and twisting his hands nervously together. "You probably wouldn't recall me, I suppose, I'm not important or wealthy or—"

The spot of green paint caught in the cuticle of one finger gave him away.

"Of course I recall you, sir," Karal replied, in a properly subdued manner. "Master Celandine, is it not? The painter?"

"The artist, yes, and I was *terribly* grieved to hear about Master Ulrich, *terribly*," the mole replied, his fingers knotting together until his hands resembled a nest of worms. "I hope—I pray—that your gracious mistress will not take this incident badly—oh, dear, no—that would be dreadful, dreadful—"

"I suppose from the Valdemaran point of view it would," Karal replied, with careful neutrality. There was something about this man...

something nagging at the back of his mind.

"Oh, I'm not from Valdemar, but it would be *personally* dreadful for me all the same," Celandine replied. "My pigments—so difficult to obtain, you understand, and before the Alliance so terribly expensive—"

A tiny thread of warning slipped down Karal's back, and his hands went cold. *He's always sending people off after pigments and colors, I remember him saying that when Ulrich sat for a portrait. He must have at least one package coming in every fortnight or so!* Could it be? Oh, surely not! This fellow was *so* ineffectual he couldn't possibly be their quarry! Everyone at court made fun of him and his pretensions of genius!

Then again, came the nagging response, *wouldn't that make him ideal for the part? How better to observe people than when they think you're insignificant?*

"—I wondered if your mistress would still be interested in that official portrait, or if she would prefer to wait until the next envoy was assigned or even have *your* little sketch turned into a portrait instead?"

Bright Sunlord! Didn't An'desha say the mage must have had something personal *in order to set the weapons, or some kind of image? This man paints portraits, he sketches people in Court circles all day long and no one ever thinks anything about it!*

:Karal,: said Altra carefully, *:I think you may have something in this one. Can you get him to take you to his studio? I may be able to find real evidence, rooting around like a cat.:*

"Perhaps," he said, assuming more dignity. "I have been given to understand that if the Alliance continues, the latter would be the most likely option."

The mole's tiny black eyes lit up, but before he could say anything else, Karal continued.

"That portrait of my—my Master, though, the one you mentioned," he continued, and it did not take any acting at all for his eyes to mist over. "I would like to have it for myself. Is it anywhere near completed?"

"Oh, yes! Yes, it is!" The mole was positively babbling. "Would you care to come to my studio to view it?"

:Excellent,: Altra applauded. *:I'll warn Florian and he can warn Kerowyn through Sayvil. Go with him now, before he changes his mind!:*

"I would very much like to see it," Karal said in complete and sincere honesty as he wiped his eyes. "Please."

The mole eagerly led the way down the hall toward the quarters of those who were not *quite* highborn, but were not servants, either. Altra padded along behind, tail in the air, pretending to be a housecat. The mole either didn't notice him or didn't care.

The mole's studio lay at the farthest end of the corridor, and Karal had a moment of trepidation when he realized that there was no way that Kerowyn could have them followed down here without it being painfully obvious. And if the mole left the studio door open, he would see if Kerowyn sent anyone down after them. Celandine might look like he was short-sighted, but as Karal already knew, there was nothing wrong with his eyes.

:*I'll shut the door behind me,*: Altra told him. :*Just enough that he won't be able to see down the corridor. With luck, he'll be so excited that he won't notice.*:

That was exactly how the next few moments played out; Celandine ushered Karal into the cluttered, crowded studio with much bowing and scraping, and Altra slipped in behind them, nudging the door closed without Celandine noticing. The place was a mess, with easels and half-finished sculptures on pedestals everywhere, supplies piled on top of furniture and spilling down onto the floor, blank canvases stretched onto frames and leaning against the walls, and dust all over everything. Karal doubted that the servants ever even tried to clean in here.

In fact, the mole was only interested in getting Karal to the area where several canvases stood on easels, covered with drop cloths. He positioned Karal in front of one of them, and made a great deal of fuss about getting the lighting absolutely right, before whisking off the cloth.

Karal did not have to simulate his reaction. Whatever else the mole was, he was also a genuine and superb artist. He had captured Ulrich in one of his rare moments of relaxation; good will and humor glowed in his face, and a half-smile played on his lips.

Karal's eyes filled, and two tears ran down his cheeks unheeded. He took an involuntary step forward; the painting only improved on closer inspection.

Celandine smiled, baring tiny teeth in an expression of greed and satisfaction at Karal's reaction.

"My—good Master Celandine, you are—" Another tear escaped down Karal's cheek, and he shook his head as he wiped it away. "There are no words. There are just no words. I *must* have this painting."

Celandine fussed over the canvas, preening, as he dusted the easel unnecessarily. "Well, I must admit, I was rather pleased with the way the robes came out. You folk who affect black—oh, forgive me, but it is *so* difficult for an artist to render properly! This particular shade of *sebeline* along the crease for instance, that is my own little secret for simulating the sheen of good black velvet—"

He nattered on, but Karal had frozen in place at the foreign-sounding word for the streak of blue-white pigment that ran along the top of one of the sleeves in the portrait. That was *not* a Valdemaran term!

:No. It's not.: The murmur of quiet noise in the background ceased, as Altra froze as well. *:Stall him, Karal! I need time to have Mindspeech with an expert!:*

"How did you make the eyes look so—so—" Karal choked out.

That was enough to set Celandine off again, this time on a much longer dissertation, about reflection and transparent colors and glazes. Meanwhile, Karal waited, the back of his neck prickling, as he tried to recall if Celandine had ever been in their quarters.

Then, as Karal leaned forward to look at the painting more closely, and noted the distinctive whorls of the background, he remembered. *He was. Not only to make the preliminary sketches, either! I found him there poking at those decorations one afternoon, complaining that every time some plaster decoration cracked, the Seneschal ordered him to repair it on the grounds that he was an artist!*

Celandine was a sculptor, who could probably reproduce anything he chose at will. He had access to plaster. He had put himself in a position to plant whatever he cared to by allowing the Seneschal to order him to fix broken decorations!

And all he had to do to be called into a particular room was to crack the original himself—before, during, or after the portrait-sitting.

:Karal!: Altra called, panic in his mind-voice for the first time since Karal had met him. *:That word, it's Imperial tongue—what's more, the pigment is only mined somewhere east of Hardorn!:*

Celandine had worked his way in behind Karal as he spoke of colors and pointed this or that effect out. The prickling on the back of Karal's neck had become an agony. He tried to watch the mole out of the corner of his eye without being obtrusive.

:KARAL!:

Karal did not need Altra's mental scream to warn him; he had sensed Celandine's sudden movement half a breath before. Karal ducked under the blow and whirled at the same time, then dodged past the easel and the painting it held, winding up facing the artist.

No—the *agent*.

The artist was gone; in his place was someone far more dangerous, and nothing at all like a mole, more like a cornered rat. Celandine's beady black eyes glittered dangerously; he had a mallet in one hand,

and a sharp palette knife in the other. The edge of the knife had a nasty, sickly green tinge, and Karal had the sinking feeling that it wasn't paint. "He'll kill me, you know," the artist said, his voice deceptively calm.

"Who?" Karal asked urgently. "What's wrong? Why would anyone kill you?" *Stall for more time. Help has to be on the way.*

"The Grand Duke. Tremane. I'm not *his* man. I'm expendable. I didn't finish the job. The little birds flew, and only pecked out the heart of one of the targets." The glitter in Celandine's eyes wasn't danger, it was madness. He feinted with the knife, and Karal winced backward. "He'll kill me; he has my likeness and my hair, he can do it. Unless I finish the job, right now."

He feinted again, and Karal flinched. He obviously knew what he was doing; he had all the moves of an experienced knife fighter. Karal's best bet was to keep him talking.

But Celandine rushed him; he ducked and sidestepped and barely managed to avoid the knife *and* the mallet blow aimed at his head.

"If I get you, I can leave you in the garden with one of Elspeth's knives in your heart," he continued. "We made copies, you know, just in case. You know the one I'm talking about."

"Actually, no I don't—"

Altra's mind-voice was frantic. *:Karal! I can't get him! You're in my line of attack!:*

Karal stepped to the side at once, but Celandine lashed out viciously with the mallet, and he stepped back again hastily.

"The one Elspeth left in the heart of *our* ambassador, of course!" Celandine said, as if he was some kind of dolt. Then he blinked. "You're playing for time!" he accused, and slashed at Karal with the knife.

:Karal! There's poison on that knife! Stay out of reach—use something as a shield.:

A shield—something Celandine wouldn't want damaged!

He grabbed one of the canvases at random as Celandine drove him back, and held it in front of him as he backed toward the windows. Celandine's mouth twisted in a snarl.

"Put that thing down, you idiot!" he screamed. "How *dare* you put your hands on—"

He never finished the sentence.

There was a crash of glass as all the windows shattered at once. Karal ducked instinctively, crouching and making himself as small a target as possible as shards of razored glass went everywhere. Celandine came up out of his fighting crouch in shock and glanced around wildly—

Then a dozen crossbow bolts hit him at once from the direction of every window; his body jerked wildly in a grotesque parody of a dance—

—then he dropped to the floor, eyes already glazing in death.

Karal dropped to the floor as well, as his knees gave out.

"Karal!" Kerowyn leapt through one of the broken windows and crashed through the easels to get to him, knocking paintings in all directions. "Karal, are you all right? Did he scratch you? Sayvil said there was poison on his blade. Are you—"

"I'm all right, I'm fine," he replied weakly. "Oh, dear Sunlord, I have *never* been as grateful for any lessons in my life as I am for yours." He hugged the painting to his chest, and took deep, steadying breaths. "He was going to kill me and leave me with a copy of one of Elspeth's knives in me. He said they got it when she left one in *their* ambassador."

He was babbling and he knew it, but he couldn't stop himself. Altra finally wormed his way through the tangle of art supplies and tumbled easels, and began winding around and around him frantically, purring loud enough to make both of them vibrate.

"Elspeth's knife?" A large man climbed over the windowsill with a crossbow in each hand; after a moment, Karal's mind put a name to him. *Skif.* He wasn't a mage, but he often sat on the Council with Kerowyn.

"Elspeth's knife?" the man repeated, scowling ferociously. "Demons take it, I *knew* that thing was going to come back to haunt us!"

Karal started to shiver, when he happened to look down to see just what painting he had snatched up as an impromptu shield.

Ulrich's warm, amused eyes gazed up at him; he froze for a moment, then burst into tears.

1 6

: *A*re you sure that you're ready for this?: Altra asked anxiously. :This is going to be very dangerous for you.:

Karal shrugged, and shook his head.

"Actually, I'm quite sure that I'm not at all ready for a confrontation like this," he admitted to the Firecat. "But we just don't have a choice. An'desha needs help; besides being afraid of allowing his emotions free play, he's locking down his anger because he is certain that if he lets it go, he'll *use* his powers to hurt whoever he's angry at. The problem with doing that is that it just makes things harder for him the next time he's angry." Karal rubbed the side of his nose thoughtfully. "He has to discover that 'control' doesn't always mean 'containment.' He's got to see that the simplest solution isn't always the right one."

The Firecat washed a paw thoughtfully. *:I saw how he was when they told him how near you'd come to being killed—both times,:* he said. *:Terrible anger—then nothing. He just turned it all inside himself.:*

"Terrible anger is dangerous when you are—or were—an Adept who specialized in destruction," Karal said grimly. "Someone has to prove to him that he can lose his temper and his self-control, vent his emotions, and not hurt anyone in the process. *Then* he'll feel safe enough to go after those very emotional memories of Adept Ma'ar and learn all the destructive magic that Ma'ar knew. Firesong thinks the Ma'ar memories are important; I *know* that they have to be the key to this situation. I can't tell you why I'm so certain, I only know that I am."

Hurry, hurry, hurry. That sense of terrible urgency made *him* as tight as a strung crossbow. The sense that time was running out on them was stronger than ever.

:But are you the best person to do that?: Altra asked, with complete logic. *:Shouldn't it be someone who's also a mage, who can defend against his attack if he should lash out? He* can *turn you into a cinder, and you haven't got any kind of protection.:* The Firecat looked up at him with large, bottomless blue eyes, full of candor and concern. *:I'm not completely certain even I could protect you against his full power, in a killing rage.:*

Karal sighed. "That's why it has to be me. It has to be someone so completely vulnerable that An'desha *knows* that person is defenseless. It has to be someone who knows An'desha well enough to make him rage with anger in a very short time. Firesong won't do; Firesong could hold his own against any attack An'desha could launch, and what would that prove? And it has to be done, because if it isn't, I think he'll be incinerated. Talia and Firesong both agree with me. If he keeps turning his anger inward, one day his power will turn inward as well, and it will consume him."

:And besides,: Altra added, *:he's your friend.:*

"That's right," Karal agreed. "He's my friend. Friends help friends. We're both strangers in this Valdemar place. Sometimes friends are all we have."

He didn't have to mention all the nights this past week that An'desha had held him while he wept out his grief for Ulrich; Altra knew all about that, since he'd been there. He didn't say a word about the thousand little kindnesses that An'desha had shown him since—and the way he had gently deflected Firesong's resulting jealousy. None of that really mattered anyway. What did matter was that An'desha needed help, and it was help that Karal could give him.

In the larger picture, if he *didn't* help An'desha, they might never have their "breakwaters" to use against the disruption-waves. The latest one had caught at least one large animal that Karal knew of, turning it into a monstrous killer that had savaged an entire herd of cattle before twenty men shot it full of arrows. Word had trickled back that the Tayledras Vales were suffering damage to their special shielding. According to Master Levy, the engineers and mathematicians had constructed a pattern of increasing power to these waves. Natoli had explained it to him, and he had felt the jaws of time closing on them. *Something* had to be done, and done quickly.

It had taken Karal the better part of the afternoon to work up the courage to face this particular trial. It had been relatively easy to steel his nerve to face a possible enemy, but to have to face a friend who just might kill him—that took a different kind of courage altogether.

Now, though, he was as prepared as he was ever likely to be. An'desha was hiding down in the tent in the garden, already shaken by a preparatory confrontation with Firesong, carefully planned and choreographed by Karal and the Healing Adept beforehand. The effects of the last disruption-wave were over, which meant there would be no interference from that quarter. Now, if ever, was the perfect moment.

As always, his eyes met the painted eyes of Ulrich in the portrait he'd hung on his wall. *I hope I'm doing the right thing, Master,* he told the painting silently. *I'm not as sure of this as Altra and Firesong think I am.*

He really didn't expect an answer from the portrait, and he wasn't surprised when he didn't get one. He tugged his tunic into place, and headed down the stairs into the garden.

An'desha had been getting alarmingly predictable in his reactions to emotional confrontation; now that Karal had the fabric-draped room— for Kerowyn did not want to risk another assassination attempt and ordered him to stay in the *ekele* for the duration, or at least until Solaris sent official word of what she intended to do—An'desha had no other refuge than the small tent in the garden. Whenever he was upset or had an argument with anyone, that was where he went.

He had been spending a lot of time in that tent, and the number of times in a given day he was retreating to it was increasing.

Karal nodded to Firesong, who was lurking just out of An'desha's hearing. Firesong's jaw tightened, and he nodded curtly back. Firesong didn't like this any better than Altra did; he liked *his* part in it even less. *He* was going to have to create a very tough mirror-shield around that tent to hold in whatever An'desha let loose.

If there're going to be any victims here, let's keep it to one. The expendable one. I am expendable. I am stupid. Here I go.

He pulled the tent flap aside and dropped down on his heels next to An'desha, who was sprawled on his back with his arm over his face, cushioned by a pallet identical to the one that Karal now used for a bed upstairs.

"Down here again?" Karal said incredulously. "What's wrong this time?"

An'desha didn't even remove his arm. "Firesong. He does *not* understand. He wishes me to sift through the memory fragments of Ma'ar again." An'desha's hands clenched into fists, and his mouth tightened, sulkily. "He will not understand. Those memories are very old, and to read them I must grow *very* close to them."

"So?" Karal let scorn creep into his voice. "I think that Firesong is right, An'desha. You aren't thinking of anyone or anything but your own self. You are, quite frankly, becoming a spoiled brat. We have been coddling you, making allowances for you, and now you have no more spine than a mushroom!"

An'desha sat up, suddenly, his mouth agape with shock, staring at Karal with a dumbfounded expression. "Wh-what?" he stammered.

"You are *spineless*, An'desha!" Karal accused. "You know yourself that what we need lies in *your* mind, and you are too frightened to even *try* to look for it!" He let his own expression grow pitiful and petulant, and pitched his voice into a whine. "*'Those memories are dangerous, they might hurt me, I am afraid of them—'* as if we all aren't afraid of much worse than a few paltry *memories*!"

"But I—" An'desha began, his eyes glazed with shock at the way Karal had abruptly turned on him.

"But *you*. Always *you*. What about the rest of us?" Karal asked. "What about all that we have been doing? What about the *losses*, the harm that we have suffered, while you have been curled here in your little cocoon of self-pity, feeling, oh, so put-upon? What about the Tayledras, who are trying to piece their Vales together again, the Shin'a'in who fear their herds of precious horses will turn into herds of monsters—what about the Shin'a'in ambassador who *died* a few days ago? What about them? What about Karse? And Rethwellan?"

An'desha was on his feet now as he tried to push past Karal. Karal shoved him back rudely, not letting him leave the tent, and evidently it never occurred to him that he could just turn and slash his way through the walls to get away. An'desha backed up a pace, and Karal shoved him again, getting right up close and shouting into his face.

"You are a spineless, lazy, selfish *coward*, An'desha," he spat. "You've been playing the poor little wounded bird for too long! I have had quite enough of this, and so has everyone else! It is about time *you* started doing something to help, instead of whining about how *afraid* you are! We're *all* afraid, or hadn't you noticed? *I* was afraid, when Celandine nearly killed me, but you didn't see *me* whining about it, did you? You don't hear Firesong whining about how exhausted he is, even though he is working on shields until he is gray in the face!"

An'desha's face had flushed to a full, rich crimson.

But he wasn't angry enough yet, and Karal kept right at him.

"You don't hear Darkwind whining about how put-upon he is, even though his shoulder still isn't healed and he is working night and day with the other mages! It's time to stop whining and start doing something, An'desha—or go find someone else to whine at, because *we* are all tired of *you!*"

An'desha's face was contorted out of all recognition, but Karal continued the verbal abuse, continuing to attack him for being cowardly, selfish, and spoiled.

An'desha's hands were clenched at his sides, and he stood as rigidly as a tent pole—

—and there were colors swirling around those clenched fists; brilliant scarlets and explosive yellows, mage energies that, if they were visible to *him*, were probably quite potent enough to flatten an entire building.

He'd seen Ulrich strike down something by magic once, and the powers gathering around An'desha's hands right now were twice, perhaps three times as bright.

He wanted to run. Every nerve in his body screamed at him to turn and flee. Every hair on his head felt as if it was standing straight on end from the power in this little space.

But instead of fleeing, he did the hardest thing he'd ever done in his life; harder than facing Celandine, harder than coming to this strange land in the first place.

He stepped back a pace, spread his hands, and *sneered.*

"Well?" he taunted. "I'm right, aren't I? I'm right, and you're too spineless even to admit it!"

And he waited for An'desha to strike, still holding that merciless sneer on his face.

The air *hummed* with power; he'd read of such things, but he'd never experienced it. Now every hair on his head *did* stand straight on end—

And An'desha's control finally exploded.

"Damn you!" An'desha screamed. *"Damn you!"*

There was a flash of orange and white, and the energy dissipated, draining away into the ground so quickly that in one breath it was completely gone.

An'desha collapsed down onto his pallet, folding up as if he was completely exhausted, his face pale and pained. "Damn you," he repeated dully, as Karal dropped down to his side in concern and a fear that he'd managed somehow to make An'desha burn himself out. "Damn you, Priest, you're right."

He looked up, as Karal tentatively touched his shoulder, eyes bleak. "You've been coddling me, and I've been unforgivably selfish."

Karal grinned, which obviously astonished him, for An'desha gaped at him. "I'm right twice," he pointed out. "I *told* you that you were underestimating yourself, believing that because you have the memories of a Falconsbane or a Ma'ar, you also have their ways. You thought that if you 'lost control' of an emotion, you'd lose control of everything. Well. You lost control of your temper, didn't you? You were afraid to learn everything that lay in your old memories, because you were afraid that if you got too angry with someone, you'd use it. You just *got* angry, and there you are, after doing nothing more than curse me—and here *I* am, unsinged, unflattened. Falconsbane would have sent me through a wall, or incinerated me. *You* are sitting there, back in control again, and your own man. Right?"

An'desha stared at him. "You mean—all that was just to prove to me that—" He reddened again. "Why, I should—I—"

Karal raised an eyebrow at him. "And?" he said impudently. "Why don't you, *Adept!*"

"Because *you* aren't worth the effort it would take to blow you through the wall, *Priest,*" An'desha retorted, a ghost of a smile lurking around his eyes. "And because it's not worth taking on your vengeful god as an enemy just so I can get some satisfaction! Damn you! Why do you have to be so *right!*"

"It's not my fault!" Karal protested. "I can't help it!"

"Pah!" The young mage mock-hit his shoulder. "You revel in it, and you damn well know you do! One of these days you'll be wrong, and I'll be there to gloat!" The ghost of a smile had become a grin. "Just wait and see!"

"I'll be looking forward to it," Karal replied, and he meant every word. A moment later, Firesong looked in on them both, with a small but loving smile on his handsome face.

After all that, though, he felt an obligation to be there along with Firesong when An'desha worked up his own courage and took the plunge into those old, dangerous memories. It became something of a vigil for the two of them; An'desha lay in a self-imposed trance, looking much like a figure on a tomb, while the two of them watched, waited, and wondered if they *might* have been wrong in urging him to this. Firesong hadn't expected it to take more than a mark or two, but the afternoon crawled by, then most of the evening, and still the trance showed no signs of ending.

"Is this getting dangerous?" Karal asked in a whisper, as Firesong soberly lit mage-lights and returned to his seat beside An'desha's pallet.

"No—or not yet, anyway," the Adept replied, although he sounded uncertain to Karal. "I have been in trances longer; for two or three days, even."

But those were not trances in which you pursued the memories of power-hungry sadists, Karal added, but only to himself. Still, nothing had gone overtly wrong yet. There was no point in conjuring trouble.

He wished that Altra was here, though. The Firecat had waited just long enough to be sure that he had survived An'desha's anger, then had vanished without an explanation. He could have used Altra's view on this; if Solaris' behavior was anything to go by, a former Son of the Sun should be much more familiar with trances and their effects than he was.

A hint of movement riveted his attention back on An'desha. Had his eyelids moved? If the lights had been candles, he would have put it down to the flickering shadows, but mage-lights were as steady as sunlight. Yes! There it was again, the barest flutter of eyelids as the sleeper slowly, gently awakened.

A moment later, and An'desha opened his eyes and blinked in

temporary confusion; Firesong poured the tea that had been steeping all this while, and helped him to sit up, then offered him the cup. An'desha took it, his hands shaking only slightly, and drank it down in a single swallow.

"How late is it?" he asked, as he gave the cup back to Karal, who poured more tea for him.

"Evening. Not quite midnight," Firesong told him.

An'desha nodded. Karal watched him covertly, and was relieved to see nothing in his expression or manner that was not entirely in keeping with the An'desha that he knew. "I discovered that we have been laboring under a misconception," he said, finally. "Before Ma'ar died, there *was* a time when he had to deal with the kind of situation we have now, although the initial destruction was of a single Gate and the spells of the area around it, and nowhere near so cataclysmic as what came later."

Firesong nodded with excitement in his eyes, and Karal leaned forward. "So what did he do?"

An'desha sipped his tea before replying. "It isn't so much what *he* did, as what his enemy did," he said. "He wasn't concerned with the effect of the waves outside his domain, so *he* simply built the sort of shield that I *think* we've been assuming we'd need all along." An'desha shook his head. "That would be a dreadful mistake," he continued. "A shield wall alone would simply reflect the waves again, and the reflected waves have the potential for causing more harm than the original waves!"

Karal sat back for a moment, and pictured the physical model that the engineers had constructed, a large basin filled with water, the bottom covered with a contour map of Valdemar and most of the surrounding area. He thought about the experiments that Master Levy had been making, dropping large stones into the basin over "Evendim" and "Dhorisha Plains" and watching the wave-patterns, seeing how those patterns interacted.

And when the waves reached the edge of the basin, the experiment was over, because they reflected from the edge and made new and different patterns that had nothing to do with the ones he was studying.

"I see it," he replied, "but—"

"But it was what Ma'ar's enemy did that was interesting—and more importantly, appropriate," An'desha interrupted. "Instead of making a flat shieldwall he literally created a breakwater, exactly what Master Norten has been talking about; something that not only stops the waves, but absorbs their force. Ma'ar studied it and knew how to recreate it, but he considered it a waste of his time and resources." He paused. "Because *he* knew how to recreate this, so do I. What's more, I also know how to recreate his 'shieldwall.' If we combined both—we can absorb the waves coming at us, *and* we can reflect the rest back at the Empire!"

Firesong sucked in his breath, and Karal sat back on his heels.

"I don't know if we ought to do that," Karal said at last, troubled by the implications. "Does the Empire deserve that?"

Firesong shot him an incredulous look. "You say that after what they've done to you?" he exclaimed.

But Karal shook his head. *"They* didn't do anything. There are two, perhaps three people who are responsible; Celandine, who got what he deserved, this Grand Duke Tremane, whoever he is, and possibly the Emperor. *They,* the whole of the Empire, is very large, and composed mostly of people who aren't even aware of the existence of Karse." He sighed. "Firesong, don't make the mistake that we of Karse did for so long with Valdemar. Don't make the Empire into a vast conspiracy of faceless enemies who are all personally responsible for what the leaders do and do not do. There are thousands of perfectly innocent people in the Empire, who do not deserve to have their chickens turns into child-eating monsters just because a few ruthless people caused us harm."

Firesong shrugged, but Karal could tell by the troubled look in his eyes that he *had* listened to what Karal had said.

"And don't make another mistake," he continued. "Don't assume that because a leader ordered something be done, that he had any idea what the consequences were going to be. Unless you have someone like a Herald or Solaris, who has a—" he grinned wanly, for he sensed Altra padding in the door just at that moment, "—a rather insistent and altogether meddling four-legged conscience always at his side, leaders are just people, and they frequently forget to think before they act."

:Indeed,: Altra said sardonically. *:A very nice speech. Meddling, am I?:*

He only reached out and scratched Altra's ears, a caress that the Firecat "submitted to" quite readily.

"That's all very well, but we still need to do something about the next wave coming in, don't we?" An'desha replied pragmatically. "Once I can think properly again, we need to get all the mages together. I can explain this once, and get the questions over with."

"Should I bring over Master Levy and Master Norten as well?" Karal asked, assuming that it would be his task to find everyone and notify them that their presence was needed.

An'desha considered that for a moment. "I believe so," he said finally. "They can find the key points where we can place our defenses to do the most good; I think their formulas will be useful there."

Karal was struck, suddenly, by the fact that An'desha sounded different somehow; it was nothing very obvious, and he wasn't saying things that he wouldn't have said before, but it was the way he said them that had changed.

He's—by the Sunlord, he sounds older, *that's what it is! He doesn't sound like a half-child anymore! He sounds—yes, and he acts—his true age!* Karal didn't say anything, but the change delighted him; so far as he was concerned, this was *all* to the good.

:One wonders what Firesong is going to make of an independent An'desha,: Altra remarked, as if to himself. The same thought had occurred to Karal, just as Altra made the comment.

Well, there was nothing to be done about it. Firesong was just going to have to cope. Whether the Adept liked it or not, Karal was certain that this change in An'desha was not going to be temporary. Firesong should be allowed a little time to recognize it and deal with it in private.

:Or not,: said Altra. Karal aimed a sharp thought-jab at the Firecat; once in a while it *would* be nice to have a private thought or two!

"I'll go tell the others that we'll have a meeting in the morning," he said, getting to his feet. "And I'll be back only when I find them all. Don't bother to wait for me."

He trotted off down the hall and down the stairs without giving either of them a chance to reply.

But was it his imagination, or did he actually hear An'desha say "We won't," and chuckle?

By the time the morning was half over, the Master Craftsmen had narrowed down the "necessary" key points for the new shields from several dozen to the absolute minimum. There would be three major, essential points of blockage, and several minor points. The minor points could all be handled by sets of Master Mages, and all of them were within a few days' ride of Valdemar.

"We have enough mages here, between Herald-Mages and the envoys, that we can post people to each of those minor points," Elspeth said, pursing her lips over her list of available personnel. "This shouldn't be a problem."

"But here, here, and here—" An'desha pointed on the map to the three major points—north, in the heart of the Forest of Sorrows—south, at the border of Karse—and east, at the place where the borders of Iftel, Hardorn, and Valdemar all met. "These are problems. The breakwaters are unstable in their first stage; they actually require the energy from a wave to stabilize them and make them self-supporting. You will *have* to have either two Adepts or one Adept and two Masters to create them, join them to the two others, and hold them until the wave comes." He studied the map, and put his finger on the third point. "This one will be the easiest, but the most vulnerable; it's like the keystone of an arch. It will need less power, and more craft. And the mages will *have* to be at the site in order to create the breakwater and join it into a whole."

Elspeth grimaced. "We only have four Adepts," she pointed out gently. "And we only have a few days to get them in place, before the next wave comes."

An'desha took a long, deep breath. "You have two Adepts, one Healing Adept—and me."

Firesong turned to stare at him, and it was as clear to Karal as the color of his eyes that he had *no* idea what An'desha meant.

"You have a Sorcerer-Adept," An'desha elaborated. "A creator. The kind of mage who actually *made* living beings. All of Ma'ar's knowledge is mine, now. I know how to build these breakwaters because in a sense, I've done it before. I can work with two Masters; you don't have to pair me with Firesong."

Firesong paled but said nothing.

Elspeth's mouth formed a silent "oh," but she wisely bent her head over her list. "Right, then—let's think about *how* we get the Adepts in place." She bit at the end of her quill, and looked at the map. "For obvious reasons, at least to some of you," she said, finally, "I think that Firesong and I should go north. We can Gate there—"

"We'll probably have help," Firesong muttered. Elspeth's mouth quirked, although Karal had no idea what he meant; evidently this was a private joke.

"Hydona and I arrre Massssterrrsss," Treyvan said. "Darrrkwind can Gate parrrt of the way, then we can carrry Darrrkwind in the basssket. We have done ssso beforrre." He cocked his head at Hydona. "Ssso, sssouth orrr eassst forrr usss?"

:You *will go south.*:

Everyone's head came up at the imperious mind-voice. Altra jumped into the center of the group, landing right on top of the location of the eastward key-point. The Firecat posed like a statue, holding a folded and sealed parchment packet in his mouth; with the exception of An'desha and Firesong, the rest of the group gasped, and Karal guessed that they were finally seeing the Firecat as he *really* was, and not in the guise of a household pet.

:You and the gryphons will go south, Darkwind,: Altra repeated. *:For reasons I am not permitted to reveal at this time, Karal and I will accompany An'desha to the east.:*

"Karal and you?" Elspeth said incredulously. "But he's not even a mage! He's not even an envoy!"

:He is an envoy now.: Altra dropped the parchment packet on the table. *:Solaris has decided. Karal will replace Ulrich. He is a full Sun-priest now, and a channel for magic as Ulrich recognized when he was a child. I am a mage. Karal, one Companion, and I will accompany An'desha.:* Altra stared her down, and she finally dropped her gaze.

"So *that's* how all those miraculous documents of Ulrich's were getting here!" Prince Daren exclaimed.

Altra favored him with a faintly approving look but said nothing.

"Wait a moment. You said one Companion," Elspeth objected. "Who is the Herald?"

:There is no Herald. Florian is unpartnered. He, too, is a mage and will use Karal as his channel as well,: Altra shot back. *:Although we may not work magic as a human can, we are mages and can support as Masters with Karal as our channel.:*

Elspeth looked back up at him, her face showing nothing but disbelief. "This is impossible!" she cried. "You're breaking all the rules!"

:And who made those rules?: he countered, just as swiftly.

Karal cleared his throat. "This is Altra," he interjected mildly. "He is what we call a Firecat; and he is—something like an Avatar. I don't think any of you are aware that there were *four* of those Imperial weapons targeted for Ulrich and myself. Altra dealt with two and deflected the third."

Everyone in this room had seen the swiftness and deadly power of the weapons at firsthand; they stared at Altra with surprise and growing respect.

"We of Karse generally consider it wise not to argue with a Firecat," Karal concluded as the silence grew. "They are often acting on orders."

:As I am now,: Altra stated. *:There are reasons for what I have said. Those reasons do not yet concern you, and may never concern you. The future is fluid and subject to change.:*

And you are being your most inscrutable and infuriating, Karal thought hard at the Firecat. Altra turned his head slightly in Karal's direction, and dropped one eyelid in a quick, but unmistakable, wink.

Elspeth was clearly fuming. "Look, you—Avatar or not, I *won't* be manipulated on some grand playing board of—"

She stopped in midsentence as Altra turned to face her directly.

:I understand,: the Firecat told her with surprising gentleness. *:Please believe me, Lady Elspeth. What I have been ordered to tell you is not meant to manipulate you all like so many game pieces—it is to ensure that you have the opportunity to* exercise *your free will.:* He sighed, and somehow conveyed the impression of a burden of terrible grief. *:The future holds the secrets, not I, Solaris, or even Vkandis. Ulrich should have been here. He was an Adept, although he seldom made that known. It would have been he who accompanied the gryphons in the east, Elspeth and Darkwind together in the south, and An'desha would have gone north with Firesong. This is not optimal; now Florian and I must serve as the suppliers of power—you have not enough Master Mages to cover all the minor points and send two with An'desha. Besides, there is another consideration. Karal is the most acceptable substitute for a—a guardian—that must be placated by a presence it will understand. The guardian is not intelligent, but it will recognize Karal. I am not yet permitted to tell you why. Be assured that when I can, I will— although—:* His ears twitched. *:—I have the feeling that by that time, you will have deduced the reason for yourself.:*

"Guardian," Elspeth muttered to herself, and her eyes dropped to the Firecat's hindquarters—or rather, where those hindquarters were set. "Bright Havens!" she exclaimed. *"Iftel!"*

The Firecat bowed his head to her. *Precisely. Check Master Levy's calculations. You will find that the middle key-point stands at the exact joining of the three countries. Because of the mages who are available at this moment, this key-point requires a certain diplomacy where that guardian is concerned. You will be working Great Magics that will become one with the border of Iftel, after all; the guardian must be reassured that this will cause no harm. Originally, this would have required two Adepts, or Ulrich and the gryphons. Now it requires a balance of four workers. Two will stand in and for Valdemar—:*

"That will be Florian, obviously," Elspeth stated. "The other would be An'desha?"

:Yes—and two will stand in and for Iftel. That must *be Karal and myself. The Vkandis Priest-mages still in your land would not be recognized by the guardian as legitimate; although they are good men and women, they are mages first and Priests only as an afterthought. Talia—:* the cat paused. *:If Karal were not here, Talia might* possibly *be an acceptable substitute, but I am not willing to risk the chance of failure. It must be Karal; he is the only one besides myself available that the guardian*

will allow to pass the border. And since he is not a mage, but is a channel, he can support An'desha with help from myself and Florian.:

"This is beginning to sound like a religious ritual," Prince Daren said, finally, with a chuckle. The chuckle died when Altra turned those fiery blue eyes on him.

:You are not entirely wrong,: Altra replied. *:The circumstances are extraordinary. If Karal had died along with Ulrich—:* he paused again *:—it is possible that Solaris herself would have been with you at this moment, at whatever cost. The situation is that grave.:*

"Oh, no," Elspeth said hastily. "No, no, no! Talia has told me quite enough about Solaris, and I don't even want to *think* about that possibility!"

Altra actually shrugged, although a cat's body was not particularly suited to that gesture. *:Think on this, then. It is also true that if you had been able to learn the magics for the breakwater-shieldwall before this last wave, the key-point would have involved only the borders of Valdemar and Hardorn. If you wait until this wave is passed, however, the next will involve only the borders of Valdemar and Iftel. You will still need Karal, which means you would still need me and Florian.:* He shrugged again. *:This is simply the way that things fell out. There is no Great Destiny involved, if that comforts you any.:*

"Great Destinies generally involve great funerals," Elspeth muttered, as if she was quoting someone. Both gryphons laughed. "All right; I can accept all this, then. Thank you for taking the time to explain."

:Well,: Altra replied, standing up again and walking carefully to the edge of the table. *:Your dislike of manipulation is well-established. Infamous, even. Had I not explained, you might well have found some way to subvert my orders entirely. In this case, that would have been a disaster for all concerned.:*

"I guess he does know you," Prince Daren whispered roguishly to his stepchild. Elspeth blushed.

"Cats," Elspeth muttered. "They always know. Why don't we get back to the business at hand, then?" she added hastily.

"I don't care what that cat is, or what it *says* it is!" Firesong said waspishly. "I do *not* like the idea of you holding the middle key-point all by yourself!"

An'desha suppressed the response that had been second nature to him; to give in to Firesong and defer to his judgment.

We can't afford that now, he thought, chillingly aware of how little time they *did* have. As blithely as Altra had spoken of "waiting until the next wave," he and Master Levy both knew that would be a very bad idea.

The wave that was approaching *would* have intersection-points in several populated areas.

He knew, as no one else did, what that would do to the humans in those areas—and not all of those populations were in places that could be warned in time.

"I don't like it either, *ke'chara*," he said instead, very quietly. "To tell you the truth, I'm terrified. I'd much rather it was you beside me; Karal has never served as a channel before, and no matter how well Altra prepares him for it, this will still be an entirely new experience for him. What's more, *I* don't like the idea of *you* being at the most volatile of the key-points! Elspeth may be an Adept, but she is very young in her power, and I would much rather that you had someone experienced beside you."

"You aren't experienced—" Firesong began, then coughed sardonically. "Of course. You have all that secondhand experience to draw on, correct?"

He had not been distracted by An'desha's own, very real, concern for *him. Ah, well, I tried,* An'desha thought.

"You were the one who rightly insisted that I learn to use those memories," he began.

Firesong interrupted him. "Oh, well, throw my own words in my face!" he replied angrily. "And what next? I suppose now that you have all this experience at your behest, I am no longer interesting to you! Shall I expect to find myself left by the wayside, with the rest of the unwanted discards?"

There was more in the same vein, and it was a very good thing that Karal and Talia had seen the signs of this turnabout in Firesong and had warned An'desha. This would have been very hurtful, had An'desha not understood what was behind it all.

Firesong, possibly for the first time in his life, was jealous and afraid— afraid that An'desha *would* simply walk off and leave him behind. He could, now. He was no longer frightened and dependent. Firesong had never been in the position of the courter, rather than the courted, and he had no idea how to deal with it.

Firesong was also afraid *for* An'desha; the substitution of two mages and a channel for a real Adept was dangerous enough to make An'desha's hair stand on end when he stopped to think about it. Only his faith in Karal allowed him to even consider it.

Karal will allow himself to be burned out before he breaks, he thought, as he let Firesong continue to rant. *He has changed, too.*

He knew what Firesong's conscious intention was—to make him so emotionally wrought up that he would give in, and let Firesong find some other solution to the situation.

There was only one problem with that idea. An'desha had spent too much time with Karal. *I suppose a sense of responsibility must be contagious,* he thought, a bit wryly.

"Aren't you even listening to me?" Firesong cried desperately. "Don't you care what I'm saying, what I'm going through?"

"Yes," he replied, reaching out to catch Firesong's hands in his own. "But more importantly, I have listened to everything you didn't say, but meant. You are afraid for me, and you think I am in great danger. You are afraid I will leave you, that I no longer care for you. You are right in the first instance, and completely, absolutely, utterly wrong in the second."

Firesong's hands tightened on his; Firesong's silvery eyes begged for something he could hold in his heart.

"I am in danger; *all* of us are in danger. If we do nothing, your people, mine, and all these friends in this adopted land of ours will suffer, and maybe die." His eyes, he hoped, told Firesong that this was wholly the truth, nothing held back. "If we try to change this plan—" He sighed. "I must tell you that I do not know what difference the changes will make. Altra swears that this is the optimal use of our powers, and that anything less will not guarantee success. With all of my so-called 'experience,' I cannot tell you if he is right or wrong, but I am willing to trust him."

Firesong nodded, reluctantly.

"*I will not leave you.*" He said that with such force that Firesong winced. "I am not tired of you, nor bored with you, nor do I find you less than my equal." He allowed a hint of a smile to flick across his lips. "I *do* find you my superior in more than you know." Now he tightened his hands on Firesong's. "I have never said this in so many words, *ashke,* and I believe it is time that you heard it."

And take this with you, to hold in your heart.

"I love you." He said it softly, simply, and with all the conviction in his body, mind, and soul, and not entirely sure that even this would satisfy him.

But the truth is often enough in itself. So it was, now.

They made an odd little group; Altra beside Florian, An'desha in his Tayledras finery beside Karal in his sober black, holding the reins of Trenor. An'desha would have to ride Florian as soon as they got through the Gate; he wouldn't be fit to sit on an ordinary horse afterward. They would need to ride for about two days to get from the place An'desha knew—where he and all the others had crossed into Valdemar from Hardorn, fleeing the destruction of the capital—to the place where all three borders met. All three groups would have to travel about two days to get to their ultimate destinations, once they Gated as far as they could. And for the first day, whichever mage had created the Gate would be altogether useless for much of anything.

Firesong and Elspeth had gone first, then Darkwind and the gryphons. Now it was An'desha's turn.

He turned to Karal, as if to say something, then turned back to the stone archway in the weapons-training salle they would all use as their Gate-terminus.

Karal had heard of Gates, but he had never seen one. And after a few moments of watching An'desha build his, he never wanted to see one again.

It wasn't that the Gate itself was so terrible to look at; it was actually rather pretty, except for the yawning Void in the archway where the view of Kerowyn's office should have been. No, it was because Karal sensed that the Gate had been spun out of An'desha's own spirit; An'desha was a pale shadow of himself, as this Gate fed upon him, a lovely parasite draining his very essence. It was quite horrible, and Karal wondered how *anyone* could bear to create something like this.

Suddenly, the gaping darkness beneath the arch became the view of a forest—a place where the forest had taken over the ruins of a farm.

"Go!" An'desha said, in a strangled voice. Altra bolted through. Karal set Trenor toward the Gate; Trenor fought the bit. The gelding did *not* want to go in there!

Karal started to dismount, then looked back at An'desha and saw the terrible strain holding this Gate was costing him. With a silent apology, he wrenched Trenor's head around and dug his heels into the gelding's sides.

Although he wasn't wearing spurs, the startled horse acted as if he was; Trenor neighed frantically and bolted through the Gate.

It felt as if the ground dropped out from underneath them. For no longer than it took to blink, Karal's body swore to him that he was falling; for that long, his senses swore to him that the entire universe had vanished and he was blind, deaf, and frozen.

Then they were through, and Karal spun Trenor around on his heels as soon as they had cleared the immediate area. He saw that this side of the Gate was the remains of a ruined stone barn, with only the frame of the door and part of a wall still standing and a view of the salle where only weeds and tumbled stones should have been. A moment later, Florian and An'desha came barreling through, and the scene of the salle vanished behind them.

An'desha swayed in the saddle; someone had thoughtfully strapped him in so that he wouldn't fall. He clutched the pommel with both hands, leaving the reins slack on Florian's neck; his face was alabaster-white, and his eyes were closed. He opened them slowly as Karal rode Trenor up beside him.

"I never want to Gate anywhere ever again," Karal said, putting such intensity into every word that An'desha sat up straight in surprise. "I *never* want to put you through something like that again!"

"It won't be so bad, next time," An'desha replied weakly. "I promise you. Next time, we will make the journey in several smaller portions, over several days."

"There won't *be* a next time, if we don't," Karal replied acidly. He looked down. "Florian, is he fit to ride?"

:Even if he weren't, I am fit to carry him. That is why he is bound to the saddle,: came the reply. *:We have no choice. Time is speeding.:*

"So we had better speed ourselves." He reined Trenor back and gestured. Florian knew the way without a map; he was the best guide they could have had. "If you would lead?"

He steadied Trenor, and Altra leapt up to the padded platform where a pillion-saddle would have been. Rris had sworn that his "famous cousin Warrl" often used such a contraption to ride behind the Shin'a'in warrior Tarma shena Tale'sedrin, and in the interest of making the best speed possible, Altra had agreed to try it. Trenor didn't seem to mind too much, although he'd tried to buck a little the first time Altra had jumped up there.

Florian swung off into the deeper woods, and if he was following a trail, it wasn't a trail that Karal could read.

Then again, I'm not a woodsman, am I?

There must have been a trail there, though, since Florian pushed through the brush and rank weeds with no real problem. He was making good time, too; not quite a canter, but certainly a fast walk.

Poor Trenor. Two days of this is going to wear him out.

But there was no choice; every mark that passed was a mark that brought the next wave nearer—and Natoli had confided to him that there were several small villages lying where interference-points would fall. The ones in Valdemar had been evacuated, of course—but there could be no such guarantees of the villages elsewhere.

They *had* to stop this wave. They *had* to be in place in time.

When we have done all we can, then it is time to add prayer to the rest. That was one of Master Ulrich's favorite proverbs. Well, they had done all they could; Karal shut his eyes, trusted to Trenor to follow Florian, and sent up fervent prayers.

Whenever Karal sensed that Trenor was tiring, they stopped for a brief rest, water, and food; other than those stops, they rode right on through the night and on into the next day. This country was all former farmland, now gone to weeds and desolation; Karal didn't really want to ask why it had been left like this. He had an idea that the answer would involve the war with Hardorn, and the little he had learned about Ancar from An'desha did not make him eager to hear more.

Hurry, hurry, hurry. There isn't much time.

The countryside was desolate in other ways, too; there didn't seem to be a lot of wildlife. Birds were few, and mostly oddly silent. Although it was late fall and frost soon crusted every dried, dead leaf and twig, there *should* have been night sounds; owls, the bark of a fox, or the bay of a wolf. The only sounds were the noises they themselves made, and that very silence was more than enough to put up the hair on Karal's neck. An'desha slept in the saddle, as he had since they left the area of the Gate; Altra was not disposed to conversation, and Florian had his mind on finding their way. That left him with nothing to do but half-doze, worry, and try another prayer or two.

When dawn came, it brought a thin gray light to the gray landscape, and matters did not improve much. Trenor was tiring sooner, now, and it hurt Karal to force him on, but he knew there was no choice. They only had until two marks after dawn tomorrow to get into place.

But not long after the sun rose, An'desha actually shook himself awake, and looked around.

"I remember this," he said quietly. "This was land that Ancar held briefly, and he drained it while he held it. It has made a remarkable recovery."

"This?" Karal replied incredulously. "Recovered?"

"You did not see it before," the Adept told him grimly, turning in the saddle to face him. "Nothing would grow; *nothing.* By next year this may be back to the kind of land it once was." His eyes were shadowed by other memories than of this place, and finally he voiced one of them. "Ma'ar made places as desolate as this. The truly terrible thing is that he

325

thought he was doing right in creating them."

"Because in creating them he served some kind of purpose?" Karal hazarded.

An'desha nodded. "He served his own people very well; he made them into a great and powerful nation. The only problem is that in doing so, he turned other nations into stretches of desolation that are still scarred by his wars today. For him, nothing mattered except himself and his own people—who were extensions of himself. He did horrible things in the name of patriotism, and thought that he was in the right. I do not *like* Ma'ar, but I understand him. Perhaps I understand him too well."

Karal heard the self-doubt creep into An'desha's voice again, and answered it. "Understanding is the essence of not making the same mistakes, An'desha," he replied. "I rather doubt that Ma'ar ever understood himself, for instance."

An'desha actually laughed. "Well, now that is true enough," he said cheerfully. "So, once again you unseat my problems before they can dig spurs into me. How far to the key-point?"

:Most *of the day, if we are not delayed,:* Florian replied—

—just as they topped a hill to find themselves staring down at a gorge many hundreds of hands below. The gorge held a river—a river so full of whitewater rapids that it would be insane to try and cross it.

:This should not be here!: Florian exclaimed.

They all stared down at the river below, all but Trenor, who took the occasion to snatch a few mouthfuls of dried weeds.

:And here, right on schedule, is our delay,: Altra said finally.

"Not necessarily," Karal pointed out quickly. "There may be a bridge. Do we go upstream or down to try and find it?"

"Upstream, I think," An'desha said, after a moment of consideration. "It takes us nearer the Iftel side that way."

In the end, they *did* find a bridge—a narrow, shaky affair of old logs and rough planks. Karal had to blindfold Trenor to get him across, after Altra tried the footing by carefully padding over first. But that put them several marks behind schedule, and it was nearly dawn before they finally reached their goal.

Karal had wondered just how they would know what side of the border was the Iftel side, and what was the Valdemar side. As the sun rose, he had the answer to that question.

"What *is* that?" he asked in awe, staring at the wall of rippling light that lay along the top of the ridge, just above them. He couldn't see the top of it, whatever it was; it wasn't air, unless there was a way to solidify air and make it into a curtain of refraction. It wasn't water, although it moved and rippled like water with a breeze playing over it, and Karal was just able to make out large masses of green and gray-brown on the other side of it that *could* be trees and bushes.

:That is the border,: Florian replied warily. *:It wasn't always like that. Before the war with Ancar, it looked just like the border between Valdemar and Rethwellan, but once Ancar tried to bring an army across it,* that was *what sprang up. Anyone who tried to cross it was forced back. Anyone who tried to drive their way in with magic—died. I've heard that there are some very select traders who are allowed to come and go between here and there, but they are a close-mouthed lot, and they won't talk about anything that they've seen over there.:*

"I thought they had an envoy at the Valdemar Court," An'desha observed.

:They used to, a very long time ago. Not anymore.: Florian let out his breath in a sigh. *:It's tradition to keep their suite ready for them, but no one has come to claim it in anyone's lifetime.:*

Karal swallowed as he contemplated that shimmering wall of—of—

Of power, that's what it is. Pure force. And I'm supposed to walk across it! And anyone who tried to cross it is dead!

What was more, he was supposed to walk across it *right now.* There couldn't be more than a mark to go until the next wave was upon them!

"Come *on,*" he urged as his hands shook. "We have to get moving *now.* We haven't got any time at all to spare!"

To set an example, he urged poor, tired Trenor into a clumsy trot, sending him down the valley, through the knee-high grass, and up the ridge. The wall just loomed larger and larger; it didn't change at all except for the continuous rippling of the surface as he drew nearer to it. He sensed An'desha and Florian at his back, but the sheer power of the wall drove them mostly out of his thoughts.

There wasn't time for finesse, for study, for anything other than what he was already doing—running headlong into the thing, and hoping that it didn't decide to kill him, too.

Fear held him rigid and made a metallic taste in his mouth. He closed his eyes and shouted at Trenor to drive him the last few spans remaining—

—opened his eyes again, just as they actually reached it, and passed into it—

Something seized and held him.

****what****

He could not move, not even to breathe. He was surrounded by light, yet could not see. He could only wait, while whatever it was that held him examined him, inside and out.

*****Priest?*****

Was he a Priest? An'desha had named him "priest," but it had been in jest. Or had it? Solaris had named him "priest," but he thought it had merely been expedience. What had he done to earn the name?

****ah****

Suddenly, it let him go. He found himself still in Trenor's saddle, looking at An'desha and Florian through a curtain of rippling light that seemed thinner here than elsewhere.

:It is thinner. That is so we can reach them,: Altra said, urgently. *:It is coming, Karal, take your position. Don't just stand there thinking,* move!*:*

He tumbled off Trenor's back and took the stance he'd been coached in, bracing himself and holding both his arms out and up.

:Now. Into the trance I taught you.:

Obediently, he spoke his keywords and fell into a light trance; not so deep that he was unaware of everything around him, but too deep for him to move on his own now. He wasn't sure what was going to happen after that; Altra and An'desha hadn't gone into it—

A fraction of a heartbeat later, he realized *why* they hadn't gone into it. If they had, he'd have been too terrified to go through with it all.

From Altra's side, a torrent of power poured into him; from Florian's, another. There was *something* in him that managed to join those two streams of energy and actually hold them—even though from his point of view, it was like the one time he'd foolishly mounted an unbroken stallion. He was not controlling the power; it was permitting him—briefly—to hold it!

Then An'desha somehow reached out to him from across the border, and the two streams of power that had been made one found their outlet.

Now An'desha did something with that energy that Karal could not see, and could only sense, very dimly, as a blind man might sense a mighty fortress being built beside him. He arched his back and closed his eyes to concentrate on holding the power steady; the longer the power "permitted" him to hold it, the more control he actually had over it.

It was not easy, and he sensed something else. If he slipped, it was going to do terrible things to him, and if he survived the experience, the likelihood that he would regret surviving was very high.

He no sooner had that unsettling revelation than the disruption-wave hit.

It was worse than all the others combined.

The ground heaved and buckled under him, as if this was the earthquake that would end the world. He went entirely blind, but not in the sense of being immersed in total darkness. Instead, there was nothing to see *but* color and light, swirls and whirlwinds and cascades of color and light. The light was something he could hear; it roared and rushed in his ears. The color had flavors; iron, scorched stone, and copper. Somewhere out there he knew that Florian and Altra were still pouring energy into him; he felt it, hot and primal, deep inside him— and An'desha needed that power. So he held to it, even when the light turned into a million serpents that threatened to crush him, even when the colors tried to wash him away, right up until everything collapsed and he was all alone in an unending darkness, and he knew he would never, ever find his way out again—that was when he faltered.

Fear overcame him; he felt the power slipping through his tenuous grasp.

I can't take this! he thought, gasping in panic. *I can't do this! This was for someone like Ulrich, not me! I can't—*

His control slipped a little more, and he flailed in confusion.

I don't even know what I am anymore.

His heart raced in panic, and he *wanted* Ulrich. He wanted to be *like* Ulrich.

Then from deep within him came a feeling of conviction, of responsibility, too strong for even fear to shake.

I have to. There's no one else.

He held the power, though it writhed and threatened to escape. He ignored his confusion, fought his panic, and held.

Then, as suddenly as it began, it was over. Abruptly, he found himself back on the Valdemar side of the barrier, kneedeep in dead grasses, staring into An'desha's eyes from a distance of no more than an arm's length. How he had gotten there, he had no clue.

:The other breakwaters are up,: Florian said, his voice so faint with exhaustion that it might have been nothing more than a whisper of Karal's own thoughts. *:All three are joined. The Iftel border is part of it all. We did it, Karal.:*

Karal sat down in the grass; Altra was already lying down beside him, completely drained, one very flat Cat. "We did, didn't we?" he said, wonderingly.

:Ah.: That was Altra. *:I believe that I will lie here for a while. A month would*

be good. Maybe two. How do you manage with the limits of these bodies?:

"I manage very well, thank you," An'desha replied sharply. "I had a taste of doing without one, remember? Don't complain."

Karal decided that Altra's idea of lying flat was a good one. He felt—he felt as if someone had filled him full of light, then drained him; as if someone had turned him inside out, left him under the desert sun for a while, then turned him rightside out again.

:There is help coming,: Florian said. *:A Herald on circuit. Just rest now, until he comes.:*

"We did it," he said again, wonderingly.

:We did. The barriers will hold for now. We have bought some breathing space.:

Breathing space. Time. He blinked, and looked up at the blue sky. Maybe a little rest. All three sounded impossibly good.

Never mind that *he* was truly going to be the Karsite envoy now, a position he didn't want, and wasn't sure how to fill. And never mind that there was a young engineer back in Haven who made him think very uncomfortable and yet delightful thoughts.

There was still the Imperial army out there—and no telling what they would do. Karal himself was now a potential major target for them. And the cataclysmic mage-storm was yet to come.

But at the moment, it doesn't matter. For now, they *had* time; and a little time—and each other—could be all they needed.

STORM RISING

A VALDEMAR OMNIBUS

BOOK TWO of
The MAGE STORMS

Dedicated to Teresa and Dejah

1

Grand Duke Tremane shivered as a cold draft wisped past the shutters behind him and drifted down the back of his neck. This was a far cry from Emperor Charliss' Crag Castle—which, though outwardly austere, was nevertheless replete with hidden comforts. Even his own ducal manor, while primitive by the standards of Crag Castle, was free of drafts in the worst of weather. Tremane closed his eyes for a moment in longing for his own home as yet another breath of ice insinuated itself past his collar. It felt less like a trickle of cold water and more like the edge of a knife blade laid along his spine.

More like at my throat. That cold breath of air was the merest harbinger of worse, much worse, to come. That was why he had gathered every officer, every mage, and every scholar in his ranks here together, all of them crammed into the largest room his confiscated headquarters afforded.

Who did they say had built this place? A Hardornen Grand Duke at least, as I recall. His own manor boasted many rooms grander than this, and better suited to gathering large groups of men for a serious discussion. The tall windows, though glazed, were as leaky as so many sieves, and he'd been forced to block out the thin gray light of another bleak autumn day by having the shutters fastened down across them; and although fires roared in the fireplaces at either end of the room, the heat went straight up into the rafters two stories above his head, where it was hardly doing anyone any good. In happier times, this wood-paneled, vaulted hall with its floor of chill stone had likely played host to any number of glittering balls and entertainments. The rest of the time it had probably been shut up, given that it was a drafty old barn and impossible to keep at a reasonable temperature. Tremane glanced up at the exposed beams and rafters above him; they were lost in the shadows despite the presence of so many candles and lanterns on the tables that the air trembled and shimmered just above the flickering flames.

The massed candles must be putting out almost as much heat as the fireplaces; too bad none of that heat was reaching him.

Dozens of anxious faces peered up at him. He was seated on a massive chair behind a ridiculously tiny secretary's desk up on the platform where musicians had probably performed. It was uncomfortably like a dais, and he was well aware that such a comparison would not be lost on the Imperial spies in his ranks. Right now, though, that was the least of his concerns. The primary issue here was a simpler one: survival.

He stood up, and the murmur of incidental conversation below him died into silence without the need to clear his throat.

"Forgive me, gentlemen, if I bore you by stating the obvious," he began, concealing his discomfort at addressing so many people at once. He had never been particularly adept at public speaking; it was the one lack he suffered as a commander. No stirring battlefield speeches out of him—he was more apt to clear his throat uneasily, then bark something trite about honor and loyalty and retire in confusion. "Some of you have been involved in other projects at my request, and I want you all to know our current situation as clearly as possible, so that nothing has to be explained twice."

He winced inwardly at the awkwardness of his own words, but there were some nods out in his audience, and no one looked bored yet, so he carried on. Officers formed the bulk of his audience, massed at three long tables in front of him, dark and foreboding in their field uniforms of a dark reddish brown—the color of dried blood. Some wag had once made the claim that the reason the field uniforms were that color was to avoid the expense of removing stains after a battle. As a sample of wit, it had fallen rather flat; taken at face value, it might just have been the truth.

To his right and left, respectively, were his tame scholars and the Imperial mages; the latter in a variation on the field uniforms, looser and more comfortable for middle-aged and spreading bodies. The former, as civilians, wore whatever they wished to, and were the sole spots of brightness here. He addressed his first summation to mages and scholars both, rather than to the officers. "Although the Imperial forces have not met with any active opposition since we pulled in our line and took a fortified position here, we are still in hostile territory. Everything to the west of us was completely unsecured when we broke off all engagements, and I would not vouch for Hardornen land to the south and north of our original wedge. Hostilities could break out at any moment, and we must keep that in mind when making plans."

Grimaces from the scholars and mages, grim agreement from his officers. The Imperial wedge meant to divide the country of Hardorn into two roughly equal parts, to be divided still further and conquered, was now an Imperial arrowhead, broken off from the shaft and lodged somewhere in the middle of Hardorn. And at the moment, he only hoped it was lodged in such a way that it could be ignored by the populace at large.

"We have been cut off completely from Imperial contact ever since the mage-storms worsened," he continued, giving them the most unpleasant news first. "We have not been able to reestablish that contact. I must reluctantly conclude that we are on our own."

There were not many in his ranks who knew that particular fact, and widened eyes and shocked glances told where and how the news hit home. They took it rather well, though; he was proud of them. They were all good men—even the Imperial spies among them.

Are any of them still in contact with their overseers in the Empire? I'd give a great deal for the answer to that little question. There was no way of knowing, of course, since anyone who was an agent for Emperor Charliss would be a better mage than he himself was. Charliss was too canny an old wolf not to cover that contingency.

Another draft of cold licked at his neck, and he turned the fur-lined collar of his wool half-cape up in a futile attempt to keep more such drafts away. It was the same dulled red as the uniforms of his men; he wore what they wore. He had a distaste for making a show of himself. Besides, a man in a dress uniform covered with decorations made far too prime a target.

"The mage-corps," he continued, turning to nod at the variously-garbed men seated at the table nearest him, "tell me there is no doubt but that the mage-storms are worsening rather than weakening. As you have probably noticed, they are having an effect on the weather itself, and they will continue to do so. That means more *physical* storms, and worse ones—" He turned a questioning glance at his mages.

Their spokesman stood up. This was not their chief, Gordun, a thickset and homely man who remained in his seat with his hands locked firmly together on the table in front of him, but rather a withered old specimen who had been Tremane's own mentor, the oldest mage—perhaps the oldest man—in the entire entourage. Sejanes was nobody's fool, and perhaps the mages all felt Tremane would be less likely to vent his wrath upon someone he had studied under. In this, his mages were incorrect. He would never vent his wrath on anyone telling him a harsh truth—only on someone caught in a lie.

Sejanes knew that, and looked up at his former pupil with serenity intact. "You may have noticed what seems to us of the Empire to be *unseasonable* cold, and wondered if we are simply seeing weather that is normal to this clime," the old man said, his reedy voice carrying quite well over the assemblage. "I assure you all, it is not. I have spoken with the local farmers and studied what records are available, and this is possibly the worst season this part of the country has ever encountered. Fall struck hard and early, the autumn storms have been more frequent and harsher, and the frosts deeper. We have made measurements, and we can only conclude that the situation is going to worsen. This is the effect of the mage-storms upon an area that was already unstable, thanks to the depredations of that fool, Ancar. The mage-storms themselves are growing worse as well. Put those things together—and I'd just as soon not have to think about what this winter is going to be like."

Sejanes sat down again, and Gordun stood up; about them, looks of shock were modulating into other emotions. There was remarkably little panic, but also no sign whatsoever of optimism. That, in Tremane's opinion, was just as well. The worse they thought the situation was, the better they would plan.

"We've flat given up on restoring mage-link communications with the Empire," he said bluntly. "There isn't a prayer of matching with them when both of us are drifting—it would be like trying to join the ends of two ribbons in a gale without being able to tie a knot in them." His face was set in an expression of resignation. "Sirs, the honest truth is that your mages are the most useless part of your army right now. We can't do *anything* that will hold through a storm."

"Just what does that mean, exactly?" someone asked from the back of the room.

Sejanes shrugged. "From now on, you might as well act as if we don't exist. You won't have mage-fires for heat or light now or in the dead of winter, we can't transport so much as a bag of grain nor build a Portal that'll stay up through a single storm. In short, sirs, whatever depends on magic is undependable, and we can't see a time coming when you'll be able to depend on it again."

He sat down abruptly, and before the others could erupt with questions, Tremane took control of the situation again.

"The latest mage-storm passed three days ago," he said. "I have been taking reports since then." He leafed through the papers he had read so often that the words danced before his mind's eye. *Give them some good news.* "The last of the stragglers from that engagement outside Spangera trickled in right before it passed. Every man's been accounted for, one way or another. The preliminary palisades were finished just as the storm hit, so we are now all behind *some* kind of wall or other." He let them digest that bit of good news for a moment, as a palliative to all the unpleasant information they'd had until now. The shutters behind him rattled in a sudden gust of wind, and the candles flickered as another draft swept the room. This time it was a puff of warm air that touched him, scented with wax and lamp oil.

Shonar Manor, the locals called this place; he'd chosen well when he'd chosen to make it the place where the Imperial Army would dig in and settle down. This fortified manor he had taken as his own had no one to claim it, or so he had been told; Ancar had seen to that. Whether he'd slaughtered the family, root and branch, or simply seen to it that they were all sent into the front lines of his war with Valdemar, Tremane did not know. Nor did it matter, in truth, except that there would be no inconvenient claimants with backers from the town to show up and cause him trouble. The walled city of Shonar itself could hardly hold a fraction of his men, of course, even if he'd displaced the citizens, which he had no intention of doing. They were much more useful right where they were, forming a fine lot of hostages against the good behavior of their fellows—and in the meantime, providing his men with the amenities of any good-sized town. In fact, they were being treated precisely as if they were Imperial citizens themselves, so long as they made no trouble. For their part, after their first alarms settled, they seemed satisfied enough with their lot. Imperial silver and copper spent as well as any other.

From the reports Tremane had gotten since the last mage-storm cleared, it was a good thing for everyone that he *did* get all his men together before it broke.

"The scouts are reporting a fair amount of damage in the countryside this time," he said, turning over another page without really reading what was written there. "This time it's not just the circles of strange land appearing everywhere. Though we've a fair number of those, and they're bigger, there *are* fewer of them emerging—but we have something entirely new on our hands." He regarded them all with a grave expression; they looked up at him expectantly. "I'm certain that at one time or another each of you has seen mage-made creatures; perhaps some of the attempts to recreate the war-beasts of the past like gryphons or makaar. It appears that the mage-storms are having a similar *changing* effect on animals and plants, but with none of the control that there would be with a guiding mind behind the magic."

"*Monsters*," he heard someone murmur, and he nodded to confirm that unpleasant speculation.

"Monstrous creatures indeed," he acknowledged. "Some of them quite horrifying. *So far* none of them have posed any sort of threat that a well-trained and well-armed squad could not handle, but let me remind you that this last storm hit us by day. What is relatively simple for men to deal with by day may become a much more serious threat in the dark of night."

What if the animal trapped had been something larger than a bull, or smarter than a sheep? What if it had been an entire herd *of something?* He sighed, and ran his hand through his thinning hair. "This," he pointed out fairly, "is going to do nothing for morale which, as most of you have reported to me, is at the lowest point any of you have ever seen in an Imperial Army."

He turned over another page. "According to *your* reports, gentlemen," he continued, nodding in the direction of his officers, "this is also to be laid at the feet of the mage-storms. I have had reports of men being treated by the Healers for nothing more nor less than fear, so terrified that they cannot move or speak—and not all of them are green recruits either." As the officers stirred, perhaps thinking of an attempt to protest or defend themselves, he gazed upon them with what he hoped was a mixture of candor and earnest reassurance. "There is no blame to be placed here, gentlemen. Your men are trained to deal with combat magic, but not with something like this—certainly not with something which is so random in the way it strikes and what it does. There is nothing *predictable* about these storms; we do not even know when they will wash over us. That is quite enough to make even the most hardened veteran ill-at-ease."

Yes, the one question none of us will ask. What if the mage-storm changes not only beasts, but men?

He smiled a little, and his officers relaxed. "Now, as it happens, this is actually working in our favor. My operatives in unsecured areas tell me that the Hardornens are just as demoralized as our men. Perhaps more so; they are little used to seeing the effects of magic close at hand.

And certainly they are not prepared for these misshapen monsters that spring up as a result of the storms. So, on the whole, they have a great deal more to worry about than we do—and that can only be good news for us."

In point of fact, active resistance had evaporated; it had begun to fade even before the last mage-storm had struck. He watched his officers as they calculated for themselves how long it had been since a serious attack had come from the Hardornen "freedom fighters" and relaxed minutely as he saw *them* relaxing.

"Now—that is the situation as it stands," he concluded, with relief that his speech was over. "Have any of you anything to add?"

Gordun stood. "Following your orders, Your Grace, we are concentrating all our efforts on getting a single Portal up and functioning. It will not remain functional after the next storm, but we believe we can have it for you within a few days, with all of us concentrating on that single task."

May the Thousand Little Gods help us. Gordun by himself could have created and held a Portal before these damned storms started. Will we find ourselves wearing skins and chipping flint arrowheads next?

He nodded, noting the faintly surprised and speculative looks his officers were trading. Did any of them have an inkling of what he was about?

Probably not. On the other hand, that is probably just as well.

Finally, at long last, it was the scholar's turn; he did not even recognize the timid man urged to his feet by the sharp whispers of his fellows, which argued for more bad news.

"W-we regret, Y-your G-grace," the fellow stammered nervously, "there is n-nothing in any r-records to g-give us a hint of a s-solution to the s-storms. W-we l-looked for hidden c-ciphers or other k-keys as you asked, and there was n-nothing of the s-sort."

He didn't so much sit down as collapse into his seat. Tremane sighed ostentatiously, but he did not rebuke the poor fellow in any way. Even if he'd been tempted to—the man couldn't help it if there was nothing to find in the records, after all—he was afraid the poor man would faint dead away if the Grand Duke even looked at him with faint disapproval.

These scholars are hardly a robust lot. Or perhaps it is just that they are neither fish nor fowl—neither ranked with the mages nor bound to the army, and thus have the protections of neither.

Odd. That wasn't anything he would have taken much thought for, in the past. Perhaps because he knew they were on their own, he was taking no man for granted, not even a scholar with weak eyes and weaker muscles.

"Gentlemen," he said, even as those thoughts were running through his head, "now you know the worst. Winter is approaching, and much more swiftly than any of us thought possible." As if to underscore his words, the shutters that had been rattling were hit by a sudden fierce gust that sounded as if they'd been struck by a missile flung from a catapult. "I need your help in planning how we are to meet it when it comes. We need shelter for the men, walls to protect us, not only from the Hardornens, but from whatever the mage-storms may conjure up. We cannot rely on magic—only what our resources, skills, and strength can provide." He cast his eyes over all of them, looking for expressions that seemed out of place, but found nothing immediately obvious. "Your orders are as follows; the engineering corps are to create a plan for a defensive wall that can be constructed in the shortest possible time using army labor and local materials. The rest of you are to inventory the civilian skills of your men and pool those men whose skills can provide us shelter suitable for the worst winter you can imagine. Do not neglect the sanitation in this; we are going to need *permanent* facilities now, something suitable for a long stay, not just latrine trenches. Besides shelter, we will need some way to warm that shelter and to cook food—if we begin cutting trees for the usual fires, we'll have the forest down to stumps before the winter is half over." Was that enough for them to do? Probably, for now. "You scholars, search for efficient existing shelters, ones that hold heat well, and some fuel source beside wood. If you find anything that looks practical, bring it to my attention. Mages, you have your assignment. Gentlemen, you are dismissed for now."

The men had to wait to file out of the great double doors at the end of the hall, suffering the cold blasts penetrating the hall as one of the shutters broke loose and slapped against the wall. The Grand Duke was not so bound; his escape was right behind the dais, in the form of a smaller door at which his bodyguard waited, and he took it, grateful to be out of that place. The short half-cape did nothing to keep a man warm; he wanted a fire and a hot drink, in that order.

The guard fell in silently behind him as he headed for his own quarters, his thoughts preoccupied with all the things he had not—yet— told his men.

The mages probably guessed part of it. They were not simply cut off, they had been *abandoned*, left to fend for themselves, like unwanted dogs.

The Emperor, with all the power of all the most powerful mages in the world at his disposal, could (if he was truly determined) overcome the disruptions caused by the mage-storms to send *some* kind of message. Tremane had never heard of a commander being left so in the dark before; certainly it was the first time in his own life that *he* had no clue what Charliss wanted or did not want of him.

There could be several causes for this silence.

The most innocent was also, in some ways, the most ominous. It was entirely possible that the mage-storms wreaking such havoc here could be having an even worse effect within the Empire itself. The Empire had literally been built on magic; distribution of food depended upon it, and communications, and a hundred more of the things that underpinned and upheld the structure of the Empire itself. If that was the case—

They're in a worse panic than we are here. Civilians have no discipline; as things break down, they'll panic. He was enough of a student of history himself to have some inkling what panicking civilians could do. *Rioting, mass fighting, hysteria... in a city, with all those folk packed in together, there would be nothing for it but to declare martial law. Even then, that wouldn't stop the fear or the panic. It would be like putting a cork on a bottle of wine that was still fermenting; sooner or later, something would explode.*

Tremane reached the warm solitude of his personal suite, waving to the bodyguard to remain outside. That was no hardship; the corridors provided more shelter from the cold drafts than half of the rooms did. Fortunately, *his* suite was tightly sealed and altogether cozy. He closed the door to his office with a sigh. No drafts here—he could remove his short winter cloak and finally, in the privacy of his quarters, warm numb fingers and frozen toes at a fire.

The second possibility that had occurred to him was basically a variation on what he, himself, had just ordered. The Emperor *could* have decreed that literally everything was to be secondary to finding a way for the mages to protect the Empire from these storms. There would be no mages free to try and reopen communications with this lost segment of the army. The Empire itself might be protected, but that might very well be all the mages could manage.

But the Empire would hardly spend such precious resources as Imperial mages on the protection of client-states. No, only the core of the Empire, those parts of it that were so firmly within the borders that only scholars recalled what names they had originally borne, would be given such protection.

Which means, he mused, feeling oddly detached from the entire scenario, *that the client states are probably rearming and revolting against Charliss. If the Empire itself is under martial law, all available units of the army have been pulled back into the Empire to enforce it. They won't be spending much time worrying about us.*

No, one segment of the Imperial Army, posted off beyond the borders of the farthest-flung Imperial Duchy, was not going to warrant any attention under conditions that drastic.

But no one born and raised in the Imperial Courts was ever going to stop with consideration of the most innocent explanations. Not when paranoia was a survival trait, and innocence its own punishment.

So, let us consider the most paranoid of scenarios. The one in which our enemy is the one person who might be assumed to be our benefactor. It was entirely possible that these mage-storms were nothing new to Emperor Charliss. He could have known all along that they were going to strike, and where, and when. In fact, it was possible that these storms were a weapon that Charliss was testing *on them.*

Tremane grew cold with a chill that the fire did nothing to warm.

This could be a new terror-weapon, he thought, following the idea to its logical conclusion, as his muscles grew stiff with suppressed tension. *What better weapon than one that disrupts your enemy's ability to work magic, and leaves land and people beaten down but relatively intact?*

There was even a "positive" slant to that notion. Perhaps this was a new Imperial weapon that was *meant* only to act as an aid to them in their far-distant fight, and it simply had a wider field of effect than anyone ever imagined.

But far more likely was the idea that, since no one knew precisely what the weapon was going to do, it was tested out here, in territory not yet pacified, so that any effect on Imperial holdings would be minimal. Tremane and his men were nothing more than convenient methods by which the effectiveness of the weapon could be judged—

Which would mean that they are watching us, scrying us, seeing how we react and what we do, and whether or not the locals have the wit to do the same. This lack of communication was a deliberate attempt to get them to react without orders, just to see what they would do.

If this happened to be the true case, it ran counter to every law and custom that made the Army the loyal weapon that it was. It would be a violation of everything that Imperial soldiers had a right to expect from their Emperor.

For that matter, being left to fend for themselves was almost as drastic a violation of that credo.

In either case, however, this would *not* be above what could be done to test a candidate for the Iron Throne. Other would-be heirs had been put through similar hardships before.

But not, his conscience whispered, *their men with them.*

That was what made him angry. He did not mind so much for himself; he had expected to be tested to the breaking point. It was that the Emperor had included his unwitting men in the testing.

There was no denying that, for whatever reason, Charliss had abandoned them. There had been time and more than time enough for him to have sent them orders via a physical messenger. This silence was *wrong*, and it meant that there was something more going on than appeared on the surface. It was the Emperor's sworn duty to see to the welfare of his soldiers in times of crisis, as it was their sworn duty to protect him from his enemies. They had kept their side of the bargain; he had reneged on his.

It would not be long before the rest of the army knew it, too. In a situation like this, they all were aware they should have been recalled long ago. Since there was no way that a Portal could be brought up that was large enough to bring them all home, Charliss should have sent in more troops to provide a corridor of safety so that they could *march* home. And he should have done all this the moment the mage-storms began, when it became obvious that they were getting worse. Then they would not only have been safely inside the Empire by now, they would have been on hand to deal with internal turmoil. That meant a kind of double betrayal, for somewhere, someone was going shorthanded, lacking the troops he needed to keep the peace because the Emperor had decided to abandon *them* here.

Or rather, it was more likely that he had opted to abandon *Tremane* and, with him, his men. He had probably written Tremane off as the potential heir because he had not achieved a swift victory over Hardorn, and had chosen this as the most convenient way to be rid of him.

And if I cannot contrive a way to bring us all safely through the winter, they will suffer with me.

That was the whole point of his anger. He had been schooled and trained as an Imperial officer; he had been an officer before he ever became a Grand Duke. This callous abandonment was counter to both the spirit and the letter of the law, and it made Tremane's blood boil. It represented a betrayal so profound and yet so unique to the Empire that he doubted anyone born outside the Empire would ever understand it, or why it made his skin flush with rage.

The men would certainly understand it, though, when they finally deduced the truth for themselves and then worked through their natural impulse to assume that anything so *wrong* could not be *true*. And at that point—

At that point they will cease to be soldiers of the Empire. No, that's not true. They will be soldiers of the Empire, but they will cease to serve Charliss.

He sat down in the nearest chair, all in a heap, as the magnitude of that realization struck him. Revolt—it had not happened more than a handful of times in the entire history of the Empire, and only *once* had the revolt been against an Emperor.

Was *he* ready to contemplate revolt? Unless he did something drastically wrong, it was to him that the men would turn if they revolted against Charliss. Was he prepared to go along with that, to take command of them, not as a military leader, but as the leader of a revolt?

Not yet. Not… yet. He was close, very close, but not yet prepared to take such drastic action.

He shook his head and ordered his thoughts. *I must keep my initial goals very clearly in mind. I must not let anything distract me from them until the men are secured to face this coming winter. That is* my *duty, and what the Emperor has or has not done has no bearing on it.* He set his chin stubbornly. *And to the deepest hells with anyone who happens to get in my way while I am seeing to that duty!*

He rose and went directly to his desk. The best way to ensure total cooperation among the men was to make things seem as normal as possible. So—to keep them from thinking too much about the silence from the Empire, he should keep up military discipline and structure the changes he planned to make to the military pattern.

He wrote his officers' orders quickly but carefully. He had already recruited a half-dozen literate subalterns to serve as scribes and secretaries since it was no longer possible to replicate written orders magically—and they would have to be able to read his handwriting in order to copy it. Now he was grateful for the "primitive" but effective and purely mechanical amenities of this manor. Nothing here had been affected by the storms. His lights still burned; his fires still heated. His cooked food arrived at the proper intervals from the kitchen. The jakes performed their function, and the sewage tunnels carried away the result without stinking up the manor. Somehow he was going to have to find men who could manage these same "primitive" solutions for an entire army.

We need men who don't need magic to get things done. Leather workers, blacksmiths—farmers, even—break all the work of running the camp down into what is and isn't done by magic, then scour the ranks for those who know how to do those jobs with ordinary labor. Now, how to see to it that these men were given the appropriate recognition so that they would volunteer their abilities...? Well, that was a simple problem to solve. *Promote them to "specialist" rank, with the increase in pay grade.* There was nothing like an increase in pay to guarantee enthusiastic cooperation.

He put the cool, blunt end of his glass pen to his lips for a moment, and felt his lips taking on a wry twist. *Money. There isn't much in the coffers at the moment. Well, that makes the plan that much more important.* Money was the other constant in the Imperial Army, and had been, from time immemorial. *Small wonder, given that our history claims we began as a band of mercenaries.* Regular pay was the foundation of loyalty when it came to the individual Imperial fighter. Troops had been known to rise up and murder commanders who shorted their pay; an Emperor had been dethroned for failing to pay the army on time and another had been put in his place because he had made up pay and even bonuses for the men directly under his command out of his own pocket.

Of course, there had never been a situation like this one, with troops abandoned so far from home, and cut off from all supplies. Under circumstances like this one, his men *might* be understanding... or they might not. It was best to be sure of them for now.

He sanded the inked orders and took them to the door of his quarters, where one of his bodyguards took them away to the corps of secretaries to be copied and distributed.

"I do not want to be disturbed under any circumstances," he told the guard, who nodded and saluted, and when he went back into his room and closed the door, he also locked it. The guard would think nothing amiss in this. Locking his door was nothing new; he often required privacy to think and plan. There was no one of higher rank here to question that "need" for absolute privacy.

This time, however, he needed privacy to act, not to think. And it was just as well that he had made a habit of privacy. No one would know what he did here, tonight.

Thanks to the Little God of Lust that my aunt was his devotee. If it had not been for his aunt, and her own need for secrecy... He sat down at his traveling desk and reached beneath it, straining a little to touch the spot behind the drawer that held his pens, ink, and drying sand. The place he needed to reach lay just past the right-hand corner of that drawer...

He felt the tiny square of wood sink as he depressed it, and he quickly removed the pen drawer, taking it out of the desk and placing it on top, out of the way. His aunt had been a woman who was very protective of her secrets—and absolutely ruthless in that protection. If he had removed the drawer first, pressing the key-spot on the bottom of the desk would have resulted in a poisoned needle through the fingertip. Within an hour, he would have been dead. The poison on that needle was known to persist in potency for two hundred years, and as for the mechanism, he was certain it would outlive him. He reached into the cavity that had held the drawer and felt for a similar spot in the back of the cavity and on the right-hand side.

Another square of wood sank beneath his questing finger, and he moved his hand to the left side of the cavity. In this case, had he not removed his hand immediately but continued to press at the spot, it would have triggered a second mechanism, and the secret drawer he was trying to free would have locked into place. Unless you knew the way to reset it, nothing short of hacking the desk to pieces would allow one to reach that hidden drawer.

That second drawer, the secret one, half the height of the original, had slid a bare fraction out of the back of the cavity. He pried it completely out, touching *only* the top edge, and brought it out of its hiding place into the candlelight. It, too, was trapped; this time with a slow-acting contact poison that was a natural component of the wood forming the bottom. He was *very* careful not to touch the bottom, only the sides. The inside was lined with slate to insulate what it held from the poisonous wood.

All of this was quite necessary, for within this drawer was an object that meant death without trial if it was ever found in his possession. Or rather, it *had* meant a death sentence. Now, well—unless there was an Imperial spy in his army with the rank and authorization to carry such a sentence out, it was—

It is less likely. I will never say "unlikely" when it comes to the power of the Emperor.

More precious than gold, more magical than jewels, more potent than drugs. It was the pure, crystallized essence of power. He took it from its nest of silk with hands that were remarkably steady, given the deadly danger it represented.

It was a completely accurate copy of the Imperial Seal, identical in every way, mundane and magical, with the original. It had been obtained at incredible risk—although the actual *cost* had been minimal, for he had made the copy himself. He could never have bought this; there was not enough money in the world to pay a mage to make this, and not enough to bribe an Imperial secretary to let it out of his keeping long enough to make that copy.

He set it carefully on the desktop, and the memory of the first time he had placed it on this very desk overlaid itself on the present.

To this day, it was the single most daring act he had ever accomplished. He was still not entirely certain what had possessed him to even contemplate such a mad action. Although he had not known it at the time, it was Emperor Charliss' policy to assign each of the potential candidates for the Throne to a stint within the Imperial Secretariat, so that they would know what the duties of their underlings were—and where the opportunities for bribery and espionage among those underlings lay. During *his* tour of duty, the Imperial Seal had come into his hands for two entire days, as he followed Charliss on a Royal Progress through newly conquered lands. Charliss had been preoccupied with the machinations of a local satrap and had immersed himself in dealing with his twisted and involved plots to defraud Emperor and Empire of their rightful portions and authority. He'd sensed possible treachery, and had entrusted the Seal to Tremane while he dealt—personally and magically—with the "problem." He'd had no other thoughts on his mind, and it might have been that he had forgotten that Tremane was a mage.

But Tremane's skill, while not the equal of the Emperor's, was still sufficient to copy the Seal. By sheerest accident, he'd had the time, the materials, and the Seal itself, all at once, all readily at hand. The temptation had been too great; he'd bent to it and had made the Seal during one long, feverish night of work.

Once he had made it, however, he had almost destroyed it in panic. Only one thing had prevented him from doing just that: the existence of this desk.

He'd inherited it from an aunt with numerous lovers—many of them dangerous to know, all of them married to other women. She'd had the drawer built to conceal missives too hazardous to keep, but too precious—emotionally or with an eye to later blackmail—to burn. It was the only place remotely safe enough to hold something as risky as a copy of the Imperial Seal.

Since that time, the desk and its burdensome secret had always traveled with him. He had used it only once, just to be certain that it *was* identical in every way to the original, and then only to seal a document the Emperor had already approved and signed, one of an entire stack of similar documents that Charliss had signed and sealed without glancing more than once at each.

Now, however, Tremane was about to forge a document that the Emperor would definitely never approve of.

On the other hand, in order to reach him to bring him to justice, once the deception was discovered, the Emperor was going to have to come to *him*. Or, at least, his minions were.

That was hardly going to be an easy proposition, all things considered. There was a great deal of disturbed and hostile territory between him and the Emperor.

It was also going to be some time before Tremane was found out, and during that time conditions were only going to worsen, which would further protect him from Imperial wrath.

Besides all that, there was no telling if Charliss could manage to track Tremane down in the first place, much less put through a Portal to haul him back for justice—or send troops across the unsettled countryside of Hardorn to accomplish the same goal.

In either case, he would prove he *could* reach them—and there would be questions about why he had not evacuated the troops if he could pursue Tremane to bring him to book for his actions. Charliss would have no excuse not to bring back the rest of the army as well as the errant Grand Duke.

If he does come after me, I would just as soon it were an overland trek. I have a notion that I could manage to escape from custody during a mage-storm if I put my mind to it. He shook his head again; he was allowing himself to be distracted by speculations. He must keep his mind on his immediate goals.

Especially since he was going to need intense concentration and a very steady hand for the next few hours.

He wrapped a scarf around his forehead to keep sweat out of his eyes; not that he was too warm, but he knew from past experience that he was going to be sweating from nervousness. He had to be able to see clearly, and he didn't want any drops falling on his pages either; Imperial scribes did not *sweat* over their work. Setting aside the secret drawer and the pen drawer, he selected a new glass pen and picked out one very special bottle of ink. While this bottle was not going to land him in any trouble, it might have caused some raised eyebrows if anyone had known that Grand Duke Tremane possessed a bottle of the special ink used for official Imperial documents, ink made with tiny, glittering flecks of silver and gold in it, to mark the letters as coming unmistakably from the hand of an Imperial scribe.

First, though, he took out a piece of paper and a silver-point pencil, and worked out the exact wording of the document he intended to forge.

It wasn't terribly elaborate—but it wasn't every day that someone came to an Imperial storage depot, authorized to empty it and the Imperial pay coffers of every scrap, bit of grain, and copper coin. The wording had to be such that it would cause no one to question it during the time he and his men were there.

This was the plan. He had one chance to ensure the survival of *all* of his men this winter—if the storage depot was fully stocked, as he expected it to be, there would be enough supplies there to see them all through, not only until spring, but possibly even well into summer. If the coffers were full, the men could be paid for long enough that he would have the time to win their personal loyalty. Even if there was no place for the soldiers to spend the money locally, their morale would be buttressed simply by having it to spend later. So now it was time.

This was the Portal he had targeted for reopening, the one leading to the storage depot lying nearest them. Fortunately, it was *in* his duchy, and he'd had to fight the temptation to use it to flee homeward, leaving his men to loot the depot and then fend for themselves. But his duty lay here; his duchy was in good hands, and there was no one there he had any real emotional ties to. And frankly, when his raid was complete, he would be much safer here than there. *Here* was a known quantity. The mage-storms may have left his home duchy a chaotic wreck, and holding a Portal open long enough to move more than just a raiding party through could be impossible.

This was a small Portal, able to take only a few men at a time, and the mages doubted that they would be able to hold it open for more than a few hours. He would not be able to use it to bring more than a scant fraction of the troops home—but he *could* use it to bring everything they needed back here.

He had a select group of experienced and trusted men from his personal guard ready to move the moment he alerted them. They were all huge; as his bodyguards, they towered over him. Before joining his guard, they had all worked as stevedores or in similar occupations. The

Portal wasn't even large enough to admit anything bigger than a donkey; what they brought out would have to be moved with the help of those tiny beasts of burden and their own muscles.

Once he had the wording worked out, he dipped his pen carefully in the special ink, and began tracing the glittering letters on the snow-white vellum.

The very act of writing with such ink on such a surface brought back more memories—of overseeing the Imperial scribes, of writing such documents himself during a brief stint as an Imperial scribe, when he had been brought to court by his father at the age of sixteen.

All the discipline drilled into him at that time came back, steadying his hand, and sending his breathing into the calming patterns that enabled the scribes to work, bent over their desks, in a state of meditative concentration for hours at a time. This did not, however, keep him from making mistakes.

An Imperial document would be flawless. There would be *no* mistakes, no blots, no misspelled words. He could not permit the tiniest discrepancy between this document and the genuine ones that would have been presented ever since the depot opened.

He made and destroyed half a dozen copies before he had a perfect one. As he waited for the ink to dry, he threw the rest, and his faint original of the wording, into the fire. He watched them burn, making sure that they were all reduced to ashes before turning back to the next and most difficult part of his forgeries.

Ordinary red sealing wax would become something extraordinary before he was through with it.

He lit the tip of the brittle, gold-dust impregnated wax at his candle and dripped it carefully onto the vellum, at the very base of the document. While it was still hot and viscous, he pressed the Seal into it, and mentally twisted the energies about the Seal and the wax together, activating it. The metal of the Seal grew warm in his hand, and the wax beneath it glowed, first white, then yellow, then the red of iron in a fire.

Carefully, he raised the Seal from the vellum as the glow faded.

Impressed into the wax was something that deceived the eyes, but not the touch. His fingers told him that the wax impression was a sketchy bas-relief, but his *eyes* told him quite a different story.

What he *saw* was the Wolf Crown, rising out of the wax of the seal as if made from that wax, scintillating with gold dust and a hint of rainbow. Was it an illusion? Not exactly. Nor was it exactly reality. It lay somewhere in between the two.

He laid the Seal back in the drawer and sat where he was, catching himself with both hands on the desk as he went momentarily giddy with exhaustion.

He had not expected that, and it took him completely by surprise. Was it the effect of the mage-storms, or only that he was much older, and under much more strain, than he had been the last time he'd used the Seal? There was no way to tell.

And it didn't matter. If he was lucky, he would never have to use it again.

If I am wise, I will never use it again!

Nevertheless, luck and wisdom had very little to do with the traps Fate might hold for him. He put the Seal back into its hiding place, and put his forgery in with several other, perfectly genuine "contingency" documents that the Emperor had supplied him with when he traveled out here. No one knew exactly what documents he had, nor how many of them there were. When he took this one out of the stack, there would be no way that anyone could say that this one had not been among them originally.

He rested a while after that; no point in unlocking the door directly; someone might sense that magic had been at work here, and he wanted to wait for those energies to fade. Besides, it gave him a badly-needed chance to rest.

Only when the last of those energies had dissipated past *his* ability to detect them did he rise, unlock the door, and tell his bodyguards to summon his escort.

While there was still daylight left, it was time to make one of his periodic rounds of inspection, and survey his small and desperate kingdom.

Tremane never walked out of his personal stronghold without an escort of half a dozen strong, superbly-trained bodyguards. Of course, at least one of these men was in the pay of the Emperor. He didn't let it bother him, but rather set himself to winning, if not their complete loyalty, then at least a moment's hesitation when the time came for them to raise the assassination knives. *That* was his best defense against Imperial agents among those he was required to trust.

As he had told his generals, the preliminary defensive wall, a wood-and-daub palisade, had just been completed a few days ago. This palisade contained not only the Imperial camp, but the entire town within its protection. The local populace was *quite* happy to have them here now, although they had not been too pleased to see them at first. A few attempted incursions by what creatures the mage-storms had left behind had shown them that they could not possibly defend themselves against these weirdling beasts, so bizarre and unpredictable.

The palisade had been easy enough to construct; dead trees had provided the framework, which was filled in with wickerwork and then covered with a particular mix of mud that hardened to a rocklike state when dried. The wall was about a hand's breadth thick, and able to withstand a certain amount of punishment in the way of direct mass impact. It was enough to keep out "dumb" beasts, but Tremane was not about to take the chance that it would have to stand up to more than that. If conditions in the area outside the palisade worsened, there could be mobs of people roaming the countryside, looking for loot, food, or shelter. Tremane was not about to risk the lives of his men against a mob when a well-made wall would take all the risk out of the situation.

Nor were unruly mobs the only possible danger. The war monsters of ancient legend had been able to take down simple palisades—or go over them—and those war-monsters had been created by magic. With more magic loosed in the land, it was possible that chance could recreate something like them. While it was still possible to build before real winter struck, his men were building; building a *real* wall, one that was constructed of sturdier, and less flammable, materials.

Normally they would have erected a second palisade of wooden tree trunks behind the wicker-and-daub construction, but the sheer size of the camp and the fact that the town was part of the camp made that notion prohibitive. He did not want to denude the countryside of trees, which was what such a palisade would require.

However, there was an abundance of limestone and other materials for making cement, so that was precisely what his walls were being made with. In one huge shelter the men cast molded bricks of cement and put them aside to dry and cure. When they were ready, they were taken to the perimeter for the next step.

Two brick walls were under construction there, behind the "protection" of the wickerwork wall. Construction proceeded in stages, with a team of men devoted to each section of the new wall. When the two brick walls were much taller than the tallest man in the ranks, rubble and earth were packed down between them, and a brick "cap" built over the rubble filling.

It would take an organized force to get over that, but Tremane wasn't done with his project even then. He planned for a curtain wall to be built on top of that, giving his men a protected walkway to use to patrol the perimeter, a protection only real siege engines could breech. Emotionally, he would have liked for the walls to be taller, but practicality told him that there was no real need for them to be that tall. No mere beast, however twisted by magic, could possibly come over the single-story wall—and if anything else came at them, it would be the men and their weapons that kept it back, not a wall.

Still, he found the three-story wall around his confiscated manor very comforting, and he would have liked for that same comfort to be shared by his troops.

Four out of every five of the men were working on the walls, and even with the wretched weather they had been enduring, they were making good progress. There was certainly no shortage of hands for what would ordinarily have been a very labor-intensive job. He'd broken up the long stretch into a hundred sections so that each team of men could see real progress being made. It gave them heart, gave them a reasonable goal to reach.

He took a tour of the brickworks, then went out to where the men were laying a course of bricks. Those who were real masons supervised the trickier bits; the rest laid bricks and spread mortar, bending to the work as if they, too, realized they might be grateful for such protection before long.

But even if Tremane had not personally felt a need for this wall, he would have had the men out doing *something* constructive. The best way to keep them from getting into trouble was to keep them busy—too busy to make up rumors and spread them, too busy to think of anything other than the good, hot meal waiting for them at the end of the day, and the warm bed to follow that.

The duties varied, and the men were rotated out through all of them unless their skills were particularly needed on one specific job. Those not actually laying bricks or making them were cutting stone, building molds, crushing stone, carrying bricks, or mixing cement and mortar.

And when the wall was complete—which looked to be sooner than he had hoped, for the men worked with a will and a speed he had not expected—he would put them to building winter quarters as soon as the design was determined. That could not come soon enough, and he hoped that somewhere among all of the books he had dragged with him on this journey there would *be* a design. Something that could concentrate and hold heat, something to take a winter a hundred times worse than any he had endured. He had to plan for the worst, then assume that his imagination was not up to the reality and add to his plans.

Perhaps—I wonder if I can't build the kitchens onto the barracks, and use the waste heat from the ovens and stoves to heat the barracks...

The thin, gray light filtering through the clouds made everything look faded and washed out, as if all the life had been leeched out of the world. Although there was no wind, the air was chilly and damp, and he was glad of his uniform cape.

There was a certain nervousness in the way the men moved, nervousness that had nothing to do with the inspection. Perhaps rumors were spreading about the newest monstrous creatures showing up in the countryside. If that happened to be the case—the men could be even more eager to see the wall completed than their commander was! *I would not be unhappy if they acquired a sense of urgency on their own. Fear is a powerful motivator, and the more motivation they have, the faster the walls will go up.*

He made a point of watching the men work at each section and complimenting the team leaders on their effort. At least the Hardornen rebels were no longer a factor. Where they had gone, Tremane had no firm answer, but he had some guesses and one of them was probably very close to being correct.

The rebels were, in the main, Hardornen farmers; the rest were young hotheads playing at being virtuous heroes. The former had crops to get in, and the latter were not numerous enough to make a head-on attack on a fortified town.

That was his optimistic guess. His pessimistic projection was far different, and he could not even begin to guess how probable it was.

There might be something out there that had eluded his own patrols; something that was concentrating on the Hardornens, who were not as well armed or armored, and not as accustomed to fighting eldritch creatures as the Imperial forces were. The Imperials were ensconced in one place, behind a wall; the Hardornen rebels had been in concealed camps scattered everywhere. It would be much easier for a clever, powerful creature to take men in a series of scattered camps than to pry the Imperials out of their protections.

On one hand, even the pessimistic guess allowed for a certain relief. If mage-warped creatures were out there picking off the Hardornens, then neither the Hardornens nor the monsters were attacking *his* men. But if that *was* the case and it was not simply that now that the Imperials were bottled up in one place, soldiering farmers had gone back to their farms, then sooner or later Tremane and his men would have to deal with whatever it was that was giving the natives trouble.

He hoped the reason for their current state of "peace" was just the harvest and the coming winter. He truly did. One thing that his scholars *had* managed to unearth was a series of chronicles and fragmentary tales from something called the "Mage-Wars." He did *not* want to have to face some of the creatures described in those faded pages. Even the names were ominous—makaar, cold-drakes, basilisks...

Perhaps some of those stories, which had thoroughly rattled his scholars, had leaked out to the men. That would account for the nervous haste—and yet the careful attention to detail—with which the wall was going up.

Try not to think of it for now. Wait until you have a chance to talk to those scholars. Perhaps there are physical defenses against those creatures suggested in the chronicles.

He only hoped that the defenses did not prove to be chimeras. Any defense that required more magic would be useless.

He completed his inspection and moved on to the troops on active patrol duty. There were always patrols coming in and out through the newly-constructed east gate; in spite of the fact that the walls were not yet up, he wanted them to be in the habit of coming and going by that route.

He was just in time to see one of his speculations made flesh.

Shouting and excited cries at the gate in one of the completed portions of the wall drew everyone's attention. Men ran toward the gates, where the shouting took on a tone of alarm; more men dropped their tools and ran to see what the matter was.

Tremane did not hasten his pace, however. The alarm trumpets had not sounded, so whatever it was that was causing the uproar, it was not an attack, and it would wait until he got there. The Commander did not, *must* not run, unless there was an attack in progress. No matter how he felt personally, he must maintain the dignity of his position, must show through his calm that he was in command of every situation. Panic, and even the appearance of panic, was contagious.

Now the gate, which had been standing open, darkened with a rush of people, both uniformed Imperial soldiers and civilians. At first, it only appeared that one of his patrols had run into some hostile farmers, but when he arrived at the gate itself, it was just in time to see stretcher bearers carrying away three badly-wounded men, and the too-quiet, covered forms of two dead.

The civilians were not under guard; it appeared that whatever had injured and killed, it had struck his men and the civilians indiscriminately.

Could it be that his worst guess was the correct one?

Heart in mouth, he looked for someone to interrogate, but the leader of the scouts found him first. "Commander, sir!" the man said, appearing right under his nose, snapping to attention and saluting smartly. "Reporting an encounter, sir!"

Tremane returned the salute just as crisply. "Report, scout leader."

By this time a cart drawn by a pair of sweating, nervous ponies had come into the compound through the gate, where a crowd of onlookers had gathered to await it. There was a tarpaulin draped over the back of it, hiding whatever it held. Someone unhitched the ponies and led them away before they bolted, which they threatened to do at any moment. Whatever was under the tarpaulin had them in a state of near-hysteria.

"We were on patrol, just past the ford across Holka Creek, when we heard shouting," the scout leader said. This was not a man Tremane knew personally; he fit the mold of the semi-anonymous Imperial officer candidates, so nondescript that they could all have been brothers of a particularly undistinguished house. Everything about them was average: height, weight, appearance. Except, of course, for their intelligence, which was much, much better than average, and their ability to apply what they learned, which was quite exceptional. The young officer continued, his words crisp and precise. "We investigated, and we found six of the locals defending against *that*—"

"That" was revealed as the men pulled the tarpaulin off the cart, showing that it was filled with a creature so bizarre that he would never have believed a description. In general, it was spiderlike; hairy with a round thorax, a rust-brown in color. It had *far* too many razor-taloned limbs, no discernible head, and a lumpy body which had been liberally feathered with arrows.

"It had already killed two horses and three men; a couple more of ours charged in before I could stop them and were wounded," the scout leader continued. "I ordered a withdrawal into safer range, then we kept hitting it with arrows until it dropped over."

"Good work," Tremane commended absently, unable to take his eyes off the monstrosity in the cart. Had it been a spider? If so, how did it get so large so fast? And if not, what *had* it been?

"Have any of the locals ever seen anything like this?" he questioned the scout leader, as they circled the cart, examining the dead beast. It stank, smelling vaguely of musk and stale sweat. No wonder the ponies had been afraid of it; the scent alone would have driven them half crazy. The rust-brown limbs were also furred, but thinly.

The scout shook his head. "No, Commander, it was as new to them as it was to us. They're very grateful to us, by the way."

So here it is; something deadly the mage-storms conjured up. Exactly what I was afraid of. Are there more of these things? I hope not.

"Take it to the scholars," he ordered. "Perhaps they can make something of it. And send word to the town, as well; there might be a priest or someone else who can identify what it is—or was."

The scout leader saluted and marched off to attend to his orders. Tremane turned away from the bizarre scene and headed for the main camp site. He still had an inspection to complete.

He walked along the rows of tents, surrounded by his guards; the few men in camp left off what they were doing and jumped to their feet, saluting smartly as he came in view. The tents were closer together than was usual in an open camp, arranged in neat rows, with the ground between kept immaculately cleaned. He noted a number of makeshift ways to keep warm already cropping up; straw or hay mattresses under the sleeping rolls, quilts made of two blankets with more hay stuffed in between. Canvas tents were no real protection against the cold; they barely screened against the wind. The more money a man had, the more blankets he'd bought, but that was no kind of solution.

The tents, despite their makeshift contents, were up to an inspection; he nodded his approval to the officer in charge and moved on.

He completed his inspection with the latrines—which had already been replaced with an efficient, if involved, system that sifted and dried the waste and turned it into grain-sized dry granules which were eagerly sought after by the local farmers for fertilizer. He didn't ask how it worked; he had a similar system on his own estate, and he had never wanted to know how *it* worked, either.

There are some things a man is not meant to know.

At least they wouldn't need to worry about their water supply being contaminated. He did *not* want to think about a plague of dysentery in the dead of winter. If even half the men survived something of that nature, he'd count himself lucky.

But as he turned his steps toward his headquarters, he found himself thinking about his estate, and his people, and wondering how they were faring. Were things better there than here? Could they be worse?

Absently, he returned the salutes of the men that he passed. He had been trying to keep thoughts of his home out of his mind, but they kept intruding.

At least I have no Duchess to worry about. For once, prudence has paid a dividend in having one less person to fret over.

Marriage had not seemed particularly wise once he became a candidate for the Iron Throne. He had not dared to marry for affection; his wife would have become nothing more than a target, a way to manipulate him, and he would put no woman he cared for through that kind of experience. He would not wed for pure expediency; his wife might well have been set upon him as a spy, or be in and of herself an attempt to manipulate him. He had kept all of his affairs strictly commercial, choosing comely and willing women from those on his estate, and setting them up with the husbands of their choice and a proper dowry after both of them tired of the situation. It satisfied the needs of the body, if not the heart, and he took care that there were no children to complicate the issue.

So although he had great affection for the land and the people of his estate taken as a whole, he had no particular concern for any single person on that estate. He felt warm fondness, in the way that a young man might have fondness for a favorite horse or dog, but nothing more passionate. He had always felt that the love of his heart was somewhere out there, distant, untouched. Gaining emotional attachment for his immediate surroundings… well, he hadn't deemed it to be of strategic advantage in the development of a Grand Duke or a potential Emperor. Prudence dictated that one should never extend himself past his ability to predict outcomes.

It was altogether fortunate, given the effect of these mage-storms, that his family had maintained a tradition of conservatism where the management of the estate was concerned.

People called us old-fashioned and sometimes laughed at us, but we'd never depended on magic to run the estate. Water was pumped by hand or by windmills, water mills ground the grain, transportation was by well-maintained roads, using horses and mules, ridden or driven. So of all of the lands claimed by the Empire, Tremane's duchy was probably one of those that was better off than most at the moment.

As for Kedrick, he's young, but he's sound, or I wouldn't have left him in charge in the first place. His current heir, a young cousin, was as well-schooled in the management of the estate as Tremane could manage before he left. Now he had plenty of incentive to do the job right; if he failed, he'd starve right along with the others.

I did everything I could for them. It will have to be enough. I certainly can't manage anything more at the moment.

Though if he could get back, *with* the troops, the duchy could certainly support that many more mouths to feed. It would be impossible to pry him out of his little kingdom with his own private army. That might be a thought to tuck away, for later consideration.

And as I recall, there was a scarcity of eligible young men round about there. It wouldn't be a bad thing, to tie the men to me by marriage...

Once back at the manor house, he dismissed four of the men and went on to his rooms with his usual two trailing along behind him. He stopped at the office where his chief aide sat behind a desk laden with lists. Young Cherin looked up at Tremane's footstep; the aide could easily have been the older sibling of the scout leader. Brown hair, brown eyes, sun-browned skin, square and unremarkable face; he was neither ugly nor handsome, but at least Tremane did remember his name, which had not been the case with his last aide. The poor boy had been so self-effacing that Tremane often forgot he was in the same room. He was so good at being inconspicuous that Tremane eventually sent him off to his spymaster for special training.

"Have you any reports for me?" he asked as the young man looked up, then jumped to his feet with a crisp salute.

"No, Commander," was the prompt reply. Tremane sighed; he'd hoped that at least one of his people would have some ideas for meeting the coming winter. But perhaps he was asking too much, too fast.

"Carry on, then," he replied automatically. The youngster saluted again and returned to his work; lacking anything else constructive to do, Tremane went back to his own suite to sit at his desk and leaf through the old reports listlessly.

A word caught his eye; *Valdemar.* It was nothing much; just a report that the Valdemarans had been working frantically on a way to block out the mage-storms themselves.

He hadn't thought much about the report at the time he'd first read it, but now as he reread it, he began to wonder about some of his earlier assumptions.

I was so certain that they were the source of the storms, he mused, staring at the fire in his small fireplace and listening with half an ear to the sounds of his men drilling in the courtyard below his office window. He found that sound rather comforting in its ordinary familiarity. *I was so certain that this was some strange new weapon that Valdemar had unleashed upon us. But according to this, they have been suffering as badly as we have. Their Queen doesn't have the reputation for being ruthless that Charliss has. So would she turn something like this loose on her own people just to eliminate us?*

She might, of course. just because Selenay did not have a reputation for being ruthless, it didn't follow that she was *not* ruthless. She might simply be a very good actress. She could be mad, too; that was hardly a novelty among royalty.

What was more, Valdemar did not depend on magic for anything. It didn't even *have* magic as Tremane knew the art. So the only hardships that Valdemar was suffering were those caused by the storms interacting with the physical world—

But there, his reasoning broke down, as he thought about the creature his men had brought in. *Only? Not a good choice of words. There was nothing "only" about that monster.*

And as a counter to the rest of his arguments, there was the entirely random nature of the storms and their effect. Why would *anyone* who was sane—and he had seen no reason to think that Queen Selenay was insane—unleash something whose effects were so completely unpredictable? If you had a weapon and you knew what it did, of course, you used it. But if you had a weapon and you had *no idea* what it was going to do—well, there was no sane reason to use it, not when it could harm you as badly as it harmed your enemies.

Now his head hurt, and he rubbed his temples with the heels of his hands. He hadn't *liked* sending that assassin in to destroy the alliance Valdemar was making. Something had told him at the time that he might be making a mistake, but he had persisted in order to make the mage-storms stop.

But they didn't stop, did they? In fact, they got worse.

Could he have made a major error in judgment? Granted, the alliance hadn't been disrupted, but at least one of the more important mages had been eliminated. Since the storms hadn't started until after that Karsite priest had arrived in Valdemar, it made sense that he was one of the prime forces behind the mage-storms, *if* they were indeed originating from Valdemar. With him gone, they should have stopped.

What if Valdemar was not perpetrator, but fellow victim?

His head hurt worse than before. If he'd had better spies—but he didn't. He'd done his best to break up the alliance with Karse, and it hadn't happened. He'd tried to scatter them, leaving them as disorganized as a covey of quail scattered by a beater. But they *weren't* disorganized, and his assassin hadn't even made an appreciable difference in their level of efficiency. Furthermore, and this was the important point, the mage-storms continued, increasing in frequency and in power.

So what if I was wrong?

He brooded on that for a while, feeling sicker and sicker the longer he thought about it. If that was the case, he had ordered the assassinations of people who could have been his allies against the storms.

Nothing like burning your bridges *before* you reached them.

I haven't heard from the assassin, and that fool of an artist would contact me if he thought he was in the tiniest danger. He shifted his position in the chair as his back began to ache and his legs to twitch restlessly. *The fool must have gotten caught, though I can't imagine how. He's probably dead by now. Even the Valdemarans wouldn't keep an assassin alive. They're probably working out ways to pickle his head and send it to High Priest Solaris in Karse.*

In fact, given the evidence from Valdemar, the assassin must have been caught before he did any damage. Only that would account for the seamless way in which Selenay and her allies were presenting themselves.

He botched the assassination, then he botched his attempt to escape. That's what I get for relying on operatives someone else puts in place.

He shook his head and checked in a desk drawer for a headache remedy. Like the Hardornens, he had other things to worry about besides far-off Valdemar. At the moment, there was nothing they could or could not do to him or the Imperial forces. And there was nothing he could do to or about them.

It was far more important to deal with the immediate survival of his own troops.

I must have those plans for winter quarters. Should I step up the patrols? What are we going to do about food supplies if the plan can't be carried out?

Could he get his men to help the locals make a really *efficient* harvest? There was always grain left in the fields, but if he sent his men out to glean behind the harvesters, there would be that much more—

It might not seem like much, but experience had taught him that many small gains often added up to a large total. If he could just find enough of those little gains, he might have enough to ensure his victory against his real enemy.

Not Valdemar, but the mage-storms, and what the storms gave birth to. *Concentrate on one enemy at a time. I can't afford to divide my attention or my resources...*

Frantic pounding at his bedroom door woke him. He had taken to leaving a single lamp burning, not because the darkness disturbed him, but because he might be awakened at any hour. He raised himself up on one elbow, instantly alert. "Enter!" he called imperiously. Keitel, Sejanes' apprentice, burst in the moment he spoke the word. Behind him trailed his aides with more lamps and his clothing. Only one thing could have brought Keitel and the aides here at this hour, in such a state of excitement.

"The Portal?" he asked, reaching for his trews and pulling them on.

"It's up, Commander," the skinny youngster blurted, every hair on his head standing up in a different direction. "Sejanes sent for the men—he said to tell you the Portal's unstable, he doesn't know how long he can hold it open, but that you'll have the time for what we need most."

"Get back to him, then; he'll need everyone to keep it open, including you." Excitement chased the last sleep-fog from his mind. The youngster nodded, hesitated for a moment, then fled the room. Tremane pulled on the rest of his clothing, his aides handing each piece to him as quickly as he donned the last. From his bedside table he took the packet of papers he had ready and stuffed it into the breast of his tunic. He jumped to his feet, stamping hard to settle his boots in place, and turning that motion into a leap of his own for the door. His aides and guards sprinted down the hall behind him; from their panting he was amused to think they were finding it unexpectedly difficult to keep up with "the old man."

Didn't pay any attention to the amount of time my swordmaster spends training me, obviously. The few guards and the like that he passed stared after him with eyes wide and mouths agape. The Commander never ran—

Except when time is against us. If Sejanes said that the Portal was unstable, he was not exaggerating for effect. Tremane cursed as his boot soles slipped and skidded on the stone floors; this would be a fine time to slip and break an ankle!

The manor was built around a central courtyard, and it was here that the mages had set up their working area. Tonight the courtyard was ablaze with light, torches in every available sconce—and in the center of the courtyard, doubling the illumination, was the Portal.

To Tremane's experienced eye, the instability was obvious; instead of a clean curve, the edge of the Portal wavered and undulated like a ribbon in a breeze. It should not have been giving off as much light as it was, either; that was a sign of wasted energy.

The mages surrounded the Portal, each adding his effort to the whole. To the untrained eye, the Portal itself, a dark hole, laced with lightning and surrounded by white fire, could easily have been a living thing. It had a feeling of *life*; in this case, a rather sinister life, and the movement of its edge added to the effect. To the trained eye, however, the Portal was an inferior specimen of its type. It was the kind of structure a group might build as their first effort at such an undertaking.

As Tremane and his escort came through the doorway and slowed to a walk, the mages surrounding the Portal managed to exert a bit more control over their creation. The boundary stiffened into a proper curving arch, and the dark, energy-laced center faded, replaced by a view of a loading platform and a warehouse wall.

The rest of the handpicked men entered at a quick-march from another door, then took their places on the cobblestone courtyard with drill-team precision. Tremane straightened his uniform tunic and took his place at their head; his aides and all but two of his guards fell back. There were no wasted orders or movements. As they had all rehearsed, the men moved in behind him as he strode toward the Portal and through it.

He had expected the usual disorientation of a Portal-crossing, but this was much worse. As his feet touched the floor of the warehouse Portal-platform on the other side, he staggered and went to one knee. His men were similarly disoriented as they came through, wavering to one side or another as if they were drunk or faint. One or two clutched their stomachs and turned pale.

He fought back nausea and regained control of himself by hauling himself erect, closing his eyes, and locking his knees until his dizziness passed.

He opened his eyes again as soon as his stomach and balance settled. He and his men stood precisely where he had expected them to be; on a wide loading platform in front of the permanent Portal, under a clear night sky. Two steps down took them to the walkway, and a ramp ran from the walkway to the large wooden loading doors that were directly before them. The walkway led to the office, and predictably there was a light in the office window. This *was* an Imperial depot; there would be a clerk on duty, no matter what the hour. Tremane pulled his packet of forged and genuine papers from his tunic.

"Stay here until you see the loading doors open," he told the men, then motioned to his guards to follow. He didn't think about the fraud he was about to perpetrate, or he might have shown some sign that not all was correct. He simply walked briskly to the office and pulled open the door, confronting the startled clerk inside with a bland and impassive expression.

He dropped his papers on the desk in front of the middle-aged, stoop-shouldered man, and stepped back, folding his arms over his chest. This place had the familiar look and smell of every Imperial office—the precise placing of desk, stool, and filing cases, the scent of paper, pungent ink, and dust, with a hint of sealing wax and lamp oil.

The clerk gingerly picked up the top paper and read it through; he examined the seal, his face reflecting growing bewilderment, and then read the second. By the time he reached the end of the stack and looked up at Tremane, his face was stiff with shock.

"S-sir—" the clerk stammered, "—s-surely this can't b-be right—"

"I have my orders," Tremane said flatly. "You have yours."

"B-but—these orders—they s-say—you are t-to strip the d-depot—"

Tremane allowed his expression to soften a little. "Friend, with all the Portals down, it's going to be impossible to get supplies in or out of here. We had to make an extraordinary effort just to get *this* one working, and it won't last past the next storm, if that. Shouldn't the supplies go to men who need them, before they rot or get spoiled by vermin?"

The direct appeal, one to the clerk's good sense and logic, had the desired effect. The man faltered, looking from the papers to Tremane and back again. "But if there are no supplies here, there's nothing for us to do—"

"That's why the last papers authorize you to take indefinite leave," Tremane explained patiently. "Strange things are occurring, and you are stationed out on the edge of the Empire, alone and unsupported. There is no reason for you to suffer this isolation when you could be sent home during this crisis. If the warehouse is empty there will be no need to guard or staff it. Your Emperor knows that you must be anxious about your families, and he knows that without Portals it will probably take you some time to make your way to them. Hence, he has given you indefinite leave."

The clerk picked up the last paper and reread it, his face clearing. After all, it *did* authorize Tremane to pay him a full year's salary as discharge pay—him and every other clerk here. "There's just the four of us, Commander. Standard depot—and we're all clerks, no—"

"That's quite all right; I brought my own men," he interrupted. "Let's just get those doors open and move out those supplies while we still can."

"Yes, sir!" The clerk jumped to his feet, knocking over his stool in his haste, and hurried over to unlatch the winch that operated the huge loading doors. By clever use of mechanical contrivances, this rather undersized and scrawny individual was able to open doors even the strongest guard would have had difficulty hoisting.

As soon as the doors opened, the men poured in. This, too, had been rehearsed, since every Imperial depot was built to the same pattern. They went straight to the most important items of food and rough-weather supplies. Once those were through the Portal, they would move to items of lower priority: uniforms, bedding, and blankets. And once those had been carried off, they would proceed to strip the depot for as long as the Portal held. Imperial depots were notorious for containing equipment so antique and out-of-date that even a historian would have been hard put to determine the function. Among these, there might be items useful to them in a time when magic had ceased to work. And if nothing else, such items could be converted to their component parts.

Meanwhile, Tremane ordered the clerk to get him the records and to open the lock room at the back of the office containing all records and the Imperial gold stores normally held to pay for deliveries from civilian merchants and for pay shipments to the troops. Out of that, he counted out the discharge pay for the four clerks, putting the small, wafer-thin gold coins up in pay packets and neatly labeling each with the man's name and his own seal.

"As of this moment, you are free to go," he said kindly as he handed the clerk his particular packet. "We can carry on from here. If you have a stable, help yourself to mounts and baggage animals on my authority."

"Thank you, Commander," the clerk replied, his face now full of eagerness. He shuffled backward, toward the door, as he spoke. "I've got a long way to travel—perhaps I ought to make an early start of it—"

He could not back out of there fast enough, and Tremane thought he knew why. Every Imperial clerk indulged in a certain amount of graft; reselling Imperial supplies and the like, recording that he had paid more for deliveries than he'd actually given out. This man wanted to get out of reach before Tremane compared the lists of what *should* be there with what actually *was*.

Little did he know that Tremane didn't care. Of course the mice would have nibbled the crust; most of the loaf was still there, and that was what mattered.

He had his own reason for wanting to be rid of the clerks. When—or if—the authorities *did* descend on this place, if there was no one here, that would confuse the situation still further. Somehow the authorities would have to decipher where the clerks had gone before they could find out whose seal was on the pay packets—assuming that the clerks *kept* the packets. He intended to take his papers with him when he left. All the authorities would have was a looted warehouse, with no idea who was responsible. Unless, of course, one or more agents managed to get "left" behind.

Even if that happened, it would still take the agents a long time to reach the capital and the Emperor. They might not make it. Conditions could be bad enough here to prevent even an experienced agent from reaching his contact. All of the spymasters relied on Portals and mage-crafted messengers to get information to and from their agents. Without those, an agent might not even know who his contact *was!*

Meanwhile, his guards were taking the gold through and handing it over to the custody of his *other* guards, to be placed under double guard and lock in the strong room. Gold was heavy; the men could not move much at a time. But, as he had hoped, there was enough there to pay his entire army for a year. That would give him the time he needed to win their personal loyalty.

Once the gold was all across, he directed his two guards to join the rest of the men in stripping the warehouse to the bare floor, walls, and ceiling. There were even stores of lumber here, and if he got the chance, if the Gate held long enough, he'd take those.

They had been at this task for long enough that the vital supplies were all through; now the men just made a human chain, passing boxes, bundles, crates, and barrels through without bothering to check what was in them. He had clerks of his own that could inventory the mass of supplies at leisure.

While they worked, Tremane helped himself to the warehouse records. What he found there confirmed his fears and his hopes; the personnel here had been in disarray for weeks, without orders, contact from their superiors, or any sign that the Empire still existed. They had no idea what was going on; all they knew was that the Portals suddenly went dead, and that there were strange things going on outside the safe walls of the fortified depot. What he found indicated a certain amount of panic on their part, and he didn't blame them. In their place, he'd have been panicking, too.

The huge warehouse echoed strangely as the contents were emptied; the torches his men placed to light their way made oddly-moving shadows among the racks and shelves. He wished there might be time to loot the small stable that was surely attached to this post—but on the other hand, the four clerks would probably need every beast there, just to get themselves and their own goods home safely. *It wouldn't do to be greedy*, he chuckled inwardly.

The Portal showed no signs of deteriorating, and this warehouse was more than half emptied. As he checked on the progress of his men, he caught sight of another door where he had not expected one, and he stopped dead to stare at it.

Another door? Could it be possible that this depot was a *complex* of warehouses?

He ran across the dusty floor and wrenched the door open. Enough light came from the torches behind him to show him a sight to make his heart leap.

Grain. Tin barrel after barrel of grain—meant for horses, for cavalry, but perfectly edible by humans.

And here was the answer to the dilemma of how to keep both town and garrison alive. This would buy him the loyalty of the town, especially if the winter ran long and hard and supplies ran short. The farmers had been complaining that the weather had been bad and the harvest poor, and he had been assuming their complaints were nothing more than the usual. Every farmer he had ever known had complained about the weather and the harvest—they always did, and never would admit to having a good year.

But what if this time the complaints were genuine? He had seen the weather and the state of the fields for himself. How could he have thought that the harvest would be *normal?*

Because I didn't dare think otherwise, or I would have given up.

Quickly he hailed half of the men over to this new storehouse, telling them to haul the grain but leave the hay bales that would also be here for the very last. Hay was not a priority, but if there was time, why not take it, too?

I need more men. It was a risk, bringing still more men—men who had not been checked beforehand—across an unstable Portal, but the gain was worth the risk. Almost certainly some of these would arrange to be left behind. There *would* be agents among them. He didn't care.

He ran out to the Portal and sent a message across with one of the guards; Sejanes was no fool and he should know how many more would be safe to send across.

He went back to the men—but now it was to join them in a frenzy of hauling. He joined the line, working side-by-side with one of his own bodyguards and a man whose name he didn't even know for certain. When the man cursed him for clumsiness when he dropped a box, and cursed him again for being slow, he kept silent. It was more important to get one more box across that Portal than it was to maintain the distinction of Commander and subordinate. He sensed, rather than saw, more men making a second line; at the time he had his own hands full and sweat running into his eyes.

He had never done so much hard physical labor in his life. His muscles and joints begged him for the mercy of a rest, his lungs burned, and his throat and mouth were as parched as if he were crossing the desert. There was no rest; his line was down to transporting the lumber at the back of the warehouse, but the other line still had grain to move.

There was light outside now; at some point dawn had arrived, and he had missed it. How had Sejanes managed to hold the Portal up so long? The poor mages would be only semiconscious for a week after this!

His line broke up at that point; there was nothing more to move. Half of them went to the sides of the warehouse to try to get the few large objects—dismantled siege engines—that could not be hauled by a single man. The rest joined the grain line, but now the grain line was actually hauling hay bales!

At just that moment, a whistle shrilled from the Portal; the signal that the mages had held it as long as they could. Tremane had drilled his men in this, too; every one of them dropped what he was holding and sprinted for the Portal at a dead run. The new men who had not been drilled took their cue from the rest. He joined them; as they reached the outside they formed into four running ranks, since the Portal was only large enough for four abreast to cross at once. Those four ranks continued to race for the stone arch that marked this side of the Portal.

Despite his care, he knew that when he called for more men, he had allowed many agents to cross over, and now some of the men would deliberately lag behind, to remain when the Portal collapsed. There would be agents of the Emperor and of his own personal enemies among them. That would be fine; no one else knew that his orders were forged.

In a way, he wished them no ill, for if this Imperial depot had been left so completely on its own, that did not speak well for conditions in the Empire as a whole. They would have to somehow find transportation, work their way across several client states, and only then would they reach anything like solid Imperial territory. Faced with such a situation, he would give up and find a place to wait out the situation; they might well do the same.

And as for the rest who lagged behind—they had worked with a will, and he could not find it in his heart to condemn them for snatching the chance to stay on home ground. Without a doubt, the Empire would need them as much or more than he would.

And every man who stays here is one less mouth to feed—as well as one less agent that might turn to sabotage in the absence of other orders.

He was one of the last men through, and the instability in the Portal was directly reflected in the effect the crossing had on him. He landed on the other side in a tumble, unable to stand, his head reeling, his stomach racked with nausea. He lay on his side in a helpless heap for a moment until someone dragged him clear.

He opened his eyes and regretted doing so; the courtyard was spinning around him and the bright sunlight lanced into his skull like a pair of knives thrust into his eye sockets. He closed his eyes again, hastily, and simply lay where he was, waiting for the sickness to pass.

"It's coming down!" someone shouted, voice hoarse with exhaustion.

"Let it go—we can't wait any longer!" That was Sejanes' voice; the old man must have counted noses and come up short. "They'll be all right over there—drop the pattern, before it burns us all away!"

He opened his eyes again, just in time to see the Portal collapse, folding in on itself until it was a single point of bright, white light that burned for a moment, then crackled out.

The illness had passed enough to let him rise; he found that he was in a corner, dragged there by some wise soul on this side of the Portal. That was a help, for with the aid of the wall he was able to get to his feet and lean against firm support until the rest of his equilibrium returned.

Finally, when he thought he could present a reasonable front, he walked slowly out into the courtyard full of collapsed men, collapsing mages, and heaps of supplies.

The guards he had left here were still standing; he sent one of them off for help. "Stretchers and stretcher bearers," he directed. "Everyone down should be taken to his own quarters and given full sick leave for at least one day. Have the Healers look at them." He looked around the courtyard at the supplies still there, and frowned. They had emptied two warehouses—why wasn't this courtyard stuffed with supplies?

The guard correctly interpreted that frown. "As soon as things started coming across, Sejanes sent for more men to move the supplies by wagon out to storage, Commander," the man said. "They'll be back shortly."

Tremane's frown cleared. "Good. And the clerks are making inventories?"

"Yes, sir. Everything is as you ordered, Commander, except—" the guard could no longer suppress his grin, "—except that Sejanes held the Portal open longer than even *he* thought possible. Commander, you did it!"

Now, for the first time in weeks, he relaxed enough to reply to the guard's grin with one of his own. "Now, let's not tempt the Unkindly Ones with our hubris. We were lucky. We have no idea how long those supplies sat there, or what condition they're in. Half of them could be useless."

The guard nodded sagely. "Indeed, Commander. Shall I send for your sedan chair as well as the litter bearers?"

Tremane was about to refuse—he had scarcely used his sedan chair a handful of times in the past year—but a sudden wave of dizziness made him reconsider quickly and nod. "Do that. I'll be over by Sejanes."

He managed to get as far as his old mentor before *needing* to sit down, and he succeeded in seating himself on a box without making it look as if he had collapsed. The old man was in about the same shape as Tremane—which in itself was remarkable, given the strain under which the mages must have been laboring. Sejanes lay flat on his back on the cobblestones, and acknowledged Tremane's presence with only a wave of one hand.

"Well, old man," Tremane said, "we did it." He was rewarded by a thin smile and a weak twinkle in the old mage's eyes.

"We did. We've bought the time you needed, my boy. And I hope you're prepared to reward your hard-working mages—"

"I'm having you all moved into the best quarters this place affords," he interrupted. "There's no reason for you to be bivouacked with your units anymore when your units can't use your services. And to head off any question of favoritism, I'll make it known that after the great personal sacrifice you have all made in this effort, you've all been rendered invalids, or the next thing to it. Therefore, you need special consideration."

"You won't be far wrong, boy," Sejanes replied seriously. "We won't be up to much but bed rest for days."

"Then bed rest is what you'll get," Tremane promised. After a few silent minutes, the haulage crew returned, and with them, his aides. He hailed his chief aide Cherin over and put him in charge of the mages.

"Put them in the infirmary for now," he said. "And find a way to reshuffle my officers so that we can get quarters in the manor for every mage who worked on the Portal. I want them all moved in before the end of the week. They're going to be invalided out of field service for now."

Cherin looked at the mages, still lying where they had collapsed, and seemed more than convinced. "There're some store rooms could be made into barracks, Commander," he offered. "We could take your bodyguards, put 'em in there, shuffle the pages and messengers into *their* barracks, put the aides in the little rooms the boys have been in, and that'll give you rooms for each mage and still let the aides have private quarters."

"And it puts the boys back in a common room where the page-sergeant can keep an eye on them. That's good," Tremane agreed, with a wry, yet appreciative smile. "Those little imps have been unnaturally good lately, but I don't have faith that the spell is going to last. See to it."

The aide saluted. "Sir!" he replied and marched off to begin the shuffling.

"You're a good lad, Tremane," Sejanes said gruffly, and closed his eyes.

At about that time, the sedan chair and its four carriers arrived, and Tremane decided it was time to let his aides do the work of getting everything organized. He gave each of them assignments and ordered them to have reports on his desk when he woke up. He climbed stiffly to his feet and took his place in his chair. The four carriers raised their poles to their shoulders and marched off to his suite as he lay back and closed his eyes.

I would like to sleep for a week. He wouldn't, though. He'd wake up as soon as his body had recovered enough to allow him to function. By then he would have some idea of what, precisely, they had looted from that depot.

He did know this much; even if, as he said, fully half of what they'd taken proved useless, he still had enough to see his men through a winter out of a Northman's nightmares. His men—and possibly even the town as well.

The future looked a hundred times brighter than it had yesterday. And as dark as things were at the moment, that was enough.

2

A stable was hardly the place one normally took lessons in protocol, but neither Karal of Karse nor his adviser were precisely "normal" as an ambassador and his tutor.

It was a cold gray day; the sky was a solid sheet of low-hanging clouds. On the whole, the stable was not an unpleasant place to be on such a day, especially not for a young man who had begun life as a horse boy. It was no ordinary stable either. This was the foul-weather shelter for all Companions now resident at the Herald's Collegium and Palace at the Valdemar capital of Haven. The stalls were mostly empty; those that were filled were preternaturally silent, since Companions seldom acted or sounded much like horses.

But in every other way, this building, as no other place in all of Haven, reminded Karal of home. The warm scent of hay, the dusty aroma of grain, the rich odor of leather (as much a taste as a smell); all those comforted him and made him relax. Although the air outside was cold, inside, sitting next to a huge brown-tiled stove, Karal was as comfortable as he would have been in his own room.

"All right," Karal said, rubbing his tired eyes. "Explain to me how the followers of all these religions manage not to slaughter each other over their differences one more time."

That warm fire behind the iron door of the stove at his back crackled cheerfully, and the relative gloom of the stable was actually rather restful to his aching eyes. It was too bad Florian wouldn't fit into his suite at the Palace, though. A hot cup of tea would have been very nice right now.

Of course, a hot cup of tea might have put him to sleep, which was not a good idea at the moment.

His adviser shook his white head until his mane danced. *:It's really very simple, Karal. The single rule that each of them* must *obey if they wish to continue practicing in Valdemar is "live and let live." You can proselytize as much as you wish, but you may not persecute, harass, intimidate, or otherwise make a nuisance of yourself. The secular laws of Valdemar take precedence over the dictates of every religion. No matter how deeply your religious feeling is offended by something allowed according to the religious practices of your neighbor, you have no right to force him to live by your rules, and no right to try to. If you can't live by that, then you are escorted to the border and left there.:*

Karal tried to imagine something like that being effective in Karse and failed utterly. *His* people would simply ignore the law and revel in their holy and God-given right to persecute, harass, intimidate, or even murder those who did not agree with them. If *their* God, in their own narrow interpretation of His Writ and Rules, said that something was wrong, then it was wrong for *everyone*, whether or not anyone else agreed even with that particular interpretation. Karsites had been cheerfully slaughtering each other over interpretations of the Writ and Rules almost as long as they had been killing those outside their borders and religion. Things had been different once, as he had found from his reading, but the current state had been holding for generations. Since Vanyel's time, in fact. Or, as Ulrich would have pointed out—since the time that the Son of the Sun had been elected by the Sun-priests and not by Vkandis Himself. "It seems too simple to work," he replied wearily.

Florian scraped a hoof on the floor, which Karal had learned was the equivalent of a shrug. *:I suppose it works largely because it was established as a law back when there were fewer people in Valdemar and all of them were of the same religion. At that point, of course, no one saw any reason why such a law shouldn't be in effect. If you plant a tree early so that it has time to grow, the roots are too deep for a later storm to tear it up.:*

A cat from the stables strolled by—a perfectly ordinary black-and-white, and not one that bore the vivid markings of a Firecat. Karal held out his fingers to the mouser, but his majesty had other things on his mind.

"That sounds like another Shin'a'in proverb," Karal observed, turning a little so that his right side could benefit from the warmth of the stove. Was it his imagination, or was it too early in the autumn for it to be so cold? "You've been tromping around An'desha too long."

Florian "chuckled"—more of a whicker. The fact that Karal was talking to a blue-eyed white horse might seem very odd to anyone from beyond the borders of Valdemar. The fact that he was talking to a Companion—or, as he would have said a year ago, a "cursed Valdemar Hellhorse"—would have been sheer blasphemy to many still in his own land of Karse. But Karal had learned more about Heralds and their Companions in that last year than he had ever dreamed possible, and now he relied on Florian's advice in the ways of Valdemar as surely as he relied on his friend An'desha's advice in the ways of magic. Both were equally opaque to him although he was familiar with the effects of magic if not the practice of it. As for the ways of Valdemar—they were all as odd as this surface congeniality among religions.

"I guess I'd be safe to assume that any time I have to deal with a priest *from* Valdemar that they're going to tolerate me, even if they don't like me." At Florian's nod, he shrugged. "At least that's easier than waiting for holy assassins to waylay me in the hallway."

:Holy assassins are going to come from outside Valdemar, if they come at all, and Kero has had a particular watch out for that sort for some time.: "Kero," of course, was Herald Captain Kerowyn, the only Herald in all of the history of Valdemar who was also the Captain of a mercenary Company. She was in charge of Valdemar's less conventional defenses—the ones that the Lord Marshal did not want to know about officially. She was also one of the—former—Great Enemies of Karse, and had been rumored to eat Karsite babies on toast for breakfast.

Karal could vouch for the toast, and Kero swore she didn't touch babies, Karsite or otherwise, before lunch at the earliest.

Florian did not actually "speak" to him; the Companion's "voice" echoed inside Karal's head. They called it "Mindspeaking" here. The locals took it for granted that Heralds and Companions talked to each other just like two human friends. One Herald could mention an appointment with a thought, and his Companion would round the corner a moment later, to bear the Herald on his way. It was odd, still, to see a Herald and Companion walk by, and witness the Herald suddenly breaking up in laughter at some silently-shared joke while the Companion whickered merrily. Heralds spoke with their minds and Companions answered, and none of it was considered the least bit unusual.

This was a magic that Karal had never even known existed before he came here—largely because in the past the Sun-priests did their best to eradicate children "Gifted" with such things. "Witchery," they called it, and hunted it out ruthlessly until Solaris took the Sun Throne.

Other Heralds had the ability to talk with each other as they did with their Companions. Some could move things without touching them, or see things at a distance. Others could see into the future or the past, and some had even stranger abilities.

All these things could be accomplished with the magic that Karal was familiar with, of course, but this was *not* the magic he knew. Sun-priests often had the ability to work "true" magic; the false priests used it to create "miracles" to deceive the gullible. Because such a power could be controlled, the Sun-priests had incorporated those with the ability to perform magic into their ranks, rather than destroying them.

The Valdemarans had the "witch-powers"; they called it "mind-magic," or "Gifts," and they were something that was inborn, though skill in them could be honed with training and practice.

Karal had gotten used to it, to a certain extent, although it never ceased to amaze him how casually the Heralds accepted these powers. And it would have been so very easy for those powers to be misused, as the power of true magic had been misused in Karse. Yet here—there were the Companions.

The only place to find training in mind-magic was at Herald's Collegium, and the only way to be accepted into the Collegium was to be Chosen by a Companion. Thereafter, the Companion acted as best friend, mentor, conscience, and sometimes stern taskmaster. The fact that the Companions happened to look like horses—always white, always blue-eyed—was incidental. Florian told him once that the initial reason Companions came in that particular "shape"—rather than, say, a dog or a cat—was because a horse was not only ubiquitous and hence invisible, but because a horse was weapon, fellow fighter, and transportation all in one. In Karsite mythology, as a sort of mirror image of the reality, the Heralds, in their all-white uniforms, were the "White Demons," and the Companions the "Hellhorses."

Florian had been "assigned" to him by the other Companions when he first arrived as the secretary to his mentor, the ambassador from Karse, Master Ulrich. Florian had assured him many times that he had *not* been "Chosen" to be a Herald, which was normally what happened when a Companion sought out a particular human and spoke to him in his mind. No, in this case, Florian was simply an adviser, someone who could steer him through the complicated tangle of life in the Kingdom of Valdemar without having an agenda of his own to pursue. Karal had no reason to mistrust the Companion's seemingly altruistic nature; after all, he had it on very trustworthy authority that Companions were the same as Karsite Firecats—particularly wise humans who had opted for rebirth in this rather odd form, the better to guide and advise those who held great power in their lands. Not being human, or having human concerns, made it possible for them to take the long, dispassionate view of things. That was the theory anyway. As Florian had once said, being solidly ensconced in a material body had a tendency to skew one's outlook sometimes. "And," he'd added obliquely, "it also depends on how many times you've been around."

Whatever *that* was supposed to mean.

Karal was graced—or burdened—with a Firecat, too, although he was not certain why. However, as wise as Altra was, he knew no more about Valdemar than Karal did. Both were somewhat handicapped when it came to understanding the land that had been Karse's enemy for centuries—as, once again, he was learning.

He dropped his head down into his hands for a moment, putting his cold fingertips against his aching temples. It helped, but not enough.

:You are tired,: Florian said with concern. *:I am not certain I should continue to drill you without some rest.:*

"I'd like some rest, too, but I'm meeting the *entire* Synod, or Assembly, or whatever it is they're calling it, tomorrow afternoon, and if I don't have the proper addresses down, I'm going to mortally offend someone." Karal sighed and massaged the muscles at the back of his neck. "I never *wanted* to be the Ambassador of Karse," he added mournfully. "I had my hands full enough being the aide. I was a *secretary*."

Florian didn't answer for a moment; he looked away, as if he were considering something. In the silence, Karal clearly heard mice scuttling around in the hay stored overhead. That was probably why the tomcat had not lingered for a scratch. *:I hesitate to suggest this—it means you would have to trust me much more than you already do—but there is a way around this particular problem.:*

"What?" Karal asked eagerly. He was perfectly willing to consider anything that might help at the moment. The "Holinesses," "Radiances," "Excellencies," and other titles were all swimming in his poor, overheated brain and would not stick to any particular "uniform." He had no idea how he was going to master them all by tomorrow. Like so many things, this meeting had been sprung upon him with little warning.

:If you'd let me inside your mind, let your barriers down, I could look through your eyes, see who you were talking to, and prompt you,: Florian replied hesitantly. *:I can show you how to let those barriers down easily enough. The problem is, I'll see more than surface thoughts if you did that. I'll know whatever you're thinking, and you tend to think about several things at once. You might not want me that—hmm—intimately in your mind.:*

Well, that was something of a quandary. *Did* he want Florian to know what he was thinking? Some of it wasn't going to be very flattering. He had already encountered some of the religious leaders of other sects here, and they had made it very plain that there was no love lost between them and the representative of Vkandis Sunlord—even if, or *especially* if, that representative was a field-promoted secretary.

Now, it was true that the followers of Vkandis Sunlord had wrought terrible things against the followers of other religions in the past. But that *was* the past, in days when the Son of the Sun had been (to put it bluntly) a corrupt and venial tool of other interests than Vkandis'. High Priest Solaris had put an end to that, to the war with Valdemar, and to the insular and parochial attitude of those under her authority regarding those who lived outside the borders of Karse. Things were different now, and there had been Sun-priests spilling their blood to save Valdemar to prove it. Furthermore, Karal was hardly old enough to have done anything personally to anybody under the old rule—despite the fact that some of these old goats seemed to hold him personally responsible for every slight and every harm worked upon their people and possessions since the time of Vanyel.

So Karal's innermost thoughts were hardly likely to be charitable.

On the other hand, if he couldn't trust Florian with those innermost thoughts, who *could* he trust?

"I think I had better accept that offer," he told the Companion. "But you ought to know you're likely to share in my headache as well."

:I don't mind,: Florian told him. *:Not at all. Now, this is what you do; it's easy, really. You know how it feels when I talk to you?:*

He nodded.

:Think of that, then imagine that you are reaching out a hand to me. When you "feel" me clasp it, your barriers will be down.:

It was actually quite easy to imagine just that, since Florian had never been a "horse" to him. He closed his eyes and stretched out an imaginary "hand" to his friend, and almost at once he had the uncanny sensation of having another "hand" enfold his. He opened his eyes, and for a moment experienced a very curious double image, the "Florian" he knew superimposed over a young man about his own age, thin, earnest, with dark hair and eyes, dressed in Herald's Whites.

The second image faded quickly, but Karal had to wonder. Was that what Florian *had* been—before?

:That's excellent!: Florian applauded. *:Can you sense the difference?:*

"Yes," he answered at once. "Now it's as if you're standing right at my shoulder and whispering in my ear."

:I'm seeing things through your eyes now. Mind you, I wouldn't advise it for the inexperienced. It's rather disorienting.: Florian chuckled, and Karal "felt" the chuckle at the same time that he heard the whicker.

:You're working so hard,: Florian continued wistfully. *:I only wish I could do more to help you.:*

"You help me a lot," Karal replied with feeling. "Just knowing that I have a real friend here helps more than I can say."

A light footstep at the door alerted him to the fact that he was no longer alone with Florian in the stable. "Only one?" An'desha asked as the Shin'a'in Adept entered the stable. "If I didn't know you didn't mean that literally, I would be sorely hurt." The teasing tone in his voice told Karal that he wasn't particularly serious.

As An'desha neared, Karal noted that he looked better than he had in days. Both of them had participated in a magical ceremony at the Valdemar/Iftel border that had been much more powerful and traumatic than either of them had ever dreamed possible. The end result of that was a temporary "breakwater" running from the northernmost tip of Iftel to the southernmost end of Karse, a breakwater that disrupted the mage-storms as they moved across the face of the land, broke them up and dissipated their energies harmlessly. It wouldn't last forever—for as the storms increased in power and frequency, they were tearing away at the new protections—but it bought them some time to come up with a better solution.

Of the two, An'desha had been the most exhausted, for he had been the one doing most of the work. Karal was not a mage; his mentor Ulrich had said once that he "had the potential to become a channel," but no one here knew what Ulrich had meant, until he was needed at the Iftel border.

Channeling must be instinctive, rather than learned. That was what other mages had said, once he described what had happened. He had recovered quickly, once they all returned to the capital of Haven and the expert care of the Healers. An'desha's recovery had been much slower.

An'desha's complexion was closer to the healthy golden tones of his Shin'a'in ancestors now, rather than the pasty yellow he *had* been sporting. There was more silver at the roots of his hair, which was hardly surprising, considering how much magical power he'd been handling. Handling the extremes of mage-energy bleached the hair and eyes to silver and blue, so Karal had been told. That was why An'desha's lover, the Tayledras Adept Firesong, had hair as white as snow before his eighteenth birthday, as it was to this day.

Karal had been told that An'desha had once been something called a "Changechild," a creature with a body that seemed part-animal, part-human; changed into that form by the spirit of an evil Adept who had taken possession of An'desha's body and twisted it into the form *he* chose, that of a cat-man. Mornelithe Falconsbane had eventually been driven out and destroyed, and by some miracle—literally a miracle, according to those who had been there at the time—An'desha's body had been returned to the form it had once held. With one exception.

An'desha's eyes were those of a cat's, still: green-yellow, and slit-pupiled. Now, though, they were growing paler, more silvery blue than greenish yellow. Again, that was the effect of all the magic An'desha had handled in setting up the breakwater.

Those were the outward signs of change. There were other signs; a calm that had not been evident before, an air of relaxation. *Confidence.* An'desha knew what he was now, and was comfortable with the knowledge. He also knew what he was not.

He was *not* Falconsbane, though he shared that evil creature's memories.

"I'm glad you know I did not mean to exclude you," Karal said with a welcoming smile.

"And I know what you meant—you are glad to have one *Valdemaran* friend. I am as much a foreigner and lost among these crazed folk as you." An'desha winked at Florian and dragged a short bench over from beside the stove. He was wearing clothing that marked him as foreign as Karal's Karsite robes, a cross between Hawkbrother garb and the quilted winter clothing of his own Shin'a'in nomads. "Firesong is complaining of the cold and swearing he will freeze to death before the first snow. Darkwind reminded him that his home Vale has winters worse than any in Valdemar. Firesong, of course, retorted that *he* never had to go out into such barbaric weather, and Elspeth chose to point out that he showed up at Darkwind's Vale riding *through* a snowstorm. *He* claimed it was because he represented his Vale and thus he *had* to make a dramatic appearance, and Darkwind said he was just posing. This became a contest of exaggerations, and no one noticed when I left." An'desha was laughing, so the "argument" must not have been that serious. "Firesong looking for pity, and he is not going to find it from a Herald and a Tayledras scout, I fear."

"Nor from you?" Karal teased.

"Nor from me." An'desha stretched out his booted foot toward the stove. "If he seeks it, I shall only tell him what he told me so very often; too much sympathy makes one look for excuses, not answers. If he does not like the weather, perhaps he should consider making a Veil to cover Haven and turning it all into a Tayledras Vale."

"Ouch! A hit, indeed." Karal chuckled, and Florian whickered his own amusement. "Poor Firesong! All hands are raised against him today."

"It is only the weather that makes him irritable," An'desha said matter-of-factly. "In that, I cannot blame him too much. Grim, gray, gloomy, and chill! I hope that the farmers are able to get their harvests in, or we all shall be wearing tighter belts come spring."

"I don't know. I haven't heard that things are any worse than previous years, but no farmer anywhere admits to a good yield," Karal replied. "I *have* heard that things have improved, now that the breakwater is up." That gave him an opening he'd been looking for. "An'desha—you were outside the Iftel border. Did you see anything when I went in?"

"How do you mean? I saw a great deal, both with MageSight and my own two kitty-slit eyes." An'desha pointed to them, then crossed his legs gracefully and leaned forward a little. The wood of his seat creaked as he moved.

Karal thought carefully and phrased his question as clearly as he could. "Did it seem to you that the magic barrier at the border actually... *recognized* me in some way?"

"Oh, there's no doubt of that!" An'desha told him firmly. "It touched and tested you before it allowed you to pass within. I Saw it myself. Short, then longer tendrils." He frowned a little as he concentrated. "The area you were in brightened, and I Saw things—it is hard to describe—I saw the energies touching you, and I knew from some of—of Falconsbane's memories that they were what he called 'probes,' ways to test someone. Though *what*, precisely, you were being tested for, I cannot say."

"But why did it recognize me?" Karal blurted. "Altra was very firm about that, remember? He said the border would only recognize *me* of all of us. So why me?"

"It wouldn't have been only you," An'desha pointed out. "He said that it had to be a Karsite Sun-priest of a particular kind. Ulrich would have been the first choice. And obviously, Solaris would have served as well."

"But what is the connection between the magic at the border of Iftel and a Karsite Sun-priest?" Karal asked, frustrated. "And just what *is* Iftel? No one can get in or out, except for a very few, all of them selected traders and Healers, and you couldn't get one of them to talk if you tortured him, which is the point, I suppose. I've asked Altra—*when* he happens to show up, which isn't often since we got back—and all he does is switch his tail and tell me that I'll find out when the time is right."

:I can't help you; I'm as baffled as you are,: Florian admitted. :Sorry, but there it is. Neither Altra nor Vkandis Sunlord have bothered to confide in this insignificant Companion.:

"I suppose we'll just have to be patient. Frankly, if your Vkandis is anything like the Star-Eyed, I'm afraid He's probably going to insist that you figure it out for yourself." An'desha shrugged. "Deities seem to be like that. If I were one, I'd have a little more pity on my poor, frustrated, thick-headed followers."

Karal had to laugh at that, and reflected again how much he himself had changed. A year ago such a joke would have had him white with shock at the irreverence, not to say blasphemy.

An'desha smiled. "Good. Finally, I've made you laugh. You should be laughing more; you look as if haven't had a good laugh in days. And why haven't you been spending any time down at the Compass Rose with Natoli and the other students? I was down there last night. They've been missing you."

"I'd like to," Karal replied wistfully, "but I don't have the time. I'm doing my old job and Ulrich's, too. And having to learn all the things he knew about protocol without having the leisure to learn them over the course of a year or more." He shook his head as Florian's ears dropped sympathetically. "It started almost as soon as we got back from the border, and it hasn't let up any. I can't just be a place-holder, An'desha, I have to be a *real* envoy, whether I'm ready for it or not."

:Too true.: Florian nuzzled him, and he absently patted the Companion's nose. And got another curious overlay of someone clasping his shoulder, and he patted the comforting spectral hand in thanks.

"Take today, for instance. *Please* take today," Karal continued. "I hadn't even finished my breakfast before a page brought me a message from our border. There's a Herald down there trying to arbitrate a dispute between some Holderkin and a set of Karsites who style themselves 'border-riders.' Neither party would accept a Herald, so it got thrown back in *my* lap and it had to be answered immediately."

"Did you?" An'desha asked with interest. "Could you?"

"In this case, at least, yes." He made a sour face. "I happen to know more than I'd like about the border-riders. They aren't much better than bandits; back in the old days, they had a habit of keeping two sets of clothing, Valdemaran and Karsite, and raiding farms on *both* sides of the border. Now that Karse is at peace with Valdemar, they can't do that anymore, so they've settled down to the odd cattle theft, or helping themselves to everything in a house when the family is away at the Temple Fair." He frowned, then took a deep breath and grinned a little. "They tried abducting the odd Holderkin girl, but often as not they couldn't tell the girls from the boys, and in either case they generally wished they'd stuck their hands in a wasps' nest instead when the family came boiling out, looking for blood. With no protection from the guards on our side of the border, and a kidnapped brat screaming blue murder, they didn't get away with *that* very often."

"So what was the dispute this time?" An'desha asked.

"The usual; cattle the Holderkin swore were theirs. Knowing what I know, I pointed out that the Herald should check the ear-notches to see if they were fresh. Holderkin don't notch the ears of their cattle because they hold them in common at each Holding; Karsites do, when the cattle are still calves, because cattle theft is in our blood, I'm afraid. If the notches were fresh, the cattle had been recently stolen, and there you have it."

:Oh, do tell him the outcome, it's rather funny,: Florian prompted.

Karal chuckled. "I got word back that *most* of the cattle had freshly-notched ears, but on just about a third of them the notches were clearly done when the cattle were young. It seems that the Holderkin were not above trying to get a little revenge by claiming the *whole* herd instead of just the ones that had been stolen."

An'desha laughed. "You should tell Talia; she'll be amused, I think."

"I shall; really, I think you're right. She certainly has no great admiration for her own kin." He sighed. "I just wish all the things I'm asked to settle were so easy to solve. Tomorrow I'm supposed to meet with the heads of nearly every sect and religion in Valdemar, and settle some disputes between the splinter sect of Vkandis that took root up here in Vanyel's time and some Sun-priests that came up from Karse during the war with Hardorn. I'm afraid I'm not going to make anyone happy with my decisions this time."

An'desha made sympathetic noises. "That is not something I would care to deal with. I remember——" He paused. "I have noted that in matters of religion logic, facts, and reason bear little weight when measured against emotion. It does not matter what *is*, when people are convinced that the very opposite is *what should be*."

"I wish that were less true. I could pile up a hundred facts in favor of a particular argument, and all would be dismissed in favor of 'but that is not what I believe.' I am afraid that my age is going to tell against me as well." He eyed An'desha's silvering hair enviously. "Perhaps I ought to have you impersonate me. Or better still, have Darkwind do it. They would respect silver hair more than black."

"Oh, why not go the whole way and ask Firesong to do it?" An'desha laughed. "I can just see the faces of those stolid priests as Firesong sweeps in, wearing *his* version of a Sun-priest's robes."

"Oh, glory!" Karal had to laugh at that idea. Firesong's clothing was never less than flamboyant. "And once he began to talk, he'd have them all so tangled in logic and illogic, and dogma and cant, that they wouldn't even remember their own creeds!"

"It is entirely likely," An'desha agreed. "And it is a pity you wouldn't dare. I believe he would probably have a wicked good time of it if you asked him to."

"Now *there* is a 'White Demon,' for certain," Karal chuckled. "I think he gets more enjoyment out of twisting people around and playing with them than any other pursuit."

"I would not say he is *that* manipulative," An'desha temporized, "But there is a streak in him that makes him want to prod at people simply to get a reaction, and the more dramatic, the better."

"He certainly has a talent for drama, whether being at the center of it or inducing it," Karal agreed, and sighed. "Well, Florian seems to have solved the problem of how I am to remember who goes with what title tomorrow, so I shall be able to get a *little* rest tonight."

"I came here thinking you would go to the Compass Rose with me," An'desha said, looking hopeful. "Don't you think that just for once the Court can do without you at dinner? They were baking sausage rolls at the Rose this afternoon, and I'm told that the new yellow cheese is excellent."

"Demon! You know I'd do anything for good cheese and sausage rolls!" These were the closest foods Karal could find to the homey fare at the inn where he had grown up, and An'desha knew it. He cast an imploring glance at Florian. "*Could* I be absent, just this once?"

Florian was not proof against what the Companion had called "Karal's lost-puppy eyes." With a shake of his head, Florian gave in without a fight. :*I'll see that it's arranged,*: he promised, :*even if I have to tell an untruth and claim you're with me. But you'd better go now, or something else is likely to come up to prevent you from going at all.*:

The Compass Rose was a tavern unlike any other in all of Haven, and possibly all of Valdemar. It wasn't so much the food—which was quite good, but by no means up to the demands of a gourmet—or the drink, which was just about average. It was the clientele.

The Palace grounds actually hosted three Collegia; Herald's, Bardic, and Healer's—but there was a fourth unofficial Collegium there as well. If one looked into almost any given classroom, there would be *four* uniform colors in evidence. A gray uniform meant that the student in question was a Herald-trainee, a rust-brown tunic identified a Bardic student, and a pale green robe betokened a fledgling Healer. But a *blue* uniform was an "unaffiliated" student. More often than not these were merely the offspring of courtiers who preferred to have their families with them rather than back on the estate or holding. Classes at all three Collegia were open to them, and they were required in these days to wear a blue uniform, although that had not always been the case. But there was always a group of students who came from common blood, who were there at the Collegia, receiving the best education possible in Valdemar, because of merit or exceptional intelligence. They usually had a sponsor, either in the Court or one of the three Circles of Heralds, Bards, or Healers.

Most of *these* were divided into two groups; pure scholars and "artificers."

The latter were the people who would go out into Haven and beyond, to invent and build—bridges, mills, roads, cunning devices which would allow one to navigate or survey the land accurately—the list of possibilities was as endless as the imaginations of those who were doing the inventing.

And most of *these* spent their "leisure" time at the Compass Rose.

So did their Masters, the teachers at the three Collegia, and those artificers who resided in Haven itself. And "leisure" time was relative, for at any given moment in the Compass Rose you could find people working out the difficulties in the gears of a new mill or a student project—planning an irrigation system or arguing over the results of the last exam—

Or finding a way to integrate magic with logic and avert the peril of the mage-storms.

The students and teachers at the Compass Rose had been just as responsible for the creation of the magical breakwater as any of the mages whose talents and powers built it. If it had not been for them, in fact, there probably would never have *been* a "breakwater" at all. The entire concept was a new one, and mages were accustomed to using only the old, tried, and proven ways of doing something.

When Karal had first arrived in Haven, he had been introduced to the daughter of the Herald who had been their guide through Valdemar to the capital, a young lady named Natoli who was one of those "student-artificers." She had taken him to the Compass Rose, for she had known that among people who are accustomed to questioning everything, a "hated Karsite" was likely to be given the benefit of the doubt until he proved himself. That had been a lucky chance, for when the mage-storms first began wreaking havoc upon Valdemar, it occurred to Karal that the inquisitive and analytical minds of those same people were the ones best suited to taking the problem apart and perhaps coming up with a new answer.

Sometimes the most vital part of solving a problem was simply getting people to think about it.

For the first time, mages and artificers spoke to one another, and a new synthesis resulted.

Unfortunately for Karal, he hadn't gotten to see the aftermath of that synthesis since his duties had kept him away from the Rose, his friends there, and from Natoli. He was afraid now that she would be angry with him for deserting her for so long. Matters had been tending in the direction of something more than mere friendship, and now she might be thinking that he was getting cold feet over the idea.

A crowded tavern was not the best place to explain himself to someone who was possibly hurt and angry—but it was better than not seeing her at all.

It was that, and not the sausage rolls and cheese, that really took him to the tavern tonight.

He couldn't tell if An'desha was aware of that or not. The Shin'a'in was very good at keeping his thoughts to himself when he chose, and the subtle differences in his eyes made his expressions a little harder to read than most people's. On the other hand, An'desha was Natoli's friend, too, and she might have confided in him.

If nothing else, he thought, as the two of them wound their way through the streets of Haven to where the tavern lay, wedged in between a warehouse and a clockmaker's shop, *it will be good to be just myself for one evening, and not His Excellency, the Karsite Envoy*. It had gotten dark early, in part due to the heavy overcast, and the chill, damp air, though windless, had gotten colder yet. The darkness seemed very thick, as if it were swallowing up all the light. He was glad both of his heavy coat and the light from the streetlamps.

They turned a corner and were finally on the cobblestone street in the merchant district. The Compass Rose stood in the middle of the block. As usual, the Rose identified itself by the hum of conversation long before they reached the doorstep. Rumor had it that the clockmaker who shared a wall with the tavern was deaf; Karal certainly hoped so, or the poor man would never get any sleep at night.

From the sound, the Rose was full, which was the usual case on sausage roll night. The tavern boasted both a carved door and a carved sign bearing the compass rose of its name, both illuminated by torches. Karal hung back, feeling suddenly shy, as An'desha reached for the brass handle and opened the carved wooden door.

Cacophony assaulted them the moment the door swung wide, and Karal felt a twinge of nostalgia. it was as if nothing had changed—the room was exactly as it had been the first time Natoli had brought him here.

Table after table was full of students—eating and talking at the same time, gesturing with rolls or a piece of cheese, making mechanical arrangements out of the cups and plates, much to the disgust of those who were trying to use those cups and plates. The tables themselves were covered with rough brown paper, because the students tended to draw on them to illustrate some point or other, whether or not the surface was suitable for drawing. There were one or two of the Masters out here, usually with a tableful of their own students, prodding them through an assignment. The rest of the Masters were in the back room, a room reserved for them alone. A student "graduated" when he (or she) was invited to take his meal back in that hallowed sanctuary; there was no other special ceremony marking the ending of his life as a student and the beginning of his life as a professional. Here there were Masters, but no apprentices nor journeymen.

The roar continued for a moment as the door closed behind them with a thud, and Karal let his ears get used to the noise and his eyes to the light. The Rose was one of the few taverns where the light was as important as the drink, since so many here were working on projects as they ate. In fact, the lighting in the Throne Room at the Palace was dim by comparison. After coming in from the thick darkness outside, the glare of light took some getting used to.

But as they stood there, and Karal tried to see if Natoli and her cronies were at their usual table, the uproar began to subside, as people saw who was standing in the doorway, and turned to poke neighbors who hadn't yet noticed. As Karal shifted his weight uneasily, the roar faded into absolute silence.

No one moved. Then, off to the right, a single person stood up, a person who had been sitting with her back to the door. She turned and peered across the sea of faces to the doorway.

It was Natoli. And for a moment, Karal considered bolting back outside. *She's upset with me, and everyone knows it… I've hurt her feelings, and now they all hate me. Oh, glory, what am I going to do?*

"Karal?" she said clearly, and her strong, handsome face lit up with a welcoming smile. Natoli was not "pretty"—but her face had such character written in every line that you never noticed. "Havens, they finally let you take a night off! It's about time! Get *over* here! Look, everybody, it's Karal!"

The place erupted again, this time with cheers of welcome, a few playful catcalls, and offers of beer, food, or both. As Karal and An'desha waded through the crowd on their way to Natoli's table, he was staggered often by the hearty back slaps and playful punches his friends aimed at him. It occurred to him then that sometimes being Natoli's friend could be as hazardous as being her enemy!

He didn't manage to get across the room without being loaded down with food and an overfilled mug that slopped every time someone slapped his back. He kept apologizing, but it didn't seem that anyone noticed. Or perhaps they were just used to stray beer going everywhere.

Natoli's table was crowded, as usual, but also as usual there was always room for one or two more. People edged over and places were made for him and An'desha, one on either side of Natoli. As he sat down, Natoli helped herself to one of the many sausage rolls that had been thrust at him and offered him a plate of cheese in return.

He shared his bounty with anyone who didn't have food in front of him, and in the course of getting everyone settled again, he lost all of the apprehension he'd felt.

"You looked like a Bardic student in front of a hostile audience when you came in," she said, quite matter-of-factly. "Problems?"

"I suppose I was afraid that you would all be upset with me for not coming here before this," he said, a little shyly. "You might think *I* thought I was too good for you, now that I'm the Ambassador. Or—something."

She raised a hand and mimed a cuff at his ear. "Be sensible. Father's a Herald, remember? Just because I don't stick my nose into Court, that doesn't mean I don't know what's going on. They've had you tied up with more meetings and business than any one person has a right to be burdened with, and we all knew it. *I made sure* everyone knew that."

He relaxed at that. "I didn't want you to think that I'd forgotten who my friends are."

"Ha." She applied herself to her meal with a grin. "You've been working, and we haven't exactly been idle. Even if everyone else in Valdemar thinks that the crisis was solved, *we* know we only put it off for a while. We're still trying to work out a solution. Master Levy thinks there won't be *a* solution; he thinks we're going to have to come up with one make-do after another, because he thinks that the problem is getting too complicated to actually solve in the time we have."

"Do the mages know that?" he asked, feeling a chill. *More temporary solutions? Doesn't that leave us open to mistakes and the results of mistakes?*

"The mages know," An'desha confirmed. "At the moment they're trying to let their minds lie fallow while they track the current patterns of mage-energy for Master Levy's crew to analyze. I think some of them are hoping that if they don't *try* to think about a solution, one will spring forth from the back of their heads, fully formed."

Natoli snorted but didn't comment otherwise.

"Well, that's not necessarily bad thinking," one of the others pointed out. "I'm not talking about wishful thinking—it's just that if you try too hard to put all the facts together, sometimes they won't fall into place. Come on, Natoli, *you* know that even happens to us!"

"I suppose you're right," Natoli admitted grudgingly. "There *is* Cletius and the bathtub, for instance. It's just that some of these mages are just *so* certain that they can vibrate their way to answers that it makes me want to drown them all."

"Let's talk about something else," Karal urged. "Something that has *nothing* to do with mages or mage-storms or the Empire. What's exciting?"

A red head at the end of the table popped up. "Steam!" he exclaimed. "*That's* what's exciting! There's no end to what we can do with it! Who needs magic? Steam will save the world!"

"Don't go too far overboard," Natoli warned. "There're problems with steampower that we really ought to consider before we have people riding all over in steam-driven carriages. You have to burn things to heat water, and that makes smoke, and what happens when we start putting more smoke in the air? There's already a soot problem in Haven from all the heating and cooking fires."

"But you won't need heating and cooking fires if we heat everyone's house with the hot waste water from the steam-driven mills and manufactories," the other argued. "In fact, we should eliminate most of the soot problem that way."

"Not if you replace every one of those cookfires with one heating the boiler in a steam carriage," someone else put in. "Natoli's right about that. We really need to think about what we're doing before we launch into something we can't stop."

"Wait a moment," Karal interrupted. "Steam *carriages*?"

"One of the Masters came up with a water pump for draining mines that was steam driven, and someone else realized that the same principle could be used as the motive power for a carriage, by basically adding wheels to the whole affair rather than having a stationary boiler," Natoli explained. She snatched a stick of charcoal out of someone else's hand and began to draw on the paper covering the table in front of them. "You see—here's the boiler, in front of the firebox; pressure builds up in here and you vent it into the cylinder—the piston gets driven back—that turns a wheel—"

As she sketched, Karal began to see what she was talking about. "But why steam carriages at all?" he asked. "Aren't horses good enough?"

Natoli's eyes sparkled, and he realized he had uncovered her secret passion. "But these go *faster* than horses, Karal," she said. "They never get tired, they can pull more than horses can without hurting themselves, and the only time they have to stop is when they run out of fuel or water."

"Huh." He could think of places where that would be useful. In the mountains, where the roads were cruelly hard on carthorses. Or any time you needed to send something very quickly somewhere. Supplies, perhaps, or soldiers. Of course these things would be limited to places where the roads were good, which was quite a limitation, when you thought about it. Using them on a regular basis meant that the roads would have to be improved and kept in repair, and that could get rather expensive...

"We're thinking about putting them on rails or in grooved tracks," Natoli continued, waving a sausage roll in one hand as she spoke. "Like the coke carts at the big iron-smelting works. The only problem is that takes a lot of metal, so where do we get all that metal? And if you used cut stone, it would wear out rapidly from the wheels. Every time you solve a problem you bring up twenty more." But she didn't look particularly discouraged. "The point is, we know we can use large versions of this in places where windmills don't work and there isn't any water for water mills. We can use the waste heat to heat houses, or even the Palace. Wouldn't *that* be a sight!"

"Wouldn't it be a sight as you get in everyone's way digging up the Palace and grounds to lay all your pipe," An'desha pointed out sardonically. He pushed a fall of his long hair back from his forehead, showing his pale eyes crinkled in smile lines. "I can't see the Queen holding still for that! Especially not in the foreseeable future."

"Oh, I didn't mean right now," Natoli said airily, waving her hands in the air. "I just meant eventually. After all, it's not as if it hasn't been done. Think of the mess it made when all the new indoor privies and the hot and cold water supplies were put in. That was in the first couple of years of Selenay's reign, and I don't hear anyone complaining about it now!"

"A point," An'desha acknowledged. "I'd like to see you folk find some other source of heat than a fire, however. Fires are not very clean."

"Some magical source, maybe?" Karal said without thinking, and blushed when every eye on the table turned toward him. "I don't really know what I'm talking about, I'm just speculating—" he stammered. "Don't pay any attention to me, I'm just babbling."

"But your babbling makes some sense," Natoli responded, her eyes lighting up with enthusiasm. "A practical application of magic! That might be the answer to my chief objection as well."

The talk turned to possible magical sources of heat then, and An'desha held center stage as he speculated on how this might be accomplished in such a way that the mage would not actually have to be there to make the source work. It led into talk of binding magical creatures, small ones that thrived on fuel of one kind or another, and it was clear to Karal that An'desha was in his element. Karal was able to watch Natoli to his heart's content, as her face grew animated during the heat of the discussion, and she tossed her hair with impatience or excitement.

"So," An'desha said, as the door of the Compass Rose closed behind them, shutting off part of the noise, which had not in the least abated. "Feeling rested and relaxed?"

Karal paused and took stock of himself and blinked in surprise. "Why—yes!"

An'desha laughed. "Good. That was what I hoped would happen. Now are you wondering why I pulled you away after Natoli left?" He started off down the street in a fast walk, and Karal followed.

"A little," he admitted, sniffing in the cold and damp. "Though I must admit once she left I got a bit bored when they all started talking about mathematics and drawing on the tables again."

"Because you and I are going to go to the *ekele*. Firesong is up to his eyebrows in some discussion involving the Tayledras, the Shin'a'in, and k'Leshya at Haven, so he won't be there. *I'm* not taking part because I've been told I'm not Shin'a'in enough to satisfy the envoy. He doesn't like halfbreeds."

"Hmph, I'm not surprised. He seems to dislike all sorts of people," Karal growled. "Well, I don't like *him*, so we're all even."

Karal walked on in silence, seeming lost in thought, then turned to An'desha. "What did you have in mind when we get there?

"You are going to soak in the hot spring, and you are going to have a nice, relaxing cup of Shin'a'in tea, and then you are going to go to your suite and sleep." It was too dark to read An'desha's face, but his voice told Karal he was not going to be argued with. "As I recall, you made the same prescription for me a time or two, and turnabout is fair play."

"So is that why you have turned into my counselor?" Karal asked, and he wasn't entirely being facetious. The events of this afternoon and evening had proved to him that An'desha had achieved an inner peace that he found enviable.

If only I could be so sure of things again!

"The turnabout? Oh, it is a part of it," An'desha said, with serene warmth in his voice. "You have done good things for me, with good reason and without. You have been kind when you could have been neutral. There is a saying from the Plains: *Every gift carries the hope for an exchange.*"

Karal mulled that over, but his thoughts about the Shin'a'in proverb were eclipsed by marveling over An'desha's calm.

That was part of the problem he had with the entire situation. He was not only acting as envoy, but as a priest—and a priest should be utterly sure of himself and his beliefs. Either a priest or an envoy should be sure and calm.

But he was being required to determine what was heresy for those of his faith here in Valdemar, and *that* was where his beliefs were collapsing around his ears. How could he make a judgment on what was heretical, when he had seen evidence with his own eyes that what he "knew" was the Truth was only truth in a relative sense?

Take the very existence of An'desha's Star-Eyed Goddess, for instance. For a Sun-priest, there was *one* God, and one only, and that was Vkandis—yet he had ample proof that was beyond refutation that the Star-Eyed existed and ruled Her people right alongside Vkandis Sunlord.

To even think that was rankest heresy by the standards of the Faith as he was taught it. But he had been taught *the old ways* and things had changed drastically since.

He'd already deferred the decision once, which had only made both parties angry at *him*. He suspected that this was the reason why he was being confronted by all the heads of religion in Valdemar. They weren't going to accept a deferred decision again.

Perhaps in his new-found confidence and serenity, An'desha could act as *his* adviser as he had once acted as An'desha's.

"Would you mind listening to a problem of mine?" he asked, as they walked side-by-side up the deserted street, toward the Palace.

"You listened to mine often enough," An'desha replied. "It only seems fair. I won't promise an answer, but maybe I can help anyway."

He explained the predicament he was in; his own uncertainty, and his unwillingness to label *anything* heresy. "I don't know now if there *is* a wrong or right, in anything. And I am put in the position of being the person that is supposed to know! It all seems so relative now," he ended plaintively.

But An'desha only chuckled. "If I were to turn and stick a knife in you now, *that* wouldn't be 'relatively' good or bad, would it?"

He had to laugh. "Hardly!"

"Work from that, then," An'desha suggested. "You've *been* reading all those old books that Master Ulrich brought with him, the ones written back before the Sunlord's priesthood went wrong. You have a fair idea what was considered heretical then, don't you? And what's more, since you have those books, and since Solaris approves of them, you can cite sources to *prove* the position you're taking, right?"

Fog rose from the damp cobblestones all around them, but it seemed that the fog in his own mind was lifting. "Well, yes, literally chapter and verse. That's true," he said slowly. "I think the problem is that I know what I wanted to say, but I couldn't think of a way to make it stick."

"You probably still won't be able to make it stick," An'desha warned. "The people you're dealing with are like that new Shin'a'in envoy that replaced Querna; hidebound and dead certain they're right."

"True, but if they don't like *my* decision, I can tell them to appeal to Solaris, and as long as I follow what Master Ulrich was trying to show me, I think she'll back me." His cheer was mounting by the moment. "I don't much care if they don't like me afterward. There are so many people in Valdemar now who don't like me that a few more won't matter."

"That's the spirit!" An'desha applauded. "Good for you. *Now* are you ready for that soak?"

"I'm soaked in trouble anyway, why not add hot water?"

"Careful with that kind of talk," An'desha grinned. "You'll make it start raining again."

Karal's backside and face were both numb. His shoulders ached; he maintained an expression of calm interest, but inside, he was yawning. *All we do is talk!* he thought, taking a covert glance around the Grand Council table, and seeing nothing but the same expressions of stolid self-importance he had seen for days. *We never actually do anything, we just talk about it!*

The Valdemaran "Grand Council" was new; an institution formed so that Queen Selenay could attend to the problems that were strictly internal to Valdemar in a forum where every envoy, Guild functionary, Master artificer, and their collective secretaries did not feel urged to put in their *own* bits of advice. She had been getting nothing done, and every busybody in her kingdom had been privy to Valdemar's internal problems. The old Council Chamber had gone back to the use for which it had been built, and one of the larger rooms in the Palace, formerly a secondary Audience Chamber for the reception of large parties, had been turned over to the new function.

Of course, everyone involved had his own ideas on protocol, which meant that the Queen and her advisers had to come up with some seating arrangement that would suit everyone. A new table had been constructed in the form of a hollow square with one side open, like an angular horse shoe. Around it were placed enough seats for everyone who might conceivably want to have a hand in the situation with the Empire, the mage-storms, or both. The table sat squarely in the middle of the otherwise empty room, and on the platform that had once been the dais was a huge strategic map of Valdemar, Hardorn, Karse, Rethwellan, the Tayledras lands to the west, the Dhorisha Plains, and south as far as Ceejay. The gryphons, when they attended, actually sat (or rather, lounged) in the hollow interior of the table, with the rest spaced evenly along the outside. No one sat at the "head" of the table, for there was no head or foot, and so everyone could feel he was equal, superior, or whatever his pride demanded.

Although the room was well-provided with lights, both along the walls and from a chandelier hanging from the ceiling, it was cold. Two ceramic-tiled stoves, one at either end of the room, had to make shift to heat the whole place. The white marble floor and white-painted walls and ceiling added to the impression of cold. Karal always dressed warmly for these meetings, and kept the pages busy refilling his cup of hot tea which he mostly used to warm his hands. Nor was he the only person to resort to such measures to keep warm; he noted that Firesong actually had the forethought to bring a handwarmer and a heated brick which he put inside a special footstool. He cast envious glances now and again at both, as he wriggled his toes in an attempt to keep them from turning into little blocks of ice.

Prince Daren acted as the Queen's voice on the Grand Council, leaving Selenay free to rule her country and not sit in on meeting after endless meeting. Meetings at which, it seemed to Karal, very little was accomplished.

That's not fair, actually, Karal thought, looking around again. *No one has ever done anything like this before. We're all having to come to terms with each other, and that takes time. We have to learn to work together before anything can happen.*

All this, obviously, meant that the Seneschal, the Lord Marshal, the heads of the three Circles, and any other Valdemaran official that normally sat on the Council often ended up attending double meetings when the Grand Council met. And any other Valdemaran functionary who wanted to look important (or actually felt he might be needed) helped to round out the field. This, of course, meant that every single meeting since the breakwater went up consisted of one person after another pontificating on how he and his special interests had been affected, what would probably happen next, and what *he* thought should be done about it. Typically, those with the most important and relevant information generally said the least.

There should be a way of cutting this nonsense out. It's taking up time. Maybe a maximum word count, enforced by cudgel?

Karal really would have preferred to be off doing something constructive, even if all he was doing was making copies of energy-flow maps for the artificers. At least that would be accomplishing more than just sitting here trying not to fall asleep, a job that grew more difficult as the time crawled by.

So far today, at least eight people had made long speeches that were only variations on "as far as my people can tell, this breakwater business is working and everything is back to normal," and the one currently droning on was the ninth. He was the particular representative of dairy farmers—and *only* dairy farmers—and they had already heard from grain growers, shepherds, vegetable farmers, fruit growers, professional hunters, the fisher folk of Lake Evendim, and poultry farmers. Each of them had gone on at length about why *his* particular group had suffered more than any other from the mage-storms, though what this was supposed to accomplish, Karal didn't know.

Why can't the farming folk find one *person to represent them all? And why can't he be someone who'll give us hard information instead of whining?*

He cupped his hands a little tighter around his tea and resolved to find out where Firesong had gotten the footstool with the heated brick in it.

They can tell the people who sent them that their complaints and troubles are on record, I suppose, he thought vaguely. *As if that makes any difference to this group. I suppose it must make people feel better to know that someone at least* knows *that they are having hard times.* It would have been much more useful for all these farmers and hunters and herders to have compared the damages this year with those of previous bad years—during the time when Ancar's magic in Hardorn was causing ruinous weather all over, for instance. Then all the foreign envoys would know how things stood here in comparison to the way they *should* be, and could offer advice or even help-in-trade if it looked as if help really was needed. They could *all* compare notes on the damages across the region, and see if there were any differences. The plans being worked out by Master Levy's artificers and the allied mages were all based on information mainly gathered in Valdemar. They were all assuming that patterns in Valdemar were similar to patterns outside Valdemar. But what if they weren't?

He'd tried suggesting that, but the people he'd suggested it to had said that gathering such information was going to take a great deal of time, and could he justify such an undertaking? He'd tried to point out why it would be useful, but no one seemed to find his arguments convincing.

Finally, the man stopped droning. It took Karal and the others a few moments to realize that he had actually ended his speech, rather than simply pausing for breath as he had so many times before.

Prince Daren nobly refrained from sighing with relief, as he consulted his agenda. Though still as handsome as a statue of a hero, the Prince was showing his age more and more lately; there were almost as many silver hairs among his gold as An'desha sported. The stress of the past several years was beginning to tell on both of Valdemar's monarchs. There were strain lines around his eyes that matched the ones around the Queen's. Like the Queen, since he was also a Herald, he wore a variation on the Herald's Whites.

"Herald Captain Kerowyn, I believe you are next," the Prince-Consort said, and although the gentlemen and ladies now seated about this square table were too well-trained to show relief in their expressions, people did begin sitting up a little straighter, and taking postures that showed renewed interest. Kerowyn at least was not going to stand there and drone about nothing; whatever she reported was going to be short, to the point, and relevant.

Kerowyn, who was the same age as Daren, nevertheless remained ageless. Her hair, which she always wore in a single long braid down her back, was already such a light color that it was impossible to tell which hairs were blonde and which were silver. And any new stress lines she had acquired would be hidden by the weathered and tanned state of her complexion, for Kerowyn was not one to sit behind a desk and "command" from a distance. She had begun her military career as a mercenary scout in the field, and that was where she felt most at home. There was not a single pennyweight of extra flesh on that lean, hard body, and every Herald-trainee knew to his sorrow that she was in better physical shape than any of them. When she wasn't drilling her own troops, she was drilling the Herald-trainees in weapons' work, and heaven help the fool who thought that because she was a woman, she would be an easy opponent. She had been sporadically training Karal, and he knew at firsthand just how tough she was.

She stood up to immediate and respectful silence from everyone at the table, Valdemaran or not.

With one hand on her hip and the other holding a sheaf of papers, she cleared her throat carefully. "Well, I don't need to go into the obvious. What we're calling the breakwater is obviously working. The mages tell me that what's happening is that rather than reflecting the waves of force as they come at us to somewhere else, this business they've set up is breaking them up and absorbing them to some extent. That's good news for us, but Hardorn is still getting the full force of the waves."

Chuckles met that, and she frowned. "As a strategist, I don't think that's particularly good for us, my friends. If the situation in there was bad before—and it was—it's worse now. We may see the Imperial forces in Hardorn getting desperate, and desperate people are inclined to desperate acts. I might remind you that they may be blaming *us* for all these mage-storms. They've made one attempt to break up our Alliance. They may decide to act more directly."

The pleased looks around the table evaporated. Even handicapped, the Imperial Army was vastly larger than anything the Alliance could put together, and everyone here knew it. The members of the alliance had been fighting the renegade King Ancar of Hardorn, separately and together, for years before the Eastern Empire came onto the scene, and their forces were at the lowest ebb they had ever been. The attrition rate had been terrible on both sides, for Ancar had been perfectly willing to conscript anything and anyone and throw his conscripted troops into the front lines under magical coercions to fight. He had intended to take Valdemar and Karse, even if he had to do it over a pile of his own dead a furlong high. Ancar was gone now, but…

"Now, one way to make sure they don't come after us is to take the fight to them," Kerowyn continued matter-of-factly. "You know what they say about the best defense being a good offense. My people tell me that the Imperials pulled everything back and they've concentrated in one spot, around a little town called Shonar. Looks as if they are making a permanent garrison there. That makes them a nicely concentrated target. Their morale is bad, and it looks as if they've been cut off from resupply and communication with the Empire. They depend on magic; right now, they don't have any. My best guess is that they're doing their damnedest just to get dug in to survive the winter. The questions I have for all of you, are—do you think we should take advantage of that, and are you prepared to back a decision to go on the offensive when that means taking what troops we have right into Hardorn?"

Half of the people at the table began talking at once; the other half sat there with closed expressions, clearly thinking hard about what Kerowyn had just said. It was fairly typical that the people who had begun babbling were the ones who were the least important and the least knowledgeable so far as a decision like this one was concerned—representatives of farmers and herders, tradesmen and Guilds, priests and the like. The rest—the actual envoys, the Lord Marshal, the Seneschal—were the silent ones, and Karal was among them.

On the other hand, he was inclined to think—*why not?* Why *shouldn't* we hit these people while they are in trouble? The Shin'a'in envoy, Jarim shena Pretara'sedrin, began to speak as Karal was considering that.

"This is our chance," he said fiercely. "Let a few bad winter storms take their toll, then let us strike while they are freezing and starving! Let us wipe them from the face of the world! If we destroy this army now, the Empire will never again dare to send a force against us. Let us take our revenge, and let it be a thorough one!"

And for once, on the surface and at first impulse, Karal was inclined to agree with him. *They murdered Ulrich,* he thought angrily. *They murdered Ulrich and poor Querna, they injured Darkwind and Treyvan and others, and they didn't even come at us as honest enemies! They sent an agent with vile little magic weapons to assassinate whoever happened to be in the way, with no warning and no provocation. Don't they deserve to be squashed like bugs for that? Don't they deserve to be treated the way they treated us—as insignificant and not even worth a fair fight? Doesn't Ulrich's blood cry out for revenge?*

But it was that last thought that stopped him because *revenge* was the last thing Ulrich would have wanted. What was being proposed meant that vengeance was enacted, not upon the perpetrator, but upon people—soldiers—who had no idea what evil had been wrought here. Ulrich had once commanded demons—and gladly renounced that power when Solaris decreed it *anathema.* The demons were the next thing to mindless, and too often, like a hail of arrows loosed at random, they killed those who were innocent along with those who were guilty.

These soldiers, far from home and desperate, were not the real enemy. The real enemy was the one who had commanded those magical weapons, and the one who had sent the assassin. They had caught the original assassin, after all. What would be the point of going after anyone else now—unless, perhaps, they in their turn specifically targeted the commander of these forces, assuming he had been the one who had ordered the assassin to strike in the first place.

Others joined Jarim in calling for action, or opposed him, cautioning that it might be better to let the full force of winter take its toll before acting. But Karal sat and clasped cold fingers before him, wondering what had happened that he was no longer able to see things involving humans as day or night, good or evil.

He knew when it had begun; something had changed when he entered the barrier at the border with Iftel, and it had continued to affect him in the days he had spent recovering from the experience. He had the feeling, always humming in the background like the blood in his veins, that he had been welcomed by something extraordinary. Karal lived in a time of wonder and strangeness, yet the feeling he had was not, at any time, that of being a spectator. He was a *part* of it all, an active player in whatever game the fates set the board for, and that feeling itself was beyond anything he'd prepared for.

I can't help it; present me with a situation, and I have to think about both sides of it. I can try to suppress it, but I cannot shut off the way I think. Once knowledge is gained, there's no going back to ignorance. I think about what the other feels. I can't stop it, and I don't think Vkandis Sunlord, Solaris, or Altra would want me to. Or Ulrich, far away in Vkandis' arms.

Ironically enough, it had been Ulrich himself who had planted the seeds of this change, back when he and his mentor had first crossed into Valdemar. Ulrich had asked a slow but steady progression of perfectly logical questions that had ultimately forced him to see his former enemies as people, and not as a faceless horde. Because of Ulrich's patient coaching, he now knew, at the deepest level of pure reaction, that the impersonal and evil army of nameless demons that lay across the border of Karse was nothing of the sort. It was Heralds and Companions, farmers and townsfolk, soldiers of the Queen and ordinary citizens; people very like those he had known all his life.

Now he could no longer see an enemy impersonally. The great and mindless "they" were nothing more nor less than people, and he saw them that way. While the others spoke of wiping out the Imperial Army, *he* saw ordinary fighting men, suffering unseasonable cold and demoralizing doubt, wondering if they would ever see home again. He even imagined faces, for the faces of fighters came to look much alike after a few seasons in the field: tired, unshaven, with lines of suppressed fear and dogged determination about the eyes and mouth.

"They" were just doing their jobs. They didn't know anything about Valdemar. Conditions in Hardorn had been so dismal when they first crossed the border, they had been welcomed as liberators. Ancar had abused his people to the point that they were happy to see even a foreign invader, if that meant that Ancar would be deposed. Now the Imperials were probably wondering why the welcome they'd gotten had turned so sour. Things they had come to depend on were no longer working, and by now word must have filtered down that no one had any contact with their headquarters back home. Strange and misshapen beasts had attacked them, and they had seen a "weapon" at work that no one understood.

If any of them had the slightest notion that their superiors had assassins working in Valdemar, a few of them might even be horrified. Certainly, since the professional soldier generally had the deepest contempt for the covert operator, they probably would be a bit disgusted. But it was unlikely that any of them knew or even guessed what had happened in Valdemar's Court, that one of their leaders had assassinated perfectly innocent people.

So why should perfectly "innocent" soldiers suffer for the action of what was probably a single man?

They were already under more privation than they had any right to anticipate.

They're far from home and all the things they know. They have no idea if they will ever find their way back again. They may not even be able to retreat in a conventional way. They must be afraid—how could they not be afraid? And winter is coming, more mage-storms. The storms created some terrifying creatures here before we built the breakwater. What can they possibly be making in Hardorn?

Since he was alone and far from home himself, he couldn't help but have some fellow feeling for them. Perhaps it was foolish, but there it was.

For that matter, it was only presumption on their part that the assassination orders originated with someone commanding the forces in Hardorn. There was no real reason to assume that was actually true.

After all, Talia and Selenay's old nemesis, Hulda, had been getting *her* orders directly from the Imperial capital, possibly even from one of Emperor Charliss' personal spymasters. Charliss was accustomed to sending in operatives who worked at an extreme distance, for with the magics the Empire used routinely, distance was no object. So who was to say that the assassin hadn't been sent directly by Charliss or someone just below him, and had nothing to do with the forces in Hardorn at all?

The Imperial Army itself had never done anything overtly against Valdemar; they had only moved to take over a disorganized and demoralized country after its own ruler had been killed—

—by Valdemarans. Valdemar *assassins*, not to put too fine a point upon it.

Don't we have trouble enough right now without adding to it by attacking the Imperials directly? We should be concentrating on the next step after the breakwater, not trying to get an army of our own halfway into Hardorn to attack someone we don't even know is our enemy!

The general din seemed to have died down a bit, and he saw an opening. With shaking hands, which he disguised by keeping them clasped on the table in front of him, he spoke up.

"I'm not certain going after them is a good idea," he said quietly. "We should be concentrating all of our effort on the mage-storms; the breakwater isn't going to hold forever—in fact, if the storms change their pattern drastically, it won't hold at all. The Imperials haven't done anything we can prove, and they are going to have all they can take with the results of the mage-storms over there. Why don't we just leave them alone, at least for now, and see what happens?" Stunned silence met his suggestions, and he added into the deathly quiet, "Our resources are limited, and things might get even worse. Who knows? They have so many mages with them—they know things we don't—they might turn out to be valuable allies."

"*What?*" Jarim sprang to his feet, his face scarlet with outrage. Karal felt his heart stop, then start up again, and he knew that he had gone pale by the cold and stiff way his face felt. "Are you *mad?* Or are you so much of a coward that you won't even face what these Imperial jackals have done to you? They slew *your* mentor, *your* envoy! Are you a fool, boy? Or—are you a traitor?" He put one hand on his knife hilt and drew the blade with a single swift motion. "Those assassin blades somehow mysteriously never touched you! Foul piece of *sketi*—have you been the traitor in our midst all along? By the Star-Eyed, I swear I—"

Karal kept himself from shrinking back only by iron will and the knowledge that Daren and the others wouldn't let Jarim actually *do* anything to him. Darkwind rose malevolently and grabbed the Shin'a'in's wrist in a grip of steel, roaring to drown out whatever Jarim was going to say.

"Stop that, you fool! Where are your senses? Drawing steel in the Grand Council, threatening the Karsite Envoy, are you *trying* to break the Alliance apart all by yourself?" He shook the man's arm, rattling the startled Shin'a'in's teeth. Karal was impressed; Darkwind did not give the impression of being stronger than any other normal man. Evidently there was a great deal about this Hawkbrother that was not obvious.

The Shin'a'in was so startled that he dropped the knife, which clattered to the table. Firesong snatched it up before Jarim could reach for it.

"The boy is only pointing out alternatives—*as is appropriate*. He *is* a priest, he *is* supposed to think beyond the obvious, and he *is* supposed to suggest peaceful possibilities rather than ones involving war!" Darkwind turned to glare at everyone around the table, and some of the representatives of other gods had the grace to look chagrined, since they had been doing nothing of the sort. In fact, they had been calling for war as enthusiastically as Jarim. "He is absolutely right; in regard to what has happened here, we have no proof as to the origin. We have speculation, but no *proof.* For all we know, our real enemy could be someone we are not even aware of, someone who set all of this up to make it *look* like the Empire was the perpetrator!"

"Oh, that's hardly likely," the Lord Marshal scoffed. "Who would this nebulous enemy be? Some hypothetical evil shaman from the North, beyond the Ice Wall?"

"Not likely, I will grant you, but possible—and we have not even discussed the possibility. I remind you, before any of you accuse our own Council members of duplicity, that *outside* influences should be the first consideration. A history-proven means of destroying vital alliances is to sow dissension among its members, *from outside, by duplicity!*" Darkwind met the Lord Marshal's eyes squarely, and it was the older man who dropped his gaze. "Furthermore, as a mage, I concur with his priority. You've all accepted the breakwater as the solution to the problem of the mage-storms, but it was never meant to be more than a stopgap measure to gain us time."

"Now that is completely true and irrefutable," Firesong drawled, toying with the Shin'a'in dagger. "Forgive me, Herald Captain, but this breakwater of ours is rather like its namesake—and the more storms that come to wash away at it, the faster it will erode. It is more like a levee made of sand than one made of stone. I know it seems to you as if this is a good time to strike at a *possible* menace, but believe me as a mage of some talent—they will have all they can handle and more as the mage-storms wreak havoc in Hardorn. If they are very, very lucky, the monsters that are conjured up will be stopped by walls and enough arrows. If they are not—" He shrugged, "—well, let me remind you that the breakwater may stop mage-storms, but it is no barrier against hungry creatures capable of decimating an army. What comes to dine on them might well move in to dine on *us* before all is said and done. As mages and artificers—" he bowed ironically to Master Levi, "—we should be searching for the next level of protection against the storms. As military leaders, *you* should be searching for ways to hold off whatever might come at us *through* the Imperial Army. The likelihood is that, if you do not, it may be our Alliance that will be smashed like a particularly inconvenient bug."

He held the dagger out to the sullen Shin'a'in, hilt first; Darkwind released the man's wrist, and Jarim took the dagger and thrust it back into the sheath. He sat down again, his face still rebellious.

Karal drew a breath of relief; at least this crisis was over, for the moment anyway. Kerowyn had simply stood there through all of it, her own expression a study in passivity.

Finally, she spoke. "On the whole," she said carefully, "I must admit that more energy should be put into finding another solution to the mage-storm than anything else. I wanted to point out the possibility that the Imperial Army *might be* vulnerable at this time. I do not want anyone to think that I am certain of that. After all, as Karal rightly pointed out, nothing is certain but those facts that we can verify for ourselves. He is also correct in pointing out that a great deal of what we think we know is only speculation. *Probability* is not fact, and I for one prefer not to send troops into battle while the home fronts are unprotected."

She sat down amid heavy silence. Prince Daren cleared his throat. "In that case," he said, with remarkable aplomb, considering that moments before, one of his allies had been stopped just short of declaring blood-feud on another, "Perhaps the next to speak should be Darkwind k'Sheyna."

Darkwind seized the verbal "ball" that had been thrown to him, and proceeded to take over the meeting. The Hawkbrother did not have his bird with him, but he stood as if he was so accustomed to the weight of the forestgyre on his shoulder that he was always ready for it. He, too, sported the all-white hair of a Tayledras Adept, for he had been Elspeth's original teacher of magic, before he became her partner and beloved. He was a typical Tayledras; strongly handsome, rather than the sculptured beauty of Firesong. He tended to much less flamboyant clothing than his fellow Hawkbrother, but when he spoke, it was with authority, and people listened.

Karal simply sat very still during most of the rest of it. It was all to the good that Darkwind managed to get across the fact that the breakwater was *temporary*, and get the attention of the allies centered on that rather than anything else, though he did not seem to Karal to be getting the urgency of the situation across to them. But Karal could not ignore the smoldering glances of Jarim, or the dismissive glances of many of the rest of the people at the table. Once again, his youth was speaking against him. People assumed that because he was young he was inexperienced. And Jarim clearly assumed that because he was not ready to rush out and slaughter every Imperial that came his way, he was, at the least, a coward.

Well, Darkwind and Firesong seem to think I've got a point. Maybe I ought to work through them instead of trying to make my points myself.

But if he did that, he'd just look ineffectual, and how would *that* serve Karse?

When the Grand Council broke up, it was with very little accomplished and nothing really settled.

As usual.

He returned to his suite feeling as if he had failed in his duty.

As he closed the door, shoulders slumping beneath his elaborate black robes, a patch of golden sunlight in the middle of the floor rose up to greet him.

:You look as if you could use a friend,: Altra observed, as what had been golden light resolved itself into a huge cat, cream colored, with reddish-gold mask, paws, and tail—and vivid blue eyes. *:Did the meeting go badly?:*

Karal managed to dredge up a ghost of a smile and sagged into a chair as Altra padded across the floor and sat regally down at his feet. At least it was comfortably warm in here, with the sunlight streaming in the windows and a fire in the fireplace. The Valdemarans took good care of their guests, and sometimes it seemed as if the one commodity that Valdemarans treasured above all others was warmth. He had a suite of three rooms, including his own bathroom—not the same suite he had shared with Ulrich, which would have been too painful to return to. That suite had been given, ironically enough, to Jarim. "It didn't *end* badly—but if you were paying any attention to the meeting, you'll know I was within a hair of having Shin'a'in blood-feud declared against me."

The Firecat blinked. *:I was eavesdropping a bit, and I must say you're certainly talented. No Sun-priest has had Shin'a'in blood-feud declared against him in the entire history of Karse.:*

Karal just sighed at this display of Altra's rather sardonic sense of humor. "It's not funny, cat. I guess the important thing is that this all proves that I am in far past my depth, here, and I might as well admit it. It's one thing to have Solaris send a piece of paper making me the envoy, but it's quite another to get people to *accept* me as the envoy."

Restlessness overcame his lassitude and weariness. He lurched out of his chair and began pacing. "I'm too young, I'm inexperienced, and if I was a place-holder, neither of those things would matter. But I'm not just a cipher. I'm supposed to be making decisions here; I'm supposed to be representing Karse's best interests. But how can I *possibly* do that when I'm young enough to be the *son* of half the people in the room, and the *grandson* of the other half?"

He was so frustrated and so very, very tired! His repressed emotions boiled over and came pouring out of him in a torrent of impassioned words. At least Altra was listening, rather than cutting him off. "The worst thing is, I know I'm too young, and *that* shows, too! Altra, these responsibilities are driving me mad! I don't want to sound as if I'm whining, but I am *not suited* to this! I thought this would only be for a few weeks—that Solaris would send someone else, someone the others would listen to. When we were trying to catch the assassin, it was reasonable to have me as the envoy. It was even reasonable when I was only interacting with the people on Selenay's internal Council—after all, Darkwind and Elspeth and a couple of the others know that I have a good idea now and then and are willing to listen to me because they know me. But now I'm supposed to be dealing with all of these other allies, and they all look at me and see a—a child!" He turned toward the Firecat and held out his hands, imploring Altra to see the dilemma he was in. "Altra, I can't do the task I was given, and there is nothing that is going to make that possible, short of aging me twenty years overnight. I'm doing my best, but this is akin to asking a blind man to sort beads by color. Trying to do what no one will let me do is going to drive me insane without helping Karse!"

Altra had remained silent during this entire outburst. When he finally subsided, Karal bitterly expected the Firecat to deliver a crisp lecture on growing some backbone. After all, that was what he had done on similar occasions in the past.

But Altra did nothing of the sort. He curled his tail tightly around his legs, and sat so quietly that not even a hair moved. His eyes had grown very thoughtful and were looking far away, to some place Karal could not even begin to imagine. His introspection was so deep, Karal wondered if he was actually *communing* with something—or Some-one—else.

After waiting a few moments for a reply, Karal took his seat again, dropping heavily into his padded armchair with a thud. Altra did not seem to notice.

Huh. This is different. He's never acted like this before...

Then, suddenly, without any warning whatsoever, the Firecat leaped straight up into the air—

—and vanished into the patch of sunlight he had appeared out of.

"Oh, now *that's* an informative answer," Karal growled to the empty air in disgust. "Thanks a lot!"

Somewhere out there, Natoli and the others were collating energy patterns, An'desha was helping them analyze the patterns, and Master Levy and his mathematicians were plotting courses. He suspected that Firesong's warning about monsters being created in Hardorn had been taken to heart, and Kerowyn's folk were inventing monsters and ways to deal with them. Somewhere in this very Palace, others were getting actual work done. Somewhere out in Haven, or beyond, artificers were trying to find a way of getting people and supplies in and out of an area quickly, perhaps involving some of Natoli's beloved steam machines.

And I am sitting here waiting for yet another Grand Council meeting. He sighed glumly and then sat up a little straighter as he realized that the Shin'a'in envoy, who had just entered the room himself, was heading, not for his own seat, but straight for Karal.

Oh, glory. Now what? A challenge to personal combat?

He made himself smile, and rose in courtesy as Jarim reached him. "Greetings, sir." *Now what do I say? "I trust you realize we are still on the same side?"* Or— *"Are you still desirous of examining my liver at close range? I fear I cannot oblige you—"* He settled for a neutral and polite, "How can I serve you?"

"You can serve me, Envoy, by accepting an apology," the Shin'a'in said brusquely—and grudgingly. But at least he was saying it, which was an improvement. "I overreacted yesterday. My people are protective of their own."

And mine are not? Is that your implication? "I understand, sir," he replied smoothly. "Please, *you* must understand that I am trying to think of the best use of our admittedly limited resources. I am trying to suggest what is useful for the Alliance as a whole. Your people never encountered the armies of Ancar of Hardorn. My country and Valdemar are low on fighting men and the wherewithal to supply them; your people are mighty warriors, but they do not send folk off the Plains very often, and they would be at a bad disadvantage. The Hawkbrothers are no use as an offensive military force, and Rethwellan has sent all it can afford. I frankly would rather that the Imperials were slowly whittled away by magic-born monsters than that *any* fighter of the Alliance perish in ridding us of them. We must survive the mage-storms ourselves, after all, and—"

"Yes, yes, I see your point," Jarim interrupted. "But it should be obvious that we are going to have to eliminate these interlopers while we have the chance. They have a long history of conquest, and no border has ever stopped them before. It is pure folly to think that they will allow anything to stop them now, save such a fierce resistance that it is clear even to them that they have met their match in us! The only way to do that is to strike now, strike hard, and remove every trace of their forces from Hardorn. Then and only then will the Empire respect us enough to let us alone!"

He was getting wound up again, and nothing Karal had said had made any difference to him. His *words* said "we" but it was obvious to Karal that what he wanted was personal revenge on the Empire for daring to murder a Goddess-Sworn Shin'a'in.

By now most of the others had arrived, and all of the Grand Council were listening closely to this exchange, obviously waiting to see how he would answer.

But any answer other than the one that Jarim wanted—full agreement—was only going to start another argument. So instead of replying directly to Jarim's statement, he turned to Elspeth, who happened to be nearest to him.

"How long do the mages believe the breakwater will remain intact?" he asked earnestly. "Has anyone an estimate?" It was one question that no one had asked yet—but it was important, because an answer might make it clear that there was no time for personal vengeance—or, indeed, any revenge at all.

"Good question," the Princess replied, arching an eyebrow at Darkwind and Firesong, who edged closer at her signal. "Do either of you have an answer—or even a guess?"

"I would prefer to err conservatively," Firesong replied—earnestly, for once, rather than flippantly. He cast a glance at Karal that looked appreciative. "I would not trust it to hold for more than four months at the most. Through the winter—perhaps. Not much beyond."

"I would give it until summer, but that is certainly no more than six months away at best," Darkwind said, nodding. "Now, given that winter fighting is difficult at best and suicidal at worst, that means we will lose the breakwater before we have any chance at attacking the Imperials."

Karal noticed that Prince Daren was also giving him a look of both appraisement and approval. Evidently he had impressed the Prince-Consort. Jarim looked startled; his eyes widened with shock. "I thought that it would last longer than that," he objected. "You only just put it up!"

Firesong shrugged. "The breakwater loses a bit more of itself with every storm, and the storms are coming more and more frequently. There is a mathematical progression to them. We *told* you that. The erosion is accelerating. Pity, but we knew when we set it up that all we were doing was buying time, and we tried to make that as clear as possible to all of you."

Firesong can say that, and say it insolently, and get away with it. Jarim respects him; I think he might even be a little afraid of him. Today Firesong was wearing stark and unornamented black, a costume that accentuated both the gold of his Tayledras skin and the vivid silver-blue of his eyes—which only served to remind Jarim that the Hawkbrothers and the Shin'a'in were related—and the silver of his hair, the reminder of the power he wielded. Firesong was very good at choosing the best costume for the purpose. Today he was obviously in the mood for intimidation. It was a talent Karal wished he had.

Prince Daren stepped forward at that point, and took over the discussion. "Ladies and gentlemen, would you all take your seats? Firesong, would you repeat what you have been saying to everyone? This is important, very important, and I want to make sure there are no misunderstandings."

Daren went to his own seat and sat down, effectively beginning the meeting.

There was some shuffling about as people found their accustomed chairs, and Firesong not only stood up, he stood in the hollow center of the table where the gryphon Treyvan was, with one hand on the gryphon's shoulder. The gryphon twitched an ear-tuft a bit.

"Some of you were part of our earlier Council when we first learned how we could, *temporarily*, protect the Alliance lands and Iftel from the battering we were taking from the mage-storms," he said gravely. "This we did, and as you are all aware, it was successful. But it was still a *temporary* solution. Like a shoreline breakwater from which this protection takes its name, it absorbs the force of the waves of the mage-storm, but at a cost to itself. It is eroded, a little more with every battering that it takes. It *will* come down, collapsing under the repeated battering that it is subject to. Just because you are not feeling the effects of the mage-storms, that does not mean they are not continuing to move in on us. Even if you, yourselves, do not feel the force of one of these storms against your body, somebody out there *will*. They bring pain and misery and destruction. They are still coming at us, and the frequency and force are increasing as time goes on. We can measure this force, and we are doing so. I estimate that the breakwater will collapse in about four months' time, Darkwind gives it a slightly longer six months. Once again, all that we did was to buy our Alliance time to concoct another solution—one that could involve magic, since our magic is no longer being disrupted by the storms. We told you this was temporary at the time we did it, and we meant it."

That was just about the longest speech Firesong had ever made, and his words were given added impetus when the gryphon nodded with every salient point.

"I have ssseen the effectsss frrrom the airrr, frrriends. They leave the earrrth rrriven in placesss. We sshould be concentrating on the brrreakwaterrr'sss replacement," the gryphon added. "And, frrrankly, on what we can do if we cannot *find* a replacssement in time. If you thought thingsss werrre bad beforrre—"

He left the sentence unfinished, hanging in the air like the threat that it was.

Although Karal distinctly remembered that this point was made before anyone left Haven to set up the breakwater in the first place, the fact that it was not the permanent solution still seemed to come as a complete surprise to many of the officials and envoys, Jarim among them.

"Well, why didn't you put a permanent solution in place?" snapped the head of the dairy farmers.

Firesong leveled a look at the man that should have melted him where he stood. "Oh, and you wanted us to wait to *find* one?" he asked, then continued. "This phenomenon was as new to us as it was to you; completely unprecedented, and we still don't fully understand it. As I recall, the mage-storms created a few killer cows before we put a halt to them," he said icily. "*As* it happens, we did the best we could at the time, to save the rest of you from as many of the effects as we could while we tried to put together something better. Would you rather we had let the storms rage across the landscape, turning more cattle into monsters?"

Perhaps the man had seen one of those "killer cows," for he paled and looked shamefaced. "Well, no—but—"

Someone else interrupted with another shouted accusation, which Firesong met with equally devastating wit and logic. Accusations and counteraccusations flew for a moment, until it was finally driven home to even the most hardheaded at the table that the mages and artificers had not somehow "cheated" them—that they had done what they could at the time. "Like a barricade of sandbags holding back floodwaters," was Elspeth's analogy.

The uproar settled into silence, and it was Jarim who was bold enough to break it.

"Well, if this is only temporary, then what *are* we going to do?" he asked testily. "Have you people made any progress at all?"

What does he want us to say? They've already told him everything they know!

Darkwind sighed, and Elspeth patted his shoulder. "Well, candidly, not much," he said wearily. "We don't have enough facts yet—"

"Why not?" Jarim interrupted. "Why haven't you made any progress?"

"We have made *plenty* of progress! It is only magic we use, were you expecting miracles?" Firesong shot back testily. "If you want miracles, speak directly to a God. Or a Goddess." That last was a shrewd hit on Firesong's part, since Jarim, unlike Querna, was *not* Sworn to the Star-Eyed. He could pretend to no special communication with his deity, no more than any other Shin'a'in had.

Karal closed his eyes and just let the words wash over him, as Darkwind and Elspeth tried to put into nonmagical terms the things that they *had* learned, and Firesong added acidic rejoinders whenever someone questioned their progress. He was not a mage, and very little of what they said made sense to him. He could ask An'desha later, when he needed to write up a summation for Solaris.

Solaris. What was she doing, back home in Karse? Was she holding onto her leadership with the same firmness as before? *Surely Vkandis Sunlord will keep Karse safe, no matter what,* he told himself, and felt a twinge of guilt for such an unworthy thought. He was supposed to be thinking on a wider stage than just Karse; it was the welfare of the Alliance that was as important as Karse's welfare.

But Karse was where his interests lay, and it was Karse's interests he was representing. So was it so bad that he took comfort in the fact that Vkandis held His hand over His chosen land?

As a priest, he *must* believe that, anyway. To doubt was to doubt the word and the promises of Vkandis...

Except that He has said in His Writ that we must rely on the intelligence and wit that He gave us, that He protects us only in extremis. What if there is a solution here and we simply fail to reach it because we do not try hard enough? Would He still protect us then?

He felt his face grow cold and pale.

The uncertainty of it all was terrifying.

Oh, glory—what was happening to him? Now was he beginning to doubt even his own God?

What could *he* do, anyway? He was no mage; he knew next to nothing about magic *or* mathematics. He could only place his trust in others, in the hands and minds of those who did understand all of this. Elspeth and Darkwind, the gryphons, Firesong and An'desha, the mages of Rethwellan recruited by Kerowyn, the fledgling Herald-Mages of Valdemar trained by all of the others, the Priest-Mages of Karse; these were the folk that needed the help and guidance of Vkandis in their endeavor—and any other deity who happened to be interested. Perhaps the best thing he could do now was to pray. At least he understood how to do *that*.

Right now, he was just very, very tired... and very homesick. *I would much rather be the secretary to* anyone, *even one of those rigid old sticks who disliked Ulrich and Solaris, than be the envoy myself. It's not that I don't want the responsibility—it's that I can't get the authority to take care of the responsibility.*

So today, rather than try to make anyone listen to him, he just took notes whenever he caught something he understood. *If I have a point I want raised, I'll write it down and give it to Elspeth or Darkwind later,* he decided. *That's still doing my duty by the Alliance as a whole, even if it isn't accomplishing anything for Karse.*

Right now, that was the only solution *he* could think of.

3

An'desha dropped another pebble into the water-table, and watched the resulting waves break up and disperse on the model. The elegant concentric rings quickly turned into a chaos of wavelets and counterwavelets amid the barriers placed there, and he shook his head in despair. He'd been told about this, but he hadn't believed it until this moment. "This is too complicated even to see, much less measure and analyze," he said bitterly. "And this is only a *model*. The reality is a hundred times worse!"

Master Levy gave him a sidelong, sardonic glance of approval. "For an unlettered barbarian who believes in curses and spellcasting, you show a surprising grasp of logic," he said dryly. "And a remarkable understanding of the difficulties of measurement and analysis in a moving system."

An'desha was not about to be goaded. "For a hard-headed statue who only believes in what he can see, weigh, and measure, you show a surprising flexibility," he countered. "And besides, you know very well that I read, speak, and write more languages than you, so although I am a barbarian, I am hardly unlettered. Now, shall we dispense with the insulting small talk and get on with this?"

But Master Levy only sighed with frustration. "At the moment," he admitted, "small talk is all I have to offer. I am venting my frustration in sarcasm. You are correct, the reality *is* too complex to calculate. I haven't been able to derive any kind of formula, and if I cannot, I doubt that anyone else would be able to."

Unconscious or conscious arrogance that last might be; nevertheless, Master Levy was right.

"There must be a predictable mathematical progression in there somewhere," An'desha muttered, staring at the table and the last of the fading ripples. "The result is geometric, so there *must* be a way to derive the formula."

"I thought you mages were all certain that magic was entirely intuitive," Master Levy said with amusement. "I confess that I was hoping by bringing you here and showing you the demonstration you might be able to intuit the formula. As one of our youngsters pointed out, intuition *is* a valuable tool, since it merely consists of being able to put together facts so quickly that the progression from premise to conclusion is no longer obvious."

"Firesong is the only one of us with that particular affliction," An'desha replied absently. "The rest of us are rather fond of logic. Though it is beginning to look as if his way of doing things may be the only answer right now."

In truth, the reason he was here instead of at the *ekele* was that Firesong had not been able to "intuit" an answer either, and was rather short-tempered as a result. Things were already strained between them as it was, and on the whole, An'desha thought that his absence would be more valuable than his presence. Let Firesong rave at the plants in his frustration.

Ever since he and Karal had returned from their journey to the Iftel/Valdemar border, there had been stress in his relationship with Firesong. It was not, as he had first feared, that Firesong was jealous of Karal—or at least, he did not consider Karal to be a romantic rival. Which was just as well; it was rather difficult to prove such a nebulous negative as "Karal is my best friend, but I am not in the least attracted to him." If Firesong couldn't figure *that* out, he was less observant and less intelligent than An'desha had given him credit for.

It had taken An'desha this long to divine precisely what the problem really was between them, and it turned out to be something rather disconcerting. Something he knew *he* wasn't going to be able to remedy, in fact.

Firesong did not seem to know how to deal with the "new" An'desha, an An'desha who was growing less dependent upon him with every passing day.

An'desha gazed down into the water-table as if the answer to his problem with Firesong lay there, as well as the answer to the question of what to do when the breakwater failed.

He doesn't seem to understand that just because he saved my life, and helped me when I was so confused that I didn't know how to cope with the smallest details, that doesn't make us automatically lifebonded. It doesn't even make us automatically best friends. I love him, and I owe him a great deal—but I do not owe him my total devotion for the rest of my life. No one "owes" that to anyone.

They had become lovers out of mutual attraction and An'desha's helpless dependence on someone, anyone, who might give him the support and security he desperately craved. And to his credit, Firesong had been very well aware that such dependence was unhealthy and infantile; he had done his best to wean An'desha away from that clutching dependence and to help him grow a real spine of his own.

But was that because he wanted me to be independent, or because I was strangling him? Hmm. Good question. Only Firesong knows the answer. Certainly being strangled is hardly comfortable, but he did wean me away as gently as possible, rather than simply shoving me away. But was that because he liked me dependent, but not too dependent? Another good question.

Now—well, the old proverb said, "Be careful what you ask for, because you might get it." Firesong had gotten an An'desha who knew who and what he was, and what he wanted to do with his life—and now Firesong was the one who was unhappy.

He wasn't exactly picking fights, but whenever An'desha said or did something Firesong didn't expect, he was visibly taken aback. Startled, even shocked, as if An'desha had turned into someone he didn't recognize. And when An'desha actually had a difference of opinion from him, Firesong would flash into a quiet and unobtrusive rage.

It never lasted more than a bare instant, and he never actually said or did anything except try to persuade An'desha that he was wrong—but that instant of rage was there. It was naked in his eyes and in the way he first flushed, then paled, then clenched his jaw hard and would not speak until the moment was over.

Firesong's solution, which An'desha had decided to emulate, was to avoid such situations by avoiding An'desha except at meals and at night.

At night, at least, they were still compatible, and it was a good tension reliever for both of them. But for how long would that last?

He shook himself out of his reverie; Master Levy was staring at him with curiosity, as if wondering what it was An'desha saw in the water-table. "Well, I'm not getting anything done here. Perhaps I ought to go take a walk and get some fresh air. Maybe I *will* intuit something that will help."

"I will go back to my angles and instruments, and see if I can't make something out of the result," Master Levy replied, but he sounded discouraged. "One of our problems is that the waves are coming from outside, yet our models rely upon waves generated from the center outward. We can extrapolate the results by formulas based on that, but it is still not an accurate enough representation."

On the whole, An'desha didn't blame him for being discouraged. What they needed was a new way of looking at this situation, a new approach. That was how they had come up with the breakwater, after all, a new approach—a mathematically-derived analysis of magical energies.

"Say… how about this?" An'desha said quietly. "A hoop that can be dropped into the water model to create a circular wave from the outer edge inward?"

Master Levy examined his hands and reflexively cleaned under his fingernails for the twentieth time this conversation. "Mmm," he murmured finally. "That could help. I will put a student-artificer on the idea immediately. There are problems with the shortness of sampling time from the wave strike to edge reflection, but perhaps a large enough hoop could be made…"

Master Levy went on in the same vein for a while. They could come up with ideas, small ones that added up, but they never felt like a master solution. Now they needed another source of inspiration. The trouble was, they had run out of new cultural influences to provide such a source of new thinking.

We need a god to help us out this time. Unfortunately, since it is not likely that we will all be wiped off the face of the world when the breakwater fails, I doubt that She is going to be inclined to help us.

He shrugged and picked up his quilted Shin'a'in riding coat, pulled it on, and buttoned it up to his chin. He left the Palace workroom in a state of absorbed introspection, but he was not thinking about the mage-storms as he walked through the dead and deserted Palace gardens.

Odd. Not that long ago I would have been worried sick if Firesong had begun avoiding me. I would have been certain he was getting tired of me and was looking for someone else to replace me. I would have been in a panic at the thought of being alone. Now—

Now it simply didn't bother him, in part because such avoidance also avoided confrontations between them.

And frankly, it wouldn't matter to me if he did find a new lover.

That surprising realization stopped him, right in the middle of the path. He repeated it to himself, and it felt logical—right.

It would not matter to me if Firesong found a new lover. In fact, it would be something of a relief. I would stop feeling obligated to please him for fear of hurtful response. A feeling like that has no place in a love affair.

Yet there was no one else *he* was even remotely attracted to! So what was prompting this sentiment?

Do I want to be—alone?

That felt right too. Oh, he didn't want to be alone forever, but a third realization came to him, on the heels of the other two.

I'm starting to find things out about myself—not just all the things in the memories of Falconsbane-that-was, but things about me. I need time to think about them. And it has to be time alone.

Poor Firesong. *He must be sensing that I want to be alone, and he's thinking it means that I don't want him around.*

An'desha shook his head and started walking again, with his head down and his hands in his pockets. If only Firesong *would* find someone else, it would make things a great deal easier on everyone.

But the chances of that happening are not very good. There aren't a lot of she'chorne *around for him to choose from, and most of them are involved with each other. And the others—* He grimaced. *I'll be charitable and say that the others are understandably warped by unfortunate early experiences. But that doesn't make them pleasant or healthy to be involved with.*

She'chorne. When was the last time he'd heard, or even thought that word? *Back with the Clan, before Falconsbane—I hadn't been making any attempts to court any girls in the Clan, so Grandmother started asking if I would at least consider courting one of the* she'chorne *boys.* Such an alliance, though it obviously would not be possible to produce children of the blood, was still considered honorable. More than that, such couples could pursue the adoption of orphans from within the Clan. In fact, many Shin'a'in Clans encouraged such alliances so that there *would* be couples available to adopt parentless children. By Shin'a'in standards, a *she'chorne* couple, with no children of their own to support, always had the resources to support someone else, thus removing the burden from those with their own children to feed.

But that wasn't what I wanted either, and she started in on how I was as shiftless and rootless as my father...

There wasn't much to examine in his relatively short "real" lifetime, but he'd been going over his memories, trying to find hints of what he was in what he had been. He'd also been examining the less-disgusting memories left to him by Falconsbane and all his previous incarnations, trying to find a common denominator.

There has to be more than one reason why Falconsbane grabbed me to settle into. By now, there must be a lot of Ma'ar's blood-children around, and at least a fair share of them should be mages. For that matter, given the way that Falconsbane and the rest used to ride out on little loot-and-rape expeditions just for amusement, there ought to be plenty of appropriate candidates out there. Somehow I have the feeling that there must be many common threads in my life and all of his... if only I can untangle them.

He'd already found one. Every single one of those previous lives had involved a person who, before Falconsbane moved in and took over, was someone who was despised or even abused by his natural family. Many of them had run away, seeking new lives elsewhere, actually seeking the implied power that came with being a mage so that they could return home and have revenge of one sort or another. That was why most of them had tried the fire-calling spell when they were alone; most of them had not yet found a teacher, yet had felt the stirrings of the power within them, and had decided to try it "just once."

I wonder if having a teacher would have prevented Falconsbane from moving in? I wonder if the presence of the teacher would have prevented him from even trying?

Possibly; Ma'ar, the original of all the incarnations, had been one of the craftiest wizards of all time. Surely he would have hedged in his search for a new body with all kinds of conditions.

But what of that common thread of abuse, neglect, and derision? What if being despised and ignored was also a prerequisite to possession? *When I ran away from the Clan, I wasn't sure what I was looking for—except a place to belong and a way to escape being forced into the life of a shaman. But I seem to remember that most, if not all, of the others were actively looking for power when they ran. Some wanted real, bloody revenge, some just wanted to "show them all," with "them" being the people who had offered scorn and mockery.*

Now, wasn't *that* an interesting thought? Had that condition actually caused them to somehow welcome Falconsbane, at least somewhere deep inside?

Being possessed, giving up your own responsibility for the sake of revenge—that's beginning to make too much sense.

He stopped for a moment, and probed deeply into some of the earliest memories of possession. *Oh... this is interesting. The first time, Ma'ar didn't just rush in and take over, he seduced! He offered instant Adepthood, no tedious apprenticeship. My, my. It was only much, much later that he became impatient and careless, and just took over in a rush.*

That initial welcome would have been all he needed to get himself well established; in the time it took them to realize what it was they had welcomed, he'd be entrenched. By then, of course, it was too late; Falconsbane would not tolerate a second soul, a second personality in "his" new body. By the time any of them thought to rebel, Falconsbane eradicated them and reigned supreme.

But I didn't want him, and I didn't particularly want power. All I wanted was—people. Someone who wouldn't *despise me, who* would *welcome me and give me a chance to prove* myself. *Was that the difference that made it possible for me to survive?*

It might have been. It was just such a tiny wedge that had made the difference in the past.

There were other reasons for his survival; he had "run," hiding in his own mind, while Falconsbane settled in, rather than trying to resist the intruder. Once in hiding, he had made no effort to try and force out the Dark Adept.

A chill wind whipped through his hair, and he shoved his hands deeper into his pockets, hunching his shoulders against the cold. These gardens were good places to be alone, once bad weather had set in. Once the last of the wintering preparations had been made, not even the gardeners ventured out here.

It's odd, but a great deal of what Falconsbane and all his other "selves" did were the darker applications of things that could *have been very admirable. It's as if they couldn't create, they could only warp, twist, and mutilate.*

That was especially true in the way that Falconsbane had manipulated people's minds and hearts, including that of his own daughter Nyara. Falconsbane was capable of inspiring true devotion from his servants, as well as devotion inspired only by fear. In fact. if An'desha went all the way back to the source of the memories, the Adept called Ma'ar, he found that Ma'ar seldom, if ever, needed to command by fear. He could, and did, manage to convince his followers that he was everything they wanted him to be, and that he truly cared for their welfare. If Ma'ar's memories were to be trusted, he had underlings who would gladly have flung themselves in front of an assassin's blade for him out of pure worship.

Compared with that, Falconsbane's sick and twisted love-hate-need relationship with his daughter Nyara was without sophistication, even crude.

I am glad that she and Skif were sent to be the envoys to the k'Leshya. Skif was growing restless with nothing to contribute, and she was not comfortable here. Neither was Need. I think she was afraid that one day Kerowyn would decide to make good on her threat to drop the sword down a well. He smiled to himself; there could not be two such supremely self-assured—not to say "arrogant"—females in the same physical location as Kerowyn and the sword called Need, without conflicts arising. It was just as well that Skif, Nyara, and Need were gone. The k'Leshya could use Skif's knowledge, and the sword knew magics even older than their own. And Nyara, of course, would be much more comfortable in a place where she was by no means the oddest looking person in the Vale.

What Falconsbane had done to her and with her just on an emotional basis was sick and demented by any normal standards. But just as intimate knowledge of the way that the body worked could be used to heal, as well as to kill and torture, could not Falconsbane's ability to manipulate minds and emotions be used for some other, benign purpose?

In some ways. wasn't that precisely what Ulrich and Karal had been doing to help *him*?

He chewed his lip thoughtfully. Did that make Falconsbane something like—like an evil priest?

Certainly on one level. A good priest is supposed to counsel and guide his followers to their betterment, and Falconsbane used similar tools of persuasion.

Bells at the Collegium rang, signaling the beginning of the dinner hour. That meant that both the Palace and Collegium libraries would be empty, and both libraries had comfortable reading areas with fireplaces—certainly much better places for continuing these introspections than the gardens, at this point! It wouldn't be long until dark, the gray light was fading into thick, gray-blue dusk, and the wind was getting colder with every passing moment. His nose and ears were getting numb, and the wind somehow managed to find every seam in his coat to blow through!

He turned his steps back toward the Palace, nodding at the guard at the garden door as he passed. One advantage of being who and what he was—he was instantly recognizable. Most guards let him by without a challenge, the way they let the Hawkbrothers and the gryphons pass.

The Palace library seemed the best choice; the reading area was smaller, and most of the people who used it were court functionaries. This was not a library filled with books of poetry, clever histories, and tales. The books here were dull chronicles for the most part, with a leavening of books on language, law, and custom. *Meaty and informative, but as hard to digest as a stone and about as entertaining.* It was tucked away between the room used for Valdemaran Council sessions and the office of the Seneschal, sharing a fireplace wall with the latter.

Only one or two lamps had been lit, but there was a bright fire going in the fireplace—and as An'desha had hoped, there was no one in the reading area. He chose a comfortably padded chair, draped his coat over the back, and sprawled sideways with one leg over an arm of the chair, staring into the fire.

So if Ma'ar and all his other "selves" were able to control and persuade people—would it be wrong to use that same power to help people? To get them to compromise with each other, for instance—would that be wrong? I wish I had some help with this... I have a feeling I'm getting out of my depth. The trouble was that he was too close to those memories; seeing such abilities and powers in action made it very tempting to assume that such things *could* be used for good purposes.

Someone once told me that even the deadliest of poisons could be used to heal—with expertise and great care, in the minutest of doses. How tiny a dose of "persuasion" was moral? He didn't know where the line should be drawn between "trying to help people," and "manipulating people."

Firesong would be no help at all, even though he was a Healing Adept. *His* powers were all concerned with the world of the material, not the world of the soul, heart, and spirit. He tended to get very impatient when An'desha strayed into the realms of what he considered to be "mystical." For all of his insistence on the intuitive nature of magic, he was bound up in the practical and had little use for mysticism.

I'd like to ask Karal, but he's already carrying so many burdens, I'm afraid to add one more to his load. It might be the one that breaks his back—or his spirit. Poor Karal! He was carrying far too much responsibility on those slim shoulders.

Perhaps that sweet lady, Talia? But—no, really, what he wanted wasn't *comfort,* it was a place to start figuring out ethical solutions.

This was the one place where his old nemesis, the shaman of his Clan, might have been useful. The old man was as rigid as dried rawhide, but he was enough in tune with the Star-Eyed that he never gave anyone bad spiritual advice that I ever heard of. And he knew his ethics... The new Shin'a'in envoy was not a shaman; he was temporary, the brother of his Clan Chief, and An'desha really didn't like him any more than Karal did. If only Querna were still alive! He wouldn't have hesitated a moment in asking *her* help.

If only I had someone, anyone, to talk to! No, not "anyone." A shaman, a priest. But I don't know which priests here to trust except Karal; I'd rather talk to someone who comes from the same background as me. How ironic! I got myself into trouble by running away from the shaman, and now I would give anything to be able to talk to one.

The fire gave a sudden flare, and he jumped as a deep, purely mental chuckle washed warmth through his mind.

:You had only to ask, little brother,: said a mind-voice he had thought never to hear again, as the Avatar of the Star-Eyed that he knew as Tre'valen appeared in the fire before him. The last time he had seen the Avatar had been when he was in Hardorn, and Falconsbane had control of his body. Although he was told that the Avatars appeared in Valdemar when they transformed him and Nyara from their feline Changechild forms to something more human, that was one appearance *he* did not remember. Mercifully, perhaps; the transformation had not been without a great deal of physical pain. Flesh was torn loose from its Adept-shaped form and resculpted, even the hairs of his body were altered in one massive rush of magical power. A gift from the Star-Eyed for his bravery, but no changes were without pain.

As Tre'valen had often before—though *never* in Valdemar—the Avatar took the form of a hearth-bound vorcelhawk that fanned and mantled its wings of fire amid the flames dancing in the fireplace. *:I am pleased that you have come this far, although the state of your heart is bringing you no peace at the moment. We have missed talking with you. I believe, little brother, that we can help you.:*

Firesong paced the floor of the sitting room of the *ekele*, looking out from time to time at the bare, wind-tossed branches of the trees outside the window. His high-cheekboned face bent with a frown. An'desha had gone off on his own—again. The young Shin'a'in was spending less and less time in the *ekele*, a complete reversal of the times when Firesong had been unable to get him to go beyond the doors of the indoor garden on the ground floor.

He's changed. He's still changing. Neither of those thoughts sat particularly well with him. He didn't particularly like the direction of those changes, and he definitely did not know how to cope with them.

It had been so pleasant when An'desha was uncertain of himself, when he looked only to Firesong for answers and reassurance in a strange and frightening world. It had given Firesong such a delightful feeling to be *needed* so desperately... No one had ever needed him like that before, although plenty of people had wanted him. That very dependence had been quite attractive.

On the down side, he had to admit it had occasionally been an annoying and even constrictive relationship, for he could not even joke and flirt with Darkwind without sending An'desha into hysterics.

But most of the time it had been very, very sweet.

His conscience said it had been more than just "sweet." *Admit it. It gave you a great deal of pleasure to have that kind of power over someone. An'desha would willingly have been your slave, if you'd asked it of him.* He winced a little; his conscience was altogether too accurate.

In those days it had been as if An'desha was barely afloat after a shipwreck and did not know how to swim, and absolutely depended on Firesong to get him to safety.

The room was exactly twelve long paces wide; ten, to avoid running into walls. *I was very content with that; with An'desha being passive, and putting all responsibility for his life into my hands.*

Well, not all responsibility. Even then, An'desha had shown flashes of stubborn will, even though the application of that will was hardly productive. Firesong's own conscience and memory reminded him of that, too.

Enough pacing! Firesong flung himself sullenly onto a couch and lay there with his hair and one leg trailing over the side, staring up at the ceiling. It was getting dark, but he did not bother to light any of the lamps, although he could have done so with a thought. His firebird looked at him curiously from his superior elevation on his perch, but when Firesong didn't show any interest in scratching him, the bondbird yawned and went back to preening himself. False sparks sparkled along the snow-white firebird's feathers whenever Aya roused all his feathers and shook them, and in repose, in this uncertain half-light, the quills of each feather glowed softly. Aya seemingly hovered in the air, his perch invisible in the near-dark, a glowing ghost of feathered light.

Firesong had lost patience with An'desha many times over when the young man had refused to delve into the memories of past existences that Mornelithe Falconsbane had left behind. Even though it was obvious that crucial knowledge of the past lay there, he *still* had refused, out of the fear that such probing would somehow reawaken the dark Adept. This was one place where Firesong had failed him; it had been Master Ulrich and Karal that had convinced him that there was no danger of his becoming another Falconsbane, much to Firesong's hidden annoyance.

On the other hand, being no priest, I had no personal experience of possession, so I had no way to convince him that I knew what I was talking about. Perhaps that was when the separation started. It was certainly one more victory to Karal.

And there is the belief, as almost all people have, that keeping a memory of someone alive keeps that person *alive. So how could An'desha* not *believe that speaking of Falconsbane would keep the evil Adept's soul alive? Even when I reassured him repeatedly that I had shredded Mornelithe Falconsbane in my own spirit-talons? Yet another failure.*

Oh, but there were more. Firesong had also failed to convince An'desha to learn to *use* those magical powers he'd been born with, and the expertise in them that Falconsbane's tenure in his body had granted him. Now *that* had been not just annoying, but it was *damned* frightening. As long as An'desha had refused to use and practice those powers, they were dangerous—because where will failed, instinct might take over.

I could not *convince him that ignoring his power was more dangerous than learning to control it. In many ways, Falconsbane had no control; he acted on impulse more often than he planned things. I tried to show him that such impulsive actions were second nature to him, and that unless he* learned *to control his power, it would control* him.

It had been Karal who had devised a plan to show An'desha that he had the self-control to use his magic without abusing it—by provoking him to the point where, if he had *not* had self-control, he would have flattened the young priest.

I have to give him this much; that was sheer, unadulterated bravery on his part. I'm not certain that I would have trusted An'desha's will and ability to control himself in that situation, and I live with him. Or used to, anyway.

Not that Firesong hadn't tried other means of convincing An'desha, but the young man could not be convinced by his lover. The trouble was, Karal could convince him, because Karal's ploys had all worked.

Damn him.

Now An'desha, emboldened by his success and encouraged by Karal-damn-him, was looking for answers from someone other than Firesong. Suddenly he was no longer content with the guidance and advice he got from his lover. He was striking out in directions—often directions of a mystical bent—that Firesong didn't like and didn't want to take for himself.

It would be my luck that he'd find a priest to be his best friend. Priests make people so—deep.

Karal was not An'desha's lover; he wasn't An'desha's type in the first place, and in the second, as far as Firesong could tell—and his instincts there were seldom wrong where the extremes of sexual preference went—Karal was at the opposite end of the spectrum from *shay'a'chern.* Perhaps that actually gave him an advantage over Firesong; An'desha knew that he had no ancillary motives for his advice.

Once again, Firesong's conscience pointed out that Firesong almost *always* had ulterior motives behind anything he tried to get An'desha to think or do. Of course, he had An'desha's best interests at heart. They just happened to coincide with his own best interests.

I can convince myself of that quite prettily. I wonder if I could convince anyone else.

He ground his teeth in frustration and stared at a lamp hanging from the ceiling. At this point it was just a dark round shadow against the lighter ceiling. Soon he would have to light the lamps, if he didn't want to have to stumble around in the dark.

So what am I supposed to do now? Am I doomed to lose him? Can't he see how I feel about him? It's not as if I haven't obviously been courting him. At least, I think I've been obviously courting him. It was a frustrating position to be in, since he'd never *had* to court anyone's attentions before; he'd always been on the other end of the courting, and others had always labored to catch and hold *his* attention.

Now, here he was, with the situation reversed. He was turning himself inside out trying to catch and hold An'desha's interest, and it wasn't working. *Now I know how it must have felt to Rainbird when I was oblivious to his overtures. The problem is, just what am I going to do about it? How am I going to get him back?*

He knew one thing that he was very good at that might work. Besides magic, of course. *I could certainly launch a seduction that would completely overwhelm him; I'd have him so swamped with sensuality that he wouldn't have the energy to even think about anything or anyone else.*

It would be a very successful seduction, too—for a while.

Unfortunately, I know precisely how long that particular tactic can work from personal experience, he thought glumly. *The "spell" of seduction only lasts as long as the seducer has energy. And the seducer is going to run out of energy before the seduced does.*

Besides, An'desha wasn't stupid, nor was his nature centered on sex or sensuality. The trouble, as far as Firesong's ambitions went, was that An'desha's mind was awake now and growing. It wasn't going to just "go to sleep" again, and a mind like An'desha's needed more than an overwhelming of the senses to occupy it for very long.

That led to another temptation entirely. Firesong was not—quite—a Mind-Healer, but he had many of the same skills, and one of his minor Gifts was that of Empathy. He knew enough that he could, if he chose, tamper with that too-awake mind and put it to sleep again, or paralyze it. *Oh, it would be so easy to take what I know and begin manipulating him. I know all of his weaknesses, all of his fears, everything that makes him twitch, everything that makes him feel good about himself.* Yes, it would be so easy to twist An'desha around—

It was so tempting—but—

His stomach twisted, and he grimaced. *Oh, that's no answer either. It's wrong, and I know it. Father would have a cat, and Mother—I know what she'd have to say if she knew I'd even thought about doing something like that to another person.* He shuddered; he had faced monsters, mage-storms and Mornelithe Falconsbane, and none of them had frightened him as much as the prospect of facing his mother with a guilty conscience.

He grimaced again, this time at his own foolishness. *I don't care what anyone else thinks about me, but may the gods help me if Mother found* that *out.*

And besides his mother—oh, gods. *What if my dear ancestor Vanyel got wind of this?* He shuddered again; he definitely did *not* want to have to deal with that. Although, given the two of them, he'd rather be forced to deal with an angry ghost than his mother in a state of righteous wrath.

He sighed, and threw his arm over his eyes, feeling as if it wouldn't be such a bad thing to be a Falconsbane and not have to worry about angry mothers or guilty consciences.

That's why their way is easier, I suppose. Well, I've got a conscience and I'm stuck with it. He couldn't use his mind and his magic on An'desha to make him pliable again. Besides being wrong, it would be stupid. No matter what he did, if he played with An'desha's mind, what he would have when he had finished wouldn't really be "An'desha" anymore. So what would be the point to all the work? If he wanted someone to be his toy, he could pick someone at random, a stableboy or page, anyone. That wouldn't be right either, and it *still* wouldn't be An'desha.

He swallowed with difficulty. *So where does all this leave me? The odd man out, with An'desha spending more and more time away from me. And I'll have to smile and pretend everything is fine.*

It looked as if he was going to have a great deal of uncomfortable time to fill as An'desha drifted farther and farther from him. But what else could he do? The single course that was open to him was confrontation, and *that* would only drive An'desha away faster.

He was not prone to depression, but now he tried to swallow a hard and uncomfortable lump of despair that seemed to have gotten lodged in his throat. *I thought I had finally found someone I could spend the rest of my life with, and once again it comes to nothing.* He felt so loaded down with melancholy he might never be able to rise again. No one understood. They looked at him, saw how handsome he was, how Gifted a mage he was, how intelligent he was, and thought that everything always fell into his hands. They didn't know, they couldn't guess, how hard it was for him to make and keep friends, much less lovers—never dreamed just how lonely he was. It was easy to find people who would fill his bed; impossible to find anyone who would fill his heart. Temporary lovers were easy to come by, but reliability was rarer fare.

I suppose the best thing I can do is to work, he thought dully. *If I keep my mind occupied, my heart generally leaves me alone.* That always worked in the past, and the gods knew that they had enough troubles now, trying to come up with the next solution after the breakwater.

I should go make myself available to Darkwind, Elspeth, and the Valdemaran artificers. That was what he *should* do, all right; it was the logical direction. But that was what An'desha was doing, which would only serve to put him in An'desha's company. An'desha might like the artificers, but they made Firesong think of bees or ants—logical, well-coordinated, but without souls. Their "magic" was a thing of gears and clockwork, regular and completely artificial.

Besides, Darkwind and Elspeth are much, much better than I am at this new approach to magic. It obviously doesn't feel artificial to them.

No. *No, I cannot learn to like these artificers. I cannot learn to think the way they do, or to admire the way they think.* Their odd, mechanical approach to what he still felt, deep down inside, was a process that was part instinct, part art, and part improvisation, robbed magic of all the beauty and the thrill he had found in it when he first began to make use of his Gift. Without beauty, what was the point anyway?

They've taken poetry and reduced it to a mathematical formula, that's what they've done. But knowing the formula doesn't mean you can produce poetry; it only means you can produce well-crafted doggerel.

The more he thought about it, the more he rebelled, soul and heart. He had *tried* to work with them before, and in the end, neither he nor they had been comfortable.

They keep trying to find ways to measure things that should be felt, *not measured. You can't take a ruler to a love affair, you can't hold up a gauge to weigh sorrow, and you shouldn't try to find a way to measure magic!*

Melancholy had weighed him down a moment before; now irritation drove him to his feet again. He pushed himself up off the couch with a muttered curse, and flung his power around the room recklessly, lighting the wicks of every lamp within the walls with an ostentatious flare. Aya started, uttered an unmusical squawk of annoyance, and settled down on his perch with all of his feathers fluffed, glaring at his bondmate through a slitted blue eye.

Firesong ignored him, although he sensed Aya's own irritation in the bondbird's mental mutterings. Well, that was as much a reflection of his own unsettled emotional state as Aya's peevishness. When his emotional state was negative, so was the firebird's.

Maybe he'd better get out of Aya's way for a while, before their mutual irritation started to get out of hand.

A hot soak, perhaps. If nothing else, soaking in the hot pool in the garden below would unknot some of his tension-knotted muscles. If he *didn't* get them relaxed, he'd have a headache before morning.

Abruptly he turned and took the spiral staircase down to the ground floor of the *ekele*. Here, frosted glass lamps like little moons placed among the foliage displayed the wonders of a Hawkbrother Vale in miniature. Luxuriant plants spread their leaves in every part of the room, which had floor-to-ceiling windows comprising all four sides. Firesong had landscaped with rocks and plants until it was impossible to tell—particularly at night—that this was a little corner of Companion's Field in Valdemar, and not a private corner of a real Vale. Finally, after much forced growth, vines covered the uprights between the windows, the trees and bushes hid the glazing, and a canopy of leaves concealed the ceiling. As he had leisure, he added tiny spots to the ceiling that absorbed sunlight by day and emitted it at night, mimicking stars.

The centerpiece of the room was the soaking-pool, fed by a hot spring brought up from deep beneath Haven by Firesong's power—the heat source was partly natural, partly magical, and shielded as well as the Heartstone under the Palace. With all of the strange effects of the mage-storms about, the last thing Firesong wanted was to discover his spring gone either boiling-hot or cold as ice.

He stripped off his clothing as he walked, leaving a trail of discarded garments until he reached the side of the pool and dropped into it. It was too bad that there were no *hertasi* here; he would have to pick up after himself. But just at the moment, he didn't feel like being careful.

According to legend, it was Urtho, the Mage of Silence, who had first discovered the way to create these pools.

Hah. According to legend, Urtho is also responsible for first discovering the wheel, taming the horse, and cooking meat. Firesong sank up to his chin in the hot water, cynically reflecting on the many legends surrounding the last of the Great Mages. Obscure legends even claimed that Urtho had achieved much of his power by inventing ways to measure magic and to use it efficiently!

As if Urtho were some sort of Mage of Artifice! I don't think so. Urtho has become whatever the speaker wants him to be at the time.

That was the argument the gryphons had last used on him—that if Urtho had used ways to measure and ration magic, couldn't Firesong?

Of course, if anyone would know whether or not the claim was true, it would probably be the gryphons and the Kaled'a'in. They alone held actual records of the Mage-Wars and the time immediately preceding the Cataclysm. The people who had become the Shin'a'in and Tayledras had both escaped without any such things. Clan k'Leshya, the Clan that had welcomed outsiders, that had supported and cared for the gryphons, that had held both Urtho's trusted chief of wizardry and his chief *kestra'chern*, had been entrusted with the care of all of Urtho's records during the escape to safety.

Well, so what if he was a superior Artificer Adept? Why should I change my ways of working—ways that have served me very well until now!—just to emulate someone dead millennia ago? For that matter, didn't my way of working take down his ancient enemy when he failed to do so? He smiled into the steam, for the first time today feeling both smug and superior. *So, there's a great deal to be said for intuition and creativity! I'll wager none of these artificers could have figured a way to safely shut down k'Sheyna's rogue Heartstone either!*

Let Elspeth and Darkwind hare off after this "new thinking." Let even An'desha take to it with a speed that left Firesong gaping at him. Time would show which was the better way. *The ways of a so-called "golden" ancient time may not necessarily be better than the ways we have developed since. "Golden Ages" are often nothing more than fool's gold, or merest gilding over dross.*

He closed his eyes and leaned back against the sculpted stone of his seat. His shoulder and neck muscles were finally relaxing in the heat, and something else occurred to him. The one thing that *did* impress An'desha now was skill and competence. That was why Karal and the Master Artificers were currently high in his esteem. Karal had evidently proved his mettle at the border, and the Master Artificers had convinced the Shin'a'in that there was a cold beauty—and certainly there was logic—in their formulae and numbers.

But if Firesong could come up with an answer that superseeded the breakwater, wouldn't *he* get An'desha's attention back?

Of course I would! He knows the ways that Falconsbane and all the rest worked, but he has never had formal Tayledras training in magic, except for the little he's gotten from me so far! And if I can prove that my way is the better way, he'll be panting at my heels to learn from me again! I'll have his fullest attention and his admiration!

Now *that* was an answer!

He'd seen the new water-table anyway, and it was obvious even to an idiot that the reflections within it were going to be too complicated to analyze. The artificers were setting themselves up for failure.

Maybe I shouldn't even try to work with that; it might be setting myself up for the same failure, to deal with a situation so complicated. Maybe I should just let the breakwater fail, then put my own solution in place, between mage-storms. Certainly the original problem had been much simpler to deal with, and the difference would only be a matter of degree. *More frequent, more powerful mage-storms, that's all. Did An'desha say something about Falconsbane-*

Ma'ar anticipating the original set of mage-storms and envisioning something to hold them back?

When An'desha came back tonight, could he somehow coax his lover into talking about that? *That wouldn't make very good pillow talk, considering how he feels about Falconsbane...*

In a strange way, Firesong actually admired Falconsbane—or rather, he admired the level of craftsmanship of which Falconsbane was capable in his rare moments of sanity.

Well, that wasn't precisely true; Firesong admired those abilities in Ma'ar, in which they had been the purest and the closest to sanity. Certainly *Ma'ar* had been able to create. He'd come up with his own forms of fighting-creatures, although he had sacrificed elegance for expediency and grace for brute power. The makaar hadn't been without intelligence, though; they couldn't have been stupid, or they wouldn't have survived a heartbeat in the air against the gryphons.

And as for Ma'ar's secret of immortality—in its way, that was the most elegant of all, although An'desha was hardly likely to agree with that assessment.

He does have the best right in the world to have an opinion on the subject, Firesong reflected sardonically. *But he's also not precisely unbiased on the subject.* Of all the people alive in the world at that very moment, there were only two who knew exactly how Ma'ar had lived long past his own death—and how every "incarnation" after that had managed to live long past the natural span without actually "dying" and being "reborn." There were drawbacks to that particular system, after all.

For one thing, it places your soul in the hands of the Powers Above, and if you've been naughty, you really don't want that to happen. For another, it seems that damn few people who undergo that particular process remember their previous lives. And last of all, so far as I know, you don't get a choice about who or what you return as.

Of course, if you were a good and virtuous person, none of these things would bother you. *However, Ma'ar was a* very *naughty boy, and he only got worse with each successive body he possessed. He* had *to remember who and what he was, otherwise he'd waste years relearning all he'd learned about magic. He had to have a choice about who he took over, or the body wouldn't have the ability to handle magic. And he certainly wanted no part of the Powers Above.*

That, at least, was Firesong's assessment. An'desha, of course, would know Falconsbane's full motivation, but Firesong doubted that An'desha would want to talk about it.

It was a clever—no, brilliant—scheme, though. And I'm in a position to recognize just how brilliant it was. Only he and An'desha knew how the scheme had worked; An'desha because he had seen it from the inside, and Firesong because he had destroyed the very foundation of the scheme.

Ma'ar-Falconsbane had avoided the hand of Fate by creating a stronghold for his spirit and personality in the Void, that place between Gates where neither the spirit nor the material could be told from one another. He had avoided *real* death by using the tremendous energy released by the violent death of his own bodies to catapult himself into that stronghold and seal himself inside until someone of his own direct bloodline matched a very rigid set of criteria and made his first attempt at the spell to create fire. *That* triggered the release of the spirit from the stronghold and flung it, with almost all of the original energy, into the new body.

An'desha said he couldn't find a single incarnation where Falconsbane hadn't either suicided or been murdered. Feh. The man must have been a masochist as well as a sadist. Either death would release shattering amounts of energy, quite enough to accomplish the trick with power to spare.

Firesong was as intimately familiar with the process as An'desha because he was the one who had tracked Falconsbane's spirit to that stronghold, ravaging the stronghold then destroying Falconsbane, utterly and completely, shredding the Dark Adept's spirit to atoms and scattering them across the Void. Presumably the Powers Above *could* put the scattered spirit back together again—but if They did, it would be for Their purposes, and Falconsbane would likely see rebirth in a form that would horrify even him.

Say, as a helpless, impoverished cripple, unable to move without assistance, deaf and blind, utterly without magic or mind-magic, who spends every waking moment in pain. Or perhaps as a slug, a dung beetle, or a cloud of gnats.

That wasn't Firesong's business. What happened to what *had* been Falconsbane was of no concern to him, so long as the Dark Adept couldn't work the trick that had kept him turning up like a clipped coin, over and over, across the decades.

Still, the trick was a clever one, and that much Firesong could admire.

And in a way—if Falconsbane hadn't been what he was, it wasn't likely that Firesong would ever even have met An'desha.

For a moment he amused himself with the paths of might-have-been, trying to figure out what he and An'desha would have done—

Well, I might have met him, but he'd have been the age of my parents, and I never did care for older men. I keep forgetting that his apparent age and his chronological age are vastly different.

The Shin'a'in and Tayledras Goddess, in the persons of Her Avatars, had literally given An'desha back the body that Falconsbane had stolen away. They had returned his body to the state it had been when he had been possessed, at the age of seventeen or eighteen; perhaps a little younger, certainly no older.

By the same token, An'desha had spent so much of that time in hiding, in a kind of limbo within his own mind, that he didn't have the personal experience to match that chronological age. Emotionally, he was as young as he appeared.

Or he was, anyway.

Firesong licked salty sweat from his upper lip as he debated getting out of the hot pool. *Maybe a little longer. The longer I stay in here, the less likely it will be that my muscles will knot up again with tension as soon as I get out.*

He *should* be thinking—if he thought about Falconsbane at all— about those fugitive memories of Ma'ar's, and the "solution" that the Dark Adept had contrived to keep his own land safe from the mage-storms that were going to occur when Urtho died. That was where, if it was anywhere, the germ of their own solution would lie.

But his slippery thoughts kept coming back to that elegant little pattern of stronghold—possession—stronghold. It was just so very clever! And no one would have ever guessed what was going on if An'desha hadn't found a way to survive the possession.

I wonder what the other criteria were for possession, besides Adept-potential. I would think they would have to be solitary sorts, or his "new" personality would have given the signal that something was wrong.

If one could somehow assure that one returned in an ethical fashion, there wouldn't have been anything wrong with the entire scheme. *Yes, but just how would one displace another's spirit in an ethical fashion, hmm?*

Still, he kept coming back to that, as he climbed the stairs to the living area of the *ekele*. If only there was a way—

Well, infants were not ensouled, to the best of *his* knowledge, until the actual birth; it happened with the first breath. What if one arranged to slip in just before that critical moment?

It would mean a certain tedious time spent maturing, but that could be gotten around, I expect. At least, I could shorten that time, although it would certainly startle the parents. I can accelerate plant growth, so why not my own? It would only be one more application of the same thing Falconsbane used to change his own body.

He combed his wet hair with his fingers as he walked, pulling it forward over his shoulder. All his adult life he had cherished a secret longing, born when he had learned about his ancestor Vanyel and the love and lifebonding that had lasted through time and across the ages with his beloved Tylendel-Stefen. As foolishly romantic as it was, *he* had longed to find someone, a lifebonded, a soul-mate. He had really thought that person was An'desha.

Unfortunately, it didn't seem that An'desha shared that conviction, and if there was one thing that Firesong was sure of, it was that those who were lifebonded were *both* aware of the bond to the point of pain if they were apart or at odds with one another. They could not be lifebonded and be having the kind of personal problems they were now.

He searched through his wardrobe for something appropriate to his mood—black—and winced when his hand brushed across one of An'desha's Shin'a'in tunics. *He's reverting more and more to the Shin'a'in.* That in itself should have told him this was no lifebond. Lifebonded couples tended to dress *more* alike, even without thinking about it. Look at Heralds Dirk and Talia—who always chose the same color when they were off-duty. Or Sherrill and Keren, who dressed like a pair of twins, even though Sherrill tended to prefer elegant lines and Keren to dress entirely in riding leathers whenever possible! An'desha seemed to be choosing clothing as opposite that of Firesong's elegant robes and tunics as possible, wearing the bright—not to say gaudy and clashing— embroidered vests, and tunics and trews trimmed in the bands of colorful wide braid that the Shin'a'in loved.

He sighed as he pulled a long, silken robe of unrelieved black over his head. No, he was going to have to admit it. This was no lifebond And the bond he did have was, quite frankly, falling apart.

Lifebonds were incredibly rare. The chances of ever finding one's lifemate were remote, no matter how much one looked.

He paused with his hand still on the wardrobe door as he was closing it when the inescapable thought occurred to him. True, the chances of finding one's lifemate were remote, *if* one only lived a single lifetime.

But what if you lived for several lifetimes?

What if you had a way to return, over and over, fully as yourself?

What if you managed to find that ethical way to return the way Falconsbane had? You could search as long as you needed to in order to find your lifebonded. And then?

Then, perhaps you could find a way to stay together forever. Vanyel and Stefen had.

And wasn't *that* a fascinating thought?

4

Grand Duke Tremane looked out of the window in his office, gazing down through the bubbly pane of its poor-quality glass at the row after row of tents sheltering supplies down in the courtyard of his fortified manor. *Security. That's what lies down there, made tangible and visible.* The tents themselves were from the supplies he had appropriated; as soon as his clerks had found them in the records and his supply-sergeants had identified the crates they were in, he'd had them unpacked and set up to hold everything that could tolerate cold and didn't need to be under guard.

The courtyard was full of tents, with scarcely room to move between them. There were more tents lined up between the manor and the camp. Some of the supplies had already been distributed. Every man in his army now had triple bedding, triple clothing, double harsh-weather gear. They could *survive* a hideous winter now without barracks, although there would be sickness, frostbite, and other cold-related problems if they were forced to. That was more than they'd had before; if the worst predictions had come true, many would have died in the cold and snow.

He still couldn't believe that he had actually succeeded with his raid on the supply depot, and succeeded beyond his wildest dreams! All the men were current in their pay, including the bonuses he'd promised for odd or hazardous duty, and morale had taken an upswing, despite the fact that the drizzly weather hadn't broken for weeks. The extras that he had rationed out to them in the way of clothing and bedding hadn't hurt either; when he'd made a night inspection after lights-out, he'd seen the men were already making use of what he'd given out. Every tent contained a cocoon of blankets, with nothing visible of the man inside it but his nose, and the snores emerging from those cocoons had sounded very content.

The gold and silver entering the local economy wasn't hurting the morale of the townsfolk either, though he was glad he'd established a policy regarding double-pricing back when he'd first occupied this place. Any merchant found charging one price to a native and a higher price to a soldier—provided, of course, that the price difference *wasn't* due to the soldier being a poor hand at haggling—was brought up before his own fellow merchants and fined four times the difference in the price, half of which went to the Merchant's Guild, one quarter to the Imperial coffers, and one quarter to the fellow who was cheated. With all this new money flowing, his men could have been robbed blind without such a policy already in place.

Now his primary concern was to use his new stock of lumber to get warehouses up to shelter all the foodstuffs he'd looted. Everything else could stay under canvas, but the food needed real protection. That was keeping those of his men not robust enough to work on the walls quite busy. Even some of the clerks were taking a hand, since there wasn't as much need for them without all the Imperial paperwork to keep up with.

We have some space to breathe. That's the biggest factor. A great deal of the tension is gone.

The unspoken feeling of threat that was driving the work on the walls was still there, and certainly the men were thinking about the foul weather, looking at their tents, and wondering if a little canvas between them and a blizzard was going to be enough. Nevertheless, *now* no one was looking at his ration at mealtimes and wondering when those rations would be cut; no one was counting arrows, lead shot, or vials of oil for lamps and heating stoves. They all had been given a reprieve, and they all sensed it.

The mages were going about their new assignment—finding a way to shield them from the effects of the mage-storms—with a renewed optimism about their own ability. The walls were going up faster than before.

And a small, select group of mages was working on a new project—to find the source of the storms.

He turned away from the window, but instead of going back to his desk and the welter of papers lying there, he took a seat in a comfortable chair before his fireplace. *I never felt the cold and damp so intensely before,* he thought, as he winced a little when he flexed stiff fingers in the warmth of the flames. *Is it age, I wonder, or is the weather affecting me that much?*

He gazed deeply into the flames and gave thought to the latest report from that smaller group of mages, a report that tended to confirm some of his own uneasy speculations. In it, they expressed severe doubt that Valdemar was the source of the mage-storms, and their evidence was compelling.

Valdemar's few mages have only begun working in groups, and are not, in our view, coordinated enough to have developed or produced these storms. If *anyone* knew about working group-magic, it was Sejanes. The old man had multiplied his own personal power far and above that of any single mage, simply by finding enough compatible minor mages to work with him, and by being careful that they never felt exploited, and so were not inclined to leave him. If Sejanes felt the Valdemarans were too new to group-magic to be effective at it, Tremane was going to accept that estimate without a qualm.

Valdemar has been feeling the same effects that we have, and it would be suicidally stupid to unleash a weapon that would work the same damage to you as it does to the enemy. Well, he'd already figured that one out, so it hardly came as a surprise.

Valdemar has never unleashed uncontrolled area-effect magic, and their overt policy, at least, would preclude such a weapon. He couldn't exactly argue with that, either; he'd studied their past strategies, and there was nothing of the sort in any of them. In fact, right up through the war with Ancar they had plied purely defensive tactics.

It was hard to believe, but the Valdemarans were something Tremane had never expected to see in his lifetime: people who were exactly what they appeared to be, employing no deceptions and very little subterfuge.

Which means I misjudged them, and I sent in an assassin for no reason. Ah, well. He wasn't going to agonize over it. He had done what he thought he had to at the time, with his own best assessment of the situation. *Expediency. We are ruled by it...* He had enough now to worry about with the welfare of his own men, and if a few Valdemarans and their allies had gotten in the way of his agent's weapons, well, that was the hazard of war.

At least, that was what he'd always been taught.

Never mind. But as for the mages, I might as well order them to stop chasing that particular hare and go after more promising quarry. If not Valdemar, then where are these things coming from? And why now?

The fire popped and hissed as the flames found a particularly knotty piece of wood. *Wood. My scholars have a good idea for shelters which requires a minimum of wood, and that is good news.*

These new barracks began with four walls of the same bricks he was building the defensive bulwarks with; heaped up against them, pounded earth, reaching to the rafters. There would be no windows and only two doors, one at either end. The roof frame and roof timbers would be of wood, but the roof itself would be thick thatch, of the kind that country cottages around here used. Each building would look rather like a haystack atop a low hillock. If snow started to build up on the roof to a dangerous weight, it would be easy to send men up to clean it off, but a certain amount of snow would insulate against cold winds. His builders liked the plan, for a fireplace in each of the outer walls that did not contain a door could easily heat the entire building efficiently.

We can start those as soon as the defensive walls are up. Thatch; that's straw, and there's certainly plenty of that. I can probably hire thatchers from the town. Brick he had in abundance, and plenty of earth. *If we have the time before snow starts to fall, I can build more of those structures with no fireplaces and only one door to use as warehouses for the foodstuffs, then take the wood from the warehouses we tossed up and reuse it elsewhere.*

Could these same buildings be used for army kitchens? He'd have to ask his people. Or better still, could he put a kitchen in each barracks, and use the heat from cooking to help heat the barracks?

And what are we going to do about bathhouses? His men were accustomed to keeping themselves healthy, and that meant clean. Perhaps he could find enough materials to build a few traditional bathhouses with steamrooms and have the men use them in tightly-scheduled shifts. *But how are we going to heat them, and heat the water?*

And the latrines, the privies; how far along were the builders on those? His men who knew about such things had assured him that they would have adequate arrangements before the first hard freeze, arrangements that would not poison the local water supplies. Would they? Was there a progress report on his desk yet? He couldn't remember.

He almost got up to find out, but the warmth of the fire seduced him. If there was a report on his desk, it would still be there later, and if there wasn't, it wouldn't materialize.

Not like the old days, when one *might* have. *The old days—huh. The "old days" were less than six moons ago.* It seemed like a lifetime ago, and he was a different man then. He had already done things that Grand Duke Tremane would never have considered.

I have burned all my bridges.

The walls would be done in a few days. Then work could start on the barracks. He wanted to get everything done at once, and despite the number of men he had, there still weren't enough—and—

And we have gold. We have gold! Why can't I just hire some of the locals? Why shouldn't I? I've seen boys standing about, looking for work. Maybe there are only boys and old men and women, but not all the work will need strength. Oh, damn. We have gold, but I need to keep it in reserve if I can, to pay my own troops. Besides, how do I get those people to work for us? Not all that long ago, we were the enemy. How do I manage to get the townspeople and my men to work together? How?

His thoughts stopped as he realized that he was planning for a long future. These new barracks weren't meant to last for a season or a year; his builders had given him plans for structures that would last for years. His sanitary men were planning for decades of use.

Oh, a long future be damned. Well, of course, they're giving me plans for good barracks. The winter is going to be worse than anything we have ever seen. Tents or flimsy structures made to last a season won't cope with the kind of winter storms we're going to see. And one of the worst things that could happen would be for our facilities to freeze up; if we overbuild, that won't happen. Probably. Maybe.

Better to concentrate on how he could hire some of the locals, how he might be able to keep the people of the town and the men of the Imperial Army from going for each other's throats. If he could just find a way to get them to work together—that was how the Empire had forged all the disparate people of its conquered lands into a whole in the first place. Young men from all over the Empire were conscripted into the ranks of the army, where they served out their terms beside young men from places they might not even have heard of before. By the time their terms were over, they all returned to their homes unable to think of men from places they didn't know as barbarians or foreigners, and capable of thinking in larger terms than just their own villages.

I can't conscript the townsfolk, more's the pity. For one thing, they wouldn't stand for it. For another, there's no one worth conscripting. Ancar took every able-bodied man away for his own army.

"Sir!" One of the aides was at the open door, calling anxiously into the gloom. Of course, he couldn't see Tremane from the door, hidden as he was in the oversized armchair. "Commander, are you here?"

"Over here." Tremane stood up and turned to face the door, and saw relief spread over the aide's features.

"Sir, there's a delegation here from the town, and they are rather insistent. They say they must talk to you now." He made a gesture of helplessness. "They wouldn't leave a message or talk to anyone other than you."

Of course they wouldn't, they never have. The townsfolk didn't seem to grasp the concept of delegation of authority. They evidently thought that unless they spoke directly to Tremane, whatever it was they had to say would never reach him. "Send them in immediately." He moved back into his office and sat down behind his desk as the aide went off to fetch this delegation. Whatever they wanted, whether or not it was really important, he would make time for them. At all costs, he must stay on good terms with these people, but he must also make it clear—though with such subtlety that they themselves would not be aware he was doing so—that *he* was the real ruler here, that he *permitted* them their autonomy. Perhaps that was why they insisted on seeing him and him only; perhaps he had done his job too well.

Or perhaps, after years of terror under Ancar, they no longer believed in anything but the witness of their own ears and eyes.

Would it be complaints this time? It had been the last, though they were complaints from those living nearest the new walls about the noise and dust. He had made it very clear at the time that while such inconveniences would pass, he was not about to slow the progress of his walls by restricting the building to the daylight hours. Since the spider-creature had been brought in, interestingly enough, there had been no more complaints about noise. It was a pity that the town had no real walls of its own; people who had protective walls usually had a firm grasp on the *need* for protective walls.

The delegation was the usual three; the mayor of the city and his two chief Council members representing the Guilds and the farmfolk. The mayor, Sandar Giles, was a much younger man than Tremane was used to seeing in a position of authority, and was quite frail, with a clubbed foot, though his quick intelligence was immediately obvious when he spoke. Thin and dark, he looked like a schoolboy, although Tremane knew his real age was close to thirty. His eyes were the liveliest thing about him; large and expressive, they often betrayed him by revealing emotions he probably would rather have kept concealed.

Both the Chief Husbandman and the Chief Guildsman were old enough to be his grandsires and the main difference between them was that the Chief Husbandman was weathered and wrinkled with years in the field, his face resembling a dried apple, while the Chief Guildsman wore his years more lightly. Both were gray-haired and bearded, both knotted and bent with the years, joints swollen and probably painful. Both had square jaws beneath the close-cropped beards, and cautious eyes that betrayed nothing.

All three took their seats, both of the Council members showing great deference to Sandar, seeing to it that he was seated comfortably before taking their own chairs in front of Tremane's desk. Tremane had always been more at ease receiving civilians in his office rather than in any kind of a throne room; the former implied a businesslike approach that he found made civilians more inclined to cooperate.

They all exchanged the usual greetings; Tremane sent for hot drinks, since he had learned that Sandar was quite susceptible to cold. As soon as the aide was out of the room again, he leaned forward across the wooden expanse of the desktop.

"Well, what is it that you need to see me about so urgently?" he asked, coming to the point quickly, something that would have been so unheard of back in the Empire that his visitors would have been shocked into utter speechlessness. "Not a complaint, I hope. Not only *can't* I do anything about building noise, I won't. We're racing the winter, and I hope by now your people know how badly *all* of us need those walls."

"Definitely not a complaint—or, rather, not a complaint about you or your men," Sandar replied, with both thin hands cupped around the mug of *kala*, though it was still too hot to sip. "If I have a complaint about anything, it would be about the weather."

Tremane raised one eyebrow, and Sandar shrugged. "I hope you don't expect me or my mages to do anything about that," he replied, amused. "I wish we could, as heartily as you do. Not that we couldn't have in the past, but—"

"I know, I know, it's these confounded mage-storms!" growled the Chief Husbandman, Devid Stoen. "Hang it all, *we* used to have three good weather-wizards that could at least give us a few days of guaranteed clear weather for harvest, and did a fine job of telling us what was on the way. But that was before that damned puppy Ancar stole the throne and conscripted 'em all! For that matter, a pair of 'em trailed back to us just after your lot moved in and started building walls—but all they can do is tell us that they can't read the weather anymore, that because of the mage-storms, they can't do a thing!"

Tremane's other eyebrow rose to join its fellow; this was the first time he'd heard officially that there were any kind of Hardornen mages in the city. For that matter, it was the first time he'd heard the rumors his spies had reported confirmed. Were they admitting it just because those mages had proved to be powerless? Had they assumed he already knew? Or was it a slip of the tongue that Stoen was mentioning them now?

"If you can't do anything, and you know my mages can't either, then what is it about the weather that brings you here?" he asked carefully. No point in mentioning these weather-mages. If it was a slip, he'd rather they didn't realize he'd taken note of it.

"Well," Sandar said, after a pregnant pause, "you must have noticed that there is a decided scarcity of healthy, strong young men around about here." His expressive eyes were full of irony as he glanced down at his own frail body.

"Hmm. It's hard *not* to notice." He lowered his eyebrows. "I'd assumed that Ancar conscripted them, and—" He hesitated, not knowing how to phrase "used them as deployable decoys" politely.

"He used them up, most of them," Sandar said bluntly. "A few came trailing back with the mages, but most of them were slaughtered in his senseless war on Valdemar and Karse. That's how I became mayor; my father was barely young enough and definitely fit enough to be conscripted, and I had been his secretary from the time I was old enough to be useful. I knew everything he'd known, so I became mayor by default."

Tremane wasn't certain which aroused more pity in him; the old pain in Sandar's voice as he spoke so casually of the loss of his father, or the resignation and acceptance of the situation. *Don't become too involved with these people, Tremane. They aren't yours, they never will be. You have no responsibility toward them beyond the immediate, and only then in ways that will benefit your troops.*

"Virtually every healthy male between the ages of fifteen and forty was taken," Sandar continued. "And it wasn't just in the towns; he sent his butchers out to every farm, not once, but repeatedly. You might be able to save your sons once, twice, or even three times, but sooner or later Ancar's slavers would find them. That left us with old men, women, and children. In towns, that's not a situation that's impossible. At a task requiring skill rather than strength, old men and women are as good as any young man, and often better. At a task that requires strength, well, there were enough skilled craftspeople in the town to come up with ways that someone with minimal strength can do the work of two or more powerful men. But out in the farms—" He shrugged.

Stoen took over. "The fact is, farms need strong people to run, and lots of 'em," he said, "And we don't have 'em. Things have been goin' downhill since Ancar took over, and that's a fact. Now we did all right this year at planting. We were lucky, we had lots of good weather, though you can't say that about other places in Hardorn. We did all right during the growing season, partly by not gettin' much sleep, partly because if you spread enough children out, they can do the work of a man. But now—it's harvest, we haven't *got* the good weather, and frankly, sir, we're in trouble. There's not a chance we're going to get more than half the crops in. We've tried, we've gotten some help from the city, but—" He spread his hands helplessly. "We can't really *pay* nobody, and people generally aren't bright enough to figure out that if they don't help out now, they're gonna be on short rations or *no* rations come spring."

"And I can't force anyone to work in the fields who doesn't want to," Sandar finished. "I can try to point out the consequences, but if they don't want to go, or say, 'let someone else do it,' I can't call up what old gaffers are left of the city constables and force people to go pull roots or gather wheat."

"Nor can I," said Master Goldsmith Bran Kerst. "Particularly not when there's money to be made selling to *your* men, sir. Can't ask someone to go pull roots in a cold, muddy field for nothing when he can be carting beer at a good wage here in town."

Rather than ask the obvious question, Tremane simply waited for them to get to the point.

Stoen sighed gustily. "The point is this, Commander. We only need help for a few days, a fortnight or two at most, but those days are critical, or the crops are going to rot in the fields. Could you see your way clear to sending some of your men to help with the harvest?"

Tremane pretended to consider it for a moment. "Let me ask you this, first. How many people in your Guilds are skilled or semiskilled builders? *We* have a problem, too. We need to get new barracks up and the walls finished before the weather gets too cold to build in." Before Kerst could say anything, he added, "They'll be paid a fair wage, of course—and work would go much more quickly with people who knew how to build than with those of my men who are fighters, not builders."

Kerst opened his mouth, then closed it again. Tremane waited for either him or Sandar to say something, then continued when they said nothing. "I'll be frank with you; I have enough supplies to last out the winter with no trouble. I don't need to purchase anything locally. Nevertheless, I am no fool, and I can foresee problems if *your* people don't have enough to support them. If your people are short of foodstuffs, there will be trouble here in my own camp before too long. Some of my men will steal Imperial stores and sell them illegally, some of *your* people will try to steal from our stores. I'll catch them, of course, and I'll be forced to punish everyone involved. I may have to order some hangings, depending on the amount of theft; I will certainly have to order some fairly harsh punishments to assure that I can keep order. This will mean—shall we just say—unpleasantness for garrison *and* town. I'd rather deal with the situation before it becomes a problem."

"How?" Stoen asked, leaning forward intently.

Tremane took a quick glance at his ledgers before answering. If the payment didn't have to be in hard cash…

"My coffers are not bottomless, but I have a certain amount of property my people don't need at the moment," he said carefully. "If I can barter that property for services—or, say, sell the property to some of the Guilds for coin—we can muster the most efficient use of all the workers in the Imperial forces *and* in the town to get all of our projects done before the snow flies. Everyone who works will be paid a fair wage, according to the skill of the job." He gave each of the men a level look, and all three of them nodded as they met his eyes. "This will put some of my men—farm workers before they were recruited into the army—in the fields. That will be efficient for you; better to have one man who knows how to swing a scythe than five who don't. People from the town who are unskilled workers will either serve in the fields as common harvesters, or on the walls or barracks as haulers and other unskilled laborers. People from the town who are skilled builders will *definitely* be on the walls or the barracks. But for every man I send into the fields, I require someone to take his place here, and I will *not* send any builders of my own into the fields."

"Regardless, everyone who works will be paid?" Stoen asked.

He nodded. "I consider it an investment in peace," he replied frankly, as he mentally blessed the Hundred Little Gods for answering his prayers in such a timely manner. This was precisely what he needed, a way to mingle his men and the Hardornens in a peaceful, productive pursuit where both sides benefited. He'd have paid double for this.

"I think this can work," Sandar said cautiously, then flashed an unexpected grin. "It is rather ironic, since *your* gold, paid into the taverns and the like, will ultimately pay for your supplies, which will in turn go back into the town in the form of wages."

"But I will have buildings and walls," he reminded them. "With any fortune at all, by exchanging unskilled workers for skilled, I will have them faster. I will even grant you this; for jobs requiring neither skill nor strength I will hire two boys—and by 'boys,' I mean children ten years old and younger—at a man's wage, and that is probably fairer than they would get anywhere else."

It was, as he knew very well, more than fair. Girls didn't normally work in the Empire, they went to school until they turned sixteen, then became servants or got married. Some few became mages, entertainers, or scholars, but seldom craftspeople. Boys who worked usually got whatever copper bits they could scrape up; if they were apprentices, they got room and board and stayed grateful for both if their masters were generous.

"I think we can agree to that," Sandar said quickly—as Tremane had thought he would. "Send a list of what you have to dispose of over to my office; we'll either barter the work of apprentices and journeymen for it or buy it outright, provided it isn't totally useless, like ornamental funeral urns or some such."

"Oh, I think I can guarantee it won't be anything of the sort," Tremane said agreeably. He was already making a mental list of things his men wouldn't need from the looted stores. Raw iron, tin, and copper bar-stock, for instance; *he* didn't have any smiths, but there had been crate after crate of the stuff in the storehouse. By now, this town must be running low on raw metals—wars disrupted trade, after all, and he hadn't seen any mines or smelters in operation around here. He had enough finished metal goods to last his men for years; he didn't need the raw material. He had more horse tack than anyone would ever need; he had cured leather by the stack, and he knew by the state of some harness he'd seen, mended with bits of rope or patched together with bits cut away from worn-out straps, that they'd welcome both tack and leather. Those were just the things he could think of immediately. No, there would be no trouble finding things these people would be very happy to see.

"In that case, we'll be getting on our way," Sandar replied, showing a bit more color in his thin face than he'd had when he came in—and a bit more hope, as well. "We'll have to send criers out all over town to round up the unskilled laborers, but Master Kerst will have an answer for you from the Guild of the Masons and Woodworkers shortly."

"Is there a—a Thatcher's Guild?" Tremane asked, wondering if he sounded like a fool for asking.

Stoen laughed. "No Guild, lad, but I'll have plenty of thatchers for you once the harvest's in. Never fear of that; most farmers know how to thatch a roof fair handily. You'll be wanting thatching straw, then?"

He nodded, relieved to have that one out of his hands. "Yes, and a great deal of it, I suppose. These barracks are going to be barnlike buildings, and a thatched roof has been recommended."

"Just leave that to me," Stoen assured him. "Thank your gods, the one thing we've no lack of is thatching straw." He sighed. "Keeps well, and there've been fewer roofs to mend these days."

The men shook hands all around, and the delegation left, escorted by the aide. Tremane remained where he was, behind his desk with his nose buried in the account of the looted stores, going through the ledgers line by line, making up his list of barter goods. He found an amazing variety of absolutely useless items—useless to his men, that is. What in the name of all that was holy would they do with a hundred pairs of women's half boots? Or three crates of gilded copper bracelets? Or regulation Healer's tunics and trews in sizes too small for any man in the force? All of those could go; since his Healers wore the plainest of clothing without rank or regiment marks, even the tunics and trews could be redyed and used as common clothing. Tools—he had enough shovels to give every man two; he certainly didn't need that many. Small hatchets, hammer-ended, made for pounding tent stakes into the ground and cutting firewood—again, he had twice as many of those as he had men. Did he really need all those tents? He certainly didn't need six decorative dress-parade pavillions!

There were things he didn't need but was not inclined to put into the hands of former enemies—siege engine components and weapons, for instance. But why on earth had the Imperial supply depot been holding six trunks of costumes for veil-dancers? Or all the scenery, props, and costumes needed for a production of *The Nine-Days King*? Or an entire field mews for thirty hunting birds, complete with imping flat-drawered cabinets?

Though I do know why it had that "special tent and accountrements for the Commander's recreation." Duke Clerance can't even field an army without his mistress, and she can't do without anything she's become accustomed to. That should certainly bring a pretty piece of coin. Best he didn't let on that it was meant for a courtesan, however. Let the ladies of the town that still had money argue over who obtained what.

There were oddments; insect veiling for swamp campaigns, white salve and suncoats for desert fighting, camp furniture for officers—a few of this, a dozen of that. Once he had his list, he gave it to his clerks to copy out in Hardornen and send to Sandar, then went about writing up the orders calling for volunteers for harvest work.

Those required very special care in phrasing. *No man receiving special pay for special skills will be accepted for harvest work.* As he'd told Sandar, he did not intend to lose a single skilled builder to pulling roots. He made it quite clear in his orders that he would not tolerate any "interference with or molestation or harassment of the women, married or unmarried, of the farms." He reiterated that Imperial Army rules regarding civilian women would hold and that there would be officers there to enforce them. He did this very deliberately; without coming out and saying so, he was telling the men that there would be attractive—or, at least, fresh-faced—young farm women working alongside them. They would know that there would be severe punishment for taking liberties with the civilians, but if a young woman and a young man decided to meet some time *after* the soldier was off-duty, and the soldier had proper leave to go off-grounds and conducted himself with respect for the lady's wishes...

Farm labor might be hard work, but it was easier than building walls, and for those soldiers conscripted from farming families, it would be much more pleasant. And certainly the surroundings—especially surroundings including unattached young women—would be much more congenial.

I might get more volunteers than I can spare. I'd better make arrangements in advance for a rotation of duties so I avoid the appearance of favoritism.

As he sent off the orders and call for volunteers to be copied and posted, something else occurred to him. Romances, serious ones, were bound to come out of this. And, inevitably, marriages.

Oh, gods. I'd better find some local priests. I have to find out what the local marriage customs and laws are. I'll have to have the men briefed. Gods, and courting customs; I don't want to have cases where one party thinks it's a light flirtation and the other thinks it's a betrothal! Maybe I had better think about partitioning one of the barracks into cubicles for married quarters. Can we afford that? Or should I just tell married couples to make their own arrangements in town? But if I do that, how do I enforce discipline? This sort of thing had never occurred to him before; wives and sweethearts were always left behind when the Army marched off. When the men had been confined to the light women of the taverns, he hadn't had to worry about all that. A lady of negotiable virtue knew what the rules were, and so did her customer. But properly brought up girls of the town and the farms—that was something else altogether—

His hands and thoughts both stilled, as he realized what he was planning.

This is not an encampment anymore. It's a permanent post. I am planning for a long future here.

That was what had been nagging at the back of his mind despite his efforts to deny it. He *could* have chosen a flimsier structure for the barracks plans, something that would last a few years. Instinctively, he had picked the strongest, most durable structure his designers had offered.

This was no longer an armed camp, it was an armed holding... He was allocating the men to serve both camp and town. He was planning for the mingling of both. He was planning for a future that included married soldiers, children, families.

Less and less of what he had learned as a military leader would apply, and more and more of what he had learned as the manager of his own estate.

If they all survived the mage-storms and the winter.

He pulled his mind and his planning back to the present. *One thing at a time. First, the walls, the barracks, and the harvest. Then worry about what comes next.*

Sandar was evidently overjoyed at the list of barter goods; late in the afternoon his messengers returned from town with answers from the Mayor and Master Kerst. The note from Sandar was good news, but the one from the Master Guildsman was even better. Master Kerst had two stonemasons and their journeymen and apprentices, four brickmasons and theirs, and a Master Builder and his. There were also assorted plasterers, woodworkers, a furniture builder or two, and others that Master Kerst felt might be useful...

Might be useful? Tremane very nearly did a dance around his desk, which would have either scandalized or terrified his aides, depending on whether they thought he was drunk or mad. He'd resigned himself to rough-finished walls in the barracks and the crudest of appointments; the men would certainly have seen worse in their time. Having skilled craftsmen available meant there would be *real* walls, a floor of something besides pounded earth, real bunks and mess tables for the men. And the answer from Sandar meant he was going to have all this without touching the stores of coin he'd taken from the Imperial coffers!

I wonder if you'd thought about bathhouses or a substitute for latrines? Kerst's note continued. *We have men who not only can advise you on both, but who have an idea or two you might want to consider.*

Bathhouses *and* latrines? He scribbled off a note in semiliterate Hardornen to Kerst directly.

Instead of the quiet dinner he usually had, he sat down that night with a tableful of men whose conversational topic was not usually considered appropriate over food.

By now, in order to deal with the locals efficiently, both his staff of chirurgeons and his builders had learned Hardornen, so the conversation was held in the local tongue. That was just as well. It was somehow easier to eat and listen to a conversation about latrines at the same time, if it was held in another language.

"—mix with wood ash and ground cob or chopped leaves, then you spread what you get out on drying racks," said one of the locals earnestly. "Depending on the weather, in a day or so you get something dry enough to bag, and that's what we've been selling to the farmers to put on their fields."

"You just need sewers and the treatment site, don't need sewage tanks, see?" finished his coworker. "Let the sand, gravel, and the rest of it purify the liquid, let it percolate through all the purifying layers, and you don't run the risk of poisoning our stream or our wells."

His own men nodded wisely. "We've been doing something like this in the cities and on the large estates, but you need magic," one of them said. "I've heard some people had a less sophisticated system on their estates because they didn't have a house mage. This will work."

"Well, it gets better," the first man said, grinning. "Bet you didn't know if you use the same system on cow dung, minus the wood ash and adding dried wood chips or sawdust, or ground woody plant waste, like heavy stalks, you can burn it."

"You have to compress it, make it into bricks, but it burns," the second confirmed. "Now, normally they'd take that cow dung and put it on their fields, but if you offered to trade them weight for weight for *your* dried sludge, they'll take it, and you'll have fuel you didn't have before. See, our stuff don't smell; it's dry and easier to handle than what comes off of a muck pile. They'd rather have ours. And we get fuel."

That got Tremane's interest. "Not for indoor fireplaces, surely—" he objected.

The two Hardornen sewage experts shook their heads. "No, and not for cooking—unless you like your soup to have that particular flavor."

"But we don't need open fireplaces to heat the barracks!" one of his own men suddenly exclaimed. "In fact—Commander, that would be a wasteful use of burnables. I just thought of an old design used in some of the houses up north—look—"

Tremane had already supplied the table with old documents taken from the depot and plenty of pens; his man seized one of each and began sketching on the back of an old pay roster while the rest leaned over each others' shoulders, peering down with interest.

"Look, you have your—your *furnace* here, below the level of the floor, and fed from outside, with a tiny little iron door. Above it, you have a huge mass of brick riddled with tiny chimneys. This works like a kiln, you heat the brick, the brick heats the barracks." He sucked on the end of the pen for a moment. "Put the door to the barracks *here*, on the far end of the wall, fill up the rest of the end wall with the brick arrangement, and there you are. Two sides sheltered by the earth, two with brick furnaces. Or only one furnace, if you want a barracks kitchen with ovens and a cooking fireplace at the other end."

Tremane looked the drawing over; it looked and sounded feasible. Put the sleeping quarters near the furnace, the common rooms in the middle, the kitchen at the other end. "It'll still have to have some arrangement like a smoke hole," he pointed out, "or all the smoke from lanterns and candles will just build up in there."

"Yes, but you'll be using more of the heat from the furnace," his man pointed out. "And you can burn dung without smelling up the inside."

"I don't see anything to object to," the Chief Chirurgeon said judiciously. "Other than the fact that it will be darker than the eighth hell in there without windows, and I'm bound to warn you that will have an effect on the men's morale and health."

"Better dark than freezing," one of the others muttered, which only confirmed Tremane's own thought.

"Health you can deal with in their diet; sprouted beans and the rest of that stuff you chirurgeons are so fond of," he replied. "And as for morale—since they'll be on duty outside most of the daylight hours, I don't see a problem—but wait a moment, though," he added, as something odd occurred to him.

The chirurgeons hadn't listed a single complaint or difficulty since they made a permanent camp here. *"You* people aren't having any problems with the mage-storms affecting you. Isn't that laying-on-of-hands healing that you do a kind of magic?"

One of the lesser Healers choked behind his hands; the Chief Chirurgeon, a tall, thin, balding fellow with an attitude of aristocratic arrogance, favored him with a frosty smile. "Firstly, although the uninformed think of healing as a kind of magic, it is *not* the sort of magic that you mages are accustomed to using," he replied, in a lofty, superior tone of voice that made Tremane grit his teeth in response. "Mind you, I am a surgeon; my skills are in the excising of diseased flesh with the knife, in the stitching of damaged tissue with needle and gut-thread. However, I have made certain that I am educated even in those healing arts that I am not equipped to perform."

As you should have been, his tone seemed to imply. Tremane simply schooled his features into mild interest and nodded. He had learned long ago to keep his temper under more trying circumstances than this. Strangling the man would accomplish nothing.

Except to make me very happy...

"So just how does this differ from the magic that I, as a mage, am familiar with?" he asked with exact politeness.

"In the first place, it is performed entirely with the mind," the Chief Chirurgeon lectured. "The only difference between a self-taught or untaught Healer and one who has gone through training is in the recognition of how to heal things besides obvious broken bones or wounds. The Healer's mind convinces the patient's body to restore itself to the perfect state it had before the injury or illness. That is why they cannot correct those who are born with deformities." He smiled smugly. "That is something only those with my skill can do."

"All right, but I still don't understand why you aren't encountering interference from the mage-storms," he persisted.

"Because the Healers don't work during a storm, when the disruptions in energy are the only things that could interfere with their talent," the Chief Chirurgeon replied, as if to an idiot. "Accelerated healing only takes place when the Healer is actively working. The rest of the time, the patient is simply doing what he would under ideal circumstances. Under ideal conditions, our bodies would always repair themselves and throw off disease; the Healer simply reminds the body of what it should be doing."

"Oh." He had some vague notion that, basically, the reason the Healers were unaffected was that they were essentially working very small, limited magics of extremely limited duration and at very close range, but he doubted that the Chief Chirurgeon would agree with his particular definition.

Evidently his subordinate didn't even care for his expression. "Healing just is *not* magic as you understand it," the man persisted. "There's an old term for healing and a number of other abilities all lumped together: mind-magic. No one these days ever bothers with most of the other abilities, except a few practitioners of some of the odder religions."

Mind-magic? Where have I heard that term used before? There's something very familiar about that term. "What *are* those other things that were lumped in with healing?" he asked, out of a feeling that the answer might be important.

"Oh," the chirurgeon waved dismissively. "They're hardly important, things many educated people think are mostly delusional. Speaking mind-to-mind without the assistance of a teleson-spell; moving objects or even people with the power of the mind alone and no Portals involved; seeing and speaking with spirits of the dead; communicating directly with deities; seeing into the distance, the past, or the future without benefit of a mirror-spell; and imposing one's will upon another." He shrugged. "Most folk in the Empire are rather skeptical about those sorts of things. It is very easy to pretend to powers that are only in the mind, and thus very subjective."

He'd been speaking in Hardornen, though whether it was out of politeness for the company or simply because he'd forgotten to switch back to the Imperial tongue, Tremane couldn't have said for certain. The locals, who had been listening to his speech with some interest, laughed uproariously at that last statement. The chirurgeon glared at them in annoyance.

"I fail to see what was so amusing," he said acidly. "Perhaps you would care to enlighten me?"

"You people wouldn't be so skeptical if you'd ever met a Herald out of Valdemar," was the reply. "They don't use your 'real' magic over there, or they didn't until just lately. *Everything* they do is with mind-magic, and they think *yours* is poppycock and fakery."

Affronted, the chirurgeon turned his attention back to his own underlings; the Hardornen builders and Tremane's men got involved in a discussion of the best placements of "furnaces" and other devices to heat the barracks, and whether or not the walls really needed to be piled with earth. There seemed to be a brotherhood of builders, of stone and wood and metal, that transcended nationalities.

That left Tremane with an interesting tidbit to mull over. The Valdemarans did everything with mind-magic? That must have been where he'd first heard the term.

So Heralds must be the people born with these abilities; somehow they have a way of testing for them, I suppose. Then they get herded up the way the Karsites collect children with Mage-Talent, and sent off for training. Clever, to put them all in service to the Crown; the Empire could do with that policy regarding mages. And they aren't used to using real magic; it's new to them, so they don't rely on it. Fascinating.

No wonder they weren't having the kind of problems with mage-storms that he was having! They simply didn't have things that would be disrupted by the storms!

There are plenty of folk in the Empire who would call that a barbaric way of life—but they can heat their homes and move their goods and we can't... So who has the superior way of life now?

Heating homes... all very well to heat the barracks with cow dung, but what was he going to cook with? "Wood," he said aloud. "We have a problem; trees don't grow as quickly as wheat, and I don't intend to denude the countryside to keep my people warm if I can help it. Have any of you any suggestions?"

The Hardornens exchanged glances, and one of them finally spoke up. "Commander Tremane, you know as well as we do the state of things here. Half the people of Hardorn are gone. Whole villages are wiped out just because some lieutenant of Ancar got offended over something someone said, farms were abandoned when the last able-bodied person gave up or was carried off. We were going to suggest that once the harvest was over, your folk and ours go out together on foraging expeditions."

He considered this for a moment. "Do I take it that there is a reasonable chance that such expeditions will be left alone by the—the loyal Hardornen forces?"

The man snorted. "The loyal Hardornen forces aren't 'forces' at all. Most of them will be getting their harvests in, *if* they can. They're battling time and weather just as we are, and they won't have the extra men we will."

He nodded; that confirmed his own ideas. "How is the harvest looking?" he asked, thinking that this man just might be honest enough to tell him.

"That's another reason for foraging," the fellow told him frankly. "The harvest isn't bad, but some of us aren't sure it will hold the town over the winter. Sandar wants to send out foraging parties to some of the farms that have been abandoned and see what we might be able to get out of the fields, or even the barns and silos." He grinned. "There's sure to be stuff good enough for your thatching straw, if nothing else."

"You'd prefer to have some of my forces along, I take it." He made that a statement; another bizarre killer-beast had been taken today, after it had attacked one of the harvesting parties. This time no one was killed, and only a few men were hurt, but no one was going to forget that these things were still out beyond the nearly-completed walls. "So what do my people get out of this?"

"We find out just who's left—after Ancar, the Empire, and the mage-storms," the man said bluntly. "You get a census of who's around here, and where. You know who's got boys or men that might be tempted to make things difficult for your men in the name of Hardorn. Some of these farmers may have extra food to trade for. We find out what the storms have done to the land. If they're changing animals, what else are they leaving behind? And when we find abandoned farms, deserted villages, your people can move in and tear down the buildings. At the worst, you've got fuel. At the best, you've got fuel and building supplies. And—well, Sandar may be hoping for too much, but he thinks if we find any camps of the men from our side, we might be able to persuade 'em that you Imperials aren't the devils they think you are. Maybe we can get you a truce, if nothing else."

Tremane kept his face expressionless, his tone noncommittal. "I'll think about it," he said, and turned the subject back toward his barracks and the improvements the locals were suggesting.

But when everyone had cleared away, and he was back in his own room with another cozy fire going, he had to admit that the proposals didn't sound bad.

Provided, of course, that this wasn't just a way to lure him and his men out where the rebels could pick them off or ambush them.

Oddly enough, he didn't think it was. The idea of harvesting abandoned fields, rounding up and butchering half-feral livestock, and tearing down vacant buildings was a good one. With locals as guides, he would not have to send out sweep searches for such places, and run the risk of incurring the wrath of farmers who had *not* abandoned their holdings.

"I never thought I'd find myself in a position like this," he said aloud into the quiet night air.

His assignment had been to pacify Hardorn. He had never counted on his pacification force becoming the equivalent of the local government, yet that was precisely what was happening.

There would be no more battles; the worst he could expect would be skirmishes against men who were increasingly short of supplies and resources. In any other circumstances he would have laughed at the idea he could trust the people of Shonar to make and hold a truce with their fellow Hardornens. He would *never* have believed the half-promises made to him tonight.

But although nothing had been stated openly and baldly, it was very clear to him that these people no longer regarded him and his men as the enemy. Instead, they represented the one source of safety and order in an increasingly disordered country. They looked at their own men, ragtag bands of "freedom fighters" who were ill-armed and untrained; they looked at the strange monsters created in the wake of the mage-storms. They turned their eyes on the Imperial forces: well-armed, well-trained, and prepared to defend not only themselves, but the town of Shonar. It did not take a master scholar to figure the odds on which ones they would trust their safety to.

There would be no more reports to the Emperor; the agents still with Tremane would not take long to assess their own position here. Not that *his* ambitions regarding the Iron Throne were anywhere on his list of current priorities. No, he was past the point of thinking in terms of "acceptable losses." There was no loss that was acceptable now, and any deaths in his ranks would be avenged swiftly and with finality.

Now came the time for concentration on the minutiae that would save them all; the heroes of the winter would be the best managers, not the best generals.

He had pestered his clerks until his office was stuffed with papers, box after box of them, rank after rank of dossiers. He had the equivalent of the sheaf of papers that followed every Imperial citizen through his life for every man in his forces, three copies. One set of files was arranged, not by military rank or specialty, but by civilian specialty; what the man had done or been trained as before he joined the army. The second set was arranged more conventionally, in alphabetical order within each company. The third set was arranged by military specialty; all the scouts, all the infantry, all the cavalry, and so on.

Now, depending on what was needed, he could put his hands on the exact men with the precise skills that were required.

He did not believe that any other commander in the history of the Empire had ever done such a thing, not even when copying records had been a simple matter of a mage and a duplication-spell. Odd, considering what a bureaucracy the Empire was—but this was an innovation, and innovation was not encouraged in the Imperial Army.

For good or ill, he was in charge; Sandar's deference to his authority and the attitude of his Council made that clear. It was the position he had aimed for, but the implication that it had been granted him meant he was now, effectively, the liege lord of Shonar, with all the responsibilities of that office toward "his" civilians.

5

Karal waited for Jarim to finish speaking, then got wearily to his cold, benumbed feet. *Why am I doing this? No one is going to pay any attention.* His face felt stiff and frozen as he addressed people that were not even looking at him—except for Firesong, Darkwind, and the Valdemaran Heralds, who at least pretended to listen.

I'm doing this because they're going to overlook the most significant statement in that spy report that Kerowyn read us, that's why. Jarim has already tried to bury it in rhetoric. "Herald Captain Kerowyn, I believe that you said in your report that the Imperial forces seem to be cooperating with and protecting the civilians of the Hardornen city of Shonar, and that the citizens of Shonar do not seem to be under any duress and are, in fact, cooperating with the Imperials. Did I misunderstand that report, or do I grasp the facts correctly?"

"That was the report from one of my operatives, yes," Kerowyn acknowledged. "Mind you, he got his information on Shonar only at secondhand. None of our operatives have penetrated that far personally."

"Nevertheless, the evidence is that the Imperials have been accepted as the authority for these people in and around Shonar. They are certainly acting in a protective manner." He swallowed and said the unthinkable. *This is it. They're going to think that I'm quite mad now. Or that I'm a coward.* "Given the appalling conditions in Hardorn, and given the fact that we know because of the reports from the Herald Captain's operatives that the mage-storms are causing more havoc on top of an already unstable and precarious situation, I believe we ought to leave the Imperial forces alone. Harassing them in any way would be counterproductive for the citizens of Hardorn." Well enough, he had said that before. But now he would go completely out on a limb. "My personal recommendation is that we at least *consider* opening negotiations with them so that we can give some aid to Hardorn without that aid being read as an attack."

Jarim predictably exploded; Talia interrupted his tirade before it began, as she stood up and repeated what Karal had said. "The envoy from Karse recommends that we at least discuss the possibility of opening negotiations with the Imperials," she said. "Doing so would give us an opportunity to render some aid to the people of Hardorn, and would certainly allow us to insert operatives in as far as Shonar. On purely humanitarian grounds, I second the envoy's suggestion and advise that we talk about this."

Although no one except Talia and Jarim had paid any attention to what Karal had said, when Talia repeated it, in practically the same words, the rest of the Grand Council suddenly took notice, and a real discussion erupted.

Jarim took no part in the talk but, instead, continued to glare at Karal from across the table. Karal just sank his head into his hand and listened to the argument and counter-argument. *I've made my contribution; nothing else I say will matter until it all comes to a vote.*

None of this was new. Despite the early apology from the Shin'a'in envoy and the outward appearance of tolerance, Jarim's hostility had not abated and had become increasingly personal. Karal was not sure why. Perhaps someone had convinced him that the Karsites and Querna had not gotten along, although the reverse was actually true. He had admired the Shin'a'in Querna. Ulrich had considered her a friend on the personal level. If Jarim knew any of this, he did not seem to believe it.

Maybe he just resents the fact that An'desha, Darkwind, Talia, Elspeth, and the gryphons like me and they don't much care for him. Or maybe he's just a fanatic.

And despite the fact that Karal made it a point never to speak up in the Grand Council sessions unless he had something of substance to contribute, no one ever paid any attention to what he said except Jarim, and Jarim paid attention only so he could immediately belittle it. In fact, Talia had taken to repeating what he said almost verbatim so that it would at least be brought up for serious consideration.

Was it just that he was so young? He'd tried everything save cosmetics and coloring his hair gray to make himself look older. He'd tried a dignified manner and cultivating a deep and booming voice; he'd tried wearing a stark black set of full formal Sun-priest robes. A more elaborate costume had been suggested to him, but he'd felt so ridiculous in it that he hadn't dared try it in public.

I felt like a walking shrine. Or an actor done up for a miracle-play.

He was grateful to Talia for her assistance, but this was no way for him to conduct his office. Before long, this kind of situation would affect not only how he was treated in this room, but how he was treated outside it. What little authority he had with his own people, the Karsites here in Valdemar, would soon be eroded by the fact that no one respected him in the Grand Council meetings.

He didn't know what else he could do. If an enemy, either of him personally or of Karse, had *wanted* to undermine his authority, they could not have organized anything more effective than what his own youth and perceived inexperience was doing.

Could it be Jarim's doing? I can't see how. The only reason anyone listens to him is because he shouts louder than I do.

His insides were nothing but one twisted, snarled knot and had been that way for days. He had been living on herb tea and plain bread, for nothing else would stay in his stomach for long. *I'd be drinking myself to sleep, if I didn't know that the liquor would only come right back up after I drank it,* he thought glumly. He'd tried sending word of his difficulties back to Karse, but all he got in return were reassuring messages full of platitudes. It was as if Solaris or her advisers weren't even reading the pleas he'd been sending—or were ignoring the content as the vaporings of an inexperienced and homesick boy.

I am homesick, but only because I can't get anything done here. I'd happily go back to being a secretary, even under an unpleasant and unfriendly master.

If he couldn't even get his own people to listen to what he was saying, what hope did he have of convincing anyone here?

He needed authority, and not even his own countrymen were going to exert themselves to see that he got it.

I want to go home. I want to bury myself in books. I'm not important; I've done everything I needed to here. Anyone Solaris could assign here would be better than me.

He closed his eyes as his stomach cramped, grimacing and quickly covering it. *Karse would have been better off if Altra had protected Ulrich instead of me,* he thought, clenching his jaw to control his expression. *Before long, I will be doing my land great harm by remaining in this office, because disregard for me will become disregard for Karse.*

He had begged, pleaded for someone to be sent to relieve him, citing that very thing, but his pleas had been ignored. Why? He had no idea.

If it had not been for Florian, Natoli, and An'desha, he would have thrown himself into the river days ago. All three of them kept encouraging him—though the one creature who might have been able to help him was conspicuous by his absence. Altra had not put in a single appearance in all that time. Karal was beginning to wonder if he had somehow offended the Firecat. Or worse, offended Vkandis Sunlord.

Perhaps he has deserted me. Perhaps Vkandis no longer favors me. Perhaps He has abandoned me for the same reason that Jarim hates me—because I see no reason to waste time, resources, and lives in persecuting the Imperials. Aren't the mage-storms punishment enough? Must vengeance go on forever? Perhaps He thinks so.

That only depressed him further, and his stomach and throat knotted more tightly.

Why was he continuing in this farce? The only reason why he didn't get up and walk out now was that he was just too tired. *Perhaps tomorrow I simply won't get out of bed. I'll cancel everything. I'll tell the servants I'm too ill to get up. The results of the day will be exactly the same...*

But he knew he wouldn't do that. It wasn't in his nature. *I wish I really was ill; I wish I could break a leg or an arm or something, so I'd have an excuse not to get up. I wish I was really, seriously ill, perhaps with pneumonia, so they'd give me drugs to make me sleep, and I wouldn't have to think about any of this.*

What a fine pass he'd come to, when he would rather be seriously injured or sick than have to face his duty and his work!

He was supposed to join An'desha and Natoli and go to the Compass Rose as soon as the meeting was over, but he didn't have the heart for it now. *I can't face the others tonight. I'm no kind of company. I'll just crawl off to my room and see if I can't catch up on some of my correspondence. I can try one more letter to Solaris...*

Maybe this was his punishment for not taking care of Ulrich as he had promised. Perhaps Solaris had decided that he should suffer for not keeping his promise. If so, it was certainly working.

Finally the debate wound down to a close, concluding, as he had hoped, that there was nothing to be gained by harassing the Imperials, and that the innocent civilians of Shonar could be harmed in the process.

The group was split equally on the subject of opening negotiations, with himself, Talia, and Darkwind conspicuously on the side of negotiating and Jarim, Kerowyn, and Elspeth the leaders against. Finally, the session came to an end, and he was free to stand up with the others and trail out. He waited for everyone except the most minor of secretaries to precede him, hoping that no one would notice whether or not he had left the room; right now, he didn't want to talk to anyone, not even for idle small talk. His robes seemed to weigh down his shoulders like slabs of stone as he finally stood and collected his notes and his gear. He stowed them all in the leather pouch he had carried as Ulrich's secretary. His neck ached, and there were places beneath both shoulder blades that were so knotted it felt as if he was being stabbed there with a dull pick.

At that moment, he was perfectly well aware that he would have exchanged his lot in life for that of the lowest servant in Vkandis' temple. He'd gladly be a horseboy in the Temple stables. He'd cheerfully tend the Temple pigsty. He'd scrub the floors for the most ill-tempered priest in Karse...

But it seemed that his misery had not yet reached its nadir, for Jarim was waiting for him just outside the door of the Council Chamber, and there were several other members of the Grand Council loitering conspicuously in the hallway. It was very clear to him at that moment that Jarim wanted a confrontation, and these jackals were waiting avidly for some entertainment.

The best way to avoid that is to avoid the confrontation. It takes two to argue, and I'm not going to give him the opportunity. He tried to ignore Jarim, keeping his eyes down and his face without expression as he attempted to ease past the Shin'a'in, but Jarim reached out and seized his arm before he could get out of the way.

"And where do you think you are going, traitor?" Jarim asked loudly, as he tried to pull loose without turning it into a physical fight. "Can't wait to get back to your kennel, dog, and howl to your Imperial masters? So eager to let them know the good news? And what bone will they toss to you for ensuring their safety? Land? Gold? Some of their magics, maybe? Not content with what your God can give you anymore? Is it so easy to betray your old master?" Jarim spat—not into his face, but at his feet. "Did you serve him only to get a chance to betray him, dog?"

Karal had expected an attack, but not this one—and not so vehemently. He froze, half paralyzed and quite unable to form anything coherent; he had no reply at all to Jarim's accusations. His head came up and he stared into Jarim's angry face, thunderstruck, and cold all over. He couldn't speak, he couldn't even think clearly. What demon possessed the man to make him so obsessed and so certain that Karal was a traitor, that Karal would have betrayed the one man in the world he had thought of as his second father?

Jarim snarled angrily at his silence; but when Karal didn't move, his grip loosened just enough that Karal was able to pull himself free. Karal's paralysis lifted, and he jerked his sleeve and arm out of Jarim's hand so violently that he staggered half a dozen paces down the hallway.

Then he stood there for a moment, chilled to the bone, staring back at Jarim and the Council members gathered beside him. Karal's mouth worked, but not his voice. Not even a whisper emerged—which might have been just as well, since whatever he might have said would have been incomprehensible babbling.

He backed up a pace instead, then another—then turned abruptly and fled, robes flying, back to his suite.

He knew that his silence in the face of Jarim's incredible accusation had only confirmed his guilt in the eyes of the onlookers. He was certain that by day's end, the rumor would spread everywhere that he had been working all along for the Empire, that he had survived the attack on Ulrich because he had been meant to by his Imperial masters. And he had no way, none whatsoever, to prove that the accusation was false.

Florian found him in the dead and deserted gardens, long past sunset. His suite had not been the refuge he had thought it, for the moment he reached its doors, it had occurred to him that Jarim knew where it was, and could very easily find him here. And if the Shin'a'in was as fanatical as he seemed to be, Jarim might well decide to deal with a traitor in Shin'a'in fashion; quickly and decisively, at the point of a hunting knife. Granted the murder of another envoy would cause him a certain amount of difficulty—unless he managed to convince everyone that he had proof of Karal's guilt. He just might manufacture that "proof," knowing that with Karal dead there would be no way to refute it.

So he had paused just long enough to snatch up his warmest cloak, a hat and long scarf, and a pair of mittens. Then he had fled to the gardens, in the hope of finding some peace there until Jarim's temper should cool. And in the somewhat desperate hope that something, anything, would occur to him to help him defend himself against his accuser. He found a secluded bench and sagged down on it, an anonymous form in a dark, hooded cloak, huddled in such a way as to discourage anyone thinking of approaching him.

It had been late afternoon when he went down; it was after dark when Florian found him, looming up out of the thick gloom as silently as a ghost. Karal saw Florian out of the corner of his eye, but he was so sunk in misery at that point that it didn't seem worthwhile to do anything about the Companion's presence. *:Karal?:* the Companion said hesitantly when Karal didn't even move to greet him. *:Karal, you're in trouble.:*

"Tell me something I don't already know," Karal replied bitterly without raising his head, speaking down at the ground between his feet.

:No, I mean real, serious trouble,: the Companion said, unhappily. *:Jarim has been going around the Court telling everyone—:*

"That I'm an Imperial agent. I know." Bile rose in the back of his throat, and he wondered if he was going to be sick right then and there.

:Worse than that, people believed him. Even Heralds. There were a great many people who couldn't believe that a foolish artist was the real agent at Court.: Florian shifted his weight, and a few pebbles rolled out from under his hooves as he scuffed them against the gravel. *:It is worse that Heralds believe him. Nothing I have said will convince them that you are not what Jarim says you are.:*

That surprised him in a dull way. "But—you're a Companion—"

:And you are not *my Chosen. They won't believe even me since you aren't my Chosen. They believe that you have deceived me.:* Florian sounded depressed, which certainly didn't help Karal's mood at all. *:I don't know what to do, Karal.:*

"Neither do I, except to saddle my horse and go home." *Or fling myself into the river, but that wouldn't accomplish very much either, although it would probably make Jarim very pleased with himself. Well, riding off would make him very pleased, too. I've certainly made a mess of this entire situation. I don't know how anyone could salvage it now.*

Florian couldn't seem to stop talking, although Karal would rather have been left alone with his own thoughts. *:I don't know who is on his side, precisely, nor how many there are. I only know for certain about the Heralds...:*

"I suppose I might as well go back into the Palace and see how many people believe him," Karal said finally. "We might be pleasantly surprised, I suppose."

:You don't sound very optimistic.:

"Neither do you," Karal replied. "But before I saddle up and go home in utter disgrace, I might as well find out just how bad things are. I'd have to report just how much of a disaster I've created, no matter what."

He rose slowly and stiffly and wrapped his cloak closely about him, walking back to the beckoning lights of the Palace on leaden feet.

As he discovered the moment he entered the Palace, things were very bad indeed.

Conversations stopped the moment he entered the hallway; as he passed through one of the reception chambers, he was surrounded by an aura of silence. People would turn to stare at him, then deliberately turn their backs on him. Once he passed, though, conversations resumed, loud enough to make certain that he heard them.

"It's bad enough being a traitor, but being a coward as well…"

"He must be some sort of mage, disguising himself. No one could be that vile and look that young."

"I'm surprised his own god hasn't struck him down dead before this."

Those were the personal comments; he was fairly certain he wasn't hearing the others—the speculations on how everything vile that was ever said about Karse must be true. How Solaris must have *known* he was a traitor—and had set that poor fellow Ulrich up as a sacrificial lamb to eliminate suspicion against Karse.

Servants pointedly ignored him as he passed, and once he reached his suite, he found it precisely as he had left it. Which meant, of course, that no servant had set foot in here to clean it, and quite probably no servant would from this moment on. They would "forget," or leave the rooms until last, then "fall ill" just as they reached his door. If he had thought things were uncomfortable when he and Ulrich had arrived, well… the hostility now was more than double. All the old prejudices were springing back to life, with redoubled vigor for having been suppressed for so long.

He stood in the doorway for a moment, trying to make up his mind about what he should do. Should he start packing and leave this very moment? He thought he had just about enough money to get to the border, if he stayed in very modest inns. He would have to be circumspect when he talked, but his Valdemaran was fairly good now; he might be able to pass for a foreign priest from anywhere but Karse.

Maybe I could talk Florian into coming with me? I might be able to purloin some Herald's Whites from the Palace laundry and pass as a Herald until I got home—or better yet, it would be a lot easier to get hold of one of the gray uniforms the trainees wear. For once it wouldn't be so bad to look young.

Would Florian be willing to go along with the scheme?

He heard footsteps down the hall, and moved inside, quickly, closing the door behind him. Maybe he couldn't get Florian to help, but the idea of purloining a uniform gave him another notion. *I can get Natoli to find someone to loan me one of the unaffiliated students' blue uniforms. Then no one will bother me. I can just say I'm going home if anyone asks, and it won't be a lie.*

He started to turn toward his bedroom, planning to start packing immediately, but a knock on his door startled him into immobility.

Who could it be? He could think of any number of possibilities, and few of them made him *want* to answer the door.

The knock came again. "Karal?" said a soft female voice. "I know you're in there; I can sense you, and I know you aren't more than two steps from the door. It's Herald Talia, and you might as well open up."

Talia? She was one of the few people he had *not* thought of. He had to obey her, actually; in the hierarchy of Vkandis she was senior to him. He reversed his turn and let her in. She blinked at the darkness, for he had not had time to light more than the single candle beside the door.

"I see the shunning has begun already," she said dryly, and moved past him so he could close the door again. He nodded; both the Karsites and the Holderkin used the ritual of "shunning," where someone who had been cast out of the community was ignored and avoided from that moment on by all the faithful. It had driven sensitive people in Karse to suicide before this; presumably it had the same effect on Holderkin.

"I'm dealing with the Heralds on your behalf," she told him, taking the candle from the holder beside the door and moving with it to the other side of the room to light the lamps for him. "I am sorry that idiot Jarim started all this; it's going to take some time to untangle it and more time to undo all the damage from his foolish fanaticism."

Karal sagged down into a chair, depression overcoming him. "It's never going to be untangled," he said bluntly. "And I'm not sure it's worth the effort to try. Even if you manage to convince the Heralds, even if by some miracle you manage to convince everyone else, you'll *never* convince Jarim. It would be better for everyone if I just go home and let Solaris send another envoy in my place."

"Jarim would win," Talia replied. "Why should you let him?"

"Why shouldn't I?" he countered. "I wasn't particularly effective *before* he started all this, and you know that's true. Even if you convinced everyone that I'm the innocent victim of Jarim's prejudice, you'll never persuade them that I have a copper's worth of sense. I'm too young; I'm young enough to be the child of anyone sitting at that table, except maybe Elspeth, and I wouldn't bet on that. No one there trusts me. I'm too young to have any experience, too young to let my emotions take second place to my reason."

She didn't immediately reply as she went about the room lighting lamps and candles, and he closed his eyes for a moment. "Herald Talia—*Sun-priest*—we might as well both admit it. I am doing neither Karse nor the Alliance any good here. I might as well go home and let someone who is competent, experienced, and new take over."

She turned then, and looked at him with a solemn expression on her face, a single curl of reddish-brown hair falling over one eye. "Have you been recalled?" she asked, the candle clasped in both hands.

"Well, no," he admitted. "But—"

"Does Solaris speak for Vkandis, or not?" she persisted.

"Well, yes—but—"

"And don't you think after all this that if Vkandis perceived your presence here as detrimental to Karse you would have been recalled by now?" she continued mercilessly. "It's not as if Altra couldn't convey your recall papers from Solaris *immediately* if that was called for. Given the situation here, there is every reason to bring you back—unless there is a more compelling reason that Solaris and Vkandis are not ready to reveal to leave you here."

When he didn't reply, she fixed him with a sharp glare. "Well?" she prompted.

He gulped, and shrugged. "I suppose so, but—"

"No 'buts,'" she said, sternly, with more authority concentrated in her tiny figure than in a hundred generals he had seen. "As a Sun-priest, I can vouch for all of that, and so can you. There is a reason why Vkandis wants you here and no one else. We may not know what it is, but there is certainly a reason."

Then I wish He'd tell me what it is. "That's fine in theory," he replied, "but just at the moment it doesn't seem to me that anyone in Haven wants me here. How am I supposed to get anything done when most of the Grand Council thinks I'm working for the Imperials, and at least one envoy wants to murder me?"

She made a grimace of distaste and walked over to the door to replace the candle in its holder. "That, I must admit, I have no answer for," she said, with her back to him. "But I think you should at least absent yourself from the Palace for a few days, and stay away from meetings. Say that you're sick—or *I* will. I'll tell Selenay that you've been so overcome with shock at Jarim's accusations that you've collapsed." She turned back, and surveyed him with a critical eye. "From the look of you, I won't be telling that big of a lie. Much more stress and you're going to be the youngest man I know with a bleeding stomach. You're well on the way to it; you haven't been eating or sleeping well, have you?"

He stared at her. "No!" he blurted, "but how did you—"

"I *am* the one with the Gift of Empathy," she reminded him. "And I've been associating with Healers for most of my life. I think you ought to see if An'desha and Firesong can take you in again. I'll have the Healers send you over some medicines. Better yet, I'll send one of the Healers there in person."

He scowled, and she laughed.

"Oh, don't look at me like that," she said. "The teas and potions for stress and a rebelling stomach are probably some of the best things you'll have ever tasted in your life. They have to be; otherwise people who are under stress wouldn't drink them, and people with bad stomachs wouldn't be able to keep them down. Go pack," she concluded. "Pack enough for about a week, and I'll go find An'desha and see if there's room in that *ekele* for a third person."

She turned and started toward the door when another knock stopped her dead in her tracks.

"Karal?" came the quiet voice from the other side of the wooden door. "It's An'desha and Natoli. We're here to help you, if you want."

Talia opened the door so quickly that she left An'desha standing there with his hand still raised for another knock, Natoli fidgeting beside him.

"In," she ordered; both of them obeyed instantly, and she shut the door behind them.

Natoli spoke before either Talia or Karal could say anything, her words pouring out in a rush. "You didn't come to the Rose and we were both worried about you because you've been looking like death and we came back here to find out if you were all right and have you *heard* what they're saying about you? They're—"

"Saying that I'm an Imperial spy and that I'm responsible for just about everything bad that's happened since I arrived yes, I know," he interrupted, and sagged down in his chair again, one hand rubbing his stinging eyes. "Some people have probably even decided that I brought the mage-storms with me by now. Or that I was somehow to blame for Ancar being born."

"You're not far wrong. There're even some Heralds prating a lot of nonsense, and not even Father can talk any sense into them," Natoli said grimly, looking at Talia with a challenging expression, as if daring *her* to do something.

Karal was a little amazed at her audacity—a simple student, challenging the Queen's Own herald? And not even a Heraldic student at that?

"I'm doing what I can, but it's going to take some time," Talia replied, and smiled thinly. "I'm beginning to understand what Herald Savil was supposed to have gone through over Vanyel when he was first Chosen. Like Vanyel after Tylendel died, Karal seems to be getting the blame for things that happened before he was born. It's going to be interesting."

Natoli gave an unladylike snort, while An'desha just looked bewildered.

"Meanwhile," Talia continued, turning to An'desha, "I'd like to get him out of the Palace for a while so that people can calm down, and I would like to see that he gets some rest before his stomach begins to bleed from all the strain he's going through. Can you and Firesong take him in again?"

"I was going to offer just that," An'desha replied. "Firesong's been off on some project of his own anyway, so he'll gets lots of peace and quiet at our *ekele*. Are you going to claim he's collapsed with shock and stress?"

"That was the general idea," Talia told him. "And if I can get a Healer to confirm that, it will simply add to the story."

"Will you please stop talking about me as if I'm not here?" Karal asked plaintively, looking from one to the other.

An'desha patted his shoulder and looked down at him with speculation, as if there were a number of ideas going around inside his head and he was just weighing them all to determine which one might be the best. "Sorry, my friend," he apologized, then took a closer look at him. "You look like you've been dragged at the heels of a horse across the Dhorisha Plains," he said, with a frown. "Herald Talia, please have a real Healer attend us as soon as we get to the *ekele*, would you?"

Karal stared in surprise; that didn't sound like the diffident young Shin'a'in he knew. That sounded more like someone who took it as given that he was Talia's equal.

She nodded just as if she accepted his status, too, and slipped out the door before Karal had a chance to object. "You stay here with Natoli; I think I can manage to pack for you," the young Shin'a'in continued sternly. "Anything I forget, you can borrow from me. If *I* have anything to say about it, you won't need anything but a bedshirt for two or three days anyway."

As An'desha disappeared into his bedchamber before he could object to *that*, Karal looked at Natoli with a face full of woe.

"Don't I get *any* choice in any of this?" he asked.

He got no sympathy from her.

"No," she said flatly. "You don't. You've done your best, and you've gotten into a mess you can't do anything about. You're tired to death, you're sick with strain, and your judgment is not good right now. We're going to take over and let you rest, so you might as well relax and enjoy it."

Be careful what you ask for, he thought, as the memory of his earlier wishes flashed into his mind. *You might get it.*

An'desha and Natoli took Karal and his bag across Companion's Field, trailed anxiously by every Companion there. Florian led the parade, which under other circumstances might have been hilariously funny. A hard frost was forming; the stiff blades of grass crackled underfoot, and their breath hung in frosty clouds in the still, cold air. Behind them followed dozens more "clouds," the silent, white forms of the Companions. They weren't being herded; An'desha would have recognized that behavior. They were worried about Karal, and although he was no Empath, their concern was strong enough it made itself palpable even to him.

The Healer was waiting for them just inside when they reached the *ekele,* her eyes closed as she breathed in the faint, sweet perfume of some of Firesong's night-blooming flowers. "Thank you for letting me come here. I know this is just a more sophisticated version of a forcing-house," she said to An'desha as they entered through Firesong's clever double door that kept cold drafts out. "But this place always seems the epitome of *magic* to me."

"You could build one of these yourself, with one of our steam boilers and pipes to send hot water through the room to heat it," Natoli told her matter-of-factly.

"You could *not* have plants this large and healthy in a matter of weeks without the magic, however," An'desha countered firmly, standing up for *his* discipline. "Here is your patient, lady Healer—" He pushed

Karal to the front, as his friend seemed inclined to lag back, trying to avoid attention.

The Healer took Karal's wrist, put her free hand under his chin so that he could not look away from her eyes, and frowned as she stared into his face. "One would think you were a much older man—or a Herald—the way you have abused yourself. Come, child," she continued, although Karal was not a great deal younger than she. "I think you should be put straight to bed."

"I am very glad to hear you say that," An'desha told her, relieved.

"Follow me, please."

Before long, Karal was indeed in bed, dosed with several potions from the Healer's bag, and blinking sleepily. An'desha had his instructions and a line of bottles of more of the same stuff with which to ensure that Karal remained in his bed and permitted his poor abused insides to heal. The Healer, who never had given her name, also left a list of what Karal was and was not permitted to eat.

"We can't do this for long," the Healer said warningly to both An'desha and Natoli. "These herbs in this row are powerful and dangerous, and they shouldn't be used for more than a week. However, I do not think that he will need to be forced to rest for more than a few days. After that, these other potions, these brews, and good, soothing foods should effect the rest of the cure."

"Provided we can keep Jarim from turning all our work into nothing," Natoli muttered. The Healer looked at her without comprehension.

"Never mind, she's just thinking out loud," An'desha told the Healer. "Thank you, we're very grateful."

"Well, *I'm* grateful that Herald Talia caught him before he had a real bleeding stomach," the Healer said cheerfully. "That's ten times harder to cure. Good night to you!"

After the young woman had gone off into the night, Natoli turned to An'desha with discontent written all over her intelligent face. "All my life I've heard about how the Healers can cure almost anything that's not congenital," she said. "I've heard how they can piece shattered bone together, how they can make wounds close before your very eyes!"

"So?" An'desha asked, heading back toward the stairs and the living area of the *ekele*.

"So why didn't she *do* something?" Natoli demanded as she followed. "All she did was look at him, put him to bed, make him drink a couple of messes of leaves, and that was it! He's been looking like grim death for days, and he doesn't look much better now, so why didn't she wave her hands around or whatever it is they do and make him well without all this resting and drinking teas?"

An'desha paused on the staircase and looked down at her, trying to think of an analogy for her. "Would you build one of your big steam engines just to convey a few pots of tea to the Grand Council chamber all day?"

"No, of course not; that's what pages are for," she replied impatiently. "What does that have to do with Healing?"

"There is no point in this Healer using a great deal of energy—energy that comes from *within* her by the way—just to perform a task that her herbs and minerals will accomplish, particularly not when Karal's life is not in any danger." He raised an eyebrow and Natoli flushed; he figured he might as well not bother to point out that Talia could well have asked for an Herbalist-Healer rather than one who relied completely on her powers. "She is simply using her resources logically. You would scarcely thank her for exhausting herself over Karal if—oh, say later tonight the Rose were to burn down and she would be unable to help some of your friends who were burned, because she had no energy left. It's a matter of proper use of resources, my friend, and not any slight intended toward Karal." He looked back over Natoli's head, into the darkness beyond the garden windows, and smiled. "Of all of the many kinds of people who may have been deceived by Jarim's foolish accusations, you may rely on it that no Healer picked by Lady Talia will be one of them."

He looked back down at Natoli, who grimaced. "I suppose I'm jumping at shadows," she said reluctantly. "And I keep forgetting that Healers are supposed to work differently than you mages."

"Not quite; you are used to seeing the Masters and Adepts at work," An'desha interrupted, as he resumed his climb, with Natoli just behind him. "Journeymen and Apprentices—and what are called 'hedge-wizards' and 'earth-witches'—also rely entirely on their own reserves of energy, unless they are extremely sensitive to the currents of energy about them. Even then, they cannot use either the great leylines or the nodes where the lines meet. Only Masters can use the former, and Adepts can use both. But there are many, many mages who do their work very effectively with no more power than what lies within them."

Natoli shook her head in frustration; An'desha turned to face her again as she stepped up into the gathering room of the *ekele*. "It all obeys rules," he chided her. "It is all perfectly logical. Do not be the equivalent of a Firesong, who refuses to believe that the energies of magic cannot obey rules and logic. It is no more illogical to say that one must be born with the ability to become an Adept than it is to say that one must be born with the ability to become a sculptor or an artificer."

"That isn't logical either," Natoli replied with irritation. "All people should be born equal."

He laughed at her. "Now it is *you* who are being illogical, assuming that because the natural world does not follow what you perceive to be the regular pacings of the world of numbers, the natural world should be discarded!"

She didn't reply, but he heard her muttering under her breath, and it was probably not very complimentary. He didn't mind; in fact, he rather enjoyed teasing Natoli, who he felt was far too serious for her own good.

Not unlike myself, in some ways. He ignored the mutters and went back to the room that had once been "his," which had been Karal's temporary refuge once before.

Karal was still awake, but even to An'desha's inexperienced eyes he was fighting a losing battle against the potions the Healer had given him. "You should sleep," An'desha said, sitting down beside the Shin'a'in-style pallet that lay on the floor. Natoli knelt next to him.

"I 'spose I should." Karal yawned hugely, and blinked. "Funny. I *wanted* to get sick, 'cause then I could just—stay in bed—and—"

"Well, you *are* sick and you *will* stay in bed and do what you're told," Natoli said severely. "There is no point in trying to fight it."

He smiled, a smile of unexpected, childlike sweetness. "I won't," he replied. "Just wanted to say—thank you."

"You're welcome," An'desha told him, as Natoli patted his hand. "Now sleep."

To prevent any more attempts at conversation, he extinguished the lamp with a thought, and got up, leaving Karal and Natoli alone in the faint light coming from the lamp in the hall.

He went down to the garden again, leaving her to find her own way out. She and Karal had not had much privacy to be together for the past several weeks, and he thought it was about time that they had a chance for a word or two before Karal couldn't fight the drugs anymore.

I'll give them a better chance later, he promised himself.

As for him—he had some ideas that might be helpful, but he also needed some privacy to put them to the test. The primary one was that he should try something he had not attempted since Falconsbane leaped from his body as it lay dying.

He waited, watching the fountain, until Natoli descended the staircase again, wrapped in her cloak. She didn't notice him, and he didn't interrupt her introspection as she let herself out quietly. Then he let the falling water lull him until he was in that half-aware state in which it was easy to slip into a trance.

Then he sought the Moonpaths.

He was not certain he would be permitted to find them; after all, the Moonpaths were to be walked by shaman, Sword-Sworn and Goddess-Sworn, not for just anyone. The Avatars had taught him how to reach them so that he would have a safe place to meet them where he could talk with them while Falconsbane slept. But now he sent his spirit *out*, and *up*, in that familiar twisting of reality—

And he was there, standing on a path of silver sand, surrounded by a gray mist that glowed with its own pearly light.

I did it! He savored his elation; he was never certain when the Avatars would show themselves anymore, and it seemed best that if he *could* go to them, he should, rather than waiting for them to come to him. Their relationship with him had changed since he had come to Valdemar; when they answered his questions at all, it was obliquely. Rather than giving him answers or teaching him directly now, they gave him the briefest of guidance, leading him to find his own answers to his questions.

Then again, his questions were more difficult to answer, and the answers were of necessity more subjective than objective. In many ways, he was now determining what he wanted to make of himself and his life by the answers he uncovered.

I am learning what I am by determining what Falconsbane was in all of his lives, and determining why he did what he did and why he thought what he thought, then deliberately taking the opposite direction.

Well, that was grand philosophy, but at the moment he had need of some of those other answers, the simple ones. He hoped that the Avatars, particularly Tre'valen, could help him. After all, the real problem lay with Jarim, a Shin'a'in—and weren't they both the Avatars of the Star-Eyed? If Jarim got a visit from Tre'valen in all his glory, and was told in no uncertain terms that he was mistaken entirely about Karal, wouldn't that solve the entire problem right then and there?

That was his hope, anyway.

He sent his thoughts questing out into the mist, hunting for his teachers and guides; it was not possible to reckon the exact passage of time in that timeless place, but it was not too long before he was answered.

The mist above the path shimmered in a double column of light; then, with a shiver, solidified into two figures. One was male, the other female; the male of the two was clearly Shin'a'in, but the female was not. Her clothing and her hair, a long waterfall of silver, marked her as a Hawkbrother, Tayledras—or in Shin'a'in, Tale'edras—as were Firesong and Darkwind. Although they looked wholly human, there was a suggestion of great wings, wings of flame, in the air behind them. They, too, glowed with their own inner light, and their eyes, as they gazed smiling upon An'desha, had neither whites nor pupils. Instead, they were the dark of a night full of stars, and in the black depths shone tiny sparks of light.

When Shin'a'in called their Goddess of Four Aspects the Star-Eyed, this was what they meant, for She and all of Her spirit-servants and Avatars had eyes like this. It was a sure way to know them, and was impossible to counterfeit—so An'desha had been told.

"Well, little brother." Tre'valen crossed his arms in a curiously human gesture and looked upon his pupil with approval. "You have not forgotten your lessons."

"I would not have dared to come here, if I had not the need," An'desha said hastily. "I beg that you will indulge me—

"Oh, we know, we know; you are altogether too diffident," said Dawnfire with a laugh. "So come, what is it that brings you here, seeking us?"

"It is my friend Karal," An'desha said. "The envoy of the Shin'a'in who replaced Querna is—is causing him great despair."

Quickly, for he had carefully rehearsed all that he wanted to say if he got the chance, he related troubles that Jarim had wrought since his arrival. Tre'valen and Dawnfire listened sympathetically, but when he had finished, their words were a disappointment.

"I am sorry, little brother, but there is nothing that we can do to help," Tre'valen said with finality. "I wish for your sake and for his that there was—but there is not. You and all the others involved in this sad situation will have to work your own way through this."

"Only if it is clear—clear to Her, that is—that we must act or the consequences will be catastrophic, will we be permitted to intrude," Dawnfire added, although her expression was sympathetic. "I am sorry."

An'desha sighed, but he did not bother to make any further pleas although their words disappointed him greatly. *I was brought up on all of the tales of the Star-Eyed and how She sends aid only when all other courses have been exhausted. I should not be upset at this.*

In fact, sometimes She did not aid at all—unless a price was paid in lives. That, too, was something he had known.

He should not have been so disappointed, but he was, and they saw it in his eyes. He thought of poor Karal, lying on that pallet, pale and too thin with trying and failing to do a job that was beyond his strength. He thought of smug Jarim, sneering at the halfbreed An'desha, radiating an unreasoning hatred whenever he looked at Karal. There was an awkward silence for a moment, then words burst from him. "She tries Karal past his endurance, and so does his own God!" he cried. "Is that fair?"

But Tre'valen only gazed at him steadily. "Fair?" the Avatar repeated. "You ask me if this is fair? And—you think that She and He are responsible for this?"

An'desha spread his hands mutely.

"Do you think that She is some sort of trainer of men, as one trains horses, heaping trial upon trial on a man to see if he shall fail, and how he bears up beneath the load?" Tre'valen asked. "Do you think that the Sunlord is a great clerk, with His ledger, noting what is fair and unfair and making a sheet of debts and credits?"

"It has been implied—" An'desha began.

"By men," Tre'valen said sternly. "By men, An'desha, who would take their own narrow views of the world and squeeze the gods into those views; who would put their words in the mouths of their gods. No. They are constrained, by Their own wills, to give us the freedom to make our own choices and live or die by them. We are Their fledglings, but when the time comes to leave the nest, They cannot fly for us. The world is what *we* make of it, for it was given to us—as your tent is what you make of it, for it was given to you. You may keep it neat and in repair, or you may let the poles break, the hides rot. That is the truth. It is a hard truth, but truth is often hard to bear."

An'desha flushed, feeling obscurely ashamed of his outburst.

"It is only when we have passed the bonds of this world that They may act—or when events have passed into realms where nothing men can do will mend them. Your events have come nowhere near that point." Tre'valen finally smiled at him warmly, and An'desha flushed again, feeling as if he had been taken gently to task for something that should have been obvious.

"There are many courses that *you* may yet take," Dawnfire suggested.

"Think of all the friends that you and Karal have, those who will not be swayed by a hateful man's willful blindness. I can tell you that the Healer already spreads her tale of a poor young man tried past endurance, and there are as many sympathetic ears as unsympathetic. You might think on what ears you may find."

Well, that was true enough, and while Karal was recovering, Jarim would not have a target for his abuses.

Unless he takes me for a target—and then, I think, it is unlikely since he will not only have to contend with me, but with Firesong, and Firesong is a past master at making fools look as foolish as they truly are. The thought made him smile a little.

Still—it would not be easy for him to move among the people of the Valdemaran Court, defending Karal's honor and honesty. He still often felt gawky and out of place except during a crisis, when he was too busy to think or feel self-conscious.

But I am Shin'a'in. Jarim cannot deny my heritage. And I, beyond anyone here, can vouch for Karal. Did I not see him with his master, and the way the two acted with one another? Did he not bring me through my own darkness? Did he not place his life in jeopardy to protect not only his land, but those of all the Alliance? I can speak to all of this, these things that others seem to have conveniently forgotten.

"You have all the resources that you need to solve this trial without our intervention, little brother," Dawnfire said as he thought through all of this. "You need only to reason out where to look, where to reach, what to grasp, and how."

Tre'valen laughed. "And know who to ask, and guess what will result, and know how to cope with the results, and after that, the universe is easy to live with, hey?"

To his own surprise, An'desha laughed along with the Avatar, his earlier shame forgotten. He realized at that moment that he felt much more comfortable with the Avatars now than he ever had dreamed he would.

"We are your friends, An'desha," Dawnfire said, as if she was following his thoughts.

He nodded, feeling the same warmth he knew in Karal's company. They *were* his friends, as well as his guides and teachers—and could it be that the distance between them, that gulf between student and mentor, was narrowing more with every moment?

"Soon enough," Tre'valen said enigmatically.

Well, that might be. What was certain was that things were by no means desperate, though Karal had reached his own limit. Karal's own reticence and determination not to reveal his difficulties had actually worked against him. Most of his friends had probably not been aware of his plight; now they knew, and now was the time to organize them to *do* something about it.

The gryphons! They like Karal—and it would take a braver man than Jarim to cross them! I need to talk to them, let them know what's been going on—

"Now you are beginning to see your options," Tre'valen encouraged. "And now, I think, you should go where you can do something about them."

"But return again, little brother," Dawnfire added, as he prepared to return to his body and the world he knew. "The Moonpaths are always open to your walking."

He gathered himself; flung himself *down*, and then *in*.

And only then, as he opened his eyes in the quiet of the garden, did he pause to think about the significance of that last remark.

The Moonpaths are always open to your walking. The Moonpaths—all Shin'a'in could walk them on the nights of the full moon, but for Dawnfire to say that they were *always* open to his walking meant that he now possessed a status, a power reserved for Sword-Sworn, Goddess-Sworn—

—and shaman.

An'desha looked in on Karal the next morning after Firesong had gone, to find him barely awake, drugged and sleepy and not really able to think well. He spoke in monosyllables, yawning between each phrase. That made him tractable, which so far as An'desha was concerned, was all to the good.

"Can't get up," Karal complained, and yawned. "Too tired."

"Then stay there; I'll get your breakfast," An'desha told his friend and left before Karal could object. He made certain that Karal ate— soft, mild foods that the Healer had prescribed—then saw to it that he drank all the potions the Healer had left. He left Karal alone with a book to make his own meal, and by the time he returned, Karal was asleep again, the book fallen from his hands onto his chest. An'desha smiled down at him and walked softly out.

Good. He should stay that way until this afternoon, and that leaves me free to prowl.

Rather than don his more colorful Shin'a'in garb, he ransacked his wardrobe to find a plain brown tunic and black trews, which he thought would blend nicely into the background. There wasn't a great deal he could do about his hair, but he thought that if he tied it back and kept to the sidelines, he should be, if not ignored, certainly less conspicuous.

He took an unaccustomed place at Morning Court, staying carefully on the edges of the crowd, near the curtains. He said nothing, but kept his ears open.

Karal was the major topic of the conversations he overheard; he had positioned himself as near to the Guild Masters as possible, mostly to see what people who could reasonably be thought to be uncommitted would say.

He strained his ears, eavesdropping shamelessly, the moment he heard Karal's name. "...the Karsite is not in his room," said the Master of the Goldsmith's Guild grimly. "The servants say he was not there last night. I fear that the Shin'a'in's accusations are too true."

"Your news is late and incomplete," replied a woman in the tabard of the Weaver's Guild crisply. "The Karsite is not in his room because he collapsed last night. The Healers have seen to him, and they say that he is ill with strain and grief." She looked at the Master Goldsmith in a way that made An'desha think there was a long history of rivalry between them.

"And this means that Envoy Jarim's accusations must then be false?" the Master Goldsmith retorted, with a broad gesture that nearly knocked the cap off of a young page next to him. "I think not! If I were an Imperial spy, I do not doubt I would be under great strain, and as for grief, we have only the Healer's word for that."

"And you doubt the Queen's Own, who says the same?" the woman snapped, crossing her arms over her thin chest. "One might well ask where *your* loyalties lie, if you choose not to believe what Herald Talia says!"

The Master Goldsmith smiled at her in a superior fashion. "I say only that it is strange that the boy survived when the master did not. I say it is strange that the boy was made envoy. It is strange that the mage-storms first appeared after his arrival, and it is strange that the boy preaches peace with the devils who are responsible for the death of his master." The Master Goldsmith was clearly not deterred by the vehemence of his fellow Master, and it seemed that Karal's plight represented a way for him to voice some agenda of his own.

There were plenty of people gathered around these two, courtiers and high-ranking tradesmen alike, all dressed in the fine costumes An'desha had come to expect for a Court ceremony of any kind. An'desha examined the faces of those within earshot of this conversation. All of them mirrored the same emotion: grim concern.

They think Karal's illness is nothing more than a corroboration of Jarim's accusations. An'desha knew that his face mirrored concern, too, but it was for a far different cause. He hoped there were enough people here who knew Karal too well to even suspect him of something so outrageous.

The two Guild Masters turned their verbal sparring match to another topic. He moved on, wondering what he should do about the situation, and circulated among the onlookers at Morning Court, still silent, still listening. Karal had his friends at Morning Court, and they were out in force—even Treyvan the gryphon made a rare appearance, and he was brief but adamant in his support.

But Jarim's adherents were far more vocal—and it was difficult to prove a negative. Karal's supporters had only their feelings and a few facts to support them; Jarim's had all the wild speculations they cared to concoct.

An'desha debated attending the Grand Council meeting, knowing that Jarim would do his best to turn it into an indictment of Karal. There had to be a way to keep him from having that official channel!

He debated it all through the Court, and finally decided to take full and unfair advantage of his position and approach Prince Daren himself.

He waited until Morning Court was over, extracted himself from the milling crowd, and presented himself at the door of the Queen's Chambers, requesting a private audience with the Prince-Consort.

He waited in the wood-paneled antechamber, watched carefully by both door guards, who clearly did not recognize him out of his normal costume. He found himself wondering if the Prince would even hear his request, or if some official, unfamiliar with his name and position and deceived by his modest costume, would simply intercept the message. *They'll probably ask me to come back later, or wait until the Grand Council meeting,* he told himself. *If it was Firesong who was asking—*

"Sir?" a page popped his head out of the door, startling not only him but the two guards. "You're to come in immediately, An'desha, sir!"

As the guards stared at one another and at him, obviously wondering who he was that he rated this kind of reception, An'desha didn't wait for a second invitation. The page opened the door, and he slipped in past the boy and into the reception room of the Queen's Chamber.

Apparently he was not the only one who was wasting no time; rather than a servant, Prince Daren was standing right there in person waiting for him, one hand stretched out in welcome.

"An'desha!" he exclaimed, clasping An'desha's hand warmly as the Shin'a'in reached for the Prince's hand. "Talia warned us what was happening last night. How is Karal, truly? She wasn't certain just how he was responding." He gestured at one of the carved chairs that stood beside a small table in the middle of the room, and An'desha took it, although the Prince himself remained restlessly standing.

"Sick and asleep, Highness," An'desha answered gravely. "He will mend his body, and the Healers say soon, but it is up to us, I think, to mend this situation. If we cannot, he will collapse again from the strain."

Daren ran a hand through thick blond hair and sighed gustily. "I was afraid that he might be sicker than anyone had told us," the Prince said with relief. "He's—he's a good boy, but much too inclined to hide his hurts, I think. Listen, I intend to overturn every attempt by Jarim to make any accusations against Karal in the Grand Council meetings. If he won't come around, I'll exercise my prerogative as the Queen's proxy and dismiss the meetings altogether." He smiled grimly. "We can afford to do without these meetings for a week or two. The real work is being done by Kerowyn, the mages, and the artificers anyway. Frankly, we've been going through with them partly because we must keep the people appraised of our progress, and partly out of hope that something new might come out of them. I must admit that I would not mind an excuse to cancel these time-wasting exercises for a while."

Greatly daring, An'desha decided to ask a question that he had no right to ask. "Highness, have you heard from High Priest Solaris? I cannot believe that she does not know of all of this. She has had her ways of knowing things immediately before this."

Daren looked at him strangely. "I have," he said, slowly. "This very morning, a message from her lay among the correspondence on my desk, and it had not been there last night, nor did a page or a messenger bring it. And I believe that you should tell Karal what I have been sent. It was only two words long." He paused, and an odd, unreadable expression passed across his face. "It said, 'Karal remains,' and was signed by Solaris herself." He shook his head. "I am not certain what to make of it, but the meaning is plain enough."

An'desha nodded. "Karal is still her chosen representative. She could simply be keeping him in place, though, until this current crisis is over so that it does not look as if she is replacing him because of guilt."

"I hope so." Daren was too well-schooled to pace, but he shifted his weight uncomfortably from foot to foot. "We have done all we can to bolster his authority, but there is only so much we can do when he has to deal with people who have not known him from the moment he arrived here."

An'desha grimaced, and quickly changed the subject. He and the Prince discussed what they could do to try to redeem Karal's reputation, but both admitted that they were handicapped by Jarim's prejudice.

"I will see what I can do to have him recalled and replaced by a Sworn or a shaman," the Prince said finally. "But that will take time, time during which he is free to poison minds."

"And we must try to find an antidote to that poison." An'desha hesitated, then shrugged. "I can think of nothing more to say or do at the moment."

"Nor I," the Prince admitted. "But thank you for coming to me. You have given me reasons to do things I had wanted to do in the first place. Jarim is not a bad person, but he is a miserable failure as an envoy. I suspect the Shin'a'in have not had much experience at selecting people to represent their interests off the Plains."

An'desha laughed as he rose to his feet and made his way toward the door. "*I* would make a better envoy than he, I'm afraid." At Daren's look of sudden interest and speculation, he added in warning, "They would never accept me unless I were to be made a shaman. I possess magic, and as such, I could never be said to represent them. No Shin'a'in can practice magics but the shaman, and there is an end to it."

"As one who practices magics and has endured more than a hundred warriors, you have an understanding that Jarim sorely lacks," Daren retorted dryly.

An'desha shook his head, thanked Daren for his time and patience, then took his leave, secure in the knowledge that the Prince-Consort would keep Jarim on a short leash.

He returned to the *ekele* to find that Karal was awake and sitting sleepily in the sun in the garden. Warm golden sunlight streamed through the eastward-facing windows, making a green-gold glory out of a scrap of lawn surrounded by flowering shrubs with aromatic leaves. Karal had made himself a soft place to sit with a rug purloined from among An'desha's things, a few cushions, and a blanket from the bed.

"What are you doing down here?" An'desha asked sternly, gazing down at him with both hands planted on his hips. "The Healer said you were to stay in bed!"

Karal looked sheepish, but he did not look away from An'desha's face. "I couldn't sleep anymore," he said. "I won't go anywhere else, and I'll drink everything except the sleeping potions, but I can't stand being so muzzy-brained." He looked pleadingly into An'desha's eyes. "I promise that I will take naps if I can, but I don't want to be forced into it. The drugs—" now he faltered, "—they're making me dream of—of the Iftel border."

An'desha shuddered; that was one experience he didn't particularly want to recall either, and he knew it had been worse for Karal. "All right. I must admit that I'd feel better knowing you weren't asleep and alone here. Herald Kerowyn has beaten enough self-defense into you that I think you can protect yourself if you're awake. Assuming anyone or anything could get past all the Companions out there." He paused for a moment. "Prince Daren asked me to tell you that he's heard from Solaris. It was a two-word message; 'Karal remains.' Maybe you can make more out of that than I can."

Karal only shook his head.

"I have a plan," An'desha continued, "but it's going to take a few days to put into motion. Meanwhile, your friends are out there defending you; you haven't been deserted. I think if I let them know that you're up to seeing visitors, you won't be alone here for long, either." At the sudden interest and veiled hope in Karal's face, he added, "I believe that Natoli in particular has plans to keep you company."

Karal's blush told him all he needed to know on that score. So, there *was* something brewing between them besides merest friendship.

Good. Very good. It's about time, for both of them. Natoli has been 'one of the boys' for too long, particularly since she isn't she'chorne *any more than Karal is.*

"And in the meantime, I have brought you books that have nothing to do with politics or wars or magic. Here." He dropped the three books he had taken from the library beside his friend. "You read them and think of nothing. I shall go off and attempt to exercise my Shin'a'in craft and guile."

Karal laughed at this, because of course the Shin'a'in were noted even as far north as Valdemar for being the least crafty and most direct people in the Alliance. "As straightforward as a Shin'a'in" was an old saying that An'desha had encountered more than once.

Perhaps that was because no one in the Alliance recognized how directness could be used as cleverly as guile... nor did they realize how telling only part of the truth could be as deceptive as telling a full lie.

* * *

For three days, An'desha left the defense of Karal's honor in the hands of Karal's other friends and concentrated on Jarim himself. It had occurred to him that there might yet be a way to get to the man; he was not unlike the Chief Healer of Karal's old Clan. Tor'getha was not a bad man, but he was quick to leap to conclusions, and quick to look for enemies outside his own folk. Yet when he was presented with enough evidence, Tor'getha had been known to change his mind.

So the first thing was to establish that he really *was* what he claimed, and not simply some rootless vagabond pretending to Shin'a'in blood as a door to opportunities. Dressing conservatively, but unmistakably in the Shin'a'in style, An'desha hovered about the edges of any group that included Jarim. Karal's actual whereabouts were not known except to those few of his friends who could be trusted with the information, so Jarim was not aware that An'desha was playing host to the young Karsite. After three days of near-constant attention, Jarim had stopped frowning and sneering whenever he saw An'desha, and was watching him with a puzzled expression, as if he was wondering just what An'desha wanted.

An'desha let him wonder; his plan depended on Jarim approaching *him*, not the other way around. He felt very much like those who hunted falcons and hawks, who would bury themselves in sand or leaves with a live, fluttering pigeon in one hand, waiting for their quarry to come and take the bait. When the hawk descended, it would be a fight to keep him—though hopefully *this* particular quarry would not realize there was a struggle going on.

At last his patience was rewarded; the quarry came to investigate the bait. Jarim intercepted him on the third afternoon of Karal's absence, just as he was leaving the Palace, heading for the *ekele*.

Jarim was actually waiting for him at the door to the path through the gardens. "An'desha. I wish to speak with you." He paused awkwardly, looking puzzled as he groped for words. Dust-motes drifted in a shaft of sunlight from the window above the door, lancing between them like a wall. "You claim Shin'a'in blood, yet you do not look Shin'a'in, for all that you ape our dress and customs and speak our tongue freely. I—" His mouth twitched as he tried to find diplomatic words and came up with no diplomatic way to say what he wanted. "I am the representative of the Shin'a'in here, and I would have no impostors claiming to be of the Clans."

An'desha smiled mildly. This was exactly what he wanted, to establish his credentials. "My father was Le'kala shena Jor'ethan," he replied steadily. "My mother was an Outlands woman, a weaver, dwelling at Kata'shin'a'in. My father, they say, had a need to wander, which took him often to the edge of the Plains, most often to Kata'shin'a'in, where he would see and mingle with the largest number of foreign folk." He licked his lips. "My mother died at my birth, and he brought me into the Clan to be raised there as a son of the Bear."

"Halfblooded, then—" Jarim began dismissively, clearly preparing to deny him true Clan status. An'desha interrupted him.

"I have more of the blood than most of Tale'sedrin," he replied boldly. "You cannot deny that. When did the Goddess create hair of gold and russet among the Clan, or eyes of green? Those are the legacy of Kethry shena Tale'sedrin, and if you would deny Tale'sedrin to be of the Blood, then you must answer to Kal'enel, for She decreed Kethryveris to be blood-sworn into the People."

Swallow that, old man. There is not a Shin'a'in on the Plains who would dare say Tale'sedrin was less than wholly of the People, yet the Clan-seed came from a man and a woman who never even heard of the People until they were full grown.

Caught without an answer, Jarim grimaced, his eyebrows drawing together into a frown. "When did the Goddess decree that the People might boast eyes as slitted as a plains-cat's?" he finally said. "Or hair bleached to silver by magic?"

Quickly, An'desha weighed all the possibilities and decided on the boldest course. "Will you close your mind because of what your eyes see, as if you were an Outclansman who believes only in what he has before his face?" he asked. "Or will you hear my tale and learn what happened when you were not there?"

Jarim reared back a little, his head coming up, his spine going stiff. He had not been challenged like this since he had arrived here, and An'desha was well aware of this. But he had phrased his challenge very carefully, appealing to blood and clan, and the tradition that a Shin'a'in would *always* hear out a fellow Clansman before he made a judgment.

Finally the envoy grimaced and jerked his head sideways. "Come to my rooms, then. I will hear you." He headed toward a nearby staircase, and An'desha followed him willingly.

Jarim's rooms were precisely as An'desha had thought they might be; spare by Valdemaran standards, with most of the furniture gone, but quite luxurious by the standards of one who lived all of his life in a tent.

At Jarim's gesture, An'desha took a seat on a flat cushion on the floor, automatically dropping into the cross-legged position of anyone born in the tents. Jarim's mouth twitched; obviously he hadn't thought An'desha could even manage the seat on the cushion, much less the posture that marked a Shin'a'in the moment he sat.

Interesting. I could almost believe that this man has not bothered to learn a single thing about any of the people here! Is that possible? Can he have been sent off so ill-prepared?

Perhaps that was why he had been so willing to jump to conclusions about Karal and An'desha. If so—and if he would listen with his mind open at least a little—this might be easier than An'desha had thought.

"What do you know of me?" An'desha demanded.

Jarim paused, then shook his head, as if to say that there was not much he could state truly. "That you claim Shin'a'in blood, that you are paired with that too-pretty Tale'edras sorcerer, that you have the white hair of a sorcerer yourself. That allegedly you had a hand in building the protections which now keep the mage-storms at bay."

An'desha closed his eyes for a moment. *He knows nothing. We assumed too much. We thought that someone would have told him about all of us, and yet he has been working in complete ignorance, using whatever he happened to pick up in conversation and working it into the skewed and incomplete view of the situation he has built with poor information.* It seemed impossible, insane that anyone would have sent an envoy off so poorly briefed.

Then again, this was a *Shin'a'in* envoy. There were plenty of folk among the Clans who viewed anyone dwelling off the Plains with suspicion. He might not have felt it necessary to actually learn anything about the people with whom he was working. He might have decided that since his only duty was to represent the needs of the People, any such details were unnecessary.

But how to tell him what he needed to know in a way that would make him believe it? *He is less like the Healer and more like that stiff-spined old bear, Vorkela, the shaman of my Clan.* Then he knew how to present his story—and Karal's—in the one way that such a close-minded individual would listen to.

He altered his position a trifle, taking the poised, yet relaxed seat of a shaman about to tell a traditional history; Jarim responded automatically to the posture without thinking, taking a counter-attitude of subservient reception.

And he didn't even realize he was doing it! The positioning of his own body would influence his mind; already An'desha had established who was to be the "teacher," and he had not yet spoken a word!

He began his own tale with the traditional opening words and cadence of such a history. And although they had been speaking in the tongue of Valdemar, he spoke now in the language of the Dhorisha Plains.

"Here is a tale; hear it with your heart, for it is as true as the Hand of the Star-Eyed and as sure."

Through half-slitted eyes, he saw Jarim start, his own eyes open with surprise that An'desha not only knew the words, but knew the cadence with which they were chanted. "In the time before the sundering of the Clans, in the time when the Clans served a sorcerer called the Mage of Silence, in the time before the Plains existed and the Shin'a'in served to guard them, the great enemy of the Kal'enedral was Ma'ar, the Dark Adept."

Only a few of the traditional histories began with those words, but An'desha was about to add to them.

"When the Mage of Silence died, it is said that Ma'ar perished with him in the Great Cataclysm that formed the Plains. This is known and chanted among the Clans; what was not known until this very generation was that although Ma'ar's body died, his spirit did not—nor did it go to be weighed and judged. Ma'ar was a sorcerer of great power and greater evil, and he had discovered a way to cheat death." Jarim now was torn between fascination and impatience—fascination, because this literally was all new to him, and impatience because he could not see what this had to do with the present day. Nevertheless, long habit held him silent, for one did not interrupt a shaman in the midst of telling a tale, even if one did not see the point of it.

"He had found a way to hide his spirit, his soul-self, in a pocket of *this* world," An'desha continued, phrasing the truth in a way that Jarim would grasp. "There it would wait until a male child of his blood proved that it had the Gift of magic power by trying the spell that called down fire. At that moment, the door of Ma'ar's hiding place would open, and he would rush forth, possessing the child and obliterating its own soul. Then he would shape the body of the child to be that of a man of full years, and he would stride forth into the world in possession of all of his old, dark knowledge and powers."

Jarim forgot himself and tradition enough to interrupt. "But—this is the blackest of sins!" he cried, leaning forward to emphasize his words, his hands clenched on his knees. "This is the purest of evil!

"And in these new shapes Ma'ar wrought more evil still," An'desha said calmly. "Taking care always to sire many children and broadcast them upon the land, so that there might always be another of his blood with the Gift for him to possess when he had worn out the body he had stolen. *We* knew him, often and often, for his hatred of the Mage of Silence extended to the People." He raised one eyebrow shrewdly, for in his memories was a particular "incarnation" that had made for much weeping among the tents of Jarim's own Clan in the long-ago. "Perhaps you know the name of Sar'terixa the Mad, whose evil caused the deaths of half of the young warriors of the Cat? That was Ma'ar, in the body he had stolen of a young mage of Kata'shin'a'in."

Jarim's lips thinned, and he nodded slowly.

"So; Ma'ar did this, and it was of great evil. The lives he stole were many, although there were times when a suitable child did not appear for generations. Then there was born to the Bear Clan a halfblood child, of a Shin'a'in father who called the boy An'desha."

Jarim's eyes narrowed, but he said nothing. This was encouraging, and An'desha continued. "Through the blood of his mother, An'desha had the gift for magic power, which is a thing forbidden among the Clans, but more than that, he was of the blood of Ma'ar's last incarnation, for the poor maiden was the child of rape although she knew it not. An'desha was a foolish boy, although he meant no harm to anyone; when he knew he had the gift of magic, he hid it as long as he dared. He feared the path of the shaman, but he feared more the loss of his gift, for in many ways he was less than ordinary, and this was all that set him apart. So he hid his gift until he could hide it no more, and then he ran away, intending to seek the Tale'edras and learn the use of his powers among the Kin-Cousins."

Jarim shook his head. "But why did he hide it and then run away?" the envoy asked in honest puzzlement. "Surely if he had gone to his leaders and told them he could not follow the path of the shaman nor give up the magic, they would have sent him there with a proper escort. It is no sin to seek the Kin-Cousins if one is unfortunate enough to bear that gift. I would send my own son to the Hawkbrothers if he wished it so badly."

Well, that was more than I expected out of him! There's some flexibility there after all!

"Thus speaks a man of generous heart whose Clan is as the flowers in springtime in their numbers," An'desha replied warmly. "Thus speaks a man whose Clan is generous, and lets the fledged bird fly where it will. But a man with only one son may not wish to see his blood leave the Plains and join that of the Tale'edras. And a Clan whose numbers are small has a fear to lose even one. An'desha would have had no choice; either he lose the power or become a shaman."

Jarim thought about that for a while. An'desha let him digest the blunt words. They did not go down well, but he finally nodded, and An'desha took that as a sign to continue.

I think it has finally occurred to him to admit that not all of the People are perfect.

"So An'desha foolishly fled, found himself alone and afraid in the Tale'edras forest, and in his fear and loneliness, tried to call fire to keep him company."

"And found himself possessed," Jarim filled in grimly.

"And found himself possessed." An'desha nodded. "But this time the case was different. An'desha did not fight, for he was not used to fighting. He fled, hiding himself deep in his own mind, and Ma'ar—who now called himself Mornelithe—*thought* he was destroyed."

Jarim settled back, wearing a look of speculation. "So An'desha lived on. Of Mornelithe called Falconsbane I know some, none of it good. It is said he shifted his form to that of a man-cat of powerful build." He quirked his eyebrow in silent inquiry, inviting An'desha to admit that this was where his odd eyes came from.

"He did, as you can see by this." He tapped the side of his head beside his left eye. "An'desha was a prisoner, for he dared never reveal his existence to Mornelithe." An'desha decided to cut some of this short. "Perhaps some day I will tell you some of what he endured and experienced. It is enough to say that it was more terrible than any human should ever endure. In the course of it all, Mornelithe Falconsbane became damaged, and also acquired as enemies the clan of k'Sheyna, the Clans of Valdemar, and Firesong k'Treva. And it was at this point that the Kal'enedral took an interest."

"That I also remember," Jarim confirmed.

"It was soon thereafter, with Falconsbane's hold and sanity weakened and An'desha able to exist with a little more freedom, that messengers came to him." *Now, how far do I go with this? Better just describe them, and let him make his own conclusions.* "They were two, spirits, one called Dawnfire and one called Tre'valen."

"That is a Clan name." Jarim raised an eyebrow still higher.

An'desha only nodded. "They came in the form of vorcelhawks of fire, as well as in human form. They taught him to walk the Moonpaths, and their eyes were the black of a starry night." He did not wait for Jarim to comment, but moved on to the end of this part of the story. "They helped him to help the others in destroying Falconsbane *truly*, and for all time. Then—although *I* do not recall this—after all of them escaped to the safety of Valdemar, they appeared again. This time, to reward him, they transformed the strange body in which An'desha now dwelt alone back to the form that An'desha had borne those many years ago when Mornelithe stole it. They left only his eyes unchanged, to remind him and others what he had been, what he had endured, and the price he had paid. And now you have heard why it is that I appear the way I do. This tale I speak, that you may recall. This story I give, that you may learn."

Jarim sat in silence for a very long time. An'desha waited patiently: silence was a positive sign; it meant that Jarim was at least thinking. The fire in the hearth beside them burned brightly and quietly, not even a hiss or a crackle to break the quiet.

And, fortunately for An'desha, Jarim's thoughts had settled, not on the transformation, but on Those who had accomplished it. "They were Avatars," he said, slowly and reluctantly. "You have been touched by Her Avatars."

An'desha just shrugged. "I make no judgments, and you may determine the truth of what I have told you for yourself. There are those who were present when I regained my true form who can describe what they saw to you. Among them are Darkwind and Firesong, whom I believe you trust."

"But if—if An'desha's body was host to the Falconsbane—he—you—are much older than you look."

"I believe," he said slowly, "that although They chose not to erase the memories, They elected to return to me all the years that had been stolen." *Do think about that, Jarim. Think about how one can look seventeen and actually hold the bitter experiences of twice that many years.*

"Now, we come to the next story, if you are ready to hear more."

Jarim made a wordless gesture which An'desha chose to interpret as agreement; his guarded expression held elements of awe, surprise, and speculation. An'desha rose to his feet, and Jarim automatically followed. "I should like to show you something, actually," he said. "Would you walk out with me for a space? Too much sitting is bad for the bones in this cold."

Jarim caught up his coat and An'desha's and passed the latter over. An'desha did not resume his story until they were outside, walking in the chill air under a pale but brilliant sky.

Once again, he told the tale traditionally as if "An'desha" was someone out of legend. "So An'desha was now in Valdemar, with his new friend Firesong. He had great power and did not know how to use it, feared to use it. He now felt things and was afraid of those feelings. Although his friend reassured him, An'desha knew that his friend had many reasons to want him to feel secure, and he mistrusted his friend's objectivity. Above all, he felt alone in this strange land, neither Shin'a'in nor Tale'edras, neither mage nor ordinary man. Further, terrible dreams foretold that there was a great danger coming to all the lands, yet he could not puzzle out what it was. He was as terrified as he had ever been, even when the Falconsbane ruled his body. Then he met a young man who was the apprentice of a priest come as envoy from *his* people." He decided not to name names; not yet. "Actually, it was Herald Talia who introduced them, knowing through her powers that both were lonely, both lost in the strange land, both in need of an ordinary friend. They came to be friends, and in his innocent wisdom, the young priest saw An'desha's terrible fears and knew the great danger that An'desha could pose if An'desha could not conquer his fears to grasp his powers."

They had reached the edge of a memorial garden, and An'desha paused long enough to take some of the greens—and in season, flowers—that were always left there for visitors to place upon graves. Holly for Ulrich, with the berries as bright as flame, and bunches of goldenoak leaves the color of butter, still on their branches.

"You see, possession is not a thing that is known among the Shin'a'in. An'desha feared that Falconsbane was not truly gone, or that he had so tainted An'desha's soul that nothing An'desha did would be pure or clean again, or that he had warped An'desha's spirit so that An'desha himself would follow in Falconsbane's evil footsteps." He glanced aside at Jarim, and saw the envoy nodding. "But such a thing *is* known among this young priest's people, for their history and magics are different, and he and his master gently taught An'desha what he needed to know, and led him by example out of the darkness of fear and into the light of understanding."

"And why did he not turn to his Avatars?" Jarim demanded. "Why did They not teach him? Would that not have been more fitting?"

"Perhaps because the Avatars saw that he had mortal teachers?"

An'desha countered. "They did not come, and in his fear he thought that this was his fault; perhaps his fear kept Them away, or They felt that this lesson was better in the hands of mortals. Perhaps this was one of those times when She leaves mortals to choose their own paths, as She so often does. I do not make judgments upon what She directs Her servants to do."

Since this was precisely what any shaman of the Clans would have said, Jarim was again left without an answer.

"So, it was thanks to this brave young priest—who risked his life to show An'desha that he was not and would not be twisted into evil by having been touched by the hand of Falconsbane—that An'desha became a mage in truth, and wholly himself." Now they were at a particular small plot, one with four holders for greenery and a single bronze plaque that held Ulrich's name, rank, title, and the years of his birth and death in both Valdemaran and Karsite. An'desha added his handful of holly and autumn leaves to the other greenery there. Jarim looked puzzled, although he knew what this place was. The Shin'a'in burned their dead and scattered the ashes; the Karsites also burned their dead, but interred the ashes. Solaris had directed that Ulrich's be interred here, as a sign that the Alliance had been bound up the tighter by Ulrich's death.

"Now, here is what An'desha saw, when he observed that young priest and his master." An'desha described in great detail the fatherly relationship between Karal and Ulrich, the affection, trust, and honesty between the two. He also described in great detail all that the two of them had done for him. And he sent a silent prayer to the spirit of that brave Sun-priest to help him choose the right words.

I will not bring up Altra. I do not know that Jarim is open-minded enough to believe in an Avatar of any other deity but ours.

"It was during this time that the mage-storms began, and An'desha knew that *these* were the terrible dangers his premonitions and visions foretold. Then it was even more important that An'desha learn not to fear the dreadful memories he carried, for it was within those memories that keys to stopping the mage-storms lay."

"Of course," Jarim nodded. "That is obvious even to me. If Falconsbane was Ma'ar, and the mage-storms are echoing back from the Cataclysm, then within Ma'ar's mind might be the secret to stopping them."

"So. And just so." An'desha took a deep breath. "There was another complication; the presence of the Empire. It is thought that *they* believe that the storms were sent by the Alliance; at any rate, they told their agent in the Valdemaran Court to act, murdering by magic as many of the members of the Alliance that they could, in order to destroy it."

Jarim was not stupid, he glanced suddenly down at the plaque, read the name again, and looked up, his eyes wide. "This is the Karsite envoy!" he cried. "The one slain along with Querna!"

"And the young priest is Karal," An'desha said calmly. "And never in all my life have I seen such grief as Karal bore. It was my turn then to comfort him, and I truly think if he had not been burdened with the responsibilities of his office, if he had been left alone with his sorrow, he would have gone mad with it, and taken a knife and joined his master in death. He and his are much like our own shaman; they do not often show their feelings. To me he showed his grief, and it was terrible."

"But—" Jarim began.

"There was one thing that he *could* do to both avenge his beloved teacher and our own Querna, and to give himself an outlet for his sorrows. He made of himself the bait in a trap to catch the killer. He very nearly died in that trap." An'desha made certain that his expression was a grim one. "It was luck and the skill of a Herald trained by Herald Captain Kerowyn alone that saved him, and you may verify this yourself from those who were there, beginning with that redoubtable lady herself."

Jarim's expression was an interesting mix; so complicated that An'desha could not even begin to read it.

"As for the rest of the tale, I shall make this short as well. Although he is no mage, he apparently has some powers that permit him to channel magic. These were needed to create the defense against the mage-storms; further, the Iftel border would allow only *him* to cross into it in order to set that protection up, and so once again he risked his life and sanity to help provide the protection for us all." An'desha raised an eyebrow himself. "This, I can verify, for *I* was there, acting as the mage in the north and east with him. I can promise you that the experience was painful and maddening, and it was worse for him than for me."

He spread his hands. "So, now you have the end of the tales."

"But—" Jarim shook his head, as if he was trying to settle all the contradictory things he had heard into an order that made sense. "With all of this—*why* is he urging peace with the very people that slew his master? If he is so brave, why is he speaking the words of a coward?"

"He is no coward," An'desha replied severely. "And as for his words—Jarim, he is a priest. He cannot speak *only* for himself, nor can he think *only* for himself. He must think and speak for the greater good. How often has She allowed things to happen that seemed ill, yet later proved to be the salvation of our People? Think of the First Sacrifice above the Plains! And I ask myself—which is the greater danger to the folk of the Alliance, the mage-storms, or an army which has dug itself in and cowers in its lair because it has lost touch with the Empire? The mage-storms, which increase in fury and frequency with every passing day, or fools who rely so on magic that they are desperate for a way to keep themselves warm this winter?"

Jarim shook his head again, but now his expression was easier to read. He was a greatly troubled man.

"Let me add one thing more," An'desha said. "Have you *ever* heard of a shaman being permitted to take Sword-Sworn black to avenge a wrong?"

Jarim's expression became blank as he searched his memory and finally shook his head. "Never in my knowledge," he admitted. "The oath of the shaman is too important for him to become Sword-Sworn for the sake of revenge."

"So why do you expect Karal to pursue revenge rather than the path of his priesthood?" An'desha countered. "Why do you expect him to seek a personal goal rather than that of his god?

He gestured down at the small plaque. "This much I can tell you; if he chose to take such a path, I think that his own master would rise in spirit and scold him for it!"

And I hope you forgive me for putting words in your mouth, friend Ulrich.

Jarim pulled at his lip, and finally closed his eyes. "I must think about this," he muttered. "You have told me almost too much to take in."

"Well and well," An'desha replied. "Now, if you will forgive me, I shall return to the path I was taking when you asked to speak with me." He glanced about at the thin sun, the dead grasses waving in a chill breeze, and shivered. "I would prefer to put my feet on the path that leads me to my warm hearth and a welcoming fire."

"And I—" Jarim said, as An'desha turned and walked away, "I shall see what path I find."

There were no more outbursts from Jarim; in fact, the Shin'a'in envoy became amazingly quiet on the subject of Karal, much to the relief of An'desha and the rest of Karal's friends. An'desha did not hope *too* much, however; Jarim was thick-headed and stubborn, and not likely to admit that he was wrong without a great deal of coaxing and many facts refuting him.

There were promising signs. Jarim did take the time to speak to those people An'desha had directed him toward; Darkwind and Treyvan, Kerowyn and Talia, and even Elspeth. An'desha did not go to them afterward and ask what was discussed, however; it was none of his business. But he knew at least that these were some of Karal's staunchest allies, and they would have confirmed everything An'desha had said. He only hoped that they were convincing.

Kerowyn, at least, will give him the real facts about the assassination and about the uncovering of the assassin, he reflected when he learned that Jarim had requested an interview with that formidable woman. *She just might be able to give him other information as well. After all, if there is anyone in this Kingdom likely to know who the Imperial agents might be, it is Kerowyn! And I know she was absolutely beside herself for having overlooked that damned artist-assassin. By the time she got done with her checking and rechecking, I don't think another agent could get into the Court even disguised as a mouse!*

It was several more days before the Healers would permit Karal to resume his duties and his rooms at the Palace; on that day, the Prince convened the first Grand Council since Jarim's verbal assault and Karal's near-collapse. An'desha decided to attend this one since Jarim was no longer sneering down his nose at the "halfbreed." In fact, when he looked in An'desha's direction now, it was with mingled respect and a touch of fear. That was somewhat amusing, all things considered.

As if being singled out by Avatars made me any wiser! If anything, I suspect it only proves that I am a bit slower than others, and need the extra help!

He debated shepherding Karal into the Palace and finally decided to let the young priest handle the situation without a nursemaid hovering about him. He did lag a bit behind while Karal took his place, filing in with the others to the meeting—so he was the first person to see when Jarim intercepted Karal at the door, and took him off to the corner for a low-voiced, urgent colloquy.

He moved quickly to a position where he could hover in the background, and he wasn't the only one! Out of the corner of his eye, he noticed Talia moving unobtrusively into place at a similar position of potential rescue, and Darkwind doing the same. If Karal needed help in dealing with Jarim, there were going to be three people tripping over each other to see that he got it!

But Karal didn't seem particularly distressed; in fact, as Jarim talked, his expression changed from suspicion to surprise to open relief.

Had An'desha's plan worked?

Finally, Jarim said, in a voice fully loud enough for the entire room to hear, "I don't understand *how* you can feel that way, boy, but—well, according to the gods of both our people, that's more to my shame than yours." He shook his head and managed a grim half-smile. "I don't understand the gift of forgiveness and I never did, but there are those who do, and it seems you are among them. It's a good gift for a man of the gods to have, they tell me. Better than the opposite. I'm satisfied, and I apologize."

He slapped Karal on the back heartily, staggering him.

"Your apology is generous, and it is gratefully accepted, sir," Karal managed, also speaking loudly enough for the rest of the room to hear. "I never wanted any conflict between us. Our people need us to work together, not tear the Alliance asunder with misunderstandings."

"Good enough." Jarim glanced at the avid faces around the room and shrugged. "I'm sorry you were ill, I hope you're better, but we've wasted enough time waiting for you to recover. Let's get on with this."

With that, he strode to his seat, leaving Karal and the rest to take theirs. An'desha moved to the Tayledras delegation with a sigh; Firesong was not there, and he rather thought Darkwind could use another voice. He knew he was right when that worthy gave him a grateful smile as he took his seat.

Across the table, Karal was getting out his papers and pens, as usual, but his color was better and that look of strain was gone.

Good, An'desha thought with satisfaction. Karal would still have detractors, for there were and probably always would be people in Valdemar who would not trust *any* Karsite, but at least now he could work without fear of persecution. And maybe, just maybe, if Jarim started treating him with respect, the others on the Grand Council would, too.

Now, let's get down to the business we should be dealing with. The mage-storms aren't waiting for us to settle our internal quarrels. And settling grievances isn't doing a damned thing about stopping them.

Time is still against us, and we still do not have any answers.

6

Firesong had found the most private place in the Palace, a place where no one ever intruded, and a place where his own magics were shielded from the outside by the most powerful shields available inside or outside of a Vale. He could disappear here for hours at a time, and he did.

It was not the place he would have thought of first as a very private spot, but no one seemed to want to spend any time in the chamber of Valdemar's Heartstone. Perhaps they found the sensation of all that power rather unnerving; the pressure of it was as palpable as hot sunlight on one's exposed flesh. Firesong liked it, but for someone sensitive, and one who was not used to being in the presence of so much power, it was probably very uncomfortable. He had been told that even those who had no Gift for mage-craft could feel the power in this room, and that in itself was impressive.

This was the most powerful Heartstone he had ever worked with; it represented the latent power of the Stone Vanyel had originally constructed and linked into the Web, and the power from k'Sheyna's Heartstone that Vanyel, now a spirit and able to work more freely with such energies, had cleverly purloined.

He opened the door—a door that was by no means obvious, even though everyone in the Palace knew it was here—and walked inside, allowing it to fall closed behind him. This chamber was identical to one directly above it that had been used for scrying for centuries. The room itself was tiny, with so many shields on it that even sound had difficulty penetrating the walls. A round stone table all but filled the available space, with four curved benches around it. A single oil lamp was suspended above the table, but it was not lit, for it was not needed. A single globe of crystal in the middle of the table itself glowed with enough light to illuminate the room perfectly. The fact that this light was merely a by-product of the power held in the Stone was astonishing. *I've never known a Heartstone to glow before. I wonder if it has anything to do with the fact that it is crystal? This is quite fascinating.*

That globe of stone was the tip of Valdemar's Heartstone; the globe was fused into the tabletop, which was fused in turn to the column that supported it, which was fused in *its* turn to the stone floor and the bedrock beneath it. If one chipped everything away, one would find a single column of fused, ultra-hard, heat-forged stone, topped by the crystal globe, extending downward into the earth until it touched the place where the rock flowed with molten heat. The end result would look rather like a charlatan's "magic wand."

Firesong felt completely comfortable and at home here, despite the fact that this room had no windows and was inclined to induce claustrophobia. He was one of two people who had been originally keyed into the Heartstone's powers, after all. Elspeth was the other, and they had both been given that particular "gift" because they were both descended from Herald Vanyel Ashkevron, who had created the Heartstone in the first place, and had taken the power of k'Sheyna's Stone to reactivate this one.

The chamber had dropped out of the minds of everyone in Valdemar during those years when, in order to strengthen the Valdemarans' reliance on the Heraldic Gifts of mind-magic Vanyel's meddling had driven the memory and the belief in *real* magic clear out of their minds. The ward-spell he had set among the *vrondi* of this land to keep true mages at bay had served well enough to protect his land from the incursions of rogue magicians at the time. The sensation of being stared at by hundreds, thousands of unseen eyes the moment one cast a spell was enough to turn even the boldest half-mad.

But that was then. Now, everything was turned about; the protections at the border were down, and there were mages from four or five lands in Valdemar. Although magic had not taken a more important role than the Heraldic Gifts, Herald-Mages were certainly playing crucial roles.

But some of that *avoidance* of this chamber must still be in effect, for in all the times Firesong had come here, he had never found signs that anyone else had so much as touched the half-hidden door. Perhaps Elspeth came here now and again, but he doubted it. She didn't need to come here to feel the power of the Stone. It was in her blood more deeply even than in his, and it sang in his veins, hummed in the back of his head. He was too used to power for it to intoxicate him.

Perhaps the power-song frightened others. That was certainly fine with Firesong, for it gave him a place to work and to think without any danger of being interrupted.

Ever since An'desha had begun drifting away, he had been searching his memory for details about Falconsbane's spirit-sanctuary and the journey he himself had taken through the Void to find it. He had many questions about the whole procedure, and rather than ask An'desha about any of it, he thought he'd rather see if he couldn't deduce some answers himself.

When he was reasonably certain that he remembered where to go and what to look for, he launched his spirit out into the Void in search of the spot where the sanctuary had been.

He hadn't really expected to find anything but a few clues at best. After all, very few magical creations ever survived the deaths of their creators, much less the creator's total dissolution. Then there was the Void itself to contend with; changeless, yet ever-changing, how could anything so foreign to it remain after it had been ripped open?

Yet when he sank himself into a mage-trance and projected himself to the general area that he thought he remembered, not only was the sanctuary still there and open, it was intact except for the damage he himself had done to it! Even that was mending, as if the sanctuary were alive and had the Power to heal.

He was able to examine it in detail and at his leisure. One of the oddest things that he noticed was that it was substantially unaffected by the mage-storms echoing through the Void. There was a bit of surface turbulence, but the fabric of the sanctuary was unaltered.

He considered that as he took his seat on one of the stone benches in the room of the Heartstone. *The sanctuary is so oddly solid, rather like the fabric of the land beneath a series of great thunderstorms. Even if the storms cause floods or landslides, beneath the movement of a little topsoil, the shape of the land and the contour of it remains the same.*

With the ease of what had become habit, he settled himself on his bench, linked his own power in with that of the Heartstone, and leaped out into the Void, leaving his body behind.

The "track" of his passage was well-worn by now; he actually left a trail of residual power that linked his body to the sanctuary. Through the swirling, multicolored energy patterns, sparkled with tiny fireflies of power and now turbulent and roiled by the passage of so many mage-storms, the trail remained steady and unchanging, though faint. Then he came to the open mouth of the sanctuary, disguised in the swirl of energies by a swirl of chameleon colors on its surface.

He settled "himself" in the comfortable womb of the sanctuary, and the very existence of that link set off a train of other thoughts, other observations. As he gazed out into the wild chaos of the Void with all of its tumbling energies, he noted two "links" back to his physical body. One was the tenuous path he had made, the traces of all of his journeys, a sparkling golden trail of faint sparks of power, a dusting of silver-gilt leading back to the Heartstone. The other was the stronger, brighter, ropelike silver link of power that tied him to his own physical self.

He'd made note of that before. But suddenly, what he noticed was that the path and the link were both comprised of energies that were completely homogeneous. That made sense, of course, for both were *his* energies; even the power he drew from the Heartstone had to become his before he could use it.

But the energies the sanctuary had been built from were *not* homogeneous. Here they were, layer upon layer, warp and weft of a hundred, a thousand different threads of power. Some of them he recognized as having the taint of Ma'ar about them, the dried-blood dark-red and muddied energies of death and blood-magic. But others were quite clear and clean, pure, though thin. How had *they* come here? They had nothing to do with Ma'ar or any of his incarnations.

Finally, he found the clue, as he found every one of those pure, clear strands of power tagged at the very ends with the muddied colors of Ma'ar. And then the entire secret of the sanctuary's construction and the life it now had of its own unfolded before him.

The link between a living creature and a place like this one, similar to the link between his spirit and his physical body, could be artificially created or inflicted upon another. And when such unwitting victims died, a great deal of their power would go along that link to wherever the link led. And for that matter, a stronger link could be forged between a mage's physical body and this sanctuary and stretched as tightly as a harp string Even if the moment of death were instantaneous, making it impossible for Ma'ar to do what Falconsbane had done and make the conscious flight along the link into the sanctuary, the release of the tension at the end linked to the living physical body would literally snap the spirit into its sanctuary, whether or not the mage himself was even aware of what was happening to him.

So here was the answer to all of the questions. By investing the power of many, many followers in this place, the willing and unwilling, the witting and unwitting, Ma'ar had created a sanctuary that would outlast everything. By creating more links to underlings throughout the ages, Ma'ar had strengthened his creation so that it actually attained the permanent quality of a node. By putting in place the strong, tight link between himself and his sanctuary, Ma'ar ensured that he would *always* come "home" to it at the moment of his death.

While the result was appalling, the concept was intriguing. *Oh, this is fascinating.* Everyone knew, of course, that it was possible for an unscrupulous, immoral mage to make use of the power of someone's life-force by wresting it away in a violent death. Violent death was what often created a link to the physical world, in fact, as the power released, combined with the dying person's wish to live, forged a bond holding the spirit to the earth past the end of his life. That was how ghosts were created; that was probably how the spirits of Vanyel, Yfandes, and Stefen had been able to join with the great Forest in the north of Valdemar. Vanyel had done consciously, and under control, what others had done by sheerest accident and panic.

Now, there was no doubt that killing someone to take the power of their life-force was wrong, evil. But what if you simply forged that link to drain it off when they died naturally? Why would that be bad? The original owner wouldn't *need* that power, and it would only dissipate back into the energy-web that all life created. That would be why so many of the power strands woven into this sanctuary were so clear and clean; this power hadn't been stolen, reft away by violence. It had simply been taken up when the original "owner" no longer needed it.

No, there would be nothing immoral about that, no more than inheriting a house or a book from someone.

Hmm. This requires a great deal of thought. Granted, it does take power to create these links, but the outcome… when your donors did die, the power would go to whatever receptacle you had created for it, where you could tap it at will. It wouldn't even need to be invested in an object like this sanctuary.

Falconsbane could very easily have used the power in this sanctuary to keep himself aware of the world, even to keep track of those of his bloodline, picking and choosing among his "candidates" until he found one about to make that crucial step, opening himself to invasion by opening himself to magic.

All the pieces of the puzzle had fallen into place, leaving Firesong with a most intriguing whole.

The view from here is enchanting indeed. Enough for one day. It certainly answers the first part of my question—how I create the same kind of sanctuary that Falconsbane did. Now he was left with the other half—how did one find a new body without stealing one?

He followed his link back to his own body, and opened his very physical eyes on the tiny stone-walled room, the stone table, and the glowing crystal.

It wasn't cold in here, or he would have gotten a great deal stiffer than he was. He stretched, getting his blood moving again. An'desha had said this morning that he would gladly take Firesong's place on the Grand Council; Firesong was not certain what had prompted that offer, although he was mildly grateful for the gesture.

Today, too, they were finally rid of Karal again—he'd gone back to the Palace and his official suite.

Today Karal was supposed to take up his duties again. And An'desha wants to be at the Grand Council meeting. Coincidence? I think not.

He frowned and rubbed the side of his nose with his finger in irritation. Karal and An'desha were entirely *too* solicitous of each other. And could Karal actually be the one responsible for An'desha's increasing independence? The Karsite had all manner of odd notions in his head; could he be imparting them to An'desha? After all, An'desha was perfectly tractable until he began spending so much time with Karal.

Well, if Karal keeps aggravating that Shin'a'in, he's going to find himself with more trouble than he can handle. It wouldn't surprise me too much if the man decided to declare blood-feud, which would certainly solve all of my difficulties with him.

A gloating, gleeful thought occurred to him. Karal's career as an envoy—as well as his life—seemed destined to be very short, given the number of times he'd been attacked and the number of enemies he'd collected. Perhaps he could persuade Karal to be a part of his own experiment with capturing the power of another's life-force. And then— perhaps he could play with the situation a bit—

No, that's probably not a good idea, he decided immediately. *And I don't want to link a Karsite Priest into anything of mine; the Goddess only knows what Vkandis would do about* that. *Nor do I really want to manipulate the situation to get Karal into difficulties, even though an accident to Karal would make certain that An'desha was in great need of comforting, and pliant with grief.*

He stretched again, grimacing at the numb state of his rump. *Stone benches. How very typical of this place! Elegance without comfort...*

He had come to realize that he was very discontented here. He hated the feeling of eyes on him every time he ventured out of the *ekele*, and so perversely went out of his way to be outrageous. Not that he hadn't been the center of attention back in the Vales, but the attention he attracted here was not the unalloyed admiration and indulgence he got back home. Here he was stared at because he was alien, flamboyant by the standards of these curiously dull people. When he gave vent to some strong opinion, people looked at him as if he had committed some breach of etiquette; often as not, when he inquired after something that *should* have been commonplace, they gave him looks that said clearly they thought he was out of his mind.

I miss the Vales, damn it all. I miss decent food that I don't have to prepare for myself. I miss my hertasi *servants. There is no reason why I should be forced to pick up and clean after myself; there is no reason why I should have to devote a single moment to anything other than mage-craft! I am a mage—why should I do the work of a menial?* Oh, he could have servants coming in, but he didn't want snoops from the Palace making free with his private areas.

He missed the way he didn't even have to *ask* for something he wanted at home; *hertasi* would anticipate what he wanted without his asking. He missed the varied temperatures of all of the springs in a Vale; here he was confined to one spring of hot water and one of cold. Most of all he missed the gentle, cultivated warmth of the Vales, the unvarying climate, the presence of flowers and fruit everywhere, at every season. His own *ekele* was a poor substitute for a Vale. It was too small, and there was no way one could pretend one was alone in a wilderness.

And I am mortally weary of the prudishness of these Valdemarans. One cannot even soak in a pool without some sort of modesty covering.

He was tired of their limited diet, tired of their limited understanding, their limits upon everything except their curiosity.

I have very simple tastes. I am not asking a great deal. Just some of the amenities of civilization, including civilized behavior.

As for the reason he was here, there were no answers and far too many limitations there as well. The mage-storms were too strong, too chaotic in their effects, to respond to the magics *he* knew, yet he could not bear to admit that they defeated him. If he had all the Adept-level mages of all the Vales at his disposal, he *might* be able to concoct a shield, but that was by no means a certainty. The storms themselves came and passed so quickly he could not study them properly, and even if he could, he simply didn't have the resources he needed.

He wanted, longed to go home, but to do so now would be to admit he had been defeated, leaving the field to those artificers An'desha was so enamored of.

Nothing in his life was satisfactory at the moment. He could not find success or contentment in his environment, his personal and emotional life, or his work. And no one cared, wrapped up as they were in themselves.

It was all so bitterly ironic! *He* had been the one they had all turned to when they needed problems solved, but when he wanted a little attention, a little consideration, they all found other things to do.

It would have been very pleasurable to find something or someone on which to vent some of his frustration.

He rested his chin on his hand and stared into the crystal globe of the tip of the Heartstone. *Frankly, it seems to me that this land and its people owe me a great deal. If it had not been for me, Falconsbane would be secure in his sanctuary even now, waiting to find another body to seize. If it had not been for me, the mission might not even have gotten as far as the capital of Hardorn. Certainly neither Elspeth nor Darkwind would have survived their encounter with Ancar, much less made it back home to Valdemar.*

So why weren't the leaders of Valdemar falling all over themselves to make certain that he was content here? Why weren't the people begging to be permitted to thank him? Why did they all treat him as if what he had done was his duty and no more? He didn't *owe* these barbarians anything! He wasn't one of their foolish Heralds, who practically stood in line for the chance to fling themselves in front of some danger!

I don't have to be here. I could go right back to the Vales at any time. I'm the most powerful Adept they have, and even if I haven't figured out a solution to the mage-storms yet, I have the best chance of doing so. I could have gone right back home as soon as everyone was safe in Valdemar after we got rid of Ancar and Falconsbane. I could leave this very instant. I wouldn't even have to go home; I could go to k'Leshya Vale instead.

With An'desha obviously *not* the lifebonded mate he had hoped for, with everyone here trying to prove they didn't really need him, maybe he *should* go.

Once I'm gone, let's see just how independent An'desha really is!

But if he left, he wouldn't have the satisfaction of seeing An'desha learn that he was not as self-sufficient as he thought.

But there might be a better idea.

I'll stay. Too much is unfinished. And perhaps I can find a way to engineer something that will prove to An'desha just how much he and everyone else still needs me. And then I'll get what I deserve!

As usual, the Grand Council chamber was too cold. Nevertheless, Karal remained in his seat after the adjournment of the Grand Council, ostensibly writing down more notes, but in reality just delaying his departure so that he could cool his temper and swallow some of his sour disappointment. Everyone else was getting out as soon as they could so that they could warm their frozen feet and noses, and he didn't blame them. It was going to be a dreadful winter.

"I'm sorry, boy," Jarim said in an undertone, leaning over and patting

Karal on the arm in a decidedly paternal manner as he rose. "I wish there was something I could do to help you.

Karal managed to smile weakly at his odd and new-found ally. Jarim seemed determined to make up for his hostility by displaying a fatherly interest in the young Karsite. To his credit, not only had he dropped all of his opposition and outrageous charges after that public apology, *he* no longer treated Karal as if he were still a mere secretary. They now sat side-by-side at the Council table, the only two who took their own notes rather than leaving it up to a secretary. Of course, in both their cases that was a matter of necessity; there were no secretaries conversant enough with the written forms of Shin'a'in and Karsite to listen in Valdemaran and write in either tongue simultaneously.

"I wish you could, too, sir," he sighed. "Unfortunately, there is nothing that I can do about my youth." There was the core problem, all right. *It* hadn't gone away, and he was still trying to convince his superiors of that.

Jarim shook his head, the small braids in front of each ear swaying with the motion. "Perhaps it is only that among my people, men your age are found leading border-scouts, and as the fathers of families. These soft and civilized sorts see your lack of years and assume, because *their* sons have no more sense than a green and untamed colt, you must be equally foolish, to their thinking." He scratched his temple with a callused finger. "They also may be confusing the evidence of their eyes and the evidence of their ears."

Karal shrugged; Jarim had summed up the entire problem most succinctly and with a surprising amount of insight. It could be, now that Karal and others were taking the time to brief him on the background of all of his fellow Councilors, that he would make a better envoy than anyone had guessed.

The Shin'a'in envoy patted his arm again, and took himself out of the room, possibly sensitive to Karal's unspoken distress.

Though he might just be anxious to get back to his own hearth-fire. He might be a toughened Shin'a'in, accustomed to spending the winter in a tent, but that doesn't mean he doesn't feel the cold as sharply as any of the rest of us.

The latest twist in the situation was that the other envoys had settled into a pattern of asking Karal for confirmation from his superiors in Karse for every single suggestion, statement, or decision. They had to see his authorization for every agreement or even statements of fact. Jarim alone was treating him as an equal, but in a way that was doing him more harm than good, given the Shin'a'in envoy's flamboyant and volatile temperament. At the moment, the only hope he had of changing anyone's opinion of him was to impress them with his diligence. He was not particularly sanguine about his chances of success.

When everyone else, including the secretaries, had cleared out, he finally packed up his own papers and left. He headed for his rooms, which once again were a sanctuary of peace, if only a fleeting peace.

The wave of warmth met him like a welcome. He closed the door carefully behind himself, and went directly to the waiting kettle on the hob. He poured hot water—now kept ready for him at all hours by orders of the Healers—over the handful of herbs in one of the mugs waiting on the mantelpiece. He had an entire series of those mugs lined up, refreshed every day by one of the servants. At least, thanks to the stomach-calming potions the Healers had prescribed for him, he was still able to eat, although he had given up his favorite sausage rolls and other spicy or fatty foods, none of which agreed with him anymore. At this rate, he would be reduced to living on turnips and cress.

Is it just me, is it only that they simply cannot accept me as their equal? he wondered as the tea steeped. *Or is it an actual and calculated affront? Can it be that now that the immediate crisis is over, many of those people on the Grand Council are trying to alienate Karse?*

He could not dismiss the possibility, and he was not feeling steady enough to judge whether it was a silly, childish fear or a real concern. He wished he had the ability to read thoughts that some of the Heralds boasted. He wished he had the ability to read *intent.*

:I wish that I did not have to make this particular request,: said a familiar, but long-absent, voice in his mind, speaking in a tone of considerable reluctance.

Karal spun around, hardly able to believe his "ears" and hardly daring to hope—but there was Altra standing behind him in a pool of sunlight, ears slightly flattened and tail twitching. There was a message-tube at his feet, but at the moment, that hardly seemed important.

The Firecat looked no different than he had the last time Karal had seen him; to all outward appearance, a blue-eyed, cream-coated feline with orange tabby markings on paws, ears, facial mask and tail, and thick, soft fur. Of course, there *was* one thing that marked him as out of the ordinary: his size. He easily stood with the top of his head even with Karal's hip.

"Altra!" Karal exclaimed joyfully, relieved beyond words at the Firecat's appearance and all that it implied. *Vkandis is not displeased with me! I have not been heretical or blasphemous! I* have *been doing what He wants here—I have not been abandoned to my punishment—*

Altra flattened his ears further, looking decidedly apologetic. *:I am sorry, Karal. We have tried to be patient, and it is not your fault, but it does not seem that you are being granted the respect that you are due here. No one in Karse wanted to undermine your position or your authority, but things are getting out of hand. Would you feel terribly betrayed if Solaris took control of the situation here?:*

Karal could not help himself; his jaw went slack with surprise for a moment. At last—at *last!*—the plummeting situation was going to be taken out of his hands and put into the hands of someone old enough to deal with it properly!

"Not only would I *not* feel betrayed, not only would I *not* be disappointed, I would be overjoyed," he replied, trying not to laugh aloud with relieved gratitude. "I thought I have made that perfectly clear in my dispatches! I am here to serve the interests of Karse and Solaris, not to indulge myself in fantasies of prestige!" He finally gave way to his feelings and laughed giddily. "I cannot even tell you how happy it will make me to be able to go back to being a simple secretary again!"

I might actually have something of a real life again!

This was the last thing he was going to admit to Altra or anyone else, but this message could not have come at a better time. His enforced idleness had given him a great deal more time with Natoli than he had ever enjoyed before, and things were developing in ways he found both pleasant and a bit unnerving. He would much have preferred to be able to capitalize on that—except that once he had resumed his duties, he had gone back to the same dull round of not having enough time to spend on anything *but* duty. It had been frustrating, to say the least.

But I'm not telling Altra that! Oh, no!

The Firecat's ears came up, and his tail stopped twitching. *:You know I promised you that I wouldn't rummage around in your private thoughts, and I haven't. So I really didn't know how you would feel about being relieved of your authority.:*

"Relieved is the correct word," Karal told him, taking his mug to the table and sitting down with the sensation that a vast weight had been taken from his shoulders. "Who is coming here as envoy? And how soon?"

:Ah—that's the thing I was told to prepare you for.: Altra replied nervously, *:But I'm not certain that I can prepare you for it. The—person—is only coming up here to reestablish your credentials in such a way that no one will be able to treat you like a nonentity without creating a diplomatic incident. And the—person—is Solaris.:*

He was very glad he was sitting down; doubly glad that he had not been drinking his tea, or he would have choked. "Solaris?" he repeated, dazed. "Solaris?"

:She wants to make a state visit.:

"Can she do that? Is she secure enough at home?" Solaris' rule was by no means rock steady; there had been several times in the past when only the intervention of events—or Vkandis—had kept her on the Sun Throne.

:Oh, she's secure.: Was that a hint of a chuckle in Altra's tone? *:Believe me in that. Karse is closer to the Dhorisha Plains than Valdemar, although it's farther away from Lake Evendim—and before the breakwater went up, things were very... interesting. There is not a man, woman, or child in Karse that does not know how this Alliance has saved them.:*

"Oh." *Now* he took a gulp of tea, as much to steady his nerves as his stomach. That was important information, but it was not something he had truly wanted to hear. Some small part of him had hoped that because Karse was so far from Evendim it might have been spared some of the worst effects of the storms. Evidently its proximity to the Plains caused nearly as many problems. He couldn't remember the model; couldn't remember how many intersections of the two series of waves happened over Karse; it was the intersection points that were the places where real damage took place—

Altra went on, ignoring Karal's furrowed brow. *:She thinks now that it is time she actually met Selenay in person—and equally time that Selenay met her.:*

"I have to admit that I find it difficult to disagree with that," Karal told him candidly. "I think it would prevent misunderstandings when things get tense again if each of them knew how her counterpart thinks." He frowned. "But I'm still not certain about this. Even if she feels secure enough to come *here*, can Karse afford to be without her? Things can happen without notice, without warning. What if a crisis arose and she wasn't there to deal with it?"

Altra looked a bit sheepish, an odd expression on a feline face. *:As to that, she's arranging things so that even most of the Sun-priests are not going to be aware that she is gone.:*

"Hansa isn't going to 'jump' with her, is he?" Karal felt his own stomach lurch at the idea. "I don't think that's a very good idea!"

Altra had the audacity to chuckle at him, irritating the young Sun-priest, although he refused to show his irritation. *:No, Hansa and I are going to establish a Gate between us, so that Solaris can come and go without depleting her own powers.:*

Oh? This was the first he'd ever heard of that particular talent! Karal allowed an eyebrow to rise. "Well, isn't *that* convenient," he drawled.

Altra sniffed derisively. *:If you had troubled to continue reading in those books that Ulrich left you, instead of bothering yourself with making letter-perfect copies of your notes to send to Karse, you would have seen that Firecats have created Gates between them in the past, when there have been two or more of them about. It is just an extension of "jumping," after all, and you could logically have deduced that. It is not—:* he added smugly, *:—an ability shared by the Companions.:*

Karal rolled his eyes at that last, but let it pass without further comment.

:And I must point out to you that we could not have put you and your mentor in place this way, because I was not here, and I could not have come here without you. I am linked to you and to no one else.:

Another interesting bit of information. Altra was certainly being generous with it today! Was he making up for his prolonged absence by dropping his secretive stance?

:We had always intended to use a Gate in an emergency to remove you—or—or Ulrich, if we had to.: At the mere mention of Ulrich, Karal felt his throat knot and his eyes sting. *:Unfortunately, it takes more time to establish a Gate than we had when—:* Altra faltered for a moment, then went on. *:Just remember that is always an option for you, if there is an untenable situation.:*

"I will," Karal promised solemnly, after he managed to clear his throat and rub the suspicion of tears from his eyes. "Now, am I to be the one to make the request for this visit official?"

:Precisely.: Altra tapped the tube with one paw, and it rolled over to Karal until it ran into his foot. He bent down to retrieve it.

:That is an official document from Solaris to Selenay, requesting her permission for a Visit of State.: Altra looked pensive. *:I hope she is as sensible as we believe, but this is bound to come as something of a shock.:*

Well, that was something of an understatement. The leader of a land that until very recently was Valdemar's deadliest enemy was now asking to come to the heart of Valdemar? "Then the sooner I get the shock over with, the better," Karal replied, drinking the last of his tea—more grateful for its stomach-easing properties than ever—and standing up. "I think I had best get on the way with this now, before something else happens."

He looked down long enough to put his mug securely on the table; when he looked up again, Altra was gone.

* * *

The Queen's Chambers were less impressive than Karal had expected. The furniture was in keeping with her station and extremely comfortable, but hardly constructed of priceless material. It showed slight signs of wear, the wood of the desk and chairs showed a few scratches no amount of polishing would remove. Karal waited, standing in front of that desk in respectful silence with his hands folded in front of him, while the Queen of Valdemar read through Solaris' letter for the third time. Her look of absolute incredulity had not diminished since the first reading.

Talia, however, did not seem particularly surprised. *Then again,* Karal reflected, *she knows Solaris, perhaps better than many of us in Karse.*

Finally, Selenay put the document down and looked up into Karal's face. For all the stress she had been through in her life, Selenay looked remarkably young. Karal could easily imagine that in her place, he'd have aged about fifty years in the past ten. "I have to admit, Ambassador Karal, this comes as something of a surprise," she said carefully. "I think I would be safe to say that it is altogether unprecedented."

"Not entirely, Your Highness," Karal said carefully. "The Crown Prince of Rethwellan has been here on at least two occasions; the Prince-Lord Martial Daren also, arriving at the head of an army."

To her credit, Selenay did not point out that Valdemar and Rethwellan had *never* been at odds, much less at war for generations. "But the King of Rethwellan has never been here," she pointed out instead. "I honestly cannot say that I can think of a single monarch who has made a state visit to Haven. In the past, when monarchs have conferred, they met at the border. This—this shows a great deal of trust on Solaris' part."

"And on yours, Highness," he felt constrained to tell her. "You have only my word and hers that she will not bring an armed force through this Gate."

But both Selenay and Talia smiled, and it was Talia who spoke. "The queen gave her greatest trust when she sent me into Karse with an escort of two," Talia said gently. "And logically speaking, it would take a great deal of time to bring an army through a Gate, one man at a time. I am sure we could do something about disrupting the Gate long before she could bring enough people in to threaten us."

"As for this," Selenay tapped the letter with her finger, "you know, of course, that I cannot possibly give you a yes or no answer immediately?"

"You must first consult your Council, if not the Grand Council," Karal agreed. "And I am certain you will have many questions, both of a personal nature and involving logistics, that you must put to Solaris."

He spread his hands wide. "I am at your disposal."

"And Altra, too, I presume." Selenay's mouth quirked in a quick smile. "Although the idea of a cat being at anyone's disposal is rather at odds with the species."

Karal chuckled; he couldn't help it, since she was far too accurate. "Altra is also at your disposal to convey messages directly to Solaris so that you can have your answers immediately. If you would prefer, he and I can wait just outside your Council Chamber; you can have your pages bring me questions and Altra can take whatever communications you wish to have sent to Solaris, bringing back the answers. We are willing to remain on duty however long this takes to get settled."

"You may regret that offer." She wrote out something quickly; an order for an emergency Council session, he guessed. Talia took it outside to a page, and Selenay herself stood up. "I think we should hold the meeting here, in the interests of security," she said, and nodded at a door just to the side of the office. "You can remain there since you have offered. I will send a page to you every so often to make certain you don't perish of hunger or thirst. Is there anything I can send one for now?"

"Hot water and the row of mugs on my mantlepiece," he replied quickly. "It is medicine I am supposed to be drinking. Or else send to the Healers for more of it." His stomach gave a lurch, as if to remind him that it would be a bad idea to forget that medication.

Selenay gave a glance of inquiry at Talia who nodded. Satisfied, she returned her gaze to Karal.

"If you would go in there, I shall see your medicines are brought," she promised, as Talia rose and walked over to the door, opening it for him with an ironic bow and a little flourish. "If you would please take your place?"

He bowed to her with no irony whatsoever, and followed her gesture to the door Talia was holding open. The Queen's Own closed the door behind him, and he found himself in quite a cozy little room, equipped with a piece of furniture that could serve as both a bed and a couch and was supplied with a blanket neatly folded at the foot of it. There was a single table, and one wall was a floor-to-ceiling bookcase full of books. A tiny fireplace kept the room comfortably warm; at the moment the light from the single window was more than adequate, but there were candles on the table for after darkness fell.

A page's waiting room, or else the Queen's reading room, he recognized, and relaxed. If the meeting went on for very long—

:Not bad. You can sleep in here if they decide to debate things for hours.: Altra faded into view; predictably, he appeared sitting on the couch. *:They probably will—and you can certainly use the rest.:*

"You don't mind my promising your services as a messenger?" That had been the one thing he'd been nervous about.

:I expected it. I'll be pleased and surprised if they can agree on this in a day. It may take several.: Altra curled up on the couch leaving ample space for Karal. Karal took the implied invitation and sat beside him. *:Karal, I am very happy to be with you again. Believe me, it was not my choice that I was away for so long. I was needed elsewhere, but if there had been an emergency, I would have come to you at once.:*

Impulsively, he hugged the Firecat who purred just like any ordinary feline and rubbed his face against Karal's. "I can't even begin to say how happy I am to see you. I've missed you, Altra, I've missed you for *yourself*, and not just for what you are."

:I'll bet you didn't miss the cat fur up your nose.: Altra batted him playfully, which practically left him speechless. He'd never seen the Firecat in quite so light a mood!

:I don't need to scold you into sense or spine anymore. You're doing quite nicely on your own, leaving me free to be your friend as well as your adviser.:

Karal blushed with embarrassment and pleasure, and was left utterly speechless. But that was perfectly all right, since Altra was quite willing to fill in the silence.

:You might as well pick out a good book and get comfortable. There will be a page along shortly with your medicine and something to eat for both of us.: Altra curled up on the foot of the sofa, the end of his tail twitching ever so slightly. *:I believe that the fish is for me. Meanwhile, enjoy your leisure.:*

Karal smiled, scratched Altra's ears, and followed that very sound advice.

In the end it took two days of solid negotiations before an agreement was reached, two days broken only by an adjournment to sleep. Selenay or Talia often looked in on Karal during the process to make certain he was all right, and to keep him briefed on what was going on with the Council. This was a meeting of *only* the officials of Valdemar, as Karal had anticipated. What he had not anticipated, although he was very grateful for it, was the attitude of Valdemar's Councilors. They were all cautiously in favor of the visit when it was first proposed to them. What they felt needed clarification was precisely how this visit was to take place.

In the end, there were precautions asked for and conference on both sides. Only Karal, Altra, and Florian would be present at the Valdemar Gate-terminus as Solaris stepped through; that was her demand, and it was a wise one, since she would be particularly vulnerable to attack at that moment. All others, including the Herald-Mages on guard against trickery, would remain at a distance.

At the edge of Companion's Field, to be precise. The few standing remains of the Temple in the middle of the Field included the arch of the doorway. That doorframe had been used as a Gate-terminus many, many times in the past, when there had been mages and Herald-Mages able to create such things. Such use tended to attune the terminus to the forces of Gate-energy, and make each subsequent Gate construction a little easier, a little more stable. An'desha had said that he thought that this very tendency of stone to attune itself might be part of the basis for the long-lost ability to create the permanent Gates of the past.

One day, An'desha swore, he intended to go all the way back to his past as Ma'ar, and try to fathom out more of those secrets. Ma'ar had never known how to make permanent Gates; that mastery had been reserved for Urtho, the Mage of Silence. But Ma'ar knew many of the secrets, and An'desha hoped that by consulting with modern mages and the mages of k'Leshya he might be able to rediscover the long-lost method of building permanent Gates.

That was on the end of a long list of other priorities, however. And given what they were all going through because of the mage-storms, Karal doubted that any of the Allies would ever be willing to rely entirely—or even regularly—on permanent Gates for transportation. Physical transportation was far more reliable, and less likely to be affected by anything short of utter catastrophe.

Karal knew why it had only taken two days to come to this agreement. The Valdemarans (although they would never admit this) were willing to trust to the Companions as an informal front line and expected Florian to warn them if anything or anyone besides Solaris herself came through the Gate. And, no doubt, the Valdemarans knew he knew, and he knew they knew he knew, and so they were all very comfortable together, for that which could not be admitted could still be tacitly acknowledged.

It took another two days to make the necessary arrangements, and somehow it was all accomplished without anyone but the Council members and those who were immediately involved finding out. That in itself was a minor miracle.

At least, it had been accomplished without anyone likely to make a public nuisance of himself finding out. Without a doubt, people with other agendas than public ones had learned of her arrival. That was why, if the Valdemarans had not insisted on the Gate being in Companion's Field, Solaris would have insisted on it being either there or in the heart of the Palace. The Companions would work equally well to guard Solaris as to guard against her.

The weather even cooperated; it was clear and sunny, though very cold, as Karal waited beside the tumbled stones of the old Temple. There had been a thick, hard frost last night; where the stones were still in shadow, they were covered with a heavy coating of white. The ruin stood in the heart of a thickly wooded grove; *the* Grove, the Valdemarans called it, and for all that it stood in the center of Haven, in the middle of the Palace grounds, there was an air of great age and mystery about it. The ruined stones were piled around the foot of a bell-tower still in relatively good repair; the only other place where there were still two stones on top of each other was the stone arch.

:Well, here we are,: Florian said as his breath puffed out into the still morning air. *:Everything is as ready as it is ever likely to be.:*

"Except me," Karal replied. He was dressed in every bit of Sun-priest regalia he or Ulrich had ever owned, and it felt as if he now labored under twice his normal weight. He couldn't imagine how any of the high-ranking Sun-priests managed to wear these things day after day.

"Why did you volunteer for this anyway?" he continued, as Altra daintily picked his way through the stones and examined the ground to find a place fit for his regal rump.

:It occurred to me,: the Companion said, with grim humor, *:that anyone from Valdemar who might consider putting an arrow through Solaris would think twice about doing so with a Companion in the way. And I intend to be in the way at all times.:*

"Ah." Karal inserted a finger in his collar and pulled on it to ease it a bit. "Well, that's certainly logical. I can't imagine anyone in Valdemar having the temerity to shoot anywhere near one of you lot."

:Thank you.: Florian had been groomed to within an inch of his life this morning, and although he was not wearing a saddle, he did have the full formal barding and belled halter that Companions normally wore for special occasions. His mane and tail were braided in multiple strands with blue and silver ribbons, and each braid ended in a silver bell. *:May I say that I hope your rigout is not as uncomfortable as mine?:*

"Oh, it is; probably more so." Karal smiled. "If it was any heavier or stiffer, I wouldn't be able to walk."

:And they say that rank is not a burden!: Florian tossed his braided mane to the wild chiming of tiny bells, and whickered his amusement. *:I could wish I was a Firecat; at least they don't have to put up with being beaded and braided.:*

The Firecat looked back over his shoulder. *:No, but when I am done, you will be glad you only need to bear beads and bells. Building a Gate is not like Jumping—well, you'll see. This is, in my opinion, a small price to pay for the great good that will come out of it.:*

With that, Altra examined the ground further, and something occurred to Karal. Altra was going to expend a great deal of energy—and concentration. He wasn't going to be able to concentrate if he was shivering. He needed to be off the cold ground, but none of them had thought to bring anything for Altra to sit on.

Wait a moment—Florian was not wearing a saddle, but he was carrying an ornamental blanket.

As he turned to ask Florian if he could borrow the blanket, Florian reached around and pulled the silver-embroidered blue blanket from his back with his teeth, clearly with the same idea in mind.

:Here. There's something appropriate about Altra sitting on a Valdemaran blanket to bring Solaris here from Karse, isn't there?:

Altra pivoted to face them again as Karal took the blanket from Florian. His blue eyes went from Karal to Florian and back again. *:Thank you,:* he said simply. *:This is why the Alliance will work.:*

:At least it is why we three make a good team, pulling as one in the same harness,: Florian said with amusement.

Altra snorted, indicating a place for Karal to lay the blanket with a tap of his paw. *:Trust a horse to say we work in harness. I would have said we were running the same prey.:*

:So you would,: Florian replied agreeably, watching Altra settle himself on the blanket. *:And you may have my share of the mice we take.:*

:And you, my share of the corn they were eating. Gentlemen, are we prepared? Hansa is ready on his side.:

It was a rhetorical question, and they all knew it. Karal gave his tunic a last tug, while Florian positioned himself very carefully beside him. They both turned their attention to the stone arch.

Every muscle on Altra's body was tense; not even his tail twitched. The stones of the arch began to glow, faintly at first, but the brightness increased with every passing heartbeat. Then, between one moment and the next, there was blackness inside the arch instead of the view of the stones and weeds on the other side.

A few tendrils of energy licked across the blackness; slowed lightning was all Karal could think of. Every hair on Altra's body stood on end, puffing him up to twice his normal size. More tendrils appeared, and still more—

Then, just as suddenly as the blackness had appeared, it vanished. But the view through the archway was not that of the ruins; it was of a wall of books and a wooden floor—and Solaris, with Hansa sitting beside her, the precise mirror-image of Altra.

The scene held for only a single moment, not even as long as it took to cough. Solaris wasted no time at all in acting, stepping through the stone archway with all the casual aplomb of one walking from one room to the other—

Except, of course, that she was stepping across a distance so vast it had taken Karal weeks to cross it. And that she, too, was in her full formal robes as the Son of the Sun, the Voice of Vkandis, the ruler of all Karse.

She glittered with gold; her robes were sewn with plates of it rather than simply being embroidered with gold bullion and braid. Her jewels of office were twice the size of Karal's. She was as covered with gold and sun-gems as the statue of Vkandis Himself. Karal wondered how she could move.

But move she did, from Karse to Valdemar and away from the Gate quickly, so that Altra and Hansa could break the connection and close it down. The instant she was clear, that was precisely what they did; the Gate went black, then vanished completely, leaving only the view of the ruins in the picturesque archway.

Altra sagged, and Solaris bent quickly to support him for a moment until he regained his strength. "Thank you, Altra," Karal heard her say very quietly. "That was well and smoothly done."

If Altra made any answer, he made it only to her, for Karal "heard" nothing. When the Firecat seemed better, Solaris straightened and turned her attention to those waiting to welcome her.

Karal quailed beneath that direct gaze, as hard to meet as the full glare of the sun at noonday on the Summer Solstice. He shivered and tried to drop his eyes, entirely overwhelmed and not just by the fact that he was in the presence of his ruler. He now had what he had *never* wanted, the full and undivided attention of the Son of the Sun. But more than that, he stood before Solaris with a heavy knowledge in his heart that he had failed her; he had broken his promise to her by failing to keep Ulrich safe.

He trembled, and her gaze softened; for a moment he saw the woman beneath the High Priest. Her mask dropped altogether at that moment; she took several swift steps forward, and before he could bow to her, she caught his shoulders in her hands, then embraced him.

"I need not be the Sun's Son just yet," she whispered into his ear as he forgot to breathe. "And Karal—I know. I know what you feel. You did the best you could, and if you can be said to have failed at all, it is because I gave you tasks suited for a score of seasoned mages and priests, not for one young man alone. The trouble is, I did not have those seasoned mages and priests to send here. I had only you, and hope, and you have repaid that hope by accomplishing more than anyone had a right to expect."

He felt caught in the silence and could not reply.

"Twice now, I have unthinkingly given you a task too great for you, and I am sorry. Can you forgive me?" She released him so that he could look into her anxious eyes. He nodded dumbly, and her eyes brightened with a suspicion of tears. "Oh, Karal," she breathed. "I miss him too!"

That was too much for him; with a spasm of heart and throat, he lost all of his control and broke down, weeping. But she was doing the same, and the two of them wept together in silence.

She regained control of herself first, though she did not push him away. Instead, she held him while he wept himself out, while the pain of loss ebbed, and released him only when *he* made a tentative move to free himself.

"Here," she said, handing him a handkerchief which she produced out of the capacious sleeves of her robes. "I had the feeling this would happen, and I came prepared." She managed a wan smile, for a moment more, no longer the Son of the Sun, but just a harried and weary woman. "The one thing these robes are good for is being prepared. I could hide a donkey, a week's provisions, and a small tent in these sleeves."

That made him laugh, as she must have known it would. He composed himself as she carefully removed the last damage from her tears and resumed her dignity. Karal blotted his own face, glad that the cold air would quickly restore him and that the redness of his eyes would be attributed to staring into the bright sun for too long. When he was ready, he nodded to her, and with Florian at her left and himself at her right, and a much-subdued and slightly shaky Altra bringing up the rear, they moved out of the Grove and toward the waiting delegation.

Selenay waited there, clearly visible among the rest in her white and gold, as impressive in her simplicity as Solaris was in her ornate robes. Beside her stood her Companion, as beaded and belled as Florian, but wearing full formal tack, including a saddle; behind her stood Talia and Prince Daren and their Companions, likewise bedecked, and the rest of the welcoming delegation behind them. Those who were not Heralds had dressed in sun colors as a tribute to Solaris; they made a bright and welcoming patch of warm color against the dead, gray-brown grass and barren branches.

It was an interesting moment; the first face-to-face meeting of two strong-willed, strong-minded women, both the rulers in their own lands, and each of them once the greatest enemy of the other. Karal felt the pressure of their gazes as Solaris approached with that graceful, gliding step he could never emulate. Neither of them had an iota of attention for anyone else.

Finally Solaris stopped, no more than a pace or two from her counterpart, both of them eyeing each other for a breathless moment of assessment.

Breathless, indeed; once again, Karal forgot to breathe. Would they hate each other? When they were so far distant from one another, personal feelings had meant nothing, but now that they were within touching distance, it was imperative that they at least be able to tolerate each other! What if they were instant enemies?

His heart pounded painfully in his ears as he waited for one or the other of them to speak—or *something!*

Finally, though, it was Selenay who broke the impasse, and she did it with a smile.

"Talia told me that we were much alike, Holiness," she said, as Solaris answered that smile with a wary one of her own. "I suspect that she was being tactful."

"Very tactful, Majesty," Solaris replied, in that peculiar, carrying voice that never seemed to rise above conversational level, yet could reach clearly to the back of the Temple. "But I would expect that level of tact, knowing Our Priestess."

Cleverly phrased; Karal marveled at how clever—in the same breath, by saying "I" first, she had given Selenay notice that they were equals and she was claiming no special precedence for herself, even as Selenay had not. But by referring to Talia as "Our" Priestess, she reminded Selenay that unlike the Valdemaran ruler, Solaris spoke with more voices than her own. Talia was a Priestess to Vkandis as well as Solaris, and where Solaris was, so, too, was her God.

"I suspect," Solaris continued, reinforcing that status of equals with another "I", "that what she truly meant and would not say is that we are *too* much alike."

She raised a long, thin, elegant eyebrow at Talia, for the first time taking her attention from the Valdemaran Queen. Talia had donned Karsite Sun-priest robes—but they were in white and silver, rather than black and gold, in token of her dual duties as Priest and Herald. Another nicely balanced gesture.

Talia blushed, as Selenay chuckled very softly, and relaxed the tiniest bit. Karal relaxed a great deal more than that; finally letting out the breath he had been holding. *They like each other! Oh, thank you, Vkandis!* Solaris was *never* that frank except with people she liked and trusted. She would never lie, but she was a past master at partial truth and dissimulation. She had to be, after all; she could not have gotten as far as she had if she was not.

Then again, although he could not speak from personal experience, Selenay was probably just as clever.

Solaris moved forward the remaining few paces and held out her hand. Selenay took it immediately, clasping it heartily.

"Now, Holiness," the Queen of Valdemar said, turning adroitly so that she now stood side-by-side with the Son of the Sun, "if I may begin the introductions. Talia you know—and this is my husband and consort, Prince Daren…"

Karal took a discreet step to the rear, placing himself in a modest position behind his ruler; at last laying all the intolerable burden of authority on the proper shoulders to bear it.

7

Dear gods, it's a frozen wasteland out there. Commander Tremane—who no longer thought of himself as a Grand Duke, nor in any other context than as the commander of his men—gazed out at the now-empty courtyard of his stronghold. It was buried beneath snow that reached to the knee, and the weather-wizard from the town said that more was coming. Even though the old wreck couldn't *change* the weather anymore, he could still predict it, and he thought he could teach one or two of Tremane's mages the trick. *Snow. I haven't had to deal with this much snow since the years I spent on my estate.* In the Imperial capital, of course, all snow was neatly steered away from the city itself, except for a dusting that looked ornamental and could easily be swept from the streets.

Winter had arrived, bypassing most of fall altogether. But with the help of his men, the locals had gotten their crops in, the foraging parties had brought in bales of hay, baskets of wheat and root crops, pecks of nuts and fruits, and even some livestock that had not gone altogether feral. The armed parties had brought back some of the livestock that *had* gone feral, in the form of carcasses now hanging frozen in a locked warehouse in the city. Ownership of those carcasses was not a matter of dispute; Tremane owned them, traded one-for-one for Tremane's half of the living animals collected. The fresh meat would be a welcome change from the preserved and salted meat in the Imperial warehouses— having it so far from camp, while it increased the chances of pilferage, ensured that the cooks would do as he had ordered, and plan meals that alternated fresh meat with preserved. He didn't want the fresh meat used up all at once, leaving only preserved. The men would complain, and rightfully, if meal after meal was nothing but the salty stews and other dishes that were all that could be made with preserved meat. It was a little thing, but in winter, and under the conditions that the men were now living in, little things could amount to great problems of morale.

It could be worse. Snow is not the worst thing that could happen to us. He was happy enough with snow, actually, because two days ago what had come down out of the sky was an ice-storm. Snow was infinitely preferable to ice that made walking between buildings into an ordeal. There were two men down with broken legs, five with broken arms, and a half dozen with broken collarbones, according to the roster.

Such injuries were not the calamity they would have been a few weeks ago, when he had needed every able-bodied person. The walls were completed; so were the new barracks. The builders had arrived at a clever and elegant solution to the heating problem—or, rather, one that made the best use of limited fuel and equally limited time for building. It was a variation on the idea of a furnace that one of his own men had concocted.

The barracks were still being finished inside, but that could be done while the men were living in them. As long as there was room to put down bedrolls, that was what mattered. They were similar in design to the plan of the earth-sheltered buildings he had looked at earlier, but instead of making the entirety of one wall into a chimney, these plans arranged for the warm air to run under the floor to the opposite wall, and there were additional chimneys built into the support posts. Directly above the furnace were brick ovens for baking and depressions shaped exactly like the huge army kettles for heating water and making soups and stews.

That meant there were *no* windows, so all light came from candles and lanterns. What the barracks lacked in light, they made up for in warmth. Tremane reflected that if a vote had been taken, the men would probably have voted against windows in favor of heat in any case.

Of course, since they had not been consulted, the men called the new barracks "the holes," or "the caves," and although they were not happy about living in such dank and poorly-lighted places, a fair majority of them admitted that the barracks were far, far preferable to not having solid shelter.

They had still been in their tents when the first ice-storm hit. They had been a great deal less happy about that, as fully half the tents had collapsed beneath the weight of the ice that had built up on them. It was amazing how quickly the last bit of building went up after that.

There was a faint but persistent smoky animal odor about the places, caused by the dung bricks and peat blocks they were burning instead of wood in the furnaces. It wasn't too unpleasant, though the men complained about that too, claiming it got into the bread and the soup. He had given orders that strong herbs be added to both to cover the scent and taste.

There were plenty of complaints; the rumor mill was positively acidic these days, but the complaints and rumors were all of the sort that appeared when people had an excess of time and energy, and none were the kind that presaged mutiny. In fact, in a strange way they were a sign of health; the natural result when men who were used to activity were confined in comfortable but boring surroundings.

I will have to find creative ways for them to use up all the energy. Wood gathering parties—hunting parties, too. But that won't take very many. Snow maneuvers? Or perhaps something in the town? But what? I don't want to have them take over the duties of the local constables this soon; that could only cause resentment.

Tremane had made certain that the men were given leave to go into town on a regular basis; there was no point in cooping them up in barracks when a mug of beer and an hour with a pliant girl would make them cheerful again. The townsfolk were getting along reasonably well with the men and vice versa; the only incidents had been caused by drunkenness, either on the part of the soldier or more rarely of one of the townsfolk, and all had been resolved. As might be expected, the man who was drunk was usually to blame, and punishment was meted out by the appropriate authority. Between them, Tremane and the Shonar council had established a list of infractions and punishments, based on the Imperial Code, that was applied to townsman and Imperial soldier impartially.

On the whole, Tremane's world was in relatively good shape, as long as he kept his gaze within the walls of Shonar.

Outside, however—

From somewhere beyond the walls, out in the snowy gloom, came a high, thin wail. *One of them.* That cry had not come from the throat of a wolf, a lynx, or a feral dog; it had come from... something else. He heard them howling and wailing at night from dusk to dawn, and the sentries on the walls reported shadows by dusk and glowing eyes in the dark, gazing up at them and then vanishing. Whatever they were, they were smarter than the spider-creature, for they had not been caught— but he pitied the farmers who had declined the hospitality of the town for the winter. It must be terrible to hear those creatures crying beneath the windows, and know that only one thin wall of wood separated you and your family from them. Did they snuffle at the cracks under the doors, and sniff at the barred shutters? Did they scratch at the walls or gnaw on the doorposts? He hoped that long before the beasts became a danger, those farmers would change their minds and pack up what they could, and head for the high brick walls of Shonar, driving their stock before them. Thus far, whatever they were, the walls were keeping them out— but every mage-storm brought more and potentially worse creatures to roam the snow-covered landscape. And the winter had just begun...

Turn your eyes within your walls, Tremane.

The roofs of his barracks, like the roofs of most of the buildings in town, were thick thatch, and pitched steeply enough that a buildup of ice merely broke free and slid down the straw rather than collapsing the roof. That had been necessity rather than wisdom, but it was fortuitous; the same storm that had collapsed half of the tents had collapsed the roof of one building in town that had been covered with plates of slate rather than bundles of thatch. Yes, with thatch there was a danger of fire, and that was a consideration. By design, though, there would be no chance of a soot fire in Tremane's barracks, for all soot built up in the roof of the furnace itself, and could be poked loose when the furnace was stoked.

Tremane's roof here was slate—but laid over stone rather than wood. This manor had been designed to last for centuries, which was no bad thing at the moment. Some of the rooms were perishingly cold, but very few of the officers or mages spent much time in their tiny closet-sized rooms. If the room was cold, one could always warm up in the Great Hall before retiring, send a servant in with a bedwarmer first, and then bury oneself in blankets with a hot brick for comfort at bedtime. There was no lack of servants now; plenty of folk were happy to serve in Tremane's manor. *Imperial coin spends better than their own now. Ours is of fair weight, and theirs has often been shaved and clipped.*

But there were few places, other than his suite here, that were truly warm. In that much, he envied his men their "caves." Many of the floors on the first story of the manor were of stone and no treat to stand on; even through thick bootsoles, cold numbed the feet. Someone had recalled the old country trick of covering the floors with a thick layer of rushes mixed with herbs to keep them sweet, and he'd ordered the floors of those rooms with no carpet so buried, which had helped with cold drafts coming up the legs of one's trews. The men on housekeeping detail and the newly-hired servants had appreciated the move, since it meant they no longer had to sweep and wash the floors on a daily basis. The only exception was in the room he was using as the manor mess hall; there he would allow no rushes, and the daily sweeping and scrubbing went on as it had in the summer.

Outside the bubbly glass of the window, snow fell in fat flakes the size of coins. You couldn't even make out the clouds when you looked up, for the sky was a solid sheet of gray-white. *Clouds? You can't even see the sun!*

His nose itched, and he sneezed convulsively as his foot crushed a sprig of a pungent herb carried up from the lower floors. He let it lie there; the stuff was everywhere anyway, and just as well. The only product of the mage-storms to pass inside the walls was not a huge, vicious monster, but a tiny, vicious monster, and a prolific one at that. It had probably begun life as a flea; it was about the same size and general shape as a flea, but it was venomous. Not enough to poison a man, but certainly unpleasant; its bite left painful boils that had to be lanced and drained immediately or they went rotten. One of the locals had found a common herb that kept them away, so now every clothes chest, every bed, and every storage closet smelled of the stuff. Sprigs of it were in the rushes, and crushed on the bare floors. Both town and barracks were coping with the plague, but there were many poor people who couldn't afford the herb and were suffering from the bites of the thing. He'd heard that the poor were carting off the discarded rushes and searching through Imperial rubbish piles for the dried-out bits of the herb. He'd left orders not to stop them. He hated to think of children covered with bites from the things...

At least the cold weather would probably kill what specimens were outside, and as for those inside—bored men were hunting the things down and keeping tallies of the kills. It might be prolific, but it couldn't last long under those conditions, unless it lingered in the slums.

So there is my life; reduced from candidacy for Emperor to a war against monsters and fleas.

Well, better monsters and fleas than other things he could name.

He had a full war sentry out on the walls; men posted every few paces with pitch torches burning between them at night. The watches were for four marks, but if it got as cold as Tremane feared it might, he intended to reduce the watches to two marks. It would be pretty pointless to make all this effort at building tight, warm barracks only to afflict the men standing sentry watch with frostbite.

Those that were not standing watch he'd assigned to finishing their own barracks. The floors were rough wood and needed to be finished and polished so they could be kept clean. There were still the partitions to put up, the bunks and storage lockers to build, walls to plaster, furniture to put together. And when they finished all that, he'd think of something else for them to do. Maybe build attic space beneath the thatch; lowering the ceiling would conserve still more heat.

And still no contact from the Emperor, not that he had expected any. Oh, it was *possible* that one of his agents could have made it back to the capital to report the looting of the warehouse, and it was possible that the Emperor would then have gotten together a score of powerful mages to open a Portal and fetch Tremane home to justice. It was even possible that Charliss would have sent a physical message with a physical, overland courier or with a troop of heavily armed men and mages. Whether or not he did so would depend on how badly the Empire was suffering the forces of the mage-storms—if indeed the Empire was suffering them at all.

But as the days had stretched into weeks, the possibility of Imperial recontact diminished rapidly. Now, with the onset of winter, there was no way that even a physical courier would be able to reach them. It would take something the size of the army he already had to do so, for travel across the winter landscape would be impossible under these conditions unless one had an army.

So now Tremane stared down at the wintry isolation beyond his windows that was an uncomfortable mirror for the state of his own spirits.

Well, I certainly have my empire now. A small one, but all mine. I doubt that anyone is likely to dispute me for it until spring.

"Commander, sir?" One of his many aides was at the door; he turned to face the boy, composing his own expression into one calculated to bring confidence.

"Yes, Nevis?" he replied, keeping his tone even.

"Sir, there is a rather—odd group of men here to see you." The boy was clearly puzzled. "Frankly, sir, I don't know what to make of them. They're none of them from the same units or even the same disciplines, but they say they wish to see you for the same reason and that they must speak with you personally."

"And they won't tell you what it is?" He pursed his lips at the aide's nod. "Well, perhaps you'd better show them in. It might be we have another nasty little insect to contend with, one that bites people in... places they'd rather not discuss."

The boy flushed, which amused Tremane; how *had* that youngster managed to climb through the ranks and still be able to blush at the idea of a flea that bit a man's privates? "I'll bring them up, sir," he said hastily, and took his leave.

Blue dusk outside the window gave little light for a meeting, and one thing they had in abundance was candles. There must have been hundreds of sealed caskets of candles, and hundreds more of the cruder tallow dips. Tremane set about lighting them himself before the delegation arrived. He'd set the last one alight and was trimming the wick when Nevis brought in the men.

They were a very mixed bag, some dozen or so of them. One mage, one of his high-ranking generals—which was probably why Nevis hadn't dared send them away without consulting Tremane—two sergeants, two lieutenants, and an assortment of scouts and troopers.

That's odd. The one and only thing these men have in common is that they were all someone's agent, and I doubt any of them know that the others are agents—

He sat down behind his desk and contemplated the sober-faced group before him while Nevis closed the door. "Well," he said finally. "I hope this is not the prelude to a mutiny."

General Bram laughed. "Hardly, Commander. In fact, that's the point, and I'll be brief. I've no doubt you already knew this, but we're all spies—some of us reported to your rivals; I reported to the Emperor. We've decided to come admit it and fling ourselves upon your mercy. You're too good a leader to throw us away; our request is that you retain us in our current positions."

Tremane was very glad that he was sitting down; agents were not normally that blunt and open. *Not normally? This is unprecedented! A mass defection to my side? I don't think that's ever happened in the history of the Empire!* "I—ah—take it you all knew each other?" he said, hoping he did not sound as dazed as he felt.

"Of course," said the mage—a minor fellow, Tremane didn't even remember his name, but he had just recently been graduated from Apprentice. "Just as you knew who we were." He shrugged. "That's the whole game-within-the-game, now, isn't it? We all knew each other, though until we all got together this afternoon, none of us knew who the masters of the other fellows were."

"Were," Tremane repeated carefully. "Not 'are'."

"Were," General Bram said firmly. "What's the point in beating around the bush, hoping to flush a bird that scuttled away hours ago? We haven't had any more contact than you have, and what's the point of serving a man you haven't heard from since the beginning of a crisis? About half the lot that stayed on the other side when you organized that raid on the storehouse were agents, too, and if our masters were ever going to contact us again, it would have been a week or so after the raid." He shrugged. "There's no point in pretending otherwise; we've been abandoned out here, and we all know it."

"Bram called us all together to talk it over, but we'd all been thinking the same thing," the mage said, scratching his unruly hair. "They're there, and you're here; you could have had the Portal opened just for you and an escort big enough to get you to your estate. You stuck with us. By our way of thinking, that makes you a better master than the ones back home."

"The gods know you're more dependable," said one of the scouts in a disgusted voice. "Anyway, we came to show you who all the agents in your ranks were just in case you'd missed any of us, and let you know we're coming over to you so you can stop worrying about sabotage from inside. That'd be like poking a hole in the bottom of the boat you're riding in anyway."

"I see." He took a moment to settle himself, for of all the unlikely events he'd endured in the last several months, this was the least likely of all. It was utterly unprecedented; agents simply did *not* go over to the man they were sent to spy on, much less come over *en masse*!

"Fact is, Tremane, you're the most popular commander I've ever seen," Bram said, with wonder and a tinge of envy. "There isn't a man out there, for all the complaints, who doesn't know you could have left us high and dry, doesn't know everything you've done since we bivouacked here has been aimed at keeping 'em all alive and healthy. It wasn't just the way you kept up their pay; after the way you went around digging the men out of collapsed tents and making sure none of 'em was hurt or frostbit, there isn't one of 'em that wouldn't serve you for nothing. I'll stake my reputation on that."

I'm a popular commander? he thought, with another twinge of bemusement. Again, it was nothing he had expected, although it was something he had hoped would happen. He hadn't a clue what made a "popular" commander, and he wasn't certain anyone did. Commanders who had not only kept up pay, but paid bonuses, had not been popular; successful commanders had not been popular. Even commanders who had made attempts to curry favor with the troops had not been popular. *I'm working them hard and I intend to go on doing so to keep them busy. I've asked them to perform tasks wildly outside their duty. I might have been keeping up with their pay, but it's no secret that the pay chests are going to run dry some time in late spring or early summer. I try to be fair and impartial when I'm administering justice, but there is no guarantee that I will always be right. I simply haven't done a thing that should make me so overwhelmingly popular that even Bram should notice.*

But if Bram and the other agents had made note of the fact that he was "popular," there was no doubt it must be true, and he was not about to inquire too closely into the lineage of this particular gift horse.

I can only hope that I continue to enjoy that popularity. The winter is young. And it's going to be the hardest winter these men have ever seen.

"Gentlemen," he said finally. "I accept both your allegiance and your request to remain in your current positions. I only ask that you in your turn continue gathering intelligence—or rather, let us call it, simple information—and report back to me directly." He fixed Bram with a stern gaze, picking the General as the ringleader of the group. "I don't want to hear about the men's private lives. I don't want to hear about simple grumblings. You are all experienced enough to know when the men are just venting frustration. I want to know about *real* difficulties, complaints that need attention, things I can *do* something about. Or serious situations I might not be able to do anything about directly, but which I must be aware of."

With thought, or even direct appeal to the men, I might even be able to cope with those. The Hundred Little Gods know that no one in the Imperial Army has tried direct appeal to the men in generations.

"Oh?" Bram replied, putting a volume of meaning into the single word.

"I have no choice," he said heavily. "I am being frank with you all, because you are all intelligent men. *We* have no choice. I believe I am the only man in this benighted place with the experience, with the *fitness* to lead here. You must think the same, or you would not be here. If I am to be the leader, I must have all the information I can get, and I must not ignore unpleasant information because I don't like it. I rely on you to bring me that unpleasant information because I am not sure my own people will, every time."

That was a bit of a lie, but a tiny lie of that nature might well cement them further to his cause. And the truth was, these men who had been used to looking for weaknesses in his leadership on behalf of another master were more likely to see such weaknesses than his own agents. They'd have had practice, after all.

General Bram nodded, very solemnly. "We can do that. Are you at all interested in any of us taking a more active role, if we see something a word or two can set right?" He smiled rather grimly. "The Hundred Little Gods themselves know we are used to looking for situations where a word or two can set them wrong."

"Yes," he replied decisively. "You aren't stupid; you know not to expose yourselves. I'll make this bargain of trust with you. You can trust me to do the best I can for every man in our forces; I will trust you to do the best you can to keep me in power." Again, he fixed Bram with that gimlet stare. "This is not a situation where the men can be permitted to rule by popular vote, for there will be things I must do that will not be popular. *My* hand must remain on the reins, mine and no other, or there will be disaster." He smiled slightly. "There is a saying that it is not wise to change drivers in the middle of a charge. I am the driver of the war chariot in this charge, and you had all better stick with me or be thrown beneath the wheels while you're grabbing at the reins."

Bram, who had led no few charges in his time, nodded. "I can agree with all of that—and I believe that I can speak for all of us in agreeing with your conditions." He looked down at his feet for a moment, then looked up again, with a peculiar expression on his face. "You are the best leader we could hope for in this situation, Tremane. You've got civilian experience we old war dogs lack; and where you get your foresight, I'll be damned if I know. And you've got two other things that can't be calculated; you've got luck, and you've got heart. We won't be rid of a leader with that combination."

Tremane closed his eyes for a moment. Of all the many things that had happened here, this was of a piece with the rest. Luck, was it? Well, he was not about to spit on luck, and he would capitalize on every piece of luck he got, but he was not going to count on it either. Perhaps that was the essence of luck.

He opened his eyes. "Gentlemen, thank you. Never forget that we must all work together to save our people here. Remember that *our* people now include these Hardornens of Shonar, although they may not yet realize that fact—and never forget that in the future, to continue to preserve all our lives, we may have to look for friends in strange places."

The General saluted slowly in answer to this, and without another word, led the delegation of former spies out and back to their posts.

After the snow cleared off, they had steady cold but sparkling and beautiful weather for two days. The weather was *so* cloudless that Tremane began to wonder if the Hardornen weather-wizard was losing his talent at weather prediction to the mage-storms. The old man kept insisting that there was more bad snow on the way, and a great deal of it, but where was it?

If they couldn't rely on the weather-wizard for predictions, it would make preparations a great deal more difficult.

The third day dawned just as clear and beautiful as the first two, and Tremane was just about resigned to the fact that the old man was slipping. Restlessness made him eager to stretch his legs in the afternoon, after a long day of dealing with the paperwork needed to keep up with the state of the supplies in the warehouses, and he decided to go in an unusual direction. Rather than taking his walk down, to make another informal inspection, he would go up, to the walkway at the top of his tower. The weather was good, the air still, the sun bright enough that even up there, exposed, he shouldn't get too chilled until he'd walked out his restlessness. The tower was the highest spot in all of Shonar; he should get a good view of the surrounding countryside outside the walls from there. He might even spot one of the furtively lurking monsters.

It was a long walk, but worth it; he left his escort at the foot of the last stair, for he intended to savor the rare experience of being outdoors and yet completely alone.

I have not been alone except in my own rooms since I accepted this post. I have not stood alone beneath an open sky since my last hunt on my own land.

The stairs came right up onto the roof; there was a small slant-roofed affair covering the last few of them, rather than a trapdoor one had to push open. He approved of the arrangement; if there'd been enough heavy snow, he wouldn't have been able to budge a trap door.

He opened the door at the top to emerge into brilliant sunlight that made his eyes water even as it lifted his heart. What was it about sunlight that made a man feel so much better? He was glad now that he'd ordered a general standing-down for all the men during the past two days; he'd heard they were doing absurd, lighthearted things, acting like schoolboys, making snow forts and having snow fights—creating snow sculptures. *I wonder if I ought to give out prizes for the best snow sculpture? Should I order a winter festival? That wouldn't be a bad notion! It would give the men something to occupy them that had nothing to do with duty!* He resolved to find out what sort of festival these people celebrated; he could make it a joint effort of garrison and town, foster some friendly competitions between the two.

Skating races, sled races—an archery contest—could we somehow adapt stickball to snow or ice?

Someone had been up here already, clearing away the snow. The brilliant sun had evaporated what had been left behind, leaving bare stone beneath his sheepskin boots. He moved forward to the edge of the parapet and looked down.

Below him were part of the manor, a few of the barracks, and beyond them, the walls. His men stood at their regulation intervals along it; not at all like statues, for he had made sure his orders included that they move about to keep themselves warm, and that each man be permitted to chat with the ones next to him provided they kept their regulation distance and didn't bunch up. Some of them were stamping their feet to warm them, others leaned on the edge of the wall, talking, and one was even making snowballs and lobbing them off into the distance, while the ones stationed at either side of him watched. They were probably wagering on how far he was throwing them. There was no sign at all from here of the night-monsters, although prints had been reported in the snow and the mages were trying to work out what kind of creature could make such prints. Tremane wished them luck; judging by the spider-creature, there was no telling what odd beasts might suffer changes into something unrecognizable.

I would rather not imagine a vole, which must eat its own weight in prey three times a day, transmuted to something the size of a cart horse.

He made a quarter-turn, and now looked out at Shonar, all of which lay beneath the level of this tower. It was not a big town by the standards of the Empire, and from here it was easy to see the signs of decline; abandoned houses where the thatch had disappeared or rotted, warehouses and workshops where walls had fallen in or been broken down. There were a lot of them; more than he had guessed, and certainly more than the Town Council would want to admit. If Ancar had not been killed, he would have driven his land into oblivion in a few more years, by taking the able-bodied and leaving behind those unable to keep towns, farms, and businesses going.

He was mad. There is no doubt of it. Irrational anger stirred briefly in Tremane's heart, but it faded quickly, for what, after all, was the point? Ancar was dead, dead as last year's grass. What was important was this; there were empty and abandoned structures in the town that could be taken over and put to good use. *That* was what he would do when the men were finished with their barracks; he'd send them into town and begin repairing and refurbishing the houses, warehouses, and workshops. Those would become Imperial property—and he would have his quarters for married couples, his workshops for men wanting to retire into a profession.

Satisfied with that idea, he made another quarter-turn to look out over more of his barracks and empty land beyond the walls.

The men down below him were drilling in an area cleared of snow; the ones on the walls doing much the same things as the men on the other side. The one difference was that two of them were having a snowball-hurling contest with improvised slings. *Now there's an idea for a festival competition Target-throwing snowballs with bare hands and with slings. There certainly won't be any dispute about where they hit!*

But as he raised his eyes past the level of the walls and out over the landscape beyond, he was puzzled, sorely puzzled. There were no mountains in that direction, so what was that long, dark line on the horizon? A forest of exceptionally tall trees? But it was so far away!

A moment later, a wind sprang up out of nowhere, and the long, dark line moved nearer—and he knew what it was.

Huge clouds, black and heavy with snow, were hurtling toward him on the wind that blew into his face. The old weather-wizard had been right!

Before he could call out anything to the sentries on that side, they had already reacted to the rising wind by leaving off their games and conversations and peering toward the horizon. It took them longer to see what he had because of his higher vantage, but as the clouds raced into their field of vision, they reacted.

"Is that a storm?"

"Looks like one to me!"

Shouts up and down the line quickly confirmed what Tremane knew, and one of the men with an alarm-horn at his belt lifted it to his lips and began to blow.

Three long, steady tones and a pause, repeated for as long as the man had breath, that was the agreed-upon signal for a heavy storm approaching. It might seem alarmist to signal the approach of a storm, but Tremane was taking no chances. He'd heard of dreadful snowstorms in the far north where men could get lost and freeze to death not a dozen ells from their own doorstep. If there were men outside the walls, hunting or gathering wood, he wanted them alerted and homeward bound before a storm hit.

Other men with alarm-horns all across the walls took up the call, amplifying it and sending it out over the snow-covered fields and into the woods.

The men drilling stopped what they were doing at a barked order; a moment later, the officer in charge divided them into one group for each barracks, and marched them off to the piles of dung bricks, peat bricks, and wood to stockpile fuel beside each barracks' furnace. Below him, Tremane saw men going off purposefully in small groups, presumably sent on other errands by their officers. He didn't even *have* to send men into town to fetch back the ones on leave of absence—they were coming in through the gates by threes and fours, secure that although their excursions had been cut short the time would be made up later.

It was all running like a smoothly-oiled clockwork, and he marveled at it. *It wasn't just my foresight; they understand why the orders are there, and they're cooperating. If a bad storm is on the way, I want our men here so that their officers can account for all of them and we can send out search parties for the missing.*

Well, *he* had better get back to his desk so his officers knew where *he* was! The clouds had already filled up half the sky to the north, and now even the men below the walls could see them. They weren't getting any lighter the nearer they got, either, and the wind was picking up. There was a damp bite to the wind, something that was almost, though not quite, a scent.

Was that lightning? He paused for a moment and stared in fascination. It was! It was lightning! He'd *heard* of lightning in a heavy snowstorm, but this was the first time he'd ever seen it!

As if to remind him that he was lingering too long, a growl of thunder reached his ears.

He turned and pulled open the door to the roof, hurrying back down to the escort of guards waiting.

"Bad storm coming," he said to them.

"We heard the alarm, Commander," the leader told him. "Is there anything you want to assign us to?"

He thought for a moment. "Just to be on the safe side, once you leave me at my office, go down to the chirurgeons and see what they'd want in the way of a snow-rescue kit and put one together for them. I don't believe there's anyone of ours likely to get caught out there, but you never know, and that's one thing I forgot to look into."

The leader of his guards saluted, and once the escort left him at the door to his office, they hurried off to follow his orders.

He walked back to his desk and sat down but restlessness was on him and it was hard to just sit there and wait while the windows darkened and the alarm call rang out, muffled by stone and glass. The one thing he could *not* do in a case like this, however, was to run off and see what was going on. If there was an emergency, he needed to be where people expected to find him.

Search parties… if I need to send out search parties, how can I keep them together, and prevent their getting lost? How can you set a trail in a blinding snowstorm?

As long as they weren't searching a forest, the men could go roped together like a climbing party. That would prevent them from getting separated. But what about a trail back to safety?

If it's still daylight… sticks? Red-painted sticks? It was too late to go painting sticks—*No, wait, we still have all the sticks from surveying the walls and a lot of chalk line.* He made a note to get both out of storage. *You might see lanterns through thick snow.* Another note. *Bells. You might hear bells. Weren't there ankle and wrist bells with those dancers' costumes that no one in town wanted to trade for?* He noted down the bells as well. The chirurgeons would know best what a half-frozen victim would need; he'd leave that part of the kit up to them.

I wish there was a better way of getting around in snow besides walking. Well, there wasn't and that was that. But if they're looking for someone who's half-buried in snow, perhaps they ought to have walking sticks to probe the snow for a body. Blunt spear shafts would do, and they might make walking easier. Wait, I'd better insist on every two men staying very close together, one to probe and one to guard, the Hundred Little Gods only know what's out there and a storm will give those howling things lots of cover for an attack.

He tried to think of anything else that rescue parties might need and failed to come up with anything else. Putting his notes into a coherent form, he called in one of his aides and sent the young man down to ferret out all the disparate rescue objects and lay them out on the floor of the manor armory.

By now it was too dark to see without a light; it might as well have been dusk rather than just after noon—except for the weirdling flashes of lightning, a strange and disconcerting greenish color, that illuminated the office in fitful bursts. He lit a twist of paper at the fire and went around his office, lighting all his candles and lanterns himself. He waited until he had finished his rounds to look out the window, and when he did, he was astonished.

He couldn't see a thing beyond the thick curtain of snow, and the snow itself slanted obliquely. The wind driving that snow howled around the chimney of his fireplace, and vibrated the glass of the window. No wonder he couldn't hear thunder now; the wind was drowning it out. The lightning strikes were not visible as bolts; instead everything lit up in unsettling green-white for a moment.

Now I know what they mean by a "howling blizzard." And I'm glad we designed the barracks around those furnaces, rather than fireplaces. It'll be harder for the wind to steal the heat from the fires. That was always a problem with a true fireplace; in a high wind most of the heat went right up the chimney. He couldn't afford that to happen in his barracks. They'd use up most of their fuel in no time.

One by one, his officers brought their reports, and he lost a little of his tension. Everyone was accounted for; the hunting and wood-gathering parties had returned before the blizzard hit, in fact they had returned even before the alarm went up. All the barracks were provisioned for a long storm; ropes had been strung between the buildings, barracks, and manor so that no one would get lost.

"You can get lost out there, sir," one of the last of the officers said, as he brushed at snow that had been driven into the fabric of his uniform coat. "Make no mistake about it. You can't see an ell past your feet once you're out of shelter. I've never seen the like."

"Well, there'll be plenty of fresh water at least," Tremane remarked, initialing the report. "Just melt the snow."

The officer nodded, then paused for a moment. "Sir, you did know most of the men in my barracks are from the Horned Hunters, didn't you?"

Since the Imperial Army made an effort to integrate all of the recruits into a single culture rather than cater to individual cultures, Tremane didn't know a thing about it until that moment. "Actually, no—wait, *they* ought to be used to this sort of weather, shouldn't they?"

He had an obscure notion that the Horned Hunters were a nomadic tribe from a land so far to the north of the Empire that they never saw summer. "Don't they herd deer and travel by sled?"

"You're thinking of the Reindeer People, sir. My lot are a sect, not a tribe. Shamanistic, animal spirits, that sort of thing." The officer coughed and looked a little embarrassed. "They sent me with a request, since we're all going to be confined to barracks for a while. They want permission to turn a corner of the barracks into a sweat house permanently. *I* don't see anything wrong with it, but I told them I had to have your permission."

"I believe this comes under the heading of Article Forty-Two—'the Empire shall not restrict the right of a man to worship—' and so on." Tremane smiled slightly. "I don't see the harm so long as they understand there won't be any ritual fasting without special permission, and if they want to undergo any prolonged dream quests, they'll have to apply for and use their leave days to do it."

The officer sighed and looked relieved. "That was the one thing I was worried about, sir, and using leave-days takes care of the problem. Very well, sir, I'll tell them. I doubt they'll have any trouble with it."

"I certainly don't have any difficulty with it," Tremane told him. "And if we get multiday storms like this all winter... well, I might even make concessions on the leave-days. If you're cooped up in the barracks, you might as well send your spirit out for a little stroll, hmm?"

The officer laughed. "May I tell them that, too, Commander? I think it would appeal to their sense of humor."

He shrugged. "I don't see why you shouldn't. If they know I'll let them have their proper rites, it'll probably keep them more content."

The officer saluted and headed back down to return to his men. Tremane toyed with a pen and wished he had an outlet for pent-up energies for all of his men that would match the Horned Hunters' dream quests. If this storm went on for too long, there'd be fights as the men got on one another's nerves. While many commanders did not like having the odder, shamanistic cults going on among the men, Tremane had never minded; provided you made an effort to understand what they wanted and see that they got it, they were generally easier to please than the "civilized" men.

There was something to be said for diversity, though it sometimes did complicate matters.

Once all of his officers had reported in, he relaxed. Now, no matter what came up, he knew where all the men were. He tried to think of ways they could fill in long days of being snowbound once the insides of the barracks were finished.

Well, now I wonder. The Emperor's Guard has their Guard Hall all hung with captured banners and painted with murals of great battles of the past, and those were all done by the men themselves. So—what about seeing if we can't dig up a few men with some artistic talent, then let each barracks decide how the inside of their place should be painted? The lad with the talent can rough things in, and the rest of the boys can color it. We've paint enough for a thousand barracks. That would encourage division pride, camaraderie—

Should he let the Horned Hunters do their barracks with religious symbols? *Yes, but only in the sweat lodge area.* That would work. And if there was another cult that wanted to do up a small shrine, he'd let them build that, too. *Better standardize a size, or they might get greedy and take over half a barracks.*

"Sir!" His aide Nevis interrupted his train of thought. "Men from Shonar with an emergency, sir!" The young man didn't wait for permission to bring them up—which was quite correct in an emergency—he had the group with him. Tremane didn't recognize any of these people, but their expressions told him they were frantic. He recognized their type, though: farmers. Rough hands, weather-beaten faces, heavy clothing perfectly suited to working long hours in harsh winter weather—they were as alike as brothers. That, and their expression, told him everything he needed to know.

And they came to me instead of to Sandar Giles or Chief Husbandman Stoen.

"You've got people lost in this, outside the walls, right?" he said before they could even open their mouths to explain themselves. "People you sent out with herds? Children?"

The one in front, delegated to be the spokesman most likely, dropped his mouth wide open in surprise. Clearly, that was a correct guess. Tremane seized his arm and led him over to the map table, clearing the surface with an impatient brush of his arm, seizing one particular map from the map stand. Nevis scrambled to pick up the discarded maps while he released the man and spread out the map of the countryside around the town his men had finished just before the first snow, anchoring it with candlesticks so it wouldn't roll up. He glanced at the man, who still hadn't spoken, and who still looked stunned.

"Shake yourself awake, man!" he snapped. "What else could have brought you here? Now show me where these people were *supposed* to be; the sooner we get out there, the better the chance of finding them before the damned boggles do!"

That seemed to bring the man around, although it took him more than a moment to orient himself to the map. Evidently, he'd not seen a map before with symbols on it instead of rough sketches of landmarks.

When he finally did open his mouth, his accent and vocabulary betrayed him as the rough farmer Tremane had assumed he was. "We didn' send 'em out too fur, sor," he said apologetically, "Kep' 'em within sight uv walls. We niver thought lettin' 'em take sheep out tedday would—"

"Of course not, you wouldn't have sent them out into danger, I understand, now just show me where they were," Tremane interrupted. "You can apologize later. Show me where they last were. Frankly, man, as fast as this storm blew up, they could have been within sight of my men on the walls and be lost now. You can't have known that would happen."

The farmer stared at the map, his companions peering over his shoulder, and poked a finger hesitantly at the white surface. "Here— there's three chillern with sheep. Here—Tobe's eldest with cows. Here— the rest uv the sheep with Racky Loder—"

"That's five children, in three parties." Tremane signaled Nevis. "Go to the barracks; explain what's happened. Call for volunteers to meet me in the armory, then go get kits from the chirurgeons. I'll lead the party going out the farthest." That would be the group going after the sheep with the lone boy in charge. He turned to the nervous farmers, who were twisting their woolen hats in their hands. "I'll want you to go with us; the children might be frightened of strangers and run away from us; they won't run from you."

Without waiting for one of his aides to help him, he dashed into his bedroom and rummaged through his clothing chests to layer on two heavy tunics and pull woolen leggings on over his trews and boots. Then he caught up his heaviest cloak and the belt from his armor stand that held his short sword and long dagger, and belted it on *over* the cloak, holding the fabric against his body. A pair of heavy gauntlets reaching to his elbows completed his preparations, which were accomplished in mere moments.

Despite the bulky clothing, he took the stairs down to the bottom floor two at a time, leaving his visitors to clamber along behind him. He waited for them at the bottom of the staircase, then led the way to the manor armory.

Despite his own expectations, he and the farmers were not to wait long for his volunteers. Men began to straggle in before he had a chance to grow impatient, and soon the armory was full to overflowing with snow-covered volunteers. It soon became obvious that he was going to get far more volunteers than he had thought.

By now Nevis was back with his three rescue kits from the chirurgeons, and with two of the chirurgeons themselves. "Nevis, stay here and send any stragglers to the Great Hall," he called. "The rest of you—we need more room, let's go."

He did not lead them; there were too many men between him and the door. He simply went along with the crowd, and only when they had reached the frigidly-cold Great Hall did he push to the front. Someone brought in lanterns; he took one and climbed up to stand on the table. "Right; we have five lost children. Hopefully the three that were together have stayed together. You, you, and you—" he pointed to three of the farmers. "You go after the three children with the sheep. You and you, go for the boy with the cattle, and you come with me after the last boy. Now, *you* go to that corner, *you* over there, and *you* stand by the table. Men, divide yourselves into three parties and position yourselves with these farmers."

He watched them separate and distribute themselves with a critical eye. He redistributed the result a trifle, adding more men to his group, which would be going farthest out. "Right. Weapons—boar-spears, long daggers and short swords. Bows are useless out there. One man is responsible for taking stakes and surveying cord and marking your trail out. When you get to the general area your children are lost in, he stays there with someone to guard, blowing a horn at regular intervals."

They hadn't had time to practice moving while roped together; wiser to use some other way to keep track of each other.

"The rest of you spread out in a line, but make sure you're always in sight of the lantern of the man next to you. if you find anything—kick up a sheep or a cow, for instance, yell for the others. The rest of you—when someone finds something, we all gather on that spot."

That should work. He continued. "Watch out for boggles; keep your weapons out. This would be prime hunting time for them. When you find the children, yell again; we'll gather, retrace our steps, and follow the horn back to the stake man. If you get lost, try first to retrace your steps, and remember to listen for the horn. You lot going after the three children, take the west gate, you going for the boy with the cattle take the north. Got that?"

There was no dissent, and the men looked determined, but not grim. "All right, then. Let's move."

He led his group out of the manor and into the driving snow, each man carrying a weatherproof lantern. Snow pounded at his face, and the wind tore at his clothing; it wasn't quite sunset, but you still couldn't see more than a few paces away; the lantern light reflected from the snow in a globe of chaotic, swirling whiteness. Now he wished devoutly for magic lights that would neither blow out nor be extinguished if they were dropped in the snow. He wished for a mage-rope that would hold the men together without interfering with their movements. He wished—

To hell with wishes. We make do with what we have. Wishes are no good anymore.

The wind and snow came at them from the side, and he was glad he'd belted his sword on over his cloak; he'd never have been able to hold the fabric closed. He led the entire troop across the practice grounds, and past the hastily-erected warehouses that held the supplies so vital to them. Many of these warehouses were nothing more than tents with reinforced sides and roofs, just enough to keep the snow off; these structures loomed darkly out of the undifferentiated blue-gray of the rest of the world. The walls were first visible as a line of spots of yellow light above a black mass—the lanterns of the men on guard along the top. The men guarding the gate looked startled to see them, but the officer in charge had a good head on his shoulders when he heard where they were going.

"I'll have my men build a beacon fire above the gate!" he shouted over the howling wind. "If we shelter it on three sides it should stay lit. And if you get lost out there anyway, have your man blow the storm signal, and I'll have mine answer it."

Well, the beacon might be invisible at fifty paces and the horn inaudible, but it was another slim help and worth doing. He nodded his agreement, the stake man tied off the end of the survey string to the gate, and out they went.

Every step had to be fought for; despite his swathings of clothing he was still freezing before they had even reached the point where they were to spread out. He and the rest of the men had swathed their faces in scarves, but every exposed bit of skin stung and burned under the pinpricks of driving snow. He frankly didn't know how the old man leading them knew where he was going, although frequent checks of his own north-needle showed him that the old boy was keeping a straight heading. He'd pulled the hood of his cloak tightly around his head, but his nose and ears were numb in no time. Now he was glad he'd had the foresight to order the men out in pairs, one with his weapon ready and one with a lantern; if there were monsters out here tonight, you'd never know until they were on top of you.

The snow had been about calf-high before the storm began; it was thigh-high now, and drifting with the wind. There'd be drifts up to the rooftops in some places by morning.

His feet were frozen and aching with cold; his legs burned with the exertion of pushing through all that snow. Convinced that the old man knew where he was going, Tremane finally handed the lantern over to him and took out his sword; the old farmer handled his boar-spear like a pitchfork, and probably hadn't the least idea how to use it.

Is it his boy we're looking for, or perhaps a relative? There was no doubt of the single-minded determination he'd seen on the man's weathered and leathery face. Now, of course, he couldn't see much of anything!

Finally, after an eternity, the man stopped. "Here's the edge of the Grand Common!" he shouted over the wind. "The boy should be somewhere out there—" He waved vaguely in an east-to-west semicircle.

Tremane waited for the rest of the search-party to catch up and gather around. "Stake man, horn man, stay here!" he shouted. "The rest of you, spread out in pairs—and remember what I said about keeping each others' lanterns in sight! I'll take farthest left flank, the rest of you fill in."

He led the old man off to the left, determined to hold down the farthest position so that he could be certain of one flank, at least. He positioned the pairs of men on his side himself, then marched off into the dark with the old man still at his side until the last lantern was a fuzzy circle of light through the curtain of snow. He turned and moved north again, slowly, and the lantern at his right kept pace with him.

He had the uncanny feeling that they were completely alone out here; that the world had ended, and the lantern to his right was nothing more than a phantom to torture him. *When did the last mage-storm hit? Gods, if one comes in while we're out here—* He'd be helpless, as helpless as a babe. Anyone with mage-power, mage-senses, was completely flattened by the storms. He tried to calculate the times in his head. *I should be all right. It shouldn't come in until tomorrow or tomorrow night.* But if he was wrong, if it came in and sent him reeling into that maelstrom of hallucination and disorientation *now*, while he was out here—

Then hopefully the old man would know enough to call for help, or drag him over to the next pair.

If I ever want to punish a man worse than simply executing him, I'll send him off in a blizzard like this one. Impossible to tell how long they'd been out here; impossible to tell where they were! There was just the burning of his legs, the burning ache in his side, the knotted shoulders, and the cold, the cold, the everlasting cold and dark and the tiny space of light around their lantern...

Then the snow in front of him exploded upward, in his face! It boiled skyward as something hiding beneath it lurched for him.

All discomfort forgotten, he shrieked and floundered back, sword ready, fumbling for his long dagger, his heart pounding.

"Baaaaaaa!" the snow-monster bawled. *"Baaaaaaa!"*

Tremane tripped over something hidden beneath the snow and fell over on his rump as terror turned to relief. He coughed twice, and the coughing turned into helpless laughter as the old man helped him back up to his feet. And now the snow all around him was moving, as more of the flock became aware of the presence of humans, humans who must surely represent safety to them in all of this mess. "Swing that lantern and call!" he ordered the old man. "We've found the flock, the boy has to be in here somewhere."

The farmer obeyed him with a will, bellowing like one of his own ewes, and soon more lights came up through the snow as the rest of the men got the message and gathered to this new spot. By now the sheep were pressed up against Tremane like so many friendly puppies, and except for the fact that they kept stepping on his feet, he was rather glad to have them there; their woolly bodies were warming his legs. More sheep came floundering up out of the snowy dark. Once again the men divided up and this time used Tremane as their center point for the search, and it wasn't long before the boy Racky was found, safe and warm, lying down between two of the biggest ewes Tremane had ever seen, with the sheepdog lying atop him.

While the old man greeted his nephew—for that was who this boy was—and the men congratulated one another with much backslapping and laughter, Tremane caught his breath and took careful note of the faces of those he could actually see. What he read there made him smile with satisfaction.

They're mine. By the Hundred Little Gods, Bram was right.

Now, if he could just keep them.

"All right, men—back to town!" he shouted over the howling wind. "I'll order hot spice-wine for all, and throw a joint on to roast!"

With a cheer, the men formed a long line, with the best tracker in front, the one most likely to read the falling traces of their passage in the snow. Tremane, the old man, the boy and the flock brought up the rear. He hadn't thought the sheep would be able to keep up, but they plowed valiantly along, spurred on by the sheepdog. And perhaps urgent thoughts of a warm byre and sweet hay, and shelter from the wind and snow moved through those woolly heads as well. They shoved right along beside the last of the men, their bleating barely audible over the wind.

The last traces of their path were obliterated by the wind, but at that point, by listening carefully, some of those with the best hearing made out the sounds of the horn calling out. By spreading out again, they quickly found the men left beside the end of the string-and-stake markers. At that point it was an easy task to make their way back to the gate, and the beacon fire over it was a welcome sight indeed.

Tremane sent the old man and his charges off to the town without waiting to hear his thanks; for one thing, he wanted those sheep out of his garrison, and for another, he wanted to know how the other two parties had fared. With a word to the quartermaster to break out some barrels of wine and mulling spices, bring in a joint of beef for each building, and send them all along to the barracks, he paused only long enough to leave his snow-caked cloak in the hands of an orderly. He ran up the stairs to his office, leaving lumps of melting snow from his boots in his wake.

Nevis was waiting for him, with a smile on his face. "The other two parties are back, Commander," he reported. "There was some injury due to frostbite, and one man hurt by a boggle, but it was a minor wound. All the children and the better part of the livestock were recovered."

The last of his energy flowed away like the melting snow, and he collapsed into a chair. "We have had *more* than our share of good luck," he said heavily. Nevis nodded vigorously.

"Have you any orders, sir?" the young man asked.

He started to say no, then changed his mind. "Yes, I do," he told the aide with a smile. "First—you and the other aides see that the men get that hot spiced wine I ordered. Second, see to it that the volunteers get spiced brandy instead of mere wine; you have sufficient authority to order it, so do so. Third—" he got up and began walking toward his bedroom, shedding wet garments as he walked, "—pick up this mess, and see that I am *not* disturbed. I intend to hibernate. Is that clear?"

"Yes, Commander—" Nevis began.

And if he said any more, it didn't matter. The closing door cut it off.

8

Firesong stood at one of the windows of his *ekele* garden, feeling the chill coming off the "glass," frowning out at the snow-bedecked landscape beyond. The first snowfall of the season in Valdemar was usually nothing more than a light frosting of white; this snow had fallen for hours, and covered the ground to an uncomfortable depth. Firesong had not troubled to leave the *ekele* since he'd last returned to it to warm his bones. *Snow. I hate snow*, he thought rebelliously, arms crossed over his chest. *It isn't worth crossing all that muck to get to the Palace, not for anything short of a terrible emergency.* An'desha wasn't in the *ekele*; he hadn't been "home" last night or the night before. Much as Firesong would have enjoyed indulging himself in a jealous fit, he knew he couldn't legitimately permit himself one. The same snow that kept him here had discouraged a weary An'desha from coming back. Firesong knew where both Karal and An'desha had been for the past two days. Karal was dancing attendance on Solaris, and when she Gated back to Karse, he was busy with Natoli, with whom he was spending most of his free time. An'desha had been working with the artificers the entire time. On nights when he worked late into the morning. he had taken to staying at the Palace—sleeping chastely enough, taking a bed in the pages' and squires' dormitory. Had Firesong cared to, he could have used a touch of magic and the still water in a basin to see exactly that, as he had the first time An'desha spent a night at the Palace.

He couldn't even be angry at An'desha anymore; the Shin'a'in was hardly to blame for the fact that they were drifting apart. An'desha's changing interests alone dictated that. He shifted restlessly from one foot to the other and his heavy silk clothing shifted softly against his skin. *He's gone mystical, and I never could handle mystics. And yet, at the same time, he keeps trying to make magic into a craft rather than an art—something controlled by formula rather than intuition.* Both of those positions were in diametric opposition to Firesong's own beliefs; An'desha could not have chosen anything more contrary if he'd planned to.

Firesong gritted his teeth until his jaw ached. *Logically* he couldn't be angry at An'desha for failing to fulfill Firesong's dream... but emotion does not respond to logic. Part of him wanted to let An'desha go with a sad blessing, but most of him wanted An'desha to be just as miserable as Firesong was.

So An'desha didn't need or want an emotional bond? That was fine for *him*, but what about Firesong? *I am not growing younger, and my opportunities become fewer with every passing year.* Shay'a'chern *number no more than one in ten; how can I hope to find a permanent partner when all like me are already paired up? Why must I go through my life like a white crow, cast out by the flock?* Hadn't he earned his rewards by now? Didn't he *deserve* them?

All right, so he wouldn't have An'desha. He was resigned to that; he wouldn't go around beating empty bushes, hoping to flush birds from them. He needed more time, youth, more years of life! *Then*, perhaps he might find his soul match, given decades to search rather than mere years.

And he knew how to do it, too.

But it was wrong. That was what Ma'ar had done, though for different reasons. Ma'ar had wanted power, and there was not time enough in one life to accumulate all the knowledge and power that Ma'ar craved.

I only want—love. Is that purpose enough to make us different?

Not unless he could find a way to get those years of life without cheating anyone else of his. There *must* be a way to work the trick without hurting anyone!

His frustration grew as he stood there, once again racking his brain, trying to find a way to make the trick viable. It was so *easy*, that was the worst part! Ma'ar and all his successive incarnations had done all of the hard work, all the really *dark* work. Now the Sanctuary was in place and self-sustaining; he had only to power it a bit further and link himself to it, and then he would have all the leisure he needed for his searches.

And even if I was old when I finally found him, I could link him there as well, and then find new bodies for us both...

Was that so wrong? Was it possible to use something built with blood and not be tainted himself? What dark paths were these thoughts leading him down?

But they kept intruding on everything he did. Solutions a bit less shadowed than the ones Ma'ar had used whispered to him. *Would it be wrong to take the body from someone who does not deserve to live? A murderer, perhaps? A blood-path mage such as one of Ma'ar's or Falconsbane's underlings?*

There was the small matter of needing a physical bond, however— Ma'ar had used the bond of blood-relationship. Could another bond serve as well? Could he inflict that bond on someone?

Aya stirred behind him and uttered a tense trill. Aya did not approve of the path his thoughts were tending—or at least, the bondbird did not approve of the little he understood. That irritated him further. Bad enough to be troubled by his own conscience, must he put up with Aya's as well?

And what does a bird know? he thought impatiently, dismissing Aya's discomfort. Was he going to have to follow the dictates of the wayward mind of a bird? He had a flash of regret for not having chosen a raptor over the flashier firebird; Vree was certainly amoral enough, and not much inclined to consider anything in the way of a conscience when plump prey or a gryphon's crest-feathers were in sight!

As if to compound his troubles, *now* An'desha came trudging cheerfully into view, up to his knees in snow, looking far too happy to fit in with Firesong's black mood. And it was too late to go up into the *ekele* to avoid him; the Shin'a'in saw him standing in the window and waved to him.

Damn, damn, damn. His black mood soured further. He did not want to be good company for anyone, least of all An'desha, but he'd better make a try at it. He put on a mask of a pleasant expression, and waited for An'desha to enter the protected area between the two doors. There was a further wait for An'desha to shake off the snow encrusting his legs inside the first of the doors, then enter the *ekele* itself.

"You'll never believe what's here!" An'desha called, as Firesong opened the second door. "The city's in an absolute uproar—there hasn't been such a carnival procession since—well, since *you* arrived! Anybody with a free moment at the Palace and the Collegia is gawking like any country cousin!"

"I can't imagine what you could be talking about, or what it is that's come," Firesong replied, curiosity piqued in spite of himself. "Well, what is it? A captured monster? Solaris parading through the city with a portable Temple of Vkandis?"

"Neither." An'desha pulled off his quilted Shin'a'in jacket with a shower of droplets from the melted snow, and grinned. "A floating barge from k'Leshya. They've been Gating their way across country with help from the gryphon's, which is why we didn't know they were coming; the gryphon-mages were taking it in turn to fly ahead, scout a remote location, and come back to build a Gate to the next spot. That let them get within striking distance of Haven without raising a fuss. Once they got there, they came overland by road the rest of the way. They were just waiting to see if the breakwater would hold before they chanced a Gate."

A barge? From k'Leshya? "Who? And why?" he blurted without thinking. "And why now?"

"To answer the last question first, *now* is because they had to. Among other things they brought someone who calls herself a *trondi'irn*; apparently she's a sort of gryphon-keeper, and she's come to make sure our four stay in good health. About a quarter of the barge is full of her stuff, or rather, the stuff for the gryphons." An'desha looked quite smugly pleased with Firesong's surprise. "There's also one of *my* people, a Sworn-Shaman like Querna, but a man. He's supposed to be here to advise Jarim, rather than replacing him, and I must admit Jarim seemed kind of relieved to see him."

Firesong got the feeling that Jarim wasn't the only person relieved to see this shaman. Another point of difference, of rift, between them?

But An'desha didn't notice his silence. "Then there's a expanded delegation from k'Leshya, about a dozen, counting the *trondi'irn*, and three more gryphons, and they've brought a lot of things Darkwind's been fussing over—" He interrupted his own description with a shrug. "I'm starving and I missed breakfast and lunch at the Collegia. Well, why don't you go see for yourself?"

"I believe I shall." Surprise gave way to a consuming curiosity. "Would you mind if I offered them the hospitality of the *ekele*? I can't imagine any of them would feel all that comfortable in the Palace."

An'desha flushed faintly. "Actually, I wanted to talk with you about that. Would *you* mind if I—moved temporarily into the Palace? I seem to be spending all my time there, and I've been offered a room in the Palace if I want it. That would—ah—leave you more room for the people from k'Leshya."

For one moment, Firesong throttled down rage. *Deserting me already?*

How dare he—after everything I did for him!

But he hid it carefully. Getting angry at An'desha would only drive him further away. Instead, he tried assuming a mask of indifference. "If that's what you really want, it's fine with me."

"I would think it will just be until we find another solution for when the breakwater goes." An'desha looked at him pleadingly, and Firesong now felt a surge of satisfaction.

So—since I agreed so easily, now he's worried? Good. Maybe I can make him jealous for a change!

He shrugged, deepening his pose of indifference. "Whatever you want. I'm going to go see if I know any of these folk, and tender my invitation."

He felt his mask slipping and turned away. Then, so that An'desha did not see any of the conflicting emotions on his face, he ran up the stairs to fetch his own cloak and boots—which fortunately were not in the bedroom. He heard An'desha following slowly and waited until the Shin'a'in was rummaging around in the bedroom, packing up, before he went back down to the garden again. Aya joined him with a trill of satisfaction, flying to take a secure perch on his shoulder as he went out the doors.

He pushed through the snow with his restless thoughts flitting from one subject to another. For one thing, he hadn't given any thought to the gryphons' health; he'd just taken it for granted that they *were* healthy. They always recovered quickly from injuries, and never seemed to be ill.

But the youngsters were about to fledge; this fall they'd been making short glides from the tops of fences and woodpiles. *Well, not quite glides. More like controlled plummets.* They still were only about half the size of their parents, so they probably had one major growth spurt coming. If they doubled their size in a year or so, from all Firesong knew of other creatures, he was certain that would put a tremendous strain on their bodies. There would be special nutritional demands to keep up with such a growth spurt. Perhaps that was why the *trondi'irn* was here...

Or perhaps it was because of Treyvan and Hydona themselves. There might be some traces of minerals or other things they needed that they couldn't find for themselves. *They are a created race, after all. The Mage of Silence made them up, and I don't care how much of a genius he was, he couldn't possibly make every detail perfect.* Humans had been around for a great deal longer than gryphons, and look how imperfect they were!

Even our bondbirds get strange ailments; that's why we each have to be an expert in the treatment of each particular type of bird. He hated to think of all the strange things that might go wrong for a gryphon.

As he broke through the trees, it was clear that there was *something* causing a great stir at the regular Palace stables. There was quite a crowd there, and something bulky and dark in the middle of them. The floating barge?

Probably. Firesong recalled very clearly how he had coveted one of those wonderful creations; coveted it as he seldom coveted any material object. Like many other creations, only k'Leshya had retained the knowledge that made them possible after the Cataclysm, largely because only k'Leshya had custody of as much of the Mage of Silence's library as had been saved. Based on the kind of covered barge that transported goods and trading families up and down the rivers of the time, the floating barges did just that—float. They generally hovered about an arm's length above the ground, but could go as high as the treetops or as low as the width of a single finger. It was possible to use magic to move them forward, but normally they were drawn by teams of horses, mules, or oxen—beasts being far "cheaper" to use than a mage. The biggest advantage was that they could carry literally as much as you could stuff into and strap onto them, for they were "without weight" and could be drawn by beasts with scarcely more effort than if they were moving unencumbered. Since they did not have wheels, they could go where there were no roads. Firesong could easily picture being able to load everything he owned into one of these barges, and traveling the world...

He hurried his pace, and saw the package-laden top of the barge rising above the crowd around it. An'desha must have come to fetch him as soon as the delegation arrived; it didn't look as if anyone had even unpacked as yet.

He joined the crowd of curiosity seekers; as soon as those nearest him saw he was there, they parted for him, enabling him to work his way in to the center. There seemed to be a lot more baggage than even a delegation of a dozen could account for—what had they brought with them?

The newcomers were instantly obvious from their costume; a blending of Shin'a'in and Tayledras style, but with a curiously antique feeling and exotic cut to it, and in colors as vivid as the flowers of a Vale. The gryphons were already in attendance, all four of them, paying close attention to three *new* gryphons and a young woman in brilliant orange and scarlet garments billowing out to the elbows and knees, where they were then confined by wrapped bands of black-and-orange embroidered straps. Beside her was a man in vivid blue and white, whose long black hair and back seemed oddly familiar.

Treyvan raised his head and spotted Firesong. "Heigho!" he said. "And herrre at lassst is that old frrriend of yourrrsss, Sssilverrrfox!"

Silverfox? Firesong froze in mid-step, as the *kestra'chern* Silverfox turned to greet him with a cheerful face lighting up with pleasure. *Why didn't An'desha tell me Silverfox was here?*

For a moment he was angry all over again, but reason prevailed. *How could he have known I even knew Silverfox? That was long, long before we met each other, and I don't recall ever mentioning the k'Leshya except in passing.*

His temper cooled again quickly, and he was able to greet Silverfox with unalloyed cheer—which was just as well, because the quality of the embrace that the *kestra'chern* gave him was very promising indeed.

"What brings *you* here, of all people?" Firesong asked as they separated. "I should have thought you would have preferred to stay in the Vale and not plunge yourself headlong into *this* inhospitable clime!"

"As to that, it's no worse than the weather outside the Vale," Silverfox replied easily. "And as to what brought me—we traditionally send members from each of the Disciplines when we put together a delegation." He nodded at Treyvan and Hydona. "The first to make an approach are always from the Silver Gryphons, of course. The Silvers are—well, I suppose you'd call them our version of Heralds. Peacekeepers, law enforcers, and so forth, but they also include our scouts. Usually they aren't actual gryphons, unless we're sending them *quite* far away. That was why Treyvan and Hydona were first selected to find the Vales, and then volunteered to come to Valdemar."

"But why a *kestra'chern?*" Firesong repeated.

Silverfox laughed. "Because the *kestra'chern* are one of the Disciplines, pretty bird!" He indicated his fellow k'Leshya with a long finger as he told off the "Disciplines." "Artisans, Administrators, Scholars, Silvers, Husbandry, Mages, and *Kestra'chern.* Actually, there are two of us *kestra'chern; trondi'irn* come under the Discipline of *Kestra'chern.* And we never send the last Discipline—that's Shaman—out with a delegation. There's no need for that, and besides," he added with a grin, "we brought Lo'isha shena Pretara'sedrin with us, so there's rather a superfluity of priestly types."

As if responding to his name, a Shin'a'in garbed from head to toe in a dark, midnight-blue turned and flashed a pearly smile in their direction, before returning to his conversation with Jarim.

A cold burst of air reminded Firesong just how ridiculous it was for them all to be standing around in the snow. "Look, I can't imagine why we're all freezing out here when we could be warm. I came to offer you the hospitality of my home. I *think* you'll all fit in; there's at least a few amenities of civilization—"

"Oh, Whitebird will want to stay with the gryphons, so that will be one less—and Artisans, Administrators, and Mages will want to set up a proper embassy suite in the Palace. I suspect you're only likely to get me, Husbandry, and the Scholar," Silverfox said cheerfully. "That's only four. And we store easily. If you've got a hot pool for soaking, the rest will probably come use it. Summerhawk of Husbandry is a marvelous cook, so they'll probably come to eat as well, but I suspect otherwise they'll want to be where the business is." He smiled apologetically. "I'm afraid they are all very earnest and intent on their duty. They're planning on spending every waking moment with your mages and artificers, developing the next set of protections from the mage-storms."

Firesong was secretly relieved that the k'Leshya mages would probably not be taking him up on his offer. He doubted any of them would think highly of his excursions to investigate Falconsbane's Sanctuary, much less that he was considering using it… He'd been able to conceal his activities so far from the other mages at Haven, largely because he was better than most of them. *I don't know that I can hide what I'm doing from mages with unfamiliar skills. Gods only know what k'Leshya has still in the way of mages we've lost. And as for what they might have developed, I can't even begin to guess.*

"We need to unpack—and I think you ought to stay for that much of it, my friend," the *kestra'chern* continued. "We brought some things along I suspect you've been missing. Our *hertasi* made you up some new clothing for one—you came here rather lightly packed, and I doubt these folk, pleasant as they are, have any notion of fabric or design!"

Firesong shuddered, recalling some of the things he'd been presented with by well-meaning tailors of Haven. *No* sense of style, and as for the limited palette of colors, the less said, the better! They wanted to dress him as a molting peahen.

"Introduce me to everyone so I can make my offer and they can decline or accept it on their own, would you?" he said, rather than commenting on the deficiencies of Valdemaran costume. "That way we can take the luggage and all straight to the *ekele* and you can get settled in properly."

"Luggage and *presents*, my dear friend," Silverfox said slyly. "I oversaw that part of the packing myself."

Firesong laughed. "Should I be greedy or polite? Being polite, I should pretend I don't have any great urgency to see what you've brought, but being greedy, that is the only reason why I would willingly stand here in snow up to my elbows while you sort yourselves out!"

Already his heart felt lighter for Silverfox's presence. And as he helped unload the barge and sort packages and bundles, something else occurred to him.

Here, presented on a platter as it were, was the perfect way to make An'desha anxious and jealous, if it could be done at all. He had one last chance to win the Shin'a'in back.

Silverfox reclined indolently in the hot pool several days later, after having given Firesong a profoundly satisfying demonstration of at least one of a *kestra'chern's* sets of skills. "I fear we have annoyed one set of your artificers with our arrival," he said lazily.

"Oh?" Firesong was feeling too pleased to be annoyed at the mention of the artificers. "How is that? From all I hear, your mages are getting along splendidly with them. It's a bit awkward cramming Treyvan and Hydona into the room so that there are enough translators, but so far as I've heard that's the only thing like a problem."

"Oh, it is the ones who are messing about with boilers and steam," Silverfox chuckled. "I must admit I fail to see the attraction; the only places *I* care to have steam are in the kitchen, in the steam-house, and rising above the waters of a soaking-pool."

Firesong laughed. "Oh, I understand what the trouble is. That girl Natoli and her friends were helping the steam fanatics when you arrived, but now they are crawling all over your floating barge, day or night. And when they are not examining the barge, they are trying to take apart some of the other useful things you brought with you. In the meantime, they have deserted the steam proponents to learn what mechanical wonders you have devised."

"That is why we brought artisans, dear friend," Silverfox retorted, with a half-smile. "So that the rest of us do not have to attempt to explain what we do not understand. So far as *I* know or care, it is *all* magic!" He laughed. "I told one of them that it is all run by magic smoke. When the smoke escapes, the object ceases to function!"

Firesong had to laugh at that, too—since most of the mechanical contrivances of the artificers normally emitted great quantities of smoke when *they* stopped working, exploded or burned to the ground, especially the ones powered by steam boilers.

"Your friend An'desha has been making himself invaluable to them, so they tell me," Silverfox added.

Firesong's thoughts darkened at the mention of An'desha's name, and he controlled his expression to avoid giving himself away. He had been paying Silverfox his exclusive attentions in the hope that if anything would bring An'desha back it would be jealousy, but to his dismay, An'desha actually seemed pleased and relieved to see him so often in the *kestra'chern's* company. His last attempt to fix An'desha's wandering attention had certainly not turned out the way he had thought it would. In fact, another kink in his plans had developed, for when An'desha was not translating for the k'Leshya, he was most often in the company of the Sworn-Shaman, which certainly put paid to any hopes of weaning him away from his growing mysticism!

Yesterday he'd decided to bury the remains of the relationship before they began to stink, although he was not at all happy about the end of it. That really only left him back in the same position he'd been in when the k'Leshya delegation arrived. Either he resign himself to a life predominately alone, or—

Or I find a way to extend that life and even my odds of finding my lifebonded.

Just as his thoughts took that grimmer turn, however, Silverfox stretched languidly, striking an unconsciously provocative pose that distracted him. Steam veiled Silverfox's head and torso, giving him an air of mystery. "You've been rather quiet and subdued for the past several days," the *kestra'chern* observed. "If I didn't know you better, I'd say you were brooding over something, but you keep saying it's only the weather. Is the weather here really depressing you that much?"

"Oh it isn't the weather, really—at least it isn't the primary problem," Firesong found himself admitting. "I do confess that I hate leaving all that snow where I have to look at it every moment, though. Back in our Vale you'd never know it was winter unless you went outside the protected area, and I generally managed to avoid that in bad weather."

"Hmm." Silverfox stretched again, arching his back and closing his eyes for a moment. "Still. There's something rather pleasant about being in *here*, where it's warm and comfortable, and being able to look out there and know that if you don't want to subject yourself to miserable weather, you don't have to. Don't you think?"

Firesong shrugged uncomfortably. "I said it wasn't the primary problem."

"So what *is* depressing you?" Somehow Silverfox had managed in all his stretching to work around behind Firesong, and began massaging his tense shoulders with strong, skillful fingers. "Perhaps I can help."

"What depresses anyone?" he countered with irritation. "I'm *shay'a'chern,* alone, surrounded by people who have paired off comfortably—Elspeth and Darkwind, Treyvan and Hydona, Karal and Natoli, Selenay and Daren, Kerowyn and Eldan—and gods save us, Talia and Dirk, who are mature parents and *quite* old enough not to be mooning over each other like a pair of romantic teenagers! Everywhere I look, I'm surrounded by hopeless romantics!"

"And here you are, a bird with a perfectly charming nest and no one to share it with." Silverfox managed to make that sound sympathetic without being syrupy. "I understand; that's enough to depress anyone."

"The lifebonded couples are the worst," Firesong continued acidly. "There seem to be more of *those* here than is decent by anyone's standards."

"Perhaps it has something to do with the fact that all the Heralds congregate here," Silverfox observed casually. "It would be rather like concentrating all the *shay'a'chern* in Valdemar and the Vales in an institution that was something like the Collegium. It makes such meetings of matching souls much more likely."

If only I could *do that...* But if he could extend his years, that would have the same effect. "Still. It's indecent, and it's irritating."

"I can see where it would be, although I find it rather charming. And at the same time, I rather feel sorry for them." In spite of Firesong's resistance to being soothed, Silverfox's ministrations were having an effect. But that last statement was positively bizarre.

"Why on earth would you feel sorry for them?" he asked in surprise. "I thought everyone was looking for a lifebonded mate! Isn't that the point?"

"I'm not looking for a lifebond," Silverfox said firmly. "I would much, much rather have someone who loved me out of pure attraction or simple affection than have someone who *couldn't help* loving me. So far as *I* can see, the difference between being in love and being lifebonded is rather like the difference between doing something because you want to and doing it because someone came along and put a geas on you to compel you to do it. You might have wanted to do it anyway, but the notion of being compelled to it makes me very uncomfortable."

He uttered a dry chuckle. "No—not uncomfortable; it makes me very rebellious. Quite frankly, if I met my lifebonded, I would try to fight the compulsion just because it *was* a compulsion. And I would insist that something more than a compulsion held us together."

"I can't see that." Firesong shook his head. "Lifebonded mates are so devoted to one another, so bound up with each other, it seems the perfect way of life to me. Being lifebonded means there are no misunderstandings, no jealousies, no incompatibilities; none of the things that cause so many problems in ordinary relationships—"

But Silverfox was chuckling in earnest now, as if he had said something very amusing. "Who told you there were no misunderstandings, no incompatibilities? Did you read it somewhere? Do you know any lifebonded couples intimately enough to say that with authority? *Believe* me, I've had lifebonded couples as clients in the past, and they have their share of both those things. The only difference between them and ordinary couples is that if *they* don't resolve problems quickly, they're going to suffer far more agony of spirit than you or I would."

"That sounds like an advantage to me," Firesong retorted stubbornly.

"Huh." Silverfox did not seem to have a response to that statement. "You seem very sure of that."

"I am." Firesong was not going to back down on this "And I can't see where 'agony of spirit' is any worse than fires of jealousy. I'd say a person would be better off if he was forced to reconcile differences; I think it's better for two people to be impelled to fix things between them than for one to suffer heartache while the other goes off blithely about his business without a care in the world. That would make life a great deal more even-handed," he finished grimly.

"Now *that* was certainly stated with conviction," the *kestra'chern* observed. "I might almost suspect you've found yourself suffering the slung shot of jealousy a time or two."

"Enough," Firesong replied cautiously. "Enough to know it's probably one of the most poisonous of emotions, and it encourages obsession. How is being so obsessed with someone that you can't get your mind on your work any better than being forced to be compatible?"

Silverfox moved his ministrations to below Firesong's shoulder blades. "You have a point. Certainly for some people it would make getting one's work done much easier. Obsession is a fairly ugly condition, and as you said, it is poisonous. It tends to warp one's outlook."

"And it is one that is hard to cure." Firesong winced as Silverfox's fingers encountered a particularly knotted muscle.

"So that is what is depressing you? Loneliness, jealousy, and obsession?" Silverfox sighed. "That is a combination sufficient to depress anyone, even at the height of summer and with all going well. Given the current situation, I marvel you are getting anything accomplished. I am not certain I would."

When did I admit that I was obsessed? Firesong caught himself, keeping himself from saying anything further. Silverfox was the most persuasive person that Firesong had ever encountered, not excluding Herald Talia. This was not the first time that the *kestra'chern* had managed to maneuver him into admitting something he had not intended to.

And despite the fact that he was anything but a nuisance, Silverfox had been doing a remarkable job of somehow being present whenever Firesong contemplated a little trip over to the Palace and the Heartstone for another visit to Falconsbane's Sanctuary. If Silverfox had been anything other than what he was, Firesong would have been dying to get rid of him by now, and he would have considered the *kestra'chern* to be a prime nuisance.

As it was, every time the *kestra'chern* turned up so very inconveniently, he managed to change the encounter into something pleasant, enjoyable. His timing was amazing; too coincidental to be an accident, but how did he *know*? How could he know? And he never made anything so obvious as an outright interception; he was just there when Firesong's thoughts turned grim, striking a casually provocative pose, or flirting cheerfully with him.

This was not the first time that he'd gotten Firesong to confess things to him, but this was the first time he'd coaxed the conversation into the dangerous grounds of emotional obsession, jealousy, and anger. This was *very* dangerous ground, in fact, since it might lead to other deductions.

Firesong restrained growing anger—not at Silverfox, but at the impossible, intolerable situation.

"It doesn't matter; there's nothing I can do about the situation, so I might as well just endure it with proper Tayledras stoicism," he lied, trying to steer things off that precarious ground and hide his own feelings.

"Ah, but it does matter," Silverfox countered. "You are a mage, and as such, your control is dependent on your emotional state. As a Healer-with-knives should not practice when his hands are unsteady, a mage should not practice when his nerves are unsteady. You know that well enough to teach it!"

Firesong's muscles knotted again under Silverfox's hands, betraying his temper to the *kestra'chern*. "I do know that, and my nerves are steady enough," he replied. "I know what I'm doing. And to tell the truth, at the moment my skills are not needed anyway."

"Oh, my friend," Silverfox sighed, releasing him. "Your body tells me a different story." He slid around to his former position, and his expression was dead sober. "The chiefest language of the *kestra'chern* is that of emotion; his chiefest skill is in the matters of the heart rather than of the mind or spirit; we leave the former to the Scholar and the latter to the Priest. *That* is what we do, but there comes a point when we cannot do our work without cooperation."

Instead of getting off that dangerous ground, they were now firmly atop it. Firesong feigned incomprehension and stifled alarm. "Why would you need my cooperation for anything more than you already have?"

But Silverfox frowned. "You already know the answer to that question. I do not know all, by any means, but I do know a few things. You are lonely and profoundly unhappy here, you live in a bower built for two but you are alone in it, you tense with anger when Karal and the artificers are mentioned, you tense with pain when An'desha's name comes up. Your heart is in turmoil, your body reflects that, and your mind must of necessity reflect both your heart and body. Even an apprentice in my art could put those facts in their proper order."

"What, is that all you have deduced?" Firesong retorted, more sharply than he had intended.

Silverfox looked directly into his eyes with unveiled candor. "There is more, but those are the things *I* can do something about, and only if you will talk about them."

"Oh, you can, can you?" Firesong hoisted himself up out of the pool abruptly, wrapping himself in an enveloping robe so that his body would not betray his thoughts any further.

Silverfox heeded his example, and followed *him* when he headed for the stairs to the *ekele*. "Yes, I can, and it is not a boast. That is my particular avocation, and I am as skilled in it as you are skilled in your avocation of mage. I have been studying and practicing my art for as long as you have."

Firesong remained silent for the time it took to climb the stairs, but turned angrily to face the *kestra'chern* when they both reached the top. "I suppose you can do something about the way that An'desha has turned away from me, then? And you can silence that interfering sprout, Karal, so that An'desha gets no more stupid ideas, no more obsession with mysticism? Things between us were perfectly adequate until *he* came along! If there is anyone to blame here, it is Karal! An'desha depended on me, not on some idiot priest from a land that considers the Star-Eyed's people to be barbaric eaters of raw meat!"

Too late, he realized that his mouth had run away with him again; he flushed, turned away, and flung himself sullenly onto the couch. He stared out the window rather than looking at Silverfox. It should be easier to keep a tight rein on his mouth if he wasn't staring into the *kestra'chern's* eyes.

If only it were possible to keep a tight rein on his emotions.

Outside the window an interlacing of stark, leafless branches against the snow reminded him of clutching talons.

A soft *shush* of fabric told him that Silverfox had taken a seat nearby, but not on the couch itself. "An'desha is not your lifebonded mate, and you knew that the moment he began to turn away from you. You also must know that nothing you could have said or done, nothing that was said to him, could ever make him into something he was not," the *kestra'chern* pointed out with cool logic. "And as for the way he no longer depends on you, is that as a result of meddling by Karal, or as a result of things you yourself did? You are a Healing Adept, Firesong—your own heart surely told you that such clutching dependence as you have described to me already was not healthy. You yourself must have set in motion the course that eventually led him away from your side; you could not betray your own avocation. Heal he must, even if it leads him away from you."

Firesong flushed again, and before he could stop himself, he had turned to face Silverfox once more, his anger smoldering within him and threatening to burst out. "But Karal's interference ruined everything! Where he led An'desha was *not* the direction I intended to take things!" he stormed. His voice rose, and his throat tightened as he clenched both his fists with barely restrained rage. "Damn him! He has *no* idea of my forbearance—a hundred times I could easily have *killed* him to get him out of our lives!" His rage rose into a killing thing. "I still could!" he shouted. "I wish I had!"

Across the room, Aya shrieked, and simultaneously, a vase shattered.

Silverfox did not even wince, but the crash of splintering glass dampened Firesong's anger as effectively as a bucketful of cold water splashed into his face. He stared at the heap of glass shards on the table with his jaw clenched.

What am I doing? I haven't let my temper rule my power since I was an apprentice mage! What's wrong with me? Where did my control disappear to?

"Firesong, if it had not been Karal, it would have been someone else," Silverfox said calmly into the heavy silence. "Given that he is half Shin'a'in, it would probably have been Querna. I cannot picture a Shin'a'in Goddess-Sworn leaving him in the unsettled state you have described to me yesterday. He was and is going to grow and mature, and short of damaging his mind, there is nothing you could have done to change that."

I admitted I want to murder Karal, and he says nothing. Doesn't he care?

"What would you have felt if it *had* been Querna rather than Karal?" Silverfox persisted. "Would that have made it any easier for you, as he grew away from you? Would you have been less angry than you are now?"

Of course he cares; he just realizes I still have that *much control left that I wouldn't murder Karal out of hand.*

Would I?

"No," he said slowly. "No. If he had turned to Querna, that would probably have made things worse. Karal is not precisely the figure of authority that Querna was; a Goddess-Sworn would certainly have turned him to mysticism much more quickly than Karal did."

Only now did Silverfox rise and take a place on the couch beside Firesong, although the *kestra'chern* made no move to touch him. "As you have said yourself, if it had been Querna who helped him answer his questions, we both know you would have lost him sooner," the *kestra'chern* said quietly. "As it was, since in some ways both An'desha and Karal were groping for the truth through the same fog of uncertainty, you held him to you longer. You cannot keep a chick in the shell, my friend, no matter how hard you may try."

Firesong had no answer for that, but Silverfox didn't appear to expect one. *Fine, so I couldn't hold him back—but why did he have to grow* away *from me?*

"There are many ways in which his spirit was scarred that you and I will never and can never understand, thanks to the Gods," Silverfox continued, his blue eyes thoughtful. "I have talked to him since I arrived here, since I became aware of your troubles."

He has? I didn't know that—

Silverfox paused and smiled slightly. "I knew at once that I was not the one to help him in his personal quest, but I did learn some things. I think, perhaps, that he will never be able to have a strong emotional bond to any one person—not because he is not capable of one, but for other reasons. He has seen how emotions can be a weapon in the hands of someone as unscrupulous as Falconsbane, and I think he will avoid emotional attachments for fear of using them himself in that way." The *kestra'chern* closed his eyes for a moment. "For him, the best and surest path may be that of the spirit and intellect rather than the heart. I could wish for your sake that this was not the case, but that is my reading of him."

Bitterness welled up in him, as much at the logic of Silverfox's words as at the conclusion. It matched what he himself had observed, all too closely. *It is true, but I am not going to rejoice over this!*

"But where does that leave me?" he asked, allowing his bitterness to well over into his words. "I spent all of my time here caring for An'desha when I might have been cultivating other possibilities. Now he has found other interests, and the possibilities I might have had when I first arrived are closed to me. Should I return to the Vales, I would find that all those of my inclination have paired off. So what am I to do? Where am I to look? He has had our time together *and* he has all that he now wants! Am I to have nothing for all my work and care but a few memories?"

Silverfox pursed his lips, then grimaced. "Well, I must admit that you have me there. You have given of yourself and your abilities here when you could easily have gone back to your own Vale or to k'Leshya. You have benefited a land and a people that are not even your own. Now, in fairness, I must point out that there are many who find your life and your position enviable, but that does not help how you feel now." He sighed. "I do not have a solution for you, or even much comfort to offer. Being exclusively *shay'a'chern* as you are limits you, and we both know it."

"And I am no pederast, to go looking for companions in the nursery because all those of my own years are paired," Firesong said sourly.

Only now did Silverfox offer to touch him, and only to place one hand on his knee. "Firesong, my pretty bird, I like you very much. What comfort, physical and otherwise, that you feel you could accept from me I gladly offer—and that is as a friend, not as *kestra'chern*. I know that it does not help—"

"But it also does not hurt." He managed to smile thinly. "I will have to find a solution for myself."

I think it is best if I leave it at that.

The sitting room of Karal's suite was warmer and quieter than the common room of the Compass Rose, and you didn't have to wade through snow to get to it. A cheerful fire burned on the hearth, and a kettle of hot tea and one of hot water hung on hooks where they would stay warm. Karal stood behind Natoli as she scribbled numbers and watched intently; he didn't understand anything he saw, but that didn't matter. Behind him, An'desha lounged on the couch, pretending to read a book. Karal knew that he wasn't actually reading, because he hadn't turned a page since he sat down.

"Damn and *blast!*" Natoli exclaimed, suddenly standing up and tossing the papers of scribbled calculations over her head in disgust. "Every time I make a calculation, it comes out differently!"

"Have a cup of tea," Karal advised, before the last of the pages had hit the floor. He took a hot pad to seize the nearest kettle, pouring a fresh mug full and dosing it liberally with cream and honey. He brought it over to her and handed it to her with a smile he hoped looked encouraging. "I know you wanted to try for yourself, but that's the same conclusion all the others, even the Masters like Master Levy have come to. Sun strike me, but they can't even agree on when the breakwater will finally erode to the point where it doesn't protect us anymore! They say it's all too complicated for any human to calculate."

She grimaced as she took the hot mug from him. "All right, Florian was watching me calculate through your eyes, and through him all the rest of the Companions that have any interest in mathematics were also watching. So what does *he* have to say?"

:Tell her what I told you the third time she went through the calculations,: Florian advised. *:That answer hasn't changed.:*

"He says that as far as the Companions can tell, the solution will have to involve Hardorn because we'll have to put something in place beyond the existing breakwater. Some of them believe that we need to make a different kind of breakwater and some think we'll have to do something new, but as the storms strengthen, we will have to move the protections outward. Others just have the feeling, too vague to be a ForeSeeing, that Hardorn will be involved in finding the next solution." That was a surprising conclusion, coming from Companions, but it was a welcome one, as far as he was concerned.

And Natoli went a step further. "We might as well *talk* about what we've all been hinting at for the past week. Hardorn and the Imperials. We need them, and we all know it, so let's start trying to figure out a way to get them without getting anyone in trouble or murdered."

:The Son of the Sun isn't going to like this, Karal.: Altra switched his tail nervously and got up from his spot on the couch to pace over to Karal.

"What about you?" Karal asked him, looking down into his intensely blue eyes.

:In the abstract, I don't object. I do not much like making allies of people who personally attacked my own charges, but in the interest of the greater good, it is probably going to be necessary. Solaris, however, will dislike such expediency.:

Yes, well, Solaris' reaction was going to extend rather beyond "dislike." But from the look on An'desha's face, the news was fairly welcome to him.

"So, what about you?" he asked his friend.

An'desha sat up. "They have snow up to the eaves, monsters rioting through blizzards, they're starving and freezing over there. Even Kerowyn isn't urging any kind of confrontation with the Imperials," he said obliquely. "You heard her this afternoon: 'Let General Winter take care of them.' And even Jarim agreed with her. *She* thinks that 'General Winter' is going to kill them, I bet. The trouble is, a lot of innocents are going to die, too."

"So, you're saying—?" Karal prompted.

An'desha spread his hands wide. "Haven't the people of Hardorn and the Imperials—even the guilty ones—been punished enough?"

Karal sat down at the desk that Natoli had abandoned and cupped his chin in both hands. "I know what you're saying, and I know what Florian is saying, but I've got another problem here. I want to know what the Imperials are going to do if they're desperate and feel they have nothing to lose? More assassinations? By Vkandis' Crown, what *better* time could they strike but when Solaris is here for a meeting? How can we keep that from happening and at the same time keep them from using an opportunity to talk to us as one to strike at us?"

"By bringing them within our protections, of course," Natoli said firmly, sitting down beside An'desha in the spot that Altra had abandoned. "If they're protected from the mage-storms, that should make them less desperate. What's more, I think we need to work with *their* mages as well as with the ones from k'Leshya. The Masters all think we need an entirely new set of observations anyway, and a new set of outlooks on magic could be what we're missing. It worked the last time."

"All very well and good," Karal pointed out, "but to get Imperial cooperation, we have to *find* someone with sense about the whole situation—someone who will think rather than react when we approach him. In point of fact, it will have to be someone high enough up in their ranks that we have a chance of negotiating with their leaders. So *who* do we find and *how* do we find him? I can't exactly send in a messenger with a flag of truce!" He snorted at the very idea. "I can't exactly send anyone anywhere! I don't have any authority to do anything of the kind!"

:Perhaps just as a point of beginning we could scry and try to find someone of sense?: Florian suggested diffidently.

"Florian says we should scry to see if we can find anyone who might listen to us. How we're supposed to do that with no target and over such a huge distance, I have no notion," Karal relayed, trying not to sound as if he thought the idea was completely lunatic. "Qualifications of 'authority and good sense' seem a bit vague to hang a scrying spell on."

"Well," An'desha said slowly. "As for the distance part, there's a perfectly good way to boost the power of a scrying spell, and that's to use the Valdemar Heartstone. I'd have to ask for permission, but if I'm careful who I ask, I think I can get it. I *am* an Adept, if rather unpracticed. I think I can manage a simple scrying spell."

:Tell him to ask Talia to ask Elspeth and he will get permission,: Florian said with authority. *:Rolan and Gwena both agree.:*

Karal relayed that information. "Are you going to use the kind of spell that makes a picture anyone can see and sounds anyone can hear?" he asked hopefully. He'd always wanted to see a scrying, but Master Ulrich had never used that kind of spell.

"It's the only one I know," An'desha replied ruefully. "It takes a lot more energy than the kind that works like FarSight, but I don't have a choice since I don't know that one."

"I'd prefer it even if you did have a choice," Natoli replied, tucking her hair back behind her ear. "With others watching, you have extra sets of eyes and ears to catch what you might miss."

An'desha smiled. "True. Right, well, that's how we'll have the power."

:As for a target, why don't you use the Imperial arms?: Altra said, unexpectedly. *:You're not likely to find that anywhere except in the quarters of someone with authority, either on the wall or on documents—we already know from Kerowyn's spies that they've taken the arms off their uniforms.:*

"Using the Imperial arms as a target—that's what Altra suggests. Can you do that?" he asked An'desha. "Then we can just observe people to see if they fit what we need."

An'desha looked blank for a moment. "I don't know why I couldn't. Given that, we can decide how we speak with our chosen contact once we actually have him."

:I'll find Talia for you.: Florian "vanished" from Karal's thoughts for

a moment. Karal discovered how agreeable it was to be able to use the varied abilities of Companions; normally they would have had to go in search of Talia, but through her Companion Rolan, they were able to "ask" her to come to them in Karal's suite. They couldn't convey anything in detail, however, since Talia, unlike most Heralds, did *not* have Mindspeech. Rolan could only "send" an image of them and convey a sense of need.

When she finally arrived on Karal's doorstep, she wore an expression of faint annoyance overlaid with curiosity. "I hope this is more important than what I was doing," she said without preamble as Karal let her in.

"I think so, Sun's Ray," he said, calling her by her priestly title. She raised an eyebrow at that, but permitted herself to be coaxed into accepting a chair and a mug of tea. "Natoli will explain what we're up to, and I hope we haven't overstepped our authority."

Ulrich used to say that it is easier to apologize than get permission. I hope he was right.

Natoli did explain, not only their conclusions but the reasoning leading up to them. Talia listened patiently, nodding from time to time, until Natoli was finished.

"You've come perilously close to overstepping your authority," Talia told him, "but you succeeded in staying *just* on the right side. I'll ask Elspeth, and honestly—I think she'll agree with you. She's become more pragmatic since the mission into Hardorn after Ancar and Hulda than I gave her credit for being."

"I think it was traveling through Hardorn, seeing how the people were suffering *then*, and knowing that it must be worse now," An'desha suggested. "She might not be in line for the throne anymore, but you can't remove the sense of responsibility that you trained into her."

Talia smiled faintly. "One hopes. Well, let's see what can be done— and I have a suggestion for a place where you can do your scrying. Directly above the Heartstone chamber is a room that mirrors it exactly, right down to having a crystal sphere in the center of a table. You could use that, and it's shielded to a fare-thee-well. We've used it for FarSeeing in the past." She put her mug down on a side table and stood up. "I'm beginning to think that the Queen ought to recognize you lot as a working entity; I'll have a word with her about that as well. You're all adults, you're all responsible, and you're all coming up with ideas, if not actual solutions. We ought to grant you enough authority that you can test out some of your ideas without constantly coming to one of us."

That last had Karal staring at her with an open mouth for a moment.

"Don't get too excited," she said, with a slight hint of a smile. "It won't be a great deal of authority. But you have a fair amount on your own, you know. You and An'desha are aliens on our soil, and do not necessarily have to answer to any authority in Valdemar for your actions so long as you don't break any major laws." She put the mug down decisively. "Now, if I'm going to catch Elspeth alone, I have to go now. I'll send you word through Rolan and Florian."

She walked to the door, and Karal opened it for her again, but just before she left, she turned and looked at him with a peculiar, penetrating stare. "You are something of a puzzle, young priest," she said at last. "You are the only person I have ever encountered that has a Companion speaking with him who was not also Chosen. I wish I knew why."

"So do I, Sun's Ray," he said fervently. "I would sleep better at night if I did."

Inside the scrying room, it was as silent as a cave. Even noises from outside were muffled to the point of vanishment. An'desha settled into his seat, now softened with a down cushion, brought by the ever-practical Natoli who could not see any reason why the four of them needed to get numb behinds from the hard benches when there were plenty of cushions kicking around in the Palace storerooms. The others took their places at equal distances around the table—in Altra's case, *on* the table, licking his back fur—and waited expectantly for him to begin the spell.

Their initial few attempts had ended in nothing more exciting than warehouses and a few barracks, for the Imperials might have taken their embroidered arms from the tunics of their uniforms, but they still had their battle banners displayed prominently in their barracks and the Imperial mark burned into the sides of crates. One or two had even begun murals including the arms on the walls as well. The trouble with this spell was that once it was set on a target, you couldn't move the point-of-view more than a foot or two from the target without starting over, and he couldn't do that more than two or three times a day. The spell might take most of its energy from the Heartstone, but it still required his personal power to control it.

"You know—I've got an idea. You might try the arms in the form of a seal," Natoli said after some thought. "That might at least get you a place where we can see a clerk in the headquarters. Then you can shift your target to him and set the spell again; sooner or later he's bound to go to someone in authority."

An'desha made a gesture of helplessness. "That sounds like as good an idea as any; we certainly haven't made any other progress."

"We wouldn't say that," Karal objected, speaking for both himself and Altra. "You found Shonar and the Imperial Army—and you didn't catch on to something over in the Empire itself. That's not bad for not having a specific target."

An'desha smiled faintly, and flexed his hands to warm up the muscles before he placed them palm-down on the table in front of him. He stared at a point a little above the crystal ball in the center of the table, and reached for the weighty power seething below him, embodied in the Heartstone of Valdemar.

There was no way of describing just how it felt to him, to seize this incredible energy, a force both ordered and chaotic, and with a rudimentary consciousness of its own. Were other Heartstones like this one? If so, no wonder Falconsbane had wanted to learn the secrets of constructing them! Nodes were powerful, even deadly, but this Heartstone was a hundred times more powerful than any node he had ever encountered. Linking himself in with it was similar to walking the Moonpaths, in that he found himself "somewhere else"; this "somewhere," however, was a crystalline structure thrumming with ordered power. Once there, he was possessed of the strength to do just about anything he chose, if only his control could hold up.

That was the real key, control, and it was what required so much of his own strength. *If I were riding an unbroken warsteed that happened to like me, and had decided to permit me to sit on her back, it might be like this. There is a sense that at any moment I might be thrown and trampled. "Ordered" does not mean "tame."*

Once he had the reins of power in his hands, he dropped his gaze into the crystal itself, setting the patterns and sigils written only in the invisible fire of magic to burn about it. He knew the moment it was all complete; the ring of power fused into an unbroken whole, and the "setting" sat empty, waiting for the target object.

This was the only purely mental part of the spell; he concentrated on the Imperial arms in the form of a wax impression, a seal such as he had often seen on other documents of importance. *This is what you want,* he silently told the spell as he set that image within it. *Go and find it, and bring us the picture of where it is.*

Distance meant very little to this spell if it had the power it needed to reach as far as it had to. He felt the spell straining to be off, a restive hound with the quarry in view, pulling at the leash.

He let it go, and immediately sensed power flowing from the Heartstone, through him, and into the set-spell. Oh, it was sweet. Now all he had to do was control the flow of power so that it was even, and sit back and watch the crystal with the others.

A red blur formed in the heart of the crystal, transparent, but three-dimensional. It could have been a reflection of something on the table, or something one of them was wearing; except that they all saw it, for they all leaned forward at the same time.

The haze of red solidified, the blurring focused, and the indistinct image became a clear, sharp picture, a blob of red sealing wax, centered by the now all-too-familiar arms of the Eastern Empire. The image showed him nothing more, because that was all that the spell had been set for; it did not even show the document the seal was on.

That was just *fine*, for now that he had his target, he could widen the parameters of the spell.

He seized more power from the Heartstone and wove it into new patterns, ones that told the spell to broaden its "gaze" and to open its "ears." Round about the crystal he set the new patterns, weaving them in and out of the old ones, until once again the energies fused into a whole.

The image changed; the blob of red wax grew smaller, down to a mere pinpoint, as it seemed to recede into the middle distance. It became a dot of red on a sheet of yellow-brown parchment; the document lay on a desk, on top of a stack of similar documents. Behind the desk sat a man in a sober and severely cut tunic and trews of that no-nonsense styling that says "military," both of which had the familiar look of the Imperial uniform. The desk itself was the only piece of furniture in a very small room, lit by a single lantern suspended from a chain above the desk. The top of the desk was littered with papers, inkwells, and all the paraphernalia of a clerk.

"*Yes*," Karal hissed under his breath. An'desha did not bother with self-congratulations; this part of the spell manipulation was too delicate. He rotated his viewpoint, slowly, taking it down and around until at last his "eyes" were in the middle of the desktop, staring up at the clerk working so diligently there.

There was no sound but the scratching of the clerk's pen and the hiss of his breathing—and, occasionally, a sniff as he took a moment to rub his nose with the back of his hand. An'desha stared intently into his surprisingly young face, a very earnest face, and one showing a fierce concentration on the work at hand. It was not a particularly memorable face for all that it was young; the clerk was very much of a "type." His brown hair was cut short, and from the precision of the style, An'desha guessed it was probably a regulation haircut. His brown eyes were neither very large nor very small, neither deepset nor bulging, neither far apart nor set too near the bridge of the nose. His forehead was not too broad or too narrow. His cheekbones were neither prominent nor flat nor buried in fat. His nose was neither hawklike nor pugged, neither thin nor spread, absolutely average in length and shape. His mouth was neither thin nor generous, his chin neither square nor pointed, rounded nor prominent. It would have been very difficult to pick him out in a crowd, but he *did* have one tiny scar crossing his left eyebrow and another marring the otherwise average chin. An'desha concentrated fiercely on those two flaws, branding the man's face in his mind.

Once he was sure he had the clerk as firmly in his mind as possible, he broke the spell, shattering the brittle energies with a single burst of power. He sagged down on the table for a moment as the shattered remains dissipated; feeling his own strength melting away with it.

Natoli and Karal were both ready for that moment; instantly they were each at his elbows, Natoli with a cup of something sweet and hot, Karal with cheese and bread. The moment of weakness did not last long. He had the Heartstone to draw on, after all, and he was soon sitting up again and restoring his physical strength while his magical energies slowly rose to near the level they had been when he began.

"Looks to me as if we got an Imperial clerk, one with enough status to handle important documents," Karal said, as An'desha drank the restorative brew and nibbled on the cheese.

"I hope so," An'desha said, doubt now creeping into his mind. "I don't know about that office, though. Would someone with any status be shoved away into that cramped little closet?"

But Karal only laughed. "Oh, certainly," he said, with the surety of one who has been a clerk himself. "First of all, this man wasn't wearing a heavy cloak or even a particularly heavy tunic—that means wherever he is it's warm. We know that Shonar didn't have a Great Lord, so the manor that the Imperials took over isn't going to be huge—and the Commander has consolidated all of his officers there. As many of them as can will be in the manor, not the barracks. His mages are probably in there, too. That's a lot of people to be crowded into one smallish manor house; any clerk that has his own office, and a warm office at that, *must* be of a fairly high rank."

An'desha nodded; that made good sense. "Well, I'm ready to try for him again if you are," he said. "If I can, I'm going to put a magical 'link' on him, so that it won't be as difficult to get him in the future."

Natoli nodded but also sighed. "We're likely to be doing a lot of watching before he goes in to see whatever official he reports to."

He shrugged. "There's no escaping that. I'd rather be watching him than watching the men in the barracks play dice and scrub floors."

Natoli laughed at that, since she had been the first to complain about watching the floor scrubbers and gamers. "I don't even know who to bet on!" she had protested. "That would at least make it a little more interesting!"

Once again, An'desha set the spell, this time with the face of his chosen clerk as the target. Once again the power settled into the familiar patterns, the energies drained through him, and an image formed in the heart of the crystal.

This time, he changed the point-of-view to one just above the clerk's shoulder, so that they were looking down at what the man was doing. "Another lesson in Imperial script?" Karal asked dryly.

An'desha didn't bother to answer, since Karal was the one who had suggested they use these opportunities for just that. They'd all learned what they could from one of Kerowyn's agents, and now from their various vantage points they were polishing and adding to what they'd learned. Predictably, Karal was the best at picking up the language; Natoli and An'desha were about even in their lower level of proficiency.

It was harder to concentrate on the spell and read than it was to do so and listen. An'desha soon gave up. "What's it say?" he asked Karal.

The Karsite licked his lips and narrowed his eyes as he peered into the crystal. "Something about snow—oh, it's a report about the last blizzard they got. I wish I knew what their measures meant, I'd have some idea how deep it is. Deep enough that he's writing orders to the barracks commanders to build arches out of snow blocks and turn the paths between the buildings into tunnels so the men don't have to keep digging themselves out."

An'desha whistled. "Sounds pretty grim."

"Huh." Karal was already on to something else. "Well, if Kerowyn is still counting on 'General Winter' to starve them out, she's in trouble. The supplies are holding up very well; they even have a warehouse full of frozen meat. Oh—I've got the name of the man in charge of the whole army, it's "Grand Duke Tremane." That's a name we've heard a time or two."

Indeed it was, and usually it was with something complimentary attached to it. The men of the Imperial Army had both a competent and a popular commander, and that wasn't always the case.

"Let's not tell Kerowyn unless we find out we can't make any headway with our idea, shall we?" Natoli suggested delicately. "I don't want her to try something that might make the Imperials nervous. I'd rather they weren't nervous as long as Solaris keeps attending Grand Council meetings."

An'desha nodded vigorously, and so did Karal. "Solaris keeps trying to get me accepted as her *trusted* representative, but I'm still too young for most of the Council members to think of as a real envoy. And as long as they are thinking that way, she's either going to have to find someone to replace me or keep showing up here herself." He sighed. "I'm tempted to think that she likes getting away. Maybe she does; she doesn't get out of the High Temple grounds anymore, so maybe this is a nice change of scene for her."

They watched the man write out several more copies of the same set of orders, until Karal and Natoli were cross-eyed with boredom and An'desha felt his control slipping with fatigue. Finally, he let the image dissolve and broke the spell.

"That's all for now," he said. "We'll have to try again tomorrow."

The next day, with their scrying session sandwiched in between other duties, was just as boring and disappointing as the first in many ways. But on the other hand, they soon learned that the orders being copied were actually straight from the hand of Duke Tremane himself—and in An'desha's opinion, they showed a remarkable amount of that sense they were all looking for in a contact. Dared he hope that *Duke Tremane* would prove to be the man they needed?

Finally, very late on the third day of their vigilant watching, the clerk was summoned out of his tiny office. They followed his image through hallways and up staircases, until he was stopped by a pair of well-armed guards outside a door. An'desha held his breath; the clerk identified himself and the guards let him pass. There didn't seem to be any kind of checks for someone spying by the means that they were using!

At long last they were about to see the Enemy himself, the author of so many of their troubles, Grand Duke Tremane—

That's him? *That's the enemy?*

"That can't be Tremane," Natoli said in an astonished voice that reflected her disbelief. "No. That's some other clerk."

But their target saluted the unprepossessing man behind the desk as "Commander Tremane, sir," and there was no doubt. No matter how much like one of his own clerks the man looked, he *was* Grand Duke Tremane.

"How can that be him?" Karal wondered aloud. "I expected a monster like Falconsbane, or some rock-faced hulk in armor. This man looks like—like—"

"Like a petty bureaucrat," Natoli supplied. "Like the man who makes out requisitions, the man who sees to it that you never have exactly what you need, or who demands to know how you could go through a dozen pens in a month."

"Exactly!" Karal replied. "How could anyone who looks like *that* have done what he did?"

"That's precisely why he could have," An'desha said slowly. "Because to a clerk, people who are not immediately around him are nothing but numbers. They aren't *people*, and it doesn't matter if you just ordered their deaths, because you don't know them and you never will—all you are interested in is that a certain result is achieved. The most evil people in the world might be such clerks, because everything is just another number to those who don't consider the implications of what they are doing, who concentrate only on making the numbers add up the right way." He shivered as old, old memories drifted through his mind. "Dying soldiers don't matter—they're 'acceptable losses.' Burned crops don't matter—they're 'denying resources to the enemy.' People starving and homeless don't matter—they're 'non-taxpayers.' All that does matter is getting the numbers to come out your way, no matter what it takes."

Both Karal and Natoli glanced at him with odd expression of interest. "How did you figure that out?" Karal asked warily.

"Ma'ar," he replied shortly. "Ma'ar thought like that—as an apprentice he was also his mage-master's petty clerk and he learned to think like that. Worse, he learned how to make other people think that way, how to reduce the enemy to a faceless, dispassionate number." He shook his head, and shook the memories away at the same time. "Well, that's how Tremane *could* order terrible things on a regular basis—but that doesn't mean he has. He can't have slipped as far into that way of thinking as Ma'ar or he wouldn't be as popular with his men. At least, I hope I'm right in that—give me some time to study him so I can switch the spell."

While the clerk was absolutely average, Tremane was not. He was not *handsome* by any means, and certainly was not An'desha's idea of the way a leader should look, but it was possible to remember his face very clearly without having to strain to find tiny flaws or other marks of identification.

Just as their clerk was dismissed, An'desha felt he had Tremane's face adequately in mind, and broke the spell.

The moment he did, exhaustion overcame him so suddenly that he actually blacked out for a moment, and came to just in time to catch himself falling face-first into the table.

He would have done exactly that if Altra hadn't made a leap across the crystal ball and inserted his body between An'desha's face and the marble table. He got a mouthful of fur, but not the crack to the head he would have if it hadn't been for Altra.

"*Browf!*" the Firecat grunted as An'desha's face hit the cat's side. Karal was beside him a moment later, pulling him up and then forcing his head down between his knees. Once he was in that position, his dizziness began to clear. Eventually he was able to sit up again.

"Th-thank you, Altra," he said as the Firecat stared at him with real concern. "I nearly knocked myself out!"

:You're welcome,: the Firecat replied in his mind, and followed the words with a swipe of a rough, wet tongue across his nose. *:I hate having to clean up blood, and you'd have split your forehead wide open if you'd hit the table.:*

He took the inevitable mug of tea from Natoli and sat there sipping it while he assessed his own condition and tried to make up his mind about what he should do next.

"I want to do another, while I still have Tremane fresh in my mind," he said after a moment.

Natoli frowned. "Is that wise?" she asked sternly.

"No," he admitted, "but it's necessary. And the two of you can catch me if I pass out again. I want Tremane; I want him before he has a chance to slip out of my mind. Once I've put a link on him, it won't be too hard to get him again."

Karal studied his face. "You think Tremane might be our man, don't you?"

He hesitated a moment before answering. "I think if he isn't our man, he'll take us to someone who is," he replied, after that pause to think. "I'm torn. I'd like to believe that he is for a great many reasons, and that's why I don't want to trust my judgment alone on this. It would be so much easier if we were able to work with the man on the top, for one thing. But I have the feeling that if I don't establish a link to him now, we might lose him."

"All right," Karal said, after a long pause of his own. "You're an adult; you have the right to decide what you're going to do for yourself. You certainly know what you're letting yourself in for if you exhaust yourself."

"Mostly one demon of a headache," An'desha told him candidly. "What I'm doing just isn't that dangerous."

In that, he was stretching the truth—or rather, not telling the whole truth. *It isn't that dangerous providing that Tremane doesn't have magical protections against little scrying attempts like mine.* That was the one thing that worried him. It was possible that his faint was due to brushing up against such protections. Actually touching them—

He didn't know. It wouldn't be fatal, not after the batterings such shields would have taken during the mage-storms. But it probably wouldn't be pleasant.

On the other hand, he had learned to trust his intuition about magic—knowing very well that in his case, "intuition" was really the result of an unconscious analysis of many lifetimes of accumulated memories, few of them directly available without an effort.

His "intuition" said that he'd better establish that link quickly. *Maybe it doesn't have anything to do with Tremane—maybe it's because of the mage-storms. The links seem to hold up well as the storms pass through, but the ability to scry past the breakwater might not hold up immediately after a storm if I don't also have a link.*

The paths that magic took were seriously disrupted after a mage-storm and it took time to reestablish them. Perhaps because he was Shin'a'in, the reason seemed clear enough to him. One of the effects of the storm was to "wash" everything away ahead of its cresting power, exactly like a wave of floodwater washed away things in its path. And, like on the floodplain, when the water receded, the roads and markers that had been there before the flood were gone. You had to build them all back up again.

At least, it made sense that way to him. He'd tried to explain it to Master Levy, but the artificer had only shaken his head. "If I could 'see' your magic, I could tell you if your analogy works past the surface into manipulation," he said frankly. "But I can't, and I can't test it, so I'll take your word for it. If I work out a way to test the analogy, I'll let you know. Who knows? It might give us another clue to solving our predicament."

Our predicament. It all sounds so ordinary when he calls it by that term.

He steadied himself, and when he placed his hands on the table, they were quite still, not trembling at all. "I think I must do this," he said quietly. "I know that I can with such friends standing by to help me."

Again, he established the spell, then the target; Tremane's face and upper torso appeared in the crystal, but he had someone with him other than the clerk. An'desha quickly widened his view. It was a middle-aged, ordinary woman, dressed roughly, but not poorly; she looked like a farmer's wife. There were no women with the Imperial Army, and this woman did not have the look of a camp follower about her.

The woman in question was absolutely hysterical, wringing her hands as tears poured down her face. She spoke so fast that An'desha, with his limited command of Hardornen, could not make out what was the matter.

Nor, it seemed, could Tremane. After several embarrassed and abortive attempts to calm her, he finally walked over to the door and called something An'desha did not catch.

A moment later an old man shuffled in, a man dressed in several layers of rich woolen robes. "...see if you can't get her to calm down enough to explain where she thinks the children might have gone, will you, Sejanes?" Tremane said in an undertone as they passed into the area of the spell's influence. "I can't make head or tail of what she's babbling, and nothing I do makes her anything other than hysterical."

The old man chuckled. "Boy," he said, in the Imperial tongue, "you never could manage a woman. Leave her to me."

Indeed, in a few moments, the old man did have her calmed down, in spite of the fact that his Hardornen was extremely limited and horrendously accented. He patted her shoulder and made soothing noises, and extracted information in usable bits between her bouts of sobbing.

Evidently she *was* a farmer, as An'desha had guessed. After the fright of seeing one of the mage-born monsters on the prowl, she had brought her family to the town to spend the winter. Restless at being more confined than they were used to, her children had taken it into their heads to make off somewhere outside the walls of Shonar. She *thought* they might have tried to go home, to their farm; several of them had left toys or wild animals that had been made into pets that either had been left behind in the packing or were considered to be too much of a nuisance to deal with in town. But she didn't know, because they had somehow slipped out without anyone noticing. She begged "Lord Tremane" to send men out to find them before the "boggles" did.

"Lord Tremane" sighed. "Take her off and feed her, Sejanes. I know how the brats probably got out; I'd bet they left with the children tending the flocks or herds. The guards wouldn't notice a few more children with the animals than usual. Tell her we'll see to it; I'll take a party out to question the herding children, and we should have our hands on her wandering brats before dark."

The old man took the weeping woman off, and to An'desha's surprise, Tremane went to the next room and began pulling on heavier clothing, boots, and weapons. "Come on, boys!" he shouted out as he struggled to fit boots over two pairs of heavy socks. "Get me more volunteers, we've got some lost children again! I'll meet them in the armory, as usual.

"And thanks be to the Hundred Little Gods," he muttered as he stamped to get the boots comfortable. "At least this time it's not during the height of a blizzard."

"Unbelievable," Karal breathed, as the Commander of all the Imperial Forces, Grand Duke Tremane, trotted down the stairs to the armory to *personally* organize a rescue party. And not just any rescue party, but one chasing after a handful of lost Hardornen peasant children. "Solaris wouldn't do this. I don't even think Kerowyn would."

"Maybe he just appreciates the excuse to get outside," Natoli said cynically, as Tremane led his group down snow-walled and -roofed tunnels. It was light enough in there; light came right through the thick snow, illuminating the interior in a blue twilight. Still, it could get very claustrophobic.

But just at that moment, Tremane's little troop got outside the walls of Shonar, and into the hard, diamond-bright sunlight, and confronted the brutal, snow-covered wilderness beyond. The only tracks were those made by the herds he had mentioned, tracks cut through snow up to the waist of a grown man with drifts going higher than his head. Moving dots off in the distance might represent the herds he had mentioned, browsing on the ends of branches and whatever greenery they could get at under the shelter of the trees. The men themselves adjusted scarves wrapped around their faces to stave off frostbite before they trekked across the snow after their leader.

"Firesong should see this," An'desha remarked. "He thinks *our* weather is bad; this is brutal!"

Before he forgot, and while the man's concentration was elsewhere,

An'desha reached out tentatively and laid his "link" very carefully on the Grand Duke himself.

He was jolted back in his seat by the reaction of Tremane's shields. Energy backlashed painfully through him for a fraction of a heartbeat, setting every nerve screaming.

In the next moment, it was over, though Natoli and Karal were at his elbows supporting him anxiously. His head throbbed in time with his pulse, and he knew he was going to have that appalling headache he had mentioned, but otherwise he was untouched.

"I'm all right," he assured them, checking the crystal to see that the spell had not been broken.

It hadn't; what was more, Tremane did not appear to have noticed his meddling. The link was in place, and he would be able to scry the Grand Duke no matter what havoc the next mage-storm wrought among the Planes.

"Do we need to see anything more?" he asked them. Natoli shrugged, and Karal shook his head. He broke the spell and let his weight sag into their hands.

That was all—and it was certainly enough—for one day. He let them assist him back to his room and make a fuss over him; they were rather charming about it, actually. If his head hadn't hurt so much, he would actually have enjoyed it.

The next two days proved equally enlightening. The Hardornen townsfolk appeared to have adopted Tremane as their new liege lord, and were perfectly happy with the situation. And as for Tremane himself, the man was taking equal care with the town as he was with his own men. He sat in on meetings of the town Council, his own Army Healers were serving the townsfolk, and townspeople were working to help finish the interiors of Tremane's barracks. Things were not working with absolute smoothness—there were conflicts to be resolved all the time— but Shonar was not rejecting the Imperials, and Tremane was not riding roughshod over Shonar.

Even Florian remarked through Karal that Grand Duke Tremane had all the earmarks of an excellent commander in anyone's forces.

There was no doubt in An'desha's mind that the man they needed to communicate with was none other than the leader himself. He was sensible, he seemed sensitive to the needs, not only of his own people but of those who had adopted him as their leader. He was a man inclined to reason and reasonableness.

There was only one small problem.

By watching and listening they had learned one thing further from the man's own lips. He, and no other, had been the one who had ordered the assassinations that had killed Karal's beloved Master, the Karsite Sun-priest Ulrich.

9

Firesong burned with incoherent outrage. *Someone* was meddling with the power of his Heartstone! Granted, it wasn't much power being drained off, but still, no one had asked *him* for permission to tap into it directly, and he might need that power for his experiments!

He hadn't been able to get past Silverfox to visit the Heartstone chamber in days, but that didn't matter as far as keeping track of what was going on with the Stone itself. He could tell what was happening to the Stone even at a considerable distance, and he caught the unmistakable traces of meddling although he could not identify the meddler. It wasn't Elspeth or Darkwind; he knew the signatures of their power. It wasn't the gryphons either, although he hadn't thought either of them were keyed to it. There were no other Valdemaran mages powerful enough to tap into the Heartstone directly. Initially, he suspected the new mages from k'Leshya, but one by one he eliminated them as he ascertained that they had not been linked into the Stone yet either.

Finally, this very afternoon as he was waiting for Elspeth and Darkwind to arrive for a consultation in the hot spring, he realized who it was—who it *must* be. The obvious answer had been right in front of him, and yet it was not really obvious at all.

An'desha. It had to be An'desha.

He was an Adept, and it would not have been at all difficult for him to persuade Elspeth or Darkwind to give him access to the power of the Valdemar Stone. He had been helping the artificers *and* Karal with the practice and theory of magic. One or the other had probably come up with some idea that required so much power that only that of the Heartstone would do.

And, of course, none of them deigned to ask *him* about it!

Of course not. Why should they? I'm only the most experienced Adept here! An'desha may think he has experience, but all of it is tainted, slanted Falconsbane's way. What's more, he has no experience in any form of working with a Heartstone.

But naturally, Karal has convinced him that he doesn't need me anymore. He thinks he has everything he needs to go sailing off on his own, I'm sure. He wasn't ready to work alone, and he wouldn't be ready for years! There is no way he could possibly be ready to work alone, especially not with Heartstone power! But Karal has probably told him the opposite—made him believe he doesn't need any help just when he needs it the most.

He paced back and forth angrily, forgetting that he was expecting visitors, as Aya fluttered and chirped in distress on his corner perch. The firebird began to send out false sparks with every flutter of his wings, trails of brilliant motes of light that cascaded from the bird's feathers like dust. Firesong ignored those signs of growing tension in favor of his own anger.

Rage seethed unchecked inside him. *Karal! That's who's to blame for this! By the gods, I should do something about him, the interfering fool boy! The Alliance doesn't need him anymore, not with Solaris coming here. An'desha certainly doesn't need his brand of advice!* Karal was the cause of all his problems—Karal was dangerous! He was meddling in things he couldn't even begin to understand, and he was encouraging An'desha to do the same. How long before he coaxed An'desha to try something more dangerous than just tapping into Heartstone power? How long before he encouraged An'desha to try to *change* it? Wasn't that how the k'Sheyna Heartstone had gone rogue in the first place? Pure primal rage colored everything scarlet, and his pulse sounded in his ears like the beat of a drummer gone mad. *I ought to get rid of him—I have to get rid of him, before he ruins everything!*

A high-pitched sound of ripping punctuated his murderous thoughts, and a decorative drape tore away from the wall. It shimmered with the side effects of the power he was projecting, falling slowly into progressively smaller shreds.

I should be doing that to Karal, that indolent, wet-eared whelp in diapers...

Firesong ground his teeth, letting the anger grow into a fury, not even concerned about the damage it was doing to his *ekele*. Let it happen! It didn't matter. The sound of splitting wood was reassuring—that was what breaking bones sounded like, and right now, wishing bodily mayhem on *everyone* who hadn't appreciated him enough felt *very* good.

The wooden legs of the serving table split lengthwise, in halves and thirds, twisting the surface this way and that before finally pitching sideways in collapse. The mugs and plates that slid off shattered before reaching the floor.

It is far and away past time I woke up!

At that moment, Aya gave an ear-shattering shriek of absolute terror, and a corner of the *ekele* burst into flame.

Firesong whirled, howling with anger at Aya's idiocy. The firebird leaped from his perch and fled into the corner to cower in fear under the last almost-intact table. Firesong snarled, deep in his throat, and willed the flames to *go out—go out now!* The fire only surged brighter when he directed his rage-edged power toward it. It engulfed the tattered wall hangings in a bright yellow sheet, producing an even thicker gout of smoke. He attempted to fling a blanket on the flames to smother them, and succeeded only in burning both his hands in the process. The pain only made his anger worse. He couldn't even think clearly.

Finally he clenched his burned fists and screamed at the fire.

"I said stop!"

The smoke belching out from the fire froze, and then receded back into the fire, flattening against it, smothering it, leaving the walls coated in the black of charred tinder. Finally, all that was left was a sweat-soaked, shaking Firesong, splinters of destroyed furniture, the haze of smoke, and a terror-filled firebird.

Firesong took a deep breath through his tight jaw, and his gaze darted around until he found Aya. He opened his scorched fists and lunged at Aya. The firebird fled.

He chased Aya around the room as the firebird hid under broken furniture, screaming in fear of Firesong. "You *damned* bird!" Firesong shrieked. "You *miserable* bird! How dare you!" His words degenerated into incoherent growls. Still shouting with anger that had built beyond his ability to control it, he cornered the firebird and prepared to strike Aya where he cowered, every feather shivering.

"Don't!"

The shout from the stairs made him pause—and that moment was all it took for Elspeth and Darkwind to bracket him.

"Firesong, that is your *bondbird*," the Tayledras scout said angrily. "*Your. Bond. Bird.* Are you out of your mind? Don't you realize that *you* are to blame? All *he* did was reflect what was wrong with you!"

"Get out!" Firesong spat. "This is *my* home and *my* bird, and I'll—"

"This isn't a home, it's a funeral pyre, Firesong. Strike Aya down, and you'll follow him," Darkwind warned, tapping a rhythm pattern with one foot that Elspeth quickly picked up—a pattern Firesong recognized vaguely from the containment spell they had all worked to confine the power of the rogue Heartstone of k'Sheyna. "I'm not bluffing, Firesong. We can counter anything you can throw at us, and we'll drive it right back into your teeth. It won't be pretty."

For another long moment, he stood there with his hand upraised, like an executioner ready to drop the ax, staring into Darkwind's implacable eyes. Those blue eyes bored into his coldly, promising that the words were not a bluff. His friends were prepared to cut him down.

Prepared to cut me down...

Firesong's burned hand shook and then unclenched as the impact of what was happening sunk in.

Then the anger drained out of him as suddenly as if they had lanced a suppurating boil. He dropped his hand and stared at it, appalled.

"Oh, gods—" he whispered in disbelief. "Darkwind—what did I do? What was I going to do?"

What kind of a monster did I turn into? What was I thinking? The Heartstone isn't mine, An'desha has every right to follow his own path, and—Karal is as innocent as Aya! Aya. What is wrong with me? Aya, my bird, my bondbird...

Sudden and profound grief took the place of rage, flooding in to fill the void the loss of anger had left behind. His knees gave out and he dropped to the floor, sobbing. Darkwind and Elspeth held their positions, watching steadily. If they continued tapping that rhythm, Firesong could not hear it over his own crying.

Aya, my bird, my bondbird Aya... you didn't mean to, you were scared, I scared you, and I was going to...

Aya raised up from his cowering, just a little, and false sparks showered off him in bursts. The firebird stepped forward hesitantly, and slipped into Firesong's arms to cuddle against him, crooning softly. Firesong apologized to his oldest and dearest friend through his tears, rocking forward and back, losing all track of time.

What did I do... what have I done...?

All the world was hazy from the tears and the smoke, out of focus, out of mind. There was a slow-moving blur on his right, large and graceful, with a sweep of long black hair. Someone dropped down beside him, but it was not Darkwind nor Elspeth. He squeezed his eyes shut, feeling them sting even worse, and looked up to find himself gazing into the compassionate and understanding eyes of—Silverfox?

It *was* Silverfox, whose eyes showed a soul more intricate than all the magic that Firesong claimed to understand and control. Firesong stared through streaks of soot-stained white hair, his arms full of trembling firebird.

"What have I done?" he cried to the *kestra'chern*. "What's happened to me? I've turned into... a... monster!" He sobbed, stricken with equal parts grief and guilt. "How could I have let myself get this way?"

Silverfox reached out a smooth, long-fingered hand, and swept the damp strands of hair from Firesong's face.

"That's what I hope to show you, my friend," Silverfox said quietly. "Your hands are burned by more than just fire. Now you are willing to see it all, and undo some of the harm you have done to yourself. Now you are ready. But it was a very near thing, and you must never forget it."

The *kestra'chern* stood up and offered his hand. Still burdened by the firebird and shaken by all that had just happened, Firesong took it. Darkwind and Elspeth stepped aside, their expressions sympathetic, and let them pass.

Silverfox led him into his own room, and sat him down on the bed. The *kestra'chern* sat beside him, though he made no move to touch him.

"Now rest a while, and listen to me carefully," Silverfox told him. "I will try to explain some of what has happened, but it may be complex. Be patient and open, and I will explain it all. Do you remember how the mage-storms affected you before they were stopped?"

He nodded, as Aya tucked his soft-feathered head beneath his chin.

"They affect every mage, but they do more to you than you were aware, you or anyone else. You are a Healing Adept; you are attuned to the way that magic affects the land around you, but not only are you *sensitive* to it, magic that affects the land *will* cause changes in you." He paused to see if Firesong understood, and continued at his nod of surprise. "That is why I am here; we found evidence in the records from the days of Skandranon that the same thing happened to one or two other mages of his era during the unsettled time after the Cataclysm, and it took them *years* to discover what had unbalanced previously rational people. The Vales have all been warned. I came here, in part, to see if any of you had been affected, because the changes are subtle and not particularly obvious. That is only part of what happened to you; you are ill, Firesong, but it is an illness that few Healers would sense unless they knew what to look for. There are subtle changes physically in your brain rather than your mind. They have made you quick to anger, slow to reason. They are things that make you see enemies and conspiracies where there are none."

Firesong croaked, "So," and then swallowed twice to steady his voice. "So... my own body and brain are no better off than the land."

Silverfox nodded and interlaced his fingers. "Thus and so. But there are other things; patterns of thought you have established that are your own doing, though these changes made them worse."

Firesong licked lips gone dry, and stroked Aya's back feathers "Looking to blame anyone but myself?" he said tentatively. "Searching for a scapegoat to be the author of all my problems?"

"Obsessing on finding a lifebond as if a lifebond meant the end to every problem in life?" Silverfox added dryly.

Firesong hung his head, thanking his Goddess silently for the fact that Silverfox had not ever learned of his plan to extend his life so that he could *find* a lifebond. *I will tear the Sanctuary down and scatter the pieces tomorrow,* he pledged Her. *I will destroy it as I should have done in the first place.*

Could it be that some of the taint of Falconsbane had lingered in that bloodstained place he had created? Could that also have been the origin of some of his madness?

If it was the origin, I still gave in to it, cultivated it, and cherished it. I, and no other. No one held me down and drove those thoughts into my head like so many spikes.

"I have been an idiot," he told the *kestra'chern* remorsefully. "Oh, Silverfox. No amount of ability or talent can make up for acting like a tyrannical madman."

Silverfox smiled warmly, reassuringly. With question and answer, riddle and verse, encouragement and reproach, the *kestra'chern* led him gently to bare his soul to the bones. And a few hours later, Firesong knew—just a little—how An'desha had felt, in *his* arms, not so very long ago.

Karal struggled with his demon, after finally asking Natoli to give him a little time to himself to think.

Tremane is the only optimal choice to approach. We can't let the people of and in Hardorn continue to suffer—and we need them. Tremane is an honorable man by his own standards.

But Tremane had also personally ordered the cold-blooded murder of not only Ulrich but several other important folk of Valdemar and the Alliance. The only reason those other attempts had not succeeded was purest good fortune. But he still had the blood of two perfectly innocent people on his hands, both of them servants of their respective deities, which could by some lights make it twice as heinous.

Karal was having a difficult time reconciling the Tremane who had ordered those deaths with the one who went out into dangerous conditions to rescue children.

On the one hand, I want to open negotiations with him. On the other, I want to make him suffer as much as I have. Then I want to kill him slowly and painfully, the way Ulrich died.

If the latter reaction was wrong, it was only human. Karal tried to think of the greater good, but he could not get his thoughts past that anger. Just as much to the point, he could not see how they could *trust* someone who would write someone else's life off as casually as erasing a name from a ledger.

If I just knew why—if I just knew that he hadn't done it in cold blood, in indifference, the way An'desha described—

If I just knew he had regretted it, even a little!

If I just knew why he did it—

He paced until he thought he was going to wear a hole in the carpet, and still got no further than that. it was already full dark, and the darkness outside was no less impenetrable than the darkness surrounding his heart.

I can't agree to open negotiations with someone I can't trust! That's pretty basic to the proposition of negotiations, isn't it?

Only one man knew why Tremane had issued his orders, done what he had done, and that was Tremane.

I have to know. I have to talk to him. Somehow.

"I have to talk to Tremane," he said aloud. Altra raised his head from his paws and stared at him as if he had sprouted fur and fangs.

:You must be joking,: the Firecat said flatly.

Karal shook his head. "I have to find a way to talk to him myself, Altra, before the others do. I have to know *why*. And I need to know if he'd do it again. What's the point in trying to deal with someone we can't trust?"

:I could give you a number of answers, but I don't think you're in the mood to hear them.:

"You've got to find a way to help me talk to him Altra, please!" Karal dropped down to his knees beside the Firecat, looking pleadingly into those blue eyes. "You're a mage."

:Not precisely in the way you mean.:

Karal ignored that. "Can't you do a scrying and make it work both ways?" he begged. "Can't you give me Mind-speech or find some other way that I can talk to Tremane?"

:I think this is a very, very bad idea, Karal.:

"I have to do this, Altra," he said warningly. "The other two won't follow through with the plan if I don't agree with it, that was the bargain. And I won't agree until I've had a chance to talk to Tremane myself, face-to-face if necessary!"

Altra looked at him measuringly. *:I do believe that you would pack a bag and walk across two countries if you had to, in order to speak with this man.:*

Karal nodded. "I won't have to, though. I'll bet Florian would help me rather than let me get into trouble. I'll bet Firesong would help me just to get rid of me!"

:Unfortunately, I'm sure you're correct.: The Firecat sighed heavily. *:Very well. Since you're so insistent, I'll help you. But I can't create a scrying spell for you. What I can do is to take you there myself.:*

Karal felt sick. "Jumping?" he faltered.

:It's the only way.: Altra cocked his head to one side and narrowed his eyes. *:It's either that, or give up the idea. At least if I Jump you into Tremane's study, I can Jump you out again instantly if things go wrong. I can also hold him and keep him from doing anything for a limited period of time, which should make it possible for you to ask your questions of him without his raising an alarm. And don't forget that I also know the Tell-Me-True Spell, so the answers you get will be the ones you say you want to hear.:*

"Jumping." His last experience with Jumping had been a dreadful one, and he had pledged that it would be the *last* time he let Altra Jump him anywhere. For one moment, Karal contemplated giving up—

No. I have to know. I can't make a decision unless I know!

"All right," he said, and was rewarded by Altra's ears flattening in dismay. "Now. Tonight. Before I change my mind."

:I'd prefer that,: the Firecat said sourly.

"I know you would," he retorted. "That's why I want it to be now."

Tremane rubbed his aching eyes and glanced at what was left of his candle. It had been a long day, and a longer night, but he and the Mayor's Council were working on consolidating Imperial Law and Hardornen Law into a single codex that both Town and Barracks would be living by. He wanted to be sure *they* understood all the nuances of Imperial Law; the laws of Hardorn didn't seem to be as specific, which was no great surprise. *Simpler society, simpler laws.*

Nevertheless, the Imperial forces had brought a more complex society with them, and in some ways the people of Shonar were going to have to learn how to cope.

And in some ways, we are. A hundred compromises every fortnight.

He wondered what time it was; well past midnight, certainly. He'd dismissed all of his orderlies, aides, and clerks several hours ago. Just because their master chose to short himself on sleep to work like a maniac, that didn't mean *they* should. It was good to work like this, deep into the night, in the quiet of a building in which most people were asleep. Outside, the only men awake were the ones on the walls. The city of Shonar slept, too—there would be no more emergencies tonight, and he could work without interruption, secure in the knowledge that he was completely alone in his offices.

But suddenly, he was no longer alone.

His skin shivered; the hair on the back of his neck stood up in an atavistic reaction to the power flaring up in this room.

Power? But it isn't time for a mage-storm!

He looked up from his papers in startlement, just as a boy in an outlandish set of elaborate black robes appeared in front of his desk, his arms burdened with a huge orange-and-white cat that to his shocked eyes looked to be the size of a small calf.

He tried to reach for the dagger on the top of his desk; tried to shout to alert the guards patrolling outside his quarters. With a chill of panicked terror, he found he could do neither.

The cat glared at him with widened blue eyes, eyes whose pupils reflected greenly at him, as he struggled against the invisible bonds imprisoning him. Its eyes narrowed in satisfaction as he gave up the unequal contest, and it began to purr audibly.

It's the cat! *That* cat *is doing this!* He stared at it in astounded disbelief, and yet at the same time he was absolutely certain his conclusion was the right one. The *cat* held him pinned in his place! What was going on here?

The boy cleared his throat self-consciously. "I am here to be asking you some queries, sir," the boy said, clearly enough, although the words in the Imperial tongue were thick with the inflections of several accents warring with one another. Tremane switched his gaze from the cat to the boy—and saw that the "boy" was not as young as he'd thought. This was a young man about the same age as most of his aides, although his slight build and childlike face left the impression that he was much younger than his years. "You will not be permitted to speak above a whisper, and only in answer to the question I ask." He looked a bit green, and his eyes were not quite focusing, as if he was a bit ill.

Questions? He wants to ask me questions? He transports himself here by magic and holds me prisoner in my own office to ask me questions? Am I mad, or is he? Who is he? What is he?

"This, my first question is. When you loosed forth the man in the Valdemar Court whom you had sent to murder folk by stealth, the man who was the art-maker, did you send him forth with instructions exact? Had you made a choice of who he was to kill?" The young man stared at him as if he would, if he could, bore a hole in Tremane's head with his eyes and extract the answers directly.

The paralysis eased a little, and Tremane found that he *could* speak. "I haven't the slightest idea what you're talking about," he tried to say, but his mouth would not speak what he intended to say! His lips moved, but he could not push himself to speak the untruth he thought. When his voice finally worked, the patterns it made were not the ones he had set it to! At first he stammered, and then he relaxed into speaking the truthful things he had tried to veil moments before.

"Not precisely," he heard himself whispering, to his own horror. "Not precisely, no. I ordered that people of a certain rank or station be eliminated. I really have no idea of the identities of people over there; my agents are simply not that good. Actually, at this point, they might as well not exist at all, since they can't get through to me with their information. I ordered that envoys and allies be removed; people vital to the continuance of the Alliance. I also ordered that the Queen be eliminated, but I frankly did not think *that* would succeed, as she is too well guarded."

He listened to himself, appalled. How was the young man *doing* this to him? His heart froze with fear—not because of the magic itself, but because of the implications. If this boy could do this, now, what would he be able to do later? Or was it the cat who was doing it?

The boy stared at him with eyes full of anguish. "*Why?*" he asked, his voice tight with emotion. "Why did you order such a thing?

I have to speak the truth. It might as well be truth of my phrasing and choice— the whole truth instead of parts. There is something more to this boy than—than an assassin, or an agent sent to capture me. Something personal; this boy would be a poor choice to send to interrogate an enemy commander, powers or not! His lack of composure betrays his extreme agitation and emotion. There is something larger here than one might first think. And with this compulsion to speak only what is true…

"I was certain at the time that the mage-storms that have been laying waste to the land originated in Valdemar," he told the boy. "They left me and my men cut off from the Empire, with weapons and protections we depend on for our lives utterly disrupted. Our supply lines were cut, our communications nonexistent, our organization fragmented. My men were in a panic, my mages helpless, and we were strung out along a line we could not possibly defend. If an opposing force had come against us, they could have slaughtered us. I was absolutely certain that these storms were a new weapon of the Alliance, made possible only because the mages of the Alliance were all working together. Disrupting the Alliance was the only way I could see to stop the storms."

The boy continued to stare at him in anguish, and although he no longer felt the compulsion to say anything more, that anguish urged him to continue.

"These are not men I had chosen, nor is this a command I would have picked if I myself had a choice," he said. "But the moment I accepted this command, these men became my personal responsibility. I *must* see to their safety, even before I see to my own. They must be fed before I eat, sheltered before I sleep, and although they are soldiers and expect to face battle and death, it is my job to see that their lives are not thrown away—if possible, to see that victories are with a minimum of bloodshed. At the time, I saw disaster overtaking us, and I had to do something before it caught us. If these storms had indeed come from Valdemar, they were a terror-weapon, and one tailored to strike particularly at *us*, because so much of what the Empire depends on in turn depends on magic. I thought, at the time, my action was justified if it saved my men. This was not something they could meet in combat or face over the edge of their shields."

Did this boy understand? At least he was listening, and Tremane was still able to speak.

"This is something I did not know when I first commanded men— when I was your age, in fact. Command is more than issuing orders, it is knowing what those orders might mean to the lives of your men and knowing that *you* and you alone are the one responsible for the outcome." These were the things he had never discussed with anyone else; in the spy-haunted milieu of the Empire, he would not have dared. "The men look to me to get them through each encounter; no man enters the army assuming he will die! They put their trust in me; I have to be worthy of that trust. To a good commander, no lives lost are 'acceptable.'"

The boy's gaze flickered, as if something he had said had touched a responsive nerve.

He gestured at the windows, as a cold blast shook them. "Look what these storms have wrought! Tell me I was wrong to fear for the lives of my men! I think that if it had not been for the walls we built here and the organization we gave them, the people of Shonar would be fighting monsters in the streets by night, and starving by day!"

The boy's eyes flickered toward the windows and back.

"As for what I ordered—my own mages have since told me that Valdemar did not send out the storms. I was wrong, I didn't wait for verification of my assumption, and as a result—I ordered something that was completely unjustified." He felt himself flushing hotly, and wondered at his own reaction. "*If* Valdemar had sent the storms, I am not certain now that what I did would have been justified either. Sending one weapon of terror in response to another is not a moral answer—but as a commander I don't often deal in moral answers, I deal in expediencies. I'm not used to moral answers, or moral questions. That is a failing of life in the Empire." He paused and added a final statement. "That is not meant to stand as an excuse, but as a reason. It is difficult to think in terms that one is not habituated to, and the center of life in the Empire is expediency."

True enough as far as it goes. There is no point in going into detail about Imperial life. Could anyone from Valdemar—I assume he must be from Valdemar—ever understand the Empire?

He had hardly admitted any of that even to himself, and he was surprised that he had poured it all out to a total stranger.

But this—young man—with the look of a priest has appeared in my office, with a cat in his arms that paralyzes me with a look. A single thrown knife, and I would be dead, and with my life goes the organization of my troops. Perhaps that is why I am explaining all of this. Perhaps it needed to be said so that I could acknowledge it to myself, too.

The cat's eyes were on his, gazing at him with such intensity he almost expected the beast to speak. The young man's face bore a thoughtful expression; the pain was still there, but it was secondary to the sense of introspection.

Finally, the young man nodded and put the cat down for a moment. Once his hands were free, he drew something from his sleeve about the size of a dagger. He placed it on the desk.

It was a message-tube.

He picked up the cat again, and stepped back a pace as Tremane stared at the tube, perplexed. But the young man's next words solved his perplexity.

"If you wish to open a dialogue with Valdemar and the Alliance," he said quietly, "place your opening message in this. It will go where it needs to. I can assure you that the Queen and the Son of the Sun will see it, once it has been judged safe."

That peculiar shivering came over Tremane again; his eyes suddenly refused to focus. And when he could see again, the boy and the cat were gone.

He shook his head violently; he could move again perfectly well. Had it all been a hallucination brought on by too much work and too little rest? Had he fallen asleep over his papers and dreamed the whole incident?

But when he looked down at his desktop, the message-tube was still there.

It was real. It happened. Someone from Valdemar magicked himself into my office, without the use of a Portal, and interrogated me.

Not only that, but he must have "passed" his verbal examination, for here was the way to end at least one of the conflicts facing him and his men.

Truce with the Alliance. Perhaps even membership in the Alliance?

Certainly the Allies were not suffering as Hardorn was. They had not originated the mage-storms, but they had a defense against them, a defense that the Imperial forces did not have.

Should I? It could be a trap. Dare I risk it?

A howling buffet of wind shook the stone walls of his office; snow actually drifted down to the floor from the triply-shuttered and glazed windows. And midwinter was not even here yet—

—and the mage-storms were getting worse. It was only a matter of time before they changed something or someone *inside* the walls of Shonar. It could have already happened, perhaps they just hadn't discovered it yet. What would he do if that happened? He didn't know; he hadn't been able to plan for it, though his new agents in the ranks told him that the men themselves had come up with an answer. If it was an animal, it would die, no questions asked. If it was one of their comrades, and he retained his mind, they would find a way to make him useful. If it was one of their comrades and he attacked them, they would cut him down like any of the other boggles.

I must risk it. There is too much at stake.

He picked up the message-tube and placed it carefully in a desk drawer; then he stood up and blew out his candle. There was also too much at stake to risk writing a document that important when he was half-drunk with fatigue.

Tomorrow he would close himself in his office and send word that he was not to be disturbed unless it was an emergency. This might be the most important letter he would ever write in his life.

:I didn't think you'd be so sick,: Altra said apologetically from the foot of Karal's bed, where he lay curled up around Karal's feet, keeping them warm. *:I wouldn't have brought you home so fast if I'd thought you were going to react this badly.:*

"It's all right," Karal replied faintly, as he lay back against his pillows. "Once there's nothing in my stomach things seem to settle down a bit more. The tea is helping. This is a nasty way to get a rest, though."

Altra had not even allowed him a single breath between Jumps, and his nausea had become a single overwhelming force that took over mind and body. The moment he reached his suite he had been forced to the bathroom, where he had clutched at the convenience and retched until he thought he was going to throw up his toenails. When he could stand without retching, he had dragged himself to the bellpull and summoned a "servant." As before, the "servants" who tended to his needs, especially at night, were actually Heraldic students. That was why he tried so seldom to bother them—but this time he had no other choice. He couldn't have gotten any farther than the chair he collapsed into if he'd been prodded with a hot poker.

The young man who had appeared had been seriously alarmed at his appearance, and had gotten Karal into bed before summoning a Healer.

"Stomach cold," the Healer had decreed—although Karal could tell she was profoundly puzzled by his lack of other symptoms. She had left him with several packets of herbal tea and instructions to drink as much of it as he could; the young man had made some up immediately and left it at Karal's bedside. He made up a snowpack to ease Karal's headache, and had also left a stern admonition to pull the bell to call him if he felt *any* worsening of his condition, or if he needed so much as a dry cracker.

"I'll be all right in a day or so, and meanwhile this gives me an excuse to be alone and think," he told the Firecat.

:If you were anyone else, I'd be surprised you want to do anything except lie there.:

Altra curled up around his feet a little tighter, and his icy feet finally began to warm up. It felt very good, and the snowpack the young man had made for his head was finally doing something about the throbbing in his temples.

"Well, that's the curse of being what you and Ulrich made me. I can't stop thinking even when I'm miserable." In fact, he was torn in so many directions that it was going to take some time to sort them all out.

I want to hate Tremane. His need to hate the man warred with the reality of the man himself, making him want to scream in frustration. It would have been so simple if the Grand Duke had been a liar, a fraud, a man who did generous things because it would put people into his debt. Unfortunately for simple solutions, Tremane was none of those things. Altra knew the Karsite equivalent of the Valdemaran "Truth Spell," and he had held it on Tremane once his first spell successfully controlled the Grand Duke's body. Tremane could not have spoken anything other than the truth as long as Altra held that spell active.

Which made things that much more difficult for Karal.

The problem was, he understood Tremane and Tremane's motives. It was just as he had said to An'desha; he was cursed with being able to see all sides to an argument, and the validity of each and every side.

I would not have done what he did, but I have never been in the position he was. And I was not brought up to power, nor in the Empire. It is my *reflex to take the moral path, and it is his to take the path of expediency.*

The worst of it was that, given what Tremane had honestly thought was true and faced with Tremane's situation, he could not in all candor say that he would not have made the same choice—and issued the same orders. By Tremane's background, what he had done *was* probably incredibly moral, as well as expedient—eliminating a handful of people, to possibly prevent the deaths of many hundreds of his own men *and* of the citizens of Hardorn.

It is easy enough to justify yourself by saying that something is in self-defense, or is called for because someone else did something heinous. He could not say that he would not have given in to that temptation.

He might never lose his dislike of Tremane's attitudes, and he might never be able to forgive him, but he understood the man, and so he could not hate him for being what he was—which was the product of a world full of more duplicity and deceit than anything Karal had ever known. How could Tremane have expected anything else *but* an opponent who would cheerfully sacrifice innocents to take out an enemy? He probably met opponents like that every day in the Emperor's Court!

It was hardly fair.

I know. Life's not fair. He sighed. *And I'm putting off stating a decision I've already made.* "You took my message to An'desha?"

:As soon as you wrote it. He'll scry as often as he can, and check the tube for a message. Just as you asked. If there's anything there, he'll send for you and you can send me to fetch the tube,: Altra told him, blinking his eyes lazily. *:Don't expect an immediate answer, though. It's probably going to take a few days before he makes up his mind, but we both know he's going to do it. He can't afford to pass up this chance.:*

A few days. Altra was probably right, but these few days were going to seem like an awfully long time.

:Excuse me,: Altra said suddenly. *:I should be going.:*

The Firecat stood up, and vanished, the weight of his body lifting magically from Karal's feet and leaving behind only an impression in the blankets.

Now what on earth could have caused that?

"Altra? Altra?" Karal called in confusion. "What—"

Someone tapped on the outer door in the next room, and opened it. Light footsteps neared the door of his bedroom.

Natoli stood in the frame of the open door, one arm loaded with books, and the other holding the doorpost.

"Hello," she said. "I thought you might be lonely. I figured I could keep you company as long as you're sick. Just don't pass it on to me, all right?"

He smiled. "I promise I won't," he said, knowing that was a promise he *could* keep. "I couldn't tell the Healer, but it's only Jumping sickness. Nothing you can catch."

"Oh, good," she said, smiling, and sat down beside him. "That's just what I wanted to hear."

Those few days are going to pass awfully quickly.

Karal and An'desha were pretending to look over some papers before the Grand Council meeting, but that was only the excuse so that the two of them could have a word before they upset everything with the little burden Altra was going to deliver.

"You're sure it's all right, the message is safe?" Karal asked An'desha in an urgent whisper. "I mean—look, there's Selenay *and* Solaris sitting together. One trap could eliminate them both!"

"I checked it, Altra checked it, and you checked it," An'desha replied.

"Really, Karal, given the propensity for nasty surprises that Ma'ar and his successive incarnations had, and all the information on them they left in my memory, you *can* trust me to find a mage-trap in a piece of paper! And anyway, Altra says that a mage-storm hit the Imperials again just before he went to get the tube. He doubts anything as delicate as a complicated trap would have survived."

"All right," Karal sighed, fiddling with his pens. "I'm just nervous."

An'desha gave him an oblique look. "You should be. I have to go sit down or it's going to look odd—we all agreed that it shouldn't look as if *we* had anything to do with this when it happens. I'll see you later."

An'desha hurried to his own seat as the latecomers for the Grand Council meeting arrived. When Tremane had finally put something in the message-tube, Altra had gone to get it, but he had not given it to them immediately. He asked them to think first about how it was to be presented.

Karal had wondered about that phrasing, until it dawned on him that if Solaris had any idea that he had gone behind her back to open negotiations with Tremane, she would probably see to it that the overture never got any further than that first message. She would also flay him alive, but that was incidental to the bigger scheme of things.

For that matter, Selenay might feel the same as Solaris about being circumvented.

The only person who knew they were going to be investigating the Imperials was Talia, and she had no notion that they intended to make contact. For all that the three of them were trusted, it was only to a point, and that point did *not* include haring off and sending messages to the enemy inviting him to come and play nicely.

That was when they all agreed that it would look as if *Altra* was the instigator. After they checked the message for any kind of trap, Altra would take it and present it himself to the Queen and the Son of the Sun at a Grand Council meeting, as if it had been *his* idea to contact Tremane. Solaris would no more question the reasoning and motives of a Firecat than Selenay would question a Companion. And she could hardly take a messenger of Vkandis to task for stepping outside his limits!

This was to be Solaris' last meeting for some time. She had at least managed to establish to the other members of the Council that she trusted Karal, and that Karal would never act or speak contrary to her will—and if other people on the Council had a problem with her will, that was another story altogether, and would be dealt with by negotiation. Although many of them obviously still felt that he was too young for his job, the same people felt confident that since he *was* so young, he would hardly dare to say or do anything contrary to orders.

So in theory, this would be the last time for several weeks or even months that Solaris sat in the seat beside Selenay. In theory. He had the feeling that once Altra showed up, the plans would change abruptly.

The members of the Grand Council took their seats, the Council session opened, and everything seemed routine, right down to the fact that his hands and feet were numb with cold. Things proceeded at the usual orderly pace, up until the moment that Selenay asked if there was any new business.

Which was, of course, the very moment that Altra showed up.

He simply appeared, dropped the message-tube between Solaris and Selenay, and vanished again.

Selenay was the one who picked it up and opened it, but both of them leaned over the paper rolled up inside. Karal knew what it said by heart.

To Queen Selenay, High Priest Solaris, and the members of the Alliance. Grand Duke Tremane, leader of the former Imperial Divisions of the Hardorn Pacification Force, acting Lord of Shonar, and Commander of the combined Hardorn and Imperial Armies, greets you. Tremane wishes to inform you that his relation with the Emperor and the Empire has been irrevocably severed. It is in the interest of both of our parties to negotiate a truce, preparatory to further negotiations, extending to, but not limited to, solidifying an alliance among all our peoples. To this end, he solicits an answer from you regarding such a truce, and such negotiations.

It was signed and sealed with the Grand Duke's personal seal, not the Imperial Seal, a nicety that Altra seemed to find amusing.

It was written in Hardornen and it didn't take long to read, although it was repeated in Karsite, the Imperial tongue, and Valdemaran. Tremane must have scoured the town to find someone who knew Karsite—perhaps a trader, or a priest. That was another nice touch, even if the grammar was atrocious.

Solaris and Selenay read it with their mouths clamped into tight, thin lines. Selenay passed it to Daren without a word; the Prince-Consort read it aloud.

And just as Karal had figured, all of hell itself broke loose when he finished.

Men and women leapt to their feet, each of them demanding the right to be heard *immediately*. Initially, as always with this Grand Council, there was a great deal of shouting and carrying on, mostly on the part of people who had very little to say. Solaris was ominously quiet, which made Karal very nervous. She sat beside Selenay in a pose so motionless she could have been a statue. He knew that pose; she only took it when she was being her most formal, taking on the full persona of the Son of the Sun, the Falcon of Light, Defender of the Faithful.

He kept quite silent, although Jarim more than made up for his silence until the moment when Lo'isha, the Sworn-Shaman, simply put one hand quietly on his sleeve and stared at him. Then he sat down abruptly and didn't speak for the rest of the meeting.

Solaris finally softened a little, but she kept casting suspicious glances at him all during the rest of the meeting, which made Karal even more nervous than before. He could deal with the Son of the Sun; he wasn't certain he could handle an angry Solaris who was concentrating on *personal* outrage.

Karal took notes diligently, avoiding Solaris' gaze whenever possible. The meeting finally ended when Selenay stood up and announced, "This is too important to decide on the spur of the moment. I'd like to dismiss this meeting so that we all have the opportunity to think over the positive and negative aspects of this proposal. We'll reconvene tomorrow; be prepared to present your analysis in an orderly fashion." With that, she gestured to Daren, and the two of them left the meeting, which meant that whatever else happened, it was no longer official.

That certainly put an abrupt end to the confusion. Karal gathered up his things quickly and made his escape while most of the other Council members were still arguing among themselves. But he noted that Solaris was also leaving by the same door as Selenay, and he only hoped that she was going to spend a great deal of time talking with her Valdemaran counterpart. With luck, he could be out of the Palace and down at the Compass Rose before she remembered her suspicions and sent someone to look for him.

But today his luck was out. Solaris was waiting for him in his suite, sitting on his couch as formally as if it was her throne.

"Shut the door, Karal," she ordered, as he stood in the doorframe in shock. Numbly, he did as she ordered, and turned to face her. His joints felt like carved granite, as he stood, unable to relax under her gaze.

"You were behind this, or at least you were aware of what Altra was doing, and don't bother to deny it," she said stiffly, as he stood with his back to the door and his knees shaking. His stomach quaked. "Altra is *your* Firecat, and he would not have attempted anything so audacious if you were not aware of it. Somehow you persuaded him this was a good idea. You and two of these foreigners have been closeted doing some form of unspecified scrying, according to Selenay. I do not require a spell to show me the truth or to put obvious facts together into a whole."

He swallowed, and nodded, admitting everything with that single gesture. His throat was too tight to get any words out, anyway.

She stood up, crossing her arms and narrowing her eyes as she strode toward him, anger in her every step. This was what he had feared most—Solaris, angry in herself. "This man ordered the murder of Priest Ulrich—*your* mentor, *my* friend, and a Black-robe of Vkandis! How could you even contemplate consorting with him? What possible reasons could you have for approaching him?"

After two tries, he at least got out an answer. "Because—we had to, Radiance," he said weakly. "Because there was no choice."

With that, she unleashed all of her formidable intellect and equally formidable anger on him in an interrogation that was as thorough as it was merciless. Karal answered her as best he could, but the next two marks left him weak, sweating, and shaking before it was all over. Solaris could be absolutely brutal when she wanted to be, and all without ever raising a hand or her voice. Her cross-examination was relentless and thorough, and during it she dissected his personality and left every personal weakness he knew of and some he had never suspected lying exposed. She prowled around him like a hunting cat, she moved to within a hair of his face to hiss directly into his eyes, and stood off at a distance as if she didn't want to get near him. She left his spirit flayed, and convinced him a dozen times over that she was about to demote him to least-senior cleaner of the Temple latrines—*if* he was lucky and she was feeling generous.

Nevertheless he managed to remain adamant and unshakable in his conviction that, repugnant as it was, they could not afford to allow Tremane to remain an enemy.

Finally, she sat down again, although she did not permit him to do so. Ten heartbeats later, she spoke.

"Let me see if I understand all your reasoning, such as it is," she said coldly. "First, you believe that the folk of Hardorn and even the men under this Tremane's command have been suffering for far too long. Second, the best indications are that the new boundaries of whatever solution we come up with when the breakwater fails must include the eastern border of Hardorn. Third, there is some thought that if we had access to the mages trained in the Empire we might be able to find that solution sooner. And fourth—" she leveled a stare at him that was as opaque as steel. "Fourth. You have come to the conclusion that Tremane can be trusted."

"He was under Altra's Tell-Me-True all the while he answered my questions. He has protected the people of Shonar, even though he didn't have to," Karal reminded her as he shivered and did not bother to try to hide the fact. "More than that, he has done things for their benefit personally, things that could not possibly be of profit to him. He has kept every pledge he made them, and every pledge he made his own men."

"Hmm." Her expression did not change.

"I would add a fifth, but it is quite subjective," he said, feeling sweat run down the back of his neck. "I believe he—regrets his actions."

"Regrets." Her mouth tightened, and she stood up again. "There are some things I must do, but as of this moment, *your* authority is in abeyance. You will remain here in these rooms until I give you leave to go elsewhere, and *where* that will be is going to depend on what I learn in the next few marks."

She swept past him; he held open the door for her, and she swept out, leaving him shaking with anxiety and reaction in her wake.

After he closed the door behind her, he went straight to his bed and lay down on it, his body as exhausted as if he had just run around the city walls, and his bones gone all to water. No need to tell him to stay here, for he couldn't have left his room if it had been on fire.

He didn't know what she was going to do next, but every possibility left him shaking with fear. Not for himself, but for her, and for everything the Alliance had done here.

Tremane watched his windows shake as another blast of icy wind hit them, a wind laden with so much blowing snow that there was no view outside. The cat had appeared as soon as he put down the message-tube; it had materialized on his desk, placed a paw on the tube, and vanished again, taking the tube with it.

They were in the middle of another blizzard. He had waited until another blizzard struck and had been active for some time before actually putting his carefully-worded overture into the tube; he wanted to be sure that he would have a time when he would be able to stay in his office for several hours, waiting for a reply. There had been no emergencies, and now the folk of the Town and Barracks were safely buttoned up in their lodgings, passing the time until the storm blew itself out. No one would need him until that happened. He could wait for as much as two days for an answer to his overture, if nothing went wrong.

Which was precisely what he was doing now; waiting. He fully expected the cat to show up alone, but with a written reply, a tentative suggestion that his overture was being considered. It was also possible that the cat would show up with the boy, though that was less likely. Negotiations took time, and many exchanges of paper, before anything concrete came of them.

He did *not* expect the answer he got—a cat all right, but with the cat was a woman, garbed in elaborate robes of gold and white, robes that he recognized from the descriptions passed to him by his spies. And now he cursed his stupidity for not recognizing a less-elaborate, masculine version of the same robes on the boy.

This was High Priest (*not* Priestess) Solaris, the Son of the Sun, the secular and sacred leader of all the people of Karse. And from her expression, she was perfectly prepared to whip that ritual dagger she was carrying out of her belt and slit his throat on the spot.

He, of course, could not move. Once again, the cat held him paralyzed.

Her eyes glared at him with a fire of rage that gave even him, a battle-hardened veteran, pause. Her face was as white as the snow outside, but her hands were steady. "You give me one good reason may, why killing you I should not be, as murdering my friend you did," she snarled, in heavily-accented Hardornen.

Not bad, considering that she probably hasn't studied it much.

His mind raced. What should he tell her? What *could* he tell her? What would she believe?

Nothing, probably.

No, there was no reason to defend himself or his actions. Coming up with excuses would not save him.

He would have drawn himself up in his chair if he had been free to. Instead, he gazed directly into her eyes. Once again, he would probably be forced to speak the truth, so why not simply do so to begin with?

"I cannot," he told her with bald honesty. "By the laws of your land and of my own, my life is certainly forfeit to you. I committed murder, if only by secondhand. I cannot justify a decision that has proved to be so very wrong, and so ill-conceived."

Her eyes narrowed a trifle, as if she had expected duplicity, or at least an attempt at it. Had she *not* put that magic on his lips that forced him to speak truthfully?

"By the same token, my best information at the time was that the mage-storms were a weapon of terror sent by your Alliance," he continued. "I sent my own weapon of terror to disrupt your Alliance. I proved by that assumption, I suppose, that my moral standards are lower than yours, since I could even *think* that you might send terror-weapons that strike at armies and civilians alike. I further proved the same thing since *I* retaliated with a weapon of terror. The Empire is a bad enemy to have, lady, and we have made worse enemies over the centuries. We are prepared to see just about any atrocity, and to meet it with the same."

Her frown deepened, but her eyes widened a little.

"But I put this to you, Son of the Sun—as a leader, I would venture to say that you have been in similar situations. Whether you would have responded in the same way, only you can say."

That hit home; he saw it in her eyes, in the way she winced slightly. But her anger had not lessened.

"For the first time in this, my life," she said through clenched teeth, "I considering am my ban upon the demons revoking, and up the demon-mages bringing to those terrible spirits turning loose upon your troops. *That* is what you have me brought to!"

He thought very carefully before speaking. "By all repute, Solaris, you are too just to levy upon the innocent a retribution due only to their leader."

Her chin rose. "So. You offer to me your life?"

He only raised one eyebrow—that much movement, at least, was permitted him. "The people of this place depend on my leadership, as do my men. Without me, Shonar and the barracks will be in chaos, for there is no single man that they will all agree on as leader. Likeliest, it would be one of my generals who triumphed; a general who would not know as much about you, and who would still consider your Alliance to be his mortal enemy. *You* are too good a leader to slay a *former* enemy who might be replaced with someone who will still be your enemy." He tried a touch of boldness. "I am not your enemy, Solaris. I told the truth in my missive. We have lost touch with the Empire, and the Empire has abandoned us. My duty to my men dictates that I see to their safety and there is no safety in continuing an aggression on behalf of someone who has left us here to rot." He managed a slight shrug. "The real enemy we both face is the force that sends these mage-storms. Isn't it better to face that enemy together?"

Her eyes narrowed to slits in speculation, although her jaw was still clenched tightly in anger.

"You have not attained and held the rank of Son of the Sun without learning the lesson of expediency, Radiance," he finished. *I believe this is the place to stop—while my luck is still holding. One more word might turn her the other way.*

"No," she hissed. "I have not."

She stepped back, and he felt relief sweep over him. She was not going to kill him—which meant that she *was* possibly going to support his bid for a truce and an alliance of his own.

Much as she might hate it, she knew that it would bring the greater good.

She suddenly waved her hand, then gestured with a clenched fist, and he felt the poor, sad remains of his shielding against magics collapse and disintegrate. What the storms had battered, her magic finished—and he felt dread clench at his guts.

"But I do curse you," she said, with a grim smile. "I curse you, with something the touch of which you have already felt. Your help we need, but know you I do not, and trust you I do not. In the Name of Vkandis Sunlord, and with the power He has granted me as His Son, upon you I lay that you will never to me lie, nor to anyone else tell an untruth, whoever questions you. *Never.*"

Chill spread through his body. *She could not have imagined a more terrible curse for a son of the Empire,* he thought numbly. *I can never, ever go home again...* Not that he could have anyway, given what he had already done.

"Feel the curse—or the freedom—of truth," she finished, her smile widening, her eyes glowing fiercely, "And then will we see what measure of man you are truly."

She swept up the cat in her arms, and vanished.

With her disappearance, the paralysis vanished also, and he sagged in his chair, gone boneless with relief and reaction.

He let out his breath, and laid his head down on his arms on the top of his desk, nearer to tears than he had been in all of his adult life. In all of his checkered career, he had never had quite so close an escape, not even on the battlefield—and in all of his life, he had never gotten out of such a situation by doing as he had, telling the truth.

Now I will have no choice, he thought, that chill passing over him again. *But—perhaps she overestimated her power. I should test this.*

"I am Grand Duke Tremane," he said aloud, raising his head from his arms, "and I am a mage of average powers, forty-five years of age."

He cursed, silently. He had *meant* to say, "A mage of astounding powers, and sixteen years of age." He had *thought* right up until the words emerged from his mouth, that this was what he was going to say.

The curse was working, and it worked even without having anyone to hear him but himself.

The curse of truth, he thought, propping his head up on one hand as a headache started. *How my enemies would laugh!*

But she was right. Now even *he* would find out just what a measure of a man he was. He only hoped he would be able to live with what he learned.

1 0

I am still envoy, I still have all my limbs, my skin has not been flayed from me, and Vkandis help me, but I am actually holding up under this pressure.

Solaris had finally gone, and the wonder of it was that no one but Karal had ever learned about that torturous interview in his suite. She left him and his authority intact and never mentioned to anyone else that the opening of negotiations with Tremane had been anyone's idea but the Firecat's. There was even a peculiar sort of respect in the way she looked at him now. Respect for standing up to her? Perhaps that was it. Perhaps it was respect for the fact that he stood behind his convictions, that he had not let personal feelings interfere with what was important for the greater good.

He did not know for certain just what it was she had done after she left him. He didn't really want to ask. Whatever it was, she had gone on to Selenay and convened a small meeting of the envoys and heads of state—that is, a meeting of herself, Selenay, Prince Daren for Rethwellan, Jarim and the Sworn-Shaman for the Shin'a'in, Treyvan for the k'Leshya and Darkwind for the Tayledras. With that smaller, much more manageable group, a basic reply to Tremane was worked out and sent, not via Altra, but via Hansa.

I don't think she's ever going to forgive Altra.

Karal had no idea what had made Solaris change her mind, but whatever it was, it pleased her enough that she tacitly forgave him for what he had done.

And, eventually, it was Hansa who Jumped back to Haven with

Tremane's chosen representative—Karal was just as glad that they would no longer be treating with Tremane personally. He did not think that he would ever be able to face the man without wanting to perform some very painful and undiplomatic experiment upon his body involving knives and large stones.

Karal had given up expecting anything, after learning that the leader of the Imperial Army looked like a clerk, so he wasn't particularly surprised when the man Tremane chose to represent him was a mage so old and decrepit it looked as if he might break up and blow apart in a high wind. But although the mage Sejanes was old, there was nothing whatsoever the matter with his mind. He was as sharp as anyone Karal had ever met. He already spoke Hardornen well enough to please some of the Hardornen exiles living at the Valdemaran Court, and he began picking up Valdemaran *and* Tayledras with a speed that left Karal gasping.

Finally, though, the old boy confessed that it was the result of a spell, one used successfully in the Empire for centuries. "If we hadn't had it already, we would have been forced to concoct it," he said, eyes twinkling. "Or our clerks' time would be taken up with learning languages and not with their real duties."

"And what duties are those, sir?" Darkwind had asked.

"Why, running the Empire, of course," the old fellow countered. "Everyone knows it's the clerks that run the government and the rest of it is all just for show. At any rate, I'm glad I'm in a place where I can cast it again, without having to recast it every few days."

Surprisingly, the old man had completely won over Solaris, perhaps because he reminded her of Ulrich. He had spent several marks closeted alone with her when he first arrived, and when they emerged again, Solaris demonstrated a considerably softened attitude toward the Imperials—and a positively friendly one toward Sejanes himself.

Well, what they had said or done was also none of Karal's business, much as it might eat at his curiosity. If she or Sejanes ever thought he needed to know, they would tell him. Otherwise, there were many things in the world he would never know the answer to, and this was just one more.

Much to Firesong's chagrin, the Imperial mages were *all* taught an analytical, logical approach to magic. Faced with overwhelming odds against the superiority of "instinct," the Tayledras Adept gave in, and subjected himself and his techniques to a similar analysis. It was just as well, considering that the information Sejanes brought with him indicated a failure of the breakwater just past Midwinter. Firesong volunteered to calculate the exact time, by intuition only, as a last effort to prove the validity of art over mathematics, but he finally acquiesced and helped with the more scientific method. Work on a solution proceeded at a feverish pace. All around them, the capital was preparing for Midwinter Festival with dogged determination, but there would be no time for festivals for the mages and artificers hunting for that elusive solution.

In the anxious concentration on what magic might do to save Valdemar and her allies from the same fate known of in Hardorn, the other projects the artificers and their students had been working on suffered the neglect of the Masters.

There were some projects that should never have gone without supervision. It was a week before Midwinter that the artificer's experimental boiler on the Palace grounds exploded.

The Palace rocked to its foundations, and everyone in the Grand Council Chamber looked up in startlement. Like the worst clap of thunder anyone had ever heard, increased a thousandfold, it vibrated the Palace and everything in it. As it shook the building, it shook everyone who heard it with sudden, atavistic fear. Of everyone in the chamber, only Karal had an inkling of what the cause was.

"The boiler!" he cried, and sprang from his chair in a scattering of pens and papers, heading for the door. He tripped over the legs of his fallen chair, caught himself by flailing his arms wildly as he staggered across the floor, and continued his run. He burst out of the door to the chamber, startling the guards no end, and tore down the hall in the direction of the Collegia.

One of the student artificers had been working on the boiler-engine project before all the turmoil about the breakwater failure began. Natoli and Master Isak had been helping him with it until the breakwater project occupied their attention; and ever since she stopped helping him, Natoli had been feeling guilty about neglecting him. He had no aptitude for the breakwater project and had been working on the boiler alone and unaided for some time. His idea was to heat the Collegia with the waste hot water from his boiler, while using the steam-piston contrivances attached to it to drive a water pump bringing water up from wells, and to do other mechanical work needed at the complex. Chopping wood, for instance; he had a design for a steam-drive wood splitter that would save servants endless time. His innovations included plans for an ingenious mechanism to supply wood and water to the boiler itself on a constant basis. That was the tricky part, and the one Natoli had agreed to help him with.

This was one of the largest steam-boilers anyone had ever built, almost the size of a man, and it was inherently dangerous. Boilers had exploded before this. He remembered the talk from the Compass Rose. If the boiler overheated, or boiled dry—if it had boiled dry and they weren't aware of the fact, and they'd then added water to it—

He burst out of the Palace doors into the daylit gardens, and floundered across the snow-covered grounds, oblivious to the cold. Other people ahead of him surged out of the Collegia buildings, heading in the same direction.

The boiler was at some distance from the Collegia, and had been set up inside its own little brick "false-tower" so as not to be a blight on the landscape. Those brick walls would have contained the explosion—

And if anyone was still inside the building, they'd have been caught between the explosion and the brick walls!

This was like a nightmare, where he ran as hard as he could, until his side and lungs burned and he couldn't even catch his breath, and he still made no progress in the knee-deep snow. By the time he reached the scene, plenty of other people had already arrived, and the injured had been taken away. All that was left to see were the remains of the boiler and the tower. The wooden door- and window-frames had been blown out of the walls in a shower of glass and splinters, and the brick walls themselves were cracked and bowed ominously outward. Some folk were throwing buckets of snow into the interior of the tower, presumably to put out a fire and cool the remains of the boiler, and every bucketful that went in produced a billow of steam and an ominous hissing.

Karal spotted one of the Masters; the one concerned with mechanics and clockwork, Master Isak. The old man was just standing in the snow, his square, lined face blank, his coat on inside-out. "What happened?" he cried, grabbing Master Isak's sleeve. "Was anyone hurt? Who was here?"

Isak wiped his forehead, his shock of white hair and side-whiskers standing out like an angry cat's fur. "The boiler itself didn't rupture," he said vaguely. "It was the offset pipe—just blew, tore the boiler out of its footing and drove it into the far wall in an instant. There were four students here, and they were all hurt, but only Justen was hurt badly. Poor boy! Poor boy! He tried to get the safety valve opened wide to let the pressure off, but it wasn't enough—he ran for the door, but—he was still inside the building when it went, the rest were already at the door

601

and the explosion blew them into the snow. Horrible... just horrible."

"Was Natoli here?" Karal demanded, shouting and shaking the poor man's arm. "Was she?"

"They took her with the rest to Healer's," Isak mumbled, staring blankly at the blood-spattered remains of the door and wringing his hands with anxiety. "The Healers have them all. I don't know anything else. They just left—"

Karal dropped Isak's arm and sprinted—or tried to—in the direction of the Healer's Collegium. Running through the heavy snow was like trying to run in loose hay; it was impossible to make any progress. And by the time he got there, they had taken Natoli off to a little room by herself and wouldn't let him or anyone else near her.

"She just has a concussion, some bruises, and a broken wrist and ankle," they told him. "But we don't know for certain, and we can't let anyone in to upset her right now. She's upset enough as it is."

Why, he soon found out—Justen, the boy she'd been helping, had lost both legs to the knee, and was badly scalded elsewhere. Only the fact that he had been blown out into the snow through the door saved him from worse burns. His clothing had been saturated with boiling water, but the snow had cooled it quickly enough that the burns where his clothing had nominally protected him were superficial, though painful.

"At least it wasn't his hands or his eyes," one of the Healers said grimly, wiping his bloodstained sleeve against his sweating brow. "As an artificer, he can get along without legs, but not without hands or sight. And considering that he was in the same room as the boiler, he could have been killed."

That was the general consensus; it could have been a lot worse. That was no comfort to Karal. *It is bad enough!* He loitered about the quiet halls, trying desperately to find someone to question, but everyone in the Collegium who was concerned with the four injured students was busy, and none of them had any time to talk to him. Anyone else he asked would only say apologetically that he knew as much as they did.

Finally, he gave up and headed for the chambers set up in the Palace where the artificers were working with the mages. Maybe someone there would know something.

No one did; there was a general air of gloom pervading the place. Some, like Master Levy and An'desha, were working grimly at the water-table or at other tasks; their set expressions and the tight lines of their mouths told him that they were trying to distract themselves with work. Others were making no pretense at work; they simply sat with hanging heads and nakedly anxious expressions, looking up with wide and hopeful or fearful eyes whenever someone came to the door.

He joined the pair at the water-table; they were trying some new trick of An'desha's that involved dropping a ring into the table rather than a single stone, and seeing how the waves reflected inward toward the center of the ring. Since the waves of the mage-storms were "echoing back" to their original center, this seemed to be the best way to simulate the effect.

They did this, over and over again, making minute changes and repeating the experiment mindlessly, then making notes in ledger after ledger. More and more people came to the room, as if aware that any news from the Healers would come here first.

Karal sat on a bench and watched the ring drop, over and over. Elspeth and Darkwind sat next to him and Elspeth put one hand gently on his shoulder; he hadn't seen them come in, but he wasn't surprised that they were here.

The walls of that tower were bowed outward, and the boiler was nothing more than metal scraps, he thought, feeling an invisible hand squeezing his heart. *How could she be all right? Pieces of metal must have been shot through the air like lances! Were they just telling me that to make me feel better?*

If only he knew! If only someone would come with word!

A box full of the round pebbles they used in the water-table lay on the bench beside him, and he began picking up handfuls and dropping them back into the box, one at a time. Darkwind began wrapping the shaft of a feather with fine silver wire, and Elspeth began methodically sharpening one of her knives. The stropping sound blended with the *tick tick* of pebbles dropping into the box, forming a peculiar and hypnotic pattern.

:*Karal!*:

Karal's hand closed hard on the pebbles; Altra materialized with lightning suddenness right in front of them.

Elspeth dropped her dagger.

:*Karal, I've just been to Natoli—she's fine. Or rather, she's no worse than the Healers told you. Concussion, cracked collarbone, bruises, broken wrist, but only a badly* sprained *ankle.*:

Karal babbled all this to the rest of the room, as quickly as Altra relayed it to him mentally. As he spoke, the atmosphere in the room changed dramatically.

:*Justen* will *live, and in fact he's already making rather narcotic-induced plans for artificial legs or a wheeled chair. His burns are painful, but they have new dressings and new narcotics from the k'Leshya that will make a big difference. Ferd's concussed and his wrists are both broken, but they'll heal fine, David broke three ribs and his arm. That's it. That's all. They're going to be all right!:*

Cheers rang out across the room, although Karal's mind was only on Natoli. He let out a whoop, and threw his handful of pebbles into the air. An'desha yelped and dropped the hoop he was holding onto to cover his head with his hands as pebbles showered down around him.

The hoop and one of the stones hit the water simultaneously, the stone falling in the middle of the area enclosed by the hoop. An'desha ignored it, vaulting across benches to join Karal in a back-slapping indulgence of relief.

But Master Levy ignored *them*, leaning over to peer intently at the water-table.

When they finally stopped acting like a pair of demented idiots, he beckoned imperiously to An'desha. "Get over here, would you? Something interesting happened this time."

Heads turned all over the room at that, and a sudden silence fell, for Master Levy never used the term "interesting" unless something of cosmic portent had occurred or been calculated. An'desha trotted back to his place beside Master Levy and picked the hoop up out of the water.

Master Levy picked up a stone.

He gave the signal to An'desha to drop the hoop, and at the same time dropped the stone into the exact center of the area defined by the hoop.

"There," he said, as An'desha leaned over the table. "Where the two sets of waves meet—you see?"

"They're canceling each other," An'desha breathed. "The water isn't exactly smooth, but it's just a minor disturbance. It jitters... it breaks up."

Darkwind rose to his feet with alacrity, Elspeth following. "Do that again!" he ordered. "I want to see this."

Others quickly gathered around the table, including those who had only come here on the chance that there was word about the injured students. The experiment was repeated over and over again, with the stone being dropped simultaneously with the hoop, a heartbeat after the hoop was dropped, and a heartbeat before. In all cases, the waves in the water caused by the hoop were at least partially canceled by the waves from the dropped stone.

And the trick worked best when the stone was dropped in the exact center of the area defined by the hoop.

"This is it," Master Levy breathed, his eyes lighting.

* * *

"But how are we going to set up an opposing force, in the proper modulation, that will cancel the mage-storm waves?"

Karal came back to hear Master Levy ask one of his typically brutally precise questions. He would rather have been at Natoli's side, but the Healers still weren't letting anyone in with the students. Now he was back, half a candlemark later, and the discussions were still going strong.

"More magic, like a Final Strike," Darkwind replied promptly. "The storms were caused by magic. We can set up a canceling force by magic, something that releases an immense amount of energy all at once. We've canceled magic before—we do that all the time to blunt effects, in containment spells—those are just spells that exactly counter the force coming out of someone or something." Now his face lit up as well. "That's our answer, for now at least! We can't replicate something that will exactly duplicate the force of the original Cataclysm, but I bet we can come close enough to buy us some more time! Or at least—"

"But—" Master Levy began.

Darkwind waved at him, and he closed his mouth on whatever he was going to say. "Or at least clip the top off those waves. I don't know how, but I know that there has to be a way. We've got mages from four different disciplines here, and if among all of us we can't find an answer, I'll eat my boots without sauce!"

"I hope you have a taste for leather," Master Levy muttered, but only Karal heard him.

"I'll reconvene the mages in the Grand Council chamber," Elspeth said, and ran off before anyone could stop her—not that they wanted to. Darkwind looked at An'desha, who shrugged.

"We might as well," he opined. "It isn't even dark yet. We have the whole night to argue."

The group, when it finally assembled, included not only the mages of the Tayledras, Sejanes, the k'Leshya mages, and the White Winds mages who were still teaching at the Collegium, it also included Karal, Altra, Lo'isha the Sworn-Shaman of the Shin'a'in, and one of the Karsite Mage-Priests who had fought Ancar, the same one who had saved Natoli's father's life. They had to use the Grand Council chamber as there was no other room large enough to hold not one, but four gryphons. Master Levy had the water-table emptied, brought to the chamber, and refilled so that he could demonstrate their discovery.

All of those present leaned over the table with extreme interest; Master Levy and An'desha demonstrated their experiment many times over so that everyone got a chance to see what was going on in detail.

"Now," the Master Artificer said, when everyone had looked his fill, "I am out of my depth. I leave it to you to determine if this model is accurate to the situation, and if so, what can be done about it."

"For a beginning, my people back in Shonar have been measuring the strength, duration, and timing of the storm-waves," Sejanes said briskly. "We have all of those that occurred right up until the moment I departed, but in the interests of complete accuracy, we should get the most recent. If my lord cat over there will take a message—"

Altra bowed his head gracefully.

"—I can get them to send the most recent of their records, and we can work out just how large an event we'll have to create for the canceling effect." Sejanes scribbled a brief message, and Altra paced across the table to take it from him. The Firecat vanished; by now the mages were so used to the way he came and went that they paid no attention.

"We do have a major problem," Master Levy pointed out. "We have, not one, but two event-centers, and one is absolutely inaccessible unless you happen to be a fish."

"That's true," said one of the human k'Leshya mages, "but the real problems are occurring where the waves intersect. Those are the places where weather disruptions are forming, where monsters are created, and where there is transportation of land. We might find that if we only have to deal with one set of waves, the effect on magic would be temporary and can be shielded against for a time if we can just cancel out the Dhorisha waves."

Master Levy shrugged and spread his hands. "I make no pretense that I understand magic; I only observe and deduce what I can."

Sejanes cackled and slapped him on the back. The old man was stronger than he looked; Master Levy actually staggered for a moment. "Hiding arrogance behind false modesty, boy? Don't bother; we all know we're in elite company, and you're included in that. Now, the question is, just what is our pebble going to be?"

"The generating force is going to have to be powerful," Darkwind said soberly. "Very powerful. I need to point out, friends, that I do not think it is going to be possible to generate anything powerful enough to counter that final wave—the echo of the Cataclysm itself. Not without creating another Dhorisha, another Evendim. And I don't think any of us want to do that."

"So far as that goes, I don't particularly want a massive explosion in the heart of my homeland," Lo'isha put in. "We rather like the Plains the way they are, and I'm not certain we can persuade the Star-Eyed to put it back if we ruin it a second time, however lofty our motives."

"No—now wait a moment," Sejanes interrupted. "The problem is that the original Cataclysm was the result of two events, both intended to do the maximum in physical damage. Remember? *Physical* damage. Your Mage of Silence wanted to destroy his enemy's entire force, *and* destroy his own Tower so that if the enemy somehow survived, he wouldn't be able to find anything to use. But if *all* we want to do is to send out a counter in the energy-plane of magic, is there any reason why we can't just do that, channel all of the released energy into the energy-planes? Frankly, tearing up huge tracts of land is rather wasteful use of power we could focus elsewhere!"

Darkwind opened his mouth as if he were going to say something, then got a thoughtful look on his face and shut it again. One of the new gryphons, a burly hawk-type, clacked his beak thoughtfully. "If we concssentrrrated the powerrr in that plane, we could do morrre with lesss enerrrgy than the Cataclyssssm itssself requirrred."

"Or more specifically, on the 'edge' between planes where the waves brush against our world, and cause the physical damage," Elspeth chimed in. The gryphon nodded firmly.

"Which brings us around to the question again, and that is *how?* We need a focused burst," Sejanes said, "and not a sustained release. Most of us are not used to thinking in those terms; the only focused bursts of energy *I'm* used to creating are lightning strikes and similar unpleasantness. Or Final Strikes, but the mage who does one isn't going to survive the experience, and I'd like to survive."

Lo'isha looked very, very thoughtful and stood up, clearing his throat and getting everyone's attention. All activity slowed and stopped, and attention went to the Shin'a'in.

"For the sake of clarity, I am going to impart something that some of you may already know," he said. "This was once a closely-guarded secret among my people, but there is a time when secrets need to be revealed. After the Cataclysm, all of the people formerly known as the Kaled'a'in—"

"Except for Clan k'Leshya—" interrupted a k'Leshya mage.

"Yes, except for k'Leshya—gathered at the edge of the crater that had once been their homeland—which was also the place where Urtho's Tower had stood. They divided over how magic was to be dealt with in the future, and became the two cousin-peoples, the Shin'a'in and the Tayledras. To the Hawkbrothers, who chose to follow the ways of the mage still, the Star-Eyed Goddess gave the task of cleansing the lands warped by the magics of the Cataclysm. To the Shin'a'in, who chose to ever after *avoid* the use of all magics save those of the Shaman, she gave another task." He paused, closing his eyes for a moment. "In exchange for this, she restored our home, and since we were vowed to use no magic, we did not experience the effects of the mage-storms of the time. The task we were given was to guard the Plains from all outsiders. This much is common knowledge. What is *not* common knowledge is the reason for the task. In the center of the Plains, at a site known only to the Sworn of the four faces of the Goddess, lie the remains of Urtho's Tower. Buried beneath the surface are the weapons Urtho did not and would not use. They are very powerful. And they are still alive and ready for use, according to our traditions. At least one of these should be the very thing that we need."

The Shin'a'in drew his dagger and laid it flat on the table. "It is time to end the Guardianship."

Jaws were dropping all around the table, Karal's not the least.

"Here is the one problem that I foresee—and given that we have our Kaled'a'in brothers and sisters of k'Leshya with us, this may be less of a problem than I had thought," the Sworn One continued. "Once we unearth the weapons' vault, which should still be intact, we will have to search through what is there to find a suitable weapon. And we will have to determine how to make it work, or how to adapt it to our need." He smiled slightly. "Needless to say, Urtho did not leave an inventory nor a book of instructions with them."

Karal realized he had stopped breathing with surprise, and forced himself to take a deep lungful of air.

Treyvan shook his feathers, and nibbled a talon. "I rrrecall a litany, much like the Tayledrrrasss litany of 'frrriendly beassstss,' that we magesss of k'Lessshya arrre all rrrequirred to learrrn."

"The 'Garland of Death,' of course," supplied one of the humans. "That *could* be an inventory and set of descriptions! But I always thought it was just a memory-exercise with a particularly morbid name—"

"And ssso it isss," Treyvan agreed. "But like ssso many thingsss in ourrr teaching, it hasss morrre than one purrrpossse, I think."

"Another problem—" said a voice from the door. Firesong strode in, with Silverfox beside him. "I beg your pardon for being late, but I was checking some calculations of my own. Ladies and gentlemen, we knew we were chasing a deadline, but I now know the exact moment of that deadline. How are we to get to the Dhorisha Plains before the breakwater collapses? We have only until a fortnight after Midwinter Day to reach the Plains—in the winter, across two countries. Then we must travel to the center of the Plains, and sort through the contents of this Vault. Just how are we to manage that?"

Silence. Then, into the silence, Elspeth spoke.

"There is a permanent Gate near k'Leshya Vale on the rim of the crater," she said. "There must be—Falconsbane vanished from there, and how else—"

"*Yes!*" An'desha shouted excitedly. "There is, I remember! I know right where it is! But how are we going to reach there from here?"

"Piffle. A trifle," said Sejanes.

Now all eyes turned to him, as he smiled broadly and presented his knowledge to them as a wise old grandfather presenting candy to a room full of children.

"We of the Empire are the Masters of Portals—you call them Gates. We can find them at great distances, we can key into strange Portals, and we can build Portals that are permanent structures. But most of all, we know how to construct them using energies outside of ourselves, or the joined energies of several mages." His smile broadened, and he spread his hands wide. "I can teach even the apprentices among you how to join together with a single Adept to construct such a Portal, and given that another permanent Portal will anchor the other end, we should be able to make it self-sustaining for a limited time. Will *that* serve as our means to your ruined Tower?"

After all the tumultuous months of bickering, near-blood-feud, fear, derision, and anger, they held more than just nebulous hope in their hands. Inventive minds, people of different cultures and backgrounds, had come together and despite the friction between them, had held on to reason. It all sounded too easy, to hear it spoken in series—and yet, the pieces had all been there. Once the need was identified, they slipped into formation like well-trained soldiers. Karal was dazed at how nearly they had escaped disaster—

We could still have a disaster, he cautioned himself. *Don't count the larks until they are safely fledged.*

But. But! If he had not overcome his repugnance and started in motion the negotiations with Tremane—if k'Leshya had waited to send their delegation—if the Sworn-Shaman had decided to leave things in the hands of Jarim—if Elspeth and An'desha had not recalled how Falconsbane had made a miraculous escape from the Shin'a'in Sword-Sworn—

Yet everything had been *there*, and who was to say that if they had not put this solution together there would not have been another one? *Altra and Hansa could Jump people in pairs. Or maybe more than pairs—Altra Jumped me, An'desha, and Florian at the same time. We might have been able to work out something with Final Strikes, only less drastic. We could have shielded the Heartstones with everything we have, waited until the breakwater failed, endured a single round of the storms, and* then *gone to the Plains.*

No, this was not the only solution, and any of the pieces that had fallen neatly into place could have been replaced by another piece—but just at the moment, it looked as if it was the best solution.

What was important was that everyone who *possessed* a piece to contribute, *had.*

Once a start at a solution had been identified, people began volunteering—or declining to volunteer—for the expedition. The usual restless souls volunteered—Firesong, Treyvan and Hydona (who would have flown through fire for a chance to visit Urtho's Tower, or the remains of it), An'desha. There were some surprises—Elspeth and Darkwind declined, planning instead to hold the shielding on the Valdemar Heartstone, and Silverfox volunteered, saying that they had better have someone along with rudimentary Healer knowledge. *Florian* volunteered ("To stand for Valdemar"). The Shin'a'in Sworn-Shaman Lo'isha was going, of course, it was his homeland. The White Winds mages declared themselves out of their depth. Altra was going.

But last of all, Karal was going though he was no mage; An'desha and Altra had both insisted on it, although he could not imagine why they needed *him. :Contingency.:* Altra had said cryptically.

He only hoped this "contingency" would not involve a situation similar to the one on the Iftel border. Acting as a channel for whatever power that held sway behind those magical barriers—whatever it was that a channel *did*—had ranked right up with all of the worst personal experiences in his life. He really didn't want to repeat it.

An'desha said that he just wanted Karal as a buffer between himself and Firesong. *That* was a role easier to handle.

He wanted to stay with Natoli, and his sense of duty warred with his wishes. If Altra wanted him to go, there must be a reason connected with his duties as a Priest. But Natoli needed him, too.

It was finally Natoli herself who solved his dilemma for him.

He went to visit her in her room at Healer's Collegium, and described all the preparations being made for the journey to the remains of the Tower. She listened with interest, as she nursed her bandaged and splinted wrist close to her body.

"I wish I could go," she said wistfully. "Even though I probably wouldn't actually see anything happening. Just think of how old that Tower is! Think of what you could learn from inscriptions there if there are any! And what if there are books preserved in there somehow—why, who knows what new tracks they would send us off on?" She sighed, and looked ruefully at the bandages still covering her injuries. "But I can't, and that's that. You're going to be traveling fast to get across the bowl of the Plains in time, and you can't have anyone along who would slow you down."

"What do you mean by, '*you're* going to be traveling fast'?" he asked. "No one's ordered *me* to go."

"No one's ordered you, but I thought you told me that An'desha and Altra both wanted you to go," she replied with surprise.

"They can *want* as much as they please," he said stubbornly. "I'm making up my own mind on this one. I've had my fill of other people making it up for me."

She frowned. "Are you going with the mages to the Plains or not?" she demanded. "If you don't want to because *you* don't want to, that's one thing, but you'd better not be wavering on this because of me!"

He was taken aback by the stern tone of her voice, and the hint of anger in her eyes. "Why not?" he asked.

"Because I won't have it, that's why!" she exclaimed. "If Altra wants you to go, doesn't that mean it's your duty to go? I won't have you neglecting your duty just because you want to keep me company! I don't expect or want that kind of behavior out of you, and you'd *better* not expect or want it out of me!"

Her vehemence left him speechless for a moment, and she filled in the silence.

"My *job* is to uncover new facts, find new ways of doing things, and sometimes that's dangerous," she continued, calming her tone of voice somewhat. "Well, look what happened with the boiler. I could have been killed!"

"I know——" he said numbly.

"So?" She gazed at him demandingly. "Would you ask me to choose between you and my work?"

If I did, I'd lose her, he realized. *She has a right to her work, her life. I don't have a right to ask her to give up any of that.*

"No," he replied quietly.

"And I don't and won't ask the same of you," she replied, as her fingers brushed restlessly back and forth along the bandages on her arm. "It's not fair and it's not right. This thing the mages are doing—it's dangerous, isn't it?"

He shivered. "More than dangerous. The Shin'a'in know where the Tower is, of course, and they've been working to uncover the entrance to the Vault since we decided what to do—but once we get in there, we'll be sorting through weapons that are very old, probably unstable, and not all of them are magical in nature. The mechanical weapons may be *very* unstable, the others think. Then when we find what we're looking for, we aren't sure what, exactly, we're going to be dealing with."

He heard himself saying "we" before he thought about it, and knew she'd noticed the phrasing when she smiled.

"So you're going." She made it a statement.

He sighed. "If Altra wants me along *and* he's being cryptic, it's because there's something he thinks I might have to do, and it's something he knows I probably wouldn't do if I had any choice." He grimaced. "I'm sure if I *don't* go, they'll find a way around any problems they encounter, but I'm also sure that it will be easier if I do go. In a case like this—the next best solution might not be good enough."

She reached for his hand with her uninjured one. "You know how you'd feel if this failed because you weren't there."

"If this fails, we're going to be in worse trouble than Hardorn is now," he corrected and shivered. "Think what would happen if the shielding all failed on the Heartstone here."

She blanched, as well she should.

"But we may be worrying at nothing," he went on. "And I may prove to be no more useful than an extra pair of hands to brew tea. If Altra *knew* I was needed, he wouldn't be giving me a choice. He said I should go as a 'contingency' measure. We've had everyone with *any* kind of

ForeSight trying to probe in the direction of this situation, and none of them can tell us anything. They say that the images are all too confused, and that there is no clear path to the future once they get past the fact that we do find the Vault and we *do* find the weapons there." As he squeezed her hand, he allowed himself a moment of annoyance. "Now tell me this—what good does it do to be a Priest or to be able to talk with Avatars if neither your God nor the representatives of your Goddess are going to give you any clues?"

Natoli chewed her lip thoughtfully for a moment. "I've been listening to you and An'desha talking about Vkandis and the Star-Eyed, and I wonder if this isn't another one of those cases where there are many choices, and since none of the choices are a Second Cataclysm, they aren't going to help. I mean—they watch while people kill people and let people die all the time, and only take a hand in things once in a while, when it will make a big difference down the road. The rest of the time, people have to do what they feel they should, and accept the results. It's that 'free will' thing again."

He groaned. "I could do with a little more guidance and a little less free will!"

"I couldn't." Once again, she surprised him. "I want to make my own decisions, and if they're the wrong ones, then I'll learn from them. I want to be an *adult*, not a child. I don't want to be led along the safe path! The safe path is never new, and the safe path never teaches you anything others don't already know!"

Had she always been like this, or had the enforced idleness given her time to think about these things? He was astonished at the clarity and fearlessness of her outlook. "A lot of people wouldn't agree with you," he replied, answering her as seriously as she had spoken. "A great many people would rather have the safe path, and be taken care of. They'd rather have all their answers assured, neatly packaged, with 'the end' put on the last page."

"Then they can look for that neat package, but it's a false one, and they're only fooling themselves." Her eyes were shining, and her color heightened with excitement. "There *is* no end to questioning, except decay. And I'm not ready to sit and rot, and neither are you."

"You're right, I'm not." He leaned over then, and dared a kiss; her lips were warm and soft and she didn't pull away. "And you're right; I should go. I'll be lonely without you, but I'll go."

Natoli squeezed his hand and whispered, "Be brave, Karal, and be careful. Come back to me."

* * *

Sejanes led a group of mixed Herald-Mages and White Winds mages who would be establishing the Gate under his direction and control; as Altra and Hansa had, they were using the old ruin in Companion's Field. "They're going to be worthless when we're done," he'd warned Selenay. "And they're going to be weak as newborn kittens for at least a day." Accordingly, she had sent along a contingent of servants with litters to carry them off when they collapsed. Sejanes had approved.

Now the expedition force stood in knee-deep snow beneath an overcast sky while Sejanes reiterated the plan. "We'll hold the Portal open long enough for you all to get through," he said, squinting into the bright snow glare. "That's all this lot will be good for. We'll reopen it in a fortnight, and you'd better be up on that rim when we do."

"You'll reopen it if you can," muttered one of the k'Leshya mages. "If they don't succeed, you'll have more than the Portal to worry about."

Sejanes ignored that—or perhaps he simply didn't hear it. "If you aren't there, we'll reopen it one more time a fortnight later, then send word to call up search parties down there." He paused and favored the k'Leshya mage with a sharp glance. Perhaps he *had* heard the mutter. "If, however, the force of your weapon deactivates the Gate at your end, you will have to find another way back here."

"In other words," Firesong said, laughing, "we walk home."

:Not precisely.:

Heads snapped up all over the group, as even those who did not have Mindspeech reacted to that voice in their heads.

A Companion stallion emerged from the trees to their left, leading a group of four more, all of them young, all nervously tossing their heads, and all wearing saddles and halters. Not the fancy tack of a Companion on search for his Chosen, but the everyday stuff a working Companion used.

:Rolan would like you to relay the rest, Karal,: Florian said, as he nudged Karal's shoulder with his nose. *:He can Mindspeak with anyone he wishes to, but it takes a lot of effort, and this will be faster.:*

"Ah—this is Rolan, he's the Queen's Own Companion," Karal said hastily.

:These are four of the fastest and strongest of the Companions who have not Chosen Heralds, and they have been picked by Rolan out of the volunteers to serve as mounts for those who need them.:

"Unpartnered Companions volunteered to carry the humans of our group," Karal interpreted. "These are the best." He knew from his own experience that no horse could ever keep up with a Companion, and if somehow the others had missed that particular piece of information, they'd soon figure it out!

:Rolan has made assignments.: The stallion tossed his head, and a muscular male with a short mane and tail stepped forward and bowed to the Sworn-Shaman. *:This is Kayka.:*

"Your mount is called Kayka, sir," Karal told that worthy, who bowed to the stallion.

"I am honored, Kayka." Lo'isha's tone made it clear that he meant his words, they were not just for politeness' sake.

Two mares with artistically flowing manes and tails tripped forward together, stopping in front of Firesong and Silverfox. *:Twin sisters, Senta and Sartra. Senta will take Firesong, and says——:*

"I can hear what she says, thank you, Florian," Firesong interrupted dryly. "And I assure you, I actually *do* know how to travel lightly. Remember? I came here with only what my *dyheli* friend could carry." He turned to the Companion and bowed to her as deeply as the shaman had bowed to Kayka, though with a touch more irony. "I am grateful for your assistance, Senta, and I appreciate your beauty."

Silverfox already had one hand on Sartra's shoulder, and appeared to be deep in mental conversation with her. The last Companion, another female, slim, with a long forelock half hiding her eyes, stepped shyly forward, and scraped at the snow in front of An'desha with one hoof.

:This is Idry.: said Florian. *:She is my younger sister, and was the first to volunteer.:*

An'desha smiled. "Then I shall be twice as glad to have her company, Florian."

"Well, that certainly solves your transportation problem," Elspeth said dryly. "If they can't get you there as fast as a gryphon can fly, it can't be done at all."

"Rrr, ssso we will rrracsse?" Treyvan asked, then gape-grinned. Hydona bumped her beak against his side.

"Excellent, I admit that I am very pleased," Sejanes called. "Now, can we get *on* with this?"

After seeing so many Gates opening over the past several days, even the heart-stopping magic of Gate-construction felt like a routine. Karal paid no attention to the goings-on, taking the time instead to make certain that his pack was secure and that Florian's saddle and halter were comfortable. It would be a long trek down to the bowl of the Plains with no place to stop on the trail, and anything loose could rub poor Florian raw. The others were taking their packs and securing them behind the saddles. Treyvan and Hydona already had their flying-harness on, and whatever gear they thought they would need was fastened to it. Jerven and Lytha, their half-grown youngsters, would be staying behind. According to Hydona, it was time for them to start serious fledgling lessons, and those were best given by someone who was not their parent.

Given what a full-time job those two were, Karal wondered if the two might not be using this as a chance for a vacation away from them!

He completed his inspection at about the same time that the mages made contact with the anchoring Gate in the ruins above the Plains. When he looked up, it was to see snow-covered heaps of tumbled stones below a sky so blue and clear it hurt to look at it, all framed in the arch of weathered stones on their side.

"Quickly, please!" Sejanes shouted. "We can't hold this all day, you know!"

Karal mounted, glad to feel a saddle beneath him again, and started for the Gate, but Treyvan and Hydona were already there ahead of him, dashing through with alacrity. He wondered why they were so eager, then remembered—Clan k'Leshya had settled there, in the ruins as well as in the old Vale! They were probably eager to see some of their old friends before taking the trek to Urtho's Tower.

He followed right on their heels, with An'desha behind him. He had never actually crossed large distances by means of a Gate before, and he braced himself for the unpleasant stomach-tumbling sensations of a Jump.

But there was nothing of the kind; he felt for a split second as if he was falling, and there was a strange darkness that was laced with fiery multicolored ribbons of power and light all around him. Then Florian's feet came to rest on the stone on the other side with a little jolt, as if the Companion had made a small hop over an obstacle in their path.

:Like that better than Jumping, do you?: Although Altra had not been with them on the Valdemar side, now he appeared.

"Much," he said shortly, as Florian moved out of the way for the rest to come through. Although snow lay everywhere, it was cleared away from the places that had once been streets in what looked like the ruins of a substantial town. Though still in ruins, there were signs of habitation here and there—places where walls showed signs of rebuilding, and farther in the distance, conical, shingled roofs poking up above the snow-covered piles of rubble. Just at the moment, there were gryphons flying in from every direction to meet their two. There were at least a dozen, but it seemed as if there were hundreds; gryphons in a group, Karal soon learned, were not quiet.

This was not a social gathering, however; the gryphons landed, had a brief conference while the rest of the party traversed the Gate, then flew off again. Without knowing where in relation to the Plains this ruin was, Karal had no idea which way they were going, but their flight was purposeful, as if they each had a task to perform.

The Shaman was the last through the Gate, and it closed behind him.

"The way isss clearrr," Hydona called from her perch atop a ruined wall. "The Ssssworrrd-Ssssworrrn arrre all along it and will rrride with usss in rrrelays. "Grryphonsss fly ahead to ssscout. The worrrrssst parrrt isss the trrrail down; icsssed, they sssay."

Lo'isha shrugged. "That is to be expected, but I am glad our white friends have agreed to bear us. I am more confident with them than I would be with even the best Shin'a'in stock."

Evidently he knew precisely where he was; Kayka set out at a brisk walk, and the rest followed, except for Treyvan and Hydona, who took to the air. Karal and An'desha took the rearmost position.

There were gryphons overhead constantly; as the trail wove in and around the ruined buildings, Karal became completely lost. He would have been certain that the shaman was, too, but with all the help in the air, that was extremely unlikely.

Soon enough, they turned another corner, and suddenly there was nothing in front of them but blue sky. They had come to the edge of the ruins, and before and below them lay the Dhorisha Plains.

Karse was a land of mountains, so Karal was no stranger to height—but it is one thing to look at something on a map, and quite another to stand on the edge of a sheer precipice and look down—and down—and down—

Intellectually, he had known that the edge of the crater that formed the rim above the Plains was hundreds of lengths above its floor. Now he knew it with his gut, and he gulped.

Florian seemed nonchalant. :*It's not that bad. Take a closer look; there's a switchback trail going all the way down.*:

He didn't really like the look of the trail any better than the long drop. It was barely wide enough for a single rider; they would have to go single-file the entire way, and may Vkandis help anyone who slipped.

:I'll see you at the bottom—unless you'd like to Jump with me now,: Altra said smugly. *:Feel like a Jump?:*

Thinks I won't take him up on it, hmm? "Sir!" he called to the shaman, "Altra has volunteered to Jump us down, one Companion and rider at a time!"

:I did not!: Altra cried indignantly, but it was too late. Lo'isha turned to them both with a look of grave gratitude, and it was not possible to back down without looking ungracious and ungraceful. That, Karal knew, was something that Altra's pride would never permit.

"If you would be so kind, Firecat," he said in his deep, impressive voice. "I do not like the look of this trail. I would rather we did not lose anyone to something that could be prevented."

Altra grumbled mentally at Karal, but accepted the task with outward grace. *:Just for that, you can go last, when I'm tired,:* he added, as he jumped up on the pack behind the Shaman.

Then they were gone—and a tiny dot appeared against the snow far below them.

It took exponentially less time, even going down pair by pair, than it would have if they'd taken the trail. And even though Altra *was* tired when he got to Karal, and his control *was* a bit shaky, the resulting Jump was no worse than the ones he'd made getting out of Hardorn. That resulted in nausea, but not the gut-racking illness that had been the result of the flight from Tremane's study.

And when he "landed" beside the others, it was clear that the Shin'a'in had been there before them, breaking a clear trail through the relatively light snow so that they could proceed as fast as possible without worrying about getting lost.

When Karal looked up, he saw circling dots that were the gryphons. When he looked outward, he saw moving dots that must be the Sword-Sworn, riding a protective patrol ahead and to both sides of them. He'd wondered how they were going to manage without supplies, for no one had packed anything in the way of food or shelter and not even a Companion could cross to the center of the Dhorisha Plains in a single day; now it came to him. The Shin'a'in and the gryphons would take care of that, if they had not already.

Lo'isha looked about with satisfaction—even if his lips were a little white. "The trail is clear, the wind is at our backs!" he cried. "Now, let us *ride!*"

* * *

After the first day, Karal looked back on the grueling trip he and Ulrich had made from Karse to Haven with nostalgia. Florian saved him as much as he could—and indeed a Companion's pace was blissful compared to that of a horse—

But this was still riding from an hour past sunup to far past sundown, in bitterly cold weather, without a break. Companions did not need rest the way that horses did, and the shaman saw fit to make use of that endurance.

The brilliantly blue sky of day became a huge black bowl studded with enormous stars by night. When the half-moon rose, it flooded the featureless Plains with white light that had the effect of making Karal feel even colder than before. But the flatness of the Plains did have one advantage—they saw the fires and torches of their resting place from a vast distance away, as the only spots of warm color in all the icy whiteness. Just looking at the pinpricks of warm yellow gave Karal enough strength to hold onto Florian's saddle. His cold fingers had long since grown too numb for any pretense of holding to the reins.

When at last they reached the shelters, they found a single round felt tent awaiting them, with torches all around it, a fire in front of it, and black-clad Shin'a'in tending a stewpot over the fire. Karal fell out of the saddle rather than dismounting; he stumbled toward the tent, and Florian followed him right inside.

Evidently the Shin'a'in were prepared for the idea that the Companions should share their shelter; the tent, lit by three oil lamps suspended from the roof poles, was divided in half, with half of the floor covered in old, damaged carpets, with piles of hay and grain and leather buckets of water on top of the carpets. Treyvan and Hydona were already there, fast asleep, curled together in a single ball of feathers with no sign of limbs or heads. The other half had bright new carpets with bedrolls laid out neatly for them, in a semicircle with a charcoal brazier at their feet. It might not have been very warm by the standards of the Palace, but compared to the bitter cold outside, it was quite toasty. There was a Shin'a'in Sword-Sworn waiting inside, unsaddling and wiping down the Companions and throwing warm blankets over them as they ate and drank. Florian joined the others. As the last human inside, Karal found the others already wrapped up in their blankets, eating bowls of stew and sipping at mugs of something that steamed. Karal didn't know what it was, nor did he care. He took the last of the bedrolls, pulled off his boots and shoved his legs down into the warmth of the blankets, and accepted the bowl and mug handed to him with a murmur of thanks.

Then he ate as quickly as he could shovel the stew in with the aid of a piece of tough, flat bread. The tea had an odd, astringent taste, but it was curiously soothing to his raw throat.

As soon as he had finished both tea and stew, the same Shin'a'in took bowl and cup away from him. The others were already curled in their bedrolls for sleep, and he followed their example. The Shin'a'in blew out the oil lamps on his way out of the tent, leaving them in darkness.

At some point before he went to sleep, Altra appeared, lying beside him and half over him, creating a swath of heat at his back. The Firecat purred quietly and said just one thing.

:Karal... I'm proud of you.:

With that added comfort—in more ways than the merely physical— he fell instantly asleep.

The Shin'a'in woke them before dawn, and they broke their fast with more stew, bread, and tea. Then they were in the saddle again, and pushing outward.

The second day was a repetition of the first, as was the third. Karal's eyes grew sore from the reflection of sun on snow, and from the red eyes that met his every time anyone—except the shaman and An'desha— turned to face him, the others must be suffering the same. The cold, dry air made his lips crack and chap, and his throat sore. After the second day, Lo'isha gave them each a little vial of aromatic oil to moisten their lips with, and advised them that they might want to anoint their whole faces. Karal took him up on the suggestion; Firesong resisted at first, but by midafternoon, with his cheeks flaming from wind-chapping, he had given in and done the same.

Karal lost track of time; he was either riding or sleeping—too much of the former, not enough of the latter. The landscape they traversed was always the same; not quite flat, but close enough for a young man from the mountains, rolling hill after snow-covered, rolling hill, with scarcely a tree or a bush in sight except where they marked the passage of watercourses or the location of a spring. The cold numbed all of him, and he never was really warm except the moment that they awoke him. Firesong looked miserable, Silverfox looked resigned, and only An'desha and Lo'isha seemed to thrive.

But then, this is—was—his home.

The gryphons rarely appeared, and when they did, they were fixated on the goal and could talk of nothing else. At last—after how many days he could not tell, that goal loomed up on the horizon.

It was singularly unprepossessing, for something they had chased across half a continent—an odd, melted stub of silvery-gray rock, poking up out of the top of yet another rolling hill.

Then, when it didn't get any closer, he realized that it must be much larger than he had thought.

Then he finally spotted the tiny dots of more Shin'a'in swarmed about the base, and the equally tiny dots of two gryphons circling it, and he *understood* how large it was.

There was a long pile of something dark against the snow at the foot of the Tower—rich, turned earth. It looked as if the Shin'a'in had been digging for something.

The closer they got, the more his skin crawled. The Tower simply didn't *look* melted, it *had been* melted. The great force that fueled the Cataclysm had made the rock of the Tower run like liquid wax. And they were about to play with forces *worse* and more hazardous than the one that had done this, weapons that the Mage of Silence, who had created this, thought were too dangerous to use!

What am I doing here? he thought, aghast.

It would not be the last time he had that thought.

They rested and slept for what remained of that day and all the next night; it would be stupid, and perhaps suicidal to enter the Vault with their minds fogged with fatigue. But the moment the sun rose, so did they, and one of the Sword-Sworn led them to the opening the Shin'a'in had been working on since this expedition had been decided on.

The old door to the Tower lay somewhere beneath several hundred tons of melted, fused rock. The Shin'a'in had taken a more direct route to the Vault beneath the remains of the Tower. There must have been hundreds of them working on it to get it done in so short a period of time.

They had burrowed down in a long slanting tunnel into the side of the hill supporting the Tower, straight to the ancient Vault wall. *That* was only stone blocks mortared together, and the mortar, after so many centuries, was old and weak. Urtho had never bothered to put any sort of armoring or defensive measures on the wall of the Vault—after all, anyone who got this far would still have to dig a hole in the full sight of the guards, the army, the Kaled'a'in, the gryphons...

Not likely.

The Shin'a'in, with advice from the miners of k'Leshya, and additional help from the gryphons, had been working nonstop; together they had made an impressive tunnel, chipped out the weak mortar between the stones, and pried out enough of the latter to create an entrance fully large enough for Treyvan and Hydona, not to mention Florian, who insisted on coming below as well. The other Companions were perfectly happy to remain outside and rest, and Karal caught them casting many glances askance at Florian as he prepared to descend the precipitous tunnel with the party of mages. They all had lanterns, but the light didn't help the feeling of being trapped beneath tons of earth and stone. The tunnel itself had been shored up quite expertly, and for a moment Karal wondered where they had gotten the timbers.

The gryphons, of course. They must have flown them in from k'Leshya.

A formidable task, equal to the task of digging this tunnel.

Karal concentrated on keeping his breathing steady, reminding himself that as long as his lantern flame burned brightly, there was more than enough air down here for them all to breathe.

At least I'm not cold. There's no wind blowing. There's no snow-glare.

How much longer does this tunnel go on?

He hadn't begun by counting his steps, but he started at that point. Fifty... one hundred... one hundred and fifty... shouldn't they have reached the wall by now?

His chest felt tight; was the light a little dimmer? The flame of his candle a little lower?

:Karal. I'm right behind you.: The voice in his mind warned him, so when a head bumped against his thigh, he didn't jump and screech. *:It's all right. There's air, and if anything happens, I can Jump you out.:*

Immediately the invisible bands tightening around his chest loosened. Of course! Altra could get him out, even if the roof collapsed! He relaxed, and the flame in his lantern brightened again. Or perhaps it had never been dimming in the first place.

"We're at the Vault."

The shaman's voice, muffled by all the other bodies between him and the Shin'a'in, alerted him so that he didn't run into An'desha when An'desha stopped.

The line ahead of him shuffled forward, step by step. "Watch yourself," An'desha warned, as the light from his lantern caught on the regular shapes of stone blocks. "There's debris in the way."

An'desha moved forward and vanished into a hole a gryphon could barely squeeze through. There was a litter of stone pieces and other debris in front of the hole, as if it had just today been made. Perhaps it had!

He stepped over the edge of the hole, following the gleam of light— and stepped into another world.

The floor was smoothly polished white stone with a pattern, a compass rose of eight points inset in it, made of a rose-colored granite. This was a large, round room with white stone walls that rose in a conical shape to a point about two stories above their heads. Hanging down from the center by a silver chain was a large sphere of crystal, which shone softly in the reflected light from the lanterns.

Karal stared at it in awe.

"What is it?" he asked. "A weapon? Something like a Heartstone?"

Firesong shook his head as he also stared; they stood in a loose circle with their mouths agape, gazing upward. Finally Treyvan laughed, and said, "Much sssimplerrr," and called out a word in a language that was not quite Shin'a'in and not quite Tayledras.

Obediently, the globe lit up from within. Karal cried out and shielded his eyes, but he needn't have bothered. The radiance was remarkably soft, and left only a faint afterimage that rapidly faded.

"It isss a lamp," Treyvan said superfluously.

Now that they could see clearly, they doused their lanterns and took a look around. This, obviously, was not the Vault itself, but probably a workroom to one side, for there was the dark gap of an open door in the wall. Firesong was the nearest, so he was the first one through it, where he stopped, just inside, blocking the door.

"Well," his dry voice echoed back, "it would be nice if I could see. What was that command?" Before anyone could answer him, he tried several versions of the word Treyvan had used, and finally hit on the right intonation. His form was silhouetted for a moment as the light flared to life, then dimmed to the twin of the first.

"I believe," the Tayledras Adept drawled, "we have found what we were looking for."

He moved out of the way, leaving space for the others to enter behind him.

Karal lagged back; for one thing, he was not sure he wanted to *see* what they were looking for. For another, he knew very well he wouldn't know what he was looking at!

So he allowed all the others to crowd in ahead of him, and trailed behind. He expected exclamations, but he heard nothing but a few whispers.

When he passed the threshold himself, he understood why.

This was a huge room, but practically empty except for four of the crystal lights suspended from the ceiling, and a single floating barge in the middle. Faint outlines in the ceiling above the barge suggested a door or hatchway there.

Around the periphery of the room were fifteen more doors, all of them closed.

Where were the weapons? Had all of them been taken away?

"The weapons must be behind each of those doors, one to a room," Firesong said authoritatively. "If *I* were holding dangerous objects, that's what I'd do with them. That way if you had an accident with one, it would be confined to the room it was in and not spread to the others."

"You begin to sound like a career artificer, Firesong," Silverfox replied. "That makes entirely too much sense."

Firesong turned to the nearest door on his right, and continued talking. "What's more, I'll bet the room we were in held a weapon that Urtho *did* use, and the reason that the barge is in here is to take large or bulky creations up to where you can—or could, I mean—move them out the doors."

"I wonder why this place even exists," An'desha said, as Firesong checked to see if the door was locked before he tried opening it. "You'd think that a force that would melt the Tower would destroy everything, wouldn't you?"

"Maybe because this was right below the event, none of the force went downward," Karal hazarded, trying to remember some of what he'd learned from the artificers.

"Perhaps the shields on the Vault disintegrated, but absorbed all of the force in the process," Silverfox guessed.

"Perhaps the Star-Eyed had something to do with it," Lo'isha said with great dignity.

"Perrrhapsss all of thossse rrreasssonsss, perrrhapsss none," Treyvan said with impatience. "Isss the doorrr locked orrr not?"

"Just stuck," Firesong replied, finally shoving it open. He spoke the word that lit the lamp and gave an exclamation of disappointment.

"Come look for yourself, but I don't think this one is going to do us any good," he said, waving them over.

Once again Karal held back, but on his own viewing, he was inclined to agree with Firesong. This room contained a conglomerate of bizarre parts, from coils of wire to animal skulls with jeweled eyes, all woven together in a crazed spider-web of colored string, ribbon, hair-thin wire, and rawhide thongs.

"Good God, why *skulls*?" Karal exclaimed, revolted.

"Perhaps because they had been used in shamanic ceremonies and so now were attuned to power of a sort he needed," Lo'isha hazarded. "Not Kaled'a'in ceremonies, but Urtho made use of the magics he had learned from many peoples, and many peoples were his allies."

"I don't know about you, but I don't even want to touch that," Firesong said as he edged back outside. "I don't know what it does, and I'm not sure it would still do it at this point—and even if it did, how much of it would fall into dust if you brushed against it?"

"Trrrue," Treyvan said, taking care to tuck his wings in as he moved back outside. With one accord, they closed the door with the greatest of care and moved on to the next room.

By the time they were finished, they had eliminated eight of the fifteen possibilities. None were quite as bizarre as the cow-skull construction, but no one wanted to take any chances on them. Two were featureless boxes that had even Treyvan shaking his head in bafflement, one was an unidentifiable object that resembled nothing so much as a spill of liquid caught and frozen in midair. Two more were delicate sculptures of wires and gemstones that they were all afraid to touch lest they fall to pieces, and the remaining three Treyvan recognized from his litany as being simple weapons of dreadful mass destruction of life and property—not at all suited to their purposes, for there was nothing magical about the energy released when *these* things were triggered.

That left seven possibilities.

With each of the objects was a metal plaque, identifying how to destroy it, but nothing else about its nature, except the single line, "You cannot use this weapon without killing yourself. Neither could I. Be wise, and be rid of it." Each plaque was signed with Urtho's name and sigil.

They gathered rubbings of all these plaques, together with a crude drawing of each object and the number of the room it was in—counting the empty room as number one and going sunwise—and sat down together in the floating barge to discuss what they had.

"We have three days to decide which device and how to work it, one day to set up and practice, and that's all," Firesong warned. "If we don't succeed by then, working with the assumption that the waves going out can be made to match the speed of the ones coming in, the breakwater will go down. Irrevocably. Without that to break up the force, the next mage-storm through here might well trigger one or more of these things."

"Sssurely not—" Treyvan said, but he did not sound certain.

"Are you willing to stand around here and wait to see? I'm not," Firesong said bluntly. "Frankly, I didn't think we'd find more than one or two of Urtho's weapons existing; I never dreamed there'd be this many that were still intact. It seems to me that if we don't succeed here, we'd better evacuate the Plains *and* k'Leshya."

"I wish I didn't feel the same way," the shaman said with reluctance. "I had not expected to find so many lethal objects here either. If one or even two were activated, the Tower and the physical containments still here would probably keep the damage to a small area—but if three or more went—" He shuddered, his face white.

"Right," Firesong nodded. "And we are making a lot of assumptions about whether they'd 'go off,' for that matter. Some of them might be the magical equivalent of a slow acid, some might simply shred things randomly for a long period of time."

"Then let's get on with this and make a decision!" An'desha exclaimed, his nervousness evident in the high pitch of his voice.

But a few hours later, it was clear that they had another problem.

Between the litany and the instructions for disposal, it was possible to deduce what each of the remaining seven objects *did*, and they were able to eliminate three more of the seven. The trouble was, when they had ranked the remaining four in order of suitability, they came to another, unexpected snag.

The language that the k'Leshya *thought* was the purest Kaled'a'in, that they had cherished—they fondly assumed—as unchanged for centuries, was anything but pure and unchanged.

"Look, we have *three* words here that all mean 'explosive'!" Firesong burst out. "*Your* version of Kaled'a'in has two of them, Treyvan, *ko'chekarna* and *chekarna*, and from the destruction instructions I think we've got a third, *ri'chekarna*! So which is right? We have to know or we're likely to get our number one choice going off right in our faces!"

"I—do not know," Treyvan said helplessly. "The language hasss ssshifted...."

"Languages do, over time," Lo'isha said ironically. "Your mistake was to assume that since the Kaled'a'in were among peoples that avoided change, your language and ways were immutable. We need a scholar in ancient Kaled'a'in—"

"Or someone with ForeSight, who could look at each of these things and determine which one we can use safely!" Karal said suddenly, as he looked directly at Florian and Altra.

The two looked at each other, as if they were consulting silently. The little group stared at both of them in an expectant hush. It seemed to take forever before Florian turned back to them, but it was Altra who "spoke," although his eyes were directed off past Karal's shoulder, as if he was concentrating on something.

:I cannot bring someone here in time. Florian cannot reach that far with his mind.:
Karal's heart fell.

"I can't build a Gate that will reach that far," Firesong reminded them. "And neither can An'desha."

"Then we arrre rrright back to the beginning." Treyvan's ear-tufts flattened against his head. "Back to language, a ssset of verrrssse that hasss ssshifted meaningsss overrr the yearsss, and guesssesss which can get usss all killed."

"No—" An'desha corrected, his eyes half-closed in thought. "We do have more than that. Mage-Sight should tell us something about the power sources, and *that* should tell us if it's something we ought to avoid."

"It might tell usss otherrr thingsss asss well," Treyvan put in, his ear-tufts rising again.

"And let usss make the bessst transsslationsss we can," Hydona added. "If we have the choicssse between a devicsse with a good trrranssslation and one with a half trrranssslation, need I sssuggesssst which we usssse?"

Firesong rubbed eyes so tired and puffy they were mere slits. In the end, there was only one device they *could* use, and it was not their first or even second choice. Karal had spent the time making himself useful while the mages pondered translations and probed the devices with every tool available to them. Precious time was lost while they did so, but none of them were wasting any time either. They hardly slept, and ate only when Karal or Silverfox put food in their hands.

And in the end, the shaman himself used his powers, ill-suited as they were to such a task, attempting to help with a selection. His "inspired guess" matched the choice of the mages.

"There's only one problem," Firesong said glumly, eyeing the unprepossessing pyramid of silvered metal. "This thing is going to kill whoever activates it. According to Treyvan's litany and what I've gleaned from the destruction information, the rest of us would be able to get far enough away to avoid incineration, but not the person setting it off. It can't be set off magically, we don't have anyone who can move things with his mind with us, and when it goes, not even Altra would be able to Jump out in time. Assuming he had two hands with four fingers and a thumb each, which he doesn't."

"Unlessss—" Treyvan prompted.

Firesong shrugged. "I don't see where that could make a difference. The fatal flaw in this thing, and the reason Urtho never used it, is that there's spillover energy in the physical plane. *Incandescent, white-hot* spillover energy."

Karal looked from one to the other. "Unless *what?*" he prompted.

Firesong grimaced, and Treyvan answered. "Unless the perrrssson trrrigerrring it isss a Mage-Channel. He *might* be able to channel the ssspilloverrr enerrrgy to the enerrrgy-planesss wherrre it isss sssupposssed to go."

"Yes, well, there's just one little problem with that," Firesong snapped. "He stands even odds of getting burned out—if he succeeds—and he'll need to be completely shielded, *and* if he loses control, he'll *still* get killed along with whoever is shielding him! That assumes we *had* someone who was tough enough to—"

He stopped, suddenly realizing that Karal had gone white as snow, and An'desha, Florian, and Altra were all staring at him. The muscles in his throat tensed as he swallowed.

"I'm a channel," he said, in a whisper.

Now Firesong stared at him, too, his mind whirling. "You're a fool if you think you can do this," he said harshly. "If you thought the Iftel border was hard, it's *nothing* compared to channeling this thing! You're not trained, you can't even *see* mage-energy—"

"But I am a channel," the young man persisted, though he was still pale and drawn. "And I've been told that channeling is instinctive, not learned."

"You're going to kill yourself!" Firesong shouted, unable to bear the tension. "You're out of your mind! *We can't help you.* You'd have to do this alone! The best we could do is shield you!"

"Is there any other choice?" Karal countered, looking each of them in the eyes. One by one, they each shook their heads. Finally, he came back to Firesong, who clenched his teeth angrily.

"Firesong—we all knew when we came here that we might not come back. We have all resolved in our own ways that we are willing to make sacrifices for even a chance of saving our homelands." Karal's facial expression looked like that of a boy ready to cry, but in the way he held his chin up and back straight, he acted like a grown man facing a moment of truth. "I know that if I have to give my life in this, I will be welcome in the Sunlord's arms."

How *dare* the whelp put him in this position? How *dare* he volunteer to get himself turned to a cinder before Firesong had a chance to get his own feelings straight?

"Damn you—" he began, but Karal interrupted him with a wan smile.

"I don't think your curse is capable of overriding Vkandis' blessing, Hawkbrother," he chided gently. "But if there is no other choice, I suggest you take it back anyway. I'm going to need all the help I can get."

"I take it back. But may *all* your children turn out like you!" Firesong exploded, unable to come up with a better "curse" to vent his feelings. He turned violently away and escaped to the empty chamber to pace. His gut was a solid knot of tensions, his neck felt as stiff as old rawhide.

How can he do this? He's right, but how can he? This is insane! An'desha will never forgive me!

Soft footsteps at the entrance to the chamber warned him that he was not alone.

"I have to, you know," Karal said quietly. "I had the feeling it might come to something like this. Altra kept saying he wanted me along for 'contingency'; I think he must have meant that there was an equal chance you'd have been able to use one of the other devices." A soft sigh. "The ForeSeers all said that the futures were so tangled they couldn't see past us getting here. There was always a chance that something else might have worked out."

"Maybe. If we had more time to study them. If I wasn't reasonably certain the wave front of the next mage-storm was going to get in *here* as well as everywhere else—this *is* the origin-point, after all. Hellfires! Where else would the energy go but here? And this place can't keep taking a battering without at least one of these devices going on its own!" He stopped pacing and turned to look into Karal's white and strained face. "I *do not want* you to do this!"

"I know," Karal told him.

"But if you're going to insist—by your gods and mine, I'm not going to stand around outside this place and leave you to do it alone." In this much, at least, he could assuage his own conscience. "I'll shield you—"

"We'll all shield him," An'desha said, coming up behind Karal. Firesong started to protest, then shrugged. It was their choice, too.

All right." He took a deep breath and tried to reckon the time passed. "How much time do we have left? I know it can't be much."

"About half a day." Karal sounded steady enough. Maybe he *could* do it. "I've been keeping very careful track. Every mark we delay means the closer the wave front will be to Haven and the Heartstone there. Tremane's people can weather one more storm, maybe two—"

"But the shielding on the Stone might go down, not to mention all the other Vale Stones, I know, I know." He suppressed a wave of irritation at Karal for restating the obvious. He let his irritation show as he answered in a growl. "All right, then, if that's the way you all want it, who am I to argue?"

An'desha looked for a moment as if he might retort, but only turned back to the main room. Karal followed him, leaving Firesong to trail behind, feeling as if he had somehow lost an argument, even though there hadn't really been one.

They spent their remaining time in rehearsal for the moment. Aya chittered at him from atop the pack as Firesong rummaged deep into the side pocket. He noticed that he was not alone in surreptitiously going to his belongings for stimulants to keep him wide awake and alert; such things were dangerous and they would all pay later—if they survived this—but every mage knew there would be times when there were not enough hours to rest before a vital working, and carried a packet or two of such things. He even caught the shaman chewing a mouthful of something with an expression of distaste that told him it was not dried meat.

Tayledras stimulants had the peculiar quality of setting everything emotional at a distance, enabling Firesong to focus on the purely intellectual project at hand. The mental exercises that sharpened the mind came to him naturally, like a musician practicing his fingerings quicker and quicker. Diagrams of light shone against his lids as he concentrated, eyes closed—symbols for Vale, Veil, Heartstone, ley-line, shield, absorber, deflector, suspensor, buffer—current and anchor, circle and square, star and sphere—they all appeared and interwove. And it occurred to him, as soon as he felt that distancing of his inner turmoil, that there was a *reason* for that pattern in the floor of every storage chamber. The compass rose.

In his peculiarly exalted state, he leaped straight from flash of intuition to a plan, with no conscious reasoning in between.

"Look at this!" he said, as they entered the chamber for a final rehearsal. "Look, the device is in the exact middle of that inlaid compass rose—it can't be by accident! This is a shielding-circle!"

An'desha tilted his head to one side and frowned. "It doesn't look like anything in my memory—" he said tentatively.

"Of course it doesn't," Firesong interrupted impatiently. "Your memories are all of Urtho's arch rival, and if there was a way to do something the opposite of Urtho, you can be certain Ma'ar took it! The positioning is perfect, and I'll bet there's an amplification-effect when we set ourselves up and begin the shielding. Look here—the angle from point to point is a factor of eight, with eight points, and sixty-four marker triangles point in. Look at the cupping of those scallops around the center—I'll bet you all my silk that they're collectors. Check the angles of deflection from point to point, and they'll all line up to buttress each other."

An'desha looked at Treyvan and Hydona for confirmation. The female gryphon wagged her head from side to side. "It could be," she admitted. "Sssuch thingsss arrre known. Urrrtho wasss known forrr being rrresssourcsseful enough forrr sssixty men, beforrre brrreakfassst. It would be in hisss ssstyle to put sssuch thingsss herrre."

"Then you two—take North and South," he ordered, feeling as if this must be the proper configuration, though he did not know why. "Florian and Altra, East and West." That put all the nonhumans on cardinal points, which made a certain sense given what the gryphons had told him about Urtho and how he cherished his nonhuman creations. "Karal, stand in the center with the pyramid. An'desha, you go between Altra and Treyvan in the Northeast. An'desha, I'll be opposite you—"

But here he stopped, for there were only Lo'isha and Silverfox left, and both were shaking their heads. "I know nothing of shielding," the Shaman began—

Then, with a sigh and a rush of wings on a wind that existed somewhere other than *here and now*, the other two places were taken. Light filled the room, and Firesong's heart leaped straight into his throat.

The last pieces of the puzzle. They have had a hand in this, too—

Standing in the Northwest and Southeast were—

No—

Tre'valen—

"*We have come to help in this,*" said one of the two creatures, part flame, part bird, and part man, with a face that had haunted his few nightmares since the moment he had found the lifeless body of the Shin'a'in shaman struck down by Mornelithe Falconsbane. *"We are still as much of your world as of Hers, and this is, after all, Her chosen land. She wishes it protected, as do we."*

Karal's eyes glowed with an emotion that Firesong could put no name to, but there was no mistaking the emotion on An'desha's face. It was pure, unleavened joy. And Firesong knew, truly, and with a settling of peace in his heart, that he had not "lost" An'desha to any human or any human arguments. There was no use arguing when someone heard the call of the Star-Eyed in his soul. That siren song was as unbreakable as any lifebond and as enduring.

The other bird-human-spirit spoke. *"An'desha knows—we have been with you, aiding where we could—but the Star-Eyed helps only those with the bravery to help themselves. We have come of our own volition, and live or die, we stand beside you."*

Lo'isha was on his knee with his head bowed, and the creature who had once been Tre'valen, himself a shaman, gestured to him to rise. The shaman did so, but wearing an expression so awestruck that Firesong doubted he would say *anything* as long as the two Avatars were there.

But as Firesong turned his attention back to the circle, he realized he knew what that look in Karal's eyes was.

It was the look of someone who knows he is about to die, but whose faith is certain and confirmed and who is no longer afraid of the prospect. "Fey," some called it.

Perhaps, as Stefen bid him farewell in the mountains of the North, Vanyel had looked that way....

But it was too late now to do anything about it. The last few moments were trickling away.

"Raise your shields!" he shouted, his throat tight, as he brought up his own. To Mage-Sight, each of them now stood within a glowing sphere of rainbow light, and as he had somehow divined, each point on the compass rose glowed as well. The light radiating from each of them reflected from the angled patterns outlined in the stone. It looked as though, if they survived this, he wouldn't owe anyone his silk.

"Link shields!" he cried out, before his throat closed too much to speak. There was a moment of faltering, then all of the shields formed into a thick ring of light surrounding Karal and the waist-high pyramid in the center. The young man closed his eyes and placed his hands carefully on two of the sides, fitting his fingers into the depressions placed there for that purpose.

But once again, as Firesong had guessed, older magics were activated by the energies of their shields. The design on the floor began to glow, sending up eight arms of light that pulled the shields with them, until they all met in a point, making a cone of radiance that echoed the conical shape of the walls around them. Instead of being merely ringed with shielding, Karal was encased in it, and the energy that he would release would be funneled straight up by the shields.

Precisely as it needed to be, to keep any harm from coming to the Plains outside.

Silverfox and Lo'isha watched anxiously; Firesong knew that the shaman would be able to see the energies they had raised, but the expression on Silverfox's face suggested that he, too, saw them, which meant that they were powerful enough even for non-mages to see. That meant he had been right; Urtho had built a mechanism of amplification into the design of the floor.

But there was no chance to gloat over this triumph of instinct and artistry over intellect and reason. It was time. He knew that, as if he were a water-clock and the last drop had just fallen.

"Karal, *now!*" he shouted, and Karal's face spasmed as his fingers closed convulsively on the trigger points of the device.

The center of the design exploded soundlessly into power. Karal was somewhere in the midst of all that—more power than any Heartstone, more power than Firesong had ever seen in his life, power that made Aya shriek and flee into the next room, that was so bright the shaman and Silverfox shouted and hid their eyes.

Somewhere in the heart of that inferno of energy, Karal struggled to hold it, to transmute it—he struggled—

And Firesong felt him failing. Not failing to *hold*, but failing in his grasp on the world, on himself, on his life. He was thinning, vanishing, evaporating in a little microcosm of his incandescent God. In a moment, he would be lost, and if anyone dared try to help him, the circle would break and they would all perish.

Over my dead body! Anger finally penetrated his drug-born and aloof indifference. Though—if instinct failed him, it might well be just that—

"Everybody! On my count, take human-sized steps forward, follow your compass point!" he shouted into the roaring silence. "*One! Two! Three!*"

The circle contracted around Karal, tightening in on him, and having the effect of focusing the energy he controlled as the rays' edges flanged and flared.

"*Four! Five! Six!*" They were all within touching range now, if they had all had hands. But that was not yet what Firesong's instincts cried out for.

"*Seven! Eight!*" They were practically on top of Karal now—the pyramid was gone, completely, and Karal was as transparent as one of the Avatars, his head thrown back, his mouth open in a silent cry, surrounded and encased in a pillar of white-hot, ice-cold fire.

"*Nine!*" He reached out and seized one of Karal's arms—without prompting, each of the others did the same, except for Florian, who touched the young man's breast with his nose, and Altra, who reared up on hind legs and placed both paws in the middle of his back.

The light!

It flared up in his face the moment they all touched Karal. He closed his eyes, but it scorched through his eyelids and flung him physically back! He felt his hand discorporate, turning into vapor—he lost his grip on Karal's arm, and felt himself tossed backward through the air, to land against the wall and slide bonelessly and helplessly to the floor.

It was over.

He couldn't see; couldn't hear.

They had won—but they had lost Karal.

Firesong fell back into darkness as profound as the explosion of light, and all feeble remaining awareness left him.

Firesong wasn't unconscious for very long, but it was certainly the first time in his life that he had been knocked out by magic—and the searing pain in his head told him just what price he had paid for tampering with such powers. He wouldn't be able to light a candle for the next week until he healed—and the next day or so was going to be pure hell. But with a shiver of glee, he realized he was *alive*.

He couldn't move for a moment; couldn't even think past the pain except for that tangle of elation and grief. *We did it—I shouldn't have done that, he might have been all right if I hadn't told everyone to close in, it's my fault—*

And—oh, gods, but who else had they lost? He forced himself to roll over and sit up, forced his eyes to open, but they were watering so heavily he couldn't see. He wiped at them frantically with his sleeve, as Aya scuttled back into the room and settled against his side, crooning.

"What in the name of Kal'enel happened?" he heard the shaman croak.

But the voice that answered was not Silverfox—nor anyone else who had been in the circle.

"I haven't a clue," Karal said, in a weak whisper. "I don't remember anything but pressing those ten trigger points."

Firesong managed to get his eyes clear, and to his utter astonishment, they confirmed what his ears had told him.

Lo'isha and Silverfox were bent over Karal, helping him to sit up. There didn't seem to be much of him inside those black robes of his—he looked as if he'd been undergoing a thirty-day Vision-Quest fast. Both of the others were handling him gingerly, as if they felt he was fragile glass.

Well, Firesong wasn't feeling any too sturdy himself at the moment...

But before he got a chance to build up even the faintest feeling of resentment, help arrived, pouring in through the tiny doorway, in the form of black-clad Shin'a'in Sword-Sworn, who quickly and efficiently gathered them all up and carried them bodily out through the tunnel and up into the scarlet light of the setting sun. He let his body stay limp, simply cargo.

The sunset was a crimson light enhanced a bit with a coruscating rainbow of mage-energy, covering the bowl of the sky, slowly fading as the day itself faded.

He let himself be ministered to, as Aya oversaw everything and scolded if they jostled him too much as they carried him, with the rest, into a warm tent. He was too weak to resist, anyway. It was all he could do to nod when they asked him if he wanted something to drink, and to accept the bowl of hot herbal tea—well dosed with painkillers that he recognized at the first sniff. Those would war unpleasantly in his stomach for a few moments with the energy boosters, but he knew which ones would win, and he was grateful. He drank the bitter bowl down to the dregs, and waited stoically for the roiling in his gut to cease. He gathered from the chattering that the area around the Tower had suddenly lit up like a tiny sun for a moment, though absolutely no physical effect other than the light had leaked over into the "real" world. Firesong had the feeling that not even that would have occurred if they had not interfered and kept Karal from evaporating...

And if I had not—An'desha might have forgiven me eventually, but I would never have forgiven myself.

Not all of the effects of their counterstorm had been so benign, however. In ruins all around the rim of the Plains, the gryphon scouts were reporting odd collapses, disappearances of structures and parts of structures; nothing modern, but only those things dating from Urtho's time.

Including the Gate they had arrived through.

As he faded into drugged sleep, he heard Treyvan sigh, and Hydona make the observation that he was already thinking.

"Well," she said with resignation. "We shall surrrely take ourrr time getting back—but therrre will be a home to rrreturrrn to."

STORM BREAKING

A VALDEMAR OMNIBUS

BOOK THREE of
The MAGE STORMS

Dedicated to the memory of Elsie B. Wollheim.

1

Karal lay as quietly as he could, keeping his breathing even to avoid jarring his head. He kept his eyes closed against the light, hoping that the snow pack across his brow would eventually ease his throbbing headache. It was hard to think through the pain that stabbed from both temples and seemed to meet just above his nose. He was only vaguely aware of the rest of his body, muffled as it was in blankets, with hot stones packed all around to keep him from getting cold. The Shin'a'in who tended him seemed particularly concerned that he not take a chill from the clammy stone floor or the snow packs on his head. If this had been Valdemar, or even Karse, there would have been other recourses to ease the fiery lances stabbing through his temples—but unfortunately it wasn't. This half-melted ruin of an ancient tower held no such amenities as Healers or herbal pharmacopoeias, and he was going to have to make do with whatever their Shin'a'in allies could come up with, at least for the present. That meant willow tea and snow packs, and hope for the best.

I can always hope for the best. It could be worse. How much worse, though—that was something he was not prepared to contemplate at the moment.

It was a headache of monumental proportions, which was only to be expected, considering that he had personally been the nexus-point for all of the energies of a weapon so powerful and unpredictable that not even the Great Mage who had ended the Mage Wars had dared to use it. It had required a magic-channel, a *living* channel. Either no one in Urtho's contingent of mages happened to be a Channel, or else the Mage of Silence hadn't wanted to risk the life of such a person in the use of this weapon—in either case, it had remained unused with a warning plaque advising against its use.

Or else he couldn't get any volunteers. Not that Karal could blame anyone for *not* volunteering. His first experience at being a Channel had been singularly unpleasant, but the second had been of a different order of magnitude altogether. He honestly didn't remember too much of what had happened to him, once the weapon had been activated. Both the Hawkbrother Adept Firesong and the half-Shin'a'in An'desha had assured him that was all for the best, and he believed them.

When both An'desha and Firesong agree on something... He had the shivery feeling that he really didn't want to know exactly what had happened. If he knew, he'd have to think about it, and that gave him a very queasy feeling.

It was much easier to lie in his bedroll and deal with pain than to think.

Occasionally the sounds of the others, moving about in their daily chores, made their way past the pain, oddly muffled or magnified by the strange acoustics of the place. An'desha and the Shin'a'in shaman Lo'isha were talking softly, their voices blending together into a meaningless murmur, as oddly soothing as wind in leaves or the whisper of water over rocks. Someone, probably the Kaled'a'in *kestra'chern* Silverfox, was cleaning cooking utensils; soft metallic clinks punctuated the soft sounds of conversation. Nearer at hand, the Hawkbrother Firesong sang absently to himself; Firesong was probably mending something. Firesong always sang when he was mending something; he said it was to keep him from saying something he would regret. He didn't much care for mending, or for any other chores—the Tayledras Adept had been used, all his life, to being waited on. Having to fend for himself was an experience that Firesong was not enjoying. On the whole, Karal was of the opinion that he was bearing up well under these pressures and added responsibilities.

So much for the human members of the group. And as for the ones who were not human—well, Karal knew where Altra the Firecat was. The furry, vibrating blanket covering him from neck to knee was Altra, not some arcane Shin'a'in coverlet. Somehow, unlike mortal cats which would inexplicably *increase* their weight when lying on a human, the Firecat had decreased his, making himself no heavier than a thick woolen blanket. Only the steady radiating warmth and the deep, soothing purr betrayed his presence.

Somewhere beyond the chamber where Karal was lying, one of the horselike creatures known to the Valdemarans as a Companion, the one called Florian, listened attentively to An'desha and the shaman. If Karal opened his mind a little, he would "hear" the voices that were only a vague music to his real ears, but he would hear them through the senses of the Companion. The bonds between himself and the Companion and Firecat were stronger now than only weeks ago. He had only to think of them to sense the whisper of their thoughts, and he was aware of their presence in his mind as a constant warmth. Something had happened during the time he could not remember that bound the three of them even more firmly together. Anything they saw, heard, or felt, he could experience himself if he chose. He didn't know if the reverse was true, but he rather thought it wasn't. *He* was the one who'd been changed, not them.

That was another thing he didn't want to think too closely about. The Firecat was not entirely a mortal creature, and the Companion, while mortal enough, like the Firecat was a human reborn into a body of magical nature. So if something had happened that bound *him* to *them*— and so very tightly that he no longer had to work to reach their minds—

He shivered, and the cold he felt had nothing to do with the snow pack on his head. *Oh, no. I can't have changed that much. This is probably just temporary, something that will go away when I'm stronger.*

He redirected his thoughts and noticed that at least now he *could* think coherently.

That's an improvement anyway.

Now where was everyone else? He kept his eyes closed and listened carefully, trying to locate them all by sound alone rather than take a chance that opening his eyes would wake the pain again.

The remaining nonhumans, the two gryphons, were busy packing up their few belongings. They muttered to each other with little hisses and beak clicks, and their talons scraped against the leather of the saddlebags they had borrowed from the Shin'a'in for their journey north. They had decided that they had been away from their twin offspring long enough, and no one in the group was heartless enough to insist that they stay. The thrill of walking where the fabled Black Gryphon had once walked was probably beginning to pall in the face of being away from their beloved little ones for far too long. And with the Gates down, it would be a long trip back, even for creatures that flew.

And it could very well be that coming as close as we all did to getting seriously hurt, Treyvan and Hydona have decided that they don't want to leave their little ones as orphans. Who could blame them for that?

Yes, he was definitely able to think more coherently now.

Coherently enough to notice my neck muscles are in knots. Hardly a surprise. Karal sighed a little, and relaxed tense shoulders into the embrace of his sheepskin-covered pack, which was now serving him as a pillow. *It's a good thing that I have clothing in there instead of books.* The snow pack *was* working after all; if he noticed that his shoulders hurt, that meant the headache wasn't overwhelming everything else.

Grand, so now I get to enjoy how much the rest of me hurts!

But as the pain behind his eyes eased, so, too, did the tension in his muscles, which were probably contributing to the pain of the headache in the first place. So annoying how all these things managed to feed back on each other!

Well, I'd be a poor Sun-priest if I couldn't make myself relax, now wouldn't I? Such relaxation techniques were part of every novice's training. You couldn't pray if you weren't relaxed; how could you keep your mind on the glory of Vkandis if you were being nagged by a cramp? He patiently persuaded his rebellious body to behave itself, getting muscles unknotted that he hadn't even known were tight. As he did so, the ache in his head ebbed further, thus proving his guess that part of the headache was due to muscle tension.

That's better. That's much better. If his head would just let him be, he might actually begin to enjoy this invalid state, at least a little. For once he felt completely justified in lying abed and letting others take care of him; the depleted state of his entire body had convinced him that he had actually *earned* a rest.

And after all, it wasn't every day he had a Tayledras Healing Adept waiting on his every wish. How many people could boast of that? He couldn't even sigh without having Firesong ask him if he needed anything, a rather odd turn of events given that Firesong was the one used to being waited on.

He wasn't at all certain what prompted Firesong's attentiveness— there were others who would certainly have played nursemaid if the Adept hadn't insisted on taking the duty—but the Hawkbrother did make a very good and considerate nurse.

I certainly wouldn't have expected that from him. It just doesn't seem like him at all.

Well, maybe it wasn't much like the Firesong *he* knew, but such a thought was as shallow as the flippant surface that was all the Hawkbrother would ever reveal to him, given a choice. He immediately chided himself for *that* thought.

That was unworthy as well as unkind. There is far more to Firesong than I will ever see. We are all trying to cope with extreme situations, and if that is the way he chooses to cope, he has a right to it.

Just at the moment, even when his head wasn't splitting, Karal was in no shape to do anything other than wonder and enjoy the attention. He could hardly move his hand without tiring himself, and simply getting to his feet to go to the privy area left him so exhausted, he could only lie in his bedroll and doze for marks afterward. That worried him; unless he regained his strength soon, he would not be able to travel. If he couldn't travel, he wouldn't be able to leave with the others when they returned to Valdemar. The impatient gryphon parents were not going to wait for the others, but the humans could not wait much longer either. If they didn't leave now, they might be caught and trapped here by winter storms.

On the other hand... it might already be too late. The Gate that brought us here is down, and if I were a mage, I wouldn't chance reopening it. We might be stuck here until spring. Even under the best of conditions it's going to take an awfully long time to walk back.

So long, in fact, that returning home might be the very worst thing that they could do at this point. The solution to the problem of the mage-storms he had depleted himself to provide was, once again, a temporary solution only. This might be the very best place for them to work on a permanent answer. They certainly had resources here at their disposal that they wouldn't find anywhere else.

For one thing, the ancient weapon that they had used to cancel the storm-waves had been only one of several available to them, and it hadn't been anyone's first choice, only the one they understood the best. Perhaps one of the others would provide a better chance. The Kaled'a'in had promised to provide a historian, a specialist in their own languages and the ancient writing they alone had preserved out of the Cataclysm. Perhaps when he arrived, he would be able to provide better translations than the gryphons.

We haven't even begun to explore this place, yet this was the heart of the Mage of Silence's stronghold. He is said to have been the greatest there has ever been, with vast resources. Can we really assume that we have seen all there is? There might be other rooms here, rooms they hadn't found yet, that might hold more answers to their problem. Maybe they would be much better off by staying here and looking, or studying the remaining weapons. It was an option no one had suggested yet, but he wondered if they all weren't thinking about it, much as they would prefer to return home.

The main problem as I see it is that we don't have anyone with us from the mathematicians and the Artificers. That alone worried him; the last two stopgap measures had been created, at least in part, by Master Levy's group of clever logicians. With the help of these scholars, all of them had been able to examine the problem from an original perspective. *We need them. Firesong might not like them, but we need them.*

He knew that with certainty; as if Vkandis Himself had placed that certainty in his heart, he was as positive of it as he was of anything in his life. This was not a problem that could be worked through unless all of the minds available contributed to the solution.

He sighed, and as he lifted a hand to move the snow pack off his eyes, he heard Firesong come to take it for him. The cold, damp weight lifted away. "Would you like a new one?" the apparently eternally-young mage asked.

He opened his eyes and shook his head—only a little, so as to avoid undoing the good that had been done. Firesong didn't look very much like a nurse; the incredibly handsome young mage had managed to pack a full wardrobe of his intricately styled, brilliantly decorated silk clothing into his single pack. Karal could not imagine how he had done it. At the moment, he was all in muted silver-blues which, at least, made it possible for Karal to look at him without pain. From his precisely-styled, silver-white hair to his immaculate leg wrappings, he was every inch the exotic mage and not at all servile. The amused smile he wore reassured Karal; if there had been anything really wrong with him, he was fairly certain Firesong would not be smiling.

"Not at the moment, thank you," he said, surprised at the rasp in his voice, as if he had been screaming until his vocal cords were raw. "You really don't—"

Firesong chuckled, surprising him. "Oh, there's a reason behind all of this," he replied with a smile. "You're ridiculously easy as a patient, and if I'm tending *you,* I don't have to do any of the more tedious chores." His voice took on the merest touch of arrogance. "I'd rather keep putting snow packs on your head than wash dishes, I assure you."

Karal had to laugh weakly. Now *that* sounded more like the Firesong he knew! "Oh, good," he said. "I was afraid that you'd suddenly been filled with the spirit of self-sacrifice, and I wasn't certain I could bear that for very long."

Now Firesong laughed, and tossed his long silver hair over his shoulder. "Keep your tender sentiments to yourself, Karsite," he said mockingly. "Out of my own self-interest I want you to stay an invalid as long as possible, and if you keep saying things like that, I might be tempted to do something to keep you that way."

"You promise, but you never follow through," Karal retorted, surprising himself with his enjoyment of the exchange. "I think my tender hide is safe from you."

"You doubt?" Firesong's brow rose, and he raised his gaze to a point somewhere past Karal; probably listening to Florian, the Companion. His next words confirmed Karal's guess. "Well, maybe you're right. A hoofprint in the middle of my face would not improve my looks—" He dropped his gaze to meet Altra's brilliant blue eyes, "—and I don't like the way that cat of yours is flexing his claws either."

:I wouldn't hurt you where it showed,: Altra said dryly, into both their minds. *:Silverfox might object to my alterations, however. But you would make a charming girl.:*

Firesong's silver eyes widened in mock fear, but there was a tinge of respect in his look as well. "Remind me never to anger you, Altra. That's a bit vicious even as a joke."

:If I thought for a moment that you were serious, it wouldn't be a joke.: The Firecat deliberately raised one paw and licked his flexed talons. Since Altra was the size of most large dogs, and his paws were correspondingly huge, those talons were wicked looking indeed.

That's not very subtle, cat, Karal thought warningly, knowing Altra would hear him.

:It wasn't meant to be subtle,: the Firecat replied in his mind only. *:There was a time when he contemplated injuring you. If he ever strays in that direction again, I want him to have something to think about.:*

Karal kept his face straight as Altra imparted that choice bit of information, so he did not reveal a reaction. That was certainly news to him.

And now everyone seems determined to protect me! But Firesong was waiting for him to say something, so before the mage could ask what it was that made him look so odd, he raised a shaking hand to rub his eyebrow. "Cats. You can't live with them, and the fur's too thin for a rug."

Altra gave an exaggerated snort of disgust as Firesong laughed aloud. "You *are* feeling better," he said, this time without the mockery. "Good. Maybe tonight you'll be able to stomach something besides that tasteless slop the shaman has been feeding you. Just try not to get well so quickly that I'm forced to wash my own plates again any time soon."

Before Karal could reply, Firesong rose to his feet to take away the dripping snow pack. He turned his head slowly to look in the direction of Florian and the others.

Sure enough, a little way past the chamber's entrance, Florian stood with his head just above An'desha's shoulder, looking at something the shaman was drawing on the floor.

He could, if he just relaxed a little, see everything from Florian's point of view. He didn't want to relax that much, honestly.

I just want my headache to stop. I want to be able to get up and do things like the others. I truly do want to stop being a burden. It isn't the place of a priest of Vkandis Sunlord to be the one given comfort, it is the priest's place to give comfort...

He closed his eyes, and tried to find some meditation technique that would at least enable him to sleep despite the pain. If he fell asleep, at least he wouldn't be quite so aware of what a nuisance he'd become.

Without any warning footsteps, he felt a touch on his arm. His eyes popped open, all he could manage in the way of a startled reaction.

He found himself looking up into a pair of extremely blue eyes, amused eyes, in a triangular face with golden skin. The eyes and the face topped a body wearing Shin'a'in garments of unornamented dark sable-brown; the color, he now recalled, that Swordsworn usually wore when they weren't engaged in one of their rare but vicious blood-feuds.

The Swordsworn had another name. *Kal'enedral. The ones Sworn to the service of Kal'enel, the Warrior.* He knew more about them now than any Karsite alive. The person sitting lightly on "his" heels would be one of the Swordsworn who had guided them here and guarded them on the way; who had, with the aid of k'Leshya, excavated a way into the Tower. He couldn't tell if this person was male or female; with the Swordsworn, it hardly mattered, since they were not only vowed to chastity and celibacy, but were by their bond to their Goddess, rendered incapable of a sexual impulse. That was a state that had no parallel in the Sunlord's hierarchy; although Sun-priests were not encouraged to wed, they were not denied that state either.

"Well, this was not what we intended when we opened our secret to you, young outClansman," the Shin'a'in said, in a clear, slightly roughened tenor voice that could have belonged to a man or a woman. The Sworn One spoke with very little accent, in remarkably good Valdemaran. Karal was relieved; his Shin'a'in was rudimentary at best. "We thought you would be here and gone again—"

The Shin'a'in paused then, as if suddenly aware that the "gone" very nearly had been "permanently gone."

Karal shrugged. "This wasn't our plan either, Sworn One," he said politely.

The Shin'a'in laughed. "True enough, and I think not even your God could have predicted this outcome. Certainly our Goddess did not! Or if She did, She saw fit not to grace us with the information. But now— well, given that the Gate that brought you here is gone, and our winter storms are closing in, we have determined that we will have to become true hosts."

At one point, Karal would have been shocked by the reference to a deity other than Vkandis Sunlord—more shocked that such a deity as the Shin'a'in Star-Eyed was spoken of in the same breath as He. Later, he would have been able to accept that, but would also have been driven speechless by such a *casual* reference to a deity, as if the person speaking had a personal relationship with Kal'enel.

Now he knew better; these Swordsworn *did* have such a relationship. She had been known to speak with Her special followers on a regular basis, and even occasionally intervene in their lives. Which was, after all, not entirely unlike the relationship Vkandis had with the Son of the Sun.

"I have been told that affairs were at such a turning point that any and all outcomes were equally likely," he said carefully, squinting around his headache. "Perhaps that is why She gave you no indication that we were to be unexpected tenants rather than guests."

"Well said!" the Shin'a'in replied warmly. "Well, then. Tenants you are, dwellers among our tents, and as such it becomes necessary that we provide you with something better than the hasty arrangements of aforetime. First, I am Chagren shena Liha'irden, and I am to be your Healer. Lo'isha is a good man and a fine shaman, but his Healing skills are rudimentary at best. I am better suited to helping you, trust me in that."

Karal could not help but show his surprise; a *Healer* among the Swordsworn? Chagren saw his expression and chuckled.

"Given our task of serving as the Guardians of the Plains, does it not seem logical that we must need a Healer now and again? I was a Healer before I was Sworn, and Swore myself in part because I was one of those who joined the battle with Ancar, and I vowed I would never again find myself unable to defend those who I had come to Heal. I petitioned. She accepted. Not *all* of us who come to serve Her so closely have tragic tales of great personal loss behind them." Then his expression changed, becoming serious for a moment. "Though there are many. Those who have seen too much to endure and remain sane often petition Her and are taken into Her ranks."

Those who have seen too much to endure— Karal glanced involuntarily at An'desha, and Chagren followed his glance. He looked back down at Karal. "Interesting. Your thoughts on that one?"

Karal blinked at the Shin'a'in's directness. "I sometimes wonder if there *is* any place for An'desha, after all he has endured."

Chagren lost that amused smile entirely, and his eyelids dropped momentarily to veil his eyes. "There is," he said after a pause, "if he chooses to take it. Among us there is no tale so strange that we cannot encompass it. Not among the Swordsworn, I think. but among the Wise, those who wear the blue of the night sky and the day's ending. They are Sworn to Wisdom rather than the Sword, and I think it is among their numbers he would feel he has come home. But that is for him to decide."

The smile returned. "Meanwhile, it is for *me* to ease some of your discomfort, while my fellows bring the wherewithal to make this into a home for as long as may be. So. You have been Healed before?"

"Not really," Karal confessed. "The one Valdemaran Healer I saw decided that all I needed was herbs and potions, not real Healing."

"A wise Healer knows when to Heal and when to let time do the Healing," Chagren replied with approval. "Well then; *this* time you shall be the recipient of true Healing, such as, I believe, some of your Sun-priests are known to practice. I require of you only that you close your eyes and relax, and that when you sense my spirit, permit it to touch yours. That should be easy enough, yes?"

"I think so," Karal replied as the headache returned with a vengeance. Any reluctance he might have felt vanished at the onslaught of further pain. He closed his eyes as instructed, and waited, slowly willing each muscle to release its built-up tension.

The moment he "sensed Chagren's spirit" he knew exactly what the Shin'a'in had meant; he felt something very akin to the sensation he had when he first communicated with Florian. And as he had when Florian had requested that Karal "let him into his mind," he let down those internal barriers he hadn't realized existed back when he had been plain Karal of Karse.

But this time, instead of thoughts and sensations flooding into his mind, a warm, soothing wave washed over him, and where it had passed, the pain was gone, leaving behind comfort and reassurance.

He opened his eyes; he thought it was only a moment later, but

Chagren was gone. In his place stood a metal pitcher and cup, and in his chamber and the rooms beyond, new comforts and a few new figures had appeared as if conjured.

There was a small cast-metal stove at his feet, and he had been heaped with more woven blankets. Several long, flat cushions arranged like a more comfortable bed than the one he currently occupied lay beside that. On top of the stove, there was a steaming pot.

Beyond his room, he saw at least one more stove and reckoned that there were probably more. Better bedding had appeared, and more amenities. Firesong appeared and glanced in the door to his chamber, and when the mage saw that he was awake, the Hawkbrother walked unhurriedly and gracefully to his side.

"You've been asleep through all the excitement," Firesong told him. "More of those Kal'enedral appeared with a veritable caravan of goods, and this place is now almost civilized." He smiled, and there was no mistaking the fact that he was pleased. "They even promised none of us will have to cook anymore, though we *will* still have to do the work of *hertasi*, I fear. That is just as well, since I do not believe I could have eaten another of my own meals, even if I died of starvation."

Karal croaked a chuckle, and discovered to his delight that it did not make his head hurt. "My headache is gone!" he exclaimed with glee.

Firesong nodded. "That fellow Chagren said it would be. I will probably be helping him the next time he Heals you. He told me what had caused your aching skull, and once he explained it to me, it was obvious—" He held up a hand, forestalling Karal's questions, "—and I will explain it all to you in detail, some time later, when we have the time for me to explain how and why a mage or a Healer is able to do what he does. Suffice it for now to say that you have misused that part of you that channels magic, as if you had bruised it by battering a rough stone around inside your skull, and that was why your head hurt. He was able to take care of the bruises, so to speak."

Karal tried to lever himself up, and found to his profound disappointment that he was still as weak as a newborn colt. "Too bad I'm not completely back to normal, but I suppose Chagren can't Heal everything at once," he answered with a sigh, as Firesong caught his elbow to help him.

"Obviously, he cannot," the mage replied reasonably. "There are some things, such as strength and endurance, that time will restore as much as he. Now, if you will move thus, and so, we will get you onto this more comfortable bed, and then you must drink what he left you, and eat, and then sleep again. For the next couple of days, making your way to the privy and back will be all the exercise you're fit for."

With Firesong's aid, Karal moved over to the pile of flat bed cushions, which turned out to be even more comfortable than they looked. The mage piled all of his blankets, rugs, and furs back on top of him, then handed him the metal cup. It proved to contain another herbal potion, but this one had a pleasantly fruity, faintly sweet taste, with a refreshingly astringent aftertaste that quenched a deep-lying thirst no amount of water had been able to satisfy. At Firesong's urging, he drank a second cup, and while he finished that, An'desha appeared with a bowl and spoon.

"Chagren promised that you would at least be able to feed yourself, so that is *your* task for the day," An'desha said, handing him both. The bowl held real soup, not the tasteless gruel that Lo'isha had been feeding him. Although his hand shook a little, he managed not only to feed himself, but to finish every drop in the bowl. An'desha and Firesong sat watching him like a pair of anxious nursery attendants all during the meal, and An'desha took back the empty bowl with a grin of triumph.

"Soon enough you will be sweeping and washing with the rest of us," An'desha said as he rose. Karal leveled a sober gaze on Firesong as the young Shin'a'in left the chamber.

"I feel as if I should be sweeping and washing for both of you, you and Silverfox together," he said with guilt he could not conceal. "I am taking up so much of your time, and contributing nothing."

"*Now*," Firesong replied sternly, "that says nothing of what you have done in the past, or will do in the future. And you are taking up very little of my time, since you sleep a great deal. Which is, by the by, what you should be doing now; sleeping, once you have another cup of this excellent beverage."

Obediently, Karal drank down a third cup and closed his eyes again, although he felt no real urge to sleep. But evidently there was something in the drink, or he needed sleep so badly that his body would take any opportunity to seize some, for no sooner had he closed his eyes and begun the first stages of his ritual of relaxation, than he was fast asleep.

Firesong waited until he was certain young Karal was deep in dreaming, then gathered up the now-empty pitcher, bowl, and cup and carried them off to be washed. The chamber through whose outer wall they had entered the Tower had been dedicated to cleaning—everything from pots to people. Judicious use of magic on Firesong's part had driven a pipe to the surface; at the surface was a black-enameled basin connected to the pipe that the Shin'a'in kept filled with snow. No magic melted the snow shoveled into the basin, just the sun supplemented by a simple horsedung fire. The pipe slanted down into the chamber where it was closed by a stopcock taken from a wine barrel, and simply turning the stopcock gave them water enough for about any purpose. Waste water went into a second pipe going down into the earth, set just outside in the tunnel. So far, it had been sufficient.

Silverfox was at the washing basin, used both for dishes and clothing, and he felt a stab of guilt of his own that the *kestra'chern* should be wasting his time and talents on so menial a task as cleaning dirty dishes. This seemed as unreasonable a task as to ask a fine sculptor to shovel snow, yet there he was, serenely working away the soil of camp life with his slender fingers.

But the handsome Kaled'a'in looked up and smiled at his approach, and said lightly, "Would that all troubles are so easily washed away as these! All things considered, I have actually been enjoying myself on this little jaunt. I could almost feel that I am on holiday here!"

Firesong handed him the dishes with a groan. "Why do I suddenly have the sinking feeling that you are one of those benighted individuals who thinks that taking himself off to the utter wilderness for a fortnight or more constitutes a *holiday*?"

"What?" the *kestra'chern* replied innocently. "And you do not?" His blue eyes twinkled as he continued. "Think of the splendid isolation, the uncrowded vistas, the joy of doing everything for yourself, knowing you need rely on no one else! Self-sufficiency! Feeling yourself unconstrained by all the rules and customs that can come to smother you!"

"Think of the lack of civilized conversation, the dearth of entertainment, the deprivation of decent food, hot baths, and reasonable sleeping accommodations!" Firesong retorted. "*I* had rather endure a bored little provincial courtier babble for an hour than listen to a brook do the same, while my toes are cold and my nose even colder, and there isn't a cushion to relax upon. And I do not particularly take joy from washing dishes and mending clothing, I promise you. Those are tedious tasks at best, and wasteful of valuable time at worst!"

But Silverfox's clever, sharp features softened for a moment. "For you, perhaps, but unless he is in a circumstance like this one, a *kestra'chern* is never free of the needs of others. For you, this place is an exile, but for me, a holiday in the wild is an escape."

Now Firesong suffered another twinge of guilt, and he sat down beside the washtub. "And even here you are not free of demands," he said, reproaching himself. "For there are my demands on you—"

But Silverfox only laughed, and shook his long black hair back over his shoulders. "No, those are not demands, *ahela*, those are mutual desires. I could say that my demands on you are as improvident, but I won't. But there is this—for once, I can act on my own desires rather than concentrate on the needs of another to the exclusion of anything I feel."

Firesong felt the guilt for this, at least, lift away from him. "I... make you feel more free, simply by being as I am? In that case, perhaps I should be more demanding!"

The *kestra'chern* laughed, as the two gryphons, loaded with their travel packs, poked their beaks into the cleaning chamber with curiosity. "Why all the rrrevelrrry?" Treyvan demanded. "Arre potsss ssso amusssing?"

"That depends on who is cleaning them, old bird," Silverfox replied. "Are you ready to depart yet?"

The female gryphon, Hydona, nodded vigorously. "Now that morrre help hasss come, yesss. If I werrre young and unpairrred, I would ssstay, but—"

"But nothing," Firesong said firmly, reacting to the anxious tone of her voice, sensing she was afraid that he would demand that she stay. "Your little ones need you far more than we do. Not that we aren't grateful."

"When the keeper of hissstorry comesss, we will be sssuperfluousss anyway," Treyvan admitted. "He will be able to rrread the old wrritingsss here much morrre clearrly than we."

It was obvious to Firesong that the gryphons were chagrined at their inability to decipher the ancient texts that had been found here, and they took their failure personally. They had all made an incorrect assumption about clan k'Leshya. They had assumed that the last clan that could truly have called itself *Kaled'a'in* rather than Shin'a'in or Tayledras had a purer form of the original tongue than either splinter group. Given that, the gryphons should have been able to decipher the ancient texts. And they had also assumed that since k'Leshya had come to dwell among the Haighlei, a people who shunned change, their language would obviously have remained as pure as it was the day that they all went through the Gates to escape into the West.

But while the Haighlei shunned change, the Kaled'a'in had not, and their language had drifted from the ancient tongue as inevitably as had Shin'a'in and Tayledras. Perhaps it had not drifted so far or so fast, but nevertheless, it had drifted, and in a direction that rendered the ancient writings as vague to the gryphons as to Firesong or Lo'isha.

However, providentially enough, there was among the pioneers of k'Leshya an individual who had not only come along to record what transpired in their new home, but one who had made a hobby of studying the most ancient scripts. While this historian was not the expert that a true scholar of the earliest days of White Gryphon would have been, he had volunteered to come and assist the party at the Tower, and he should prove more of an expert than the two gryphons.

That was the theory anyway. Very little in this strange situation had gone according to theory.

"I will be sorry to see you leave," Firesong said sincerely. "You both have been very patient about this, but even I can tell that gryphons aren't comfortable underground."

Hydona didn't say anything, but Treyvan shivered, all of his feathers quivering. "It hasss not been easssy," he admitted. "And all that hasss kept me here at timesss isss the knowledge that the grrreat Ssskandrranon walked thessse sssame chamberrsss."

Firesong nodded with understanding; not that long ago, he would have said the same thing in the same reverent tones about visiting the Heartstone Chamber in the Palace at Haven where his own ancestor Vanyel had once worked. That, however, had been before he had been kidnapped by that same ancestor and shoved, willy-nilly, into the affairs of the Kingdom of Valdemar. Being conscripted by a stubborn spirit to the aid of a place and people that were hardly more than misty history to him had given him a slightly more jaundiced view of "honored ancestors" than most folk had.

Oh, I'll leave them to their illusions. Skandranon is not likely to stick his beak into our affairs now, thank the gods; if he was going to show up the way Vanyel did, he'd be here already. If that was all it took to help them bear the feeling of being buried alive here, their illusions are valuable.

Besides, Skandranon had died peacefully, in extreme old age, surrounded by a vast flock of worshipful grandchildren and great-grandchildren. There were no stories of a haunted forest in which uncanny things happened connected with *his* legends, and his long line of descendants had legends of their own.

But Firesong couldn't help but wonder now and again just what his own ancestor Vanyel was planning. He'd given no indication that he planned to—as it were—move on, once the dual threats of Ancar and Falconsbane had been dealt with. By now he must have recovered from the effort of taking down the Web—and Vanyel at full strength had been powerful enough to wrest away control of a Gate *he* had not erected to transport five humans, four gryphons, a *dyheli*, two Companions, and two bondbirds all the way from a site at the edge of the Dhorisha Plains to the heart of the Forest of Sorrows beyond Valdemar's northern border. There was no telling what he might still be capable of.

I think I know why he didn't confront Falconsbane directly—but I would not have given odds in favor of Falconsbane if Vanyel—and Yfandes and Stefen—had been given leave to deal with him themselves.

"Do we take it that you arrre ssstaying, then?" Treyvan asked.

Both Firesong and Silverfox nodded, but it was Silverfox who answered. "That's why that caravan of Swordsworn showed up with all the new equipment. We just now told Karal, but that is only because he hasn't been awake long enough to listen to anything complicated. The Kal'enedral pointed out that we were lucky that we didn't encounter any winter storms coming in, but we can't count on our luck holding. If we're caught, we would have to do what the Shin'a'in do—dig in, hope we don't freeze to death, then settle in for the rest of the winter. Once the trail out is obliterated by a storm, there's no reestablishing it. If we're going to be stuck, I'd rather be stuck here, where we can continue to research what Urtho left behind. I'm looking for secret doors, or concealed rooms, while the rest figure out what the effect of the cancellation wave we sent out will be, and how long it will last."

"I think you are wissse," Treyvan said gravely. "I do not think that Karrral would sssurrvive the trrrip, much lessss a grreat sstorrm."

"Nor do I, and that was why I voted to stay," Firesong said, then added with a sigh. "Even if it means living like a brigand until spring."

Treyvan gryph-grinned at that, and gave him a mock cuff with a tightly fisted claw. "Peacock!" he chuckled. "You arrre jusst dissscontented becaussse therrre isss no one herrre but Sssilverrrfox to admirrre yourrr handsssome face!"

"No, I am just discontented because I am not especially fond of sewing split seams and scrubbing pots, which is a perfectly reasonable attitude," Firesong retorted, and made shooing motions with his hands. "Be on your way; I'm sure you can't *wait* to get back to cries of 'but *Papa* said we can!', 'But Andra's mama lets her!', and 'do I *have* to?'"

When he wished to exercise that talent, Firesong could be a wicked mimic, and he so accurately rendered a childish whine that both gryphons' ear-tufts went back in alarm.

"Perrrhapsss Hydona could go ahead of me," Treyvan ventured, then ducked as his mate leveled a killing gaze on him, "orrr perrrhapsss not. Well, why not; we faced Ancarrr, we faced Falconsssbane, we faced the Imperrrial Arrrmy and the mage-ssstormsss. What arrre two merrre childrrren againssst that?"

"Worse than all of them put together, because they'll always get what they want?" Firesong suggested, and Hydona turned her deadly glare on him. "Of course, my opinion is hardly valid!" he amended hastily. "After all, *I* don't have children!"

Hydona snorted, but looked mollified, and Firesong wisely opted to keep the rest of his opinions to himself. "We'll all miss you," he said instead. "But you've done more than your duty, and children need their parents. Fly safely, friends."

"Thank you," Treyvan said simply.

Even though the Shin'a'in had labored to open the hole in the outer wall to give them all a wider door into the tunnel, it was still a squeeze for the gryphons to get through, burdened with their packs as they were. As a courtesy, Firesong sent a mage-light on ahead of them, though Treyvan was perfectly capable of making his own. Not that they were going to get lost in a straight tunnel, but the light might make the tunnel itself seem less confining.

Silverfox sat looking after them for a while after they were gone. "You know," he said finally, "they were the only creatures I ever envied when I was young."

"Gryphons in general?" Firesong asked. "Or those two in particular?"

"Gryphons in general," Silverfox replied, turning back to his dishtub. "The main thing was that they can fly, of course, but besides that, they are just marvelous creatures. They grow their own wonderful costumes of feathers, they are armed better than any fighter with those talons and that beak, and they can take on virtually any task except those that require unusually fine dexterity. They can even become *kestra'chern*! So I envied them."

"And now?" Firesong asked.

"Now I'm old enough and experienced enough to have seen the price they pay for all those gifts. You'd be amazed at how delicate their digestion is, they are devastated by certain diseases that are only an inconvenience to a human, and their joints tend to stiffen up and get quite painful as they age. I'm still of divided opinion about whether or not the drawbacks are worth being a gryphon," he added, "but I no longer envy them."

"I never did," Firesong said softly. "I only envied myself," and left it at that.

"...and the Mage of Silence brought all of the armies back to his stronghold here, in Ka'venusho," Chagren said, pointing with his charcoal stick to the appropriate place he had drawn on the floor. Karal nodded, and concentrated fiercely while Chagren related the rest of the history of the Mage Wars. He'd heard it all once from Lo'isha, of course, but Chagren had actually *experienced* a compressed version of this history. That had been during a special moment in his training, when he went to Kata'shin'a'in and entered a holy building that housed something he called the Webs of Time. Karal's grasp of language was not quite good enough to give him a clear idea of what *physical* forms these Webs were in, but Chagren said that they held the memories of those who had made them, and that under certain specific conditions, those memories could be awakened and experienced. Karal was disposed to believe him; after all that *he* had seen, what was one more supernatural marvel?

The gryphons had already given him their own version of the story, more heavily weighted with the heroism of the Black Gryphon, of course. Even Silverfox had a slightly different tale, as handed down among the Kaled'a'in *kestra'cherns* from Amberdrake, Tadrith Wyrsabane, and the generations since them.

"... so that is why this place was hallowed for us, even before we knew there still were working weapons here," Chagren finished. "Mind, I said *hallowed*, not *holy*. We of the Plains do not count any human 'holy,'' not even Her Avatars or the Kal'enedral. The Mage of Silence was a good man, a fine man, and flawed as all men are. What made him different from most other men was that he saw his weaknesses and spent all his life trying to keep them controlled, so as not to harm others with them; that he devoted a larger percentage of his life to the wellbeing of others than most ever even think of doing. What made him dangerous were the things he never troubled to control: his curiosity and his desire to meddle and change things for the sake of change itself."

Karal digested that; it was interesting to hear the various versions, not only of the story of the Cataclysm, but the way the three cultures viewed Adept Urtho. To the gryphons, at least, Urtho was the ultimate Great Father, which was hardly surprising, since they knew he had created them; to Silverfox he was both a familiar figure of history and a figure of semi-veneration, less than a god but far more than human. To the Tayledras, he was a figure of the misty past, and they recalled very little of him; most did not even know his name, and called him only "The Mage of Silence." To most Shin'a'in he was not even that—

Except to the Kal'enedral. To them, he was a man; powerful, good of heart and soul, but one who could not resist meddling in things he should never have touched. Without a doubt, that was because their version was flavored with their own form of prejudice against magic. Even Chagren was not immune from that prejudice, though he suffered from it less than some.

The Shin'a'in had been assigned the guardianship of the Plains by their Goddess Herself, although most of them were not aware that there really *was* something here that needed to be guarded from interlopers. Certainly, being a Goddess, She could simply have removed the weapons and dangers entirely had She chosen, but deities work in ways that are often not obvious even after centuries of scrutiny. It must have taken a direct edict from the Shin'a'in Goddess to get her chief servants, the Kal'enedral, to open the Plains and this Tower at its heart to strangers. He could hardly imagine what their reaction must have been to learn that they would be opening the Tower to *mages*.

Their faith must be very great, he thought, with wonder. *Look how long it took me to accept that Heralds and Companions were not demonic—they gave over their fears in a much shorter time.*

Or if they had not given up their fear, they had certainly worked past it. He had encountered no hostility from these people, only the wariness he himself felt, faced with strangers from a strange people.

Then again, perhaps the Kal'enedral had been very careful about which of their folk were permitted to aid the foreigners.

"I could do with a little less change myself," he said with a weak laugh. "But the mage-storms aren't giving us much of a choice in that."

Chagren grimaced, his aquiline features making the expression more pronounced. "Yet another mischance that some would lay at Urtho's door. Had he not made the choices he did, some would say that none of this would be happening now."

Interesting choice of words. Could it be that Chagren is taking a wider view of things? "But not you?" Karal asked delicately.

Chagren looked for a moment as if he was not going to answer, then shrugged. "But not me. I am not certain that Urtho's great enemy Ma'ar would not have unleashed worse upon the world; after all, look what havoc Falconsbane and Ancar wrought, who were lesser mages than Ma'ar. Then again, my *leshy'a* teachers had... experience with mages."

Now that was a new word; he thought he vaguely recognized the root. Something about a soul. "What kind of teachers?" he asked, to test his guess.

"I suppose you'd call them 'spirits' although they can be quite solidly real if She wishes," Chagren replied matter-of-factly, as if he spoke with ghosts every day. Well, perhaps he did.

"At some point in the lives of most Swordsworn they encounter one or more *leshy'a Kal'enedral.* There have even—" He broke off his words, and stared past Karal for a moment, and half-choked. His eyes widened, and he gave a slight bow of his head. "I believe, Outlander," he said in an entirely different and very respectful voice, "that you are about to find out for yourself."

Karal turned, to find that another of the Swordsworn was standing in the doorway; this one was very clearly a woman, but also very clearly a warrior in every fiber. She was dressed entirely in black from head to toe, and wore a veil or scarf across the bottom half of her face. A sword and long knife hung from her belt, and she bore the weight easily, negligently. In two paces she had crossed the chamber and stood at the side of Karal's pallet, looking down at him.

She could have seemed frightening, intimidating from her clothing alone, and yet there was nothing menacing whatsoever about her. Competent, yes; certainly imposing—but Karal would have had no hesitation in trusting her. Her blue eyes above the black veil were both amused and kind, and he sensed that she was smiling.

"Forgive me that I can't rise to greet you properly, Lady," he said with deepest respect.

"Oh, not at all," she replied, and her voice had a very odd, hollow quality to it, as if she were speaking from the bottom of a very deep well. "As I understand it, you're rather indisposed at the moment."

He narrowed his eyes, as he began to see, or sense, that there was something unexpected about her. She reminded him of something very familiar; in fact, there was some indefinable aura about her that was like—like—

Sunlord! She's—not—

"I must presume," he said carefully after a deep breath, "that Sworn Ones such as you who choose to instruct further generations do not bother to take a physical vehicle such as a Firecat or a Companion." *She's a spirit, that's what she is! Like An'desha's Avatars, only more here. More real.* He felt positively giddy at his own daring, looking a spirit right in the eyes like this, and speaking to her as an equal!

"Say rather, *are chosen* rather than *choose*, and you have it rightly, young priest," the spirit replied, a hint of a chuckle in her hollow voice. "Though I have to admit that She has toyed a time or two with the notion of Black Companions. Or perhaps, Black Riders."

Since Karal could well imagine Florian's indignant response to *that* idea, he had to stifle a smile of his own. *Black Companions? Oh, the Heralds wouldn't like that at all!*

"I believe you've met a kinswoman of mine," the spirit continued. "She left her mark on you, which leads me to think that she regards you favorably. She's a hard one to please."

He tried wildly for a moment to think of who the Kal'enedral could mean. "Ah—you—Querna?" he hazarded, trying to imagine how that rather aloof lady could have left any kind of a mark on him.

The spirit laughed aloud at that. "No, young Clan-friend. *Kerowyn.* I see you've lined up anything that could serve as a weapon, hurled or otherwise, so that you can reach everything in the order you'd need it. That's the sort of 'mark' I mean. She's trained you so deep it's a habit."

Startled, he looked down involuntarily and saw he'd done just that, with the things he'd have to throw at the farthest point of his reach and his dagger right at his elbow. He flushed. What must Chagren be thinking now, that he distrusted them all? That they had let a potential assassin into their midst?

"Oh don't be embarrassed, boy," the spirit chided gruffly. "That's one of the best habits to be in. What if someone unfriendly got in here? What if one of our more fanatical brethren decided that She had been deceived by you lot, and you all had to die? Don't you know what we say? *Know where all the exits are. Never sit with your back to the door. Watch the reflections. Watch the shadows. Keep your hands free and your weapons loose.*"

Sunlord! he thought desperately, *I'm being bombarded with Shin'a'in proverbs! What a terrible way to die!*

He meant that lightly, but it seemed that the Kal'enedral intended to continue until she had recited every proverb on the subject of self-defense that the Shin'a'in ever invented. "*Never sit down to eat with your sword at your side—strap it to your back for a faster draw. Better an honest enemy than a feigned friend. When—*"

"*Who is wisest, says least,*" he interrupted, desperate to cut through what looked to be an unending stream of proverbs. Were Shin'a'in all like that? Even Kerowyn tended to spout Shin'a'in proverbs at the drop of a hint. And a spirit Kal'enedral probably knew every proverb ever composed!

The spirit laughed aloud again. "Well said!" she applauded. "Keep that sense of humor, and you might just survive this. Chagren, take special care of this one; he's deeper than he looks."

Chagren bowed low. "As you say, teacher," he replied.

Karal wasn't prepared for the spirit's departure; he barely blinked and she was gone. A chill ran up his backbone, but he was determined not to show it.

"If you see a Swordsworn in black with a veil," Chagren said slowly, "it is *leshy'a.* There have been some few here among the rest of us. We think they come to ensure your safety... or ours. It's debated which."

"It's more likely both," Karal said, feeling a bit dizzy. "Kerowyn's kin to *her?*"

Chagren shrugged. "So she says. That is something new to me, but the *leshy'a* are not inclined to talk about their pasts. Often we do not even know their names. She is my first teacher of the sword, and came to me the night that I was Sworn—" He broke off what he was saying to shake his head. "I am babbling. And *you,* young outland priest, can consider yourself as having passed a kind of examination. None of the Sworn are likely to question *your* right to be here ever again."

With that rather surprising statement, he turned and left the chamber, leaving Karal alone with his thoughts, which were, to say the least, very complex.

Although there was one thought that was not at all complex.

So my right to be here will no longer be questioned. That's all very well for me, but what about the others?

* * *

Firesong sighed as he regarded his much abused shirt with a frown. His favorite sorts of garments were not meant for rough living and a camp existence.

"Glaring at it won't put the hem back up," Silverfox remarked around a mouthful of pins. "You might as well give up and do it the hard way."

Firesong growled under his breath, but took up needle and thread grudgingly. "All very well for you to say," he complained, "but you've been able to trade off sweeping and scrubbing the sleeping room to An'desha in return for cleaning his dishes. And you've traded Lo'isha massages for cleaning and airing the bedding. *I* haven't got anything anyone wants to trade for! Valdemar, barbaric as it was, is looking better all the time!"

Silverfox chuckled. "It could be worse; we could still be eating your cooking. I believe that our kin-cousins are being very generous in taking over the larger portion of the work."

Firesong growled again. "You only say that because you can do things even the Kal'enedral are interested in. I'm a *mage*, that's all I know, and they don't want a thing I can do for them!"

Silverfox put down his needle to look up at him with sympathy. "You aren't just a mage. You are a lover, but you are so exotic to them that they could more easily entertain fantasies of bedding clouds. If there is *really* something you detest, would you please tell me and let me do it, or barter a massage or something to one of the Sworn and have him do it? You are a mage, *ashaka*, and I feel in my bones that soon enough you will have more important things to worry about than hems and ripped seams."

Firesong started to reply, then shook his head and laughed at himself. "Why is it when you say things like that, you manage to deflate my self-importance rather than inflating it, and simply fill me with dread?"

Silverfox merely tilted his head to one side, and replied, "Do I?"

Let's change the subject, he thought. *I can do without too much introspection.* "Magic is working more reliably now that the counterforce is evening out the storm-waves. It is still a horrid mess, but I think I can get a Gate up to the rim of the Plains soon; if I can do that, we can at least ask for a few more things to make life tolerable around here. How much would k'Leshya be willing to part with in the way of amenities, do you think? I haven't had a real bath in weeks and neither has anyone else. A big tub would be very welcome, even if its real intention was to water horses. A copper boiler to heat water would be even more welcome."

Silverfox looked thoughtful. "There might be a fair amount they could send us, both of leftover Tayledras gear and some of our own. And you know—if we could get a Gate open, we could get some *hertasi* volunteers to come through. They can't cross the Plains in winter without a great deal of hardship, and I wouldn't ask it of them. But they could come through a Gate, provided they were sure we could keep them warm enough over here."

Firesong closed his eyes for a moment in longing. Oh, how he missed his little army of *hertasi* helpers! If he had just one or two, he wouldn't have to do another tedious chore for himself again. They loved to do exactly the sorts of things he wanted to avoid here, and could probably show even the natives some lessons in organization.

"Before we try that, we ought to see if we can find out what Sejanes and the rest back in Haven have found out about Gating," he replied, after another moment of cautious thought. "Not that I wouldn't be willing to give up a lot for a couple of *hertasi*, but I wouldn't want to put them at any risk. It's one thing to toss a tub or a sack of meal through; it's quite another to risk a living being."

Silverfox nodded, and bit off his thread. "Should we send Karal back if we can get a Gate up that's safe for a living creature? He'd be better off with k'Leshya."

Once again, Firesong hesitated. *Now there's a question. He would be better off in a place where he could be properly cared for, but—how many more of the devices here need a Channel? What are we going to have to do in order to counter that final Storm, the one that's the reverse analog of the original Cataclysm?* "You can ask An'desha and Lo'isha if you like, but I have the sinking feeling we still need him. If he decides he's willing to stay here, we should let him." He took a few more stitches and knotted off his own thread. "I think he's going to insist on it. Sometimes that child makes me feel ashamed of myself. I sit here wailing and moaning because I have to pick up after myself, and he's fretting because he's too weak to help." He shook his head.

"Maybe that's *why* he's a priest and you're not," Silverfox said gently. "He seeks to give of himself even when there's nothing left to give. It hurts him, but it also makes him feel effective. We can't all turn out that self-sacrificing. Lady knows *I'm* not—"

He was interrupted by the sound of someone running. "Heyla, you two!" An'desha poked his head into their chamber. "Come to Karal's room. Altra made a Jump to Haven and he's back with word from Sejanes!"

Both of them dropped their mending and got to their feet, hurrying toward Karal's chamber—which once held the "weapon" that had discharged all of its formidable power through him. Firesong hadn't mentioned that to Karal yet; when they had elected not to move him, he had deduced that since all the chambers looked alike, Karal probably wouldn't notice which one he was in. *I'm not sure how he'd react. He might not care—or it might make him very nervous and unhappy, being in the same room where he nearly died.*

When they arrived at the chamber, they found Lo'isha, a few of the Kal'enedral, Florian, and An'desha already waiting there, with Altra on Karal's lap and an unopened message tube beside them.

Firesong blinked, and realized that after all the time of working with the mages and Artificers back in Haven, he'd been unconsciously expecting to see more people. *So it's just us now. I don't know if I like that. I hate to admit it, but those Artificers had some good ideas.*

"I hope this message is written in Valdemaran, but it probably isn't," Karal said. "I know enough of Imperial tongue to translate, though, if you want me to."

"Go ahead," Firesong said, motioning to him to pick up the tube. "I don't even read Valdemaran that well; you're the best reader we have except for Florian."

"And I can just picture Florian trying to unroll the paper!" Karal chuckled, though Firesong noted that Florian came to look over Karal's shoulder, probably to help with the translation.

If only Aya could read foreign tongues! he thought with envy. *We could each specialize in a language; it would be so convenient!*

Karal broke open the tube and extracted a roll of paper; he unrolled it with an accompanying crackling sound.

Evidently it *was* in Valdemaran; Karal's frown faded and he began reading immediately. Probably Florian was prompting him.

The letter began abruptly. "*Greetings, and* do not attempt to make or use a Gate. *We have already tried and the results were Unfortunate.* That's with a capital 'U' by the way."

Firesong winced. *I was afraid of that.*

"Things must be more unsettled than we thought," An'desha said with alarm. "My little magics have been working so well I thought certainly that the larger ones must surely be all right.

"That might simply be a function of where we are," Firesong reminded him. "For all we know, there are upper shields on the remains of the Tower, strong enough that we could do almost anything in here and not be affected by what's gone on outside."

Karal cleared his throat to get their attention again. Firesong turned back to him and nodded, and the young man continued. *"I fear this means you are exiled for the duration, colleagues. We built a small local Gate as soon as we could after you unloosed the power of your Device, and we attempted to transfer a few small nonliving items through it. I am glad now that we opted for caution and made those items of a nonliving nature, for the result on the other side was rather messy. Parts were recognizable, and that is the best I can say. Many suffered from desiccation, aging, or physical compression. Altra's Jumping seems to cause no such problems for the moment, even when he 'carries' someone with him, but he reports that it is becoming more and more difficult to Jump as time passes."*

At this, Altra himself raised his head and spoke up. *:I find that the distance I can Jump decreases as time passes. I am afraid that within a few weeks I will not be able to Jump across a given distance any faster than a Companion could run across it.:*

Firesong let out the breath he'd been holding in. *I wonder if I ought to go back to k'Leshya after all? I'm not sure I can continue to live like this and not begin to lose my temper, if not my sanity.* "Well, that's not welcome news," he said as casually as he could. "Is there anything else?"

Karal scanned the letter quickly. "Once the bad news is out, he gets a lot more formal and technical; the short version is that Altra can probably bring one or two people from Haven to here before he can't Jump anymore, but that we need to work on a way to communicate with Haven—maybe using scrying. Magic that doesn't transfer or move anything physical seems to work better than magic that does. I just hope that if there are shields protecting this place, they wouldn't interfere with scrying, too."

He handed the letter over to Firesong. "Here, you can get all the details yourself later; most of what he says only partially makes sense to me."

"I'll study it later," Firesong promised. "The question now is, what are we going to do? If we're going to have Altra bring someone over, we'd better do it soon."

"If we can get them," An'desha said slowly, "I'd like both Sejanes and Master Levy here."

Firesong rolled his eyes up at that, but had to grudgingly agree. "If they'll put up with the unpleasantness of Jumping, they *would* be the best choices," he sighed. "Sejanes has an entire magic discipline that is foreign to us, and Master Levy——" He paused for a moment, reminded himself to be charitable, and chose his words carefully. "Master Levy has a very unique way of looking at our problems. If not him, then we should have at least one of the Master Artificers here. Even I have to admit that we could not have accomplished anything here without their help."

An'desha and Karal both nodded vigorously in agreement, which made him feel a bit sour, but he had to admit that, without the Artificers, they would be working without a resource as valuable as the presence of an Adept. *We need that utterly different viewpoint here. And Master Levy might even be as intelligent as he thinks he is.*

:Master Levy and Sejanes have already volunteered,: Altra put in unexpectedly. *:I was just waiting to see if you would welcome them here. I can go back for them now, if you'd like, although it will take a few days to get there and back with them.:*

Now Firesong was startled. A few days? Altra's Jumping distances *had* been severely curtailed! "If it's going to take you days, I think you had *better* start back now," he told the Firecat. "I don't want to think how much faster the situation could deteriorate if we wait."

The Firecat nodded, and vanished from Karal's lap. Only Lo'isha looked at all dubious when Altra was gone.

"What's wrong, shaman?" Firesong asked politely, seeing Lo'isha's troubled gaze.

The Shin'a'in shrugged. "I am only wondering if we should have asked permission of our hosts before we brought more folk in. Hopefully, they will not be offended by the addition of two more strangers."

Curiously, that slight objection had the effect of hardening Firesong's decision. "If we'd had them here in the first place, we *might* have a permanent solution instead of a temporary one," he said stubbornly. "I, for one, *want* them here. Wind and weather, Lo'isha, if you're worried that they might somehow overpower us and escape with secrets of Urtho's forbidden magic, Master Levy doesn't know the first thing about practical magic, and Sejanes is so old that if you spoke a harsh word to him all his bones might break under the force! They're hardly a threat, singly *or* together!"

"Oh, I agree, but it is not my opinion you must have," Lo'isha began, then shrugged again. "Or, well, perhaps it is. I suppose I have as much authority here as the Kal'enedral." He grimaced. "Much as I dislike taking on authority, I suppose it is time that I did so."

Since it was Firesong's opinion that it was more than time that he did so, he simply nodded and held his tongue.

Karal looked fatigued, and Firesong stood up abruptly. "I am going to search for another hidden room. I have the feeling that this place hasn't even begun to divulge its secrets to us. Anyone care to join me?"

Urtho may have been one of the most brilliant and compassionate minds in history, but his architects were no small geniuses themselves. Firesong already had found one small, hidden room by carefully probing the floor of the "washing" room when he noticed that water, dripped in a particular place, drained away through cracks invisible to the unaided eye. It hadn't held anything—in fact, it had probably performed the task of simple storage—but now he knew that there *might* be more such places under the floors here, and he had the feeling that if he just looked hard enough, he might find more than just storage areas.

"I'll help," An'desha said unexpectedly.

He smiled. "Come along, then," he replied. "I'm trying the skull chamber next."

The "skull chamber" was the one in which they had discovered a bizarre contraption that looked like the leavings of half a dozen Artificers and shamans all jumbled together with the remains of a few feasts. The centerpiece was a highly ornamented cow skull, and none of them could even begin to guess what the device was for. They would have been afraid to dismantle it, except that the delicate construction had already fallen apart in several places already, and the shock of their magical working had made it fall completely to pieces without any other ill effect.

Rather than use magic, since the chamber itself reeked of mage-power, Firesong was using perfectly ordinary senses; taking a cue from the water drainage, he had a skin of water with a bit of ink in it to make it more visible, and he dribbled it over the floor, watching to see if it moved or vanished.

With An'desha helping, the two of them were a lot more effective than he was by himself. It was very boring work, and he had expected An'desha to start a conversation, but he had not anticipated the subject.

"You're thinking about going back, aren't you?" An'desha said. "To k'Leshya, if not your home Vale."

He didn't reply at first; he pretended to be paying close attention to the water on the floor. "I'm not used to this sort of living," he said, refusing to answer directly. "It's harder on me than it is on you."

"I won't debate that," An'desha agreed. "And I hope you don't think I'd put any blame on you for leaving. The gryphons did."

"But they have two children who need them," he snapped. "I don't. I haven't any excuse for leaving except wanting to be comfortable again!" He felt irrationally irritated at An'desha for voicing all of *his* excuses, as if he were so transparent that An'desha had no difficulty in anticipating what he wanted to do and his rationalizations.

The trouble was that every time he looked at Karal, he felt ashamed of himself.

"It's not as if you haven't done more than most people would have already," An'desha said gently. "First you faced down Falconsbane—"

"Mornelithe Falconsbane was a challenge, but no more than that," he replied stiffly. "It's not as if I was alone in facing him."

"It's not as if you had any real reason to," An'desha pointed out inexorably. "Valdemar wasn't your home. Falconsbane didn't threaten the Vales. You'd done your duty in training Heralds to be mages, and then some. You could have gone home once you'd done that much."

"Leaving whom to face Falconsbane?" Firesong demanded, his face flushing. "One of those half-trained Heralds? Elspeth? Darkwind, perhaps? None of them could have freed *you*. I'm not certain even Need could have freed you *and* dealt with Falconsbane."

An'desha simply nodded quietly. "But when it was over—you could have gone home then. You could even have taken me with you, and things might have turned out differently. You've long since gone past anything anyone could call your duty, Firesong. No one would fault you if you were too tired of all this to go on."

"And how am I going to compare to someone like Karal if I do that?" he demanded, flushing still further. "Too tired? How would I look, quitting now, next to someone who literally put his life in jeopardy over this?"

"You make him sound like a would-be martyr," An'desha chided. "Karal is quite a few things, including stubborn, occasionally bigoted, and now and then incredibly naive, but he's no martyr. And neither are you, nor any of us."

"So?" Aya must have felt his distress; the firebird sailed in the chamber door, adroitly avoided the snare of wires and junk, and landed on his shoulder. He petted the bondbird reflexively in a blind search for comfort. "If he's not a martyr, then—" He stopped, aware that his voice was getting high and strained.

He took two or three deep breaths. "An'desha, I don't know why you're baiting me this way."

Then, in a moment of blinding insight, he *did* know.

He's forcing me to think things through, so that I come to a real decision, instead of letting some unfinished business and an entire bundle of emotions sway me back and forth.

An'desha nodded, as if he saw all that written on Firesong's face.

I can't make a decision because I'm trying to demonstrate that I'm somehow better than Karal. And I can't make it out of guilt either.

So why am I staying?

"What Karal does is up to Karal, but—well, I'm not too old to take a youngster like him as a good example." He smiled weakly. "You all need me, just as you need Sejanes or Master Levy, or Altra. I'm staying because even though I'm tired and I hate living here, it would be wrong of me to go off and leave you without my skills. I don't want to die in the cold and filth, but if I must, I will. It would be wrong to abandon all those people who are hoping we'll find a solution to the final Storm. It would be wrong to break my word to the people I promised I would help. Are those reasons good enough for you?"

An'desha laughed at that. "Don't think to bait me, Firesong; I was coached by an expert to steer you through your own thoughts and motives."

He scowled at that. "Are you happy with the result?" he growled.

"The question is not whether I'm satisfied, it's whether you are," An'desha countered. "And if you are, it is not for me to object. If your decision will interfere with other concerns, then that must be dealt with then."

He stood up and moved over to another section of floor. Firesong felt an imp of perversity rise inside him, and he knew he had to have the last word.

"And I didn't mention the best reason of all yet," he said silkily. Surprised, An'desha turned back to face him.

"What reason is that?" he asked, as if the words had been pulled from him unwillingly.

Firesong smiled. "Silverfox wants me to stay," he replied. "Can you think of a better reason?"

2

Elspeth sighed, her breath streaming out in a fog of ice-crystals, and pulled the ends of the scarf wrapped around her neck a little tighter. Once again she sent a little thought of gratitude back over her shoulder toward Valdemar and the tireless k'Leshya *hertasi* who had fashioned her current costume. The little lizard-folk who had arrived with the bargeload of envoys from Clan k'Leshya had taken one look at her winter wardrobe and taken it upon themselves to refashion it, as if they didn't already have enough to do. The *hertasi* of k'Sheyna had already made her Herald's Whites in the style of the Tayledras, but those had all been of summer-weight fabrics. These new *hertasi* had remade her Whites in wool, fur, and leather, layered in silk according to patterns designed for her by Darkwind. These had been her Midwinter gift from him to her, and a welcome surprise they had been indeed, for they were certainly needed. Winter Field Whites *had* been designed for harsh weather, but not as harsh as the unprecedented weather currently holding Hardorn in its icy grip.

And Hardorn was where she, Darkwind, and a small group of mixed Valdemaran Guards and Kerowyn's mercenaries found themselves headed shortly after Midwinter Festival.

There hadn't been much choice; it was clear that Valdemar was going to have to send some form of envoy overland to Grand Duke Tremane, once it became impossible to put up any more Gates. Elspeth had been present when that last Gate had been attempted; the mangled crate that had come through had looked as if it had been turned inside out, and nothing in it was recognizable. It was just a good thing that the crate had only contained a few things for Sejanes and that they had been cautious enough to test the Gate with mere cargo before sending anyone living through.

But travel to and within Hardorn was not easy by any standard, even those of one who had journeyed from Valdemar to the Dhorisha Plains and patrolled the weirdling lands being cleansed and protected by a Hawkbrother Vale. In all of her life she had never seen snow this deep. The road they followed into Hardorn had been kept clear for traffic, but only enough to permit a cart pulled by two horses to pass. And even then, the wheels of the cart would scrape the walls of snow now and again. Every ten leagues a wider place had been cut, so that carts going in opposite directions could pass, but otherwise the snow was piled up on either side of the road until it reached shoulder-high on a horse. In places where the snow had drifted deeper than that, it could be taller than a rider's head. And the cold, the *wind*—In many ways, she was grateful that those tall snowbanks were there, because without that shelter they'd be facing a wind that bit as cruelly as any blade, and carried right down to the bone. *Hertasi*-designed tunics with fur linings and riding coats of sheepskin with the wool turned inside were the only things that made this journey bearable. She was quite grateful that the mysterious, industrious lizard-folk had been able to outfit the entire company with such coats before they all left.

"Why the sigh?" Darkwind asked, his breath puffing out in frosty clouds with each word. His bondbird Vree clung to the padded horn of his saddle, with no sign of discomfort whatsoever—except that his feathers were puffed out all over his body and his head was pulled down tight against his shoulders, so that he resembled a fat ball of wool with a beak. But then, Vree was a forestgyre, and Darkwind had once told her that they had come from stock adapted to harsher climes than this. Darkwind himself cut an odd figure, and not just because of his Hawkbrother costume or the bondbird on his saddlebow; Darkwind's mount was neither a horse nor a Companion, but a creature as intelligent and as foreign to Valdemaran eyes as a gryphon. It was a *dyheli*, a white *dyheli* at that, and the representative of his own race to Valdemar. His name was Brytha, and he had brought Firesong from k'Treva to k'Sheyna, then from k'Sheyna to Valdemar, and now consented to bear Darkwind on this current mission. Why? She didn't know; Darkwind didn't know either, and the *dyheli* seemed disinclined to explain. They were both grateful to him; although not the equal in endurance and speed of a Companion, the *dyheli* was better suited to this mission than a horse, more sure-footed and vastly more intelligent. The rest of their party rode tough Shin'a'in-bred horses, especially selected for endurance, shaggy as dogs with blunt, blocky heads.

"I'm sighing because I've decided that the one thing I will never say again is to say 'never again,'" she replied with a crooked smile. "Because as sure as I say it, I'm forced to repeat the act I swore never to repeat."

He chuckled ruefully, without needing any explanation. Neither of them had ever thought they would be riding back into Hardorn again. Their previous visit, although memorable, had not been particularly pleasant, either for them or for the Hardornens. When they had finished, mad King Ancar and his adviser Hulda were dead at their hands, mage-caused storms were lashing the countryside, the capital was in a state of total chaos, and the Imperial Army (taking advantage of the moment) was pouring over the Eastern border. And although very few Hardornens were aware of the fact, Elspeth and Darkwind were directly or indirectly responsible for most of the damage and chaos they left behind them.

Not that the Imperial Army was our fault, but that's just about the only thing we can say we didn't have a hand in.

And after the invasion came the real mage-storms, triggering incredibly vicious weather and unleashing real horrors on the unsuspecting countryside. *Those* were not the fault of anyone living, but they did make life in Hardorn even more miserable than anyone had ever dreamed possible. So riding into Hardorn didn't seem particularly likely *or* sane a few moons ago.

But that had been before Duke Tremane offered alliance; before it dawned on everyone in this part of the world that the mage-storms were a greater menace than anything mere humans could unleash on each other. Now things that wouldn't have occurred to anyone as possible scenarios were being hastily put into motion.

"Have you noticed something? The weather might be vile, but the land isn't suffering anymore," Darkwind observed. "It's not exhausted and ill anymore, it's just sleeping, waiting for spring. I don't know about you, but that was one of the reasons why I didn't want to ever come back here again."

Elspeth nodded, and so did her Companion Gwena, the bells on her bridle chiming crisply in the sharp, icy air. *:Without Ancar draining the land of its power, things are returning to normal,:* Gwena replied. *:The land, and presumably the people, are no longer sickening. And much as I hate to say it—the blood and life-energy of all those poor folk killed in the invasion may have sped that recovery.:*

"That's a horrible thought," Darkwind observed with a shudder, for Gwena had made certain to include him in her Mindspeaking.

Elspeth shivered; intellectually she knew it was probably true, but it was horrible all the same. "That just sounds entirely too much like something Falconsbane would have come up with," she said reluctantly. "But then again, Falconsbane simply perverted things that were perfectly normal and good. And I suppose it would be even worse to think that all those people died and their life-energy went for nothing, or worse, was used by someone like Falconsbane.

:Mages and those with earth-sense have known for centuries that this is the reason why the countryside blooms after a war,: Gwena observed dispassionately. *:It isn't just that things seem better, and it isn't just that the people are ready to greet any positive signs with enthusiasm. It's because the lives lost go back to the land, and when the war is over, the land can use them to heal itself.:*

"We can at least be grateful that Grand Duke Tremane is *apparently* more interested in allowing the land to heal than in using that power for his own means," Darkwind replied, as he turned for a moment to stare off into the east. He said nothing more, and Elspeth thought she knew why.

They had only the word of three youngsters and Tremane's own people that he was to be trusted at all. Just at the moment, *apparently* was the only word any of them could use with regard to the leader of the Imperial forces. Those few facts that they had about Tremane were not much comfort.

Tremane had been sent by his master, Emperor Charliss, to conquer a weak and chaotic Hardorn for the Empire of the East. This assignment was to prove him worthy (or not) to be the Imperial Heir. The Imperial Army had taken roughly half of Hardorn before it stalled, held in place by Hardornen fighters, in mostly uncoordinated groups ranging in size from tiny bands to small armies, united only in their determination to oust the interloper. Since they were fighting on their own ground, they had the advantage once the front lines stretched out and the Imperial forces were thinned by distance. Nevertheless, if nothing had changed, Tremane would probably have been able to reorganize, regroup, and complete the conquest, possibly even carrying it into Valdemar.

But things *did* change, and in a way that no one could have foreseen; the change had come from a direction no one would have looked, for it had come out of the distant past.

We never do consider the past, do we? But we should have. Wasn't Falconsbane a revenant of that past? And shouldn't that have warned us to turn our eyes and thoughts in that direction? But then again, how can we truly plan for everything, every possibility? Even if we knew all of the threats at any one moment, the defenses for half of them would negate the preparations for the other half. We are better off being resourceful than omniscient, I think.

Once, before there had ever been a Valdemar, in a time so distant that there were no records and only the vaguest of hints about it in the great library of the Heralds, ancient wars had ended in an event known only as the Cataclysm. And until Elspeth had met with the Tayledras of legend, the Shin'a'in of the Dhorisha Plains, and the last, lost Clan of the true Kaled'a'in—progenitors of both the Hawkbrothers and the Shin'a'in—that was *all* those in Valdemar had known. Now, though, with the help of histories both arcane and mundane, the full story had been put together.

Elspeth considered that story, as she did every time she had the leisure to do so, intent on extracting the least bit of useful information from it. Despite the huge amounts of power involved, there were still human motives and actions behind what had happened so long ago. Even madmen would act according to their needs, so the more that one considered events of history, the more one could deduce what those needs had been—and once one understood the needs and motivations of the people involved, one could expound upon what else might have happened, or realize that an obscure detail was actually something significant in context.

There had been two Adepts back then, perhaps the most powerful that the world had ever known, called Urtho and Ma'ar. Ma'ar, the scion of barbarian nomads, had been infected with the mania for conquest, at first for noble reasons of uniting clans to keep them from annihilating each other. Urtho, the epitome of civilization and scholarship, had resisted him. But despite the best efforts of civilization, Ma'ar, Adept and Blood-Mage, had triumphed—

But only for a moment. In the very hour of Ma'ar's victory a dying Urtho had brought defeat to his very door, with a pair of devices that released the bonds on all magic within their spheres of influence. One he triggered in his own Tower; one was sent to Ma'ar. The devices acted within moments of each other, and the results were both devastating and utterly unpredictable.

When it was over, there were two enormous craters where Urtho's Tower and Ma'ar's palace had stood. The first became the Dhorisha Plains; the second, Lake Evendim. And the interaction of the two series of shock waves created terrible mage-storms that had raged over the land for a decade or more, raising mountains and flattening them, disrupting magic, causing living creatures to change and warp out of all recognition, even transplanting entire sections of countryside from one part of the world to another.

Eventually the Storms faded, to be forgotten in the ensuing centuries, assumed by all to have been gone forever. But the forces released by the

Cataclysm were stranger and stronger than anyone guessed, and now the mage-storms had returned, echoing back across time from the other side of the world, growing stronger with every new occurrence.

That was what had changed the situation Tremane had walked into, changed it out of all recognition. The situation in Valdemar had been bad, but not a complete disaster. Valdemar had only newly rediscovered true-magic, and did not depend on its power for anything. The other effects of the mage-storms, the vicious and unpredictable weather, the warping of living creatures, and so forth, could all be dealt with in one way or another. But for Tremane's forces, dependent on magic for everything from communication and supply lines to the means to scout the enemy and cook their food, it was a disaster as they found themselves completely cut off from the Empire, effectively blind and hungry as a fighting force. As for what was going on in the Empire itself, that was anyone's guess. Tremane had initially assumed that the Storms were a new weapon unleashed by the Alliance of Valdemar, Karse, Rethwellan, and the Shin'a'in/Tayledras clans. He had reacted accordingly—and in a direction entirely typical of the Empire, where treachery and assassination were so commonplace that children were given bonded bodyguards as cradle-gifts. He had sent an assassin to break up the Alliance.

That was the single act that Elspeth and any other Valdemaran found so difficult to think past. Valdemar had *not* attacked Imperial forces. Neither Valdemar nor any of her allies had shown any sign of aggression other than increasing the guard on the borders and covertly helping to supply the Hardornen loyalists. Tremane had no reason—except for the obvious fact that Valdemar was not suffering from the Storms as badly as the Imperials were—to think that this was an attack by Queen Selenay or her allies. Nevertheless, he had treated it as one, and had sent a covert operative armed with magic weapons to kill anyone of any importance at or in Selenay's Court.

The man had succeeded only insofar as murdering the envoy from Karse and the one from the Shin'a'in, and wounding several others. That was bad enough, but was sheerest good fortune that it wasn't worse, and no one made any mistake about that. If the assassin had waited until the predawn hours when people were sleeping in their beds, he would have succeeded in killing everyone from Selenay down to the gryphons.

Herein lay the heart of Elspeth and Darkwind's current problem. Now they were supposed to trust a man who used assassins against those he only *suspected* of aggressive action.

Elspeth found it difficult to think beyond that fact, even though Tremane had won over to his side the last person likely to ever forgive him—young Karal, the secretary and protégé of the envoy of Karse, Sun-priest and Mage, Master Ulrich. Tremane had even somehow convinced Solaris, Son of the Sun and High Priest and ruler of Karse, of his sincerity and his wish to make amends, though only the gods knew how he'd done that.

Well, he hasn't convinced me, and he hasn't convinced Darkwind, she thought stubbornly. *Whatever spell of words or personality he put them under, I hope it's going to be more difficult to work the same "magic" on us. I know mind-magic, and Darkwind is so foreign to Tremane's experience that he might as well be another species altogether. And what's more, I wouldn't be in the least surprised to discover that Kerowyn slipped half a dozen special operatives into our escort. Two sides can play the assassination game, if it comes to that.*

She hoped that it wouldn't, but she had enough experience now to make her plans around pessimism rather than hope. She didn't officially *know* that Kerowyn had planted her own agents, but she knew the Skybolts, and they were, one and all, "irregulars." Their skills were not those of straight-on fighters, although they could act and fight as a disciplined skirmishing unit and had in the past.

On the other hand… Solaris has Hansa, the other Firecat. If she wanted to kill Tremane, there is no way he could stop her. So maybe that fact alone will make him behave himself from now on.

That was certainly something else to consider. The Firecats possessed the ability to "Jump" themselves and anyone in physical contact with them from one location to another, and Elspeth was not entirely certain what their range was. Certainly it was good enough that Altra and Hansa served as messengers between Solaris and Selenay, and between the party in the remains of Urtho's Tower and the mages and Artificers in the Valdemaran capital of Haven. Solaris was perfectly capable of placing an assassin of her own right under Tremane's privy to poke a knife up into him if she so desired, and for that matter, there was no reason why Hansa himself could not kill a man if he chose. Although Firecats had the ability to *look* like common cats if they wished to, in their true form they were the size of enormous hounds, and their claws and teeth were correspondingly long and sharp.

Elspeth blinked at the images that thought conjured up. *My thoughts are certainly taking a grim turn today. Maybe I'm concentrating on spilling blood as an antidote to all this whiteness. Dear gods, it's cold—and we haven't seen another human soul since our guides left us.* ·

They'd been lucky when they'd reached the Valdemaran Border. A couple of Hardornen exiles—vouched for by Kerowyn's agents—had cautiously decided it was safe to return and acted as guides up until this morning in exchange for two pouches of currency and two packs of supplies. Now, though, they would have to go on without guides, because the husband and wife had gone as far as they intended.

Last night the party had reached the village from which the couple had originally fled. Even though it proved to be deserted, abandoned, like the other villages they had passed on this road, the two wanted to stay; even in thick white desolation they had a dream of a time in the future when there would be children running and playing in a verdant town square.

Their journey thus far had been an unnerving one, riding through a landscape devoid of humans. Elspeth could only wonder what had happened. *The land might be healing, but where are the people?* True, Ancar had decimated the population, but why hadn't they met with *anyone* on this road? Why were all the villages they passed through completely deserted?

The abandoned villages raised more questions than were answered, for everything had been taken except the heaviest of furniture, and there was no sign of violence. Was this the result of systematic desertion or systematic looting? Who was cleaning off the snow? Were the Hardornens hiding from an armed and possibly hostile group? Given the fact that this was a nation racked by war, that was possible. But *why*, when there was a Herald of Valdemar riding conspicuously in the front?

Perhaps because at a distance there's no reason to assume I really am a Herald. It's not that hard to get a white horse and a set of white clothing.

"What are our plans for stopping tonight, or do we have any?" she called back to the leader of the troop. They hadn't provisioned themselves for camping, though they had brought all their own food, assuming that rations might be short given the horrible mage-weather Hardorn had endured. It was a good thing they had, or they'd have had a choice between starving and (literally) eating crow.

"In theory there's a town ahead that used to have a weekly market and five big inns," the leader replied, his voice muffled by the scarf swathing his face. "Whether or not it's still tenanted—" he shrugged. "Someone's been keeping the road clean for traders, and I'm hoping it's them."

So was Elspeth, fervently. She was not looking forward to spending another night in an abandoned, derelict building. There was always one building that could be made to serve, and there was certainly no shortage of firewood, but she had always been glad of the presence of the others around her. She'd found it hard to sleep at night, with her shoulder blades prickling as if unseen eyes watched her. No one had actually seen or heard anything that could be taken as a ghost, but such places *felt* haunted.

She couldn't begin to imagine how Rusi and Severn could bear to stay back there in what was left of their village. Granted, there was plenty of material to make more than one of the houses sound and weathertight again. And granted, they were well-equipped to do just that. But the aching emptiness of the abandoned village would have sent her screaming for Valdemar within a week.

It was more than she could bear to think about right now. *I've done a great deal that people think is brave, but I'm not that brave.*

But that was also assuming that the land around the village was as deserted as it looked. When the mage-storms created killing weather and murderous monsters, would it have been safer and smarter to fortify the farmsteads and stay where the food was, or to come into the village and trust in numbers and weapons but chance the food running out? It wasn't a decision Elspeth had ever needed to make, and she hoped it was one nobody in Valdemar would be forced to face.

For that, all their hopes rested with that tiny group in the middle of the Dhorisha Plains, in the ruins of Urtho's Tower. If anyone could find an answer, it would be them. Although Elspeth and Darkwind were both Adept-class mages, Elspeth was relatively untutored and Darkwind had abandoned magic for so many years that despite his considerable prowess he still considered himself out of practice. As mages, they were of no help to the researchers who had gone to the Tower. They might be of some use with the Imperials, and they *would* be of great use as envoys.

She knew that Queen Selenay had debated long and hard before deciding to send Elspeth and Darkwind as envoys from the Alliance to Tremane. The Queen hadn't wanted to send Elspeth, but Elspeth was the only logical choice—she could make autonomous decisions, she had been trained both as a Herald and to wear the crown herself— she was the next best thing to Selenay when it came to being able to think *for* Valdemar. Elspeth had proven that she had good judgment, and because she was no longer the Heir since her abdication, she was of little value as a political hostage. Moreover, she had been trained by Kerowyn to defend herself against assassins; she could take care of herself in an ambush or an even fight, and she was as suspicious as even that redoubtable woman could have wished.

Then there was magic, in which she was an Adept; Tremane was no more than a Master, though of a far different magical discipline than the one she had been trained in. Very few of the Heralds of Valdemar were mages at all, much less Adepts, and although their Companions would be able to help them to some extent in matters of magic, it was no substitute for being mages themselves.

All that might not have been enough, except for Darkwind; he was an Adept as well, and of longer standing than she. He had been a Tayledras scout, which made him something of a fighter as well. He would have refused flatly to accompany anyone else; he was not a Herald, and his loyalties were to her, not Valdemar. Whereas she would hardly have gone anywhere without him, of course, and together they were a formidable pair.

Between her own qualifications and Darkwind's, there simply was no one as "right" to go on this mission as Elspeth, and if she had been anyone else's daughter, Selenay would not have hesitated for a moment to send her.

To give Mother credit, she didn't hesitate long. Elspeth was actually a bit pleased at that; Selenay had been treating her less as a daughter and more as—as an adult, and Elspeth had gotten the feeling, more than once, that when the Queen forgot to think of her as her daughter, she acted naturally. In a way, given the Queen's behavior of late, Elspeth had been a little surprised that her mother had given second thoughts to the mission. *I wonder if some of what has made her hesitate in the past was more guilt than anything else.*

Could it have been? Elspeth and her mother had never been comfortable with each other. *No matter how hard she tried, she always saw my father in me. In so many ways, I was more Talia's child than hers.* Now Selenay had the twins, children she could give her whole heart to; could she be feeling guilt that she *didn't* have that same maternal bond with Elspeth? Was that why she had always overreacted when Elspeth did something that might put her in jeopardy—because she felt as if she should have been *more* worried, more emotionally involved than she was?

An interesting theory, and one I'll never learn the truth of. I certainly couldn't ask her *that, and the only other person who would know will never tell me. Talia would never betray anything she learned of Mother's heart, and rightly so.* Elspeth gave herself a mental shake. Did it *matter?* Not really. Except that—if that was indeed the case, she wished she could convince her mother that it didn't matter. The last thing that the Queen of Valdemar needed was one more thing to feel guilty about. She already carried enough guilt for twenty people.

And I would rather be Queen Selenay's friend and fellow Herald than her daughter.

But the thought did present one explanation for some of Selenay's contradictory behavior, and it was certainly worth keeping in the back of her mind. She could watch for evidence of her own, and it would be interesting to act on that theory and see what happened.

Meanwhile, there was a long and difficult job ahead of her, and there was a danger they might all *freeze* to death before they even got to it if they didn't find some Hardornens soon.

"How much farther do you think this town is?" she called back over her shoulder. She glanced back to see—what was the Guard-Captain's name? Vallen, that was it—to see Vallen shrug, the movement barely visible beneath his multiple layers of fur, sheepskin, and wool.

"Soon, I think, but that is just a guess," he replied. Despite the scarf he wore about his face, his words came clearly over the muffled hoofbeats of their various mounts, over the creaking of the packed snow beneath those hooves. He gave his horse a nudge with his heels, and took the lead position as Elspeth and Darkwind moved aside to let him by.

Elspeth stood in her stirrups for a moment to peer up the road ahead, but if there were any signs of habitations such as plumes of smoke that could have been rising from chimneys, they were invisible against the uniformly gray-white sky. The sun was nothing more than a fuzzy, lighter spot about halfway down to the horizon.

She settled back down in her saddle; the way the road wound about, it wasn't possible to see very far ahead, and they only got a view of the countryside when the snowbanks allowed. *We could be right on top of this town and we'd never know it,* she thought.

Minutes later, the road gave another turn and dropped away in front of them. The snowbanks themselves inclined down to about waist-height. As if conjured up in a scrying crystal, the watched-for town appeared ahead of and below them, down in a shallow valley, the houses sticking up out of the snow like so many tree stumps in the snow-covered forest.

This was not the first time a town had appeared before them, but now, for the first time, there *were* signs that the place was inhabited. Some of the houses were nothing more than snow-covered lumps, but some had been cleaned of their burden of white. Thin smoke wreathed up out of about half the chimneys, to be snatched away by the wind before it climbed up to form a plume. There were a few figures moving about on the road near the town, and it was clear from the purposeful way that they moved that the party had been spotted, if not anticipated.

The place looked marginally better than the deserted villages they had already passed. Perhaps half the buildings were in disrepair; one or two had collapsed roofs, and it was hard to tell under the snow how badly some of the others had suffered. She had to guess that only the buildings with smoke rising from them were actually lived in, and she caught her breath at the thought that Ancar and all the other troubles visited upon Hardorn had literally cut the population in half. *Maybe more,* she reminded herself. *How many deserted villages did we pass through?*

Were conditions like this everywhere? If so—well, she did not envy any leader the task of trying to bring this country back from such devastation. *If Tremane can get the Hardornens to accept him, he has more work ahead of him than I'd care to take on.*

A group of about a dozen people had formed up ahead of them on the road, barring them, at least for the moment, from entering the town. They were as bundled up in clothing as Elspeth's group was, making it difficult to tell anything about them, including their sexes; but in spite of that handicap, she thought that their stances showed a mix of fear and belligerence.

Fear? When had anyone ever *feared* her? They weren't so deep into Hardorn that the natives should be unaware of what a Herald was and what one stood for. How could they fear a Herald? Had Ancar created that fear in them so strongly?

She sensed the fighters behind her surreptitiously loosening their weapons, placing hands casually on hilts, and increasing their watchfulness. So it was not her imagination; they sensed hostility, too. Vallen reined in his horse and allowed her to take the lead; Darkwind signaled the *dyheli* to drop back with his head even with Gwena's flank. Elspeth brought them all to a halt about a length away from the "welcoming party" by gesturing with an upraised hand.

"We are peaceful travelers from Valdemar," she said in their own tongue, pulling her scarf down so that they could see her entire face—

though she did wonder if they'd believe the "peaceful" part with so many weapons in evidence. "Who is in charge here?"

Two of the figures looked at each other, and one stepped forward, though he did not reveal his face as Elspeth had. Now that Elspeth was closer to them, the ragged state of their clothing was painfully evident. Their coats were carefully mended, but with patches that were not even a close match for the same material as the original.

"Me. I'm in charge, as I reckon," the foremost man said gruffly, and he folded his arms clumsily over his chest. He had no weapon in evidence, but Elspeth did not take that to mean that these people were helpless. If *she'd* been in charge, she'd have archers with drawn bows at every window.

She did not look up to see if her guess was correct.

"What're you here for?" the man continued. His arms tightened and his posture straightened. His voice rose, angry and strained. "If you think you people in Valdemar are going to come in here and take us over, us and our land—"

"*No*," Elspeth interrupted, cutting him off more sharply than she had intended. The man's nerves had infected her, and she took a deep breath to steady herself. "No," she repeated with less force. "We—Valdemar—has no intention of taking one ell of Hardorn land. Until Ancar attacked us, we were always the loyal friend and ally of Hardorn, and we intend to return to that status now that Ancar is gone."

He laughed, but it was not a sound of humor. "Ha!" he jeered. "You *say* that, but why should we believe you?"

"I swear it on my honor as a Herald!" she countered quickly. "You must know what that means, at least! Surely you have not lost faith even in that!"

This all had the feeling of a test, as if what she said here would make all the difference in how they would be treated from this moment on.

Do they have some way to communicate with other communities still? She couldn't imagine how anyone could cross this frozen wasteland faster than *they* were already doing, but the party of Valdemarans was confined to the road, and perhaps the natives had some way of cutting across country to spread news. Perhaps the old signal-towers were still working.

That could be the answer. And it could be how they knew we were coming.

"I swear it as a Herald," she repeated. "And as the envoy of the Queen. Valdemar has no designs on Hardorn, nor do any of the other parties to the Alliance."

—though Solaris had to restrain a few hotheads in Karse. Or rather, Vkandis did—

"We're only traveling," she continued smoothly. "We'd appreciate your hospitality for the night, though we did bring our own provisions. We know how difficult things have been for you, and we didn't want to strain anyone's resources."

There was a long silence, during which the man peered at her closely, and finally nodded, as if satisfied with what he saw. "That outfit's kind of outlandish, but you've got the horse, blue eyes and all, and *that* can't be faked." He shrugged, then, and made a gesture that she suspected told those hidden archers that all was well. "I guess we still believe in Heralds—mostly since Ancar tried so hard to make us think you was some kind of witchy crew that had traffic with demons. I'll take your word as bond for you and the rest of this lot, but you better remember that *you* stand personal surety for them."

She nodded, trying not to show how unsettled his words made her feel. This was, literally, the first time she had ever encountered anyone this close to the border of Valdemar who *didn't* accept and welcome a Herald with trust. What had happened to these people to make them this way?

:Ancar is what happened to them, dear. They will be long in trusting anyone ever again,: Gwena said quietly. *:It may be that this generation never will.:*

"So where are you going, then?" the man asked, still wary.

"Tell him the truth, *ke'chara*," Darkwind said softly in Tayledras. "Don't dissemble. We might as well see now what kind of reception we're going to have while we still have the provisions to turn around and go home. We can't afford to fight our way across this country to get to Tremane."

She nodded slightly to show that she'd heard him; he was right, of course. If they couldn't get to Tremane's headquarters without fighting, there was no point in going on. "We're on our way to a town called Shonar," she said carefully, wondering how much or little he knew.

He knew enough; the man rocked back a pace. "You're going to Tremane?" he demanded. "The Impie Duke?"

She couldn't tell if he was angry or not, but she was already committed to the truth, so she nodded.

"We're the Valdemaran envoy to Tremane," she replied. "He—he wants to join the Alliance. Things that we have learned make us inclined to trust him to be honorable."

We hope.

There were murmurs from the group behind the man, and Elspeth took heart from the fact that they didn't sound angry, just thoughtful. The man himself considered them for a moment, then waved his followers aside. "We need to talk, Herald from Valdemar," he said with a touch of formality. "And there's no point in doing it in this cold. Come along; the inn's still in repair and heated, even if the innkeeper's gone, and if you've got bedrolls to sleep in, there's beds to put them on. If you can tend to yourselves and feed yourselves, we can give you fair shelter for the night."

That was the most welcome statement she'd heard yet on this journey, and she allowed Gwena to fall in obediently behind the man as he led the way to the inn.

The inn *was* in good repair, as promised, and so were the stables. The group dismounted in the inn-yard and led their mounts and the pack animals inside a stout building with a surprising number of animals in the stalls.

They must be keeping all of the horses and ponies in the town here, she realized after a look around. *That makes more sense than scattering them, one and two to a stable.*

The Hardornens quickly set to, throwing down straw from the hayloft to make up the remaining stalls for the visitors. As it turned out, they also had hay, though no grain to spare; that was fine, though. The Valdemarans had brought a string of *chirras* with them, loaded down with their supplies. The *chirras* did perfectly well on the hay alone, and there was plenty of grain in the supplies for the horses, Gwena, and the *dyheli*, Brytha.

Everyone in the party pitched in to help in the stables; Elspeth's cardinal rule, learned from Kerowyn, was that the welfare of their beasts came before the needs of the humans, and no one disagreed with her.

With the horses, *chirras*, Brytha, and Gwena warmly bedded down and fed and the sun setting behind the veil of gray cloud, they all trudged into the inn carrying their baggage.

Once inside, they stood in a tight group for a moment, looking carefully around. The common room, a large chamber with a huge fireplace at one end, stout wooden floor and walls, and smoke-blackened beams supporting the roof, had none of the air of neglect and decay that Elspeth had feared.

She guessed that the villagers had turned the place into their informal meeting house, for the place was too clean to have been swept out just for their benefit. The other door, the one that led into the street, kept opening as more and more people came in, and it looked to her as if most of the adults were gathering in the common room. They had all brought firewood with them as well, which relieved one question in Elspeth's mind—it would have been difficult for the Valdemarans to supply firewood for themselves.

The fellow in charge had not yet pulled off his coat, but he had removed the scarf from his face. He pushed to the front of the crowd, and waved a mittened hand at the staircase, and his weathered, careworn features were kinder than Elspeth had expected.

"Rooms are upstairs, take your pick," he said. "When you've settled yourselves, come down here where we can talk."

Several of those waiting came up the wooden staircase with their guests, bringing firewood to leave beside each hearth before returning downstairs. They didn't say anything, but Elspeth got the impression that was more because they were taciturn or shy than that they were hostile. With fires warming the chambers that had fireplaces, and bricks heating up to warm the cold bedding of those in chambers that didn't, the Valdemarans finally trickled downstairs to meet the eyes of their erstwhile hosts.

Elspeth took the lead, the rest following her. The natives watched Elspeth with covert curiosity, but the moment that Darkwind descended the staircase, they gave up any pretense of politeness and just stared, mouths agape with amazement. The corners of Elspeth's mouth twitched, but she managed not to laugh out loud at their expressions.

I doubt they've ever seen anything like my Darkwind. He must seem like something right out of a minstrel's ballad to them.

Darkwind really was quite a sight, with his long silver hair, his strange, exotic clothing, and the enormous bondbird on his shoulder. When he reached up a hand to Vree, casually lifted him off his shoulder, and cast the forestgyre into the air so he could fly across the room and take a perch on a beam, every Hardornen in the place ducked, and several looked as if they were afraid the bird was going to attack them.

For his part, Vree was on his best behavior, perching where there wasn't going to be anyone sitting directly beneath or behind him. That was extremely polite of him, for if he fell asleep, his instincts would overcome his training if he had to "slice." And a bird the size of Vree could produce an amazing amount of hawk-chalk.

She waited for Darkwind to reach her side, and took his hand in hers. "This is Darkwind k'Sheyna, a Hawkbrother from one of the Hawkbrother Clans in the Alliance," she said, as matter-of-factly as if she had said, "This is Thom, a farmer from the next valley." Their eyes bulged at that, and she didn't blame them. Even in Valdemar, up until recently the Hawkbrothers had been nothing more than a very spooky legend—what must these Hardornens think?

"He is my fellow envoy, my partner, and my mate," she continued. "Representing the Hawkbrothers, the Shin'a'in, and other interests. As I said, we are traveling to Shonar, to Grand Duke Tremane, as official envoys of Valdemar and other members of the Alliance."

The fellow who had taken charge of the meeting nodded. He had by now divested himself of his coat, and wore the clothing of a craftsman—a blacksmith, if Elspeth was any judge, by the scorch marks and mended places that might have been burn marks. He looked much shabbier than any blacksmith Elspeth had ever seen in Valdemar, where they tended to be the more prosperous citizens of a town.

Perhaps he is the most prosperous man here. What a thought! If he's as shabby as a beggar, how are the others faring?

The fact that he was the blacksmith would be the reason that Ancar had not "recruited" him for the army, given that he was able-bodied and neither too old nor too young to fight. A town this size depended on having a blacksmith, and the local smith would need to have more skill than an apprentice.

"I'm Hob," the man said, and gestured to one of the tables. If he'd been fed as well as he should have, his face would have been round, like an old, weathered ball. He was not starved-looking, but his bones were showing; just a hint that these people had seen bad times, as if she didn't already know that. "If some of your people want to go fix up your food, we'd like to talk with you and your—your mate, there."

"We'd be happy to share what we have," Elspeth began, flushing a little with guilt, but he shook his head.

"We've got enough to hold us, so long as spring don't wait to midsummer," he said. "And you'll need every bit you've got to get to Shonar. Thanks to, ah, some good advice, most folk between here and there have enough, but there's none to spare. I doubt you'll find anyone that can sell you so much as a sack of oats, and even if they would, it wouldn't be for money."

Elspeth looked back over her shoulder to Vallen; he nodded, and with a gesture sent four of the guards off to the kitchen. The rest took seats with, and carefully *around*, Elspeth. Darkwind remained at her right hand, and she was not in the least deceived by his casual pose. If anyone so much as raised his voice in a way he considered threatening, the offending party might find himself facing the point of a knife or being held in the bonds of a most uncomfortable tangle-spell or racking paralysis.

And that's assuming I didn't act on a perception of threat first, for myself.

Hob sat across the table from Elspeth, and rubbed his nose, as if wondering how to begin. Finally he just set his shoulders and blundered in. "You say you're going to Shonar. How much do you know about this Tremane?"

Not long on tact, but I doubt he's used to being the leader of these people. He probably hasn't had much occasion for tact. Elspeth shrugged. "What we know is this; he's brought in his entire force to Shonar, and he's broken off all hostile actions with Hardornen loyalists. From what we've been told, he's going out of his way to avoid conflict with loyalist groups, which, you'll admit, in this weather isn't exactly difficult."

Hob snorted in agreement.

"Not only has he expressed an interest in joining the Alliance, he loaned us several of his mages to help us with—" she hesitated. How much would he understand if she told him about the mage-storms? "—with the magical problem that's at the heart of all the weird things that have been happening."

"The monsters? The weather? Them *circles?*" Hob's eyes widened and he grew quite excited. "Tremane helped you with fixing *them?*"

"He did, and he continues to," Elspeth replied. "It's a bigger problem than you may realize. It isn't just Hardorn that's been plagued by all these calamities. It's Valdemar, the Pelagirs, Rethwellan, Karse, the Dhorisha Plains and, we're guessing, just about everywhere else, right out to the Empire. The Alliance, with Tremane's help, managed to fix things temporarily, in the area covered by the Alliance nations." She decided that it might be best not to mention Solaris' personal interview with the Grand Duke; after all, she only knew that it had occurred, not what had been said. "As for the rest that we know about Tremane, we have been told that the citizens of Shonar and the surrounding area have come to look upon him as their protector. We have heard that he has been doing good things for them."

"Aye," Hob said slowly. "We've heard the same. We've heard that them as was fighting against him have come over to his side, that he's been acting like—like we was his people. And now he's helping you in Valdemar?"

She nodded. He pursed his lips and exchanged glances with some of his fellow villagers. They weren't very good at hiding their expressions; what she was telling them agreed with some of what they had heard, and they were surprised to have an outsider confirm what they'd clearly thought were hopeful but unlikely rumors.

"We've heard as how things are pretty fat in Shonar, all things considered," he said finally. "We've heard that it's because of Tremane. We've heard he set his men out helping with harvest, building walls around the town, doing other things like that 'sides taking down monsters."

She spread her hands in a gesture he could read as he chose. "We've heard the same things," she said. "I don't know yet how much truth is in what we've heard, but I'm certain that your sources are completely different from ours. I can tell you this, not all of our sources are Tremane's people."

"And when two people say the same thing... aye." There was a great deal of murmuring behind him. He chewed on his lower lip. "All the same—"

"All the same, it's possible that he is putting on a good face for us, hoping to lure us into accepting him," she said, as bluntly as he would have. "We don't *know*, and we won't know until we get there."

Hob traced the grain of the wood of the table with his finger and avoided her eyes. "All the same, lady—we need a leader. There's nobody left of the old blood; damned Ancar saw to that."

"And people have been talking about accepting the *Duke*?" That was more than she had expected to hear, on *this* side of the former battle lines. "A foreigner? An Imperial?"

"The Duke, not his bloody Empire!" someone said in the back. "We heard his Emperor left him hanging out to dry when the troubles started; we heard he's not Charliss' dog no more."

"Hell, he couldn't be, could he, if he's comin' to you with his brass hat in his hand, looking to get into the Alliance?" Hob said, looking hopeful. "He's proving himself for Shonar; if he proves himself for Shonar, why not for Hardorn?"

"But what if he doesn't just want to be your leader?" Elspeth asked softly. "What if he wants to be your King?"

Hob hesitated a moment, then shrugged. "That's all cake or calamity tomorrow, isn't it?" he said philosophically. "We got to get through the winter first." He favored Elspeth with a shy smile. "I can tell you this, there's one way we'd take him."

"Even as a King?" Darkwind asked quietly.

He nodded, slowly. "Even as a King. He'd have to swear on something we'd trust that he wasn't Charliss' man. Then he'd have to swear *to* Hardorn. And he'd have to do what Ancar, his father, even what his grandfather never did." He paused for effect. "He'd have to take the earth, in the old way."

Elspeth shook her head. "That's nothing I know of," she replied.

Hob smiled again. "The earth-taking—that's old, lady. Older than Valdemar, or so they say. What's old is sure, that's the saying anyway. They say them as takes the earth can't betray it. There's still a priest or two about that knows the way of earth-taking. If this Tremane'd take the earth and the earth takes him—well, there's no going back. He's bound harder and tighter than if we put chains on him."

Elspeth kept her feelings of skepticism to herself. After all she'd seen, there was no telling whether Hob was right about this "earth-taking" of his or not. "Well, you can believe that Valdemar has no interest in taking the rule of Hardorn away from the people; what *you* do about it is your business," Elspeth said carefully. "Our business is to see if what we've been told is true, and to advise the Alliance if it is not."

He nodded, and did not add the obvious question of how she expected to get herself and her party out in one piece if Tremane turned out to be playing his own game. That wasn't his problem, and she couldn't blame him for not volunteering to help if things got difficult. The people of Hardorn had all they could do to survive, and they had nothing to spare for foreigners out of Valdemar.

Comforting aromas of cooking food emerged from the kitchen, and Hob took that gratefully as his escape from the conversation. "Looks like your people have your food ready; we'll go leave you in peace with it. You can leave in the morning when you choose—and—ah—" he flushed a little, "you'll have better welcome farther along. Signal-towers are still up, and there's still a few as know the old signals. We'll be passing along that you're all right, that you're going on up to Tremane. Nobody'll hinder you; there're enough places with four sound walls and a roof that you'll get shelter at night."

As he stood up, Elspeth remained seated, but raised a hand toward

Hob. "And does the Grand Duke know that the towers are still working?" she asked.

He laughed, which was all the answer she needed. So Tremane was *not* aware of this rapid means of passing news along. That could be useful, if it turned out he was playing a deeper game than they thought.

Hob and the rest of his people filed out, leaving the Valdemarans alone, and Elspeth turned first to Vallen as the kitchen crew put bowls of stewed dried meat and preserved fruit, and plates of travel biscuits onto the table. "Well?" she asked. "What do you think?"

He sat down across from her in Hob's place and picked up a biscuit and a bowl before answering. "This matches what we'd heard and didn't really believe," he said slowly, dipping his bread into his gravy, and eating the biscuit with small, neat bites. "Tremane sounds too good to be true. Altogether an admirable and unselfish leader." There was a faint echo of mockery in his voice.

"So does Selenay, if you look at things objectively," Darkwind reminded him. "And yes, I know Tremane has no Companion to keep him honorable, but I'm not sure one would be needed in this case. At least for now, he's in a precarious situation. With the way things have fallen out, his position and his level of personal danger aren't that much different from the average craftsman in Shonar. He needs them as much as they need a leader; if they fall, it won't be long before he does, too. If they rebel, he has no population base to support his troops. This summer, they were fighting against him, and it wouldn't take much mistreatment to make them turn on him."

Elspeth nodded, agreeing with him, although Vallen appeared a bit more dubious. "He has armed troops, loyal only to him," Vallen pointed out.

"He'll have a hard time feeding those troops without farmers," Elspeth replied. "And he can have all the silver he needs to pay them, but if they haven't anywhere to spend it, their loyalty will start to erode. You can't keep an army under siege, starving, and far from home without losing it."

Vallen speared a bit of meat and blew on it to cool it. "All I can say is this," the Guard-Captain said, after he'd eaten the bite. "It's not all that difficult for a charismatic leader to sway the people immediately around him with words instead of deeds. It's a lot more difficult to do that with people out of the reach of his personality. They're inclined to look for something to corroborate what they've heard, and if there's nothing there, they forget him."

"But you're surprised at what you're hearing from Hob," Elspeth stated.

Vallen nodded. "Very. And not the least because a few months ago, these people would have fought with everything they had left to get rid of the man. *Now* they're considering accepting him as a leader. Doesn't it sound as if they've heard and learned something very compelling over the past few months? I just hope that what they've heard has more substance than twice-told tales."

Elspeth sighed and nodded, as she and everyone else applied themselves to their food. This was the first warm meal they'd had all day, and their supper last night had been hastily prepared over a smoky fire in the remains of a half-ruined house, not cooked in a proper kitchen. As the gnawing hunger in the pit of her stomach eased, and the warmth from their dinner filled her, she became aware of just how tired she was. When she glanced around the table, there wasn't anyone except Darkwind who wasn't leaning his head on his hand as he ate. She felt the same way; worn down by the cold, and quite ready to go to bed as soon as she finished the last bite. Darkwind seemed in his element, and she would not have hesitated a moment in trusting the entire expedition to him.

Some of the others looked quite ready to fall asleep over their plates. "It's the cold," Darkwind said quietly. "Don't worry, this is normal. It's being in the cold from dawn until dusk, without a chance to warm up, then going to bed in cold beds and unheated rooms. Tonight will make a difference, with a good hot meal and warm beds; tomorrow everyone will end the day without being quite so exhausted. If we can get shelter like this for the rest of the trip, our people will revive in no time at all."

He ought to know, and *she* should have remembered. Then again, perhaps she was not at fault for forgetting; when she'd worked beside him as a scout and border-guard at k'Sheyna Vale, they'd lived *in* the Vale. They'd return from their shifts on patrol to an *ekele* in the midst of a garden spot, as warm as a midsummer day. Before that, he'd refused to live inside the Vale, and there might well have been times when he'd returned home to a chilled *ekele*, or might even have remained overnight camping in the wilderness. Just because she had never personally experienced such hardship, that didn't mean he hadn't.

"Let's go to bed," Vallen said abruptly, after jerking his head up suddenly for the third time as he nodded off in spite of valiant efforts to stay awake. "I can't keep my eyes open anymore."

"I'll clean up; I'm good for that," Elspeth volunteered, and smiled at the look of surprise from Vallen. What, did he think she considered herself above such chores? Or had he forgotten that at the last several stops, she'd taken her turn at gathering fodder from the ruined barns, putting together makeshift stalls for the horses and *chirras*, and gathering clean snow for water? "I was a Herald-trainee once, or don't you recall? I've scrubbed my share of pots in my time, and I think I can manage without breaking anything."

Darkwind picked up empty bowls, knives, and spoons without comment other than a wink. Sometimes they both forgot the way other people saw them. She caught Vallen staring after Darkwind with an even greater look of surprise than he'd shown when she volunteered to clean up.

Does he think Hawkbrothers magic their plates clean? Oh, well, he probably does, and it doesn't occur to him that it would be harder work to clean a pot by magic than to do it by hand.

She gathered up what Darkwind couldn't carry, and both of them went into the kitchen.

This had been a particularly fine inn once, with a pump supplying water to the kitchen; the cooking crew had left water heating on the hearth. Both the regular Guards and Kerowyn's mercenaries were used to every aspect of this kind of mission; when it came to cooking, they were nothing if not efficient. It didn't take long to clean the bowls and cutlery and the two pots they had used for heating the food.

"I keep having second thoughts about this trip," Elspeth said quietly.

Darkwind nodded. "I can understand why you would feel that way, but I believe we are doing one of many things that could be the right path," he replied, carefully wiping out a pot and putting it away. It was a typically Tayledras response. "We must remain in contact with Tremane; that much I am certain of. *How* we do that—well, this is one way. There would have been others, but this is the way we chose, and I do not think we have chosen amiss."

"At least in this case, we'll have our own eyes and ears in Shonar," she sighed.

He smiled. "And tongues as well! We can also advise, if Tremane chooses to listen to us."

The pots, bowls, and utensils had all come with them, and she repacked them in the bags with the supplies. "Given the way things have been going so far," she observed, "it's only too likely, I suppose, for something entirely unexpected to happen out here. And in that case, the Alliance had better have people in place to observe and reassure…"

Darkwind slipped his arm around her shoulders, turning his hug into a way to turn her toward the door to the common room. "And to fix, transform, leverage, and otherwise turn things for the better. Tremane, according to Kerowyn, comes from a culture in which treachery is commonplace," he reminded her. "If anything unexpected *were* to occur, that would be the first explanation that would come to him."

She shook her head, and let him draw her toward the door. If she hadn't been too tired to think properly, she might have been able to make some kind of rational discussion out of this. As it was—

"You know, I almost feel sorry for Tremane," she admitted reluctantly as they mounted the stairs to their room. Rank did have privileges, and she had laid claim to one of the rooms with a real bed and a fireplace; it had probably been one of the expensive chambers when this had still been an inn. She was looking forward to sleeping in a bed, warmed by a hot brick at its foot.

Well, maybe not sleeping, at least not for a little while. I do have Darkwind here…

"I *do* feel sorry for him," Darkwind said unexpectedly. "And I believe I know why young Karal forgave him. Just because he has been forced to deal with daily treachery does not make him a treacherous individual. We do not know what he is really like, except that we may guess somewhat through his actions."

This speech had taken them up the stairs and to the space just outside the door to their room. Elspeth opened the door, drew him inside, and stopped the rest of the speech with her lips on his.

"I have had quite enough of Tremane to last me until morning," she said firmly, as he responded as she had hoped he would, by pulling her closer and simultaneously closing the door to their room. "I think we can afford not to think of him, for a little while, at least."

"Oh, at least," he agreed, and then said nothing more with words for quite some time.

Hob was as good as his word. From that time on, they began to see and interact with the people of Hardorn—those that remained, at least—and were given the limited hospitality that this sad land could afford. Elspeth continued to be surprised at the suspicion with which the Valdemarans were met. It didn't make any sense to her that the natives should persist in considering them the harbingers of another invasion. If they had been a real invading force, they would have had a small army at least. If they had been the advance scouts of an invasion, they wouldn't have come so openly.

She gradually decided that the reason had nothing to do with logic. Ancar had already poisoned his people's minds about the Valdemarans, and some of that poison still lingered. At the very beginning of his war with Valdemar, when his people had not yet been aware of the kind of man he really was, he had told them that his war was justified, that the Valdemarans were responsible for the murder of his father and most of the High Council, and that the Queen of Valdemar intended to annex Hardorn as a subject state of her own land. Later, of course, Ancar proved even to the most naive of his countrymen that he was never to be trusted, but some of his lies still remained in the back of peoples' memories. Perhaps they no longer even recalled it was Ancar who had spread those lies in the first place.

And to folk who themselves were never warlike to begin with, and who were now suffering privations worse in their way than even their life under Ancar, an armed force like hers—obviously well-trained, well-fed, well-armed, and in top condition—must look very much like an army. These folks hadn't yet seen the Imperial Army; they'd only heard rumors of it, how large it was, how incredibly *professional*. Away from the conflicts at the border, they had never seen anything larger than the garrisons Ancar bivouacked in their villages to insure their cooperation and to collect taxes. Perhaps their imaginations couldn't encompass the idea of an army, how large one had to be. Yet here was her force, quite large enough to take over every town in its path, and they didn't have to *imagine* what it was like, for it was real, and right in front of them.

The natives usually came around after a short meeting, such as she and her troop had had with Hob. At that point, the Valdemarans were treated like travelers instead of conquerors. Villagers would recall the old, hospitable customs, and would usually open the inn, the temple, or a Guildhall to them. Then there were warm beds, warm rooms, and once in a while, a bit of fresh meat to add to their own rations. There was no trouble with finding firewood this winter—not with half (or more) of the buildings in any given community standing empty and falling down. Sensibly, the survivors had moved into the best homes and kept them in repair, and were using the rest for materials and firewood. They might be on short rations, but they were going to spend the rest of the winter in warmth.

And that, Elspeth realized, (as she and her party continued to brave the cold that penetrated even the warmest of clothing and left them aching by day's end), was what would save these villagers. They could get by on less food, as long as they were warm enough. They might emerge when the snows melted as gaunt as spring bears, but they would be alive, for the cold would kill more quickly than short rations.

But the nearer they got to Shonar, the more people seemed cautiously impressed with Tremane, or at least with the stories they were hearing about him. Once the terrible, killing blizzards caused by the passing waves of mage-storms had subsided into more "normal" winter weather, he had begun making tentative overtures toward those who lived out past the area he had secured for himself and his army. He had sent his men out to clear the roads and keep them clear; he had encouraged such small trade as there might be in the dead of winter. If the rumors were true, he had also sent his men ranging in a limited fashion on monster-killing expeditions.

Supposedly, anyone within a three-day range of Shonar could come and request his help with killing a monster, provided that they knew either where it denned or what its range was. The Grand Duke evidently had no intention of sending parties of his soldiers off to wander about in the snow, trying to find a monster, and possibly making targets of themselves. Tremane would send out a team of twenty of his trained soldiers, all armed to the teeth and experienced in fighting mage-born aberrations, and all the natives had to do was lead them to the monster or to where it might be trapped or cornered. The soldiers did the rest; the natives got the privilege of deciding what happened to the carcass. Often, if it looked remotely edible, they would ask the Healer who traveled with the group to determine if it was safe to eat, and the Healer invariably obliged.

In addition, once the monster or monsters were disposed of, the group would remain long enough to conduct a hunt of feral stock, which was generally not all that difficult to find. Half of what they killed they took back to Shonar; the remaining half they left to feed the natives. Since this was always more than the locals had before the hunt began, no one protested when Tremane's men claimed the "Imperial share." And in addition, while the hunts for monsters or feral cattle were going on, the Healer who always accompanied the expedition would tend to any illness or injuries among the natives.

In short, when the Imperial group returned to Shonar, they left behind a stockpile of much-needed meat, people who had received medical attention the like of which they had not seen since Ancar took the throne, and land that was now safer, if not as pastoral and tranquil as in generations before. If any new monsters appeared, the natives had only to request help again, and the entire scenario would be repeated.

Tremane would *not* give aid against wolves, bears, or bandits; the first two, it was said, he had decreed were perfectly well within the means of the natives to deal with. And as for the third—he claimed that he could not tell the difference between bandits and "patriots," and he was not going to try. This was a bit hard on the Hardornens who were suffering from the depredations of fellow humans, but perhaps it gave them incentive to track down those who had once been their neighbors and reintroduce them to a law that had been long absent from Hardorn.

All of this was very impressive in tale and rumor—more impressive in that the stories were remarkably consistent—but Elspeth waited to see what was being said nearer to Shonar.

Finally, they came within that three-day sphere of Tremane's influence, and they saw for themselves that the stories of Tremane's "philanthropy" were true.

Unexpectedly, they had stepped from a road cleared just enough to let a single cart pass, to one which had been completely shoveled free of snow right down to the earth or gravel of the roadbed—and one which obviously was kept free of snow. They saw for themselves the trophy heads (or other parts) from the monsters that Tremane's men had tracked down and killed. And they heard from the natives who had been fed and Healed out of Tremane's bounty just what a good and just leader he was.

No one was mentioning the word "King" yet, but Elspeth sensed that it was not far from anyone's thoughts. How could it be, when in the face of the worst times that Hardorn had ever experienced, this man was slowly imposing order and sanity on the face of the land? And it wasn't the arbitrary, selfish order of a tyrant, either; they'd seen enough of that under Ancar to recognize it if they saw it. This was law and order that they could live with and be at peace with.

Elspeth couldn't help but contrast their lot with that of their fellow countrymen who did not have the advantage of living within three days of Shonar. Reluctantly she had to admit that if she were in their boots, she'd have felt the same way.

More than that, she found herself agreeing with most of what he'd done and ordered here. A few things represented laws or customs from the Empire that *she* wouldn't have imposed, but the rest—it was just the hand and the mind of someone who was concerned about the welfare of the people and knew how to derive the greatest good from a limited amount of resources.

The day before they were to meet with Duke Tremane himself, Elspeth and Darkwind were approached by a solemn group of Hardornens as they ate their evening meal. This time the innkeeper still tenanted his inn, but it had been a long time since he had actually served guests. He had offered a chance for Elspeth and Darkwind to have a quiet dinner together, without the company of their escort, and the prospect was too enticing to turn down.

He put them in a small, private dining room, with the troop seated in the larger room outside. Elspeth had not realized how much she had missed being able to talk to him without worrying about the ears of others. There were things she had wanted to discuss that needed to wait until they were alone in their room—*if* they were alone, since they often shared their sleeping quarters with the others.

They lingered over their last drink, making the most of this private time—and that was when the innkeeper interrupted them.

"Town Council would like to talk, sir, lady," he said diffidently, poking his head into the room. "Alone here, if you please?"

Elspeth sighed. She did *not* please, but there was no point in saying so. "If they must," she replied, allowing some, but not all, of her annoyance to show.

The innkeeper vanished, and the delegation must have been waiting right outside, for they trooped through the door immediately.

"We won't take up much of your time, Envoy," said the best-dressed of the lot, a fellow who still boasted the velvets and furs of earlier prosperity. "It's just something we'd like you to—to say for us, to Duke Tremane."

"Not a complaint!" added a second, only slightly less elegant than his fellow. "No, not a complaint! Something he might want to hear, maybe—"

"There's been talk," the first interrupted, with a glare at the second. "We've heard the talk. Oh, I was Guildmaster for the Wool and Weavers Guild for this whole region—"

Which explains the finery, Elspeth thought.

"—and Keplan here was Master for the Leather and Furrier's Guild. So, as I say, there's been talk, and people have come to us with it. Duke Tremane's proven good for us, and there are some that want to make him our leader." The Guildmaster waved his hands expansively. "Some who are even saying—King."

The second interrupted his fellow Guildmaster. "Now, we've sent out word, *looking* for some of the old royal blood of Hardorn. We've got ways of sending word out farther and faster than you'd believe. And there's no one, not one person of the old Royal Family left alive."

"I can't say that amazes me," Elspeth told them dryly. "Ancar wasn't one to tolerate rivals. And he wouldn't let a little thing like the age or sex of a possible pretender stop him from removing someone he wanted out of the way."

The Woolmaster coughed. "Ah. Aye. And woe betide anyone that got in the way back then." He looked up hopefully to see if Elspeth agreed with this attempt to exonerate himself for not attempting to interfere. By that, she inferred that at least one opportunity *had* occurred, and he hadn't even tried.

But who am I to judge? I wasn't there, I don't know what happened. If he took the coward's path, his own guilty conscience may be punishing him enough by now.

"You were saying that there isn't anyone of the old royal blood left," she prompted. "So?"

"So—well—there's some consensus that we might offer Duke Tremane the Crown. With conditions." He held his breath and waited for her reaction.

"An interesting proposal," Darkwind said quietly. "I presume that the conditions would be unusual, since you mention them at all."

The Woolmaster switched his attention from Elspeth to Darkwind. "They could be," he said. "It's—well, it's something our old Kings hadn't done for generations. It's—"

"He'd have to take earth-binding," the furrier burst out. "We've got a priest of the old beliefs, one that knows the ceremony and can make it stick. He'd have to bind himself to the earth, to Hardorn, so that anything that hurt the land would hurt him!"

The Woolmaster stared at his fellow, appalled, but Elspeth only shrugged. "It sounds like a sensible precaution on your part," she told them. "And if the opportunity presents itself, we will convey your message to the Grand Duke. But we can't promise anything, and we certainly can't promise that he'll agree to any such thing."

"That's all we ask, Envoy!" the Woolmaster said, waving at his little group and backing up himself, with a great deal of haste. "That's all! Our thanks!"

As he spoke, he herded the others out in front of him, and with the last word, he shut the door to the dining room behind him.

Darkwind looked at Elspeth, and she grimaced. "Well," she said, into the heavy silence. "That was certainly interesting."

"And it leaves the question begging," he replied, with a rueful smile. "Just how *would* one present such a proposition to Tremane?"

"I think that we can wait until we ride into Shonar itself, and we get a chance to see what the Empire represents—as molded by the hand of Grand Duke Tremane," she replied. "That in itself will tell us whether or not there's any point."

Despite the icy wind cutting through her coat, Elspeth sat back in her saddle and stared until her eyes hurt from snow glare. "I can't believe they raised all this in a single season," she muttered.

:*And without magic,*: Gwena reminded her, shifting her weight in tiny increments to keep muscles warm. :*Granted, they did have a great deal of incentive—the possibility of hostile Hardornen troops attacking, and the certainty of monsters—what did that fine young man call them?*:

"Boggles," Elspeth replied absently, taking in the reality of a two-story-tall wall, and not a wooden palisade, mind, but a *brick* wall. This edifice circled not only the entire city of Shonar but the much larger camp and garrison of the Imperials, *and* an open sward that had once been the town's grazing commons as well. A monumental task? Without a doubt.

Then add to that the equally monumental task of constructing barracks buildings for the Imperial forces before the snow fell, and it became a job to stun the mind in its scope. How had he gotten all that built? Where had he found all the laborers?

"We're very proud of our work, *Siara*," said the "fine young man" in Imperial uniform who had met them half a day out of Shonar and escorted them in. *Siara* was evidently the generic title of respect applicable to either sex that the Imperial military used when the person doing the addressing did not know the true rank of the one being addressed. It was probably the equivalent to "sir;" mercenaries generally addressed their officers as "sir" regardless of gender, a perfectly sensible approach of which Elspeth approved.

"We all worked on the walls and the barracks, every man of us," the young soldier continued, his cheeks flushed in the cold. "Except when some of us went to work on the harvest, and then we traded work with townsfolk. However many it took to make up the work that one of us could do, that's what Duke Tremane traded, so the walls and the barracks could keep going up."

:Sensible. Did you notice? The boy says that Tremane "traded" work for work, not that he conscripted workers.: Gwena's head was up as she made her own survey of the walls. *:Granted, it wouldn't have been very smart to conscript workers for a wall you're building for your own protection, but that hasn't stopped rulers in the past from doing things equally stupid.:*

Elspeth nodded; no point in confusing the poor fellow by answering someone he couldn't hear. The Imperials were already confused enough by her insistence on special treatment and housing for Gwena and the *dyheli* Brytha, although they had agreed to such a condition before a single Valdemaran set foot on the road to Shonar.

Darkwind cleared his throat gently. "As impressive as these walls are, I suspect our fellow travelers are as cold as I am, and we are not growing any warmer for standing here."

The young soldier snapped to immediate attention and stammered an apology. "Of course, *Siara*, forgive me! We'll be on our way at once!"

He nudged his own horse awkwardly with his heels, sending it ambling toward the gate ahead of them. He obviously (at least to Elspeth's eyes) was not used to riding, and the horse was certainly not a cavalry mount; thick-legged, jugheaded, and shaggy, it probably belonged to a farmer who didn't have any need for it in this season. He was probably grateful he hadn't had to ride out too great a distance to meet them; he handled the reins as if afraid the steady old gelding was going to rear and bolt at any second. The horse had no intention of doing so, he was just perfectly happy to be heading back to the city, a warm stall, and a good feed. She wouldn't hurt the poor boy's feelings by laughing at him, but she was very glad for the scarf wrapped around her face, concealing her mouth.

The guards patrolling the top of the wall looked down at them with interest as they approached, though with no sign of alarm. There was some nudging and pointing when those nearest caught sight of Darkwind's *dyheli*, but that was to be expected.

For her part, Elspeth saw absolutely nothing to make her instincts issue an alarm. Except for the uniforms, these men could have been any force in any of the Alliance nations watching the envoy of one of the other Allies ride in. There was no show of hostility from them, and no sense of entrapment on her part. They went through the gate without a challenge, and followed their guide through the main street of the city. It was strange, after all these weeks of not hearing their mounts' hooves do more than thud dully on the creaking snow, to ride once again to the peculiar music that Gwena's silver hooves made as they chimed against the cobblestones once they passed the wall, punctuated by the staccato clicking of Brytha's cloven toes. Townsfolk, evidently warned of their coming, gathered along the side of the street to cheer and wave welcomes and stare at Darkwind. She was reminded of the way they had last entered towns in Hardorn, as part of a traveling Faire. They hadn't stood out then in the midst of so much outlandish, gaudy, somewhat tarnished finery; probably onlookers had assumed that the *dyheli* had been an ordinary horse or pony in disguise. Now Darkwind had everyone's undivided attention, and to his credit, he seemed just as nonchalant as if there was no one gaping at all.

They passed several good-sized inns, and several more buildings that might have quartered them, and came out on the other side of the town. They were heading in the direction, not of the moundlike barracks buildings, but of a stone edifice rising at least four stories in height in the main, with towers of five or six stories above that. It seemed they were to be quartered in this fortified manor Tremane had appropriated as his headquarters; Elspeth wondered how many clerks, officers, and other underlings had to be reshuffled to make room for them. She was not going to be parted from her escort, and she doubted that Tremane was going to be foolish or naive enough to expect anything different, and that would mean displacing a fair number of people.

"The previous owner had a very small stable actually inside the manor," the young soldier said, as they approached a second set of walls about the manor. "The entrance is on the courtyard, and it is situated beside the kitchen. The Duke's Horsemaster said he thinks it was for very valuable mares in foal. There are four loose-boxes, and it's warm enough for people to sleep in at need. Will that do for your— ah—mounts?"

He looked questioningly at Brytha and Gwena, as if he still didn't understand what all the fuss was about.

For her part, Elspeth was just grateful that they'd not only found a decent place for the nonhuman members of the delegation, but that it was gong to be within the same building complex. "That should be perfect." Now it was her turn to hesitate. "We're going to want to see to them before we are taken to our own quarters, or even meet with Grand Duke Tremane for the first time. I hope he will understand."

The soldier's nod made it clear that he *didn't* think Tremane would understand, but that he was prepared to put up with the peculiarities of the Valdemarans.

Gwena chuckled in Elspeth's mind. *:Never mind, dear. The only person we have to persuade of my intellect is Tremane, and that won't take long. And it can wait until tomorrow; he's going to have enough shocks today as it is. Frankly, I'm more interested in a nice warm mash and a rest in a warm place than in meeting Tremane anyway.:*

Gwena surely was easier to live with these days. *Or maybe I've finally grown up!* Elspeth chuckled to herself, allowing herself to relax the tiniest amount. If there had been anything untoward, Gwena would probably have sensed it.

The walls about the manor were much, much darker than the walls around the city. These had been made of cut stone, like the manor itself, a dark gray that somehow stopped just short of being depressing. There were more guards on the top of these walls as well, but again, their manner was casual. While these men were professional, and ready to act on a moment's notice, their manner led Elspeth to think they did not consider themselves to be under any particular threat.

They entered a gate with an iron portcullis, but instead of passing under the walls into the yard between the walls and the manor, they went into an arched tunnel which actually passed under the walls of the manor. Torches dispelled part of the gloom, but not all of it. Elspeth did not miss noting the murder-holes in the ceiling above them, nor did anyone else in their party. The holes were spaced so closely that if the gates on either end of the tunnel were dropped, there would be no escaping boiling oil or other unpleasantness coming out of those apertures. This would have made her a great deal more nervous had the manor not predated Tremane's arrival.

Not that he wouldn't *use* them, he just had not put them there in the first place. The nasty mind that came up with them was a native Hardornen.

Possibly one of Ancar's ancestors...

The delegation split exactly in half once they were in the courtyard.

Half of Vallen's troop took the luggage to what was going to become their ambassadorial quarters, and the other half remained with Darkwind and Elspeth while they saw to the comfort of their mounts. Elspeth was just a little irritated at the too-obvious guardians, but she was experienced enough to realize they were a necessity. Until they really knew the situation here, it was better to be too cautious and formal, and reinforce the Imperials' perceptions of herself and Darkwind as people of diplomatic importance—which, of course, they were.

Her irritation was short-lived, for Vallen and his people made themselves useful instead of decorative, and things were soon settled in the stables to the comfort and satisfaction of everyone. One of the Imperials had remained to take them to their quarters, and with their own guards trailing behind, she and Darkwind followed him across the cobblestoned courtyard to one of the many entrances opening onto it.

"We've given you this tower," he said diffidently as he led them to a staircase, his Hardornen stilted, and painfully correct. "Duke Tremane hopes it will suffice your needs."

"I believe it ought to," she replied, as they climbed to the first residential floor. The half of their guards that had gone on ahead were already making themselves at home. This was quite a spacious room, furnished with beds and chests and not all that dissimilar from barracks in Valdemar. The second floor was identical to the first, but untenanted at the moment.

They continued to climb the staircase which wound around the outside wall. "These will be your quarters, sir and lady," said their escort, as they reached the third level.

They were standing in a public reception room set up on the third floor, with a table and chairs suitable for conferences, with writing tables and an arrangement of three comfortable chairs beside the fireplace.

"Your bedrooms and a study are on the fourth floor, and there is a storage room on the fifth," their escort said. "I am one of Duke Tremane's aides, and I will be at your disposal."

As Elspeth and Darkwind explored their personal quarters, he explained very seriously that they did not really want to use that top floor for anything except storage; it had no fireplace and was exposed to the winds in every direction. After poking her nose up there and seeing a thin layer of frost on the stones, Elspeth agreed.

Tremane gave them a decent period of time in which to get settled and into presentable clothing. Elspeth very much missed the comforts of the Palace at Haven; a hot bath here meant heating water over the fire in kettles, and pouring it into a tub the servants brought into the bedroom. The rest was just as primitive, and she wrinkled her nose at the sight of the chamber pot. But the alternative could be worse... and it wouldn't be the first time she and Darkwind had made do.

Finally, when they were presentable, Tremane sent another of his aides to invite them to dinner with him.

As good a time and place to open relations with him as any. When Darkwind gave her a little nod, she accepted for both of them, and they followed the young man down the stair and into the main body of the manor. They traveled down a dark and faintly chilled hallway for some time, with their only light coming from lanterns mounted in brackets at intervals along the wall. Finally they reached another stair, and the aide led them up into what was clearly another tower. In fact, if this tower held Tremane's quarters and was laid out in a similar manner to theirs, they could probably look right into his bedroom from their own.

An interesting thought, and one which showed a measure of trust from Tremane. If one could look, one could also shoot...

They discovered, as the aide ushered them into a room that corresponded to their own reception room, that this was to be an informal meeting. The table was set only for three, with a single aide standing by a sideboard full of covered dishes. Tremane was already waiting for them, and Elspeth scrutinized him carefully, even as he was looking both of them over with the same care.

She would not have taken him for the brilliant military leader he was supposed to be. He didn't look anything like a professional soldier—but then, neither did half of Kerowyn's best fighters. He was losing his mouse-brown hair, and what remained was going gray. His intelligent face showed signs of age and strain both.

Tremane embodied contradiction. His shoulders were firmer and broader than any clerk's, but there were inkstains on his right hand. He wore a sword as one for whom it was a standard piece of attire, but there were lines at the corners of his gray-brown eyes that people got when they habitually squinted, trying to read in dim light. On the one hand—scholar. On the other—fighter.

He stood up after a moment, as if they had surprised him by arriving sooner than he had expected, and extended his hand. Elspeth found his expression impossible to read; closed, but somehow not secretive. A gambler's face, perhaps, the face of a man unwilling to give anything away.

But what his face might not reveal, other signs might. His clothing was a variation on the Imperial uniform, but with none of the fancy decorations she normally associated with someone of high rank. There was just a badge with a coronet and another with what might be his own device. Nowhere was there evidence of the Imperial Seal or Badge, although the badge of a crossed pen and sword looked as if it had been sewn in place of a larger badge.

Come to think of it, no one I've seen wears the Imperial Badge. That, more than anything else, told her he really *had* given over his allegiance to the Empire. Soldiers set a great deal of store by what device they fought under; if the Imperial Seal was gone, so was their loyalty to what it represented.

The lack of decoration, though—military men took pomp and decoration for granted. What did that lack of decoration say about Tremane? That he was modest? Or that he wanted to appear modest?

Tremane extended his hand to her, and she clasped it, returning his clasp strength for strength. He didn't test her, but his clasp was firm and so was hers. "I am pleased to meet you at last, Princess," he began. She shook her head, and he stopped in mid-sentence, tilting his head a little to the side in what was probably a habitual gesture of inquiry.

"Not *Princess*, if you please," she corrected. "I renounced that title some time ago in favor of other responsibilities. 'Envoy' will do, or 'Ambassador,' or even 'My Lady,' although I do still hold lands and title that are the equivalent to yours, Grand Duke. No one in Valdemar even considers me as being in line for the throne anymore."

Must not let him think he's being slighted by having someone sent to him who is of lesser rank.

"My partner and spouse, Darkwind k'Sheyna, is an Adept; his people do not have any equivalent titles specifying nobility," she continued. "But we judged his status as a mage to be significant in place of a title."

Tremane nodded, released her hand, and took Darkwind's. The two men gazed measuringly into one another's eyes before releasing their grips.

"I am very pleased to meet you both at last, and I would deem it an honor if you would dispense with titles and simply refer to me as 'Tremane,' as my people in my home lands did," the Grand Duke replied, softening his formal manner with a slight smile. "Would you take a seat? I fear you will find my fare somewhat plain, but these are not the times for overindulging."

It was Darkwind who replied, as he held out a chair for Elspeth. "I could not agree more, Tremane," he said. "But it does appear that the folk under your command are prospering better than most in Hardorn."

Tremane waited until both of them were seated before he took his own chair. "That is as much a matter of luck as anything else," he replied. "Luck, in that we have one resource that Hardorn lacks—manpower. There is enough to be scavenged if you have enough able-bodied men."

Tremane's aide offered Elspeth a simple dish of vegetables baked with cheese, and she nodded in acceptance. As he finished spooning a portion onto her plate and turned to Darkwind, she took up the conversation. "Nevertheless, you have impressed those natives here who live within your sphere of influence."

Tremane took a sip of his wine. "One of the virtues of the Empire is that its leaders are well-trained," he said, after a moment. "Its vices are many, but it *is* well-governed. At the best of times, its citizens had little to complain of."

"And at the worst?" Darkwind asked bluntly.

Tremane bowed his head for a moment. "So much power is easily abused," he said finally, and applied himself to his food, ending the conversation for the moment.

When it resumed, they spoke of inconsequential things. Tremane was a decent conversationalist, though not a brilliant one. He was *not* a courtier, or at least, not someone who devoted most of his time to such pursuits. But he was also too careful to be blunt, too practiced to say anything that might cause him or his people damage. He was a survivor of a very dangerous Court, and he had learned his lessons in that Court well.

When they bid their host a cordial, if guarded, good night, Elspeth knew only one thing for certain.

Grand Duke Tremane was a man who kept his own council, and it would be difficult to penetrate the walls he had built about himself. He would clearly protect his honor by maintaining silence at judicious times, and practicing deflection when possible. Anyone who attempted to divine this complex man's deeper motives would find themselves with a nearly impossible task, yet that was precisely the task Elspeth and Darkwind faced.

3

Emperor Charliss sat enrobed in his heavy velvets of State, amid the grim splendor of the panoply surrounding his Iron Throne. He endured the burden of the Wolf Crown pressing down upon his brow, ignored the content of the peoples' chatter, and watched his courtiers vainly attempt to conceal their jittery nerves.

Outwardly, this Court was like any other, except in degree. Gossip, flirtations, negotiations, assignations, betrayals, confidences—the highborn, ranked and wealthy, all danced their dances just as they had for years, as their fathers had, and as their grandfathers had. Over the years their forms of jockeying and presentation had gone from custom to manners to mannerism, tempered by fashion and fear. Today, each attempted to hold their clothing and their overly-expensive accessories in their practiced ways, but their true state showed in their stilted movements, the nervous glances toward his dais, and in the faintly hysterical edge to their voices as they murmured to one another. His Court had always been noted for flamboyance of dress, but fewer and fewer of his courtiers were taking the time and care needed for truly opulent displays, which showed more clearly than any other outward signs that their minds and energies were directed elsewhere. They were afraid, and people who were afraid did not concern themselves with inventing a new fashion or impressing an enemy with their wealth.

Below the dais, people milled in the patterns dictated by rank and custom, but he was acutely aware of the holes in the patterns. The Court itself held little more than half the usual number of attendees. How could it be otherwise? Those who could leave for their estates already had, despite the fact that the Season was well underway.

This was wildly contrary to custom; *no one* who pretended to power or importance left the Court in winter. Summer was the time when the highborn of the Empire retired to their estates, not winter. Winter, that time of the year when snow and ice barricaded the isolated estates, one from the other, was the time to take one's place at Court and engage in revelry and endless intrigue, while one's underlings dealt with the tedium of estate caretaking, and become immersed in the round of social intercourse known as the Season. Those with youngsters to marry off brought them here to display them to the parents of other youngsters or potential older spouses. Those who wanted power jockeyed for position; those who had it campaigned to keep it. Those who pursued pleasure came here to pursue it. Only the impossibly dull, preoccupied, or solitary remained in their homes during the Season.

But not this winter.

When the first of the mage-storms had come sweeping out of nowhere across the Empire, disrupting or destroying all the magic in its path except that which was heavily shielded, the Emperor had been angry, but not seriously alarmed. Such a powerful work of magic could not have been easy to create, and he had not expected that the senders would be able to repeat it at any time soon. Granted, it had taken down every one of the Portals that were the fundamental means of long-range transportation across the Empire, but it had been possible to set them back up again in a relatively short period of time. The Storm had caused inconvenience, but no more. He had never had any doubt that the mages of the Empire would restore conditions to normal, and then he would deliver a punishment to the fools who sent such a thing. This punishment would send terror not only through their ranks, but into the hearts of anyone else even peripherally involved.

But then, without any warning, the *second* Storm had passed over the face of the Empire. That had been impossible, by the rules of all magic as he knew it. And then came a third. And after that Storm had passed, still *more*, and the intervals between them kept decreasing, even as the magnitude of the damage that each wrought increased.

The courtiers might not have been aware of the damage that was being done in the Empire as a whole, but they were certainly aware of the impact on their own lives. Mage-fires heating their rooms and baths no longer functioned. Mage-lights vanished, and had to be replaced by inferior candles and lanterns, normally only used by laborers to light their hovels. Meals, even in Crag Castle, were often late, and frequently cold. One could no longer commandeer a Portal to bring something from one's home Estate. There were servants enough that discomforts were rectified to a certain extent—but not entirely. Those in the Court that had no truly *pressing* need to be here, and who had the intelligence to see what might happen if conditions continued to deteriorate, found reasons and the means to get home.

By now it was next to impossible to maintain anything of a magical nature without exhaustive work on shields, and every time another storm-wave passed, those shields were so eroded that they required intensive repair. Transportation within the Empire was at a standstill, and communication sporadic at best. Physical constructions such as buildings and bridges that had incorporated static magics into their construction had crumbled. Every structural disaster created more disruption and fear, and sometimes involved great loss of life. Nor was that the only physical effect of the storm-waves; great pieces of land had been changed out of all recognition, and bizarre monsters were appearing as if conjured out of the air itself. Migrating birds had altered their patterns, or flew entirely lost. Wide-leafed plants as tall as men, stinging to the touch, grew inexplicably from stonework and soil alike, and all over the capital and nearby provinces, vines strangled horses in the night. Carcasses of creatures that looked like nothing of this world were brought in as proof that these Storms were only making their world stranger and more horrifying with each passing day.

By this time anyone who stood the slightest chance of reaching his or her Estate by purely physical means had left the Court. At home, a courtier would at least have reasonable foodstocks at hand, and many had Estates that relied on old-fashioned, nonmagical, purely physical sources of heat, light, and sanitation. One irony was that the poorer and less pretentious of the courtiers, who had not had the spare means to spend on magical amenities in their estates, were now the least uncomfortable of their peers. As perilous as life on the Estates could become now, with monstrous creatures attacking without warning or provocation, the wise and forethinking knew it was not only possible, but probable, that life in the capital would become far more dangerous. How long before food riots set the disaffected against the wealthy?

Charliss gazed upon his courtiers through narrowed eyes, and his normally inscrutable face betrayed some of his annoyance. He wondered if these who were left realized just how perilous life here could become. There were a remarkable number of very foolish people here now; people he had heard saying some amazingly silly things. "I come here to the Season at Court to forget the world outside these walls," one woman had said testily in his hearing. "I don't care to hear anything about it while the Season is on; I have more important things to think about—I have balls to attend and five marriageable daughters to dispose of!"

But the world outside the walls of Crag Castle was vanishing, even as that woman danced and displayed her offspring, and no amount of willful ignorance was going to change that. Already those outlying provinces of the Empire that had but lately come under the rule of the Iron Throne had revolted, regaining their independence. Charliss did not know, in most cases, what had become of the Imperial forces that had been stationed there. Some few had made their way back to lands that were still within Imperial sway, but others had vanished into the silence. Perhaps they had revolted along with those they were supposed to rule; but more likely they had been slaughtered, or had merely surrendered and were now prisoners. *He* did not know, nor did anyone else. Reluctantly, he was forced to admit to himself in recent days that his Empire, powerful and vast, had one particular fatal flaw. It was entirely optimized toward controlling any and all threats from inside itself—from riots to political intrigue to civil war—but was pathetically unprepared for outside disrupting influences such as these Storms.

Within the Empire itself, with transportation reduced to the primitive level of horse and cart, matters were degenerating much faster than he could prop them up. Food was the most critical item, usually imported into the cities all winter long from the Estates that supplied it; foodstuffs were running short as even Imperial storehouses were emptied. Food *was* getting into the cities, brought by individual farmers or carters a sledgeload at a time, but there were not only distances to consider, but the dreadful winter storms as well. Prices for perishable items were trebling weekly, with the cost of staples following suit, though more slowly since he had ordered Imperial stockpiles to be put on the market to stabilize prices. In some cities food riots had already broken out, and he had ordered the Imperial troops to move in to quell the unrest by whatever means necessary.

At least on the Estates, which were used to supporting themselves, there was plenty of food in storage, and most nobles had their own personal forces to maintain order. There would be more cooperation than competition among their dependents and underlings, if a lord or lady was a wise governor of his or her property. If not, well, they would get what was coming to them.

There had already been extensive rioting in those cities where major public aqueducts, maintained by magic, had collapsed, leaving the entire city with no source of fresh water. He had been able to repress news of those riots, but he was not certain just how long he would be able to repress news of food riots if they became widespread. Somehow, when news was bad, it always managed to spread no matter how difficult the circumstances.

It was not the weight of the Wolf Crown pressing down on his brow that made his head ache, it was the weight of the misfortune.

Why am I the Emperor upon whom all this is visited? Why could it not have waited for my successor?

One bizarre effect of these disasters on the citizens of the Empire—as if there were not enough bizarre effects already—was that strange religious cults were springing up all over what was left of the Empire. It seemed as if every city had its own pet prophet, most of them predicting the end of the world—or at least of the world as the citizens of the Empire had known it. Every cult had its own peculiar rites and proposed every possible variation on human behavior as the "only" means of salvation. Some preached complete asceticism, some complete license. Some advocated a single deity, some attributed spirits to every object and natural phenomena, living or not.

Some sent the most devoted out to sacrifice themselves to marauding monsters in the hopes of appeasing whatever had sent those monsters—but of course nothing was ever appeased but the appetite of the particular monster, and that was only a temporary condition. Needless to say, *those* cults did not long survive, for either their followers grew quickly disillusioned and abandoned their leaders, or they grew quickly angry and fed their leaders to those same monsters.

The cults neither worried nor really concerned Charliss, even though many of them had recruited untaught or ill-taught mages, and were raising impressive, though short-lived, power. He left it to his own corps of mages to deal with that power or drain it. He left the day-to-day emergencies in the hands of his underlings, mostly from the military. He had more personal concerns; most of his attention these days was taken up with his own wellbeing, even his own survival, both of which were in great jeopardy. He had *depended* on reliable and consistent magic to maintain those spells keeping him alive and healthy after two centuries of life, and magic was neither reliable nor consistent anymore.

He *could* die before he was ready, and he had come chillingly close to it more than once. That, above all, was something he wanted no one to learn.

Many of his courtiers were mages, and he wondered how tempting it would be for one of them to take advantage of his precarious situation. He was under no illusions about the ultimate loyalty of his courtiers; he had once been one of them, and like them, his ultimate loyalty had been only to himself. There were two sorts of folk out there in the Great Hall now; those who were still here because they were fools, and those who were still here because they saw opportunities. The latter were drastically more dangerous than the former, and he never forgot that.

He had been able to keep his own existence from being eroded by keeping the heaviest of shields upon himself, but he required an increasing number of lesser mages to do that, and he lost more ground every time another wave of Storms passed. Not even his corps of mages knew just how delicately his life was hanging in the balance.

At the moment, he had managed to keep the fact that there was even the slightest thing wrong with him a secret. His courtiers did not seem to notice any difference in his appearance, but it was only a matter of time before some sharp-eyed individual—or one with a good network of informants—learned that all was not well with the Emperor by assembling all of the small hints into one concise answer. The moment that happened, the panic in the cities would be replicated in miniature in the Court, unless Charliss could quickly exert total control over every courtier here. How could he do that, when every spare iota of time and energy was spent bolstering his failing reserves? He felt events slipping like sand between his fingers, and his very helplessness raised a rage in him that was as powerful as it was futile.

My Empire is disintegrating beneath me. Soon I may not have an Empire; I may consider myself fortunate to still retain a Kingdom—or a city—or my life.

But he did not despair. Despair was an emotion for weaklings and failures, with no place in the heart of the one who wore the Wolf Crown. Anger, a cold fire in his belly, rose in him until he felt he had to find a direction for it or burn away.

The realization of how his anger should be channeled rolled in and struck like a thunderbolt in his mind. He knew *precisely* where to place the blame for this situation, and his anger pointed like a poisoned arrow into the West and the home of his enemy.

Valdemar.

There could be only one source for his troubles, for the mage-storms and all they had wrought. Nothing like this had ever happened before he sent Tremane to finish taking Hardorn and consider taking the Kingdom of Valdemar which lay beyond Hardorn. Valdemar did not *have* magic as the Empire knew it, and yet they had defended themselves successfully against all of Ancar's magical attacks. The rulers of Valdemar had prevented his own agents from penetrating its borders for decades with great success; only a handful had obtained any intelligence, only three informants had ever gotten into the Court itself. Two of the three had not been mages, which had seriously hampered their effectiveness, and the third had been forced to forgo magic while she remained within the borders, which had the same effect. Valdemar had allied itself with foreigners as weird as any of the monsters currently springing up everywhere—with the grim Shin'a'in and the alien Hawkbrothers, with the monotheistic fanatics of Karse. Valdemar would be the only power to have come up with so completely unpredictable a weapon. The fact that—at least at last report—Valdemar and her Allies were not suffering the effects of the Storms only confirmed his "revelation." Surely only the people who had sent out such an encompassing weapon would know how to defend against it affecting them as well.

Besides, Valdemar had murdered his agents and envoys. That, he had personal proof of, for they had fallen through the Portal from Hardorn with daggers bearing the Royal Seal on the pommel-nuts. His advisers differed in their opinions on whether or not this had represented a deliberate provocation, an act of war, or simply a challenge, but there was no difference of opinion on whose hand had done the deed. It had to be someone actually in the Royal Household, either the Heir or the personal agent of the Queen, not just any provocateur or Herald.

Tremane, parked on the very doorstep of Valdemar, had agreed with that assessment, but the measures that *he* had taken to disrupt the Alliance had gone seriously amiss.

Or had they?

It could be that he had never taken those measures at all, that he had concocted the story of his tame assassin out of whole cloth. Had he been planning to defect to the Valdemaran Alliance all along, in the hope that they would give him a Kingdom, when he saw that he could not win the war with the Hardornen rebels?

That would make very good sense, considering that Charliss had made the promise of the position of Imperial Heir contingent on whether or not Tremane won Hardorn—the *whole* of Hardorn—for the Empire.

Given the choice between coming home in disgrace—barely retaining his own Duchy—and winning himself a Kingdom, it could have been an easy decision.

All this was speculation, of course, but Charliss did have certain facts to guide him. Without question, Tremane had revolted, looting an Imperial supply depot, declaring to his men that the Empire had deserted them, and making common cause with the Hardornens he had been sent to subdue. Chances were that the Valdemarans had persuaded him, perhaps had even given him the idea to revolt in the first place. Tremane had been the best choice Charliss had from among those to whom he had offered the opportunity to earn the Heir's Coronet.

Tremane was no fool, but nothing in his makeup had given Charliss the impression that he could be induced to revolt. He was intelligent, but not particularly imaginative. Yet one agent who had made his way across country against impossible odds had painted a very clear picture of Grand Duke Tremane's traitorous words and deeds.

That betrayal was as bitter as any experience in Charliss' long life and reign, and it would not go unpunished. It was a pity that Tremane had left no potential hostage in the form of a wife or child at Court, and that his Estate was so far away on the borders of the Empire that reaching it to despoil it was about as practical as going after Tremane himself. Of course, Charliss could and would assign it to someone else, but that was an empty gesture, and both he and the recipient would be well aware of that. No one would be able to get there until late spring at best, and if the Empire continued to fall apart, they might as well not try.

Still, a gesture would have to be made, hollow or not. These people below him, fools though they were, would have to be shown once again that he *was* the Emperor, and he was not to be trifled with.

He signaled to his majordomo, who rapped his staff three times on the marble of the floor to gain the Court's attention. Nothing disturbed the icy tranquillity of the majordomo's demeanor; men had been cut down by the Imperial Guards at his very feet and he had not turned a hair. Arrayed in a splendor of purple velvet and gold bullion embroidery, and bearing the wolf-headed Imperial Staff which stood taller than he was, no mage-made homunculus or clockwork manikin could have been more controlled than he.

So completely did his office subsume him that Charliss did not even know his name.

Silence fell immediately with the first rap, so that the next two echoed down the hall with the impact of Death himself rapping on a door. All eyes turned at once to the Iron Throne, and Charliss stood up to face them all, his heavy robes dragging at his shoulders. He braced his calves against the Throne, grateful for the invisible support.

He could have had the majordomo make the announcements, but that would lessen the impact, and it might give the impression that he was no longer vigorous. He could not have that, especially not now. He must appear to be as powerful now as the day he took the Throne.

His voice echoed portentously out over the crowd of courtiers, amplified and rendered more imposing by clever acoustical design around the dais. "Intelligence has reached Our ears that gravely grieves and angers Us," he said sternly into the silence. "We have received news from an unimpeachable source that Tremane, Grand Duke of Lynnai, has turned traitor to the Empire, to his vows, and to Us."

The gasps of surprise that rippled through the Court were not feigned, and only confirmed Charliss' impression that those courtiers still remaining were for the most part not among his brightest and best. He scanned for a few particular faces, men and a few women who were numbered among his advisers—and there was no surprise or shock registering there.

Good. It's agreeable to know that I haven't chosen any complete idiots.

"There can be no doubt of his intent or his thoughts," Charliss continued, as the gasps and murmurs died down again. "He has orchestrated the looting of an Imperial storage depot for his own profit, including the contents of the exchequer there, monies intended to pay the faithful soldiers of the Empire their just and well-earned stipends."

He cast a glance at the stiff figures lining the walls. *Ah, my own guards are looking black at that one. Good. Word will spread through the rest of the Army, and may the Hundred Little Gods help him if he shows his face where a single Imperial soldier can find him.* Of all the truths in the Empire guaranteed to preserve life, limb, and prosperity, this was the truest: *Pay the Army, pay it well, and pay it on time.*

Charliss permitted a touch of his anger to show on his face and in his voice. "He has declared his allegiance to the Empire at an end, and has subverted his troops, entrusted to him, to renounce their oaths as well. He has broken off hostilities with the rebels of Hardorn, has entered into unlawful and traitorous alliance with them, and is acting in all ways to have set himself up as King of that benighted land."

Shaking heads and avid looks told him that every one of the power seekers still gathered here was hoping for profit from Tremane's downfall. Well, in the void left when a great tree fell, little trees could climb to reach the sun. Even in these strange days, that might still come to pass.

Now, however, was the time to alert these idiots to their danger. "Worst of all, he has entered into alliance with the vile and duplicitous monarch of Valdemar, which nation has sent unprovoked assaults by magic lately against this, Our peaceful Empire." He paused for a breath, steadying himself against the Throne under cover of his robes. That last was only supposition, but even those with intelligence networks the near-equal of his could not be certain of that, and really, would not care. Tremane had no friends here; those who had been nominally his allies would be scrambling for new men to attach themselves and their fortunes to. And proving that the current misfortunes had a recognizable origin might consolidate some of these idiots into a cohesive whole. There was nothing quite like a common enemy to make a force out of disparate and bickering parties.

Now to show them that the old lion had teeth. He put on his most dreadful look, the one that left even hardened guards with trembling hands and quaking knees, and made his next words thunder out like the pronouncement of some barbarian god. "We therefore declare Tremane of Lynnai a traitor, his title and lands forfeit, and his name anathema! We pronounce upon him the sentence of death, to be executed by any that have the means and opportunity! Let no loyal citizen of the Empire aid him, on pain of that same sentence; let his name be stricken from the rolls of his family, and let the House of Lynnai die with his father! Let his name be chiseled from monuments of battle, be erased from the records of the Empire, and let it be as if he never was born!"

That was the harshest sentence possible to pronounce within the Empire, and no few faces below him turned pale. For most of these people, this erasure was worse than a sentence of execution, for it extended Tremane's punishment into the Hereafter. If and when Tremane *did* die, he would have no immortality, for without some record on earth of who and what he had been, his soul would vanish at the moment of his death, or would wander aimlessly in the cheerless, empty limbo between earth and the afterlife, without any knowledge of who it had once been...

Or so it was believed. When a citizen of the Empire believed anything, he believed in the immortality of records; when he worshiped anything, he always included his ancestors. To remove someone from his rightful place among his ancestors was to remove a piece of the very cosmos.

Charliss smiled grimly. *Now they know I haven't gone soft, just because I was prepared to name a possible Heir.*

He allowed his expression to soften. "We know that this has come as a great shock to all Our loyal subjects, the more especially as the Nameless One had been put forth as the potential Heir to the Imperial Crown. Such a betrayal harms you as well as Us, by threatening the security of the Empire. We would not see Our children distressed by the taint of betrayal mingled with uncertainty. Therefore, We now do name Our successor, and bestow on him all those lands, goods, and titles that were once the property of the Nameless One."

The looks of greed and avidity were back—though only briefly, and quickly controlled. At this moment, no one knew who Charliss was going to name, least of all the recipient. Once Tremane had been designated, Charliss had taken pains to show no partiality to anyone else; he had wanted to give Tremane as fair a playing field as possible in a Court as filled with intrigue as this one. And besides, by not showing favor to any one person, he had virtually opened up the field—if Tremane failed to conquer Hardorn—to *anyone*. The scrambling and jockeying had been most amusing when he'd had the leisure to take note of it. Every one of his advisers had the potential to be named Heir as far as anyone knew, and several of his mages as well. Those who thought themselves in the running were moving up through the crowd, almost without realizing that they were doing so, attempting to place themselves nearer the Throne, where he could see them better.

But his thoughts were wandering; the suspense was about to send one or two out there into a fit of apoplexy.

He had to end the suspense, although there would be several who were shocked or affronted at his choice. Nevertheless, Melles had been his second choice before he sent Tremane off to conquer Hardorn, and Melles had remained in that position all along. "We therefore do name as successor and Heir, the most worthy and knowledgeable adviser and most loyal servant of the Empire, Court Baron Melles."

He had just named Tremane's most fervent and implacable enemy. And if *anyone* was going to put in the astounding effort it would take merely to attempt to execute the Imperial death sentence on Tremane, it would be Melles. There was real hatred between the two of them, a hatred more powerful than Charliss had witnessed in a very long time. There was not much room for hatred in the Imperial Court; it was better to keep emotions superficial, for today's enemy might be tomorrow's ally.

Melles had been standing just to one side of the dais, visible, but unobtrusive, as was his normal habit. He was a slightly better-looking version of Tremane in some ways; thinner and not as muscular, with none of the physical attributes of a fighter. He was not balding; his hair was darker, and he was two or three years Tremane's junior. Otherwise, though, they could have been cut from the same cloth and sewn by the same tailor. Both of them had cultivated the art of being ignored and overlooked, though Charliss suspected that their motives for this differed greatly. He *knew* what Melles' motives were; now, in retrospect, he could guess at Tremane's.

Melles was not a hereditary noble like Tremane; he was a Court Baron, a man with a title but no lands, as his father had been before him. Melles' wealth came from trade, as did the wealth of most of the Court nobles, although the commodity that Melles bought and sold was quite unlike that of his livestock-brokering father. It was no secret that an ambitious tradesman with enough ready cash could buy a Court title for himself, and with further applications of his wealth could arrange for the title to be inherited by his son. There was no shame in this—though many of the Court nobles were extraordinarily touchy about their titles, and many of the landed gentry made no secret of the fact that they considered the Court nobles to be purest upstarts. There was some friction between the two factions, although it was quite astonishing how quickly that friction vanished when a family with title but no fortune was presented with the heir or heiress to a fortune with no title as a matrimonial prospect.

Was that how the enmity had begun between Tremane and Melles? Had Tremane, or Tremane's father, snubbed Melles or Melles' father? It seemed unlikely that such hatred could spring from so trifling a cause. Oddly enough, Charliss could not imagine Tremane being rude to anyone, not even to someone he held in contempt. Tremane had always been too clever to make such enemies casually.

Well, it didn't really matter now. Whatever the cause, it served the Emperor's ends.

Baron—now Grand Duke—Melles moved forward out of the knot of courtiers at the very foot of the steps leading to the dais. He stood alone for a moment, then walked with solemn deliberation up the three steps permitted to one of his new title, bowing his head and going to his knee at the fourth. Charliss motioned to the guard at his right to bring up the coronet of the Heir from the niche at the side of the dais where it had resided since Charliss himself had resigned it to put on the Wolf Crown.

Although the acts of this ceremony appeared spontaneous, it was anything but. It was another dance, the steps dictated by the custom of ages past, every move choreographed centuries ago. Only the participants in the dance changed, never the steps themselves.

Even the guard who brought the coronet to Melles had rehearsed just this action a thousand times, even though there was no telling *which* guard would be directed to retrieve the circlet, nor who it would be given to. It was simply a part of an Imperial Guard's duty, rehearsed along with every other part.

The guard performed flawlessly, handing the circlet to Melles, who in accordance with tradition, solemnly crowned himself, just as he would crown himself with the Wolf Crown when Charliss died. Power and authority in the Empire came from within the man, and were not bestowed by the hands of priests, and in token of that, every Emperor and Heir bestowed the trappings of power upon himself.

Once crowned—not that the coronet was all that imposing, just an iron circlet in the shape of a sword, with a topaz matching those in the Wolf Crown set as the pommel-nut—Melles stood up, and bowed to his Emperor. Charliss surveyed him with satisfaction, thinking that he probably should have chosen Melles in the first place. Unlike Tremane, Melles was a powerful Adept who could, with a few decades of practice, be Charliss' equal in magic. Given that, and despite current conditions, it was just barely possible that Melles *would* contrive to bring back Tremane's head.

Charliss mentally resolved to resign on the spot if Melles managed to pull that one off. Not that he considered it *likely*, but such diligence would deserve a reward, and there wasn't much else Charliss would be able to give him.

And if he can do that, he'll be strong enough to take the Wolf Crown from me. It would be better to resign it with grace, and concentrate on keeping myself alive.

No matter how powerfully his enemies among the courtiers would gladly have plunged daggers into Melles' heart at that moment, not one of them would betray himself. "Go and take your well-deserved congratulations from Our Court," Charliss directed with cool approval. "We will discuss your new duties and privileges later."

Melles bowed, and backed down the steps. There was no throne for the Heir, nor any special place for him at Court ceremonies. Emperors of the past had not deemed it necessary or advisable to give their Heirs too much power or the appearance of it lest they acquire an addiction to it and crave more. As Melles turned at the foot of the steps to face those thronging to greet him, Charliss decided that the Emperors of the past had been very wise. Melles could certainly be one of those who would crave more than his just due.

Charliss decided to keep him on a short leash, as he watched the dance of power begin swirling about this new center.

One Tremane was enough, after all.

* * *

Melles had often thought, of late, that there had been so many upheavals that there was nothing that could evoke the feeling of surprise in him anymore. And although his intelligence network was extraordinary—in fact, it had been one of *his* spies who had brought word of Tremane's defection back to Crag Castle—he really had not expected to be named Charliss' Heir.

According to his own calculations, he wasn't the logical candidate, even though there were personal considerations involved. Since the onset of the mage-storms and the consequent disasters spread over the entire Empire, it had seemed to him that the Emperor would have to name someone who had absolutely no enemies at Court whatsoever. Whoever came after Charliss would have to cope with a much-reduced Empire, revolt everywhere, a possibly hostile Army; he would have to somehow convince the worst of enemies to act together and forge alliances until the Empire was stable again. Melles had far too many enemies who would rather die than work with him in any way; Tremane was not the only one, nor was he even the most deadly. Melles was a man who made enemies far more easily than allies. On the whole, he preferred enemies, for it was much easier to manipulate them than allies, and there was never the risk of disillusion when they realized they had been manipulated.

Friends were quite out of the question; a friend was a potential hole in one's armor, and he had not permitted himself such a weakness since he became a man. Then there was the matter of his position and duties under Charliss, which did not endear him to anyone. He could not think of a single person who *liked* him in the entire Court. Many feared him, some admired him grudgingly, others tolerated him as a necessary evil, but no one *liked* him.

But there they all were, flocking to fawn on him as if they couldn't wait to become his best friend. Some of them, in fact, might very well have plans in that direction, foolish as such plans might be. He was, after all, surrounded by fools; they wouldn't be here now if they weren't.

He smiled and accepted their congratulations with an expression that suggested that he would be eager to become their best friend. Why not? Even fools had their uses, and just like the Emperor who had bestowed his new title, he had never been the kind who threw away a potential tool.

The men thronged about him first, jostling one another in their eagerness to say something that he might remember later, reminding him of past favors they had done for him, offering favors for the future. It was quite astonishing, the sort of things they considered to be "favors;" he could not for a moment imagine why *anyone* could think that invitations to incredibly boring social gatherings featuring meaningless entertainments would ever be sought after.

And the *women*! They were worse than the men! If they were unmarried, they were pressing about him with looks and poses that were just short of open invitations to do as he pleased with them. If they were anything other than blissfully, happily married (and there were damned few of *those* at Court, especially now!) they were behaving the same. If they had daughters of anything resembling marriageable age—and plenty of these women had very liberal ideas about what constituted "marriageable age"—they were alluding to their daughters' admiration of him, and dangling invitations on their behalf.

As if any of them had the faintest notion who I am or what I look like—

No, that was unfair. Not all of these people were here because they were blind idiots who wouldn't have their Season spoiled by a few petty disasters. Some were here because they couldn't get back to their Estates, others because of their positions as Imperial Advisers, and some because they had no Estates. There were young girls—and not so young girls— who knew very well who he was and what he looked like, as they knew the identities, properties, and titles of every unwedded man expected to be at Court this Season. That was part of *their* duty, as they and their parents went about the serious business of husband hunting. He might not have been very high on their list of desirable matches until now, but they knew who he was.

And if he made an appearance at a private party, a musical evening, or other entertainment, each of them would proceed with grim determination to try to convince him that nothing would make him happier than to take *her* as his lawfully wedded soon-to-be-Empress.

That no less than an hour ago most, if not all, of these maidens would have cheerfully confessed that the idea of wedding him made them ill was of no consequence now.

Look how these same women throw themselves at Charliss, the old mummy! It isn't his handsome face that makes them act like shameless cows in season around him. Furthermore, Melles was well aware that if he had evidenced any preference for young *men* he would still be under siege from these women and their parents. After all, he would still be expected to *try* to produce an Heir of his body. The fact that only about half of the Emperors of the past had been the physical offspring of their predecessor didn't matter, he would still be expected to try.

And if some of what I've read in the private Archives is true, some of them went to some fascinating extremes in trying...

Well, that didn't matter either. He wasn't a lover of men or boys, and not of little girls either. But he would wait until he wore the Iron Crown himself before he took a wife, and when he did, his first choice would be an orphan with no living family left whatsoever, just for spite!

"Yes, of course," he murmured to one of the women—after being certain that he was not agreeing to anything of importance. It would be a grand joke on all of them if he selected his bride from among the common citizens. It would certainly be easy to find an attractive orphan there!

He whispered an aside to one of the other advisers, a man who had been a disinterested ally in the past. *This is all going to my head. There will be time to think about women later; now is the time to concentrate on consolidating my base of power, and determining what can best be done to get the Empire through this crisis.*

Pleasures of all sorts would have to wait until the Empire was stable. Perhaps sometime in the future there might even be an opportunity to execute the Emperor's sentence of death on Tremane. But that time was not now, and he would wait for it to come to him. Hatred was an emotion that brought him a great deal of energy and entertainment, and he enjoyed it.

It was not for nothing that his enemies often compared him to a spider sitting in the middle of a web. If there was one virtue he possessed, it was patience, for patience was the only virtue that eventually brought rewards.

Now that the dance of courtiers and Court was over and the business of the Empire had been disposed of in Council, Melles got his private audience with the Emperor. Private? Well, not precisely; the Emperor was never alone. But no one of any pretense to wealth or rank in the Empire ever really noticed servants or bodyguards—

Unless, of course, that person was Melles, or someone like him. To the Emperor, without a doubt, they were invisible. To Melles they were possible spies.

The subject of conversation, as befitting the position and duties of the new Heir, was the state of the Empire. Melles was not particularly surprised to discover that Charliss had less information on this subject than he did. The Emperor had not been concerned with the day-to-day workings of his Empire for decades; he had been able to leave that to his underlings.

In Melles' opinion, he no longer had that luxury. "My Lord Emperor," Melles said patiently. "It seems to me that you have been insufficiently acquainted with the desires and needs of the common man."

They compare me to a spider in its web, Melles thought dispassionately, as he watched the old man glare at him over the expanse of a highly-polished black marble table. *They should see him when he is not playing his role. He looks like an ancient turtle deciding whether or not to stick his nose a fraction more outside his shell.*

Inside the sheltering back and arms of the Emperor's thronelike chair, that was precisely what Charliss resembled. And, like the turtle, Melles suspected that the Emperor really *did* want to pull himself back into his shell entirely.

He did not seem disposed to learn, or deal with, the basic changes in the Empire, and that fit with Melles' plans. *So what I need to do is to persuade him that not only is that a good idea for him, but also that he can trust power in my hands.* Melles already had a great deal of power; he had been in charge of dealing out whatever punishments the Emperor deemed necessary for many years now. Not quite an Executioner, and considerably higher in status than a mere lawkeeper, when something unfortunate occurred to a member of the Court and the Emperor took special notice of it, everyone knew whose hand had been behind seeming accidents or twists of fate. Melles' value to the Emperor lay in making certain that it was impossible to prove anything when such accidents occurred.

The "accidents" weren't always supposed to be fatal, or at least not fatal to the physical body. Sometimes ruin suited the Emperor better than death, whether it be the ruin of a reputation or of a fortune. A ploy that Melles particularly favored was to contrive romantic liaisons that were entirely disastrous; it was amazing what people would do to prevent their follies from becoming widely known when that folly involved sexual favors, infatuation, or a combination of the two.

"Just what exactly do you mean by that?" the Emperor asked querulously.

Melles spread his hands wide. "I mean, Lord Emperor, that the common man is an extremely simple creature. You are thinking of him now in terms of the mob, which is a being with many arms and legs and no head, and as a consequence behaves in ways no rational man can predict. *I* am thinking of him as he is before he devolves to that mindless, intractable state." He tilted his head to one side; that had been a much longer speech than he usually gave to the Emperor, and he had learned to make certain that the Emperor always had openings in which to insert his own comments.

"So what is the so-called common man, when he isn't in a mob?" the Emperor mocked.

Melles was not about to let his own mask of serenity slip. Such mockery was as much a test as Tremane's assignment had been.

And I am not likely to be lulled by the illusion that I am the Emperor's only executioner. If he perceives me as a failure, I will not live long enough to rebel.

He inclined his head a little; not quite a bow, but enough to acknowledge his subservience even as he "corrected" the Emperor's ignorance. "As I said, Serenity, he is simple. What he needs—desires—those things are just as simple. First of all, he wants the roof over his head to be sound and the food on his plate to be abundant. He wants that food to arrive every day. He wants to be left alone to pursue his work and the pleasures of his bed, home, and table. If you give him these things, he is not inclined to argue overmuch about the *means* required to deliver them. If he is deprived of them, he is likely to welcome whatever measures are taken to restore them." He raised a single finger to emphasize his next point. "Most, if not all, of your common citizens have been so deprived, and see only a steady decline in the quality of their lives, but if measures could be taken that will restore many of their comforts, those things they consider so important to their lives…"

"I see your point," the Emperor replied, with no more mockery in his voice. He sat in silence, only the movement of his eyes betraying his alertness. He could have been a grotesque statue, if not for those glittering eyes. The Emperor did not fidget, did not visibly shift his weight in his chair, or perform any of the other tiny, unconscious movements of lesser beings. Partly it was a matter of training, for such utter stillness enhanced his image of supernatural power; partly, or so Melles suspected, it was simple good sense, to conserve his waning energy and resources.

Finally, the Emperor spoke, his voice low, deep, and grating. "You want me to give you the authority to order whatsoever you think is necessary to restore order at the level of the streets."

Melles nodded, very slowly, as those powerful eyes, blazing with the deadly life of a finely-honed blade, pinned him to his seat. He could not, dared not, return that glare. He was not here to challenge the Emperor, he was here to get the old man to share out some of his power. But he also wouldn't get anywhere if he didn't admit what he wanted. It was an interesting observation by one of his tutors that there were only three classes of people who could afford to speak the unvarnished truth—the very bottom, the very topmost, and children. The lowest classes could afford it because they had nothing to lose, the highest because there was no one who could call them to account for it, and children because they held no power and hence were no threat. Melles had never forgotten that observation, nor did he forget the implications of it. The Emperor could speak pure truth; Melles could not. When the Emperor asked a direct question, Melles had better be careful how much of the truth he told.

But there was another factor here. At the best of times, when the Emperor had been in his prime, he hadn't had time enough for everything. No great ruler did; that was why they had underlings and delegated their authority to those they thought could be trusted with it. Now, the Emperor was old, his powers waning, and he had the very personal and pressing matter of preserving what was left of his life to concentrate on.

The real question, the one Melles had no answer to as yet, was just how close to the end the Emperor was. That would tell him how reluctant Charliss would be to give up power to his Heir. Would he clutch his powers and possessions to him, or release them to clutch at life itself?

Those sharp, chill eyes measured him, and missed nothing in the process. "Very well." The voice was as cold as the eyes. "Have the orders written, and I will sign and seal them, granting you authority over city guards, militias, and authorizing you to make use of the Army in quelling local disturbances. That will be enough to see if you have the insight into the common man that you claim." A thin, humorless smile stretched the Emperor's lips. "If you succeed, I shall consider granting you more."

He waved a hand at the Emperor, in mute disavowal of wanting any other powers. "That will be sufficient, my Lord Emperor, I assure you. I wish only to restore order; without order, these seeds of chaos will spread to engulf us all."

Charliss only made a wheezing grunt full of cynical amusement. "I doubt that you intend to limit your grasp. But this is all you will get for the present. Go to the clerks and draw up the orders."

That was clear dismissal, and he took it as such. He stood, bowed with careful exactitude, and walked backward until he reached the door.

The Emperor's eyes were on Melles every step of the way, and the slight smile on the Emperor's lips would have chilled the blood of a lesser man.

He reached behind him and opened the door without looking at it, backed through it, and closed it without taking his eyes off the Emperor. As the door closed, the Imperial eyes were still fixed on him, still measuring, still watching him for a hint of insubordination.

As the door shut with a decisive *click*, Melles let out his breath, slowly. *That went better than I had any reason to hope. He's still sane; if he stays that way, I can handle him.* He turned and stalked silently down the cold gray marble hallway with its high ceilings and austere decorations of captured weaponry from ages and wars long past. Like the room he had just left, the hallway was chilly enough to make him wish he had worn heavier clothing. Ostensibly, it was due to a failure in the enchantments of heating, but in fact it was deliberate, to discourage loitering. The hallway was meant to impress one who walked it with his own insignificance, and its acoustics underscored the message well.

Here, so near to the highest seats of Imperial government, the Audience Chamber, the Council Chamber, and the great Court Hall, one necessary adjunct to so much power was a highly-trained cadre of Imperial clerks to make decisions into orders. Nothing could function without written orders. Articles, commands, and doctrine, no matter how seemingly small, had no official life until they were quantified as documents. These pieces of paper were so vital to the working of the Empire, they were like water, food, or air to a soldier, and an official document would carry more power in its words than any courtier posturing and spouting similar verbiage.

And of course, there was such a group of vital clerks, a small army of them, ensconced in the one comfortable chamber on this floor, between the Court Hall and the Council Chamber.

An efficient Empire was one dependent on (though not run by) clerks, though they might not know it; their masters did, and always had, and took care to ensure the comfort of these all-important workers in the hive of Imperial rule. Large windows, screened against insects, let in cooling breezes during the heat of summer. And although the heating-spells had failed elsewhere in Crag Castle—legitimately—measures had always been in place in case of such a failure in the Clerks' Chamber. There were three great fireplaces on the wall shared with the Council Chamber, and two more on the one shared by the Court Hall, all of them burning merrily. Charcoal footwarmers sat under desks, and those all-important fingers kept warm and supple with metal handwarmers on each desk. Each clerk had his own oil lamp to read and write by, and there were pages assigned to this room only, to bring food and drink whenever called for.

Some—always among the "new" nobility who were not yet acquainted with the way things worked—grumbled at this treatment of "mere" clerks. What they were not aware of was that these clerks weren't "mere" anything, and most of them were higher in rank than the grumblers. Here the offspring of the noblest families in the Empire paid their service, even those intended eventually for the Army. They were accustomed to preferential and comfortable treatment, but that did not mean they did not earn it by their labors. There was never an hour when there were not at least six clerks on duty here, and there were twenty between dawn and dusk. Only the most skilled and most discreet served here, and their ability to remain closemouthed about what passed over their desks was legendary.

To open the heavily-guarded door and enter this haven of heat and light was a decided relief; Melles felt tight muscles relaxing under the influence of the gentle warmth. It was still early enough in the day that all twenty clerks were in attendance; Melles scanned the rows of desks, and went straight to the first unoccupied clerk he saw.

The young man he chose sat, like all the rest, at a large wooden desk with everything he required arranged neatly on top of it. A stack of rough draft paper, a smaller stack of Imperial Vellum, inkpots containing red and black ink, blotting paper, blotting sand, glass pens, and his handwarmer were all arranged in a pattern he found personally the most efficient. Off to one side was the book he had been reading, which he had immediately laid aside when Melles neared him. The only sign of individuality was a small egg-shaped carving of white jade in a motif of entwining fish.

The clerk himself was nondescript, unmemorable, as all of them were. They were taught how to be forgettable and self-effacing before they came to this duty. Here, they were a pair of hands and a brain full of specific skills, interchangeable with every other clerk in the room. Melles alone among his acquaintances had never taken a turn in this room, but that was because he had been serving Empire and Emperor by learning another set of skills entirely.

While the clerk made rapid notes, he dictated the orders; the clerk first made a rough copy, checking it word for word with him, then from the corrected rough, made a final copy on Imperial Vellum incorporating all the changes. Melles was being very careful in how he phrased these orders, giving himself precisely the amount of authority that the Emperor had specified and no more. Three more clerks were summoned to make copies at this point, for a total of five copies in all.

As yet, obviously, the orders were nothing more than paper. When he had finished, the clerk summoned a page from the group waiting and chattering on a bench beside the fire and sent him to the Emperor with the finished documents. The page would not walk down the corridor that Melles had just left; he would use a special passage between this room and the Emperor's chambers reserved only for the pages, so that he could not be stopped and questioned or detained.

Melles did not go with him; he was prohibited from doing so, nor would the Emperor's guards permit him to approach with documents to be signed in hand. This was to prevent him from somehow coercing the Emperor into signing and sealing them, or being tricked into doing so before he had read them. All these convoluted customs had their reasons.

At length, the page returned, and the glitter of the Imperial Seal on the uppermost document told Melles that all had gone well; the orders were approved with no changes. Had there been changes, the page would have returned with one copy, not five, which would have had the Emperor's revisions written on it. The rest, one of the Emperor's guards would have burned on the spot, so that the Seal could not have been counterfeited on them.

Melles accepted his copies with a bow of thanks, and left the room. The chill of the hallway struck him with a shock, despite being prepared for it, but he didn't hesitate for even a moment. Now his first priority was to get one copy of the orders into the hands of the Commander of the Imperial Army. The cooperation of the Army was needed before he attempted any of his ambitious plans.

He had been careful to phrase his orders in such a way that the Commander's authority was not being subsumed by his own. The last thing he wanted was to make an antagonist out of General Thayer. The General made a very bad enemy, one who never forgot and never forgave. The orders as he had dictated them gave him the authority to coopt regimental groups or smaller, depending on need, but only if they were not currently deployed on some other duty. *If I can't quell a riot with less than a regiment, I won't quell it with anything larger. That's not a threat to Thayer, and it means I won't be countermanding any of his standing orders to the Army as a whole.*

With luck, he wouldn't need to use Imperial soldiers very often, but luck had not been with anyone of late. He already knew that he would have to disperse at least one riot in each city by giving the soldiers orders to kill. It would be the first time in centuries that Imperial soldiers had been used against civilians, and it would come as a tremendous shock. He hoped that the shock would be great enough that he would not need to repeat the lesson. The loss of civilians meant loss of taxpaying workers, and at this point the Empire could not afford to lose much in the way of taxes.

The Imperial Commander had quarters here in Crag Castle, as every Emperor since the Third had preferred to have the Commander of his Armies where he could keep a watchful eye on him. The Third Emperor had originally been the Imperial Commander, and he had not approved of the Second Emperor's choice of Heir. He had taken matters into his own hands the moment that the Second Emperor was dead, and had decided not to give his own Imperial Commander the kind of opportunity that he had taken advantage of. The rest had followed his wise example.

As Melles moved down various corridors and staircases, he passed through narrow zones of warm air alternating with much more extensive zones of chill to positively frigid air. Since the denizens of Crag Castle were now relying on fireplaces and other primitive providers of warmth, heating was unreliable and often unpredictable. There would be illness in the Castle before the year turned to spring; illnesses of the kind more often associated with poorer folk.

The times are... interesting. And likely to become more so before the end.

The corridors themselves never varied in decor, only in size and height; they continued to be built of the same gray marble, and continued to feature only captured weaponry as decoration. Once Melles left the area of the Emperor's Quarters and the official chambers of government, the hallways he traversed became much narrower, and the ceilings dropped to a normal level, but that was the only way to tell that he was not within the quarters of the Emperor himself.

The Imperial Commander was one of the highest-ranking officials in the Council, so his chambers were correspondingly nearer to the Imperial Chambers. Only those of the Heir—which Melles' servants were currently engaged in arranging to suit him—were nearer. The Commander's personal bodyguards stood at attention to either side of the door, showing that the great man himself was inside, as Melles had expected. Melles would shortly have a pair of those guards outside of his own chambers, now that he was the designated Heir. They were not just to protect the life of those they were assigned to, they were meant as protection for the Emperor. The Imperial Guards were an elite group, trained and spell-bound to the service of the Emperor. No force on earth could turn them against Charliss, and if either the Heir or the Imperial Commander proved troublesome, well... only the details of burial would prove troublesome once their guards were finished with them. It *was* possible to break the spells sealing them to the Emperor, and it was possible that the Storms themselves had already done so. The only way to be sure would be to approach them on the question of eliminating the Emperor, and if the spells were intact, that could be a fatal mistake.

Tremane had managed to leave his pair of Imperial Guards behind him when he went off to command the conquest of Hardorn, probably because the Emperor had not expected trouble from him away from Crag Castle. Perhaps, if Charliss had insisted that Tremane take along his watchdogs, things might have turned out differently.

Or perhaps not, except that the Guards would have solved our problem by dispatching Tremane for us, and I would still be Heir. There would still be mage-storms to contend with, the Empire would still be falling to pieces, and all else would be following much the same paths. The only change would be that they would have one less danger to worry about—Melles knew, as no one else in the Court did, that it was by no means certain that Tremane *had* allied himself with Valdemar. In point of fact, he hoped fervently that this was not the case. These mage-storms were bad enough, random and untargeted as they seemed to be; if the mages of Valdemar had at their disposal an expert, one who knew everything there was of any importance about the Empire, what would happen then? What if the Storms could be targeted accurately, to cause the most disruption and damage? If Tremane really *were* to ally himself with Valdemar, that might be what they would have to deal with.

As for what such a revelation would do to the Emperor—

When he was fit and not beset by so many problems, he would simply have been angry, gotten over it, and would dismiss his anger until someone brought him Tremane's head. Now, I cannot be sure, because it is possible that he, like the Empire, is disintegrating, and his sanity will crumble along with his physical body.

He nodded to the two guards, who saluted and stepped aside for him as he displayed the Imperial Seal on the documents he carried. He knocked once on the door, then opened it and stepped inside.

He entered an anteroom, lushly carpeted, with battle-banners on all of the walls, but holding only a monumental desk, three comfortable chairs, and a single servant dressed in a compromise between military uniform and private livery, who was obviously one of Thayer's secretaries.

"I have Imperial orders for the Commander," he told the bland individual behind the desk. "And if the Commander has time for me, I should like to discuss them with him."

Conciliate, be polite and humble. It costs nothing, and keeps the peace.

The secretary immediately rose to his feet, and held out his hand for the orders. "I will deliver the orders to him directly, High Lord Heir," he said smoothly. "Please take a seat. I believe I can assure you that the Commander will always have time to discuss matters of the Empire with you, for he left standing orders with me to admit you to his presence regardless of other circumstances."

As Melles suppressed his surprise, the secretary took the paper from his hand and exited quickly through the doorway behind his desk. Melles took a seat, examining the fingernails of his right hand minutely as a cover for his thoughts. He had been aware since he became a member of the Council that Thayer was an astute politician, but he had not known how astute. Most of the other advisers were still scrambling to decide how to handle Melles now that he was officially the Heir. That Thayer had left standing orders with his underlings to admit Melles at any and all times was an interesting development, and Melles wondered if it meant that the Commander was prepared to cooperate with the new Heir on all levels. If so, that would make Melles' tasks incalculably easier.

To have the Commander of the Imperial Army in my pocket... half the power of the Empire will be divided between us. And the rest, well, that can wait.

The secretary returned before Melles needed to find some other object to examine. "Please follow me, Great Lord," the young man said as he bowed deeply. "The Lord Commander is eager to speak with you without delay."

Melles rose to his feet and followed the secretary into the next room of the suite, this one very similar to the antechamber. The Commander had excellent taste; he had carpeted over most of the floor with one of the rich, plush rugs of the Biijal tribes of the Eastern Islands, some of the more attractive captured battle-banners hung on the walls, and there was a good fire going in the fireplace. Like the antechamber, this room held little in the way of furniture, just another monumental desk, several comfortable chairs, and two smaller tables. Oil lamps served for illumination in place of the mage-lights that would ordinarily have been here; with darkness falling, these had been lit and burned brightly.

General Thayer was waiting, the Imperial Orders in his hand, standing beside his desk rather than sitting behind it. In the silent protocols of the Empire, he was receiving Melles as an equal rather than Melles arriving as a supplicant. This was another good sign; Thayer was not going to challenge his authority at all.

The General could have taken his place in the ranks of his own forces; though his hair was as gray as granite, his body was as hard and tough as that stone. The very few fools who had challenged Thayer to single combat over one pretext or another had not survived the experience. Enemies and friends alike compared him to a wolf—enemies compared him to a ravening, insatiable hunter, friends to the powerful pack leader. Gray as a wolf he was, and his teeth and wits were just as keen.

That sharply-chiseled face wore a friendly, welcoming expression today, however, and although Melles knew the General to be an astute politician, he also knew that Thayer was no good at all at hiding his feelings. As surely as his mind was a great asset, his face was a great handicap in the game of politics. To counter that handicap, Thayer made every attempt to play the game in writing and appeared in person only when policy permitted truth.

The General extended his free hand toward Melles with a smile as the secretary bowed himself out, and Melles took his hand with an answering smile.

"By the Hundred Little Gods, I was hoping you'd come to me first before any of the rest!" Thayer grated. A hilt-thrust to his throat as a young man had left him with a permanently marred voice. "Congratulations, Melles. The Emperor finally made a good choice. Tremane was a little *too* popular with his own men to make me entirely easy in my mind about him."

"Whereas I am so equally unpopular with everyone that you find me more acceptable as Heir?" Melles raised one eyebrow delicately, and Thayer barked a laugh.

"Let's just say that when the Commander discovers that one of his generals is *popular*, it makes him wonder why that general is cultivating popularity." Thayer bared his teeth in a smile as Melles nodded his understanding. "Sometimes it happens that popularity is an accident, but more often than not it's been deliberately sought. You, however—"

"I, who am known as 'Charliss' Executioner' need not trouble himself about such trifles as popularity." Melles softened the comment with a wry smile. "I would rather have respect than popularity."

Thayer answered that sally with a lifted brow of his own. "In that, as in other things, we are like-minded. The Emperor, may he reign long, is not the only one who needs to worry about underlings with ambition, and I am glad enough to see Tremane eliminated. So, about these orders—your idea?"

Melles nodded, carefully gauging Thayer's reactions before saying anything. He need not have been concerned; it was clear that Thayer could not have been more pleased had he dictated the orders himself.

"Damned good idea! Come sit down so we can talk about this in detail." The General waved him to one of the chairs beside the fireplace, and took another, tossing the orders onto the desktop but making no move to place himself behind the desk. Melles took his seat, and the General moved his own chair nearer to that of the Heir before sitting in it. "Damned good idea!" he repeated. "Declare martial law, and you'll have the cits up in arms and starting a revolt in the streets, but bring in the Army without actually *calling* it martial law, and they'll fall in line without a whimper if you can restore order." He coughed. "Give them back their easy lives, and they'll call you a god and not care how you managed it."

"My idea is to use the smallest number of soldiers that I can to crush disturbances absolutely," Melles said cautiously. "I don't want people to begin muttering that we've called out the Army on them; I believe that is one thing the citizens of the Empire won't tolerate. If you'll look at those orders, you'll see I've been given direct command of city guards, constables, and militia. The way I see it, if I use those forces in the front ranks, and only use the Army regulars to back them up and add strength to their line, I'll get the effect that I want without it looking as if the Army is taking over."

"Good. Sound strategy," Thayer confirmed. "Out in the provinces they expect the Army to put down trouble, but the cits think they're above all that. Put down the first riots efficiently, kill a few of the worst troublemakers, and I don't think you'll have any trouble reestablishing order. I was hoping someone would figure out that we're in for a spot of domestic trouble and would plan on dealing with it."

And of course he didn't dare suggest it himself. Charliss would see that as a direct threat to his own authority, and I would have been asked to find General Thayer a—retirement. Thayer knows it, too. He nodded, and leaned back in his chair, feeling much more confident with Thayer as an open ally. "It's not common knowledge, but there have already been small disturbances, and I expect larger ones as food runs short and hardships build up," he said easily. "If we're ready—and ruthless in suppressing the troubles to come—I think the citizens will accept what we do as a necessary evil."

"Yes, as we've said, find a way to get them their meals and peace and the cits will accept anything short of burning down the city," Thayer retorted with contempt. "Now, how exactly do you want me to help? You want a special regiment detached to go wherever it's needed, or—" Thayer paused, looking eager, but a bit reluctant to put forth his own ideas. "Well, I'm a military man, I don't have any experience in riot control, but—

"You have an idea of your own," Melles said, leaning forward with interest. "Please. I'd like to hear it."

"We've still got limited communication mage-to-mage with all the military bases, and you know there's at least one near every large city," Thayer told him. "Now, if *I* were to move a certain number of men, a company, say, into each city—if *you* were to get the militias and city guards and so on organized in the way you want beforehand—well, as soon as a riot started, your city militia would naturally go take care of it, and just as naturally the captain of the company would offer his help. Your militia captain would accept it, and why not, they're both in military brotherhoods, as it were. With the backing of the Army, I don't see any reason why we couldn't squash any riot. And technically, since I doubt every hothead in every city would take it into his head to riot on the same day, you wouldn't be exceeding the number of men you asked for." He grinned slyly. "You see, they'd only be under *your* command for the duration of the riot; after that, they'd come back under my authority."

Melles allowed himself a dry chuckle. General Thayer was obviously a past master at the fine art of manipulating loopholes, and his strategy was an application of the very orders that he had written that he himself had not considered.

But then, I didn't have any reason to suspect that Thayer would make quite such an eager ally.

"That, General, is a brilliant plan; quite perfect for all our purposes," he replied, allowing approval to creep into his voice. The General smiled, a smile with just as much steel in it as warmth.

"Good. We're agreed on it, then." Thayer nodded decisively. "Now, in return, I'd appreciate it if you could do something about some domestic orders for me—not exactly requisitions, more like assignments. It all still comes under the heading of restoring domestic order."

"I'll do what I can." Melles had expected this; trading favor for favor was the accepted way of doing business in Imperial politics. He wouldn't commit himself until he'd heard precisely what Thayer had in mind, but Thayer knew that already.

"Put the Army in charge of all intercity transportation of supplies." Thayer looked him straight in the eyes. "As it is, stuff's being moved inefficiently, *what* gets moved is random, and carters are getting fat no matter what. The Army's suffering, because we're having to pay through the nose, just like the cits are. Conscript the carters, take over the Cartage Guild, make 'em subject to Army discipline, and we'll cure what's causing some of your riots in short order. Every dog in the Empire knows what's going on, and they'll be happy to see the Cartage Guild get what's coming to them. The cits are as tired of the profiteering as I am."

And you and your officers will get fat on the profits, instead of the Cartage Guild. Melles saw right through that one, but Thayer was right about several things. Transportation *was* a hit-or-miss matter right now, and the profits that the carters were making were obscene. Putting the Army in charge would reduce profiteering to an acceptable level, and get transportation organized. And there *had* been unrest over the profiteering; at least one of the riots had destroyed a Cartage Guildhall and the buildings near it.

No, there will be no weeping if I conscript the carters, their beasts, and their vehicles.

The question was, could he get away with that assignment, as an interpretation of the orders that Charliss had just signed?

He unrolled one of his own copies and scanned it quickly, then looked up into Thayer's flat brown eyes. "I think this particular set of commands gives me that authority," he said, knowing that the Emperor wouldn't care so long as he could keep anyone from lodging complaints against it. And since Thayer was going to have pressing reasons to prevent complaints… "When I send out copies of the original orders, I'll see to it that this particular amendment is added."

Thayer smiled with satisfaction. "I'll have my mages get to work," he promised. "By tomorrow night, there'll be companies picked; by the next day I'll have them moving into barracks in the cities. Don't worry; I'll send orders to select steady men, veterans, men who won't panic, won't shoot unless they're ordered, and won't exceed their orders. I'll send captains who have every reason to keep peace, steady men, not sadists who enjoy breaking heads."

Army efficiency, he thought enviously. *It's a beautiful thing to see working.* "My orders will have to travel by signal and sometimes courier, but they'll get to most of the Empire in a fortnight," he replied, and stood up. "It will be a pleasure working with you, Lord Commander," he finished, holding out his hand as the General stood up.

Thayer took it in another firm handclasp. "An equal pleasure here," he said. "And a damned sight better than working with one of the infernal groat-counters, let me tell you!" He followed at Melles' elbow, quite pleased to accompany his visitor to the door.

Melles knew what he meant; several of the possible candidates for Heir were men less of vision than of caution. Few of them would have the imagination to foresee the riots he knew were bound to come, much less to plan how to quell them. "Just remember—we want our actions to be as unobtrusive as possible—so that the citizens welcome the sight of soldiers in the streets rather than fearing it."

Thayer opened the door to the antechamber for him, nodding vigorously. "Exactly. I'll draw up a set of riot orders for you; you look them over and tell me what you want changed." He waved Melles through. "Grevas, see the Lord Heir out, would you? Lord Melles, I can't thank you enough for coming here yourself."

"Think nothing of it; I am glad that we could reach an understanding so quickly." Melles passed into the antechamber where the secretary received him with a deep bow of respect, then hurried to open the door for him. He waved his thanks at the underling, and entered the cold hallway feeling as if he had done a good day's work indeed.

Now, what else? Orders to requisition food if it's necessary, and it will be. And orders to requisition extra beasts and vehicles from the Estates, placing them in the hands of the Army. Have to specify rules about requisitions; taking a farmer's only cart and horse is only going to be counterproductive. Put one of my secretaries on it. Mertun—he was a farmer's son. That would be enough for now; too many orders all at once, and it would cause more unease and unrest than already existed.

And I need to consolidate my personal position. That, fortunately, was mostly a matter of reinforcing his own standing orders to his special operatives. Those operatives would act as needed, and bring him the information he required. And insofar as power in the Council of Advisers and the Court went—well, most mouths would smile and utter compliments, and he would accept them. Action would speak the real truths, and his operatives would ferret out what those same mouths said in private.

There was a single exception to all of that. If the Army could manage to keep their lines of communication open, it meant that they were able to get some magics to work. *Probably those of short duration; and that may be the secret. That, and a great deal of power forcing the magics through. I have power, and I have more than one mage in my own pay. I simply hadn't thought to apply great power to small goals, but maybe those goals are not so small after all, now.*

He hurried down the corridor to his new quarters, only a short distance from the General's, and found his own Imperial bodyguards waiting at the door for him. They opened the door for him with great ceremony, and he was greeted on the other side by his own servants, who surrounded him and began fussing over him immediately with great ceremony and a little fear.

Impatiently, he waved most of them away. His new quarters were fundamentally identical to his old, except that the rooms were a bit larger, the furnishings (those that were not his personal gear) more luxurious, and the suite itself was situated better with regard to conveniences. In the time he'd spent conferring with the Emperor and General Thayer, his servants had removed all signs of the former occupant, and had made it seem as if *he* had always lived here. His own carpets were on the floor, his tapestries and maps on the walls, his books in the cases and on the tables. He went straight to his desk to draft the orders—or rather, elaborations—that were to be appended to the Imperial Orders he had with him. When he had finished, he handed the rough drafts to his own secretary, along with the four copies of the Imperial Orders he still retained.

"Take care of these—and have Mertun specify under what conditions a man's beast and vehicle are to be exempt from requisition," he ordered. His secretary bowed and took the papers out. Only then did he permit himself to relax, putting himself into the care of his valet. His secretary would see that three sets of the Orders got into the hands of the Imperial Clerks for distribution and dissemination. One set would remain here, for use as a reference.

He walked into his private chambers at the direction of his valet; with his own furniture here, in the same positions as in his old rooms, he could almost convince himself that nothing had changed.

Almost. *It's begun. I have started the avalanche; there will be no stopping it now.* He allowed his valet to extract him from his stiff coat of heavy, embroidered satin and help him into a much more comfortable robe. Within a short period of time he was settled in a chair beside a fireplace, with food and drink and a book on the table at his right hand.

He stared into the flames, amused and bemused by everything that had happened today. It had certainly been an *eventful* day, and one he would remember for a long time.

Nevertheless, his day was not yet over. He rang for his valet, and when the man appeared, murmured a certain phrase that meant his operatives were to be contacted and called in, one at a time. *My agents will have to watch for some new things now, as well as the old. My mages—well, if the Army can accomplish communicative magics, perhaps there are a few things that we can accomplish, too.*

It occurred to him that although vengeance on his old enemy Tremane was probably out of the question, at least he ought to be sure just exactly what Tremane was up to. Scrying was another magic of limited scope and duration, and it was just possible that enough could be learned by means of scrying to warn him if Tremane was actually a danger to the Empire.

He settled back, sipped hot spiced wine thoughtfully, and waited for the first of his spies to appear. No, much as he would like to, he could not dispose of that annoying Tremane—but he could not ignore the man either.

And in the kind of war *he* waged, the best and most reliable weapon was knowledge.

It was time to wield that particular weapon, and with more finesse and care than he had ever exercised before.

4

The cavernous interior of Urtho's Tower was remarkably quiet with the gryphons gone. An'desha hadn't quite realized until now how much sound the gryphons produced—like the constant click of talons on stone, the windlike bellows-sound of their breathing and the rustle of feathers. He'd gotten used to those whispers of sound, and without them, his own voice seemed unnaturally loud despite the sussuration of other activity.

"Look here, it's really quite logical," An'desha said, with one finger under the line of characters—the same words, written in three different languages. Karal peered at them, his forehead creasing with concentration. "This is the Hawkbrother, this is the Shin'a'in, and you can see how similar—"

A muffled *thud* interrupted him, followed by the sound of alarmed and complaining voices. Startled, he looked up, past Karal and into the central room of the Tower.

He knew those voices, although he had not expected to hear them today. He got up and moved to the doorway, just to see if he was somehow mistaken.

He wasn't. The aged Imperial mage Sejanes, in his robes of oddly military cut, was a strange contrast to Master Artificer Levy in his practical, yet luxurious, black silk and leather. Both of them, however, looked pale and ill and much the worse for their travel. Walking ahead of them was Altra.

"By the Hundred Little Gods!" said Sejanes, every hair on his gray head standing straight out. "If I *never* have to travel this way again, it will be too soon!"

Master Levy swallowed, looking to An'desha as if he were fighting to keep his stomach from revolting. His face had a greenish tint, and the knuckles of his clenched fists were white. "I... quite agree with you, Sejanes," he said in a strangled voice. "I believe that, given the option, I will walk home."

Altra looked at both of them with unconcealed contempt, stalking off into Karal's side room to bonelessly flop down onto the foot of Karal's pallet. An'desha followed him. An'desha didn't "hear" the Firecat say anything, but Karal pulled his mostly-untouched bowl of stew over to the cat, who gratefully inhaled it as if he hadn't eaten in weeks.

Meanwhile, Firesong, Lo'isha, Silverfox, and two of the Shin'a'in hurried over to greet the aged mage and younger Master Artificer. There wasn't much in the way of furniture here, but Silverfox brought both of them folding stools to sit on, and they sagged down onto that support with evident gratitude. An'desha didn't blame either of the newcomers for their reactions; he knew from personal experience that they were not exaggerating their exhaustion and illness.

An'desha had traveled once in the care of Altra the Firecat, in the creature's bizarre distance-devouring method of transportation called "Jumping," and he would not particularly care to experience it again. The Firecats were somehow able to cross great distances in the blink of an eye, and could take with them whatever or whoever was touching them. The experience was a gut-wrenching one, similar to a Gate-crossing, but repeated over and over with each Jump. The closer together the Jumps were, the worse the effect was. The amount of cumulative effect varied with each person, but from the look of these two, Altra hadn't paused much between Jumps and this latest journey had been quite a rough ride for them.

An'desha watched for a moment, but Firesong, Silverfox, and the rest seemed to have the situation well in hand. Sejanes clearly needed to go lie down, and Master Levy to sit down and have something to settle his stomach. After a brief rest, both of them were taken into the vacant side chamber that had earlier served as the gryphons' nest. Karal, meanwhile, was fussing over Altra, who, for the first time in An'desha's experience, was looking rather shopworn. Evidently the trip hadn't been easy on him either.

He remembered what Altra had said about the fact that even Jumping had become much more difficult. "Are you feeling all right?" he asked the cat, as Karal hovered over him anxiously.

:I have felt better,: the Firecat replied dryly. *:But I believe that with a short rest and food, I shall be fine. The currents in the energy-fields are vicious. It has become very dangerous to Jump even a tenth of my usual distances. I do think that from here on in I, too, would prefer to walk where I need to go, given the choice.:*

The clacking of hooves on the floor signaled the arrival of the Companion Florian. *:Oh, don't be ridiculous, Altra,:* the Companion said mockingly. *:Of course you won't have to walk. You'll convince one of us to carry you.:*

Altra ignored him, pretending to concentrate on the vital task of licking the bowl clean. That didn't take too long, and as soon as the last hint of gravy was gone, he curled up in such a way that he wouldn't be in the way of Karal's feet if the young Karsite needed to rest. *:I'm going to sleep now,:* the Firecat said with great dignity, and he closed his eyes firmly, still ignoring Florian's jibe.

Florian made a whickering sound that was so like a chuckle that there was no doubt in An'desha's mind what the Companion was thinking. "Oh, leave him alone, Florian," he told the Companion. "At least for now. You can't deny that he has done more than his share for some time to come. If Gating is dangerous, how could Jumping be less than hazardous?"

:True enough,: Florian replied equitably. *:You are correct, An'desha, and I am at fault here. Altra has served heroically, and I should not have teased him, especially not when he is as exhausted as his passengers. I beg your pardon, cat.:*

:And I grant it, horse,: came from the seemingly-sleeping Firecat.

Florian stepped over and touched his nose to the Firecat's fur in a conciliatory gesture, then backed off to the chamber entrance. He stood with one eye cast toward the main chamber, and the other watching over Altra and his friends, before finally quietly clopping off.

"Well. We have everyone we need," An'desha said to Karal. "Except perhaps that Kaled'a'in scholar we have been promised. We can certainly resume investigating the other devices we found."

"I keep thinking that there are more rooms and chambers we haven't found yet," Karal replied, lying back down on his pallet, taking care to not to disturb Altra.

"There probably are," An'desha told him. "We've found signs of at least four more places where there might be storage chambers or even a passage to a lower level. The problem is that we haven't been able to get them open. Perhaps Sejanes or Master Levy will be able to help there." He smiled at his friend. "To tell you the truth, I suspect it will be Master Levy; I have the feeling that the tricks to getting these hatches open are purely mechanical."

Karal smiled back. "I think you may be right. That would fit well enough with what Treyvan was able to tell me about the Mage of Silence. It would be like him to put a mechanical catch in a place of magic, knowing that anyone who came here intending mischief would probably be expecting magic and not be prepared for mechanics."

An'desha chuckled. "And that would certainly put Firesong's nose out of joint. Poor Firesong! At every turn, it seems as if his great powers as an Adept are less and less important!"

Karal nodded and rubbed the back of his neck in thought. "It must be awfully difficult for him to face each day. Just look at what has happened. He went from being the brightest star in the skies to... finding his powers unreliable and lessened, with new methods to do what he used to do coming up every day. Some of them are even contradictory to what he has known as fact all his life."

An'desha frowned and nodded. "Sometimes I feel like I cheated him out of his glory by being who and what I am, but I know that none of us dictated or could have predicted the way things would unfold. I owe him my life, by the Star-Eyed's grace, and I am grateful to him, but I wish that he could feel the happiness now that he used to enjoy in the Vales. And as for things being contradictory—you've been experiencing much of that yourself, spiritually. So have we all, I think." He paused, fingers tented as he carefully considered his next words. "Still—Master Levy says that all things in our world, no matter how illogical they may seem, are still consistent under unseen laws. The spirits I have spoken with on the Moonpaths have implied much the same—that magic in all its forms works under those laws as surely as rain, wind, and beasts do. Perhaps Firesong, and all of us, are learning new aspects of the laws we have been subject to all our lives."

"With Master Levy here to confound us all with his teachings on universal laws, you'll need me for a secretary again," Karal said as he smoothed down his warm robes, brightening considerably. "I'll be glad to be useful again."

An'desha nodded with sympathy; he knew how idleness, even enforced, had fretted his friend, and he would also be glad to see Karal feeling as if he were contributing his share. Realistically, Karal was not able to help at all with brute-force physical tasks, but the role of secretary was perfect for him.

He would have said something, but he noticed that Karal seemed very tired, and it occurred to him that the two of them had been working quite steadily on comparing Shin'a'in, Tayledras, and Kaled'a'in writing ever since breakfast. Mental work could be just as exhausting as physical labor, even for those, like Karal, who had a knack for it.

"Why don't you look after Altra for a while?" he said, cleverly using the Firecat as an excuse to get Karal to rest. "I'll go see if our hosts want to know anything about Sejanes and Master Levy."

Karal nodded, and caressed Altra with one hand while he closed his eyes. An'desha collected the empty stew bowl and made a mental note to get something more suited to Altra's tastes from the Shin'a'in.

He left Karal beginning to doze, Altra already asleep, and Florian watching over them both, and went out into the main chamber in the center of the Tower. Master Levy, already recovered, was examining the floor of that chamber on his hands and knees. He looked up as An'desha entered.

"Has anyone looked at the floor here?" he asked.

"We looked, but we didn't see anything," the Shin'a'in replied. "Why? Have you found something?"

"Perhaps." Master Levy got to his feet. "When I was still studying, I used to earn spending money by designing and helping to build hidden doors and chambers for wealthy or eccentric clients. I think there might be something here."

"Huh." An'desha looked closely at the floor, and had to shake his head. "I'll take your word for it. Do you think you can get it open—if there is anything there?"

"Perhaps," Master Levy repeated. "I'll have to examine it later, when I'm not exhausted. This is all sheer nervous energy, you see, plus a rather stupid wish to seem in better physical shape than old Sejanes, and it's all about to run out. I'm going to get a bowl of that stew I smell, and then I am going to sleep for a day."

An'desha laughed, as Master Levy shrugged ruefully and with self-deprecation. As the Master Artificer drifted in the direction of their little charcoal stove and the bubbling stewpot atop it, he started back toward Karal. But halfway there, he turned, a little surprised, as a soft voice hailed him.

It was one of the few black-clad Kal'enedral, and with him was another wearing dark blue. The one in black he knew; Ter'hala, an old man whose blood-feud would technically never be completed, because the one who murdered his oathbrother had been Mornelithe Falconsbane. It was doubly ironic that An'desha and Ter'hala had become friends over the past few days. Ter'hala knew who and what he had been, of course. An'desha, understandably nervous, had asked him why he continued to wear black; Ter'hala had laughed and said that he was used to the color and too old to change.

"Ter'hala!" An'desha greeted him. "Who is your friend?"

The Kal'enedral sketched a salute of greeting. "This is Che'sera, young friend. He wished to meet you."

An'desha bowed slightly. "I am always honored to meet one of the servants of the Wise One," he said politely, though he could not for the life of him imagine what had brought so many of the reclusive "Scrollsworn"—as he called them, to distinguish them from the true Swordsworn—out of Kata'shin'a'in and their stronghold there. "We are all truly grateful for the hospitality and tolerance you have shown to us."

I wonder if the reason is that we've just added two more meddlers to the group, and one of them is a mage from a completely unknown land, he thought, though he kept his thoughts to himself. *Not that I blame them. We're the interlopers here; the Star-Eyed gave them the keeping of this Tower and its secrets, not us.*

Che'sera returned his bow. "I am pleased to meet you, An'desha," he replied, his voice so carefully neutral that An'desha could not read any second meaning into the words. "It is not often that one of the Plains who goes to become a mage ever returns again."

"It is not often that the shamans permit him to return," An'desha replied, as calmly and carefully as he could, although he could in no way match the lack of inflection in Che'sera's voice. "Until only recently, mages have been forbidden the Plains, even those of the People."

"Well, and you can certainly see why," Che'sera countered immediately, gesturing at the Tower remains about them. "This would all have been a great temptation. Can you say, had you become a mage of the Tale'edras, that you would not have been tempted to try to use one of these weapons against the one they called Falconsbane?"

An'desha shuddered. He still had far too many of Falconsbane's memories of the life he had led using An'desha's body for comfort—and behind those memories marched others, a seemingly endless parade of atrocities stretching back into a dim past as ancient as this Tower.

"I would," he admitted slowly. "I would have been tempted by anything that might have brought the monster down. Anything that would have saved others from the horror he wrought."

Che'sera shrugged. "And yet it took *how* many of you, working together, to simply use the energy of one of these weapons rather than the weapon itself?"

"And yet you permit us here now." An'desha allowed one eyebrow to rise.

"We do, and that is in part why I wished to speak with you," Che'sera told him. "May we speak privately, you and I, for a little while, Shin'a'in to Shin'a'in?"

Now An'desha was considerably more surprised, and not at all certain what Che'sera had in mind. This was the first time in his reckoning that any of the Shin'a'in here had addressed him in such a fashion; most seemed uncomfortable with the concept of a Shin'a'in who was also a mage, and some seemed of the personal opinion that his half-foreign blood made him more alien than Shin'a'in. "Certainly, if that is what you wish." He nodded toward the sleeping chamber. "My friend Karal is asleep in there; he will not hear us, and if we speak quietly, we will not disturb him. I fear that is the most privacy I can offer, as it is in somewhat short supply here despite the vastness of the place."

Che'sera nodded. "That will do," he said, and gestured to An'desha to lead him onward.

An'desha did so, walking with great care past Karal and Altra, although neither stirred, nor in fact gave any indication that they were alive except for their steady breathing. At the moment he was suffering from mixed feelings; he was both curious and apprehensive to hear what Che'sera wanted to say that required privacy.

He gestured at his own pallet, waiting until Che'sera took a seat at the foot before seating himself.

"So," he said, wondering what he was letting himself in for. "What is it you wish of me, Sworn One?"

When Che'sera left him at last, he sat back against the gently-curving stone wall and simply thought of nothing for a while. He felt as if Che'sera had taken his mind, had turned it upside-down and shaken it, examined it, poked and prodded it, turned it inside out, and then, when he was finished, put it all neatly back in place with the ends tucked in.

He had probably been the most skillful interrogator that An'desha *or* any of Falconsbane's many incarnations had ever encountered. *You know, I suspect that at this point he could predict my reaction to virtually any situation, and do so with more accuracy than I could!*

Although his questions had covered virtually every subject, Che'sera seemed particularly interested in the Avatars. That was the one thing that hadn't surprised him, since virtually all of the Sworn had wanted to know about Dawnfire and Tre'valen sooner or later. Some of them here had actually been present when Dawnfire, trapped in the body of her bondbird, had been transformed into an Avatar in the first place. It had occurred to An'desha that as far as *he* was concerned, such a transformation was a poor substitute for returning Dawnfire to her proper human form. But then again, perhaps that had not been possible; granted, the Star-Eyed had been able to undo most of the changes Falconsbane had run on An'desha's own body, but that was in the nature of restoring something to its rightful state, not changing it into something else altogether.

Perhaps all that She would have been able to manage would have been transformation into a tervardi, *one of the bird-people, and that might have been a truly cruel "reward" for her, since the* tervardi *are frail and not very humanlike. At least this way, she is still fundamentally herself and she is anything but frail.*

He also sensed that there were other complications to the story that no one had told him about. And there was, of course, the factor that Dawnfire had been mourned for dead, and her human body buried when the bond to it was snapped by Falconsbane. It didn't necessarily do for a deity to resurrect people; the question would inevitably arise: "Why this one and not *my* father, mother, sibling, lover." Better, on the whole, not to do any such thing. Look at all the effort that the Companions went to in order to preserve the secret of their own nature, and they weren't even returning as humans!

Just such philosophical questions had arisen in the course of Che'sera's questioning—though on his part, rather than Che'sera's—and the Sworn One had neatly deflected them. Perhaps it had been because Che'sera wanted him to think of possible answers for himself; there had been that kind of feeling as the conversation progressed.

And in all of that, I didn't learn a thing about Che'sera himself. Now that was truly unusual, since Falconsbane had been a rather skilled interrogator and some of that expertise was available to An'desha. Given the proper occasion, that was one of Falconsbane's abilities that An'desha did not mind coopting, but he had not been able to insert so much as a single personal question of his own the entire time the two of them spoke. Che'sera was most unusual, even for the Sworn.

An'desha rubbed his temples, feeling as if he should have a headache after all that Che'sera had put him through, even though he did not.

Activity, that was what was called for. There were dishes to wash, there was clothing to mend, and there were all manner of things to be done. Or perhaps he ought to go look at the food supplies the Shin'a'in had brought, and see if there was something more that could be done with them than the seemingly endless round of soups and stews they had been presented with thus far. He wasn't precisely a grand cook, but he did have experience in dishes that no one else here did.

He rose and went in search of something useful to do.

The clothing and kitchen work had already been taken care of, but as it turned out, there was something new he could concoct in the way of dinner for them all. There was fresh meat, brought in by Shin'a'in hunters; there were beans and a few other winter vegetables such as onions, and there were spices and dried peppers. That particular combination reminded him of a recipe Karal had made up for him once, when they'd been too late to catch dinner with either the Court or the Heraldic students. He diced some of the meat and hot peppers and browned them together, added onions, beans and sweet spice, and set it all to cook slowly. While all of those ingredients had been used before, no one in the group had ever used them in that combination. It would definitely be different from anything the Shin'a'in had been cooking, and that was what he was looking for.

It had taken a long time to dice the meat as finely as the recipe called for, and having his hands busy allowed his mind to rest. His mind wasn't the only thing resting, however, and although Karal was still sleeping, others were awake again. At about the time he finished with his concoction, Master Levy was out in the main room on his hands and knees, looking intently at the floor, and prying at invisible cracks with some very tiny tools he took from a pouch at his belt.

An'desha washed up the utensils he'd used for his preparations, dried his hands, and went out to join him, though no one else seemed at all interested in what he was doing. "Is there anything I can do to help?" he asked, sitting on his heels just behind the Master Artificer.

"Well, there *is* something here, all right," Master Levy replied in an absent tone. "This is a movable stone, and I would guess that it drops down and fits into a slot carved into the rock. It may take me a while to figure out the release, though. Tell me something, do you have any idea if this mage thought in patterns, in *numbers* of things? As in—oh, the Karsites think in terms of one, seven, or eight—if they build a device with a catch, it will either have a single trigger-point or seven. That's because they have a single God, but in the usual representations of Vkandis as the sun rising, there are seven rays coming from it and in the ones of the sun-in-glory there are eight rays. The Rethwellans almost always use three, for the three faces of their Goddess. Most Valdemarans use three or two, three for the same reason as the Rethwellans, or two for the God and Goddess. It's not a conscious thing, it's just the kind of patterns that people establish as very small children."

"You might try four," An'desha said, after a moment of thought. "Urtho shared the Kaled'a'in faith, if he shared anything religious with anyone, and that's the same as the Shin'a'in. Except where it's free-flowing and curvy, there's a great deal of square and diamond symmetry in the decorations around here."

Master Levy grunted what sounded like thanks, and seemed to widen his scope of examination a bit.

Finally he sat back on his haunches, stretched all his fingers and shook his head. "Shall we see if we're supremely lucky and we're not dealing with a random placing?" he asked An'desha, his saturnine face showing rather more humor than An'desha was used to seeing from him. "If your guess is right, I think I've found all four trigger points; if *mine* is right, this far inside his Tower Urtho would not have bothered to be terribly clever about hiding his additional workrooms and the catches won't be difficult. I don't suppose you've got a clue about an order in which to push four trigger-points, do you?"

"If you're not supposed to push all of them at once, you mean?" An'desha thought again. "East, South, West, and North. That's the order in rituals, with the Maiden being in the East and the Crone in the North."

"That sounds as good a guess as any. Let's see what happens."

Master Levy reached out with one of his tools, but An'desha shot out a hand to stop him. "Wait a minute!" he stammered. "If you do this wrong, is anything likely to—well—go wrong? Will the ceiling fall in and crush us, or poison gas start seeping in here, or something?"

Master Levy paused. "There is that possibility," he began, and laughed at An'desha's expression. "Oh, for Haven's sake, it's not very likely he'd put something like that *in the floor* now, is it? Where it might be triggered by accident just by people standing on it?"

An'desha flushed, embarrassed. "I suppose not," he replied, letting go of Master Levy's hand.

The Master Artificer continued his interrupted task, depressing a small spot in the stone of the floor. An'desha noted with fascination that it remained depressed so that if one had placed a coin on the spot, it would be flush with the rest of the floor. Master Levy then touched a second, and a third, both of which also remained depressed after he touched them, and although An'desha had not been able to spot the second place, once he had the distance between the first and second, he was able to deduce the locations of the third and fourth spot before Master Levy touched them. An'desha held his breath in anticipation when the Master Artificer pushed on that last place.

Nothing happened for a long moment, and An'desha sighed with disappointment. Master Levy however, had his head cocked to one side, and as An'desha sighed, he stood up, looked fixedly at a place in the pattern of the floor shaped like an octagon, then stamped sharply down on one corner of it with his boot heel.

With a reluctant, grating sound, the stone moved a trifle, dropping down by about the width of a thumb.

Master Levy stamped downward again, and the stone moved a bit more. "It's stuck. Old, you know," he quipped. He continued urging it with carefully-placed blows of his heel as it dropped down about the distance of a man's hand measured from the end of the middle finger to the wrist, then began to slide sideways. Once there was a sliver of a gap between the octagonal stone and the rest of the floor, he got down on hands and knees again, and peered at it.

By now, thanks to the sounds of stamping and the grating of stone-on-stone, he had attracted the attention of everyone in the Tower who was not asleep. "Will you look at that!" Silverfox exclaimed, as the curious gathered around. "We never guessed that was there!"

"I am looking at it. I think I'm going to need something to pry with," Master Levy replied. "The mechanisms are rather stuck, which shouldn't be too surprising considering their age. I'm afraid once I get this open, it's not going to shut again."

"I don't see a problem with that," Firesong said, dropping down on his heels to peer at the stone himself, beside Master Levy, while Silverfox went off to get a pry bar from a Plainsman. "If there's anything down there worth bothering with, we wouldn't want to close it, and if there isn't, we'll clean out the trash and use it for sleeping quarters or something."

Master Levy grunted and nodded his head as he felt along the crack with great care, then put his nose to the crack to sniff at it gingerly. "I don't smell anything that shouldn't be down there," he said after a long moment while he concentrated on the scent with his eyes closed. "And I always did have the best nose in my year-group. When the students were experimenting, my Alchemy Master always used to count on me to know when to evacuate the workroom if something went wrong."

"Comforting, considering there might be a mechanism to release poisons into the room below, if not this one," said Sejanes, coming up to the rest with his hair all rumpled from sleeping. Silverfox arrived at that moment with the pry bar and shook his head at the Imperial mage.

"Not Urtho, and especially not in his own Tower," the *kestra'chern* said decisively. "He was a compassionate and considerate man, safe and resourceful but not vengeful. He would only create wards to protect things, not to punish. He wouldn't have taken the risk that a curious *hertasi* or some other innocent might set such a thing loose."

Sejanes looked skeptical, but didn't say anything. Silverfox, however, read the look correctly.

"You're not dealing with the Empire, Sejanes," he said. "You're not dealing with people looking to gain in rank by whatever means it takes. Urtho's personal servants and close friends were loyal enough to die for him—and many did, to his sorrow. Here in the heart of his personal stronghold, he would not have used safeguards that could harm his own people as well as intruders."

Master Levy inserted the tongue of the pry bar in the crack, and pulled.

The stone grated, and moved slightly, then kept on moving for a little after Master Levy stopped pulling. Now the gap was about as wide as a large man's palm.

"Do we want to investigate before we open this any further?" the Artificer asked Silverfox. "I defer to your judgment, since you seem to know more about the master of this place than anyone else here."

Silverfox looked pointedly at An'desha, who shook his head in answer to the silent question. "My knowledge is tainted, since it comes from his enemy," he said at once. "Ma'ar is far more likely to have underestimated a foe he considered sentimental and soft."

"It wouldn't hurt to drop a lantern down on a string," Silverfox said to Master Levy. "Then at least we'll be able to see what we're dealing with. For all we know, this is just a well, and not any kind of a storeroom or workroom."

"A source of water other than melted snow from the surface would be welcome," Lo'isha murmured quietly. Master Levy heard him, and nodded in answer to both statements.

This time it was An'desha's turn to go off and rummage for a lantern and some appropriately strong string. They hadn't needed lanterns since they arrived here, although the Shin'a'in had brought some, just in case the magical lights failed. The magic lamps hanging from the center of the ceiling of each room had been quite enough to serve their needs and showed no signs of being harmed at all by the mage-storms that made magic problematic outside the Tower. An'desha dug one of the lanterns out of a pile of articles no one had found a use for, and got some string from the kitchen area. He filled the lamp with oil, trimmed the wick with thread clippers from a sewing kit, and lit it before bringing it out to the rest.

Master Levy made the handle fast to the string and lowered the lantern down into the cavity while the others crowded around. An'desha couldn't see anything from his vantage, and neither could most of the Shin'a'in.

"Well?" called Che'sera. "What's there?"

"Stairs, mostly," Master Levy replied. "So this isn't a well. I believe I see something like furniture at the bottom, but the light doesn't go very far down."

"It's not dimming in bad air, is it?" An'desha asked anxiously, vague memories of tomb openings intruding from one of Falconsbane's previous lives. "Even if there are no poisons, the air could have gone bad from what's been sealed inside."

"No, it's burning brightly enough. It's just a long way down to the next floor and the light is between me and what's down there," Master Levy replied. "It is an issue of contrast and visual acuity. Well, no help for it. Back to hard labor."

He inserted the tongue of the pry bar and continued to lever the stubborn stone out of the way, while at least a couple of the observers looked at each other, wondering why the Artificer used such flowery terms to say he couldn't see well. Suddenly, with no warning whatsoever, the frozen mechanism gave way. The stone slid beneath the floor into hiding, and Master Levy, taken completely off guard, fell over backward, the pry bar dropping out of his hands and clanging end-over-end down the staircase.

Only An'desha remained to assist the winded Artificer to his feet; the rest of the spectators made a rush for the stair with Firesong in the lead. In mere moments they had descended out of sight; then Firesong spoke a single word, light poured up from below, and muffled exclamations were drifting up through the hole in the floor.

"You might say 'thank you!'" Master Levy called after them, and sighed, rubbing his hip where he had landed. "We may as well go find out what they've discovered. I only hope it isn't Urtho's treasury; there isn't a great deal of good that gold and gems would do us in this situation."

"Urtho's treasury would have books, not baubles," An'desha assured him. "But we ought to go down, too, before they all get carried away in their enthusiasm."

Master Levy went with An'desha following him, taking the stone stairs carefully, for they were quite steep. They also went down farther than he expected, for the stone floor of the room above was at least as thick as his hand was long, perhaps a little thicker, which accounted for the fact that it hadn't rung hollow and had sounded like solid stone to their footsteps. It looked as if this room had actually been hollowed out of the bedrock after the Tower itself had been built.

Although the air was a bit stuffy and very dusty, with a hint of strange metallic scents, it was not at all damp. Nor was the room as gloomy and ill-lit as An'desha had anticipated. There were more of those magical lights everywhere, and as An'desha looked around, he had no doubt at all just what Urtho had used this room for. It was a workshop, with everything necessary for an inveterate tinkerer who was interested in literally everything.

Needless to say, the room was very crowded, despite the fact that it was just a little smaller than the main room above. This was not a mage's classical workroom, a place where *only* magic took place, and few if any physical components were needed. This was a place where anything and everything could be worked with, played with, investigated. Here was a bench with an array of glassware and rows of jars that had once held chemicals both liquid and solid—most of the former long since evaporated, leaving only dust or oily residue in the bottoms of their bottles. There stood another bench with a small lathe, clamps, a vise, and tools for working wood and ivory, and beside it a similar bench with the tools for shaping soft metals, and a third bench with the tools for cutting and polishing lenses, glass, and crystal. Looking incongruous beside that was a potter's wheel and glassblower's pipes, and along the back wall were a forge, a kiln, a glassmaker's furnace, and a smelter. They probably had once shared a chimney, long since blocked up by the destruction of the Tower above. There were more benches and work spaces set up, but from the staircase An'desha could not tell what they were, only that most of them had been in use up to the day of the Cataclysm.

An'desha simply stood and stared as the others wandered about, looking, but not touching. Master Levy, on the other hand, looked supremely satisfied by what he saw, as he surveyed it all from the staircase.

"Now this is much more in my way of doing things," he said, folding his arms across his chest and looking over the workshop with approval. "I believe I could have liked this Urtho."

On all of the benches—*all* of them—were projects in various states of completion. It was difficult to tell what some of them had been intended to do, if anything. There were pages of notes arrayed neatly beside each of these projects; it appeared that, in his workplace at least, Urtho was a tidy and methodical man. Firesong stood beside a particular bench laden with some very odd equipment indeed. He gazed on these pieces of paper with longing, although he forbore to touch them.

"This is maddening," he complained, hovering over a small sheaf of scrawled manuscript. "I'm afraid even to breathe on these things for fear that they'll fall to dust, but I think I may die if I can't read what's on the next page!"

But something about the way the "paper" looked stirred echoes in An'desha's deepest memories; he descended the last few stairs and made his way over to what appeared to be a small jeweler's workbench. There was a half-finished brooch there, nothing magical or mechanical, obviously *just* a piece of jewelry in the shape of a hummingbird to be inlaid with a mosaic of tiny agate-pieces formed into stylized feathers. "Wait," he muttered. The original design lay next to it, and after a close examination of the sheet, An'desha picked it up.

Silverfox stifled a gasp, and Firesong bit off a protest. He waved the intact and flexible drawing at them to prove it was not hurt by handling.

"Pick up what you want," he urged. "It's not paper. Or rather, it isn't like the paper we know and use now. It's a special rag-paper treated with resins so it wouldn't disintegrate. You can write on it in silverpoint, crayon, or graphite-stick, but not ink; ink just beads up and won't penetrate."

"Really?" Master Levy walked to the bench nearest him and picked up another piece of the paper. "Very useful around chemicals, I would guess."

"Very useful around anything that might ruin your notes," Firesong observed, snatching up the papers he had stared at so covetously. "Oh— now *this*—oh, my—" He held the papers up so that Silverfox could peruse them, too, as between them they tried to decipher Urtho's notes in ancient Kaled'a'in, using the Hawkbrother tongue Firesong knew and Silverfox's modern Kaled'a'in as guides.

Che'sera looked at them curiously, but Lo'isha laughed at their immediate absorption. "Oh, we have lost them for a time," he said indulgently. "I know that look. The weaver is one with the loom!"

"Not entirely," Firesong responded absently. "But I will be very pleased when this scholar of Silverfox's shows up, so he can help us with this. If these notes are right, this *may* be the answer to our isolation here." He waved a hand at the bench and what looked to be a pair of mirrors serving as the lids to a matching pair of boxes. "These are completed, or all but some cosmetic frippery, and they're *supposed* to act like a pair of linked scrying spells, except they don't use true-magic, they use mind-magic. Apparently it can work over unknown, incredible distances. Somehow they amplify it so that it only needs *one* person with mind-magic to make both boxes work, or so I think this says."

That made every head in the place turn toward the Adept, and he finally looked up from the notes he was sharing with Silverfox, shaking his hair out of his eyes. "Got your attention then, did I?" he asked, with a sly smile.

:If these devices use mind-magic, they won't be disrupted by the mage-storms,: commented a mental voice from above, and Altra flowed gracefully down the staircase, taking a seat on one of the steps at about head-height to the humans. *:That would be more than merely useful. If we learned*

how to use them, I could take one to Haven; if we learned how to make them, I could take another to Solaris. And I certainly have enough mind-magic to make them work, no matter who wishes to use them.:

"I thought you said that you didn't want to Jump anymore," Firesong said sardonically. An'desha chuckled.

:I don't want to, but devices like these could replace that aspect of my duties as well as give us the resources of all of Master Levy's colleagues at Haven,: the Firecat replied with immense dignity. *:For that matter, if we could concoct a third device, I would not necessarily have to Jump it to Solaris; Hansa could come and get it instead.:*

An'desha hid a smile at the unspoken implication behind Altra's statement, an implication that Altra felt his colleague and fellow Firecat had been getting off a bit too easily in the transportation department.

:Our ability to Jump is partly true-magic, partly mind-magic,: the Firecat continued, for once without any hint of irony or mockery in his mind-voice. *:It is growing hazardous for passengers to Jump with us, as Master Levy and Sejanes discovered. It is no longer comfortable for us to Jump very long distances, and I was not exaggerating earlier about how I felt when we arrived. I was exhausted and drained, not a common occurrence until now. I can predict a time very soon when it could become actually inconceivably dangerous for us to Jump. But if we have a way to communicate with Haven and Karse—such a thing would be beyond price.:*

"I *had* deduced that for myself, thank you," Firesong replied with a touch of acid. "If you can just conjure up that Kaled'a'in scholar, we have a chance of learning how to use these things before the time comes when you can't take one back to Valdemar."

"The scholar will be here soon," Che'sera put in, looking up from the glassware bench. His dark-blue clothing reflected richly from the surface of the dusty glassware. "The main problem has been that since his assistant is a—what do you call the lizard-folk—?"

"*Hertasi*," Silverfox interjected. The handsome *kestra'chern's* face lit up at Che'sera's words. "Ah, so it *is* Tarrn who is coming! Oh, that is very good; he may be frail, but he is the finest scholar in the ancient version of our tongue outside the lands of White Gryphon, and a good being as well." Silverfox seemed immensely relieved by what Che'sera had said, and that in itself made An'desha feel as if they were all beginning to make some progress at last.

"Yes. It seems the problem has been to find a way to bring both of them in a gryphon four-harness carry-basket and still keep the *hertasi* warm without magic." Che'sera left the glassware-bench, and moved back toward the staircase. "When I left, a means had been devised, and they were planning on arriving within two or three days of when I expected to be here. They had only to manufacture this device, whatever it was, and then they could leave. I would have told you earlier, when I first arrived, but you all seemed quite busy, and I had business with An'desha that I wished to conclude before I dealt with anything else."

"That is even better news!" Now Firesong seemed much happier as well, so much so that he forbore to comment on that last statement. "I vote that if we can't, on superficial examination, find anything more important to investigate than these devices, we'll concentrate on those for our immediate goal. If we can communicate with all of the mages and Artificers on a regular basis, it will be as good as being at Haven with all the advantages of being here in the Tower to implement what we deduce."

He looked around at the rest of the party, most of whom shrugged with indifference or bafflement. "You and Sejanes should be the ones to decide. I'll be of very little use without a translator in any event," Master Levy said with great candor. "At the moment, I have nothing really to work on, as I believe we need to develop a new set of theories to match the changed conditions. Those, I feel, must come from things we can learn by studying the Cataclysm itself and Urtho's own methodologies. So until the translator arrives, what I can and will do, is attempt to find out if this place holds any more secrets in the floor."

"Very little use!" Firesong actually snorted. "After you were the one who *found* this place! No false modesty, thank you, Master Levy!"

"I may be of some slight assistance here below," Che'sera said, with great caution. "I shall examine those objects that seem to partake of the nature of the shaman, and see if I may make something of them. We Shin'a'in lost some things when the Cataclysm destroyed our land and sundered the Clans. I may be able to rediscover some of what was lost, and that may be of some help."

Hah! An'desha thought with triumph. *Now I know what you are, o mysterious one! Both Sworn to the Old One and a shaman! Now, is it a need to keep an eye on all these mages that brings you here, or was it the hope of keeping us from finding things that the Clans would rather we didn't learn? Is it an interest in what you might find within the walls of this Tower, or is it something else altogether? Myself, perhaps?*

It could be, but he was not going to have the hubris to assume that the latter was the case. There were plenty of reasons for the Kal'enedral to want a shaman here; most of the Sworn were not *leshy'a* with a direct link to the Star-Eyed, though they could all walk the Moonpaths when they chose. Although An'desha had seen more than one or two of the Veiled Ones about, they had never stayed for very long, and he had the feeling that they were not "permitted" to take a physical form for too long—perhaps just long enough to serve some specific need, or be in themselves a kind of message.

The Moonpaths... perhaps I ought to go walk them myself. I haven't seen or spoken to Tre'valen and Dawnfire since we burned out that weapon of Urtho's.

Firesong looked up, as if distracted for a moment, and cast a speculative look at An'desha. "You know," he began, "it is all too fortuitous, that we find these things."

An'desha smiled a little as he noticed Che'sera looking at him in a similar way. He heard himself saying, "It is the way of the Star-Eyed to provide such opportunities for those who will help themselves. If I were you, I'd be careful with these new finds, for She is unlikely to hand over easy answers. The mind that controls the hand must use the tool wisely, and all tools can harm their user."

Firesong grunted, and actually looked for a moment as if he could be considering those words in the way a Shin'a'in would acknowledge the cryptic advice of a shaman as being worthy of meditation. Then the Adept shrugged a little and made off with the sheaf of notes.

An'desha looked about the workshop to see what the others were doing; Che'sera cracked a slight smile and rejoined Lo'isha, huddling together over a workbench's treasures in the far corner. Sejanes was examining the bench with some of the equipment that An'desha could not immediately identify. Firesong and Silverfox were halfway up the staircase in no time, with their papers in their hands, chattering to one another and ignoring everything else about them. Master Levy was already back up on what An'desha was now thinking of as the "ground" floor, and Karal was probably still asleep. There might or might not be other Kal'enedral besides Che'sera about; they preferred to spend much of their time in the camp on the surface, and since he had arbitrarily taken care of dinner preparations, there was really no need for any of them to be inside the Tower at this point. This would be as good a time as any to walk the Moonpaths undisturbed.

He went up the stairs as quietly as he could, nodding to Altra on the way. The Firecat nodded back with immense dignity, then turned to follow Firesong and Silverfox, tail waving like a jaunty banner. Evidently *he* wanted to hear what they were up to, probably because they were the most interesting creatures in the Tower at this, moment.

An'desha turned his steps in toward the sleeping chamber. Karal was, indeed, still asleep. He noticed as he paused in the doorway that Master Levy was in the side chamber where An'desha and Karal had found indications of another trapdoor. The Artificer was back down on his hands and knees and peering at the pattern in the floor. Florian was beside him, occasionally tapping a hoof on the stone at his direction.

An'desha tiptoed past Karal to his own sleeping place. *You know, if I look more as if I'm taking a nap, I'm less likely to be disturbed.* He pulled off his boots and curled up in his bedroll, arranging himself in what he thought was a very natural-looking position.

It occurred to him as he closed his eyes that he was being very secretive about this, when there really was no reason for him to do so. *On the other hand, I don't think I want Che'sera to know everything I'm doing until I know more about him.* If Che'sera turned out to be as rigid and inflexible as Jarim first was, or as hidebound as the shaman of An'desha's home Clan, it would be easier to keep away from him and his demands if he wasn't aware of everything An'desha knew or could do. *All I've told him is that the Avatars appear to me, not that I can go look for them. I think I'll keep it that way for now.*

He settled himself comfortably, then slowed his breathing and began the combination of relaxation and tension that marked a Moonpath trance. This, for those who were not trained in the technique, was more difficult than it sounded; too much tension and the trance state would never be reached, too much relaxation brought on a nap rather than a trance. Once he hovered on the edge of trance, with all of his attention focused, and nothing from the "real" world intruding, he sent his mind going *in*, and then *out*, in the pattern that Tre'valen had shown him, that felt like so very long ago.

He found himself, in his vision, standing on a path made of silvery sand that sparkled with a subdued glimmer, in the midst of an opalescent mist that swirled all around him. Or rather, he *seemed* to be standing there; this body was an illusory one, and he could change it to another form if he concentrated on it. This was a comfortable form, one he didn't have to think about to maintain, and it didn't seem reasonable to waste time and energy changing it to something else. He still was not certain if the Moonpaths themselves were an illusion; he had never bothered to test his surroundings to find out. The mist had no scent, and was neither cool nor warm; the sand beneath his feet neither so soft as to impede his steps, nor so hard as to be noteworthy.

"Tre'valen?" he called out into the mist, his voice echoing off into the distance in a way that had no counterpart in the real world. "Dawnfire?" The mist swirled about him, following his words with eddies of faint colors that faded within moments.

He had no answer immediately, but he didn't expect one. The Avatars were not in existence to serve and please *him*, after all, and he was well aware of that. Instead, he moved out along the path of soft sand, occasionally calling the names of his friends quietly into the mist. Eventually, if they were not occupied with something more important, they would come to him.

And so they did. They came winging through the mist in their bird shapes, forms the shape of a vorcel-hawk, but the size of a human, and with the sparkling, fiery, multicolored plumage of a firebird. He knew they were coming before they arrived, for they lit up the mist in the far distance like lightning within a thundercloud as they flew toward him, their flight paths spiraling around each other, leaving a double helix of light through the fog in their wakes.

Here they did not need to backwing to a landing as they would if they had taken "real" hawk-forms in the world. They simply slowed, then went into a hover above the path, then flowed into the vaguely avian-human shapes they normally wore to speak to him. Tre'valen was dressed as the Shin'a'in shaman he had been before he became the Star-Eyed's Avatar; but Dawnfire, though clearly Tayledras rather than Shin'a'in, wore a simple tunic that could not be readily identified as coming from any particular culture. Her long silver hair moved slightly, like the mist that swirled slowly about her. They both seemed to be completely ordinary humans—except for their eyes.

Not eyes, but eye-shaped windows on the night sky... the darkness of all of night spangled with the brightest of stars. So beautiful....

It was said that Kal'enel Herself had eyes like that; in this way She marked these two as Her Avatars, a way that could not be mistaken for anything else.

"Younger brother!" Tre'valen greeted him warmly. "It is far too long since we have seen you, but I pledge that we have not been idle in that interval!"

"Not all that long for a mere mortal," he corrected with a smile, "but a great deal has been happening to us as well. I was not certain if you knew about what we have uncovered and learned, and besides that, I wanted to make sure that you two were all right after the Working."

Not that I could have done anything if they weren't.

Dawnfire shrugged fluidly. "Poor young Karal bore the brunt of our Working, and we two were only a little drained," she said, and extended a cool hand to him, which he took in brief greeting. "It sounds as if you have not been idle either—you in the Tower."

That confirmed one of his guesses, that the Avatars, for all their power, were neither omniscient nor omnipotent. They were bound by some physical laws at least. Was that because they were not really physically "dead," as the spirit-Kal'enedral were? Or was it because they had been granted wider powers by the Star-Eyed?

"Would you like to tell me what you can, or hear what news I have first?" he asked.

"Your news; I suspect that much of what we have to tell you will be mere confirmation of what you already know," Tre'valen told him. "We have been ranging far in the world and in the Void, to see what changes the Working wrought on the energy-patterns of the Storms, and how far-reaching those changes were. I fear I bring no startlingly good news."

An'desha nodded, and detailed everything that had been happening since the "Working" of which Karal had been the channel; from the effect that being the focus of so much energy had wrought on the young Karsite priest, to the departure of the gryphons and the arrival of Sejanes and Master Levy, to the comings and goings of so many Kal'enedral, to Che'sera's intense interest in *him*. Lastly, he described the events of the afternoon, the opening of the hidden trapdoor and the discovery of the workshops below.

They both listened with concentration and apparent interest—and surprise when he described the workshops. *So, the existence of the workshops is something that the Star-Eyed did not tell them, though Her agents have certainly been about. Interesting.*

"There may be answers there," Tre'valen said at last, and for a fleeting moment, his face took on that "listening" expression that Karal wore when either Florian or Altra Mindspoke him. An'desha wondered if the Star-Eyed *might* be speaking to Her Avatar at that instant, and his next words might have been a confirmation of that. "Certainly Firesong should pursue the investigation of the mind-mirrors; they should not be difficult to revive nor to duplicate, and they will serve you all in the days to come."

Oh, my; even more interesting. Perhaps my intuition about the Star-Eyed's providence was well-founded.

Dawnfire placed one long hand on Tre'valen's shoulder and, with a rueful expression, admitted, "This is the only concrete advice we can give at the moment. Would it were otherwise, but the future is still trackless and without a clear path. And even our Goddess is bound by constraints She cannot break, so that we may all work out our futures with a free will."

An'desha sighed, but saw no reason to doubt her. "So we are still muddling our way through a point when there are many futures possible? I had hoped after the Working that we would at least have gotten our feet on a clear path again!"

Tre'valen looked uneasy. "The danger has only been postponed, not negated, but luckily the forces involved have not worsened," he told An'desha. "You knew that the Working was not a solution to the mage-storms, only a reprieve, and that has not changed."

"We have been tracking the results of the Working since the initial release of the energy contained in Urtho's weapon." Dawnfire took up the thread of conversation. "The effect is all that one could have wished over Valdemar, the Pelagirs, Karse and Rethwellan and even Hardorn. The waves that you sent out *are* canceling the waves of the mage-storms, but—only to a point."

"What point?" he asked instantly, sensing that this was important, although he did not know why yet.

"Just beyond the border of Hardorn in the East," Tre'valen told him. "Also South, just at the borders of the Haighlei Empire, and around White Gryphon and its environs, but *they* know how to deal with the effects. And in any case, the Storms are weak there. North, well into the Ice-Wall Mountains. To the West, well, that is Pelagir-wilds and the Storms will hardly change *that*. It is East that concerns us, for the Empire is the recipient of the worst of the Storms, and they are causing great havoc there, among those who depend so much upon magic."

An'desha gave that some thought. "That could be good for us, or bad," he said finally. "Given what the Emperor did to us, I'm not at all sad to hear that they are having troubles. I'd rather that the Empire was so busy trying to hold itself together that they had no time to think of us, but Duke Tremane thought we were the source of the Storms, and what if the Emperor's people assume the same and retaliate?"

Tre'valen nodded. "Precisely. Warn your friends, An'desha, and when the mind-mirrors are working and in place, use them to warn Valdemar. Such things could be possible."

Could *be possible, he says. Yet if I understand the constraints the Avatars labor under, pointing out something specifically as* possible *may be the only warning they are allowed to give of a future they have seen. Or perhaps not...*

Despite the unpleasant information, An'desha felt a warm glow of satisfaction. The Avatars avoided giving direct advice most of the time, but he was getting better at deducing what they wanted him to think about, and what information was the most critical to the current situation.

"What about the Storms themselves?" he asked. "Eventually, they're going to become strong enough to overcome the counter-Storm we sent out, aren't they? That's why we knew what we did was only going to be temporary—" He watched Tre'valen's face carefully and took his cues from the faint changes in expression, as he suspected he was supposed to do, "—so eventually, what happens? We're getting a—a reversal of the original Cataclysm, am I right? That was why we used this spot for the Working, because it's the place where the waves converge. Eventually the Storms are going to overcome the Working, and build up to something very bad?" He swallowed uncomfortably as Tre'valen's slight nod told him he was on the right track. "So then what? Obviously, the Storms that got set off aren't going to—go back into the weapons and things they came from. Do we get the Cataclysm all over again?"

Tre'valen shook his head, but not in negation, and Dawnfire spread her hands wide. "That is just what we do not know," she admitted. "And I confide in you—neither does She. There are too many possibilities, and some of them rest on very subtle factors. We do not yet know what the mages and Powers of the Empire will do, and that will have an effect. There are many things that you could do here, all of them effective, but in different ways and with differing results. *Probably* there will be another, lesser Cataclysm, unless you here manage to do one of the things that could avert or absorb it. There are many things you could do; you could do nothing whatsoever, as well, and from any action that is taken there are the possibilities of prosperity or ruin in varying degrees. Whatever happens, that is all we can tell you for certain."

He groaned. "That is not much comfort!" he complained. "But I suppose that it gives me enough to tell the others for now."

Tre'valen managed a ghost of a smile. "We never pledged to bring you comfort, younger brother," he chided gently. "Only enough help that you need not make your decisions blind, deaf, and ignorant."

"Let me ask about something closer to home, then," An'desha replied. "Che'sera. What is Che'sera to me, or I to Che'sera? Sooner or later he will deduce the source of my information, whether or not I actually say where it comes from in his presence."

Tre'valen's expression softened with affection. "What is Che'sera to you? Simply enough—a teacher, if you should decide, for yourself, that you wish to learn what he has to teach. And what are you to Che'sera? Largely, affirmation. He has been searching for someone to pass his knowledge on to, and he hopes that you will be that person. But it must be your decision, and he will not urge it upon you. He is—a good man, and much in the same way of thinking as Master Ulrich was; Karal will be like him, one day."

So. There it was, out in the open at last; his invitation to become a shaman. And not, perhaps, just any shaman, but one Sworn to the Goddess in her aspect as Wisdom Keeper. He sighed, wishing that he could be as certain of what he wanted as Karal was. But at least now he knew that Che'sera was neither a fanatic nor inflexible. That took a few worries from his shoulders, at least.

"You will be seeing more of us in days to come," Dawnfire told him, her sweet face full of seriousness. "I promise you, An'desha, we will tell you and help you all that we can; we see no good reason to leave you without aids and guides in this—"

Tre'valen looked out into the mists suddenly.

"—and right now, we must go," Tre'valen interrupted her. "There are more things we must investigate and watch for you. Fare well, younger brother! Time is running, and it is not on our side."

And with that, An'desha found himself alone again on the Moonpaths, as if the Avatars had never been there. With no further reason to remain, he sent his awareness dropping slowly back into his physical self, going *down*, then *out*—

As he slowly woke his senses, he heard Karal stirring at last, and smelled the distinctive scent of the meat and bean mixture he had prepared earlier. His stomach growled, and he opened his eyes.

"I brought you some dinner," Karal said, looking at him intently as he handed An'desha a bowl. "You were with *them*, weren't you?" Karal hooked his thumbs together and made flapping gestures with his fingers by way of definition.

He saw no reason to deny it, and nodded as he sat up slowly, and accepted the bowl and spoon from Karal. "They didn't tell me anything we didn't already know, or at least not much. I'll let Firesong and Sejanes know as soon as I've eaten."

Karal looked better than he had in days, and An'desha wondered if that was all due to the work of the Shin'a'in Healer, or if the Avatars had a hand in it. He suspected the latter, and not for the first time wondered what the link between Vkandis and the Shin'a'in Goddess was. The Avatars seemed quite drawn to Karal, and he to them.

On the other hand, they are very compassionate by nature, and he certainly deserves compassion and sympathy.

"Florian and I are going out for some fresh air. Do you want to go with us?" Karal invited nonchalantly. "I'm tired of being down underground like a hibernating bear; I want to see the sun before I go mad." He shook his head. "I can't imagine how that mage was able to stand being cooped up in here."

"You may see the sun, but you won't feel it," An'desha cautioned. "It's so cold that if you pour out a cup of water it'll be ice before it hits the ground."

"So I'll bundle up," Karal shrugged. "I've felt cold before. Karse isn't exactly a pleasure garden in winter, and up in the hills, there's snow on the ground for half the year. I'm beginning to sympathize with the gryphons; if I don't see some open sky, I'm going to start babbling."

"Then I'll go with you." It didn't take An'desha very long to pull on a heavy tunic, a second of the same weight, then his quilted Shin'a'in coat over it all, but Karal needed a little more help getting all that clothing on. He was quite steady on his feet, however, which An'desha took to be a good sign of his recovery.

By now, Master Levy was deep in his prodding and poking of the floor, and he jotted down measurements and diagrams in one of his notebooks. Silverfox and Firesong were sitting on their heels, the pages of notes neatly stacked in front of them, regarding another sheaf of their own notes with some dubiousness. "Where are you two going?" Silverfox called as the three of them passed by.

"We're going out for some fresh air," Karal replied. "Why don't you join us? We'll go frighten the Shin'a'in into thinking what you found in the workroom turned us all into monsters." He made a hideous face and Silverfox laughed.

"Fresh air? Not a bad idea." Firesong raised his head as Karal tendered his invitation. "We aren't making much more out of these notes. Maybe a little sun will wake up my mind. Go on out, we'll catch up with you."

An'desha noticed at once that their hosts had been at work on the tunnel to the surface—the opening they had made into the side of the Tower was large and quite regular, without any debris of broken masonry to trip over. The tunnel was also wider, though no higher, and there had been some extensive work done in shoring it up since the last time he'd come through it. It was *still* claustrophobic, but on this trip he no longer had the feeling that the tunnel was going to collapse and trap him at any moment.

He sent a small mage-light on ahead of Karal; he couldn't see past Florian's rump, so a mage-light was hardly of much use to *him*. Altra had declined to come, saying that he had seen quite enough of snow, and was planning another nap in Karal's bed.

He scented the outside before he saw any indication they were nearing the entrance. Although the air below remained remarkably clean, and the scents that lingered, thanks to some small magics on his part and Firesong's, were all pleasant in nature, there was a fresh quality to the outside air that nothing below could duplicate. Some of that was due to the cold, but not all.

The other thing they could not duplicate below was the light. As he stumbled out into the late afternoon sunlight, he squinted and put out a hand to steady himself against Florian's side. There wasn't a single cloud in the sky; the great bowl of the sky itself was an intense and blinding blue, and with all of the glare reflected off the snow, there was as much light coming from below as above.

Karal stood to one side, taking in huge gulps of air, his pale face taking on more color with every breath. Florian trotted off and kicked up his heels friskily.

Seen from the outside, the Tower itself was hardly more than a snow-frosted stub of melted-looking rock protruding from a snow-covered, rolling hill; the only projection above the otherwise flat Plains at all, not prepossessing except for its size. Because they had dug a long, slanting tunnel to reach the wall of the Tower below, the entrance came out quite some distance from the remains of the Tower itself, and it was at the foot of the Tower, precisely above the point where they had broken into the walls, that the Shin'a'in had pitched their tent-village. The round felt tents, white and brown and black, made a very orderly and neat array against the snow, so neat and orderly that it looked like a model rather than a place where people were actually living and working.

"Whoof!" Firesong exclaimed from behind An'desha, as Florian frisked and gamboled in the snow with Karal laughing and throwing snowballs for him to dodge. "Very bright out here! I shouldn't wonder if you could get a worse sunburn than in high summer!"

Silverfox ducked as Karal turned and lobbed a snowball at them. Karal laughed, and the *kestra'chern* pelted after him, swearing vengeance, while Firesong looked on indulgently.

"So," the Adept asked quietly, while Karal and Silverfox took shelter behind facing snowbanks, and hurled missiles at each other. "What did your Avatars have to say for themselves?"

An'desha flung him a startled glance, and Firesong chuckled at his expression. "You have a certain quiet glow after you've gone visiting them," the mage told him. "It's not terribly obvious, but it's there if you know what to look for. So? What did they have to say? Anything useful?"

"Mostly that nothing has changed that much. We've successfully bought some time for ourselves and our friends, things outside the areas we protected are deteriorating quickly, and eventually even our time will run out," An'desha said, wishing his news was better.

Firesong nodded, unsurprised. "And when our time runs out, we'll get—what? A replication of the Cataclysm? After all, everything is supposedly converging here."

"Maybe. Even They don't know for sure." An'desha sighed. "If She has any idea, She's not saying anything. If you want my guess, the gods are doing what They always do—unless and until *all* life is threatened with catastrophe, They'll see to it we have the tools and the information to find our own solutions, then leave us alone to find them. The Avatars think the things we're finding in the Tower will help us, but—"

"But there's no clear 'future' to see or even guess at." Firesong looked surprisingly philosophical. "I'm determined to see this as an opportunity; for *once* in my life there isn't a god or a spirit or the hand of fate or prophecy or anything else demanding that I trace a certain pattern on the pages of time. We're going to make our own future here, An'desha, and nothing is going to interfere with us to make it go some other god-ordained way. There's a certain satisfaction in that, you know."

"I suppose so," An'desha replied; he would have said more, but Silverfox suddenly broke off the snowball fight to peer into the north, and point.

"Look!" he exclaimed with glee, as Karal dropped his final snowball without throwing it to squint in the direction he indicated. "Gryphons! Yes! They have a carry-basket, and I think they've brought Tarrn!"

An'desha shaded his eyes and narrowed them against the glare, and finally made out four sets of flapping wings with a half-round shape beneath them. He couldn't think what else would have that particular configuration except four gryphons and a large carry-basket.

"Come on!" Silverfox crowed. "Let's go meet them!"

He set off at a run; Florian loped up and half-knelt beside Karal, who pulled himself onto the Companion's back. The two of them quickly overtook Silverfox; Firesong cast an amused glance at An'desha and indicated the others with a finger.

"Shall we trundle along behind?" he asked.

"It would only be polite," An'desha pointed out. "And besides, the Shin'a'in have cleared a perfectly fine path between here and there. It would be a shame not to use it."

They followed in Silverfox's wake, though at a more leisurely pace. By the time they arrived at the Shin'a'in tent-village, the gryphons and their passengers had already landed and been taken into one of the tents. It was easy to tell which one; there was only one that was large enough to hold four gryphons at once, and only one whose pallet of snow had been churned by gryphon claws.

Dark-clad Kal'enedral nodded as Firesong waved to them, then went about their own business. An'desha pulled the entrance flap aside, and he and the mage entered the tent, being careful to let in as little cold air as possible. It took quite a bit of time for An'desha's eyes to adjust to the darkness inside the tent after all the snow glare outside; he stayed where he was while he waited, listening to the chatter of at least half a dozen creatures all speaking at once.

He looked around as soon as he could make anything at all out; he didn't recognize any of the gryphons, but he hadn't expected to. They were all arranged at one side of the tent, and it came as no surprise to see that they were eating—or rather, gorging. Not only would they have to recover from the stress of carrying their passengers all the way from k'Leshya Vale, but they would have to recover from the stress of dealing with the cold as well.

Karal was conversing with the gryphons, occasionally helping them where the quarters were too cramped for them to move themselves. Silverfox, however, was engaged in a highspeed conversation with a gray-muzzled, but jaunty-looking *kyree*.

This odd creature, vaguely wolflike as to the head and coat, but also vaguely catlike in body shape and proportions, was easily the size of a small calf. An'desha knew more about *kyrees* from personal experience than from Falconsbane's memories, as Mornelithe Falconsbane in all of his incarnations had very little to do with the creatures. An'desha, on the other hand, was quite familiar with Rris, the *kyree* representative to the Kingdom of Valdemar and the Alliance. Rris might look like this old fellow many years from now; his muzzle was quite white, and his head was liberally salted with paler hairs among the black. He was tired, but clearly in good spirits, and he chatted with Silverfox like the old friend he probably was.

Or to be more accurate, Silverfox chattered; the *kyree*, who could only Mindspeak, nodded and made replies in his own inaudible fashion. Until Tarrn chose to "speak" in the "public" mode, no one would hear him except those he chose.

With him, bundled in so many layers of quilted clothing he resembled a roll of brightly colored Kaled'a'in bed coverings, was a *hertasi*. He was practically sitting on a brazier, since the lizard-folk were very susceptible to cold. It wasn't that they were cold-blooded, precisely, it was that they were not able to control their own body temperatures very efficiently. Opinions were divided on whether *hertasi* had been created by Urtho or by an accident involving magic, but in either case their physiology had some flaws, and this was the major one. The poor thing could very easily lose limbs to the cold, or would go involuntarily into a kind of hibernation. Layers of clothing would not necessarily help this, especially not during a long journey in bitter cold, hence the brazier now and whatever other measures the Kaled'a'in had taken. All that could be seen of this *hertasi* was the end of the snout and a pair of alert, bright, and apparently happy eyes peeking out of the depths of the hood.

A great deal more of Tarrn was visible. An'desha knew *kyree* from his acquaintance with Rris, but he had not had much opportunity to get to know any *hertasi*. A few had come with Silverfox and the Kaled'a'in delegation to Valdemar, but he hadn't had much to do with them. And of course, Falconsbane was universally despised by both races, in all his lives, so *he* would hardly have had any congress with them.

At just that moment, the *hertasi* spoke up; the *hertasi* associated with the Kaled'a'in tended to vocalize far more often than they used Mindspeech, the exact reverse of the habits of the ones associated with the Hawkbrothers.

"I believe I am thawed enough to make the dash for the Tower," he said, in a high-pitched voice with hints of a whistling sound underlying the tone.

:Excellent, Lyam,: the *kyree* replied. *:They tell me our baggage is already there, waiting for us. If we truly make a dash, you won't get too much of a chill.:*

"Florian says he'll be happy to carry Lyam, if Lyam thinks he can cling on," Karal spoke up. "Florian can get him to the tunnel mouth faster than he can get there on foot." He turned toward the *hertasi*, polite but a little uncertain in addressing such an odd creature. "A Companion's gait is very smooth, and I've never heard of one losing a rider, and you should see one run!"

"I have never tried riding, but if I can get from White Gryphon to here without the loss of limb or tail, I think I should be able to survive an attempt on a Companion's back," the *hertasi* said with warm good humor. "And almost anything is worth not having to walk through snow myself!"

"We ssshall ssstay herrre overrrnight," one of the gryphons said. "Thisss issss verrry comforrrtable, and we do *not* want to go underrrgrrround even to sssee the Towerrr!" The others nodded with agreement.

"It isss wonderrrful to be wherrre the grrreat Ssskandrrranon once wasss, but *he* did not have to crrrawl underrrgrrround," said another, flicking his wings nervously. "I do not know how Trrreyvan and Hydona borrre it."

The *kyree* didn't shrug, but An'desha had the impression that if he could have, he would have. *:Suit yourselves; you will have to make do with my descriptions, then.:*

"Yourrr dessscrrriptionsss will be asss if we werrre therrre," the first gryphon said firmly. "I will fly the ssssky that Ssskandrranon flew, and that will be enough forr me."

Tarrn stood up, and shook himself thoroughly. *:One more dash, then, and we will be where no kyree or hertasi has set foot in thousands of years!:* He seemed to relish the prospect with scarcely-restrained glee, and the air of a creature a quarter of his apparent age. *:Well, friends, let us take these last few paces at the gallop!:*

Firesong, who had known many *kyree* and *hertasi* in his life, was comfortable with these two immediately. Tarrn had all of the warmth and wisdom of Irrl, one of Firesong's academic teachers, and Lyam had a great deal more assertiveness than most of the normally-timid Vales-bred *hertasi*. Although Firesong loved to be petted and made much of by his own *hertasi*, he had always found the shyness of the Vale *hertasi* something of an irritation. Someone once suggested that their manner was reflective of the deep trauma they had suffered during the Cataclysm, and that worried him deeply; if that was so, how would they react to another such event?

They'll cope, I suppose; it's the thing they do best. I don't know how they manage.

Both *kyree* and *hertasi* were at heart cave- and den-dwellers, and both of the new arrivals were obviously comfortable in the Tower. They settled into the same room shared by Karal and An'desha with every evidence of content. They had not yet moved in their luggage, but the Shin'a'in had brought appropriate bedding material for both of the new guests— and extra warming pans for both beds. As far as personal belongings went, the two had traveled much lighter than he had expected. Their main luggage consisted of boxes of very special writing materials; books of tough paper with waterproof metal covers that locked over the contents like protective boxes, and ink that would never run once it had dried, even if water was spilled directly on it. Tarrn was a historian; not a traditional *kyree* historian like Rris, who memorized and recited from memory, but the kind of historian like the Chronicler of Valdemar, who attempted to personally view as much as possible of epochal events, and to note the honest and bare facts in record-books called Chronicles. Only when those hard facts had been listed would Tarrn then make his own interpretations of the events, written separately in Commentaries. Tarrn was very serious about his calling; he would rather have the fur pulled out of his tail until it was as naked as a rat's than put a personal interpretation in the Chronicles.

Actually, that wasn't precisely true. Tarrn would dictate, for, having no hands, he could not write. Lyam would do the actual writing. Lyam was Tarrn's third secretary in a long life as a historian, and his relationship with the *kyree* was obviously based on affection and mutual respect. Normally it was Lyam who cared for the *kyree's* needs, but with Lyam just now the one who was in need, Tarrn was seeing to it in a quiet and dignified manner that Lyam got first priority.

Lyam needed warmth more than anything else, and Karal volunteered to take care of him. Firesong had an idea that he knew why, too. At heart, Karal still considered himself to be the young secretary who had ridden to Valdemar from Karse, and he must be feeling a great deal of empathy for Lyam.

That's good; they are both strangers in strange places, and it will do them good to have a friend with the same—outlook? Status? They have a lot in common, anyway.

Tarrn, however, was quite ready for work, and looked it. He had been consulting with Silverfox all the way here from the tent-village. Firesong could not imagine where he was getting the energy.

He approached Firesong with Silverfox still in tow as soon as Karal took Lyam off to be wrapped up in warmed blankets and given something hot to drink.

"Firesong, Tarrn wants to speak with you privately, before we get to work," Silverfox told him, with a quizzical expression. "He says he has something for you, but he can't tell me what it is."

The *kyree* nodded his head as Firesong turned to look down on him with surprise. *:Indeed, Firesong k'Treva,:* Tarrn said with grave courtesy. *:I have. Would you come with me to where they have brought our belongings?:*

"Certainly," Firesong replied with equal courtesy. "Would you prefer that I Mindspoke with you?"

:That will not be necessary, but thank you,: Tarrn replied, turning and walking slowly toward the heap of bundles that the Shin'a'in had left just inside the main room of the Tower. *:It is not that this is a secret matter,:* the *kyree* continued. *:It is simply that I have not been given permission to say anything to anyone else before I discharged my obligation.:*

"Oh?" This was getting odder with every moment. Firesong couldn't think of anything or anyone among the Kaled'a'in of k'Leshya Vale who would have had anything to send to him.

Tarrn stopped beside the pile of belongings. *:If you will please remove the three bags of Lyam's clothing there—:* he indicated the drab bundles with his forepaw *:—you will find what I brought you beneath them. It is wrapped in blue wool, and it is very long and narrow.:*

Firesong easily moved the three packages, revealing a long, narrow packet wrapped in blue wool cloth and tied with string. Firesong picked it up.

And it Mindspoke to him.

:Hello, boy.:

The grating, decidedly *female* voice was all too familiar to him, although it was not one he had expected to hear ever again.

"*Need?*" he gasped, as he tore at the wrappings, trying to free the blade within. Lyam must have wrapped it; the string was tied in a complicated knot-pattern only a *hertasi* or a *kestra'chern* could admire. He finally pulled off the string, the fabric fell away, and there was the ancient spell-bound sword. She looked precisely as she had the last time he saw her, strapped to Falconsbane's "daughter" Nyara's side as she and Herald Skif rode out of Valdemar to become Selenay's envoys to the Kaled'a'in and Tayledras, and possibly to the Shin'a'in as well.

"Need, what are you *doing* here?" He hadn't been taken so completely by surprise since—since he'd been kidnapped by his ancestor Vanyel!

:Nyara doesn't require me anymore; she's better off on her own,: the sword said to him. *:There's nothing at k'Leshya that she, Skif, or the Kaled'a'in can't handle. You, on the other hand, are dealing with very old magics. I am very old magic, and I still recall quite a bit. I helped you once before, and I'm hoping I can help you again.:*

Firesong held the sword in both hands, and stared at it. It was very disconcerting to be Mindspeaking with what should have been an inanimate object. A sword didn't have a face to read, eyes to look into, and it was difficult to tell if *it* could read his expressions.

But there's something about all this that doesn't quite make sense yet.

"I find myself wondering if there is something more to this than just an urge to help us here," he said finally. "You've never put yourself in nonfemale hands before."

:Hmm—let's say I've never done it deliberately, but it has happened, and it was usually with lads who had the same taste in men as my "daughters.": The sword chuckled, but he sensed there was still a lot more than she was telling, and he decided to press her for it.

:Try again,: he said sternly in Mindspeech. *:You're avoiding my question.:*

A sword could not sigh, but he got that sensation from her.

:All right. I could tell you to work it out yourself, but why waste time? You've got mage-storms disrupting magic; you've managed to get them canceled out for the moment, but we all know this is only a temporary respite, not a solution. I'm magic. I've managed to hold myself together this long, but each Storm gets stronger, and sooner or later I'm going to lose to one. I don't know what will happen when I lose, but it's going to happen.: She paused for a moment. *:Worst case is that I'll go up in fire and molten metal, the way the sword was made. Best case is that the magic will just unravel, and there won't be anything here but a perfectly ordinary sword.:*

He had never once thought that Need might be affected by the Storms; she had always struck him as being so capable, so impervious, that it never occurred to him that she might have been in trouble.

This bothered him. *:I can't promise anything,:* he said soberly. *:I don't even know if we're going to survive the end of this ourselves.:*

To his surprise, the sword laughed, though rather sardonically. *:You think I don't know that? If I go pfft, I don't want little Nyara to see it happen. She had enough troubles in her life and she shouldn't lose an old friend and teacher in that unexpected a fashion. Besides, if I'm going to go, I want to do it while I'm trying to accomplish something. How could I miss a chance at getting my hand in on what you're trying to do? It's complicated, it's dangerous, it's challenging, it's irresistible.:*

"If you say so," he said aloud, but strapped the sword on anyway, for she required *his* presence to be able to see and hear clearly. Without a bearer, it took incredible effort for her to perceive anything, and at that it was only dimly. He didn't often carry a blade, and she felt very odd, slung across his back in Tayledras fashion. "An'desha will probably be happy to see you, but you're going to have to explain yourself to the rest. They don't know anything about you."

And the gods only know what the Shin'a'in are going to make of her. Yes, Kethry had carried her, and Kerowyn after that, but still—she was yet another creature of magic inside the heart of the Plains. How much more were they going to be willing to allow?

:I can't wait,: Need replied, with a bit less irony than he expected. *:There's something rather amusing about the reactions people get the first time I talk to them.:*

Amusing? Oh, gods. Firesong buried his irritation at this particular complication in an already complicated situation; after all, Need was right about her abilities. She *did* know much older magics than anyone here, and that included An'desha. That might be crucial at this point, for there could be something ancient and long-forgotten that would give them all the clues they needed to solve this situation. She was a powerful mage in her own right—something near to an Adept, or she never could have made the magics that bound her human soul to an iron blade. He, An'desha, and Sejanes were the only true mages here; having Need with them gave them a fourth.

And if she is right, and the mage-storms overwhelm her along with the rest of us, she won't have to worry about how *she unravels. If she dissolves into flame and melted steel, we here among all these dangerous machines of power will have far more to worry about than her.*

On the other hand, dealing with Need's irascible personality was not going to be easy. He rubbed his temples, feeling another headache coming on.

She Mindspeaks; perhaps I can get Tarrn interested in her. When he is not translating for us, wouldn't she be fascinating for a historian?

He could only hope that was the case, because he had the feeling that Need was not going to give him a choice about becoming her bearer. In this all-male enclave, he was probably the closest she was going to come to an acceptable bearer, for, by now, even the female Companions they had ridden here on had begun the long journey back to Valdemar.

"Well, we might as well get this over now," he said aloud, as Tarrn watched him with interest. "I assume, sir, that you have made the acquaintance of my metal friend, here?"

:*I have, and I hope she will continue to impart her tales of the past to me here, when our work permits,:* Tarrn replied gravely, which made Firesong feel a little more cheerful about the situation. At least he wouldn't be burdened with Need's presence and personality *all* the time.

"Well, most of my other colleagues here don't even know she exists, so we'd better introduce her to them before she startles one of them into dropping something critical by Mindspeaking to him without warning." Need remained silent after that little sally, which either meant that she agreed with him, or that she was insulted and was plotting revenge.

:*An excellent plan,:* Tarrn replied. :*Carry on.:*

He gathered them all together by the simple expedient of going into the central chamber, clearing his throat, and announcing, "Excuse me, friends, but something rather—unexpected—has come up that you really ought to know about."

That certainly brought everyone who understood Valdemaran boiling out, and the few Shin'a'in who didn't know the language followed the rest out of sheer curiosity.

Silverfox was the first to arrive, and stared at him as if he'd grown a tail. "Firesong," the *kestra'chern* began incredulously, "what are you doing with a sword?"

He removed Need from her sheath, just in case the leather and silk hampered her ability to Mindspeak at all, and held her out in front of him, balanced on his palms, as the others arrived. "Well, that's what I wanted to tell you all about," he said, flushing a little. "It seems we didn't get *two* additions to our little group here, we got three. I'd like you all to meet Need, those of you who haven't already encountered her."

"Need!" An'desha had only just emerged from the sleeping chamber, but there was no doubt that *he* was glad to see the mage-blade. "What is *she* doing here? This is wonderful!"

Firesong's expression must have been a bit sour, for An'desha took one look at his face and laughed. "Oh, it's that way, is it? You're the chosen bearer?" He looked down fondly at the blade. "Firesong is *much* too certain of his own expertise, dear lady; I trust you can teach him that there are other people here who are just as expert in their crafts as he. I warn you though, he looks much better this way than in a dress."

:*Don't be so hard on him, boy,:* the blade replied, amused. :*Leave that job to me. I've got more experience at it.:*

By now all the rest had gathered around, and were staring with varying degrees of fascination and puzzlement at the sword. "What is this?" Sejanes asked, brows knitted.

"Is this by any chance *the* famous sword called 'Need' that the ancestress of Tale'sedrin Clan once wore?" asked Lo'isha, as the other Shin'a'in gathered in a knot behind him, murmuring. "The one carried by our Clan-sib, Herald Kerowyn?"

"The same," Firesong all but groaned. "To answer you, Sejanes, Need is a magically-made sword with the soul of its maker bound into it, and she is unbelievably ancient. Either she or Tarrn can probably tell you the story of *why* she did such a daft thing—"

:Hardly daft. Reckless, yes, and probably less than wise, but at the time we didn't have many options, and all of those were worse than what I did. Of course, I could have just folded my hands and done nothing at all, but—let's just say that went against my conscience and my nature.:

Those who didn't know what she was went wide-eyed with startlement at the sound of her projected mind-voice.

"The point is, she's from a time that actually predates the Mage Wars and the Cataclysm, at least so far as we can tell, and that makes her an expert in magics much older than the ones we know," Firesong said, noting as he spoke that An'desha's eyes were unfocused, which probably meant he was talking privately to her. "She has volunteered to come help us, since her last bearer no longer requires her tutelage."

Master Levy rubbed his chin with one hand as he looked down on the sword with speculation. "What happens if and when the mage-storms overwhelm us here?" he asked. "If she *is* magically made—"

:Then unless I can manage to shield myself, which I'm not certain I can, I either go quietly or dramatically, and I don't know which it will be,: Need replied bluntly. *:These Storms disrupt the patterns of magic so deeply they may as well be spells of Unmaking. But that would happen whether I was here or somewhere else, and I'd just as soon be trying to accomplish something. I told you, I'm not one to sit with folded hands, even if I still had hands to fold.:*

"Wait a minute," Sejanes objected, speaking directly to the sword, glimmering with reflected light from above. "If you predate the Mage Wars and the Cataclysm, how did you survive *them*?"

:In a shielded casket in a shielded shrine in the heart of the triply-shielded Temple to Bestet, the Battle-Goddess,: she replied promptly. *:And when the Cataclysm was over, the shields on the shrine and the casket were gone and I felt as if I'd been drained to the dregs. It took me years to recover, and by then I'd been moved to the armory since no one could figure out why I'd been put in with the Goddess' regalia in*

the first place. If I were inclined to such things, I'd have been indignant.:

Sejanes nodded. "It would be difficult to find such a situation again," he observed, stroking his chin with one hand. "Indeed, it is quite surprising that you were in that situation during the first Cataclysm."

:The only reason they had shields like that was because of the war with Ma'ar. I don't know of any Temples now with that kind of protection,: Need went on. *:Or to be more honest, I don't know of any that would offer me shelter. I might as well be doing something useful, and I just might be able to save myself while doing it.:*

"Do you fear death so much?" Karal asked softly. Light rippled across the surface of the sword, as if Need reacted to that question.

Firesong expected a sarcastic reply, or none at all, but was surprised by both her answer and her sober tone.

:I don't fear death, youngling,: she said, with great honesty. *:What I'm afraid of is more complicated than that. I don't want to vanish without fighting, I don't intend to just lie down and accept "death" passively. There is the possibility that I could meet my end violently, and if that is the case—:*

"Then it would be better here," Sejanes said with finality, as a chill crept up Firesong's spine. "If there is a second Cataclysm and the effect penetrates this place, *your* demise will be insignificant compared to the violence that will be unleashed."

Light rippled along the surface of the blade again. *:Good. You'd already considered that.:* Need sounded relieved. *:I'd hoped I wouldn't be the bird of ill omen forced to point that out to you.:*

I would rather hope we can pull this off right to the very end, thank you. "No, just the one who forced us to think about it a little earlier than we wanted to," Firesong sighed.

Now she gave him one of her typical sardonic chuckles. *:Consider it incentive to find a solution,:* she told him.

Now, of course, those who had never met Need wanted to speak with her; Firesong handed her over to An'desha for that, although he was quite aware that she was not going to change her mind about her choice of a bearer. Somewhat to his surprise, Karal separated himself from the group for a moment and approached him.

"I'm not quite sure what to say, except that I know it isn't going to be easy or very entertaining to have Need literally on your back while we work our way through all this," Karal said quietly. "I've had teachers like her. They were very good, but not easy to live with, and you have my sympathy, for what it's worth."

"Thank you, Karal," he replied with some surprise. The last thing he had expected was sympathy or understanding from the Karsite!

"Just trying to—oh, I don't know." Karal smiled crookedly. "Believe it or not, I like and admire you, Firesong. We irritate each other sometimes, but who doesn't? And I never properly thanked you for what you did for me."

Firesong found himself blushing hotly, something he hadn't done since boyhood. "Oh, please," he replied, for once at a loss for words. "Don't thank me, we all—"

Karal shook his head. "I know very well what all of you did, and I won't mention this again since it obviously makes you uncomfortable. I just want you to know that it's appreciated and you are appreciated. And—well, I think I've said enough."

Considering that Firesong didn't think he'd be able to flush any hotter, Karal was probably right. When the Karsite rejoined the group talking to Need, it was a decided relief.

:Ahem.:

This time the mind-voice was Tarrn's, and Firesong was very glad to hear it.

"Can I help you, sir?" he asked, looking down at the *kyree*, who was in turn looking up at him with amused golden eyes. The white hairs of his muzzle contrasted strangely with the youth in those eyes.

:Since virtually everyone else is involved with speaking to our metallic friend, why don't we go have a look at those notes Silverfox says you are so concerned with? If this device is what I believe it to be, then the translation will be a simple one, and we may have some answers within a quarter-day.:

"Really?" Firesong's eyebrows rose.

:Mind you, this is likely to be the only *case where the translation will be so easy,:* Tarrn cautioned, *:and that is only because I am familiar with similar devices used by our gryphons. I think this is probably an improvement on those devices, allowing visions as well as thoughts and—:* He stopped, and shook his head until his ears flapped, *:—and we really ought to just see for ourselves before I make too big a liar of myself. Shall we?:*

Firesong got the notes and spread the pages out on the floor in one corner of the main chamber. He and the *kyree* bent over them in intense concentration, with Lyam taking notes beside them, and before very long, Tarrn *was* able to determine that the device was nothing more than an improvement on something he called a "teleson."

At that point, Silverfox joined them again, and by the time supper came and went, they had worked out not only the way to activate the devices, but also how to make more.

Provided, of course, that there were sufficient parts to do so. There were some esoteric components that needed to be prepared beforehand, and Firesong wasn't certain whether or not there had been any of those components among the parts in bins on the workbench. Both Tarrn and Silverfox were of the opinion that, although the Kaled'a'in could probably make more of these components eventually, it would take a great deal of trial-and-error to do so, given the vagaries of the way the language had changed over the centuries.

"Well, let's confine ourselves to activating the two we have," Firesong said at last, sitting back on his heels and stretching muscles that had cramped in his shoulders and back. "If they work, then we can see if we can make a third and get *it* to work. With communication open back to Haven, that will give us more than we'd hoped for; open it to Sunhame, and we're doubly advantaged. We can worry about being able to build more of these devices from scratch later, when we have the leisure."

"That seems a good plan to me," Silverfox concurred, rotating his head and neck to stretch out cramps of his own. "Let me go and get one of the devices and bring it up here, and that way we can actually test it over a little distance." He looked around. "We'll need someone with Mindspeech up here. That would be Tarrn, I suppose."

:That seems reasonable,: the *kyree* said agreeably. *:We will also need a mage— Sejanes, perhaps—to activate it.:*

"And I'll go down to the workshop and activate and man the other device down there," Firesong said, getting to his feet. He and Silverfox descended the stairs down into the workshop; Silverfox took one of the two devices from the bench and carried it carefully up the staircase again.

The instructions for activation had been quite unambiguous and equally simple, phrased in language that not even the passage of time had altered. Even a child, had he both true-magic and Mindspeech, would have been able to follow the instructions. It was obvious from the notes now that the reason these devices had not been put into use by Urtho was that *anyone* could "eavesdrop" on conversations held with their aid. That rather negated their value in a time of war. Urtho's notes had made it very clear that Ma'ar had many folks Gifted with Mindspeech in his ranks, and that he used it as he would any other tool.

Firesong only hoped that communications sent through these telesons would not be *forced* into the minds of those with Mindspeech; if that were to be the case, their use would be severely limited. Having to maintain ordinary shields was one thing; having to put up shields against something like coercion in order to block these communications out would be very uncomfortable. And for those who were untrained and unaware of their Gift, it would be impossible.

I don't want to drive people mad by having them suddenly forced to listen to strangers talking in their heads!

Well, there was only one way to find out for certain.

A very little magic was needed to help activate the device, and none to maintain it once it was active. There was nothing for mage-storms to disrupt; the device took Mindspeech and amplified it, using some resonance of an arrangement of crystals. The trick was, even those who normally would not be considered to have Mindspeech would be able to use it also; it only needed *one* so Gifted on one of the two telesons in order for the trick to work.

That would mean that Master Levy could talk with one of his fellow Artificers through the intermediary of a Herald, or a mage so Gifted could speak with Sejanes, who was not.

Hmm. And if the device isn't urgently needed, young Karal can talk with Natoli. The idea delighted him; now and again he had the urge to matchmake, and this was one of those times. It might be the strangest courtship ever on record, but if it worked—

Worry about that when you can get this ancient construction to operate! he scolded himself, and bent his concentration to doing just that.

A moment later—well, it *seemed* to be working. So far as he recalled the notes, it *looked* as if he had activated it. But—

:FIRESONG?: If it had been a real voice and not a mind-voice, the shout would have deafened him. As it was, it was excruciatingly painful!

"Aiii!" he shouted, clapping his hands over his ears, even though he knew that wasn't going to make a difference.

:Sorry.: That was a more normal "volume," although there was no sound involved. *:Is that better?:*

He didn't recognize the mind-voice; it certainly wasn't Tarrn. It also "sounded" rather odd, and he couldn't tell why. *:Who is this?:* he sent back cautiously, so as not to blast *their* minds.

:Sejanes. I must say, this is an interesting way to speak.: Firesong blinked for a moment, both to clear his thoughts and to try to pinpoint just why the mind-voice felt so strange. The mental images—

Wait, that's it. There are no mental images! There's no emotional flavor, no images, no leaking over of other thoughts! This is just like speaking, not like Mindspeech at all.:

779

And that, for those who were not Gifted and not used to sorting through the wealth of additional information that came along with mindsent "words," would be a good thing. *:I believe we have a workable pair of prototypes,:* he sent back with glee.

His elation was matched by the others. After making certain that both devices were working according to the notes, and that all of the components were well-seated, the consensus was that they had earned a real respite.

But before they took that well-earned rest, everyone, Gifted and not, had a try at the teleson pair. The notes were correct; so long as one of the operators was Gifted, the result was the same, crisp, clear Mindspeech with no overtones of anything else. If both were Gifted, then the results were different; precisely like "normal" Mindspeech. To Firesong's relief, there was no "spillover" from the devices to those who were Gifted, although, as Urtho had indicated, the Gifted *could* "listen in" with perfect ease when the devices were in use.

Right now, that might be an advantage. It certainly wouldn't hurt to have more than two people at each mindsent conference.

Altra had recovered enough from his last Jumps to take the device to Valdemar immediately, and insisted on doing just that, then and there. He saw no reason whatsoever to delay, and every reason to make all speed.

:With every mark that passes, it is more difficult to Jump,: he said firmly. *:Why wait? It will be easier to Jump with an inanimate object, but "easier" does not mean "easy." I want to get this over with!:*

There were no dissenting voices, so as soon as the mindmirror teleson had been wrapped in a cushion of quilts to keep it from any possibility of damage, Altra left, saying that he thought he would return in four days.

"We'll know if the device still works or if it works at the distances that Urtho claimed in two days, of course," Sejanes observed as they all prepared for sleep. Not that any of them really thought he would get much sleep after all the excitement that day. "In two days he'll be in Haven, and then it will just be a matter of getting one of the Heralds to try calling us."

He crept into his own bed—the only one that *was* a bed, since it was not possible for him to get into and out of a pallet on the floor.

"Or one of us can call them," Karal pointed out, and yawned. He was already in his bedroll, with Florian curled up at his back, taking the place of Altra as a living bedwarmer. "You know, I was really excited a couple of marks ago and I thought I'd never be able to get to sleep, but now—" He yawned again, and looked puzzled, "—now it seems as if this is an anticlimax."

Firesong had the answer to his puzzlement. "Well, we're all worn out—it's been a very busy day—but there's more to it than that." He tied up his long hair to keep it from knotting up while he slept.

:*Permit the old pessimist,*: Need interjected. :*It's not an anticlimax, child, it's that this hasn't been the climax you think it should be. We have a new tool, and nothing more. If those devices hadn't worked, we would have gone on without them. We will find the answers here, if there are answers to be found, but the teleson is not one of those answers, and that is why it feels as if what we accomplished with them is only a minor addition to our work and not a major part of it.*:

"Ah." Karal's face wore a sober expression of understanding. "I see what you are saying. We're not at the end of our work, just the beginning, and it's not even close to the point where we can celebrate. Well. That's a little disappointing, but at least we haven't fallen back."

"Exactly," said Firesong. "Which is all the more reason why you *should* get a good night's sleep. We'll need everyone in the morning." He leveled a sober look at Karal. "Especially you. I think we'll have work enough to make you and Lyam wish there were four of you."

"I'll be glad to get back to work," Karal said, with a weak smile, and on that note, Firesong extinguished the lights with a word, and it was not long before even he was fast asleep.

5

What is the Shin'a'in saying? Darkwind asked himself, as he watched Duke Tremane trying to make out careful plans for the time when the mage-storms finally overcame the latest efforts to stave them off. *Ah, I remember. "The best plans never survive the first engagement with the enemy." How has the Empire done so well when they insist on having detailed plans for everything?*

The three of them sat around a small table in the Grand Duke's personal quarters, a table currently quite full, what with papers, glasses of water, and maps strewn across it.

"What do you two think?" Duke Tremane asked, setting aside the plans he and the Valdemarans had been discussing, and leaning over the table. As he looked up at them, his gray-brown eyes seemed anxious. "My scholars haven't been able to unearth any more information about the Cataclysm, and my mages have not been able to predict anything that these mage-storms have done."

Elspeth grimaced. "I don't know that much either, I'm afraid," she replied honestly. She glanced over at Darkwind, who shrugged slightly.

"I can only tell you of the effects the Cataclysm had, according to our records and traditions," he told the Grand Duke. "Those effects were widespread and all-encompassing. *All* magic was disrupted, from the Ice-Wall Mountains in the north to the borders of the Haighlei Empire in the south, and in an equal distance east and west of what are now Lake Evendim and the Dhorisha Plains. If any shields survived the Cataclysm, I am not aware of it, but I must add that the Kaled'a'in groups my people are descended from had none of the greater mages with them."

"So shields might survive?" Tremane persisted, fiddling nervously with a pen.

Oh, how he wants to have some way to get his sort of magic back! Now that this area of Hardorn was buffered from the worst effects of the mage-storms, Tremane had given orders for some judicious use of magic to take some pressure from scarce resources—mostly burnables. The barracks and headquarters were all heated and lit with mage-fires and mage-lights now, and about half the time food was cooked using mage-fires in the stoves. It did make things more comfortable, especially in the barracks, which had been heated with dried dung, and were hardly illuminated at all. But Darkwind and Elspeth could both tell how much the Grand Duke wanted to be able to use magic for all of the things he was used to; the only trouble with that idea was that it just wasn't possible to do so. For one thing, magical energy ran thin and low here; Ancar had depleted it sorely, and it would take a long time to recover. There was enough for lights and fires—but not for something more complicated, such as blind scrying, or creating mage-walls to keep the "boggles" out. For another, Hardorn was only *buffered*; there were still slight effects, and those were increasing, a little at a time, with every passing day.

Darkwind spread his hands wide, shaking his long, silver-streaked hair back over his shoulders as he did so. "That, I cannot tell you. The people to ask would be the k'Leshya, and they are somewhat difficult to reach at the moment."

He caught Elspeth's face taking on that slightly vacant look that meant she was Mindspeaking to Gwena, and he waited for her to say something. Tremane was always forgetting that Gwena was "present" in spirit, if not sitting at the same table, and the Companion would hardly forgo a chance to remind him.

"Gwena says that she can relay an inquiry to Skif's Cymry at k'Leshya Vale, and get the answer back in a couple of days," Elspeth said, her dark eyes crinkling at the corners, telling Darkwind that she was holding back laughter. Gwena had probably said far more than that, probably about Tremane and his faulty memory, but this *was* a diplomatic mission and such things would not be diplomatic to relate. "There are enough mages there that surely someone will know the answer. And she says if not, then she can relay on to Florian at the Tower and see if An'desha knows anything."

Not every Companion had that long-distance capability; in fact, there were only two in all of the world as far as Darkwind knew. One was Gwena, and the other was Rolan, the Companion of the Queen's Own. They were special; "Grove-born," the Heralds called it, and claimed that instead of being physically brought into being in the normal way, they simply appeared, full-grown, out of a grove in the middle of Companion's Field. They had unusually powerful abilities in mind-magic, and through most of the history of Valdemar there had never been more than one Grove-born Companion at once. But then again, this was, by all accounts both sacred and secular, a crucial point in the history, not only of Valdemar, but of this entire part of the world, and if ever there was the need for a second Grove-born Companion, this was the time.

Tremane chewed on his lip, and ran a hand over the top of his balding head. "You know," he said cautiously. "The fact that those weapons they are looking at in the Tower survived at all might indicate that some shields held, wouldn't it? Surely there were very powerful shields on that Tower at the time of the Cataclysm."

"And it might only indicate that things at the heart of the Cataclysm had some natural protection, like things in the eye of a whirlwind," Elspeth reminded him, twisting a silver-threaded chestnut curl around one finger. "I wouldn't count on that. I also wouldn't count on any of us, singly or together, being able to replicate shields created by the mages who lived back then. These were people capable of *creating* living beings—gryphons, basilisks, wyrsa—and I don't know of anyone living now who would even attempt such a thing."

Darkwind cleared his throat softly to regain their attention. "To get back to your question about the effects of the original Cataclysm—afterward, the natural flows of magic energy in those areas changed completely, and we can only assume that the same thing will happen again. And as for the physical world—well, we Hawkbrothers are still healing the damage that was created in the wake of the original Storms. If you think the monsters that you've seen so far are bad, wait until there are hundreds, thousands of them, when the number of warped and changed creatures equals or exceeds the number of normal creatures." He drummed his fingers on the table for a moment as he made some quick calculations. "To give you an idea, it has taken us something like two thousand years to clear an area approximately half the size of your Empire of dangerous creatures and even more dangerous magic."

Tremane brooded over his stack of paper for a moment. "So your suggestion would be…?"

Elspeth and Darkwind exchanged another look, and it was Darkwind who replied. "If our group at the Tower can't do anything—warn everyone you can reach, create what shields and shelters you can, assume that they won't hold, and endure. Make your plans after you see what the effects are this time."

The Duke made a sour face, but did not respond. Elspeth tried some sympathy.

"Duke Tremane, I know this is difficult for you, but at least you are in command of an area in which much of the magical energy has been drained away, and which never relied on magic to get things done in the first place," she pointed out. "You can count on most buildings staying up, most bridges standing firm, count on fires heating your barracks as they always have, candles lighting the darkness, and food cooking properly in a well-made oven. Hardorn is prepared for everything except what the final Storm will do to the physical world—and in a way, you can even prepare for that, simply by knowing what the last Cataclysm did."

Tremane sighed, and rubbed one temple with his fingers. "Yes, I know this, and I also know that this is not going to be the case in the Empire. Things were falling to pieces so badly that when I mounted my raid on that Imperial warehouse complex, the men there hadn't heard from their superiors in weeks, and now—I can't even imagine the state of chaos the Empire must be in. It's just that things were difficult for us before, and the one comfort I had was that I couldn't envision them getting any worse. Now I have to, and plan for it, somehow."

Elspeth shook her head emphatically. "You can't *plan* for this, Tremane. All you can do is to warn people of what they *might* expect, and put things in place that will give you information once the worst happens. The signal-towers, for one thing. They work almost as well as Companions, and you ought to make it a priority to get them manned by people who know how to use them. You ought to make it a priority to get more of them in place if it is at all possible! If every little village had a tower, the way every village has access to a Herald, you'd be able to get help to people long before a messenger could have reached you."

Darkwind nodded. "Don't plan for specific events; doing that will inevitably prove to be an exercise in futility."

"Plan for flexibility, you mean?" The Duke considered that for a moment, and nodded. "All right, I can see that." Then he sighed. "And plan for communication, put ways of bringing in information in place while we still can. That's good, as long as the trouble spots are places where there are still people living. But if they aren't, there could be a nest of something brewing, some monstrous creatures, say, and we wouldn't know about it until the creatures had wiped out an entire town. Maybe not even then."

He rubbed his forehead, and Darkwind saw the shadow of physical pain in his eyes, in the tense muscles of his homely face. "I just wish there was a way to watch the *land*," he said fretfully. "I used to be able to get my mages to scry entire stretches of countryside, and that's what I'd give my arm to have working again."

Darkwind exchanged another look with Elspeth. *:What do you think? This is the best opening he's ever given us.:*

:If we can make him believe in earth-sense,: she replied, with some pessimism. *:Still, you're right. It isn't just the best opening, it's the only opening he's ever given us.:*

:You, or me?: he asked.

:Me first, just to open the subject. I'm the local royalty, the local Herald, and the local expert in mind-magic. I could be expected to know about these things, and know if the Hardornens were just making something up. You pick up if you see an opening to insert something you know.:

He folded his hands on the table in front of him as she cleared her throat. "Duke Tremane," she said. "I may have a solution to that particular problem, and oddly enough it is a part of a proposition that the Hardornens outside your domain wanted me to make to you on their behalf." She smiled apologetically. "I think you probably were anticipating that the loyalists might ask us to serve as their envoys as well as envoys for the Alliance. We promised we would put their proposal before you at an opportune time, but we promised nothing else; that seemed harmless enough."

He looked up sharply, and a little suspiciously. "A proposition? What sort of proposition?"

Elspeth bit her lip and looked down at her strong, well-muscled hands for a moment. They were hardly the hands of a pampered princess, and Darkwind had a suspicion that Tremane had noticed this. "Well... it's a rather interesting one. It seems that they've been watching how you manage things here, and you've frankly impressed them. There seems to be a general consensus that under certain very specific circumstances, they would not only be happy to arrange a truce with you, but they would be willing to offer you the crown of Hardorn itself."

He looked as if she had hit him in the back of the head with a board. It was the first time he had ever actually shown surprise. "The *crown*? They'd make me their *King*? What about their own claimants?"

"There aren't any," Darkwind said crisply. "Ancar was very thorough when it came to eliminating rivals. We were told that there weren't even any claimants on the distaff side; apparently he didn't in the least see any reason to exclude his female relatives from the purges, nor children, nor even infants. From all anyone can tell, he went back to the fourth and fifth remove of the cousins. By the time he was finished, well, you have as much right to the throne as any of the natives, that's how thin the royal connections are."

We learned most of that when we were here last, but I don't think it would be politic to mention that little trip.

Tremane didn't exactly pale, but he did look a little shocked. "And I thought that politics in the Empire were cut-throat," he murmured, as if to himself. Then he blinked, and collected himself. "So, just what *are* these specific circumstances you were talking about? And how will all this give me intelligence about what is happening to the land?"

Elspeth toyed with her glass of water. "This is where I am going to have to ask you to stretch your imagination a bit, Tremane," she replied. "You know that mind-magic exists, now that you've seen the members of our party use it."

He nodded cautiously.

"You also have your own Healers who use Healing magic, which is similar to, but not identical with, mind-magic," she continued. "And you know that neither are affected by the mage-storms which are disrupting what we in Valdemar call *true*-magic."

"I'm following you so far," Tremane said with a nod.

"'Well, as near as we can tell, there is another form of magic which is *like* mind-magic and *like* Healing-magic, but isn't exactly either of them," she told him, leaning forward earnestly. "It's called earth-magic, and it seems to have entirely to do with the land, the health of the land, and restoring that health. We think that's what hedge-wizards and earth-witches use, rather than true-magic; people who are trained in those disciplines—so they tell me—also refer to their power as earth-magic, and they call what you and Darkwind and I are accustomed to using by the name of *high*-magic."

:Right. So you tell him about Hawkbrother Healing Adepts while I figure out how to segue this into the earth-binding ritual.:

Darkwind nodded very slightly and caught up the conversational ball. "We Tayledras have specialized Adepts, called Healing Adepts, who have the ability to sense the poisoned places, the places where magic has made things go wrong, and fix them again," he told Tremane, who was sitting back in his chair with an odd expression that Darkwind could not read. "And if you need evidence of how well this works, it is in the fact that we *have* restored so much of the land to the pre-Cataclysm days. The special ability that makes this possible—Elspeth's people would call it a *Gift*—is something we all call the earth-sense."

"It's not just Tayledras Healing Adepts and earth-witches that use this. Both the King of Rethwellan and my stepfather Prince Daren have earth-sense, in fact," she said, taking the narrative back. "It seems that the Gift has always been in the Rethwellan royal line. They haven't needed it for generations, but it's obvious how useful it is when you know that even though Daren was not familiar with Hardorn and not ritually tied to the land here, he could *still* sense what Ancar had done to it when he came here to help Valdemar drive Ancar out. That actually proved to be of tactical value, since it gave us an idea of where Ancar was finding all the power he needed."

Tremane nodded, his brows knitted intently, and seized on the phrase that they had both hoped he would. "Ritually tied to the land?" he asked. "Just what does that mean?"

"The monarchs of Rethwellan—and I presume, of Hardorn—have always taken part in a very old ritual known as *earth-binding*," she told him. "Because we in Valdemar do not have that particular ritual, I can't even begin to tell you how it works, or why, but when it is over, every major injury or change to the land is instantly sensed by the monarch. Ancar obviously never participated in that ritual, or he could not have done the things he did—I suspect that, as in Rethwellan, the earth-binding is part of the Hardornen private rites that take place just before the public coronation. Ancar crowned himself, without the usual rituals, so—" She shrugged. "My stepfather says that those who even have earth-sense latently can have it aroused by such a rite."

"The point here is that the people of Hardorn have found some of the priests of the old ways who know that ritual," Darkwind continued, as she glanced at him to cue him to take up the narrative. "*They* think that if you were to be tested for earth-sense and had it even latently, that would qualify you for the Hardornen crown. And if you were to undergo the earth-binding ritual, thus awakening the earth-sense and binding you to Hardorn, you would be a—a *safe* monarch for Hardorn, because you would be unable to harm, abuse, or misuse your land the way Ancar did."

"Because harming the land would hurt me." He lifted one eyebrow skeptically.

:*Is he going to laugh?*: Elspeth sounded dubious, and Darkwind didn't blame her. This was such a primitive, unsophisticated concept—for someone from the Eastern Empire, so sophisticated in the ways of magic that its power was used for practically everything, this must seem incredibly savage and crude.

But he didn't laugh, and in fact, he seemed to be thinking the concept over. "Can you tell me anything else about this earth-sense? Just what does it entail? How do you learn to use it?"

"Among my people, it isn't very complicated," Darkwind told him. "You don't so much learn to use it as you learn to keep it from using you. It's rather like Empathy in a way, or extremely strong Mindspeech. You actually learn how to shut it out so that it doesn't affect you all the time."

"Interesting. I can see how it would be inconvenient to be affected adversely by the very condition you are attempting to remedy." His brows creased in thought. "And does it go the other way? Does the physical condition of the King affect the land?"

"Havens, no!" Elspeth exclaimed. "For one thing, the King is not exactly as—as *monumental* as a country! It would be like a flea stepping on a horse. For another, it's only a sense, like the sense of smell, and..." She trailed off in confusion as Darkwind shook his head.

"I hate to have to contradict Elspeth, but that's not entirely true, Duke Tremane," he said, feeling the need to be totally frank. "Under certain *very* specific circumstances, the health of the King who is bound to the land can affect the land. He can, in fact, sacrifice himself—give up his own life—to restore the land to its former health. This is something that my people know, and that the Shin'a'in not only know, but have even, very rarely, practiced. I must also say, however, that I personally do not believe that the Hardornens ever practiced that form of earth-binding. As with all crafts, there are scores, even hundreds or thousands of ways to do them, and nothing that they told us gave me any indication that they even know such a possibility exists. And I must also point out that to be valid, to have any chance of working, the sacrifice must be a *self*-sacrifice, entirely voluntary, and indeed eagerly sought by the sacrificial victim." He managed a thin smile. "Hauling one's King to the stone of sacrifice and spilling his blood upon the ground only serves as a sort of gruesome fertilizer to the local grass; it won't change anything else without that will to be sacrificed."

Tremane's brows crept halfway up his forehead as Darkwind imparted that choice bit of information, but he made no comment. After a moment, he stood up.

"I'd like to go think about this for a little," he said. "I assume you have a way of contacting someone if I make a decision?"

"I can find a contact,: Gwena said firmly in both their minds.

"We do," Elspeth told him.

"Then give me—about a mark," he replied. "I'll send for you, if you have no objections."

Since it had been a very long time since breakfast, and this would provide an excellent excuse to send their Imperial aide in search of food, Darkwind had no objections whatsoever, and neither did Elspeth. With a polite exchange of bows, they retired to their own quarters, leaving him sitting back in his chair, staring at the ducal ring on his finger, clearly deep in thought.

They were about halfway through a solid, if uninspired meal of bread and cold sliced meat and pickles, when Gwena announced that she had found the contact she had promised. *:Go to the Hanging Goose Tavern after dark,:* she told Darkwind. *:It will have to be you, since I don't think that Elspeth would be welcome in this particular tavern, and if there are two of you, he might suspect a trap.:*

Elspeth exchanged a wry glance with Darkwind and shrugged, applying herself to her food.

:You want to speak to the bartender who dispenses the beer, not the one who handles the harder drinks,: she continued. *:You tell him, "I drink my beer very cold." He is supposed to reply, "That's an odd habit," and you say, "I picked it up in the West."*

He'll nod and ask you what your message is. He has a perfect memory; he'll pass it on word for word. If Tremane decides to take the gamble, I suspect you'll have your delegation, priest included, within a few days. Maybe sooner. They might have moved someone into a village nearby, hoping you would be able to offer him the proposition soon after we arrived.:

"I rather suspected that the loyalists had agents in the city," Elspeth said, as she ate the last bite. "I couldn't imagine how they knew so much about him just from 'hearing things.' But this sounds as if the network has been well in place for some time. It takes a long time to find someone with a perfect memory who is trustworthy enough to act as a message drop. It makes me wonder if this tavern wasn't a contact point for... other things." She smiled suggestively at Darkwind.

He chuckled. "I am just a poor Hawkbrother scout with no knowledge of you city dwellers and your ways," he protested. "What other things?"

"Smuggling, maybe. Possibly intriguing against Ancar. And I'll *bet* the reason Gwena doesn't want me to go there is not because I wouldn't be welcome alone there either." She grinned at something Gwena said only to her. "I thought so." She reached out and patted Darkwind's hand. "The ladies working in this tavern will be selling more than just strong drink and food, my poor, uncivilized Hawkbrother. I suggest that you make it very clear to them that you aren't interested in their wares, or you might bring something inconvenient and uncomfortable home with you that would require a Healer's help to clear up."

He grinned back at her, and was trying to think of a clever retort when Tremane's aide came to fetch them.

The Grand Duke was waiting for them when they arrived, looking no different than when they had left him. They took their seats and waited for him to speak.

"Frankly, I am not entirely convinced that this earth-sense you told me about really exists," he said after a moment. "And I honestly do not think, if it exists, that *I* happen to have it. It just seems all too very pat and too coincidental that out of all the people who might have been sent here, *I* would happen to have this sense which is needed at this particular time." He frowned a little. "It's rather too much like something a tale-seller might make up."

"Possibly," Darkwind replied. "But you might consider it before you dismiss this proposition out-of-hand. If you take as your premise that earth-sense *does* exist, and that the extreme form of it could only be... induced, let us say... by this ritual, then the lesser, or latent forms would be very useful to anyone who was in a position to rule even a small area. Having such a thing could explain why some landowners are more successful at managing their property than others—why some landowners have an uncanny ability to gauge what is going on with their property and people, and why some have remarkable hunches that always prove correct."

"I can see that," Tremane acknowledged.

"So, given that, it is logical to assume that those landowners whose lines were so Gifted would be more prosperous than others, would accumulate more property, and would eventually rise to higher and higher positions of power over the many generations," Darkwind persisted. "And in short, it would actually be *logical* to assume that a man who had been a ruler of property or even a King would be so Gifted, because his predecessors could not have prospered so well without it."

Tremane laughed out loud; it was the first time that Darkwind had ever heard him laugh, and he liked the sound of it. He often judged aspects of peoples' character by their laughter; Tremane's laugh was open, generous, and not at all self-conscious.

"I think that if you had not been born among the Hawkbrothers, you would have become a diplomat, a courtier, or a priest, Master Darkwind," he said finally. "You certainly can turn a fine argument. Now, hear me out, if you please."

Darkwind and Elspeth both nodded, and Tremane set forth his own reasoning.

"You must know, and *they* must know, that with or without this *earth-sense*, if my men and I can recreate order here—as we already have done, you might note—people will come to my banner without the title attached to it. That is the great secret of Imperial success. We wait until a land is disorganized and demoralized, and then we move in, offering peace, order, and prosperity. Usually people welcome us. Then, when they see the high level that Imperial prosperity represents, word spreads, and the lands we move on generally are half-conquered before the Army itself ever reaches them."

"That makes rather too much sense," Elspeth put in dryly.

He nodded his acknowledgment and continued, tapping his index finger on the table to emphasize each point. "You must make it very clear to these people that no matter what happens, I intend to go on holding this particular piece of Hardorn from now on, for myself, my men, and those Hardornens who have accepted my rule and my order without any of this earth-binding business."

"I think they are already well aware of that, Tremane," she answered just as frankly. "But I will make sure that arrangement is openly acknowledged on both sides. To be honest with you, there is no way that you can be dislodged with the few resources these Hardornen loyalists have at their command. That would take an army. The only armies large enough are those commanded by the Allies, and we are here representing the Allies in a gesture of peace and goodwill, so I don't think you need concern yourself about losing your hold on this place."

"Good. Just so that we're all clear on that." He toyed with a corner of a piece of paper for a moment. "I can't say that I really care for the idea of subjecting myself to this ritual. It all sounds terribly primitive, somehow. But perhaps even if *I* don't believe I have this so-called earth-sense, the priest will be convinced that I do, and will let me go through with this ritual even if it is meaningless. Frankly, if that happens, it would be the easiest and quickest way to get all of Hardorn under my wing, and it would be done with absolutely no bloodshed." He smiled; an oddly shy smile, and Darkwind had the feeling that it was a rare smile, as if Tremane had even less to smile about than to laugh about. "How could I possibly turn away that kind of opportunity?"

"In your position, I certainly would not," Darkwind told him. "Well, is that the whole of your message?"

Tremane nodded. "And if you'll excuse me, I have matters regarding my men to see to. My aide can escort you back to your quarters, and if there is anywhere in the city you need to go, he can give you the proper directions."

:*That won't be necessary,*: Gwena said.

"Thank you," Darkwind replied, without giving any indication that he would take Tremane up on his offer.

Once again, after a polite exchange of bows, they departed for their own quarters. Elspeth had a thoughtful look on her face, but waited until they were alone again before saying anything.

She stood with her back to the cast-iron-and-brick stove holding the mage-fire, warming herself at it. A real fire also burned on the hearth, and between the two, their rooms were as comfortable as any in Valdemar. But the hallways of this fortified manor were still cold, despite the addition of such stoves, and they both tended to get chilled going from their quarters to Tremane's.

There was no doubt that this was one of the worst winters that Hardorn had ever experienced, even without the effect of the magestorms. The main difference in the weather now that the mage-storms had abated, according to their aide, was that now there were only snowstorms, not killing blizzards, every two weeks or so. With the incredible blanket of snow covering the ground, the sun couldn't even begin to melt it before another layer fell.

The modified Heralds' Whites that the *hertasi* had designed for her seemed particularly well-suited to the icy landscape outside. She wondered what the Imperial soldiers thought when they saw her; did they believe that her costume was meant to reflect the season, as Tayledras scout gear did?

"You know," Elspeth said finally, in Tayledras. "This situation has some interesting parallels in the history of Valdemar—the Founding, specifically."

"Oh?" Darkwind joined her, hands outstretched to the warm stove, wishing that there was something like a Hawkbrother hot spring or soaking pool about. It never seemed possible to be entirely warm except in bed. He responded in the same language. "I wasn't aware of that."

"Well, Valdemar was fleeing the Empire rather than serving it when he and his followers trekked out in this direction, but when he got to the point where Haven is now and started building, he actually built beside an existing village," Elspeth replied, turning to face the stove and rubbing her hands together. "The locals there were not entirely thrilled with having a foreign power moving in, although they never actually *opposed* him. But once they saw the advantages of coming under his protection—and the way in which his own followers were treated—they began to act the way the Hardornens are with Tremane. And eventually, of course, they insisted that he call himself a King." She chuckled. "That was really rather funny; it seemed that every little petty ruler for leagues in every direction was calling himself a 'King,' and his own people were embarrassed to be led by a mere Baron. They had a crown made up, called in a priest to concoct a ceremony, and had him crowned before he had a chance to object. I gather that he was rather startled by it all."

Darkwind laughed. "That may be the first time I've ever heard of someone being tricked into becoming a King," he responded. "But you're right, I do see the parallels there."

She stared at the stove, frowning. "I think we can assume that Tremane is going to be offered the Crown, no matter what."

"I think that is a foregone conclusion, yes, lover," Darkwind admitted. "Even if he doesn't have earth-sense, the priest may perform the binding anyway, just to make him eligible. I think he was right about that."

She sighed and nodded. "The next question may be how we arrange for there to be the same checks on the King of Hardorn that there are on the Son of the Sun, the King of Rethwellan, and the Queen of Valdemar. Solaris has to answer to Vkandis, Faram has both the earth-binding and his family's sword to contend with, and Selenay has her Companion." She chewed her lip. "Then again—we may already have those checks partially in place. Solaris *did* curse him with speaking only the truth, after all."

"Yes, but not the whole truth," he reminded her. "There are ways of lying simply by not telling *all* of the truth."

She grimaced, and turned away from the warmth to pace the room as she often did when she was thinking. "You may think I'm going mad, but I'm beginning to agree with young Karal; I think this man has a basically good nature. That entire interview about the assassins when we first arrived…"

Darkwind nodded, for he had come away with the same impression out of that interview; that Tremane was a man who would bear the dreadful burden of indirectly ordering the deaths of innocent people, and he would feel guilt about that for the rest of his life. *Real* guilt, not feigned. And it didn't matter that he had good reason at the time for his actions; what mattered was that he himself had changed over the course of these several months. What had been acceptable to him before no longer was.

But Darkwind also was aware that the man could be a very good actor. Most rulers were, to a greater or lesser extent.

"I still have some reservations," he said after a moment. "What occurred in the past is immutable. He *has* done terrible things to us, and without any provocation. Perhaps he has regrets now, but I find myself wondering if he might not revert to his old ways under pressure."

She sighed. :*I think we'd better continue this conversation in a way that can't be overheard,*: she cautioned.

:*Good idea. Sejanes had some magical way of learning Valdemaran and other tongues; there might be someone else here who can do the same thing.*: Granted, there might not be enough mage-energy for them to do so, but why take the chance? :*We Tayledras are more suspicious than any other race, I think, but I wish I knew if it was Tremane's better nature that had been subverted by the expediency of the Empire, or his expedient nature that has chosen to disguise itself as a good heart for—well—!*:

:*He's in a position to do everyone more good than harm right now,*: Gwena pointed out, joining the conversation.

:Gwena's right; and in fact, that's exactly what he has done,: Elspeth seconded. *:Look at his record:* granted, *he coopted the best structure in the area for his headquarters, but other than that, he lives a relatively lean life for someone who is basically the uncrowned king of this area. He eats exactly the same food as his men, he isn't wasting precious resources on extravagant entertainments for his own benefit; in fact, he's pouring a lot of those resources back into the community here. He never asks his men to do anything he wouldn't, and he's usually out there leading them in person.:*

:He thinks first of his men, then of the local folk, then of their land and their beasts, and then *of himself,:* Gwena put in. *:That is the pattern that I'm seeing, and honestly, while some of that might be expediency, it can't all be explained by that.:*

Darkwind chuckled. *:I'm glad he's not handsome; I'd be jealous. He's managed to seduce both my ladies away from me.:*

Elspeth picked up an inkstand and pretended to throw it at him; he ducked.

:Consider yourself kicked,: Gwena retorted.

:Honestly, ke'chara, *I would like to give him the chance to prove himself, and the way he handles the next crisis—which is going to be very, very bad, I think—will tell us what he's really made of,:* Elspeth replied.

Darkwind chewed on that thought a while before replying, wondering if they were all making a terrible mistake. He *wanted* to believe in Tremane, and in the idea that the man was finally allowing himself to behave in a moral fashion rather than a calculated one. How must it have felt, to spend most of one's life having to plot each and every action without regard to whether or not it was ethically right? If he himself had been in that position, he'd have been driven mad.

:All right,: he said at last, *:but I have one proviso.:* His jaw tensed as he hardened his mind. *:If he proves treacherous, and a danger to the Alliance—if he is going to cost more lives—we take care of the situation ourselves.:*

:You mean, kill him.: Elspeth nodded, very slowly. *:I don't like it—but I don't want another Ancar, much less another Falconsbane. He's used to using magic, and it would be very tempting to resort to the blood-path to get the power he's used to having.:* She shivered, and so did he; they had both seen far too much of the results of that path. *:We've done this before, and I'd rather the blood were on our hands, I suppose, than find that even more innocent blood had been spilled.:*

It was a nasty moral trap; when was murder acceptable? But that was the moral trap that the Tayledras had always been in. Darkwind himself had faced it many times—warning trespassers three times, and assuming that if they did not heed the warning, they were in Hawkbrother lands

795

for evil purposes. How many would-be enslavers of *tervardi* and *hertasi*, mages hunting for yet more power for the wrong purposes, and would-be murderers of Hawkbrothers had he eliminated over the years? Enough that he had lost count.

Elspeth only had a handful of deaths on her conscience, but she was prepared to add another if the need was there.

:And with any luck, we'll all discover that our pessimism is unfounded,: Gwena said cheerfully. *:I'll tell you what; I will see if I can tell whether or not Tremane has earth-sense, while you make contact with the loyalists. Darkwind, my dear, we need to rummage through your wardrobe and find something in it that will not scream* foreigner *to every person in the town.:*

:What do you mean, we, *horse?:* he asked her.

Darkwind found his messenger—and Gwena's careful probe of Duke Tremane uncovered only a verdict of "maybe." Four days later, their aide knocked tentatively on the door to their quarters just after they'd finished breakfast. "Excuse me, Envoys?" he said, when Darkwind opened the door to him. "I don't want to interrupt, but there's a religious gentleman below who says that you called for him?"

Elspeth turned in surprise. Despite Gwena's assurance, she hadn't really expected an answer to their message this quickly. The man really *must* have been fairly close by; that argued for certainty on the part of the Hardornens that they had made Tremane an offer he would find irresistible.

"We have been expecting him, Jem," Darkwind told the young man. "We just didn't know when he would arrive. If you are reasonably sure that it is safe to do so, please show him the way up. Otherwise, if you are not happy with a potential breach of security, we can arrange to meet him in the town."

Jem flushed. "Oh, no. He's just an old man—it won't cause any problems. I just didn't know if you wanted to be bothered with him, if he might be a charlatan or—" He flushed even redder, realizing that he might have inadvertently insulted all of them.

"That's fine, Jem. Please show him here, and arrange for something hot for all of us to drink. And perhaps more food, he might not have broken his own fast yet," Elspeth said, in her kindest tones.

The aide bowed a little, still red with embarrassment, and left quickly. Tremane's aides were far more used to military situations than to the diplomatic ones they now found themselves hip-deep in. Elspeth found it rather charming, actually; military men were, in general, much easier to deal with and much more straightforward than civilians.

The old man and the second breakfast arrived at the same time; Elspeth privately thought that she wasn't too surprised Jem had taken him for a possible charlatan. There was nothing at all remarkable about him. His hair, gray and a touch on the shaggy side, looked as if he had not put scissors to it lately. His build was that of a long-time clerk whose parents may have been merchants or tradesmen of modest means. His face, square, with a small beard, was lined with care, yet had smile-creases bracketing his mouth and eyes. His robes and cloak were clean and serviceable, but hardly impressive, he wore no liturgical jewels, and his manner was unassuming and cheerful. All of which, in her experience, meant that he was probably a very *good* priest; good priests, like good leaders, gave more to their followers than they kept for themselves, and were not particularly conscious of appearances.

They introduced themselves and offered the old man, who called himself Father Janas, their hospitality. As Elspeth had anticipated, he hadn't eaten, and he applied himself to the food with a hearty appetite. They kept conversation to a minimum until he had finished; once he had taken his cloak off, it was fairly obvious that, like most Hardornens, he had been sharing in the hard times. He wasn't emaciated, but he was thin enough that he had probably been on the same short rations as his followers.

"Oh, that was lovely," he said at last, when he had finished, and leaned back in his chair cradling a cup of hot tea laden with honey. "I'm afraid that my besetting sin is that I cannot resist good food." He laughed. "Since we are supposed to be concentrating on the spiritual world rather than the secular world, I suspect I shall be chided for my failing sooner or later by those to whom I must answer."

Darkwind smiled at that. "I would rather say that you were showing proper joy and respect for the bounty of the earth," Darkwind replied, and the old priest chuckled, a twinkle in his eyes.

"Well, shall we deal with the reason that I am here, rather than engage in rationalizing my shortcomings?" he asked, after taking a sip of his tea. "As I assume *you* suppose, I have come to test Duke Tremane for earth-sense, which will mean that I will awake it if it is there; and once I have done so, I will bind him to Hardorn. Now, nothing I have been vouchsafed has given me any indication that he does or does not have the sense, and I am quite sure that *he* has no idea what is going to happen; do either of you?"

Elspeth shook her head. "We don't use that Gift in Valdemar, or, rather, if we do, it isn't used by Heralds, Bards, or Healers. And those are the only ones whose training I'm familiar with," she said. "My stepfather has it, but we've never discussed it much, and *he* was never formally bound to Valdemar. I've heard of other latent Gifts being awakened as a theoretical possibility, but no one in my lifetime has ever tried such a thing."

Darkwind shrugged, as the priest turned to him. "The Tayledras Healing Adepts all develop earth-sense along with their other abilities," he replied. "It doesn't come on them all at once, and if anyone has it latently, we've never bothered to awaken it. I haven't any idea how someone would react in such a circumstance."

Father Janas raised an eyebrow. "It can be rather dramatic," he said cautiously. "Assuming that one has it latently, rather than having a very weak version of the sense, that is. We have always conducted this particular ceremony several days before the actual coronation of our kings, precisely because of that. It sometimes takes the recipient a good deal of time to get used to his new ability, if heretofore it has only been latent and when actuated proves to be very strong."

Elspeth nodded. "Rather like suddenly being able to see, I suppose," she offered. "Well, that is all very well in theory, but you are here to put theory into practice. How soon would you care to see Duke Tremane? Are there any preparations you would like to make, any vestments you need to change into before you are presented?"

Father Janas smoothed down the front of his robe self-consciously. "Much as I wish I could present a more impressive picture, I am afraid that I am wearing my best—indeed, my only vestments." He licked his lips and looked apologetic. "Ancar did not persecute priests and clerics directly, but he found many ways of doing so indirectly. I do not think you will find a single religious organization in all of Hardorn surviving at better than a subsistence level, and many simply vanished altogether as old members died and no new ones came to replace them." He shook his head sadly. "At any rate, it is all moot; I have no preparations to make, and I should prefer to see the Duke as soon as possible, as soon as he has the time free."

Darkwind rose to request their aide to take a message to the Duke. Elspeth had some other ideas, however.

She wrote a short note while Darkwind was talking with Jem, and asked the aide to take the message down to Tremane's chief of supply on his way back from delivering their request for an audience to the Duke. Jem looked baffled, but agreed; he was obviously not going to question why the envoy wanted to send a note to the supply sergeant.

"Just what are you up to?" Darkwind asked her, as they closed the door behind his retreating back and returned to their guest.

Elspeth seated herself before replying. "Tremane told me that he and his men had virtually gutted an entire Imperial warehouse complex," she told him, as well as their guest. "Now, given how the Empire likes to regiment things, even though there is no *official* Imperial religion, I am betting that somewhere among all the uniforms brought back are at least a few standard Imperial Army Chaplains' robes, or something of that nature. And I'm also betting that they look pretty much like every other priest's robes I've ever seen, precisely because an Imperial Army Chaplain would have to be able to conduct the rites of several religions, hence the uniform robe will be as bland and as *general* as possible."

"I follow your reasoning so far," Darkwind said, still puzzled. "But why should the supply sergeant let us have one of these uniforms, if they exist?"

She grinned. "I've been talking to the townsfolk. I know that it is Tremane's standard procedure to sell anything in stores that is not immediately useful to his soldiers if a civilian wants to buy it. You'll find a lot of townsfolk outfitted in surplused uniforms of some of the odder auxiliary disciplines, if you know what to look for. I asked specifically if I could purchase a set of chaplain's robes if there are any, and asked him to send them up as soon as he found them." She turned to the priest, who was a little flushed. "We'll have plenty of time to alter them into something approximating your own vestments before Tremane has time to see us."

Father Janas looked even more embarrassed. "Really, that's too good of you—"

She interrupted him with a cautionary hand. "You're being generous and forgiving; I know that this was a bit high-handed of me. But we may be more anxious to settle this than you are, and I'd prefer not to leave anything to chance. The Grand Duke isn't even certain that he believes earth-sense exists; I suspect his attitude is more that he is humoring us than anything else. We all want him to agree to go through with something he already considers to be mummery, and we want him to agree to do it *now*. The better the impression your appearance will make on him, the more likely he is to do that."

Darkwind nodded thoughtfully. "Actually," he put in, "using an Imperial uniform may serve us better than if you had come with your own vestments. He has lived with the chaplains. He is going to respect the uniform and what it represents without realizing he is primed to do so."

Father Janas uttered a faint laugh in self-deprecation. "Well, it is certainly true that most people rely on one's outward appearance for their first impressions, and I am afraid my appearance is hardly likely to inspire confidence."

His admission only deepened his obvious embarrassment, and Darkwind quickly changed the subject to that of the conditions over most of Hardorn. The priest was only too willing to talk about the hardships people all over the country had and were suffering, and the spirit with which they were enduring those hardships.

"Everything you saw as you journeyed here is representative of conditions everywhere in this land," he said, with real sadness. "People are not starving, but they are hungry. They are not freezing to death, but they are cold. There is not a single soul in this country that did not lose at least one member of his family to unnatural death in the last five years, and as you saw, entire towns and villages have been emptied. Temples and other places of worship are deserted, or tended by a few old men like myself. Worst of all, we have lost most of a generation of young men, and no matter how much better things become, how can we possibly replace them? Who will be the parents of our next generation of citizens?"

There are several thousand young men, none of whom will ever be able to return to the Empire, camped right here, Elspeth thought. *And most of them would be perfectly happy to become the parents of the next generation of Hardornens. I wonder if he's thought of that? I know Tremane has.*

At length Jem returned with the answer from Duke Tremane; he would be free immediately after lunch to receive the priest, and if necessary, could clear a good portion of the afternoon for the interview.

"That would be wise," Father Janas said, as Darkwind deferred to him. "Please return, tell him this would be very much to my liking, and ask him to do so."

Jem went back with the reply. Not long after he left, one of the many locals who had been hired to run errands within the Imperial complex arrived with a large, neat package and a handwritten bill. Elspeth accepted both, made a face at the mildly extortionate price the supply officer was charging, but rummaged in her belt-pouch for the correct number of silver coins anyway. They were Valdemaran rather than Hardornen or Imperial, but the price had been quoted in silver-weight and not a specific coinage. Given the circumstances, she doubted that anyone would care whose face was stamped on them so long as the weight was true. Those she sent back with the errand boy, as Darkwind handed the package over to Father Janas.

Just as she had suspected, the official uniform of an Imperial Chaplain was, once the rainbow of specific accoutrements for various religions and liturgical events were set aside, virtually identical in cut to the threadbare robe Father Janas already wore; it was even a very similar gray in color. He retired to the next room to change, and returned looking much trimmer.

Darkwind surveyed him with a critical eye. "Just what form does your deity—or deities—take?" he asked the priest. "Forgive me, but I think we need to make you look a little more impressive."

The priest looked confused but answered readily enough. "The Earth-father and Sky-mother are usually represented by the colors green and blue, and by a circle or sphere that is half white and half black, but—"

Darkwind had already turned to the pile of multicolored stoles and other accessories, sorting through the plethora of plain and appliqued fabrics, and came up with one stole that was green, and one blue. Quick work with his knife gave him four halves, two of which he handed to Elspeth. She had already divined what he was up to, and had gone into the other room for her sewing kit; a few moments later, she draped a stole about Father Janas' neck that was green on his right side and blue on his left.

But it was still too plain, and she took it back from him. While she cut half-circles of black and white fabric from two of the other stoles to applique to the ends of the new one, Darkwind left for their bedroom and returned with a bit of his personal jewelry. "This probably isn't much like something you would ordinarily wear," he said apologetically. "But it will probably do for now, and Tremane isn't going to know the difference between Hardornen and Shin'a'in work."

He handed a copper medallion on a tanned leather thong to Janas; Elspeth recognized it at once as the sort of token the Shin'a'in carried to identify themselves or their allies to Tayledras. She had once carried a similar token, meant to identify her to Kerowyn's kin, as well as to any Tayledras she might have encountered. This one was engraved with a swirling, abstract pattern on one side, and a deer on the other.

But a leather thong simply would not do. Now it was Elspeth's turn to go back to the bedroom and rummage through her jewelry.

Copper. What do I have that is copper?

When they had left, she had simply tossed everything she owned into a bag, including some of the pieces meant to go with the costumes that Darkwind himself had designed for her. A glint of copper at the bottom caught her eye, and she untangled an interesting belt made of a heavy copper chain entwined with a light one. She purloined the light chain to hang the medallion from, then as an afterthought, suggested to Father Janas that he use the heavy chain for the original purpose of a belt. That was the final touch that he needed, for the robe had been just a bit long on him; now with the new robe, stole, belt, and medallion, Janas presented quite a different picture from the man who had arrived.

He seemed to feel the change as well; he seemed less weary, stood a little straighter and with confidence matching his natural cheer. All in all, Elspeth reckoned that they had put in a good morning's work.

"It isn't precisely canonical," Janas told them. "But as you said, no one here is going to know that, and it *does* look—well—much more respectable, in the sense of *worthy of respect.* I can't begin to thank you enough."

"Thank us if all of this bears fruit," Elspeth replied firmly. "And speaking of which, here's our lunch."

As usual, it was rather plain fare, but there was plenty of it. Jem seemed startled by Father Janas' transformation, but treated him with more deference than he had shown initially, thus confirming Elspeth's feeling that the effort of reclothing the priest was more than justified. Jem lingered while they ate, which all of them read as an indication that Tremane was impatient to have the interview over with quickly. Spurred by that, they made quick work of their meal.

:I think we should let Janas take the lead in this now,: she told Darkwind.

:I agree; it will establish his authority from the beginning. After all, officially, we're only involved in this peripherally. We were never more than the informal intermediaries,: Darkwind replied.

Elspeth signaled the priest with a slight nod as she set her cup aside. He read the hint as adroitly as she had thought he would.

"I think we are ready to see Duke Tremane if he is ready for us," Father Janas said to the aide, standing up and settling his new vestments with an air of brisk competence.

"He is ready for you, sir," Jem responded with all of the respect that any of them could have asked. "If you would care to follow me?"

He then looked for a moment with confusion at the two envoys, as if he had, for that instant, forgotten that they were involved. Clearly he was uncertain whether they should be properly included in the invitation.

Father Janas solved his problem. "I have asked the Alliance envoys to accompany me," he said smoothly. "If Duke Tremane has no objection."

Jem's face cleared as Janas took the question out of his hands, and he bowed slightly to all of them. "Certainly, sir. If you would all please come with me?"

All during the quick walk to the Grand Duke's private quarters, Elspeth was conscious of an increasing feeling of irrational excitement. *Something* was going to happen; she wasn't quite certain what it was, but this visit was not going to pass without an event of some sort.

I wish there was something more of ForeSight in my family than just an ability to get an occasional hunch, she thought fretfully. *It would be nice to have some warning when a mountain is about to drop on us.*

At last they were finally closeted with Tremane, seated across from him in three chairs arrayed before his desk. This was not to be the less formal (Tremane was never *informal*) sort of meeting that she and Darkwind had been having with him of late; he had arrayed himself as the Grand Duke, the Commander of the Army, and the local Power. He wore his uniform, minus the Imperial devices, but with all of the other decorations and medals to which he was entitled. He had both a crackling fire in the hearth and a mage-fire in a stove, imparting a generous warmth to the room and a fragrant scent of pine resin to the air. Sunlight streamed in through the windows, whose heavy velvet curtains had been pulled back to let in as much light as possible. He had a choice of chairs to use here, and he had selected the heaviest and most thronelike for his use; the desk separated them from him like a fortress wall made of dark wood.

She was very glad now that she had gone out of her way to dress Father Janas appropriately. If he had entered this interview looking as shabby as he had when he had arrived, he would have begun on an unequal footing with Tremane. As Darkwind had speculated, she could see Tremane responding to the implied authority symbolized by a "uniform" he recognized, and Father Janas assumed his rightful position as an authority equal to his.

As for Elspeth, she was acutely aware of everything around her, her senses sharpened by her anticipation. Her feeling was so strong that it was amazing to her to see that Duke Tremane was concealing a certain amount of polite boredom under a smooth and diplomatic courtesy.

If Janas was put off by Tremane's attitude, he didn't show it. "Duke Tremane," Father Janas said, "you know why I am here. Those who have led the struggle against Imperial subjugation have heard of your defection from the Empire, seen how you have governed and protected the people here, and have come to the conclusion that *you*, at least, are not necessarily an enemy to Hardorn."

Tremane nodded at this recitation of the obvious, and waited for him to continue. Behind him, a knot in the wood on the fire *cracked* explosively; no one jumped.

Janas had clearly rehearsed his speech many times, until he was comfortable enough with it that he didn't have to think about it. "The consortium of loyal fighters believes that, since there is no one man who has been able to become their clear leader, and since no one in Hardorn commands the resources that you do, you may be the appropriate person to take up the defense of this land against outsiders and current adversity." He smiled thinly. "I will not mince words with you, Duke Tremane. These men are willing, given other conditions, to allow you to purchase the rule of Hardorn with the resources and men that you command."

He seemed a bit surprised by Father Janas' bluntness. "That would seem reasonable," he replied with care. "And I am certainly willing to put those resources into Hardorn."

Father Janas nodded. "So I have been sent here by those men to discover if you are both fit and willing to lead this nation and help to defend it against those who would subject it to the rule of a foreign power—*including* the Empire." Janas tilted his head in inquiry. The fire popped again, scattering sparks, as he waited for an answer.

Tremane's reply was brief but polite. "I would welcome the opportunity to prove my worth, but I would like to point out that I am not, and never have been, a traitor to any cause. It was the Emperor and the Empire who abandoned us here; *we* broke none of the oaths that we had given. But now that those vows are broken, we see every need to hold fast to the oaths that we gave to each other. And if, in keeping those vows, we aid the people here, that is all to the good. Times are perilous, and whenever loyalty is found, it should be rewarded with loyalty." His face hardened. "But any new responsibilities that I assume must work *with* my vows to my men."

"There will be no conflict." Janas nodded, and there was a great deal of satisfaction on his face. "In keeping with our traditions, the ruler of Hardorn must be possessed of the quality we know as *earth-sense*, and be bound to the land if he has that quality. In order that your consent to be tested is informed, I shall explain precisely what that means."

He went into a much more detailed explanation than Elspeth or Darkwind had done, and in Elspeth's opinion, Tremane was a bit too cavalier about the entire thing. *She* had not been certain until this moment that the test for the earth-sense involved actually awakening it if it was latent. And Tremane was clearly preoccupied with some other thought as the priest explained that if he showed the symptoms of having the earth-sense, he would be expected to undergo the earth-binding ritual immediately.

Perhaps his own statements to Janas had reminded him of things he needed to deal with among his own people; perhaps it was only that he was not inclined to spend his time on something even peripherally connected with religion. She had the feeling that Tremane was a man who gave secular respect to religious authority, lip-service to the rituals, and otherwise gave no thought to the subject. And he considered the entire business of earth-sense and earth-binding to be essentially religious in nature, a matter of faith rather than fact.

:He has already made up his mind that nothing is going to happen,: Darkwind commented, as he watched Tremane's attention wandering. *:He is good enough at reading people to know that Janas thinks he can be a good leader for Hardorn, and I suspect he thinks that is the only "test" he needed to pass. I think he has decided that Janas will make a couple of mystic passes, then declare he has the earth-sense, mumble a few phrases, and say that he is bound to Hardorn, all without anything he can detect actually occurring.:*

:I think he's making a mistake, if that's the case,: Elspeth offered. *:I wish he'd listened a bit more closely because I don't think he really knows what he might be getting into.:*

Well, it was already too late to say anything, for Tremane nodded with relief when Janas finished, and said, "Please, I am quite ready if you can begin now."

And Janas was not going to give Tremane a chance to change his mind, for the priest stood immediately.

"If I may come to your side of the desk, sir?" Janas asked, and at Tremane's nod, moved around the desk until he stood behind Tremane's chair, and placed the tips of his fingers on Tremane's temples before Tremane had a chance to object.

The priest closed his eyes and opened his mouth before Tremane could pull away from the unexpected touch. Elspeth started, literally jumped, as what emerged from Janas's mouth was not a chant, but a single, pure, bell-like tone.

The sound resonated through her, filling her ears and her mind, driving every thought from her head and rooting her to her chair. She couldn't have moved if the room had suddenly caught on fire. She couldn't even be afraid; the tone drove out all emotion, including fear. It had exactly the same effect on Darkwind, who stared at Janas with round, vaguely surprised eyes.

But it did *not* have that effect on Duke Tremane.

Beneath Janas' hands, the Grand Duke stiffened, and his own hands came up to cover the priest's, but not as if he was trying to tear Janas's fingers away from his head. His eyes closed, and his hands were clearly holding Janas's hands in place. His own mouth opened, and a second tone, harmonizing with the first, emerged from *his* throat. The effect of the two tones together was indescribable, and even as Elspeth experienced it, she was unable to analyze it. She was suspended in time and place, and nothing existed for her but the two-note song that resonated with every fiber of her body and soul. In fact, every sense was involved; colors intensified and became richer, and there was a scent of growing things and spring flowers filling the air that could not possibly have been there.

How long that went on, Elspeth could really not have said. It took no time at all, and it took forever. The moment when it stopped was as dramatic as that when it had started, for suddenly Tremane's eyes opened wide, then rolled up into his head; his mouth snapped shut, cutting off the tone. He let go of Janas' hands, and he collapsed over his desk as if his heart had suddenly given out.

Elspeth was still frozen, unable to stir. Janas stopped his singing—if that was what it was—the moment Tremane fell forward. For a moment he stared at the Grand Duke in something like shock, shaking his hands as if he had touched a burning coal.

"Well," he said finally, "he *certainly* has earth-sense."

Before either Elspeth or Darkwind could move, the priest pulled Tremane back up into the support of his chair, and shook him gently until he awoke.

"Is—" Darkwind began, half standing. Janas waved him back.

"Duke Tremane is simply suffering from the confusion of having a very *powerful* new ability thrust upon him," the priest said in a preoccupied voice. "But there is nothing wrong with him, I promise you. In fact, he may well be more *right* than he has ever been before in his life."

Tremane was clearly still dazed, as Janas reached for a letter opener on the Duke's desk, seized one of his hands, and stabbed the tip of his index finger with it. He was so dazed, that he acted as if he hadn't even felt the point of the blade piercing his skin.

Janas held onto the Duke's hand so that Tremane couldn't pull it away, and reached into a pouch on his belt, pulling out a tiny pinch of earth. He inverted Tremane's maltreated finger over the bit of dirt, and squeezed until a single drop of blood fell and mingled with the soil.

"In the name of the powers above our heads and below our feet, I bind you to the soil of Hardorn, Tremane," he intoned, letting go of Tremane's hand and seizing his chin instead. "In the name of the Great Guardians of the people, I bind you to the heart of Hardorn," he continued, and took up the pinch of mingled blood and earth. "In the name of Life and Light, I bind you to the soul of Hardorn, and by this token, you and the land are one."

He held out the bit of blood-soaked earth to the Duke's mouth. Tremane opened his lips to receive it, and fortunately, he swallowed it rather than spitting it out, which would probably have been a very unfortunate gesture and a terrible omen.

Janas stepped back, watching the Duke narrowly, and Tremane blinked owlishly at him for a moment. Then, without any warning, he made an odd little mewling cry and clapped both hands to his head, covering his eyes with his palms.

Now Elspeth started to rise, but the priest waved her back as well. "It's quite all right," he said, with immense satisfaction. "I can't begin to tell you how well this is going. He has the strongest earth-sense that I have ever seen in someone for whom it was latent until now—and just at the moment, he's a bit disoriented."

"Disoriented?" the Duke said from behind his hands. "By the Hundred Little Gods, that is *far* too mild a description!" He sounded breathless, as if he had been running a long and grueling race. "I feel—I feel as if I have been deaf and blind, and suddenly been given sight and hearing and I haven't the *least* notion what the things I am experiencing mean or what to do with them!"

He brought his hands down away from his head, but it was quite clear from the bewildered expression he wore and the dazed look in his eyes that he was undergoing sensations he had never experienced before. "I think I may be ill," he said faintly. "I feel terrible. I'm going to be very, very sick in a moment."

"No, you won't," Janas soothed. "That's not your own body you're feeling, it's Hardorn. The land is sick, not you; sick and weary. Separate yourself from it; remember how you felt when you woke up this morning? *That* is you, and the rest is the land's ills."

"That's easy for you to say, priest," Tremane replied feelingly. "*You* aren't in my head!" He was pale and sweating, and his pupils were so wide that there was scarcely any iris showing.

But Janas had already gone to the door and had called for Tremane's aides. "The Duke is not feeling well," he told them. "He needs to be taken to his bed and allowed to sleep. I think it would be wise to cancel any appointments he has for the rest of the day."

Both aides looked alarmed at the state of their leader, and one put a hand on the hilt of his weapon and cast a doubtful glance at Janas, suspecting, perhaps, that the priest had somehow poisoned the Duke or inflicted a disease on him.

"It's all right," Tremane reassured them. "I think I've just been overworking. It's nothing serious."

As if that had been a coded phrase to tell the aides that nothing the visitors had done had caused his condition, both aides relaxed immediately and went to assist their leader to stand. "You know that the Healers have been warning you about overworking yourself," one of them scolded the Duke in a whisper that the foreigners were probably not supposed to hear. This was an older man, the Duke's age or even a few years senior to him, and the aide clearly considered it his responsibility to take Tremane to task. "Now look what's happened to you! You can't work yourself half to death and not expect to pay for it!"

"I'll be all right, I just need to sleep," the Duke said vaguely, and although he was not paying a great deal of attention to his surroundings or his visitors, he no longer seemed quite so disoriented, at least to Elspeth. It seemed more as if he had focused his attention inward, in a state of partial trance.

His two aides helped him into the other room, and Janas nodded at the door. Taking the hint, Elspeth and Darkwind rose and followed the priest out.

"Don't you need to be with him, to give him some kind of instruction?" Darkwind asked anxiously as they made their way along the cold corridors back to their own quarters.

The old man shook his head; he still had that air of great self-satisfaction. "No, he already has the instruction; that was what I was giving him at the beginning. It's all there for him to use, he just needs to sort things out while he sleeps. Don't worry, we've been doing things this way for centuries, not just with our monarchs, but with priests whose earth-sense is also latent. But I must say, this is probably the *most* successful ritual I have ever done!" He rubbed his hands together with unconcealed glee. "Now we'll have to get word across the country what has happened, plan for a coronation, find something like a crown—oh, there are a hundred arrangements we'll have to make."

He shook his head, interrupting himself, as they reached the door of their quarters. "I hope you won't think me rude, but I am going to *have* to leave immediately. There is just too much I have to do, and not a great deal of time to do it in. We'll be sending important people here soon, as liaisons with our new monarch. In the meantime, I think I can count on both of you to help him through the next day or two."

"I can certainly help *explain* what he is feeling," Elspeth replied, but with a little doubt, opening the door and waving him inside ahead of her. "I suspect it might be like the first time I was—ah—blessed with Mindspeech."

"Exactly, exactly!" Janas said, as he gathered up his old robe and made it into a neat bundle. Then he looked down in confusion at the clothing he was wearing, and for a moment, certainty was replaced with uncertainty. "Ah—I—"

"Consider the new vestments a gift from the Alliance," Darkwind said, divining his question before he could ask it. "And please feel free to approach us if any of your other liaisons might need similar outfitting."

Janas turned, taking his hand and shaking it with gratitude. "Thank you, thank you for all your help!" he said, brimming with so much effervescent pleasure that Elspeth could not help but smile back at him. "Now, I really must be off, there is absolutely not a moment to waste!"

He hurried to open the door to the hallway; fortunately, one of the sentries at the door intercepted him and offered to find an aide to escort him out. He accepted absently as he pulled his shabby cloak on over his new finery, and the last that Elspeth saw of him, he was explaining to the aide some of the preparations that would need to be made to get ready for Tremane's coronation as the new King of Hardorn.

Elspeth closed the door behind them, and joined Darkwind who was sprawled bonelessly on the couch. She suddenly felt as if *she* had been running an endurance test, and collapsed beside him.

"Well," he said finally. "I confess I am at a loss for words."

"I have a few," she told him, putting her head on his shoulder. "But mostly, I can't begin to tell you how *relieved* I feel."

She turned her head so that she could see his face, and he smiled into her eyes. "You know how the Shin'a'in are always saying to be careful of what you ask for," he chided gently. "And you did *ask* for some sort of check on Tremane's behavior as a leader."

"I did." She took a deep breath, and let it out slowly. "I can't say that I'm at all *unhappy* about how this has fallen out. This means the probable end of conflict inside Hardorn. They're going to have a real, competent leader. He is going to be incapable of misusing the land or the people, and I have the oddest feeling that he won't even be able to *think* about going to war with anyone unless Hardorn is threatened first."

Darkwind kissed her forehead, then rested his head back against the back of the couch, staring up at the ceiling. "At the moment, I feel a great deal of sympathy for him. This may not be a punishment commensurate with what he did to our people, but he is going to be suffering real and sometimes serious discomfort for quite some time if I am any judge of these things."

"Because of the state of the country, you mean?" she asked.

He nodded. "Absolutely. You heard Janas; Hardorn is sick, injured, and only now beginning to recover. *He* gets to experience all that, until the land is healed again. What's more, when the mage-storms start up again, whatever they do to the land, he'll feel as if it's happening to him!"

She chuckled, a little heartlessly. "I wonder what having bits of the countryside plucked out and transplanted elsewhere will feel like?"

"Nothing *I* would care to share," Darkwind said emphatically.

She contemplated the prospect, and it didn't displease her. And she knew someone else who would find the new situation very much to her liking.

"I wonder how long it will take to get word of this to Solaris?" she mused aloud.

:*Not long, trust me*,: Gwena replied. :*And, oh, to be a fly on the wall when it does!*:

As the official-unofficial liaisons to Tremane on behalf of the rest of Hardorn, Elspeth and Darkwind found themselves dealing with a dozen requests the next morning that were the direct result of Father Janas' work the previous day. "You know, it is just a good thing that all this is happening in the dead of winter," Elspeth remarked to her mate, as she dealt with yet another request for "Royal Patronage" from a merchant in the town. "If we were in the midst of decent weather, we'd have half the country trying to get here for this coronation Janas wants to arrange."

Darkwind had handed most of the correspondence over to her, for the Hawkbrothers had no equivalent to royalty and the pomp and display that went with such personages. He shook his head. "I feel as lost as a tiny frog in the midst of Lake Evendim. Or a forest-hare in the middle of the Dhorisha Plains," he said ruefully. "Now I know what your people mean when they speak of feeling like a 'country cousin.' I haven't any idea what half these people *want* from Tremane."

"Frankly, neither have they," she replied dryly. "Royalty is rather like a touchstone to those who are accustomed to kings and queens and the like. One judges one's own worth by one's worth to the king, whether or not the king is himself a worthy person. All these people are attempting to gather about Tremane in the hope that some of the glitter will rub off."

She would have said more, but at that moment, there came a knock on their door. When Darkwind went to answer it, much to her surprise, Tremane himself stood in the doorway, guarded by his older aide, and looking a bit wan.

"Might I come in?" he asked. "Something in these memories of mine says that you might be able to help me. Sort things out, that is."

Darkwind waved him in; the aide remained behind, but with a look that said he would station himself at the door and not move until Tremane left again.

The Duke took a seat on their couch, and Elspeth made a quick assessment of him. For once he was hiding nothing; she suspected that at the moment he simply was unable to. He was still quite unsettled, disoriented, and distinctly wild-eyed. She handed him a fragrant cup of *kav*, a beverage the Imperials favored that she had also begun to enjoy, as much for the effect it had of waking one up as for the flavor.

"You know," he began plaintively, "when you came here, I told you that I accepted this mind-magic of yours, but to tell you the truth, I didn't entirely *believe* in it. You could have done everything you claimed simply by having two well-trained beasts and a clever set of subtle signals. Spirits, putting one's thoughts into someone else's head—that was all so much nonsense and only the really credulous would have given it much credence…"

His voice trailed off, and Elspeth nodded. "Now, for the first time, you are in the grip of something you can't explain. Right?" she asked.

He nodded, looking oddly vulnerable and forlorn. "Magic is *supposed* to be a thing of logic!" he protested. "It has laws and rules, they are all perfectly understandable, and they bring predictable results! This is all so—so—*intuitive*. So unpredictable, so messy—"

Darkwind started to laugh, and the Duke looked at him suspiciously. "I don't see what is so amusing."

"Forgive me, sir," Darkwind choked. "But very recently a friend of ours, who truly and with all of his heart believed that *magic* was wholly a thing of intuition and art, having nothing to do with laws and logic, was confronted with the need to regard magic as you and your mages do. And he sounded *just* like you do now—the contrast is just—" He choked, trying to swallow his laughter, and Elspeth, who recalled quite well how Firesong had sounded, had to work very hard not to join him. That would not have done Tremane's spirit any good at the moment.

"When you have gotten used to this, I think that you'll find it has its own set of rules and logic, and you'll be able to deal with it in a predictable manner," she soothed. "This is simply as if—as if someone had dropped *all* of the rules of mathematics and geometry into your mind, and expected you to deal with them. You're overwhelmed with information, and I promise you that will change."

Darkwind managed to get himself under control, and took a seat next to the Duke. "I'll help you as much as I can," he pledged. "I am probably the nearest to an expert, until Janas or someone like him comes back here."

Tremane let out a sigh, and began slowly trying to ask questions for which the vocabulary was as new to him as the concepts. Elspeth listened carefully, adding what she could, and relaying when Gwena had any useful information to add.

:*Poor man,*: she said to Gwena, though not without a touch of faintly vindictive amusement. :*The only thing more unsettling to him right now would be for the ghosts of his ancestors to come back to haunt him, or for a Companion to Choose him.*:

:*Oh, now there's a thought,*: Gwena replied, and at Elspeth's reaction of alarm, sent a chuckle of amusement of her own. :*Don't worry. The only way that Tremane would ever be Chosen would be for most of the population of Hardorn and Valdemar to be swallowed up by the earth, and even then, I wouldn't put high odds on it.*:

:*At least now he'll believe us when we say you've said something.*: That was a satisfying realization.

Then something else occurred to Elspeth. *:Darkwind,:* she told her mate, *:I think this is best treated as something like Empathy. Janas may have put the rules for dealing with it in his mind, but if the Gift is so very strong, he may be so overwhelmed by the sensations that he can't actually relate them to what is happening. Try taking him through ground and centering, then shielding, just as you would someone with strong Empathy.:*

He nodded slightly, and changed his angle of attack on the problem. To Elspeth's way of thinking, this was actually going to be easier than dealing with someone with Empathy; there would be no changes in what he sensed as people around him underwent emotional changes. Since what he felt from the land was quite steady, with no sudden increases in intensity, once he learned to shield he would not have to learn to strengthen or weaken his shields.

In fact, he wouldn't want to; he *needed* to know when the land was harmed, and he couldn't do that if his shields were too strong.

She watched the two of them as Darkwind coaxed him through his first exercises. She came to the conclusion, watching his rapid progress, that there was more to what Janas had given him than mere instructions; once he had a grasp of the technique Darkwind was showing him, it didn't take him long to apply the technique correctly.

:Too bad we can't teach every young Herald the way Janas "taught" him,: she remarked wryly to Gwena.

:It would take an ability most Heralds haven't got,: Gwena replied frankly, and a bit enviously. *:For that matter, most Companions haven't got it either. I didn't realize until now just how remarkable old Janas is.:*

Oh, really? That made her reexamine the priest and his mission in an entirely new light, and wonder just what his real rank in the hierarchy of his religion was. Something equivalent to the Son of the Sun, perhaps? Probably only someone like Solaris would be able to tell for certain.

The only conclusion she could make was that the Hardornens had left nothing to chance in this venture, and had gambled a great deal.

But she kept all of this to herself; it wouldn't matter one way or another to the situation, and Tremane had enough on his hands right now with this new ability *and* the responsibility of becoming a King.

Becoming a King. What a strange idea that is. I can't think of any ruler in this part of the world who has been picked by his people since—since Valdemar. The parallels were coming closer all the time.

Tremane absorbed all that Darkwind showed him like dry ground absorbing rain; slowly the lines of anxiety and strain left his face, and the signs of disorientation and illness eased from his posture and expression. Finally, he sighed and closed his eyes with relief.

"I feel—normal," he said, as if he had never expected to feel that way again.

He opened his eyes, and Darkwind smiled with satisfaction. "That is precisely how you should feel," the Hawkbrother told him. "You shouldn't have to think about those shields for them to be there, since you are already acquainted with setting magical shields. They should remain in place until you take them down or weaken them yourself. *Now* the only things you will feel will be when something happens to Hardorn, for good or ill; you'll sense the change as soon as it happens."

Tremane colored a little, and coughed. "I seem to recall some injudicious words to the effect of *wanting* an ability that would give me that information."

Darkwind's smile turned ironic, but he didn't say anything. He didn't have to.

Surely every culture has a variation on the saying, "Be careful what you ask for, you may get it."

"Well, sometimes the Hundred Little Gods display an interesting sense of humor," Tremane sighed.

"They've displayed it more directly than I think you realize," Darkwind told him. "Are you aware that thanks to this 'gift' that Janas bestowed on you, that you are *literally* bound to Hardorn? You can't leave, at least not for long."

Tremane shot him a skeptical glance. "Surely you are exaggerating."

Darkwind shook his head. "I am not. You will not be able to go beyond the borders of this land for very long. Janas was not speaking figuratively as we both assumed when he made his explanations to you. I know enough of magical bindings to recognize one on you, and I doubt that anyone can break it. This is the magic of a very primitive religion, meant to ensure that a ruler could not get wandering feet and go off exploring when he should be governing."

Elspeth watched Tremane's face; though normally opaque, this experience had left him open—not as open as an ordinary person, but open enough for her to read his expressions. "What you're saying is, this *earth-binding* they put on me ensures that there is no possibility of going back to the Empire."

Darkwind held his hands palm up. "The most primitive magics tend to be the strongest, the hardest to break. Perhaps a better word would be *primal.* I suspect this one may date back to the tribes wandering this area before the Cataclysm. It was a fascinating piece of work to watch; no chants, no real ritual, just a tonal component as a guide for invocation, and of course the mental component. Simple but powerful, and that argues for a piece of work that is *very* old, and so proven by time that it is, in fact, a benchmark by which later magics could be judged." As Tremane sat there, with a dazed look in his eyes and a numb expression, Darkwind warmed to his subject. "It really does make sense. If you have a tribe that has recently settled, given up nomadic, hunting, and herding ways and gone into agriculture, it stands to reason that your best leaders, the ones who are likely to be the most successful at defending your settlement from other nomads, are the people most likely to want to go back to the unsettled ways. If you want to keep them where they belong *and* give them a powerful incentive to hold the land in trust and not plunder and ruin it, you'd bind them to it."

"I get the point, all too clearly," Tremane interrupted dryly. "Seeing as I am the one blessed with this particular application of 'primitive' magic, and now am prisoner in an all too clear way." He rubbed his head with his hand, absently. "No disrespect to you, Darkwind k'Sheyna, but speculation about the origin of this bit of religious arcana is moot, and it can probably wait until the happy day when everything is settled again and you and Janas can argue about history to your hearts' content."

Darkwind was not at all embarrassed. In fact, he graced Tremane with the expression of a teacher whose student has missed the point of the lesson. But all he said aloud was, "Duke Tremane, if you wish to know how and why a magic works the way it does, you must learn or deduce its origin and purpose. In complex spell-work, the causes, triggers, paths, and effects are not always obvious, and are often fragile. In more primal spell-work, the variables may be fewer, but they are not necessarily any more obvious. You cannot unmake a thing—supposing you should choose to do so—without knowing how it is made."

"Supposing I should choose to do so..." Tremane's voice trailed off, and he stood up to go look out the window. "I am not, by nature, a religious man," he said, with his back to them.

"We rather gathered that, sir," Elspeth put in, her tone so ironic it made Tremane turn for a moment to give her a searching look.

"There is not much in the Empire that would make one believe in gods, much less that they have any interest at all in the doings of mortals," he said, looking straight into her eyes. "Tangible effect is the focus in the

Empire. Results and tasks of the day take a distinct precedence over thoughts of divine influence or the spirit world. The closest thing to a religion of state is a form of ancestor veneration, which takes its higher form as the honoring of previous Emperors and their Consorts, who are collectively known as the Hundred Little Gods. Not that there are exactly a hundred, but it's a nice, round figure to swear by."

"I'd wondered about that," Darkwind murmured.

"Nor have I in the past been one to put credence in either predestined fate or omens. Nevertheless," he continued, "since arriving here, I have been confronted, time and time again, with situations that have literally forced me into the path I am now taking. I find myself beginning to doubt the wisdom of my previous position regarding destiny."

Elspeth could not resist the opportunity. "If you would care for some further proof that your previous position on the divine is faulty," she offered, "I am sure that High Priest Solaris would be happy to arrange for a manifestation of Vkandis Sunlord."

It was wrong of her, but after all that Tremane had been responsible for, she could not help but take a certain amount of vengeful pleasure in the way that his face turned pale at the mere mention of Solaris' name.

"That won't be necessary," he said hastily.

"As you wish," she murmured, with an amused glance at Darkwind.

:Well, talk about fire to the left and torrent to the right—not only does he have Solaris' curse of truthfulness on him, but the Hardornen earth-binding: Gwena sounded unbelievably smug, but for once, Elspeth was in full agreement with her. *:I do believe that Grand Duke Tremane is going to be very cooperative with the Alliance from now on—because if he isn't, he hasn't got the option to escape and he knows it.:*

:And I just thought of another good reason for putting the earth-binding on your King: Darkwind Sent silently, as Tremane turned back to the window. *:If you bind him to a place so that he can't escape from it, he has to rule well, because he certainly can't ignore what he is immersed in.:*

:Let's hope that's one of the things he's thinking about right now: Elspeth replied. *:He is a skilled leader and an intelligent man, and he is certainly a pragmatic one. It should dawn on him soon just how deep in he is right now, and then he will have to accept it and deal with the tasks at hand. For the sake of the Alliance as well as of Hardorn, I want him to know he has no other option but to rule wisely and honestly. We can't afford anything less.:*

6

Paper rustled quietly, the only sound in the cold, cavernous room. Baron Melles read the last page of Commander Sterm's report with a smile of satisfaction on his lips. Jacona, the throne city, was now effectively secured. Although the capital of the Empire was not precisely under martial law, his soldiers shared the streets and the patrols with the city constables, and both were happy to have the situation that way. He had tried his plan out here, where everything was directly under his careful supervision, and his ideas had all worked. They had not worked *perfectly*, but he had never expected perfection; they had worked well enough that he and Thayer were both pleased.

As he had predicted, the price of staple food supplies had increased as the availability had decreased, to the point where the average person either could not find or could not afford two out of three meals. That was enough to trigger food riots, his first shoot-to-kill order, and his second tier of plans. Jacona was already divided into precincts, with an elected official, the precinct captain, responsible for arranging local matters such as street repair with the city. That made organization much easier. The citizens of Jacona were now under strict rationing, with so many ration chits per commodity per week each, as arranged and administered by their precinct captains. Price controls went into effect with the rationing. No one was starving, and prices, while high, were no longer as extortionate as they were. Food supplies from the surrounding countryside had been assured, and those ration chits guaranteed that everyone would have access to a minimum diet. The chits did *not* cover luxury items, only staples, permitting those with higher incomes the ability to buy what they chose.

Naturally, there would be some citizens who would choose to barter away their own chits and even those of members of their families for cash or other commodities, such as alcohol. And, naturally, the Empire officially took no stand on this, so long as those who were involved were adults.

A child was different, and precinct captains were on orders to watch for children begging for food. If they found a child starving, and if its parent could not produce its ration chits or enough food to cover the household, the child (and its ration allocation) would be taken away and put in an Imperial orphanage.

That would be the end of that; once taken away, a parent could not retrieve a child, and it became the ward of the State. Once it turned fourteen, if male it would go into the Army; if female, underdeveloped, or sickly, an Army auxiliary corps or a workhouse—unless it showed extraordinary ability and qualified for higher training. But that was child welfare, and had nothing to do with rationing.

Naturally, there were luxuries and larger rations available for cash, and the Empire took no stand on this, either, so long as the commodities for sale on the gray market were not purloined from Imperial stores. Meals and services continued normally in the homes of the wealthy, although household expenses had doubled in the past few weeks. From what Melles had learned from his agents, prices on the gray market had stabilized, which meant that the wealthy would simply have to work a little harder to maintain their wealth. Many of them had already begun investment in coal, wood, and other fuels, or speculation in food items. There were a few with new-built fortunes in the city, because they had seen the trend of things and had moved accordingly. There were a few who were ruined, because their stock-in-trade consisted of small items that depended on magic, or because they were dealers in items like Festival costumes that no one wanted to buy under the current conditions. But so far as Melles could see, aside from these few unlucky or clever individuals, nothing much else had changed.

There were no more riots after the first serious one that gave Melles the excuse to issue his shoot-to-kill order, and which had resulted in the death of a dozen fools who happened to be leading it. There were occasional demonstrations, and a great many speeches on street corners, which were officially ignored. There were also no more collapsing buildings, or loss of service because magic had failed. This was because there were no more services left—or buildings still standing—that depended on magic.

There was plenty of work, though, and the one large change was that unemployment simply did not exist anymore. Those who demonstrated or made speeches did so when their working hours were over—unless, of course, they happened to be one of the few wealthy eccentrics who did not need to work to have an income. Where magical aqueducts no longer supplied water, and there were no communal wells, brigades of otherwise unemployed citizens with buckets brought fresh water from reliable sources to fill newly-constructed below- or above-ground cisterns. An entire newly-formed corps of citizens with handcarts now collected garbage, cinders, and ashes from fires, and animal waste from the streets and yards. Fortunately, the sewers were nonmagical in nature, and still functioned reliably.

Life in the city was not back to the way it had been, and never would be again until these mage-storms were over, but the ordinary citizen went to work, received his pay, ate regular meals, and slept securely at night. If he was colder this winter than last, or a little hungrier, well, that was the case for all of his neighbors, too. But not only were his streets kept clear of dangerous riots, they were also kept clear of vagrants and beggars—for vagrants and beggars swiftly found themselves in Imperial workhouses or work gangs, cleaning the streets and carrying water for the good of the ordinary citizen. This made the ordinary citizen happy. What made him even happier was the fact that Imperial workers were toiling day and night to find ways to restore more of the things that he had come to take for granted in the days of reliable magic. Already some things had been replaced—safe stoves that could burn a variety of fuels, from dried dung to coal, were now being made available at a moderate price from Imperial workhouses. Imperial bathhouses and laundries had been established, so that if a man could not afford to heat water for regular baths and laundry, he *could* still have those baths and get his clothing clean for a few copper bits. The average citizen could look forward to eventually regaining the kind of comfortable life he had lost.

And if he had to give up some of his freedom to get that life back, well, all but a few malcontents thought that was an acceptable loss. Some folk even welcomed these new workhouses and work gangs, and were happy to see soldiers patrolling the streets and sweeping up those with nothing better to do than to make trouble. It was true that crimes like assault, robbery, rape, and burglary had dropped to almost nothing after the deadly-force patrols had been deployed on the street level.

Well, assault, robbery, rape, and burglary by citizens against citizens have dropped to almost nothing. No one in his right mind is going to report a soldier or constable for such a crime. And if there is no report, there is no crime, and hence officially no problem.

So far, everything that he had set in motion in Jacona was working well or would be with a few slight adjustments. Now was the moment to plan the next steps. He put both elbows on the desk, tented his fingers together and rested them lightly over his lips, thinking.

He stared at the flame in the oil lamp on his desk that replaced the mage-light that had once burned there. The desk itself had been placed near to the antiquated fireplace, which held a better, more improved version of the official stove, a contrivance of ceramic and steel that burned coal rather than wood. More Imperial cleverness, that; coal fires burned hotter and longer than wood, and although the smoke coming from them was dirtier and might cause a problem one day, this new "furnace" invention would get them through the winter. All the fires in the Palace and in most of the homes of the noble and wealthy had these furnaces, and the coal mines, which once produced only fuel for the smelting furnaces for the metal trade, now sent huge wagonloads into the city on daily deliveries. A variation on this furnace heated the boilers that once again delivered hot water into the bathing rooms of Crag Castle and other edifices—and also supplied the hot water for the Imperial bathhouses and laundries. Interestingly enough, this entire situation was proving to be surprisingly profitable for the Imperial coffers, for not only was the Empire collecting more tax money, since taxes were based on profits, but the Empire was also something of a merchant, selling heating- and cook-stoves and the services of the bathhouses.

Theft of coal was punishable—like all theft—by being sent to a work gang. So were the crimes of inciting to riot, participating in a riot, looting, chronic public drunkenness, vandalism, vagrancy, and delinquency. Any crime against property rather than against a citizen now bought the perpetrator a stint in hard labor rather than gaol or the Army. The new policy made for quiet streets.

Tremane would never have ordered all of this; Tremane didn't have the vision or the audacity, and perhaps not even the intellectual capacity to mastermind such sweeping plans on such a broad scale at such short notice.

Melles continued to stare at his lamp flame, but nothing in the way of inspiration occurred to him. He reached for another, much shorter report, and leafed through it again. Perhaps before he thought more about the next stage of his plans, it was time to deal with his covert operations.

All in all, once the food riots were quashed, there had been fewer complaints than he had anticipated, and very little civil unrest. That came as something of a surprise, because he had assumed there would be a higher level of resistance to his new laws than there actually was.

So, all that meant was the good citizens of Jacona were being very good, going where he led like proper sheep.

There were, of course, a few wild goats out there still—the inevitable underground "freedom" movement, which he had also anticipated. How could there not have been? There were always those who would not be hoodwinked into accepting restrictions on their freedom, no matter how one disguised those restrictions.

The Citizens for Rights group correctly identifies you as the source of all of the new edicts and punishments, the report, written by the head of his network of low-level agents in the city, read. *They assume that the Emperor knows nothing, and that with enough work they will be able to draw his attention to your abuses and have you ousted. Failing that, and assuming that you somehow have the Emperor under your personal control, they plan on a general citizens' uprising to overthrow the entire government.*

That was also precisely what he had anticipated; not only did it not alarm him, he was actually rather pleased that he had predicted the development so accurately. His agent was not particularly worried, but he wanted more instructions about what to do now that he had identified the movement, its goals, and its members.

He picked up a pen and took a clean sheet of paper from the tray at the side of his desk. He wrote in code without having to think about the translation; he'd had enough experience at it that he could write directly to any of his agents in the correct code. This was a content-sensitive code, rather than an encoded letter; to all appearances, this missive was a perfectly ordinary letter about commonplaces, from a servant in the Palace to a relative in the city.

What it really said, however, was something else entirely.

Do nothing to openly disrupt the movement against me. As for the general citizens, continue to feed them misinformation; concoct tales of my helplessness in the face of the Emperor's growing tyranny. Make them think that I am trying to stem the Emperor's excesses and that Charliss himself is directly responsible for everything they object to. What I want is to hear that even the members of the Movement are starting to call me "The Peoples' Friend." Continue to identify all new members of the Movement, and if any really effective leaders emerge, identify their weaknesses and find ways to handicap them without actually removing them. Keep me informed at all times.

He started to seal up the envelope, then thought of something else and added a second page.

There are always bureaucratic mistakes; men taken up in a street-sweep who were actually on their way to work, outright victims of some soldier's personal feud. These people will know of each and every one—send me the particulars so I can arrange for investigations and turn a few loose with restitution. If any of them have young children suffering hardship without their father, mark them especially.

Now he sealed and addressed the letter and put it in the tray for his house agent to take to the appropriate drop. That last addition was nothing less than inspiration; all he would have to do would be to have one of the clerks deal with the paperwork to free the man, and send the family a little money, some luxury food items, and a basket of sweets for the children, and Melles would be a hero on the street. And he needn't trouble himself about petitioners plaguing him either. Now that he was officially the Emperor's Heir, the layers of bureaucracy between him and the citizen on the street were so many, so complex, and so labyrinthine that the average citizen would die of old age before he completed all of the paperwork required for an audience with him. This would only generate a little more work in the way of petitions, and there were plenty of low-level Imperial civil servants to take care of additional petitions.

Perhaps another man might have sent soldiers to arrest every member of the Movement—but another man did not have the depth of experience that Melles did. As long as he knew who belonged to these organizations, who were the real leaders and workers, and what their failings were, he was better off leaving them all in place. In times like these, insurrectionist movements were like cockroaches; squash one and a hundred more would hatch behind the wallboards. Rebels actually tended to thrive on a certain level of persecution, since persecution validated their cause in the eyes of others. In fact, many of them absolutely required feeling persecuted—and speaking loudly of it—in order to validate their own meager existence, since obviously only a Great Good would be opposed by a Great Evil. What made this even funnier, in a cripple-pitying sort of way, was that they would only proclaim their oppression to those peers least likely to disagree with them.

Melles, of course, played one facet of the same game on a much higher, more sophisticated level. People invariably polarized their views when they were given little information about a situation's complexities. If someone was not for your cause, then they must be against your cause; if not black, then white; if not day, then night. While the perennially-oppressed would use this tendency in human behavior to generate sympathy from others, Melles used it to steer public reaction. His actual plans and coups were more complex than could be briefly discussed by any layman, and he used fronts—like the labor groups and the police—to act as buffers and visible representations. He created simple concepts for laymen to absorb and react to, while giving little information about the greater, more complex goings-on. Thus, even the most clever leaders of rebel movements would be basing their actions upon incomplete information at best, low-end rumor at average, and utter fabrications at worst. Worst for them, anyway; for Melles it was simply human behavior according to schedule.

No, he would watch them, occasionally nurture them, frustrate and thwart them, and use them, but above all, he would let them have their little "committee meetings" and make speeches and inflame one another. That kept them quiet and mostly harmless. The more they ranted about being suppressed under improving conditions, the less anyone would listen to or believe in them.

It was better to remove the occasional competent and dangerous member than to go after the entire group. If he could not manage to do so in any other way, the really dangerous ones would tragically die while defending themselves against a street thug or a house robber. Then, before the person could be martyred, various carefully-contrived "secrets" about them would turn up during "investigation" of the death—evidence that they were child molesters, for instance—to spoil the probable public outrage there would otherwise have been, and that distaste would carry over to be associated with any of the person's movement. It would only take ten or twenty such instances for the general citizenry to feel relieved that these troublemakers were gone.

On the whole, he enjoyed the amateur "freedom fighters" as delightful entertainment, and if no group had sprung up, he would have had to start one just to have an organization to attract the real troublemakers. The most dangerous would be the very few individuals who realized that groups were obvious targets, and determined to undermine the authorities on their own. If he could catch someone like that, it would be by accident.

But the insurrectionist groups had their uses, not the least of which was that they gave the hotheads a place to vent their spleen. When they were making speeches, they were not setting fire to a storehouse of records, counterfeiting and giving away food chits, or breaking into a work camp and freeing prisoners.

Better a thousand fools' ineffectual speeches than a single food riot.

He moved that report from the "pending" tray to the "completed" tray, and turned his attention to the next in line. If conditions had not been so dire, he would have been positively gleeful; never had he possessed so much power over so many, and the sensation brought an intoxication he had not expected.

Report after report, from the heads of his specialized covert operations rings around the city, indicated that events were proceeding with as much smoothness as anyone could reasonably expect. The only things that could not be planned for were the effects of the mage-storms, and he hoped he had made enough allowance for the chaos those could cause. The precinct captains were political creatures, and although they were elected, he could replace them at his discretion. They could and would lie to save their jobs. The Imperial Commander was less likely to lie, yet still might shade the truth to conceal problems. His agents, however, were carefully picked and trained and they never reported anything but the facts, no matter how unpleasant. That was their job; he rewarded the truthful and got rid of those who were not—sometimes permanently, if they had been in a delicate or sensitive position. These reports confirmed his impression that the city was his: pacified, and lying quietly in the palm of his hand.

That was good, because he had no intention of leaving the capital, and he wanted it secured so that he could turn his attention to the Empire beyond without worrying about his personal safety and comfort. The power that gave him his authority was *here*, and although by now he could carry out his plans if the Emperor changed his mind and made someone else the Imperial Heir, it would be much more difficult to do so. He had the Army, but that might not be the case if the Emperor appointed a new man—and to subdue the rest of the Empire, he needed the Army.

Now that he knew what was working with Jacona, he knew what would work outside the capital. He returned to the longer report that he had set aside; this was the condensed version of what was going on in the Empire itself.

In the immediate vicinity, the countryside could reasonably be declared "pacified" as well. The sources of disturbance were those of chaos rather than man's intention—terrible weather and roving monsters rather than rioters. Within the small towns and villages, people were in no danger of going hungry, but they were terrified. Physical storms could sweep down at any moment, bringing snow that could bury a village to the eaves, winds that could rip a building apart, blizzards combining the two that lasted for days at a time. That was bad enough, but in the midst of the storms, terrible, malformed creatures came ravening into their very streets, monsters that no one recognized or knew how to kill. On the estates, things were sometimes even worse, for most nobles did not keep many retainers who were trained to fight; this close to the capital, keeping a small private army was generally frowned upon. So there had already been a case or two of a storm burying an estate, and before the servants could dig it out again, a bloodthirsty creature had appeared that kept them all penned inside—and in one case decimated the entire estate.

One less annoying minor noble to endure.

The Army was handling that situation with all the efficiency that anyone could ask for. Melles was both pleased and surprised to learn that General Thayer had deployed squads of monster hunters *before* ever implementing the requisition orders that Melles's secretary had drawn up. With scores of monstrous beasts hanging from hooks on display in village squares and estate courtyards, people had not only been happy to "donate" the items the Army requisitioned, they had even come forward with additional help. Some truly antique equipages had been made roadworthy—but also some very clever work had been put into the hands of the Army as well. Some genius of a village blacksmith had come up with a way to fasten runners on the wheels of carriages after locking those wheels in place, so that instead of having to wait until snow had been removed from the roads, carts could skim over the top of it. Practically speaking, what that meant was that the Army supply trains bringing food into the city could use roads with a single, narrow track cut for the horse or mule rather than needing to clear the entire road.

Pity that the wicker snowshoe for horses didn't really work, then we wouldn't have to clear the roads at all, or even use the roads. It is ironic that the poor are turning out to be the saviors of the wealthy, for only they had the knowledge of how to do things in completely nonmagical ways.

Other than that, life in the countryside was not at all bad; certainly better than in the city. Firewood was immediately available. So was food, in a greater variety than the cities were seeing now. Life on the estates was even better, and Melles was fairly sure that those nobles who had fled back to their possessions were by-and-large congratulating themselves for having had the wisdom to do so.

So much for life in the immediate vicinity of the capital. Now for the other large cities...

With a few variations, it seemed that what had worked for Jacona would work for any large city in the Empire. He had to make allowances for local religion in a few places, and for one brand new cult in Deban that had virtually taken over the entire city, but for the most part, there were not too many changes he needed to make.

Finally, he finished the last of the replies he needed to make to Thayer and to his own agents in the field. His hands were cramped by the time he was done, and one of the servants had come in to check the fire and add coal twice. Despite the fire, the room was icy; for all its luxurious fittings, it was less comfortable than a warehouse.

Perhaps a sheepskin cover for his desk chair would help, and a charcoal brazier for under the desk. Better still, he ought to have his valet bring in the same kinds of amenities that the Imperial clerks used. He flexed his aching fingers and rose, feeling the cold in every stiffened joint. He knew with grim certainty that his battle with the encroachments of age was failing. Before all this nonsense with the mage-storms had begun, he had started on his own minor rejuvenation magics. He resented the fact that they had failed him now, at a time when he most needed his body to be in perfect health. He simply could not afford any distractions, yet what were all these aches and pains *but* irritating distractions?

Reminders of mortality?

He went to the heavy gilded and carved sideboard where the blown-glass decanters of liquor and special, cut crystal glasses were stored. His nose and feet were so cold they were numb; perhaps a drink would restore circulation and make him feel warmer. He was well aware that the warmth that came from liquor was a false, fugitive thing, but he wanted the comfort of it just now, and the pain-deadening effects that would ease his aching joints.

His valet entered, impeccable and correct in his livery of black and purple, just as Melles poured himself a small glass of potent, doubly-distilled brandy. The liquor gleamed in the glass with the deep glow of fine rubies, as Melles held it up to the light, admiring its color. The valet waited until Melles acknowledged his presence with a nod before speaking. "His Imperial Highness has called a Court, Lord Heir," the man said smoothly, one arm already draped with a suit of court robes in anticipation of the fact that Melles would need them. "Would you care to change your clothing here, or in your more private quarters?"

Melles sighed. This was the last thing he needed right now; he was tired and cold, and really wanted a moment or two to warm up and rest before he dealt with another crisis. But Bors Porthas would not have interrupted his working hours if this had been some bit of social nonsense; no, this must be something serious, and he had better steel himself to meet it.

"Here will do." No one was going to walk in on him unannounced, and Porthas, bland, self-effacing, incredibly competent Porthas, would have brought everything Melles would need with him. The balding little man with the thin, expressionless face was a miracle of efficiency, but that wasn't too surprising. He'd had plenty of practice in more demanding service before Melles retired him to this, his own retinue. In fact, there were a great many of the higher nobles of the Court who would have recognized Porthas' face as that of their own valued personal servant, forced by sudden illness to retire... A fair percentage would have been shocked into speechlessness, and a few would have gone pale, recalling that they had sent floral tokens to the funeral of this particularly faithful servant.

Porthas looked remarkably healthy for a man who had been dead at least three times, and rendered forever incapable of leaving a bed on another five occasions. He looked ageless, in fact, and Melles was aware that not only could Bors Porthas perform every possible duty that would be asked of a valet, he could also still meet and beat many men younger than he in a bout of swordsmanship. As for his other talents—he was the only person Melles would entrust with certain jobs besides himself. That trim body was as efficient as the mind that was housed in it, and just as lithe.

Melles sometimes wondered if, after all the years of serving as Melles' agent, the life of a "mere" valet was stultifying. But then again, Porthas was no "mere" valet, any more than Melles was a "mere" courtier; he was the coordinator for all of Melles' agents, in the city, outside of the city, and most importantly of all, within Crag Castle. He and Melles alone knew the real names and identities of all of Melles' agents. And in the rare event that Melles would need to have a "removal" performed with precision and absolute secrecy, if he could not for some reason perform it himself, he would entrust it to Porthas. There was no one else besides he who was anywhere near Melles in level of expertise at their mutual profession. And he actually seemed to *enjoy* being a valet. Perhaps, after all his other activities, serving as a valet was restful and amusing.

He was certainly nimble enough at assisting Melles into the cumbersome court robes he despised. In sartorial matters, Porthas was not Melles' equal; he was Melles' acknowledged superior, and Melles was only too happy to give way to his expertise. When the last fold and crease had been arranged to Porthas' liking, Melles thanked him— without overdoing it, but making sure that the man knew that his service was noted and valued. With a smile of satisfaction, Porthas gathered up the discarded garments and retired to Melles' private chambers.

The long walk down the castle corridors, accompanied by the silent and ever-present Imperial Guards, allowed him to rid himself of some of his irritation. He knew that there was something in the air when he entered the Throne Room; nervous whispering did not cease at his entrance, as it often did, and the Iron Throne itself was vacant.

Melles made his way up to the foot of the Throne and his own proper place as First in the Court. General Thayer was already in attendance, with a frown on his face that told Melles he had no more idea than anyone else why the Emperor had called this particular Court into session. The General was also in full regalia, ceremonial breastplate gleaming over the somber livery of Imperial Army full-dress uniform, his ceremonial helm with its jaunty crest of purple horsehair tucked under his left arm, from which position he could fling the useless piece of pot-metal at a would-be attacker while he pulled his not-so-ceremonial sword with his right hand. On one occasion, the General had actually stopped his attacker with the helmet before the man ever came within reach of his sword.

"Have you heard anything?" he asked Melles under his breath. Melles shook his head, and the General swore several pungent oaths, his face darkening. "I don't like this," he said. "Charliss never used to call full Courts without notice. He's been closeted with a messenger or an informant—and now he calls a full Court. He's not acting rationally anymore, and the Hundred Little Gods only know what he can inflate out of tiny rumors. If he's heard something—"

"It won't be about us," Melles said smoothly. "We are proceeding splendidly, and the law-abiding citizens of the Empire are very happy with us, and with the Emperor. Look at the reports—look at the streets! And he signed every law, edict and change to procedure we've instituted with his own hands. Whatever he has heard, it will concern someone else's activities, and not ours."

At just that moment, Emperor Charliss appeared, draped in his own ceremonial robes, moving slowly toward the Iron Throne flanked by two of his guards, with four more following. Melles was shocked at his appearance, although he doubted that anyone other than a highly trained Adept would notice the level of deterioration in Charliss' protections and rejuvenation magics. It only showed in small things—in the careful way that Charliss moved, and in the signs of pain and illness around his mouth and eyes—but it was very clear to him that Charliss was losing his personal battle against age and the mage-storms. And as Thayer had said, only the Hundred Little Gods knew what that deterioration was doing to his mind.

In the past, the Emperor's mind had been the very last thing to go; all of the Emperor-Adepts had died with their minds clear even as their eyes closed for the last time. But that was in the past, with magic working properly; what if the reverse was happening, and Charliss' mind was decaying faster than his body? What if the poisons of age were pouring into his brain, acting like insidious drugs on his thinking processes?

The Emperor surveyed his Court with cold eyes, then placed himself in the chill embrace of the Iron Throne, and regarded his assembled Court again, as if searching for signs of insurrection. Finally he gestured, and a single, weatherbeaten man in the garb of an Imperial soldier stepped out from behind the screen of guards, moving down the stairs to stand below the Iron Throne.

"One of Our agents has returned from the west," the Emperor rasped. "And meanwhile, there have been petitions and questions brought before this throne. Some among you doubt the wisdom of Our declaring a second heir, saying that the rumors concerning the Nameless One are only that, and that We should wait until We had real proof before We acted. We have brought you all here to witness this report, so that you may see that the Emperor rules over you because he is wiser than you."

The man stepped forward, went on one knee before the Throne, and began reciting a report in a dispassionate and unaccented voice. His report was virtually identical to everything that Melles already knew, and he didn't pay a great deal of attention to it. Granted, he had not realized that Tremane had looted the Imperial supply depot in Fortallan quite so *thoroughly*—the man had practically taken the very walls of the place, and Melles had to give him credit for the sheer audacity of the undertaking—but it was still hardly what he would call *news*. Charliss himself had known all of this; he'd made it public when he'd declared Melles as his new Heir, and there should have been nothing in these words to cause the Emperor to feel the need to call a formal Court just so everyone could hear it.

In fact, there was something odd about the fact that Charliss felt the need to address the petitions and questions of Tremane's few friends in the Court. Charliss had always ignored such voices of dissent in the past. It wasn't at all like the Emperor to behave in such a fashion, anymore than it was normal for him to sit and listen to a report he'd already heard several times over. Nevertheless, Charliss was clearly agitated by what he heard, and grew more so with every word the agent recited.

Then the man reached the part of his report that was actually new information—a speech that Tremane had allegedly given to his troops, the contents of which were very clearly treasonable. Melles was fairly certain that the speech was accurately reported, in no small part because the agent kept referring back to notes he had taken, held in a small book that he took from his belt-pouch.

Melles paid very close attention to that speech, once he realized this was the reason that Charliss was so agitated. As the man spoke, the Emperor's hands clutched the arms of the throne, and he leaned forward with his eyes narrowed, cold rage in every nuance of his posture. This was a problem; the old Charliss would never have betrayed the fact that something angered him, but this was not the old Charliss. If the Emperor lost his temper violently in public, it was possible that his competence might be called into question. If that happened, his choice of Heir might also come under fire. The last thing that Melles needed right now was a Court on the verge of deposing the Emperor and finding a new and more tractable Heir.

Supposedly, Tremane accused the Emperor of violating his own sacred oaths to the Army. He accused Charliss of being the one who created the mage-storms, as a mad experiment in weaponry of mass destruction. He told his troops that Charliss deliberately sent them all out to be left in the area of effect of this new weapon, just to see what would happen to them. He claimed that Charliss had then deserted all of them, leaving them to face mage-storms and hostile enemy troops on their own, with no supplies, no pay, and no reinforcements. Lastly, he declared that they would have to make their own way, for the Empire no longer cared what became of them.

A strong speech, and one that Tremane might well have believed himself. Certainly, with no clear source for the mage-storms, one could make a case for them coming from the Empire rather than the insignificant little nation of Valdemar. Given that the Empire had centuries of tradition of magic use, and Valdemar, so far as anyone knew, had none, it would be far more logical to assume that combat-mages within the Empire had originated the mage-storms. In fact, if Charliss had actually possessed such a weapon, he might very well have used it in exactly the way he was accused. The Emperor was guilty of such callousness so often that a great part of his anger might stem from the fact that he had been accused when for once he was actually innocent.

Then the agent dropped real news, rather than just relating a speech.

By working a team of mages together, his group had managed to get a clean scrying on Tremane until the last mage-storm had passed through. They had proof, besides the speech, of Tremane's perfidy. He had made common cause with Valdemar and her allies against the Empire. He had joined the Alliance, and would soon be crowned the new King of Hardorn, the land he was supposed to have taken for Charliss. And one of the stipulations that the Hardornens had insisted on was that he and his men, Imperial soldiers, would defend Hardorn against any further attempts by the Empire to invade and conquer their land.

It was at this point that Charliss exploded with fury, halting the recitation in mid-sentence.

Melles and Thayer exchanged a startled glance, for neither of them had ever seen the Emperor react in this uncontrolled a fashion. And the moment that the Emperor paused for breath—which was, thanks to his poor physical condition, after no more than a dozen rage-filled words— they both stepped up onto the dais and flanked him.

"*I* will handle Tremane, Lord Emperor," Melles said before Charliss could start again. "That is why you chose me, and believe me, he will live just long enough to regret his actions."

"And *I* will deal with the traitors who decided to cast their lot in with him," Thayer rumbled. "They are Imperial soldiers under my command, and as such, they will be executed by Imperial hands." Charliss looked up at them both, face still contorted with rage, and started to rise.

Melles again exchanged glances with Thayer, and nodded at the side door that led from the dais to the Imperial quarters. Melles moved his head in agreement, and each of them took one of Charliss' arms to help him to his feet.

"The Emperor wishes to confer with us as to the appropriate punishment for these traitors," Melles proclaimed, as they got Charliss up and standing between them. It wasn't a good answer, but it was better than saying nothing, and far better than letting the courtiers make something up for themselves. Before Charliss could say anything else, they had him moving, and once they had him started in the right direction, he continued until he was back in his austere, gray marble, high-ceilinged, private chambers. Wisely, the guards did not hinder them, perhaps because they knew that if Charliss went into a spitting, foaming rage in public, it would not do anyone any good except the rumor mongers.

Once Melles and Thayer got Charliss into a seat, however, the temper tantrum they had prevented from occurring in public broke out in private.

Charliss hissed, spat, pounded the arms of his white-leather chair, and probably would have thrown things if he'd had the strength to rise. Flecks of foam dotted his withered lips, and the pupils of his eyes were dilated. The guards stood at the door, eyes straight ahead, pretending to be deaf.

Most of what he babbled was incoherent, and it was painfully clear that Charliss had completely lost control of his formidable temper and of his ability to think. If it had not been for the fact that he was so angry he couldn't even control his voice, his shouts would have informed everyone in Crag Castle just how out-of-control he actually was.

But between his rage and his physical state, his voice didn't get much above a hoarse growl, and much to Melles' relief, he also could not get out of his chair to pace—or to destroy the contents of his chamber, as he had once or twice in the past decades. He could only beat impotently on the padded arms of the chair as he cursed Tremane's name and lineage back to the days of the First Emperor.

He and Thayer took turns trying to soothe the Emperor with promises of personal revenge and Imperial justice, not that any of those promises had any likelihood of being fulfilled. The agent had made it quite clear that there were no more "loyal" Imperials with Tremane's troops; for one reason or another they had all defected over to him. The only way to get at Tremane now would be to send a magical assassin—and that would take the combined abilities of several mages. In light of all of the other pressing needs there were for the little magic that could be made to function, a magical assassin would be an extremely stupid thing to waste time and energy on.

While it was Thayer's turn to distract the Emperor, Melles sent one of the guards for his physicians, and looked around for something that might serve to blunt the Emperor's anger—or at least anesthetize him. This was a fairly public room, filled with gray- or white-leather chairs arranged in small groups, with a white desk of bleached wood that was too clean to be used very often off in a corner, and rugs made of bleached sheepskin scattered about on the white-marble floor. There was a sideboard of gilded gray marble to Melles' right that was even more impressive than the one in Melles' rooms; it was loaded down with crystal decanters of liquors he recognized and those he did not. What, in the name of the Hundred Little Gods, would a drink as yellow as a buttercup or as blue as a berry taste like? Or one as green as new spring grass?

Or did he really want to know?

Probably not. If Charliss was used to entertaining the minor rulers of his possessions here, he would probably keep a stock of every vile concoction that every pelt-wearing barbarian ever invented in the name of "something to drink." Over the years, Melles had sampled a few of these, and he was not eager to renew his acquaintance with any of them. There were some things man was not meant to know—or imbibe.

By carefully sniffing the necks of each of the likely bottles, he found a decanter of the same potent brandy he himself had been drinking when the formal Court had been called. He poured a much larger portion than he would ever have drunk himself, and took it to the Emperor.

Charliss seized it in a clawlike hand and downed it without even blinking, then threw the glass across the room, where it hit the wall and shattered, leaving sparkling shards and a few ruby-red drops of bloodlike liquid on the white floor.

Melles raised an eyebrow at Thayer, who shook his head. Evidently the General figured he had the situation in hand and didn't need to turn the Emperor over to Melles just yet. Melles nodded, got another two glasses of the wine, kept one for himself and brought the other to Thayer. Then he stood back until Thayer needed him.

His enforced idleness gave him plenty of time to think about the Imperial agent's report. Tremane had shown more intelligence and initiative than Melles would ever have given him credit for, and on the whole, Melles was impressed. He would never have gotten the troops to stand by him, if he had not come up with a story to convince them that it was the *Emperor* who had deserted *them*. It was an adept use of polarity. And to somehow manage to make peace with the Alliance and convince the very people he had been fighting against to make him their new ruler—well, that was nothing short of a miracle. Melles would have given a great deal to know how Tremane had managed that particular feat.

Despite the fact that he hated Tremane with an unholy passion and would happily have seen him slowly drawn and quartered over the course of a lengthy dinner, Melles knew that in Tremane's position he would have done exactly the same things. For all the faults that Tremane had, stupidity wasn't one of them. He wasn't as brilliant as Melles, but he was not stupid either. He was lucky, though, and he had used all of the facts he had to make some reasonable conclusions. Melles had access to all the Imperial records, and he knew for a fact that Charliss had not given Tremane support or orders for months before the looting of the Imperial depot. Once Tremane's magics began to fail, he would have found himself fighting an unsupported war in unfamiliar territory, surrounded by enemies. He would have had no advantage over the enemy without magic to help. By the time the winter storms began, it would have been impossible to retreat across country to the Empire. So just what *did* Charliss expect Tremane to do at that point? Die in place, like a loyal fool out of the old Chronicles? Men like that had gone extinct in the days of the First Emperor, probably because they kept doing stupidly loyal things that bought them early graves. Charliss could not have concocted a better scheme to get rid of Grand Duke Tremane if he'd tried—except, of course, if he had appointed Melles to do away with him.

Not that Melles would have minded at all if Tremane *had* been such a loyal fool, but the fact was that he was loyal, like most men, only to a point. And after that point, he saw no reason to repay betrayal with more loyalty. And his luck must be phenomenal, for he had managed to pull an amazing victory out of a well that looked to hold only the bitter water of defeat.

But then, Tremane always had been unaccountably, inexplicably lucky. Fortune always smiled on the man and doubled the effects of his adequate competence. That was part of the reason why Melles hated him.

The liquor had enough effect on Charliss to get him to stop babbling; he still pounded the arms of his chair, but now he focused on Thayer, detailing the excruciating punishments he wanted Tremane and his men to endure before they died. Thayer did not bother to point out that Tremane and his men were quite out of reach of any Imperial punishments; he simply nodded gravely, pretending to pay attention, when in fact he was probably just hoping that Charliss' Healers would arrive before the Emperor erupted into incoherence again. Finally the physicians did arrive, and in a moment they had taken over from Thayer, swarming over the Emperor, pressing medicines on him, urging him to calm himself. Since Charliss' energy had been fading as the strong dose of liquor took effect, he was finally ready to listen to advice, to take those medicines, to allow his servants to take him to his bedroom and put him to bed. Thayer and Melles took the opportunity then to make their escape.

Thayer was in no mood to talk. "I was dragged away from writing out orders for troop movement in the provinces," he told Melles brusquely.

"And I need to get those orders out, whether or not Emperor Charliss has other duties he needs me for."

Melles nodded, hearing and understanding the things that Thayer had not said. It would be best to get as many orders out as possible, quickly, while Charliss was otherwise occupied. It was all too clear that the Emperor was no longer entirely sane or stable. The problem was not that he was disintegrating; Melles and Thayer between them could very easily take over if he dropped dead this very night. The real problem was that he was not disintegrating fast enough.

Until he either abdicated or died, the Imperial Guards would make sure he *remained* the Emperor; that was their duty, and not only were they trained and sworn to it, they were *geased* to it. He would not be the only Emperor to have gone mad in the last few months of his life; the Empire had survived such rulers before, and truth to tell, with the difficulties facing the Empire now, being ruled by a madman was the smallest of its problems. At the moment, his obsessions were harmless enough. As long as he insisted on pursuing the twin goals of the destruction of Valdemar and the punishment of Tremane, Melles would be perfectly content. If all that happened was an occasional interruption of work, it would be a small price to pay to have the Emperor harmlessly occupied and out of the way of real business. Charliss was an Adept, and he did have an entire corps of mages who answered only to his demands—and it was entirely possible, if he decided to sacrifice all attempts to keep his anti-senescence magics working, that he *could* find some way to destroy Tremane, Valdemar, or both. Granted, such powerful magics would probably kill him and most of his mages, but that was to be expected, and it wouldn't bother Melles in the least. *He* did not intend to worry about anything as far beyond practical reach as Tremane, and Valdemar was even farther than that.

The real danger to Melles and all he needed to accomplish was that Charliss might recover his senses and his priorities enough to decide to meddle in what Melles had planned. That would mean nothing short of disaster, for the Emperor had his own nets of agents and spies that rivaled the ones Melles had in place, and he would know very soon just what Melles was doing, overtly and covertly. Most of it, of course, was simply good strategy, but there was that tiny fraction designed to make Charliss into a villain and Melles into a hero, and Charliss would probably not care too much for that.

Charliss would also have his own plans—which would not be a bad thing, if the Emperor was still sane. But he wasn't, and the situation was only going to get worse as time went on. If he began to meddle, he could easily undo everything that Melles and Thayer had worked so hard to establish.

Something would have to be done to keep that from happening.

All that flashed through Melles's mind as he stood in the frigid hallway with General Thayer. He nodded slowly. "We both have work to do," he replied. "We need to get our structure too solidly in place to dislodge by any force."

That was an innocuous enough statement, but a brief flicker of his glance toward the closed door of the Emperor's quarters brought an answering glimmer of understanding to Thayer's eyes. "Jacona's under control," Thayer replied. "It's the rest of the Empire that we need to think about now. And with your permission, I'll get to my part of it."

Melles clapped him on the shoulder. "And I to mine; after all, what *is* the Empire but soldiers and civil servants of various rank?"

The General nodded in agreement, and the two of them went their separate ways; Melles hurried his steps to his own apartments with the determination to get enough in place that no matter *what* mad schemes Charliss came up with, it would make no difference.

He returned to his suite to find the ever-attentive Porthas waiting, ready to remove the uncomfortable court robes and replace them with loose, fur-lined lounging robes and sheepskin slippers. When he raised an eye at that, Porthas shrugged.

"I assumed that my lord would be working late into the night and would not wish to be disturbed. I had arranged for a meal to be brought here, and declined invitations on my lord's behalf for a card party and a musical evening." Even as Porthas spoke, he assisted Melles out of the heavy over-robe.

The moment that Porthas mentioned the card party and "musical evening"—the latter of which would probably be some idiot's wife, unmarried sisters, and unbetrothed daughters, all performing popular ballads with varying degrees of success—he shuddered. The card party wouldn't have been much better; when he played cards, he played seriously, and it would be a dead certainty that he would have been paired with an unattached female who either bet recklessly or was too timid to make a bid.

"You were correct, Porthas," he replied, as the valet eased him into the comfort of loose robes heated on a rack in front of the fire. "And I do have a great deal of work to do."

Charliss' actions today had given him the spur that he needed to make some fairly bold moves. That long report on the state of the rest of the Empire had left him with uncertainty earlier, but it was clear now that he had no time to waste.

First, the Empire; second, the Court. Thayer would have no part to play in that second act of consolidation.

He sat down behind his desk, and pulled paper and pen toward him. As he had already anticipated, local leaders throughout the Empire had already secured *their* immediate territories wherever possible. In places where the situation had not yet been secured, he had only to expand his existing arrangements, and he wrote out those orders first. The drafts would go to Thayer before they went to the clerks for copying, just to make certain that they weren't going to step on each others' feet, but the plans were simply extensions of what was already going on around Jacona.

Porthas placed a cup of hot mulled wine at his elbow; the fragrance of the spices in it drifted to his nostrils. He reached absently for it and sipped it, holding it with one hand while he wrote with the other.

The real challenges would come in dealing with those local leaders, people who had made themselves the top wolf in their own little territories, and would not care to hear from a bigger, tougher wolf than they were. Somehow he would have to persuade them that he had authority and power, perhaps in excess of what he *really* had, and that it was in their best interest to begin taking orders from him.

If he couldn't achieve that objective, he was going to have to eliminate them without direct confrontation, and put someone more amenable to authority in their places.

He put the cup down, out of the way, while he contemplated his options.

The real trick would be to get rid of them in ways that would not be traced back and connected with him. Getting rid of people was never difficult. It was doing so without leaving any tracks or signs pointing to who was responsible that was the hard part. Those clever, perceptive, and skilled enough to trace blame were few but devastating, and all plans had to be made with the assumption that such a sleuth would be investigating, though the odds were slim.

As with cards, duels, and death sports, look at the odds—but consider the stakes.

He picked up the report, leafed through it, and scanned the list of those local leaders and their brief dossiers again; his agents were good, and it was possible to get some idea of who would cooperate and who would not just from the thumbnail sketches of their personalities that had been provided to him. He had a short list of assassins to chose from, "special agents" who were adept at making deaths look like accidents or illness. It was going to be difficult to get them into place, given the current conditions, but it would not be impossible. With the help of the Army, he ought to be able to get any individual to the right location within a few weeks.

It would probably be a good idea to place his best agents on his most likely targets immediately, rather than waste time attempting to persuade some provincial idiot with an overblown sense of his own competence. If the blow came before he even contacted a given fool, it definitely wouldn't be connected with him. That would leave the agent free to take on a second target if attempts at persuasion of someone worth saving failed.

He switched ink and paper, to the special colors of both that would tell these operatives that he had a job for them. The note he sent would be commonplace greetings, of course; no special agent would ever trust primary instructions that came written. This was a gamble on his part, for many of these people were freelance workers. When they heard what he had to say, they might even turn *him* down; although they would be paid more for these targets than any of them had ever gotten for a job before, getting to their targets through the miserable conditions that existed now could be a real problem. And again, that was the privilege of an agent who was as good as these were; you couldn't persuade an artist to make a masterpiece by standing him in front of an easel and threatening him with death. It might be possible to pick off one or two of these provincial leaders with ordinary assassins, and if he came up short on the number of agents he needed, that was what he would do.

But he really would prefer it if all of these operatives found the jobs enough of a challenge to take them on. They were very good. He, above all, should know; he used to be one of them, as did Porthas, and he had even trained some of them in technique.

There was nothing like being able to call on old school ties...

As he wrote out his list of "invitations," it occurred to him that he actually did have a way to fulfill the Emperor's demands and "bring Tremane to justice," provided that the "justice" came in the form of a swift, sure blade or the sharp bite of poison. There were three of these assassins—four, if he counted Porthas, though he did not intend to do without that worthy's talents right here, who could and possibly *would* go to Hardorn and eliminate Tremane. Magical assassination being out of the question, physical assassination would take a year or more, but it could be done.

He paused to consider it, even though the idea did not appear to be a particularly good one. There was a certain amount of personal satisfaction to be had if he could somehow kill Tremane. *How* had the man managed to wheedle his way into the hearts and minds of the Hardornens? It did not seem fair that his old enemy should come through a situation that *should* have destroyed him, only to be made a King. Granted, he would never see his home again, and granted, Melles was going to be an Emperor, not a mere King. Nevertheless, the prospect was galling. It would have been satisfying to bring him down altogether.

Porthas took away the cup, and left a fresh one and a plate of sliced fruit, bread, and cheese in its place. This was a subtle hint that he should eat something. He took the hint, and ate without tasting any of it.

He weighed all the considerations. Given that the agent sent out would be brilliant, crafty, and given every resource, the likelihood of anyone from the Empire reaching the center of Hardorn was remote. Success would be remoter still, for an agent of the Empire, without the magical aids that would enable him to study the people and conditions surrounding his target, would be operating blind in a foreign land. He would stick out like a single red fish in a school of green fish.

In a way, it was possible to sympathize with the Emperor's obsession. Tremane *should* be dead at this point. Normally, he did not give in to his own emotions, but there was a sick anger in the bottom of his stomach that twisted and bit as if he had swallowed a viper, and it would probably never give him rest. He wanted Tremane dead, and he wanted to do whatever it would take to get him there.

But even when he had been an operative himself, he had known that there was a point past which it was inadvisable to pursue your target, no matter what your employer said or offered. This was one of those times.

He got up from his desk and poured himself another drink, ignoring for the moment the cup of mulled wine; not brandy this time, but a thick cordial with no alcohol in it, made entirely of syrup and stomach-soothing and gut-deadening herbs. He went back to his seat, let himself down into the embrace of the chair, and tried to convince his heart of what his head knew were facts.

When the enemy is "dead" to the world one inhabits, he might as well be dead in totality.

That was something his teacher had told him, and it was as true now as it was then. Tremane might as well be dead; his lands and possessions were confiscated, his name erased from the records, and he could never return here again. He would have to be content with a petty kingdom in a land of barbarians.

Pursuit of Tremane was a waste of resources, which were in very short supply, especially good operatives. There was no point in wasting a man who could serve Melles better elsewhere. It was time to bury the past vendettas with Tremane's name.

There was no point in following the Emperor into madness.

Every time a mage-storm washed over them, anyone with any pretensions at being a magician felt it; there had even been clever daylight robberies timed to coincide with the onset of a mage-storm, when the owner of a building would be incapacitated. The Storms were bad enough when they came during the daylight hours, but when they occurred at night, when everyone was asleep, they were worse, for they became part of one's dream and turned those dreams into nightmares.

Melles woke up in a sweat, clutching his blankets, out of a nightmare of tumbling through empty space. But the waking reality was no better, and he hung onto his bedding with grim recognition of what was behind the dream. Complete disorientation, nausea, the feeling that he was on the verge of blacking out and yet could not have the relief that unconsciousness would bring—this was a mage-storm to him, and he was profoundly grateful that Porthas and his guards were not mages and did not feel these effects.

At that, his own bouts with the Storms were not as bad as those of some of the other mages he knew, though he had not ventured to ask the Emperor how he weathered these things. He had a theory that the amount a mage suffered was directly proportional to the amount of magic he had tried to work in the interval between the Storms. If magic was tied to its caster, and the Storms disrupted magic, it stood to reason that when the Storms hit, they would give trouble to mage and magic together. As a consequence, he had tried to keep from working any magic at all, even giving up his own rejuvenation magics when they had not survived disruption.

When the Storm finally passed, and his dizziness and nausea vanished as they always did, he let go of the covers and tried to relax back into his goosedown mattress. With any luck, the Emperor would be "indisposed" today after his bout with the Storm, and with further luck, the mage-storm would send his mental and physical state plummeting again. It was too much to hope that the Storm had killed him, but it was certainly possible that this time he might wind up bedridden.

That would be an excellent thing, for then Melles would have to stand proxy and speak *for* him. It might even be possible to frighten him into stepping down and making Melles the Emperor. He would not hope for it, and he would not urge it, for the Emperor might well take such suggestions very badly. It was a fine dream, though, and one he was loath to give up.

He closed his eyes and tried to relax in hope of resuming his slumbers, but it was of no use. He could not get back to sleep again. He opened his eyes and stared up at the canopy of his bed, or rather, at the darkness within the sheltering curtains of the bed. No light penetrated those thick velvet curtains, nor would it until morning, when the servants pulled back both window and bed curtains to wake him. Now that there was no magical way to heat Crag Castle, one needed those heavy curtains around the beds to keep the drafts out, just as one needed goosedown comforters and featherbeds, and many blankets. Even then, he often woke with a cold nose.

He was not a heavy sleeper, nor a long one, and never had been. Some would say that a guilty conscience kept him awake, or the memories of all of his victims, but the truth was simpler than that. Sleep, in his profession, was a dangerous necessity, the one time when he was completely vulnerable and had to entrust his safety to others. He had trained himself to wake completely at the slightest disturbance, and once he was awake, his mind leaped into activity whether or not there was any need for it. Once he was *that* wide awake, it was difficult to get back to sleep again.

He wondered what time it was. If it was near enough to dawn, it was hardly worth fighting to get back to sleep only to be awakened again.

He shifted his weight, and a scent of pungent herbs filled the still air. Porthas had ordered the servants to add those herbs to the bedding, in anticipation of problems when the vermin-repelling spells failed. That was yet another example of Porthas' foresight; he'd seen some of the Councillors scratching surreptitiously at the last meeting of the Grand Council, and suspected fleas, since these were some of the same courtiers who kept dogs or other pets and insisted on having them here at Court. Vermin spread, with or without pets to spread them, unless one took precautions.

Fleas at Court! Well, they were not the only bloodsucking vermin here, only the most honest about it. In some ways, Melles would have preferred fleas to some of the other vermin he had to deal with on a daily basis.

That led his thoughts immediately to the current problem facing him: the Court. He had always known there would be some opposition to him as the Emperor's Heir, but he had not thought that all of his enemies would forget their own differences to unite against him.

His only solid ally was Thayer; in Thayer he had the Army—but *not* the Imperial Guards. Those were answerable only to the Emperor, and led by Commander Peleun, who was *not* a great admirer of Melles. How Peleun had managed to climb to the heights he had while still retaining a fair number of illusions about honor and fidelity was quite beyond Melles, but he had, and he was already causing some trouble. He didn't care for the idea of a former chief assassin as an Emperor— although Melles was following in a long and distinguished, if not openly acknowledged, tradition. He had preferred Tremane, who at least pretended to honesty, and had a fine career in both the civil service and the military behind him.

More important than Peleun, however, was Councillor Baron Dirak, who was in charge of the Imperial Civil Servants. *He* had been one of Tremane's staunchest allies, still defended him openly at Court, and was not at all pleased with Melles' rise to power. He'd had some hope of wedding a sister to Tremane, and was very bitter about losing that chance for power.

Either of these men alone could have caused him some small difficulty, but with both of them allied, things could become serious. And if his sources were correct, they were maneuvering to get Councillor Serais, head of the tax collectors, into their corner.

He had to consolidate his power in the Court. There were other candidates for the Iron Throne, many of them just as qualified as Melles. It was entirely possible that someone could send an assassin out after Melles. Peleun probably would be horrified at the thought, but Dirak would consider it, and there were others who knew how to contact the same list of "special agents" that Melles used. Melles hadn't been able to contact them all, and that meant there were at least a few top-level assassins unaccounted for. Peleun could use *his* power as the head of the Imperial Guard to allow anyone he wished in to see the Emperor at any time, and given the right set of circumstances, the end result of such an interview could be a brace of guards arriving to put Melles under arrest. With the Emperor's mind so unbalanced, it wouldn't be too difficult to persuade him that Melles was not enthusiastic enough in his pursuit of Tremane. That alone would be enough to get him arrested and replaced.

If he was arrested, his enemies would have the leisure to concoct as much evidence as they pleased to prove whatever they wished, and he would not be able to interfere. It was possible, of course, that Porthas would take up the reins and act in his absence, but Melles preferred not to count on such enlightened self-interest. It was far more likely that Porthas and all of his special employees would offer their services to what they perceived to be the winning side.

He was secure in the city; Jacona was quiet, and entirely his. He had issued his orders and sent out his assassins and negotiators along with Thayer's troops; within a few weeks he would know how successful he had been at taking the rest of the Empire under his rule. Now, while he was waiting for word from the countryside, would be a good time to consolidate the Court. That was one thing that his enemies never counted on; that he would continue to work on another aspect of his projects while waiting for results from the previous phase. They always started on a phase and waited to see what would happen before going on to the next, but that was a costly way to operate.

As for the Court—he would order no assassinations, at least not yet, and only use it as a last resort. If anyone died in the next few weeks, even if it was completely an accident, he would be the first to be suspected of initiating foul play. But he had always used the knife as a tool, not an end, and the skills that had made him the Emperor's most successful agent included blackmail, information brokering, and—of course—rumor creation. He didn't need to kill anyone to be effective. It was more effective to keep a small but omnipresent *fear* of death in peoples' minds than to actually deliver the blow itself.

Peleun, Dirak, and Serais; he would concentrate on those three, who were outwardly his enemies. The little fish were probably waiting to see who came out the victor, and the bigger fish, the equals of those three, had not yet openly taken sides.

Peleun's weakness was his fortune, or rather, his lack of one; he didn't have a solid financial situation and he had been speculating lately in commodities. He had been doing very well, in no small part because he knew just what commodities were going to be in short supply, thanks to his contacts with the Army. The Army, of course, had taken over the Cartage Guild, and although the Army did not own or profit directly from the cargoes carried, there were Army records of what had just come in that Peleun could easily get access to before the goods ever came on the market. Everything had to go through inspection, weighing, and taxation before so much as a grain of wheat could be sold, and that took several days, enough time for Peleun to purchase goods that were going to be scarce before anyone else knew that supplies were going to temporarily dry up until the next cargoes came in. That was a great weakness in the current market situation, for there was no telling what might come in besides staples. There was no way to effectively communicate back to the farms and estates, so at some point, it might be impossible to find an apple, and at another, there was nothing in the way of fruit in the market *but* apples. All Melles had to do would be to see that Peleun saw the wrong records, or completely falsified records, and within a few weeks he would be a ruined man.

Dirak was a very nervous gentleman, timid and altogether afraid of his shadow; perhaps that was why he had gone into civil service in the first place. The current situation had him gulping handfuls of calmatives on a daily basis; surely there was something that Melles could do to further destroy his nerves?

And as for Serais—did he but know it, he was the most vulnerable of all. Some quick work among the Imperial tax records, and hundreds of thousands of gold pieces that had never existed in the first place would "vanish" from the treasury. Of course, the errors would eventually be uncovered, but it would take a great deal of work and require referring to all the original tax receipts, and Serais' reputation would be completely ruined by the time it was over. With any luck, he was probably skimming a little off the top anyway, and when Melles was through, that would have been uncovered as well.

That wouldn't be enough to keep the Court completely under his thumb, though. He had to give the malcontents within the Court another target than himself, just as he had done for the malcontents in the city. It could not be a target for *blame*, however, but a target of profit and reward. It would be very dangerous to *blame* the Emperor for anything, and there was no point in spreading rumors accusing anyone else of wrongdoing, when those rumors might well be turned on him. No, with all the uneasiness in the Court, offering people hope and profit would be far more effective.

What would happen when the mage-storms were over? What, exactly, would the Empire need? How could those courtiers who remained here profit from the end of the Storms? If he could give them a direction—even an entirely specious direction—that would get them too busy to concern themselves with him.

Last of all, he and Thayer should work together to at least make his position *look* unassailable. Perhaps by tempting one of his three targets to attempt to persuade the Emperor to do something—something that Melles could come out against—something that Melles would *know* the Emperor would never even consider. Reliable rumors that the Emperor was actually in favor of the given action would spur the target onward. By urging something the Emperor was against, the target would label himself as a troublemaker and potential traitor in the Emperor's eyes.

He smiled to himself. And what better action could there be than urging clemency for Tremane?

He felt his eyes growing heavier, and his body relaxing. He had a plan. In the morning he would implement it.

Now he could sleep.

Melles smiled and nodded graciously as one of Viscount Aderin's six unmarried daughters blushed and dedicated her performance on the great-harp to him. He watched her attentively—which had the effect of making her fumble her fingerings—as she labored through a rendition of an old chestnut entitled "My Lady's Eyes."

Musical evenings were the best cure for insomnia that he knew, but attendance at this one was important. If one was going to plant information, this sort of gathering was the place to do so—a room full of very minor nobility, all of them hungry for advancement, all of them so eager for a crumb from the tables of the great that they would listen to and believe practically anything. They would never divulge where their information originated, in the hope that those they imparted their choice bits to would think that it originated with them and give them credit for enormous cleverness.

And none of them could be directly linked to him. He did not mix with them socially, except at extremely large gatherings like this one, which he had been urged to attend by the Emperor's Minister of Protocol. He was not related to any of them. No one had any reason to assume that he had any reason to *give* them information. For all intents and purposes, he was here to survey Aderin's daughters as possible marriage fodder, not to chat with Aderin's friends.

In fact, the girls weren't that bad. Three of the six were discreet and submissive, able to entertain without embarrassing him, unlikely to try to put themselves forward, attractive enough to satisfy him, and tractable enough to smile and ignore any little excess of his own. He could do worse, and very well knew it. This was probably why the Minister of Protocol had suggested the gathering, at least in part. There was some nervousness among the Ministers about the fact that he was not yet married and showed no signs of wanting that particular state. There *had* been a single Emperor in the past who had been uninterested in the opposite sex, and there had been trouble during his reign that he could have resolved with a marriage of state but had not done so. This had eventually led to a costly minor war, and at the moment, the Empire could not afford a *cheap* minor war.

Of course, he could always make the ministers happy by doing what the Sixth Emperor had done. With his reign starting on a shaky note, and unwilling to offend anyone by picking one girl over another, he had handpicked the daughter of a mere Squire, a very plain, very quiet child, and had educated her to be the perfect Empress. She had offended no one in his Court, because she had deferred to everyone; she had every skill needed in an Empress. Even the fact that she was plain had been valuable, because it was quite clear to everyone that she was the Emperor's place-holder and hostess, and nothing more. The Emperor had been able then to appoint dozens of royal mistresses over the course of his reign, all of them enjoying the same status, and he had threaded his way through many intrigues on the basis of which mistress he chose to favor at any one time.

That might be the best solution of all. And if he *had* to make a state marriage eventually, well, the Emperor could divorce his wife and remarry within a day and a night, and an insignificant place-holder would have no family to make trouble later. In fact, such a girl would probably be very happy to retire from Court with a generous settlement.

As he caught himself playing with the various possibilities of such an arrangement, he sternly brought his attention back to the real reason why he was here. He was going to plant rumors, and he had better get about it before people began indulging themselves a little too heavily in the mulled punch to properly remember what they heard.

Before the evening was over, he had started a whisper-campaign about Serais and the "missing" tax money, had suggested several lines of profit to be pursued when the Storms were over, and had hinted that when *he* was Emperor, those who confined their attention to conservative ideas and relied on "what always worked before" would take second place to those with innovation and creativity. Since these folk were among the lesser nobility, they had less access to rejuvenative magics, and hence the average age here was much lower than for the Court as a whole. Melles knew that the one thing he could do to attract the support of little fish like these was to suggest that he would be more receptive to fresh, new ideas than his predecessor. This indicated that there was room at the top—and that some old, tired titles might find their Council seats and Ministerial offices taken by those who had been languishing in their shadow.

It had been a profitable evening. And in addition, he had managed to deflect any accusation that he was actually pleased at Tremane's downfall by pretending to a low level of disappointment in "his old childhood friend," thus lending another layer of obscurity to his motives. Now there would be a substantial number of people with the impression that he and Tremane had been friends for most of their lives rather than rivals. So when he laid the trail to suggest that the Emperor might be willing to consider clemency for the Grand Duke, there would be people ready to believe the suggestion since it came from him.

This very evening, a bright young fellow who'd brought himself to Porthas' attention by his brilliance with both forgery and "fixing" account books had been smuggled into the tax office and was ensuring Serais' downfall. Peleun had invested everything he had to spare, and some that he did not have, in smoked ham, bacon, and fancy sausage, certain that the cargo that had just arrived from Tival was frozen fish, not meat. Tomorrow the double caravan of smoked ham, bacon, and fancy sausage that had arrived from Tival would go on the market, and Peleun would be very lucky if he could hold onto his house in the city.

And as for Dirak, well, Melles had something very special in mind for him. Besides being nervous, Dirak was devout—or perhaps it was better to say that he was superstitious. He was about to be the recipient of a great many omens of bad fortune, together with many minor mishaps that might lend further credence to those omens. If Dirak did not collapse with nervous exhaustion before the end of a fortnight, Melles would be very much surprised.

Melles was feeling pleased enough with the way that things were going that he dismissed Porthas early when he returned to his rooms.

Porthas had been responsible for setting up most of what Melles had planned for his three enemies, and he was looking a bit worn, at least to Melles' critical eye. "I can take care of myself for once," he told the man. "I'm going to work for a few more hours, then go straight to bed."

"I would argue with you," Bors Porthas replied, rubbing his hand across his eyes, "but I'm too tired. I know my limits, and I've just reached them."

Melles uttered a short bark of laughter. "Good! I was beginning to think you had no limits, and I was wondering when you were going to set yourself up as my rival." He was only half joking about that; it was something anyone in his position had to consider.

Porthas snorted. "No fear of that, my lord. *You* are a target. *I* am not. To my mind, my position is the better one. Please sleep lightly and put an extra guard on your door, my lord. And *don't* try to dress yourself until I arrive to select your robes for the day. I do not want a repetition of the day you wore the sapphire tunic with the emerald trews. I would not be able to live down the shame."

Melles acknowledged the advice with a wave of his hand, and Porthas bowed himself out.

Since he would be doing without his valet's silent attendance, Melles set his desk up with everything he might need to work before he ever sat down. A servant would come in to mend the fire, but otherwise he would be left alone at his own orders until he chose to go to bed.

He had been working steadily on follow-up orders for his agents in Jacona involved with the freedom movement, and similar, but more general orders for similar agents in other cities of the Empire. He had noticed that the room seemed to be getting colder, and had been about to ring for the servant, when the servant finally came in, bearing a metal hod of coal.

He started to turn his attention back to his work, when something about the young man's posture sounded a mental alarm in his instincts.

He was already out of his chair and had slipped free of the cumbersome outer robe as he dove toward the floor, when the first knife hit the back of the chair and stuck there, quivering.

He rolled to his feet beside the fireplace and snatched up a fireplace poker as the youngster threw a second knife that he dropped down from a hidden sheath in his sleeve. Melles easily dodged that strike, too, and his lip curled with contempt. Arm sheaths—that was a trick for sophomores and sharpsters! And against *him*! What kind of fools were they sending after him anyway?

"You might as well hold still, old man," the young one whispered, pulling another knife from somewhere behind the back of his neck as he went into a lithe crouch. "You're going to die anyway, so you might as well make it easier on both of us."

Old man! Who did this young idiot think he was? But the stupid speech—*so* melodramatic and such a waste of breath—told him the kind of assassin he faced. He had to deal with nuisances like this one at least once a year; youngsters who thought they were better and faster than the old masters, and would use any excuse to take them on. He would have to kill this cretin; he had no choice in the matter. If he didn't make an example of the fool, others like him would think he'd gone soft and keep coming at him. Killing the boy would mean that the others would leave him alone for about another year.

But anger boiled up deep in his gut, and not just because some young freelancer, ill-trained and without even a nodding acquaintance with discipline, had decided to show that the master had lost his touch. No, this boy would never have come here if he had not been brought into the palace by someone who belonged here. That meant he'd been hired.

And *that* was an insult that was hardly to be borne. How *dared* someone send a rank amateur against *him*? Did they think his reputation was inflated? Did they think he could no longer hold his own against even a boy like this one?

Were they that contemptuous of him?

They were about to discover that it was not wise to tease the old basilisk; they would learn that it was only pretending to sleep.

He rushed the boy, startling him into skipping backward; he was used to the flickering shadows cast by flames instead of mage-lights, but the boy obviously was not. As he passed his desk, he feinted with the poker and picked up the tray of sand he used to dry the ink on his documents. The boy's attention was on the poker, not on Melles' other hand. Before he could get out of reach, Melles flung the contents of the tray into his eyes, then threw the tray itself at him. The boy deflected the tray clumsily with one arm; it hit him and clattered to the floor. He could not deflect the sand.

So far neither of them had made enough noise to attract the attention of the guards at the door, and Melles had no intention of calling for help. If the guards came, they'd kill the fool before Melles had a chance to find out who had sent him.

Blinded and in pain, the boy still had a few tricks left; with his eyes watering, he threw the dagger he held at the last place Melles had been standing, and rubbed at his face with one hand while groping behind his neck for another blade. Of course, Melles wasn't where the boy thought, but had dropped down below the level of a thrown blade. He lunged forward before the boy could register where he was, and swept the poker out in a savage backhanded blow at knee-height.

He shattered the boy's left kneecap, and the boy went down with a strangled cry.

"Who sent you?" he hissed angrily, as he stood up slowly, absently pleased that he was not at all winded. The daily workouts with Porthas had been more than worth the effort.

The boy responded with a curse about Melles's sexual preferences, rolled out of the way of another blow, and got his fourth knife into his hands at the same time.

"No matter what you've heard, I don't take any pleasure in that particular pastime," Melles said coldly. By now, his eyes had watered so much that the boy could see again, although his eyes were bloodshot and swollen. Melles was in no mood to take chances, even though he was facing a partially disabled foe, so he watched the young fool warily. The boy did not writhe or take his eyes off Melles, though the pain from his shattered knee must have been excruciating. "I suggest you tell me who hired you, and save yourself a great deal of pain."

The boy inched away, sliding over the slick floor, while Melles moved cautiously toward him. This time the curse was a bit more colorful and less accurate. Melles sighed, and shook his head, as the boy got into a standing position with the help of a chair. What did he expect to accomplish from there? He couldn't walk; his leg wouldn't hold him. And if he couldn't walk, his balance would be off. Didn't he know that? Was he so desperate he'd try anything, or did he really think he had a chance to escape?

Melles backed up, keeping his eyes on the boy at all times, until he reached his desk. Without needing to look to see where it was, he pulled the boy's first knife out of the back of the chair, weighed it in his hand for a moment to get the balance, and threw it.

It hit precisely as he had intended, in the boy's gut with a wet *thud*; the boy dropped to the ground again with a gurgle, unable to twist out of the way in time, as his own knife clattered to the floor. Perhaps the fool had thought he was going to try for the trickier hand shot. That was stupid of him, if he had. A gut wound hurt more and wouldn't kill immediately.

Melles walked over to the boy and stood looking down at him, with the poker held loosely in one hand. The boy had both hands on the hilt of the knife, trying to pull it out; his breath came in harsh pants, and his eyes were glazing with agony. "Who hired you?" he asked again.

The boy looked up, and spat at him.

He sighed. He was going to have to spend more time than he wanted on this, squandering time that could have been better spent on his orders, but there was no help for it. "You're going to tell me sooner or later," he said, without much hope for sense from this arrogant idiot, who *still* didn't think he was going to die. "You'll be better off with sooner."

This time the boy responded with a suggestion for an unpalatable dietary supplement. Melles brought the poker down on his other knee, and proceeded dispassionately to inflict enough pain to extract the information he wanted.

In the end, he managed to get what he wanted without too much of a mess, and the answer made him even more disgusted than he had been at the beginning of the futile exercise.

Duke Jehan. An idiot with just about as little sense as the cretin he'd hired.

And it was not for any great ideological reason, nor because Jehan was avenging Tremane, or trying to put one of the other candidates in the Heir's suite. No, it was because Jehan had somehow gotten the impression that if he managed to assassinate enough candidates, *he* would manage to be put on the throne because he was Charliss' second cousin!

Apparently he'd thought that if he used assassins to do his work for him, no one would connect him with the deaths! Melles had no idea who Jehan thought *would* get the blame if Melles himself was gone, but perhaps this would-be King of Assassins had gotten his order of targets reversed and had gone after the last on the list first.

He finished off the mewling thing on the floor with a single thrust of the boy's own knife, threw the knife down next to the body, and wiped his hands with a napkin, contemplating his next move. It wouldn't be enough to make an example of this boy, or Jehan would think he'd gotten off undiscovered and try some other way of ridding himself of his rivals. Melles had acquired immunity to most of the common poisons, but that didn't mean he wouldn't get sick if someone slipped a dose to him. That would cost still more valuable time, and might incapacitate him long enough for one of his *real* rivals to get in to the Emperor. No, he was going to have to give Jehan a real fright, and make him into an example for anyone else at Court idiotic enough to try something like this.

In the end, it took all of his skill to pull the job off—not to get into Jehan's quarters without arousing anyone, but to get past his own guards. The nurse who was supposed to be watching in Duke Jehan's nursery was easily incapacitated with a needle dipped in a poison that sent one into a deep sleep rather than death. Jehan's oldest son, slightly more than a year old, sat up in his crib and looked with wide eyes at the stranger who came to lift him out and place him on the floor. He didn't do anything more than babble, though, when the stranger gave him several pretty toys to play with.

Melles dropped the body, wrapped in a bloody sheet, into the crib in place of the child, and left the child himself sitting on the floor, happily absorbed in the bladeless daggers that had been intended to kill Melles.

That was a somewhat melodramatic gesture in and of itself, but Melles had the feeling that anything less wouldn't get Jehan's attention. He'd considered leaving the daggers whole rather than snapping the blades off, but if the baby was as stupid as its sire, it would probably have managed to kill itself with one of them. While that would have been no loss for the Court or the world, Jehan would have been so overwrought that the lesson would be completely lost on him. And killing babies, or allowing them to be killed, was bad for one's public image.

Melles slipped back across the palace and into his own rooms again, feeling drained and no less disgusted. He had lost most of the working hours of the night—and this late, although he had easily gotten the blood off the stone floor with the sheet, he'd used up all the hot water in his suite to do so. He'd have to wash himself in cold water; one more mark against Jehan.

He put himself to bed, chilled and angry, but at least he was physically tired enough to sleep.

And hopefully, his little present would prevent Jehan and several others from sleeping for many nights to come. It wasn't much in the way of revenge, for him, but for now it would do.

7

"Amazing!" Silverfox shook his head and stepped away from the teleson crystal, tossing his long, black hair to one side. "If I had not seen this, I would not believe it was possible."

"I couldn't agree more," Karal said. He had been watching over Silverfox's shoulder as the *kestra'chern* spoke with Treyvan. The round crystal lens mounted on top of the teleson had held a perfect image of the head and shoulders of the fascinated gryphon, and a thin but distinct echo of his voice emerged from the matte-gray metal box that held the crystal cradled in a quarter-moon-shaped depression on its surface. This was even more impressive than the time An'desha had done long-distance scrying on Grand Duke Tremane.

This was a distinct improvement over the original sets. A little fiddling and the addition of the crystals on each set as well as the mirrors— simple polished lenticular lenses that any glassworker could make—had made it possible to have images and the audible voices of the two users. All that had been in the notes that Lyam and Firesong had interpreted, but the crystals had never been installed. Perhaps that was why the sets had been on the workbench.

Karal gazed wistfully at the device, which was now being used by Sejanes and one of the new Mage-Gifted Heralds. "This is quite amazing. I wish you didn't have to have Mindspeech to use it."

"But you don't—" Silverfox began. "Or at least only one of you does."

Karal only sighed, very quietly. Silverfox looked at him askance, with a question in his blue eyes, but it was Sejanes who guessed what lay behind Karal's comment.

"You'd like to use this to speak to that young lady of yours without any of us eavesdropping, wouldn't you, lad?" he said shrewdly. Karal blushed and didn't reply immediately, trying to think of an answer that was noncommittal enough without being an actual lie.

"Well, *you* need to use it to confer with the others back in Haven," he said, nodding in the direction of Sejanes, Firesong, and Master Levy. "That's important."

"And you aren't. Is that what you're saying?" Sejanes graced him with a skeptical look.

"What you are talking about is important," Karal replied, knowing that any declaration of how unimportant *he* was would only be met with a counterargument. "Idle chatter with Natoli isn't. It's not as if I really need to hear about what scrapes our friends are getting into, or who's passed to the back room at the Compass Rose."

Sejanes didn't counter that particular response. Instead, he provided a different answer. "We won't be using this device all the time. Personally, if there is a way, I don't see any difficulty with you using it to catch up on news with the young lady." He tilted his head at Firesong, An'desha, and Master Levy in unspoken inquiry. All three of them nodded their heads, completely in agreement with him.

"We all know that you would give it up to one of us if we even looked as if we *thought* we might want to use it, Karal," An'desha told him. "If you could think of a way that you can make it work without an eavesdropper, there's no reason why you can't use it, too. It's not as if you're going to wear the thing out, or use it up."

:Pish. I can Mindspeak. And so can Florian.: Altra wrapped himself gracefully around Karal's legs and looked up into his face. *:For that matter, so can Need. We certainly wouldn't embarrass you, would we?:*

"The Firecat says that he, Need, or the Companion could hold the connection for Karal," Firesong told all of them.

Karal started to protest, then shut his mouth, realizing that he was wrong on all counts and he might as well be quiet. The others wouldn't need to use the teleson all the time, Altra and Florian already shared most of his secret thoughts so why not these, and there could not be any harm in talking a little to Natoli now and then. His cheeks and the back of his neck grew hot. "As long as you don't mind," he said diffidently.

A snort from Firesong was the only reply to that statement, as a Herald in the teleson watched and listened with polite interest.

"*Shall I see if Natoli can be found later?*" the far-off Herald asked. "*If there's no one at the device, one of the Mindspeakers can project to you until Need, the Firecat or the Companion can come hold the connection.*"

:I would think that would be quite satisfactory.: Florian told Karal. *:And I think you ought to tell him that, so that he can arrange for Natoli to come as soon as the mages are finished.:*

"Ah, Florian thinks that would be a good idea," Karal said, trying to control his blushes. "Thank you."

He hurried away to find something to do before he got himself into any further embarrassing situations.

The most useful thing he could do was to serve in his proper place as a secretary, and right at this very moment the only person who needed the skills of a secretary was Tarrn. The *kyree* was down in the workroom, carefully describing everything before Firesong and An'desha took it all to pieces. Lyam had already made scale drawings of each workbench, and now he was making notes while Tarrn dictated. He gratefully gave up his place to Karal, even though the notes would now be in

Valdemaran rather than Kaled'a'in. Tarrn didn't miss a beat, changing his Mindspeech from Lyam to Karal as soon as Karal held the notepad and graphite-stick. Karal rubbed his nose to keep from sneezing; they had stirred up quite a bit of dust just in walking about. It was amazing how much dust found its way down here once the hatchway was open.

"Why are you doing this, sir?" Karal asked, when they completed one bench and moved on to another. "I'm just curious."

:A number of reasons,: the *kyree* replied pleasantly. *:Later, if we are trying to put together another device, we will know what pieces were laid out on which bench in what order. We will have a historical record of how the workshop looked if we ever wish to reconstruct it. In this way, if for some reason the contents of the workbenches are ever jumbled together, we will know what tool goes with what project. It is not always intuitively obvious.:*

Karal nodded, and made another note on the identity of an object. All of that made perfect sense, but it would never have occurred to him to make such detailed drawings, or to measure the distance an object was from the edge of the bench.

:In a case like this, young scribe, records are always important,: Tarrn said. *:The more, the better. Once anything is moved, it is changed forever; perhaps that might not be important, but at the moment, we can't know that. The thing is to make drawings and notes on everything, and several exact copies of the documents we find:*

Karal laughed, which seemed to surprise the *kyree*. "It is a good thing that Urtho was a neat man, or you would be copying foodstains, I think, along with diagrams."

The *kyree* opened his mouth in a wide grin. *:It would not be the first time. I am a mere historian; how am I to know what is a diagram and what was a long ago spill of wine? Perhaps a semicircle of dark brown may not in fact be a ring from the bottom of a mug, but rather a notation of where a teleson lens should go?:*

Lyam, now freed to go make more of those exact copies of the documents and notes they had discovered resting on the benches, trotted up the stairs. Karal had been amazed to discover just how much he had in common with the little lizard-creature over the past several days. Lyam was good-natured, patient, uncomplaining, and about the same age as Karal. Like Karal when he had first arrived in Valdemar, Lyam never expected to be anything more than a secretary. Lyam was probably right, but if anything was to happen to Tarrn, it would be Lyam who would apply the things he learned from the historian to complete a given task.

Tarrn, on the other hand, was a little easier to work for than Ulrich had been, largely because what Tarrn wanted and needed were simple things. It was quite possible for Karal to anticipate Tarrn's descriptions just by looking at the bench, although Tarrn often had a more succinct way of describing something than Karal would have come up with. And Tarrn, although he did have an air of quiet authority, was not as intimidating as Ulrich had been. Since he was physically much shorter than Karal, and since he looked like a friendly, shaggy sheep-herding dog, it simply wasn't possible to be intimidated by him, no matter how intelligent and knowledgeable he was. On the other hand, he seemed just a bit wary around Karal, which was not too surprising. The Karsites had a reputation for being extremely insular people, and it would be logical to assume that Karal harbored certain prejudices about fourlegged "people." Tarrn could not have known about the Firecats, of course; very few people outside of Karse even knew such things existed.

The work went slowly but steadily. Tarrn had refused to allow anyone else to carry away anything after Firesong had taken the telesons and their notes. Since there wasn't anything down here that was needed immediately, the others had given in to his demands with good-natured humor. Since then, the meticulous description and drawing had been going on every day. Tarrn permitted people to remove articles from the benches only after he had finished with them, but since it wasn't always obvious when he was done with a bench, so far no one had moved much of anything.

Now they were down to the final bench, and Tarrn seemed very pleased with all that had gone before. This bench was virtually empty except for a few pots of dried-out paint and ink and some brushes and pens. :*A scribe's bench, I would guess*,: Tarrn speculated. :*Look at the height of the stool—how close the inkwell and the pots are to the front of the bench. Urtho never sat here, I'll wager.*:

"I doubt that any human did," Karal replied, noting the distances down on the diagram. "This is a backless stool, where all the other seats are tall chairs, and to me, that says that whoever used this bench might have had a tail. The seat tilts slightly forward and has an angled, rounded cut-in toward the back, so I'd say it was a *hertasi* that sat here. Probably Urtho's personal scribe or secretary."

:*Impressive deduction. I suspect you are correct,*: Tarrn replied. :*And this is good, since it means Lyam can use this bench for his copying work instead of taking an awkward position on the floor. Well, that is all we need from here. Do run up and tell the others that they can come loot to their hearts' content, would you please? Then if you would, tell Lyam about all of this, and could you help him move his supplies down here?:*

Tarrn gave the order carefully, phrased as a very polite request, as if trying to avoid giving insult. Karal would have obeyed him no matter what his attitude had been, but Tarrn probably wasn't taking any chances about hurting his feelings since they all had to live together in a very crowded environment. Lyam was very happy to transfer his work from the floor upstairs to the bench downstairs, and Karal helped him carry his effects. As Karal had thought, the backless stool was at the perfect height for the little lizard.

"This will be good," Lyam said, hissing his sibilants a trifle as he tested the seat. "The stool is perfect." The brushes proved to have failed to withstand the rigors of time; Lyam examined them, pronounced them useless for scribing, and added that nothing had changed much in the art of brushmaking over the centuries. It did give Karal a sense of awe to hold in his hand something that had last been held so long ago, but Lyam was right; the brush could have been made last week except for the fact that the bristles were crumbling.

"I admit to having a special regard for the tools of my trade," Lyam confided. The paint and ink in the pots were useless as well and were consigned to part of another bench to await their fate. Lyam and Karal cleared the top of the scribe's bench and set it up to Lyam's satisfaction. It did not escape Karal's notice that the graphite-sticks, silverpoint sticks, ink, pens, and brushes that Lyam arranged were in nearly the same places as those that had once served that long-dead scribe. Together they swept and cleaned out the corner, so that there would be no dust or dirt to smudge Lyam's new-made copies.

"Ah!" Lyam finally said with satisfaction, stretching his tail out and flexing his stubby hand-talons. "This is good, good light, and a good position! I can be very happy here, I think! Thank you, *gesten*."

"You're very welcome. Really." Karal paused a moment as it struck him again, in a moment of astonishment, that he was chatting amiably with what could be loosely described as an intelligent dog and its lizard secretary, in the ruins of a magic-blasted tower once ruled by a legend. His musings were interrupted as the lizard secretary held up an ancient brush so that the tarnished ferrule shone dully in the workshop's light. "You know, simply by virtue of where this brush has been found, it could be worth enough in trade to feed my family for a season, but its highest value is in what it makes us think of when we see it."

The *kyree* looked over at the *hertasi* with a look of pure pleasure, saying nothing. Lyam held the old brush reverently in both hands and continued. "An artifact of Urtho's own workshop. This is history itself, Karal, as great as any carved monument or temple. History is in the small items as much as the huge ones. When we see an edifice, we see what the ancients *wanted* us to see, and that is important, but we find out so much more from what was so familiar to them that they thought little of it. And one day, perhaps historians will look back at our clothes, our brushes, and our everyday things, and learn who we were, too!"

:Now you know why I enjoy Lyam's company so much, Karal. He is truly a brother in spirit!: Tarrn's mind-laugh was joyous.

"Oh! I—well. It is easy to be overcome by all of this. It is wonder itself we are immersed in here," Lyam muttered, embarrassed, as he gingerly set aside the brush that had been the focus of his oratory. Karal and Tarrn exchanged knowing looks with each other. Even across time, species, and cultures, the enjoyment of history's "wonder itself" could be shared.

Karal left Lyam bent over yet another copy of the ancient notes; this batch seemed to be the jewelry designs. He would have offered to help, but although his drafting ability was up to making sketches of benchtops and their contents, it was not up to making copies of intricate jewelry patterns.

When he went back upstairs, Tarrn came with him, and immediately engaged himself in conference with Firesong and An'desha over another copied set of notes. Firesong and An'desha were chattering away, with odd breaks in the conversation as they listened to Tarrn's Mindspoken replies. Master Levy had replaced Sejanes at the teleson, and was talking to someone Karal did not recognize, but who wore Trainee Grays instead of Herald Whites. Sejanes, who was standing behind Master Levy, simply watching the conversation, turned at the sound of Karal's footsteps and waved him over.

"I understand from Firesong that you were the Channel for the last effort here," Sejanes said, when Karal was within earshot. The old mage looked at him expectantly, motioning him to follow as he moved away from the teleson and Master Levy's intensely technical conversation.

Karal nodded, wondering what Sejanes wanted. "Not that I have any idea of what a Channel is or does, sir," he added. "I'm afraid I put my faith in what I was told, that Channeling is instinctive." He felt very diffident, telling such an experienced mage that he had no idea of what he had been doing. He hoped that Sejanes wasn't going to be annoyed at him for mucking about with things he didn't understand.

Sejanes pulled on his lower lip thoughtfully. "That's true in a limited sense," he finally replied. "You could perfectly well go on that way; many Channels prefer not to know anything about what causes what they're doing. But there are things that can be learned that would make the experience easier for you, and perhaps less frightening. I could teach you, if you wanted to learn; that's why I asked about it. It could make an important difference in how you feel afterward."

Karal's mouth went dry, and he swallowed as a tremor of fear passed through him. How could he tell this old mage that the very last thing he wanted was to have anything to do with more magic? On the other hand, Sejanes seemed to understand how horrible it had been for him, and if there was a "next time," wouldn't it be better to undertake it fully prepared?" Well, sir, if I had a choice—I've done it twice, and I'd really rather not ever do it again. But if I have to, anything that would make things easier would probably be a good idea. So I guess I ought to take you up on your offer."

The old man chuckled at his lack of enthusiasm and patted his shoulder, as if to reassure him. "There's no shame in that reaction," he told Karal. "I've never Channeled myself, but I've spoken to those who have and they would probably agree with you on both counts. I can't blame you a bit. Yet if we're going to start, I suspect we ought to do so before you lose your nerve about it. If you have some time to spare, we could begin now."

Karal shrugged with a nonchalance he in no way felt. "I'd rather not put it off and take a chance that I might need to channel power in the next few hours. The way my luck runs, I would need what you *might* have taught me if I hadn't delayed because—"

He stopped himself before he admitted how frightened he was, but Sejanes saw it anyway. He left his hand on Karal's shoulder a moment longer. "I told you, it is no shame to be afraid, young one," he said in a low, reassuring voice. "Channels hold power as great as any Adept, and sometimes greater; the only difference between them is that Channels don't actually use what they carry. And perhaps that is what makes it harder for them. They are used by the power, rather than using it. What sane creature ever gives up control if he does not have to?"

Karal shuddered; he wouldn't ever *want* to use all that power. It would be more responsibility than he ever cared to handle under any circumstances, no matter how dire. "That's—that's quite a thought, sir.

We—we of the Sunlord give up control to Him as a matter of faith. But we are still afraid sometimes, and He only helps those who try hard to deal with difficulties themselves. And I'm afraid I don't know much about magic at all, if it comes right down to it."

"Good. Then you have little or nothing to unlearn. And, yes, your faith will help you." Sejanes led the way to the chamber they were using for storage, purloined a couple of empty buckets and a pair of folded blankets for cushions to sit on, and took Karal over to a quiet corner. When they had made rough stools out of the upturned buckets and rested the cushions upon them, he began. Karal experienced a disconcerting sense of familiarity and an equally disconcerting sense of disconnection; Sejanes sounded like every good teacher he had ever studied under, but the surroundings were nothing like the classrooms of the Sun-priests where he had done all that study. And if he closed his eyes, Sejanes sounded so much like Ulrich except for the accent that it was uncanny.

"Mage-power, as we know and understand it, is an energy that is given off by living things in the same way that fire gives off heat and light in the act of consuming wood," he said, his manner easy and casual, his tone exactly the same as if he were describing the weather and not a power that could wreck kingdoms. "It tends to want to gather together, and tends to follow well-worn paths. In that, it is more like rainwater than fire."

"And mages can see this power?" Karal asked, though his mouth was dry with nervousness.

"That's what makes someone a mage," Sejanes replied. "I can see that power any time I make the effort to—and someone like Firesong has to make an effort *not* to see it."

Karal glanced over at Firesong, who looked no different from any other absurdly handsome Hawkbrother, and shook his head. Seeing power all the time... was it like seeing things with an extra color added? Was it like seeing particles and waves swirling all around you like swimming underwater? And when the power got too strong, did it blind you, like looking into the sun?

"Now, the power itself obeys rules," Sejanes continued. "When the threadlike paths, or tiny streams, merge together enough to make them of a different magnitude of strength, we call them 'ley-lines.' These *tend* to be straight, at least in the short term, and that, besides strength of power, is what makes ley-lines different from the trickles that feed them."

"Is it the strength that makes them straight?" Karal hazarded.

Sejanes looked pleased. "We don't know for certain, but that is the theory," he said. "It makes sense; a trickle of water will meander more than a powerful river. We think that after a certain point, the power can cut through the world taking the shortest distance which, as Master Levy will tell you, is always a straight line."

Karal nodded; no wonder Sejanes and Master Levy got on so well!

"Now, sooner or later, since power is attracted by power, these lines will meet. The places where two or more ley-lines meet forms something called a 'node,' where power collects." Sejanes looked at him expectantly.

Karal hazarded another question. "It can't collect indefinitely, though, can it?"

Sejanes looked *very* pleased. "No, it can't, and it will either be used up or drain away into the Void, and we honestly don't know what happens to it after that."

Karal seemed to recall An'desha telling him something about a third option, something that the Hawkbrothers used called a Heartstone, but that was a complication he didn't need right now. *First, learn the rules, and worry about the exceptions later.*

"Now—about using power," Sejanes continued. "Mages can use the power that they themselves produce. Mages can use the power given off by things in their immediate vicinity. Mages can also store power for later use in reservoirs; those can be available only to a single mage, or can be a group effort, built by group contributions, for as long as the group lasts."

"Everybody?" Karal asked, more than a bit alarmed by the notion of a barely-trained Apprentice being able to use such power.

"Oh, no!" Sejanes chuckled. "No, fortunately, lack of training and practice provides some control. The common titles for levels of ability refer to what power they can tap, and not their absolute skill. As with any venture, some people are more skilled than others, but I digress. Apprentices can only use their own power or what is immediately available around them below the level of a ley-line. Journeymen can use ley-lines. Masters can use those reservoirs. If a mage is part of a particular school, he is given the key to the reservoir built by the mages of that school at the time he becomes a Master. At that point, part of his duty every day is to feed the reservoir as much power as he has time to gather. Eventually, over the years, with these reservoirs being filled more often than they are drained, they are ready for anything the Masters might need, but that power is tame, like water in a still pond."

"Because it isn't flowing anywhere?" Karal asked, and was rewarded by Sejanes's nod. "But what about nodes?"

"That," Sejanes said with a shading of pride, "is what only Adepts can do. Adepts don't need to bother with the reservoirs, though they sometimes do simply because they are so still—for very delicate work, for example, such as Healings. Adepts can tap into and use the raw power of the nodes. The stronger the Adept, the larger the node he can control. Ley-line power is harder to control than reservoir power or ambient power, because, as you guessed, it is 'moving,' so to speak. But node power fights the user, because it is moving swiftly, sometimes in more than one direction and is wild and unconfined. Have you understood me so far?"

Karal nodded; so far this all seemed very straightforward. Perhaps Altra would also be able to help him with this, since the Firecat seemed something of a mage.

"Last of all of those who handle mage-power come the Channels." Sejanes nodded at Karal. "As I said when I began, the one thing that all life-path mages have in common is that they have what the Valdemarans call the Mage-Gift, and that ability enables them to actually see magic power. Channels, however, usually do not have Mage-Gift, or if they do, it isn't very strong."

"Why?" Karal asked.

Sejanes rubbed the side of his nose. "I don't know if there is a reason. There is some speculation that this is partly a protection for them, and partly a protection against them. The ability to sense magic power might be blinded the first time a Channel was used by very powerful magic. And if you can sense something, you can use it, so it might be better for all of us that anyone who can handle power stronger than any Adept would even *dream* of touching cannot actually use that power himself."

Again, Karal nodded. If you went on the basic assumption that any Karsite would—which was that it was Vkandis who granted such abilities—such a system of checks and balances made complete sense. Vkandis would not have placed extraordinary power within the capacity of mere mortals without some curbs on the system.

The explanation might also simply be that the act of attempting to actually *use* that much power rather than just direct it could be fatal. If mages who were also Channels died before they could wed and bring forth children with the Gift, such a combination wouldn't last for long.

Look what happened to those with mind-magic in Karse. They'd been gathered up and given to the Fires for generations, and as a result, just before Solaris took power, there were so few such "witches" and "demons" that there hadn't been more than four or five Fires a year, with a single victim apiece.

Sejanes looked down at his hands for a moment, gathering his thoughts. "Think of a funnel; the wide end catches scattered drops of water or small pieces of matter, and focuses it down into a small, directed stream. That's what a Channel does, and roughly how a Channel does it. And because a Channel actually forces the power going through him to flow through a 'smaller space,' he increases the force of that flow and its 'speed,'" if you will. So what a Channel needs to work perfectly is someone to guide the power in, however wild it may be, and someone to direct it as it goes out again. Remember that directing something—much like shunting a stream a few degrees—is much easier than using it."

Karal nodded numbly as Sejanes continued.

"Magic is much like water, Karal, but it is far more versatile. It can be manipulated by force of will, by natural aptitude, by specialized devices, and by other ways. Water, essentially, can only get things 'wet,' if I may use a crude analogy. Magic, however, can get things wet, turn things to dust, set them ablaze, make them into stone, give them life, put them somewhere else, and so on. But magic in its wild forms works in very gradual and subtle ways. It is not until magic is manipulated by someone that it has 'quick' effects. Without mages, magic takes its natural course."

"Like a river," Karal offered. "And mages make water wheels and dams and bridges."

Sejanes leaned back, apparently impressed. "That," he said slowly, "is essentially it. Yes. That is what we do."

Karal bit at his lower lip and offered, "And what happened here, is that long ago there was an explosion in the magic that—scooped a hole out. And the water—I mean, the magic—is rushing back to fill the hole."

"Close," Sejanes nodded. "Very close. You are a bright young man, Karal. Now, back to just what you are. A Channel. For whatever reason, a Channel collects power that is brought 'to' him, and directs it in a more purely directed, less stormy fashion."

"That's all there is to it?" Karal exclaimed. "I am a funnel?"

Sejanes smiled. "That's all the *theory*," he chided gently. "But now comes the practice that will help you keep parts of yourself from interfering with or even fighting that stream of power. And it will be all the harder because you will be dealing with something you yourself can only sense dimly, like playing blind-man's bluff with an unruly stallion. And to continue that analogy, I'm not going to show you how to catch and ride the beast, because it will kill you if you try. Instead, I'm going to try to teach you how to keep 'yourself' out of its way."

At the end of the lesson, Karal was quite certain that Sejanes' analogy of a game with an angry horse was the correct one. The inside of his head felt bruised, somehow, though certainly not as bad as he had felt after the first time he'd acted as a Channel. The lesson was over when Sejanes clapped him on the back and told him that he had done very well for his first attempt.

"You aren't the worst Channel I've ever seen, and we tend to use them more than you Westerners do," the old mage said cheerfully. "I don't know if the ability occurs more often in the Empire or if we Imperial mages are so lazy that we'd rather use Channels than focus power ourselves, and so we make an active effort to look for the ability. But you aren't the worst, that's for certain, and you've come to the lessons late in your life, so that's encouraging."

:Faint praise, but better than none, I suppose,: Altra observed, wrapping himself around Karal's legs. *:Natoli is waiting to talk to you.:*

"I'm going to assume that since my lord Altra is here, that your young lady is ready to speak to you," Sejanes observed. "Go on, off with you. By the by, you'll toughen up as you practice; this should be the worst training session you'll ever endure."

:You'll notice he said training *session,:* Altra observed, as Karal got up from his stool and followed the Firecat. *:That doesn't say anything about the real thing.:*

That hadn't escaped Karal's attention, but he really didn't want to dwell on it, not when he was finally going to get to see and talk to Natoli.

Karal took his place on the empty stool in front of the teleson; Altra draped himself over Karal's feet, and the Herald in the crystal winked, and stepped away. A moment later, Natoli moved into the place he had vacated.

She looked as if she had recovered from the boiler explosion. Her hair was a little longer than it had been when he left, and she looked at him as if she had forgotten why she was there. Suddenly he felt very shy.

"Hello, Natoli," he said awkwardly. "You look in good health."

He winced as he listened to himself; was that any way to speak to a girl he really wanted to be able to kiss?

"You don't," she said bluntly, peering at him. "You're too pale, and too thin. What have you been doing to yourself?"

That was so very typical of her that he had to laugh, and relaxed immediately. "As to the first, we've been living underground, and we mostly don't get to see the sun. And as to the second—have *you* ever tasted Firesong's cooking?" He shuddered melodramatically, and she laughed in return. "Seriously. We're mostly eating as the Shin'a'in do; it's not that bad, just a little odd."

"And you don't often see a fat Shin'a'in," she said shrewdly. "Things were quiet until Altra showed up with this contraption. We Artificers all wanted to take it apart, of course, but when we were told that the first person to try would be skinned, we gave up on the idea." She grinned. "We'll have to make do with trying to duplicate it from those manuscripts. If we can, we'll send one by fast Herald-courier to Solaris, and then you'll get to talk to *her* on a regular basis."

"Must I?" he asked weakly. He was not ready to face Solaris just yet. He wasn't sure he would be for quite a while, actually. Her Radiance was not a comfortable person to speak to, face-to-face. For that matter, she wasn't a comfortable person to communicate with, letter to letter; he always had the feeling that he was reading something intended for an audience rather than a personal letter.

"First we have to duplicate it," she pointed out, and smiled. "You know, I'm very glad to see you again. Sometimes, in the middle of the night, I'd wake up, and I'd wonder if you were—quite real."

Oddly enough, he knew exactly what she meant. "It's hard to imagine someone being real who's that far away," he agreed. "It's as if they never existed except in your mind."

She flushed a little, and looked away for a moment. "Anyway," she continued awkwardly, "we've been busy, though it doesn't have anything to do with the important things." She sounded wistful. "There's just nothing we *can* do right now to help with what you're doing, so we're back to the old projects like bridges and steam boilers."

"There's nothing wrong with that," he countered. "Don't these things have to be done no matter what disaster might be looming?" He managed a crooked grin. "If everything else falls apart, your bridges will be there to get people across rivers that can't be ferried or forded. Surely that's worth something."

She shrugged but looked pleased. "At least what we're doing is useful," she admitted. "It's odd, though. The folk around and about Haven have the funniest attitude; you can tell them and tell them that the protection we've given them from the mage-storms is only temporary, but they act as if it's permanent. They aren't doing anything to prepare themselves for the worst, they aren't even thinking about it." Now she sounded and looked very frustrated. "When you ask them why, they just shrug and can't give you an answer, or they say something stupid, fatalistic, or both."

"I think," he said slowly, "that ordinary folk just can't imagine anything awful happening to *them*. It always happens to someone else."

"Well, you'd think after years of war and bandits and all they should know better," she replied acidly. "At any rate, now that things have settled down, they aren't at all interested in asking us about things they can do when the Storms come again, they just want to know how long it is going to take before a bridge will be up. Or if the steam boiler is likely to explode again."

"I hope *you're* on bridges," he said, trying not to show alarm. "And not steam boilers."

"Actually, I'm on metal stress," she replied, running her hand through her hair absently. "I get to make some very interesting and loud noises. We're trying to make tougher alloys, but I don't want to bore you with what we're doing. I spend some time in the forge, because at the moment, work on steam boilers is stalled until we can find a better way to make the boiler itself."

He sighed, resting his chin on his hands. "It wouldn't bore me, but I'd be lost," he admitted. "Sejanes is trying to teach me some specific kind of exercises for working with magic, and those would probably mean about as much to you."

"Probably." The conversation died for a moment. "Still, I hope you aren't—I mean, I don't want you to think that—" her face twisted with frustration. "Just, if you're doing something dangerous, don't take more on yourself than you can carry all right?"

He smiled. "As long as you promise to do the same," he replied, and she laughed.

"Grain for the gander is good for the goose, hmm? Well, I'll promise to try but my judgment is sometimes faulty."

"So is mine, so don't hold it against me." His smile took on an ironic edge. "We can't all be infallible Sons of the Sun."

"Oh, even Solaris admits to fallibility," she chuckled. "Believe it or not."

"Solaris?" he chuckled. "That would be an entry in the annals, especially if she admitted that she was fallible to you polytheistic barbarians."

"But she did!" Natoli protested, and as he continued to regard her askance, she looked surprised. "Oh! I'll bet no one told you, any of you! You will not believe what has happened with Grand Duke Tremane!"

As she outlined the astonishing developments in Hardorn since the arrival of Elspeth and Darkwind, Karal felt his eyes growing larger and larger. No one had seemed to think that any of this was significant enough to pass on to any of the other members of his party—

Which is probably because they all have their own preoccupations and not a one of them thinks anything is important outside those preoccupations! But you'd think someone *would have said something to Sejanes!*

"We have a Herald and a Companion stationed down in Karse in Solaris'—court, I suppose you call it—" she added.

"Conclave," he corrected.

"Conclave, then. We sent him down so that we could get information to her by way of his Companion and Talia's Rolan." She laughed. "Actually, it's not just a 'Herald,' it's my father, and he seems to be enjoying himself. Anyway, we sent her word about this, and the reply she sent back was: 'Since he has voluntarily placed himself in the hands of a higher judge of character than myself, I feel impelled to point out that Natoli, An'desha, and Karal were correct in their assessment of his basic character, and I was at least in part swayed by nothing more substantial than emotion.' What do you think of that?" She grinned, as if she had somehow won a great prize. Then again, winning a concession like that from Solaris would have been a great prize, particularly as it was her father who had sent the message on to Haven.

It's a small thing, but she just proved to her father that she doesn't have to be a Herald to accomplish something important, he realized. *And maybe she just proved it to herself as well.*

"I think she didn't use the ecclesiastic plural, which means that she was speaking for Solaris and not for the Son of the Sun," he told her, but he felt very pleased, nevertheless, for the sake of his own people. Historically, it was a tremendous temptation for the Son of the Sun to always think of himself as speaking for Vkandis, until even the most minor personal opinions were incorporated as doctrine. Solaris appeared to have overcome that particular temptation. "Which is not a bad thing."

"No, it's not." She appeared to have run out of things to say, and another awkward moment of silence descended. "I suppose you'll want to go tell all this to Sejanes...."

He did, but he also didn't want to go, even though he didn't really have anything to say. The silence lengthened and became more strained. She glanced to the side, and her expression lightened a little with relief even while it darkened with disappointment. "Oh, here's someone for Master Levy. If Altra will hold the teleson open while you get him—"

"Of course!" he said, feeling both emotions himself. "Natoli, take care of yourself! And I—I miss all of you."

He didn't dare say that he missed only her, but he hoped she got that impression from his hesitation. "I—we miss you too," she replied, with a smile more shy than usual, and vanished from the crystal. Karal ran to get Master Levy, who nodded and hurried to the device carrying a sheaf of notes as if he had been expecting to be summoned back.

Karal glanced around and couldn't find Sejanes in the upper rooms; he listened carefully and heard the old mage's voice coming thinly from the workshops below. He hurried down the stairs to find Sejanes chatting away comfortably with Lyam, though Tarrn was nowhere in sight.

"Sir!" he called. "I've got the most amazing news about Duke Tremane!"

"Well," Sejanes said, chuckling softly. "Well, well, well." He was inordinately pleased with Karal's news, and Karal could not help but wonder why.

That's an odd way to react, considering that Tremane has acted quite unlike a proper Imperial officer. "I thought you might be upset, sir," he ventured, tilting his head to one side. "Aren't you?"

"Upset? No, this is rather good news, all things considered," Sejanes replied, and chuckled again. "It seems that my former pupil has learned at long last that there are things that do not always answer to his logic. I am quite glad to hear this, truth be told. This is going to be a very good thing for everyone concerned."

Karal kept his inquisitive expression, hoping to prompt more information from the mage, and Sejanes enlarged on his statement.

"I am pleased for Hardorn, for that sad, maltreated land could not have found a better caretaker." He blinked, and his eyes fixed on some distant point beyond Karal. "I am pleased because Tremane could not have found a better trust than Hardorn. He was wasted on the Empire; he has the misfortune to be that rarest of Imperial creatures, a man of high rank who still maintains a shred or two of integrity and compassion. That is not to say, at all, that the military is composed of heartless men; far from that, in fact. He might have done well had he remained within the military, but as Emperor, he would have been a victim of one of three unpleasant fates—eaten alive by those conspiring to use him, murdered, or corrupted."

"That much I can see," Karal replied. "It's quite logical, but..." He faltered, unsure how to ask what he wanted to know without being rude. Imperials were not—quite—irreligious, but they were hardly as devout as even the average Valdemaran. And when compared with the average Karsite, they were positively atheistic!

Sejanes seemed to understand what he wanted to know. "Not all citizens of the Empire are so immersed in practicality as you think." His gaze softened and turned inward for a moment. "Those most likely to become cynical, believers in nothing that they cannot see, are the career courtiers. Those least likely—probably the folk who live nearest the land, and those who live by magic. My young protégé was poised between the cynic and the believer, and he could have taken either path. He may be the rarest of all, one who can see the truth in both."

Karal wanted badly to ask just what Sejanes believed in, but he sensed that Sejanes would not tell him now. He might never. That was his right, of course. And it would be horribly impolite of Karal to ask him. If he ever wanted to tell Karal, he would.

"It is my own opinion, that whatever else has happened, Tremane has discovered that there are those other paths. Perhaps that will open his mind to those other possibilities." He rubbed his eyes for a moment, as if they were tired. "And I am pleased that he has an outside governor in this earth-binding, something to—shall we say—keep him from succumbing to other temptations."

"He is that weak, then?" asked Lyam, with the careless tone of one to whom Duke Tremane and his men were no more real than the folk in the Chronicles of a thousand years ago.

They might not be. The Kaled'a'in are so different from the Imperials that they must seem equally unreal to each other.

"Not weak," Sejanes amended, and his wrinkled brow knitted, as he searched for words.

He's trying to explain Tremane to a couple of youngsters for whom the Empire is only a name, who cannot even imagine the levels of intrigue that someone like Tremane must negotiate every day. Karal waited for the aged mage to find the right words. *And he can't know that the Temple of Vkandis is—or was, anyway—as much a hotbed of conspiracy as any court. I don't think Lyam could ever understand the stresses that Tremane must have been under, but I do. I wonder if Tremane ever got tired of it all, and wished for things to be simpler?* "No, he's not weak," Sejanes repeated. "The trouble is that certain habits, certain ways of reacting, become ingrained. It would be all too simple to revert to the ways in which business is conducted in the Empire, without thought for what was good for Hardorn. That, more than anything, would be the temptation; to take the way that is easiest, rather than the one that is best for the people and the land, and doubly so when resources are low."

Lyam looked baffled, but shrugged, accepting what Sejanes said for the moment.

Karal nodded. "Trying to do things the way he was used to would probably get him in great difficulties in Hardorn, wouldn't it?" he asked. "It might even break up the peace, and he might not know why that had happened. Now, he hasn't a choice, you see; he'll *know* what is best and he'll have to do it, or he knows how he'll suffer for it. And you know," he continued, feeling a certain amount of surprise at the insight, "the thing is, since people will know he *can't* do anything selfishly or maliciously, they're likely to be easier on his mistakes, if you take my meaning. They'll be more likely to forgive and explain."

Sejanes flashed a mildly surprised but appreciative look at him. "Exactly so. And I am very fond of Tremane; I should like to see him as happy as anyone burdened with power and the ability to wield it can be. He has a strong sense of responsibility, and this may be the one opportunity of his lifetime to exercise that responsibility with people who are likely to appreciate the care he will take." Once again, Sejanes' gaze turned inward. "He had his estate, of course, but those on it were used to being ruled gently. The folk of Hardorn were subjected to every ill imaginable. That will make them grateful to a gentler hand."

Lyam uttered the breathy equivalent of a laugh, showing very sharp, pointed teeth. "He will be finding himself burdened with more than power, I think. Earth-sense is as jealous a mistress as responsibility."

"But the earth-sense and his own responsibility will work in harness amicably, rather than pulling him to pieces between them," Sejanes countered. "Had he risen to power in the Empire, he would have spent every day being torn among fear, duty, responsibility, expediency, and the right. I think it might have driven him mad. I know it would have changed him into something I would no longer recognize."

The *hertasi* shrugged again. "Good, then. We take what small victories we can. I hope that all this gives him aid if we cannot stop the Storms.

He shall need every help he can muster to protect these people who are now depending on him."

"It might." Karal knew something about earth-sense, though few Sun-priests had it. The ability was much valued among the farmers of the Karsite hills, where the soil was poor and the weather chancy. If you knew that it would be a bad decision to plant corn this year in a particular field, and a good one to plant clover, you might prosper when your neighbors failed. And if you shared your expertise with your neighbors, you might all be able to pay the tithe in goods instead of your own flesh-and-blood, come harvest time. It wasn't *exactly* a witch-power, and it wasn't *exactly* one of the things that would get you sent to the Fires, but it also wasn't the sort of thing that you spoke about to the Sun-priests. The Sun-priests in their turn were careful not to *ask* about it, and all was well.

"Another small victory, then." Lyam nodded decisively, and seemed to think that a change of subject was in order. "This Natoli, who gave you this word—is she kin to you? Or something else?"

That was not the subject the young Karsite would have chosen, and Karal felt himself blushing furiously, as Lyam's quick eyes and quicker wit filled in the truth. "Ah—" the little lizard said, not without sympathy, his head bobbing. "She is to you what Jylen is to me, I think." He sighed gustily. "I do miss her company, but I would not have her here. She could not have endured the journey, and I think she would have felt herself useless, which is a bad thing for anyone to feel."

"Natoli would have felt the same," Karal admitted. "Oh, *I* feel useless about half the time, and it makes me want to bite something. I'd rather not think how she would react."

"Nor I, Jylen." Lyam laughed. "A trimmer tail there never was, nor a more graceful snout, but neither belong to a maid with an overabundance of patience."

He shared a glance of fellow-feeling with Karal, and the young Karsite experienced a definite warming in the relationship between them.

"Well, Sejanes, I will take my leave of you," Lyam told the mage. "And of you, Karal. My stomach has an overly-intimate embrace with my spine, and I think I shall venture Firesong's cooking and see if it is as terrible as you claim. Surely he learned *something* from his *hertasi*!"

"It's not Firesong tonight, it's An'desha," Karal assured him. "And he and the Shin'a'in have agreed to share that particular chore from now on."

"Thanks to the Hundred Little Gods!" Sejanes exclaimed with clear relief. "Even enduring Shin'a'in butter-tea is preferable to eating what Firesong cooks!"

"In that case, I will haste my steps!" the *hertasi* cried. "In case the other starvelings aloft decide to leave me with naught but scrapings!"

He scrambled down from his stool and scampered up the stairs with a staccato click of toenails on stone. Sejanes cocked an eyebrow at Karal.

"What about you?" he asked. "I was under the impression that young men were never quite fully fed."

It was Karal's turn to shrug uncomfortably. His stomach was still in something of a knot, and he wondered if Natoli was always going to affect him that way. If so, he was destined to grow much thinner.

"Lucky in love?" the old man asked, softly, and with a kindly and sympathetic manner. "Or unlucky? Either one can be hazardous to the appetite."

"I—I'm not sure," Karal replied, feeling his cheeks burning. "We don't know each other that well…"

Sejanes reached out and patted his knee. "Uncertainty can be just as hazardous. But I take it that she *is* a trusted friend?"

"Oh, yes, absolutely," Karal said fervently. "There isn't anyone I would trust more."

:Humph.:

Karal glanced hastily down at his feet, where Altra lay coiled around the legs of his chair, hitherto unnoticed. How had the Firecat gotten there? The last Karal had seen, Altra had been sprawled on the floor near the teleson.

"There isn't a human I trust more. I trust her as much as I trust Altra and Florian," he amended hastily. "And for a great many of the same reasons."

:Better. Not perfect, but better.:

"That is an excellent beginning, then," Sejanes said, his tone just as serious and his demeanor as sober as if he was discussing the next solution to the mage-storm. "One should always begin with friendship, rather than a more ardent emotion. The former will last, if the latter does not. And one should also have enough in common with a young lady to be her friend. Unless, of course, it is a case of a prearranged attachment, and in that case, there is little that one can do besides hope that one's parents, guardians, or other adults involved have *some* notion of what might appeal to one in the way of a lifetime companion and attempt to find those things that one has in common with her."

Karal had to chuckle at Sejanes' careful way of putting things. He was delicately trying to learn if Karal and Natoli had been joined to one another by parental agreement, or if they might be violating other such agreements with their own acquaintance. "It's not prearranged, and I also don't think her father, Rubric, will mind that we're—ah, friends—since he's the one who introduced us in the first place. He's the Herald who's been sent into Karse as the liaison with Solaris. I think that Natoli doesn't make friends easily."

Sejanes brightened. "This sounds more promising with every word you add!" he said with real enthusiasm. "And your feelings at the moment? Attracted, but confused?"

"Very much so." Karal was as amused as he was embarrassed. Sejanes was certainly taking a very active interest in this situation! And if Karal had not known him, it would be very tempting to dismiss his interest as that of an interfering, old-maidish busybody.

But Sejanes had never interfered in anyone's private life, as far as Karal knew; he was hardly old-maidish, and gave no evidence of being a busybody, although he had intervened to offer to teach Karal something of magic. No, this concern seemed to arise out of some genuine interest in Karal, in the manner of a master with a protégé.

Just like Ulrich, his former master.

"You remind me in some ways of some former students of mine," Sejanes said quietly, echoing his own thoughts. "And you can tell me to go to the dogs if you think I'm prying where I have no right, but I hope perhaps I can give you useful advice about Natoli." He grinned conspiratorily. "I have had a number of lady friends over the years, and most of them were as highly intelligent as she seems to be. I believe I can remember what it was like to be young!"

Karal stared at him in mingled surprise and gratitude, for he'd had no one to ask for such advice. An'desha was mostly concerned with Lo'isha and the other Shin'a'in, when he wasn't working, as they all were, with the dangerous magics here. Florian and Altra weren't human, and although Lyam apparently had a lady friend, neither was he. Firesong—well, *his* advice would hardly apply to Karal's situation, even if he wasn't already wary of asking the Tayledras anything personal. He didn't know Silverfox well enough, he was *not* going to ask romantic advice of Natoli's teacher Master Levy, and the Shin'a'in were none of them approachable enough. The idea of coming to Sejanes would never have occurred to him.

But Ulrich would have helped me…

Ulrich would have given him the same advice his father would have given him, or an older brother if he'd had one. Vkandis did not require that his priests be celibate, only chaste outside of marriage. Ulrich had told his pupil more than once that he had been romantically attached twice, and that only outside circumstances had prevented him from making either of those women his wife.

Karal knew a bit more than just that, though it was still bare bones. In the case of the second lady in his life, Ulrich and his intended had an extreme difference of opinion over the internal politics of the priesthood, and had not spoken again, not even after Solaris became Son of the Sun. The first time, early in his life, the lady had suffered a short but fatal illness, leaving him brokenhearted for many years.

Ulrich himself had never told Karal the stories; he'd learned of both from some of the Red-robe priests who were longtime friends and colleagues of his mentor. They had meant to compassionately keep him from inadvertently touching salt to Ulrich's open wounds, and warned him of the things he must not press unless Ulrich himself broached the subject.

But that had not prevented Ulrich from giving him some preliminary advice about girls, and the possible pursuit thereof, though at the time he had not been at all interested even in the idea. Perhaps Ulrich had a premonition that one day, he would need that advice.

But it was far more likely that Ulrich had simply been offering what he would give any lively young person who was his protégé; the suggestion that he himself had enough experience in matters of romance to offer advice. That set the scene for what was inevitable, and would have prevented him from going to his less-experienced peers for advice that had as much chance of being harmful as helpful.

Now Sejanes was offering the same thing, and Karal was only too happy to accept the offer.

"Thank you, sir," he said simply. "Do you have any ideas about what I should say to her?" He smiled sheepishly. "Don't think that I'm ungrateful, but talking with her is all I can do right now, given our current distance."

"That may be just as well," Sejanes replied mildly, but with a twinkle. "And yes, I have a few suggestions."

That was precisely what he wanted to hear.

* * *

Karal and Lyam scribbled on identical sheets of foolscap, seated side by side on a pallet bed, both of them taking full notes of this meeting. The entire group sat on pallets in a rough, three-sided square around the teleson, which was situated in front of Firesong. This was a new version of the old Council sessions that they had held in the Council Room of the Palace at Haven, and he wondered how many of the Councillors on the other side were gazing at the teleson with bafflement. Surely the device must seem to them as strange as any of the Storm-changed beasts that had been displayed for their edification. A tiny image of Queen Selenay gazed solemnly at them from the crystal lens. She had just asked Master Levy if he had any more information on when the mage-storms would begin again.

"I can't speak for magic, but I can for mathematical probability, and that has given us the ability to predict what is going to happen up to a point. The mathematics is relatively clear on this," Master Levy said gravely. "The cancellation effect of the power burst that was released from here is gradually eroding; we'll be seeing the resumption of stormlets in four days, but I don't think that even the most sensitive mage will detect them unless he is looking for them. That's all we know right now, and Treyvan will be in charge of the mages who will be looking for the stormlets and attempting to measure their relative strength. Once we have the resumption of stormlets that actually affect the physical world, we can measure how much they increase in strength and decrease in interval. We'll be able to calculate then how long it will take before the Storms have major physical effects again, and how long until they are dangerous. Once they are dangerous, however, they will build up to a repetition of the one released at the original Cataclysm. I have absolutely no doubt of that."

In the crystal of the teleson, Selenay nodded gravely. Although she alone was visible, the Haven teleson sat in the middle of the Council Chamber, surrounded by a full Council at their horseshoe-shaped table. All of them were able to hear what Master Levy said, although they only saw Firesong.

"Now we come to the question of the last Storm and the effect here, where all of the force will be concentrated. Here is where Need, An'desha, Sejanes, and I have performed our own calculations, and we're not optimistic," Firesong said with uncharacteristic restraint. "It is not good, Majesty. Although the shields of this place survived the initial, *outward* release, we do not believe they will survive the impact of the energies converging on this place. We think the shields will go down, and all the weapons that have not been rendered harmless will go then, and that will be bad."

"By 'go', just what is it that you are saying?" asked one of the Councillors around the Haven teleson. "And just what precisely does 'bad' mean?"

Karal restrained a nervous titter. How would you explain "bad" to someone whose idea of a catastrophe was a major forest fire, a great flood, or a landslide? How do you get him to believe that it was possible to release forces that melted rock towers and dug craters the size of some countries?

"I wish I knew," Firesong admitted. "We don't know what most of them were intended to do, only that they were weapons deemed 'too dangerous' to use. It would be supremely ironic to discover that they cancel one another out, but I gravely doubt that we can count on that. Certainly the area of destruction will cover the Plains, and since we have enough warning this time, the Shin'a'in are evacuating."

The Shin'a'in are evacuating. The Shin'a'in, who never, ever left the Plains. Would that tell the inquisitive Councillor just how grave the situation was? Karal didn't know.

"Whether the effect will carry as far as Valdemar, I couldn't say, although if I were in your place, I'd count on it." Firesong held up a hand in warning. "And don't ask, 'What effect?' because I don't know that, either. We're trying to find out, but we're dealing with weapons created in secret by a secretive mage and the only notes are in a language that was current two millennia ago. We're doing the best that we can, and having more people here would only slow things down, but what we do may not be enough, or in time."

Karal noted the grumbling on the other side, but no one said anything out loud. *Probably because, as Natoli said, they just don't believe it can happen. Sheer stupidity on their part, but there it is.* In a way, he couldn't blame them; they were new to true-magic, relatively speaking. For most of them, the terrible things that Ancar's mages had done were only stories, and the first time they had seen anything like magic was when the mage-storms began. Nor could they imagine a force that could turn a flourishing country into a smoking, glass-floored crater. He noted that down, in a sidebar. Tarrn had told him that his observations could be important, so long as they weren't of a personal nature, and to note them down.

Most people don't believe that a disaster is coming, or that it can affect them, even when they're told repeatedly.

He was tremendously grateful that *he* no longer had to represent

Karse at the Council; one of the Sun-priests who had fought with the Valdemarans against Ancar had come north at the same time that Natoli's father had gone south. He had never been comfortable in such a position, had never felt particularly capable of handling it, no matter what Solaris herself said. And certainly about half the other members of the Council had doubts now and again about his competence and even his integrity. But that Sun-priest had certainly seen magic and believed in it with his whole heart. Perhaps he could help convince the doubters.

"What about the weapons themselves?" someone else asked intelligently. "If we can get rid of them harmlessly, we'd be able to lessen the danger by that much. Is there any way of dismantling them?"

"When *Urrrtho* sssaid he could not?" That was Treyvan, his voice indignant. "When he left a warrrning to that effect? Arrre you mad?"

Ah, the things a gryphon can get away with saying, just because he's larger than anything or anyone else! Karal was glad that Treyvan and Hydona were there to say all the rude things that needed saying.

"We are proceeding very slowly in our understanding of these devices," Firesong said smoothly. "If there is a way to dismantle them, we will. We *may* be very lucky; at least one of them simply disintegrated with age, and time might have done what mortal hands could not."

It was interesting to Karal how Firesong had taken on the role of spokesman for the group. Not that anyone else had rushed to volunteer, but Firesong was by nature a bit lazy, and not apt to take on any more responsibility than he had to.

Then again, if Florian or Altra had held the teleson link open, the Councillors would have seen only Karal, the Companion or the Firecat, none of which were good choices for inspiring respect. Sejanes had no mind-magic, nor did Master Levy. An'desha did, but he was no better choice than Karal, although thanks to his magic-whitened hair, he looked a bit older than Karal. Need could have gotten respect, but if Need had held the link, they'd all be seeing Firesong anyway. At least people respected Firesong; even feared him a little. One good thing; his acidic wit made a fine weapon to wield against intransigent or argumentative Councillors.

Then again, it is a chance for Firesong to be seen, appreciated, and admired, and who else has he had as an audience lately?

"First we have to discover *what*, exactly, they are supposed to do. Then *how* they do it. Then we might be able to judge if we have the ability to disarm them," Firesong explained patiently. "If you think of them as enormously complicated traps with a weapon in the middle, this will make more sense to you."

"But—" someone began, and stopped.

"Fortunately," Sejanes picked up smoothly, "this study does not at all interfere with our studies of the mage-storms, because that is taking place up there, among you. Here we are still operating on the assumption that we may have to trigger one of these weapons to counteract the final Storm. We already know which are the best choices, and together with the notes we found in the workshop below, we are studying them to see if the same solution we found the last time is viable this time."

"And what if you *can't* find an answer?" That voice sounded strained and somewhat panicked. So there was at least one person on the Council who was taking this threat seriously! Karal only hoped it was not someone who was inclined to take a panicked view of everything. Getting people to organize their own defense would be easier if they did not think of the person goading them to it as a chronic overreactor.

"You really ought to be operating on the assumption that we won't, and that all we have done is to buy you time to prepare," Master Levy replied truculently. *He* was very impatient with the Council, and had said as much before this meeting began. "We told you that in the beginning. When I left, the Artificers were devising a formula to predict the pattern of the circles of damage."

"We're still working on it," said another voice. "The model isn't perfect, but we expect to have an answer before the stormlets start, and we'll check its accuracy with measurements as the stormlets increase in strength. By the time there's real damage, the formula will be tested and ready for use."

"So, there's your answer. If we can't come up with a simple solution, you simply keep people and livestock out of those dangerous areas, drain as much power as you can out of that stone under the Palace and shield it with everything you have, and wait for the final Storm to pass." Master Levy's tone said the rest; that any idiot should have been able to sit quietly and figure that much out for himself.

"While you all sit there safe and sound in the Tower?" someone else accused angrily.

That was a mistake. Karal braced himself for the riposte. Firesong was not in a good mood, and there was going to be blood on the Council table in a moment, even if it was metaphorical blood.

"Safe? Sound?" Firesong asked dangerously. "Where did you come by *that* incredible notion? Would someone please remove that man for incompetence and put him in the kitchen washing pans where he belongs? If *I* were the lot of you, I'd throw him off the Council. I do believe in encouraging those of lesser ability, but I think that appointing a congenital idiot to a Council seat is going too far."

There was an indignant spluttering on the other side, then a certain amount of commotion; Selenay continued to look serene, but her attention was not on the teleson. It was maddening not to be able to see what was going on.

"Well?" Firesong asked, when the noise had ended.

"We will take your recommendation under advisement," Selenay replied urbanely, and clearly as much for the benefit of her side of the gathering as for Firesong's. "You are correct in one thing, if a little less than tactful; this Council can no longer afford to seat members whose attention is so concentrated on minor details within their own sphere that they are paying no attention to the greater dangers that threaten us all."

"Here here," said another voice, one that Karal recognized after a moment as Kerowyn's.

Oh, my! That was unexpected! And Karal could think of three or four Council members who matched that particular statement, too! It seemed that after treachery and invasion and war and Alliance and more war and mage-storms, even Selenay's patience had begun to run short.

And about time, too. It was all very well to say that those three or four had been loyal during the worst troubles, and that loyalty deserved reward, but there was a limit. It was not wise to let the shortsighted continue to have authority in a situation like this one. Better to find them some position with rank and privileges and no authority, if Selenay still felt impelled to reward them. Right now, being too shortsighted could very well cost lives.

She might not see any reason to continue to reward these people; and that wouldn't be all that bad either. Sometimes the hand of censure needed to be used in order to make people believe it *would* be used, even against those who thought themselves above censure. In the words of the Shin'a'in, "Use the whip to get the horses out of the burning stable."

He was tempted to add that to the notes, but those were the kinds of purely personal observations that Tarrn had warned him against, and he kept them to himself.

:There are two Councillors that ought to be given the sack right here and now,:

Altra observed with irritation. *:One of them is not entirely certain he believes in the intelligence of Companions. How can we expect him to plan for a magic-fed disaster? And the other is so wrapped up in why his district needs protection more than any other that he'll waste valuable time and probably try to divert resources he's not entitled to.:*

Altra didn't have to describe the offending members; Karal knew them well enough from that notation of their personalities. *:It's Selenay's Kingdom and Selenay's Council,:* he reminded the Firecat. *:If you'd like to make a recommendation as a Karsite representative, I'd do so privately to her. I'm sure that she would have no difficulty speaking with you after this is over.:*

:I'm not such a fool as to make one publicly!: Altra snapped, and shook his head until his ears flapped. *:Now I'm more than ever pleased that you're out of there. You don't need to have to deal with these idiots; they'd probably start blaming you for the Cataclysm! And I don't need to be there either; I'd be tempted to wind around their ankles as they started descending a staircase, and be certain of getting them replaced by someone with a bit more reasoning ability than a brick of cheese.:*

He managed to send a mental image of himself coiling around the legs of the stupidest of the two Councillors, and of the man pitching down the staircase in a very comical fashion.

:Bloody-minded today, aren't we?: Karal observed.

:Vkandis help any rodent within a league of here,: Altra replied. *:When this session is over, and after I've spoken to Selenay, I'm going hunting.:*

:You won't have to go far,: Karal told him. *:The Shin'a'in were complaining about mice in the horse grain. Think you can lower your dignity for a bit of mousing?:*

Altra just snorted.

The Council session proceeded with admirable dispatch after that particular outburst. For his part, Karal admitted to himself that he was acting in some ways precisely like those unfortunate Councillors who could not or would not believe in the disaster threatening just below the horizon. *He* was conducting some parts of his life—as in, pursuing his interest with Natoli—as if nothing whatsoever was going to happen to change that life. And he was not going about in a state of barely-suppressed panic either. But the truth was that what he and Natoli did or did not do was not going to make a bit of difference to the Storms or the resolution of the problem, assuming there *could* be one. Neither was going about in a cloud of fear going to help resolve their difficulties. Fear wasn't an emotion you could sustain for weeks at a time either, so why try to keep himself in a continual state of near-panic?

But what he could do, he was doing, and at least one of his

observations might turn out useful. It had occurred to him that the workshops had remained pristine and intact—more so, even, than the stored weapons—and that there might be even more shielding on them. Or perhaps there was a natural property of the stone, as there was of silk, that insulated everything inside from the effects of magic. Since they had always kept the hatchway open, there was no way to tell, and no one really wanted to volunteer to be shut inside just now.

Natural or not, it would have made sense to have the workshops protected from the possible effects of the weapons stored above—the more so as the workshops could serve as a shelter in case something up here went wrong. Or, alternatively, if something went wrong down *there*, the weapons stored up here would be unaffected.

But the workshops would make the safest place for those who were not involved to wait out the last Storm—and perhaps, for *all* of them to do so, if it turned out that there was nothing they could do. There was room enough for all of them, their supplies, and their attendant Shin'a'in friends to wait in a fair imitation of comfort. It would be difficult for Florian and the Shin'a'in horses to get down the staircase, but not impossible. The one drawback the place had was that it was at a level lower than the tunnel in—and if the stored weapons were affected—they might find themselves literally sealed inside, as the rock melted and ran or the remains of the building shook itself apart.

But if they waited in the tunnel or on the Plain outside, there would be no escape. He'd already discussed using the workshops in this way with the Shin'a'in, and they had agreed with him, going so far as to carry half of the supplies down there and store them, and making plans to evacuate the camp above into the workshops when the time came.

And as for the folk of the surrounding land, well, for the first time since the Sundering of the Clans, Shin'a'in and Tayledras were living together. More than three-quarters of the Clans were off the Plains and distributed among the nearest Vales. Some others had chosen to go to trade-cities and the like, where they had contacts or relatives.

Those remaining were heading south rather than north or west, taking with them all of the breeding horses and other herds, for only the baggage beasts and personal strings could be accommodated in the Vales. They were under the escort of the fighters of Kerowyn's old mercenary company, the Skybolts—those few who had retired or elected not to remain in Valdemar. They had returned to Bolthaven and formed a smaller company with the sole duty of guarding the Bolthaven mage-school run by Quenten, the town of Bolthaven, and the annual Shin'a'in Horse Faire. The herds would be safe in the wide and gentle Rethwellan valley below the fortified mage-school, as they would be safe in the hands of those who had benefited from the generosity of Kerowyn's Shin'a'in relatives in the matter of most excellent Shin'a'in-bred mounts.

Before too many more days had passed, the Plains would be empty of almost everyone but the little group here in the heart of the crater that was the Dhorisha Plains. A stranger would, for the very first time, be able to cross from one side to the other without hindrance.

Not that anyone would be stupid enough to try. The weather alone ought to prevent such an idiotic course. Only the Shin'a'in knew where game lurked in the winter; only the Shin'a'in had fuel sources and tents made to withstand the killing blizzards the Storms had brought. And in a landscape of endlessly rolling white hills with no landmarks, it would be suicide for most to try to navigate across the bowl of the Plains.

Besides, the Kal'enedral who were left were not your normal border-guards. It was not too bloody likely that anything would move into the Plains that they didn't know about the moment the breach-of-border occurred. And under the current circumstances, it would not be wise for anyone to assume that the Star-Eyed was not personally watching the borders. She would not even have to intervene directly in the event of an intruder; simply dumping a foot of ice on the cliffs ringing the Plains would prevent anyone but a skilled ice climber from getting down into the Plains proper. And dumping another foot or two of ice and snow on him while he was climbing, or arranging for an avalanche along the cliff, would see to it that not even an expert ice climber set a single living toe on the Plains below.

Good heavens, I'm as bloody-minded as Altra! Karal realized, as he serenely contemplated the notion of intruders turned into ice sculptures. But then again, they couldn't really afford to be anything less than ruthless now. The escort of Kal'enedral who remained to care for them had put their lives in the hands of their Goddess to do so, and knew it. Not only was there a good chance that the Tower would not survive the final Storm, but they were defending an indefensible position.

The Kal'enedral had defended the Tower in the past by keeping people far away from it; if there was a "lowest geographic point" to the crater that was the Dhorisha Plains, this Tower was probably cradled in the bottom of it.

Most of the Swordsworn had remained with the Clans, and rightly, to protect them during the evacuation. What if someone deliberately chose this moment to come looking for the Tower with a mind to stealing one or more of the weapons still in it? There would not be much that anyone could do to stop him if he came with sufficient force. It would have to be someone who was completely mad, but as the existence of Ancar and Falconsbane proved, there were people who were that mad, that power-crazed, to take such a chance.

But given all that this little group of seekers represented, the Star-Eyed would probably take care of such an expedition Herself—and if She didn't, it was just possible that Vkandis would.

Just as he thought that, a lull appeared in the discussion, and Karal decided to do more than add an observation to his notes. "It has occurred to me just now," he said slowly, "that there is a source of possible protection, at least for those of you outside the Tower."

"What's that?" someone asked warily.

His ears burned, for he might be stating the obvious, but it seemed stupid not to mention this. "Ah... prayer," he said diffidently. "Divine intervention. I mean, have you had people really *concentrating* on asking for help from other sources?"

"That is no bad answer," Lo'isha interjected, before anyone else could say anything. "If our Star-Eyed is like your gods, that could be a fat hare to pursue. You see, She only responds to peril quite impossible for mortals to deal with, and *only if asked*. Otherwise, She allows us to handle it ourselves. Your gods may only be waiting to be properly asked."

"Vkandis has traditionally been the same way," Karal confirmed. "I don't know what the gods do in Valdemar, but what is the harm in finding out?"

"None, of course," Selenay said gently. "And in our own pride and insistent self-reliance, we often forget that option. We would not be asking for aid for ourselves against other peoples, after all. We would be asking for aid for all peoples against an implacable force we don't completely understand. Thank you, Karal, for not being afraid to state what should have been obvious. I will have the various notables draft up notices to their Temples to that effect."

Now Karal blushed, but with pleasure, and Altra's deep purr, vibrating his feet, was all he needed to gauge the depth of the Firecat's approval. He glanced sideways at Lo'isha to find the Shin'a'in gazing at him with a thoughtful smile that broadened when their eyes met.

Well, let's see if they're still pleased with me after this...

"Please, Queen Selenay?" he added. "Don't exclude the Empire in those prayers. The *people* of the Empire haven't done anything to hurt us, and by now they must be in terrible straits. They've been suffering the mage-storms all this time, and from all Sejanes has told us, they need magic, they use it everywhere. For you, it would be as if fire suddenly stopped giving off heat."

She nodded very slowly, with just a touch of reluctance. "I will remember to phrase it that way," she promised. "And to remember that we have no quarrel with all of the people of the Empire, only with those who harmed us."

He stole a second glance at Lo'isha, then one at Sejanes. Lo'isha still seemed pleased with him, and the old mage positively beamed.

And what about Altra, Vkandis' own representative?

:What of me? I think you have done a very good thing.: Altra's purr did not let up at all. *:You manage to keep in mind that a nation is made up of people, most of whom have little or no control over what their leaders do. That is twice now, that you have urged mercy, and that is very good.:*

Even for Vkandis, notorious for being a vengeful god?

:Especially for Vkandis; please remember that religions are made up of people, most of whom have very little control over what their priests decree is doctrine. Keep in mind that given that the priests and the people have free will and the means to exercise it, gods may not always be able to control their priests either. So what the priests say, and the people believe, is not always the whole truth.:

Karal blinked at that. Altra evidently decided Karal was ready for a little more doctrine smashing.

:Time for a parable. Think of a very wealthy, very reclusive man with a dangerous reputation; say a former mercenary. Assume he lives in a town but seldom leaves his home. Nevertheless—and not wanting people to think he is trying to buy good opinion—he sends his servants out secretly, day after day, to help the worthy poor, the sick, the helpless. Then one day while he is coming in his front gate, a woman with a baby is attacked by ruffians, and he reacts as he was trained, draws his sword, and cuts them all down in the blink of an eye. Say that later, in the inquiry, it was learned that those same ruffians were old enemies of his, looking for his new home. Now what are the townsfolk going to say about him?:

Karal knew very well what they would say. They would know nothing about the countless acts of mercy and charity that defined the man, they would know only the single moment of public bloodshed. At the least, they would call him vengeful, they would fear his temper, and might avoid his company. If there were those who envied him, it might even be whispered that he arranged for the attack on the woman in order to have an excuse for killing the gang. And although there would be a shred of truth in the stories of vengeance, it would by no means be the entire truth.

:Vkandis—any god—is far more than His people make Him,: Altra continued. *:It is the responsibility of the priest to lead them to that understanding, so that they do not attempt to limit Him to what they know.:*

That was what he had been groping for, these past several weeks! All the pieces for understanding had been there, but he just hadn't put them together in so elegant and simple a whole.

:And just at the moment, the meeting is going on without your note-taking,: Altra added, bending to clean a paw with fastidious attention to detail. *:Life is attention to both the large and the small, little brother. Pay heed to the sun, but watch your feet, or you'll fall ingloriously on your nose.:*

He bent hastily to his paper, with a soft chuckle inaudible to anyone else.

The meeting went on for far too long, but Firesong managed to annoy enough useless Councillors to guarantee that the next meeting would be much shorter.

It would have to be; Firesong had also cut short any attempt by the Councillors to turn the meeting into an accusation-and-blame session (with most of both being aimed at the group in the Tower). That, Karal found difficult to believe the first time one of them started. They seemed to be cherishing a variety of bizarre ideas about what was going on here, not the least of which was that *they* would be safe when the final Storm hit, and those outside the Tower would be the ones in the most danger.

"What was wrong with those people?" he asked Lyam in amazement, as the members of their own group broke up and went off on their interrupted studies. "Where did they get those ideas?"

The young *hertasi* shrugged, his tail beating softly against the floor where they both sat, organizing their notes and putting up their writing supplies. "They think we wallow in luxury here, that we spend all our time in idle pursuits and speculations that have no bearing on work or reality. They half don't believe in the Storms; they think we've got a fabulous life here and we're prolonging our stay here to continue to enjoy this glorious place and our freedom from work and responsibility."

Karal glanced around at their "luxurious surroundings," taking in the elegant appointments. Well, the inlaid stone floors were certainly beautiful, and there wasn't a ceiling like this one in all of Karse and Valdemar combined. But in between—

True, the Shin'a'in pallets were colorful, and comfortable, but they weren't the equivalent of anything in the guest quarters at the Palace at Haven. And as for the rest, he didn't think that a single one of those Councillors had ever eaten, slept, or lived like this, and he didn't think any of them would ever want to. It wasn't as bad as the poorest Karsite inn workers endured, and in some ways it was a *little* more comfortable than the conditions of Vkandis' novices, but those highborn Councillors would probably think they'd been exiled to hard living at the end of the world.

And what they'd make of butter-tea, I don't know. They might consider it a form of penance.

"I don't know, Lyam," he said, finally. "Is this some sort of delusionary illness they're under?"

The lizard did not have many facial expressions, but he could and did cock up a brow ridge. "Actually, it's distance. A fair number of our people back in White Gryphon assumed that because we had been given k'Sheyna Vale that we must be living in the midst of incredible luxury. Anything that's far off must be better than anything at home, you see." He snorted. "Actually, if you want luxury I'd recommend the courts of the Black Kings. I've been there, so I know. Silk sheets, private gardens, food worth dying for—now *that* is what I would call luxury!" He smacked his lips, or what passed for lips.

Karal sighed and shook his head, and Lyam patted his back. "Cheer up! The ones who think we're shirking are all idiots, and Firesong is going to get them to go away. If that Queen of theirs doesn't find them something harmless to do to keep them occupied, that is. I know his kind. He'll keep chipping at them until they quit."

Karal chuckled at Lyam's all too accurate assessment. "He can be diplomatic when he wants to be," he felt impelled to point out.

"Of course he can, but diplomacy is for when you've got time, and that's the one thing we're short of." Lyam shook his head as his expression turned grave. "Karal, I'm going to get serious for a moment; I want you to tell me something, and be honest. You've worked with these people—Firesong, An'desha, Sejanes, and all—for a long time. Can they do this? Can they really find an answer to the last Storm? Or should I look for a deep, dark den to hide in and hope it doesn't get melted shut behind me?"

Karal closed his eyes for a moment, taken by surprise by the sudden question. Perhaps that was why Lyam had asked it, so that he wouldn't have a chance to prevaricate.

"If anyone can, they can," he said at last. "An'desha holds the actual memories of Urtho's enemy Ma'ar, who was the second-most-powerful mage of the time of the Cataclysm. I just don't know if it's possible for mortal creatures to save this situation."

Lyam sighed. "I was afraid you were going to say that." He slumped abruptly, and looked up at Karal with an unreadable expression. "Let's talk about our girls," he suggested. "You and I can't do a blazing thing to help *them*, so let's talk about our girls, eh?" In a mercurial change of mood, he grinned, showing a fine set of pointed teeth. "Nothing like girls to get your mind off your troubles."

"Or give you a different set of troubles to think about!" Karal laughed, only too happy to oblige.

Tarrn found them both commiserating over the way that females had to approach any difficulty sideways, like a crab, instead of meeting it head-on, a trait it seemed both *hertasi* and human females shared. He stood within earshot for some time, simply listening, with his pointed ears pricked sharply upward, evidently waiting for a natural break in the conversation before interrupting.

:*Lyam, have you any notion where the Shin'a'in stored the gray bag of books we brought with us?*: he asked. :*I find I need a reference.*:

"It's easier for me to find it than tell you where it is," the *hertasi* said, leaping to his feet. "Stay right here; I'll bring the whole bag."

He scampered down the stairs to the workroom, and Tarrn turned his attention to Karal. :*You and my apprentice seem to be getting on well,*: he observed mildly.

"We have a great deal in common, sir," Karal replied politely. "As you probably noticed."

Tarrn's mouth dropped open in a lupine grin. :*Young women, for one thing. Alas, I fear I could never give you reasonable advice on that subject; my kind are neuters, but by birth rather than by oath, as our Shin'a'in friends are.*:

That left Karal more confused than enlightened. "All *kyree* are neuters? And where do the Kal'enedral come into it?"

It took Tarrn a few moments to explain that, no, all *kyree* were not neuters, but that the neuters tended to be the scholars, tale-spinners, poets, and historians. Then it took him a bit longer to explain the oaths of the Sworn, and how the Goddess herself rendered them literally sexless, which was why it was so very difficult for anyone to be accepted by Her into Her service.

Karal was not precisely appalled, but he was certainly baffled. "I can't imagine why anyone *would* want to be Sworn!" he said to the *kyree.* "I mean, I beg your pardon, but—"

:Don't apologize; I don't regret being neuter, and over the years I've often considered myself fortunate not *to have to put up with what you do,:* Tarrn replied thoughtfully. *:As for the Sworn, whether Swordsworn or Goddess-sworn, I can well imagine any number of circumstances where a human would find the burden of sexuality intolerable. Such tales that brought them to that condition may be sad, even horrible, but at least among the Shin'a'in they have a refuge. And for some—well if their life has been spent entirely in the sphere of the intellectual, then there is no sacrifice.:*

Karal took a moment to look for An'desha, and finally found him, deep in conference with Lo'isha and another black-clad Shin'a'in. "I suppose I can think of at least one case where memories might be intolerable," he said slowly.

Tarrn followed his gaze. *:The thought had occurred to me as well. If we live…:*

If. There was that word again, the one he thought about all the time, but did his best not to mention. "Are we likely not to?" he asked soberly.

As if called by his gaze, An'desha left the other Shin'a'in and walked over to them, just in time to catch Tarrn's reply.

:I don't know.: Tarrn was quite sober. *:I came here knowing that there was a good chance we would not, and so did Lyam. It is possible that what we record will serve to help others cope with the next Cataclysm in another millennia or two. Or it may help the survivors of this one. It seems that the only way we can be assured of survival is through the mechanism you yourself suggested.:*

"Divine intervention?" he said, dryly. "Ah, but there's a catch. We can't count on it; if we do, we *certainly* won't get it."

An'desha nodded as he sat down beside Karal. "That is the way of things with the Star-Eyed, at least, and this is the heart of *Her* land. If we were to call upon anyone, it should be Kal'enel. But Lo'isha says that She has been silent of late, as if She is no more certain of what is to come than we are."

:So what are we to do?: Tarrn asked. *:When the gods themselves are silent, what is a mortal to do?:*

"I don't know," An'desha admitted.

"You might try calling on old friends," suggested a helpful voice from above their heads, as brilliant golden light flooded down upon them.

Tarrn jumped straight up in the air and came down with his eyes wide and his hackles up. Lyam, whose head was just poking up out of the hatchway leading to the stair to the workroom, had to grab for the edge of the hatch to keep from falling. Even Karal, who had seen this phenomenon before, and An'desha, to whom it was familiar, gaped with astonishment as they rose to their feet.

Swooping down from the ceiling in a spiraling dance that involved Firesong's ecstatic firebird Aya, were a pair of man-sized hawks with feathers of flame. They landed with the grace of a dancer and the weightlessness of a puff of down, and the moment they touched the ground, they transformed into a man and a woman who still had a suggestion of bird about them. The man was dressed as a Shin'a'in shaman, but the woman was all Hawkbrother.

The Shin'a'in present all reacted the same way; they did not drop to their knees or grovel, but went rigid with the profoundest respect, and with naked worship in their eyes.

:What—is—this?: Tarrn managed, every hair on his body standing straight out.

"I am Dawnfire, and this is Tre'valen," the woman said, looking down at Tarrn with a smile. Her eyes were open wide, as were his, and they were perhaps the strangest thing of all about the two, for those eyes were the bright-spangled black of a star-filled night sky. "We're old friends of An'desha."

Altra and Florian appeared from one of the farther rooms, and made their way across the floor to the little gathering, and it seemed that they were the only creatures in the building capable of moving. They paused a few paces away from the bright creatures, and both made little bows of greeting in unison.

"Tre'valen and Dawnfire are Avatars of Kal'enel, Tarrn," An'desha said, very quietly. "And although I would not have claimed the privilege of saying they were my friends, they have been very good to me."

Tre'valen laughed. "Well, claim it or not, we are your friends, little brother. And more than that, we're here to help you as much as we can."

That astonishing statement broke the spell holding everyone frozen in silence, and everyone in the Tower converged on the pair except for Karal, who sat abruptly down.

We have Altra for Vkandis, Florian for the gods of Valdemar—and now this. What is that Shin'a'in saying? Be careful what you ask for?

Well, he had asked for Divine aid; whether it would be enough remained to be seen.

8

"All I know is this," King Tremane said, rubbing his temple in a gesture of nervous habit. "I haven't even tried to light a candle magically for weeks, but my mage-energy is going *somewhere*. If you can tell me where, I'll feel a great deal better."

Darkwind nodded, squinting a little against the brilliant sunlight streaming in through the windows of the King's Tower. That was what everyone called it now—"the King's Tower," as Shonar had become, by default, the new capital of Hardorn. It was a small and slightly shabby residence for a King, but Hardorn itself had seen better days. It would do Tremane no harm to be seen putting the welfare of his new country above his own comforts.

After a frenzy of make-do preparations, there had been a tiny coronation ceremony, wherein Duke Tremane had become King Tremane, and had been presented with a crown that (like the country) was rather the worse for wear. It even appeared to have been flattened before someone managed to wrestle it back into shape.

Still, it *was*—at least now—the authentic crown of Hardorn, and there was something to be said for that.

Tremane had accepted it graciously, worn it for the coronation, then immediately went to his private possessions and had a few things melted down and made into a very slim, gold band with minimal ornamentation that bore a remarkable resemblance to his ducal coronet.

That, in turn, had borne a remarkable resemblance to the slender coronet that Selenay wore, but Darkwind didn't see any reason to mention that. Frankly, the thin band looked dignified on Tremane's balding head, as opposed to the heavy crown. Even if it hadn't been battered, the original crown still looked rather silly, at least to Darkwind's eyes.

Crowns. This conference isn't about crowns. He turned his attention instead to Tremane's statement. "I think," he said slowly, "that your energy is going into the land—at least in making queries of where and what problems there are—and that *where* it goes tells you what places are most damaged. I suspect that those places producing monstrosities are the most heavily damaged, which is how you have been managing to pinpoint their lairs. You can probably stop the drainage if you choose."

Tremane considered that for a moment, then shrugged. "On the whole, I don't see why I should bother. It isn't a critical drain, and it isn't paining me or making me physically weaker. The only things I might want to do magically are things the earth-sense is giving me anyway. I just wanted to know *where* my energies were going; it could have been due to something more sinister."

That was astute of him, and a reflection on the changes in his thinking that he did not immediately assume it *was* something sinister and begin looking for an enemy. "Tayledras Healing Adepts can send their energies out to damaged land deliberately," Darkwind told him. "And they can redirect energy from elsewhere, using themselves as a conduit. You seem to have many of the same abilities, given to you by the earth-sense, rather than by accident of birth or because of training."

"Interesting," Tremane replied, his brows knitting slightly with thought. He leaned toward Darkwind as something occurred to him. "You know, there's another thing; I had assumed that I'd have earth-sense for all of Hardorn, from border to border, but every time one of those groups comes in to give me their—their pledge—it seems as if I can sense more than I could before. It's difficult to explain; it's as if I knew the place was there, but it was blank or shadowed to me. It's analogous to seeing into a room that was darkened and is now illuminated."

"That may be precisely what is happening," Darkwind admitted. "When someone has an affinity for a given area—usually a homeland, or at least the village they grew up in—a magical link naturally forms between them and the place. Location and divination spells work just a little easier when they involve that person's home area as a target, for example, over places the person may have been to only once. When these people open themselves up to your rule, they may also very well be opening up their home-affinity connection to you, too. Or, well, it could also be that the earth you take from them in the seisin ceremony links you to that place. It's fairly obvious to me that the seisin ceremony itself is a primitive piece of contamination-magic. As for details of how you can use that to advantage, I don't know; you'd have to ask someone who already has the sense."

He hadn't missed the hesitation before Tremane picked the word "pledge." Poor Tremane was enduring a great deal of personal embarrassment for the sake of these people, if only they knew it. Little groups were trickling in all the time to swear fealty to their new king, and they were using an ancient ritual they referred to as "seisin," a ritual probably as old as the earth-taking ritual. There was no doubt in Darkwind's mind that it was just as potent as the earth-taking, and just as primitive.

And it profoundly embarrassed the urbane and efficient Tremane, as most "primitive" rituals would embarrass him.

Nevertheless, it was effective, and he didn't think he needed to point out to Tremane that the reason he could sense another new area every time his new liegemen swore to him was that he literally was adding to the area he had "taken." It was entirely possible that the pinch of earth he had ingested at the ceremony that gave him this new power had been carefully made of a bit of every soil the priests could get their hands on, for that very reason, thus adding in the extra power gain from contagion.

"Speaking of your new subjects, Tremane, there's another group coming in at the gate now," said Elspeth, who happened to be standing by the window. "They're pretty heavily armed and I see someone with a pennon at the front." She frowned and shaded her eyes with one hand, looking down into the courtyard. "Is that—yes, it is, four sets of strawberry-leaves. It's a baronial coronet on the pennon-head. Congratulations! You've hooked one of the few big fish remaining in Hardorn."

Darkwind barely suppressed a smirk. *:For the first time since I've been with you, ke'chara, I've just seen a Herald... act as a Herald.:*

Elspeth just made a short choking sound, while Gwena tittered in their heads.

Tremane sighed, but it was with visible relief. "I'd better go right down and greet them properly, then," he said. "Can we resume our meeting later?"

"No reason why not," Elspeth said for both of them. "We'll meet you down there with Gwena and the full panoply. If you've gotten a baron, we'd better confirm your treaty and association with the Alliance."

Darkwind smiled; this was not, by any means, the first time that Gwena, he, and Elspeth had dressed up and assembled to impress the new liegemen. It had rather startled some of them to see a "horse" indoors, until they saw Elspeth's white uniform and realized that it wasn't a horse at all, but a Companion.

Tremane laughed unexpectedly; it seemed to Darkwind that the new King laughed quite a bit more than he would have expected, perhaps because he had a strong sense of humor about himself. "You should hear the things my housekeeping staff has to say about hoofprints in the wood floors. Do you have the same problem in Valdemar?"

"Sadly, all the time," Elspeth told him. "We've never found a way to prevent them, and we've tried everything." She moved away from the window with her arms crossed over her chest and a twinkle of amusement in her eye. "A silver piece says this one will be more impressed by Darkwind and Vree than by Gwena and me."

"I'll take that bet," Tremane responded easily. Darkwind stood up, smiling mostly to himself. Tremane had become much more relaxed around them since the earth-taking ceremony, treating them more often as colleagues and equals than as foreign ambassadors. Darkwind thought he knew why, although he doubted if Tremane himself was aware of the reason.

The land "knows" Elspeth and Gwena; the Valdemarans have always been good stewards of the land and good friends to Hardorn since Vanyel's time. It also "knows" me, since serving and healing the land are what the Tayledras were born and bred for. Because the land knows and trusts us, it is making Tremane feel comfortable around us and inclining him to trust us as well.

Tremane's new link with Hardorn was going to affect him in any number of ways that he was not always going to be conscious of, but Darkwind didn't see anything but good in that prospect. Very occasionally Tremane grew momentarily disoriented by some new information the earth-sense threw at him, but for the most part he was coping well. Eventually, as Hardorn recovered from the damage that had been done to it, Tremane would find that the land sustained *him* in moments of stress, rather than the reverse.

There was a knock on the door, and Elspeth joined Darkwind as Tremane's aide—now styled his "seneschal," though he still acted and probably thought of himself as a military aide-de-camp—entered diffidently.

"Sir—I mean, Your Majesty—there is a party below who—"

"I know, I'll be there directly," Tremane interrupted. "You know the drill by now; go see to the arrangements, and as soon as I look appropriate I'll be down. Blasted crown," he muttered, as the aide saluted, recollected again that Tremane was a King now and not a military commander, and bowed himself out. "Where did I put it this time?"

"Where you always put it, Tremane," Elspeth laughed. "Locked up in the chest."

"Right, with the robes that are too damned heavy to wear and not warm enough to make any difference in the Great Hall." Tremane swore with annoyance under his breath, and Darkwind wondered how he would ever have survived being made Emperor if he disliked the panoply of rank so much. "I won't miss winter one tiny bit. Thank you; I'll see you in the Hall and we can get this nonsense over with. Again."

"Oh, this time it looks as if it will be more than worth the effort," Elspeth assured him, as she preceded Darkwind into the hallway.

"Will it?" he asked her, as they descended the staircase to their own quarters.

"I think he'll be pleasantly surprised," she said. "I don't know much about Hardorn heraldry, but I think this new fellow may be the highest-ranking native to survive Ancar, and that means he'll be bringing a fair piece of the country with him. Not to mention his escort, and they looked as if they probably represent some major armed forces."

"So how old is this baron?" Darkwind asked. He had a good reason for asking; the surviving nobles of Hardorn tended to be mostly very old, or very young. The former had survived by being no threat to Ancar, and the latter by being hidden by their relatives, usually with reliable farmers or other family retainers.

"I'd say early teens; fourteen, fifteen at the most," Elspeth replied.

"Hence the reason he'll be more impressed by a Hawkbrother than a Herald. He may not even know what a Herald *is*, until someone tells him." Darkwind shook a finger at her. "You're stealing Tremane's silver, you little cheat."

"Then he shouldn't bet with me. He ought to know by now that I never propose a bet unless I'm certain of the outcome." She nodded at the guards on either side of their door and opened it herself. Their own guards from Valdemar stationed inside the door brought their weapons up until they saw who was entering; then they grinned sheepishly and returned to a deceptively relaxed posture.

"Is that any way to treat a monarch?" Darkwind asked her, and sighed as he began climbing the stair to their private quarters. "Never mind; forget I asked. I suppose it won't hurt him."

"I never treat Tremane casually in front of anyone else," Elspeth reminded him, taking the narrow staircase a little behind him. "This is calculated behavior; it shows him that I consider him my equal and will treat him as such. And as Mother often reminds me, the fact that I abdicated in favor of the twins does not make me any less a princess. It's not a bad thing in this case to have one of the Blood Royal acting as ambassador."

"True, all of it." The next floor was the purview of their guards and staff, who were currently lounging about, engaged in various off-duty occupations in the main room of their circular suite. Elspeth and Darkwind both waved at the rest of their entourage as they passed through, but did not stop on that floor. He continued the conversation. "Well, I take it you think this latest delegation is worth bringing out the full formal gear."

"Every feather, bead, bell and bauble," Elspeth said firmly. "Full Whites for me, and the circlet, with badges *and* medals. And don't pretend you don't like to dress up, my love."

"I wouldn't dream of it." The scent of the balsam incense he used both to perfume the air of their private quarters and to discourage pests met them as they reached their own floor. "Unlike you so-called 'civilized' peoples, we Tayledras know how to create clothing that is impressive, functional, *and* comfortable."

"Don't put *me* in that 'civilized' category!" she protested. "We Valdemarans feel precisely the same way! Well, we Heralds do, anyway, and that category includes the ruling family."

"Impressive?" He raised an eyebrow even as he went to the chest containing his clothing and raised the lid. "I'll grant you the functional and comfortable, but you Valdemarans have no sense of style, or at least, you Heralds don't. You horrified my poor *hertasi* with your uniform, you know. They thought you were wearing the sacks your clothes were supposed to be carried in."

They "argued" about clothing, style, and decoration happily all the time they were changing into their formal clothing, she into the Whites that he had redesigned, with the additions of rank, and he into the most elaborate outfit he owned, although by the standards set by Firesong, he was rather drab. His draped clothing of scarlet, gold, and warm brown was augmented by a sculpted leather tunic with a padded shoulder, and when he was dressed, Vree left his perch by the window and lofted straight to him, to land on the shoulder with a fraction of the impact he would have used in making a landing on a perch. Having Vree on his shoulder instead of his wrist served a double function. First, no falconer would ever have let one of his birds sit on his shoulder; that was a tacit invitation to facial scarring or losing an eye if something startled the bird or if it suddenly decided that this was a good time to strike out for freedom. This marked him to the knowledgeable as a Hawkbrother with no doubt. Only a bondbird could be trusted to sit this way, with no jesses, no hood, and no means of "control" over him. And second, if the exotic clothing would not set him apart from the rest, then Vree, who was much larger than any forestgyre or other gyrfalcon these people had ever seen, certainly would.

Elspeth, who had a lifetime of rapid changes-of-outfit to fall back on, waited with an exaggerated expression of boredom for him to finish his belt adjustments. "Bring your head over here," Elspeth commanded, the feathered and beaded ornaments meant to be braided into his hair dangling from one hand. She already wore the beaded feather he had given her as a token of love, one of Vree's own primaries, braided into her own.

"Should I leave the rest of me here?" he suggested. She made an exasperated *tsk*ing sound, and pushed him down into a chair. Vree flared his wings to stay balanced. She wove the feathered cords deftly into his long hair, as cleverly as if she had been born in an *ekele* rather than a palace.

"There," she said, bending to kiss him, then rapping him lightly on the top of his head with her knuckles. "Now you're presentable."

"So I am. And so are you." He rose and headed for the door, this time taking the lead down the stairs. The entire procedure, from the time they entered the room to this moment, had taken a fraction of the time it would take Tremane to get ready. But then again, they were not going to have to be laced into ceremonial armor either.

Their own entourage was so used to this by now that there had been no need for Elspeth to ask anyone to go get Gwena, drape her with her ceremonial barding and bells, and bring her to the Great Hall. The Companion was already waiting for them when they arrived at the side entrance they would use to get in place before either Tremane arrived or the delegation was allowed to enter. The members of Tremane's staff were quite used to seeing a "horse" wandering about the halls now, and let her go her own way when they saw her. Waiting with her were all of the dignitaries that could be hurried into formal clothing or uniforms on short notice, though there was always a chance that not all of them were what they were dressed up to be. Once, after most of Tremane's staff had gone to a meeting with the town council, Darkwind recalled, someone had actually borrowed an Imperial officer's tunic and a handful of medals and coerced the cook into it for one of these ceremonies! Since the folk coming to pledge their loyalty were likely never to set eyes on Shonar again, it did no harm to anyone to have impersonators fill in the ranks of Tremane's Court if it was necessary, to give the impression that every petty lordling with a handful of men was being given the highest of honors.

This time the reverse was true, for not only were all the real Officials present, but the mayor of Shonar, Sandar Giles, had been on his way for a meeting with one of Tremane's underlings when he saw the procession of armed men heading for Tremane's manor. He'd sent a now-exhausted runner hastily back to the town for his mayoral finery, and now stood waiting with the rest while the servants did what they could to make the Great Hall bearable.

"One of Tremane's mages is in there, warming the place up," Sandar was saying to Tremane's aide, who was looking distinctly uncomfortable in his nonregulation, heavily embroidered tabard. It looked like—and probably was—something that had been found in an attic and been pressed into service as the "official" clothing of His Majesty's Seneschal. A great deal of the Court garments had been made out of salvaged material or dredged out of attics. For that matter, Sandar Giles' outfit showed a touch of the moth's tooth around the squirrel-fur trim and the woolen hood, as if he had gone to storage for his grandfather's mayoral outfit.

Small wonder Tremane has difficulty taking all this seriously. His "court" is hardly up to the standards of even his old ducal household, I should imagine. Elspeth and I are the only ones who are not threadbare and much-mended.

But none of the various delegations that had come riding or walking in to Shonar had looked any better, and most had looked much worse. By the current standards of the country, Tremane's Court probably looked remarkably prosperous.

Before this is all over, we may look back on these times fondly, as the days when we were all doing well. It was a grim thought, but one which he and Elspeth often shared. If the mage-storms could not be held back—

Well, there was nothing to be gained by dwelling on that now. Under Tremane's direction, people were readying themselves for worse to come, and Hardornens, unlike Valdemarans, were perfectly willing to believe in "worse to come." Once the ceremony was over, but just before the delegation left for home, Tremane would give this new lot their directions on surviving the final Storm, as he had every other delegation so far. That those directions were mainly guesses hardly mattered; they would have direction and confidence that he had the situation on the way to being under control.

The door opened, and a thin, gawky man came through it, a fellow with thinning hair, who squinted at them from behind a pair of glass lenses set in a lead frame that rested on his nose. "It's warm in there now, and it should last through your ceremony," the mage said, and made shooing motions as if they were a bunch of hens he wanted to drive before him. "In with you now! The sooner you get the ceremony over with, the less likely that the spell will wear off before it's over!"

None of them needed a second invitation; the hallway was freezing, and the promise of warmth was all the encouragement they required to move quickly.

Elspeth and Gwena hung back until the others were inside, and Darkwind remained with them. Gwena was quite careful whenever she came inside the manor, and despite the complaints from Tremane's household staff, she left very little sign of her presence after these ceremonies. Some of the Hardornen warriors, who forgot to remove spurs or came striding in wearing heavy, hobnailed boots, did worse damage than Gwena, who picked up each hoof neatly and set it down again with the greatest of care.

Gwena was arrayed in the "riderless" version of Companion full dress; no saddle, but with a blue and silver blanket cut like her barding, decorated at all the points with silver bells, a blue-dyed leather hackamore with silver tassels at the cheekpieces, and reins bedecked with more silver bells. Had there been more time to ready her, the decorations included even bells and blue ribbons to braid into her mane and tail, but she had to be content with her mane and tail flowing freely.

"You look lovely, as always," Darkwind told her.

:Thank you,: she replied coyly, and gave her head a tiny toss so that the bells chimed. *:I'm afraid we four are making a more impressive show than Tremane's own Court, but that can't be helped.:*

"At least we are making our support unmistakable," he pointed out, as they took their appointed places among the rest.

There was some shuffling as the dignitaries of Tremane's Court sorted themselves out, then the young Seneschal nodded his head and the main doors were flung open to admit the latest delegation.

At the head of the procession was a youngster—no boy, but young, too young to need a razor—of about fourteen. Under his scarlet cloak and tabard, he wore full armor that had seen hard use, and his eyes were far too old to belong to that young face. The dented and slightly tarnished baronial circlet about his brow did not detract from the painful dignity with which he carried himself, and by his build and the muscles beneath the armor, he was clearly no stranger to real fighting. Behind him, more men in full armor followed in pairs, ranging in age from powerful graybeards to men only a little older than the boy-baron. One of the two immediately behind the boy carried a small wooden box. They paraded in slowly, surveying every person there with suspicion, and Darkwind smothered a smile as the boy's eyes lit on the Alliance envoys, widened, and flitted from Elspeth to Darkwind and back, finally remaining on Darkwind.

:I won,: she Mindspoke unnecessarily.

The entire delegation came to a halt at the foot of the low dais. By now, several of the Shonar artisans were at work on a real throne for Tremane, since the original throne of Hardorn had been lost in looting and fires, but it would not be finished for another week or two. In place of a real throne was a prop throne, made for an Imperial theatrical production, and modified by those same artisans. They had sanded off the gilt paint, which had probably looked fine at a distance but only looked cheap and shoddy up close, and had removed all of the glass-paste jewels set into the back. What had been carved wolves adorning the back were now hounds, the Hardornen symbol of fidelity. The swords making up the legs and arms, and interlaced on the back below the hounds, had become tree branches, and the wood had been rubbed with oils and polished until it shone. The shabby cushions had been replaced with brown velvet purloined from drapes taken from storage. However, in the course of all the recarving, the wood had been pared down in some places to a precarious extent, and Tremane had been warned to be very careful when sitting on it. Everyone was going to breathe a sigh of relief when the new throne took the place of the old. It could be taken for a terrible omen if Tremane's throne collapsed beneath him in the middle of one of these ceremonies. Tremane had good-naturedly commented that having a fake Imperial throne recarved into a fragile Hardornen throne was entirely appropriate.

Tremane kept the delegation waiting just long enough for them to get a good look at the rest of his Court, and to take in the banners on the wall behind his throne, which represented those who had already come in and brought him their pledges. Most of those who had sworn their oaths had taken their banners from the arms of the former nobles of the region, although more often than not there had been no one who actually qualified to take those arms. Tremane had solved that quickly enough by confirming the delegates in their places as the new lords, and bestowing the old titles upon them as soon as their pledges were confirmed.

Sadly, besides a number of ancient titles going begging, there was plenty of empty land lying fallow and abandoned, but Tremane had plans for that, too. Once summer arrived, it would be settled, and former Imperial officers who were ready to retire would be ennobled and put in place as overlords. They would be allowed to take with them as many Imperial soldiers as wished to retire to farming and had found brides among the Hardornens; these would be given freehold-grants on reclaimed farms. Thus, the newly ennobled would have garrison and work force in one, and the newly wed couples would have more of a base for their start than most. After that particular announcement, the number of engagements and handfastings had skyrocketed, and if some of the good farmers and fathers of Shonar had been a bit reluctant to welcome Imperial sons-in-law at first, their reluctance had evaporated when they learned of the royal bride-price the foreign sons-in-law would bring, thanks to the foresight of their new King.

Darkwind hid a smile as the young Baron kept taking covert glances at him, as if the youngster had never seen anything so outlandish in his life. Darkwind had been told that rumors of his presence and powers were circulating out beyond Shonar's walls, rumors which got more and more fantastic with every league distant from the city. He wondered what the boy had heard, to make him look so wide-eyed.

There was a bit of a stir at the door just off the dais, and Tremane's majordomo stepped inside.

The majordomo rapped three times on the floor with the butt of his staff. "His Majesty, King Tremane of Hardorn!" the man announced in ringing tones, his clear, commanding voice showing precisely why he had been plucked out of the ranks to fill this position. "And his Majesty's Chief Advisers!"

Tremane and his four Chief Advisers filed in with ponderous dignity. Of course, his Chief Advisers were also members of his bodyguard, but their weapons were not carried in an obvious fashion, and there was nothing about them to advertise that fact. Tremane wore his ceremonial armor, the Hardornen Crown, a tapestry tabard with his own arms (requisitioned from his former squire), and was draped in a fine cloak of silk edged in heavily embroidered silk trim purloined from the same curtains that had provided him with material for the seat cushions of his throne. The cloak was also part of the props for some unknown play; it was ridiculously long and required the services of two small boys recruited as pages to carry the trailing end.

Both pages were from the group of five children that Tremane and his men had rescued from the grip of the first killing blizzard; Tobe and Racky were their names, and they took their duty as Tremane's pages very seriously. They had been nicely outfitted in page costumes cut down from Imperial officers' uniforms by their mothers, who nearly burst with pride at the notion that their boys were serving the new King.

Tremane took his seat gingerly, which translated into a ponderous sort of dignity to outside eyes. The pages arranged his royal mantle out before his feet, like a peacock's tail, just on sanity's side of preposterous, and retired to their positions behind the throne. The young Baron tensed as Tremane nodded to him.

"Baron Peregryn, I understand that you are from Adair," he said quietly. "You are a very welcome addition to the Court."

Darkwind watched the boy and his entourage to see if they noticed the relative informality of Tremane's address. After much consideration, he had decided to completely do away with the royal plural, because Ancar had been so rabid in its use. Darkwind saw two of the older men exchange brief nods, and it seemed to him that they wore expressions of satisfaction.

The young Baron took two steps to the foot of the throne and went immediately to one knee, and the rest of his entourage followed his example in dropping to theirs. "I have come to offer you my pledge, King Tremane," the youngster said, in a high tenor that trembled only a little. "And in token of this pledge, I bring you seisin of my lands, and those of the men pledged in their turn to my service."

Young Baron Peregryn reached behind him without looking, and the man carrying the small wooden casket placed it in his outstretched hand. Darkwind watched their movements carefully, analyzing everything they did, and making some guesses about the relationship the Baron had with his men.

He is the acknowledged leader, no matter how young he appears to be, and he and the older men have worked and fought together a great deal. They trust him—and he trusts them. He has youth, enthusiasm, and charisma, and they have experience, and they all work to weave these things together. This one will be worth watching for stories and songs of noble deeds.

The boy opened the casket and held it out to Tremane, who took a double handful of soil from within and held it for a moment.

"Thus do I, Tremane, King of Hardorn, take seisin of the lands of Peregryn, Baron of Adair, and of those who are pledged to him," he proclaimed in a voice suitable for a battlefield oration. He dropped the soil back into the casket, and held out his hand to Tobe, the older of his two pages. Tobe handed him a small dagger, and with his face completely unflinching, he slashed his palm shallowly, held his hand over the casket, and allowed his blood to run into it and mix with the earth inside.

"Thus do I, Tremane, King of Hardorn by acknowledgment of the soil of Hardorn itself, give the pledge of my body to the lands of Peregryn, Baron of Adair, and of those who are vowed to his service." The other page, Racky, took the dagger and handed him a linen cloth, which he used to bind the wound across his palm. Meanwhile Tobe took the casket from Peregryn, mixed the soil and blood thoroughly with a miniature spade, and then used the spade to divide the moistened soil between the original casket and a small box. Tobe handed the casket back to Peregryn, who received it with the same reverence as he would a holy relic. Tobe gave the box to the Seneschal, who would take it to the cellars of the manor and add it to the urn of soil already there.

All of this mixing and dividing gave Tremane a chance to recover from the shock of adding yet another stretch of land to his "senses." Darkwind knew that by the time he reached his own quarters again the slash would be completely healed—and now was the moment when he would confirm his right to be King by telling Peregryn what, if anything, was wrong with his lands.

"If anything?" No, there will be a great deal wrong, there. Adair is supposed to be in the north, and there would have been reflections off the Iftel Border before Firesong and the rest instigated the Counter-Storm.

Tremane's eyes had the glazed look that meant he "felt" something very strong, which probably meant very bad. "Your lands, Baron Peregryn, include a small river valley, bounded by a lake, a hill shaped like a sleeping cat, and a forest of pines," he said slowly, as if he were talking in his sleep. Peregryn's eyes widened, and several of the men behind him began whispering urgently together. "Beneath that hill there is a cave, and within that cave there is a place where magic is pooling and stagnating. Living there is a beast, changed by magic into a monster. You cannot kill it directly; it will cost too many lives. You cannot poison it. To kill it you must feed it a cow which has been fed on datura-flower for three days. It will gorge itself, and the action of the flower will make it sleepy and it will go to the cave to hide. You must then collapse the cave or brick it up, sealing it inside."

Tremane went on, reciting the locations of several more pockets of trouble, together with suggested solutions for eliminating the problems. Peregryn wouldn't be able to implement all or even most of those solutions until summer, but at least now he and his men knew where all the trouble spots were, and would be able to deal with them one at a time. As Tremane spoke, more and more of Peregryn's men began whispering together, their expressions taking on the slightly stunned look of men who were hearing something they could not believe, and yet *could* verify. Evidently several of Tremane's revelations matched problems they already knew about—and knew that Tremane could not have learned by any normal means. Finally, Tremane fell silent, then blinked, shook his head a little, and his eyes cleared of their daze.

"I trust that will help?" he said dryly. He would remember everything he had said, of course; this was not a true trance, more of a state of intense concentration. And behind him one of his clerks had been taking down every word and would give Peregryn a copy before he left. If Peregryn was unable to deal with any of the problems Tremane had identified for him, there would be a record of what the problem was and where, and eventually Tremane's own men would move in to take care of it.

"More than simply 'help,' Your Majesty," Peregryn replied shakily.

He would have said more, but one of the men of his group, overcome with fervor and enthusiasm, leaped to his feet, brandishing his sword over his head.

"Long life to King Tremane!" he shouted, his voice actually cracking with excitement. "All gods bless King Tremane!"

That goaded everyone else in the entourage, and eventually Peregryn as well, to get to their feet in an eruption of cheers. Tremane remained sitting on his throne—in part, Darkwind knew, because he couldn't stand just yet—and bent his head to them in gracious acknowledgment of their accolade. Some of the oldest men were openly weeping; these were the ones who eventually thrust themselves forward, flung themselves at Tremane's feet, and kissed his hand with tears streaming down their faces. It was a moment of extreme and powerful emotion, and Tremane himself was not unmoved by it. The King took great care to clasp every man's hand, using both hands, listening to him babble, until he was ready to rise again and let another take his place. It was quite obvious to Darkwind that Tremane recognized these old warriors for what they were, and knew how difficult it was to get any sort of accolade from them, much less this kind of emotional outburst.

These older men always proved to be those who had survived the purges and who had expected to die without ever seeing Hardorn return to peace and prosperity. Darkwind knew very well why they wept, and so did Tremane. "I have given them back their dreams and their hope," he had said, a little in awe himself, after the first time this had happened. "They see a future now, where their grandchildren can expect to grow up without fear of being murdered on a royal whim."

And he was right; that was precisely what those old men saw: a future, where before had been only darkness and doubt.

It took some time before the young Baron and his men managed to calm themselves down, and more before all of the appropriate ceremonies had been fulfilled. Tremane apologized for having to house them in a barracks; they hastened to assure him that they would have been perfectly willing to camp in the snow. Tremane directed his supply sergeant—who now bore the impressive title of "Procurement Adviser"—to bestow upon his new liegemen the "usual gifts" and they made a token protest. The "usual gifts" were all surplus items, so much in surplus that their value in the town would be seriously depreciated if any more came on the market. Surplus Imperial clothing, surplus hand tools, surplus weapons. Some of Tremane's people had argued against that last, pointing out that he would be arming those who had lately been his enemies. But Tremane felt, and Darkwind agreed with him, that giving them weapons demonstrated his trust in them. It was a gesture worthy of a King.

Besides, these new liegemen *needed* the weaponry that Tremane gave them. Their own supplies had been depleted in their war against the Imperial forces. If they were going to rid themselves of their land's boggles, they needed weapons.

This wasn't at all altruistic. Practically speaking, Tremane would rather that *they* went after their boggles instead of turning to Imperial soldiers for help. They knew the lay of their own land, where a boggle might lair, where it could run. His men wouldn't, couldn't. Better to let the local experts handle it, if there was any chance they could.

By the time the presentation was over, Baron Peregryn and his men were, however, so happy they were beside themselves. They never even noticed that Tremane had gone pale, and was sweating, his hands clenching the arms of his throne so hard that the knuckles were white.

:*He isn't getting up, because he can't,*: Elspeth said, her Mindvoice sharp with alarm. :*It's more than simple disorientation this time. It's really striking him hard.*:

:*What's wrong?*: he asked, hoping she'd know.

:*I can't tell, and neither can Gwena.*: There was frustration there as well as alarm. *:All I can tell for certain is that he's in nearly the same state as he was when his earth-sense was first awakened. This has something to do with the earth-sense itself, and something to do with this new area he's taken seisin of.:*

Neither of them dared move to help him, not while the Baron and his people were still present; Tremane was clearly attempting to conceal his weakness and it was their responsibility to follow his wishes. He reached for her hand as she reached for his; their hands closed on each other and they stood waiting, tensely, while the last of the amenities were played out.

Finally the Baron and all of his men trooped out, to be accommodated overnight in one of the barracks. In the morning, Tremane would meet with them again and give them warning and instructions concerning what everyone here was now calling the "Final Storm," and what to do to weather it. Then, when everything had been organized for their return, they would go back home with a small caravan of supply sledges. Only after the doors closed behind them, could Tremane fold his body over his knees and his own people rush to help him.

But he waved them away before they could do more than ask him what was wrong.

"I'll be all right," he said, and Darkwind let out the breath he had been holding, for he *sounded* normal, just a bit shaken. "It's nothing physical, and I don't believe it's anything to worry about. Just— something unexpected just happened; let me sit here for a moment or two more while I get over it." He looked over at Darkwind and smiled ruefully. "Quite frankly, it feels as if someone just dropped me off a very high cliff, and I stopped just short of the ground."

Elspeth knelt at his side, and Darkwind joined her. "It's the new Barony, isn't it?" she asked. "It's something there. Is it the Storms starting again?"

As if her questions gave him a focus for his own sensations, he seized on them. "Yes. No. Yes, it's Adair, and no, it's not the Storms. I don't know what it is, but it's not—no, wait." His eyes took on that far-off gaze again. "It's the border, the northern border. Adair is on the northern border, and something has happened up there. Something important. Something that changes everything."

"What—" one of Tremane's generals began, but Tremane just shook his head, dumbly.

"I don't know," he repeated. "I just know—it's something completely new."

"What's on the northern border?" someone else asked, and looked at Elspeth for the answer.

She had one for that question, but she had turned as pale as Tremane. "Iftel," she said, and her hand clenched tight on Darkwind's. "Iftel. The one place in this part of the world that *no one* knows anything about."

"So that's the message?" Tremane said, his eyebrows rising. "Just that? Nothing more?"

With his recovery, the meeting among Darkwind, Elspeth, and Tremane that had been interrupted had been moved back to the office in his quarters, but by now they had all forgotten whatever it was they had been talking about, for a message had come by way of signal-towers from the north. Unfortunately, it only confirmed that something had happened, and gave them very little other information.

"That's all there was, sir—Your Majesty—" the aide recovered from his mistake. "Just that the border with Iftel suddenly opened, and a new delegation of something friendly was coming down here to meet with you. I'm afraid," he continued apologetically, "that the signal language is not very specific."

"The signal *did* say they were friendly, though? You're sure you're not misreading that?" If Tremane's voice was sharp with anxiety, Darkwind couldn't blame him.

"No, sir, that much is *quite* clear," the aide said with certainty. "The old man at the signal did say that the term used was one that he hadn't seen very often, but that it was definitely noted as being friendly."

"Thank the gods for small favors," Tremane muttered, and sighed, running a hand over his chin. "Well, now I know what it—ah—*feels* like to have the Iftel Border open up. That's useful information. But how whatever is coming expects to travel in this winter weather, I can't begin to imagine."

"Peregryn and his men did," Darkwind pointed out. "There's no reason to suppose others can't, but it will take time for them to arrive, perhaps weeks on foot, ten days by horse."

"By then, I might even have a throne I can sit on without worrying if it's going to break and drop me on my rump," Tremane sighed, then laughed. "Listen to me complaining about a flimsy throne! As if that was the worst thing we have to face!"

"A delegation from Iftel," Elspeth mused, twisting one of the rings she wore around and around. "They've always allowed a single envoy from Valdemar inside their land, so long as it was a member of the Merchant's Guild—but never anyone from the Mercenary's Guild. And they would never permit Heralds inside." She shook her head. "The envoy never would tell us much, only that they 'preferred peace' but weren't particularly interested in any exchanges with us."

"Very insular," Darkwind commented, quite well aware that this was a case of the goose complaining that the swan had a long neck. *One can hardly call the Tayledras anything but insular.*

"They could have good reason for being insular," Tremane pointed out. "When was the first time people of Valdemar encountered them?"

"Quite some time after the Founding," Elspeth admitted. "Their barrier was already in place then, at least according to the Chronicles. It was a merchant who was first allowed inside, and it has mostly been merchants who crossed it since." She smiled deprecatingly. "They may be insular, but like the rest of us, they enjoy buying things." Darkwind hid his own smile. for that last shot had been meant for herself. She had been unable to resist spending some of her own money on a few odd trifles that had turned up in the loot of the Imperial storehouse.

"So they could have encountered someone or something extremely dangerous before they ever saw you," Tremane pointed out, his eyes speculative, as he probably tried to envision what could have been so terrible that it caused an entire country to erect a magical barrier to keep out intruders. That it was a barrier that had survived centuries and baffled the magic powers of Ancar, Falconsbane, and the Empire alike made it all the more intriguing.

"They probably did," Darkwind put in. "In those early days, there were terrible things that far north. There was at least one Tayledras Vale somewhere about there, and *our* Chronicles report that at some time while they lived there, they encountered and defeated a Dark Mage much like Ancar's servant Falconsbane, but with a larger following."

He did not add that this mage probably had actually been Falconsbane in one of his earlier incarnations. Tremane neither knew about Falconsbane, nor likely cared; the only person still concerned with Ma'ar-Falconsbane was An'desha, and only because An'desha still held those critically-important memories. But as for the rest of them...

Falconsbane is dead, with the past, and this time he will stay that way. And about damned time, but we have more important things to worry about. The sober glance that Elspeth cast his way said virtually the same thing. For now, the situation was grave enough that even isolated Iftel was opening her borders and sending representatives to them; there was no leisure to dwell on the past.

"I don't know what, if anything, these representatives of Iftel might offer you," Darkwind cautioned.

"If nothing else," Tremane mused, "perhaps we can get them to part with the secret that makes up their Border. It's shielded them from the worst of the Storms so far; it might be able to shield us as well."

"Provided these people arrive here before the question becomes academic," Gordun, Tremane's chief mage, reminded him dryly. "It's a long way to the northern border and the going is difficult; by the time they get here, the Final Storm could have left us in ruins here."

Tremane nodded ruefully. "A good point, though it was an entertaining thought while it lasted. Well, that brings up the next decision; what shall we tell our newest Baron tomorrow about the Final Storm?"

"Hide, and finish your card games quickly?" one wag suggested. There was a general, strained laugh, and then the discussion moved into the serious channel of what to do in the immediate future. Eventually, late that night, precisely what should be told to the Baron and his entourage had been worked out; enough to make him understand the gravity of the situation, but not so much that he would panic. Panic would be bad for Peregryn and his people as well.

Over the course of the next couple of days, the Baron got his pick of surplused supplies, was given a review of troopers interested in resettling up north, and got his briefing and warnings about the Final Storm. He and his own advisers were philosophical about that last; there was nothing they could do to stop it, and they could only hope that the physical effects were limited to places with no human populations. During the first of the storms, caught both by the initial storm waves and the reflected waves from the Iftel Border, they had suffered more damage than anyone yet reporting in. "We have already had a half-dozen people unfortunate enough to be caught in one of the things we are calling 'change-circles,' and they were changed even as beasts are," Peregryn said, with a shrug of deeply-felt helplessness. "The fortunate died."

"And the unfortunate lived," added one of his advisers grimly. "Though often, that was not long, when they made the mistake of approaching others for help. It wasn't always their bodies that changed, at least not outwardly."

Tremane exchanged a significant look with Darkwind. This was something he and his people had thought of at about the same time the potential for trouble occurred to the Allies. But while those in Valdemar had been concerned with prediction of where the change-circles would occur, and thus preventing people or large animals from being caught in one, the people in and around Shonar had planned on what to do *when* a human became a monster.

Until this moment, that had been nothing more than a possibility. Now they knew that there *were* transformed humans somewhere out there in the north, and it was time to put some of those plans into action in case the hapless victims trekked south. Tremane wrote something on a small slip of paper and passed it to a page to take to his clerks. The orders, already written out, would go into the troops' daily briefing. In essence, they were simple enough: *Humans have been caught in the Storms and changed. If a boggle shows intelligence and no aggression, be wary—but leave it alone long enough for it to show its intentions.*

There had been some debate on the subject, with a minority objecting to the mere idea of giving a boggle the chance to attack first, and a second minority wanting to make attempts to communicate with every boggle that even paused for a moment before attacking. Finally, to end the debating, Tremane had exercised his royal prerogatives and decreed the language of the order, which predictably did not entirely satisfy anyone, not even Tremane himself.

Darkwind had noticed, however, that Tremane had applied enough of the Imperial manner not to care if anyone was satisfied (including himself), so long as his decree did the job for which it was intended.

Neither of them could ever have guessed the immediate effect of that simple order.

Not more than two days after sending Baron Peregryn and his entourage and gift sledges off, during yet another ceremony of seisin— this time for the benefit of a very old Squire who had sent his informal pledge some time earlier, but who had not felt equal to taking the winter journey until now—they learned exactly why the signal-towers had said that some*thing* was coming down from Iftel.

No one there could have expected just what the some*things* were.

Tremane had just added his blood to the soil that old Squire Mariwell had brought with him, when a great clamor arose up on the walls of the manor. Darkwind started and looked up automatically, although he wouldn't be able to see a thing through the stone walls and ceiling. With great presence of mind, Racky took the casket of earth from Tremane's hands, mixed the contents quickly, divided them and handed the old man his own casket back, while all about him, his elders were behaving skittishly, staring and muttering among themselves, hands on empty scabbards. Before Tremane could send someone to find out what the cause of all the ruckus was, and right after Racky pressed the casket of soil back into its owner's shaking hands, one of the King's bodyguards came bursting into the Great Hall, his face as white as the snow outside.

"Boggles over the castle!" he cried. "Oh, by the gods! Great, huge, flying boggles! So many they cover the sky! Oh, gods, help us..."

Elspeth held up her hand to shade her eyes, and squinted up at the dark shapes hovering in the brilliant blue sky above the courtyard. It was too soon yet to say just what these "boggles" looked like, other than the fact that they were winged, but there was something about those black V shapes and the way that they swooped and soared that looked tantalizingly familiar.

They remind me of Treyvan and Hydona, but they don't fly exactly the same way. Could they be gryphons? There've been rumors of gryphons in the north for years now...

"Remember your orders, men," Tremane called to the nervous sentries on the walls and towers above. "No shooting without provocation."

Pray they don't take simple swooping as provocation!

"There're exactly twenty-one of them," Darkwind said absently from her right, as he peered upward into a sky blindingly bright. He bit his lip and she sensed that he was thinking hard for a moment, then his eyes narrowed as if he had just made a decision. He extended his gloved hand to Vree, who transferred his perch from the shoulder to the gauntlet with that intensity of gaze that told Elspeth he was getting silent instructions from his bondmate.

A heartbeat later, Darkwind flung Vree upward, and the bondbird pumped his wings skyward, heading straight for those twenty-one mysterious Vs. "I'll know in a moment just—" He began, his eyes half closed.

Then, unexpectedly, he laughed, the sound echoing across the otherwise silent courtyard and making just about everyone in Tremane's escort jump and stare at him as if they suspected he had gone mad. He brushed his snow-white hair back from his forehead, and pointed up at the "boggles," then at Vree, who had reversed his climb and was making a leisurely descent.

"Tell your men to put their weapons away, King Tremane," Darkwind called, holding out his gloved fist for the returning forestgyre. Vree flared his wings, ruffling Darkwind's hair, and landed as lightly as a bit of thistledown, settling his talons gently around the leather-covered wrist. "I suspect that's your delegation from Iftel up there, and if they can see half as well as my old friends Treyvan and Hydona can, they aren't about to land until there's no chance that they'll wind up becoming feathered pincushions."

:They are gryphons, then?: Elspeth asked, feeling a strange thrill of excitement. *:Could these be more of the "missing Companies" from the days of the Mage Wars?:*

:Could be; even with the distortion of looking through Vree's eyes, these gryphons don't look quite like the ones we've seen. Millennia of separation from the parent stock would do that, I suspect.: Darkwind continued to peer upward as the Imperial guards reluctantly put down their weapons at Tremane's shouted orders. *:It's either that, or some unbelievably clever Adept managed to duplicate the gryphons we know, and I doubt that's possible.:*

Whatever was or was not possible, it was soon obvious that Darkwind was right about the gryphons' eyesight. As soon as the last spear was grounded and the last arrow put back in its quiver, the hovering specks above descended with a speed that put Vree to shame, and made Elspeth recall what her mother's falconer had once said: *"If you want to know what the fastest bird in the world is, ask the falconer who's just had his prize peregrine carried off by a stooping eagle."*

Not only did the gryphons descend with breathtaking speed, they did so with artistry. They dropped in a modified stoop that followed a tightly spiraling path down into the relatively small courtyard, one after the other in a precise formation, like beads on a string. As the first of them backwinged hard, kicking up a wind that drove debris all over the courtyard and made those who had not been prepared for the amount of air those huge wings could push shield their faces, Elspeth wanted to applaud the theatrical entrance. The huge creature landed on the cobbles of the court as lightly as Vree on Darkwind's glove, touching down with one outstretched hind-claw first, then settling neatly an eyeblink later, posed and poised with wings folded, like a guardian statue in the middle of the expanse of stone.

The next followed a moment after, and the next, until the remaining twenty were ranged in a deliberate double half-circle behind their leader, all in the same precise, regal posture.

As Darkwind had indicated, they did not look *quite* like the gryphons of k'Leshya. These creatures were heavier of beak, neck, and chest;

like eagles, rather than stocky and broadwinged like hawks, or lean, large-eyed, and long-winged like falcons. In color they were quite unlike the gryphons of k'Leshya, who were as varied in color as the creatures they had been modeled after. These gryphons were a uniform dark brown from beak to tail, a color with some patterned shading in a lighter brown, but nothing nearly like the malar-stripes or masks of the falconiform gryphons, or the variegations of the hawk-gryphons, with their bright yellow beaks and claws. The effect was very impressive to someone who had never seen any two gryphons who looked precisely alike; as if someone had deliberately made up a wing of gryphons that matched in every way, like a matched set of horses in a parade group. They looked every bit as intelligent as Treyvan and Hydona, and their yellow eyes watched every move made by the humans before them with calculation and speculation. The heavier beaks made their faces look oddly proportioned, at least at first, but Elspeth found herself swiftly growing used to the new variation.

Each of them wore a harness and pack very similar to the ones the Kaled'a'in gryphons often wore, made of highly polished leather of a rich reddish-brown, with polished brass fittings. The apparent leader also wore a neck-collar and chestpiece that looked as if it had been derived from armor some time in the far distant past. Now it served only to bear a device of three swords, hilts down, points up, with a single heraldic sun above the middle. Elspeth glanced at Darkwind, who shook his head slightly; whatever it signified, he didn't recognize the symbology.

The gryphons waited, motionless except for the rising and falling of their chests, watching for someone among the humans to make the first move. The Imperials and Hardornens, one and all, stared back at them, faces pale and limbs rooted to the spot. Elspeth thought of her first sight of gryphons, and couldn't blame them for not moving. Here were creatures, twenty-one of them, with sickles on their front and hind claws, and meat hooks twice the size of a man's head in the middle of their faces—she wouldn't have been eager to rush up and embrace them in the name of brotherhood either.

"I suppose it's up to us," Darkwind said, a touch of amusement in his voice. He stepped forward, Elspeth a scant pace behind him, Gwena following at Elspeth's side, until he stood in comfortable speaking range of the leader, who regarded him with the unwavering, scarcely blinking gaze of the raptor.

"Welcome to Shonar, capital of Leader Tremane of Hardorn, in the name of the Alliance," he said in careful Kaled'a'in. "I am Darkwind k'Sheyna, representative of the Clans of the Tayledras of the Pelagirs, the Shin'a'in of the Dhorisha Plains, and the Kaled'a'in of k'Leshya Vale and White Gryphon. This is Elspeth, daughter of Selenay, ruler of Valdemar, and Companion Gwena, representatives of the peoples of Valdemar, Rethwellan, and Karse. Behind me are Leader Tremane, of Hardorn, and his officials and advisers."

Elspeth knew only enough Kaled'a'in to follow what Darkwind was saying; she could not have hoped to make the same speech herself. Kaled'a'in was handicapped by not having a word for "king;" the closest was "leader" or "ruler," and it gave no sense of the size of what was ruled. Darkwind's three peoples freely borrowed whatever local term applied, but she suspected that he was afraid that the gryphons before him would have no idea what the Hardornen titles meant. The chief gryphon listened attentively and with great concentration, and waited for a moment after Darkwind had finished to see if he would add anything. When Darkwind said nothing more, but made a slight bow, the gryphon opened his beak. He replied in a clear enough voice, but his words were in a form of Kaled'a'in so drastically different from anything she knew that she could only recognize the origin and not what the envoy said. Now it was Darkwind's turn to listen, closely, and with immense concentration, brows knitted into an unconscious frown as he followed the carefully enunciated words. She did not venture to break his concentration by Mindspeaking to him.

:I don't suppose you're picking up anything from them, are you?: she asked Gwena, as Darkwind made a reply of which she only understood half the words, none of them in sequence. She guessed that he was elaborating on who was what, and to whom the gryphon needed to apply for reception of his delegation.

:Not a thing, they're shielded, and shielded hard,: came the helpful reply. *:It would be useful to have an Empath with us at the moment, but I don't think there's anything other than a fairly reasonable level of anxiety in them at this point.:*

In the gryphon's reply, Elspeth caught the word, "Hardorn," and Darkwind's face cleared. "It would be a great deal easier if you *could* speak in the language of Hardorn, sir," he replied in that tongue. "I fear that time has changed the language you speak from the one taught to me."

"A grrreat deal of time, young Brrrother-To-Hawksss," the gryphon rumbled, with evident amusement. "A verrry grrreat deal of time by anyone's measurrre. I am Tashiketh pral Skylshaen, envoy from the land you know as Iftel to the court of King Tremane, who we have been told has been chosen for his office by the land, as it was in the old days." He waved a huge taloned hand in an expansive gesture at the twenty gryphons poised behind him. "This is my wing. These are the representatives of the twenty *hrradurr* of Iftel, courageous and worthy of their offices, who each won the right to fly in my wing in the *bahathyrrr.*"

The *hrradurr* were evidently subdivisions of Iftel—though what the *bahathyrrr* could be, Elspeth could not even begin to guess. She made a quick hand-gesture behind her back, hoping Tremane would take the hint and come up to be presented, but he was already moving before she gestured. With quick wits, he had already anticipated what was needed the moment that the gryphon began to speak in Hardornen.

He walked forward with grace that could only be trained into someone who began learning the peculiar "dance" of court movement at a very early age. When he reached Darkwind's side, he bowed his head in a slight acknowledgment to Tashiketh. The gryphon in his turn made a deep obeisance to the King, then carefully extracted a packet of folded papers from a pouch at the side of his harness and handed them to Darkwind who in turn gave them to Tremane.

"The land of Iftel sends greetings to Hardorn's new ruler, oh, Tremane, once of the House Imperial," the gryphon said, in his strangely accented Hardornen. "We have been sent by the Assembly of Peoples and He Who Made The Barrier to bear the greetings of our Assembly and our Peoples, and to offer you our personal assistance in current and future difficulties. We are," he added, with a lift of his head, "authorized to assist you in any way."

Elspeth could guess at the thoughts running through Tremane's head at the moment, though he gave no sign of them as he gravely thanked the Ambassador for his greetings and his offer.

He can't take this offer seriously. Likeliest is either that Tashiketh is not aware of what he is actually promising, or that this is a polite custom of Iftel, a standard speech, and the offer is not meant to be anything more than an expression of polite esteem.

That, of course, was only logical. As welcome as the aid of a full wing of gryphons would be, how could an ambassadorial delegation be expected to perform *any* services that did not directly benefit their own land? And certainly there was no reason to believe that such a blank card had been given to King Tremane to fill in as he cared to. He could, conceivably, ask them to do something too dangerous for his own men to try. If they were harmed, he would have to face the consequences, but it made no sense to think that Iftel would be willing to put its citizens in danger.

Of course, Darkwind and I and our entourage are perfectly willing to put ourselves in danger—and do—but that's because we aren't really just envoys, we're representatives of the Alliance and we're performing as Hardorn's military allies as well as our other duties. In a sense, we're a very small military unit as well as ambassadors.

The next thing that *must* be running through Tremane's head as he surveyed the half-circle of twenty-one very *large* gryphons, was where on earth was he going to put them?

He *couldn't* put them in the stable nor in one of the barracks, surely he must see that. The stable simply wasn't suitable, even if her Companion and Darkwind's *dyheli* Brytha were willing to put up with it, and the earth-sheltered barracks buildings would probably give creatures of the air great screaming fits of claustrophobia. She considered the gryphons, their size, and their probable needs. They *would* all fit in the Great Hall; could that drafty barn of a room be made habitable as well as elegant? Each of the several towers of the manor would probably hold four or five gryphons in each of the topmost rooms, which were mostly used as armories and weapon storage for the sentries that were posted there; would the gryphons consent to being split up? If they would, there was at least access to the air from the trapdoors in each of the tower roofs. Fortunately, thanks to the spacious barracks now available, and the fact that a large number of staff persons (mages, Healers, and other auxiliaries) were now housed in the city rather than in the manor itself, the overcrowding that had been making life so difficult in the early days here had been overcome. There *was* room in the manor for the gryphons, at least on a temporary basis. But from Tashiketh's speech, this was intended to be a permanent delegation, and they would need permanent housing.

Tremane made a graceful, rambling speech of welcome, probably while he was trying to think of housing options.

There are still some unused buildings in Shonar. Would the gryphons be willing to be housed in an "embassy" in the city?

But if they did, what would they use for servants? Gryphons required a lot of tending; there were any number of things that they couldn't do for themselves. Lighting fires, for instance; talons were not good at manipulating firestrikers, and feathers were dismayingly flammable. The gryphons of k'Leshya had specially trained *trondi'irn* to see to their health and wellbeing; Treyvan and Hydona had done without such help, officially at least, for several years—but the k'Sheyna *hertasi* had helped them unofficially. What would these gryphons do? Did they even guess that the people of Hardorn and the Empire were unready to host them?

Tremane finally ran out of things to say, and so did Tashiketh. They stood on the cobblestones and looked politely at one another for a moment, and it was Tremane who finally broke the silence.

"Now I must confess that I and my people are simply not prepared for anything other than strictly human ambassadors," he said, in a burst of that un-Imperial frankness that was becoming a welcome characteristic of his. "We were somewhat thrown off-balance when the Alliance sent two nonhumans, the Companion Gwena here, and her collegue the *dyheli* Brytha, who intends to present himself to you later. We were completely unprepared for them, but they were gracious and generous enough to accept the stable as perfectly adequate, though it was scarcely that."

Gwena bowed in graceful acknowledgement of the compliment, and Tashiketh glanced at her curiously, then returned his attention to Tremane.

"To be honest, Ambassador Tashiketh, I do not know what we are going to do for the comfort of you and your entourage," Tremane confessed ruefully. "I can only think of three possibilities, and none of them are ideal. There are four tower rooms that might do, if you'd be willing to split up into groups of four or five?"

At Tashiketh's headshake, he went on doggedly. "Then there is only the Great Hall, or taking a building in the city itself—"

"But that was what we had intended to do, take a building and make of it our permanent Embassy," Tashiketh interrupted gravely. "We have brought with us the hire of the building, of staff. We knew that your resources are stretched, and had no intention of straining them further. If we could just spend a few days here, somewhere, that would be enough, surely. As soon as we have established our own place, we will remove to it."

If Tremane sighed with relief, he was schooled enough not to show it. "We shall be happy to house you in the Great Hall for as long as it takes for you to establish your Embassy," he replied with commendable ease, as out of the corner of her eye, Elspeth saw the young Seneschal breaking away from the rest of the group and pounding at a dead run toward the nearest doorway to put Tremane's intentions into effect. She hid a smile; that was one benefit of having a staff composed entirely of military people. Instead of arguing that something couldn't be done, they ran off and made it happen.

"If you would be so kind, then, I would ask you to send a messenger to some representative of your city, that we might establish ourselves as quickly as possible?" Tashiketh asked, and she thought she caught a sly glint of humor as he added, "And in the meanwhile, perhaps you have someone who would conduct us in a tour? This is the first time I have seen a wholly human city; the differences are apparent even at a distance."

Elspeth tried not to choke, for this was *so* clearly a diplomatic gesture to ensure that Tremane's people had time to get suitable quarters for the gryphons ready! Tashiketh and his wing must be exhausted and were probably also ravenous; to ask for a tour under those conditions bespoke a consummate diplomat. *:Volunteer to give him the tour yourself; I'll go help advise Tremane's people on the care and feeding of gryphons,:* she quickly told Darkwind, who smoothly volunteered his services as soon as she made the suggestion.

The Iftel delegation and their reception committee quickly broke into three groups; one of humans, one of mixed humans and gryphons, and one of gryphons only. Tashiketh, Darkwind, and an escort of amused Valdemaran Guards and two solemn and militant gryphons went off for a brief tour of the grounds as built and fortified by Tremane's people. The rest of the gryphons stationed themselves in the courtyard like a group of sober and businesslike young Guard-trainees to wait for their leader's return. Gwena returned to the stable by herself, as Elspeth went with Tremane and his people, and volunteered her expertise as soon as they were out of gryphonic earshot.

Within a relatively short period of time, the Great Hall had been stripped of the trappings of power and refurbished as temporary housing for twenty-one gryphons. This turned out to be a great deal easier than she had thought it would. Remembering what Treyvan and Hydona had done, Elspeth and the Supply Sergeant went over the lists of surplus and stores, until they found enough equipment to make the gryphons reasonably comfortable, then she commanded a squad of sturdy fighters in carrying out every bit of furniture. Stage curtains and painted backdrops were sent for, to help keep the chill of the stone walls at bay, and a rainbow of rugs brought in to soften floors. Every featherbed that could be spared was brought in once the rugs were down and the draperies up, until there were twenty-one good "nests" covered with as many thick blankets and throws as a gryphon could want. Twenty of the nests were arranged along the walls, with the twenty-first up on the dais, and hastily-rigged curtains put up that could partition off that part of the room to make an individual chamber. As privacy, it wasn't much, but at least it was a good gesture in that direction, and if Tashiketh preferred to keep the curtains open, he could.

The largest soup kettles available were brought and filled with fresh water for drinking, with large, deep soup bowls arranged on a table beside the kettles in case these gryphons preferred to drink from a small vessel rather than plunge their prodigious beaks into a larger one. That took care of drink, and Elspeth advised the cook what kinds of raw meat, fowl, and fish best suited their new guests. The room looked quite odd by the time they were done, but strangely, not at all shabby. There was a curious sort of harmony in the painted canvas scenery backdrops, separated by velvet stage curtains, covering the walls, and between the bewildering variety of rugs, blankets, and throws covering the floor and the nests, the end effect was something like being inside an extremely luxurious tent.

:We're ready,: she told Darkwind, as the last of the carpenters cleared their ladders and equipment out, and the first of the kitchen staff began arriving with whole sides of beef and baskets of fish.

:That's good, because I'm running out of things to show them, and I doubt they're going to be able to express even polite interest in warehouses and latrines.: Darkwind sounded distinctly amused, and Elspeth had the feeling that Tashiketh was proving to be quite good company.

She cleared out herself, leaving the young Seneschal to do the honors on behalf of Tremane, and decided that she had best report what she had so cavalierly ordered to the King himself.

But someone had already gone to fetch him, for he met her at the door, with his escort and hers in tow.

He surveyed the transformed room with some surprise and a great deal of relief. "Bless you, Herald Elspeth," he said with feeling. "I'd have had my carpenters trying to cobble up gigantic cages or floor perches, or something of the sort—which wouldn't have been a disaster, but it would have delayed things while Tashiketh explained what they really needed. Will this be warm enough, though?" he added, looking at the hangings with a slight frown of uncertainty. "This place is notoriously drafty."

"It will do," she replied. "Their feathers keep them as warm as our winter cloaks do, and they really only need to stay out of extreme cold and drafts. The hangings will block the drafts well enough, and they *can* wrap themselves in rugs and blankets to sleep. Add charcoal braziers carefully tended, and they should be fine. They'll need one of your Healers—a good, brave person, who will find them a challenge and not something to be afraid of—and about four servants to run errands, watch the braziers, and fetch things at all times."

"A Healer?" Tremane asked with surprise, signaling to one of his aides. "Why a Healer? They look healthy enough to me."

"Gryphons have peculiar strengths and weaknesses; the ones I know always try to have a specially trained helper around them to keep them healthy," she explained. "A Healer is the closest we have to that, and I expect that Tashiketh will be willing to explain their needs." She coughed, hiding her expression behind her hand. "The hardest part will be finding a Healer and a handful of servants brave enough to come tend to 'boggles.'"

But it was Tremane's turn to smile knowingly. "Not as hard as you might think, Elspeth of Valdemar," he said lightly. "We of the Empire are made of sterner stuff than that."

And so it proved; Tremane had not one, but *two* Healers eager to have access to the gryphons, and there was no problem in getting volunteers from the ranks for the light duty of acting as servants to the Ambassador and his entourage. As soon as Tashiketh and his corps had been installed, pronounced themselves "delighted," and dined, they had their Healer and their servants waiting for orders.

Tashiketh had displayed surprise when he saw the quarters, if an onlooker knew what to look for; he had shown more surprise and pleasure at the quality of the hospitality. He dismissed the would-be *trondi'irn* and three of the four servers as soon as he and the others had eaten, with thanks and the information that they all needed to rest after their journey. He asked the fourth server to stay, to watch the braziers, and in case any of them required something after they retired, which the man was not at all loath to do. The other three made themselves comfortable in a niche in the hall close by, and got out the inevitable dice.

"Are they going to sleep, really?" Tremane asked Darkwind as the King and his small entourage left the gryphons to their privacy.

"Probably so," the Hawkbrother replied. "Even given that they flew here in order to reach us, that was a tremendous distance they covered in a very short time. Judging by the amount they ate, they're going to sleep the sleep of the sated until well past sunrise tomorrow."

Tremane ran his hand over the top of his balding head, looking, at the moment, nothing like a King. "I thought that having earth-sense dropped on me was confusing," he said slowly, looking honestly bewildered. "They're huge and like nothing I've ever been near before. *Now* what do I do? How do I treat them?"

"You have dinner with Elspeth and me, and you simply accept them as any other foreign ambassadors," Darkwind advised. "This is a great honor, yes. It is also the first time Iftel has sent out representatives who were not human. This can't be any easier for them than it is for you. You may not be used to having gryphons as ambassadors, but *they* aren't used to being ambassadors in the first place."

Tremane looked at him oddly for a moment, then began to laugh. And if there was a faint edge of hysteria to his laughter, Elspeth couldn't blame him.

Tremane's men trampled their way purposefully through the snow, hauling burdens, readying sledges and animals, shouldering packs and weapons. Darkwind guided Tashiketh and his ever-present gryphon-guards through the gates and toward the worst of the congestion, stopping often to allow someone with a more urgent task to get past them.

"What is all this excitement concerning?" Tashiketh asked, watching the activity swirling around them with curiosity brimming over in his large golden eyes.

"I was about to explain it to you," Darkwind replied, quickly stepping out of the way of a man burdened with an entire bundle of spear shafts. "We had a very unexpected and unpleasant message last night."

"Ah! Now I regret vacating our palace quarters so soon!" the gryphon said brightly. Tashiketh and his own entourage had established themselves within two days of their arrival in an old inn very near the manor, cheerfully vacated by the owner at the sight of the odd, octagonal gold coins offered for its purchase by the treasurer for the gryphons. They had chosen the inn because of its large rooms on the second floor, each of which had its own balcony, and several of the staff were quite willing to stay on and serve such relatively undemanding masters. Now Tashiketh and his escort of two moved between the inn and the manor every day, taking part in daily Court and Council sessions, showing extreme interest in everything Tremane did. So far, they had neither interfered in the business of Hardorn nor done anything other than tender an opinion when asked for one. It was Darkwind's thought that they were acting in very similar fashion to the way that Treyvan and Hydona had behaved when they first came to k'Leshya Vale—willing to offer advice, but making no move to push in where they might not be wanted.

But the cause of this particular uproar had occurred very near midnight, long after the gryphons had retired for the night. The gryphons Darkwind knew did not find it necessary to be purely daylight creatures, but Tashiketh and his group had not been trained from their youth to be explorers and navigators of the unknown, and their experiences here were probably wearing them down. Between the cold and their strange surroundings, they felt much more comfortable taking to their own, warm quarters after dark, and not stirring out until daylight. So when the messenger pounded in on an exhausted horse last night, reporting that one of Tremane's newly-sworn liegemen was under attack by one of his neighbors, the gryphons were blissfully asleep. In the excitement, no one had bothered to wake them or even send them a message, and by the time anyone thought of doing so, it was already daylight and Darkwind was on his way to the gates to escort Tashiketh inside.

There was nothing in the simple attack of one set of humans upon another that would have alerted Tremane through the earth-sense, so the attack came as a complete surprise. A substantial amount of last night had been devoted to planning a defense, and with dawn the men in the chosen barracks were roused, briefed, and moving by the time Tashiketh appeared at the gates.

Darkwind, who met the gryphons here every morning, explained the situation to him. Tashiketh stopped, just out of the way of traffic, and stared at him in perplexity.

"But it will be very difficult to fight in this season, will it not?" he asked, very slowly. "And with the possibility of the mage-storms resuming soon, that could make it more difficult yet."

Darkwind nodded. "How could it not be?" he replied. "But if King Tremane does not come to the aid of this liegeman, then every other bandit who thinks to make himself King in place of Tremane will think himself free to do what he wills."

"But why did Tremane not call upon us?" Tashiketh asked, with a surprised and even injured expression. "Did we not offer to be of all assistance to him? And would his enemies not find the sight of a gryphon wing descending upon them enough to terrify them into submission? Why, look how frightened his own people were when they *knew* that we were coming—how much more so must his enemies be?"

Now it was Darkwind's turn to stop in his tracks and stare at Tashiketh with shock and incredulity. "But you are ambassadors!"

"We are *allies*," Tashiketh replied firmly. "Even as you, Brother-to-Hawks. I am not only the Ambassador, I am the leader of this force, which members have drilled and trained together. Is it not preferable to quell disturbance with the application of a small force, rather than to wait and meet war with a greater one?" He clicked his beak and then gryph-grinned, in the way that Darkwind was so familiar with in Treyvan. "Besides, we are bored. It will be good to show our fighting prowess. It is what we are born, bred, and trained for."

"I thought that there was no fighting in Iftel," Darkwind blurted, as activity swirled all around them. "I thought that your Border prevented any such thing!"

Now Tashiketh sobered. "Simply because we do not make war on other nations, nor permit those nations to make war upon us, that does not mean that we do not prepare ourselves for war or for the day when the Barrier might fail us. I cannot tell you how long we have trained..." He shook his head "All my life, all the life of my father, and his, and his, and so far back I cannot begin to count the years. We have always trained and contested, and will always train and contest. And when the need is there, we fight."

Then he roused up his feathers, and moved so quickly that Darkwind was left behind, completely unprepared. "Come!" he shouted. "We go to this King, and we tell him in a way that will make him believe!"

As Darkwind knew, even when on the ground, gryphons could move very quickly when they chose. He was left behind as Tashiketh and his escort charged into the manor, bent on offering themselves as potential victims on Tremane's altar. And he was afraid, terribly afraid, that Tremane would accept them.

But when he reached the council chamber, he found that although Tremane *had* accepted their offer, it was with conditions—and reservations.

"Tell the men to stand down," he was ordering as Darkwind entered. "I'll try Tashiketh's way, but—*but*—" he said, turning to the exultant gryphon and raising his voice. "You, sir, will obey the orders of your commander, that is, *me*, and you will make the preparations that I tell you to and adhere to the conditions that I set."

Darkwind could hardly believe the transformation that a few moments had made in the dignified gryphon. Tashiketh and his two escorts were wildly excited, hackles and ear-tufts up, eyes flashing as their pupils expanded and contracted rapidly, their talons flexing against the wooden floor and leaving gouges that would be the despair of Tremane's housekeepers. These were no longer the strange ambassadors of an even stranger culture, these were warriors, and he wondered how they had kept their nature hidden beneath those serene exteriors.

"We have the time, if you and your wing are determined to fly a warning against these people, to *take* the precaution that is needed to prepare you," Tremane said sternly, every inch the commander. And now Darkwind wondered at the transformation in the King as well. Here and now, there was no uncertainty, no hesitation. *This* was the Imperial Commander, a man who knew both planned warfare and scrimmage fighting, the man who had been entrusted with the conquest of Hardorn. "There is time enough for you to see what maps we have of the area and speak with those of Shonar who have relatives in the contested area. I would have you see my armorer, so that he can make you breast- and side-plates to protect you from arrows, and helmets to defend you from slung shot, if there were time enough." Tashiketh opened his beak to protest, and Tremane swiftly overruled him. "Not a word, sir! *I* am your commander, *I* have been fighting these people, as you have not, *I* know what they can and cannot do, and *I* will decree the terms under which you will fight. I will not dictate your tactics, sir, for that is your purview, but I can and will decree what I need for your safety!"

He looked so black and angry that Darkwind thought for a moment that Tashiketh would take offense. But one of the two escorting gryphons muttered something under his breath, and Tashiketh burst into laughter.

"What did he say?" Tremane asked, his anger fading.

"He said, 'What a surprise, to find after all these centuries, a commander who is more concerned with saving our blood than spending it!' And he is right." Tashiketh bent his head in submission to Tremane's will. "We will follow the wishes of the commander who does not waste anything. I'll send Shyrestral to bring the rest, and we will see your maps and plans rather than improvising solely upon what we find there."

In so short a time that Darkwind was astonished, the gryphons were lined up in three ranks for a none-too-hasty briefing. Only one somewhat bewildered man, who had only visited the place once, could be found to tell the gryphons about the lay of the land in that area. He found himself overwhelmed by the gryphons' relentless questioning over details of the region's wind currents.

On the fourth day after the messenger had arrived, the gryphon wing flew off to confront the enemy, and Darkwind and everyone else watched them fly off with mingled hope and dread. The gryphons seemed full of confidence and good humor; they might have been going off on a pleasure jaunt.

Except that their behavior showed Darkwind very clearly that their hunting and killing instincts were roused. When they were not moving, they were intensely alert, heads up, eyes taking in everything, bodies poised. When they moved, it was with bewildering swiftness and utter sureness, as deadly and beautiful as the dance of warrior and sword. They took no notice of the snow beneath their claws, of the cold breeze; their eyes were on the blinding blue sky, and they could not wait to be up and out. When they took to the air, they leapt up, catching the shivering wind in their talons and conquering it.

"You're sure they will have a chance?" Tremane asked, as the wing vanished into the blue distance. "I keep feeling as if I'm sending them to their doom."

"Gryphons were originally created as fighters," Darkwind replied slowly. "Very versatile ones. It's in their blood, and a millennium or two isn't going to change that."

"They may have been created as fighters, but are they trained?" Tremane said, his voice sounding strained. "I know what my men can do—but these creatures? Granted, their opponents aren't as well-equipped or skilled as my men, yet it only takes a single well-aimed arrow to kill someone. And you tell me that Iftel has kept war away from her borders for as long as the Valdemarans have known them. How can they be ready for this? Surely—"

"Forgive me for interrupting you, but has Tashiketh told you how his twenty wingmen were chosen?" Darkwind replied, before Tremane could voice much more in the way of anxiety.

The King shook his head.

"I thought not. Let's go inside where it's warm," Darkwind told him, as the sharp wind cut through the seams of his coat and chilled him. He shivered involuntarily and stamped his numbing feet to warm them. "I believe I'm about to surprise you."

The group retired to Tremane's study; several of his other staff members, who had overheard the exchange, had managed to tag along. The gryphons had excited a great deal of interest among the Imperials and Hardornens alike, and Darkwind didn't at all mind assuaging some of their curiosity. It was a close fit for all of them, but Tremane gave no hint that he wanted any of them to leave.

"I've managed to learn a bit about the way things are done in Iftel, at least as far as the gryphons are concerned," Darkwind told the group, once they were all settled in a circle of chairs, Tremane's only a little larger and more elaborate than the rest. "It's not the peaceful paradise you and I might have imagined."

"Oh?" Elspeth said. "But they won't even let the Mercenary's Guild establish a Guildhall there!"

Darkwind could only shake his head. "I don't know of their origin, but because of what I have learned from Tayledras history and some Kaled'a'in information, I have a few guesses. Tashiketh either doesn't know the answers, or has been ordered to pretend that he doesn't, so this is speculation."

Tremane uttered a scornful little cough. "Darkwind, at times your insistence on hedging is maddening. *Tell* us! Don't keep saying it's only your opinion."

Darkwind chuckled, not at all offended. "Certainly. I think that the citizens of Iftel are descended from some of the forces that were cut off when the Mage of Silence's stronghold was overrun. There were gryphon-wings with several of the armies, and since female gryphons by and large are a bit larger and heavier than the males, females always fought alongside males, often their mates, so there would have been a breeding population."

"You mean some of these gryphons are female?" one of the generals blurted, looking completely taken aback.

Darkwind laughed. "You didn't even look between their haunches, eh? Yes, some are female. Probably half; males also spend as much time tending the young as females, since they feed their young the way young hawks are fed." He raised an eyebrow at the general's stunned expression. "Oh, come now—you didn't think anything with a beak like that could suckle milk, did you? *I* wouldn't want to see the result if one tried!"

The general winced, and Tremane himself made an expression of sympathetic pain.

"As for the concept of females being poor fighters, I would not venture that opinion around Herald Captain Kerowyn of the Skybolts if I were you," Elspeth added crisply. "She is likely to invite you to have a practice session with a few of her ladies—or worse, with her!"

Darkwind watched the general in question as he took a second and third glance at Elspeth, finally *saw* the calluses and muscles, and realized that Elspeth was not the pampered princess he had thought. "So much for physiology; I am assuming that they *must* have come from Urtho's people, because gryphons are created creatures, and I can't imagine where else they could have originated. We know from Kaled'a'in stories that some of Urtho's people were cut off from their own forces—they knew what was going to happen when the enemy overran the last stronghold," Darkwind continued. "I guess that they threw up hasty Gates—Portals, to you—and just tried to get as far away as possible. They succeeded, and ended up in fairly hostile country and then the Cataclysm happened and the Storms began. At some point, *something* put up the Barrier; Tashiketh isn't being very forthcoming about that either. The problem with putting a wall around you, though, is that it walls you in as well as other people out. So, in order to keep from killing each other or losing such self-defensive abilities altogether, the Peoples of Iftel organized their aggressions."

Tremane looked troubled. "Organized? How?"

Darkwind sighed, for he was of two minds about what he had learned. He understood *why*, and sympathized, but he wasn't happy about *what* they had chosen to do. "Games, but games that verge on being blood-sport. If Tashiketh is telling the truth, no one *has* to participate, but in the highest and most competitive levels, there is real possibility of serious injury and even death. Serious wargames; Tashiketh says that in his part of Iftel there are several deaths among participants in every round of competition. That was how his wing was formed; every single one of these gryphons is the winner of contests in his district that pitted him against opponents of his own and other races, coming at him singly and in a group, and using weapons that were merely *blunted*, not rendered harmless."

Tremane blinked. "Oh, he said, thoughtfully. "Interesting. They aren't as inexperienced as I assumed."

"That isn't all, of course," Darkwind went on. "Each preliminary winner was required to participate in intellectual contests as well; what those were, I don't know for certain, but they probably included memory tests and logic puzzles. Tashiketh was the overall winner of everything. And the reason that the delegation is made up entirely of gryphons is that only gryphons would have been able to get here before the Storms started again. Now you know the gist of everything that I have learned or guessed."

Tremane and the others seemed somewhat taken aback by the fact that the right to be an ambassador had been determined by a series of often-deathly-violent contests, but Darkwind privately thought that was a more logical means of choosing someone for an important post than some other methods he had heard of from supposedly "civilized" lands. Picking someone to whom you owed a favor, or someone whose family was important, or worst of all, giving the job to whoever paid the most for the honor—all those were recipes for sheer disaster, and whoever used such means probably got the disasters he deserved. Granted, most ambassadors didn't have to compete in highly dangerous war games, but then, most ambassadors weren't also authorized to participate in their allies' real conflicts, either. He just wished that the contests weren't so lethal.

"Are *you* confident in their ability as a fighting unit?" Tremane asked him bluntly. Darkwind nodded.

"I know *my* gryphons, and I know that these are well-trained," he replied. "I also know they aren't stupid. I don't think they would have been nearly so eager to volunteer if they thought your opponents had working magic."

"Ah!" Tremane exclaimed, and chuckled. "I see. They don't expect to come within range of a normal distance-weapon, is that it?"

"Probably not; *they* can stay out of range of arrows and drop large, heavy objects down on the enemy." Another of the generals started to chuckle, as if he found the idea vastly amusing. "Or spears, or firepots—"

"Or any number of things that are inconvenient when crashing through one's roof," Elspeth interrupted, before the good gentleman could wax eloquent. "But telling you that they were going to do *that* would not have sounded nearly as heroic as they wanted to appear."

"So, we will let them believe that we are still cherishing the illusion that they flew off to battle talon-to-sword with our foes," Tremane said firmly. "If they *choose* to tell us what their tactics are, we will then praise their cleverness. Otherwise, we will be effusive in our praises of their bravery. In either case, they will succeed in making it clear to troublemakers that *we* have a formidable ally that they do not; they will accomplish what they set out to do, which is to win this single scrimmage, and that may be all we need. I would rather have a bloodless victory than any other kind."

"I've taken the liberty of ordering a congratulatory feast of wild game, sir," the Seneschal said diffidently. "I was afraid that if we left it too long, we would never get the meat thawed in time."

Tremane nodded his agreement absently, which relieved the poor lad, who was still afraid to order anything on his own that might have a serious impact later. In this case, ordering a feast *might* lead to a shortage later. Darkwind privately doubted that, having seen the stores of frozen meat himself, but it was a possibility. Perhaps more than a possibility, when he recalled the sheer mass of food that Treyvan and Hydona could put away without hesitation. But now that Tremane had given his approval, the young Seneschal clearly felt much easier in his mind.

I do miss Treyvan and Hydona, and their two little feathered fighters. I miss tumbling and playing with the little ones, and feeling Hydona preen my hair, and watching Vree dive after Treyvan's crest-feathers. And I miss their deep voices, their affection, and advice.

"Now, gentlemen and ladies," Tremane said, his tone turning somber. "Let us consider what we must do if our allies fail."

"It isn't likely, I don't think," Darkwind offered. "A single gryphon, half-asleep, can defeat a squad of fighters with less effort than it takes to preen. This is a group of twenty-and-one, fully awake and eager!" Several of the attendees laughed, looking quite convinced of that by what they had seen of the creatures. "But you're correct, of course. Preparations should be made for less than total victory."

The rest of the day was spent making plans for just that contingency, but as sunset reddened the skies to the west, the victors came winging home, quite intact, and with the foes' leader's personal banner, a letter of surrender, and a pledge that he would come in person to swear his allegiance, all clutched proudly in Tashiketh's talons.

The cheers that rose to greet them as they replicated their previous graceful landing in the courtyard were prompted as much by relief as by joy in the victory, but they didn't need to know that.

Darkwind assured one and all that a tired gryphon was a starving gryphon, and Tashiketh's second-in-command nodded firmly. At the feast, to which the tired gryphons were immediately ushered, Tashiketh formally presented the surrender and pledge, and then modestly revealed the secret of their victory.

"First we dropped rocks through their roofs," he said, with a faintly cruel chuckle. "Then we dropped *one* firepot on a thatched outbuilding, and circled in three subwings of seven each. After six passes, we threatened to drop more. That got their attention long enough for us to claim that we were a mere fraction of the winged army that King Tremane could command if he chose. And I hinted that we weren't too particular about waiting for provisions to arrive in a case like that, and were inclined to help ourselves. The idea of *hundreds* of us descending out of the sky, smashing big holes in every roof, setting fire to things, and snatching and carrying off who-knew-what to eat, had them in a panic. If that idiot leading them hadn't surrendered on the spot, I think they might have killed him and served him to us on a platter with a good broth on the side!"

Several of the generals laughed heartily at this, and even Tremane smiled. Darkwind thought it best to interject a cautionary note.

"It won't do to make them think you're going to carry off children for snacks," he warned Tashiketh under cover of the laughter. "How could they trust a King who'd let his 'monsters' feed on children?"

"No fear of that," Tashiketh soothed. "I made sure we were eying the sheep when I said that, and added a bit about how tasty fresh, fat mutton was, and allowed as how we could decimate their every flock and herd in a matter of days and just feel stronger for being so well fed. For a people on the edge of starvation, accepting surrender in place of that sounds very appealing. Our rules of combat have always stressed that we're not to intimate that we eat thinking beings. We might not have done this in earnest before, but we've had plenty of training."

"Good." Darkwind relaxed enough to chuckle. "I wish I'd seen their faces when you told them that you were only the vanguard. And of course, *they* would never know when you were bluffing."

"It wasn't all bluff," Tashiketh said smugly, then suddenly took an extreme interest in his food, as if he realized that he had said too much.

Well. Well! Darkwind took an interest in his own meal, as if unaware that Tashiketh had let fall something important. *So Iftel has more interest in Tremane's welfare than I thought. Enough that they would back him with a significant force? It certainly sounds that way.*

If they would send an army to help him, what else would they be willing to offer? The secret of the Barrier? Other secrets?

And how much of that would be of any use against the coming Storms, especially the Final Storm?

Or would so little be left after that last blow that none of this would matter?

"You could not possibly have conceived of anything more likely to have turned you into the Army's favorites," Elspeth told Tashiketh, as a roar went up from the watching crowd. Five of Tashiketh's subordinates climbed, crawled, flew, leaped, and contorted themselves across a torturous obstacle course under the bright noontime sun. It was cold enough to numb feet encased in boots and several layers of stockings, but that hadn't prevented the now-usual crowd from showing up as soon as the contest began. Typically, the former Imperial soldiers had gathered to watch, cheer—and then bet on the outcome. This was probably the most exciting entertainment in the entire country about now.

There was not a great deal in the way of entertainment in Shonar, in spite of the presence of the King here; every time the one and only Bard in the town composed a new song, the tavern where he played was crowded to capacity for days, and the soldiers did their best to enliven otherwise dull days and nights with mixed results. One of the highest-priced items to be had among the soldiery was a deck of cards. But now there was a new and novel source of spectacle in their midst, one with all the finest attributes of a fair, a race, and a real contest. Since Tashiketh never participated except to practice alone, the outcome of any given competition was always subject to the whims of chance, which made it perfect for wagering. That in turn made it more attractive yet, if that was possible.

"Would it harm me in your esteem if I confessed that this was a deliberate choice, making our contests public affairs?" Tashiketh asked Elspeth, gravely.

"Hardly. I would simply congratulate you on your intelligence," she replied promptly. "The only question I have is why stage these obstacle things at all? There are other ways of keeping you all in fighting trim."

"Because we must. Our hierarchy changes as the results of the contests change, and as our own ranking changes, so will the rankings of our various counties. And *that*, at year's end, will decree where discretionary tax funds are spent." Just as he made that surprising assertion, Tremane joined them, relatively anonymous in a plain brown soldier's cloak with the hood pulled up against the bite of the cold wind. Tashiketh did not turn his head or appear to notice, but a few moments later, he addressed the King directly.

"So, King of Hardorn, I am given to understand that you are exceedingly curious about my people. I finally have leave to answer your questions, for you have proven yourself to be an honorable ally and worthy to hear the full tale of our land." Now Tashiketh moved his head to gaze into Tremane's astonished face with mild eyes. "Ask," he said. "The time for secrets is past."

Whatever Tremane's faults, an inability to think quickly was not one of them. "Darkwind k'Sheyna believes that your people were descended from one part of the armies of the mage his people served, specifically the one called Urtho," he said. "Are you?"

Tashiketh laughed, a deep rumble that came from somewhere down in the bottom of his chest, and he roused his fathers with a shake. "Yes. The shortest version of the tale is this. Our several Peoples were all serving the Third Army. Urtho made it his policy to group all the folk of a particular land into one Army, rather than dividing all of them amongst his Armies. However, the humans of the Third, serving a God who decreed that those who had magic power should be His priests, had no mages of their own. They had no prejudice against working with those of other faiths, and so had a group of mages assigned to them, mages who had nothing whatsoever in common with them, not even nationality. Also attached to the Third were a wing of gryphons with their *trondi'irn*, a pack of *kyree*, a surge of *ratha*, a knot of *tyrill*, and a charge of *dyheli*."

What am I hearing? Tyrill? Ratha? *How did they get into this story?*

"And these are your Peoples of Iftel?" Tremane asked.

"What is a *ratha*?" Darkwind asked, at the same moment.

Tashiketh wasn't the least perturbed by being bombarded with questions. "These are our Peoples, yes. *Ratha* are from the far north, and are to the mountain cats what *kyree* are to wolves. *Tyrill* I think you know already, Brother-To-Hawks."

"Only by legend," Darkwind replied, feeling a bit dazed. "They were one of Urtho's last creations, a larger race of *hertasi*, and there weren't many of them."

"But, oh, they breed with such enthusiasm!" Tashiketh laughed, tossing his head so that the freshening wind ruffled his feathers. Behind him, another cheer rose (together with some groans) as one of the other gryphons did something clever. "They learned it from us gryphons. There are plenty of them now! Well, to make this as brief as possible, the Third, whose emblem I wear, was cut off from Ka'venusho at the time of retreat. They chose to Gate to the remotest place the mages could think of, hoping they would be beyond the reach of Ma'ar and the destruction that would ensue when Urtho's Tower was destroyed by its master. But there was a problem."

"Not enough power," Tremane guessed shrewdly.

"Nowhere safe to go?" asked Elspeth.

"No Adepts," hazarded Darkwind.

"A little of all three," the Ambassador explained. "Their Priests— the humans—had remained behind in their own land to protect their people. The only Adept with them strong enough to raise a far-away Gate was someone who, at the time, was thought to be a barbarian shaman from the far north. They had to go to the remotest place *he* knew of—his home, not the gryphons' home, nor that of their human charges, not anywhere near it. There wasn't much choice; they took the escape that was offered, ending in the north of what is now Iftel. They thought to wait out the destruction, then be reunited with the others. But no sooner had they all gotten across, than something terrible happened, worse by far than anything they had expected."

"The Cataclysm," Darkwind said aloud. "The Tower *and* Ma'ar's stronghold destroyed, and the interaction of the double release of terrible forces."

"And needless to say, they did not know the cause for many years. They only knew that things were impossible, that there would be no way to find their friends and fellows, that there would be no way for the humans of the Third to find *their* way home. And almost as bad, it soon became obvious that they had not gone far enough; they ran into a fresh Army of Ma'ar's." Tashiketh shook his head. "It must have seemed as if they had come to the end of the world, that everything evil had won against them, and was about to annihilate them. Battered by the mage-storms that followed, on the verge of attack by superior forces, and unable because of the high number of wounded to travel to someplace where they might escape the worst of the effects, they did the only thing they had left to do. The humans prayed to their god, Vykaendys—"

That name struck Darkwind like a blow to the head. "*Who?*" Darkwind blurted, as Elspeth's eyes widened.

"Vykaendys," the Ambassador repeated. "The Holy Sun, from whom all life—"

Elspeth interrupted. "Ambassador Tashiketh, do the humans of your land use a different language from the gryphons?"

The huge gryphon nodded. "The sacred language is different," he replied. "The shared language is a combination of several tongues, and Old Gryphon is very like that tongue you spoke to me when first we met. Do I take it you wish to hear something of the Sacred Tongue of Vykaendys?"

"Please," said Elspeth and Darkwind together.

Tashiketh rattled off a few sentences, and Darkwind looked to Elspeth, who had a better command of languages than he did.

She listened very closely, as her eyes widened further until the whites showed all around. "I'm not a linguist," she said when he has finished, "but I would say that this is to Karsite what the Iftel gryphon tongue is to Kaled'a'in."

Darkwind whistled. *:No wonder Altra kept insisting that the Border would only recognize himself, Karal, Ulrich, or Solaris! The God of Iftel and the God of Karse are one and the same! Isn't that going to put a Firecat among the pigeons?:*

Gwena chose that moment to add her own observation. *:Oh, this is interesting indeed. Solaris doesn't know this, but Altra does. I wonder why and why he hadn't told her?:*

"They prayed for protection, right?" Elspeth asked the Ambassador. "And the god established the Border to keep their enemies out?"

"Precisely," Tashiketh agreed. "And of course Vykaendys did exactly that, answering their prayers. He is the one who ordained that we send our representatives beyond the Border to help as we could with the current crisis. He sent us to Hardorn once He knew that Hardorn again had a King who had been bound to the land. Otherwise, given the gravity of the current situation, we would, of course, have been sent into Valdemar. All creatures must work together to survive the last Storms, but Vykaendys is pleased to welcome the land that lies between the two that He governs, as a brother-country rather than an enemy-state."

Elspeth shook her head. "Of course," she replied.

:I can't help wondering what Solaris is going to make of this when she finds out about it,: Elspeth added to Darkwind. *:Although, in retrospect, it's fascinating, the ways in which gods answered the prayers of their followers—the Star-Eyed creating the Dhorisha Plains for the Shin'a'in who had renounced magic, and granting the Tayledras the power to protect themselves with their magic while they healed the land a bit at a time. And now the Sun Lord, creating a barrier around Iftel—:*

Darkwind wondered if He had done something similar for Karse just to hold through the Cataclysm itself. The Karsites were certainly close enough to the source of the Cataclysm to have needed such protection. *But wait; the Sun-priests are mages. Maybe the Sun-priests are their equivalents of the Tayledras, and Vkandis gave them access to great power to protect themselves the way the Tayledras did.* The greatest dangers after the Cataclysm lay in the monsters that had been created. Could *that* be where and why the Sun-priests got the ability to summon and control demons so effectively? Now *that* was an intriguing thought!

There was no way of knowing without having Karal to ask, and even then it might not be canonical information. But Altra was obviously privy to noncanonical truths, and if he was inclined to share them with nonbelievers—

If he is, we might learn more than we ever wanted to know.

But Elspeth had been thinking further ahead than he. As Tremane asked more detailed questions of Tashiketh, she drew Darkwind and Gwena into a close mind-link.

:What are the odds that we can involve gods in all of this?: she wanted to know. *:Vkandis, Kal'enel, either or both? The power of a god might save us.:*

:Or it might cause a whole lot more trouble than any mage-storm, however powerful,: Darkwind warned. *:We can't know.:*

:But I can ask Florian to ask Altra,: Gwena said. *:And perhaps he can ask An'desha as well.:*

Darkwind shook his head doubtfully. *:Don't count on any real help,:* he told them. *:The Star-Eyed is disinclined to interfere, Vkandis may be fundamentally the same. They may be able to help us only after the disaster strikes, and be unable to do anything to prevent it from coming—because we have that power, if only we make the correct choices, and They will not take that right to choose from us.:*

Gwena nodded mentally, but Elspeth's mind-voice seethed with frustration. *:But how can we make the right choices if we don't know what they are?:* she fumed.

:If we knew what to do, then they wouldn't be choices, they would be plans,: Darkwind chided gently.

He didn't blame her, and he didn't have the heart to tell her that the "right" choice, from the point of view of a god, might not be the one that prevented a second Cataclysm. Gods tended to take a much longer view of things than mere mortals, and what they considered to be good in the long run might be pretty horrible for those who had to live through it.

I'm sure that Baron Valdemar's people heartily wished him to the bottom of the Salten Sea during that first winter in the wilderness, he thought soberly. *And certainly it was terrible for the last Herald-Mages of Vanyel's time to be the last of their kind. But in the long run, those were good things for most of the people of Valdemar.*

This was probably not the time to point this out to her, however.

:All we can do is what we've always done,: he told her with utmost sincerity. *:We must do our best. Then, even if things turn out badly, we will know it was not from any lack of trying on our part.:*

She sighed. *:I do wish you weren't right so often,:* she said forlornly. *:I rather enjoyed being able to rail against Fate and the Unfairness Of It All.:* But she pulled herself a bit straighter and nodded. *:Whatever happens, we'll survive it, and we'll build on what's left.:* She glanced around, and her mouth twisted wryly. :*All our peoples do seem to be rather good at that.*:

He squeezed her hand in agreement. :*And we will do it together,* ashke.: He could not help thinking about the group at the center of Dhorisha, picking through the remains of the Tower, without experiencing a feeling of chill. Whatever happened—yes, he, Elspeth, and the others here would probably survive it.

But what of his friends in the Tower? Would *they*?

As he turned his attention back to the conversation at hand, his stomach gave a sudden lurch, his eyes unfocused for a moment, and he felt very much as if the ground had dropped out from underneath him. Then the world steadied again, but as he looked from Tremane to Elspeth and back, and saw the same startled look in both their eyes turn to sick recognition, he knew what had just hit him.

The mage-storms had begun again. Hints of their building power were beginning to overcome the Counter-Storm. They were not strong enough yet to cause any problems, but it was only a matter of time.

Darkwind understood.

This was the first sign of the coming Final Storm, and their respite before it struck would be measured in, at best, weeks. Their survival was in doubt, and even if they did survive, whether they would prosper afterward was in deep question. There were hundreds of variables, and just as many major decisions. There were key uses of power and defense, solving of mysteries and understanding of connections. Like each segment in a spiderweb, the failure of any of those elements could collapse it all, and cost every one involved—everything.

9

"What is wrong with your friend Firesong?" Lyam asked Karal in a whisper, as Firesong went off to a remote corner of the Tower to brood—or as he called it, "meditate"—for the second time that day. "The others are all working together over the notes for the cube-maze, but he keeps going off by himself, he says to think. Is that usual for him? Is he ill, do you think? Or have the frustrations begun to weigh upon his soul?"

"I'm not sure," Karal replied, although this behavior of Firesong's wasn't particularly news to him. Living together as closely as they all were, it wasn't possible for any of them to deviate from normal behavior without the others noticing. And Firesong was certainly acting oddly—

though not with that selfish oddness that made him so dangerous before.

There were several signs that this bout of solitary brooding was far different than the last. For one thing, Aya kept cuddling close to him, tucking his head up under Firesong's chin while Firesong held him and scratched gently under his wings, and it had been Aya's avoidance of his bondmate that had been one sign that his temper and thoughts were tending in dangerous directions. He wasn't tinkering with odd magics either; he was sitting in out-of-the-way corners, staring into space, as if Firesong sought the privacy in his mind that he could not get in the Tower. But those bursts of "meditation" always seemed to end in a sharp and thoughtful glance at Karal, and given some of the past difficulties between them, that didn't make Karal feel entirely easy about his possible thoughts.

"Huh," Lyam said, and scratched the top of his head with a stubby, ink-stained talon. "Well, he doesn't seem to be getting much done, and he's giving me collywobbles with the way he just sits and stares. If he's gotten into a blue funk, maybe one of you ought to shake him out of it."

Karal made a face. "I'm not sure any of us want to *shake* Firesong out of anything, but I suppose it can't hurt if I talk to him. If there's a problem, maybe Silverfox could help him with it, or something. Or maybe it's a problem he doesn't want to get Silverfox involved with, and maybe I could help him." He made a face. "After all, I'm supposed to be a priest, and that's the sort of thing that priests are supposed to do, right?"

Having said that, he knew he had talked himself into the position where he was going to have to do something about the situation. Lyam nodded encouragingly to him at that last statement, so before he could find a reason to put it off, he got to his feet and trailed off after Firesong.

Altra invited himself along, sauntering casually at Karal's heels. As Karal glanced inquisitively down at him, Altra blinked guileless blue eyes at him. *:I thought I'd come along, too, just in case you needed me,:* the Firecat said idly. Karal did not ask "for what?" since he knew the answer already. There wasn't a great deal that Altra couldn't shield him against, if Firesong turned angry or dangerous, or both.

He found the Adept in the chamber containing one of the mysterious contrivances (one made of wire, odd plates of some sparkling material, and gemstones) that looked far too delicate to warrant the label of "weapon." Aya was with him, cuddling inside his jacket. Aya's long tail trailed comically down from beneath the hem, as if the cascade of feathers belonged to Firesong. The Adept stared at the softly glowing stones with an intense look on his face. He turned to face the entrance when he heard Karal's deliberate footstep, but he did not seem particularly surprised to see the Karsite.

Karal approached him gingerly, but there was nothing in Firesong's slight smile to indicate anything other than welcome. As he edged around the wire-sculpture weapon, Karal tried to think of a lateral approach to the subject, and failed to come up with a good one. So he decided to go straight to the heart of the matter, and make no attempt at being clever.

"You've been wandering off by yourself for the last couple of days, and we're a little concerned about you," he said bluntly. "It didn't seem right to go behind your back and pester Silverfox to see if you were all right, so I decided to ask you directly. Is there anything wrong?"

"Other than everything?" Firesong asked archly. "We *are* in a very precarious position here, you know."

"Well, yes, but——" Karal fumbled. "I mean——"

"There's nothing wrong, or rather, nothing wrong with me, Karal," Firesong interrupted, with a smile for his bondbird, as Aya stuck his head out of the front of the Adept's jacket, saw who it was that Firesong was talking to, and tucked himself back inside. "But I'm glad you came to find out, because I have a few questions that really concern only you. Here, sit." He patted the floor beside him, and Karal lowered himself down warily. "Karal, Karse and Valdemar fought a generations-long war, and I can understand that anyone from Karse might feel very negative about certain figures of Valdemaran history, but you are bright enough to reason things through for yourself and not just take everything you are told in without ever examining it. So, given that, here's a history question: what do you know and what do you think about Herald-mage Vanyel Ashkevron?"

Karal stared at him, a bit confused by the abrupt change of subject, for the initial question Karal had asked about Firesong had nothing whatsoever to do with a figure of ancient history like Vanyel Ashkevron.

But it was a very interesting question, given all of the changes Karal's own life and thoughts had been going through. It might, on the surface, seem like the question had no relevance in any way to the situation in the Tower, but he knew Firesong better than that, and Firesong *had* to have an ultimate purpose in asking it.

"I'm going to have to think aloud, so bear with me," Karal said, finally. "As you probably guessed, according to *our* history, Vanyel

Demonrider was absolutely the epitome of everything that was terrible about Valdemar. Every child in Karse used to be told that if he was bad, Vanyel would come and carry him off. He was a Herald, a rider of a demon-horse, and the implacable enemy of all Karse stood for. He was a mage, which was anathema, of course, and he had the audacity to be a very powerful mage, one who could turn back the demons that the most highly skilled Priest-mages could raise, which made him even worse. And if that wasn't bad enough, it is said by some chroniclers of the time that he could break the compulsions that the Priests put on their demons and send them back against their own summoners, which made him the King of the Demons so far as our people were concerned."

"That's your history," Firesong replied, watching Karal with peculiar intensity. "How do *you* feel about it?"

"I'm getting to that." Karal rubbed the back of his own neck, trying to sort out his thoughts as he loosened tight muscles. "I do think it's supremely ironic that the worst accusations about Vanyel have to do with him riding a demon-horse and being a mage, when our own Priests were mages who summoned demons and controlled them."

Firesong's sardonic smile had a note of approval in it. "No one has ever dared to claim that the causes of warfare and the sources of prejudice are ever rational." He scratched Aya under the chin, and was rewarded by a particularly adorable chirrup. "And religious fervor is often used as an excuse for a great many socially unacceptable behaviors."

"That's religion as an excuse. Sometimes it seems to me that when religious fervor enters the mind, the wits pack up entirely and fly out the ear," Karal replied a bit sourly. "But worst of all is when powerful, ruthless people use the religious fervor of others to further their own greed."

Aya poked his head out of the jacket again, as if he found what Karal was saying very interesting. Altra settled himself at Karal's feet, and there was nothing in the Firecat's demeanor to make Karal think his own religious guide disapproved of anything he had said so far.

"All that is true in my experience," Firesong replied with one of his brilliant, perfect smiles. "Though I'm not *that* much older than you. So, what do you think Vanyel was really like?"

Karal shrugged. "Of course, I am sure that he must be a very great hero to the Valdemarans; the fact that my people considered him to be such an evil enemy would make that a simple conclusion to come to. Given that he was fighting what *I* now know to have been very power-hungry and entirely amoral men, most notably one of the worst Sons of the Sun we ever had in all our history, I suppose that he was only doing his duty to protect *his* people against the rapacious land grabbing of mine. I—cannot say that I like that thought. It fills me with shame, in fact." He paused, and a final thought floated to the surface, one that seemed to define the situation. "I can only say that not even his enemies in Karse ever tried to claim that *he* led any armies over the border into our land, and the same cannot be said of the Karsite commanders. Now, I can't pretend to tell who was right and who was wrong in those areas where both sides claimed to have been attacked first, or were provoked into attacking, or where magic, sabotage, and assassination were allegedly employed, but I can tell that the Valdemarans never took armies into Karse, but my people certainly waged war up into Valdemar."

"Very even-handed," Firesong replied approvingly. "No side is always in the right. Now, we'll change the subject again. I need a religious opinion from you. What do the Sun-priests have to say about ghosts?"

"As in, what?" he asked. "Unquiet dead? Haunts? Spirits who return to guide?"

"All of those," Firesong said, making a general gesture. "Some religions deny that any such manifestations exist, and some religions are written around them as a form of ancestor worship. What does the Writ of Vkandis say?"

"The Writ says very little." He frowned, trying to think of what it *did* say. "Now that I come to think of it, what it *does* say is rather interesting. According to the Writ, no one who is of the Faith, whether the purest soul or the blackest, could possibly become a ghost. Anyone born or brought into the Faith *will* be taken before Vkandis and judged—'sorted' is the word used in the Writ. *And the good shall be sorted from the evil; no spirit shall escape the sorting. The evil will be cast into darkness and great despair, into fear and pain, to repeat their errors until they have learned to love and serve the Light of Vkandis. And the good shall be gathered up into the rich meadows of Heaven, to sing His praises in the everlasting rays, to drink the sweet waters and bask forevermore in the Glory of the Sun.* That's the actual quote. There's a great deal more about who shall become what rank of angelic spirit, and what each kind does, but I have a suspicion that all of that is a clerkly conceit. I've got an earlier version of the Writ that doesn't have any of those lists in it."

"Some people even have to have their afterlife ranked, arranged, and organized," Firesong chuckled. "I hate to say this, but being gathered up to lie in a meadow sunbathing and singing for all eternity is *not* my idea of a perfect afterlife. I should be screamingly bored within the first afternoon."

Karal laughed. "Maybe not for you, but think about the poor shepherds who were the first Prophets, living in the cold, damp hills of Karse, with rain and fog and damn poor grazing most of the time."

"I suppose for them, rich meadows and sun forever would be paradise, wouldn't it?" Firesong raised his eyebrows. "All right, so Karsites can't become ghosts—but what about other people?"

"Well, that's not in the Writ. But there is a tradition that the unblessed dead become the hungry, vengeful ghosts who roam the night. That's why most Karsites won't venture out after dark without a Priest to secure their safety." But Firesong's question had asked about more than mere Karsite tradition, it had been about what Karal himself thought. "As a Priest, I *can* exorcise ghosts, in theory. I'm supposed to be able to send any unblessed spirit to the sorting even if they aren't of the Faith, if they want to go. The Writ is kind of vague about what happens to heathens who have the misfortune to worship someone besides Vkandis. Most people assume that they'll be sent to eternal punishment, even if they are *good* people, but the Writ really doesn't *say* that, it just says that they will be sorted and sent to 'their places.' It doesn't say what those places are. For all *I* know, those places could be right here on earth."

Tre'valen and Dawnfire are ghosts of a kind, and if what Lo'isha and An'desha have been saying is true, then some of the Kal'enedral *are ghosts, too. Or if they aren't ghosts, they certainly aren't physically alive the way Florian and Altra are. So there's no reason why Kal'enel couldn't have "sorted" them Herself, and decreed that their "place" was here.*

"Well, what about the Avatars?" Firesong asked, echoing his thoughts. "Do they count as ghosts?"

"If they aren't, I wouldn't know what else to call them," Karal admitted. "And even if they aren't 'blessed' in the Karsite sense, they are anything but evil or hungry. They certainly aren't vengeful either, so there's no reason for me to interfere with whatever they are doing." He thought a bit harder. "The thing about exorcism is that if you want to be exact about it, there are two kinds. One kind just throws the ghost out of whatever it's possessing and bars it from coming back—it can still go possess something else somewhere else. The other kind blesses the ghost, opens a path for it so it can see where it's supposed to be going, and gives it some help to break the last bonds with the world and send it on its way if it's ready. But it has to *be* ready. Most Priests combine both kinds, hoping that once the spirit is cast out, it will see the Light and realize it shouldn't be here, but I've also seen reports about spirits that just seemed confused about the fact that they were dead, and in that case, the Priest only used the second kind of exorcism."

"All very well, but suppose you were to see something that you knew was a ghost—not an Avatar, or anything obviously under the direction of anyone's god. What would you do about that?" Firesong asked. "Would you feel that you *had* to do something about it?"

It was a good question. According to some Priests, he would *have* to try exorcising anything that looked or acted like a ghost, but that would include the Kal'enedral and the Avatars, and he dashed well knew that he wasn't going to even *breathe* the word "exorcism" around them! "Personally, I suppose I would try to exorcise anything that was harmful, send on anything that was ready, and leave everything else alone."

He still didn't see what relevance any of this had to their current situation, but presumably Firesong had some idea where he was going with all of this.

Firesong appeared to make up his mind about something, for his expression became a bit more animated and less contemplative. "Look," he said. "I've been asking you all these questions because I need your help, yours and Altra's, and there are some religious problems involved. I made the—acquaintance—of some real ghosts, and you wouldn't mistake them for anything else. One of them is an ancestor of mine. Physically, they're bound to a place up north, right up at the northern border of Valdemar."

Oh, no... he must be afraid that when the Final Storm hits, these ghosts of his are going to be destroyed or hurt in some way. Karal interrupted him. "Firesong, I hope you weren't planning on asking me to exorcise them. I mean, I'm sorry that one of your ancestors is physically bound to the earth, and if I could, I would be glad to help him, but I don't think it's possible. I told you, all I would be able to do without the spirits being ready, is to force them out of the place they were bound to. Even so, I doubt I could do anything for them at such a great distance."

Now it was Firesong's turn to interrupt him. "No, Karal, that was *not* what I had in mind!" he exclaimed, but he seemed more amused at the conclusion that Karal had leaped to than annoyed. "Hear me out. An'desha, Sejanes, and I all agree that we simply need more *mages* here at the Tower, powerful mages, and we're just not going to get them here to us in time. We need Adepts at the least, and every Adept within physical range of the Tower is needed right where he is. We can't build Gates to bring in human or nonhuman Adepts from farther away, and

Altra can't bring in anyone *mortal*—but what about ghosts?"

Ghosts. One of Firesong's ancestors. North of Valdemar. And an Adept. The trend of the questions suddenly formed into a pattern, and Karal stared at him in mingled horror and fascination. "This ghost—this ancestor—it wouldn't be Vanyel Ashkevron, would it?" he asked, his voice trembling in spite of his effort to control it. He felt the hair on the back of his neck rise. Discussing Vanyel Demonrider in abstract was one thing. Seriously discussing bringing him here was another!

He wanted to beg Firesong to tell him that it was *not* Vanyel Ashkevron he was talking about, but one look at Firesong's face told him differently.

:I think it would be a very good idea, Karal,: Florian said diffidently. *:Vanyel is an Adept. If it is possible, I think it should be done.:*

"I won't ask how this came about," Karal said flatly. "I won't ask how *you* discovered that Vanyel Demonrider was still… in existence." He closed his eyes and shook his head. "I cannot believe I am hearing this."

:Boy, if you require more votes on this, you have mine,: said the sword Need. *:I've met the man, though I doubt he'll recall it. He and Stefen would be a tremendous asset to the group here. They* might *even give us that edge we need to beat this thing.:*

Firesong smirked. "The sword is saying that we need an edge. How appropriate. In any case, the Avatars actually suggested it. There are some things in the cube-maze notes that suggest we're going to need— well, more skilled people than the last time. The only way we can think of to get the spirits down here is to send Altra," Firesong said. "We think that Vanyel, his Companion, and his friend can link themselves to something small enough for Altra to transport."

"We?" Karal asked weakly. "How many of you discussed this?"

"All of the mages," Firesong told him. "That included Need and the Avatars. And we all agreed. We think we're about to find our answer on the cube-maze device, which is our first choice, but we need more help to make it work."

Karal looked down at Altra, who gazed back up at him with interest. "And what do you have to say about this?" he asked the Firecat.

:Seriously? I think it might work, but I don't know for certain. I'm not a mage as you think of one, but the others seem convinced. There is only one consideration, and that is why they wanted to talk to you.:

"So you were already a party to this?" Karal sighed. "I might have known. What's the consideration?"

:A very practical one. This borders on interference; if I were to just do as you ask, I would be exceeding my own authority. In order for me to do this, we would need

permission from a higher authority, and I cannot be the one to ask for permission.:

"I have the feeling that you are not referring to Solaris when you speak of needing permission from a higher authority." Karal bit his lip.

:You are correct, and you are the only Sun-priest here,: Altra said calmly. *:So you are the one who must make the petition. I cannot, and I cannot do such a thing without that permission. I may advise, guide, and run limited errands up to a point, but this is past that point. I hate to sound like a copper-counting clerk, making a fuss about a technicality, but if these spirits were Karsite and not Valdemaran, there would be less of a problem.:*

"Because of the old enmity?" Karal asked, surprised. "But it was the Sunlord Himself who ordered truce with Valdemar in the first place!"

:No. Because these spirits were bound where they are for a reason, and I don't know that this reason has been fulfilled. They may not even know that. Now, even if their purpose is not yet fulfilled, they could choose to come here anyway, disobeying the One who offered them the task. But without first receiving permission of Vkandis, I cannot choose to help them come without the risk that I would be disobeying as well, and I do not choose to take that risk.:

"I wouldn't ask you to," Karal replied. "I suppose that means I don't have much choice in the matter."

:Judging by the way your friends are staring at you, I would say not.:

Karal looked up, already feeling pressured and guilty, to meet three sets of eyes—

Well, Need didn't *have* eyes as such, but he sensed her looking through Firesong's, and Florian stood in the doorway, gazing at him with a completely heartrending expression in his huge blue eyes.

The combined weight was too much to bear. "I'll have to go outside," he gulped, and managed not to stagger as he passed Florian.

He remembered somehow to find his coat, heavy boots, and gloves and pull them all on, but the trip up the tunnel was a complete blank in his mind. He knew very well what he had to do; he'd witnessed many petitions offered up by Solaris and her most trusted Priests, and had studied the form as part of his own education in the priesthood. Like many of the core portions of the Sunlord's Faith, a petition to Vkandis was deceptively simple.

The only requirement was that a petition must be made in the full light of day. In the Great Temple, this was accomplished, of course, by virtue of the many windows cut in the upper dome. Here, of course, Karal had only to walk outside. As befitting a religion founded by poor shepherds, who had little but what they could carry on their backs, or perhaps the back of a single donkey, there were no special vestments or vessels, no trappings of any kind. The only vessel needed was the Priest, and the only "vestment" a pure and single-hearted belief that the prayer would be heard. It might not receive a "yes," but it *would* be heard.

Karal, more than many, had every reason to hold that faith in his heart. He knew that Vkandis would hear him; did he not have Altra with him to prove that? His only question was if *he* was ready, was worthy, to be answered in any way, even with a "no."

He walked a little distance off into the snow, putting a tall drift between himself and the Shin'a'in camp, until there was no sign of activity but his own footprints trailing behind him. Beside him was the Tower, looming over everything, as it loomed over their lives. All around him was the dazzling whiteness of the snow, no less than knee-deep in some places, and deeper than that in most. This was a thicker snowpack than he had ever seen before.

It was also thicker than the Shin'a'in had ever seen it before, or so he'd been told. This was a terrible winter, and it could so easily get worse—assuming that the Plains themselves survived the Final Storm and what might happen to those ancient weapons still in the Tower.

Even if I'm not worthy, the cause is, he finally decided, and turned his face up to the sun, spreading his arms wide.

Some took great care with each word when they made prayers for a particular purpose, but Karal and his mentor Ulrich had never seen the sense in that. "They are like courtiers, trying to find the most unctuous phrase in hopes that their prince will throw them a bauble," Ulrich had said in disgust. "There is nothing in the Writ about making fine speeches for Vkandis' ear. Vkandis understands us far better than we could ever find words for."

So Karal simply stood with every bit of him open to the light of the sun, the light that stood for the greater Light, and let that Light become all that he was. He kept his petition to the bare facts.

This is how we stand. This is what we have been doing. This is what we need to do. We know that this will not guarantee our success, but we think it is necessary. Will You grant Your permission for Your servants to do this?

This was the first time he had ever made such a prayer alone, and he trembled all over at his own audacity. He made of himself nothing but the question, and waited, like an empty bowl, for the answer.

The sun burned on in the endless blue of heaven, as he struggled to lose himself in the Light. And in the moment that he actually did so, Vkandis showed His face.

The sun blazed up, doubling, tripling in size; he felt the light burning his face even as he held his gaze steady and unflinching.

You can bear the Light. But can you bear the place where there are no sheltering shadows?

The sun split into two, three, a dozen suns, surrounding him in a circle of suns, creating a place where there could be no hint of darkness and nowhere to hide. The suns settled upon the earth around him, dancing upon the face of the snow, but neither melting nor consuming it. Still he waited, all fear burned out of him, empty of everything but faith and the waiting, and he breathed steadily and deeply once for every dozen heartbeats.

You can bear being without shadow. But can you bear being only in Light?

The dozen suns blazed up again, and began circling around him, faster and faster, until they blurred into a solid ring of white light. Then the ring flared and he had to cover his eyes for a moment; and when he looked again, he stood, not in the snow of the Plains, but in the heart of the sun, with light above and below, and all about him, in the heart of the Light and the Light became part of him.

But this, he realized, was not a completely new experience. Although he had not had the memory until this moment, *this* was what had happened when he acted as a Channel for the release of the great energies of the first weapon they had triggered. The Light had taken away his fears then, and it did so again, then illuminated every corner of his heart. Yes, there were faulty places, poorly-mended places, even spots of faint shadow—Karal saw and acknowledged those, as he renewed a pledge to see them made good. *But*, he said silently to that great Light, *what I am does not matter. This thing that I ask is not for me, nor even for these few who are here with me. This is for all our peoples; and for peoples we do not even know.*

The Light answered him with a question of its own. *Is this also for those of the Empire?*

He replied immediately, and simply.

Yes.

Had he not already pointed out that most of the people living in the Empire had nothing to do with the terrible things their leaders had done? Why should they not be protected?

Even your enemies? came the second question.

He answered it as he had the other. *Yes.*

If protecting his enemies was the cost of protecting the innocent, then so be it. Fanatics said, "Kill them all, and let God sort them out." He would rather say, "Save them all, and let God sort them out, for we have not the right to judge."

There was a timeless moment of waiting, and the Light flooded him with approval.

Then that is My answer, came the reply. *Yes.*

The Light vanished.

He found himself standing in the snow, his feet numb, his eyes watering, with his entire being filled with the answer. He was a scintillating bowl full of *Yes,* and he carried that answer back to the Tower as carefully as an acolyte carried a bowl of holy water.

"You don't remember anything?" Lyam asked, alive with curiosity, as he helped Karal carry a new set of notes up to the storage chamber. Karal shook his head regretfully, and watched where he was putting his feet. The last few steps out of the workroom were worn enough to be tricky.

"All I remember is going out into the snow. After that—nothing, until I woke up again with the answer." He made an apologetic face. "Sorry, I know you'd love to note all of this down, and it's not a priestly secret or anything, but I just can't remember what happened."

The *hertasi* lashed his tail, perhaps with impatience. "You could have just gone out, come back, and pretended to have the answer," Lyam began. "Not that *you* would have, but—"

"That wouldn't be as easy as you think. I might have fooled anyone but Florian and Altra, but *never* either of them," Karal replied firmly. "And I'm not sure it would have fooled Need; I think she was a priestess before she was a sword, and if she was, she'll have ways of knowing when people make up answers they say are from their gods."

"If you say so," Lyam said, though his tone was dubious.

"And it wouldn't ever have fooled the Avatars," he continued forcefully. "How could it? How could you *ever* fool them about something like that?"

Lyam conceded defeat at that; although he might not be completely convinced of the supernatural nature of Florian, Altra, or Need, he was *entirely* convinced that the Avatars were something altogether out of his experience. He regarded them with a mixture of his usual intense curiosity mingled with awe and a little uncertainty. Karal found that mildly amusing. He had the distinct feeling that right up until the moment the *hertasi* first met the Avatars, little Lyam had been something of an agnostic—willing to admit in the reality of something beyond himself, but not at all willing to concede that it had anything to do with him and his everyday world. Like many another historian before him, Lyam was only convinced by verifiable facts. That was what would make him a good historian, rather than someone who was content to repeat all the same old erroneous gossip. The *hertasi* and his mentor Tarrn believed passionately in the truth, would do anything to find out the truth, and would probably do anything to defend the truth. They might find exonerating reasons for a friend who robbed another of property, but if that friend falsified historical documents or concealed relevant facts, they would show him no leniency.

Karal and Lyam arranged the notes in order with the last batch and sealed up the now-full box and put it with those holding Tarrn's precious chronicles. "If you've got a moment, could you give me a hand?" he asked Lyam. "You're better at handling hot rocks than I am."

"That's because you humans are poorly designed," the *hertasi* replied with a toothy grin. "You should have nice thick skin on your hands, preferably with a toughened outer hide or scales, so you can pick up things without hurting yourselves."

"Remind me to ask for that option, the next time I order a new body," Karal countered, as Lyam followed him into the bedchamber. "Then again, isn't that why you were created?"

"To make up for your human shortcomings?" Lyam laughed. "Why, *yes*. Someone besides divine beings needed to. And just try getting some ghost or Avatar to cook a good meal or mend clothing! We're indispensable!"

Karal laughed with Lyam, and had decided, given the sad condition that Altra had been in when he'd come back from delivering the teleson to Haven, that he would be prepared for a similar situation. When Altra returned from the Forest of Sorrows, he would find food, good water, and a warm bed waiting for him, already prepared and standing ready. The guess was that Altra could return at any time after two days had passed, so in the afternoon of the second day Karal had arranged for all those things. The moment Altra returned he could eat and sleep without even having to ask for food or a warm bed. Karal kept heated stones tucked into the bed he'd made up, and as the warm, meat-laden broth he prepared got a little thick and past its prime flavor, he was usually able to find someone willing to eat the old while he prepared a new batch.

Lyam had been the latest beneficiary of Karal's cooking, and so he wasn't at all averse to helping Karal place more heated stones into the bedding. "So, what do *you* think of all this?" the *hertasi* asked. "Doesn't it seem kind of strange to be bringing in *ghosts*? I've never even met anyone who'd ever seen a ghost before this, had you?"

"It's no stranger than the Avatars, and they're ghosts, I suppose," Karal replied honestly. "I've never seen a ghost either before I got here, but it really doesn't bother me."

Lyam rolled his eyes with disbelief. "How can you be so calm about this? Firesong is planning on bringing a *spirit* here, and an ancient hero at that! Why, that would be like—like calling up Skandranon, or—or Baron Valdemar, or—or the first Son of the Sun! Aren't you excited? Or scared?"

Logically, Karal knew he should be both those things, and yet he couldn't manage to dredge up any real feelings about the situation. It just didn't seem real enough to him, or perhaps it was only as real as he'd gotten used to. It was not that he was precisely numb about these sorts of events, it was just that long ago he had crossed over his threshold of amazement and now things were only a matter of degree. "Vanyel Ashkevron lived a *long* time ago, Lyam," he said after a long moment of thought. "I know that you're quite passionate about history and to you things that happened hundreds of years ago are as vital as things that happened last year, but honestly, I can't get very emotional about this. Especially not after having met living people who were considered to be very serious enemies of Karse before the Alliance, and discovering that they were really quite like people I knew at home. You know, I'll believe these spirits are going to be here when they arrive, and until then, I don't see any reason to get excited."

"What do you mean, you discovered enemies of Karse were like people you knew?" Lyam wanted to know, as he tried unsuccessfully to juggle three recently-smoking stones. They thudded one by one onto the ground and he scuttled after one that was rolling away, then tucked the last of the hot rocks into Altra's bedding. He flicked his tail as his only comment.

"I actually *know* people who lost family members to Captain Kerowyn's mercenaries, and then she turned into one of my teachers when I got to Haven," Karal told him. "I found out that she didn't actually eat babies, and she wasn't any more of a monster than any good military commander. And another one of my teachers was a gentleman called Alberich, who actually deserted Karse and his position as a Captain in the Army. He was Chosen, by a Companion who smuggled himself right into Karse! They called him 'the Great Traitor' before the Alliance, and yet I found out later that he was instrumental in bringing the Alliance about. If you believed everything you heard, he was half demon and half witch and was perfectly capable of any atrocity you could name. He turned out to be a great deal like Kerowyn, except maybe his sense of humor is darker than hers."

"Interesting," Lyam said, his eyes lighting up. "I don't suppose you'd be willing to tell me about all that?"

He reached into the pouch that never left his side and took out a silverpoint and paper as he asked that, and Karal didn't have the heart to refuse him. He told the story of his own journey into Valdemar, which seemed to have occurred a hundred years ago, and to some other person entirely. He answered Lyam's questions as best he could, and as honestly as he could, even when the answers made him look rather stupid. Since Lyam was very interested in the details of his thoughts as his opinion of Valdemar and its inhabitants changed, he was as open as possible.

In many ways, he was a bit surprised at the change in himself as he tried to explain himself to Lyam. The talking and questioning helped to fill the time and allay his anxieties, too, and for that reason alone he would have been glad of Lyam's company.

There was always the possibility that all of this would be for nothing; Altra could go and request help, even present Firesong's personal petition to his ancestor Vanyel, but that didn't mean that the spirits were going to cooperate. For one thing, they might not be who they claimed they were. For another, they might not be very interested in helping old enemies. After all, Altra was a representative of Vanyel's old nemesis—and for Vanyel, what was ancient history to Karal was very much a part of his personal memory. This could all be a plot. They could be constructing a trap to hold the spirits here, far from Valdemar and the border they were supposed to be guarding.

The spirits might also be unwilling or unable to leave what had been their home. They hadn't in all this time, so why would they now? They might simply not be able to *help*, and why make the long and dangerous journey to the Tower just to sit and do nothing?

They might not be willing to take the chance that this might start out to being a need for their services, but turn into a situation where Karal could eliminate them entirely. After all, once they were *here* and in his power, Karal might change his mind about them and take it into his head to try an exorcism.

Then shortly after dawn on the third day, Altra returned, and all the doubts were resolved.

Karal was in his bed, and Lyam shook him out of a dark, deep, and dreamless slumber. It took him a moment to understand what the *hertasi* was trying to tell him.

He scrambled out of his bedroll and pulled on his clothing from the night before as soon as it penetrated into his sleep-fuddled mind that Altra was back. He filled a bowl with the hot, rich meat broth he had waiting on a little charcoal brazier, and followed Lyam out into the main room.

Not only was every member of their own party gathered around the Firecat, but a goodly number of the Kal'enedral as well. And if Altra had looked worn out when he brought Sejanes and Master Levy in, he looked positively flattened now. He lay on the floor, panting and disheveled, surrounded by people who all seemed to be talking at once. Without paying any attention to anything else, Karal pushed in among the others and placed the bowl of hot broth under Altra's nose. The Firecat cast him a look of undying gratitude and plunged his face into it, taking great gulps of the liquid rather than lapping it up daintily as he usually did.

:They need a physical link to the real world,: he said as if he was continuing an earlier statement. Karal reflected that being able to Mindspeak was a great advantage in mealtime conversation; you could go right on talking and no one would ever accuse you of bad table manners. It was also fascinating to him that Tarrn, Altra, and Florian could all make their thoughts heard even by those, like Sejanes and Master Levy, who did not have the Gift of Mindspeech themselves. *:So there it is; and I do wish there had been an easier way to transport that bit of wood here than by having me fetch it. It will take them a bit of time to use it to bring themselves here, so be patient. If I'd had to bring them as well, I would have run the risk of losing them in the Void. Besides, Vanyel doesn't particularly care for Gates, and Jumping is a lot like Gating, especially now.:*

"Why wouldn't an Adept care for Gates?" Sejanes wondered aloud when the Firecat's Mindspeech had been related to him.

"*Let's just say that I had some unpleasant experiences involving Gates in the past,*" replied a new voice, a pleasant and musical tenor that had the peculiar quality of sounding as if it came from the bottom of a well, a quality that it shared with some of the Kal'enedrals' voices.

Karal looked where everyone else was looking, but saw no new person there, only an old, decrepit, weather-beaten wreck of a musical instrument. It might at one time have been a lute or a gittern or some such thing; there was no trace at all of its original finish, nor its strings or tuning pegs, and it had probably not been playable for centuries. If this was the physical link that Altra had brought with him, it was certainly a peculiar choice.

"On the whole, I would just rather not have to deal with Gates at all if I have any choice in the matter," the voice continued, and the air above the old instrument began to shiver. *"You'll have to give us a few moments here, as my new friend Altra said. None of us are used to drawing our energy from ley-lines and nodes anymore, and we're rather out of practice."*

"We're in no hurry, Ancestor, and we have had some interesting experiences involving you and Gates ourselves," Firesong replied calmly, as the hair on the back of Karal's neck began to crawl of its own accord. It had been all very well to tell Lyam that he was neither excited nor afraid when the arrival of these spirits had been an abstract concept, but now...

Now there was an atavistic chill running down his spine, a cold lump in his stomach, and the knowledge that he would really rather be anywhere but here, as the shimmering air developed three glowing forms, which took on substance even as he watched. First, there were only two vaguely human shapes and another, larger one that might have resembled a horse. Then the shapes became more defined and detailed, although they never actually attained the solidity of the Kal'enedral or the fiery substance of the Avatars.

Maybe that was why he was suddenly afraid; the *leshy'a Kal'enedral* looked just like any of the others, and the Avatars were so exotic as to fit in the same categories as Firecats and other manifestations of the gods. But there was nothing solid about these, nor so alien that he could bear them because they were so new to him.

The first to become really clear was a strikingly handsome man, and if this was Firesong's ancestor Vanyel, it was obvious where he got his beauty. There was no color to any of these spirits, so Karal could not have told if the clothing this spirit had chosen to "wear" happened to be antique Herald's Whites or not, but the cut was like nothing he had seen in his lifetime. The spirit had long hair, though not as long as Firesong's or Silverfox's, and "wore" no jewelry of any kind. He searched the group gathered around him, and his gaze lit on Karal and remained there. In spite of the ghost's smile, Karal was *not* reassured.

"*So this is our young Sun-priest,*" the spirit said, as Karal froze. "*If I ever have the opportunity, remind me to tell you of another young servant of Vkandis that I met, who proved to me that not all of the folk who used Vkandis' Name to justify their actions should be lumped together into a single category.*" The spirit's smile widened—quite as winsome a smile as anything Firesong had ever produced—and some of Karal's chill melted away. But not, by any means, all of it. For some reason—perhaps simply that these beings looked, acted and *sounded* exactly like what they were supposed to be—Karal found Vanyel entirely unnerving.

As the second spirit manifested, Karal didn't find him any easier on the nerves, perhaps because he couldn't seem to make up his mind whether to look like a muscular, square-jawed fellow who was a bit taller than Vanyel, or a slight, triangular-faced, large-eyed lad who was shorter and more slender than the Herald-Mage. Just looking at him made Karal feel dizzy, and when the third shape came into focus, it didn't help any, for it wavered between the form of a Companion and that of a determined woman with a firm chin and the look of a hunter about her.

:If you all don't mind, I'd like to see that bed Karal has been keeping warm for me,: Altra said firmly, and when Karal looked down, he saw that the Firecat had polished off every drop of the broth, and was on his feet, swaying a little.

"*You go ahead, my friend,*" Vanyel said genially. "*We three need to have our first consultation with the mages, and having too many people trying to explain things at once is not going to get us anywhere. We will try to keep the noise down so you may rest better.*"

Since Altra did not look at all steady, Karal picked him up bodily and carried him to that waiting bed, with Florian pacing alongside him, offering a shoulder for support. Lyam cleared the way ahead of them, quite authoritative for such a short fellow. Altra was quite limp with exhaustion, and Karal wondered if he should say anything forbidding Altra to make any more Jumping expeditions. Did he have the right to demand such things?

:That's the last. That is absolutely the last,: Altra said weakly as Karal laid the Firecat in his warmed bed. *:I know you aren't seeing any physical manifestations of the Storms right now, but believe me, where I have to go, they're there. It was like trying to swim a river in flood, and cats are not particularly suited to swimming, let me tell you. I do not have the strength to try that a second time.:*

"Good, because I was going to ask you not to," Karal replied. "I don't think I could stand losing you."

:Well, you won't. That's the advantage of having a Cat instead of a Horse as a partner; we don't go running off to sacrifice ourselves at the sound of the first trumpet call,: Altra said, feebly winking at Karal on the side opposite of Florian. *:We're sensible. And right now, my sensible side demands some cosseting. I want sleep:*

:Oh, do go right ahead and sleep,: Florian said with mock-indignation. *:Don't mind us, we just want to gather worshipfully around your slumbering form and tell stories about your bravery and virtue.:*

:Fine, you do that, and about time,: the Firecat replied in the same spirit. *:Just don't wake me up.:*

And with that, he closed his eyes, his even breathing seeming to indicate that he *had* fallen straight asleep.

"Well, what do *you* think?" Karal asked the Companion, certain he was about to get a litany of praise thinly disguised as a lesson in Valdemaran history.

:I think that I'm hoping our latest visitors remain unmanifest most of the time,: Florian replied promptly, his uneasiness quite apparent in his mind-voice. *:Yfandes gives me the—what's Lyam's term for it?—the collywobbles, that's it. They're all three dreadfully intimidating.:*

"Really?" Karal arched an eyebrow at him. "I didn't think you could be intimidated by anything!"

:I can, and she's it.: Florian was quite serious, and it was Karal's turn to put a steadying hand on his shoulder. *:Not even a Grove-Born gives me the urge to kneel and knock my head on the ground the way she does!:*

"Well, don't do that," Karal advised. "For one thing, you'll hurt your head. For another, I'm sure you have nothing to feel inferior about."

He knew how Florian felt, though, and he sympathized. Hopefully these newcomers would stay invisible; if he couldn't see them, maybe he wouldn't keep having the urge to do some bowing and scraping of his own.

"Ghosts and spirit-swords, Avatars and *leshy'a Kal'enedral*—we have more not-mortal things around here than we have mortal ones!" he complained. "And when you add in bondbirds and *hertasi* and *kyree* and Companions, the weird creatures outnumber ordinary humans to the point where we're a minority!"

:It could be worse,: Florian pointed out pensively. *:This could be a Vale. Or k'Leshya Vale! Then you'd have* dyheli *and* tervardi *and gryphons, and I don't know what all else. Only the gods know what weird pets the k'Leshya brought up out of the south with them.:*

Karal just sighed and sat beside Altra with his chin on his hand. "The worst part of it is that a mind-talking horse is the most normal of all the folk around here!"

Florian only whickered, and mind-laughed weakly.

Fortunately for Karal's peace of mind and Florian's sense of profound inferiority, the three newcomers mostly remained "unmanifest" to save energy, and simply tendered advice to Firesong by means of Mindspeech. Karal had the feeling that Vanyel was a little hurt that the Karsite was so nervous in Vanyel's presence, but there was no help for it. Karal himself wasn't entirely sure why Vanyel made him so edgy. It might simply have been that the Herald-Mage was everything that Karal was not, but without the somewhat inflated self-esteem of his descendant Firesong. It might have been unconscious residue from all the "Demon Vanyel" stories he'd been told as a child. And it might only have been that Vanyel was so obviously everything that a Karsite feared about the night, and although Karal had been working with stranger beings, Vanyel's presence was simply the one bit of strangeness that was too much.

He had his own problems that were similar to Florian's—the fact that of all of them, *he* was really the most ordinary, and aside from his ability as a Channel, apparently the least necessary. He was not brilliant like Master Levy nor a mage like Sejanes or Firesong; he could not translate the ancient texts as Tarrn and Lyam could, nor had he the knack of amusing everyone and helping them see solutions to their problems as Silverfox did.

It was Silverfox, however, who made him realize that the things about him that were the most commonplace were the ones that made him the most valuable in this group of those who were out of the ordinary.

"I'm glad we have you here, Karal," Silverfox said to him the next day, as he shared stew that Altra had not been awake to eat with the *kestra'chern.*

"Me?" he said with surprise. "Why?"

"Because your strength is that you are forced to handle wildly extraordinary events and people—and you just *do* it, without complaint. You set the rest of us an example. After all, if you can handle all this, *we* should certainly be able to."

Karal made a face. "I think I'm being damned with faint praise," he replied ironically.

"It isn't meant to be faint praise," Silverfox said earnestly. "What I mean is that you are finding great strength and grace inside yourself, and you prove to the rest of us that we should be able to do the same." He gazed into Karal's eyes with intense concentration. "You keep us centered, reminding us that there is a world out there beyond these walls. You give us perspective in this rather rarefied company, and help keep us all sane." His smile was just as charming as anything Firesong could conjure. "In your own way, my dear young friend, you are a constant reminder of everything normal and good about the world that we are trying to protect."

Karal blushed; that was all he could do, in the face of words like that.

:He's right, you know,: Altra seconded. :It isn't the great mystics and saints who do the real day-to-day work of keeping people's faith firm, it's the ordinary priest—the good man who goes on being good, no matter what he has to face. Ordinary people know in their hearts that they could never withstand the trials that a saint undergoes, but if they see a person who is just like they are, and watch him bearing up under those trials, they know that they can do it, too. And as for the great ones, when they see an ordinary man bearing extraordinary burdens, they are inspired to take on far more than they might otherwise do.:

Now he was blushing so hotly his skin felt sunburned.

"Meanwhile, we *are* having to face a crisis," Silverfox continued, his smile fading as he sobered. "And it is coming on us swiftly. Firesong wanted me to tell you that they're going to use the cube-maze, after all."

That cooled his blushes in a hurry, and he nodded. Silverfox reached for his chin and tilted it up, looking deeply into his eyes, then nodded as if satisfied by what he saw there. "You know that this is the best choice of all of them," he stated. "Firesong says that of all the weapons, this offers the most gain." He said nothing about risk, but he didn't have to, for Karal already knew that the risk of using any of those weapons was great, and they really could not know how great until they triggered one.

Karal nodded. "And I knew that it was quite likely I would have to work as a Channel again. It's all right; I'm not afraid this time."

Strangely enough, he wasn't. "He wanted *me* to tell you, so that you would know he doesn't intend you to have to bear any more than any of the rest of them." Silverfox's ironic expression filled in the rest—things best left unsaid. Karal knew, though, that Firesong would not be able to lie successfully to the *kestra'chern*, and Silverfox would not allow him to put Karal in for more than an equal share of peril. In a sense, Silverfox was vouching for the Adept.

Karal shrugged awkwardly. "The cube-maze was their first choice the last time, they just couldn't come up with enough information to make it work. I'd *rather* be channeling for something that is their first choice, rather than their third or fourth."

He didn't pretend to understand half of what the mages were talking about, but the device they called a "cube-maze," which resembled a pile of hollow cast-metal cubes stacked rather randomly atop one another, was supposed to have had a nonliving core to do the channeling. Either Urtho could never get the thing to work correctly in the first place, or else the core was no longer functioning. In either case, there was no one here that was capable of making a device to act as the channel. That meant Karal was the only hope of making this thing work. It *might* work better with a living channel; that might have been one of the reasons it had failed in the first place. A living channel could make decisions; a nonliving channel couldn't.

Like the other devices here, the cube-maze didn't look anything like a weapon. It was rather pretty, in fact; there was an odd sheen or patina to the blue metal surface that refracted rainbows, like oil on water. One of the truly strange things about all of these weapons was that none of them looked alike. It was difficult to imagine how the same mind could have come up with so many dissimilar devices.

"Karal!" Master Levy hailed him from the main room. "The teleson is free, and Natoli is on it."

Silverfox cut short Karal's attempt at excusing himself politely. "Go, off with you!" the *kestra'chern* said. "You can talk to me anytime, and I'm not half so pretty as Natoli is."

That last comment made him blush all over again, but this time he didn't care. His long-distance romancing of Natoli appeared to charm everyone. They all stayed discreetly out of the way when he spoke to her, and they all seemed to go out of their way to give him occasions to talk to her on the teleson.

Altra followed on his heels, to act as the facilitator for the conversation. It was amazing that Altra didn't ever tease him about anything that passed between himself and Natoli, but even Altra apparently regarded the growing relationship as a private matter between the two of them, and not for any outsider, not even a Firecat, to intrude upon. No matter what either of the two said to each other, Altra never commented on it, either during the conversation or afterward. In fact, Karal was able to completely forget about Altra's presence most of the time.

But Natoli had disturbing news for him that had nothing whatsoever to do with their personal matters. "Elspeth and Darkwind reported that they are already getting Storms in Hardorn," she said gravely. "They aren't dangerous yet, but it's only a matter of time before things degenerate. We have already started preparations here to handle whatever comes up."

"That's probably why the mages and all finally made up their minds which device to use," he told her. "I suppose Master Levy must have agreed on their choice, since he is the one doing the mathematical modeling for the solution." He hesitated, and looked down at his hands a moment, then looked back up and told her the truth. "I'm going to have to be a Channel again."

She didn't say anything, but her face grew pale and she bit her lip. "Well," she finally managed, "that's what you're there for. You have to do your job, just as I have to do mine." She rallied a bit. "Speaking of my job, I'm in charge of some of the emergency plans. We're going to have to evacuate the Palace at the very least, and maybe even parts of Haven, just in case that node under the Palace goes unstable. All the highborn have gone home, and as of today they've dismissed the Collegia and sent the trainees home as well. Even the Healers have dispersed. The trainees that don't have homes to go to are supposed to go off with their Masters if they're Bards, off to one of the Houses of Healing as Healer-trainees, or riding circuit with full Heralds if they're still in Grays. It's a little crazy around here, since things still have to get done, and it's getting to be that whoever has a pair of hands free just does whatever it takes. They say that the gryphons will stay until the last moment and set spells to keep out looters, then they'll fly away. It'll be a relief when everyone is actually gone."

He didn't have to ask why she was still there; she could not sit back while others were in danger any more than he could. She would probably remain there until the very end because that was what her father would do. Herald Rubrik was in Karse, so perhaps she felt it was up to her to take on the familial duties. "Well," he replied. "You do what you have to, right? If your job is to be there, then you need to do it." Clumsy words, but he hoped they told her what he wanted to say—that he still would never ask her to stop doing what she considered to be her job just to be "safe." If there even *was* any place "safe" anymore. "I want you to know that I really don't think any of us here are in any more or less danger than you are," he continued, trying to give her reassurance. "The one thing I *am* concerned about is that after the last time, the others here are all so fiercely determined to protect me that I'm more afraid for them than I am for myself."

She smiled tremulously. "You would be anyway. Just promise me that you'll let them take care of you. Not at the expense of getting the job done, but let them protect you from what they can."

"If you'll do the same," he demanded. "Before you go flinging yourself into exploding boilers, wait and see if someone more suited to that particular job is already doing it! You know, it just *might* be that, capable as you are, someone else would manage that particular rescue a little better than you!"

"You drive a hard bargain," she retorted, and shook her head, a little of her old humor returning to her eyes. "All right, I promise."

"And so do I," he pledged softly, and basked in her smile.

The wind of a full-scale blizzard howled and whined outside the windows of his suite, and icy drafts forced their way past windows and thick curtains, but Baron Melles didn't care. Enveloped in one of the heavy woolen tunics that had become fashion out of necessity, with a second layer of knitted winter silk beneath that, he brooded pleasantly over the reports of his network of spies within the households of the members of the Court. Virtually every one of those pieces of paper reported a new attitude toward him on the part of anyone of any importance.

Fear. He was delighted at their reaction. They might hate him, they might envy him, they might (rarely) even admire him for his ruthlessness—but they all feared him now, and feared to have even the appearance of opposing him.

He shifted his weight in his chair, and repositioned his feet on the warming pan beneath his desk. His last object lesson was more effective than he had thought it would be, and had spread far beyond the immediate household and friends of his target. Clearly it was *much* wiser and more expedient to show that the children of his would-be enemies were vulnerable than it was to threaten the enemies themselves. And as for those who had no children, well, there wasn't a single one of them who didn't have *some* other person for whom they cherished tender feelings. Anyone who would threaten a child obviously would have no difficulty with targeting an aged and infirm parent, or a sibling, or a lover. Even Tremane had dependents he would have been very upset at losing—that old mage, Sejanes, for one.

It was ironic in many ways, for it would have been very easy for any of them to make him or herself invulnerable. There had not been another person besides himself here at Court who had read and understood the lesson old Charliss had given to them in the course of his own life: *Trust no one, care for no one, depend on no one.* They had all persisted, even in the face of obvious disadvantages, to fall in love, make friendships rather than alliances, and allow themselves the cracks in their armor that *relationships* made.

Tremane never knew that he made me what I am today, even as he made me his enemy when we were cadets. He betrayed me to the Colonel, and ruined my career in the Army. And for what? Because I was doing what everyone else wanted to do, but didn't have the intelligence or the audacity to try. I trusted him because he said he was my friend, and he betrayed me. Without that, if I had remained in the cadet corps as he did, I would not have seen Charliss' example for what it was.

He had stopped being a sheep that day and had become one of the wolves—as any of them could have. Well, that was all their own fault, and their stupidity, and that was why he was the Emperor's Heir and not one of them.

Not even the memory of that long-ago humiliation of being cast out of the corps could spoil this triumph. He had finally achieved the goal he had set for himself that day—to make anyone of any importance look at him and fear. It was in this mood of unusual good humor that General Thayer found him, and destroyed his mood with a single sentence.

His valet Bors showed the General in; Thayer wore a regulation Army cloak over his uniform tunic, and fingerless gloves to keep his hands warm. Melles greeted him with pleasure, although he did not rise.

But Thayer had not come to make a social call. "Melles, we're in trouble," he rumbled. And as usual, the General came straight to the point without even waiting to take the chair that Melles offered him.

Where had that come from? "How can we be in trouble?" Melles asked, with more than a bit of surprise. "We've got order in the smaller cities, and the larger ones are coming around. Food is getting in, and you're even making a small profit. Rioting has stopped in most places, and the subversives are beginning to be regarded as lunatics. We might have lost the lands Charliss brought under the Imperial banner and some of the provinces, but—"

"But the Army doesn't want you in charge," Thayer replied, bluntly. "That last little trick you played was one too many. The word from the field is that they don't intend to establish order just to put a baby killer on the Iron Throne. Word of your power play has been traveling farther and faster than either of us thought it would. I don't know how, but in spite of everything, virtually everyone I've contacted already knows all about it, and knows that you were the one who put the body in the crib." He scowled. "That was a stupid ploy, Melles. Your average soldier may be a hard man, but the one thing he won't put up with is threatening a baby."

Melles frowned. "But there was nothing to link me with that incident," he objected.

Thayer snorted with utter contempt, as the wind rattled the windowpanes and a draft made the candle flames flicker. "Please. Not everyone is an inbred idiot, especially not in the Army. You're an assassin, however much you pretend not to be; everyone knows it, and everyone knows you're the only one who not only could have done what you did, but who is cold-blooded enough to follow up on the threat if you had to. And I repeat to you; the Army won't support a baby killer, and there's an end to it."

A cold anger burned in the back of Melles' throat, as cold as the howling winds outside. "That's fine sentiment from people who kill for a living," he said with equal contempt. "I'm sure they ask the age of every peasant with a boar-spear who opposes them in the field, and make certain to leave insurgent villages untouched in case they *might* kill a few children."

Thayer's face flushed with anger, but somehow he kept his temper even in the face of Melles' provocative words. "I could point out that the Army operates under certain laws, and that when a soldier kills someone, he does it openly, under conditions where his opponent has an equal chance of killing *him*. But that would be specious and we both know it—and it's not the point."

"Oh?" Melles asked sardonically. "And just what is the point?"

"The point is that the average soldier *believes* all those things," Thayer said, pounding the desk for emphasis. "Whether or not they are true. Truth has no bearing on this, and you damned well know it. The average soldier thinks he is going to defend the honor of the Empire against *adult* enemies, and that makes him feel superior to any assassin, and vastly superior to someone who not only threatens the safety of a child, but threatens a child of his own people."

"Never mind that this same noble soldier would skewer the children of a rebellious village without a second thought or a moment of hesitation," Melles grumbled, although he saw the logic in Thayer's argument. Thayer was right. The truth didn't matter here, and he, who was a practiced hand in manipulating perception, should have known that. "Very well. What's to be done?"

Thayer sighed, and finally sank into the chair Melles had offered. "I don't know," he admitted. "It's not only the Commanders that are talking rebellion, it's the Generals, and the rank and file, and they aren't amenable to the kinds of coercion you can use on the nobles of the Court. Unless we can do something about this, we're going to lose them, and the moment Charliss becomes a Little God, they're going to put someone of their choice on the Iron Throne and you and me in the ground."

Melles ground his teeth in frustration, for Thayer was right. Although, unlike Tremane, he had never gotten out of the cadets to serve in the military forces of the Empire, he knew the structure and makeup. The Generals were mostly men who had made a career of the military, as had their fathers before them. Their wives were the daughters of similar men, their families all related to other military families. They employed former military men as guards and servants, employed the wives of such men as maids and housekeepers. Their positions were embedded in multiple layers of protection, and they could not be dismissed or demoted out of hand. The High Commanders could be eliminated, for they were mostly nobles like Grand Duke Tremane, but there was no getting rid of the Generals. They were like a wolf pack; you couldn't separate a victim, for none of them stood alone, and if you made a move against one, the whole pack would consolidate long enough to tear your throat out before going back to their own internal jockeying for power.

"You can't touch them, Melles," Thayer warned in an echo of his own thoughts. "If you try, they'll destroy you. They won't put up with that kind of threat, and they'll close ranks against you. Press it too far, and they'll call a coup against you. Not even your personal guard can protect you against an entire Company coming to kill you."

"It's gone right down to the rank and file, you say?" he asked, his thoughts swirling as wildly as the snow outside.

Thayer nodded, and Melles cursed them all in his mind. He couldn't even order every General within reach of the capital to come to a meeting, seal the room, and kill them all at once. If he tried, the entire Army itself would rise up in revolt. It was only when the Generals were corrupt and hated by their men that you could get away with a tactic like that.

"We're only in trouble, we aren't defeated yet," he said at last, as a few ideas began to form out of the chaos. "They might have good communications, but I have better ones. I have a few more throws of the dice coming, and *I* can pick the dice." He began to smile as he saw how he could completely subvert the entire problem.

Thayer regarded him curiously, and with a certain grudging admiration. "Have you got something up your sleeve that you haven't told me about?"

He nodded. "I'm not even going to try to deny their rumor, instead I'm going to give them something else entirely to think about. I always have more up my sleeve that I haven't told anyone about," he replied smugly. "And you should never underestimate the power of the clerical pen."

"What you can't find, you can manufacture, hmm?" Thayer hazarded. "Just what, exactly, do you have in mind? Are you going to give them a different enemy to concentrate on?"

Melles just laughed. "I won't have to manufacture anything. With enough records to search, I can find just about anything I need, and you know yourself that this Empire creates enough paperwork to fill entire warehouses. Give me a few days and I can find all the right evidence to convince the Army that I'm the one they should be supporting, show them that having a so-called 'baby killer' on the throne is the *least* of the things they should be worrying about, and in the meantime, I can woo them."

"Woo them? Like reluctant girls?" Thayer made a rude and suggestive noise, but Melles wasn't offended, now that he had the bit in his teeth.

"Wait and see," he responded, plans already growing in the back of his mind that would probably astonish the older man. "Just wait and see."

Thayer was not convinced, but was certain enough of Melles' competence to be willing to buy him some time to work on the schemes that he promised. Thayer stood up, saying so in as many words.

"Just remember that I can't give you too much more time," he warned. "And it's going to take a great deal to overcome the way they feel about the baby incident. I'm still not certain you're taking that seriously enough."

"Just remember what I told you about the common man and what he needs and wants," Melles replied. "Then remember that the Army is composed of those same common men—just with a little more training and a bit of discipline."

"Hmm." Thayer looked thoughtful at that, and took his leave. As soon as he was gone, Melles called in all five of his private secretaries.

They were all men, like his valet, of varied talents and some interesting training. All five of them were so nondescript that no one would ever notice them in a crowd. And all of them were adept at getting into even the most carefully guarded records, simply by knowing how to impersonate virtually any type of clerk in the Empire and how to forge anything but the Imperial Seal. When a clerk arrived with appropriate documentation and a request to see something, or even to carry it away, it took a hardier and more independent soul than existed in the Imperial Civil Service to challenge him.

"You—" he said, pointing to the first in line. "I want you to go over the military pay records, find out all the units with pay in arrears, and who is in charge of their pay." He pointed to the next two. "You and you—go through the records of the units sent to take Hardorn. I want you to match up the requests for supplies and reinforcements with the orders issued to fill those requests. I also want the record of every request that was denied, and on whose authority." He pointed to the last two. "You two get access to Emperor Charliss' private papers, or at least the ones that are in the Archives. I want all the correspondence between Tremane and Charliss from the time he left for Hardorn to his last known message. Go!"

The five clerks departed, scattering like quail before the hunter. He didn't need to give them any further orders about *how* to get access to those papers; one of the reason that these men were no longer *in* the Civil Service was that they had initiative. Neither initiative nor creativity were rewarded in the Imperial Civil Service, and those with both often grew frustrated and looked for employment elsewhere.

Melles next called in his private treasurer.

"You get down to the Imperial Exchequer. I want to know how much out of the military budget can be spared in hard coin and how much in goods. Tell the Exchequer that I suspect the Army's pay has been bollixed up, and we may have to make good in a hurry if we don't want trouble on our hands." He thought for a moment, and dredged up the relevant fact from his memory. "If he balks at telling you, just say something about the road budget; it doesn't matter what, just work it quickly into the conversation."

The man nodded, grinning; every Imperial Exchequer skimmed a certain amount off the top, it was expected, so long as they were clever enough not to get caught at it. But if they *were* caught, the penalties were severe. Melles knew precisely where the current Exchequer was skimming and even had a rough idea of how much; he had made it his business to know, planning to use the information at the right moment. There could be no better moment than now. A good card was no better than a bad one if you never played it.

The treasurer left, and Melles called in his final choice in this campaign of seduction, one of his odder employees. This rather elegant specimen was ostensibly Melles' personal poet and playwright, but although the man was mediocre creatively, he was an absolute genius at propaganda. Melles didn't use him often, but he was, like the valet, the appropriate scalpel for certain types of surgery. Melles was doubly fortunate in that the man enjoyed the writing of manipulative propaganda almost as much as poetry. He had told his patron once that when he wrote the former, he considered that he was writing a different kind of drama, one in which the words manipulated the actors, instead of the other way around. He enjoyed seeing how his works played out on the larger stage of the real world.

And as a peculiar kind of reward, Melles regularly financed the production of poetry readings in opulent surroundings, seeing to it that the right critics were flattered, fed, and given enough strong and exotic drink to make even the worst drivel seem inspired.

"I hope you aren't in the throes of creation," Melles said cautiously, for this was one individual who could not be coerced, only persuaded. But his loyalty to Melles was based on firm self-interest and was utterly trustworthy. When bought, he stayed bought—and no one aside from Melles himself knew that he was anything other than a peculiar affectation. It was expected that someone of Melles' status patronize the arts in some way, and a poet was the cheapest and least intrusive sort of artist to have on one's staff. "I have a rather extensive job for you," he continued. "I hope you aren't preoccupied."

The man smiled urbanely and crossed his legs with conscious elegance. He was something of a dandy and rather fancied himself as a popular man with the ladies. His salary from Melles enabled him to cut quite a figure of sartorial splendor among not only his peers but also his superiors. "What do you need my skills for? As a repairer of reputation? I've been planning what to do for you since the moment the rumors began to fly." He shook his head, and then waggled his finger in mock-admonition. "My dear patron, you have been very injudicious. This could ruin you yet, if it isn't carefully handled."

Melles did not make the retort he felt hovering on his tongue. The man was worth his weight in gold, and was arrogant enough to be quite aware of it. Instead, he got right to the point. "It isn't the Court I'm worried about; they're ineffectual enough, and like sheep, they'll follow anyone with the right bell around his neck. No, it's the Army that's giving me trouble." He leaned forward over his desk, to emphasize how serious he felt the situation was. "They've decided they don't care for the idea of someone with my ethics on the Iron Throne."

The poet pursed his lips. "That could be troublesome. I don't know quite how to handle the Army—unless you already know what you want to say?"

"I do. Believe it or not, I want you to report the exact truth." Melles smiled thinly at the poet's surprise. "We're going to concentrate on the plight of my old rival, Tremane," he continued lightly. "I want you to spread the story of how he and his command were abandoned out beyond the farthest reach of the Empire. Be creative; go on about the horror of being sent off to die in utterly unknown lands. Find the right words to convince people that *I* had nothing to do with the abandonment of Tremane and his men in Hardorn. Then convince them that I had no idea that I would be Charliss' next choice for his successor. Say that I feel that the times are so radically changed that I have changed with them. Say I personally am so busy trying to keep the Empire together that I have no interest in pursuing my old vendetta against Tremane himself."

That last could get him in a certain amount of difficulty with the Emperor if Charliss got wind of it, but he was willing to take that particular chance.

The poet pursed his lips in thought. "It's a novel approach," he admitted. "And it just might distract soldiers from the stories of dead bodies in baby cribs. After all, you didn't actually kill the *baby*, you only dumped the body of an assassin there. Whereas Tremane and his men were abandoned in Hardorn; that's without a doubt and with no particular reason to leave them out there."

"That's exactly what I'm looking for," Melles encouraged. "And soldiers have more in common with other soldiers than with brats in cribs. They will have empathy for Tremane's forces. Why weren't they called back while it was still possible to construct Portals that worked between the Storms? Don't place any blame yet, but raise as many questions in peoples' minds as you can, particularly in the Army."

"I can do that," the poet said decisively, losing a great deal of his languid pose as his own imagination set to work. "I'm very good at questions. What about answers?"

"I'll give you more to work on when I have facts," Melles promised. "For right now, this will be enough. Get people talking, get their minds on something else besides my little jokes." He signaled that the man could go.

"Gossip and rumor, opiates of the dull, can for the clever be the stuff that dream are made of," the poet said sardonically, as he smiled, standing up as gracefully as he had sat down.

"My dreams, at any rate," Melles chuckled, watching the man's elegant way of walking—elegant, but not at all effeminate. It was rather like a wolf at the stalk, and he made up his mind to copy it.

The first of his seekers came back within hours with an accurate account of the Army pay records. As he had suspected, since every district governor was individually responsible for seeing to it that the units within his jurisdiction actually were paid (even though the pay actually came out of the military budget), there were several instances where pay was in arrears, sometimes significantly. As he went over the figures with his own accountant, the secretary he had sent to interview the Imperial Exchequer also returned.

That gave him his first move in the new game.

He waited until the next day, then descended on the major figures of the Imperial Civil Service, trailing a string of clerks all bearing stacks of paper. With great fanfare and a fine speech written by his pet poet, he "revealed" the terrible injustice that had been done to the loyal soldiers of the Empire.

"But it is not your fault," he continued, before anyone could get angry at having yet *more* work heaped on him. "You are doing the best you can in terrible circumstances!" He went on at some length, praising the overworked clerks for sticking at their jobs even when they had to wade through blizzards to get to their desks, shiver in the drafts when they arrived, and fight worse weather to go to a cold home with short rations once they returned at the end of a long day's work. "I have brought you the help of my *own* clerks to see you through this crisis," he said, as his men took over empty desks or any other flat space with a chair. "I am sure you do not want our brave soldiers to suffer, but I do not want you to suffer either!"

With that, he set off a frenzy of paper pushing to get every soldier's records and pay up to date. Some of the pay had to be made in goods rather than coin, but he made certain that the clerks arranged it so the goods in question were more valuable on the gray market than the actual pay they were substituting for.

It was all taken care of in a single morning; not too difficult, when he doubled the existing workforce and had all of them concentrate on the one task, putting all other work temporarily aside. He then formally went to the Commanders and promised to personally make up for the other deficiencies that had cropped up, usually in the way of resupply. He made a great show of embarrassment, as if he had only now discovered these problems. He didn't know if anyone believed him, but he made a point of assigning his own people to make certain that existing problems were corrected and further ones reported to him so that he could see that they were dealt with.

As he had hoped, although there was some suspicion that he was trying to buy the Army's favor, he began to get some grudging acceptance. This was especially true once the stories began to circulate of how he had uncovered all these problems personally.

Then his poet went to work, sending out his insidious little stories and questions, making the ordinary Imperial soldier wonder just what "supposed mistake" could have left Tremane's people out in the cold, so to speak. An added bonus came when he got word back that the rank-and-file had a few other, unanticipated questions. Such as a question of whether the late pay was really just bureaucratic bungling, or if Certain Parties had ordered the pay held back as a form of punishment. After all, if Grand Duke Tremane and all his men could be abandoned, what was a little delay in paying out wages?

But the crowning touch to the entire plan finally went into effect when Melles' clerks found that correspondence between Charliss and Tremane. And he could not have manufactured a better final letter than the one that arrived for the Emperor's personal perusal just before the Portals went down and stayed down.

It was bad enough that Tremane had begged, over and over again, for critical supplies that were never sent, for more men, and especially for more mages. But it was the final letter that made Melles positively gleeful both from the standpoint of seeing his old enemy brought low, and for the strength of the "ammunition" it gave him.

For in that letter, which was accompanied by strategic maps, Tremane begged the Emperor to allow his men to retreat, vowing that he himself would remain behind and attempt to hold what had been taken with a corps of volunteers. He pleaded with the Emperor not to visit punishment upon men who had done nothing to deserve it, and to permit them to escape while it was still possible to hold Portals to the Empire open long enough for them to pass through.

And although Melles himself was no strategist, it was painfully obvious from the maps that Tremane's position was utterly untenable. No one, not even a military genius, could have saved the situation.

In a handwritten directive, the Emperor ordered his secretaries to make no response to this desperate plea, on the grounds that Tremane would have to solve the situation in order to prove his worth, thus condemning Tremane's forces with him. At that point, the best outcome for them was exile—and the worst was massacre.

He took that letter with the note in the margin to General Thayer, who in turn leaked the information to his own Commanders, who sent it on down the line. He managed to conceal his triumph in a show of distress so perfect he even fooled Thayer.

By this time the Army was outraged. The Emperor had betrayed them, betrayed the sacred bond that was supposed to bind the Emperor and the men who served him. The rumors of Melles the "baby killer" were forgotten in this new, and far more personal outrage, and even the lowest private began to recall how it was *Melles* who saw that the pay was put right, and *Melles* who made sure the supply wagons got through.

Melles, and not the Emperor. And in that moment, he had them.

That was the point where he got an odd invitation from General Thayer; an invitation to dinner, but not in the Palace. This was to be a private dinner, in an upper room of a very well-known and luxurious inn usually frequented by wealthy bachelors who didn't care to keep staff or cooks.

There were just a few things "wrong" with this invitation—the most obvious being that Melles was not and had never been part of the social circle that made use of this particular facility. The inn itself was suffering some of the privations of every other eatery; the fare now was far from the former standards, and in fact was inferior to anything he could get in Crag Castle. And it was halfway across the city; the mage-storms struck twice a day now, with the result that the weather was utterly unpredictable, and there were often "things" prowling the streets, animals and even humans changed by the Storms into misshapen creatures that bore little resemblance to what they had been. The once-rats were bad enough, but the other creatures required that one travel with an escort of heavily-armed men after dark.

He turned the invitation over and over in his hands, considering it.

It could be a trap, of course, designed to get him where he would be vulnerable and eliminate him. But somehow, he didn't think so. To meet in a public tavern in so remote a place suggested a need for secrecy. The private salons of these large inns had separate, outside entrances, so that people could come and go without being seen. This had the earmarks of a conspiracy.

I had better go. If anyone is going to make an attempt on the Emperor—assuming that is why they want me—I had better be in a position to advise them.

It wasn't the best plan, but it was better than allowing them to make an attempt that would fail, and would alarm Charliss. The Emperor was already unstable, and it wouldn't take a great deal to set him off on a campaign to purge the Court.

And if necessary, I can always turn them in myself, proving my loyalty to Charliss. That would be the court of last resort, however, if he could not persuade them to hold off until he was ready. Betraying them to Charliss would cost him so much difficulty once *he* was Emperor that such a move was not advisable unless there was no other possible course of action.

There was the possibility that this invitation was the setup for an assassination attempt on him, but he didn't think that they would be that stupid. An assassin himself, as they well knew, he would be a very difficult man to take down. Granted, a large number of men could overpower him, but as he had already proved, he was, despite all appearances, still perfectly capable of defending himself and killing or maiming several of them before they managed to kill him. Such an affair would be noisy and leave many witnesses who would have to be silenced or eliminated. He would have his own men with him, who would also have to be silenced or eliminated, and those men would have the superiors they reported to and families of their own who would miss them. It would turn into a nightmare of murder, and be impossible to cover up. They had to be aware of all of that.

With great reluctance, he called his valet and ordered clothing for the cold, arranged an armed Imperial escort to take care of the hobgoblins, alerted his personal bodyguard, and ordered a carriage-on-runners; nothing else could handle the icy streets now. People had to step up from their doorsteps to the street instead of down, for there was rock-hard, packed snow to the depth of the knee on most of the streets, snow that would not be gone until spring.

He was just glad that he had invested every bit of his mage-craft in shielding; mages who had not done so were in a state of near-collapse every time a Storm passed through. He barely noticed; he got a headache just before each Storm, a bit of disorientation during it, and a touch of nausea afterward. Nothing was bad enough to even interrupt his reading. But another Storm was due about the time he expected to be on the street, and anyone who was likely to be severely affected by the Storms could find himself in deadly danger in a situation of that nature. A person walking alone could collapse and freeze to death, he could be set upon and robbed, and a person riding in a conveyance could *still* freeze to death without his escort noticing.

He wondered how many marginally Talented mages had been caught and hurt or killed that way. *If so, that simply cuts down on the number of idiots with mage-power,* he reflected, as he pulled on a second set of gloves over his first set, and worked his feet into heavy sheepskin-lined boots. It was difficult to be both dressed for warmth and for elegance, and he opted, at least in his outermost garments, for the first.

The journey to the inn was something of an unpleasant ordeal, and he wondered at the number of people who still continued to make their daily trips from home to place of employment, went out shopping, or indeed, did *anything* that took them out of doors. The weather was hideous, as it was more often than not now. There was the usual blizzard blowing, driving snow deep into the fabric of one's clothing, making it impossible to see the linkmen bearing lanterns who lit the way for the driver, if they got more than a few paces ahead of the carriage. And yet there *were* other people out on the street, including some women, which amazed him. His escort changed places regularly, so that some rode while others walked.

When they were about a third of the way to his destination, a pack of hobgoblins attacked—hairy things that scrabbled through the snow on all fours, drooling and howling with hunger, their ribs clearly prominent even through their heavy brindled coats of fur. This time, it appeared that they were Changedogs, rather than Changechildren, which made it a bit easier on the escort; the men had a difficult time killing things that cried like babies and had human eyes or faces. It wasn't too difficult to beat the pack back, leaving a few bleeding, fur-covered bodies in the snow. So far, Changed creatures were routinely less intelligent than the creatures they had been changed *from*, and Changedogs were probably the most stupid of them all; they kept charging straight ahead even when that tactic clearly did not work. The exception was Changerats, which were more cunning and vicious, and swarmed in packs of several hundred. There were laws about Changed animals and people now; if your pet or relative was Changed, the only way to keep it (or him) was to take it to an Imperial examiner who would verify that it was no danger to humans or livestock. There were a few Changechildren being kept and sheltered by relatives. Most were actually killed by their own families the moment they Changed, for the horror stories circulating about the bloodbaths some of the Changed had wrought in their own households did not encourage compassion. A few who found themselves Changed had killed themselves. Most of the Changechildren who roamed the streets as hobgoblins had come *from* the streets—were beggars, thieves, and other street people who had no relatives to eliminate them and no interest in anything other than survival.

The rest of the journey was spent nervously watching for another pack of attackers. When they finally did arrive at the inn, it was fully dark, and in the interest of keeping his employees satisfied enough to keep their mouths shut, he distributed a generous purse among them so that they could entertain themselves in fine style in the common room while he met with Thayer and Thayer's guests in the private room above.

His men entered the common room at the side entrance; he entered the main entrance, stepping out of the screaming wind and snow into a sheltering foyer, softly lit and blessedly warm and attended by a discreet footman. Music played faintly somewhere; a full consort of wind and string instruments. The footman directed him up a staircase to the right to another foyer, this time attended by one of Thayer's personal servants, who took his snow-caked outer clothing and directed him inside the door behind him.

He was not at all surprised to see that besides Thayer, virtually every other important military leader in the area of the capital was there already, waiting, with an excellent supper (as yet untouched) set up on a sideboard. All eyes were on him as he entered, and the murmur of talk that had been going on stopped for a moment, then resumed.

He took his place beside Thayer, was introduced to those he did not know personally, and Thayer's servants proceeded to serve all of the guests. He watched them carefully, and noted that they only served him food from dishes that everyone shared, and only after stirring up the contents within his sight, so that there could be no "special" little spot that had been prepared for him with poison. He kept his approving smile to himself, and pretended not to notice. Dinner conversation was not precisely light, since a great deal of it had to do with the roving packs of hobgoblins and suggested means of eradicating them, but it had nothing whatsoever to do with politics. There was another peculiarity of Thayer's servants; they never handled knives themselves, deferring to Thayer for carving of meat, and they were unarmed. As for Thayer's guests, they were *conspicuously* unarmed. Everything that could have been done to reassure a professional killer that he was safe among them had been done.

So, it wasn't to be an assassination attempt after all. That meant it was a conspiracy.

And the moment that the meal was over, the dishes cleared away, the wine poured and more left in decanters on the table, and the servants sent off, the conspiracy was revealed.

They wanted to be rid of Charliss before he did any more damage, and they were perfectly willing to send him on to Godhood a little sooner.

He listened to them with great patience, making no comments, only nodding occasionally when they seemed to require it. They were understandably angry at many of the things that had been going on, and his revelations concerning Tremane had essentially been the trigger for all their pent-up frustrations. They were quite prepared to eliminate the Emperor themselves, and had a good, solid plan for doing so. He told them as much, and commended them for having a plan that took care of almost every aspect of the situation.

"*Almost,*" he repeated with emphasis. "But I would be remiss if I did not point out the major flaw in your plan. And I do not blame you gentlemen for not considering the aspect I have in mind."

"'Which is what, exactly?" asked General Thayer, who was acting as the primary spokesman.

"Magic." He held up a hand to forestall any objections. "I know that, given how your own mages are acting with the increasing severity and frequency of the mage-storms, that mages seem an insignificant aspect to you. Please believe me; they are not. You have determined that the spells binding the Imperial Guard to Charliss are broken and have not been replaced; that is good news, but those are not the only magics you need to worry about. Charliss himself is a powerful mage, and his power is augmented by an entire corps of lesser mages whose minds have been his for many years. They spend themselves to ensure *his* continued prosperity, and that is what you are not seeing in dealing with your own mages, who would do no such thing. Surely you gentlemen recall seeing Charliss' mages before—that group of rather blank-eyed individuals who trail about after him like so many adoring, mindless maidens trailing about after a handsome warrior?"

He looked around the table, and saw to his satisfaction that, although there was disappointment in their faces, there was reluctant agreement there as well, and nods all around.

"At the moment, Charliss is only moderately inconvenienced by the Storms, as opposed to the vast majority of mages, who are prostrated by them." He steepled his fingers together thoughtfully, and considered his next words. "As a mage myself, let me explain to you, if I may, the true effect the Storms are having on mages—and that is primarily in our *choice* of actions. The choice for a mage at the moment is simple: preserve all of your own power for shields, or work other magics and have each Storm that passes send you to your bed for hours, recovering." He saw more nods, as the Generals recognized the effects he had just described. "Because Charliss is using the power from his corps of mages, he can shield *and* work other magics, and not suffer. That is what makes him dangerous, still. You might well get past his guards, even past his personal bodyguards; you might get past the protections put in by his personal mages, but by then he will be alerted and you will never get an assassin past his own defenses."

There were still a few of the Generals who were not convinced; Melles saw it in their closed expressions.

"There is one more factor to be considered here, and that is what would happen afterward," he continued. "The old man still retains the loyalty of too many people—including most of the truly powerful mages of the Empire—who consider me to be an upstart. As it happens, most of them favored Tremane, who was a personal favorite of the mages who taught him, many of whom are now quite influential. I do not know if the truth of what happened to poor Tremane would turn their opinion against the Emperor, but if you remove him now, you will not give that truth a chance to work in their minds."

Now he had all of them; the last of the skeptical looks was gone, replaced with resignation.

"Please wait," he said, at his most persuasive. "The Emperor has made no attempt to say or do anything about the truths that are spreading about his treatment of Tremane. I suspect this is because he is living in a very narrow world of reasoning at the moment. He wants revenge on Tremane for 'betraying' the Empire, and he may believe that people assume he cut Tremane off after that 'betrayal' rather than before. The Hundred Little Gods know that by now he may even believe that himself!'"

A couple of the oldest of the Generals pursed their lips and looked just a touch regretful; some of the youngest only looked smug. Both expressions were probably prompted by the same thought—*how far the Emperor has fallen!* The old were thinking that Charliss' mental deterioration could easily be something they would experience if they were unlucky; the young were thinking only that it was terrible for someone that old, in that state, to still be in power.

Melles continued, seeing that he was bringing them to the line of thought *he* wanted them to follow. "Charliss looks physically worse with every day that passes. He may die soon on his own; his life is sustained by magic, and that is eroding no matter how desperately he shores it up. Let things take their natural course." He allowed himself a small, modest smile. "After all, I *am* the one who is really holding the reins now; Charliss is too busy concentrating on survival. Waiting will harm nothing in the long run. With time, I may be able to persuade those same mages that Charliss is using them with no regard for the cost to them, and no regard for the *real* enemy we face—the Storms."

Thayer looked around the table, and seemed to take some kind of unspoken consensus from his colleagues. "Very well," he said. "We will hold our hands. We agree that the real danger to the Empire is the mage-storms and the continuing refusal of the Emperor to adequately deal with them. *You* must see what you can do to convince the mages that Charliss is no longer capable of dealing with the true priorities of this situation."

He sat back in his chair and nodded. This was exactly how he wanted *everything* to fall out, and he relished the moment even as he relished a single sip of wine. If he were to prosper as Emperor, the Empire itself must survive and prosper; in order for that to happen, he *must* redirect the energies and attention of the Empire on the Storms and their effects. Just now, the energies and attentions of the Empire were seriously divided between one selfish old man who had outlived his usefulness, and the struggles to survive through worsening conditions. Either Charliss must go, or the Empire, for only one would survive through the Storms.

"I will deal with the mages, and believe me, we *must* have them," he said. "Remember, Tremane is our key. Even as the Army realized that Charliss had betrayed and abandoned one of their own, I believe that with time, I can persuade the mages of the same."

"Good." Thayer held out his hand. "Strange times make for strange allies, but sometimes those are the best. The Army is with you."

"And I," Melles pledged, with no sense of irony, "am with you as well. It is a pity that poor Tremane did not have as many firm allies."

Elspeth had just finished describing the latest results from the group in the Tower, as relayed from Rolan to Gwena, when Tremane's face suddenly went white. "Gods," Tremane said through gritted teeth. "Here comes another one."

He meant another mage-storm; he felt them first, as they traveled over the face of Hardorn. They made him tremble all over, churned his stomach, and muddled his head. But that gave Elspeth, Darkwind, and Tashiketh time to brace themselves before the onset of the Storm hit them as well. At the moment, the effects were still not *too* bad, although every mage endured some unpleasant physical symptoms in direct proportion to how powerful he or she was. But the circles of changed soil had already begun to appear again, and it could not be too much longer before the weather shifted back to the terrible blizzards that had ravaged the countryside, and before more "boggles" appeared as living creatures were changed by wild magic. They were just glad they had the formula to predict *where* those circles would appear.

Elspeth grasped the arms of her chair and clenched her own jaw; it didn't help, it never did, but at least it gave her something to do while the Storm rolled over her. Meanwhile, Father Janas watched them all with worried, wondering eyes, for he was no mage, and felt nothing when the Storms came.

This was a short, intense Storm. When it was over, she let out the breath she had been holding, let go of the arms of the chair, and put her head down on her folded arms on the table.

"Oh, I do not *like* that," Tashiketh sighed. "I do not know how you bear it."

"You bear what you must," Darkwind replied philosophically. "And there are worse things to contemplate than having one's lunch jump about in one's stomach."

"And that brings us back to the topic we were discussing," Tremane said, his clenched hands slowly loosening as color returned to his face. "I do not wish to cast aspersions upon the ability of your friends, Lady Elspeth, but I feel we *must* assume that the party in the Tower will not find a solution to the Final Storm. My concern is and must be for this land and these people; how am I to protect them? Is there any way that I can take in the damage myself, instead of having it come upon the land? Can I use earth-magic and the earth-binding to instruct the land to heal itself and to prevent the creatures here from being twisted out of all recognition? Have you any ideas at all?"

Father Janas shook his head. "You could take the ills of the land upon yourself, my son, but not for long before it killed you. You cannot bear what the land could and live."

"I don't have any ideas yet, but we have several kinds of magic that we can incorporate," Elspeth mused aloud. "Tremane, I don't think the damage to the land is going to be that terrible, but what I am afraid of is that the nodes are going to—go to a critical point where they cannot be controlled. That they are going to become rogue. I'm very much afraid that the Final Storm is going to turn them into something like the rogue Heartstone that Darkwind and I dealt with."

"That is my concern also," Tashiketh agreed. "I fear that is precisely what may occur, and such a thing would be very like having a continual Storm in one place. As power fed into it, it would continue to grow. This would be a very bad thing."

"Shelters, shields," Darkwind muttered, frowning and glaring at nothing. "The trouble with such things is that they are *going* to fail; I don't know how we could possibly make them strong enough to survive what is coming."

Elspeth got up and paced restlessly beside the windows. The weather in Hardorn had deteriorated again, but it was not yet as foul as it had been before the last protection went into place. They were currently between snowstorms, and the sun shone down with empty benevolence on the dazzling fresh snow. Elspeth was not looking forward to the resumption of blizzards, but at least the increase in the number of snowstorms was keeping the number of curiosity seekers down. Virtually everyone who *could* come in himself to pledge to Tremane had, and a few days ago, their old friend Father Janas appeared with another casket of earth, collected from all of those who wished to pledge themselves and their land to their new King and could not come in person. Now Tremane "felt" virtually every part of his realm, which was both an advantage and a disadvantage. He knew where every trouble spot was, and when a Storm began its march across the face of Hardorn, Elspeth was personally quite glad that it was Tremane who experienced the sickness of his land, and not her.

But now the system of signal-towers was fully functional again, and at least warning could be sent out when something did go wrong out in the hinterlands. The precise locations of where the circles of altered land would fall were sent out well in advance of the Storms by means of the towers. If things were not precisely under control, at least they were in a better state than they had been. There was *one* authority in Hardorn again, and resources were not being wasted on warfare. A few skirmishes with Tashiketh's gryphons had put an end to further fighting.

There was still the pressing problem of how to protect the nodes and the Tayledras Heartstones. She was all too conscious of the Heartstone right under the Palace at Haven; if *that* went rogue, it could very well destroy the Palace, all the Collegia, and perhaps a good section of Haven as well. The loss of life would be horrendous. The Palace complex had been partially evacuated, but with mixed results and quite a bit of ongoing confusion. She had seen enough magical destruction in the capital of Hardorn; she had no trouble envisioning the same level of destruction visited on her own home.

She started to shake, just thinking about it, and turned her gaze to look out the window for a moment so that no one in the room would see her face and the expression she wore. As so often happened these days, her timing was just right. She was the first to see and recognize the latest arrival to Tremane's court.

The procession was just entering the courtyard as she glanced down at the gates, and the glitter of the sun on shining metal and blinding gold and white trappings caught her eye first. Then she saw the standard, and who rode beneath it, and she gasped, catching the attention of everyone else.

"Oh, gods—" she said, feeling as if she had just been struck a numbing blow to the head and had not yet felt the pain. She wondered wildly for a moment if she was hallucinating; there was no way that she should be seeing what she saw out the window. "Oh, ye gods, this cannot be happening! This is too strange even for me."

"Elspeth?" Darkwind said, catching the timbre of her voice without knowing what caused it. "*Ashke*, what's wrong?"

The chair legs grated on the wooden floor as he hastily shoved his seat back. He got up and hurried to her side; unable to speak, she simply pointed out the window.

His eyes widened, and he choked, completely unable to get even a word of exclamation out.

"King Tremane," Elspeth managed to say as Darkwind was struck dumb. "You have a very important visitor, and I think you had better get down to the courtyard *now*."

"Why?" he asked, a little resentfully, for he had gotten rather tired of meeting so many delegations in the cold over the past several weeks.

"You should just—do what she says," Darkwind managed to croak.

Tremane looked skeptical. His tone took on an edge of sarcasm. "Who's here? The Emperor?"

"No," Elspeth replied. "Solaris, High Priest of Vkandis and Son of the Sun and her entourage." She glanced down again. "And the Firecat Hansa," she added.

Behind her, there was a muffled curse, and the sound of a chair clattering against the floor as it fell over, and by the time she had turned to see what Tremane was doing, he was already gone.

"We'd better go down there, too," Darkwind finally managed to get out. "We should be there to welcome her." She nodded, and gestured to the fascinated gryphon to accompany them.

By the time they reached the courtyard, however, Tremane had already given Solaris as respectful a welcome as anyone could have wished, even the Son of the Sun and the Mouth of Vkandis, given that she had arrived with no warning. And she in her turn had remained polite, which was all that Elspeth could have hoped for, given the circumstances.

"I have been traveling for many days at the express orders of Sunlord Vkandis," Solaris was saying, as Elspeth got within earshot. "It was, I believe, at precisely the moment when you were bound to the land of Hardorn that—"

Then she caught sight of Tashiketh—who had reared up on his hind legs and was holding his foreclaws extended in a peculiar manner that was obviously a ritual salute. And Solaris stared at the gryphon with a look of shock and complete disbelief on her face, her hands automatically moving to form a similar salute.

That's odd; she's seen gryphons before. So why is she looking at Tashiketh as if he were some new kind of creature?

As she stared at him in complete disbelief, Tashiketh intoned something in that odd gabble that Elspeth thought sounded like Karsite. Evidently, so did Solaris, who blinked and stammered something back. It was the very first time that Elspeth had ever seen the Son of the Sun taken aback by anything.

:Evidently Vkandis has a streak of the practical joker in Him after all,:

Darkwind commented with a touch of amusement. *:Otherwise, He would have warned her.:*

:Perhaps this is meant to be an object lesson. That just because she is the Mouth of Vkandis, she doesn't necessarily know everything about the Sunlord,: Elspeth answered.

Tashiketh replied, and Solaris responded. Evidently they were going through a set series of greetings and responses. Finally the little ritual came to a close; Tashiketh dropped back down to all fours again, and made a very courtly bow.

She looked from Tremane to Tashiketh and back again. "How long, sir, have you had this gentleman at your Court?" she asked very carefully.

"Since a few days after I was bound to the earth," Tremane replied. "Tashiketh informed us that he and his entourage were sent because of that particular event."

"As was I," Solaris murmured, still staring at Tashiketh. "And now I know *why* I was sent here, rather than being told to send representatives as I did to Valdemar."

:I have the feeling that it wasn't just to consult with Tremane,: Darkwind said wryly. *:Now she knows that her God has been sharing his attentions. This could be rather amusing.:*

The Firecat Hansa, who was sitting very patiently on the front of Solaris' saddle, reached out and patted her on the shoulder with his paw. *:We are about to have a blizzard descend, Sunborn,:* he said politely. *:If you would all be so kind, good people, it would be best if we could move inside.:*

As with his compatriot Altra, Hansa could apparently make himself "heard" in Mindspeech even to those who did not share that Gift. Elspeth saw startled looks all over the courtyard, as even Tremane's guards experienced someone talking inside their minds for the first time in their lives.

"I beg your pardon, Sir Hansa, of course we can," Tremane said instantly, and with commendable aplomb. "Allow me to conduct you to appropriate quarters myself." At that moment, to confirm Hansa's prediction, the warning horns blew from the walls, signaling that a physical storm was moving in quickly from the west.

And Tremane did escort them, probably thanking his Hundred Little Gods that he had set up one of the towers as guest quarters for important folk and their followers. The last set of guests had just vacated the premises; the tower was clean and waiting for the next set. It was a matter of moments to take them there, turning over the entire tower to Solaris and her relatively small entourage. Although Darkwind excused himself,

Elspeth went along as the official representative of Selenay, and because she was anxious to talk to Solaris if she could. Solaris' escort consisted of a few *very* professional and tough-looking guards, and several Sun-priests. Just as the last of their baggage came up from below, the blizzard Hansa had warned was coming did indeed descend, and Tremane took his leave of them to see that the usual precautions were in place.

The moment he left, Solaris dropped some of her detached and "official" manner. Looking at Elspeth and Tashiketh, she raised an eyebrow in an inquiring manner. "Would you care to remain while my people get us settled in? I should be glad of the company; it has been a stressful trip."

"I think we would both be pleased to remain, Holiness," Elspeth said carefully, and Solaris laughed, tossing her cloak aside and removing the heavy gold collar she was wearing. A robed attendant took both and carried them away.

"Just 'Solaris,' little sister," the High Priest replied. "There are few enough who can call me by that name, and you are certainly one who has that right." She removed a few more pieces of regalia and set them aside, then sank down in the chair nearest the fire while the wind shook the walls. Hansa immediately leaped into her lap and settled there. "Do take a seat, Elspeth," Solaris continued. "Sunborn Tashiketh, I am not certain *what* to offer you."

"The floor will do, Most Holy," the gryphon said with careful courtesy, and settled himself there as Elspeth chose another chair. "I hope you will forgive me, but how is it that you did not know that Vykaendys was—"

"Was watching over both our lands? I suspect it is partly because that knowledge was lost while corrupt Priests held the Sun Throne. As to why Vkandis did not choose to reveal this fact to me until now—" She spread her hands wide. "The God moves in His own way, and in His own time. Presumably He had a reason for sending me here to be hit over the head with this revelation."

"I suspect that He sent you here for more than that reason, Most Holy," Tashiketh replied respectfully.

"If you are here, *who* is holding the Sun Throne?" Elspeth blurted, unable to restrain her curiosity. "I thought you couldn't leave for any length of time, that there were still those you did not entirely trust."

"Oh, *that* is a tale in itself, and some day I will tell you all of it, but in short, I am here because Vkandis Himself sits on the Sun Throne at this very moment," Solaris said. As Elspeth started with surprise, Solaris nodded. "I mean that quite literally. It is the second great Miracle of my reign; the great statue of Vkandis came to life again during a Holy Service over which I was presiding, then ordered us all to follow and walked out of the Temple, shrinking as He moved, until He reached the throne room, where He took the throne."

Solaris spoke so matter-of-factly that she might have been discussing the terrible blizzard outside, rather than something that was, quite clearly, a miracle in every sense of the word. Elspeth was as fascinated by her attitude as by what had happened. She saw no reason to doubt anything that Solaris told her, for Solaris would not have left Karse without a compelling reason and an unshakable guarantee that her Throne would be waiting for her when she returned.

"When He had seated Himself, He let it be known that I was traveling into Hardorn on a life-or-death mission at His behest, and that in token of the fact that I was His true-born Son, He would be holding the Sun Throne until I returned," she continued. "He swore His protection to Karse against the Storms. At that point, the statue became a statue again except, of course, it was literally rooted to the Sun Throne. It wasn't an illusion either; the great statue is quite *gone* from the pedestal, and the smaller version in place on the Throne. And in addition, there is a peculiar barrier around Karse itself. People can come and go through it, but it is quite visible, and it seems to resemble the barrier around Iftel that Karal described to me." She smiled a bit wryly. "Now it seems clear *why* it resembles that barrier. The Sunlord has had practice."

Solaris might *seem* to be matter-of-fact, but as Elspeth listened and watched, she realized that Solaris was profoundly moved and awed. Elspeth found this a great deal easier to understand; how could anyone *not* feel awe at such an occurrence?

"I doubt that anyone will have the temerity to claim your place, given that particular demonstration," Tashiketh said dryly. "And so Vykaendys directed you here?"

"Precisely, and it was not the easiest journey I have ever undertaken, though not the worst either. Our robes earned us respect and safe passage, though no one really recognized us as Sun-priests." One corner of her mouth twitched. "I will admit it came as something of a shock to learn that Tremane had been Bound to Hardorn. That puts him on an equal basis with me, in some ways, and it was not what I would have expected to see happen. Still, it is probably good for Hardorn." She laughed softly. "I also have a confession that I might as well make to you both. I am taking a certain amount of sadistic pleasure in this. He is going to suffer physical discomfort, even terrible pain from time to time; he agreed to this, he even volunteered for it, and I think that between this and his *geas* of Truth-speaking, he just might be able to atone for his actions in the past."

"He spoke to me in private of what he had done, sending the assassin," Tashiketh admitted. "I believe he regrets his actions more with every passing day."

"Well, he should," Solaris said firmly. "I cannot even begin to describe the anguish he caused, not only to myself and Karal, but to those who knew and cared for all of his victims. But although I am not prepared to forgive him yet, I am willing and ready to work with him. I *am* an Adept of a peculiar bent, as I suspect you have guessed. I think we may be able yet to find ways to protect ourselves through this crisis."

"I hope so," Elspeth said fervently. "I *hope* so."

"With Vykaendys' help," Tashiketh replied with absolute certainty, "we shall."

1 0

Firecats had a real cat's ability to make a person feel as if she was a particularly stupid student and the cat was a teacher fast losing patience. *:Vkandis' protection is temporary,:* Hansa said firmly, looking for all the world precisely like the Cat statue at the feet of Henricht, the first Son of the Sun. Poor Henricht, even as a statue, looked singularly unprepossessing; the Cat, however, looked as if *he* should have been sitting on the Sun Throne. *:It cannot last through the Final Storm. The nodes in Karse are as vulnerable as any. The protection is only meant to prevent people and beasts from Changing, and to prevent the greater part of the priesthood from falling ill twice and thrice a day.:* He bent his head then, and washed a paw with great daintiness. *:You and your priests will have to do your share like everyone else. If nodes go rogue, you will be dealing with the unfortunate results.:*

Solaris sighed, but not with disappointment. Elspeth thought that her sigh sounded more like someone who had just heard unpleasant news she had nevertheless expected.

"Shields," Darkwind muttered, pacing, as Vree followed his movements with interest from his perch in the corner. "That has to be the key. But *how* do we create a shield that will hold through even the Storms we have now?"

Elspeth pummeled her mind for something she remembered out of—a Chronicle? No, it was a story that Kerowyn had told about one of the mages her grandmother had trained. "Why only *one* shield?" she asked. "Why not layered shields, shields within shields? Kerowyn told me about something like that; the mage layered lots of weaker shields instead of one strong one, and kept replacing them from the inside as they were taken down from the outside. If you could do that, keep replacing the innermost shield every time the outermost was destroyed—"

"Interesting, and yes, it has been done before, and quite successfully," Darkwind said, knitting his brows in thought. "Multiple shields *are* more effective than one strong shield. But we can't put a mage beside every node, and if we don't, how could we keep replacing shields as they came down? You can't shield from the *outside* once the initial shield is up, and how would we do it from the inside? That is the problem of course, and a spell—or series of spells—would have to be crafted for that."

"If we could. How would we continue to supply the energy to create the shields in the first place?" Tremane objected. Solaris gave him a withering look. "You would be sealing the perfect energy source *within* the shield," she replied, with an unspoken "fool" hanging off the end of the sentence. "That would be the least of our problems. And if the energy were to be exhausted and all the shields fail, well, an exhausted node would be no more dangerous than no node. If there's no power to act upon, there will be nothing to go rogue."

"Apologies, but things work somewhat differently where I am from, and we did not handle magic wells that way," Tremane offered. Tremane did not take offense at her manner, perhaps because she was at least participating in these experimental sessions and demonstrating that she was not going to take out her animosity toward him on Hardorn and its people in general. He grimaced as if he was getting a headache. "Then if we could simply find a way to keep a node spawning its own shields until the energy ran out—"

"This is all very nice in theory," Elspeth pointed out impatiently. "But even if we could do that, we haven't the time or the resources to run about the countryside slapping a shieldspell over every node!"

"Well, actually, we wouldn't have to do that, at least not here—" began Tremane.

"There are Priests enough in Karse to shield every node there," said Solaris at the same time.

"And that works for Hardorn and Karse," Elspeth frowned. "But what about Valdemar? And the Pelagirs? And elsewhere?"

"Hmm," Tashiketh rumbled, moving his gaze from Solaris to Tremane and back again. "There is an answer to that question already in our hands."

Hansa and Father Janas switched their gazes between the two rulers also, as Solaris and Tremane exchanged a very peculiar look.

There was something rather odd going on there, and Elspeth hadn't a clue to what it was all about, but the tension between those two suddenly increased a hundredfold.

"I do not *like* you," Solaris burst out, as she abruptly got to her feet and stood, glaring at Tremane. "I do not like you at all! Ever since you and your heathen army came here, you have stood for everything I find detestable—expediency above honor, craft above wisdom, guile above truth, self-reliance above faith! I do *not* like you!"

And with that, she gathered her robes about her and swirled out, Hansa padding in her wake. The heavy silence that followed her outburst made even their breathing seem loud.

"What in hell was that all about?" Elspeth asked, bewildered. She had never seen Solaris lose control like that before.

Tremane looked at the door that Solaris had closed—not slammed—behind herself. "I'm not sure," he replied, "but it might have to do with a solution that involves a personal compromise on the part of the Son of the Sun." He appeared to make up his mind about something and stood up. "If you four can work on the problem of a self-renewing shield-spell that can take power from a node-source without the intervention of an Adept, I will go and speak with Solaris, and see if my guess mirrors actuality rather than just an outburst of frustration."

He nodded at all of them, and left as well.

Darkwind snorted. "A self-renewing shield-spell that takes power from a node without an Adept. At least he was only asking the impossible!"

But Elspeth wasn't so certain. "Don't Tayledras Heartstones do self-renewing spells, like the Veil? And they don't need an Adept around to make *them* work."

Darkwind started to object, then got a thoughtful look on his face. Tashiketh rested his beak on his foreclaws, looking expectant. "They do," Darkwind replied slowly. "And I was about to say that nodes aren't Heartstones, but Heartstones *are* a kind of node. Let me think about this one for a moment."

Father Janas simply shrugged. "I haven't the least idea of what you're all talking about," he said cheerfully. "Tremane asked me to sit through this because I know how the earth-binding and earth-magic works. Other than that, my friends, I'm fairly useless. But it does seem to me that for your controlling factor, you could *use* earth-energy, the very slow and subtle energies that underlie everything, the ones even hedge-wizards and earth-witches use. Those are fundamentally unaffected by the Storms."

Tashiketh raised his head and nodded eagerly; Darkwind looked at Father Janas as if he had unwittingly uttered something profound.

Elspeth had come late to magic and thus undergone a forced-growth process like a hothouse plant. She had never actually worked with such primitive energies as Janas described. But the theory seemed reasonable to her, and both Tashiketh and Father Janas obviously were familiar in detail with how those magics operated. "Well, why don't we just pursue that particular hare until we either catch it or it goes to cover?" she asked decisively.

"It is these energies with which Vykaendys created the Shield-Wall," Tashiketh said thoughtfully. "This is why there is less magical energy to spare within Iftel itself than there is in other lands. It is constantly going to renew the Shield-Wall. If this works, there will be little energy to spare in any of the lands when the Final Storm has passed."

"And the alternative?" Elspeth replied. "I don't think any of us want to contemplate *that*. Most of us have been doing without a great deal of magic ever since the Storms started, and I doubt that it is going to be too much of a hardship."

"Except for the Vales," Darkwind sighed. "But as you said, the alternative is a great deal less pleasant." He regarded the three of them with an expression so mournful that it almost made Elspeth want to laugh. "I will need your help in asking me very stupid questions, for we will somehow have to unravel the processes by which Tayledras make Heartstones and link them into spells like the Veil. I am so *used* to being able to do such things that I cannot tell you *how* I do them. This," he concluded with resignation, "is going to be a very great deal of difficult work, all of it mental."

He was right; it was. They were still only in the earliest stages when Solaris and Tremane returned, and Darkwind remarked via Mindspeech to Elspeth that since there were neither knife wounds nor signs of violence on either of them, the talk must have gone well. Neither of them said anything, and both of them acted as if they did not particularly wish to discuss what had occurred.

The group was not able to get beyond the most basic of understandings that day, nor for several more days, although they all worked feverishly to put together their solution. Only Tremane did not spend every waking hour of the day deep in research and testing; Solaris remarked cryptically that he didn't need to, since his presence was only necessary when they had a solution ready to try. Whatever had passed between them had cleared the air considerably, for Solaris had stopped making her acidic comments and was even distantly friendly to him at times.

Perhaps, not so ironically, it was the discipline and methodology they had learned from Master Levy and the other Master Artificers that enabled them to dissect magic logically, apply the laws they had learned, and find the fundamentals that allowed the magic to work in the first place. Finally, they had all the pieces of a solution; thanks to Darkwind, they all knew how to make a node behave like a very weak Heartstone and how to tie one into a self-sustaining spell. Unlike a Tayledras Heartstone, nodes could only support *one* such spell, but one was all they would need. They knew how to use earth-energy to power the second spell that would control the first, triggering the spawning of a new shield when the outermost collapsed. Now came the question to which they had no answer, unless Solaris and Tremane already knew it—how to reach every node at the same time.

Then, at last, Tremane rejoined the group.

"Earth-binding," he said succinctly. "Every Tayledras Vale will be able to control the nodes in the territory of that Vale; Solaris will be able to reach the nodes in Karse, the King in Rethwellan the nodes in his land, and so forth. Those leaders will have to undergo the ritual, but the gods know it's simple enough, and once they do, they can *immediately* protect their nodes."

Elspeth looked askance at him, but Father Janas nodded. "I thought so," he said with satisfaction. "This is one of those few times when the King can affect the land, rather than vice versa."

"I am not looking forward to this," Tremane added bitterly. "When we take this to the next level and involve the entire country, it is going to be extremely unpleasant. But it isn't going to kill me, and I would rather spend a week recovering from the aftereffects of this than have my people face a single node gone rogue. So, let us test our theory on the nearest node to Shonar, and if it works, we will then make all of Hardorn into our second test."

Something about his tone made Elspeth think that the effects of the full-country test were going to be something worse than merely "extremely unpleasant;" she had the feeling that this was going to require every bit of courage Tremane possessed. But there was nothing she could do about it, and she knew very well that her mother would have willingly sacrificed herself in the same cause, as would Solaris, or any other good ruler.

The test on the single node was far less difficult than Elspeth had envisioned; first the controlling-spell was set in place, then the node itself was altered to allow for the linkage of a shield-spell directly to it. This was the part that only an Adept could do, so it was up to Darkwind as the most practiced of all of them in this particular kind of magic, while Solaris "watched" with single-minded intensity.

Then, when everything was in readiness, Darkwind triggered the spell, just before the next Storm came through.

If Elspeth had not been "watching" at the time, she would never have believed that it was possible, for between one moment and the next, the node disappeared, and in its place was a shielded spot into which ley-lines fed but nothing came out. Then the Storm swept in, and they all waited out the effects.

When they had recovered and were able to "look" again, the node was exactly as it had been before the Storm, shielded and safe.

Tremane looked very much like a man who has received both incredibly good news and incredibly bad news at the same time. "Well," he said, "we know it works."

"How soon do you want to try protecting all of Hardorn?" Father Janas asked him gently.

"Now," he said decisively. "We have until late tonight before the next Storm comes in, and I don't want to be able to sit and brood on this."

Solaris sat straight up and looked him in the eyes. "Tremane Gyfarr Pendleson of Lynnai, don't you *dare* sit there and pretend to be a martyr! What you are about to endure, *I* will also have to, and Prince Daren of Valdemar, and Faramentha of Rethwellan, and whoever it is in Iftel—"

"Vykaendys-First Bryron Hess," Tashiketh said helpfully.

"The Son of the Sun in Iftel, and a half-dozen Hawkbrothers and at *least* one Shin'a'in," Solaris concluded.

:Not to mention as many other leaders we can reach as we think will have lands in jeopardy,: Hansa added helpfully. *:There will be a great many leaders with dreadful headaches before this is all over.:*

"Exactly! You will not be alone in this, and although you may feel fear because of the justifiable guilt you bear for your other actions in the past, I can assure you that the land will *not* let you die!" She rose to her feet, full of anger and some other emotion that Elspeth could not put a name to. "If you are afraid, then be a man and admit it, and let us help you through it! *You* should know that if you are too afraid, the land will resist what we are about to do. We may not be able to overcome that resistance, for the land takes its cues from you."

:That's Solaris talking, but it's also something else,: Darkwind said, in Mindspeech tightly focused and tense. *:I wonder if Tremane realizes it?:*

:Vkandis?: Elspeth asked, but even as she said it, she knew that it was the wrong answer.

:Since when does a male use all of someone's names to scold him?: Darkwind asked, a little of the tension ebbing. *:No, Solaris is acting as a Mouth for a different power, and I suspect that if you asked Father Janas, he'd be very familiar with it. Probably her annoyance with Tremane and her familiarity with being a Mouth opened her up to acting as an inadvertent channel for it.:*

Elspeth sent silent agreement, after casting a quick glance at the priest, who was watching the little scene with a faint smile on his lips. Darkwind was right. Only a woman—a mother—would scold someone using every one of his names. And wasn't the earth often referred to as Mother? Looked at in that light, there were some subtle physical changes in Solaris that gave more clues. For one thing, she looked more—feminine—than Elspeth had ever seen her.

The scolding did what it was supposed to do, which was annoy him enough to make him willing to admit to a weakness; and in a way Elspeth could feel very sorry for poor Tremane, who hadn't asked for any of this, and had borne up very well under it all. He stiffened his back, looked up into Solaris' eyes, and said, with quiet dignity, "You are right, Solaris. I am terrified. I am accustomed to using power, not having it use me, and the prospect of giving up control over myself to *anything* gives me the horrors. Doing it with the lives of thousands of innocents in the balance is terrible beyond my ability to articulate."

Whatever had Solaris let her go, and the anger faded as she sat down. "It isn't so bad, being used by this kind of power," she said softly. "You will be exhausted when it is over; perhaps a little ill, though I don't think it will be very bad. I think the power will use you gently, if you don't resist it. Sometimes giving up control in a greater cause is the noblest thing one can do in one's life." She hesitated a moment longer, then it looked as if some wall inside her gave way. Her expression changed completely. "Perhaps you are rightfully afraid that some of us, who have grievances with you, may not protect you with a whole heart. You would have been correct in fearing that not very long ago; I might not have moved to help you if I saw that you were in danger." She took a deep breath and plunged on. "That is no longer true; I forgive you, Tremane of Hardorn, and if it is any more comfort to you, young Karal, who has greater cause to hate you than I, forgave you before I did. The man who loosed the assassin that murdered our friend was an Imperial Commander, subject to the orders and whims of an Emperor with no morals and no scruples, and you are no longer that man." Now she looked shamefaced for a moment. "The Sunlord himself told me that I must forgive you if we were to succeed, but until this moment, I could not."

Tremane looked at her with astonishment, and offered her his hand; she took it in a firm handclasp that said far more than words could have. "Thank you for that; I know what it cost you," was all he said.

Then he released her hand and looked at the others. "Well? Shall we begin?"

As far as Elspeth was concerned, there was very little for her to see or do, other than to feed mage-power to Darkwind, who in his turn did things with it that she could neither see nor follow, although she knew in theory what he was doing. She was what they all called the "anchor" and she brought in the power, directed, and refined it. Tremane searched for the node, and "held" them all there when he found one. Darkwind built the node into a matrix that would permit a single spell to be linked into it. Father Janas constructed the controlling spell that triggered the main spell, using the loss of a shield as the guide for activation. Solaris built the main spell, which created the nine nested shields using power from the node, and Darkwind linked it in. Then, once that node "disappeared" because it was now shielded, Tremane moved their viewpoint on to the next node. In the end, by the time they were done, Tremane was so completely exhausted that he could not even move, but as Solaris had promised, he was neither ill nor in pain. They had worked through him to reach every node in Hardorn and replicate the same shields and spells they had tried on the first node. This was the only way they *could* have reached all of the nodes without going to them physically; in a sense, since Tremane was bound to all of Hardorn in a very *physical* fashion because of the blood and soil he had ingested, they actually were working there physically.

They completed their work just as the next Storm came through, and had the satisfaction of seeing their work hold. And Tremane got a small reward out of it after all; since the nodes were no longer being battered by the energies of the Storm, *he* was suffering only about half of the physical effects he had been enduring with every Storm-wave. This made him feel half again better.

"That in and of itself made this all worthwhile," he said weakly, but with a smile, and then they sent him off to bed.

"He feels as though he will sleep for a week, but it won't be more than a day or so," Father Janas said with weary satisfaction. "He'll be back on his feet and hard at work shortly. Now do you need anything to alert the peoples in your homes?"

"I will send two of my fastest flyers—mages both—back with the exact instructions in the morning," Tashiketh rumbled, his eyes alight with pleasure at their success. "And if you will permit me, Most Holy, more will convey you and Hansa back to your own land to save you as much time as possible; as many of your escort as care to remain here can, I suppose, and the rest can follow you at their own pace."

Solaris gave him a puzzled look. "I would appreciate it no end, but how do you intend to do this?" she asked. "I assume you mean me to fly with them, but I can't imagine how that could work properly."

"A basket, suspended between them. It is perfectly safe," Tashiketh assured her. "There are some minor spells on the basket to make it and the contents light; you can renew these easily enough, and the only thing you will need to take care with is that you go to ground during Storms."

"Our gryphons use the same means," Darkwind seconded. "It's safer than you'd think. You'll be able to cross into Karse within a few days, even with having to land twice or three times a day as a Storm passes."

"Then I thank you, for I will have to seal off the Temple as well as our nodes, and whether or not Tremane will believe that, it will be a harder task than this." Her words were still a little sardonic, but she smiled, and Elspeth sensed that Solaris would no longer be able to say in truth that she hated Tremane of Hardorn.

"And you?" Father Janas asked Elspeth and Darkwind. Darkwind answered for both of them.

"It is already accomplished," Darkwind said, his voice heavy with tired content. "Gwena has sent the word to Rolan; Rolan has sent it on to Skif's Cymry, who will detail it to the Kaled'a'in of k'Leshya Vale. *They* will see to it that Tayledras and Shin'a'in alike have the information, and our nodes and Heartstones will be protected within days. Messages will go from Valdemar to every White Winds mage in every land, and from there—wherever the word needs to go."

"Your Companions are useful friends," Father Janas said with envy. "Perhaps there will be room for them in Hardorn in the future." He looked shyly at Solaris. "And there should be room for Temples to the Sunlord as well, I should think. When it all comes down to it, what is done for the cause of Good is done in the name of every Power of the Light."

She smiled; the first open, unshadowed smile that Elspeth had seen on her face since she arrived here. "And on that very optimistic note, I shall thank you and beg leave to go to bed myself," she said, getting to her feet. "Hansa and I have a long journey in the morning."

"Room for everyone," Darkwind echoed, as he and Elspeth walked slowly to their own quarters. "That is not so bad a way to conduct one's land."

"I know," she replied saucily. "We've been doing it that way in Valdemar for some time now."

And now, at least, we have some assurance we will continue to be able to, she thought. *And now we can spare some prayers and energy for Karal and the rest where they are. May all our gods help them, for we cannot.*

Emperor Charliss sat in, not on, the wooden Throne in his private quarters, and plotted revenge, for revenge was all he had left to hold him to life. His mind was clear, despite the hellish mix of drugs his apothecary had concocted on his orders, to dull his pain and sustain his failing body. That was because the mix included drugs to keep his mind from becoming clouded. Outside his quarters, a physical blizzard raged, as it had raged for the past three weeks. The mage-storms, too, passed through Crag Castle several times every day, leaving most mages shuddering with the aftereffects. He wasn't suffering from that difficulty, though; or if he was, it was insignificant in the light of the degeneration of his body.

Although he did not appear to take any notice of what was going on outside this suite, such was not the case. He knew very well what Melles was up to; discrediting the Emperor even with the Imperial Army, spreading truths, half-truths, and lies to make it appear that only Baron Melles had the welfare of the Empire in his heart. He was also quite well aware that Melles was doing a fine job of holding the Empire together, even if it was with devious and dubious means. He knew that Melles was using the Emperor's treatment of Tremane as a weapon to bring the feuding political factions of the Empire together under Melles' control. It was a ploy that would not have occurred to Charliss, but in retrospect, given that Melles was detested by at least a quarter of the Great Players in the game of Empire, and feared by another quarter, the only way he could have united them was to find a common enemy they could hate worse than him.

None of that mattered, for he no longer cared what Melles or any other living man did. His priorities were different, and much more personal.

The spells that kept his worn-out body going, that reinforced failing organs, were themselves failing. Each time a Storm came through, he lost more of them and was unable to replace all the spells that were lost.

He saw no way of being able to save himself; he was dying, and he knew it. He could no longer move under his own power anymore; his servants carried him from bed to Throne and back again, all within the confines of his private quarters. The long, slow decline he had anticipated had accelerated out of all recognition.

He was not afraid, but he *was* angry, with the kind of calculating, all-consuming anger only a man who had lived two centuries could muster. He had been cheated of the last, precious years of his life, and he knew precisely where to lay the blame for it.

Valdemar.

He had sent his scholars on a search for that benighted land and its origin, and had learned things that gave him all the more reason to assume that it was *Valdemar* that had unleashed these Storms across the face of the land. Valdemar had been founded centuries ago by rebellious subjects of the Empire who had escaped into the wilderness too deeply to follow. But time and distance were no barriers to revenge, as he himself very well knew. The rulers of Valdemar had probably been plotting this attack against the Empire ever since their land was founded. A plot such as this one would have taken centuries to mature, centuries to gather the power for. These Storms could not have been generated by anything less than the most powerful of Adepts working together in concert; such a weapon was fiendishly clever, diabolically complicated.

In the end it might have been his own actions in reaching for the land of Hardorn that triggered the long plots of Valdemar and gave them the opportunity to destroy those who had driven them out of their homes so long ago. He should have read the return of his envoy from Hardorn, dead, with the blade belonging to Princess Elspeth between his shoulders, for the serious warning it really was. *You're too close, and we'll finish you*; that had been the real message. Like a nest of bees, he had ventured too near, and now the insects would swarm him and destroy him.

It didn't really matter what the cause for their actions was, nor did it matter whether he could have done anything to prevent this. The Storms had been unleashed, *he* was dying, it was all the fault of Valdemar, and he was going to see to it that Valdemar didn't outlive him—at least, not in any form that the Valdemarans themselves would recognize. Like a wild bear making a final charge, in his death throes he would destroy those who were destroying him.

He had everything he needed; all of the magic of the local nodes, plus all that of his coterie of mages, plus a great deal he had hoarded in carefully-shielded artifacts. Every Emperor created magical artifacts, or caused them to be created; he could drain every one of them. Every mage he had ever worked with, whether he was one of Charliss' private group or not, had a magical "hook" in him, one that tied him back to Charliss. The moment Charliss cared to, he could pull every bit of that mage's personal power and use it as if the mage was one of his personal troupe. The smartest of the mages had, of course, discovered and removed that hook—but most of them hadn't, and Charliss could use them up any time he cared to.

But his own time was rapidly running out. The shields protecting those hoarded objects weren't going to last through too many more Storms, nor were the resources of his mage-troupe, nor of the mages he had hooks in. If he was going to use this power, it would have to be soon.

He sat supported by the tall back and heavy arms of his mock Throne, and contemplated the methods of vengeance. What could he do to finish them, these upstart Valdemarans? What form should his attack take? He wanted it to be appropriate, suitable—and he wanted it to do the most damage possible.

What would the best allocation of his resources be? *It's obvious. Release all the power at once*, he decided. *Release it as the wave-front of the Storm passes, and use it to augment what the Storm does. Make it the worst Storm that the face of this old world has ever seen.*

The results of that should be highly entertaining, and since he would release it as the Storm passed from east to west, most of the Empire would be safe.

But Valdemar—ah, Valdemar would have no idea that the blow was coming.

The results of such an enormous release of power would be devastating—and amusing, if he lived to watch it, and to collect his information.

Everything from Hardorn to far beyond Valdemar, and from the mountains in the north to the south of Karse, would erupt with Nature driven mad. The weather was already hideous; this would make it unbelievably worse. Earthquakes—there would be earthquakes in regions that had never known so much as a trembler, as the stresses in the earth built to beyond the breaking point. Fire—volcanoes would erupt out of nowhere, pouring down rivers of molten rock on unsuspecting cities. Physical storms would spawn lightning that in turn would ignite huge forest fires and grass fires. Blizzards would bury some areas in snow past the rooftops, while floods would wash away the country elsewhere, and mudslides make a ruin of once-fertile hills. Mountains would fling themselves skyward, and the earth would gape as huge fissures opened underfoot. Processes that normally took millennia would occur in a single day or less. There would be no place that was safe, no place to hide. And when the wrath of Nature was over, the Changed creatures would descend on the demoralized and disorganized survivors.

It would be everything he could have wished for. He just wished he was going to live long enough to properly gloat over it; once the energy was released, Charliss would have no more magic to sustain him, and he would die. But so would most of his enemies. Anyone and anything that lived through it all would probably wish for death before too long.

Tremane would be caught in all of this, of course, which would give him revenge on the faithless traitor—revenge that Melles had been too cowardly or too lazy to take. Lazy, probably; Melles never had been one to pursue targets that were out of his immediate reach; he could always manufacture excuses to obviate any need to do so.

Well, he would take matters into his own hands, then.

It was possible that the extra energy released wouldn't just wipe Valdemar off the world—it might rip through the Empire and its allies as well. The chaos he was about to unleash could have far-reaching effects.

He didn't care. He was long since over caring about things that meant no immediate improvement in *his* wellbeing.

Why should my Empire outlive me? he asked himself, seething with resentment over the fact that the Empire as a whole was not willing to make the sacrifices to sustain him. *I gave them my life and my attention—my entire life. Was I appreciated? Beloved for being stern with them? No. Not at all.*

They took and took. Now they pay for their greed. They should have thought ahead and appeased me.

And there was no reason to make life any easier for Melles either. Let him patch something together from what was left, if, indeed, there was anything left. Let Melles see if he could actually do something with the crumbs and shards. It would serve that effete bastard right.

He smiled slowly, thinking of how Melles would react. The Baron had been progressing *so* well in imposing order on the chaos left in the wake of the Storms. He must feel so proud of himself, and be so certain that he had everything under control now. It would be delicious to see how he crumbled as everything he had worked so hard for vanished before his eyes.

Revenge; on Valdemar, on Tremane, even on Melles for daring to succeed—that was all Charliss had left, and he would take it. By the time he was finished, the known world would be driven down to the level of cave-dwelling, nomad-hunter survival. If Melles reclaimed anything at all as an Empire, it would be an Empire no bigger than this city.

I will destroy it all. His hands clutched the arms of his chair, and he felt his dry lips cracking as his smile widened. When he set off the final cataclysm, when he ignited nations to form his funeral pyre, he would prove he had been the greatest and most powerful Emperor to ever live.

No one would ever surpass him as he burned the world to light the way to his grave, and the darkness that followed would be a fitting shroud.

Karal felt peculiarly useless at this moment in time, although in a little while he would be just as important as anyone else in the Tower. He watched the others making last-minute preparations, and wished wistfully that he could use the teleson to talk to Natoli; it might have relieved his nerves. He sat quietly where he'd been told to sit, immersed in a peculiar mixture of terror, resignation, and anticipation. He knew he could do what they were going to ask of him, but he couldn't think past that. Even when he tried, he was unable to imagine a single moment *after* their task was done. Was that only because he was frightened, or because once it was over it would *be* over for them, forever?

He was still acting as the Channel for this "weapon," but this time he would not be in the physical center of the group. This time the main participants—himself, Firesong, An'desha, and Sejanes—would stand in a square formation around it, and it didn't seem to matter what direction each stood in, so long as they were spaced equally around it.

There was another difference this time. Each of the "mortal" participants would be shielded by those who were not. Karal had Florian and Altra; An'desha would be protected by the Avatars, Firesong by Need and Yfandes, and Sejanes by Vanyel and Stefen. Yfandes had attached herself to Firesong without comment, perhaps so that each of the participants would have two protectors. Aya was to be kept strictly out of the way, in the care of Silverfox, with the rest of those who were not participating. *They* would all be in the workroom below, with the hatch closed. Firesong and Sejanes had determined that the shields on the workroom were as much purely physical as magical. There were properties in the stone that insulated from magical energy. The workroom had been cleared of anything remotely magical in nature, and stocked with tools, food, and water, so that if the worst happened and the survivors were sealed inside, they had a chance to dig themselves out.

The cube-maze was the exact opposite of whatever device was used to unleash the Cataclysm in the first place, and the Adepts had surmised that it had been created as a fail-safe. As they now understood it, all of Urtho's magic had been released at once when he dissipated the bonds of all of the spells on everything that was not inside the specially shielded areas of the Tower. At the same time, a similar device had done the same to all of Ma'ar's magic in his stronghold, thus creating the Cataclysm as the two reacted together in violent and sometimes unexpected ways. They had partly replicated that when they set up the Counter-Storm.

This time, if their research and planning paid off, they were going to reverse that; they were going to open up something that would swallow all of the magic energies converging on this spot and send it all out into the Void. At least, they hoped that was what would happen. They didn't know what was going to happen at the other original release point, but Ma'ar had not been the tinkerer that Urtho had been, and had not been known for having workshops to experiment in. There were probably not any of the dangerous devices there that there were here— and in any case, the site was at the bottom of Lake Evendim. Whatever happened there would take place under furlongs of water, and far from any populations of human or other beings.

No one knew what would follow when they closed the device as the last of the energies were swallowed up. They all had some theories. Master Levy insisted that since no energy could be destroyed, it would all go elsewhere; his suggestion was that it would become a kind of energy-pool in the Void that mages could all tap into. He also warned that resistance to energy flow usually manifested as heat, and there was a very real possibility that despite their best efforts all here would be charred to death partway through. This earned the mathematician a few sour looks, which were returned with an apologetic smile. Both Lo'isha and Firesong were of the opinion that all the energy would come right back into the "real" world, as if a flood was swallowed up and came back out of the sky as rain, like the water in a fountain, endlessly cycling from pond to air and back again.

Whatever happened, the only certainty was that all the old rules of magic would go flying right out the window. No one even knew if all of this energy was ever going to be accessible anymore. They might end up with a world that was fundamentally without magic, though that was fairly unlikely.

As Urtho had said in the placards that he had left, this would have been a suicidal device to use as a weapon; once it was opened, it would have proceeded to swallow all the magic in its vicinity—in fact, it was quite likely to drain all the rest of the weaponry in here dry—and it might even have swallowed up the mages who opened it. But with the tremendous energies of this Storm breaking over it, the device would probably have all the energy it could possibly handle.

The plan was to take down the Tower shields and open it as the Final Storm hit, feed it all the energy of the Storm until it couldn't take any more or melted down, and close it again under control if it was still active.

Storms were coming in all the time now, and although the Tower shields were still holding, they had been forced to evacuate the remains of the Shin'a'in camp some days ago as a blizzard like none of their hosts had ever seen before raged across the Plains. Similar weather ravaged Valdemar, Karse, Hardorn, the Vales—

Probably everywhere else, too, Karal thought, listening carefully. *And it's supposed to be spring out there.* If he paid very close attention, he could ignore all the sounds coming from inside the Tower, and was able to pick out, very faintly, the howling of the winds outside. You couldn't even stand out there, the wind would knock you to the ground in a heartbeat. It was a good thing that they had evacuated the Plains weeks ago; tents wouldn't take this kind of pounding, and no horse, sheep, or mule would survive exposed to a storm like this.

As for the Vales—Firesong said that the Tayledras were incorporating the magic that shielded nodes with the one that formed the Veil that protected each of their Vales. Hopefully, these would hold; if not, they would have to live as the scouts did from now on, exposed to the elements, without their little lands of artificial summer.

Karal wished he knew what was going on in Karse; Altra would only say that Solaris had the situation well under control, and that most of the people were being well cared for. He hoped that his family was all right, though since they were living in a fairly prosperous village, they should be. The ones in real danger would be the remote farmers and shepherds who, isolated and alone out in the hills and mountains, might not have gotten warning in time to get to adequate shelter.

He hadn't thought about his family in a long time; the Karal that had helped his father in the inn's stables was another person entirely, and he knew that if his mother or father were to pass him in the street, they would not recognize him. And he would have nothing whatsoever in common with them. He had always expected to change as he grew up—but not this radically.

He tucked up his legs and rested his chin on his knees, thinking wistfully about all he had left behind—all he would leave behind if this effort failed. When it came right down to it, there were only a handful of people who would actually miss him if he didn't come out of this, and most, if not all, of them would recover quickly enough. Natoli probably wouldn't exactly *recover*, but she would manage, and go on to make something good out of her life. And meanwhile, he would have done something important with *his* life, and there weren't too many people who could actually say that. The thought, though bleak, was curiously liberating.

He had made his good-byes to everyone except those who were still in the Tower itself, down in the workroom; he still had time, and this might be the moment to take care of that little detail.

He got to his feet and slipped down the stairs, hoping to find Tarrn and Lyam alone. He was lucky; Lo'isha, Master Levy and Silverfox were still up above, with the handful of Shin'a'in who were still here, wedging doors to other weapon rooms open and helping to drag the cube-maze out of its little room into the main one. No matter what else happened here, they were at least going to accomplish one thing Urtho could not; they were going to render every other weapon in the Tower inactive.

Their industry left the workroom mostly untenanted. Only Aya sat nervously on a perch in the corner, while Lyam and Tarrn puttered about, storing things away more efficiently.

He stood uncertainly on the stairs, and it was Tarrn who noticed him first. *:Well, young one, it is nearly time,:* the *kyree* said, looking unusually solemn.

"I know," he replied, sitting down on the bottom steps. "I came to tell you both that I'm very glad I knew you, and I learned a lot from both of you."

They left what they had been working on to join him. "I am very pleased to have been your friend, Karal," Lyam said earnestly, taking Karal's hand in his own dry and leather-skinned claw-hand. "I hope we will be able to continue that friendship after Tarrn and I have gone back to k'Leshya."

:And you figure prominently in my Chronicles, young scholar,: Tarrn said gravely, with a slight bow of his graying head, giving Karal what the young Karsite knew were the two most important accolades in the *kyree's* vocabulary—being called a scholar and being told he had a prominent place in the history Tarrn was writing. *:In days to come, cubs will be astonished that I actually had the privilege of your friendship.:*

An awkward silence might have started then, but at that very moment, Silverfox came trotting down the stairs, followed by all the rest. "It's time, Karal," the *kestra'chern* said, and gave Karal a completely unselfconscious hug. "They're waiting for you."

"Good luck, boy," Master Levy called, and cracked an unexpected smile. "Don't disappoint Natoli; she's expecting you to take careful notes and tell her all your observations."

Lo'isha only clasped his hand warmly and looked deeply and gravely into his eyes, and the rest of the Shin'a'in paused long enough to give him the nod of respect they normally only accorded to Lo'isha.

Each of them in his own way was saying farewell—giving him what encouragement they could—without doing anything that might unnerve him or shake his confidence. He knew that, and knew that they knew it as well. And he knew that he *should* be afraid, but somehow all his fear had passed away as he made those farewells, as if each of them was taking a little bit of it with them, so that he could be freed to do his task.

He walked quickly up the stairs; Firesong and An'desha waited up there to lower the hatch down into place, once again sealing it behind shields both magical and physical. The cube-maze was the first thing he saw as his head came up out of the hatchway; placed in the center of the room, it was curiously dwarfed by the sheer size of the place.

It looked very pretty, a piece of abstract art, gleaming with blue and purple reflections in the light from overhead. Sejanes was already in his place, flanked by the two wisps that were Vanyel and Stefen.

Dawnfire and Tre'valen, looking far more solid, waited on either side of An'desha's position, and another white wraith stood beside the place where Firesong would stand. Firesong already had Need in a sheath on his back, and as he took his stand, he drew the mage-sword and held her.

An'desha moved to his place between the two Avatars, a closed-in expression on his face, as if already concentrating on what he was going to do. Sejanes had his eyes closed and his hands cupped in front of him. As Karal took his own place, flanked by Florian and Altra, Firesong made a little movement that caught his attention, and as he glanced at the Hawkbrother, Firesong gave him a wry grin and a one-handed sign for encouragement. Somehow, that made him feel better than he had all day, and he set his feet with more confidence.

As the terrible energies broke over them, Firesong was to open the device, and hold it open; next to being the Channel, his was the most dangerous task. An'desha and Sejanes were to act as funnels and control the energies as they converged on Karal, keeping a steady flow. Surges would be particularly dangerous; if a surge of power overwhelmed Karal, he might block the flow. If that happened, it would feed back on all of them. It was also the job of Sejanes and An'desha to "homogenize" the incoming energies by mixing them, for a flood of only one kind might do the same thing. Karal would actually transmute them before feeding them into the device.

"Are we ready?" Firesong asked, looking around the circle at all of them. Each of them nodded, and Karal saw for a moment, in each of their faces, the same resignation that he himself felt.

They all think in their hearts that they are going to die. They're putting on a brave face for the rest of us.

And he did the same. Despite all their care and planning, this could go horribly wrong, and if it did, it wouldn't just be *one* of them that would take the brunt of the punishment, it would be all of them.

:Here it comes,: warned Altra, and then there was no time to think of anything else.

Charliss waited, tense with anticipation as he had not been in decades. This would be perhaps the most powerful spell that had ever been cast in the history of the world since the Cataclysm; it would certainly be the most powerful spell ever cast in the history of the Empire. And for all that, it was such a deceptively simple thing—just a spell that released all of the energy of every magical object and person within Crag Castle that Charliss had any control over. This would probably kill all of his mages. If it didn't, it would certainly leave them disabled for many weeks, and might well destroy their minds. That had a certain piquant pleasure to it, for this spell would definitely kill its caster, and Charliss was not at all averse to taking an escort with him when he died.

The only emotion within his breast now was rage; it left no room for anything else. It really left no room for any thought but revenge.

He might well be the last Emperor, and that thought had the sweetness of revenge. More so since no one would ever know that he was the one who had done this—those few who knew he was spell-casting thought it was of the usual sort, that he was trying to extend his life a little longer.

They would probably blame Melles for this, since the mages who would die would all be mages closely allied with Charliss. That was even sweeter. Melles would have all the blame as the man who had destroyed the Empire, and Charliss would acquire the virtues that Melles did not have in contrast. Melles would be the terrible villain, and Charliss the saint that he destroyed.

What a subtle revenge!

The only thing that would make it better would be to know for certain that he was taking Tremane down with him. But never mind. One couldn't have everything—and if Tremane didn't actually *die* in the catastrophe that Charliss unleashed, he might well be among those who wished he had.

Charliss gathered the threads of his power in his hands, and waited for the Storm to break.

It was a strange little gathering, here in the Great Hall of Tremane's manor. Tashiketh and the four gryphons that were left with him, part of Solaris' escort of Sun-priests that had remained behind to help, Elspeth and Gwena, Darkwind and Vree, Brytha the *dyheli*, all of Tremane's mages, the two old weather-wizards from Shonar itself, and Father Janas, all arranged in concentric circles around Tremane. Anyone with even the tiniest bit of Mage-Gift was here, and they would all be working on a single task; to create and hold a shield. If they could hold it over Shonar, they would—if that proved impossible, they would try to hold it over the castle, and if that failed, just over themselves.

The scene looked and felt unreal and dreamlike, but Elspeth was doing her best to control a fear that was as deep and all-pervasive as the fear in a nightmare. For once, the menace looming over Elspeth was invisible, implacable, and faceless. There was no villain, no Ancar, no Falconsbane; only a terrible thing that had been loosed millennia ago and was now coming home, too ancient, impersonal, and powerful to grasp, yet too real not to terrify.

Nevertheless, the danger was real enough, and it would be worse if the group in the Tower failed. There had been a blizzard howling across the face of Hardorn for the past three days, the strangest such storm that Elspeth had ever seen. Greenish lightning somewhere up above the solid curtains of snow illuminated the entire sky in flashes, yet revealed nothing but white. There were reports of whirlwinds, and of spirits riding the wind, strange creatures blowing before it. None of these reports had been verified, but Elspeth would not discount any of them.

Every time that Storms came through, the effect was worse—although every one of the node-shields held with no apparent problems. But this Storm was going to be worse, much worse, than any of the previous lot. This was the return of the initial blast that had caused all of the storms, so long ago.

As for what would happen if the group at the Tower failed—no one could predict that, except that it would be terrible. Nature already raged out of control; could they deal with *years* of this?

Never mind. It was out of her hands, and that was what felt the most unreal of all. She had never been in a position where she was utterly helpless to do something about her own peril before, never been in a case where she had *no* control over what was going to happen. She felt demoralized and impotent, and she didn't like it one bit.

Darkwind squeezed her hand, and Gwena rubbed her soft nose against Elspeth's shoulder. Well, at least she wasn't facing this alone; no one else in this room had any more control over the situation than she did.

"It's time," Tremane said hoarsely. "It's coming."

And now it was too late to think about anything but joining mind, heart, and power with the others, disparate as they were, and shield and hold with grim determination...

"*Now*," Firesong said between his clenched teeth, as the Storm broke over them. Around them, the stone of the Tower rumbled and groaned, like a carriage-spring being twisted beyond its ability to return to normal. This time was unlike all the previous experiences with the energy of the Storm, in that it had a distinct sound—a hollow, screaming roar accompanied by a steady increase in air pressure. Firesong held Need up between himself and the cube-maze, spoke some apparently private words to the sword, and did something to the taut fabric of magic that Karal half-saw, half-felt—

Then the cube-maze scattered motes of light along its surfaces, toward the apex of the topmost cube, and a ring spread outward to the farthest edges of the device—and all inside that ring vanished, and in its place was what could only be described as a great Darkness. The Void. The Pit.

Karal sensed it pulling on him and let it; Florian and Altra held him anchored as he let some inner part of himself meld with that awful darkness in the center of their circle. Then there was nothing but Light and Dark; the Pit in the center, and a coruscating, scintillating, rainbow-hued play of light and power all about it. Karal felt part of himself opening to it, sensed that he had become the conduit to send that power down into the Pit, which swallowed it hungrily but did not yet demand more than he could feed it.

All of his attention was on the Pit before him; he sensed explosions of energy behind and to all sides, and the energies around him oscillated furiously.

He tried to contain them and shove them into the dark maw, but the Pit had reached the limit at which it could accept them.

He heard shouting; it sounded like An'desha's voice, but he couldn't make out what the Shin'a'in was trying to tell him. Off to his right, a shining shape emerged from the chaos of swirling, flashing light, growing brighter with every moment.

It was Firesong, with Need glowing white-hot in his hands. He trembled in agony but refused to give in to the obvious pain of his blistering flesh.

Melles paused outside the Emperor's doorway—for once unguarded, thanks to the complicity of the Emperor's personal guard. With the *geas* binding them in loyalty to the Emperor now quite gone, they were all of them able to think for themselves, including Commander Ethen, who had replaced the now nerve-shattered Commander Peleun. In the past several weeks, they, too, had seen and heard enough—not quite enough to take things into their own hands, but enough to make them willing to leave their posts for a carefully staged "emergency."

There was no sound in the white-marble corridor except for the ever-present screaming of the wind. Even sheltered inside their glass chimneys, the candle flames that had taken the place of mage-lights flickered in icy drafts strong enough to have earned the name of "breeze." But these gusts were no zephyrs, and the blizzard out there wasn't half as powerful as the Storm now breaking over them was likely to *make* it.

The Emperor was going to be utterly engrossed in his spellcasting; over the past several days, Melles had made a point of going in and out of the Emperor's chambers and the Throne Room on one pretext or another during a Storm, and he knew that Charliss was completely oblivious to everything around him when he was spell-casting.

If the Emperor had put half the effort on holding his crumbling Empire together that he was spending on maintaining his crumbling body, Melles would not have felt so impelled to remove him now.

If he had done so, Melles would not have half the allies he now had either.

He walked boldly into the Emperor's quarters, as he had any number of times over the past few days, as if in search of an official paper or something of the sort. He ignored the unconscious mages sprawled over the furniture in the outer room, taken down either by the Storm itself or the Emperor's ruthless plundering of their energies.

The Emperor would not be here or in his bedroom; Melles already knew that Charliss had ordered his servants to carry him into the empty, cavernous Throne Room and place him in the Iron Throne itself. He made a tiny hand-sign to the two bodyguards standing on either side of the door, a pair of bodyguards from his own retinue, inserted into the Emperor's personnel with the collusion of the Guard Commander. They acknowledged his presence with a slight nod and stood aside. He opened the door to the Throne Room carefully, a fraction at a time, as he sensed the Storm building to an unheard-of fury and a new and oddly-flavored spell building inside the room in concert with it.

He wasn't certain *why* the Emperor had taken to casting his magics while in the embrace of the Iron Throne, wearing the Wolf Crown, but it made his own task easier. There would be no witnesses and a dozen entrances through which a murderer could have made his escape, assuming that there were even any murmurs of foul play. He frankly doubted that would be the case. People were far more likely to point to all of the loyal bodyguards on duty, each within eye- and ear-shot of the next pair, and believe the report of suicide.

Despite the roaring fires and a half-dozen charcoal braziers around Charliss' feet, the room was icy, but not still. Charliss could already have been a wizened corpse, hunched over in the cold embrace of the Throne, eyes closed, white, withered hands clenched on the arms. Only the yellow gem-eyes of the wolves in the Crown watched him, and he fancied that there was a look of life in those eyes, as they waited to see what he would do. But wolves protected only cubs and territory and they had no interest in protecting individuals once those individuals were detrimental to the welfare of the pack. They would not hinder Melles in what he intended to do.

There was a tightly-woven, furiously rotating spell building up around the Emperor, a spell somehow akin to the Storm outside. Did Charliss think to tap the power of the Storm now to bolster his failing magics? If so, he *was* mad.

The spell neared its peak. After years of watching Charliss spell-cast, Melles knew the Emperor's rhythms and patterns. If he was going to strike, he had better do so now. He slipped a sharp dagger, pommel ornamented with the Imperial Seal, out of the hem of his heavy, fur-trimmed tunic. He had purloined this very dagger out of the Emperor's personal quarters two days ago; it was well known to be one of Charliss' favorite trophy-pieces and virtually every member of the Court would readily identify it as his and no one else's.

Now. Before Charliss woke from his self-imposed trance, realized his danger, and turned all that terrible energy on *him*.

As only a trained assassin could, Melles flipped the dagger in his hand until he held only the point between his thumb and forefinger, aimed, and threw.

The dagger flew straight and true, with all the power of Melles' arm and anger behind it. With a wet *thud*, it buried itself to the hilt in Charliss' left eye. The Emperor was killed instantly, left with a slack-jawed version of his self-absorbed expression.

But the spell he had been about to unleash did not die with him.

For one instant, Melles felt the chill hand of horrified fear clutch his throat, as it had not in decades, and he waited to be pounded to the earth as the rogue spell lashed out at him.

The gathered energies, with no direction, and no controls, whirled in a vortex of light around the Emperor's body for a moment, obscuring him. Rays of light shot upward, punching holes through the darkness, leaving scorched spots in the ceiling. Other sparks jumped and careened, arcing back to the sword points arrayed in ominous fans behind and around the Iron Throne. The crackling sparks disappeared with a flash and a soft sizzle. Then suddenly the vortex stilled, and a moment later, the gathered energy invested itself in the Iron Throne, leaving it glowing for a moment before returning—apparently—to its original state.

Melles let out his breath in a hiss, walked tentatively over to Charliss, and reached for the Wolf Crown. He touched it for just a moment, and he could have sworn that the pack-leader on the front of the crown grinned at him.

Then he removed the dagger from the dead man's eye; a thin trickle of blood followed the removal of the blade, but it took less force to pull it out of the skull than Melles had feared. The corpse of the former Emperor was already falling to pieces. He examined the wound; it could be made to look less serious. He made a few more facial wounds with quick stabs, as if Charliss had cut himself about the face in a mad frenzy. Then he placed the dagger in Charliss's hands, clenched both the flaccid hands around the hilt, pressed the point to the Emperor's breast, and shoved, piercing the heart.

He checked to make certain that he had not gotten any blood on himself, more as a reflex than anything else; he had been a professional for too long to have made so foolish a mistake.

Then he strolled casually out the door, nodding to the guards as he passed. In a few more moments, they would go in, find Charliss, and report that the Emperor, distraught and deranged by his failing magic and crumbling health, had committed suicide.

And long live the new Emperor, may he reign a hundred years.

Karal was on his knees. Altra was beside him, a glowing cat-image under his groping hand. Florian stood braced between him and the Pit, a horse-shape of Fire against the darkness. To his right, looming out of the swirling, fluctuating energies, Firesong still stood like a blinding statue of a warrior with upraised sword—a high keening sound that somehow penetrated the roar in Karal's ears came from Need, as if the sword had somehow acquired a voice. To his left, there was no sign of An'desha, but two bird-human shapes with feathers of flame wove a restless web all about a shadowed core. He couldn't see Sejanes at all across the Pit.

He sensed the energies around them were winning. They couldn't feed the Pit fast enough, and their protectors were burning out.

And yet, he was no longer afraid. Even if they didn't survive, they *had* fed enough of the terrible power into the Pit to prevent a second

Cataclysm. As he gazed on the burning image of Florian, great peace descended on his heart, and he faced the terrible, glorious, mystical fire without flinching. Once again, he stood in the heart of the Sun and knew he was welcome there. He opened himself up to it fully, and lost himself there, past fear, past pain, past everything but the Light.

And then his awareness of self evaporated, and there was nothing more.

The light was gone; the Light was gone. There was nothing but darkness, yet Florian's image still continued to burn against that dark.

He was lying on his back. His groping hands encountered rough blankets over him, then warm fur.

"I think he's awake," said Lo'isha in a low voice.

He coughed, cleared his throat, and replied, "I am awake. How is everyone? Did the light fail?"

His question was answered with the kind of heavy silence that only occurs when someone has unwittingly asked a question that has an answer that will make him very unhappy.

"Firesong has been… hurt," Silverfox said gently. "An'desha and Sejanes are quite all right, only tired."

He tried to sit up, and felt hands on his chest holding him down. "How badly hurt is Firesong?" he asked urgently. "Can I see him? Where's Florian? Haven't you got any lights going yet?"

Again, that awkward silence, and then the answer came to him, to his last question at least, as Lo'isha asked, very softly, "What can you see?"

"Nothing," he whispered, stunned. "Only—Florian—"

"It seems that those whose guardians were entirely spirit fared the best," said Lyam in that dry way of his.

The fur draped over his legs moved. *:Florian is gone, Karal,:* Altra said, in the gentlest tones that Karal had ever heard him use. *:I am the only one of the protectors to survive the experience. I am sorry.:*

Karal moved his head, and still saw nothing but darkness and the fiery image of Florian in reverse silhouette against it. He swallowed, as the full impact of realization hit him, and felt hot tears burning their way down his face. Florian—gone? Protecting him? He blinked, but nothing changed in what he saw—or rather, what he didn't see.

"You see nothing, Karal?" Lo'isha persisted. He shook his head dumbly.

"What about Firesong?" he asked, around a cold lump in his gut and a second lump in his throat. "Is he—like me?"

"No, but—the sword, Need—she exploded in a mist of molten metal in his hands. His face and hands are badly burned." That was Lyam. "I just sent Silverfox back to him."

Although tears of mourning continued to trickle down Karal's face, he nodded. "Good," he managed. "I don't really need a Healer…" He let his voice trail off, making a kind of question out of it.

"No, Karal," Lo'isha said, with a comforting hand on his shoulder. "I'm afraid a Healer won't do you any good right now."

"Then, just leave me with Altra for a bit, would you?" he asked, and after a while, he heard them get up and move away. He felt Altra settle on his chest and legs, and began gently scratching the Firecat's ears. Tears slid down his cheeks, and Altra continued to rasp them away.

:Karal?: Altra asked, after a long silence. He answered the Firecat with a fierce hug.

"Just stay with me," he whispered.

:I'll never leave you, Karal,: Altra promised. *:Never. Not for as long as you live.:*

Firesong remembered the exact moment when Need lost her battle to shield him, which was right after Yfandes had evaporated into motes of energy. She had screamed—a warning, he thought—and he had let her go and flung one arm over his eyes to protect them. All he remembered after that was pain.

He hadn't ever lost consciousness, and right now, loss of all awareness would have been a blessing. Silverfox had given him something that turned the terrible agony into bearable agony, but he still *hurt*. Almost as bad was the knowledge of what had happened to him. *He* knew what he looked like—and worse, he knew what he was going to look like. No Healer would be able to keep scar tissue from forming, and his face—

He struggled to keep back tears, tears of pain, tears of loss. *Yes* he had been vain, and why not? His face had won him all the lovers he had ever wanted, and now no one would ever give him a second glance.

A touch on his arm made him start and open his tightly-closed eyes. "*Ashke,* I am here," said Silverfox, his face full of concern. "Are you in pain?"

"Better to ask, what *doesn't* hurt," he replied, trying to make a feeble joke of it. "I am trying not to scream; it is very impolite, and would frighten An'desha."

"We have sent the Kal'enedral out for stronger pain drugs," Silverfox told him tenderly, resting one hand on the part of his arm that was not burned. "They should be back soon. The blizzard stopped, and the snow is melting, and in a little we will have gryphons or horses here to take you to k'Leshya. Kaled'a'in Healers are very good." He hesitated, then added, "It is a pity they are not good enough to help Karal."

That snapped him out of the slough of self-pity he was wallowing in. "What about Karal?" he asked sharply.

"I think—he has lost his sight." Silverfox looked away for a moment.

Lost his sight? For one bitter moment, Firesong actually envied him. Better to lose his sight than to go through life, scorned and pitied, to have people look away from you because they could not bear the sight of you—

But even as he thought that, he rejected the thought with anger at himself. *You fool,* he told himself scornfully. *You vain, self-important fool! You are alive with all your senses; you are neither crippled nor incapacitated, and you still have Aya.*

As if to underscore that last, the firebird trilled a little from his perch beside Firesong's pallet.

Poor Karal, came the thought at last. "Poor lad," he sighed. "Florian, and this—" then involuntarily whimpered as the movement sent pain lancing through the burns on his face. He felt tears start up, and soak into his bandages.

Silverfox cupped his hands at Firesong's temples, and stared into his eyes with fierce concentration. As Firesong looked into his eyes, some of the pain began to recede, and he almost wept again, this time with relief. "I will be glad—" he gasped, "—when those pain drugs arrive."

"They cannot arrive soon enough for me," Silverfox muttered, then managed something of a wan smile. "You are being much braver than I would. I cannot bear pain."

"It is not too bad, except when I am alone," Firesong said, still gazing into those warmly compassionate eyes.

And somehow, those eyes softened further. "In that case, *ashke*, I will never leave you," the handsome *kestra'chern* said softly. "If you think you can bear to have me here."

And for a moment, Firesong forgot any pain at all.

An'desha lay curled up with his face to the wall, and Karal could tell by his shaking shoulders that he was weeping silently. The view through Altra's eyes was rather disconcerting, given that Altra's head was about at knee-height, and he had to look up to see peoples' faces when they stood. But at least now, with Altra glued to his leg and lending him the view, he wasn't bumping into things, nor tripping over them.

Karal knelt down beside An'desha's pallet, and put a hand on his shoulder. "If you keep this up much longer," he said, trying not to dissolve into tears himself and make things worse, "you're going to be sick."

An'desha only shook his head violently, and Karal tried to remember exactly what it was that Lo'isha had told him.

"*An'desha blames himself for the loss of the others, especially the Avatars,*" the Kaled'a'in had said. "*You must persuade him to walk the Moonpaths, or—or it will be bad for his soul, his heart. I have not been able to persuade him.*"

The older man had left it at that, but there was no doubt in Karal's mind that he knew how An'desha had managed to help him through his own crisis of conscience. Altra had seconded the Shin'a'in's request as soon as Lo'isha was off tending to some other urgent problem. After that, how could Karal have possibly refused?

"There wasn't anything you did or didn't do that would have made a difference for the better," Karal persisted. "How could there have been? We tried to do more than Urtho could, and it *still* came out better than we had any reason to expect!"

"I should have known about those other weapons," An'desha said, his voice muffled by his sleeve. "I should have known what they'd do when they started to fail."

"How?" Karal asked acerbically. "Those were *Urtho's* weapons, not Ma'ar's! How could you have known what they were going to do? ForeSight? When not even the ForeSeers were able to give us decent advice?"

One red eye emerged from the shelter of An'desha's sleeve. "But—" he began.

"But, nothing," Karal said with great firmness. "You aren't a ForeSeer, and you don't have Urtho's memories, you have Ma'ar's. And if you'd go walk the Moonpaths, you'd find out from the *leshy'a* that I'm right."

An'desha winced, blanching, which looked quite interesting through Altra's eyes. "I can't—" he began.

Karal fixed him with what he hoped was a stem gaze, even though he couldn't feel his eyes responding the way they should. "That sounds exactly like what someone who's been thrown says," he replied. "What do you do when a horse throws you?"

"You get back on," An'desha said faintly, "but—"

"You've already used 'but' too many times." Karal patted his elbow. "Try saying, 'all right,' instead."

"All right," An'desha replied obediently, then realized he'd been tricked. Karal wasn't about to let him off.

"Go," he said, and got unsteadily to his feet again. Instead of looking down, he sensed that his head was in a position of looking out, echoing Altra's head-posture. "Go walk the Moonpaths. I want you to, Lo'isha wants you to. That ought to be reason enough, right there."

Having finished what he had to say, and having partly tricked An'desha into agreement, he left and returned to his own pallet, far from the others, where he sank down onto it, exhausted by holding back his own emotions, and cried himself to sleep.

"*Karal.*"

He looked around, startled. He wasn't in his bed in the Tower anymore; he was standing in the middle of—of nowhere he recognized. There was opalescent mist all around him, and a path of softly glowing silver sand beneath his feet. Not only that, but it was his own eyes that he was looking out of, not Altra's.

Where was he? This wasn't like any dream he had ever had before. In fact, it was rather like the descriptions that An'desha had given him of the Moonpaths. But that was a place that only Shin'a'in could reach, wasn't it?

Wasn't it?

"*Of course not,*" said that voice again, teasingly familiar. "*Anyone can come here, they just see it differently. But Altra thought that after all you've been through, you probably wouldn't want to visit SunHeart for a little.*"

This time, when he turned around, there *was* someone there—or rather, four someones, two male and two female. Two of them, the ones standing hand-in-hand, with vague bird-forms swirling about them, he recognized immediately.

"Tre'valen!" he exclaimed "Dawnfire! But—"

"*Oh, heavens, you didn't think we'd burned up or some such nonsense, did you?*" Dawnfire laughed. "*It takes more than a storm of mage-energy to destroy a spirit! We just lost the parts of ourselves that held us in your world, that's all.*"

"You did?" said someone else, incredulously. "That's all?" Karal found, without any surprise at all, that An'desha had somehow come to stand beside him. "But, why didn't you come back when I called you then?"

"*Because—well—we can't.*" Tre'valen actually looked shamefaced. "*I'm afraid that we overstepped the bounds of what we were actually permitted to do to help you. The Star-Eyed wasn't precisely put out, but...*"

Dawnfire interrupted him. "*You'll have to come here to meet us from now on,*" she said ruefully. "*But if you're going to be a shaman, you ought to get all the practice you can in walking the Moonpaths anyway.*"

"All I can think of is how glad I am that I didn't—" An'desha began, but it was the strange young man that interrupted him this time. He looked very familiar, but Karal could not imagine why. Thin and not particularly muscular, but with a build that suggested agility, he had sandy brown hair that kept flopping into his blue eyes, and a friendly, cheerful manner.

"*Nothing you did or didn't do made any difference in what happened to us, An'desha,*" the young man said. "*Part of it was purest chance, and the rest was that we took on more than we had any right to think we could handle and we managed to carry it off anyway. We dared. Right, Karal?*"

At this point, Karal had an idea that he knew who the young man was, and he gave voice to it. "Right—Florian," he replied, and was rewarded by a wink, a flash of a grin, and a nod. "But if this is where all of you came—after—where are Vanyel, Stefen, and Yfandes?"

"*Free of the forest for one thing, and high time, too, if you ask me,*" Florian replied. "*And probably if you ask them. I suppose it seemed like a good idea at the time, but I suspect they were stuck there a lot longer than they thought they would be.*"

Karal hadn't the faintest idea what Florian was talking about, and some of his bewilderment must have shown on his face. Florian chuckled.

"*Never mind,*" he said. "*Basically, they've made decisions about their destinations, and they didn't have a lot of time to make sure they got properly placed, so they've already gone on. I can't tell you what they decided, but it's going to be fine. As for me,*" he continued with a wink, "*I've made mine, too, but I wasn't so picky. It should be obvious if you think about it, but don't tell any Heralds, all right?*"

Karal nodded solemnly; Florian's decision *was* obvious, though he doubted that his friend was going to look anything like he did at the moment when he returned to the world.

Then again, maybe he would. Karal branded that face into his memory. If in fifteen or twenty years' time, Karal—or rather, Altra—saw a Herald who looked like this, they would both know who it was.

I'd better remember that he won't remember, though, and not go rushing up to him and greet him as my long-lost friend.

Even though that would be precisely what he was.

"'Florian—" he faltered, and continued. "I've never had a friend like you."

"*Well, you'll have one again in time,*" the irrepressible Florian interrupted.

Evidently he was in no mood for sorrowful good-byes or recriminations. He cut short any other attempts at speech by embracing his friends. *"Now, you go back to Valdemar and get into as much mischief as possible with Natoli, and I'll go take care of my business, and eventually we'll meet again. It's not 'good-bye,' Karal, it's 'see you later.' All right?"*

What else could he do but agree, and return the hearty embrace? With a cheery wave, Florian faded into the mist, and was gone, leaving Karal behind with tears in his eyes and a smile on his lips.

Now he was alone with An'desha and the old woman.

This must be Need, he realized, listening to her give An'desha some tart and intelligent pieces of advice. *"And as for you, young man,"* she said at last, turning her clever gaze on him. *"I heartily agree with that young scamp, Florian. You're too sober by half, and just because you can't see things for yourself, that's no reason to go back to that gloomy country of yours and sit in a corner and mope. Go get into mischief with that young lady of yours; I had plenty of apprentices like her in my time, and I suspect she'll keep you hopping and she won't let you feel sorry for yourself."*

"Probably not, my lady," he replied politely, thinking that her assessment of Natoli was remarkably accurate for someone who didn't actually know her.

"Now, since you asked earlier, as for me, I'm taking a long-delayed rest. Maybe you'll see me and maybe you won't, but I'll be damned if I ever go sticking myself into a piece of steel again!" She gave both of them a brief hug. *"Now, you both stop ruining good pillows with salt water, and go and get some living done."*

And with that, she turned and stalked off into the mist, leaving him and An'desha alone. Tre'valen and Dawnfire had already vanished while their attention was on Need.

"Now what?" he asked.

He looked at his friend, who shrugged, but with some of his old spirit back. "I suppose we'd better do as she says," An'desha said. "You know her. If we don't, she's likely to turn around and kick us out." He toed the soft silver sand for a moment, then added, "I'm glad you made me come here."

"I'm glad you let me," Karal replied, and smiled, feeling more peace in his heart than he had ever expected to have again. "Now, let's go home."

Karal looked back through Altra's eyes, over the tail of his Shin'a'in riding horse, a lovely and graceful palfrey. It felt very strange not to be riding Florian, but he supposed that he would get used to it after a while.

Firesong rode behind him, supported by a saddle that the Shin'a'in used for riders who were ill or disabled, watching everything around him with his eyes shining behind the eye-holes of the mask covering his half-healed face. Firesong's mask was a wonder, not only because it was as extravagant and beautiful as one of his elaborate robes, but because he and Lyam had made it of materials they had scavenged from things in the Tower during the fortnight they had waited. With a base of leather and adorned with bits of crystal, wire, and feathers that Aya himself had carefully pulled from his tail and brought to Firesong while he still lay half-healed in his bed, it probably would have fetched a small fortune from a collector of such things. But Firesong was dissatisfied with it, and was already designing new ones.

All around them, the Plains were blooming in a way that the Shin'a'in said they had not seen since the Star-Eyed Herself walked there. One could hardly see the grass for the flowers, which painted the landscape in wide swathes of color. The land had gone from deepest winter to the heart of spring, all in the space of a fortnight. Through Altra's eyes, Karal took in the incredible beauty with a sense of awe and wonder. According to the messages that Altra had brought from Solaris in Karse, all their friends in Haven, and Elspeth in Hardorn, the phenomenon was not confined to the Plains. All the world was in blossom, as if to make up for the ravages of the Storms.

Sejanes and An'desha had been working to discover just how magic operated, and as soon as he was able, Firesong had joined them. It had not been long before they discovered that there were no ley-lines anymore, no nodes, no huge reserves of mage-power. Magical energy had been dispersed fairly evenly across the landscape; and there wouldn't be any large magics for a very long time. That meant no Gates, of course, but it was no hardship to ride through a countryside where the sun shone down with kindly benevolence, where birds serenaded every step of the way, and there was such an all-pervasive perfume of flowers, both night- and day-blooming, that it even permeated their dreams at night. And once the clever Kaled'a'in found the means to make the carry-baskets light using the small magics that still worked, they would make the rest of their journey by air.

Karal had been given the choice of going home to Karse—a shorter journey by far—or back to Valdemar. But when all was said and done, it had not been a difficult choice. One of the first messages from Solaris had been strictly for him, commending his actions, and asking him if he would, as a personal favor to her, resume his work in Valdemar both as the Karsite envoy and as the head of the Temple outside Karse. "With the visible evidence of your sacrifice," she had written, "no one in Valdemar will question your authority. Additionally, you will be dealing with the representatives of Iftel—creatures I confess I find somewhat unnerving. The Sunlord has decreed some odd things in Iftel, and I frankly do not think that outside of you there is a single Priest in the entire Temple who could treat these peoples as anything other than heretics. I do not want to offend these new brothers and sisters in any way, but I fear that if I assigned anyone else to Valdemar and Iftel, there would be blood spilled before long. However, if you want to come home, I will understand, and find a way to cope."

The message had come on the day when they were all deciding whether to go to their homes or back to Haven.

Tarrn and Lyam had elected to return to k'Leshya, which was no surprise at all. Silverfox and Firesong, however, were going with them. Karal had half expected Firesong, at least, to want to return to his own people, but the Adept had smiled behind his mask and simply shaken his head, the crystals and bits of metal dangling from the mask tinkling softly.

"No one remembers what I looked like before in k'Leshya," he said quietly. "And—besides, Silverfox wants to be there, and it *is* a familiar Vale." It was plain in his voice, burned lips or not, that being with Silverfox was the primary reason.

An'desha rode with them, but he would not be leaving the Plains. He had elected to remain and study with Lo'isha, taking the vows of the shaman. Karal had been surprised at that as well, especially as he had been earnestly practicing magic alongside Sejanes and Firesong during the time that they waited for their hosts to put a caravan together for them.

"There is no prohibition on magic among the Shin'a'in now," An'desha explained with a chuckle. "There is no reason for one. I suspect that Lo'isha has it in mind for me to be the teacher to the new mages among us, in time. I should like that," he finished softly, with a tone of contentment in his voice that Karal had never heard before. "Ma'ar in all of his incarnations gave nothing of himself. I shall perhaps be able to balance that, eventually."

So Lo'isha and An'desha would leave them at the edge of the Plains, and Silverfox, Firesong, Tarrn, and Lyam at k'Leshya Vale. Master Levy and Sejanes were going on, of course, and they would be joined by the Heralds who had carried the messages from Haven telling the mages and rulers of other lands how to keep their nodes from going rogue.

And Karal would be going with them. After all the advice from the spirits on the Moonpaths, he was hardly surprised when Natoli sent him a message of her own, asking him to come back to Valdemar. "I can be your eyes, too," she had written. "And you can be my good sense, which I seem to have a distinct lack of. I think I need you." Confused grammar, but not confused thoughts. He had been afraid for a little that despite the surety of others, she might not want to see him as less than he had been; he knew now that he should have given her more credit than that.

So he *would* be going on with Master Levy and Sejanes; back to duty, back to love. But most of all, back to a place he was already thinking of as home.

Altra would stay with him to provide him with "eyes," but he had the love of friends, awareness of himself, and hope for the future to give him vision, vision without sight, perhaps, but as true and clear as anyone could imagine.

ABOUT THE AUTHOR

Mercedes Lackey is a full-time writer and has published numerous novels and works of short fiction, including the bestselling *Heralds of Valdemar* series. She is also a professional lyricist and licensed wild bird rehabilitator. She lives in Oklahoma with her husband and collaborator, artist Larry Dixon, and their flock of parrots.

www.**mercedeslackey**.com

THE COLLEGIUM CHRONICLES
Mercedes Lackey

Follow Magpie, Bear, Lena and friends as they face their demons
and find their true strength on the road to becoming full Heralds,
Bards and Healers of Valdemar.

Book One: Foundation
Book Two: Intrigues
Book Three: Changes
Book Four: Redoubt
Book Five: Bastion

"Lackey makes a real page-turner out of Mags' and the collegia's
development… this book's outstanding characters, especially
Mags, will greatly please Valdemar fans." *Booklist*

"The tone, characterization, and rampant angst recall
Lackey's earliest Valdemar books… this is a worthy entry
in the overall saga." *Publishers Weekly*

"Lackey's Valdemar series is already a fantasy classic,
and these newest adventures will generate even more acclaim
for this fantasy superstar." *Romantic Times*

THE HERALD SPY
Mercedes Lackey

Mags was a Herald of Valdemar. But he had once lived the brutal
life of a child slave. When he was Chosen by his Companion
Dallen, his young life was saved, and he slowly adjusted to being
well fed, educated, and treasured as a trainee in the Herald's
Collegium at Haven. Singled out by the King's Own Herald,
Mags would thrive in his secret training as a spy. His unusually
strong Gift—an ability to Mindspeak and Mindhear anyone, not
just others who were Gifted—made him a perfect undercover
agent for the king.

Closer to Home
Closer to the Heart
Closer to the Chest (October 2016)

"A welcome addition to the Valdemar canon…a fast, page-turning
read." Shiny Book Review

"You can feel Lackey's passion for her characters…funny and
entertaining." The Qwillery

"Mercedes Lackey is a master storyteller and *Closer to Home* is a
masterful, satisfying visit to Valdemar." Bitten by Books

THE ELEMENTAL MASTERS
Mercedes Lackey

Mercedes Lackey's bestselling fantasy series set in an alternative Edwardian Britain, where magic is real—and the Elemental Masters are in control.

The Serpent's Shadow
The Gates of Sleep
Phoenix and Ashes
Wizard of London
Reserved for the Cat
Unnatural Issue
Home from the Sea
Steadfast
Blood Red
From a High Tower
A Study in Sable

"Fantastic… this is Lackey at her best." *Publishers Weekly*

"Intriguing and compelling." *Library Journal*

"Colourful characters… great fun." *Booklist*

"Innovative historical fantasy." *Romantic Times*

TITANBOOKS.COM

For more fantastic fiction, author events, exclusive excerpts,
competitions, limited editions and more

VISIT OUR WEBSITE
titanbooks.com

LIKE US ON FACEBOOK
facebook.com/titanbooks

FOLLOW US ON TWITTER
@TitanBooks

EMAIL US
readerfeedback@titanemail.com